Cecily,
I hope you ⌣ ⌣ ⌣ ⌣ ⌣ ⌣ ⌣ ≥ˡ.
Make sure you have a
glass of wine to pair it with.

Love ya,
    WHISKEY
      EMERSON

EAST OF HELL

WHISKEY EMERSON

Illustrations by Charlie Spencer

www.mascotbooks.com

East of Hell

©2021 Whiskey Emerson. All Rights Reserved. No part of this publication
may be reproduced, stored in a retrieval system or transmitted in any
form by any means electronic, mechanical, or photocopying, recording or
otherwise without the permission of the author.

This is a work of fiction. Names, characters, businesses, places, events, and
incidents are either the products of the author's imagination or used in a
fictitious manner. Any resemblance to actual persons, living or dead, or
actual events is purely coincidental.

For more information, please contact:
Mascot Books
620 Herndon Parkway #320
Herndon, VA 20170
info@mascotbooks.com

Library of Congress Control Number: 2020922555

CPSIA Code: PRFRE0121A
ISBN-13: 978-1-64543-228-9

Printed in Canada

For Ryan

PREFACE
NEW YORK CITY, JANUARY 1888

A dark, overcast sky lingered in the early morning hours, foretelling of a short day when time blends together in a blur of grey and shadows. White, fluffy snowflakes trickled down from the low hanging clouds, settling delicately onto the surrounding rooftops, and the air was hauntingly static and dense. The courtyard of the Tombs was crowded for such a bitter January day, though it was no surprise, considering how widespread the publicity following the capture of Danny Driscoll had been. According to the papers and the New York City Police Department, Danny was caught red-handed for the murder of Beezy Garrity, though his original target had been none other than the notorious gangster Johnny McCarty. McCarty and his own organization were giving Tammany Hall a run for their money on the streets of Midtown, and Richard Croker wanted to crush the infamous gangster's power before it was too late. Tammany Hall had almost entirely won New York City, the only exception, politically, being the consistently stubborn Swallowtails, and once McCarty was out of his way, Croker could finally claim victory over his most treacherous criminal rival. Nowadays, everyone was in Croker's pocket, sucking off the tit of the Hall just for a little extra cash and to avoid any conflict with the most powerful man in the city…

Everyone except the Madame and her underground web of renegades.

Louis stood near the entrance and watched the onlookers pass him by as they searched to find a spot in the masses, all of them bloodthirsty and jeering at the prospect of seeing one of the foremost thugs and terrorizers of lower Manhattan sent to meet his maker. Sadly, Danny was the least of Louis's worries. In the last few months, the Whyos had gotten out of control, and it was obvious Croker's sway over the gang and his comrade Walsh was running thin. The hit on McCarty had been discussed amongst Croker, Will, Louis, Esther, and Walsh on multiple occasions, but no real plan had ever been put into motion, meaning the hit was unsanctioned. Personally, Louis didn't believe that Danny killed Garrity, regardless of how rogue the Whyos' recent antics had been. He knew Danny, had spent time with him, much to Louis's own disdain, and to pull off something of this magnitude would require a number of resources Danny absolutely did not have. There were only two viable explanations: either Walsh killed Garrity mistakenly and pinned the fall on Danny, or Walsh framed Danny for some sort of disobedience against him. Louis's gut told him it was the latter.

The Dannys still held face as the runner of the Whyos, but they reported to Walsh, and the gang never managed any sort of hit or venture without his permission. With Danny Driscoll out, Danny Lyons and Kitty would be at the helm. It was only a matter of time before the gang would disintegrate, and the thought gave Louis chills. He and Will discussed the notion often—if Kitty and Danny were usurped, nothing would stop Walsh from a complete takeover of the gang, and that would put Walsh in charge of all organized crime south of Midtown. No matter what he said aloud, Louis sensed that if Walsh were to gain that territory as well as a small army of delinquents, his allegiance to Croker would come to an end. New York City would be burned to the ground, and total anarchy would ensue.

It was then that he spotted her, slinking into view from an alleyway across the street. She was undistinguishable from a young man, sporting a pair of brown trousers, leather boots, a worn-out wool sweater, and a heavy long jacket whipping out behind her in the fierce winter wind. Her face was smartly covered by the bill of her newsboy cap, and her hair was still as short as the day Will cut it off years ago; those beautiful green eyes would be a dead giveaway that she was, in reality, a female, though very much changed from the Esther he'd befriended at the tender age of ten. Since the time her training began, her physique transformed, and so did Esther. She was no longer thin or petite; instead, her arms and legs were sinewy, toned from the vigorous activity and exertion of her muscles on a daily basis. Blending in and being invisible were what kept her alive, a vast contrast to the parties, dinners, and social gatherings she used to attend with Celeste in her teenage years. Her family and friends consisted solely of Louis, Will…and unfortunately, Richard Croker. Drawing near, Louis caught a hint of the small shiner under her left eye from sparring with Will earlier that week; the substantial scar on her neck from Timothy Adams also stood out, to anyone looking for it. The memory of that murderous bastard made Louis's cheeks hot, regardless of how much time had passed, and he tried to forget everything they'd lost because of Timothy.

Pausing beside Louis, Esther delicately slipped a few things inside his jacket pocket and sighed heavily. When he glanced at her, he saw she had tears in her eyes, and he was stunned.

"I never wanted to come back here, but I guess it's time to let it go."

"What do you mean?" Louis asked.

She kept her eyes straight ahead. "Four years since we lost Danny…our Danny…all for nothing. All for fucking nothing." Esther shook her head. "I gave you some things for the Vault. The Madame will be happy with it, I think, but I haven't gotten close enough for the safe combination yet."

"Keep trying," Louis said, trying to be empathetic. "You are already giving more than you should, you know that."

"I know," she admitted. "I guess my conscience needs me to give as much as I can so it doesn't die away completely. Croker will be by to see her soon, so make sure you let her know. It's an election year and he has some ideas on how to…well…wipe out the competition."

"Things Will and I don't know?"

"Yeah. You know how he gets. I am his confidant…bastard thinks I'm like a goddamn daughter to him." Esther scoffed loudly. "How can people be so fucking twisted like that? I don't understand it."

It was a rhetorical question, so Louis moved on. "Did we finally get the details?"

"I think so."

"And?"

The little color in Esther's face drained away. "He set this up, Louis."

"Walsh? He set Danny up?"

She nodded. "It was all a ploy."

"Fucking son of a bitch!" Louis murmured loudly, accidentally catching the eyes of a few members of the audience. He hastily recovered his wits and lowered his tone. "What happened?"

"I don't know. I got most of it out of a belligerent Kitty last night, while I carried her home from the fucking bar after starting a fight with McGloin's old cohorts. From what I can tell, Walsh asked Danny to do something that Croker deliberately told the Whyos to stay out of, and Danny refused Walsh's order. Next thing you know, the police were out looking for Danny and Beezy was dead. No one knows how the authorities got the idea it was Danny who murdered him…it's not like they caught him with the damn murder weapon in his hand at the scene of the crime…they found him holed up in a whorehouse in the Bowery, for Christ's sake, high as hell on opium!"

"So, you confirmed the evidence was planted?"

"We can assume as much."

"Jesus Christ." Louis took a deep breath. "I sometimes wonder what could possibly motivate Croker to keep that bastard around."

"What makes you think it's Croker that's keeping Walsh around?" Esther remarked quietly, shuffling her stance. "I'm beginning to think his power over Walsh is a façade. And that, above anything else, is fucking terrifying."

The crowd around them suddenly started to roar as Danny Driscoll was led out of the Tombs in the direction of the platform, where a stoic priest and the hangman waited for him. Wanting to make a show of it, the officers escorting Danny took their time, allowing him to get pelted with vegetables, rocks, or anything the crowd thought fitting to lurch at the man who stood as the scapegoat for the decades of gang violence in New York. Louis observed closely and could perceive in Danny's eyes that he was already long gone from this world, probably having suffered far worse during his days in jail than any of them would ever come to know.

With the noise, Esther's gaze went to Driscoll, and while her eyes never wavered, Louis suspected it was not easy for her to witness. Although she always tried to hide it, deep down, Esther had some enduring goodness in her heart, a small flicker of hope that she might actually escape this life. She had come a long way since her own time at the Tombs; her training with Louis and Will was absurdly tough, as Croker demanded she learn and succeed faster than a human being could ever be prepared for. Much to Croker's delight and Will and Louis's surprise, Esther persevered at an astonishing rate, becoming more skilled and more lethal than either of them could have predicted. Her first kill was the hardest, yet she pressed on afterward, not once thinking back and regretting what she'd done. The Esther standing in the Tombs' courtyard was fast, clever, and when necessary, vicious. Louis was beyond proud. Will was too.

In her usual fashion, Esther was currently armed with a dag-

5

ger strapped around the outside of her hip, mostly concealed by her jacket, yet her boldness in not worrying over its exposure was a clear sign to troublemakers that she was not to be fucked with. A glint from Esther's hand caught Louis's attention, and he was shocked to realize she'd brought her brass knuckles with her. Learning to fight with those had taken her nearly two years to master, evidenced in the heavy scarring on her fingers, hands, and wrists from the sharp metal. Now, however, Louis felt sorry for anyone who ended up on the wrong end of her fists.

It never ended well for them.

He grinned. "Was I supposed to have come ready for an altercation?"

Esther's intensity eased at his words, and she smirked. "I always come ready. You taught me that."

Danny was center stage as the priest read him his final rights, and the audience was bellowing so loudly that Louis fought to hear Esther speak.

"Do you think he'll have us put down Walsh?"

Louis shrugged, wanting to seem nonchalant, when really, the idea made him uneasy. "Don't forget, Walsh still has Kitty and Danny Lyons standing in his way. The gang is loyal to them first. If he tried to pursue a coup, the progress he's made within the Whyos would go up in smoke. It's probably the sole reason he hasn't killed them."

"And probably why he had to frame Driscoll, to get rid of him."

The executioner put the noose over Danny's head, and finally, Esther turned to face Louis, her expression serious.

"We can't do this without Thomas," she whispered desperately.

He stared back at her. "I know."

Esther's eyes flickered from left to right, checking for anything suspicious. "We've talked about this. After everything that's happened, you said he'd come back and finish this with us. You said he wouldn't have a choice, and that he'd even been training like we had."

6

Louis put his hands on the sides of Esther's shoulders to steady her emotions. "He'll be here soon. His time is drawing closer, and the Samurai has been training him like I foretold. Soon, Esther, I promise you that."

"How can you be sure?"

After a small hesitation, Louis thought it best to reply with the truth. "Edward wasn't the only friend I had at Amberleigh," he confessed. "That's all I am going to tell you. But trust me, all right? Soon."

With another nod, Esther seemed appeased, and she returned to Louis's side as Danny shouted out his last words, which were completely inaudible over the swarm of people shouting. The moment his lips stopped moving, the black sack was shoved down over his head, and the mob hushed for the final scene of Danny Driscoll's life. Dramatically, the executioner moved to the lever and gave it a pull. Danny fell downward, followed closely by the sound of his neck snapping, which caused the crowd to let out a giant cheer.

Louis and Esther departed together, and she slipped her arm through his, her head leaning against his arm. "What do you think is going to happen?" she inquired softly.

"When?"

"When Thomas does get here…what do you think is going to happen?"

He kissed the top of her head. "I am not sure. If my contact is not exaggerating, I'd say we'd finally be getting the miracle we've needed to win this. And if I were Croker…" Louis's voice trailed off.

Esther peered up at him. "What?"

"Well, Esther, I'd be scared shitless."

She gave his arm a squeeze and released, banking to head north as Louis headed south. "I am late to meet Richie, but I don't have any jobs tonight, so I'll pick up mutton for dinner. You find us some wine."

Louis grinned and gave a small bow. "We'll see you at eight."

PART IV
NEW YORK CITY, MAY 1888

CHAPTER XXX.

"The longer Hewitt sits in office, the more votes that nativist bastard takes away from Grant. I should have never caved to those Democratic pieces of shit. You were right, Madame. And you know that's not easy for me to say."

The Madame grinned behind her almost empty glass of whiskey. "I told you conceding to those Swallowtail pricks would get you nowhere," she said plainly, shaking her head. "You thought putting their man in the mayor's chair would win them over. All it did was cause the Hall more fucking problems than it needs. You need to get labor on board and befriend the 'working man' again, and toss these Swallow imbeciles aside as quickly as you can. They're a dying breed, Richard."

Croker finished his small pour in one gulp and got to his feet, moving toward the drink cart for a refill. "I know," he sighed, grabbing the decanter. He poured a much larger portion this round. "Grant will get it, and we'll have ourselves a mayor that backs Tammany and our operations. But if we lose—"

"You won't lose."

"If we lose, Madame, we can say goodbye to all our power. You will go back to your small-scale enterprise of extortion and bribery, and I will be kicked to the curb by my compatriots. There are no two ways about it. I already have a hoard of assholes wanting to investigate me and the Hall for a public hearing—"

"Richard—" she tried to interject.

"A goddamn public hearing!" he exclaimed, a hint of panic in his voice. "And I can only hold them off if I get a big player to take over for Hewitt as mayor, or I'll be nailed to the cross and crucified."

"Oh, for Christ's sake, don't be so fucking pessimistic," she declared. There were moments when men acted no better than melodramatic schoolchildren. "I've got eyes on Frederick. I am hosting a bunch of union reps in a few days and I'll see what I can get on them. What else do you need me to do that you don't already have Louis or the lunatic taking care of down south?"

"We need votes."

The Madame was a little puzzled. "And how the hell do you think I can help with that?"

"I've got the camouflage already set—we've got the mob south of the park because of the Whyos and the saloons." Croker walked back toward his armchair across from the Madame and sat, staring at her intently. "The labor party I can get, but I need the upper class."

She scoffed loudly. "My darling Richard, you will never get the upper class. Not entirely. To win those bastards over, you need to do more that appeals to them—parties in the park, picnics, balls, all the superficial bullshit they love and you hate. Right now, you are only passing by because you attend what you are invited to, and because you allow your investors to throw fundraisers. You need to be the one hosting. You need to be the one everyone sees. They all know you are the Grand Sachem. Fucking act like it."

Croker's cheeks flushed with anger. "You will mind how you speak to me."

The Madame laughed. "You are upset because I've struck a nerve…and because, once again, you know I'm right."

Croker didn't respond, and she rose, going for more whiskey.

12

"You are letting your personal history as a lower class migrant get the better of you, Richard. I was right about Hewitt. I was right about the Swallowtails. I am right about this. Douglas and Celeste can only do so much to push your agenda with your coveted wealthy targets. You have the slums, the immigrants, the Irish. Now you have to work for the old money, which I, of course, can help with, if provided further compensation. I have clients that have been coming here for two decades, all of which live on Fifth Avenue. I can work that angle."

"How do you plan on doing that?" he asked, still visibly irritated with her, though curious.

"The way I've done it since the beginning: blackmail."

Croker rolled his eyes. "Not everyone has something to hide, Madame."

"On the contrary, Richard. Everyone has something to hide. That's what makes my line of work so interesting…and so effective."

As he sank into his chair, the Madame left Croker with his thoughts momentarily, filling her whiskey glass. For as much as she despised him, the Madame did enjoy their one on one talks, particularly because after four years, he was finally taking her opinion seriously. The politics and community welfare bored her, and the difficulties he dealt with at the Hall were petty and irrelevant in comparison to the bigger picture of what was going on in New York; yet she dealt with it because it was her way in. After losing Thomas to England, the Madame made a choice; the Vault, which over the years she so strategically termed her ever-growing stash of acquired dirty secrets, was now serving a different purpose. All the information she'd extracted in her professional career was being openly shared with Croker to use to his advantage politically. In return, a new Vault was formed, one which became the hiding place containing every single piece of material she and the others could secure on Richard Croker, information that might bring about his downfall. Somehow, the Madame had become his favorite "off the record" advisor. Her knowledge of the way New York operated was beyond compare, and unlike so many others, she was candid—extremely fucking candid. While she secretly prayed the upcoming election might complete the task of destroying Croker for her, the Madame knew better. Grant was a shoo-in, and would be the first Irish mayor in the city's history. Instead, she prepared as best she could, waiting with a small thread of hope that, if and when Thomas did come back, her work of assembling the Vault would assist in crushing Richard Croker.

He cleared his throat while the Madame slid into her throne once again, giving Croker the floor. "We need Frederick gone. Legislatively speaking, he's the last thing standing in my way, and when we get Grant into office, he can appoint another judge to fill Frederick's shoes. Can we make that happen?"

"It's already in the works," she replied, leaning back and resting her feet on the top of her desk. "Celeste and Douglas have been putting together all sorts of—"

"No," Croker uttered quietly. "I mean…gone."

Her left eyebrow rose. "I haven't been sanctioned for a hit from you since we started working together."

"That's correct."

"Even when I've asked." She had a sip of her drink, trying to wash the bitterness out of her mouth. "I was under the impression you took care of that firsthand, either with Will and Louis or the lunatic. Why else is it that my personal bodyguard is spending so much time running your bullshit errands instead of helping me with mine?"

Louis had gone to great lengths to convince Croker that he was his man first, the Madame's second, and to everyone involved, he seemed to be. In reality, however, Louis did more to build the Vault than any of the others combined, though she had to make it appear to Croker that Louis's absence was noticed as often as the opportunity presented itself. This made Richard feel more confident with her…as if he had more power over her than she recognized, which, for the Madame, was quite amusing.

"When I send the boys to take care of something, it's not to this magnitude," Croker admitted somewhat reluctantly. "A direct hit on anyone outside the Points hasn't been done since…well, since…"

"Since you murdered Edward Turner," she blurted out.

A flash of rage emerged in Croker's expression. "Are you trying to provoke me into a fight? Because I'm sincerely considering leaving before you end up hurt."

The Madame dramatically held up her hands in surrender— she'd pushed him a little too far. "Please. That was not my intention."

He rescinded, shaking off his aggravation, but the Madame couldn't resist asking the question that had been bothering her for years; the chance to hear the truth outweighed any other possible negative repercussions.

"Richard, can I ask you something? I swear it will never leave this room, and I ask with the sole objective of wanting only to improve our…affiliation."

"I don't see how I can stop you." He finished his whiskey.

The Madame shifted in her seat, not certain what to expect when the words left her lips. "You didn't actually order Walsh to kill Edward Turner, did you?"

Richard Croker's face contorted in such a way that the Madame immediately got her answer, though she paused to listen to what he had to say before she reacted.

"Why do you presume this?" he queried her.

"Because every time his murder is brought up, you start acting like a defensive prick. And I mean that with absolute sincerity."

Following a minor hesitation, Croker set his glass on the side table. "My aim for Edward Turner was to send him running from New York, perhaps cripple him emotionally and physically…enough so that his family would never dream of coming back. Alas, sometimes when your strength comes from the bastards the Whyos produce for muscle, controlling a situation such as that one becomes…difficult."

The Madame's throat went dry. "What happened?"

"More whiskey first."

She nodded, got to her feet, and retrieved the decanter, bringing it back over to where he sat. "It was the lunatic, wasn't it?" she pressed, pouring the beverage into his glass.

Croker couldn't look her in the eyes. "I think he was hoping to make a statement. It was when he first became involved with the Whyos. He wanted to assert his leadership position…to make them afraid of him. I brought some of their best fighters to beat the living hell out of Edward, and in truth, he beat the living hell out of them. I couldn't stop him. With every one of the Whyos down, Walsh stepped in and ended it right in front of me."

"And you had to play along like it was your idea, because if you didn't—"

"Exactly."

The Madame was quiet for a few seconds as the reality about that horrendous day sank in; Croker continued on, oblivious to how this news changed everything.

"Don't get me wrong, Madame. I've had quite a few people killed since I've gotten into my political career. I've even killed a few myself back in my angrier, youthful years. But unlike Edward Turner, each one of those sons of bitches had it coming, and I've never killed anyone of Lord Turner's caliber since that day. Which is why, with Frederick, I need it done right."

The Madame rested against the front of her desk and took a drink from the decanter bottle. "Fucking hell, Richard."

"Madame, if you can't handle this—"

"I can handle it, godammit!" she asserted strongly, and then immediately took a deep breath to steady her voice—the intelligence about Walsh had unmistakably struck her hard. "I apologize, that was unnecessary. I can handle it. I assume that what you're asking me to do is set up Judge Frederick the way I set up Douglas in killing Charles Adams."

"Precisely what I am asking. Louis and Will can carry it out, but I need you to put the big pieces together, so when that son of a bitch is found dead, the story lines up. Seamus and Samuel can do the investigation to make sure there are no loose ends."

"And a suicide is out of the question?"

Croker chuckled dryly. "Anyone who has ever met Judge Frederick would know he's too cocky of a prick to ever off himself."

Instantly, the clock in her office struck six. Croker downed what was left of his whiskey and got up. "Time for me to be going. Madame, remember, what I told you here today is clandestine. No exceptions."

She had another swig. "Right."

Straightening his vest and jacket, Croker paced lightly toward the doors to her office, then halted, his demeanor changing. "Ah! I nearly forgot. I have a recent discovery I will be sending your way. I am aware I have been hogging your precious Louis for my 'errands,' as you call them, and for that reason, I have found someone who will be a reliable replacement as your fill-in bodyguard. He just got to town, and he's young, smart, and trigger-happy. Being a hit runs in his blood…a family trait. For what you need in regards to The Palace, he is a perfect fit."

The Madame groaned. "If he's such a perfect fit, why the hell don't you just give me Louis back and send this toddler around with Will?

A smug look came to Croker's face. "Well, let's just say it would cause a few internal issues amongst my men. This is the way it is for now; expect him to come by tomorrow night. Good day, Madame."

Once Croker had left, the Madame drank more to calm her nerves, feeling perturbed about the way their evening discussion concluded. While another guard was just what she needed, something in the way Croker spoke made her increasingly suspicious that whoever ended up on her doorstep would be a lot more trouble than she bargained for. And with so much looming on the horizon, the

Madame certainly didn't have the patience for any more wearisome bullshit taking up her precious time.

An hour later, with The Palace in full swing preparing for the night's usual festivities, Celeste arrived, appearing upbeat and determined. The Madame was finding it increasingly difficult to recall the girl Celeste had been prior to their alliance. When Celeste marched into her office four years ago and declared she would take over Esther's role at The Palace, the Madame hadn't really believed her, assuming it would be a matter of weeks before Celeste would give up. The girl had spirit, the Madame couldn't deny that, but she wasn't quite sure Celeste had the forte required to fulfill said proposition. Very rarely in her life did the Madame have to eat her own words; in the case of Celeste, she was more than happy to find she'd been proven wrong.

Absolutely wrong.

No naivety remained. There was very little sweetness or vulnerability unless Celeste wanted to come across that way, which she did amongst her upper-class society friends. Her focus lay with achieving whatever it was the Madame asked of her, and Celeste had not once left any room for disappointment. Where Esther had struggled, she flourished; without any attachments to friends or care for those she spied on, Celeste was able to do what Esther was not and separate herself entirely from her circle. There was no remorse for the people who had cast her aside when her luck was down, no empathy for the bastards who'd befriended her solely due to money and status. In a strange way, Celeste took pleasure in what she did, and if her past was not enough motivation, there was the unrelenting conviction that she was continuing Esther's legacy.

The Madame wasn't sure which of the two girls she'd grown to respect more.

Sitting in front of her now, the Madame eyed Celeste intently. She'd gotten remarkably clever in their years together. Almost overnight, Celeste started to alter her style, dressing a bit more provocatively and in the most expensive fabrics she could get her hands on. To the Madame's delight, Celeste made the Madame go with her for a second opinion whenever she deemed a new dress was necessary for her wardrobe, wanting her advice and input. Currently on her cheeks and on her lips was the smallest hint of rouge, just enough to accentuate her previously unpainted face, and it was remarkable how such subtle changes made Celeste go from relatively plain to stunning. On top of that, her air and style of walking transformed from polite and well-mannered to confident and charming, making her all the more approachable. Celeste was smarter, far more observant, and quick-witted, and it was comical to witness how much it alarmed and thrilled Douglas to see this new version of his daughter.

"So, I beat Father here, then?" she asked the Madame, sinking into the loveseat with an alluring smile. "Please tell me you have wine open."

The Madame pointed to the drink cart. "Of course, darling. Your father should be here any minute."

For the last four years, Celeste and her father had worked closely with the Madame in a fashion similar to that of Esther, and with their aid, the Madame was at the top of her game. Not only was she gaining favors and money for secrets, but she was also making substantial progress in popularity amongst the upper class, or at least as much as she could as a high-end brothel owner. People sought her out for financial advice, loans, investment opportunities, and in a few unusual circumstances, safe passage out of the country. Amongst the wealthy, Douglas spread the word that the Madame would provide covert solutions to any problem for the right price. She took at least four appointments a week, though in the afternoon, so she could attempt a few hours of sleep after her late working nights. On occasion, even Croker had sent her a few clients. It was a wonderful cover—she appeared as if she were expanding her business, thus eliminating Croker's old suspicions, while pursuing her true motives for his destruction when no one was watching.

Celeste stood up and went over to pour herself a glass of wine. "It's getting warm outside already. Can you believe it? After the monstrous blizzard we had in March?"

"Hardly. Although I can't say I am sad about it. Hold on, I'll grab my whiskey and join you in the sitting area. We've got some planning to do."

"So, the talk with Croker went as predicted?"

The Madame shrugged. "Yes and no. There will be one major alteration to our planning. Bastard doesn't like to tiptoe around, that's for damn sure."

Celeste flopped down onto the loveseat, wine glass in hand. The pastel pink dress she wore beautifully accentuated her curvaceous figure, and her long blonde hair hung down in near perfect curls, glistening from the light rain outside.

"Tell me what happened," she requested, taking a sip.

"First things first. You have your invitations to the Admiral's Ball?"

Celeste grinned. "Father and I were amongst the first to receive them. We already have a small party planning to attend with us."

"I am glad to hear it," the Madame replied, rising to her feet and pouring a whiskey from the decanter. "You are taking the Captain, I presume?"

Her cheeks flushed ever so slightly. "Yes. He only just returned a few weeks ago. A lot of long, hard years fighting the Indians out West has changed him. He's...motivated to settle down, and has made no secret of that."

"Really? So, he has made his intentions to marry you clear?"

"Abundantly." Celeste shook her head. "God damn him. I don't know, Madame, I just don't think I can marry Jonathan. It feels so wrong."

The Madame paused. "Because of Esther?"

"No, it's not even that. There is also the large part of me that does not wish to marry again. And I…I just don't love him."

"Well, Celeste, if there were any benefits to being married, I would push you that direction. However, considering the son of a bitch you dealt with the first round, I understand your disinclination."

They each took a gulp of their drinks.

"Tell me about Croker," Celeste entreated her again.

The Madame moved to sit by Celeste. "Darling, it is trickier than we presumed. He wants us to kill Frederick."

"Why doesn't he just have Louis or Will do it?"

"Clever girl," she remarked. "Croker needs us to set up a hit for him to make sure there are no loose ends. Frederick is not the sort of man to take his own life, no matter how fucking bad his conditions may get. Did you make any progress in digging?"

Unexpectedly, Celeste beamed at her, her eyes sparkling. "I sat next to Judge Frederick's wife, who was extremely drunk, at the Bernards' dinner party last week. I am having Father look into it, but she mentioned they were in financial debt. Bad financial debt, with some not-so-great people. She revealed it to me only because she thought there might be a way to discreetly come to an agreement to pay it off through a third party…I wonder whomever could she mean?"

It was hard not to adore Celeste when the Madame truly felt she was becoming an extension of herself. "I love when you bring me good news. Go on."

"She heard Father mention to another friend of hers months ago about your services and never thought anything of it. I am meeting her for tea tomorrow to secure it for us."

The Madame's jaw dropped. "Tea already planned?"

"Why not? He has been the target for a few weeks now. I saw my way in and jumped at it when I had the chance."

"This is a big win for us, darling, and I am beyond impressed," the Madame praised. "You did brilliant, Celeste. Absolutely fucking brilliant."

"Thank you," she responded gratefully, though the Madame could see something was bothering her.

"What is it, Celeste?"

She was thoughtful for a moment. "I've never been a part of... of killing someone...other than that awful night when Esther shot Timothy."

"We are going to be setting Frederick up in a very similar manner to how your father was set up. Are you going to be able to deal with that?"

This, oddly, seemed to bring her around. "Yes, I can definitely deal with it. Sorry. I am not sure why I let myself get so affected." Celeste took another drink of wine and straightened her shoulders. "Man is a prick, anyhow."

"That, I completely agree with." The Madame had forecasted Celeste's reaction, and primed her own methods of persuasion to coax her out of remorse. "Listen, darling, this is the final step. When we complete this task together, you will cross over the last threshold, and you will be one of us permanently. It's an eat or be eaten world we live in. I need to know you can stomach the road ahead."

Celeste appeared somewhat cantankerous that her loyalties were being questioned. "I can stomach the road ahead," she maintained humorlessly, her tone without reservation. "I know what I signed up for."

"That's my girl. All right, so our plan will commence. You will have tea with his wife, and you will offer to set up a meeting for Judge Frederick and I without his wife. Through my own methods of influence, I'll make sure the bastard does not inform Mrs. Frederick that I promise to fix this debacle for him."

Celeste was confused. "You're not going to fix it?"

The Madame held up a hand. "Hear me out, darling. I will assure Frederick that I will negotiate on his behalf to pay off his collector for a small interest fee. I don't want the wife to know the whole story—if she firmly believes that I refused to assist them with their debt and her husband's corpse pops up, there will be no queries as to who went after him."

"And we blame the murder on who he actually owes."

"Precisely."

"Frederick will think you're taking care of it confidentially, and he will be the only one to know, and we get off scot-free."

"Right again."

The wheels in her head were turning before an entertained look came to her face, and Celeste held up her glass to the Madame and saluted her.

"Touché, Madame. Touché."

After Celeste and a tardy Douglas left, the Madame took to organizing her night ahead, calling in her cast of beautiful and highly skilled whores to go over the client schedule. With her design for Frederick taken care of and Croker mollified, she had her own business to run, and that didn't happen by itself. George manned the front door as scheduled in Louis's consistent absence during the weekdays. She'd forewarned George they'd have fresh meat to train, thus meaning they might actually see more of Louis until whoever this mystery man Croker sent could be judged to be reliable. On the busier weekend nights, Croker obliged the Madame's request to have Louis at The Palace; nevertheless, during the other more leisurely days of Monday to Thursday, George was her go-to man, which was mildly disconcerting for her. It wasn't that George proved weak or unreliable—he just simply wasn't Louis. Thankfully, even on the nights when she was marginally anxious, Claire took the time to remind her that she could assist whenever the situation called for it. Having a girl on her staff who knew how to handle drunk bastards and a shotgun as adeptly as Claire was well worth the extra money the Madame paid her for it.

Halfway through the list of customers for the evening, the doors to the Madame's office burst open, and Dot strolled in with Marcy trailing closely behind her. From the look on Dot's face, she was none too pleased.

"Hardy is on my personal list for tonight?!" she exclaimed. "Hardy?!"

Dot had the night's clientele list in her hand and was waving it over her head, eyes furious. Marcy made a grab at Dot's arm, which Dot lurched away from Marcy instantly. There was a red handprint on Marcy's cheek, an obvious piece of evidence to prove Dot was no longer listening to reason—if Marcy couldn't get ahold of her, no one could.

"Madame, I'm so sorry," Marcy initiated. "I tried to stop her!"

"This is fucking bullshit!" Dot declared, slamming the list on the Madame's desk. "That prick hasn't been one of mine in over six months, and I'll be damned if—"

The Madame stayed tranquil. "You will lower your tone this moment."

"I refuse to take Hardy!"

"Dot, if you don't shut your fucking mouth—"

"I want you to change it!"

"Dot," the Madame hissed, "I swear, if you don't shut your fucking mouth, I will hurt you so badly you won't be working for weeks. And you'll be fully docked pay."

24

Dot froze, the pink tone of her skin going pallid. Slowly throughout the last few days, Dot's attitude had become a recurring problem; the Madame had hoped things would sort themselves out, or that the girls would take care of it for her. This was not particularly unusual—every once in a while, one of the Madame's whores got too cocky and overstepped her boundaries. Dot was no exception to this, and if Marcy couldn't put an end to it, that was when the Madame had no other choice but to threaten the girls into submission. She hated the thought of having to physically punish any one of them to make a point, yet there were only two languages these women understood: money and pain. A double blow liked docked pay and a beating was enough to scare Dot into shutting up.

"Marcy, go and get Paige, please, so we can discuss the night's festivities. Dot, sit your ass down."

With a nod, Marcy disappeared and closed the doors behind her, leaving Dot at the Madame's mercy. There was no faltering—Dot sat down in the chair directly in front of the Madame's desk, her eyes cast toward her toes, still pouting.

The Madame drew her feet off the top of the desk and to the ground, her irritation unveiled. "What the fuck has gotten into you, coming in here like you are the one making all the goddamned decisions?"

"Madame, I—"

"Did I say it was your turn to fucking talk?!" she yelled. "You have yet to be granted permission to speak freely with me, and these last few days, you've done nothing but regress! You've been throwing tantrums like you're a small child, acting as if you are better than some of the others, and let me tell you, Dot, you are not. You are so unbearable, the girls can't deal with your bullshit, so now I have to get involved. If this happens again, darling, I will fulfill my promise. You will have your ass kicked and I will not allow you to work for three weeks, minimum. Is that fucking understood?"

It was harsh, but whores needed to remember their place, and

Dot's behavior necessitated a wakeup call. The Madame adored Dot, in spite of her occasional overconfidence. She was their clientele savant: graced with an incredible memory, Dot never forgot a face, and recalled every one of their customers individually the second she laid eyes upon them. With fair skin, hair as black as the night sky, and dark brown eyes, she was quite a catch, though unfortunately, the Madame struggled to keep her slender frame as voluptuous as most of the others. Marcy had notified the Madame a few days prior that Dot was growing more exacerbating, foreshadowing this evening's events. Regrettably for the Madame, something unexpected happened after her reprimand, something that always made the Madame exceptionally awkward.

Dot began to cry.

"I'm sorry, Madame. I am...I am...!" she bawled, tears bursting out.

The Madame was so appalled, she could barely hold a straight face while Dot sobbed.

"Hardy was just so...I liked him enormously, and he just...went onto another girl because I'm not...I'm not..."

The Madame suppressed an eye roll. "Dot, darling, when is your next cycle?"

"Tomorrow," she sniffed, wiping her cheeks on the hem of her dress.

Trying not to laugh, the Madame went over to pour Dot a glass of wine. "I will grant you that sometimes we act irrationally during our monthly visitor. But what in the hell has gotten into you about Hardy?"

"He just...he switched to Jasmine and didn't even tell me...I had to find out from her that...that..."

"Spit it out, for God's sake," the Madame commanded, pulling the cork out of the bottle.

"He didn't want me anymore," was all she managed, and she exploded into despair.

The Madame poured the wine and strolled over to Dot, handing her the glass. "Is this because you like Hardy, or because of your ongoing rivalry with Jasmine?"

Dot sniffed and took the drink from the Madame. "I don't...I don't know...he really was kind to me..."

"Dot, darling, you're taking Hardy. You are also going to work out whatever fucking bullshit is going on between you and Jasmine. Tonight. Is that understood?"

She took a gulp of wine. "Yes, Madame."

"You're also going to make a note that when your next cycle approaches, your conduct will not resemble this past week's, or my promise still stands. Do I make myself clear?"

"I'll fix it. I'm sorry. She just...I work so hard and..."

"We all know Jasmine can be a fucking bitch, Dot," the Madame clarified, moving back around to her spot behind the desk. "Hardy isn't the first client she's stolen. But you're better than acting like a cunt yourself because of it."

A knock came to the door.

"Come in, Marcy!" the Madame bellowed.

Marcy and Paige entered, nervously eyeing Dot as they sat on either side of her.

"Are we ready to discuss tonight?" Paige asked, her gaze on the Madame.

"Dot realizes her actions have been a fucking humiliation to The Palace, and we're moving on," the Madame announced. A small whimper came from Dot, though the other three women pretended not to notice. "Are the reservations prepared?"

"Of course, Madame," Marcy affirmed, taking the wine glass out of Dot's hand and having a sip for herself. "The girls know their assignments and rooms. Dot will be at the bar doing her usual greetings. Hardy is the last appointment of the night."

"Lovely. Paige? The bar is fully stocked?"

27

She smiled. "Glasses are clean. Gambling tables are ready. We are good to go."

"All right. Take Dot and get out of here. Time for real work to start. Let me know when—"

"Madame?"

A different voice came from the doorway. It was Claire, and from the expression she wore, the Madame sensed they needed a moment alone.

"Dismissed, you three, and close the doors when you go," she said to Marcy, Paige, and Dot.

Marcy rose and set the half-full glass of wine on the Madame's desk, and then the girls hastily obliged, leaving the office.

When they were gone, Claire marched directly to the Madame's desk. "I've got a problem." She tossed a piece of paper in front of the Madame, who picked it up to read it. "Son of a bitch has found me."

"I know you're still in New York City. I am coming to get you and bring you home. You can't hide from me any longer."

"How the fuck did this happen?" the Madame pressed, vexed. "I thought Louis made it perfectly damn clear to that bastard that if he came near you, he'd be killed."

"Apparently, it only enticed him further," Claire articulated quietly. "What do you want me to do? Do you want me to leave The Palace? I can disappear, Madame, you know I can."

"Christ, no. I fucking need you, Claire, you're the only one of my girls who has a level head. You're staying put. If he shows up, we'll kill him, as he's been warned."

"I don't want to put anyone in danger," she stated plainly. "He's my brother, and my responsibility to put down if necessary."

The Madame peered directly into Claire's eyes. "Do you want the chance to be the one? After what he's done to you?"

Claire took a shaky breath. "Yes, of course I do. For my parents, for my sisters, and for my own peace of mind."

"I'll give Louis the tip that Marcus may be an issue again. He'll keep an eye out for him." The Madame handed Claire back the note. "Darling, it's going to be fine. We're not going to let him get to you."

"It's not that, Madame."

"What is it, then?"

Claire picked up Dot's wine glass and drained what was left. "The last time I saw him, he was covered in my family's blood. I'm not afraid of him. I'm afraid for him, and what I'll do to him when I finally get the chance."

The Madame smiled ominously at her. "Now, that's my girl."

At three minutes past four, while she basked in the darkness of her office, smoking a cigar, the Madame heard the familiar, gentle creak of one of her windows unlocking and opening. The night had concluded nicely: the last of her customers had just been escorted out, Louis stopped in for a whiskey around two, and Samuel had just gone home after a passionate rendezvous, to get a few hours' sleep following a long night at the precinct. Everyone at The Palace slept, save for her.

They met like this every four to six weeks, never communicating in between, to keep their covers intact. If Croker ever discovered them, the Madame wasn't sure what the outcome might be. But until that moment came, she and Esther would continue reuniting in secret to share information and plot Croker's imminent destruction.

"You're late," the Madame teased, once she spotted Esther's shadow crawling inside. "How does a whiskey sound?"

"Like heaven," Esther answered, lifting her leg in and through the glass, then locking it closed. "You'd think that would get easier as time goes on, but I swear it only gets fucking harder."

The Madame gave her the up and down. "Running around the Points with the Whyos?"

"How can you tell?"

"I can smell Kitty's stench on you from over here," the Madame told her. "I honestly can't fucking believe she thinks men find that captivating."

"I'm not sure captivating is what Kitty goes for," Esther retorted with a grin as she straightened up.

From a distance, even the Madame wouldn't be able to recognize Esther; her hair was kept staggeringly short, her beautiful face tucked under a newsboy's cap to hide any residual femininity, and her now-muscular arms and legs were buried beneath a pair of brown trousers, a brown vest over a white cotton shirt, and men's lace-up leather boots. The scar on her neck from Timothy Adams was prominent on her skin, jagged and deep, like the mark he'd left on all their lives. In the Madame's opinion, she was filthy—in the general New York sense, Esther was cleaner than most. Her existence relied upon her ability to blend into the crowd and not draw anyone's notice; amongst the Whyos, it depended solely on her wiliness and skill. The Madame glimpsed at her knuckles. They held their accustomed bruised shade of blue and purple, with deep, dark gashes to match, and the Madame got to her feet, heading to grab the ointment Marcy made to help Esther's hands heal.

"I hope you left your weapons at home," the Madame stated dryly, seizing the ointment from a side table and making her way over to Esther, who had crossed the room and was preparing them drinks. "Put this on. Marcy concocted it. Should help the bruises."

Esther complied. "My hands needed a break. I've only got a dagger tonight. Not expecting any issues, I hope?"

The Madame picked up her glass of whiskey and motioned for

them both to sit on the loveseat. "None that I'm aware of, though clearly, you've been bashing some bastard's skull in."

"It's been a tough couple of months, Madame," Esther confessed, lowering down beside her and sipping her whiskey. "My... number...has risen, trying to keep things under control. It's getting worse."

"How high has it gotten?"

"Are you sure you really want to know?"

"Darling, please."

"Since our last meeting, it's been five."

The Madame's jaw dropped. "Jesus fucking Christ, Esther!"

"Don't look at me like that," Esther stated dismissively, her body language defensive. "I'm the one who has to fucking kill people."

For the first time in a lot of years, the Madame didn't know what to say. She had a drink and sighed, endeavoring to put her shock aside.

"I'm sorry I overreacted," the Madame whispered.

Esther's head fell. "It's not you. Like I said, it's just been getting worse."

The Madame set her glass aside and took Esther's hands in hers, massaging the ointment in. "Tell me."

"Walsh is the biggest problem. He's got Lyons and Kitty convinced it's he who owns Croker and not vice versa, and I have to admit, Madame, I kind of believe it. Kitty is...infatuated with Walsh, so much so it's disturbing. Lyons worships him, despite holding the position of authority in the gang. Everybody else is getting to the point where they do whatever he tells them to and don't ask questions. He's even been talking about promoting anarchy and rioting against the coppers...like suddenly, there is principle involved. It hasn't stuck yet, most of the Whyos just say he's a loose cannon, but it's only a matter of time before Lyons gets pushed out and the Whyos are Walsh's. Then...I don't know what's going to happen."

"And you were with Kitty tonight?"

"I had to meet her at The Morgue a few hours ago. Walsh and Will were with Croker, and Louis was here, so I had to clean up a bit of a mess."

The Madame had an idea of where this was going, and she rose to retrieve the whiskey bottle for them. "What kind of mess?"

"New bartender was skimming off the top, essentially taking from the Hall and the Whyos. When this shit happens, Whyos aren't allowed to touch anyone if the Hall is involved too, so I had to go and make a fucking point." Esther thanked the Madame as she refilled her glass. "He was the fifth since I saw you last."

The Madame closed her eyes, pained for ever making Esther do this. "That's why your knuckles are so banged up, then."

"Yeah. Try undoing the itty bitty locks on your windows when your hands are swollen," Esther chuckled. "I'm fine. Really. I'm used to this now, and you know that. The ointment is a major help, though. My hands already are feeling better."

"Good," the Madame responded, releasing her. "I heard a bit of information today I wanted to pass your way. Directly from Croker's mouth."

Esther was intrigued. "And?"

The Madame's left eyebrow rose. "Well, it adds fuel to the fire on your Walsh theory. Croker never gave the order for Walsh to kill Edward Turner."

Esther stared at her. "W-w-what?" she stammered. "But he has told everyone he did!"

"He didn't. It's a cover to maintain his position. I think you're right, darling. I doubt he has any real control over Walsh."

"If that's the truth…we are in a lot of fucking trouble…" Esther downed more whiskey. "Have we…heard…anything?"

"As a matter of fact, yes. My contact at White Star wrote a note to me last week. It seems the Turners' have booked passage to return to New York."

Esther tried to mask her excitement. "When?"

"There's a steamer coming in on Friday. They're on it. I have a feeling they want to be here for the Admiral's Ball at the end of the month."

"All of them?"

The Madame knew why she asked. "Unfortunately, no, not Mary, darling. However, Lucy, William, Tony…and Thomas, they'll be here in a matter of days."

Esther didn't move an inch, and the Madame wasn't sure if she ought to address the elephant in the room or stick to business—she found a way to do both.

"Esther, you cannot forget the deal you made with Croker. Your life depends on it. You can't be seen going to Thomas, or any of the Turners, under any circumstance, and you'd better believe Croker will have a tail on Thomas and anyone who frequents their residence."

Her words eased Esther out of her trance. "Right. You're so right. Did you tell Croker this when he was here?"

The Madame sneered. "You must be fucking joking."

This made Esther laugh. "Good. I can't wait to see the look on his face."

"Dare I even ask your thoughts on Thomas being home?"

To the Madame's surprise, Esther by no means shied away from the topic. "I did this…I made my deal with Croker praying, with the small amount of heart I had left, that it would bring Thomas back to me." Esther pulled out a cigarette, lit it, and looked the Madame square in the eyes. "I never stopped loving him. The question is whether or not he can love me when he finds out what I've done… and who I've become."

This was a supremely gratifying moment for the Madame, and she didn't mask it. "Darling, you have earned my utmost respect. I hope you know that."

"I do." Esther smiled at her again. "In the beginning, it was hard. Now…I'm not ashamed of who I am. I did what I did for my own reasons. I don't regret it."

"Never regret, Esther," the Madame directed, enjoying a swig of her whiskey. "I've always taught you that. There are some things I want to share with you that Louis and I discussed earlier this evening. Things you may not be aware of yet, but that I think you need to be aware of."

"Enlighten me."

"It's in regard to Thomas. You are informed he's being trained by the chink back home to become proficient in the way his father was."

"Yes, of course."

"What you don't know is the extent of that training. From what Louis has uncovered from his…contact…Thomas, like you, has become a far different version of himself."

Esther was pensive as she took a drag of her cigarette. "Louis mentioned his master was a warrior in Japan and China."

"That is correct. And—"

In a flash, Esther held up her hand to stop the Madame, her eyes wide and ears listening attentively. She held her finger to her lips, and whispered almost inaudibly, "Someone is here."

Without a sound, Esther got up and placed her whiskey glass on the side table. "Keep talking as if you're talking to me," she murmured under her breath, and like a ghost, Esther evaporated into the darkness.

The Madame coughed aloud. "Sorry, darling! Got something caught in my throat. Now, as I was saying, I think we need to be prepared…"

She wasn't sure what happened; the only thing the Madame could hear was a small scuffle of shoes on the carpet and then the low groan of a man being hit somewhere he doesn't prefer. Suddenly, out of the corner marched Esther, with their intruder's wrists twisted behind him in her left hand and her dagger in her right hand held at his throat. With a swift kick, she knocked the man to his knees, his temple bleeding from where she must have initially struck him. Esther wasn't the slightest bit frazzled; in fact, she almost appeared tickled.

Will and Louis really had impeccably trained her.

The Madame got to her feet. "Jeremiah, what the fuck are you doing listening in on my conversations? Did you come up the back staircase?"

Jeremiah was unnerved. "Madame, please! I swear to God and on my life, I only just walked in! I was trying to determine whether or not it was a…a talk I could interrupt, or whether I should go, and then this…this boy came out of nowhere and…assaulted me!"

Esther sneered. "Boy," she remarked, shaking her head.

Jeremiah's eyes shifted, and when he saw it was indeed a female, an even greater look of horror came to his face.

"I'm sorry! I'm so sorry! Please…I didn't mean any offense. Madame, I was just coming to give you a report on the girls and their health. That's all!"

Jeremiah Hiltmore, Douglas's illegitimate son and Celeste's half-brother, was the new attending physician for the girls at The Palace after the old Doc caught tuberculosis and died a few months prior. While Jeremiah had assisted the Madame in her preliminary efforts against the Hiltmore family years ago, that time had long passed. Through Celeste's careful scheming, Douglas and his son were able to work out the complications of their relationship, and Douglas paid for Jeremiah's education to become a doctor. He was an incredibly gifted young man, and he was great with the girls. The Madame paid him more than she should, but she didn't mind giving Jeremiah extra when only negroes and whores would allow themselves to be seen by a black doctor.

She glanced at Esther. "Let him go."

A wave of relief hit Jeremiah's face as Esther released him.

"Thank you, Madame. I am so…so sorry! Please, if I can make it up to you—"

"You can fucking make it up to me by only coming to my office during normal business hours unless asked otherwise," the Madame declared. "Now, get the hell out of here, Jeremiah, before I goddamn change my mind!"

Not needing to be told twice, Jeremiah scrambled as fast as he could down the back staircase. Esther watched him go, shaking her head.

"He couldn't have run any faster," she giggled, moving toward her previous spot by the Madame.

"Remind me never to piss you off, darling," the Madame remarked. As she sat, her eyes found the clock, and she sighed wearily. "We are out of time. You've got to get the fuck out of here before anyone else notices."

Esther nodded compliantly and, rather than heading to the sofa, she changed direction toward the window. "You can keep that doctor under control, I am assuming?"

"You mean make sure he doesn't tell anyone he got his ass kicked by a girl? I'd say you took care of that one on your own."

"True." With practiced hand, Esther unlocked the Madame's window. "Keep an eye on Celeste," she reminded the Madame as she shifted her legs outside the pane of glass. "I'll keep the Whyo bastards in line as best I can."

"Watch out for Kitty," the Madame advised. "That cunt doesn't like any competition, and you constantly show her ass up."

"I know. Goodnight, Aunt."

The Madame felt a pang of adoration. "Take care of yourself, Esther."

Louis arrived the next evening at The Palace in a much more chipper mood than normal. Per Croker's instructions, the new muscle hire he was sending to the Madame was due to report in, and the Madame wanted to be certain whoever this punk was got put in his place from the start. Louis was there to spend time with him, train him, and see to it the new guy understood the rules of The Palace—or more importantly, the rules upheld by the Madame. Louis ambled into her office with an air of contentment, one he could see the Madame wasn't expecting, and it immediately piqued her interest.

"What the fuck has gotten into you, then?" she greeted him, whiskey in hand.

He went to the drink cart. "My contact confirmed the report you received from White Star. The Turners will be here Friday."

A flood of elation rushed over her. "And just when the hell are you going to tell me who this contact is?"

"You know I can't tell you that."

"Bullshit," she replied, annoyed. "We are supposed to be in this as a team. You are withholding information—"

"Oh, will you sit down and just be happy for once?" Louis interrupted, pouring his own drink. "Thomas is coming home. And I am doing this to protect you and my contact, not as a personal slight against you, for God's sake."

She had a large gulp of whiskey. "Fine," the Madame granted. "Is George going to join us this fucking century, or is he down chasing Claire around again?"

"He'll be up here soon. I told him to wait for our new employee downstairs. What did Croker say about this kid? He never mentioned it to me or to Will…or to Esther, for that matter…"

"Worrisome, isn't it?"

"You could say that again."

"I hate when that bastard gets ideas," the Madame commented. "He's one hell of a politician. But he's too fucking astute. Something isn't right, we can all smell it."

Louis took a swig from his glass. "We're going to find out shortly."

Within minutes, a knock came to the door, and George's voice echoed in the office. "Madame? I am here with the new…recruit."

"Come in!" she ordered, finishing her whiskey and then pouring more.

The doors opened and George walked in, followed closely by a familiar-looking young man wearing a long coat and Pendleton hat. Two guns were holstered on either side of his waist, and a cigarette hung casually out of his mouth. He had a little scruff on his overtly handsome face, and it wasn't until the Madame heard Louis drop his whiskey glass that she started to piece it together.

"Madame," George addressed her, "this here is—"

"Ashleigh Sweeney," the man introduced himself, his Southern accent overwhelming. He strutted directly to the Madame's desk and held out his hand to shake hers. "It's a pleasure to finally meet ya, ma'am."

Unhurriedly, the Madame held out her hand to shake his, though she was completely stunned at what she saw. "Mr. Sweeney, it's good to meet you. You understand why you are here, I assume?"

"Sure do," he replied. "I can promise you, ain' nobody goin' to mess with you long as I'm hangin' 'round. I follow orders better than anybody, long as I'm paid."

"A family trait, I think," the Madame said to herself under her breath. "Wonderful. Mr. Sweeney, this is Louis. He will be showing you the ropes around here. If you are up to par, we will discuss your contract and payment accordingly. Louis?"

Louis hadn't moved an inch. Instead, he gaped at Ashleigh, dumbfounded. Ashleigh, however, politely strode to him and again held out his hand.

"Nice to meet ya, sir. I heard a lot 'bout ya as a boy."

This barely brought Louis to the present. "You're…you're Will's son? You are Will Sweeney's…son?"

"Yes sir," Ashleigh confirmed. "Ma'am, you mind if I pour myself a drink here?"

"You will call me Madame, not ma'am. This isn't the fucking Confederacy. And yes, you help yourself."

Ashleigh grabbed a glass and filled it. "Figured this might come as a bit o' a shock to ya," he directed at Louis. "Dear ol' Daddy was s'pose' to be dead. Found out the hard way he's been hidin' out in New York."

"The hard way?" the Madame asked.

Ashleigh ignored her question. "Mr. Croker recruited me when he heard I was followin' close in Daddy's footsteps. Not sure how, exactly, but a man of his found me down in Texas…big, dark, eerie lookin' fella with glasses. Told me to come to the city and see for myself. So, I did, and now here I am, Madame, workin' for my daddy's boss without him knowin' yet. Strange, innit?"

"Croker ought to have told you that you are contracted to me and not to him from this point onward."

"I got no problem with that," he consented. "Didn' like that man too much. I like to look a man in the eye and know he's tellin' the truth. Croker ain't that sort."

The Madame grinned. "I am glad we agree on that. Well, Mr. Sweeney, if you are anything like your father, I think you've found your next job, but if you fuck up here, you're out. Do I make myself clear?"

"You bet."

"George, take Wi—I apologize. Take Ashleigh downstairs and get him situated. Louis will be right behind you."

George motioned to the door and Ashleigh followed, bowing slightly on the way out. The Madame turned to Louis, who still hadn't moved.

"You didn't know about this, did you?" she asked him.

Louis shook his head. "He's never mentioned anything like that.

He said he was married for a while, but that she was insane and he left. No mention of a…a son…"

"Are we even sure Will knows he has a son?"

"Well, we're going to fucking find out, aren't we?"

"I just have one question," she went on, rising and walking over towards him. "Why would Croker send Walsh to get Ashleigh? Why would he go so far when he knows it will cause internal strife amongst his own damn people?"

They both knew the answer the moment the words left her mouth.

"Croker didn't send Walsh," Louis stated, handing her the whiskey decanter. "Esther was right. We always thought Croker was the puppeteer behind the monster. Turns out, it's the monster pulling the strings."

"He wanted to cause turmoil—to fuck things up."

"Yes, he did. And it's only going to get worse."

The Madame, too, had a drink from the decanter. "Fucking hell."

"What did you do with the body?" Walsh pressed.

Danny Lyons shrugged. "Hudson. He'll wash up, but no one will know who the fuck he was. When she was done, bastard was beyond recognizin'."

The Morgue was empty, closed down for the night, so Walsh, Kitty, and Danny could meet in private without the rest of the gang interfering. When Walsh heard that Esther was ordered to kill the pilfering bartender in front of the rest of the gang, he had to admit that even for her, it was bold. She'd wanted to assert her power and ferocity amongst those who felt she didn't belong, and Walsh understood the Whyo gang well enough to know they could be convinced of anything with the right amount of violence and rhetoric. Most were imbeciles, begging to follow command as long as they got to rape, murder, and thieve as they wished. Their induction was meant to wean out the weak ones—only those who had killed were allowed to be a Whyo, and it had earned them an odd collection of the worst sort of men…and women. Walsh had become a god amongst them, but with the Hall funding their operations and Esther a part of their every move, he was beginning to grow tired of waiting.

Waiting for the castle to crumble.

"I've got a new guy who wants the job," Kitty told him. "He saw what happened last night, so he knows what'll happen to him if he tries to cheat us."

"Is he one of us?" Walsh asked her.

Kitty glanced at him nervously. "Not…not officially…"

Walsh gave her a look that made her noticeably cringe. "For shame, Kitty. He's got to pass induction, or he's out. This has been a rule since the start." He sighed, annoyed. "You disappoint me."

"It's not her fault." Danny interjected, coming to Kitty's aid. "I suggested him. He was an old buddy of Driscoll's. He'll do the induction. Just tell him who."

Walsh stared at the two of them, disgusted. They were pitiful excuses for human beings, each desiring nothing more than to impress him because they were scared of him. *They should be.* He'd wanted so many times to kill them both, to strangle the life out of them and watch them die with pleasure, but he couldn't. *Not yet.* He needed them because he needed the gang. *They'll die too.* Gradually, he'd climbed the ladder, biding his time—he'd joined Croker years ago, knowing that if he could persist, eventually he could dispose of that deplorable ass as well. *Soon.* Croker thought he had a hold on Walsh, but the reality was becoming more and more obvious to those around them, and Walsh was thoroughly enjoying it. *Pathetic bastard.* His plan was coming to fruition…a plan he'd made even before he joined Croker, though Walsh had to admit torturing the Madame for a few years had been entertaining for him. *Arrogant whore.*

41

He smiled. He would kill her too one day in the near future, and it would be an utter delight. *Then they'll know they can't escape.*

"Bring him to me," Walsh said. "I'll oversee his induction."

Danny nodded obediently, his face pale.

"What do we do about the bitch?" Kitty brought up next. "Having her around is like having that fucking politician laugh in our face."

"Yeah," Danny agreed quickly. "A lotta the boys are even afraid of her. This gang ain't about the high-class pricks—it's about us livin' our own lives the way we want."

Walsh couldn't argue. "I agree we need to get rid of Esther. But you need to leave that to me. Whenever you two try to handle things on your own, you make a fucking mess, and I'm tired of cleaning it up."

"I can do it," Kitty asserted. "She's not that tough."

"She would beat the life out of you without breaking a sweat," Walsh remarked coldly. "I said I will handle it. This is a part of the plan, and if either of you wants to challenge me, be my guest."

I dare you.

Neither Kitty nor Danny spoke a word, and Walsh went on, "Good. Danny, you will bring your prospect to me tomorrow, and we'll find out if he's Whyo material."

Understanding this was meant as a dismissal, Danny got up and left The Morgue.

When the door slammed shut behind him, Kitty got up and went to the bar to pour herself more whiskey. "Have you reconsidered my offer?" she baited him flirtatiously.

"I expected you to leave with him."

Kitty snorted. "Men all have the same needs. You aren't any different." She moved coyly back over to him and sat in his lap, stroking his inner thighs. "I promise I'll do whatever you like. Let me."

I'd rather watch the life slip from your eyes.

42

"You will get off of me. Now!" he roared, and Kitty jumped to her feet, her whiskey falling to the ground.

"I…I wasn't…" she mumbled, her body shaking. "I only just… just…"

He glowered at her, then an idea struck him. Perceiving this as an opportunity for a little fun, Walsh's countenance transformed from one of irascibility to menace.

"No…please…"

"Shh…you said you would do whatever I liked," he mocked her. "Come here."

Her trembling increased as she inched in his direction. Walsh patted his lap, indicating for her to sit back down, which she did timidly. She knew there was no other option.

"P-p-please…"

Walsh grasped his left sleeve and shoved it up past his elbow, revealing his deeply scarred arm. "What did I tell you before?"

Tears were forming in her eyes, and her bottom lip began to tremble. "You…you s-s-said that if I asked again…you would… you would cut me as badly as…as you were…I'm sorry I didn't…I didn't…"

He pulled his sleeve back down; immediately, Walsh had the blade at her jugular, his right hand clutching a chunk of her hair to hold her steady. "If you ask me again, I won't just hurt you. I'll cut your throat, and I'll thoroughly enjoy it. Now, hold out your arm."

Kitty wept, her tiny sobs causing the blade to faintly nick her neck. "Please…" she begged, but then, seeing he wouldn't relent, Kitty held up her arm and closed her eyes.

She screamed as he gave her two long cuts on the top of her forearm, enough to cause searing pain, but not deep enough to cause her to bleed to death.

"For the two times you've asked," he declared when he was done, and then tossed her onto the ground. Wiping the blade on his thigh, he sheathed it and strode over toward the door.

Kitty cried on the floor in a heap of pain. "I just wanted you to…to…how c-c-could you hurt me for just…just…"

"You've forgotten, Kitty," he called back cruelly. "I can hurt you because I don't give a damn about you, and because I don't feel."

Walsh turned to leave when another thought struck him. Sure, he found Kitty's sexual advances pathetic—repulsive even—but like everyone at his disposal, she was a tool who could be used to his advantage. There was only one person standing in his way of owning the Whyos, one person who held the loyalty of the gang over him, and that was Danny Lyons. If he could ruin whatever relationship Kitty and Danny currently had by fucking her, it was well worth the few minutes out of his day, regardless of how distasteful he found it.

Locking the door, he spun around and strode back to her, kneeling on the ground as he pulled a handkerchief out of his back pocket. Wordlessly, he cleaned up the deep cuts he'd only just created with great care, as if this was some kind of olive branch or apology. Kitty watched, stupefied to a degree that couldn't warrant any reaction other than compliance. When he'd gotten the bleeding to calm, Walsh pulled the dagger once more, causing Kitty to leap out of his clutches, but he instantly held up a hand and gestured for her to be still, and she did so reluctantly. Cutting the bottom of his pant leg, he sliced away two pieces of cloth and then again put the dagger away. He moved to her and wrapped both of Kitty's cuts, her tears drying in the process.

It embarrasses me how easy you are.

When he was done, she stared at Walsh for a few seconds, and finally whispered, "Thank you."

It was the only invitation he needed. Immediately, Walsh kissed her furiously, and Kitty returned his eagerness, wrapping herself around him as he lifted her from the floor and set her up on the bar.

He tore her clothes off of her body and she did the same, and within seconds they were stripped bare. Kitty reached down to stroke him, yet there was no reason to—he was more than ready. Without warning, he flipped her over and entered her, not wanting to look at her while he finished.

He didn't get off on her, or the memory of any woman before her. He didn't get off on the domination, or even the desire of wanting a fuck, though it occurred to him it had been awhile, and he thrusted harder, not sure if her cries were from pleasure or pain. He got off on the notion that, bit by bit, he was drawing nearer to his checkmate.

One by one, you're all going to die.

CHAPTER XXXI.

It was a humid and rainy May day, and Athena was none too pleased to once again be cooped up indoors. Thomas's attempts to subdue her with food were not going as he wished, and he honestly couldn't blame her for being irritated with him. She was kept hooded for much of their journey across the Atlantic, and Thomas only let her fly from the railing of the steam ship onto his arm on a handful of occasions; moreover, and much to Athena's dismay, Thomas refused to let her off her leash, and she'd showed her annoyance with threatening snaps of her beak. After arriving in New York City, he'd hoped to let her fly as soon as possible; instead, the relentless pouring rain kept them trapped inside the house, making Athena antsy while William, intimidated by the bird's rowdiness, refused to go into Thomas's study, where she and Thomas spent the majority of the daylight hours.

Thomas held out a small sliver of dried dove breast to her, and Athena snatched it greedily, causing him to smile.

"The moment these spring storms stop, I'll get you out," he promised her, leaving Athena on her perch for a bit of privacy while consuming her meal.

Only three days ago, William, Lucy, Tony, and Thomas landed in New York, and they were settling into the new house Thomas bought on Fifth Avenue, just a few blocks south from where William and Lucy's old mansion had once been. Thankfully, their journey was uneventful and short-lived, and Thomas struggled to hide his readiness to be home. Those nights on the ship when Thomas found he couldn't sleep, he continuously worked his muscles to stay strong, running through various exercises Hiro taught him over the years.

Tony, too, shared Thomas's enthusiasm to be in the city, and when the pair of them were restless, they chose to seek isolation and repeatedly go over their objectives and strategy. Tony's brother, who ostensibly was his contact in the underbelly of New York, had written multiple letters to discuss a meet point once the Turners were settled in, so that Thomas could begin his work. William and Lucy weren't clueless to the changes Thomas had undergone at Amberleigh, but they didn't push him to divulge what it was he was hiding. Thomas was convinced they either thought he had slightly lost his mind, or that he was following in his father's footsteps, with Edward's previous missions as a for-hire vigilante. Either way, he couldn't keep the truth from them forever, and he planned on telling them everything when the timing was right.

Just as Thomas sat down at his desk, Tony knocked and entered, taking a slight bow. "Are you needing anything for lunch, Lord Turner?"

"Not just yet, Tony, thank you," Thomas replied, flipping through the more recent numbers for Turner S & D. "How is everything going with hiring the staff?"

"I am trying to find the most discreet people I can," Tony assured him, walking a few paces into the room. "There's actually a woman I am considering hiring who used to work for the Hiltmore family. Shannon is her family name. She claimed she knew you when you were young."

Thomas instantly forgot about work and peered up at Tony. "Black dress, hair in a tight bun?"

"That would be her, Lord Turner."

A familiar sense of nostalgia hit Thomas. "Hire her, Tony," he directed, "and ask her who she might recommend for the household workforce. Even the kitchen. She runs a tight ship and doesn't tolerate any bullshit, and that's exactly what we need. I don't want rumors flying around about my...recreational activities..." Thomas paused for a few seconds, chuckling. "That old broad used to take care of Esther when she was young. I think I'm just surprised she's still alive. How did she look?"

Tony thought on it. "In good health, sir. I doubt she could keep up with you, but she seems to have more than enough energy to handle the job."

"Perfect. And you're set to meet your brother tomorrow?"

"Yes, sir. We are meeting in the early afternoon. Is there a particular excuse you would like me to use for Mr. and Mrs. Turner's benefit?"

"Whatever you'd like, Tony," Thomas said. "Just make sure it's not overtly dodgy. Can you grab William on your way to the kitchen and tell him to meet me in the study?"

"Lord Turner, you know William is not going to be pleased—"

"For Christ's sake. It's just a bird! I don't see what the goddamn problem is. Tell him to get his ass in here, all right?"

Tony suppressed an entertained grin. "Of course, sir. Right away."

When Tony was gone, Thomas glanced over toward Athena, who appeared to be taking a nice snooze on her perch in the aftermath of her meal. He couldn't wait to get out of the house and fly her; more importantly, he couldn't wait to finally start the real job he'd truly been training for. The last four years of his life were spent with three distinct goals: to become indestructible, to become lethal, and to become invisible. Through copious amounts of blood and sweat, Thomas made himself all three of those things—he was a greater fighter than his father, more perceptive and cleverer than Hiroaki, and deadlier than the best sharpshooters in the world with his Griswold. What's more, he had Athena. Her coaching was a consistent uphill battle, until one day, nearly a year after finding her, their minds synced and became one. Since that day, Athena was Thomas's primary ally, and with Hiroaki's help, the peregrine had blossomed into a brilliant hunter, both on her own and at Thomas's side.

Thomas got up from his desk and went over to pour himself a drink. There was so much road that lay ahead, and a challenging one at that. He'd chosen to take on the destruction of one of New York City's most powerful organizations, and on the top of his list was their leader, Richard Croker—a man who imprisoned and tortured his mother, killed his father, and destroyed the life of the woman he loved. Croker had ruled over the Madame and Louis for far too long, bullying them into submission and killing innocent people in the process of his rise to power. No one could stand up to him. No one could stop him.

No one except Thomas.

In the distance, Thomas noted William's familiar trundle of footsteps down the hall, and poured a whiskey for his cousin as well. Without fail, William came barreling through the door, waking Athena and sending her into a fit of shrieks.

"Jesus Christ!" William bellowed, hands covering his ears as Athena bated hard and screamed in protest to her interrupted slumber. William stayed in the doorway. "You bloody see why I don't come in here?!" he yelled.

"Relax, William," Thomas pleaded calmly, striding over to Athena and hooding her. Within seconds, her squawking came to an end, and Thomas turned back to William. "You really wonder why she doesn't like you? You might as well have kicked the door down."

"No, it's because she's a bloody menace, that's why," William retorted, removing his hands from his head. "Why didn't you leave her at Amberleigh with Hiro?"

Thomas rolled his eyes. "We've already had this talk, William." Moving again to the cart, he grabbed their drinks and handed William his before returning to his chair. "Sit down. I've got some things to discuss with you."

Though reluctant, William did as he was told and took the chair opposite Thomas's desk. "What is it we need to go over?"

Thomas had a sip of his drink. "I want you to come back on at Turner S & D as a consultant advisor. And resume your post as the head of the board."

The room went silent.

"You...you want me to...to what?"

"You know the American market better than anyone," Thomas carried on, "and now that we are in New York City, I think having you back would only be a positive addition to the team."

"Thomas, Bernard is the head of the board. What do you think he's going to say when you fire him?"

"Don't be ridiculous, William. I am not firing Bernard. I am giving him a raise and sending him to San Francisco to expand Turner S & D even further."

William's eyes grew so wide, Thomas thought they might pop out of his head. "When did...did...how did you...?"

"Bernard's son is already there. I can decipher from his letters he is itching to go now that his wife has passed, so I will send him out to commence distribution negotiations. Shouldn't be too difficult or too risky, with the native population more docile nowadays."

"And I'll be the head of the board?"

"Yes."

William downed his whiskey. "I suppose I have been a little idle as of late..."

Thomas beamed. "I'm so happy you're in agreement! Lucy and I both thought it would be a good change for you."

"Lucy?! She knows about this?"

"William, Lucy is nosier than any person I've ever met. When I mentioned moving Bernard to California, she was the one that suggested you might want your old position back."

Though he couldn't hear William's words, Thomas was quite certain he was cursing his wife under his breath.

"When are you planning to tell Bernard?"

"Tomorrow evening. We've been invited over to his home for dinner. I have an inclination it will be welcome news."

Before William could respond, another knock came at Thomas's study door, catching him off guard.

"Come in, Tony!" Thomas called.

The butler entered and bowed. "Lord Turner, there is a detective here to see you. Detective Ellis."

Confused, Thomas got to his feet. "That's a little strange. Did he mention why?"

"No, sir, but I've left him upstairs in the library. Should I tell him you are unavailable?"

Thomas looked to William and shrugged. "No, that's fine, Tony. Tell him I'll be right up."

Tony took his leave.

"You already have a detective here to see you?" William asked, teasing. "We've only been here three days and already you're causing a ruckus."

Thomas, on the other hand, was skeptical. "Can we finish this later, William?"

"There's nothing to finish," William remarked, standing and holding out his hand. "I'll take the job."

Thomas grasped his hand and shook it. "Thank you, William. We'll hammer out the details later. Make sure you tell Lucy about dinner tomorrow, and also to go buy herself a new dress. On me, of course."

Detective Ellis was sitting in the great room, appearing extremely edgy and apprehensive as Thomas strode in. While he'd noticeably aged, Samuel Ellis was still one of the most handsome men Thomas had ever met, even if the city's hardships these last few years had markedly taken a toll, as was evident from the crow's feet around his eyes.

This, however, was not a social visit. Thomas could sense from the moment he walked into the room that much had changed since their last encounter at The Morgue, where Samuel labored to keep Thomas in one piece upon viewing his father's mangled corpse. There was no warmth—only agitation and nervousness, like perhaps he was being watched. What was unsettling to Thomas was the inkling that perhaps the Madame hadn't sent Ellis this time. Not once since their initial meeting fourteen years ago had the detective ever seemed so manic in his presence, and Thomas suspected he was about to find out why.

"Detective," Thomas welcomed him, stretching out his hand to greet Samuel, "it's such a pleasure to see you alive and well."

Ellis gaped at Thomas for a few seconds, and then remembered his manners and shook Thomas's hand. "Forgive my manner, Lord Turner, you...your appearance...it just startled me how...how..."

"Much I've grown up?" Thomas suggested.

It was true. Thomas's figure, above anything else, was much different than it had once been. His already broad shoulders were thick with muscles, and his arms, legs, and chest sinewy and strong; this just happened to be in addition to the last two inches he'd grown in his later twenties. His countenance donned a tougher furrow in his brow that left no remnants of youthful adolescence, and his air and character were far altered from the man Samuel Ellis had seen last.

Thomas fought off a smirk when the detective persisted in silence. "What is it I can do for you, Samuel? I would say come in and have a whiskey, but I doubt from your…readiness…that this is a social call. Is anything the matter?"

Samuel cleared his throat. "I wanted to drop in and give you my best. And also, if you don't mind, ask what has brought about your return to New York? I assumed, when you left us five summers ago, you wouldn't be back."

"You mean after my father was murdered and I took his body home to England?"

The detective's face went white. "Your father was killed in an accident, Thomas."

"Of course he was," Thomas agreed contemptuously. "But before I answer your question, might I inquire as to who is standing on my stoop?"

"His name is Detective Murphy. He's been my partner the last two years."

"And he didn't want to come inside with you and introduce himself?"

Ellis's eyes indicated he was about to lie. "I requested to have this meeting alone, you being an old friend and all."

"I see." Thomas motioned to the leather armchairs a few feet away, and they went over to sit down. "So, you wish to know why I've returned," Thomas carried on as Tony miraculously emerged with a cold whiskey for both of them and then speedily disappeared. "Business beckons, my dear detective. I am planning on expanding westward, and now that I have a trustworthy man in London, I can be here and send another trustworthy man from New York to San Francisco."

"Meaning you will be here for some time, then?"

Thomas had a gulp of his drink. "There are a lot of untied ends in New York I need to take care of, in regard to my company and otherwise."

"Well, I am happy to hear the company is doing so well, Lord Turner."

54

"Detective, please. Call me Thomas. How is the Madame?"

Samuel at last had some of his whiskey. "She's…well…her. The Palace is flourishing, and her connections are better than ever."

"And you two are still seeing each other?"

Ellis's cheeks went from white to red. "We have our…understanding…yes."

Thomas smiled. "I am sincerely very happy to hear that."

Ellis sat his glass down and stared into Thomas's eyes. "What are you really doing here, Thomas? Why are you doing this to yourself, when you have a life and a home in England? There's nothing left here for you but misery."

"On the contrary, Samuel, this is my home. There is more here for me than you realize."

"I just don't…"

"Don't what?" Thomas beseeched him.

Samuel sighed heavily. "The Madame doesn't tell me everything, but I am aware of certain developments when it comes to your… motives…" Hastily, Ellis glimpsed outside to Detective Murphy on the stoop, who was occupied with his cigarette, and then back to Thomas. "That man outside was appointed to keep an eye on me. We are all being watched and bullied like goddamn sheep, and the Madame is in the worst of it. I know you know the truth, so listen to me. He's Grand Sachem now. He runs this whole fucking city. I hope you understand just what sort of war you're taking on." Samuel stopped to take a big breath. "She's been waiting for this for so long, and if you're everything she says you are, you might really have a shot at vengeance. For both of you. She doesn't have that power, but you do."

Thomas finished his whiskey. "Why are you telling me this, Samuel?"

Ellis picked up his glass and did the same, his voice now in a whisper, "Because I want you to know I've got your fucking back. I'm on your side. There's some scary shit happening in our city, Thomas, and sadly, our worries go beyond…him."

"What do you mean, 'beyond him'?"

Ellis's jumpiness flooded in again. "Look, just be careful. I've got to get going." The detective got to his feet. "Thank you for the whiskey, Lord Turner."

Thomas rose and pulled Samuel in for a hug. "Tell her to come see me," he uttered softly.

"When?"

"Tomorrow night, late, when she can get out unseen."

Ellis released him and took his leave, and Thomas watched as he ushered along Detective Murphy, who looked far too unseemly to be a man of the law. Murphy rotated around and regarded the mansion with scrutiny, then proceeded to follow in Samuel's wake.

Detective Ellis's visit had been quite unexpected, leaving Thomas both enthralled and contemplative. His excitement stemmed from the realization that there were more on his side than he initially suspected; nonetheless, what engrossed his thoughts more than anything else was Samuel's declaration that Richard Croker wasn't their biggest problem.

Thomas recognized that there must be a big piece of the riddle he, Hiroaki, and Tony missed, and he needed to find out what it was sooner rather than later.

The rain ceased just after tea time, and Thomas found he was unable to shake off his earlier encounter with Detective Ellis as well as the notion that tomorrow evening he would reunite with the Madame. He paced back and forth in his study, and before long, could no longer stand being locked between the walls of his new home. Athena, sensing his restlessness, started to stir on her perch—she, too, wanted nothing more than to escape their confined environment and stretch her wings. Needing fresh air desperately, Thomas grabbed for his glove, Athena's leash and jesses, a few scraps of hen breast, and at last, the peregrine herself, then made his way outside. Lucy and William had gone out for lunch and to explore the new additions to their neighborhood in the city, and Tony would still be interviewing potential employees in the servants' quarters of the house. Thomas was free to escape with Athena to the northern part of Central Park, where there would be fewer people and more open country for his falcon to hunt.

There were lots of stares as he marched across the street with Athena on his arm, though most were filled with fascination and awe at such a beautiful bird. Falconry was by no means a foreign concept to the upper class, particularly during the spring months in the country, but he doubted many people on the Upper East Side of Manhattan had ever witnessed a man fly his hunter in Central Park. Rather than staying on the gravel path on the edge of the road, Thomas ventured straight into the park, hoping to expose Athena to her new atmosphere of city life in a piecemeal fashion and not utterly terrify her. On several occasions, she had traveled with Thomas to London prior to their New York departure; he'd done this to break her into the overpowering noise and distractions of city life. Having Central Park so near to his home would be a blessing for the peregrine; Athena was a hard judge of character who certainly wasn't shy of picking favorites, and if she intuited fear in an admirer, she immediately displayed her dislike.

Once they were amongst the trees, Thomas and Athena were alone, most likely as a consequence of the overly rainy morning. The ground was wet and soft under Thomas's boots, and every few minutes, he and Athena were sprayed with a light shower of water from the tree branches overhead; neither of them minded. In England, the pair had endured harsh weather and rapid change in the skies for years. A little water was nothing, and gratefully, the sun was be-

57

ginning to peek out from behind the grey sky. It would be a beautiful afternoon, one great for flying, and Thomas was certain Athena
would pinpoint and strike her prey fast.

It took them some time to complete their hike north, yet when
they arrived, Thomas couldn't spot another soul over the great expanse of open land laying beneath his feet. A few trees were scattered about, and Thomas carefully took a few minutes to scout for
other birds of prey. In the two circumstances, other wild raptors had
found Athena and tried to eat her; she had out-flown them and, as a
result, made them her meal instead. However, those instances deeply frightened Thomas—Athena was only so tough, and the thought
of losing her in such a way made chills run down his arms. He'd become painstakingly wary wherever they flew, monitoring the skies
constantly and walking the grounds of their hunts two or three times
before any pursuit. This particular ground in Central Park, he'd discovered a day after their arrival, at first believing they might have to
leave the city for her to hunt in her natural climate.

He'd only had to look outside his front windows to realize that
wouldn't be the case.

Athena let out a small purr of anticipation, her talons readily
loosening their grip on Thomas's glove hand. With a grin, Thomas gave a consenting hum and untied her jesses. Patiently, Athena
waited until she was loose, and with Thomas's signal, she took off in
a flash. Up, higher and higher into the sky she crept, and then shot
down between the trees, stretching her resilient wings after weeks of
stagnation. Thomas observed her, eternally amazed at her graceful
abilities and stamina as the falcon proved over and over to be the
fastest creature on earth.

Suddenly, Thomas's senses perked up. Approaching from his left,
perhaps fifty yards away, was a man in a long jacket headed straight
for him. He could tell in the way the man carried himself that he
had abilities, in a similar category to Thomas's. As the man drew

near, Thomas suspected he was used to sneaking up on others, and a few years ago, Thomas would not have known anyone was near until the man was right beside him. Not wanting to indicate to this stranger that he was aware of his advancement, Thomas continued to focus on Athena and pretended to be consumed by his falcon.

Not a minute later, the man halted a few feet from Thomas.

"She's a swift little girl," he remarked. "Reckon you've only had her a few years?"

Thomas whipped around, feigning shock at the stranger's emergence. "Why, yes! We've had four years together. Are you a falconer yourself?"

Thomas, while masked in politeness, instantly sized up the man, someone he was sure he'd never met before. He was tall, though not much above average, and stood with an intimidating confidence that undoubtedly scared off men of softer dispositions. There were two guns holstered on either side of his hips, and he showed no shame in their exposure as his jacket whipped out behind him. He spat tobacco on the ground and smiled, a dashing smile, making Thomas believe that early in his life, this man must have had no issue with winning over women. Unfortunately, he was deeply scarred on his face, from what weapon Thomas couldn't ascertain, and he stood in a way that communicated he was not to be trifled with. This man had fought numerous battles throughout his life, killed many without regret, and now presented himself to Thomas in the open with no intention of hurting him or a challenge. He was, apparently, just there to talk.

"When I was a youngin', I would train red tails," the man told him, as if Thomas were an old friend.

Wanting to extend the conversation without worrying over Athena, Thomas signaled her, and she quickly dove and resumed her post on his arm.

"My name is Thomas Turner," Thomas introduced himself,

holding his left hand out to shake in salutation. "Who are you, my good sir?"

"Ya mean Lord Turner, I'm sure," the man corrected him, and bowed rather than shook Thomas's hand. "Name is Will Sweeney. It's an honor to meet ya, Tommy."

His gaze narrowed. "Pardon my asking, but how is it you know me, Mr. Sweeney? Only those who are my closest friends or family ever call me Tommy."

Will's clever smile faded, and instead he became strangely melancholic. "I shouldn't be here," he remarked quietly, considering turning to go.

"Wait!" Thomas retracted, realizing who this man was, and Will hesitated. "You're...you're Louis's old friend, aren't you? The Cat?"

"That's correct," he admitted. "I'm the one he's been partnered with. Ya know, with Croker and all."

"I see." Thomas peered at Athena, itching to go for the hunt, and he obliged, releasing her to scour for prey. "So, tell me, did Louis send you?"

"Actually, brother, he has no damn idea I am here, and I'd really like to keep it that way, if ya don' mind."

"Sure," Thomas consented, watching Athena out of the corner of his eye as she stalked from overhead. "Can I ask you why it is you sought me out?"

Will spat tobacco on the ground and moved nearer to Thomas. "I came here to...well...fill ya in on the shit storm we are findin' ourselves in. I saw the detective stop by your place earlier. He's a good man. Trapped, like we all is."

"He elaborated on that," Thomas disclosed. "You're obviously here for a similar reason, I presume. To advise me to be careful, to see with your own eyes if Louis's account of who I am is correct, and to warn me about how there are bigger problems than Richard Croker."

"So...ya haven' heard the account of the lunatic yet, brother?"

"Lunatic?"

Athena dived into the field and caught whatever it was she'd been shadowing. Motioning for Will to come with him, Thomas set out in her direction.

"I'm here for the lunatic. The lunatic who killed my father, incarcerated my mother, and...and...well..."

Will kept an even tempo with Thomas. "Well what?"

"Esther's gone," Thomas mentioned, trying to hide the fact that he knew she was still alive somewhere, "and Croker is at fault."

"Look here, Tommy," Will pronounced, "I know ya want to send Croker to his grave. Ya might have to get in line for that one. But the more ya start barkin' up this tree, the closer you're gonna get to Walsh, and ya need to be aware of just who this son of a bitch is."

They came upon Athena, who was thoroughly enjoying a meal of pigeon.

"Walsh?" Thomas queried. "Who is he?"

Will looked from left to right, and spoke so that Thomas could barely hear him. "He's a fuckin' psychopath. He's the one been torturin' the Madame for years, scarin' the shit out of anyone who won' support Tammany when Croker asks, always spyin' on us to make sure we're...cooperatin'. Worst part of it is, he's the leader of the goddamn Whyos in the Bowery." He let out an ironic chuckle. "Fuck if I know how that happened."

"Why are you telling me about him?"

Despite being an inch or two shorter than Thomas, Will stepped forward and grabbed his shoulders to make a point. "'Cause he's the one that even she..." He paused, and very hurriedly, Will recanted and cleared his throat. "Sorry. He's the one that even we...me and Louis...is 'fraid of. Bastard has some kinda sickness...it's like he can' feel pain or any of that shit. That's at least what the rumors are...can' feel anythin'. Enjoys torturin' folks and don' mind killin'."

"Neither you nor Louis have minded killing," Thomas emphasized. "What makes this guy so special? A high pain tolerance?"

Will glared humorlessly at Thomas. "Croker ain' got any fuckin' control over him, Tommy. He pretends he does, but he ain'. Walsh does what he wants, and it's only a matter of time 'fore he turns on the Hall. He's a fuckin' wild dog, and I just wanted ya to know what sort of man you'd have to be dealin' with, is all."

Athena let out a small squawk to indicate she was finished. Thomas squatted down, lowering his arm for her to hop back on, and he tied her jesses.

"A man who doesn't feel pain, and who Richard Croker can't control." This was new. "You sure we can't get him on our side?"

There was no humor in Will's face. "Walsh don' got no side," he asserted harshly. "Maybe I ain' made myself clear enough here, brother, but this man is a demon of hell. He likes watchin' the world burn, and he don' give a fuck who he hurts. Worst yet, he has a special kind of fascination with your dear old Madame. Not an army in the world could protect her from that bastard, ya understand? He's a fuckin' ghost. He's everywhere and nowhere at the same time. And he hasn' screwed up yet."

Thomas became grave, finally allowing the reality of what one of the best hitmen in the world was trying to tell him.

"Well...shit." With Athena secured, he rose to his feet. "I get it. You don't want me to be blindsided, and I cannot tell you how much I appreciate you confiding this in me..." His voice trailed off as his thoughts raced. "This must have been what Samuel was referring to this morning."

"Detective Ellis? Yeah, that poor bastard is stuck with Richie's goon on his tail all day long. Can' imagine that's any fun."

"Ah, so the other Detective was one of Croker's, then?"

Will managed a small smirk. "Figured that one out, did ya?"

"Doesn't take a professional to spot someone who is as out of place as that man was," Thomas replied. "So, how does this end, Will? We pretend we never met around the others?"

"Others?"

Thomas scoffed. "Don't play fucking dumb with me. You, Samuel, the Madame, Louis…I know what the hell this is," he professed. "Everyone is in position, ready to strike. Now I'm here to get this thing rolling, and you better believe we'll be fighting side by side soon enough." Thomas let out a heavy exhale. "A lot of us are going to die doing this, Will. You know that, right?"

"I know," he concurred candidly. "I honestly couldn' give a damn. Been ready to die a long ass time, brother."

"Good." Thomas commenced walking back toward the tree line, and Will followed. "I fly her every day or two. When you want to talk, just come find me out here. How's that?"

"That'll do," Will confirmed. "Lord Turner, it's nice to finally meet ya."

"Tommy, Will. Call me Tommy."

Will grinned and took a small bow. "Ya wanna know what's so funny 'bout this?"

"What's that?" Thomas pressed.

"We got this ragtag group o' miscreants runnin' around this city, all walks o' life. And it's all her doin'."

"All walks of life? What do you mean?"

He chuckled. "She's even got Miss Hiltmore workin' things from Esther's old angle. Ya know, spyin' on them rich pricks like yourself."

"Celeste?" Thomas was completely surprised. "That's just not possible. You must be mistaken."

"Nah, it's true, Tommy. You'll believe it when ya see it. When she lost Esther, that girl took it to heart, and has become a fiend of her own. You'll see." Will took another small bow and spun around. "Until next time, Tommy!"

As he watched Will go, Thomas too initiated his slow trudge home with Athena, the day's revelations mounting higher and higher with the passing hours. A visit from Detective Ellis, a close encounter with Louis's longtime partner in crime, a new thug to worry over, and the strange idea that Celeste Hiltmore was possibly following in

Esther's footsteps. It was an excessive amount of new information for Thomas and Tony to add into their equation, though aside from the surfacing of this man named Walsh, most of the news worked well in his favor. He noted the fear in Will's words as he spoke of Walsh and what he was capable of; still, for Thomas, until he came to this challenge face to face, he wouldn't let rumors pollute his conviction. Assurances from Will aside, Thomas alone was aware of his strength. Will, Detective Ellis, and the others would find out in due course.

Halfway home, Thomas felt something tinge the back of his neck. Turning to stroke Athena in a practiced motion, he was able to move his head just enough to spot what appeared to be a young man tailing him with a newsboy's cap tucked neatly over his head, just enough to cover his eyes. Now conscious of yet another visitor, Thomas kept an eye on his pursuer, making sure to keep his pace steady and not lose whoever this man might be. Whoever this new-comer was, he easily kept up with Thomas, and on approach to his residence, Thomas hoped that after much practice, Tony would be ready to follow through on one of the dozens of protocols they prac-ticed in England.

Taking his time up the stoop, Thomas started to loudly whis-tle the call sign, and as he reached the front door and opened it, he was ecstatic to witness Tony rushing to meet him.

"Got her," he assured Thomas, a glove ready on his right arm as he hastily untied Athena's jesses. "What have we got?"

"Trailer," Thomas whispered, closing the door and peeking out the adjacent window once Athena hopped onto Tony's arm without complaint. "I'm going in pursuit. Do we have my camouflage ready?"

To his left, Tony opened a closet door in the entryway with his left hand and pulled out a plain white cotton shirt, the Griswold, and bowler hat. "Ready."

Thomas tore off his jacket, tunic, and cravat, and pulled the cotton shirt over his head. The Griswold he stuffed into the hidden

holster already fashioned into the side of his trousers, and speedily, he slicked his hair under the bowler hat and moved back to the
window, canvassing the street. His pursuer was only just making his
move to leave the premises, giving Thomas the perfect opportunity
to turn the tables on him.

"Get Athena to my study," he told Tony, opening the front door
ever so slightly. "She should sleep soundly for the rest of the night.
And if anyone asks—"

"You're out for a stroll with a young lady you met," Tony affirmed. "Make sure you don't compromise your distance."

"I won't."

Thomas slipped out the front door and snaked down the stoop,
the anonymous figure heading south at a healthy stride. Diligent in
his chase, Thomas struggled but managed to trail the young man for
an exhaustive forty blocks, staying far enough behind not to catch
attention, though close enough not to lose him. A half an hour later, when they reached Fourteenth Street, the man took a hard left.
Thomas did the same and, upon getting his bearings, realized the
man was, in all probability, headed for Tammany Hall. As he turned
the corner onto Fourteenth, however, Thomas was astonished to
find the man had disappeared from the roadway. He raced ahead,
his gaze scanning to and fro, searching for any sign of the spy without a clue as to where he might have gone. Thankfully, just prior to
reaching Fourth Avenue and about to give up hope, Thomas halted in his tracks, hearing a muffled noise down an alleyway on his
left. Trotting over and peeking around the brick corner, Thomas's
breath caught in his chest.

His pursuer rested alone, back against the same building Thomas was also leaning upon, squatting down on the ground about thirty
feet from him. Eyes straight ahead, his once-stalker had no inclination of Thomas's presence, and she sobbed softly with her newsboy's cap in a heap on the ground next to her, wiping her eyes with

her hands. Her tears were not out of sorrow or grief—there was an odd smile on her face, indicating some kind of happiness, and she wept openly, shaking her head as if in disbelief.

Eyes wide, Thomas gulped down a lump forming in his own throat, the scene utterly crushing him: her black hair was cut short like a boy's, and her figure was much different than the one Thomas remembered from years ago. She was more beautiful than he remembered, her green eyes still sparkling, and she wore a nasty scar that extended from her jawline to below her cotton shirt. To anyone other than Thomas, Esther would be unrecognizable, but that did not apply to him.

His stomach knotted mercilessly with guilt.

Thomas observed her for a few more seconds until he couldn't stand it any longer, and he went on his way, stifling his emotions as well as the drive to run to her and hold her in his arms. This was the most crucial time, where exposure could jeopardize his whole mission, and in spite of the fact that Thomas now had his answer as to where Esther had gone, his sentiments must be kept in check. Pacing toward Fifth, he took deep breaths in and out, the tremor of his broken heart echoing in every step. A wave of denial caused Thomas's fists to clench, followed by the overbearing logic Hiroaki spent years instilling in his mind. There was no refuting what he'd just seen, and it horrified him to a degree that sent goose bumps all over his body.

Bewilderment and frustration blossomed while he hailed a carriage and leapt inside hurriedly, directing the driver up Fifth Avenue. Esther was supposed to be far away from New York, either in hiding or in a place no one from the city might happen to come across her, and yet, he had seen her with his own eyes; she had, no doubt, been trapped into working for Tammany Hall along with the others. Did Louis know…did the Madame? It was impossible to predict the depth of her involvement. Her new manifestation was so unlike the Esther he'd fallen in love with years ago; he assumed her physical appearance had been altered to aid in blending into the crowd, particularly since she was dressed to resemble a young man rather than a young woman—he himself had made that assumption not an hour before. Esther had followed him...she followed him and was hiding after her pursuit, crying notable tears of joy at his return... and that made his heart skip a beat. His reservations over Esther's feelings for him were gone: she still loved him, and he still loved her, despite having to acknowledge he too was a far different man than he'd ever dreamed he'd become, and Thomas felt his defenses of her escalate exponentially.

Thomas was seized by the overpowering notion that he had to save Esther, added in along with the others, and it motivated him to a degree that bordered on what Hiroaki would deem as unacceptable provocation. When he arrived home at last, Tony wouldn't believe this news, and together, they'd have to assess Thomas's day of surprises and configure the new factors into the grand scheme of their plan.

But Esther,,,what had happened to her and why was she here? Thomas knew he would find out in time, though it didn't decrease the unrelenting pain he felt in his heart. Like his father, Thomas left the love of his life in New York City to rot and should have come for her long ago. If he'd only known...if he'd only come sooner...

"No," Thomas said aloud with his head in his hands, trying to dispel his agony. "You are here. Esther is alive and you are going to save her. You are not your father, Thomas, you didn't abandon her."

Thomas felt his words choke as he uttered them again and again to himself, the carriage swaying from side to side as it carried him home in despondency. "I am not my father...I am not my father...I am not my father..."

Thomas didn't sleep that night. He tossed to and fro in his bed for what felt like a tortured eternity until he finally got out of bed, pouring himself a brandy and moving to sit by the embers burning in the fireplace. It didn't matter that he hadn't known about Esther, it didn't matter that he couldn't change the past. What suddenly mattered more to Thomas than the mission or any of the others, including himself, was saving Esther; the guilt washed over him and consumed him like a sickness. He wouldn't let her fate, or his, fall victim to being put second behind a cause Thomas wasn't even sure he could win in the first place. No...Esther was his priority, and then came everything else.

For years, he'd prepared, and in those years, Thomas slaved to prove himself capable of taking on the underbelly of New York single-handedly, only to discover there were many more variables in the ever-changing equation. The numbers on his side were larger than they'd fathomed...encouraging even...and they spoke of a network of individuals camouflaged within various occupations and spread out enough to make an impact. The overpowering negatives, however, were what preyed on Thomas's heart. First was the anonymous, shadowed figure implied to be worse than Croker himself, a person who alarmed the toughest men Thomas had ever known. Second was Thomas's horrific discovery of Esther's mysterious existence in the city as well as her perceived involvement with Tammany Hall.

In regard to the unknown man, Thomas already requested Tony press his vaguely-discussed brother for answers and follow whatever trail left by the Whyos they could dig up. When it came to Esther, Thomas was at a loss. She'd followed him to Central Park while he flew Athena, she'd seen him come face to face with Will Sweeney, and in the aftermath, Esther tailed him home, in an area he was certain she shouldn't trespass. All of New York City thought Esther had been hung for the murder of Timothy Adams years ago, and any contradictory information regarding her execution was bound to get her into trouble. Nonetheless, Thomas had to admit that he himself did not recognize her, though he didn't really believe anyone other than himself would have. He was conflicted, and desperately wished to seek Esther out, wondering whether she too was a part of this unspoken network the Madame managed to string together. But he couldn't. He had to wait. He'd already waited almost five years, and another few weeks would feel like nothing in contrast.

Dawn came, and yet Thomas's trepidations did not fade with the darkness. On these occasions at Amberleigh, he had been able to retreat to the lower floors of the manor, where he would pick up his hammer and not stop beating the metal until his feelings were resolved. To his dismay, there was no place in his home on Fifth for Thomas to resume his longtime hobby, a hobby he used as a release of his consistent vexations and frustrations. He could make an attempt to do more exercises, bury himself in work, or even go for a run on the outskirts of the city limits, as he had similar to his training on the property of Amberleigh, though he knew it would bring him no reprieve. Thomas was despondent, clutching at straws for any solution to ease the consternation. It was useless.

Out of the blue, an idea sparked, and Thomas sprang from his seat and dressed quickly. Rather than his typical suit, he threw on the more casual clothing he'd sported the previous afternoon in his pursuit of Esther, also opting for his extremely worn leather boots with the built-in sheath for Lawrence's old blade. Prior to leaving his rooms, Thomas eyed the Griswold, and decided for the next few hours he could do without it. He proceeded to put on his long jacket, and Thomas left a note for Tony on his side table, bidding that Tony push his meetings back to sometime after lunch. With that, Thomas took off out of the house, trying not to make a sound, though not without grabbing cigarettes for his long walk south.

The streets were relatively vacant with the sun still low in the sky, and Thomas was able to avoid attention from the very few people he passed, his attire assimilating him into the middle and lower-class crowd once he was free of uptown. A chilly breeze caught his neck, and Thomas popped the collar of his jacket while pacing through Midtown, the general state of living growing more crowded and sullied with each block he passed. Thomas moved with purpose, not keenly observing the things around him only because he already found his disposition disconcerted, and any addition to that weight would be too excessive. It had been years since Thomas truly explored the immigrant neighborhoods of New York, a place that in his youth felt like home, and not much had changed other than the number of people seemed increasingly dense. He'd mentally prepared for this—for embracing the emotion of returning to the more depraved parts of the city, and remembering what it was like to struggle…for seeing the devastation he never appreciated in his adolescence and was now all too aware of…for throwing himself into the worst ghettos of the world and fighting back against the beast New York had evolved into.

Not a soul in the masses acknowledged Thomas's presence during his trek, and when he arrived at his old master's place of business, Thomas halted across the street, gaping for a few minutes. Nearly fifteen years had gone by since he'd last seen Lawrence, and the chances he was alive were quite minimal, but a small piece of Thomas had hope. He took a deep breath and crossed the road, ducking under the giant canvass that hung over the archway into the portico, the smell of the fire already hitting his nostrils. The flames to his right were burning hot, and the work table to his left was prepared for a long day of horseshoes, with the farrier's tools scattered about and giant pile of steel ready to go. Glancing around, Thomas noted he was alone and walked toward his old station, grinning as he recalled how warm Lawrence had been with him on his last day. He closed his eyes, feeling more at peace than he had in months, like at last he'd finally come home to the one place the world made sense to him.

"Excuse me, sir, can I help you with something? Horseshoes?"

Thomas was overjoyed to hear Lawrence's booming old voice behind him. "I just thought you could use a hand here," he said, turning around slowly. "You're getting to be pretty old, you know."

Lawrence had aged in Thomas's absence. His thick beard was peppered with grey, and he'd lost a few pounds, though he retained his girthy figure. The smoke, as it did with most blacksmiths, formed deep wrinkles on his forehead and around his eyes, and while he couldn't see his legs, Thomas was certain from his gait that Lawrence was battling gout. Everything else, however, remained the same: his huge leather apron was tied snug across his front; the scent of beer and sausage rolled pungently in Thomas's direction; and he wore no more than his cotton shirt and slacks, a small sweat stain already forming on his chest.

Thomas couldn't suppress a laugh as he shook his head. "You haven't changed a day. I can smell you from over here."

Lawrence peered at Thomas, unable to believe what he saw.

"T-T-Tommy?" he stuttered, taking a few steps forward. "Is... is that...you?"

His hand gripped onto the working table, as if he might topple over in astonishment, and Thomas paced to Lawrence and wrapped his old master into a tight embrace.

"You told me I could come back whenever I wanted," he reminded Lawrence. "I thought I'd take you up on the offer."

Lawrence gave him a huge squeeze, making Thomas, even at his strongest, lose his breath.

"Well it's about goddamn time!" Lawrence cried.

Thomas could feel Lawrence's tears wet his shirt, and his spirit soared, a tiny piece of himself falling back into place. After a few seconds, Lawrence released him and looked straight into his eyes, beaming.

"We've got a bitch of a day ahead. Your apron is in the corner." He gave Thomas a cheerful slap on the back. "Let's get to work!"

The day flew by. It was late afternoon before Thomas realized he'd missed most of his meetings, and not a single fiber of his being cared in the slightest. Together, Lawrence and Thomas shoed horses for over eight straight hours, tripling Lawrence's earnings, and then retired, catching up over Lawrence's own homemade lager while Thomas enlightened him over just what had happened to him over the years. This, of course, excluded the true reasons for his return to the city, as well as his plan to take down Richard Croker, though Lawrence was astonished at his story. Thomas didn't leave anything out; he was amazed to find he was eager to open up to Lawrence, not shying away from his more painful memories of Edward or Esther, and was ecstatic to relay that his mother was, in fact, alive, but those details he didn't elaborate on either. Four o'clock was nearing and Thomas had to be home to dress before his dinner with Francis Bernard, and he had an inclination Tony and William would be furious with him for disappearing for the majority of the day. Thomas promised Lawrence he'd be by once a week to work, refusing to take any compensation for it other than Lawrence's beer, and headed home, grabbing a coach the minute he found a vacant one a few blocks north.

The second Thomas crossed the threshold of his front door, William's aggravated words began echoing down the foyer: "Tommy, is that you?!"

"Yeah, it's me! Sorry. Had an errand that unexpectedly took the whole day!"

Loud footsteps approached, and Thomas was instantly ambushed by both William and Tony.

"Sir, let me take your coat," Tony stepped ahead, silencing William momentarily. "I rescheduled your meetings over the next few days. When I received your note this morning, I assumed you had... underestimated...how long you'd be gone."

Thomas shuffled out of his jacket. "How did you know to do that, Tony?"

72

"Based on what you took with you, sir. And what you didn't take, as well."

With that, Tony took off down the hallway.

"Right," Thomas mumbled.

"And just where in the bloody hell have you been?" William implored him, annoyed. "You smell like a goddamn...wait...what is that..." His nose sniffed like a hound dog, and he peered at Thomas. "Blood sausage?"

"I went to see an old friend of mine, William. My former master, Lawrence. We've come to an arrangement so that I can work with him and have some time with my hammer while I'm in New York."

"Normally I wouldn't give a damn, Thomas, but we've got a big night tonight!" William asserted. "I thought we needed to strategize how to handle Francis. Oh, and this bloody abomination arrived today." William reached into his pocket and pulled out what appeared to be an invitation of some kind. "We are invited to the bloody Admiral's Ball. Lucy got to it first, so there's no way we can get out of this one. Damn her."

Thomas chortled, taking the envelope from William. "Es and the Hiltmores used to go to this event," Thomas reacted, attempting to sound casual, despite any mention of Esther tugging at his heartstrings. "It's the biggest party of the summer. We are absolutely going."

William's jaw dropped. "Are you...you're not seriously...you have always hated these things, Tommy!"

"We discussed this on our way here," he prompted. "Remember? For business, I want to make an even bigger name for us here. The only way we can do that, William, is by actually having a presence within the culture of the city."

"Did I hear talk about the Admiral's Ball?" Lucy drifted into the conversation, gliding toward them down the hall. "Boys, can we move to the sitting room? There's no need to linger by the door."

When they'd settled down with brandy, Lucy broached the subject again. "Thomas, did I hear you say we were going to the ball?" She was trying to mask her enthusiasm, and doing a terrible job at it.

"You bet, Luce," Thomas confirmed, having a sip of his drink. "And you can expect that we will be quite a bit more active on the social front. I also want you to plan a party at the house for Friday, a kind of homecoming, if you will."

William's expression was full of disdain. "A party?!" he exclaimed.

"Oh, shut up, William!" Lucy squealed, clapping her hands together. "I cannot wait, Thomas. I will send out cards immediately to some of our old friends. Would you like for me to invite Miss Hiltmore and her father?"

"I suppose the faster I embrace seeing them, the better off we will be," Thomas conceded. "Go ahead, Luce. The more, the merrier."

William was turning a deep shade of purple. "And I have…no say in any of this?!"

"Nope," Lucy remarked cheerfully, hopping to her feet. "I am going to ready myself for tonight. Thomas, you ought to do the same, you smell like old beer and smoke! Tony?"

Tony was there in a flash. "Yes, Mrs. Turner?"

"Make up a bath for Tommy. With extra rose petals."

"Of course, Mrs. Turner. Sir?" Tony directed his attention to Thomas. "I do have a few things for you to look at regarding business today."

"Time for me to get moving as well," he said to William. "Meet for a drink in the study before we head to the Bernard's ?"

William glared at him. "You aren't giving up on me liking this bloody bird, are you?"

Thomas shrugged. "I'll meet you in an hour," he affirmed, heading out of the sitting room and toward the staircase with Tony in his wake.

Once the pair of them were alone in Thomas's rooms, Thomas made a whiskey for himself and for Tony, and the two slumped down into the armchairs by the fire.

"Upon realizing you would be gone for the day, I took the liberty of spending most of the afternoon with my brother," Tony stated, taking a large gulp of his whiskey. "I've got new information that will help us fill the holes from yesterday. There's much more than we imagined."

"I could only assume as much. Start from the beginning."

"I'll proceed in order. In reference to Detective Ellis's new partner, I have come to understand this gentleman is named Seamus Murphy, and has worked with Tammany Hall for years. He was somehow appointed as a detective, mainly with the intention of keeping an eye on Samuel Ellis, but he is also one of Richard Croker's oldest friends, and by far the most loyal."

"Shit," Thomas muttered. "All right. Next one."

"Mr. Sweeney works for the Hall, alongside the Madame's old bodyguard Louis. They are the strongest Croker has aside from this other man, who goes by the name Walsh, though both Will and Louis are much older than most other men in their profession."

"Any word on what kind of shape Louis is in?" Thomas asked.

"As far as my contact is concerned, he's as good as he's always been," Tony declared. "This Walsh is the man who has become the problem. Apparently, he's…uncontrollable."

"Uncontrollable? And he works for Croker?!"

"He does, Thomas. I believe the issue is that he is Tammany Hall's tie to the Whyo gang, and they're devoted to Walsh, not Croker. He has a bad habit of leaving bodies in his wake, and lacks sentimentality. He has additionally taken an unfortunate liking to the Madame and to The Palace."

"So, this bastard is an asset and a problem for Croker," Thomas thought out loud. "We could use that to our advantage, but first I need to see how this guy operates in the flesh. Where can I find him?"

"The Points." Tony reached into his vest and pulled out a piece of paper, which Thomas observed was a handmade map of the southern tip of Manhattan. "Down at The Morgue or The Dry Dollar with the Whyos." Tony pointed to a square that was bolder than most of the others. "The Morgue is a bar that is their headquarters, but they split time. I'd guess a stop at The Dry Dollar would be a good start."

"Classy," Thomas commented sarcastically, admiring the incredible specifics drawn in the diagram. "Jesus, Tony. This is brilliant! Your brother helped you with this?"

"He said it would be the key to finding our way in and out of hell unscathed, sir."

"Tell him I owe him and will see to it he is compensated," Thomas articulated. "And anything on…Esther?"

Tony hesitated, reluctant to share. "Sadly, I only know one thing about Esther, Thomas, and it is that her involvement and who she is are definitively meant to be a secret. My brother was unsure of who I referenced when I asked; however, when I gave him the particulars of her appearance, he himself only knows she works for Richard Croker, and is his representative amongst the Whyos."

"His…representative?" Thomas was baffled. "It sounds like she is…well…"

"Like I said, sir, I have no real news on her. Though it was mentioned that she has a nasty reputation. Not many people will cross her, and everyone in that gang is well aware of who she is."

"Tony, there is only one possible way you have a nasty reputation amongst a group of degenerates like the Whyos."

Tony's eyes went to his whiskey glass, and he proceeded to finish the contents. "Try not to think on it, Thomas. It won't bring you solace."

He shook his head, indignant. "How many people do you think she's done in?"

"I don't know." Tony sighed. "I'm not sure I want to."

"Fuck." Thomas set his glass aside and got to his feet, running his hands through his hair. "This is my fault. This is all my goddamn fault, Tony."

"Take a breath, Thomas," Tony advised, standing and resting his hands on Thomas's shoulders. "Think back on your training. Don't let guilt cloud the present. What's done here is done, and the only thing that matters is the path ahead. Only you can do this. You have to concentrate on your objective. You will save Esther… you will save everyone you care about from this quicksand, but only if you keep your wits."

Thomas inhaled and exhaled slowly. "You're right. I've let my drive be swayed by my emotions. Thank you, Tony."

Tony removed his grip. "Of course, sir. Now, might I recommend you bathe and change for the night? You've got a long evening ahead, and Lucy will be extremely unhappy if you continue to smell like Lawrence's beer and the fire pit."

Dinner with Francis turned out to be easier than Thomas anticipated. One mention of the idea that San Francisco might be in Turner S & D's prospective future and he had his pen out, ready to sign the contract to take over expansion on the West Coast. Francis was eager to see his son and his son's family, and to start fresh on the Pacific now that he resided in New York alone. His late wife's illness prevented them from traveling the long distance across the country to their son for a number of years. When the mention of William's reinstatement arose, Francis couldn't have been more thrilled, firmly believing that Thomas would have a difficult time taking over New York and the eastern seaboard on his own. Thomas heartily agreed— what they weren't aware of was that this was exactly Thomas's reasoning behind his push to have William back. By day, Thomas would be a businessman; however, by night, he would have other affairs to attend to, and wanted to make sure his company was in the right hands while he pursued Croker and the Hall. Not to mention William was bored and becoming somewhat intolerable in his stagnation...at least according to Lucy.

Dinner passed, followed by cigars and brandy, and as the midnight hour approached, Lucy, William, and Thomas staggered out to a coach to head home. William and Lucy were both in high spirits, chatty and eager for this new phase of growth with the hopes that they would be able to travel to San Francisco themselves one day. A customary wager formed between them on how quickly Francis might remarry, and just how young she would be, while Thomas's pulse began to quicken with the notion that the Madame ought to be waiting for him at the house. He'd told Ellis to send her, but just because he asked didn't mean she would comply. In spite of this, he'd forewarned Tony, who expected the Madame's arrival in the early morning hours. Still, Thomas wondered what sort of reunion he was walking into, or more importantly, what version of the Madame had blossomed in the years he'd spent away.

William and Lucy hopped out of the coach first as Thomas delayed to pay their driver, and he trailed the two of them inside. Unexpectedly, Tony was not at the front door to greet them, immediately sending alarm bells off in Thomas's mind, though William and Lucy appeared not to notice and headed straight down the hall toward the great room. All at once, they stopped where they were, staring at something Thomas couldn't see. A screech rang out, one Thomas knew was from Athena, and he raced forward, pushing past them to see what in the world they were both gaping at.

There sat the Madame by the fireplace with Thomas's glove on, Athena merrily unhooded and perched on the Madame's arm with the jesses perfectly tied. Her shrieks of displeasure were at the sight of William, who was deaf to the bird's cries as he considered the scene, motionless. Lucy, too, was seemingly frozen in place. The

Madame gave Athena one stroke of her wing and the hawk was instantly pacified, settling back into her position and glaring menacingly at William.

"I am sorry to say that she really doesn't like you, William," the Madame pronounced, her eyes traveling from Athena to the three Turners in the doorway. She smiled radiantly. "It's a pleasure to see you all alive and well once again."

She was magnificent to behold. With the exception of a few growing hairline wrinkles on her face, Thomas noted that she had barely aged in his absence. The Madame was styled as if she were off to have dinner with the mayor, donning a beautiful dark green dress with her hair fashioned impeccably onto her head. Her lips and cheeks were rouged, and on her shoulders rested a sparkling black shawl and a flawless pair of diamond earrings that must have cost a small fortune. With Athena as an ornament on her arm, the Madame looked like something out of a dream; in front of her, resting on the coffee table, was a full glass of whiskey and a bottle next to it.

"Good evening!" Tony's voice came from down the hall as he raced to meet them. "I apologize for the delay, we had a small issue with one of the...the..."

Tony's gaze found the Madame, and he joined William and Lucy in being utterly astounded.

"Hello, Tony," the Madame said nonchalantly. "I hope you don't mind. I helped myself to the whiskey and found this marvelous creature in Thomas's study. I thought she should get out for a bit." Using her free hand, the Madame picked up her whiskey and took a very large gulp.

Thomas cleared his throat. "Tony, why don't you take William and Lucy upstairs?"

There was a moment of silence, then Tony snapped back.

"Yes, sir, right away," Tony declared. "Shall I bring you some brandy?"

79

"The whiskey will do just fine for me," he said, "but please do come back and collect Athena. Thank you, Tony."

Nodding, Tony hastily ushered William and Lucy upstairs; their expressions were beyond confused as they complied with Thomas's request. When they'd gone, Thomas grabbed a glass from the drink cart and went to sit in the vacant armchair beside the Madame and Athena, pouring himself a whiskey.

"She hates most people, you know," Thomas acknowledged to the Madame. "Unless I am the one to do the introduction, Athena despises strangers."

"I guess I am not a stranger to her, then," the Madame countered. "I hope it was all right by you that I broke her out for a few minutes. I had my new guard devise a distraction to get rid of Tony so that I could make myself at home."

"New guard?" Thomas asked. "Where is Louis?"

The Madame had another sip of her drink. "We'll discuss that another time." She set the glass down, gazing merrily at him. "How are you, Thomas?"

He couldn't help smiling at her. "I am happy to be home."

"We couldn't be happier for you to be here."

Taking a swig of whiskey, Thomas relaxed. "My homecoming has been pretty interesting, in more ways than one."

"How so?"

Tony emerged in the doorway with his own glove on and marched toward the Madame, steering Athena onto his own arm. "I will leave you for the night, sir, unless you ring for me."

"No, go and get some rest. We'll pick up tomorrow where we left off."

Tony turned to the Madame. "Have a great evening, Madame. It was lovely to see you once again."

The Madame bowed her head faintly, smiling. "Good night, Tony."

When they were alone, Thomas persisted, "I've had three encounters with three different...associates of yours...sorry...ours."

The Madame's left eyebrow rose. "Who other than Ellis have you seen? Although clearly, you found Lawrence. I can smell him from over here."

Thomas smirked. "I guess I didn't do as good of a job bathing as I thought. I went to see him today. It was the best day I've had in years."

"I am happy to hear it." She pulled out two cut cigars, one for each of them, and Thomas grabbed matches from his jacket pocket for her. "So, I am assuming you met Seamus," she stated after a few puffs.

"He sat outside my front door," Thomas revealed, taking his own cigar and lighting it. "I don't blame him for not having the courage to come in."

"He shouldn't have fucking been here," the Madame snapped angrily, though not directly at Thomas. "The fucking audacity of that bastard..."

"It's all right," he assured her, and Thomas lit his own cigar. "Once Ellis and his babysitter were gone, I went to the park to fly Athena, where I came face to face with Will Sweeney."

The Madame was legitimately amazed. "W-what?"

"That's how I felt too," Thomas disclosed, exhaling a cloud of smoke. "And he told me the same story Ellis tried to about some scary bastard who works for Croker causing a lot of the damage with that Bowery gang."

The Madame sat silently for a few seconds, and when she spoke, Thomas noted a small shudder in her words. "His name is Walsh. He's worked for Croker for...years. Only in the last five or six has he become increasingly...maniacal."

"What has he done?" Thomas pressed. "If I am supposed to

be careful with this bastard, I need to know what I'm dealing with, and yet no one seems to want to tell me."

The Madame took a drag of her cigar. "There are only rumors. We'll get to those. First, I'll give you the facts. After the war, a lot of gangs ran rampant in the Points until somehow, they strangely became welded together into one, or at least one ruling over all the others. Their original founders were the motherfuckers who ran me and Louis out of the lower west and sent us uptown, though they didn't really become as dangerous or as unpredictable until recent years. Croker originally sent Walsh in to be his contact with the gang…" She stopped mid-sentence and threw back the rest of her whiskey. "Instead, that son of a bitch took over the gang by picking off two of their leaders and scaring the rest of them into submission. There's still one left, but he follows Walsh around with his tail between his legs."

"So, he has access to a substantial amount of bad people who will do whatever he wants," Thomas supposed aloud. "That's soothing. But if that's the worst problem, Madame, I think we can work around it."

"That's not the worst problem. You need to hear his history, and the rumors."

"By all means, enlighten me."

"The rumors are just that…rumors. However, I have people I trust more than my own fucking self who have confirmed the eeriest of them."

"People like Esther?"

Shocked again at his knowledge, the Madame's face went white beneath her rouge. "How do you know about Esther?"

"She was the third person I saw yesterday," Thomas confessed, leaning forward and refilling their glasses. "She followed me, and then I tailed her down to the Lower East Side."

The Madame was furious. "I fucking told her," she spat through gritted teeth. "She knew if she came up here…God damn her! If she got caught, she'd be fucking dead, and she just had to do it anyway." The Madame gazed at Thomas, her eyes like fire. "Do you realize what could have fucking happened if she were caught on Fifth?! Everything she's done would be for nothing!"

This was not the reaction he'd anticipated. "Please! Calm down. Why don't you explain to me what it is that's going on before you lose your nerve?"

"Lose my nerve?" the Madame hissed. "The only reason she's had to become what she has is for you, Thomas."

"Had to become what?" Thomas asked her curiously, wanting answers. "I mean, I am not arguing with you. I saw her in the alley. She's an entirely different person, but I want to know what it is she's doing with Tammany Hall."

The Madame's countenance hardened. "You'll see it with your own fucking eyes soon enough," she uttered, and then biting her lip, her anger softened. "I am not upset with you, Thomas. You have to understand. We've been waiting for you to return for,,,for fucking years, We've all done our part to set the stage, and now it's your time. We need you to do what we can't, and I promise I'll provide whatever tools you need."

"I want to know who is on my side," Thomas stressed, wishing desperately to ask her more about Esther, though realizing the Madame had already, in her opinion, disclosed more than she should.

She looked around, as if afraid they would be overheard. "You have The Palace. You have Will. You have Esther. Ellis, of course. And Louis."

It was a list of names he only needed confirmed. "What is this I hear about Celeste Hiltmore being one of yours?"

"The Cat tell you that one?"

"It wasn't Ellis."

The Madame was charmed. "She's a work in progress."

Out of the blue, a young man stepped into the doorway of the sitting room, his appearance so familiar, though Thomas couldn't figure out where he'd seen him before.

"Madame? I think it's best we get goin'. I want you back at The Palace 'fore too late, and ya know I hate leavin' Georgie there on his own."

Thomas's mouth dropped open. "Holy shit…"

"Thomas, this is Ashleigh Sweeney," the Madame introduced, speedily putting out her cigar and rising to her feet. "Ashleigh, this is Lord Thomas Turner, my…" the Madame let her voice trail off and looked at Thomas, as if testing him, "my…nephew, as we used to say."

Ashleigh strutted forward, openly wearing two guns on his belt, and held out his hand. "Honor to meet ya, Lord Turner."

"Are you…by chance…"

"Yeah, I'm his boy," Ashleigh established, a little annoyed as he rotated to the Madame. "Like I said, Madame, time to get movin'."

Thomas reached into his vest and pulled out his pocket watch. "I also need to get moving. Time went by faster with Francis than I thought it would."

The Madame paused. "Where the fuck are you going at this hour?"

"I've got my own work to do," he mentioned offhandedly. "And I need to have Tony lock the house down before I leave."

Ashleigh eyed him closely. "Workin' at this hour? What sorta thing you doin', then?"

"Later, Ashleigh," the Madame dismissed him in a way that shut her new guard up. "Thomas, just one thing. About the…man we were speaking of."

"What about him?"

"One of the rumors is that he…he doesn't feel."

Thomas was confused. "Feel? Feel what?"

"Anything," the Madame replied darkly. "Keep that in mind while you're out…working. What are you arming yourself with?"

Thomas sniggered, the irony almost making him laugh. "I thought you'd never ask."

It was six in the morning, the sun just peeking over the horizon as four officers struggled to drag the body out of the Hudson River. It was a cool, spring daybreak, with a heavy set of fog hanging over the surface of the water under a clear sky, the stench of fish and garbage more mild than usual because of the temperature. The body was swollen from its time in the water, but the minute Seamus examined the corpse, he knew there was no possible way this was a drowning. The clothes clinging onto the flesh were wet and tattered, and the fish had eaten bits and pieces from the skin. There were no shoes on his feet, no way to tell who this man had been or where he'd come from, only that he was dead as a fucking doornail. Prior to being flung in the river, he'd taken one hell of a beating. The contusions and bruising, though old, were unmistakable. It made Seamus grimace.

The four officers dropped the body on the shore as Ellis and Seamus walked toward it.

"Who called it in?" Ellis asked them, scrutinizing the corpse as he squatted down beside it.

"Got caught underneath some poor bastard's boat," one of the officers announced, moving away from the smell of rotting death and holding a handkerchief over his face. "Sent his son to the precinct the minute they got back to harbor."

"Whoever this guy was," Ellis thought aloud as Seamus drew nearer, "someone killed him before he went in the water." He spun around, gazing at Seamus callously. "Want to take a look and make sure this isn't one of yours? Otherwise, I'm calling it in."

"Oh, fucking hold your horses." Seamus waved him off, crouching beside him.

85

"He's unrecognizable," Ellis remarked, shaking his head. "God-damn Whyos probably beat him to death and tossed him."

"Go have a cigarette and try to keep your head," Seamus jeered under his breath.

The officers were standing a good twenty feet away from the body now, but Seamus was growing tired of Ellis giving him grief at every corner. Two years ago, when Detective Samuel Ellis was becoming harder for Richie to control, Croker had done something Seamus couldn't quite wrap his head around. A few favors, some forged documents, and Croker's own letter of recommendation put Seamus Murphy on the police force as a new partner for Detective Ellis. It was a dream come true for Seamus, who had always wanted to be a man in blue, and Ellis couldn't have been more furious. With the threat of losing his job as well as his credibility, Ellis cooperated after a few weeks of forceful protest. In those two years, they had finally found a kind of balance, though in the last couple of days, something in Samuel had changed, following a stop they'd made to see none other than Mary Daugherty's son in the flesh. Later that afternoon, Ellis swore to Seamus and Richie that he was doing his own digging, and found Thomas was only there for business purposes, with no mention of his mother, Richie, or the Hall. But his attitude changed—he'd become more obstinate with Croker and an even bigger pain in Seamus's ass at the precinct. This recent arrogance would only be tolerated for so long before Seamus would personally see to it he had an attitude adjustment.

"I'll look him over," Seamus asserted strongly. "Better you aren't here."

"Fine." Ellis stood up. "This is out of line, Seamus, even for them." He spat on the ground, pulling a cigarette from his pocket as he walked away muttering, "Fucking barbarians…"

When he'd gone from view, Seamus moved hastily and grabbed the left wrist of the man's lifeless body, and sure enough, on the inside was the small symbol every Whyo currently had carved into their skin. It was a W, though whether it stood for Whyo or Walsh Seamus, he wasn't sure. Walsh was the sick bastard who'd started the idea, and it was how Seamus was able to identify whether or not to get rid of the body for good or actually take it into the station. At least that's what he claimed, yet to Seamus, his gut told him it was more along the lines of a cattle brand for Walsh to claim them. The Whyos were never brought in, of course, mainly to cover Tammany's tracks and their link to the gang, and while it was extreme, it had made Seamus's clean-up task easier.

But as Seamus examined the body, something struck him as odd. Walsh would end every "lesson" by blade, and the majority of other Whyo deaths were gunshot or stab wounds. This man was literally beaten to death with something hard...something small, yet with incredible force...

It was then that he figured it out.

"Oh, fuck me," he breathed, looking the body up and down. "Little girl struck again."

Seamus hated to admit he liked Croker's "assistant," as they were asked to call her. She was a tough bitch and intimidated him enough to not second guess her input at their meetings. Half her time was spent with the Whyos, watching Walsh and representing Richie; the other half was with Sweeney and the French goon, muscling politicians, government officials, or anyone who needed a push to keep Tammany rising. Seamus wondered if Croker was aware, and assumed he had to be—she would never do anything without his say so.

He sighed, getting to his feet. "Grab the kerosene," he ordered the four officers. "We gotta do this one fast."

The officers complied, and Ellis reappeared. "Burner, then?" he asked, unfazed.

"Yeah. Wasn't one of Walsh's though."

"Drunk brawl? Gambling debt? Opium addict? The options are endless, Seamus."

Seamus rolled his eyes. "Give me a fuckin' break, would ya?" He grabbed for his own cigarette. "It was the girl again."

Ellis froze. "Esther?"

"You know we don't call her by that name," Seamus reminded him, "but yeah. It was the assistant."

Without warning, Ellis reached over and took the cigarette from Seamus as he lit it, though Seamus was more amused than pissed. "What's gotten into you, then?"

Ellis took a long drag of the cigarette. "Sometimes I just wonder how it all came to this," he said softly.

Seamus smiled, taking out another bit of tobacco and lighting it. "Richie," he stated blandly, "King of fucking New York made this whole thing happen."

A strange expression formed on Ellis's face. "Yeah, yeah you're right," he settled. "King of New York."

The officers returned, coating the lifeless corpse in oil from the gaslights, and lit it on fire with matches. The six men stood and watched it burn to ash in the sunrise, covering their mouths and noses from the smell.

As Ellis observed the destruction of evidence, that look didn't fade away, and he mumbled too quietly for Seamus or the others to hear: "But every king falls. Every king falls."

CHAPTER XXXII.

"At this point, I think having anyone in office other than that na-tivist prick Hewitt would serve us well," Francis Bernard boomed. "So what if Grant's a Catholic? Overall, he's a better man for mayor!"

The Admiral's Ball was just getting started, gradually filling wall to wall with everyone Celeste had ever met in high society dressed to the nines, and while the thought of being there with an agenda was not new to her, she was nervous. While her friends and acquain-tances were present only to socialize, Celeste was there to work; one task in particular would be tricky to see through. Laura and her hus-band Ralph stood on Celeste's right, Captain Bernhardt on her left, and Douglas had, just minutes before, approached with Francis Ber-nard, his son, Francis Jr., and Francis Jr.'s wife, Sylvia.

Celeste wore a brand new silk gown, the front decorated with a violet and lilac brocade, the full skirt of the dress billowing out wide around her. Carefully, she'd styled a feather into her hair, donned her usual long white gloves, and fought to breathe through her cor-set, which was always tied far too tight. The short sleeves rested just off her shoulders, and she bore an exquisite amethyst necklace, the colors complementing her gown perfectly. It was no secret amongst their party that Celeste was the most beautiful girl in the room, and she carried herself in such an easy, confident way that she caught the attention of every man she passed by. At times, Celeste had to ignore Laura's begrudging looks in her direction. Her once-maid had come into her own fortune, yet Laura struggled to ever own a room the way Celeste did, and over the last few years, jealousy had turned their once-close friendship into a courteous acquaintance-ship. It didn't matter. Celeste now occupied her time with pursuits other than simply existing in the superficiality of wealth and Fifth Avenue, and she found them far more rewarding.

Until her father and the Bernard family joined them, Captain Bernhardt and Ralph had compared horror stories of the American West; Celeste happily embraced the reprieve of such daunting and gruesome tales of the savage Indians amongst new company. With champagne in hand, the conversation turned and stuck on the most popular topic of the season: the upcoming mayoral election.

Douglas chuckled at Francis's remark. "I couldn't agree more, Bernard, but what's it matter to you, anyhow? In a matter of days, you'll be heading to California!"

"What's the matter, Douglas?" Francis teased. "Jealous?"

"As a matter of fact, I am!" he admitted. "I am even more jealous that I didn't take the opportunity to invest in Turner S & D when I had the chance!"

Francis slapped him on the back playfully. "There is always room for more investors, Douglas! You should have come to the party they threw! I know, I know, you had other business constituents in town, but you still might have a chance! The Turners should be attending the ball this evening. I am sure Thomas would be happy to have you on board!"

"When do you expect the Turners?" Celeste cut in.

"Any minute now! The other night at dinner, Thomas was resolute that they would arrive on time, much to William's disdain." He had a gulp of his whiskey. "They promised to attend if only to see me before I ship out with Junior and Sylvia!"

Douglas held up his glass for a toast, and the group saluted Francis. "We are most happy for your family to be closer, and for the prospect of such a business opportunity. I just never thought I'd see you leave New York! It is home, after all. Celeste? Any interest in San Francisco?"

She had a sip of champagne. "Like you said, Father, New York is home! Do you ever miss the city, Sylvia?"

"On nights like these!" Sylvia pronounced jovially. "I really do love the West though. There's something almost romantic about it, really. I think—"

"Romantic?" The Captain chided abrasively, disrupting Sylvia. "There's nothing romantic about the lives that have been repeatedly lost to keep you safe on your journey to and from California, Mrs. Bernard."

Everyone in the group became embarrassed, and Celeste tried to hide her grimace at his words.

"Jonathan, let's go grab a drink," she suggested, taking his arm and escorting him away from the others.

Weaving through the crowd, Celeste was upset with herself for putting Jonathan in such a situation. Since he had returned from the frontier, it was evident Captain Bernhardt's time fighting had changed him. He was bitter, angry, and grappling with the lives he'd taken as well as the lives of friends he'd lost. Jonathan's face, though still alarmingly attractive, had hardened with the difficulties of the last few years, and he rarely wore any expression other than a frown. When it was just the two of them, Celeste had a way of helping to alleviate that, using her charm and wit to make him smile and forget those horrors, at least for an hour or two. However, what scared her was the notion that Jonathan wasn't improving; if anything his resentment had worsened, and she worried constantly about what might provoke him next.

They reached the bar, and Captain Bernhardt immediately ordered a whiskey and her another champagne.

"I apologize, Celeste. Really. That was out of line and I just...I snapped."

"Jonathan please, you of all people know you do not need to apologize to me." Celeste took her flute from the barman and raised her glass to him. "I am just glad you are home in one piece."

He held his glass to hers, and Celeste impulsively had a drink.

Jonathan stared at her for a few seconds. "Would you marry me, Celeste?" he blurted out.

Upon hearing this, Celeste choked on the champagne halfway down her throat. She started coughing violently, fending off an assortment of randomly worried guests as her mind raced at what Captain Bernhardt had just said.

"Christ, are you all right?" he asked her as she recovered.

Celeste managed to shake off the last of her fit. "Jonathan you just...you just asked me to..."

"To marry me, yes."

Celeste took another breath to remain composed. "But...you've only just returned!"

"When I was gone, you were the only thing that got me through the worst of days," he confessed, setting his whiskey down and taking both her hands in his. "I've been a miserable bastard since I've been home, and you are the only thing that makes me feel human again. We would be so happy together, you and I, and I just...Celeste...? What are you looking at?"

Judge Frederick and his wife had just arrived at the ball and were descending down the main staircase in their direction. Celeste didn't have time to deal with Jonathan—but she couldn't cause a scene either.

She gazed into Jonathan's eyes. "Please allow me the night to think it over. I am just...so overwhelmed with the party and the... the surprise of your proposal," she told him as sweetly as she could.

Noticing the disappointment in his face, Celeste knew she had to do better to pacify the situation. She leaned in close, fighting every one of her impulses not to lie. "Jonathan I...I love you...you know that."

His countenance transformed instantly, as if that alone answered his question. "I love you too," he whispered.

"Let's continue this conversation tomorrow.afternoon," she requested. "Would that be suitable?"

"Are you abandoning me for a while?" Jonathan asked her, though thankfully not crossly.

"Just a few connections I need to speak with," Celeste answered. "I'll be back in an hour or so. Have a champagne ready for me?"

Jonathan nodded, cheerier than she'd seen him in days, and Celeste gave him an encouraging wink as she moved toward the Fredericks.

"Goddammit, Celeste," she scolded herself inaudibly, closing in on the Fredericks. "What the fuck are you doing? You can't do this to him. Pull it together..."

"Celeste, my dear!" Mrs. Frederick greeted her, holding out her arms to kiss Celeste on both cheeks. "We are so pleased to see you. Might I say, you look absolutely stunning!"

This same woman was one of the many who'd openly condemned Celeste's family after they lost their fortune, and her warmth was purely the result of needing Celeste and the Madame's assistance to pay off her husband's debt. Appreciating what was in the future for the Fredericks, Celeste felt no pity about her role in what was to come. Judge Frederick had fiercely advocated to keep Douglas locked away during his appeal; as far as Celeste was concerned, they'd earned their fates.

"Lovely to see you, Miss Hiltmore," Judge Frederick chimed in, bowing to her as Celeste curtseyed ever so slightly. "Is your father here, too? I must pay my respects after I say hello to an old friend."

"He's visiting with Francis Bernard and Ralph Calhoun, Judge," she informed him. "He would be delighted to see you."

"Ah, yes. I need to give my regards to Francis before his departure."

Celeste pointed him their direction. "They are standing through this small crowd; you can't miss them."

With a nod, Judge Frederick took off, though Celeste lingered with Mrs. Frederick for a few seconds.

"How did everything go?" she asked softly.

"He has a meeting with her in a few days," Mrs. Frederick muttered. "I cannot tell you how much you have helped, Celeste. Thank you so much for your discretion in the matter."

Celeste beamed at her. "If there is ever anything you need, please don't hesitate," she offered kindly.

Right on time, Douglas was there to save her. "Daughter, might I steal you for a moment? Good evening, Mrs. Frederick, you are a vision!"

She laughed and waved him off, and Douglas took this as a cue to pull away from further talks with her.

"He was beckoned outside by another man I'd never seen before," Douglas updated her hastily. "The back balcony. Go quickly! I'll be close behind with Mrs. Frederick so that you aren't caught."

Celeste stepped lightly through the main hall toward the balcony, pulling her cigarette wand and matches out of her purse. Because there were so many guests still arriving, the balcony was mostly deserted save for the far right corner, where Frederick was speaking with a man who Celeste couldn't clearly make out. In a flower pot, she dumped the matches from the box into the soil and, at a practiced, leisurely pace, walked toward them in an effort to overhear as much as possible prior to reaching them.

Twenty feet away, she could make out sentences. First was Frederick.

"...can't put together enough proof of anything. Grant is going to be elected, and when he is, Croker will have full jurisdiction over the city."

"So, you're saying until he's fully in power, we can't do anything to stop him?" the second man asked, dismayed.

"Unfortunately, yes. He hasn't made a big enough mistake to merit the kind of investigation you seek. I can't back an investigation if there's no solid evidence."

Celeste was too close not to speak up, and she'd heard enough. "Pardon me, gentlemen!" she interrupted, causing both of them to jump upon spotting her. She shook her empty matchbox. "I seem to have run out. Would one of you care to lend me a light?"

Judge Frederick reached into his pocket, taking out a match to strike. "Here you are, Miss Hiltmore." His politeness was forced through frustration at being interrupted by her, and Celeste could sense an introduction would have to be instigated by her.

She held out her hand. "Good evening, sir, I don't believe we've met. My name is Celeste Hiltmore."

The unknown man took her hand half heartedly. "Charles Henry Parkhurst," he established, letting go of her not a second after he took her grasp. "Judge, I must be going."

He gestured toward the doorway with his eyes, causing Judge Frederick to rotate around and observe his wife standing with Douglas, searching for him. After spotting her husband, Mrs. Frederick waved, and she and Douglas began to stroll toward them.

Not a second later, Parkhurst tipped his hat and left instantly, bounding past Celeste's father with his head down. When Douglas and Mrs. Frederick reached the judge, Douglas held a whiskey out for him.

"Good evening, sir," Douglas greeted. "That gentleman was certainly in a hurry! And definitely not dressed for the ball."

"A constituent with a case," Judge Frederick stressed, visibly irritated.

"I thought you had gone on to find Douglas!" Mrs. Frederick stated, letting go of her escort. "Who was that man, dear?"

"Like I said, someone who is just working on one of my cases. It was an urgent matter we needed to settle."

"That would explain his hasty departure," Douglas added, a touch of condescension in his tone. "Well, Mrs. Frederick, I am happy I could assist you in finding your husband. I am sure you have quite a few other guests you need to visit!"

Mrs. Frederick was not aware that Douglas was being somewhat contemptuous. "You know he is right, dear," she said to her husband. "We ought to get to the main ballroom."

"Right," he agreed. "Good to see you, Douglas."

Celeste's father smiled derisively. "You too, Judge."

No one said a word, the tension heightening, and finally, Douglas held his arm out for his daughter. "I hope you two enjoy your night!"

Celeste had a drag of her cigarette and took his invitation, slipping her arm through her father's as they moved away from the Fredericks.

"And?" he muttered when they were out of earshot.

"They were saying something about Croker. I can't be sure. Judge Frederick claimed he couldn't back an investigation without more evidence, and the man he met with was upset by that. I don't know what it means."

"The Madame says if Grant gets in, Croker will be appointed as city chamberlain, and he'll have the whole city at his disposal," Douglas shared, halting and turning to her. "That would mean no more Swallowtails, no more political opposition. People don't like the sound of that, especially the upper class." Douglas put his free hand onto Celeste's, which was resting on his forearm. "No wonder Croker wants Frederick out. We'll go see the Madame after the ball and let her know we've confirmed Frederick is still attempting to undercut Tammany."

Celeste exhaled a cloud of smoke, glimpsing around. "Have they arrived yet?"

"Not yet. Soon."

"Do you think he'll do it, like the Madame predicted?"

"The Madame is almost never wrong," he reminded her. "You need to let Thomas know we are on his side...that we're on the Madame's side. Understood?"

"I will."

Douglas pulled her in and kissed her forehead. "Be safe," he cautioned, and together, they made their way inside to join their party.

As they drew near to their group, Celeste and Douglas were frantically beckoned over by Francis Bernard, and upon resuming their spots amongst their friends, Celeste's jaw dropped. There, in front of her, stood Thomas Turner, Lucy Turner, and William Turner in the flesh, already with drinks in hand and laughing with Francis Jr. and Sylvia. Her gaze warily found her father's, who was just as astounded as she that in the brief amount of time they'd been absent, the Turners miraculously appeared and found the Bernards.

"Good evening, Mr. Hiltmore, Celeste," Thomas addressed them with a deep bow. "Celeste, you remember Lucy and William, I presume? Mr. Hiltmore, these are my cousins, Mr. and Mrs. Turner."

He was not at all how she remembered him, and suddenly, Celeste felt absurdly unprepared for her assignment.

"Thomas!" she squeaked, her voice almost a full octave higher than normal. "I cannot believe it is really you!"

Celeste curtseyed, and Douglas smoothly took the lead. "Lord Turner, it is an honor to see you in good health. We were so sorry we couldn't make it to your dinner party last week, but I had clients in town we were forced to entertain instead, much to our disappointment."

"You missed a hell of a good time," Francis declared, slapping Thomas on the arm. "Though I have to say, Lord Turner, I was hoping to once again have the pleasure of seeing the infamous Madame I met a few years ago."

"Perhaps next time," Thomas articulated carefully with a small grin. "Mr. Hiltmore, I am delighted to see you as well. I thought you'd be interested in hearing that my new head of house was, in fact, your previous head of house."

Celeste's jaw dropped. "Mrs. Shannon?"

Lucy clapped her hands together. "Yes! We adore her, even if she can be extremely…"

"Strict?" Douglas suggested, chuckling. "She has a way of bringing everyone in the house under her rule. I must say, Lord Turner, how did you find her? I did not realize she was still…well…in the business!"

"Our butler found her," William revealed to the party. "Thomas couldn't believe it either, Mr. Hiltmore. She's a feisty one, that old broad."

"Has she taken to hiding the whiskey yet?" Douglas entreated William.

William's face lit up. "Just last night! Couldn't bloody believe she had the audacity—"

"William!" Lucy cried, grabbing his arm to restrain him, but not before the entire group burst into laughter.

Jonathan remained silent, and Thomas noticed. "Captain, how the hell are you? I heard you were on the frontier for quite a few years, keeping the railroads and territories safe."

"I was gone for too long, Lord Turner," he replied coolly, making it clear he did not wish to discuss the topic or speak to Thomas at all, for that matter.

Again, Celeste grew apprehensive, for Jonathan held a grudge against Thomas, believing wholeheartedly it was Thomas's fault Esther was dead; yet, from his expression, it was obvious Thomas didn't realize this.

Taking the hint, Thomas dropped it, and held up his empty glass. "Ah, damn. It seems I'm dry of whiskey. Anyone need a refill?"

For a half second, Celeste hesitated. Thomas's newfound disposition was intimidating, even for her, but she didn't have a choice. Boldly, she stepped forward.

"I could use another champagne, Lord Turner. I'll come with you."

She could sense he was unsure if he should accept her offer to accompany him, yet there was no polite way to tell her no. Instead, Thomas held his arm out to her, and awkwardly, they sauntered toward the bar.

"You are looking lovely, Celeste," Thomas complimented her, though without much enthusiasm.

Celeste gave him a dashing smile. "Thank you, Lord Turner."

At the bar, neither of them spoke to each other as Thomas ordered their beverages. A few friends passed by and Celeste cordially greeted them with a tiny curtsy, though she made sure her body language was not inviting of a conversation. When Thomas turned around with her flute of champagne and his whiskey, Celeste gestured in the direction of the open balcony, and Thomas didn't say a word. He courteously took her arm in his again and they went outside.

A few men were smoking cigars where she'd previously found the judge and his cohort, another group of guests chatted nearby the doorway, and to their left lingered a handful of older ladies talking at such a high volume, Celeste was certain no one would overhear whatever she and Thomas conferred. What made her increasingly nervous was that Thomas somehow expected her to isolate him; she wondered if he also had some things to say to her in return.

They stopped at the railing, and Thomas leaned onto it, taking a sip of his whiskey while he stared out over the city.

"What is it, Celeste? We don't have much time. This is definitely not an ideal place for us to have an open and honest dialogue."

She'd gone over this moment in her mind for weeks, wanting to be a professional and get down to business without dwelling on the past—suddenly, Celeste didn't care about any of it. Finally, she had the chance to communicate her feelings about the worst winter of their lives, and that became far more important than the Madame or The Palace.

"I know about the wires," she revealed, moving closer to him. "I know you tried to stop it, the execution. I hadn't known that, or I would have written or reached out to your family. For years, I was so, so hard on you...you know...afterward. And then the Madame told me what happened, and that you tried to save her...that you still love her..." She took a breath to steady herself. "My opinions were wrong. I want you to hear me say that I was wrong...about you, about Esther. God, I am so, so sorry Thomas. If I could take it back—"

"Do you have a point with this, Celeste?" Thomas pressed.

"I'm fighting the same battle you are," she stated strongly, her resolve building. "You can pretend to be cold and unfeeling with me, I've never earned any better from you, and it honestly won't affect me or my pursuits. Me...my father...we are a part of The Palace now. I am not the same Celeste you once knew and I...I just...I wanted you to know that."

Thomas was silent for a few seconds, and then to her disbelief, he grinned and swiveled to face her. "Well," he said, his tone becoming friendly, "I'd heard you were taking after the Madame. I didn't believe it until now."

Celeste relaxed, smiling. "I guess you could say she's rubbed off on me."

He gave a small nod and looked back the way of the city. "A lot of things are going to change around here." He pulled out a cut cigar and matches from his dinner jacket. "It is nice to have you tell me upfront where your loyalties lie."

"I wouldn't have it any other way."

"I am happy to hear it."

"You must know he's going to be here soon," she muttered as Thomas lit the cigar. "Are you going to…well…let him know you're here?"

Thomas paused and let out a small laugh. "He already knows I am in New York."

"Yes, but he doesn't know you'll be at the ball."

"I suppose she would have predicted my purpose tonight. She wants you to witness it then, I presume?"

"She knew you'd want to send a message."

Thomas took a long drag of his cigar, his eyes moving over her shoulder. "Well, it seems you'll have a full report to give her then. That bastard is making his way toward the balcony."

Celeste whipped around to see firsthand that Thomas was right: Richard Croker, along with a few other gentlemen, was walking out to the balcony, a glass of brandy in one hand and an unlit cigar hanging out of the corner of his mouth.

"I told you. He has no idea you're here…" Her voice trailed off. This was it.

"Stay here," he commanded. "When I make the signal, come to me."

"Signal?" she implored. "What signal?!"

"You'll know."

Thomas threw back his whiskey and straightened up. He handed his empty glass to Celeste, who could only stand there and gape at him. Striding forward, Thomas had such a threateningly self-assured level of poise, it drew the eyes of the increasing crowd around them, making this a very public happenstance. Richard Croker was speaking with the man on his left, completely unaware of Thomas's approach until they were only two feet apart, and both parties halted. At the exact moment Croker's regard fell on Thomas, the guise that struck Thomas's face was unmistakably that of a predator ready to strike, and she smirked.

Croker was unreservedly aghast.

"Excuse me, Mr. Croker, I am so sorry to bother you, but I wanted to reintroduce myself." Thomas took an extremely low bow, cigar in hand. "We met a few years ago at a party. My name is Lord Thomas Turner of Amberleigh. I am the owner of Turner S & D."

A hush of whispers spread through Croker's group of constituents, and gradually, also amongst the party goers on the balcony.

"Why yes, Lord Turner, I do remember meeting you," Croker managed to spit out, and held out his hand to shake Thomas's. "You have come back to New York for a visit, then?"

Thomas complied with the salutation. "We have moved home permanently," Thomas announced. "I have just purchased a brand new residence on Fifth, and we are expanding business to the west. While I love England, I just couldn't stay away when there is so much here for me to do."

Their eyes were locked on each other. Despite the courteousness of their words, there was nothing but hatred in Thomas's eyes, and to Celeste's delight, panic in Croker's.

"I am thrilled to have such a successful New Yorker here in our grand city to make his fortune," Croker articulated loudly so that everyone might hear. "We need more rags to riches stories like yours, Lord Turner. Please let me welcome you home with an invitation to come down to Tammany Hall for a whiskey sometime next week, and see if I might convince you to join our board."

"I'll be gone on business, but perhaps another time," Thomas contended while Celeste nonchalantly moved closer to their discourse so she stood only a few feet away. "I've heard that Tammany may have a man in the mayor's chair before long."

"We can only hope!" Croker replied. "So far the numbers are in our favor."

Thomas's left eyebrow rose. "A dream come true for the Hall, I must say."

"If we win, we will finally have the power to shape this city into what it should have been years ago!" he voiced, a few shouts of agreement echoing from the group behind him. "A win for Tammany is a win for all! There won't be any more Swallowtail pricks to stand in our way and we can progress forward at long last."

A sneer formed on Thomas's face. "Progress with a foundation undoubtedly built by Irish immigrants in your early days at the Hall, Mr. Croker. Like my mother, for example, who worked for you in her younger years."

"Ah, yes...that was a very long time ago..."

"But it was at the start of your career at Tammany."

Croker hesitated, not sure how to respond to Thomas's insinuations, and in Croker's silence, Thomas lowered his tone and carried on "There may not be Swallowtails, Mr. Croker, but I know this city well enough to understand it has a way of keeping balance on its own. Even if it comes from...unexpected places."

A look exchanged between them, one Celeste would never forget, and for what felt like an eternity, both men glowered at each other wordlessly.

Thomas twisted toward Celeste with his hand outstretched, and then concluded his and Croker's banter. "Pardon me, but I've kept Miss Hiltmore idle too long, and we should be getting back to our party."

"Yes!" she agreed, rushing to his side and taking his arm. "Father will be wondering where we've strayed off to, I think."

"Thank you for the friendly homecoming and invitation, Mr. Croker," Thomas concluded. "It was a pleasure. I am sure we will be seeing more of each other in the future."

"I have...I have no doubt," Croker answered through gritted teeth. "Good evening, Lord Turner, Miss Hiltmore."

Celeste politely took a small curtsy and she and Thomas strutted inside, Celeste's heart beating so fast she could barely contain herself.

"Jesus Christ, Thomas..."

"The message has been sent. Please do relay it as best you can to the Madame, and thank you for being such a perfect exit piece."

"You're...you're welcome..."

Without warning, Thomas stopped and muttered so softly Celeste almost didn't hear him: "How is she?"

Initially, Celeste thought he was referring to the Madame, yet after a brief suspension, she understood who it was he really meant.

"I can't be sure," she mumbled. "I don't get to...see her. She leaves me paintings...I have a whole collection...you ought to see them, Thomas, they're...beautiful."

Thomas's jaw twitched, and he commenced walking again.

Trying to keep her voice down, Celeste found once more she couldn't prevent herself from speaking. "She's all alone, Thomas. And scared. I can see it in how she paints. I know that sounds ridiculous, but I just...I can tell."

Thomas's countenance became pained. "I'm going to get her out of this, Celeste. I swear to you I will."

"I know you will. So does she."

Celeste couldn't quite figure out what it was, but something about Thomas made her feel safer than she had in years—likely a combination of his confidence in what lay ahead and their intertwined history, though the two of them had not personally been anything other than acquaintances, linked together by Esther. They both loved Esther above all else, and in a strange way, it bonded them together regardless of their many differences. In that sensation, Celeste also understood she could never marry Jonathan; she loved him, yes, but she was not in love with him. If she ever were to commit to another man, he would have to make her feel the way Thomas did right now—like no harm in the world would come to her as long as he was there at her side. She wanted a partner, not to be someone's wife, and there were very few men in the world who could comprehend what that meant.

"Just what the hell do you think you're doing?!" an angry voice came from behind Thomas and Celeste as they neared Douglas and the Bernards.

Thomas and Celeste halted and circled around to see Captain Bernhardt, who'd evidently chosen to start drinking heavily the moment they'd left the group. As a consequence, he was angry and very drunk. A glass of whiskey was in his wavering hand, and he was having trouble standing steadily on two feet. To Celeste's horror, people were gawking at them.

Before she or Thomas could react, Douglas jumped in the middle. "Come along now, Captain, let's get you some fresh air."

He tried to wrap his arm around the Captain's shoulders, but Jonathan instantly batted him off.

"Get your hands off me!" he bellowed, causing Douglas to withdraw.

Jonathan proceeded to focus his attention on Thomas, pointing a finger at him. "You think just because you're some lord you can come and take away another one of my goddamn fiancées? Huh?! What sort of man are you?!"

"Jonathan!" Celeste hissed, shuffling to him. "Stop it right this minute!"

He glared furiously at her and shoved her toward Douglas, who caught her in his arms. "You've done enough! Parading around here with him like I didn't just ask you to marry me!"

Celeste felt her cheeks blaze red with mortification, yet Thomas remained where he was, watching Jonathan closely. "Why don't you calm down, Captain, there's nothing going on here. Celeste and I have been friends since we were very young."

"Yeah?!" he shouted, then downed his whiskey and threw the

glass on the ground, glass shards exploding on the floor. "Well, that's what Esther said, too. And now she's dead, and it's your fault, you son of a bitch!"

The entire ballroom was dead quiet, every guest seemingly frozen in place as they viewed the drama unfolding. Celeste, too, couldn't fathom Jonathan's lack of propriety at the biggest event of the summer, not worried about her reputation, but rather what this might do to her work for The Palace. Her eyes went back to Thomas, who, to her surprise, was so enraged it was taking every ounce of his resolve to stay composed. She realized if someone else didn't step in, trouble would unfold.

Her father recognized it, too. "You have to fall on the blade this time," Douglas suggested in her ear. "Thomas cannot be seen acting violently in public."

"But Father—"

His grip on her tightened. "You have to do it, Celeste. For all of us."

Celeste bit her lip and pulled free of Douglas's arms, flicking her hair back and marching for Jonathan. Without thinking twice, she went right to him and slapped him hard across the face, acting utterly exasperated.

"How dare you?!" she shouted at the top of her lungs. "You ask me to marry you and then treat me in such a way?" Celeste threw her arms in the air theatrically. "I can't marry a man who doesn't trust me!" Spinning to Thomas, she curtseyed for the final time that night. "I apologize, Lord Turner, for you being treated so rudely upon your return to New York City. Please forgive Jonathan; he has had way too much to drink. Father? Take me home this moment. I cannot stand to be here another second longer."

Douglas was instantly there, pulling her arm through his; together, they promenaded out of the main ballroom as the crowd watched in awe, though the ballroom remained completely noiseless until they reached the exit.

"Good work, daughter," Douglas praised her the moment they were safely tucked away in a coach, heading for The Palace. "You did what needed to be done. The Madame and Thomas will be grateful."

There was a small moment of silence.

"Jonathan proposed to you? Why did you not tell me?"

"He proposed to me right before the Fredericks arrived," Celeste affirmed. "I barely had time to process it!"

She pulled a cigarette and her smoking wand from her dress, and Douglas immediately had a match lit in his hands for her.

He fell back into the seat of the coach. "God damn him for doing that to you."

"It's all right, Father, I'll handle it."

Douglas shook his head. "I think you already did." He glanced at her, looking serious. "Did you want to marry him? It's recoverable if you want it to be."

"I…" her voice trailed off as she put her feelings into words. "If I married him it would be for the wrong reasons. I love him, but I'll never make him happy, and he won't make me happy either."

"You're both broken birds when it comes to love. You don't think you could mend each other? I have an immense amount of respect for the Captain and, with the exception of tonight, I do believe he would take great care of you. Although the drinking would need to be cut back significantly."

Celeste took a long drag of her cigarette. "Father, I'm not giving this up. And I'd have to do that to be Jonathan's wife."

Douglas studied her. "You really want to keep doing this?"

"Yes, I do," she contended, meaning it more than she'd ever meant anything in her life.

Her father grinned. "You're well on your way to becoming the strongest woman I know."

Celeste beamed at him, exhaling a cloud of smoke. "Someday, Father, I will be."

"Well, I'll be damned," the Madame declared. "It's no wonder Richard wants this bastard gone. Clearly he has a vendetta against the Hall, and it's not letting up any time soon."

Douglas stood over by the empty fireplace nursing a whiskey, while Celeste sat opposite the Madame's desk in the loveseat with Louis, sipping wine.

"I don't know the name Parkhurst," Douglas thought aloud, shaking his head. "He's not a society man, which means he could be a lot more troubling than the average finger pointer."

"Well, if he's not a fucking Swallowtail, he must be clergy reformer," the Madame added. "And we would know if he was a Swallow." She took a gulp of her whiskey, followed by a large drag of cigar. "All right. We have everything ready to set in motion. Let's eliminate Frederick and give Richard some reprieve. Meanwhile, Louis, start looking into this Parkhurst character. I want to know everything about this prick sooner rather than later."

"Yes, Madame," Louis replied, pulling out cigarettes for himself and Celeste, and again, she daintily retrieved her smoking wand from her dress.

Douglas finished his drink and left his glass on the mantle. "I am spent. Celeste? Let's grab Jeremiah and head south."

"Not just yet, Douglas," the Madame stressed. "I need Celeste longer. Go ahead home and I'll send her back with Louis when we are finished."

He nodded, moving towards the door of the office. "Absolutely. Celeste? I'll see you in a few hours. We'll have breakfast late."

Celeste smiled. "Sounds lovely, Father."

When Douglas had gone, the Madame let out a heavy sigh. "All right, darling. Tell me everything."

"Croker was astounded to come face to face with Thomas; shocked—scared even. He couldn't believe what he was seeing, and when he tried to extend an invitation, Thomas instantly declined with the utmost courtesy. It was a perfect first play for him."

The Madame smirked, leaning back in her chair, amused. "Oh, Thomas...I am so, so proud of you..."

"What did you tell him?" Louis inquired eagerly. "You spoke with him for a few moments just the two of you?"

"Thomas understands that Father and I are on his side," Celeste conveyed. "And he's...he's very worried about Esther. He says he's going to save her."

The Madame's amusement faded. "He's the only one of us who can," she admitted, then speedily buried her sentiments. "Did he mention anything else?"

"No, we didn't exactly have a proper goodbye," she told them. "The Captain saw us together and was drunk enough to cause a commotion." Celeste downed some of her wine. "He blames Thomas for Esther's death. And, of course, he now thinks that I am romantically pursuing Thomas less than an hour after he proposed to me."

The Madame's left eyebrow rose. "He proposed to you?"

Louis's jaw had dropped. "At the ball?"

"Unfortunately, yes, and I told him I had to think about it."

"Do you want to marry him, Celeste?" Louis asked kindly.

She looked to the Madame. "No, I don't think I do."

"Might I ask why?"

Celeste turned to face Louis. "I don't want that kind of a life, Louis. I want this life. If I did want to go back to being a society woman, I would have done so rather than work for the Madame in the first place. Marrying Jonathan wouldn't make me happy, and would cripple me in the worst possible way."

Louis reached over for the wine bottle and poured a little more into Celeste's glass. "Well, I can't say I am shocked to hear you say that. Madame?"

"Celeste knows my thoughts on the matter," she remarked, taking another drag of her cigar, "and I fully support her choice to tell the Captain she doesn't fucking want him. He's a goddamn disaster after being on the frontier all those years, and the last thing she deserves is to be married to another abusive head case."

Louis changed the subject back to Esther. "When is the last time you've received a painting?"

"Months," Celeste confessed. "I've been worried because usually she leaves them at closer intervals." Her eyes went to the Madame, reading the expression on Louis's face. "She hasn't come by in a while, has she?"

The Madame was vexed. "She has, but it was a short visit, and not one that was very fucking comforting. Her kill count is on the rise, and against Croker's orders, she's been following Thomas."

Celeste nearly dropped her drink. "She's been...been what?!"

"We're trying to get a handle on this, Celeste," Louis assured her, "but Will and I can't confront her about it and give Thomas away."

"Nobody knows except us and Thomas," the Madame added. "The only reason we do is because Thomas fucking told me when I went to see him early last week. If Croker does find out, she'll be up shit's creek. Though she's so goddamn stubborn, she probably wouldn't listen to us anyhow."

"I'll make her care!" Celeste nearly shouted, her distress overpowering her self-control. "She hasn't sacrificed her life to this son of a bitch to give up now!"

"This isn't news to us, darling," the Madame acknowledged forcefully, wanting to squash the argument. "And yet, I will add that if there is one person other than Walsh who can sneak around Croker, it's Esther. Now, Louis and I will get this little problem under control. You have to finish off your end with the Fredericks and fucking hold yourself together. Do you understand me, Celeste?"

She took a deep breath, biting her tongue. "Yes, Madame."

The Madame put out her cigar, set down her whiskey on her

desk, and got up, walking around to where Celeste sat and lowering down beside her.

"She's going to be fine, darling. I can promise you we won't let anything happen to Esther." The Madame put a hand on Celeste's shoulder. "Go home, get some rest. It's almost dawn. I have a feeling you'll have a visitor tomorrow wanting an answer for what happened at the ball this evening, and you're going to need quite a bit of fortitude to handle that bastard."

Celeste scoffed miserably. "Between the two of us, I think Esther and I might destroy poor Jonathan."

"That's his problem, darling, not yours."

Celeste sighed, and she and the Madame rose to stand. "Send word on how your meeting with the judge goes," she requested. "And I'll let you know as soon as I hear from his wife."

"You'll be the first to know," the Madame declared. "Louis? Take Miss Hiltmore home and make sure she gets there in one piece." The Madame moved elegantly back to the throne behind her desk. "Goodnight, Celeste. Oh! Make sure you remind your father to extend an invitation to the Turners for social occasions from this point forward."

"The Turners have always hated social occasions, Madame," Celeste said, confused. "Is this some sort of new angle Thomas is trying to work?"

The Madame picked up her whiskey glass. "Something like that. Just mention it to your father, please. Goodnight, darling."

By the time Louis had her home, the sun was climbing over the eastern part of the city. He and Celeste chatted about Esther and the Captain on their way to Hotel St. Stephen while they smoked cigarettes, though Celeste was finding it challenging not to break their "don't ask, don't tell" policy regarding Esther's life in the underground. It was arduous, as time went on, to attempt to comprehend just who exactly her friend had become in her years serving

Richard Croker and working with the Whyo gang of Manhattan, and Louis often emphasized the woman Celeste had once known was a completely different person. Someday, Celeste hoped they would meet again, if only to relieve the pain of missing her dearest friend. There were so many unknown variables hanging by a thread, ghosts lingering in every shadow, ready to strike at any given moment. Celeste recognized who was on her side, but she still couldn't quite figure out who their enemy was other than Richard Croker.

She bid Louis adieu and walked inside the hotel. Mrs. Ryder snored loudly at her post in the front lobby and Celeste snuck by softly, hoping not to wake her as she tiptoed over to the far staircase that led to her residence. Her head swam with the events of the Admiral's Ball, from Jonathan's proposal to Thomas's return to New York City, and of course, on to Esther and the very thin ice she stood upon. Halting on the stairs, Celeste shook her head, stopping herself from letting the things beyond her control fester. What she needed was a few hours of rest and to try and put these matters from her mind. She ascended the remaining few steps and once more tiptoed down the hall to her door, which she unlocked without a sound and slipped inside.

The living room was dark, and Celeste went straight for her bedroom, already going through the motions of loosening her corset to remove her long, flowing gown by herself. She opened and then closed the bedroom door behind her, sucking in a deep gulp of air as she felt the strings of her dress release. Moving toward her vanity, she went to splash fresh rosewater on her face, washing away the drama of the night and feeling cleaner and lighter in the process. She reached for the towel beside the bowl and dried her skin; as she turned around, Celeste froze where she stood, the towel falling to the floor.

There, in her open window, rested a peregrine falcon, watching her with sharp, all-seeing eyes. The bird stared at her hard, her irises an intense color of gold, as if dissecting every aspect of Ce-

112

leste's person. At first Celeste was startled, yet that faded with the strange impression that the beautiful raptor was protecting something, and firmly held her ground as her talons dug into Celeste's window pane. For nearly a minute, the peregrine remained steady where she was, so motionless Celeste started to wonder if the falcon was actually alive. Then, with a giant swoop of her wings, the bird disappeared from sight.

Celeste delayed a moment before scrambling to the window, locking it shut while she scanned the street below for the falcon, but with no luck. Her heart was racing in her chest, and Celeste felt mystified. Never in her life had she seen a bird like that up close, so exquisite and yet so fierce, Celeste continued to sense her lingering presence. The bird hadn't been wild—she was trained, and she had been in that window for a reason. That reason, however, Celeste could not guess, and she put on her night clothes wondering just how safe she was. Once in her bed, Celeste sat up one last time, and she peeked over toward the now locked window, speculating that perhaps in her exhaustion, she had imagined the whole thing.

But there, on the bottom of the window pane, were the scratches left by the raptor's talons, as if to remind her the falcon was out there somewhere, watching her.

After a few hours of rest, Celeste woke up and joined her father and Jeremiah for breakfast; both, like her, were desperately in need of coffee. The three of them sat down and were served a meal of toast and hard boiled eggs, with thick slices of ham fresh out of the frying pan.

Every once in a while, Celeste would catch one of the staff members raising an eyebrow at Jeremiah's equal treatment in their household, and she would see to it that they were either reprimanded or fired. Years ago, when Celeste learned of her brother's existence and

113

his aspirations to become a physician, she implored Douglas to fund his son's education. For a while, Jeremiah went and studied abroad in London with some of the finest medical doctors in the world. Unfortunately, the United States was far behind the open-mindedness of Europe, and Jeremiah returned home to be scorned, finding work only in the negro hospitals. The Madame took pity on Jeremiah and employed him to take care of her girls, paying him almost double for one visit what he made at the hospital in a week, and Celeste was so grateful for her generosity.

What had been problematic was reuniting her father with Jeremiah in the first place, and somehow restraining her brother from strangling the life out of Douglas.

When Celeste had originally written to Jeremiah, he politely returned her correspondence, making it clear he didn't want to be anyone's charity. Nonetheless, when Douglas offered to finance his entire education to a degree even most white doctors couldn't dream of, the proposition made Celeste's proposal harder and harder to say no to. Eventually, she persuaded Jeremiah to come to New York and hear her out; following multiple rejections of the idea, Jeremiah did comply. The awkwardness and the anxiety at their gathering were unlike anything Celeste ever experienced. Jeremiah had a tough countenance to read, asking Douglas questions and making accusations that Celeste's father by no means could avoid. To his credit, Douglas was humbled with regret and admitted to Jeremiah his wrongs, rightfully taking the blame for his monstrous actions in his youth. But he then was able to charm himself into his son's favor, using his longstanding skills as a lobbyist to advocate for his cause. Douglas wanted Jeremiah to have the best education possible, he wanted to be a part of Jeremiah's life, and most importantly, Celeste needed a brother to watch out for her and keep her safe when Douglas wasn't around. After a week of initiating talks, these get-togethers concluded with Jeremiah consenting to Douglas's monetary assistance and agreeing to take steps to get to know his father and his sister, though he wasn't entirely convinced he could put the past in the past.

It took years, but Jeremiah did find a way to forgive Douglas, and had recently moved into their residence at the hotel. For Celeste, it was the greatest win of her life, as she was at last able to rid her conscience of the demons regarding her family history, or more accurately, the misdeeds of her mother.

When their breakfast concluded, Douglas skipped out to a meeting with a few investors; Jeremiah also left, to make rounds with his patients at the negro hospital. To her relief, Celeste would have the afternoon alone to contemplate just how to handle Captain Bernhardt. Once she'd seen her brother and father out for the day, she made her way to her sitting room for a cigarette to clear her head.

Opening the door, Celeste gasped. On the floor at her feet, her maid was unconscious, and Celeste ran to her, attempting to wake the poor girl while simultaneously checking to be sure she was still breathing.

"She's fine," came a voice from across the room. "When she wakes, she will barely remember what happened."

Celeste felt her whole body go numb, a twinge of chills running down her spine. She knew that voice. She hadn't heard it in so long, and the sound of it was such a shock, Celeste could barely grasp how this was possible. Slowly, she stood and looked to the source, her hand flying to cover her mouth while tears started forming in her eyes. There, in the doorway, stood her best friend, her sister—her Esther.

Celeste ran to Esther and threw her arms around her. "Es!" she cried, feeling uncontrollable sobs escape her. "Oh, Esther, I just...I just..."

Esther hugged her friend close. "I missed you too, Celeste," she said. "I couldn't stay away any longer."

They held each other, and when Celeste was able to get control over her emotions, she let Esther go and beheld her transformation.

"Would you be offended if I told you I think you're stronger than the Captain is?" she teased with a big smile. "You're as solid as stone!"

Esther grinned. "I'll take it as a compliment."

Always the hostess, Celeste motioned for them to move over to sit, darting over to grab them each a glass of wine and cigarettes.

"How long do I have you?" she inquired, uncorking the wine and snatching glasses from the shelf.

"A half hour, maybe more."

Celeste grabbed two already rolled cigarettes. "And no one knows that you're, well, here?"

"No one knows. Not even Louis. This has to stay between us. The Madame is already furious with me."

"We have so much we need to talk about in such a short time," Celeste declared, sitting down across from Esther as her friend retrieved matches from her jacket. They each took a big gulp of wine, gawking at each other.

"You are so changed," Esther declared. "I honestly can't get over how different you are."

"I'm changed?" Celeste guffawed, temporarily setting aside her glass of wine and lighting her cigarette. "Don't even get me started on you, Es."

Esther couldn't hold a straight face, chuckling while she lit her cigarette. "How the fuck did this happen to us?"

"I don't know, but I don't hate it."

"Truthfully, me either."

The room went quiet as the two girls relaxed, falling right back into the comfort of their friendship as if no time had passed.

"So, you've seen Thomas?" Esther asked after a time.

"Last night. He came face to face with Croker."

Esther's eyes lit up. "What I would have given to witness that."

"Croker is rattled, Es. He was caught with his pants down. And the best part is, he has no idea what Thomas is capable of."

Esther was thoughtful. "We need to keep it that way. Thomas is the last piece to this, and we need to keep him guarded on every front. I will handle the Whyos and Croker, but you'll need to handle the social aspect of everything."

"I am all over it." Celeste took a breath. "Es, why did you say the Madame is furious with you? When I was there yesterday, she mentioned you haven't been by to see her in a few weeks."

"Well, we all know I can't lie for shit." Esther took a long drag of her cigarette. "It's because I have been tailing Thomas, and the Madame found out about it."

Her mouth fell open. "Jesus Christ, Esther!" Celeste exclaimed. "Croker will kill you if he finds out!"

"He won't find out, I can promise you that."

"How do you know that? How do you know that...that Walsh freak isn't stalking you and tracking your whereabouts?"

Esther rolled her eyes. "Don't you think I am smarter than that by now?" Angered, Esther got to her feet and went over to roll another cigarette. "I only go when I know Walsh is engaged elsewhere. And I've only done it a handful of times, just to get a read on what's going on with Thomas."

She didn't speak for a few seconds, and Celeste could sense Esther's irritation was fading. When she rotated back with a newly lit cigarette, it had passed.

"The ironic thing is that now, I think Thomas is following me," she observed, taking a drag and exhaling smoke. "I can't be sure, but I swear, it's like I can feel him watching me. I can't really describe it."

Celeste had a drink of wine. "He has. It's how the Madame found out you were following him in the first place."

Unexpectedly, Esther snorted, amused. "I should have known he was better than me."

"Better than you, hah!" Celeste exclaimed. "We'll see about that, Es."

With a smile, Esther returned to her seat beside Celeste. "I'm tired, Celeste. I am so tired. I need help. I can't keep doing this by myself."

"We have each other. That's what has been getting me through this, and finally, we can actually start the work we've been preparing for." A thought occurred to her. "Can I ask you a very personal question?"

"You know you can."

"Do you still love him?"

Esther looked directly into her eyes. "So much it scares me."

Celeste sighed. "I wish I knew what that felt like," Celeste thought aloud, finishing her cigarette. "Es, I have to tell you something."

"Anything."

"The Captain asked me to marry him last night."

This didn't surprise her. "What did you say?"

"That I had to think about it. I don't love him enough, Es. I've already been the wife once, and I don't want that again. I love my life. I love who I have become. I don't want to be a New York City socialite again—I want to have a purpose. I'd never have that being Mrs. Captain Jonathan Bernhardt."

"Then say no, Celeste."

Celeste grabbed Esther's cigarette and took a long inhale before passing it back. "You're right. There really isn't another way around it." Celeste gazed at her friend, the awful scar from Timothy's blade visible on Esther's neck, jagged and menacing in its appearance. "How bad is it?"

"How bad is what?"

"How bad is…existing and doing what you do? How bad is it?"

Esther reached for her wine glass. "How much do you want to know?"

"Everything."

Her friend's face wretched up into an aggrieved expression. "You're going to lose sleep if I tell you."

"Oh, please. There's no rest for the wicked, Esther."

Esther smirked, then her mien grew dark. "It's like nothing you could imagine. I mean, Louis, Will, and I take care of each other, and we train most mornings, but I have to pretend to be the loyal dog of a man I despise. We run his errands, intimidating people… muscling for the Hall. I pretend to betray those I love. I have to hurt and kill people to keep the Whyos in line, and Walsh is constantly trying to stir them up. I am Croker's only real link to the gang anymore, and recently I've gotten more nervous about when the day comes that they decide they don't want to be aligned with Tammany Hall. The situation is volatile."

Celeste tried to camouflage her horror. "How many people have you…you…"

"More than I want to admit."

"How many?"

Esther peered directly into her eyes. "I made myself stop counting at twenty, but that's not really the worst part."

Celeste's stomach dropped at hearing the number. "What's the worst part?"

She was hesitant to respond. "The worst part is just that it doesn't bother me, the violence. I'm so…numb to it. I wish I cared. But I don't. It's just that there are so many secrets to keep, and I don't know how much longer I can keep them all straight."

Celeste knew what she needed to hear. "Thomas swore to me he'd get you out of this. He swore he would save you."

A sad smile came to Esther's lips. "The question that haunts me is how I will handle life after this. What kind of life can I live after doing the things I've done?"

"Thomas will have the same burden," Celeste promised her.

"And if anything, it will be something you two can solve together. Or...choose not to solve."

From her reaction, it was clear Esther hadn't considered this. "Thank you, Celeste."

When they'd finished their wine, Celeste had an idea to brighten Esther's day. "Can I show you something?"

"Of course."

Celeste got to her feet and Esther followed; she led her to a closed door. Pulling the key from her dress pocket, Celeste unlocked the door and pushed it open, walking inside with Esther at her heels. Inside the small room, a floor-to-ceiling window lit up the walls, every inch of which were covered with the paintings Esther had left for Celeste over the years that they'd spent apart. Esther was flabbergasted, her eyes wide as she took in the collection of her work all together. Each piece was brilliant with color, reflecting the sunlight in such a way that the flora seemed alive, as if it was jumping off the page.

Celeste moved to stand beside her friend and took Esther's hand in hers.

"It's been so difficult to be without you, but every time I missed you, I would come in here with a glass of wine and remind myself that you hadn't gone anywhere. The best consolation was the knowledge that our separation was only temporary."

Esther didn't say a word, then, out of the blue, grabbed Celeste, and hugged her tight. Celeste wrapped her arms around her best friend in return. She wasn't sure if she imagined it, but Celeste thought she felt her friend sob softly just once, and then once more retreat into silence. The pair held each other for a time, Esther's paintings warming them from every angle.

At last, Esther's grip eased, and Celeste released her in turn.

"I have to go," Esther indicated reluctantly. "I've already been gone too long."

"When will I see you again?"

Abruptly, the maid on the ground stirred, catching both of their attentions.

"Soon," Esther assured her. "I've got to be going."

As if enough wasn't happening already, a loud and desperate banging came echoing in from the front door.

"Celeste?" Captain Bernhardt's voice was easy to recognize, and Esther's panicked eyes went to Celeste's. "Celeste, we need to talk! Are you there? Your doorman said you were in."

"Fuck," Esther cursed under her breath.

From the commotion, the maid woke and sat straight up, though, miraculously, she was facing the opposite direction of Celeste and Esther. In a flash, Esther had the door to the room closed and was at the window, unfastening the latch.

Her friend moved so speedily, Celeste was having trouble keeping up. "What do I do, Es?"

But Esther was already halfway out the window. "Close this behind me and pretend nothing happened," she ordered, and for a second, their gazes met. "I'll see you soon, I swear to you."

Celeste nodded and watched in awe as Esther launched herself from the windowpane over to the gutter on the side of the hotel, a leap that soared at least seven or eight feet. Masterfully, Esther shimmied down the drain and then dropped to the ground, taking off into the street without glancing back. Immediately, she was another blur amongst the crowd.

In a hurry, Celeste closed the window and straightened up, taking a deep breath before she returned to the sitting room. She found her maid still sitting on the ground, rubbing her head in confusion.

"Good gracious!" Celeste cried, rushing to her in contrived alarm and dropping down beside her. "What happened? Are you all right?"

"I have no idea!" the maid conceded. "One minute, I was off to get you a bit of tonic for your head, the next, I just...I just..."

Celeste rested her hand on the maid's cheek and peeked into

her eyes as if examining her for some sort of ailment, only to once again be overrun with the knocks and pleading of Captain Bernhardt from outside.

"Celeste? I can hear you from out here!"

"My apologies, Captain, one of the maids has fainted!" Celeste bellowed, trying to control her annoyance. "I will be right there."

Promptly, he ceased, and Celeste helped the maid to her feet. "Are you up to fetching us a bit of wine?"

She thought about it for a moment. "I believe so."

"If you feel poorly in the least, I want you to take the rest of the day. Understood?"

"Yes, Miss Celeste."

The maid scampered away, and Celeste half-heartedly made her way to the door.

"Sorry for the delay, Captain," she said, unlocking the door and opening it casually. "I am not sure what happened to her. Poor thing has probably not eaten enough today."

The Captain stood before her, agitated, though attempting to disguise it.

"It's fine," he countered, while his tone indicated otherwise.

Celeste beckoned him in to take a seat. The maid, with color rushing back to her face, brought them each a glass of wine and sat them on the table.

"We need to discuss last night," the Captain stressed firmly.

"What would you like to discuss about it?"

He gaped at her. "Are you serious?"

"I only meant which part, Jonathan."

"Which part?" His antagonism rose, and Celeste felt her defenses heighten.

"Yes. There was one part where you proposed, and another where you—"

"Your behavior was despicable! I just, I couldn't believe that you would—"

"That I would what? Talk with an old friend upon his return to New York?" Celeste snapped, her manner taking on a ferociousness that startled both the Captain and the maid, who slipped out and down the maid's passage. Celeste, too, was astonished at where this angry passion was stemming from, but couldn't restrain herself. "You publicly humiliated me at one of the biggest social gatherings of the year, all because you were too goddamn drunk! Again!"

Jonathan's ears turned red in shame. "I will admit to having a little too much whiskey, but you cannot tell me that your actions after I had only just proposed were acceptable."

Celeste scoffed. "We aren't engaged, Jonathan. You are not the master of me. I am the master of my own person, and if this is any indication of how our marriage would be, you ought to know better than to think I could ever tell you yes!"

Sinking down into his chair, Jonathan was crestfallen. "So, your answer is no, then?"

"My answer is pending whether or not you start to become the Jonathan you were before the war, or if you remain this person I don't even recognize." Snatching up her wine glass, Celeste took a large gulp and sat across from him, wanting to calm herself down and struggling to do so.

"Well, it's not like you are the same either, Celeste."

"Where are you going with this, Jonathan?"

"You aren't the same either! You...you curse! You take abnormal hours for a woman of your station! You dress provocatively... you have your nigger brother actually living in this apartment with you—"

"How dare you!" Celeste interrupted him, enraged.

The Captain waved her off heatedly. "It's not normal, so don't you dare defend it!" he shouted, reaching for his drink and downing the contents. "And what's worse is that you scorned these ridiculous parties before I left, and now they are the center of your life once again! What happened to the Celeste who just wanted to be happy?

Who hated the public eye? When did social standing take control of your life? I mean, Jesus, you act just like your mother used to!"

Celeste lowered her gaze to her drink, on the verge of losing her nerve altogether. "Get out of my apartment," she murmured, "or I cannot hold myself responsible for the damage I might do to you."

It was then Jonathan grasped how far he'd overstepped his bounds, and his antagonism became indignity. "Celeste, please, I didn't mean that. I was just upset and lost my temper." He got up and went to her, kneeling beside her. "I love you. I really do. I am sorry that I offended you. I was...I just..."

She scowled at him, her eyes narrowing. "Get. Out. Or I will make you regret it."

He stared at her in disbelief, and then did as she asked. Standing up, he went to the door, turning around before he left.

"Did I ruin everything?" he asked, pleading.

"I don't know yet."

Jonathan left the apartment and closed the door. Celeste had another big sip of wine, pensively considering his words. In her heart, she sensed this was exactly how Esther felt with the Captain as well. How could she marry a man who didn't know her or understand her intentions? There was no way on God's green earth Celeste would allow another man to govern her life, and from what she could tell, that appeared to be the future she had with Captain Bernhardt. It wasn't that he didn't love her—he would do anything for her, Celeste was sure of that. However, the things he'd said about her brother, about her conduct...to Celeste, they were unforgiveable. She scorned the memory of her monstrous mother, and Jeremiah, no matter what color his skin might be, was her blood and her equal.

Celeste needed to get out of the apartment; finishing her wine, she leapt to her feet and readied herself to head north to The Palace.

"Becky?" she called, and the maid was instantaneously in the doorway. "Go downstairs and hail me a coach to go to the Upper West."

124

"Yes, Miss Celeste."

Marching to her room, Celeste splashed water on her face to try and wash off what had been an utterly perplexing afternoon, and then lightly applied a bit of rouge to her lips and cheeks. Minutes passed and Becky returned, assisting Celeste into her jacket and fetching her gloves.

"What time should I expect you?"

"You are dismissed for the day," she stated, "under the condition that you do not discuss with anyone the conversation I had with Captain Bernhardt."

The maid was stunned. "Miss Celeste, I would...I would never..."

"I know you enjoy telling stories to the others in the kitchen," Celeste confronted her nonchalantly. "And some of it I could give a damn about. But not this, Becky, or you'll find employment elsewhere."

Anxiety formed in the young girl's eyes. "I won't say a word, Miss Celeste."

"Good. Now run on home and get some rest."

Celeste swept out of her front door and down the stairs to the lobby, her carriage waiting for her outside. The driver helped her into the cab, and after giving him the address discreetly, Celeste pulled the curtains on the windows. As the coach rocked along on the bouncy road, Celeste discovered she was in a strangely good mood in spite of her interaction with the Captain. Seeing Esther reminded Celeste of what her true priorities were and what mattered most in the strange world that had become her existence. She cared for Jonathan's well-being, but she sadly realized anytime she thought on to the future, he was not a part of it. There was no telling what would happen to her in the days ahead, and Celeste was enthralled by that type of mystery and chance. Once already she'd attempted a mapped-out life of normalcy, and that had turned out to be the worst mistake she'd ever made. Like a weight lifting off her shoulders, Celeste found herself coming to peace with the notion that she would not accept Jonathan, and in the end, he'd probably be better off for it.

When she'd made it to The Palace, Celeste paid her driver and strode over to the gate as George's familiar face emerged at the front door, smiling at the sight of her.

"Back already?" he joked. "She'll be happy to see you. She's been bored today."

"How could you tell she's been bored?"

"Because she's been unbearable."

With a laugh, Celeste closed the gate; halfway down the front path, she froze. An eerie sensation came over her, and for a reason she could not surmise, Celeste noticed herself looking up toward the roof. There, staring directly back at her, was the same peregrine falcon she had seen last night, and a rush of goose bumps trickled down her arms.

"What is it?" George inquired.

But Celeste did not move. Was she hallucinating? Was it an omen? Where had this creature come from, and why was it following her?

Then, in the blink of an eye, the raptor was gone once more.

"Celeste?" George entreated her, hurriedly moving out to her as his hand reached for his holstered pistol. "What is it? What did you see?"

"I saw a bird," she conveyed quietly, her eyes not leaving the place where the falcon had just been.

She could feel George ease up, hands descending to his sides. "A bird? That's what caused you to turn so pale?"

There was an odd pit in her stomach. "That's the second time I've seen that bird today."

"Are you sure? Could have been a different bird but the same kind?"

His tone was filled with doubt, so Celeste shook it off. "Never mind, Georgie. Let's go see the Madame."

"You sure?"

She gave him a sideways glance. "Come on. I'm fine. Really."

As they meandered up the main staircase, George piped up again, "We got someone new on our crew, Celeste. I didn't like him much at first, but he's a smart son of a bitch."

"Someone new?" she asked. "The Madame hadn't told me she was recruiting."

"She wasn't. Croker sent him. Said it was a conflict of interest to have him, and the Madame needed another hit around since Louis is always running Croker's errands."

"You like him?"

"He's good with a gun. And polite."

"Polite, Georgie?"

"You'll see."

He opened the doors to the Madame's office, and as they walked inside, they encountered the Madame berating a man Celeste had never seen before. Nonetheless, the moment their eyes met, Celeste's heart began to beat uncontrollably.

"...try to be a little more fucking discreet when you're about town!" she thundered, and when she realized she had other visitors, the Madame smiled. "Please tell me this is a social visit. This goddamn day has been dragging on like it's never going to fucking end."

"Yes, Madame," Celeste replied. "I needed some company."

The Madame pointed toward the new hire. "This is Ashleigh. During the week, he will be filling in for Louis, since Croker can't seem to manage hiring his own fucking people."

Ashleigh appeared to be just as stunned by Celeste as she was with him, and after a moment of pause, he remembered his place and marched over to her.

"Ashleigh Sweeney, ma'am," he greeted her, taking her hand and kissing it gently.

The whole room around them blurred away, and Celeste could barely breathe. Abruptly, as the words he had spoken sank in and his familiarity struck her, she understood why George had mentioned his presence at the Hall was a conflict of interest.

"You're related to Will, then?"

"I'm his son."

Celeste's eyes grew wide. "His son?"

The Madame got to her feet and went to the drink cart, fetching a bottle of wine. "His goddamn son. Strange how these things happen."

Ashleigh took a step back from Celeste and went to grab two wine glasses for the women to drink from.

Polite, like George mentioned, Celeste thought.

She took a seat near the fireplace, and the Madame did the same while George left them to return to his post. Ashleigh, on the other hand, placed their wine glasses on the coffee table and moved over by the door, stoically standing guard. With his presence and the sudden swirl of emotions she felt, the idea of discussing Captain Bernhardt with the Madame became awkward. Needless to say, she didn't have much of an option. If Ashleigh was going to be a permanent fixture, there was no way around discussing these things in front of him.

"Jeremiah is at the hospital, I presume?" the Madame supposed, pouring them wine.

"Yes, and Father had a few meetings. I had a visitor this afternoon."

"Oh?"

"Captain Bernhardt showed up, demanding an answer."

Adding to her bewilderment, Celeste could have sworn Ashleigh twitched at the mention of this.

"After publicly humiliating you?" the Madame sneered. "For God's sake, the man has no boundaries. Have you told him your decision, darling? Or are we going to wait and see if the trauma subsides and he stops behaving like a drunken asshole?"

"I can't marry him," Celeste declared before she could stop herself, and from nowhere, the fury at his remarks returned. "He came at me, patronizing me, saying I've become like my fucking mother!"

The Madame nearly dropped her wine glass. "Did you just…"

"Don't start with me," Celeste shushed her, feeling again some stirring of confidence that was managing to take over her brain. "He has no idea what I am really doing, who I really am. He said my priorities are different than they used to be."

"Well, they are, darling."

"You know what scares me?"

"That Esther and I had this exact same conversation a few years ago?"

"Exactly." Celeste took a sip of wine. "He called Jeremiah a…a…"

The Madame held up a hand. "You don't need to go that far with your language. One step at a time. Let me guess. That bastard doesn't understand why you treat him as an equal?"

"He thinks Jeremiah shouldn't live with us."

"What a fucking prick," she thought aloud, taking a large gulp of wine. "That's what happens to men who are brainwashed in the army, thinking the natives and the slaves are second class citizens. It's a load of bullshit. Your brother is the smartest physician I've ever come across, and the best working girls I've ever had haven't been white. Fucking ridiculous."

They sat there for a moment without speaking, mulling over the situation.

"Please tell me you told him off," the Madame suggested, gazing at Celeste with sparkling, humorous eyes.

129

Celeste couldn't help herself—she laughed. "I am not sure when I started to become so outspoken, but it's a menace!"

"It was bound to happen. I'm just glad you sent that son of a bitch home with his tail between his legs."

A tiny chortle came from Ashleigh's direction, and the Madame spun her concentration to him. "Something funny over there, Young Sweeney?"

He revolved towards her. "I just woulda loved to witness that, Madame. Watchin' her tell off some racist bastard would be mighty entertainin'."

Celeste felt her cheeks flush bright red. "Thank you, Mr. Sweeney," she mumbled.

He smiled at her, and if it was possible, Celeste blushed even more. "Call me Ashleigh, ma'am."

A quick study, the Madame glanced from Ashleigh to Celeste and back to Ashleigh, an amused expression forming on her face.

"Well, then. Thank you for your contribution, Mr. Sweeney. If you don't mind, would you run down to the kitchen and find out if dinner will be ready this century?"

Ashleigh took a small bow and left the office.

When he was gone, the Madame began laughing again. "Oh, for Christ's sake, Celeste!"

"What?"

"Don't 'what' me, you little coquette! There was so much fucking sexual tension in this room, you could cut it with a knife! Oh, if Louis were here, he would completely lose his shit. You and Will Sweeney's son...what a match..."

"No...Madame, it's not like that..."

The Madame reached over for the wine bottle and filled their not-nearly-empty glasses. "Well, the boy couldn't stop swooning over you. It's the most personality I've seen out of him since he started working here."

Having more of her drink to calm her nerves, Celeste tried not to think on it. "How do I handle this thing with the Captain? I need to do it in a way that won't hurt him."

"Darling," the Madame said, her tone becoming sincere, "no matter how you do it, you're going to hurt him. But you can't keep putting yourself through this. You can't save him."

"I don't want to save him. I just wish I didn't feel so guilty."

The Madame considered this. "This is because of Esther, too, isn't it?"

"A little. Not that it's having any effect on my feelings toward Jonathan. I think a part of me wanted to take care of him because of what happened between the two of them."

"She never loved Jonathan," the Madame responded matter-of-factly. "She's only really loved Thomas in that capacity. Captain Bernhardt, unhappily for him, has very good taste in women, and to his own fault, doesn't have the capability of understanding them. You would be fucking miserable married to that man, no matter what he would try to do for you, and the sooner you got this over with, the sooner you can move on."

A knock came on the door, and Ashleigh strode in. "Madame, dinner's just 'bout ready, and I told 'em to prepare a plate for you as well, Celeste. Figured you'd be stickin' 'round to keep the Madame company."

"Why, how thoughtful of you, Mr. Sweeney," the Madame professed mockingly. "You are going to stay for dinner, darling?"

"If you'd like, Madame."

"I don't think I am the only one who would enjoy your company," she muttered so that only Celeste could hear. "Shall we head to the dining room?"

Ignoring as best she could the Madame's teasing, Celeste agreed, yet not without a small sliver of hope that perhaps she had caught the new hire's attention and the whole encounter wasn't only in her head.

Dinner went by fast, and at its close, Celeste was horrified when the Madame ordered Ashleigh to escort her home. Celeste protested incessantly, but the Madame wouldn't be swayed, claiming that it was too late for her to venture out alone. With a wink, she had George hail them a coach, and reluctantly Celeste left The Palace and climbed into the carriage with Ashleigh, praying the darkness would conceal how red she was with embarrassment. The two sat across from one another, and for the first few minutes, neither of them said a word.

Ashleigh broke the silence. "So, if ya don' mind me askin', what kinda role you playin' in this whole grand scheme of hers?"

Celeste reached in to pull a cigarette out of her dress; before she could reach for matches, Ashleigh already had a lit one in front of her. Trying to stay cool, Celeste leaned forward and allowed him to light her cigarette, and she took a long drag.

"I help the Madame secure rich clients with my social connections," she conveyed, "and I spy for her at larger parties and gatherings to get her as much information as possible."

"I see," he responded. "Do you mind if I ask ya somethin' else?"

"Not at all."

"I feel like there's somethin' I'm missin'. What's the endgame here? She just a power hungry one? Is it more 'bout the money?"

"Why do you want to know?"

"I just feel like it'd give me a better idea of what in the hell is goin' on at that place. I ain' stupid. I know when there's another agenda people are followin', and it's written over the faces of all y'all."

Celeste exhaled a cloud of smoke into the cab. "No offense meant, Ashleigh, but until the Madame shares that kind of information with you, it's not my place to fill you in on our operations."

"All right," he accepted, resting back against the bench. "If it makes ya feel any better, I ain' a big fan of that Croker bastard. Far as I'm concerned, he's the worst kinda man to be workin' for."

"You're working for him and the Madame, I presume?"

"He sends me a small stipend for my time," Ashleigh granted. "Ain' much. The Madame promised me more when I prove my loyalty. Not sure how I'll be goin' about that, but I'm sure an opportunity will present itself."

"If you want to show loyalty, the best thing you could do is stop taking Croker's stipend."

"Seems silly to do that 'fore the Madame agrees to up my pay."

"Well, there's your first lesson. With us, at the end of the day, none of us give a shit about the money."

From the look on his face, Ashleigh was shocked by her language and her honesty. "This is comin' from a young lady with quite a bit o' money brought in from her father's lobbyin', or so I hear."

A touch of outrage swelled in her chest. "You don't know anything about me, Mr. Sweeney, so I suggest you take your judgments elsewhere. My position in society and my life appear the way they do because I want them to and so I can successfully work for the Madame with enormous success. I've had trials throughout my years that would give you nightmares. So, if you think you can sum me up as a rich daddy's girl, you can go to hell."

"Whoa, whoa, whoa. I wasn' tryin' to make any assumptions about anythin'. I was just statin' the obvious based on meetin' you and your dad, how you is dressed, and where ya live. All valid pieces of the puzzle." He grew pensive for a time, then persisted. "So, you're the one Louis told me about."

"What do you mean?"

"You're the one who was married to that Wall Street prick. The one your friend shot, and she got hung for it. That's the story, right?"

Hearing what felt like her past life summed up in such a way made Celeste's skin crawl. "Yes, that's the story."

Anytime Timothy was mentioned, Celeste had to fight off an overwhelming bout of nausea with the dark memories of abuse she'd endured.

Ashleigh could tell he'd brought up something painful. "Did I cross a line? I apologize if I made ya upset."

She took another deep inhale of her cigarette. "It's fine," she said curtly.

"Guy must have been fuckin' blind, if ya ask me."

From the other side of the coach, she peered at him quizzically, not catching his implication.

"I just meant, ya know…bein' married to you and not…well… appreciatin' it."

Her residual impatience with Ashleigh vanished, and once more, her heart beat faster. "Thank you."

They arrived at the Hotel St. Stephen shortly after, and Ashleigh opened the door and hopped down first, holding his hand up to help Celeste down. She took it obligingly, noting how strong and calloused his palms were. When they were on even ground, she rotated to him, gave him a small curtsy, and gracefully floated in the direction of the hotel entrance.

"I'm goin' to take your advice!" he shouted after her.

She twirled around. "My advice?"

"I'm goin' to stop takin' pay from Croker. Like ya mentioned, it shouldn' be 'bout the money."

Celeste smiled broadly. "It's a good start."

He was reluctant to let her go. "Will I be seein' ya again soon?"

"This week, I'm sure."

"All right, then. Have a nice evenin'. And Celeste?"

"Yes?"

"Don' marry that guy. You deserve better."

Celeste was speechless. With a bow, Ashleigh climbed into the coach and left her standing there, bewildered.

"Miss Hiltmore?" the doorman queried, holding the door for her. "You coming inside?"

She stared after the carriage as it barreled down the roadway.

"Miss Hiltmore?"

"Yes, yes, I am." Celeste walked forward and inside, baffled.

"You have a good night, Miss Hiltmore?" the doorman went on as she shuffled by.

"I did, thank you."

Scaling the staircase to her room, Celeste still couldn't work through what exactly had happened on her ride home; however, there was one thing she did know. Ashleigh was going to be a concern for her, though whether it was good or bad, she couldn't quite yet determine.

"Someone gonna tell me just what is goin' on here?" Will asked, agitated at being kept in the dark. "Been a long week, an' I ain' exactly in the mood for surprises."

As requested by the Madame, Louis had brought Will to The Palace, where they planned to at last tell him about Ashleigh's newfound presence in their lives. When Louis had realized just who Croker had hired and sent to the Madame as his weekday replacement, he went after Croker hard, particularly when he'd discovered Will had no idea his long-lost son was in the city. Croker, in his usual fashion, had been dismissive about the affair, but Louis could see right through the act. Walsh had found Ashleigh on his own accord to cause a rift amongst them, and Louis wasn't going to allow that bastard to win this round. Together, he and the Madame formulated a plan to reunite father and son, though without knowing their backstory, neither of them had any clue what to envisage.

The Madame grabbed whiskeys for Louis and Will. "We just wanted you to meet the new guard at The Palace," she explained, handing their drinks over. "This group needs to remain solid with certain…people returning to town."

Will took the glass and had a gulp of his whiskey. "I can' even

135

imagine what Richie is like right now. Louis, you been by to see him yet?"

"Not yet," Louis admitted, taking a seat. "I figured you, Esther, and I would go tomorrow."

"Yeah, better we stay a team. He's gonna be unbearable. Poor bastard."

Louis endeavored to mask his anxiety and also had a sip of his drink—even the Madame remained uncharacteristically unobtrusive, behind her desk. It didn't take long before Will grasped something was amiss.

"Really, what is this, brother?" he beseeched Louis, turning toward him. "Some kinda intervention?"

A knock came on the Madame's office door.

"Come in!" she hollered.

Will's countenance transformed from slight annoyance to absolute disbelief. In marched his son, and when Ashleigh finally noted who it was gaping at him from the loveseat, he halted instantly in his tracks.

Though father and son weren't completely identical in their appearance, they carried themselves in a manner that made them indistinguishable from one another. Guns on their hips, long jackets billowing behind them, hair tied back, and Pendleton hats on their heads. Unlike Will, however, Ashleigh had a cigarette in his mouth rather than chewing tobacco. As they stared at each other, Louis watched them closely, hoping with every fiber in his being this hadn't been a giant mistake.

Will's face then became slightly irritated, and he finished his whiskey. "What're ya doin' here, boy?"

Louis shot a glance to the Madame, and she gestured for him to remain where he was.

"Got a job," Ashleigh remarked evenly. "And apparently, you ain' dead after all."

136

"Your momma tell ya I was dead?"

Ashleigh became defensive. "Nah. Sent word out for ya when she killed herself. Figured you woulda come back if you was alive to claim your son, but never heard a lick from ya. So, I assumed you was dead."

The room went ice cold.

"She killed herself? How?"

"She had another one of them episodes and went off the rails. Found her in the barn. Hung herself."

Will was impassive. "Never heard nothin' about it. Otherwise, I woulda come for ya."

Ashleigh scoffed. "Right." He motioned to the drink cart. "Madame, ya mind if I pour myself one?"

"Not at all," she answered. "Did you get Celeste home in one piece?"

"Course," he replied, pacing directly for the whiskey decanter.

Once he'd gotten his drink, the Madame stood up. "Look, gentlemen, the reason we brought you two together is a fucking obvious one. Now, if there is going to be a conflict here, I want to know about it and get it settled, because I'm not going to have a goddamn circus of drama at my establishment when we have enough issues to deal with."

"I don' have any issue here," Will asserted. "But I can guarantee ya the boy does."

"I knew ahead of time what I was in for," Ashleigh remarked. "I knew you was gonna be here and we'd be seein' an awful lot of each other. But yeah, Madame, I do have a fuckin' problem. Two, actually. So, let's get this out on the table."

The Madame descended into her chair. "The floor is yours, Ashleigh."

He threw back his whiskey. "First thing is first." Ashleigh pointed at Will. "We may be workin' in close proximity, but we is not friends, ya hear me? So, don' go thinkin' things will go back the way they

137

was, because it ain't happenin'. I'm here to work and do my job. I don' want nothin' from you."

Will was about to fire a retort at his son, but Louis touched his shoulder and shook his head, causing Will to reluctantly withdraw and listen.

"That is understandable," the Madame approved. "And I think Will can understand that as well. What is the second issue, darling?"

To everyone's astonishment, Ashleigh looked to the Madame. "I 'preciate the job I have here. I don' know what is goin' on under the surface, but you didn' hire me 'cause I was stupid. I talked with Miss Hiltmore this evenin', and she advised me that as long as I'm takin' a stipend from that Croker bastard, I ain't ever gonna find out the real deal. So, I'm tellin' you firsthand, I ain' takin' no more money from that son of a bitch. I don' like him, I don' respect him, and I got no reason to have no loyalty to him."

Louis couldn't believe what he was hearing. "You are going to drop your connections to the Hall and sign on with The Palace? Permanently?"

Ashleigh twisted toward him. "Yeah. That's the way it is."

Another long silence, until the Madame spoke up: "Little Sweeney and Big Sweeney, I need you out of my office," she declared. "Louis and I need to discuss this proposition. Can you two handle sitting down at the bar without fucking murdering each other for ten minutes?"

Ashleigh didn't say a word, only strode out of the room. Will got to his feet and finished his drink, then set the glass on the side table. Like his son, Will left the room without saying anything to the Madame or Louis, and slammed the door shut behind him.

"Jesus fucking Christ," the Madame sighed, leaning back in her chair and throwing her feet onto her desk. "I mean, it went better than I'd predicted. But what's this about Little Sweeney wanting to drop his pay from the Hall and come on board here?"

Louis rose and went over for more whiskey. "If he's anything like his father, he's sharp. He's figured out there is more here than just an upper class brothel. The question is how much should he know...and can we trust someone like him?"

"You heard it from him yourself. It wasn't Croker who recruited him. It was Walsh. To fuck our heads up."

"Yes, and while that stands, I still can't wrap my head around this. He's only been here a few weeks, and he wants to pick a side?"

Without reason, the Madame smiled broadly. "He wants to pick her side."

Louis was lost. "Whose side?"

"Celeste's."

Louis moved back over to his spot and sat again. "When in the hell did he meet Celeste?"

"Tonight. He was pretty infatuated with her."

"Most men are," Louis added, humorously. "You think that one little thing is what turned him?"

"No, I don't."

"What else, then?"

She took out a cigar and matches, cutting and lighting her tobacco. "No matter what Little Sweeney says, he loves his daddy. He's what, in his early or mid-twenties? He's more or less become the exact same man his father is. If he really fucking despised Will, he would have never taken this path. He wants to be his father. He wants to be near his father. He's just all fucked up in the head about Will leaving him to rot with his crazy mother."

"Well...fuck..."

The Madame nodded. "Sometimes, we forget that the simplest explanations tend to be the right ones. Now, we are going to start him slowly. I don't want him knowing the full scope of this shit until we know he is trustworthy."

"Yes, Madame."

"And have Esther keep an eye on him."

"Of course."

She had another sip of whiskey. "Celeste is smitten with him as well."

Louis rolled his eyes. "You can't be serious. That one?"

"I couldn't believe it either! Guess that's what happens when you go from being courted by boring gentlemen to hanging around the underbelly of this city."

"I better go make sure they haven't shot each other," Louis told her, getting up. "You don't think that'll be a problem for us, do you?"

"What? Celeste and Little Sweeney?"

"Yes."

"On the contrary, Louis, I think it will bond that boy to us for good. Wait and see for yourself."

He walked to the doors.

"Oh, and while we're on the topic, send up Samuel when you get downstairs," she called after him. "He'll be down in the bar."

Louis left her office, a big smirk on his face. Celeste had likely saved them from catastrophe, and at the same time, would have a devoted dog to assist her in what she desired and bail her out of difficulties whenever she needed it. It amazed him how Celeste was becoming more and more like the Madame every day; the thought of it made Louis worry for anyone who decided to cross both of them. If Ashleigh did turn out to be a bad seed, neither the Madame nor Celeste would let it slip by. The young Mr. Sweeney had no idea how deep in he already was, and Louis could only pray he was up for the challenge.

If not, he wondered who might strike first: the Madame, or Celeste.

CHAPTER XXXIII.

"Mr. Croker! Mr. Croker! Larry Addler from *The Evening Post!"*

Croker found him in the crowd. "Go ahead, Mr. Addler!"

"With the election just around the corner, does Sheriff Grant have any tricks up his sleeve to sway voters?"

"Other than the fact that he's Irish?"

The swarm of reporters laughed at Croker's quip, then frantically took to scratching down his joke and preparing for whatever he said next.

"In my personal opinion, ladies and gentlemen, Sheriff Grant's greatest qualification is that there is no need for tricks or magic or propaganda. Let's face facts. Hewitt's personal philosophies are hindering his ability to run this city, and we've all suffered because of it. We need a young man at the helm of our ship to keep up with the times. The old ways haven't worked, they will not work, and it is time for a new generation to steer us to success!"

Thus far, the press conference was going just the way Croker wanted. It was only early June, but Hugh Grant was gaining traction in his push to be the mayor of New York City, with fundraisers popping up left and right and an increasing interest from the public, partially due to Grant's young age. At only thirty-four, he was enormously prosperous and wealthy, and the Protestants were losing their minds trying to convince the people of New York not to fall for the Hall's semantics. Grant, however, had a way with his Irish people. He was well-mannered, devilishly handsome, and regardless of being a frequenter of The Palace and known bachelor, he made sure to be seen attending church every Sunday. In his earlier years, Grant graduated from Columbia Law and dabbled in real estate prior to being elected to the board of aldermen at age twenty-eight, and three years later, he was city sheriff. Now, he was Croker's hand-picked poster child for the future of the city, and if he could get Grant elected, Croker would officially own Manhattan.

"Mr. Croker! Terrance Hanley, sir! *The Sun!*"

"Yes, Mr. Hanley?"

"Are you worried that Sheriff Grant's age might sway voters that he's not qualified to serve as mayor?"

Croker let out an entertained scoff. "Mr. Hanley, being mayor of this city during such a revolutionary time has absolutely nothing to do with age!" he boomed in return, a sly smirk on his face as if the question were utterly preposterous. "We've had fat, old men with three lifetimes worth of political experience running New York City for decades, and where has it gotten us? Nowhere!" Croker pounded his fist on the podium to make his point, his expression hardening. "Hugh may be young, but he is a New Yorker, and he understands the way this machine works. Youth has vision, youth has determination, and youth is far less corrupted than those who have sat in the mayor's chair before him!"

He'd set this one up perfectly, and waited for the query to come. He'd been preparing for it.

"Mr. Croker! Samwell Priestly, *New York Times!*"

Of course, it had to be Samwell Priestly. That bastard loved to defame and challenge Richard Croker of Tammany Hall on his policies and tactics at every opportunity he could grasp, yet Croker had not once fallen into one of Priestly's traps. If anything, he had a track record of making that idiotic little Protestant bastard look like an ass in front of the others. And Croker enjoyed that.

"The floor is yours, Mr. Priestly!" Croker called, courteously.

Priestly cleared his throat—he really thought he had Croker in a bind. "Can you explain to the *New York Times*, sir, how the previous accusations made against Hugh J. Grant for bribery will affect his mayoral campaign?"

The look on his face was smug when their eyes met. Nevertheless, Priestly's confidence vanished when Croker smiled at him boldly, and shook his head.

"You all are very aware of the fact that this organization has gone above and beyond to clean up its act throughout the last twenty years, and with the help of my predecessor, John Kelly, God rest his soul, we were able to once again make Tammany Hall an institution of merit and honor! Therefore, when I tell you that neither myself nor the Hall has any interest in being associated with the kind of illicit activity Mr. Grant was falsely accused of, I mean it. Tammany has done its own private investigation into this indictment of bribery, and we discovered it was pieced together by those wishing to hurt Grant's reputation. Because of how competitive real estate law has become in our grand city, these accusations were concocted in an effort to slow down Hugh's roaring train of success. At that point in his career, Hugh was dominating the industry. John, being the man of integrity he was, would not have dreamed of selecting Mr. Grant for any form of public office if he thought Hugh was corrupted. So please, Mr. Priestly, do not do John Kelly the disservice of spitting on his grave. Sheriff Grant is an upstanding citizen who simply wants to serve his people and his city to the best of his abilities, and we at Tammany Hall think he's just the man to put right so many of the wrongs of his predecessors."

A cheer came up from a small crowd forming behind the reporters, with more people gathering each passing second to hear what

Croker had to say about the election. This praise, to Croker's delight, muted whatever sort of retaliation Priestly might have come up with, and Croker smoothly pointed to another reporter for the next question.

"Mr. Croker! Billy Rains, the *New York Herald*! What position, if any, will you seek if Mr. Grant is elected mayor of New York City?"

While Croker knew the answer, he shrugged. "I want to win this election first, Billy, then we'll discuss appointments! Next?"

"Mr. Croker! Mr. Croker! Curtis Chapman, *New York Tribune*! What are your plans for the city after the horrendous and deadly winter blizzard we had last March? Is Tammany Hall assisting the city in infrastructure improvements?"

The rest of the press conference passed effortlessly, and by the time it concluded, what had once only been reporters and a handful of onlookers evolved into a crowd of nearly one hundred people outside of Tammany Hall, every one wanting to hear Richard Croker speak. Inquiries started to shift after the newspapers got their fill of information about Grant, moving on to how, like everything else, Tammany was going to help fix New York City following the treacherous winter season. For nearly four years, Croker had been Grand Sachem, stepping into John's shoes after his retirement and untimely death, and Croker found he was only just starting to get the hang of things. The Hall had their hands in every jar, and there could never be a dull moment if they wanted to continue to maintain power. With Grant as mayor, it would be the final stepping stone for Croker. Hugh had already promised Richard that if he were elected, he would give Croker free reign as city chamberlain to do as he pleased with zero interference on his part. All in all, it would provide the Hall and Croker an entire city workforce at his disposal; over a thousand people to do his bidding whenever he pleased, and no negative repercussions.

There was no room for failure—Grant had to win.

Croker waltzed back inside the Hall and up the stairs to his office, content that the publicity would cast a favorable light onto Hugh's campaign and the future he could provide New York. Outside his office, Brian was waiting for him with a handful of new incoming messages.

"Great job, sir!" Brian congratulated him, giving him the papers. "You really shut Priestly up with that bit about Mr. Kelly!"

"Thank you, Brian," Croker replied, not minding the brown-nosing in the slightest. "All in a good day's work!"

"Your assistant is waiting for you in your office," Brian informed Croker, resuming his post at his desk. "She hasn't been in long."

"Wonderful," Croker remarked. "Make sure we are not disturbed by anyone. Will you do me a favor and tell my wife I won't make it home for tea before the Rockefellers' party this evening?"

"Of course, sir."

"Thanks, Brian."

While glancing at Brian's notes, Croker entered his office to find Esther sitting in the chair across from his desk, smoking a cigarette and sipping whiskey. When she heard the door open, she whipped around and waved him over.

"I just poured you a drink and left it on your desk," she told him. "You put on a hell of a good show out there."

Croker strolled to his chair and set his notes aside, his spirit lightening as he joined her. "I am glad it is just you. Did you see the look on Priestly's face? And the crowd…I really don't think it could have gone better." He reached for his whiskey. "How did this morning go?"

Esther, too, had a gulp from her glass. "I don't know this for sure, but I think something is going on with Walsh and Kitty."

He nearly choked. "Something as in what, exactly? They're fucking?!"

"I…I think so…"

Croker was stunned. "I don't even know how to respond to that…"

145

Esther had a drag of her cigarette. "The dynamic has changed. Danny is still running the show, but Kitty has everyone cozying up to Walsh, and is even spitting some of his fucking rhetoric about expanding the gang—hating the rich, fighting police. Richie, if this gets much worse, I am not sure how safe I'm going to be with the Whyos. Walsh is out to get me."

"Esther, please, don't overreact when there isn't a reason to," Croker reproached. "I would put him in the goddamn Hudson if he did anything of the sort. Danny Lyons is still loyal. I'll up his pay to be sure of it."

"There is already a huge target on Danny's back. Kitty doesn't see it, but I do. Walsh is biding his time, and when the time comes, Danny will be gone. And Kitty. Walsh doesn't give a shit about her. He's using her to manipulate the gang."

"You know you need to get control of this, then."

Esther reluctantly nodded. "Get me a bonus for Danny and I'll meet with him this afternoon to tell him our end on things. If he is less of an asshole to me around the others, that'll catch on, and it'll at least level the fucking playing field."

"And you need to kiss Kitty's ass."

Esther's face went sour. "Oh, for God's sake, Richie, I'm already doing every fucking thing she asks!"

"I don't care. You have to do this. If we lose the Whyos, we lose big income, and then it's your head I'll be coming after."

She scowled at him and finished her whiskey. After a few seconds of silence, Esther relented, rolling her eyes.

"Fine," she yielded. "I'll take care of it."

"That's more like it."

Croker had come to rely on Esther for far more than he should. Four and a half years ago when he saved her from the noose, he had no idea their partnership would become what it currently was. Like everybody else involved, Croker underestimated just how skilled she would become under the instruction of Will and Louis, who'd trained her so impeccably that now they could barely keep up with her. At the point in time when Will and Louis had deemed Esther ready to work for Tammany, Croker assumed that there might be a touch of bitterness on her end—perhaps a small sliver of resentment for her circumstances and the history between Croker and those she believed were her family. To his astonishment, this didn't appear to be the case. From the very first day she'd strutted into his office, Esther had been hard-working and dependable, never voicing a complaint that was not valid and willing to work her way up the ranks. In the beginning, Esther strictly worked cases with Louis and Will, and gradually earned Croker's respect to such a degree that he started sending her with Walsh to work with the Whyos. Walsh was not keen on this bargain: despite not admitting it verbally, Croker knew he hated the idea of the Hall having someone watch him so closely. Walsh had reluctantly conceded to Croker's orders, but not without passive retaliation.

The first rule of being a member of the Whyo gang was that prospects must pass their "initiation," and that initiation was murder. It didn't really matter who or why—it was a rule implemented by the previous generation and therefore non-negotiable. Esther was no exception, even if she was not interested in officially becoming a part of the gang. Still, Walsh ambushed her on that first night without Croker's knowledge, much to the fury of both Will and Louis, who had not yet prepared her for ending a life. Once again to everyone's bewilderment, Esther did not disappoint them; moreover, Croker recalled that even the sinister Walsh had an air of surprise upon disclosing Esther's lack of hesitation to do what he'd asked. When the victim was presented in front of a jeering Whyo crowd at The Morgue, Walsh had offered Esther his blade, only to have her decline politely. Instead, Esther didn't protest and killed a man of Walsh's choosing with her bare hands. Well, her bare hands and those menacing brass knuckles she used on anyone who stood in her way.

Years had come and gone, and Croker's "assistant," as their

small circle had taken to calling her, kept him informed of everything that the others did not. She often shared intelligence with Croker that he knew would get her in hot water with Will or Louis if they ever found her out. While at first Croker was unsure of where the road with Esther might take him, he'd come to believe wholeheartedly that she felt she owed him her life following her salvation, and any previous allegiances to others were secondary to the devotion she had for Croker. His confidence in both Tammany and himself were greater than ever, mainly because he had an unstoppable weapon, one who would do whatever bidding he asked of her.

"So, I'll try and smooth things over with Danny and Kitty," she reiterated, hopping up to pour more whiskey. "What else? As much as I love keeping tabs on everyone, you know I get a little bored."

Croker leaned back into his chair as she brought the decanter over. "I have two new thoughts."

"And those are?" she asked, filling his glass.

"First, I want you to start tailing Lord Turner."

Esther didn't flinch, but he saw a little color leave her face. She set the decanter on his desk and resumed her seat, her countenance more contemplative than timid.

"This would then retract my ban of Fifth Avenue?" she asked, her eyes moving from her whiskey glass to Croker.

He'd expected more of an emotional reaction from Esther, considering such a tumultuous past with Lord Turner; on the contrary, she appeared composed, more interested in weighing the angles and the dangers of her assignment rather than any unresolved feelings.

She really was his.

"Yes," he declared. "You look nothing like your formal self, and I have no doubt you are careful enough after all your training to handle such a task."

"Is this because of your encounter at the Admiral's Ball?"

Croker shrugged and moved to grab a cigar. "He threatened me in the most peculiar way, and I cannot help remembering how his father fought those Whyo bastards. And Louis…Louis, before he truly crossed over, vowed years ago that if he returned, Lord Turner would try to destroy me." He delayed, thinking over his words, and cut his cigar. "He may be worth a fortune, but money, in his case, won't win him more power than I've gained. What do you make of his threat?"

Esther had a sip of her drink while he lit his cigar. "Honestly, I think you can expect that he will try to work against you politically…that he'll try to muscle you out of those fucking elitist asshole—"

"Esther…"

"Sorry. He'll probably try to muscle you out of committees, social events, the usual, but what else can he do, Richie? You're in a goddamn fortress here. You have two of the best hitmen in the world, the freak, me, the biggest gang in New York, and the entire police force on your side." She chuckled, shaking her head. "He's got nothing. His father is gone. Mary is in England. The only cards he has left to play are petty and inconsequential."

"I still want you to keep tabs on him."

"I'll add him to the list," she responded. "I have a feeling he will be at the Rockefellers' tonight. They only live a few blocks from one another, and as much as I hate to tell you this, I think Thomas is worth more than they are at this point."

Croker sighed. "I realize that. And don't forget there's that fundraiser for Grant next week…ah, well, it's not like I don't have enemies already. Have you gone to see the Madame lately?"

Esther pulled out another cigarette, lighting it gracefully. "I'm overdue. Mainly because I've been trying to figure out what the hell is going on with the Whyos."

"You need to go and see her so she doesn't get suspicious."

"I know. I'll go tonight. She doesn't know, Richie, don't worry. I've done a very good job playing the burdened sufferer for her crimes."

"You are certain—"

"Certain what?" she cut him off, her gaze somewhat threatening.

"You're sure Will and Louis have no idea?"

"If they did, I would have fucking told you, Richie. And if Louis ever finds out I've been spying on the Madame for you, it'll be the end of our friendship, and neither of us can afford that. So, what's the second thing?"

Croker had been preparing to tell her for days. "I want you to take out Frederick."

Esther's eyes went wide. "Me? Alone?"

"Yes, you, and alone."

Instantly, Esther was uncharacteristically unsure of herself. "Richie, I've killed plenty of people. But I've never done a hit on a prominent member of society. I don't know if…"

"You're ready," he insisted. "You've been ready."

"Have you talked with Will and Louis? They're the professionals. They've been the ones who have trained me."

"I will discuss it with them soon. I wanted to tell you so that you could start preparing yourself, mentally and physically. They will obviously help you with the planning, timing, and the little details. You, however, will carry out the hit."

She finished her drink. "If you think I am ready, then I'm ready."

"She is not ready." A firm, eerie voice came from the doorway, and both Croker and Esther looked to spot Walsh indignantly standing at the entrance to the office; how long he'd been there, Croker couldn't say.

Croker's head tilted to the side curiously. "What makes you say that?"

Walsh strode into Croker's office and sat in the chair next to Esther's, not acknowledging her presence. "Will and Louis coddle her. She is not ready and will fail. I thought we agreed that Louis would see to this one, under the Madame's jurisdiction."

"Well, I changed my mind." Croker had a long drag of his cigar. "This is not up to you, Mr. Walsh, it is my call. And while I respect your opinion, you will mind that accusatory tone. I am your employer, not your fucking subordinate."

Walsh's demeanor didn't lighten. "Then I want to oversee the hit."

Esther leapt to her feet. "Absolutely fucking not! Richie, you just told me——"

"He just told you that you were ready, though you have yet to prove yourself in this regard, Esther," Walsh stated aggressively, continuing to only stare at Croker. "Do you really want to send her in and fuck up this hit? She will, and you can't afford to leave your organization in the hands of some cunt who only hits hard because she wears metal on her hands."

Before Croker could do anything, Esther acted. In a flash, she lunged toward Walsh and cracked him hard across the face, the blow so impactful that Walsh's chair flipped sideways and sent him wheeling down onto the floor.

"Esther!" Croker barked, standing quickly. "Stop it! Now!"

She stood over Walsh, glaring heatedly down at him as he slowly got up, first to his hands and knees, and then to his feet. Walsh had his back to her and, standing up straight, rotated around to face Esther. His hand moved up to his jaw, which was quite clearly dislocated; without flinching, Walsh snapped it into place, his dark, threatening eyes locked on her. Croker's heart was beating so fast in his chest, he thought he might have a heart attack, panicked and at a loss as to what exactly he should do next.

"If you ever do that again," Walsh muttered, so quietly Croker could barely make out his words, "I will skin you alive and relish in your screams, you little bitch." He turned to Croker. "I believe my point has been made. She is a loose cannon. Who knows what might happen during the hit that could throw her off, and do you really want to take that kind of risk?"

Esther was in total disbelief, and gazed at Croker, her beautiful green eyes furious. "It's your call," she spat out at last.

Croker sat down and put his cigar between his lips. "Walsh will oversee the hit."

Without a word, Walsh nodded and paced out of Croker's office. Esther continued to stand gaping at him, and it was then Richard realized that she'd struck him with her brass knuckle on. Blood was seeping out of Esther's knuckle—she'd hit him as hard as she could, and somehow, Walsh had barely looked like he'd been slapped. Esther observed his glances and took her brass off, picking up her whiskey glass and grabbing the decanter off his desk.

"Do you have any idea what you just did?" she questioned, her hand shaking with rage as she lit another cigarette.

"I saved your life," Croker responded defiantly.

"No," she retorted. "No, you just told him that you will choose him over me. And I've lost a fucking huge amount of ground."

Croker still couldn't process Walsh's state. "How was he not incapacitated by that? He ought to have been reeling in pain."

Esther exhaled a cloud of smoke and threw back her whiskey. "He doesn't feel anything, Richie," she said.

"Don't be ridiculous. Doesn't feel anything?"

"He doesn't."

He waved her off. "That's just those fucking absurd rumors swirling around to maintain his reputation."

"Whatever you say, Richie." Esther got to her feet. "You have a party to get ready for, and I have errands to run."

Croker almost laughed at her theatrics. "Oh, don't take this personal, Esther. With your little performance, it's a miracle he didn't retaliate and seriously hurt you. I did you a goddamn favor. Quit pouting and see to it this gets done."

She didn't say anything, only began heading for the door.

"Wait!" he shouted, grabbing a pair of his own wraps and hopping to his feet. Croker walked over to where she lingered, giving the bandages to her as an olive branch. "He does not rank above you, you know that."

She took the wraps, yet her demeanor didn't soften. "I want you to swear to me that if it comes down to it, you'll pick me over him. Swear to me."

"I swear to you," he lied.

The frown faded, and Croker was pleased to know he'd mended her wounded pride.

"Be safe, you hear me?" He pulled a cash incentive out for Danny Lyons and held it up for her to take with her. "Go give this to Lyons. Let's round up everyone late tonight. And I mean everyone. We need to talk over the future as a group. Understood?"

It irritated her, yet she nodded, taking the money. "I'll make sure it's done."

She left the office, and Croker watched her go.

"Some pets are worth the extra effort," he chortled under his breath.

He went to resume his spot at his desk and halted dead in his tracks. There, with her talons wrapped around the sill of the open window behind his desk, was a peregrine falcon. She glowered at him, eyes unblinking, as if restraining herself from attack, and for what felt like hours, Croker didn't move, entranced by the raptor's gaze. Then, from no direction he could decipher, came a sharp, piercing whistle, and the bird vanished as if into thin air.

"What in the hell?" he muttered, marching to the window to peer outside.

It was pointless. The peregrine had disappeared, leaving Croker with the unsettled sensation of being watched. He flopped down into his chair and relit his cigar, wondering if he had imagined the incident after the shock of witnessing Esther attack Walsh in front of him.

"That falcon looked at me like she wanted to kill me," he remarked aloud to himself, puffing the life back into his tobacco. "How peculiar..."

Croker made it home with just enough time to change from his suit into his tuxedo and have a cocktail with Elizabeth in their sitting room before heading to the Rockefellers' for the night's festivities. The children remained upstate for the time being, being cared for by their governess and tutors, so that husband and wife could enjoy a few days together alone in the city. Elizabeth looked beautiful in a royal blue silk gown, donning the sparkling diamond necklace Croker had bought for her a few weeks ago as an anniversary present. Her long, dark hair was perfectly curled and styled in a bun with several tendrils hanging loosely onto her shoulders—he loved it this way, giving her an enthralling and glamorous visage. There were so many things he adored about his wife, though the one thing Croker was most grateful for was that Elizabeth never was one to question Croker on his work, nor lecture him on his alleged conduct; she was devout and knew her place, never wavering in her unremitting support of her husband and his person. If Croker had learned anything throughout his climb to Grand Sachem of Tammany Hall, it was that in order to succeed, his aides and his underlings must be steadfast and reliable to their very core. His wife was no exception, but with Elizabeth, he never had a reason to worry. She'd been with him since the beginning, and would be with him until the end.

Once they'd enjoyed a glass of champagne, Croker and Elizabeth hopped into their coach and made their way east to Fifty-fourth Street to the Rockefellers' residence. A few years ago, after moving from hotel to hotel, Elizabeth had finally convinced Richard that they needed a permanent household for when the children were in town, and begrudgingly, Croker had bought a four-story manor on the Upper West Side, where the homes were a little less extravagant and therefore a little cheaper. While he had the money to purchase a plot of land and build a brick and limestone masterpiece from scratch, Croker didn't have any interest in wasting his hard earnings

154

on a home he would only spend time in when his family was present. Instead, he spent most of his days at the Hall, and even on occasion found himself getting a few hours of shut eye on the couch rather than stomaching a half hour carriage ride to his bed.

As Elizabeth prattled on about the latest with the children, Richard tuned her out, reflecting on the dialogue he'd had with the Madame a few weeks prior, when she'd made it clear the only way to win the wealthy over was to grovel at their feet; regardless of whether he hated the idea or not, he'd recognized she was right. Flattery wasn't exactly his forte, which he blamed on his ego from the labors of building his empire, rather than inheriting it; however, the Madame truly had upheld her promise of assisting in Richard and Elizabeth's assimilation.

Very suddenly, following only a handful of parties and events, Croker found he and his wife were now officially in the inner circle of the upper classes, and this he owed largely to Douglas Hiltmore. Douglas, who had once been the most despised man in New York City, had somehow managed to regain his prominent and well-respected reputation through an incredible talent of tact and wit, which Richard coveted himself. Using that talent, both Douglas and his daughter Celeste had gone above and beyond to spread Croker's name amongst their contemporaries, bringing in Tammany as a sponsor to a few parties and making the necessary introductions between Croker and the investors of Wall Street.

Still, what irked Croker about the Hiltmores was Celeste's prior connection to his assistant, Esther, as well as to Lord Turner; despite knowing he had Douglas in his pocket, Richard wasn't quite sure about the trustworthiness or loyalty of Douglas's daughter.

Upon arriving at the Rockefellers' residence, Richard and Elizabeth were promptly greeted by John D. and his wife, Laura. Their interaction was warm and friendly, and Croker studied his hosts carefully to ascertain whether or not there remained any condescension in regard to Richard and who he was. With a strong shake of his hand, John D. congratulated Richard on his handling of the press conference earlier in the day, and then proceeded to compliment Elizabeth on her stunning diamond necklace. With their courtesies done, Elizabeth took Richard's arm and they proceeded to find a waiter for some champagne, and Croker was unable to mask the satisfied grin on his face. He'd done it at last.

The Rockefellers' home was one of the largest in Manhattan. As Elizabeth and Croker waltzed into the main lobby, they came face to face with an already enormous number of guests drinking flutes of champagne and grasping at waiters as they pranced by with finger food. Over their heads was a gaslight chandelier more brilliant that Croker had ever beheld, illuminating the entire room around them. It was an early nineteenth century cut-glass and ormolu chandelier, and while it was similar to the popular French style of the day, Rockefeller had clearly added a handful of unique attributes to the piece, most notably that it was so large it might crush half the party if it fell. A string quartet could be heard in the next room playing, still notably in the first movement with their sonata, and Croker was pleased to smell the familiar aroma of cigar smoke nearby. Instinctively, he reached for his own tobacco inside his dinner jacket pocket, and in practiced fashion, Elizabeth produced a box of matches for her husband.

Before they could move onto the great room and take in the rest of the general splendor, Douglas Hiltmore and his daughter Celeste approached the Crokers, each sporting a charming disposition.

"Richard, how are you?" Douglas asked, stretching out his hand.

Croker took it cheerfully. "Never better, Douglas. Never better. You remember my wife, Elizabeth?"

"Why, yes, of course." Douglas turned to Elizabeth, took her politely outstretched hand, and bowed gracefully. "Mrs. Croker, that necklace is breathtaking!"

She beamed, enjoying the attention. "Thank you, Mr. Hiltmore! An anniversary gift from my husband."

"Have you met my daughter, Celeste?" Douglas gestured to her while Celeste stepped forward and curtseyed low, smiling radiantly at Elizabeth.

"It's an honor to finally make your acquaintance, Mrs. Croker," Celeste said genially. "I've had the great fortune to hear so many great things about you from your husband. How is the Upper West treating you?"

"It's lovely!" Elizabeth exclaimed, and Croker could sense his wife warming to Celeste. "I was so thrilled when Richard finally committed to purchasing a home. We had been living in and out of hotels for years. The children needed a permanent home in the city, and where better than right next to Central Park?"

"That sounds like the perfect location for you and your children," Celeste agreed. "Father and I have often wondered if we should find ourselves our own property again, but we are so spoiled at the Hotel St. Stephen, I don't think I could possibly bear to leave."

"One day, when you have a family, perhaps," Elizabeth replied with a wink.

"Richard, how did the conference go this afternoon?" Douglas interjected. "I heard Tammany made a strong stance for Grant, and that it was received well!" He lowered his voice so only their party could hear, "Did that Priestly bastard try to come after you again?"

With a gasp, Celeste slapped him playfully. "Father! There are ladies present!" She laughed, shaking her head. "I can't take him anywhere. Really!"

"Don't worry," Croker declared. "Elizabeth is used to it. With my Irish roots, she's usually the one scolding me. Priestly did try to get us with those damned allegations of bribery again, but I think I have kept him at bay for the time being." He peered down at his flute of champagne and noticed he'd finished the contents. "I'm going to grab a refill. Douglas, will you watch the girls while I grab another?"

"Dutifully! Another for me as well, Richard."

With a nod, Croker backed away and headed the direction of

the nearest waiter, wading through the robust and boisterous crowd. After retrieving two drinks, Croker paused a few feet away from his wife and the Hiltmores, masked by the other partygoers, while he watched Celeste vigilantly. He couldn't put a finger on it, but there was a quality in her countenance that was both familiar and unnerving to him, and though he knew Douglas and his daughter held a close relationship with the Madame, something about Celeste was inexplicably menacing. She was a beauty, and carried herself in a way that caught every man's eye. Notwithstanding, she remained effortlessly courteous to everyone she encountered, always smiling with a type of magnetism that made others, including his wife, like her instantaneously. At that very moment, the two women were deep in discussion, giggling like two schoolgirls; Croker was almost astonished at how Elizabeth had been won over so swiftly, when normally it took four or five occasions with new friends to make her open up.

No, something about Miss Hiltmore just didn't add up, and Croker was determined to find out what it was.

Returning to Douglas's side, Croker handed over his champagne. "The ladies seem to have taken a liking to one another," he observed, clinking glasses with Douglas.

"That's just Celeste," Douglas remarked with pride. "She has a way with people that cannot be taught."

"I can certainly see that." Croker had a gulp of his champagne. "How is the Madame doing this week?"

"Well," Douglas answered, turning so they were face to face. "She mentioned the two of you haven't really had a chance to speak since the Admiral's Ball."

"You mean since the return of her beloved 'nephew?'"

Douglas smirked. "I am not going to lie, I was hoping that would be more notable to you than the public embarrassment my daughter suffered as a consequence of Captain Bernhardt's drunken state." He had a sip of his drink. "So, it's true you two had a confrontation?"

"In a matter of speaking, yes. What's your interest, Douglas?"

"Well, I thought that would be obvious. I, like the Madame, feel that I will be mediating some troubled waters."

He wasn't sure why, but Croker swore that in spite of the fact that Celeste was holding an entirely different conversation with Elizabeth, she was listening to every word that came out of his mouth.

"My goal is to mend the broken fences, Douglas, especially in the case of a man like Lord Turner. He could be an incredible asset to this city, to the Hall, and to me in the long run. So yes, any mediating you and the Madame feel is necessary to put whatever grudge he holds against me to rest, I am all for it. Perhaps a meeting, the four of us sometime? At The Palace?"

Douglas was taken aback at Croker's up-front white flag, but he conceded, "I'll start making the arrangements first thing tomorrow. However, I will tell you this, Richard: he is rumored to be coming by this evening. Apparently, he and John D. have become fast friends, and are in talks on partnering for gasoline and kerosene distribution."

Croker rolled his eyes. "You really think Rockefeller cares about transatlantic distribution of oil?"

Douglas's tone took on a whisper: "No, it would be only in the states. From what I've heard, Cornelius Vanderbilt II is considering handing over the distribution end of his railroad industry to Thomas and Turner S & D, or at the very least, some kind of extended partnership between the two."

Croker nearly dropped his champagne. "You cannot be serious."

Douglas eyed him closely. "Does it look like I'm fibbing, Richard?"

Croker's internal dialogue then consumed him. In a matter of days, Lord Turner had already buddied up to two of the biggest tycoons in the city, and on top of that, had commenced business negotiations to further his wealth and the reach of his company throughout the United States. With Rockefeller and Vanderbilt II backing Turner S & D, Richard suddenly felt unusually out of his league. This wasn't the gangs, the government, or Wall Street. These were the families that made America what it was, and Lord Turner was very strategically placing himself on their level. He tried let it go, and took a quick breath to get his bearings; nonetheless, Croker found that whatever confidence he could muster up was limited, because no matter what he had convinced himself or the others of, Richard would never feel at ease amongst the upper class, especially with the knowledge that he truly needed them to have continued success at Tammany Hall.

"I do hope I am not interrupting you all," came a voice from Croker's left.

He and Douglas spun to find Captain Jonathan Bernhardt bowing low in salutation, and he wasn't alone. At his side was an eager-looking gentleman Richard was almost sure he'd met previously—he was middle-aged and balding, with a thick mustache that held a white-grey hue, yet from his gait, Richard sensed something familiar. Then, it slowly came together: the tiny scars on his face, the cauliflower ear…

"Captain, it is a pleasure," Douglas greeted, though Croker knew from his friend's expression it was more the opposite.

The Captain rotated toward Croker. "Mr. Croker, I don't believe we've had a formal introduction. My name is Captain Jonathan Bernhardt, sir. This is my associate, Virgil Archibald, who is the—"

"Christ, Virgil!" Croker cried. "How are you, old friend? It's been years!"

The Captain was just as astounded as Douglas while Virgil and Richard embraced. "My dear Richie," Virgil said with a grin, "fancy catching you in a place like this!"

"I ought to say the same! Douglas, Virgil and I used to box competitively together. That is, until he did the smart thing and started managing. And now he owns all of the rings in Chicago."

"All the legitimate ones, at least," Virgil asserted with a wink.

"What are you doing back in New York?" Croker persisted. "Last I heard, you were making quite an empire out there!"

"Business! Wanted to check in on how the boys up here were running their rings!"

"Marvelous!" Douglas exclaimed. "Captain, how is it you and Mr. Archibald are connected?"

The Captain was grabbing two flutes of champagne off a hastily passing tray, and handed one to Virgil. "Virgil's friend Casper has been teaching me to box a little. As a method of dealing with the stress after my time out West. We met a few days ago when I was hitting, and miraculously spotted each other upon arriving at the Rockefellers'."

"And how's he faring, Virgil?" Croker pressed.

"Unbelievably well. Reminds me a lot of you when you were young, Richie."

"Impressive," Douglas stated weakly, spinning around to fetch his daughter. "Celeste, come and greet the Captain! You didn't mention he would be here tonight!"

Celeste's face was bewildered. "I had no idea you would be attending the party, Jonathan," she attempted to cover, though it was obvious she was not thrilled at his presence either.

Taking a small step back to allow the confrontation to go on, Richard looked at Virgil, who copied his retreat.

"What are you really doing here, Virg?" Croker muttered under his breath. "How in the hell did you get an invitation to a party at the Rockefellers'?"

Virgil shrugged. "Married a Turlington. We live like royalty in Chicago." His eyes strayed off of Richard's, scanning the room. "You still hitting with Edmond?"

"Edmond would kill you if he knew you were in New York."

"This isn't his town, Richie, it's yours, and would you really let Edmond hurt your old pal Virgil?"

"I'd let him beat you to a fucking pulp, you thieving rat," Croker snapped. "You need to get out of this city tonight. I don't care if your wife does own the swampland of Chicago."

Virgil's ice cold stare found Richard's. "You think the magnificent people of high society would like to hear about how many men you've killed, Richie? Do ya?" he huffed, tickled at this idea. "All it takes with these folks is one rumor, and you're done. You figure that out yet? All I gotta do is tell Sydney to put a bug in Laura Rockefeller's ear, and you'll never be invited back. And you can kiss your career, your politics, and this new image you have goodbye."

Croker could feel the heat rising from his cheeks. "What the hell do you want?"

Virgil's glare subsided, and he looked almost pleading. "I want to come home."

"Out of the question."

"Talk to Edmond. Tell him I've changed. We could run Chicago and New York together."

Now it was Richard's turn to be threatening: "You were the one that fucked this up, Virg, not me. Edmond was your partner and you screwed him and ran off with everything."

"Correction. He was my goddamned trainee," Virgil countered, throwing back what was left of his champagne. "I want you to set it up. I don't care how you do it, but you will. If Edmond can't be convinced, I'll play fair and let it be. Do this, or I'll make sure you and Elizabeth never attend one of these parties again."

Without a word otherwise, Virgil left Croker stewing, and Elizabeth moved to him and took his hand.

"What did he want?" she whispered, glancing around to be sure the Captain was still occupying the Hiltmores.

Croker sighed, wrapping his fingers through hers. "Bastard wants me to help him get back in touch with Edmond."

"He must be mad!"

"I wish he was," Croker replied. "I have to do it, Lizzie. His wife is Sydney Turlington, and he threatened to use her position in society against us if I don't. We've only just gotten this far. I can't afford to lose this ground. Not now, when I so desperately need the edge."

He was thinking of Lord Turner, but Elizabeth was unaware of this, and took it as Richard referring to the upcoming election.

"All right, Richard. Do what you need to do, just be cautious. Remember what Virgil did last time."

"You don't need to remind me, Elizabeth. It's burned into my memory for good."

He kissed her hand and proceeded to pull it through his arm as they strode toward the Hiltmores. Thankfully, just as they rejoined, the Captain departed in a sulk, and any lingering awkwardness seemed to vanish amongst the party.

Until about thirty seconds later, when the music came to an abrupt halt and Lord Thomas Turner of Amberleigh was announced.

The Turners entered with all eyes upon them, and from the manifestation he openly displayed, Lord Turner was very aware he was the focus of the party and utilized it. On Lord Turner's right was his cousin, William, and on his left stood William's simple yet striking wife, Lucy, who Croker recalled happening across years ago, when he'd first encountered the family face to face. The three of them strolled in wearing large, spirited smiles, and Lord Turner raised a flute to their audience and nodded his head as if thanking them for the reception. The crowed mirrored the gesture, with whispers circling to and fro, and then, instantly, music and talk resumed where it had been not a half of a minute prior. Croker couldn't decide if he was more disgusted or impressed. If this was his opponent, Croker felt he definitely had bitten off more than he could chew. Lord Turner was already beloved by the rich and powerful, that much was evident, and their interest in him seemed only to grow with each passing second. If they truly couldn't find a middle ground, Croker would have to make small, discreet moves against Lord Turner, in a manner that would not exactly ruin him or Turner S & D, but instead cause enough doubt about Lord Turner's true character to give this doting crowd pause rather than unconditional courtesy.

Croker was just about to turn back and engage Douglas about Grant's fundraiser next week when Elizabeth grasped his arm, and he revolved toward her to find her gaze locked elsewhere. As his eyes searched for what she was staring at, Croker recognized what it was that made her react in such a way, and Croker felt his own body tense in a similar manner. Lord Turner, William Turner, and Lucy Turner were heading straight for them. There wasn't much time to prepare. All Croker could do was muster up a welcoming and good-humored grin in the hopes that the others around him at the party would witness that Lord Turner and Richard Croker were familiar acquaintances, if not friends. It would increase the magnitude of his status amongst a group of people he so desperately needed on his side. In reality, Croker was perplexed, because the last time he'd spoken with Lord Turner, their affiliation was by no means one of cordiality or esteem.

Without Croker realizing it, Douglas maneuvered nearer to him so the two gentleman were standing side by side, with Elizabeth and Celeste directly behind them. As Lord Turner drew closer, he held out a hand to Douglas.

"Douglas, great to see you," Lord Turner pronounced happily, then turned to Richard, who was attempting to equip himself for whatever Lord Turner threw his way. "Mr. Croker, it is also lovely to see you again."

He held out his hand, and Croker took it enthusiastically. "You as well, Lord Turner. Douglas and I were just discussing the incredible progress and expansion of Turner S & D in your short time here."

Lord Turner appeared pleased. "Yes, well, we have been making great strides now that my cousin William is once again running most of our operations. Mr. Croker, I don't believe you've met William Turner?"

William didn't smile, though he politely saluted, acknowledging the introduction. "Pleased to meet you, Mr. Croker. I've heard...a lot about you."

A somewhat difficult silence followed, and was speedily abated by Lucy, who outstretched her hand for Richard to take. "Mr. Croker, I do believe we met a few years ago, outside of a party Douglas hosted?"

To Croker's relief, Esther's name was not mentioned. "Ah, yes, I do recall! I believe we were all escaping outside for some fresh air." He kissed her hand. "It's wonderful to make your acquaintance once again. This is my wife, Elizabeth."

The two women greeted each other cordially, and then William and Lucy casually left their assembly in search of a whiskey for William.

Celeste came forward after allowing the introductions to conclude. "Lord Turner," she greeted him with a small curtsy, "are you thinking of attending the fundraiser Father and I will be throwing with Mr. Croker for Grant next week?"

"I was actually just going to bring that up with Mr. Croker myself," he declared, his attentions focusing onto Richard. "From what I've heard, Grant is a shoe-in, but I would be honored to contribute to the campaign, Mr. Croker. I am half Irish, after all."

Croker observed him ever so closely, searching for any hint of malice in his words. When he found none, he decided that perhaps the moment had come to try to form a working relationship with one of the wealthiest men in New York. If this was a façade, and if a grudge did still exist, Croker would deal with that at a later date. For now, business came first, and he needed Grant in office.

"Please, Lord Turner, call me Richard," he beseeched him. "The Hall would be thrilled to have you at the fundraiser and as a sponsor of Grant. We need as much support as we can get. I never trust the polls, Lord Turner, and I want to see to it this city starts moving in the right direction. With men like Hewitt in the Mayor's chair, who seriously lack a vision of the future, we have no opportunity to improve our city."

"Well, if I wasn't already sold, I am now," Lord Turner stated. "You can count me in."

He and Croker clinked their glasses together to cheers, and after a sip of their drinks, Celeste spoke up: "Elizabeth, there is someone I would like for you to meet. Would you accompany me?"

"As long as more champagne is involved," she said.

"Ladies, follow me, I'll take care of your beverage needs," Douglas assured them. "Lord Turner, Richard, I'm sure I'll see you later?"

"Absolutely," Lord Turner confirmed.

Celeste glanced at Lord Turner. "Thomas, will you come by tomorrow? We've just had a new addition to our art collection I think you would enjoy."

An expression formed on Lord Turner's face that Croker couldn't quite deduce, though his composure remained intact. "I'll be by around two?"

"Perfect."

Croker and Lord Turner watched as Douglas led Celeste and Elizabeth away and into the great room, where the string quartet was beginning their third movement.

"I hear you've been having some issues in the Bowery," Lord Turner mentioned casually, finishing what was left of his drink. "Though you seem to be making enormous progress north of Midtown."

The tone in Lord Turner's voice had completely altered, and Croker swiftly ascertained that unlike their previous civilities, this was going to be the true exchange between the two men. And how Lord Turner knew anything about the Bowery was enough to put him on his defenses.

"That's the territory of running a city," Croker articulated softly, so they wouldn't be overheard. "It never is smooth sailing. There's always work to be done and progress to be made."

Lord Turner stepped closer to Croker, his tone low. "Progress, meaning the innocent lives you've ruined in your own pursuit of power?"

Croker's own demeanor sharpened. "I have done the best I can with what I have, and if ambition is my curse, then so be it. What's done is done. Not all of us are so fortunate to have an endless amount of money at our disposal, like you, sir."

Lord Turner grunted. "And yet, here, at the largest mansion in New York, you are groveling at the feet of the money you so despise."

"I don't see you contributing to your old neighborhood, Lord Turner. For someone who thinks so much of himself, you think you'd give back to your own people."

A smirk came to his face. "Don't you worry, Mr. Croker. I'll be down in the Bowery, cleaning things up on my home turf sooner than you'd like."

Croker shook his head, wanting to make an effort to salvage the situation. "So, this is how it's going to be, is it? You'd rather be at odds with me over some belated grudge than work together and do some good for your city?"

"Belated grudge?" Lord Turner let out a low chuckle and whispered ominously, "You imprisoned my mother for almost a decade, and on top of that, you killed my father, you son of a bitch. A belated grudge? Are you fucking daft?"

Croker looked him in the eyes, and against his better judgment, let out a defeated sigh. There was no recovering from his past connection to Mary Daugherty, but there was one piece of information that might change Thomas's mind about his father. He had to take the risk of letting the truth out. And what's more, he had to get the vote.

"I didn't kill your father, Lord Turner."

"What?"

"I didn't kill your father. I didn't even give an order for him to be killed. It happened against my command."

"Then why did you tell everyone you were responsible?"

"Because I couldn't have people thinking I didn't have control

167

over my own goddamned brute squad. Not with so much at stake and with my chance at Grand Sachem riding in the balance. So, I didn't deny it."

Lord Turner glowered at Croker. "I don't believe you."

"You don't have to. But I am certain if you ask her, she'll tell you that I'm being truthful."

Three gentlemen advanced and addressed Lord Turner, giving Croker a minute to collect himself. When they were gone, their dialogue resumed.

"Who did it, then?" Lord Turner spat. "This wild dog you have running around with the Whyos?"

Croker's jaw dropped. "How…how do you know…"

"It doesn't matter," he waved him off. "And you can give me whatever excuses you like. My 'belated grudge,' as you call it, still stands, and not just because of my mother and my…late father."

"What other reasons could you possibly have?"

"More than you could ever grasp, Richard. You should know better than anyone that my family stems far beyond my own blood, and I would do anything to make sure the injustices they've suffered at your mercy are compensated in full. And all of their tragedies—all of my tragedies—begin and end with you. It doesn't matter who held the blade—you're the ringleader here, and your whole circus is going to come tumbling down, piece by piece."

They glared at each other for a few seconds.

"So, that's the way it is, then?" Croker presumed haughtily.

"Privately, yes." With a shrug of his shoulders and a twist of his head from left to right, Lord Turner recovered his lighthearted and merry manner, a genuine grin forming on his lips as if nothing were out of the ordinary. "Publicly, I will not say a word against you, and like everything you covet in this world above Midtown, it will be superficial and counterfeit."

Suddenly, Celeste was at Lord Turner's side, and she slid her arm through Thomas's while giving Croker the coldest look he'd ever received from a woman.

"Enjoy the party, Richard," Lord Turner said enthusiastically, and together, he and Miss Hiltmore left him in the middle of the crowd.

Croker delayed for a few seconds, stunned as he watched them go, deliberating just what in the hell it was that he was missing, because the math regarding Lord Turner was undeniably not adding up.

"Does someone want to take a fucking guess as to how in the hell some rich bastard from England knows about things we have only discussed in this office?" Croker barked, spit flying from his mouth. "You want to know what that means? That means one of you bastards has been breaking code and spilling our plans. And when I find out who it is, I'm going to kill you myself!"

For the first time in ages, they were all there: Esther, Walsh, Will, Louis, Ellis, Seamus, Sullivan, and O'Reilly, and not one of them said a word as Croker berated them in his office.

"I don't give a shit if one of you is protecting the other. You tell me right now who it is, and your ass is off the hook." He glowered at them, waiting.

The clock in the corner of the office rang out loud as it struck two, though they were by no means wrapping up this congregation anytime soon. Croker wasn't leaving the office until he got answers, and he had one more surprise in store—one that was going to change his operation entirely.

He snatched the whiskey decanter off his desk and filled his empty glass. "I know one of you knows something. You aren't leaving until you fucking spit it out."

He observed each of them, searching for signs of guilt. Closest to Richard was Esther, seated in one of the two chairs across from his desk, looking unperturbed and smoking a cigarette. He knew it wasn't her, yet he wanted her there to start diffusing the ongoing rivalry between her and Walsh. Walsh was off to the side, leaning against the wall, and in a similar fashion to Croker, examining the others for weakness. Will and Louis were by the drink cart, each with a whiskey in hand, also with an air that indicated they had nothing to hide. In the back were Ellis and Seamus, both having arrived last, and though he couldn't be sure, Croker was almost positive he'd never mentioned anything about the Bowery to Ellis, therefore eliminating him as well. Sullivan was in the chair beside Esther with a cigar, gazing at Richie with confusion, and O'Reilly lingered just off to his side with his arms folded over his chest.

Someone had to know something.

Out of the blue, Walsh straightened up and walked to where Esther sat, placing his arm on the back of her chair. "I have a theory."

Croker grabbed for his own cigar. "By all means."

Esther had whipped around, glaring at Walsh being so close to her, and he smiled down at her maliciously. Then, he peered back up at Richard.

"Your little assistant has been making visits to The Palace, Richie."

Right on cue, as promised.

Every man in the room except for Richard was completely shocked, their gazes moving straight to Esther, and Will and Louis glanced at each other in fear.

"I followed her. Guess the Frog and the Cat didn't do as good of a job as you thought."

Croker glanced to Esther, motioning that she had the floor, and to Walsh's feigned disappointment, Esther then stared up at him, unsmiling.

"Croker knows I've been visiting the Madame," she barked, "and it was supposed to be a fucking covert task I was taking on without any of the others knowing, you stupid son of a bitch."

"It's true," Croker supplemented. "With my permission, Esther began visiting with the Madame again so that I could cover all my bases at The Palace."

"And just how can you trust her?" Walsh pressed. "How do you know she's not playing you?"

Croker took a long drag of his cigar. "Well, to be fair, I wasn't ever sure until now."

Esther spun toward him in shock, and Croker elaborated: "If there was foul play, Walsh, I am quite certain Louis would have known about her seeing the Madame, and that would also mean Will knew. From the looks on their faces, I am absolutely sure this is the first they've heard that Esther has been in contact with the Madame at all."

Both men were so appalled, it made Croker almost laugh aloud, and Louis didn't hide the fact this deeply upset him. He slammed his glass onto the drink cart and marched out of Croker's office before Richard could tell him not to, and so he let him go and gestured for Will to follow him out. When they were gone, Croker got to his feet.

"I want to make this perfectly clear. Whatever happens in this office stays in this fucking office, and if some kind of breach like this happens again, you're all done for." He pointed to Walsh. "I don't care about what sort of issues you have with my assistant, but you both will put this fucking bitterness to rest with the upcoming hit on Frederick. You hear me? It's dividing us, and I don't need your immature bullshit causing me any more trouble. One more stunt from either of you, and you're in the Hudson." He looked directly into Esther's eyes. "And I'm not exaggerating."

"Understood," she muttered quietly, finishing her cigarette and rising. "Can I go clean up the mess that's been made? Louis might not talk to me after this."

He gave her an approving nod and Esther left hastily, while Walsh sat in her now-empty chair, his demeanor apathetic.

"The rest of you can go," Croker announced. "This has gone a wholly different direction than I anticipated. But I think my point has been made. Yes?"

The remaining assembly concurred aloud and slowly took their leave, though as Croker expected, Walsh stayed right where he was.

"Did that have the outcome you desired?" Walsh asked snidely.

"Let us hope so," Croker responded, sinking back down into his chair. "I realize that you had to take a hit on that one, but I am grateful for your participation." He exhaled a cloud of smoke into the air.

"How do you see things going from here?"

"With the trust broken between Louis, Will, and Esther, this should be an easy cover. I can't have Esther gallivanting around with Lord Turner in town."

Walsh nodded. "So, I get rid of her on the Frederick hit, and we will tell Louis and Will we got her to lay low until the heat passes?"

"It's a sufficient story," Croker added. "No one will go looking for her. If they do, we just say she must have disappeared to get away from me and New York. How could anyone argue otherwise?"

"I have to say, Richie, even for you, this scheme is a little sinister."

Croker took another drag of his cigar and exhaled smoke. "Like I told you earlier, I can't afford to have loose ends anymore. My appreciation of Esther and what she's done for this organization is outweighed by the threat I face with a man like Lord Turner. And their goddamn disastrous history is not something I need muddying up the progress we've made."

"I agree with you," Walsh assented. "We're going to lose some guys in the process. She's a tough bitch."

"Just make sure you bring Lyons with you. Let's get rid of him while we can. And make sure whoever else attends the execution is replaceable."

Walsh caught on to his insinuation. "Meaning you want me to make sure I am the only one who knows the truth?"

"Precisely." Croker had another drag of his cigar. "I only need one devil to do my real dirty work, Mr. Walsh, and that's you. Esther's always been a liability, and we've got to cut the dead weight before it starts really slowing us down. Just remember one thing."

"Yeah?"

"We never had this conversation. Which means if you fail, you fail alone. And I'll deny it to my grave that I ever fucking told you to kill her."

Walsh didn't flinch. "Plan on taking it to the grave, then, Richard."

It was just past three-thirty in the morning when Ashleigh spotted a dark figure approaching The Palace from the south, still over fifty yards out but closing in fast. Celeste had been there for the last two hours with the Madame, talking over whatever it was she and her father uncovered earlier in the night, including something about a peace meeting between the Lord who lived across the park and Richard Croker. The Madame sent Ashleigh down to relieve George, who'd been on duty for almost a day straight. Ashleigh had been reluctant to leave, perhaps because Celeste looked absolutely intoxicating, though he thought it might be for the best to leave them so he could control himself. Anytime he was around her, Ashleigh couldn't stop imagining what was lying beneath her dress, and consequently, he tended to lose focus on his job. Now, however, as he fixated on another possible visitor, he was dumbfounded as he watched the man leap over The Palace's six foot tall iron fence with grace, heading straight for the back windows, where the Madame's office was located.

Instantly, Ashleigh was on his feet, slamming the front door shut

173

and bolting it behind him. Taking the steps four at a time, he raced up the main staircase, ripping both his pistols from their holsters at once and running as quickly as his legs would carry him. Without hesitation, he burst into the Madame's office, guns out, ready for whatever fight might await them.

He stopped in his tracks. Instead of a trespasser, he happened upon Celeste, the Madame, and a third person sitting down by the fire—whether it was a boy or a girl, he couldn't quite be sure until she spoke.

"So, this is the new Louis?" the mystery woman asked, smiling at him. She wore a newsboy's cap, trousers, a white cotton shirt, and a buttoned-up brown vest, obviously wanting to pass as male rather than female on the streets. Her arm was resting on the loveseat behind Celeste, and he noted that her knuckles were mildly bruised, and additionally observed there was a slight green hue to the damaged skin tone. On her neck was a gruesome scar that stretched the entirety. While he was smitten with Celeste, Ashleigh was amazed at how beautiful she was. Even without hair.

He didn't lower his pistols. "All right, ma'am, who in the hell are ya?" he asked. "And jus' how in the hell did you get your ass up and through them windows?"

The Madame threw her hands up into the air. "Oh, for fuck's sake!" She sighed heavily and poured Celeste and the other girl whiskeys before turning to the bald one. "Well, darling, I think it's safe to say you are now the worst kept secret in New York."

"It's about time we told him anyway," Celeste mentioned, having a sip of whiskey. "Ashleigh has proven to be loyal, I think." She glanced over and winked at him, and immediately he lowered his guns.

"May I?" he entreated the Madame, and she nodded.

Ashleigh went over to the drink cart and grabbed a glass, then joined the other three in a vacant armchair. He stared at Esther.

"So, if ya don' mind me askin' again, who are ya?"

"My name is Esther," she told him, "and I am supposed to be dead."

Ashleigh was puzzled, and the Madame took over.

"Years ago, a girl was wrongfully convicted of murdering Celeste's husband, and was supposed to hang for it."

His eyes grew wide. "You're her, then?"

Esther nodded. "I've been working for Richard Croker to pay off my...debt. The deal was originally not to tell anyone other than him, Louis, and your father that I was alive, but that plan changed."

"Wait, then who was it that died for ya? I mean, someone died that day, right? Got hanged?"

No one spoke, and Ashleigh could sense this was the wrong question to ask.

"Let's not talk about that," Celeste said quietly. "It's something we can discuss another time."

He let it go at her request. "So, if you are Croker's girl, how'd ya end up back here without gettin' yourself in a load of shit?"

"At first, I was coming back in secret, though I managed to make Croker think I could play both sides. Tonight, things went a little too far, though, and I'm...I'm worried."

"Worried 'bout what?" Ashleigh pressed.

"Something just isn't right. I can't explain it."

"How did Louis do? Did he make it passable?" Celeste interrupted.

"He and Will did great. Croker definitely believes they had no fucking idea I was seeing the Madame." Esther had a large gulp of her drink. "I wish I could figure out what in the hell is going on under the surface, but I've got to keep playing along."

"If I know anythin' 'bout Louis, or even my dear ol' daddy, they won' let nothin' happen to ya," Ashleigh attempted to console her.

"It's not that, Ashleigh," the Madame insisted. "Your daddy and Louis were the ones who trained her all these years. It's that we

175

have to pretend like we don't see it coming and hope Esther doesn't get trapped in a situation she can't fucking get out of."

"Ah, shit," he mumbled, finishing his whiskey. "Ain' nothin' you can do, then, 'cept prepare for the worst. Louis and my daddy are damn good at what they do. I'm sure you'll be ready for anythin'."

"Right," Esther matched halfheartedly.

"That includes the lunatic," the Madame emphasized.

Ashleigh again was lost. "Lunatic?"

"The bastard they sent down to find you in Texas," Celeste replied.

"That crazy prick? He the one that worries ya?"

The Madame gave him a threatening stare. "While I realize you haven't been around all that long, Mr. Sweeney, know this: if you ever talk about that man with such a cavalier fucking attitude in my presence again, I will make you regret it."

"He's a freak of nature," Esther added, trying to ease the Madame out of her anger. "I've seen him in action. It's bizarre…it's like he can't feel anything. I hit him full on with my brass, and he barely batted a goddamn eyelash!"

Ashleigh thought for a moment. "They all got a weak spot."

The Madame snorted. "Thanks for the contribution, Little Sweeney."

"Nah, really. Boy got glasses, don' he? That son of a bitch comes after you, just fuckin' take out his eyes."

All three women gaped at him, speechless.

"Well, fuck me," the Madame uttered, then reached over to pour Ashleigh a bit more whiskey. "I think you earned yourself another round."

An hour later, Ashleigh and Celeste were nearing the Hotel St. Stephen. Being such a late hour, the Madame had insisted, in her usual fashion, that Ashleigh escort Celeste home, and he'd hailed them a carriage a few minutes after Esther departed. Most of the ride had been in silence, principally because Ashleigh could tell Celeste was utterly exhausted, though as she dozed in and out of consciousness, her head fell onto his shoulder. They were only a few blocks out, and before Ashleigh could stop himself, he gently took her hand in his and kissed the top of her head. At first, he wasn't sure if Celeste was aware, and he chided himself silently for taking action. He was about to release his grip when he felt her squeeze his hand softly and nestle closer to him as the carriage rocked from side to side. For the last few minutes of their journey, Ashleigh couldn't remember a time when he'd been happier.

When the carriage pulled in front of the hotel, Ashleigh opened the door and exited, helping Celeste down from the coach. Being so tired, she took a misstep onto the hem of her dress and tripped, falling directly into Ashleigh's arms. He caught her in midair and stumbled a few paces, but recovered fast.

"Oh my God!" Celeste cried, embarrassed as he set her on her feet. "Are you all right? I can't believe I fell! I'm just a mess…"

"It's all right," Ashleigh reassured her. "I'm just glad I was there to grab you."

"Well, thank you."

They stood there a moment, gazing at each other, and then abruptly, Celeste curtseyed. "Goodnight, Mr. Sweeney."

"Ashleigh," he reminded her.

"Right. Goodnight, Ashleigh."

He beamed at her and she smiled back, then made her way into the hotel. Ashleigh didn't know why, but he stayed where he was, going over what just happened in his head again and again. This was an opportunity he'd let slip by—he should have kissed her, or done something to insinuate it so she knew his intentions. Striding to and fro for a few seconds, he couldn't take it anymore. He didn't care if it was inappropriate or out of line—Celeste wasn't that type of girl, anyhow. This was his chance, and even if it was a little late, he had to give it a shot.

The hotel lobby was empty save for a snoring landlady, unconscious with a book of poetry on her chest, and Ashleigh went directly for the stairs. When he got to Celeste's floor, Ashleigh suddenly heard the sound of a man hollering at someone; whatever the interaction was, he could sense it was going to turn ugly. Turning the corner, Ashleigh spotted, at the end of the hall, a man had a woman cornered and was verbally assaulting her, not allowing her to pass him by.

Then, he felt his stomach drop when he realized that woman was Celeste.

Ashleigh sprinted to her, grabbing for his pistol, and by the time her assailant realized someone was approaching them, it was too late. With one swift thrust, Ashleigh threw the man against the wall of the hallway, pinning him there with his left forearm against the man's chest and the pistol aimed at his temple.

"Get off of me!" the man bellowed. "Get off of me this—this instant!"

He tried to break Ashleigh's hold, and he would have been a worthy adversary had he not been piss ass drunk.

"Jus' what in the fuck do ya think you're doin'?" Ashleigh hissed. "It's the middle of the night and you're attackin' a woman at her place of residence?"

"She owes me an answer! She—she owes me…"

Ashleigh didn't flinch. He struck the man across the head with the butt of the pistol hard, leaving him dazed for a few seconds.

Celeste was recovering her breath, hand clutching at her chest. "Ashleigh, it's okay."

"No, it's not fuckin' okay!" He cocked the gun, and the man's face went pale.

"Please, this is a mis—a misunderstanding…" the man slurred.

"Who are you?" Ashleigh demanded.

"C-C-Captain Jonathan Bernhardt."

Ashleigh turned to Celeste. "This is the fucker who wants to marry ya?"

Celeste didn't say anything, only nodded.

Ashleigh was horrified, and centered his attention back on Captain Bernhardt. "You listen to me, ya prick. I don' care who you is, or what this lady is to you, you talk to her again or touch her like that again, and I will fuckin' end you."

Ashleigh let him go and pushed him in the direction of the stairs, aiming his gun at the Captain. "Get the hell out of here 'fore I decide to teach ya that lesson without a second chance."

The Captain staggered. "Celeste?! You're just going to let this asshole do this to me?"

Celeste's expression was filled with contempt. It was then Ashleigh observed that her dress was torn on the sleeve and at the waist, her forearms were forming deep bruises from where he'd held her wrists, and though they were gone now, she'd had tears in her eyes.

Enraged, Ashleigh paced toward the Captain, the pistol aimed at his forehead. "You get the fuck outta here and don' come back. Ya hear me? Or I will kill ya."

At last, the Captain relented and turned around, heading for the stairwell. Ashleigh trailed him down to the lobby and watched him walk out the front door, not once lowering his weapon. When the Captain disappeared, Ashleigh put away the gun and returned upstairs to find Celeste holding her arms around herself, shaking with shock.

He marched right up to her and wrapped his arms around her. "Jesus Christ, am I glad I came up here," he said quietly, and felt her arms slip around his waist.

"I didn't know what to do. I thought he was going to...to..."

She pressed her face into his chest and cried, and Ashleigh was beyond relieved he'd gotten there in time.

"It's all right. That bastard won' touch ya again, I swear to you, Celeste. I won' let him near you."

Celeste looked up at him, their eyes meeting. Within seconds, they were kissing furiously, for how long Ashleigh couldn't say, and as things escalated, he had to pull himself away from her to prevent things going too far.

"What is it?" she asked, fearing she had done something wrong.

Ashleigh grinned. "We can' do this out here," he told her. "Not with your brother and your father inside."

"Jeremiah is working a long shift at the hospital, and my father leaves first thing in the morning on business in Virginia," Celeste informed him. "So, if we can't do this out here, why don't you come inside with me?"

He cupped his hands around her face. "This is gonna get complicated real fast, ya know."

Rather than answer, Celeste kissed him again, hard, and Ashleigh reciprocated.

Not a minute later, Celeste was unlocking the door and leading him inside. He trailed her noiselessly through the sitting area and into her bedroom, bewildered at how fate had a funny way of making things happen.

Ashleigh didn't leave until after lunch the next day, knowing he was in deep water with the Madame; he honestly didn't give a damn. One night with Celeste was worth a thousand lifetimes in hell, and he couldn't wait for more.

CHAPTER XXXIV.

Dawn had come and gone hours ago, and yet Louis
and Will were insistent on a long morning of training Esther. While
she appreciated their effort and relentlessness, Esther had reached
a point where her muscles and her energy were very nearly deplet-
ed. They were on the top floor of an abandoned wax factory on the
east side of the village, one they had successfully been able to exercise at for almost six weeks, though soon they'd need to find another location. The three of them had never been able to stick to the
same spot for more than two months; thankfully, Will had already
scouted out a few abandoned buildings for their next site just south
of where they currently were.

Esther took a few big breaths, hoping to get more fluidity in
her aching limbs. Their sparring had become exceptionally intense
throughout the last week in anticipation of her hit on Judge Frederick, with Louis and Will wanting her to be as physically well-equipped
as possible. She was happy for the push, as she'd grown to love physical challenges in her years learning from Will and Louis; however,
Louis was starting to try her patience. Esther was exhausted, and
had sustained multiple hits from both of her mentors that would
leave her far more bruised and sorer than normal, although in re-

turn, she'd done her own damage to the two aging hitmen. Louis, it seemed, had a sprained wrist and hopefully no more than one or two battered ribs from Esther's knee repeatedly digging into his torso. Will's knee was bothering him, an old injury he'd never been able to shake off, though this was the result of repeated use rather than a hit by Esther. The only real harm done to Will that morning was a jab from Esther he'd deflected, though his arm was off by a few inches, and thus resulted in a large shiner on the corner of his cheekbone. Her own body was throbbing from beaten kidneys, an overwrought shoulder, and a twisted ankle sustained trying to land on her feet after Louis tossed her off of his back. They needed to wrap up before one of them got seriously hurt.

But Louis wouldn't let up, and in spite of her aggravation, Esther knew it wasn't just because he was nervous about Frederick—it was Walsh.

"Again," he announced.

Esther was leaning against the wall by a window facing the river. Will sat on the ground ten feet from her, attempting to recuperate, and Louis paced to and fro, his chest heaving from their last round.

"Louis, I ain' got nothin' left, brother," Will declared, sweat dripping down his face. "And Es is torn up enough, don' ya think? We don' wanna overkill here."

Esther stayed silent.

"We'll go one more round," Louis asserted, cracking his neck from side to side and shuffling his shoulders. "Esther, we are going to finish with a double today."

Her jaw dropped, and Will cursed aloud.

"Louis, I can barely stand as it is!" Esther cried.

"I don't care. One more. And a double."

Will peered over at her with sympathy, then clambered to his feet. "One double, brother, and she's done, ya got me?"

Louis gave Will a scathing look, but Will was steadfast. "Just tryin' to keep everyone in one piece, is all."

Ignoring him, Louis centered in on Esther, coaching her. "You can do this. I want you to remember what this feels like—when you have nothing left and you still have to fight."

Internally, she was battling to suppress her exasperation. "Fine," she conceded, popping her knuckles.

"Use your anger at me against me. You know how to do it."

Esther hopped a few times from side to side while Will and Louis got into position, swinging her arms forward and back in a vain attempt to bring life into her body.

"Who ya want first, brother?"

"I'll initiate," Louis offered. "When I call it, Will, you interject. We will swap one more time, then double Esther."

"Five rounds?"

Louis nodded. "Five rounds."

"Fuck," she murmured to herself.

"Es, you got this," Will encouraged her. "Big breaths. It'll be over before ya know it."

"I know." Esther inhaled and exhaled, then held her fists up in proper form. "All right, Louis. Count it down." Taking a few steps forward, Esther turned the direction of the river, blinding herself from any attack she couldn't catch in her peripheral vision.

"Five…four…three…"

She counted the final two in her head, and right on cue, Louis slammed into Esther square in the hip, sending her reeling to the left. In a maneuvered roll, Esther caught herself, managing not to fall to the ground and risk being exposed. Somersaulting to her feet, she whipped around to face Louis head on, and he came at her hard. She ducked under, avoiding a calculated punch, and once he reached the end of his swing, Esther struck Louis right in his injured ribs. To her disappointment, he didn't flinch. He spun rapidly, and she found his left elbow rocketing directly for her nose. Just in time, Esther's forearm defensively blocked the hit, though she felt the repercussion radiate all the way down to her toes. Revolving under his arm while she kept it in her grasp, Esther pulled Louis into her and then pushed with every ounce of energy she had left in her legs. He fell backward a few footsteps, trapped behind her while she contracted her knees to her chest. With a giant heave, Esther lurched their residual weight downward as hard as she could and tucked, sending Louis flying over her head and onto the ground.

He didn't call for the switch—instead, Louis was instantly upright again. Striding toward her, he threw a jab, which Esther managed to redirect, then another and a roundhouse kick to her waist. In that second, Esther grasped his leg directly around his joint underneath her arm and in turn, kicked Louis as hard as she could in his balls with her left leg. He keeled over, and Esther took the opportunity to knee him in the nose, not hard enough to break it yet enough to send a message.

Without needing the cue, Will came at her next, though he at least had the courtesy to attack Esther head-on. He made a downward strike with his right arm, throwing her on the defensive, then a left hook which she barely caught, and promptly she foresaw that what was to come next would hurt her badly. In a flash, Will undercut her in the chest, and Esther felt her breath abandon her. Combatting her baser impulses to retreat, she took two strides in withdrawal, narrowly avoiding a follow-up jab to her jaw that surely would have dislocated or broken it, and straightened despite the searing pain in her lungs. Will did not stop, and their jabs clashed together, one throwing a punch and the other repelling the strike, back and forth until Esther could feel her muscles scream. Out of the blue, and in a moment of distraction at her weakness, Will managed to send her backward a few feet and, before Esther could get her arms up to shield herself, a spin kick hit her smack in the cheekbone and sent her writhing to the ground.

"Pause!" Louis bellowed, giving Esther a few seconds to recover. "Esther, you have to anticipate the assault. Read his body. You cannot focus on what you feel—you have to focus on one thing, and one thing alone."

Esther rose up, feeling blood in her mouth, and spat it onto the ground. "Winning." It was a miracle she hadn't lost a tooth.

Once she resumed her stance, Louis lunged at her again, and this time Esther used her anger to her advantage. She slid underneath Louis's clutches, his long arms nearly seizing her but missing by only an inch or two. Once behind him, Esther leapt high and struck the bottom of Louis's neck with all the might in both her fists, then landed perfectly onto her feet. Momentarily, he dropped to one knee, and Esther jumped onto his shoulders, her thighs wrapped tight around his head, and proceeded to hit the bald Frenchman once, twice, three times, until he got ahold of her and tossed her sideways into the wall. She hit with such force she felt the wall crack, and Esther toppled to the ground. Aching, she didn't linger, knowing that Louis would kick her senseless if she did. He approached with rushed strides, and Esther rolled away from Louis and manipulated her feet underneath her, hopping upright. He moved for the tackle and managed to withstand her strikes to his face and shoulders, getting his arms wrapped unbreakably around her trunk with the intention of slamming her onto the floor.

Using a hurried maneuver of her foot, Esther tripped Louis enough to get him off balance and lead him to the wall, which was only a yard or two away. Careering them both to create momentum, she hurdled her legs up to get the soles of her boots onto the wall, and the second she made contact, thrust into a backward flip and freed herself of Louis. Before Louis could whip around to face her, Esther kicked him square in the flank and sent him headfirst into the wall.

It did not sound pretty.

As she rotated around, Will was already on her. Where Louis

had failed, Will succeeded by having the element of surprise, and managed to wrestle Esther to the ground in one swoop. Within seconds, he had Esther in a headlock, and after a few attempted kicks to free herself, she realized she only had seconds until she blacked out. Plunging her arm up and over her head, Esther's palm jabbed into Will's face directly under his nose, and she felt his arms soften. Immediately, she slipped loose and rolled away, hopping upright and bracing for the final round, where she would have to beat both Louis and Will together.

They stood next to each other, both bleeding and tired, while Esther took the opportunity to catch her breath. Then, in a flash, Esther charged and slid, knocking Will to the earth with a low spinning sweep kick. Louis moved fast as Esther was on her knees, though with her left forearm she caught his strike and repeatedly went on to hammer into his torso with her fist, and a final blow to his throat caused him to recede, gasping for air. As Will scrambled to get up, Esther was already ahead of him and took two bounding strides his way, using his bent legs as a mount to climb up atop his shoulders. She wrapped her right leg like a hook around his right shoulder and, before he could make a grab for her, plunged backward and spun underneath his raised right arm. With practiced skill, Esther's left leg went straight through her gyration, smashing him in the face with her heel; the force from the swing threw her directly into the charging Louis. Clutching his shoulders mid-launch, Esther was able to bring Louis down to the ground, landing crouched and ready for her other assailant while Louis was temporarily undermined.

In a last-ditch effort, Will attempted to climb to his feet, and Esther recognized their battle was coming to a close. With one big lurch, she flew into an aerial kick and blasted Will so hard, he toppled to the ground in a heap, groaning. Louis, too, was struggling to stand up, except Esther was in a groove, moving too fast for him to predict what she might do next. Diving toward his right leg, she brought him to the floor once again within seconds and twisted herself underneath him, effectively locking Louis into an unbreakable triangle bind.

"Tap out," she panted, using every ounce of power she had to hold him. "I won't let you go until you tap out."

She squeezed her legs tighter, and after a few seconds of struggle, Louis gave the signal and Esther released him. The three of them lay on the floor panting for air for a few minutes, no fight or energy left in their spent muscles and limbs. Esther went over the play-by-play in her head as she felt her heart rate at last start to slow, and was overcome with a smug tinge of satisfaction. Not only had she been victorious, but it also solidified her confidence that she was finally ready to take out Frederick, even if Louis and Will still had their doubts.

Will pushed himself upright, bloodied and wincing. "Jus' how in the hell did ya swing under my arm like that?" he asked. "I ain' never taught ya nothin' like that."

Esther, sprawled out on the ground, chuckled. "Something I just thought I'd try."

"Pretty damn good move, if ya ask me. Louis? You alive over there, brother?"

"Mmm," was the only answer Louis could muster, and like Esther, he remained lying where he was.

"Gonna go get us some water from the pump," Will informed them, moving first to his knees, and eventually managing to get himself upright. "Be right back."

He limped over to the fire escape after grabbing their two vacant buckets, shakily climbed through the window, and was gone from sight.

"Good work today," Louis commended her, unmoving. "Christ. I don't know if I'll be able to breathe for a week after all those hits. Had to make a point, didn't you?"

Esther tilted her head and looked over at Louis, smiling. "Of course I did."

He laughed, then grimaced from the pain. "No…laughing… don't…make me laugh…"

"All right, I won't," she promised, scooting over to the wall and using it to help her stand. "You need me to get you on your feet?"

"No, no, I just could use a few minutes. I'm not what I once was."

Esther walked over and squatted down next to him. "I still think you're pretty fucking great. You almost had me in that choke."

"Yeah, well, you did get me in that choke."

"I learned from the best."

A grin formed on Louis's lips. "That swing was pretty incredible."

"I do it all the time scaling buildings in the Bowery. I figured, why not implement it into my sparring routine."

"Well, I think you certainly surprised Will with that move," he remarked, rolling to his side and then pushing himself up to sit.

They were silent for a minute or so, no sound except for the noise echoing up from the street, until Louis spoke up: "How do you feel about Frederick?"

"Ready," she affirmed. "Even if I do have to leave my brass out of the occasion."

"It could be tied back to you if you don't."

"Trust me, you don't have to justify that aspect of the hit to me. I want it to be as clean as possible."

Louis was striving to rise, and regardless of his previous assertions, Esther went to his side to aid him and pulled him to his feet.

"I appreciate that," he thanked her, clutching his ribs. "You fucking decimated my chest."

"I'll lay off bludgeoning your trunk for the next week," she teased.

"Just remember, Esther. If anything feels off, you bail. The bottom line is Croker wants the judge dead as soon as possible. But you know Walsh. It's never easy with him."

"If he's up to something, I'll sniff it out," she promised. "That son of a bitch has it coming sooner rather than later…"

"Water!" Will shouted from the fire escape and waved them over, both empty buckets in his hands now full to the brims.

Louis and Esther ambled over to Will, scaling out over the ledge of the window, and the three of them passed one bucket around, draining the contents, followed immediately by the second. When their water was consumed, Esther set the buckets aside and grabbed her newsboy cap, which she'd left on the windowsill, and placed it back onto her head. Will did the same with his Pendleton hat, then proceeded to reach into his pocket and produce a flask of whiskey, whilst Louis grabbed for two cigarettes for himself and Esther. The three of them lowered down to sit onto the fire escape, handing the flask to and fro, legs dangling off of the ledge, with Esther in the middle and Louis and Will on either side of her.

"What'd I miss?" Will asked, retrieving some tobacco to chew from his pants pocket.

"Just talking about the hit," Louis divulged. "We didn't get into exact specifics."

"I think we do like we've been discussin'," Will stated. "You'll have to use a blade, Es. Otherwise, everyone'll know it was you and your brass."

Louis lit a cigarette for Esther, handed it to her, and lit one for himself. "Let's be fair. There will be speculation that this was a hit. The idea is to make it so that there is no evidence to prove Frederick's death was done by us."

"Right. I need to make it seem like he was done in for the money he owed," Esther established, taking a long drag of her tobacco.

"That's it," Will agreed, shoving the chew in his lip.

Esther turned to Louis. "Shouldn't be too hard, right?"

"Not at all," he promised her. "We'll go over the specifics and outline every detail starting Monday. You'll need to tail him a few days, get his schedule down, and most importantly, you need to picture yourself doing it over and over again flawlessly. It'll help make you less nervous when the time comes."

Esther took a large gulp of whiskey from the flask, enjoying the burn as it hit her stomach, before broaching another subject that was pestering her: "Why do you two think Walsh pulled that stunt at the meeting?"

Will went first. "I think that bastard wants to isolate you. He don' like you babysittin' him down with the Whyos and knowin' what he's up to. Croker oughta know better than to think Walsh is trustworthy without you 'round to keep him honest."

"He wants to isolate me so I don't have a say in anything?"

"More or less."

Louis took over. "I agree with Will. Unless Walsh is up to something we haven't figured out yet."

Esther handed the flask to Louis. "I don't know why, but my gut is telling me that he's going to try something with this hit."

"Like I said before, if anything seems off, you bail on the hit. You never carry one out unless every single variable is painstakingly in place."

"Yeah, but what is Croker going to do to me if I fail my first hit and try to blame it on Walsh?"

"Louis and I will take care o' that," Will assured her. "We ain' gonna let nothin' happen to ya, ya hear me?"

Esther was curious. "What do you mean?"

The two men looked at each other. "Let's just say, we've been doing this long enough to know how to handle this type of a situation," Louis explained. "We will have every one of our bases covered."

She hated to admit that this put her much more at ease. "I don't know what I would do without you two," she confessed. "Really. I don't."

Will put his arm around her, and she leaned against him.

"Not sure what we would do without ya either, Es," he said sincerely.

Louis reached up and took Will's hand as it rested on Esther's shoulder, and she smiled at their affection, feeling happy for the first time in weeks. She loved Will and Louis more than she could ever express to either of them—they'd been her mentors, her friends, and her entire life throughout her years of isolation. The three of them had become a family. In the beginning, they'd been discreet about their relationship, perhaps afraid that Esther would make judgments or look down on them for it. Ultimately, she confronted Will and Louis about it, offering her blessing and that whenever they wanted privacy, she would find a way to give them that. Since that day, the two men had been open with her and didn't hide as they had before, and in a strange way, it bonded them together even tighter than Esther could have imagined.

She finished her cigarette and tossed the butt down into the alley. "I've got to get down to the Bowery," she acknowledged reluctantly. "It's nearing lunch and they want to talk about their new brothel on Ninth. Something about needing more fucking opium than it already gets."

Will gave her a squeeze and let her go. "Jus' don' let that cunt give ya a hard time."

"Let's just pray my bribe worked and Lyons will be on my side for once," Esther stated expectantly. "Thanks for the great morning, guys. How do you feel about meeting me at The Dry Dollar in an hour or two?"

"Count us in," Louis confirmed. "And Esther, you're more than ready for this. We've both got the bruises to prove it."

Will held her brass knuckles up to Esther as she rose from her spot. "Bring these in case ya need to bust that bitch's head in."

Esther smirked. "Wish I could, but now that she's fucking Walsh, I'm not sure I can touch her."

Will chuckled. "Don' kid yourself, Es. That sick bastard wouldn' give a damn if you killed her in front of him, long as he got to watch."

As Esther climbed down the fire escape, Will's words echoed in her mind, because a small part of her believed that no matter how disturbing his observation was, Will was probably right.

Kitty, Danny Lyons, and Walsh were waiting for her at The Morgue, and Esther was shocked and mildly repulsed when she walked in to find Walsh and Danny seated down at a table with whiskey while Kitty massaged Walsh's shoulders. Clearly, Kitty wanted everyone to understand that she and Walsh were more than just partners; to Esther's relief, Danny didn't seem to care in the slightest—if anything, she sensed he probably felt relieved to be rid of the burden of Kitty and her manic tirades that erratically came and went. As Esther marched to them, Danny surprised her once again: he had an empty glass waiting for her, and upon Esther's approach, poured out a share of whiskey and slid it toward the empty chair for Esther. To her delight, Kitty was visibly aggravated by this welcoming gesture.

So, the bribe had worked.

"Training went late, then?" Walsh inquired, his tone patronizing.

Esther lowered down into her chair and downed her whiskey. "You could say that," she let out a deep breath and leaned back. "So, this is about the brothel on Ninth?"

"We're gettin' more opium requests than we can fill," Danny clarified, then finished his own whiskey before pouring another round for himself and Esther. "I wanted to send in a request with Mr. Croker to up the amount of opium we're receivin'."

"How much more?"

"Double," Kitty proclaimed, provocation in her voice. "Walsh said it shouldn't be a problem."

Esther's eyebrows rose, and she had a sip of whiskey. "You want double what you are already getting just for one brothel?"

"It's not just one," Danny went on. "A lot of our places are gettin' hounded for more of it. We just want to up our game, is all."

Esther turned to Danny. "So, you want to start competing with the celestials for opium dens? Is that the idea?"

He nodded, and Esther peered over at Walsh. "Have you mentioned this to him yet?"

Walsh shrugged. "I told him they needed more and that you and I would get the details this afternoon."

"You realize this will have Tammany at odds with Chinatown?"

"Who gives a fuck about Chinatown?" Kitty blurted out, leaving Walsh and stepping closer to the table.

It was then Esther noticed her arm was bandaged underneath her sleeve, and Esther had a sick inclination as to where it came from.

Kitty carried on, "We can handle the chinks. They don't got shit we can't solve with a few bodies in the gutter. And, they hate leaving Chinatown for anything."

Esther was fighting to keep her cool. "It's not about that, Kitty. It's about the political repercussions that might ensue as a result. Walsh and I just need to make sure it's something the Hall doesn't care about or isn't already involved in, and we'll get you the opium."

Kitty crossed her arms. "Since when do the Irish care about chinks?"

"Easy, Kitty," Walsh interjected. "The Assistant is right. We can't make a solid guarantee to double your weekly supply without Croker's say so."

"I will get you an increase regardless," Esther said to Danny. "So, you can at least count on that. It's just how much of an increase we'll have to talk over."

Danny seemed content. "Works for me."

Kitty, on the other hand, was outraged. "Since when do you take her fucking side?" she roared at Danny. "This ain't about the Hall! It's about the gang!"

"Fuck off, Kitty," Danny spat back. "We are doin' things smart for once. Girl is gonna get us more either way, so what the hell is up your ass?"

Esther's eyes went to Walsh, who stared back at her for a few seconds. His gaze gave her goose bumps on her arms, and she could tell that rather than interrupt their argument, he wanted to see it play out for entertainment's sake.

"You didn't used to give a fuck what she said!" Kitty kept yelling. "You used to want to do this whole thing our way!"

"Yeah, well, things change, Kitty. Now, sit down and shut the fuck up. Walsh? Get ahold of her, would ya?"

Walsh looked at him blankly, and this increased Kitty's rage. She slammed her fists down onto their table.

"That's not the way this works, you prick," she jeered at him.

"Okay, that's enough," Esther inserted herself, setting down her whiskey glass and standing up. "Kitty, this isn't personal. We are trying to do this as collaborators—it has nothing to do with you or the gang."

Kitty glanced from Esther to Danny, and back to Esther. "So, let me guess. I stop fuckin' Danny and you jump in to take my leftovers. Is that what it is? Hmm? Is that why you two are suddenly so goddamn friendly?!"

Esther was completely taken aback by the accusation. "What the hell are you talking about, Kitty?"

Suddenly, Kitty picked up their dingy wooden table and flung it to the side, shattering their glasses and the bottle of whiskey all over the floor. Esther should have known this was coming, but her infuriation at Kitty overpowered her composure.

"What the fuck, Kitty?" Danny yelled. "Quit tryin' to start shit for no reason!"

Kitty took a few strides toward Esther and got directly in her face. "You ain't got no place here. We don't want you, and we don't need you."

Esther rolled her eyes and discreetly slid her hands into her pockets, shimmying her fingers into her brass knuckles. "You want me gone? That's fine by me. I'm only here because I represent Richard Croker, who you, the Dannys, and Walsh all chose to partner with years ago. If I walk, you will lose the support of Tammany Hall, and the Whyos won't last a fucking week without Croker. Walsh?" She peered at him over Kitty's shoulder, her temper on the rise. "Unless you plan on telling Croker later about how you didn't speak up for the Hall, I suggest you fucking back me up."

She'd put him between a rock and a hard place, and didn't give a damn. Finally, he sighed, still sitting in his chair despite the table being in three pieces on the ground.

"Let it go, Kitty."

"Like hell I will," she muttered, pulling a blade from her belt and pointing it at Esther's face. "I don't care who you work for. I am going to—"

But Esther was done listening to Kitty run her mouth. With lightning speed, Esther snatched Kitty's wrist with her left hand and pummeled the blade from Kitty's grip with her right, the knife falling to the floor. Using the back of her hand, Esther proceeded to smack Kitty hard across her right cheek, not caring that the brass would leave a few deep gashes. The force knocked Kitty to her hands and knees, and she made one vain attempt to rise, which Esther halted with a swift kick to Kitty's ribcage. Now pacified and curled up on the ground, Kitty held her cheek with one hand and clutched her torso with the other, glaring at Esther, though obviously petrified of what might follow.

Esther picked up the knife, tossing it around effortlessly in her hands. "Kitty, I don't know what this vendetta is that you have against me, but it's going to fucking stop. I am not here to do anything except make this alliance between the Whyos and Tammany work." She squatted down beside her, and to make a point, slammed the tip of the blade into the floorboard so that it would be nearly impossible to remove. "Stop making this difficult, or I promise I will very quickly make life unbearable for you."

She stood, and felt Danny move beside her.

"She's right, Kitty. You're just doin' this to be a pain in the ass. You're way over the line here."

"I agree," came the unforeseen opinion of Walsh, who also was on his feet and walked over to join them. "The Assistant and I are here as mediators. I am one of the gang and also one of the Hall. She represents Croker and his interests. This cannot go on peaceably if you don't stop misbehaving."

Esther tried not to alter her countenance with how she felt hearing those words come from Walsh's mouth. She wasn't sure why, but something about him and the entire situation at The Morgue was leaving a bad taste in her mouth. After bribing Danny, she'd expected him to be easier to deal with, yet this was becoming a little too easy. Throughout their history with the Whyos, Walsh never supported her in a dispute—not one time, even when Esther's life had been on the line. Such an unprecedented turn of events where both Walsh and Danny chose to oppose Kitty together with Esther was too good to be true, regardless of the reasoning, and she sensed that there was something going on under the surface she wasn't privy to just yet.

The Madame's voice spoke up in the back of her mind: *They're trying to make you comfortable so you don't see it coming. And something is fucking coming. Something that will not end well for you. Get your guard up.*

Esther crouched down and helped Kitty to stand, trying to make it appear as if she were falling for their misdirection. "Cold meat on your face. You shouldn't need stitches."

Esther then spun around and made her way to the exit.

"Where ya headin'?" Danny called after her.

"I need a drink."

"We got more whiskey at the bar," he offered.

"I'll go check on The Dry Dollar," she retorted, walking out the door of The Morgue with every fiber of her being unsettled.

Keep your wits, darling. They're all out to get you.

Repeating the encounter over and over again in her mind, Esther found it extremely disconcerting that for motives she had yet to uncover, Danny—and Walsh, for that matter—were teaming up with her against Kitty. Or, at least, that was how they wanted Esther to see it, and what was worse was the notion that perhaps Kitty was in on the deception as well.

Gliding through the streets and pulling her cap down over her face, Esther shuffled along rapidly, wanting to get to The Dry Dollar in a hurry so she could inconspicuously talk the whole incident over with Will and Louis. Thankfully, she didn't have to visit Croker today, which was a relief considering she wasn't sure how she would broach this subject with him in the first place. Irrespective of her importance to Croker, the one thing Esther would never forget was what the Madame had told her down in the Tombs just hours before her scheduled execution, and that was never to trust him. He would toss her aside the minute he found her a burden or if she happened to be a prospective liability in the future. Nonetheless, another side of her also speculated whether this was entirely Walsh's doing, and that maybe his purpose was to send Esther to her grave in such a way that Croker might not blame him for it. She would probably never know the full spectrum of the truth, and that idea alone was frightening. But the Madame was right: she needed to get her guard up. Esther was a survivor, and this was definitely not the time to get soft.

She rounded a corner to take a shortcut across town to The Dry Dollar, hoping to avoid the claustrophobia and smell of summer traffic that was growing worse every day, as the mid-June sun only got hotter and hotter. Taking a familiar alleyway, Esther snaked down the corridor when, without warning, someone grabbed ahold of her and pulled her into a vacant back entryway. Her aggressor slammed her against the wall with incredible strength, one arm against her shoulders and the other hand over her mouth to stifle a scream. They were shaded in darkness, and Esther's eyes struggled to adjust while she battled unsuccessfully to free herself. The man was larger than Esther, his features masked by the shadows and what appeared to be soot rubbed around his eyes, making him unrecognizable, and he waited a few seconds, eyeing the street for followers. She wanted to ask just what it was he was delaying for, but after another moment passed, the man swiftly ripped his hand away and leaned in, kissing her.

Immediately, Esther realized who it was, and when he gave her the chance, she threw her arms around him.

"Thomas!" she exclaimed, a rush of exhilaration filling her that she had never experienced. She held his face in her hands in disbelief, and kissed him again.

After half a minute, he reluctantly pulled away from her. "Es, we don't have time right now. You need to listen to me."

She took a step back, startled. "Don't have time? What are you talking about?"

"Please just listen to me."

It was then she was able to take in his general appearance, and even for Esther, it was somewhat astounding how different of a man Thomas was. He was taller than he'd been years prior, and filled out to such a degree he would probably make Louis seem average-sized. He wore regular boots and slacks, though around his waist she noted a small pouch, jesses, and a heavy leather glove, and inside his vest was a holstered revolver. A bowler hat rested on the ground at his feet, one she assumed he'd been wearing until he nabbed her out of the alley, and his face was heavily sooted, as if to disguise himself from anyone who might recognize him. On his shirt were blood stains, blood that wasn't his, and his knuckles were bruised and scraped.

She gazed into his eyes. "Whose blood is that, Thomas?"

"It's Whyo blood. Esther, listen—"

"Why do you have Whyo blood on your shirt?"

Thomas became impatient. "That's not important right now," he declared firmly, taking her shoulders in his hands. "Look, Es, you've got to start looking for a way out."

Esther was confused. "A way out of what?"

"You need to get away from Croker. From the Whyos. All of it." Thomas shook his head, frustrated. "You aren't one of them, and you need to get out before they find out you've been playing both sides."

"Thomas, you don't know what you're talking about."

"Yes, I do, Es. Look, I know what that bastard is up to, and you can't—"

"Don't you dare tell me what I can and can't do!" she cried furiously. "No, Thomas, you don't know what you are talking about. I have no fucking place to go where he won't hunt me down if I run away. There's no other option for me until we can find a way to bring him down!"

"You can't do that alone, don't you understand?" he shot back.

"I've been alone for the last five years, you ass!" she barked. "I did this for you! And this is how you repay me? By once again treating me like a goddamned child?"

"I know you did this for me, and that's why I am here!"

"Is it?!"

He tried to calm her and draw her into him, but she pulled away.

"Esther, can you just—"

"You are so fucking selfish, you know that? I can't believe you came all this way just to—"

"Esther!" He shook her hard, finally startling her into silence. "Look, Croker and Walsh are both trying to kill you."

Her mouth fell open. "What—what did you just say?"

Thomas exhaled. "I can't be sure on exact timing, but I know for a fact Walsh is planning to kill you after you finish off that judge. But it's worse…"

"How did...where did you..."

"Croker," he told her. "I've been listening in. He told Walsh to do it."

In an odd way, this didn't totally shock her. "You...you said after the hit, right?"

"After the hit," Thomas confirmed. "But I think I bought you some more time; you just have to hear me out."

"Tell me."

"I've just done something that will have the Whyos and Tammany Hall on their defenses. Because of that, you need to circle your own wagons. Get Louis and Will back to working with the Whyos in the Bowery with you, and their plan will completely fall apart."

She nodded, not fully understanding yet trying to keep up. "Get Louis and Will to the Bowery—got it. Thomas, how will I know when to do that?"

A bemused smirk came across his face. "You'll see it with your own eyes soon enough. Just keep Louis and Will close by, and in the meantime, I'll keep tabs on what Croker decides to do. Fucking bastard."

"Wait." She held up a hand to stop him. "How in the hell do you know all this?"

"I've been spying on Croker," Thomas confessed. "I've made three attempts at trying to break into his office, and the last one almost got me caught by that oaf Sullivan."

She studied him closely. "How?"

"That's neither here nor there at the current moment." He paused, peeking out into the alley, making sure the coast was clear. "We don't have much time. I don't trust that Walsh isn't following you as we speak." Brusquely, Thomas kissed her hard and let her go. "It doesn't make sense, I realize, but it will. All right?"

"All right." Esther hated that they had to go separate ways. "I'll do what I can. When can I see you again?"

"Days. I'll find a way and send word."

She kissed him hurriedly. "Be careful."

For a few seconds, Thomas didn't let her go, holding onto her tight. "You be careful."

Esther smiled at him and took off—if she stayed any longer, she'd never be able to leave. With longing burning in her chest, she turned to glance back at him one last time, yet the alley was empty, as if the entire encounter had been a dream and nothing more.

And she kept moving, like she always did, with her eyes on the road in front of her.

As she neared The Dry Dollar, Esther could sense that something was amiss. Foreboding clouds darkened in the skies as a light rain began to fall, and Esther squinted through the small shower, taking note that not a single candle was flickering inside the bar. There were no signs of movement, no one coming or going, though the door was cracked open ever so slightly. Esther's eyes skimmed around and found the street strangely deserted, with only a handful of people in sight. Normally in the afternoon The Dry Dollar had at least a dozen or so customers, and while they were mostly Whyos, that didn't make a difference. The bar seemed abandoned, and Esther's knuckles habitually gripped into fists around her brass knuckles while she cautiously strolled toward the entrance.

When she reached the door, Esther took a deep breath and softly pushed it open, slipping inside noiselessly. What she saw made her retreat a few steps, blinking repeatedly to be certain she wasn't hallucinating.

Straight in front of her lay the bodies of Strat and Johnny, and while Esther could barely make out Strat's raspy breath, she noticed Johnny's neck had been snapped like a twig. Ahead and to the right on the staircase, Teal was sprawled out at the bottom, in all likelihood tossed from the top considering the state of his banged up body and the groan he made upon hearing Esther enter. The piano had been used to decimate the skull of a Whyo she didn't recognize, perhaps because his head was so smashed, and Esther prayed for his own sake that the man was dead. She could see his brains from where she stood, and there were piano keys scattered around his corpse. Draped over the balcony was another victim with a pistol still in his hand—it was Finn, and he had a bullet between the eyes, shot down before he could get a round off himself. To her left and seated at a stool at the bar was the barman, Horatio; though Horatio seemed alive despite his unconscious state, he had deep scratches on his forearms like he'd been attacked by an animal. He was hunched over like he'd been placed there after being attacked, his right hand twitching slightly. On the ground at his feet lay Don, also with a bullet between the eyes, a knife on the ground beside him that was clean of blood.

"H-help…" came a plea from somewhere upstairs. "S-s-someone…help…"

Esther shook her head, snapping out of her stupor.

"Where are you?" she shouted, leaping over the groaning Teal and taking the steps three at a time. When she got to the top, there lay Naylor, beaten to such a bloody pulp it would be a miracle if he was still breathing, though the cry wasn't from him. She rotated left and found Paulo sitting against the wall holding a broken arm against his chest, a gunshot wound in his abdomen.

Esther rushed to him and dropped down to her knees, examining the wound and discovering that it was only a graze. She ran over to Naylor, tore the shirt off of him, and returned to Paulo, wrapping it tight around the open wound to create a tourniquet and stop the bleeding.

"It's not deep," she consoled, tying the shirt as tight as she could; Paulo bit his lip to try not to scream out in agony. "You're going to be fine, Paulo. Let me see your arm."

Reluctantly, Paulo released his arm and, trembling, held it out for Esther to examine. The sight of it nearly made her gag—he had a bone through the skin, the result of an arm bar taken to the subsequent extreme. Will had taught her how to temporarily set a break, though she'd never had to actually do it before, and turning away for a second, Esther took a deep breath to compose herself.

Revolving to him, Esther motioned to the arm. "I am going to have to set this. It's going to be…really fucking painful. But if I don't, it could get worse."

Paulo was resigned to his fate. "Do it."

Esther tugged the belt from her waist and placed it between his teeth. "So you don't bite your tongue off."

His dark eyes were grateful for this. "Mmm!"

Positioning herself on the other side of Paulo and laying him on his back, Esther firmly held his upper arm in place with her knees on either side of it. She supported his elbow firmly with her left hand and, placing her own forearm on top of his, his hand at her elbow, Esther closed her eyes and thrust with all her might. The snap of the bone sent Paulo reeling, yet Esther could see she'd gotten it more or less back into place, though the wound began to hemorrhage fast. Hastily, Esther tore another shred of the shirt away from Paulo's bandage around his waist and tied the open fracture as best she could. When she glanced at Paulo's face, Esther noted that he'd passed out from the shock, and hoped he'd wake up soon so she could find out just what in the hell happened at The Dry Dollar. Five dead and four so badly injured they might never fully recover—what sort of fight happened here?

And just like that, Esther remembered Thomas's shirt. She remembered the blood stains, the battered knuckles, the smell of gunpowder, and the revolver in his vest.

"Holy fuck," she uttered to herself, standing up straight and realizing that this was entirely the result of Thomas, and he'd come out almost completely unscathed.

Teal started coughing at the bottom of the staircase, and Esther made her way down to him after she sat Paulo up against the wall.

"Teal! Teal, hold still, let me help you."

Teal, conversely, was already pushing himself upright, blood in his teeth, his expression contorting in discomfort with every breath.

"Jesus fucking Christ," he mumbled, gazing around the room and then up at her. "Is everyone dead?"

"Not everyone," she revealed. "What hurts?"

"Took one to the face, one to my gut, then went down and the bastard kicked me so hard in the head, everythin' went black. Last thing I remember is—is hearin' a bird or some shit. Screechin' loud."

"A...a bird?"

He glowered at her. "I know it sounds crazy, but I ain't makin' this up!"

Esther knelt down. "I wasn't accusing you of lying. I just want to know what the fuck happened."

Teal thought about it, the memory faded from the kick to his temple. "Guy came in...couldn't see his face...fired two shots...maybe three, I can't remember...I met him at the top of the stairs...he musta tossed me..."

"Can you remember anything about him? Anything at all?"

"He had...dirt all on his face...round his eyes and such. Bowler hat. Some old gun I recognized...think it was one of them ones from the war..."

"Can you stand?"

With Esther holding him, Teal was able to get to his feet.

"Listen, Teal, you need to go get Danny. He's down at The Morgue. Go get him as fast as you can." She shoved some coins into his hand. "In case you need a coach and can't walk it."

"Wait, wait just a sec..."

"What is it?"

"Guy...he asked Horatio about...about Walsh...wanted to know where he was..."

Esther froze. "What did Horatio say?"

"Naylor and I was watchin' him from the balcony. Horatio just told him he wasn't in tonight. But then he kept pressin' him, wanted to know where he could find him..."

"And?"

"Horatio just told him the truth: You don't find Walsh. He finds you."

Esther ushered him to the door. "And that's when the shooting started?"

"Right after the guy told Horatio to give Walsh a message."

She nearly tripped over Strat, who was starting to tussle. "What was the message, Teal?"

"Somethin' like...tell the...the lunatic that...that I'm comin' for him. What the hell does that mean?"

Esther opened the front door of The Dry Dollar. "We'll talk about it later. Go get Danny and get your ass back here. Fast!"

When Teal had stumbled in the direction of a coach, Esther bolted inside and locked the door, wanting to round up the wounded and, eventually, make a pile of the dead. She checked the clock at the top of the stairs. It was nearing three. Louis and Will would get here any second to meet Esther for a drink, and she was beyond grateful they'd made plans to meet her here after the incident at The Morgue. She would need all the help she could get trying to piece this one together, and cleaning up after Thomas was going to be one hell of a task. Danny would be out for blood the moment he witnessed the carnage, leaving Esther, Louis, and Will to do whatever they could to cover Thomas's tracks.

Strat was her first to inspect. Esther went to him and rolled him over gently, his haggard breathing worrying her that perhaps it was already too late for him. Pulling him so that he was lying on his back, she examined his body for wounds, noting that his eyelids twitched as she adjusted his arms and legs. Strat had been attacked one on one, and his face sported multiple contusions from strikes; Esther assumed his diaphragm had also been damaged in the process, hence the difficulty with his breath, although to her astonishment, he seemed to be improving now that he wasn't crunched up on the ground. From what she could gather, there were no broken bones, but whatever hit he sustained to his upper abdomen had been crippling.

"Strat?" she whispered, tapping his cheek lightly with one of her hands to try and get him to come to. "Strat. Can you hear me?"

He nodded, and gestured at his throat, his eyes staying closed.

"Did he hit you in your windpipe?"

Again, Strat nodded, then slowly his eyelids flickered open. One of his eyes was red and had a severely popped blood vessel, the other its normal shade of light blue.

Esther scanned the area of his throat, noting the bluish tinge from paralyzed vocal cords.

"It's going to be at least a few days before you can talk again," she told him. "He fucking blasted the hell out of your throat."

Strat coughed a few times, grunted in agreement with her, and pointed toward Horatio.

"He's next. I've just got to get you upright first. Can I help you up and put you in that chair over there?"

Strat leaned toward her, holding his arm up for Esther to slip under, and using all the vigor left in her legs, she got Strat and herself up to stand. Shuffling carefully, Esther got them over to a vacant chair by one of the few unbroken tables, lowering him down softly into a seat.

His eyes searched the room, and he looked at Esther. "Dead?" he mouthed noiselessly.

"Johnny, Finn, Don, Naylor, and whoever that son of a bitch is by the piano," she said, flicking her head that way. "Paulo is upstairs, unconscious after I set his arm. Teal went for Danny once I got him moving."

Shaken, Strat's eyes grew big. "One guy," he mimed, holding his index finger up. "One."

"That's what Teal said, too. Hold on, let me go check Horatio."

Before Esther could get to him, Horatio was already regaining consciousness. His gaze, though not fully normal, registered Esther as she approached him. Slowly, unable to support himself, Horatio's body started to slide sideways, but Esther ran to him and caught him mid-fall, straightening him on the bar stool, balancing his body against the bar.

"What—what happened?" he uttered, rubbing his left hand against his forehead in agitation. "I can't remember a goddamn thing."

Then, his eyes fell upon his decimated right arm, and as if it all unexpectedly came back to him, Horatio flailed in a panic and collapsed onto the floor, unfortunately landing on the dead body of Don.

"Fuck!" he screamed, still thrashing about, and Esther crouched over and grasped his shoulders, holding him steady.

"Horatio! Look at me!" she insisted loudly, wanting to get his attention away from the corpse while she dragged him a few feet away. "Horatio! Get ahold of yourself!"

"What the fuck happened?!" he yelled at her, eyes fixated on Esther.

"Well, I was kind of hoping you would have something to share with the group. I showed up here and found this place fucking destroyed. Five are dead, Horatio. Five!"

"I just...I don't..."

He was frantic, and Esther needed him to focus. She slapped him hard across the cheek and waited, allowing Horatio a brief moment to recuperate.

"I need to know what happened, Horatio. And you're the only one who talked to the bastard who did this—the only one. First, let's start with what he said to you and what he looked like."

He was racking his brain, clamping his eyes shut in an effort to recall the event. "He was…really tall. Dressed normal…broad shoulders. Bowler hat. But he had…something was on his eyes…"

Esther inched closer, wanting to encourage him to keep going. "What did he say to you?"

"He ordered a drink…whiskey…had one or…or maybe two… then asked me about…about Walsh." Horatio glimpsed at Esther. "He wanted to find Walsh!"

"And what did you say?"

"That that was impossible…that Walsh finds you…and he said…he told me to tell Walsh…no, wait. He didn't say Walsh. He called him 'the lunatic' or…or something…but hell we all know who that is…"

"What was the message?"

Horatio's face lit up. "Yeah! That was it. He told me to tell Walsh…sorry. He said to tell the lunatic he was coming for him, and that there'd be no mercy. And then that's when…" All the color drained from Horatio's face. "That's when the thing attacked me."

This was new to Esther. "What thing? What are you talking about, Horatio?"

"It was a falcon."

Esther nearly laughed. "A falcon?"

But Horatio was fully serious, and he held his tattered right arm up to her gaze. "The thing burst through the window and went right for me. It would have taken my head off if I hadn't got my arm up in time. It…it attacked me with its talons…"

"So, what knocked you out?"

"I don't know…I think I fell back and hit my head…" Horatio reached around with his left hand and felt the nape of his neck, and flinched. "Shit! Yeah…hit my head…"

A loud pounding came from the front door of The Dry Dollar, and Esther left Horatio, jogging towards it in the hopes that it was Will and Louis.

"Who's there?" she called.

"It's us," came Louis's voice. "Why is the front door locked?"

Swiftly, Esther unlocked the door and flung it open, steering them inside and immediately closing and locking it up once more.

"We've had an...an incident."

Will and Louis could only gawk.

"What in the name of..." Will thought aloud, their eyes tracing the damage done to The Dry Dollar and the bodies and blood strewn about.

"Was it another fucking brawl?" Louis asked.

Esther huddled both men in close to her, checking to be certain the injured parties were far away enough that they wouldn't be overheard.

"Thomas," she uttered, so quietly she could barely hear herself.

Their expressions were stunned.

"How do you know, Es?" Will pressed.

"I can't tell you now, but I do. Teal went to get Danny and we've got five dead, four ruthlessly injured. Louis, what are you smiling at?"

His eyes sparkling with delight, Louis glanced at Esther, Will, and back to Esther again. "If this is a taste of what Thomas can do...nine against one?" A small chortle escaped his lips. "The war is finally underway. And I couldn't be happier we're on his side."

Detective Samuel Ellis marched into the Madame's office as the evening at The Palace grew busy, nearing the bewitching hour of midnight and thus in full swing. Louis's replacement, the new handsome gunslinger, showed him upstairs, and Ellis was amazed at how much he resembled his father after years of them being separated.

Without a word, the boy closed the doors behind Ellis to give them privacy, which Ellis appreciated, given the night he'd endured in the aftermath of some kind of onslaught against the Whyos.

In their usual manner at the end of the week, he and Seamus had gone to visit Croker with their various updates from the precinct; thankfully, the week had been relatively slow for the detectives. None-theless, when Brian showed them into Croker's office, Seamus and Samuel could sense that something was awry. They walked inside, intruding on an intense discussion between Danny Lyons, Walsh, Esther, Will, and Louis, evidently about something at The Dry Dollar that afternoon. Danny and Walsh were seated across from Croker, while the other three lingered close to Croker's desk, standing together and nursing whatever happened to be in Croker's decanter.

For a few seconds, Samuel wondered if they ought to come by later, but Croker gestured for them to sit near the fireplace as Danny Lyons continued his discourse.

"...tellin' me to stay calm when some fuckin' maniac is out there killin' my boys?! I don't give a shit what you think about this. I'm puttin' a bounty on this son of a bitch tonight."

"A bounty on what, exactly?" Louis questioned, drinking some of his whiskey. "Some guy with a gun, a bird that attacks people, and dirt on his face?"

Danny leapt to his feet to go after Louis, but Will stepped between them.

"Now, listen here. We understand where you're comin' from, Danny. Somethin' is gonna be done 'bout this, but we got nothin' to go on right now. You'll have hunters bringin' in all sorts of folks, just wantin' to collect the cash and not givin' a shit about who it is you're really after."

This seemed to momentarily pacify Danny, and Esther pulled a cigarette from her vest.

"The real issue we have here is that we have four guys in bad shape who all tell the same story—that this was one guy who took out nine at The Dry Dollar on his own and, from what Teal told me, left the bar without injury. This isn't a fucking human we're dealing with. Paulo is one of the toughest bastards I know, and he's beat to shit from whoever invaded The Dry Dollar."

"Uh, Richie?" Seamus spoke up from beside Samuel. "Can someone tell us what in the hell happened today?"

To his surprise, it was Walsh who rotated around and answered, "We had someone come into the bar asking for me and then took out everyone in The Dry Dollar. Five dead, four incapacitated."

"Holy shit," Seamus exclaimed.

"You said it was one guy?" Ellis pressed. "And that everyone's story is the same?"

Croker let out a heavy exhale of agitation. "Apparently, yes."

Seamus went to get a drink. "What's this about a bird?"

"Guy had a bird with him that attacked some of the men there," Croker went on in astonishment, running his hands through his hair.

Samuel's eyes went to Esther's. "Attacked the men?"

He could see her battling to suppress a grin.

"Yeah," she confirmed. "Horatio's arm got torn to shreds by talons."

The room went quiet for a few seconds; not one person there was truly able to wrap their mind around what occurred at The Dry Dollar.

"Well, what the hell are we supposed to do now?" Danny asked the group.

"We have to wait," Walsh stated blandly.

Danny was confused. "Wait? Wait for what?!"

"He's going to attack again, Danny," Esther clarified for him, taking a drag of her cigarette.

"Again?"

"Yes, again," Walsh reiterated. "Which means we are going to have to make sure each one of us is armed at all times. The bars, brothels, everything will have at least fifteen boys every day, no exceptions."

"Louis and Will need to be back down in the Bowery," Esther quickly interjected, and Samuel saw Walsh's head whip her direction, an expression of vehemence on his face.

She didn't waver, and glared right back at him. "Walsh, we need everyone we have to help sniff this son of a bitch out so he doesn't cause any more problems. We don't want word getting out that some guy is killing people at Whyo hang outs. It'll cause panic, and we'll all lose a shit-ton of money."

"She's right," Croker agreed, pointing to Louis and Will. "Until this issue gets resolved, I want you two working with the Whyos and Walsh to keep anyone else from getting killed. I don't know who the fuck this prick is, but I want him gone as soon as possible. Got it?"

They both nodded.

"Sure thing, Richie," Will approved.

"Good. Let me know when you nail the son of a bitch, and then we'll let the Whyos decide what they want to do with him."

A satisfied grin came to Danny Lyons's face. "Much obliged for that, Mr. Croker."

The five of them then departed from Croker's office, leaving Seamus and Samuel behind. Samuel moved closer to Croker, assuming the seat Walsh had abandoned, while Seamus flopped down into the other after refilling his whiskey.

Croker was cutting a cigar. "Please tell me things have been uneventful on your front. I'm honestly not sure if I can handle one more fucking problem right now."

"Slow week, Richie," Seamus established. "Nothin' out of the ordinary, really."

Croker peered at Samuel. "Detective Ellis? Anything to add?"

"Nah. Seamus is right. Been a slow week for us."

"Thank Christ."

"I am interested in one thing, though, Richie."

He lit a match. "What is it, detective?"

Ellis leaned forward. "How did this guy attack The Dry Dollar? Was he armed?"

Croker had a few puffs and looked at Seamus. "He had a gun and a bird. He shot a few of the boys right between the eyes; bashed one skull in so badly no one really is sure who it fucking was yet. The bird attacked Horatio and distracted a couple of the goons while this bastard picked the rest of them off."

Samuel wasn't stupid—he was well aware of who the mystery attacker was; however, nothing had prepared him for hearing that Thomas's first ambush was such a hard hit that it had everyone's tails between their legs, and he found it greatly satisfying.

As he recalled this interaction for the Madame, she just shook her head, smiling.

"Five dead? I have to say, that was a far higher count than I thought he had the balls for during his first round in the Bowery."

"With Louis and Will back in the Bowery, Walsh wouldn't dare do anything to Esther. At least for the time being. So, until after this hit on Frederick, I'd say she's in the clear."

He went over to the drink cart and poured them each a whiskey.

"So, do you think Croker is actually aiming to get rid of Esther?" she questioned him. "Or is this just another one of the lunatic's set ups?"

"I really don't know," Samuel admitted, grabbing the decanter. He'd been trying to figure that out for himself, with little success. "I've never seen Croker try to sabotage Esther in any way. That has been Walsh, and only Walsh. But, to be fair, based on Croker's history, I wouldn't put it past him, Madame—which brings me to an issue I have been wanting to bring up for some time."

He went over to her and handed over her drink before resuming his spot in the chair across from her.

"What is it, Samuel?"

"This is escalating, and it is not going to let up any time soon."

She had a sip from her glass. "And you're worried?"

"Even if we use the information we've collected on Croker to sabotage him, if he wins this election, I'm not sure we'll be able to make the impact we want."

The Madame thought about what he'd said. "You're worried that with Grant giving him the reins, we won't be able to fucking touch him, and I can't argue with you there, darling. The only way we could tear him down is if we had more substantial and consequential material, and that means getting into that fucking safe."

"You said Esther was getting closer?"

"My belief is that if she cleanly kills Frederick, she'll get access. Croker's made it clear to me this is her final test of whether or not she's supremely loyal to him."

Ellis downed some of his whiskey, wanting to lift her spirits. "We've just got to be patient. The bright side is that if Grant is elected, Croker will have power, but he'll be consistently under scrutiny, and his tactics won't be acceptable the way they are now. We've been waiting years for him to make a mistake. I think if he's going to do it, it'll be in the very near future."

This appeared to have Samuel's desired impact, but to his surprise, after a few seconds, the Madame let out a small laugh.

"What is so funny, Madame?"

She rested back into her chair, gulping down her whiskey as an ironic smile came to her lips. "You know, at this point, it's not Croker that keeps me up at night. I despise that son of a bitch with every fiber of my being for what he's done to my family, and we'll get him, I know we will. Or if we can't, I'll simply put him in his grave and accept the consequences of that action." She finished the contents of her glass. "No, the one thing we cannot fucking control is Walsh, and whether or not he chooses to stay with Tammany or tries to break from Croker and take the Whyos with him."

"What do you think would happen if he did?"

The Madame got to her feet and went to the drink cart for another round. "Fucking hell, I don't know. One thought is that he just runs the Whyo operations in the Bowery and causes constant trouble for Richard; another is that he disappears; a third, and the one that seems most likely, is that he goes on a fucking vendetta and kills a lot of people."

Ellis got up to refill his cup as well, and when he got to her, he put his hand on her shoulder. "He wouldn't last long, and we'd have you guarded."

The Madame poured Samuel another. "I want you to look into something for me."

"Anything."

"The only way I'm going to get a fucking handle on the lunatic is if I can get a better understanding of who in the hell he is."

Ellis understood. "You want me to do some digging on Walsh…"

She nodded. "He appeared out of thin air, working for Croker when he was no more than nineteen or twenty. I remember his first visit as if it were yesterday."

"Where do you want me to look?"

"Everywhere north of the Mason-Dixon line on the East Coast. Send out wires to whoever you can. I want to know if he's been incarcerated before, in jail or in an institution."

"You know who'd be better at this?"

"I already reached out to Sally. She's sent word to John and the agency. Between the two of you, I figure one of you will find something on Walsh we can use."

They each had a gulp of their drinks, and Samuel could no longer refrain from touching her. He brushed the hair away from the Madame's face and then pulled her in close, gazing directly into her eyes.

"I've never told you this before, but I love you."

He didn't allow time for her to respond. Instead, Samuel kissed her, and they melted together like they always did, forgetting the dif-

ficulties of the world that surrounded them for the hour they spent
tangled up on the floor of the Madame's office.

CHAPTER XXXV.

Louis lit another cigarette while he waited impatiently outside the servant's entrance of the Turner residence, trying to distract himself from the strange and unfamiliar sensation of anxiousness in his chest, despite knowing Thomas was not at the house. Late June was closing in, and already this was Louis's third occasion at the Turners' without any of the family members cognizant that he was there; for the time being, it was probably for the best. Not even William was privy to the deep history buried between Louis and the Turners, and if he was, he certainly did a good job keeping that knowledge to himself.

When Thomas escaped from New York City with Mary years ago, for the first time in decades, Tony had reached out to Louis with the intention of working together to assist Thomas in his undertakings, and Louis could not have been more eager. The only issue was whether or not they could, or should, ever tell Thomas the story Edward had made them promise never to divulge to anyone.

The dilemma, of course, was that this oath was taken long before Thomas came into the picture, and now Tony and Louis were struggling to find a reason not to tell him.

He'd had the nightmare again the previous night—Louis was

beginning to have them more frequently, and he guessed it was because Tony's existence was once again prominent in his life, and because the devastating memories Louis wished to bury deep down were not remaining repressed. With a long drag of his tobacco, Louis closed his eyes, taking a moment to reflect on the recollections of pain and suffering that, for nearly a decade of his youth, destroyed most of the good he had in him.

Smoke. Heat. Lungs aching. The stench of scorched wood. The burning of his eyes. The roar of the fire so loud Louis couldn't process a thought clearly. He was on his bloody hands and knees, scrambling over embers to find his brother. And…the house…falling apart in front of him…beams crashing, the roof caving…everything being devoured by flames. He'd left England because he wanted to give his brother a new life, free of the burden of Louis and the awful memory of the night of the fire. What Louis hadn't understood in his adolescence was that he was still far too young and naïve to take on the world alone, and that perhaps he should have heeded Arthur's insistence that he stay at Amberleigh.

But that was lifetimes ago.

Suddenly, the servants' door burst open, and there stood Tony, looking flustered but pleased to see him.

"Been here long?"

Louis shook his head. "Nah."

Tony leaned out of the doorway and peered left and right, then gestured for him to come inside.

"We don't have a ton of time," he stressed, leading Louis down the passageway to Thomas's study. "William has been lurking around the house today, although he did at last retire to have a cup of tea about ten minutes ago."

"I thought he was supposed to be downtown with Thomas?"

Tony sighed irritably. "He was. Their meetings ended ahead of schedule because Thomas was able to get the contracts signed without much negotiation."

They turned a corner at the end of the hall.

"Well, I can't say that is a shock. So, where is Thomas?"

"I have an inclination he stopped by to see Lawrence on his way home."

This made Louis smile. "Good. And Lucy?"

"Some kind of social obligation."

Another few seconds, and the pair made it at last to Thomas's study, where Tony closed and locked the doors behind them. In the unlikely incidence that they be found out, Tony wanted to give Louis enough time to slip out of the window before he was forced to open the doors, while Tony would give the excuse of securing the doors as an "old habit." Upon their entry, Athena gave them each a somewhat startled glare, the threat of a screech imminent; Tony, however, was well practiced, and he quickly gave Athena a small snack to subdue her, which always did the trick. Once the peregrine was content and calm, Tony went to the drink cart and poured them each a small whiskey. Louis lowered down in one of the armchairs across from Thomas's desk, and Tony did the same. They clinked glasses in salutation, downed the contents, and finally got to the task at hand.

"So, from your perspective," Tony entreated him, "just how bad was the damage at The Dry Dollar?"

"From my perspective, monumental," Louis revealed, setting his glass aside. "Danny is pissed. Croker is pissed. And no one except Esther, Will, and I have any idea what the hell is actually going on."

"And I am assuming they've increased their forces as a result?"

Louis nodded, grabbing for another cigarette and lighting it. "Thomas will need to be ready. He won't be able to get in and out unexpected like that again. Everyone will be armed and willing to shoot whatever bastard walks in, no matter who he is."

"We have that covered," Tony told him. "The only reason he did what he did on the first round was to send a message."

"A message?"

"Well, one message with two goals," Tony corrected himself with

219

a small smirk. "Obviously, Thomas wanted to let this Walsh character know he finally has someone seeking him out that he did not foresee coming into the picture. And in that process, he was able to get this whole situation with Croker and Walsh wanting to kill Esther under control. Not to mention the fact that now Croker feels he is losing on both sides of town."

Louis eyed Tony. "What do you mean by both sides of town?"

"Thomas has made it clear to Croker he has no interest in being a puppet of Tammany Hall, and it hasn't gone over well."

"About damn time."

"Louis, do you have an extra one of those?" Tony pointed to Louis's cigarette, and Louis obliged, grabbing one from his shirt pocket and handing it over to Tony.

Tony thanked him and took a drag. "How is the girl?"

"Esther?"

"Am I allowed to call her that?"

Louis released a small chuckle. "You are, but you're one of the few. She's fine. With me and Will back in the Bowery, we can keep a close eye on her."

"Care to fill me in on this hit?" Tony asked.

"It's a judge. Not one of us feels good about it."

"What are the odds it is a set-up?"

Louis got to his feet and snatched up their glasses, heading to refill their whiskey. "If I am honest, the odds are extraordinarily high, but we've got something up our sleeves. The Madame, Will, and I have put a backup plan together so that if Esther is in danger, we get her out of New York City and the three of us disappear for good. Croker wouldn't dare follow all three of us, especially if we take out Frederick for him in the process. If anything, it would be a blessing for him to get rid of his dirty laundry and start fresh with new muscle that doesn't know his secrets. No matter what, I won't let that son of a bitch hurt Esther." Louis grabbed the whiskey decanter and poured them each a generous share. "I know you can't tell Thomas that, but do your best to imply what you can so he doesn't get distracted."

Tony exhaled smoke as Louis sauntered over with their glasses. "I'll certainly do that. How is the Madame?"

Louis handed over Tony's drink. "Dying to slit Croker's throat. But she knows she can't." Louis stopped, pensive. "I'm beginning to have doubts, Tony."

Their gazes locked. "Tell me."

"Our endgame. The point of everything our tiny syndicate is working toward. Initially, we went in on this with the sole intention of hurting Croker slowly and deeply, and in time removing him from this earth. We've spent years doing this—collecting information, finding people to out him, infiltrating his inner circle. How long are we going to keep trying if there is no real end in sight?"

"Your question is, more or less, what if we can't kill Croker?"

Louis shook his head. "I can kill Croker whenever I want, Tony. I could walk into his office this afternoon and shoot him dead. I've been fighting this war a long time already. My question is, what is the point? At what cost will we see this through, knowing it will probably kill all of us and another Croker will come along and take his place the second he is dead?"

There was a pause. "I don't know, Louis. Only time will tell. The fight Thomas is fighting is not one I fully understand. I'm just doing what I promised Edward I would do, and that's protect this family as best I can. But Hiroaki probably said it best, and I think it's what Thomas lives by when he has doubts like you are having. He would always stress to Thomas, 'If not you, who will stand up to him?' It resonated with Thomas, and that's what he has been building his defenses around—that he is the only one who can stand up to a man like Croker, and so he will. No matter the cost."

"What if the cost is Esther?"

Tony's face fell. "Then I think we would suffer watching him deteriorate in a far worse manner than Edward. So, let us hope it doesn't come to that."

Louis finished his whiskey. "He hasn't seen me; hasn't tried to see me." For the first time in years, Louis felt his throat tighten with emotion. "I don't know what I've done to deserve this fucking punishment from him, but I can't stand it. It's fogging my ability and my concentration to do my job properly."

"Thomas's silence is giving you these uncertainties?"

"Yes, more than anything else."

Tony leaned over and put his hand on Louis's shoulder. "He doesn't know you're my source, Louis, or that you are my brother. We can't tell him. Not right now. He'd feel betrayed and this whole endeavor would be at risk."

With a hard swallow, Louis gulped down his grief. "I just don't know how to be patient, but you're right. With Croker already arming his defenses, and with a man like Walsh lurking around, we can't—"

Out of the blue and interrupting Louis mid-sentence, Athena started to shriek from her perch, bating as if startled by something. Then, without warning, Louis and Tony heard a key in the lock, and with a hasty glance at one another, realized it was too late for Louis to run. The door swung open, and there stood William, a cup of tea in hand, utterly speechless at what he was witnessing.

"I...er...Tony?" he stuttered when he at last found the words to speak. "Just...what exactly is going on in here?"

Quick as a whip, Tony turned the tables on William, leaping gracefully out of his chair and bowing smoothly.

"Good afternoon, Mr. Turner! Louis was bringing by an invitation from the Madame for Lord Turner, as well as a small treat for Athena. I had Louis accompany me down to the study so he could report back to the Madame that the falcon was delighted with her gift. A very tasty hen breast that was devoured almost instantly. Would you like to give her the final piece?"

Carefully, Tony managed to place himself in front of the empty whiskey glasses sitting on a small side table between his and Louis's chairs, as well as the ashtray.

"Does Thomas allow you to be in here?" William beseeched him suspiciously.

"Of course, sir! I tend to Athena while he is away, otherwise she becomes restless. Is there something I can help you with?"

William stared at Louis for a moment, and then turned his attentions back to Tony. "No, but thank you, Tony. I was, well, oh bloody hell. I was coming in to try and get a little whiskey. That—that woman is starting to drive me goddamned mad!"

"You are referring to Mrs. Shannon, sir?"

"Of course I bloody am! To the point that I would come down and face this—this *bird* just to taste a bit of freedom!"

Louis had to bite his tongue to keep from laughing, and cleared his throat as he rose from his chair. "Well, I should be getting back to the Madame, who will be happy to hear her favorite pet enjoyed the treat. A pleasure to see you, Mr. Turner, and I apologize for startling you. Tony, I know my way out, and give Lord Turner my respects."

Without another word, Louis walked toward the maid's passage and departed, hoping his brother could fend for himself against the not overly witty William, though it was obvious Mr. Turner didn't need much workaround. He was embarrassed at his own intentions for being there to get around Mrs. Shannon's antics, and that would make handling the situation easy for Tony.

Louis made it out of the Turner residence without encountering another soul, and once he neared the road, chose to make his way to The Palace on foot rather than hailing a carriage.

For years, Louis had been devastated by his break of friendship with Thomas, and aside from the very long and detailed letter

Thomas requested with the truth about Richard Croker, they hadn't spoken since Edward was murdered. Initially, Louis believed he'd been more than fair with Thomas, who sought to take out his anger on Louis and the Madame when they'd been fighting against Croker to keep him alive. It was why he was so unreserved in the letter he'd sent to Thomas of their involvement, as well as the admittance of Edward's participation at The Palace to keep Esther safe when there had been a target on her back. What confused Louis was why he was the only one being punished—why he, out of everyone, was still being kept in the dark, despite doing everything he could to help Thomas. He was battling to refrain from bitterness, to keep a level head and listen to Tony for once and be patient. But it was hard, mainly because Louis was heartbroken over it.

As he sauntered through Midtown, Louis grabbed another cigarette, thinking again on the dream and on how he and Tony had gotten to where they were.

The Turners hired Louis and Tony's parents as groundskeepers a few years after the family migrated over from France, and initially they'd lived in the servants' quarters of the house. When Tony was two or three years old, they moved to the village not far from Amberleigh, where Louis and Tony were subsequently raised and also where the two boys went to school. On the weekends, they would be brought up to the Amberleigh estate to assist their parents with the labor of the land, though in the meantime Louis, Arthur, and Edward became fast friends, with Tony falling into their group antics as he got older. When Louis reached adolescence, he was offered a position of employment for the Turners working the property, and he and his father worked the land together up until the night of the fire. A neighbor left a candle burning just a few doors down from where they lived in the village, and Louis woke in the middle of the night coughing on smoke, unable to see anything while sweating profusely from the heat of the flames. He managed to find Tony, who lay unconscious on the floor after what Louis assumed was smoke inhalation; as the fire closed in, Louis got his brother outside just in time to watch the entire house collapse. His parents had still been indoors, and though the exact cause could never be determined, they were killed in the accident along with seven others. Louis was sixteen years old, Tony eight.

Against the wishes of Arthur, Louis left Tony with the Turners and went to America, cutting off all ties from the family, and even his brother. He had so much anger and pain from the guilt of leaving his parents to die, and Louis had somehow convinced himself that their deaths were on his hands. Distraught, Louis wanted to free himself from this affliction, and to liberate Tony from having to tolerate the presence of a brother who would indisputably serve as a reminder of all Louis and Tony had lost. With the little money he had, Louis bought a ticket to New York City, and within weeks, was gone. On the streets of the Points, after nearly starving to death on multiple occasions, Louis found a new family amongst his fellow orphans, including a much younger and much more volatile Will. From there, everything fell into place.

It seemed that at last, Louis had an outlet for his anger through violence, and discovered his indifference to death along with an aptitude to compartmentalize his sentiments so that his conscience would not get in the way of his survival. When Edward came to New York years later, Louis had just lost Will to the law, or so he had believed, and despite his years as a criminal, Louis eagerly wanted an escape from gang life. Edward sought him out, at first wanting to reunite and make peace with the past; Louis could still recall the shock on Edward's face when he did finally find Louis. Edward struggled to come to grips with just who and what Louis had become, and he didn't quite know what to make of this new version of his friend, a man who was like a brother to him for most of their youths. Then, Edward was in love, and constantly fretting over Mary's safety. He and Louis found a solution, and without much convincing, Louis got himself a job protecting the Madame as her personal bodyguard.

Before leaving for the war, Edward asked Louis to keep an eye on Mary, and so he had, even after Edward disappeared. As a consequence of losing Edward, Louis embraced his job with the Madame wholeheartedly and continued to guard Mary and Thomas closely. What struck Louis as ironic was that if Mary had never taken the job with Tammany Hall years ago, not a single one of them would be where they were right now—and life would have been far, far different for every soul involved. Would Edward still be alive and with them? Would Thomas have found his father in England? Louis fought off those lingering "what ifs" because that was all they were. Their fates had been set in stone when Mary signed on with Croker, and he had no doubt she punished herself for that every day.

By the time Louis reached The Palace, the girls were bustling about in preparation for the evening, and Louis marched directly up the stairs and into the Madame's office. She was at the drink cart when he walked inside, and with a wide grin, poured him a glass and glided over to him.

"Well, this is a surprising but appreciated visit! I wasn't expecting you until tomorrow, but I could use the company."

Louis took his drink from her and smiled in return. "You look radiant."

She was donning a scarlet dress that left little to the imagination, and the Madame's eyes were sparkling, though it was no matter. Louis's compliment did not divert her focus.

"You look troubled." Her head tilted to the side inquisitively. "Please tell me something hasn't fucking happened that I don't know about."

Louis scoffed, "Of course not. Only melancholic regarding, well, the past, I suppose."

He took a seat over by the empty fireplace, and the Madame followed suit.

"I met with my contact today."

The Madame's left eyebrow rose. "And?"

"Thomas is hitting Croker on both fronts. It's only a matter of time before that bastard realizes the ground is shrinking beneath him."

"And you're back in the Bowery, keeping an eye on Walsh and Esther?"

"Will and I both are. And like we discussed, if the hit on Frederick were to be a set up by Walsh, we follow through with the plan."

The Madame nodded, taking a gulp of her whiskey. "I put Ellis on Walsh."

"I thought you might. And you got in touch with Sally?"

"She was here two days ago," The Madame confirmed, leaning back into her chair. "I explained the situation and she was planning to send a wire to John that afternoon. He's apparently in New Orleans, hunting down some old Confederate family with a torture house where they lure negroes. You wouldn't believe some of the shit they—"

Louis held up a hand to cut the Madame off. "Please, for the love of God, spare me. I don't want to know."

"I told you, it is fucking awful. But back to Frederick—you are confident this hit can be done efficiently?"

"It'll be over in a few days. We have absolutely everything we need for the set-up. Will and I are going through the motions with Esther, and she's more than ready. Even if something were to happen, we have every aspect covered. Not even Walsh could fuck this up for us, especially now that Thomas is in the Bowery wreaking havoc on the Whyos."

Louis took a sip from his glass and reached for a cigarette, speaking aloud before he could stop himself, "Madame, he hasn't come to see me. Or sent for me."

The Madame, too, had a drink. "It's not because he doesn't want to, Louis. Give it time."

"It's already been weeks."

"Stop fucking torturing yourself. It's not what you think."

"How can you possibly know that?"

"Goddammit, Louis. Just trust me."

Her tone was firm, and he dropped the subject, not wanting the Madame to see his disappointment. "So, other than our digging on Walsh and the Frederick hit, what have we got? My source with Parkhurst at least gives us an idea of what to expect from him."

"That clergy bastard is the least of my worries right now."

"What don't I know?"

"Oh, it's just the usual fucking catastrophes." She downed the rest of her whiskey. "The one that is starting to worry me is Claire."

Louis felt his neck get hot in rage. "Is that prick trying to find her again?"

"He is, and we are pretty sure he's en route to New York to try and, well, there's no way to know the type of shit he's going to pull. Then again, it could all be a farce like it was last spring. That son of a bitch has done this whole empty threat thing before."

"Or Marcus could show up here and do some fucking damage," Louis stressed. "Madame, do you want me to be here for a time? Will and Thomas can handle the Bowery. We need to keep the girls safe from that sadistic fuck."

She let out a big exhale. "As you can imagine, George is too fucking emotionally involved to handle this well. And Ashleigh is good. He's not you, but he's good. The concern I have is you know Marcus…you know what Marcus is capable of and what he's done… Ashleigh doesn't. You've already run this shithead off once. If you can spare the time…"

"If you need me, Madame, I am yours."

"Thank you, Louis."

"What do you think digging on Walsh is going to do? I mean, it'll show us his weak spots, of course, but at the end of the day, the answer is simple. We need to do mankind a favor and just kill him."

"I'm not getting the background for me," the Madame declared.

"We can't touch him. Not you, not me, not anyone involved with Croker without risking Esther."

Her intentions clicked. "You want Thomas to go after him."

"I think he's the only one who has the ability to see it through."

Louis put out his cigarette. "And this has to do with the theory that Walsh doesn't feel pain?"

"That, and his connections with the most dangerous gang in New York as well as Richard Croker and Tammany Hall. Every one of us is in too deep, all except for Thomas, and no one has any fucking idea it's him running around the Bowery stirring up all this goddamn trouble. If one of us is going to end the lunatic, it will have to be him; not to mention that we aren't getting any younger, Louis."

"Do you really think Richie would be that upset?" he pressed. "We might be doing him a favor."

"Do you really want to fucking chance that?"

Louis acquiesced, "So, we have Thomas get rid of Walsh. Then what do we do about Croker?"

The Madame smirked shrewdly. "One thing at a time, Louis. Let's put this goddamn lunatic in the ground. With Walsh gone, with everything riding on this election, Croker is going to make a mistake. If we're lucky, it'll be sooner, and we can watch that son of a bitch lose the empire he's built on the foundation of our due diligence."

A knock came at the door.

"Come in, Ashleigh!" the Madame bellowed.

Ashleigh stepped inside the Madame's office, and Louis noticed he looked paler than normal. "Madame, Marcy is ready to discuss the evenin' with ya."

The Madame stood and went to sit behind her desk. "Where's Claire, Ashleigh?"

"George was helpin' her restock the bar, Madame."

"All right. Louis? I'll see you back here tonight after you're done with Croker's errands."

Ashleigh was puzzled. "Louis is comin' back here tonight?"

"For the time being, Louis will be assisting with the security of The Palace when he can. If you have a fucking problem with that, tough."

Ashleigh almost seemed relieved. "Fine by me, Madame."

Louis took his leave, marching out of the office and down the main stairs of The Palace. When he reached the front door, he could feel someone nipping at his heels, and whipped around to find Ashleigh standing there.

"Can I have a moment, Louis?" he asked, staring right into Louis's eyes, causing Louis to be more than a little uncomfortable.

"Can it wait a few hours? We'll have plenty of time to catch up tonight once I am back at The Palace."

When Ashleigh's face grew downtrodden, Louis relented. "I have time for one cigarette of a conversation. Then I'll have to be on my way."

Ashleigh's countenance transformed. "It won' take more than a second. Just need some advice, is all."

Louis motioned for them to go outside, and both men sat on the stoop as Louis lit a cigarette for himself and handed one over to Ashleigh.

"Is this about Will?"

"No! No, it ain't about Daddy." He seemed to grapple with the words, "It's 'bout…Miss Hiltmore."

"What about her?"

"This stays between us, all right?"

When Louis nodded to give his consent, Ashleigh went on, "Well, we spent the night together, and I ain' heard from her since. Last time she came into The Palace, she was talkin' like she might reconsider marryin' that Captain asshole I caught nearly assaultin' her the other night."

Louis's jaw dropped. "What the hell did you just say?"

Ashleigh nodded. "Madame didn't tell ya, then? Yeah, was worried so I took Miss Hilmtore home, and—ain' important how it happened but—I went up to make sure she got into the hotel and up to her room all right and, well, I found that Captain prick tossin' her around outside her room."

"So, you scared him off and then slept with Celeste."

Ashleigh took a long drag of his cigarette. "Yeah."

"And she's pretending like it never happened?"

"More or less. It's makin' me insane, Louis. I don' know what I oughta do. Fuckin' ridiculous. I shoulda never let it happen."

Louis deliberated how best to proceed, and resolved to give Will's son a chance. "Let me give you a bit of advice. Celeste has been through an ordeal. A horrible husband, a public hearing, her best friend sacrificed on her behalf…but don't let her fool you, she's much tougher than she looks. At the end of the day, I can promise you that Celeste won't marry the Captain. It's not what she wants."

Ashleigh exhaled smoke. "Ya sure 'bout that?"

"I am," Louis assured him. "Let this thing ride out. Keep some distance. She's just trying to figure out how she went from Fifth Avenue to helping the Madame run the backdoor business of The Palace. Or better yet, how she went from being married to a Wall Street man to fucking a hitman." He had to stop himself from chuckling. "I know Celeste well. She wouldn't have slept with you if it didn't mean something to her, Ashleigh."

Ashleigh seemed to accept this and let it settle with another exhale of smoke. "How's my daddy doin'?"

"In general? He's the same," Louis admitted. "A little fucked in the head with you here, but it hasn't changed much of anything."

Nodding, Ashleigh looked out towards the street. "Ya know, I never blamed him for leavin'. Might seem that way, but my momma was…not right. Will did the best he could."

This shocked Louis. "What was it, then?"

"It was that he didn' take me with him, and now I'm stuck carryin' the weight of my momma hangin' herself…things I'll never forget seein' firsthand and feelin' responsible for. I wanted to escape just as badly as he did."

Louis could grasp he was in uncharted territory. "I think he thought he was the real source of the problem, Ashleigh."

"Nah, he took the coward's way out," Ashleigh asserted, putting his cigarette out. "And he wanted a chance to fly away. He did the same to you, ya know."

"That was different."

Ashleigh turned towards him. "Was it, Louis?"

"Yes."

"Explain how."

Louis, too, put out his cigarette and got to his feet. "Because they would have killed us if Will hadn't done it. He thought he was doing what was best for both of us, and at the time, it was the only way for us both to survive. Don't hold a grudge against him, Ashleigh, because I can promise you whatever anger you hold on to, it won't fix anything. He's punished himself enough. He just doesn't know how to make amends."

He held out a hand and pulled Ashleigh up to stand. "I'll see you in a few hours, and make sure George gets his head on straight before I get back."

As he strode away, Louis was overcome with a strange sense of melancholy, and could comprehend why almost immediately: his conversation with Ashleigh reminded him of the countless talks he and Thomas would have during his youth. With a heavy heart, Louis realized that more than being upset with Thomas for his absence, Louis missed him. There was no real way to know why Thomas had yet to visit his oldest friend, a man tied to him in a far deeper way than Thomas appreciated, but Louis needed to follow his own advice and not hold onto his resentment. In time, they would be reunited, and until the right moment presented itself, he would keep doing whatever he could to aid Thomas in his mission.

He would never have a child of his own. Edward's one and only son was the closest he would ever get, and Louis would be damned if he'd let Edward down now.

"Louis, you're late!" Croker teased.

When Louis finally made it downtown to Tammany Hall, Croker, Will, and Esther were waiting for him in Croker's office, each already a whiskey or two deep.

"Grab a whiskey. I was just telling these two that I've got a big job for you to handle tonight."

Will and Esther were already seated across from Croker, so, after pouring himself a drink, Louis stood in between their armchairs.

"Before we get rolling, I've got a favor to ask," Louis introduced hastily, not certain how Croker would take his request to spend more time at The Palace when he thought the Whyos were under siege.

The air instantly grew stale, as it always did when someone asked Croker for anything other than what he proposed. Will and Esther rotated around slowly, each giving Louis somewhat disconcerted looks, neither of them aware of what was going on.

"Go on, Louis. What is it?"

"We, I mean, the Madame is having a tiny personnel problem at The Palace, and could use some extra security for a few days."

Croker's blue eyes narrowed. "What sort of personnel problem is that crazy bitch having now? It never ends with her, does it?"

Louis chortled, taking a sip of whiskey from his glass. "No, sir, it doesn't. We've got one of the whore's brothers threatening to do her harm, and the Madame is afraid he'll try and show up there."

"Why the hell does the Madame give a damn about one whore?" Croker asked, sneering in amazement. "Christ, she really is something."

Esther leaned closer. "It's Marcus, isn't it?"

"This man in question…well, Richie, it's not just about him

threatening her. He's a murderer, unpredictable and dangerous. This son of a bitch killed their entire family one night trying to cover his tracks, and has been on the run from the law ever since, leaving a trail of bodies in his wake."

"How in the world is somebody like that able to hide from the Marshalls?" Will questioned in bewilderment.

"Well, you did the same until I paid them off, Sweeney," Croker remarked, amused as he cut a cigar. "Sounds like a mess, Louis. You can have two weeks, but if shit blows up in the Bowery again, I'll be more than a little unhappy. Got me?"

"Thank you, Mr. Croker. The Madame will be grateful to be lent my services."

Croker lit his cigar, moving on from the topic immediately, "The job tonight needs to be flawless."

"Who are we muscling?" Esther pressed, easing back into her chair once again. "Politician? Coppers?"

"Neither," Croker clarified. "You're going to set up Greyson for me."

"As in Greyson, one of the key members of the board for Tammany Hall?" Esther inquired cagily.

"That's the one," he confirmed.

"So, what sorta set-up we talkin' 'bout, Richie?" Will interposed. "He won' leave the Hall voluntarily, I can promise ya that."

"Exactly," Croker continued. "You three will go and plant evidence at his home, evidence that will be found shortly thereafter by Seamus and Ellis."

Esther's trepidation lessened. "What kind of evidence?"

"That, my friends, is confidential, but it's damning enough that Greyson will be booted off the board and I can at long last get that bastard out of my hair."

"Why do you need all three of us?" Louis spoke up. "Seems like Esther could do this without me and Will and not even break a sweat."

"Until we figure out just what the fuck is going on in the Bowery, everyone is teaming up for all errands," Croker declared. "The amount of damage done to The Dry Dollar by whoever that bastard was is bad enough, and I am not going to risk my three best handlers to some trigger happy prick we can't seem to find or identify."

"To be fair, Richie, he was lookin' for Walsh and nobody else. We got no proof it was him goin' after the Whyos or us."

Croker ignored Will. "I am playing this one close to the chest. With Greyson gone, it'll get rid of the lingering opposition when Grant is elected mayor of New York City. It'll give me total control of this institution, and I won't have to keep justifying my plans to that self-righteous ass. And between the three of you, I know it'll get done."

Esther appeared tickled. "So, Walsh couldn't find him yet, then?"

A flash of irritation crossed Croker's face, then vanished. "He will find whoever this son of a bitch is, and when he does, he has my permission to take him apart, piece by piece. But like I said, I don't give a shit what you're doing—you don't do any jobs alone until this thing is resolved. No objections."

Reaching into the top drawer of his desk, Croker pulled out an envelope and slid it over to Esther. "Here's what you need."

"Where do you want me to put it?"

"On his desk. Take everything out of the envelope and strew the papers about amongst others. We don't want it to look blatantly like a set-up."

Esther grabbed the documents. "Consider it done."

Croker held onto the envelope a moment, causing Esther to pause. "Be careful, and watch your back," he instructed her, and released the envelope.

When they were outside and a few blocks away from the Hall, Esther, Louis, and Will ducked into a narrow alleyway. Esther pulled out a cigarette, and Louis quickly struck a match to light it for her.

"You see now why I am suspicious?" she asked them, exhaling a cloud of smoke. "Normally when he's trying to appear like he cares, he doesn't do it in front of anyone. He must be trying to set me up." Esther took another drag.

Will glanced at Louis, who did his best to communicate his own thoughts without words. "We don' know that yet, Es. But whatever it is, he ain' lookin' to do it tonight, 'cause if he didn' want this Greyson set-up to go through, he also wouldn' have asked me and Louis here to hang 'round with ya."

"I agree with Will. Ironically, you are probably the safest one out of all of us right now with Thomas running around after Walsh."

Esther snorted. "Yeah, I guess you're right." Her gaze was distant as she stared at the ground. "I just want to get the fucking hit over with."

"At this point, Es, it's only a matter of hours," Will said, with a tone that was meant to be supportive. "It'll be over 'fore you know it."

"Right." Esther did not appear comforted, yet she moved on from the issue and concentrated on the task at hand. "I've got the documents tucked into my jacket. Let's get uptown…looks like it might rain."

She tossed her nearly spent cigarette aside. "Ready?"

Louis winked at her. "We're with you."

Will led them back to the street, where they hailed a coach to the Upper East Side. It took them a few tries, as most drivers kept on right past them when they saw three muscular and rather intimidating men wanting a lift, but ultimately, Louis took to holding out straight cash and flagged one down. Esther hopped in first, then Will, and Louis last, who directed the driver up toward the southeast entrance to Central Park. Louis was no novice to this game—leaving a trail was the easiest mistake to be made, and he'd had decades of practice covering his tracks. Once they got to the park entrance, he would let Esther run point, as he wanted to provide her with confidence going into Frederick's hit that she was more than capable of succeeding by herself.

There were no misgivings in Louis's mind that Croker was up to something—the scope of it, he couldn't determine, and there was no denying from Thomas's account that Esther really was in danger. The only thing Louis wanted was to get through the next few weeks, and while he hadn't yet shared this with Will, Louis was seriously considering the option of taking Esther on the run, regardless of the outcome of the hit. If there was one thing Louis had grown to appreciate about this war, it was the notion that there really weren't going to be any winners. He'd leave Thomas to take out Walsh and attempt to knock the crown off of Richard Croker's head, and in the meantime, Louis and Will would keep Esther safe for him. God knew she'd already paid her dues, and while her contract with Croker still had years left to grind, he didn't give a damn. Esther had more than earned her freedom, and she'd hurt a lot of people to get there.

Esther continued to smoke in the cab, and as the coach swayed to and fro, Will's eyes locked with Louis's. "What's goin' on in that brain o' yours, brother? I can see the wheels turnin' even in the dark."

"Nothing," Louis stated. "Just thinking on the day."

He scoffed, "You are so full o' it."

"Really! I was just thinking about the meeting." Louis tried to stay stern, but Esther's interest was also piqued.

"Bullshit," Esther spoke up, a playful grin forming. "I can see it, too. What are you really thinking about?"

Will looked at Esther. "He's got his goddamn plottin' face on. Means he's goin' to proposition us to somethin' later."

With laughing eyes, Will gazed back at Louis, who gave him a glowering squint. "Hey...don' gimme that 'you just betrayed me' glare. This is what happens when ya know somebody for as long as we have, and Esther's smarter than shit—prolly saw it 'fore I did."

Esther straightened up and crossed her arms over her chest. "Louis..."

"Fine." Louis reached into his pocket for his own tobacco. "I think the three of us should run. After the hit."

Whatever Will had expected, this clearly had not been it—his jaw fell open. "Run, like our plan for leavin' New York, run?"

Esther also gawked at him. "Where...where would we go?"

"I have a couple of ideas. Will, the Madame, and I put together a plan in case Croker tried to do anything to harm you. We can go—the three of us. I can get word to Thomas so that when he's done, all he'll have to do is come for you."

"But—but, Louis...I don't...I don't know..."

"Esther," he pleaded, leaning closer to her, "this may be the only shot we have at getting you out alive. Even if nothing is going on with Croker, we still have Walsh to worry about, and the state of the city is going to get far worse before it gets better."

"Ya think Douglas and Celeste could be ready for us in a few days?"

"If I told them tonight, I have no doubt. The Madame has already prepared everything for us on her end."

Esther was taken aback. "Wait—the Hiltmores? How are they involved?"

"They're gonna give us safe haven 'til our scent has run off. Then, we bolt from the city. That way, ain' gotta worry about runnin' fast, just gotta be smart."

"Croker doesn't know I've visited Celeste," Esther thought aloud. "He doesn't know that she knows I'm alive..."

"Exactly," Louis established, "it will be the very last place he looks. The Madame will have it the worst, but she knows how to handle Richard."

"No, this is too much..."

With a smile, Louis tried to be soothing. "Esther, it's done."

Her eyes got misty. "But why? Why all this for me? My life means nothing."

Will scooted over to her and wrapped his arm around her shoulders. "On the contrary, Esther, you mean more to us than just about anybody. That includes the Madame, Celeste, Douglas, Thomas—you saved all o' us. Now, it's our turn."

"I can't ask you to do this. It's too much."

"No, Esther," Louis added, "it's happening. And this way..." His voice trailed off, and Louis smiled at Will. "And this way, Will and I can also finally be free. Together."

"Don't you think he'll follow us?" Esther entreated them. "Don't you think he'd figure it out and send Walsh to skin us alive?"

"Pretty sure, between the two of us and Tommy, ya ain' got nothin' to worry about, sweetheart," Will professed.

Louis thought he saw relief cross Esther's face, though he couldn't be sure in the darkness. The three of them rode the rest of the way in silence, and Louis took Esther's lack of retort as an acceptance of their strategy. The most incredible part of this ordeal was that neither he nor Will were concerned in reference to the hit itself. Esther was ruthless when it came to her work, and it was something that Louis admired and, at times, feared in her. What was disconcerting was the haziness of the aftermath, especially with Croker as guarded as he'd become following Thomas's assault on The Dry Dollar. Once Frederick was taken care of, there was no telling what was in store for any of them, and Louis hated when unknown variables played such a huge part in the equation.

"Southeast entrance!" the driver yelled, snapping Louis back to the present as the coach came to a halt.

Opening the door of the coach, Louis got out and paid the driver while Will and Esther did the same. The three of them proceeded to walk into Central Park and headed west. Greyson's house was two blocks south of the park, off of Sixth Avenue. This meant that Will and Louis would tail Esther, only to be sure no one was watching them too closely or that the mysterious attacker of The Dry Dollar wasn't trying to sabotage Croker yet again. The rest of the night was in her hands, and ought to be relatively easy, considering Esther had already completed countless tasks like this one on her own.

At Fifty-seventh and Sixth, they halted to chat briefly, and then wouldn't speak until they made it back to that very spot in a quarter of an hour. It was a warm and overcast night, with a humidity hanging in the air causing Louis to perspire mildly. There were no stars to be seen—just a giant, grey blanket over the sky, thus making it easier for them to see in the dark in the flicker of the gaslights. A customary number of carriages and pedestrians made their way through the street, no one looking twice at the three of them; despite their being extremely out of place for the upper-class part of town, an older couple out walking their poodle bid them good evening as the went by.

When every pedestrian was out of earshot, Esther turned toward Will and Louis, her big green eyes sparkling from the gaslight above, hat tucked tightly over her feminine face.

"Time to go," she announced. "I'll be in and out of the second story window fast."

"If you run into anyone, choke out only," Louis ordered, pointing to her brass knuckles. "You won't be needing those for the next few minutes."

Concurring, she slipped them off and into her pockets. "If you spot anything suspicious, double whistle. If I need to get out, single whistle."

"Piece o' cake," Will articulated warmly.

With a deep breath, Esther spun around, streaming toward her destination. Louis and Will followed ten paces behind her, as was their custom, observing any activity in the surrounding area with a watchful gaze. Not a single person took notice of Esther, though Louis, in typical fashion, claimed a few stares of his own, chiefly due to his rather large size. He could hear Will sniggering softly, and fought hard not to join him, as he, too, found it relatively humorous. The duo crossed over Fifth-seventh and got beyond Fifty-sixth when Greyson's mansion came into view, and Will and Louis paused at the same time.

Effortlessly, Esther was climbing her way up to the second floor along the gutter, taking her time so she didn't make a sound. When she reached the second floor, Esther shimmied from window to window along the slight edge of stone protruding from the outside wall until she reached the closest window. It was the second window she needed to access, and Louis observed from the ground as Esther positioned herself for her next move. With her arms braced against the outside of the pane, she squatted down into her legs, and with a mighty lurch from all four of her limbs, thrust herself airborne and sideways six feet over to her target. Her hands caught the top of the second windowpane first, which she gripped with every ounce of her strength to not fall to the ground. Slowly, she lowered her feet to the tiny stone ledge, and within seconds had the window unlocked and slipped inside, the only evidence that she was there being the slight opening between frame and glass.

Louis and Will scouted the surrounding block, splitting up to cover more ground, and met again at the same spot a few minutes after. There was no one to be found. Anxiously pulling out his pocket watch, Louis checked the time, only to feel Will's hand touch his forearm. He peeked up in time to witness Esther descending down from the second floor dexterously, almost like gravity did not exist and she weighed nothing more than a feather. The moment her feet hit the ground, Louis breathed a sigh of relief, and he was hit with an overwhelming sense of pride. From their first day to that very night, Esther's determination and skill constantly astonished Louis, and he loved and respected her all the more for it.

They lingered, letting Esther pass, and once again when she'd conquered ten paces, they trailed her, holding formation until they met across Fifty-seventh and within Central Park under the cover of a nearby tree.

"Easy," Esther announced as they came upon her. "You boys want a drink?"

"Thought you'd never ask," Will consented, and together, they walked off in the direction of The Palace.

"Now, wait just a second," came a familiar voice from ten yards away.

Immediately, the three of them circled around, and it was with great irritation that Louis beheld the man who shouted out to them. Walsh.

He strode toward Esther, Will, and Louis, and Louis detected Esther's hands slip effortlessly into her pockets then out again, the glint of brass catching his eye. Will's grip went to his pistols at his waist, and Louis instinctively went for the dagger sheathed on his belt. Not one of them had anticipated Walsh to ambush such a small errand; nonetheless, Louis was very aware, regardless of not comprehending where the inclination came from, that this confrontation was not sanctioned by Croker. Walsh's demeanor was remarkably more foreboding than normal, and he carried himself confidently, which made Louis's hair stand on end. Something wasn't right, and in times like these, Walsh tended to have the upper hand. In a physical battle, Walsh was outnumbered by far; however, this was not about a fight.

It had to be something far worse.

"What the hell are you doing here, Walsh?" Esther called.

He smirked behind his round spectacles, his dark eyes malicious. "The plant on Greyson went well?"

"Matter o' fact, it did," Will asserted through gritted teeth. "Why don' you answer the lady's question, Walsh. We all know Croker didn' send ya."

Walsh let out a small chortle. "No, no, he most certainly didn't. In truth, I came on my own accord."

"Why?" Louis demanded.

242

"Because I want you to send a message to the Madame for me."

"If you think I am going to do anything for you, you can go fuck yourself, you bastard," Esther spat. "Leave the Madame alone, or I swear to God—"

Walsh held up his two hands, as if in surrender. "My dear Esther, I am only reacting to being provoked."

"Provoked? Jus' what in the hell you on 'bout, Walsh?"

"Please tell the Madame that if she insists on digging into my past, it will not bode well for her," Walsh articulated with malevolence. "I don't take kindly to people prying into my business, especially her."

Louis pulled the dagger from its sheath, ready to spar. "Is that a threat against the Madame?" he asked. "Because if it is, let's end this right here. Right now."

Walsh rolled his eyes. "Not a threat, but a warning."

Louis was finding it difficult to restrain himself. "If you so much as go near The Palace—"

Yet, Esther beat him to the punch. In a blink, she was bounding forward before she threw herself at Walsh, tackling him to the ground and proceeding to get two horrendously hard strikes on Walsh with her brass knuckles. While surprised by the onslaught at first, it didn't take Walsh long to react. Unfazed by the blows, he countered her in two moves, flipping Esther around and onto her back, hitting her hard. Within seconds, he had his hands over her windpipe, choking her ruthlessly, and also managing to withstand Esther's repeated heavy hits to his chest and arms with her brass knuckles. It was in that second that Louis appreciated the rumors must be true—the only way he could continue to persist during a beating that brutal was if he couldn't feel it. Without hesitation, Will and Louis ran to pull him off of her, yet instantaneously at their approach, Walsh was on his feet, his own blade drawn and pointed at them.

"If you two were not here, I could have done far, far worse," he hissed, spitting down onto the gasping Esther. "She is lucky to have you, but when Croker finds out you two are fucking, I can't say it will last long."

Louis's whole body went numb, tense with panic. Will, on the other hand, was furious, and drew both pistols, pointing them directly at Walsh.

"You can shoot me, Will. But if you do, that son of yours will be gutted before the night is through. I've got an entire gang of men at my disposal with strict instructions of what to do if I don't return tonight, and they are all eager to comply."

Will cocked his pistols. "You're full o' shit."

"Are you willing to risk his life to find out?"

Louis was at a loss. "Will, let him go."

"We gotta kill this son of a bitch, brother."

"I know we do, but not if it means losing Ashleigh. You'll never forgive yourself."

It took a moment before Will gave in. "Fine." He un-cocked both guns and holstered them, eyes not leaving Walsh.

"Like I said, please deliver my message," Walsh reiterated, glowering down at Esther. "And if you ever touch me again, I will kill you."

Esther sat up, wheezing a little, and smiled at him ominously. "You...made a mistake..."

He tilted his head, puzzled. "And just how did I make a mistake? By letting you live? I can certainly change that."

"I...we know...your weaknesses..." she huffed, getting to her feet.

"And what are my weaknesses?"

When Esther couldn't find her voice, Louis said it for her: "Well, we know one, and that is you can't feel."

Walsh jeered at him, "I would hardly call that a weakness."

"Uhh, Walsh? Ya got somethin' stuck in your back."

Esther's smirk blossomed, blood oozing out of her cracked lip. "Might want to get to a doctor."

Walsh reached around and felt Esther's tiny boot blade stuck into the flank of his torso. "You little bitch," he snarled, taking a step towards her, yet Will's reflexes were faster. His guns were drawn, cocked, and once again pointed at Walsh.

"I think it might be time for you to be movin' along. You don' want that thing gettin' infected, and if ya pull it out, ya might bleed to death 'fore you can get down south to have Kitty patch ya up."

"You should be...happy," Esther acknowledged. "I didn't go... for the kidneys...but I will...next time...just like you did to...to Edward..."

Walsh's face contorted up into a somewhat terrifying manifestation, and without saying another word, he took off and out of sight.

Louis rushed to Esther's side. "Jesus fucking Christ. Are you all right?"

"Just bruised," she whispered. "I could use...that drink..."

Will was checking her arms and legs, grimacing at her bruises. "How deep did ya get him?"

"Not deep...enough to do a little...damage and scar..." She looked into Louis's eyes. "I can't believe...he knows...what are we going to...to do...?"

"Nothin'," Will stressed. "He ain' got no hard evidence, which means we is fine for the time bein'. Jus' need to be careful. Can ya walk, Es?"

"Yeah, I can."

"Good. Let's get ya to see Jeremiah. He might have somethin' to help."

Louis held out his arm for Esther to help her walk, which she took obligingly. Suddenly, a small flicker of movement in the tree branches above them caught Louis's eye. As he glimpsed up, still ambling along with Esther, Louis scanned the tree and was greeted with the familiar gaze of two beautiful, hazel eyes, piercing through his own like knives. Squinting, he made out the figure of a bird— no, not a bird, a falcon...

"Athena?" he whispered, unconsciously coming to a halt.

But like a mirage, the eyes and shadow disappeared, and Louis was left flabbergasted, wondering if he'd hallucinated spotting her.

"What is it?" Esther asked, releasing his arm and glancing up into the tree where Louis's gaze was focused.

Louis moved along, and she did the same. "Nothing," he said, "just a little jumpy after our encounter with the lunatic. Let's get to The Palace."

After a few steps, Louis peeked over his shoulder again. Standing in the shadow of the tree was the figure of a man leaning against the trunk, with a falcon perched naturally on his arm. There was no way for Louis to make out his face, but he didn't have to. The man then straightened up and bowed, the way Louis and Will used to bow at each other when they were young. Before Louis could do anything in response, the man whipped around and strode off toward Fifth Avenue, the opposite direction Louis, Will, and Esther were heading.

That was all it took to relieve Louis of the burden he'd been carrying, and every one of his misgivings was replaced with hope. The Madame was right—she always was.

"This is outrageous!" Daniel Greyson bellowed at the top of his lungs while two officers escorted him to the paddy wagon. "I demand to know on what grounds I am being brought in for questioning! I have done absolutely nothing wrong!"

"Then you will be in and out of the station in no time, Mr. Greyson," Detective Ellis remarked candidly. "We have received a tip that a number of tax officials knowingly helped you evade payment, and if that is the case, you could be facing serious fines and possibly a stint at the Tombs."

They were outside Daniel Greyson's mansion on Sixth Avenue, and because of his incessant yelling, Greyson was catching the attention of his neighbors and putting on quite a show. Upon hearing Ellis say the Tombs, Greyson stopped dead in his tracks, his face losing some of its color in disbelief. The two officers on either side of him ushered Greyson onward, but Greyson's eyes stayed on Ellis.

"This is insanity!" he yelled. "I have never in all my life bribed a tax official!"

Ellis wasn't sure if the evidence Croker planted in Greyson's office was real or fake, though either way, Richard had found a way to get Greyson booted off the board of Tammany Hall. He'd easily be convicted of tax evasion, but with no jail time—only financial penalties and a massive bruise to the man's ego. While he hated to admit it, Samuel could understand why Croker despised Greyson: he was a pompous asshole and, even in his pretentious morning robe and matching smoking slippers, he still managed to demean police when it was his own integrity on the line. Ellis watched one of Greyson's escorts open the paddy wagon door for him, and reluctantly huffing, Greyson climbed inside before being joined by the two coppers. With a wave, Samuel motioned to the driver to go ahead and leave, and he did so without another word.

Ellis stayed put until the paddy wagon rounded the corner, then made his way back up to the front door, where Mrs. Greyson and the rest of the household staff loitered anxiously in the front lobby.

"Please...Detective..." Mrs. Greyson began with an air of contempt as she approached Samuel. "What is it that's going on here? Why is it necessary to barge into our home on a Sunday morning if you are only taking my husband in for questioning?"

Samuel could tell just from a once-over that Mrs. Greyson was probably going to be more of a pain in the ass than her husband, her attitude of entitlement one he wholeheartedly resented about the upper class.

Not caring if it provided gossip later, Samuel spoke so that everyone in the lobby could hear: "I am sorry for the intrusion, Mrs. Greyson; however, it was necessary and the order was given by our captain. Daniel Greyson is being investigated for tax evasion, and we were trying to be courteous to your…" Ellis paused a moment, looking toward the wide-eyed staff behind Mrs. Greyson. "We were trying not to…cause a scene, per se. Unfortunately, your husband's objections notified the entire block anyway."

Sniggering came from the group, and Mrs. Greyson spun around, giving her staff a look of sheer fury before turning back to Ellis, her cheeks crimson. "How dare you take such liberties with me! Do you have any idea who my husband is?!"

"Yes, ma'am, I do. And like I said, my captain gave us the order for this morning. I believe it is a matter of urgency."

This did not appease her, and she huffed at Ellis's reasoning, "It's improper and rude to make such wild accusations of a man of Daniel's standing!"

Without warning, Seamus appeared in the doorway to the dining room, a smug grin on his face. "Well, I am sorry to say, Mrs. Greyson, that we found evidence to suggest otherwise. So, can you please stop harassing my partner?"

Mrs. Greyson was flabbergasted while Seamus and Ellis marched out of the house, not wanting to have to converse with her any further.

"Found it, then?" Samuel inquired while they sauntered down toward their own vacant coach.

"Yeah, course I did. She did a good job too, the Assistant. Made sure it was convincing…there's a whiskey glass stain on it in the exact shape of one of the glasses on his drink cart…just brilliant, if you ask me. Got a whole bunch of other papers and letters as filler, so Greyson's lawyer can't peg this as a set-up."

He handed the collection over to Samuel, who slipped it into his jacket pocket and stepped up into the carriage, Seamus after him.

"Ready, Collins!" Ellis yelled up to their driver, and in seconds they were on the move, heading to the precinct.

Seamus pulled out two cigarettes and handed one over to Samuel. "Greyson is a real bastard, eh? Fuckin' rich people..."

Ellis took out matches and lit his tobacco. "Seamus, I've been meaning to bring something up with you, and it's a subject you probably won't like very much."

Seamus's countenance grew curious. "What is it?"

"Look, I'm not trying to rag on anyone or get you at odds with Croker or anything. It's just, well..."

"Well, spit it out, would ya?"

"You've gotta start watching your back more, Seamus."

"What are you on about?"

Samuel sighed in frustration, taking a drag. "You have to see the big picture here, all right? I've been a cop most of my life. I know how this shit works and I watch my own ass. But you're new to the game, and while you're buddies with Richie, you also gotta realize you're also walking around with a giant target on your back."

"You're saying I shouldn't trust Richie? Hell, he's like my brother, for Christ's sake. You're way off the road here, Ellis."

"It's not Richie I worry about."

"Then who?"

"The Whyos," Ellis told him. "They are out of control, and they hate the police more than they hate the rich, and it doesn't matter if you think you're protected by the Hall. You're not protected by them on the street—no one other than Walsh knows your connection to Croker, and Whyos gain more notoriety amongst their faction if they kill boys in blue."

Seamus didn't buy it. "Little paranoid there, Ellis?"

"Better to be paranoid that oblivious, Seamus. You're one of us now, whether you want to admit it or not. And being a detective has consequences that draw a firm line in the sand between us and everyone else working for Croker."

The coach went silent, and Samuel was certain he'd made his

point. Seamus was a prick, and Ellis got tired of being stalked by Seamus and having to babysit him all at the same time. Nonetheless, at the end of the day, Ellis was stuck with him, and with the Whyos becoming a radically increasing problem in the Bowery, it was only a matter of time before their antics started to creep uptown. Croker wouldn't put a stop to it as long as it didn't affect business or the election, and Samuel could already predict how Croker might spin the gang's expansion into a political issue that only Grant could solve with his new ideas and forward thinking. Another factor urging Ellis to warn Seamus was his perpetual dread of Walsh and what he was capable of with so many thugs at his disposal. So far in his digging for the Madame, Ellis had uncovered absolutely nothing—there was no record of Walsh anywhere prior his joining Tammany Hall, and that made Samuel tense. He hoped that the Pinkertons could find something to give them some answers, but until then, it was guesswork.

When they arrived at the station, Ellis and Seamus popped out of the carriage.

"I gotta head south to meet Richie," Seamus revealed. "I'll see you first thing tomorrow."

"Tell him everything went smoothly," Samuel requested, motioning for the coach to wait so Seamus could use it to trek to the Bowery. "What are you doing with Richie?"

"Some asshole from the old days has popped up and started making a fuss about wanting to team up with Edmund. Me, Sullivan, and O'Reilly are gonna talk to Edmund and Richie about what they wanna do next. Edmund hates the guy—stole all his money and ran off to Chicago."

"Well, Edmund's not exactly the sharpest tool in the shed," Ellis observed. "What's this prick doing back here, then?"

"Hell if I know," Seamus admitted, taking a step up into the coach. "I'll fill you in tomorrow. You gonna drop the stuff with the captain?"

"Of course."

"Right. Night, Ellis."

"Night, Seamus."

Samuel had climbed five stairs when Seamus yelled out to him, "I know you're right, ya know. About the whole Whyo thing."

Ellis rotated around, moving up the steps backward. "Just trying to help, Seamus."

"I know you are, Ellis." He was quiet for a moment. "See you tomorrow."

Samuel waved goodnight and twisted forward while he kept ascending, feeling slightly strange about the interaction they'd just had. In a way, he'd gone from utterly despising Seamus to painfully tolerating his presence, and while he in no way liked Seamus, there was something about working with another person in such dangerous and risky circumstances that bonded them together. Samuel meant what he'd said—he was worried about Seamus because, like many people before him, he made the mistake of trusting that Richard Croker would stand by his side no matter what storms they faced. The Whyos would be another storm, and down the road, Ellis wasn't so sure Croker would remain the shielding and understanding friend he'd been to Seamus in the past.

Only time would tell.

CHAPTER XXXVI.

The Madame poured herself a large whiskey at her desk, leaning back into her chair and propping her feet up in an effort to get more comfortable. Comfort, however, was something that seemed less and less attainable for her these days, even with a loosened corset and a cigar on the horizon. By this time next week, the worst of this fucking hurricane would be over.

It was late in the afternoon, and the Madame had spent much of the morning vainly trying to sleep off the long Friday night she'd endured; between hosting a rambunctious night at The Palace and Will, Louis, and Esther coming around for drinks and news, there'd been no time until the sun rose for her to take a breath. While things at The Palace had gone magically, in their typical fashion, earning the Madame the most capital on a night yet that summer, there had been one tiny bit of bad news: Walsh, it seemed, was striking back against The Palace, and had nearly killed Esther as a result. The ensuing damage was disturbing, and Esther futilely tried to hide that she was not only in an excruciating amount of pain, but also that her accumulating injuries were ruthlessly taking a toll on her body.

There were two things left that the Madame had to see through, and both would happen by the time the sun set that following Sunday evening. First and most importantly, Esther would kill Judge Frederick—the Madame had met with the judge just a few days prior, and managed to convince him that his wife's safety depended on her ignorance of their deal, and additionally, that within the month she would settle his debts, and he would make cash payments to her directly. While originally the plan had ended there, Richard recently came by for a visit with a special request, wanting to get rid of an old acquaintance of his in the process, so the set-up took on another element of scrupulous planning and execution. For Esther, though, it was no matter. The Madame had the necessary materials to plant once the hit was done, and that would be the end of Judge Frederick.

The second undertaking was getting Esther, Louis, and Will out of New York City. She and Douglas spent countless hours piecing together the details, and with Sally's help, the Madame had no misgivings she could get the three of them to safety as long as everyone played their respective roles correctly. In the aftermath, the Madame would hand the remainder of the grunt work with Walsh, the Whyos, and Croker over to Thomas. When Walsh was six feet under, the Whyos were running scared, and Croker found himself on trial, the task that she'd set out to complete the day she'd met Richard Croker would finally come to an end. Still, until then, sleep was a luxury she couldn't really afford.

A knock came to the door.

"Yes, Ashleigh?" the Madame called, taking a large gulp of her whiskey.

Ashleigh peeked his head in. "Two o' these boys from Tammany are here. Say they got a message from Richie."

The Madame dropped her feet to the floor and straightened up. "Send them in."

Ashleigh pushed the door open, and in strutted Sullivan and O'Reilly, both appearing way too at ease for the Madame's liking.

"Good afternoon, gentlemen. How can I help you?"

Each took a seat in one of the armchairs across from her desk.

"We's here for Richie," Sullivan informed her. "Wanted to pass along that the big…er…fundraiser was a success."

She put on a smile. "Lovely! And he put my contribution to good use?"

"He did, Madame," O'Reilly took over. "They made nearly double what he thought they was goin' to."

"Well, this demands a celebration! Ashleigh?"

Like Louis in the beginning, Ashleigh had rapidly learned to read the Madame's moves well and was already one step ahead of her, striding toward the drink cart to get Sullivan and O'Reilly each their own share of whiskey. Once Ashleigh delivered their drinks, the Madame and her guests toasted to the Hall, then they resumed their seats while Ashleigh returned his post by the door.

After downing his whiskey, Sullivan set the glass aside. "We got another thing to discuss wit' ya."

"And that is?" She hated the way Sullivan looked at her. If he wasn't one of Croker's, she'd have already gauged his eyes out with her dagger.

"Says he's gonna come by tomorrow to talk, but he wants ya to do some fuckin' peace talk…with the nephew."

"My nephew?" the Madame questioned derisively.

"Lord Turner," O'Reilly corrected, finishing his drink. "He was at the fundraiser. Evidently showed a lot of support and donated even more than you did, Madame. Croker wants to settle the bad blood, and thinks you and Hiltmore can fix the rift. Richie told us that Hiltmore had already offered it to him."

What these two bastards didn't realize was that the Madame had already arranged for Thomas and Richard to have said meeting the following afternoon.

"Douglas and I have discussed it on multiple occasions," the Madame confirmed, pouring a little more whiskey into her cup. "Should I have him here tomorrow night as well when Richard stops by?"

O'Reilly nodded. "I think Richie'd appreciate that."

"Tell him to consider it done, then! Is there anything else?"

The stench of the two men alone was enough to make the Madame's good graces waver in their diligence, irrespective of them being Croker's goons.

"Nah, that's it," Sullivan affirmed, rising to his feet. "We get an employee discount here? Ya know, workin' wit Richie and all?"

It took every ounce of her composure not to show her disgust. "I'll tell you what. If you boys ever want to come by on a week night, I'll give you a special price as long as I have girls available."

This seemed to make Sullivan's day, and he nearly skipped out of her office without another word. O'Reilly then got up, stood there awkwardly for a few seconds, and proceeded to hastily pace out of the room in Sullivan's wake, visibly unsure of how to end their visit.

"What a bunch of fucking imbeciles," the Madame said to herself under her breath.

After seeing them out, Ashleigh returned up to her office with a snide grin on his face. "I swear on my momma's grave, them two is lucky to have jobs, 'specially that son of a bitch Sullivan—man is dumber than a rock."

This caused the Madame to laugh aloud. "You read my mind, Little Sweeney."

She flicked her head toward the drink cart, indicating Ashleigh could grab himself a whiskey if he so desired, and he obliged.

"Those two bastards have been a pain in my ass since the first day they walked in here. And for Christ's sake, you'd think they'd fucking bathe once in a while!"

Ashleigh snorted mid-pour. "Not everybody is fortunate enough to work for The Palace, Madame, and have a bath at their disposal."

"Oh, don't you dare side with those pricks. Croker pays them enough goddamned money for them not to smell like pigs."

"I can't disagree with that. I know what Daddy makes." Ashleigh grabbed his glass and went to join the Madame. "I assume Miss Hiltmore is arrivin' soon?"

She glanced toward the grandfather clock. "A few minutes. She should be here at half past four."

Ashleigh let out a heavy sigh. "Right."

"If she was going to marry him, then she would have said yes by now," the Madame stated firmly. "Can you get your head out of your ass and work? Or is this going to be an ongoing problem?"

"Whoa there! I didn' say nothin' about it! And it sure as hell ain' been affectin' my work."

"Good."

Ashleigh didn't say anything else, projecting a somewhat self-conscious air until the Madame decided that perhaps now was the opportunity to bring up a subject she'd been meaning to with the young Mr. Sweeney.

"Ashleigh, the next time I have a meeting with Lord Turner, you are to sit in on the meeting. Is that understood?"

"You—you serious?"

There was a valid reason for such a speedy initiation. In a few days, Louis would be gone for good from The Palace, and most likely from her life. She needed Ashleigh to get a better grasp of the big picture, because while she hated to admit it, the Madame needed him, and more importantly, she needed to trust him.

"Yes, I'm very goddamn serious. There is another part of this equation I have been waiting to share with you, and if you are as good of a hit as I think you are, you're going to need to have an idea of just what the fuck is going on."

Ashleigh finished the contents of his glass. "You mean aside from Esther bein' alive and you wantin' to kill Richie?"

"That's correct."

"Well," he chuckled, "whatever ya got, I ain' goin' nowhere."

"Fine. Now, get downstairs and wait for Celeste."

"Aw hell, can' Georgie show her up?"

The Madame threw him a scathing gaze, and Ashleigh stood

up, put his empty cup back on the drink cart, then strutted out of her office.

It wouldn't be more than five minutes before Celeste arrived, giving the Madame just enough time to grab a bottle of wine and glasses for the two women, and she relocated to the sofa so they could be seated next to one another. There was so much to explain to Celeste in such a very limited amount of time, and the Madame hoped she could cover all her bases prior to commencing a Saturday night at The Palace.

In his usual way, Ashleigh knocked twice and opened the door for Celeste, and to the Madame's relief, she noted he appeared alleviated despite his ongoing consternation regarding Celeste. He waited for a nod from her, and after Celeste walked into the Madame's office, Ashleigh left and closed the doors behind him.

In sharp contrast, Celeste was flustered and flushed in her cheeks, though she managed to look positively radiant in a sky blue dress she'd only just bought. Her hair was loose, and the customary touch of rouge was absent from her face, but the Madame was well aware of how stressful these last few weeks had been on her, and the next would be much worse. She uncorked the bottle and smiled at Celeste, patting the spot beside her.

"Sit down and relax," she commanded, pouring the wine into the glasses. "You look like you've run the whole fucking way here from downtown!"

Celeste shook her head, picking up her wine. "I haven't slept. I think I am more nervous for these next few days than anyone else is."

"Because of Frederick?"

"Because of Esther."

"Ah," the Madame observed, putting her hand on Celeste's knee for comfort, "Esther will get the hit done, and by the time we meet here, the worst of this will be over as long as everyone holds up on their end."

Celeste had nearly chugged down half her glass. "Everything is ready. Father and I will be here at eleven sharp and position the carriage in the back alley. Father will stay and carry on the meeting between Thomas and Croker with you. I will escort Will, Louis, and Esther to St. Stephen. No one is to be seen, especially not Louis."

"Perfect," the Madame declared, hoping to give rise to Celeste's spirits. "Listen, we do need to discuss a bit of a change about the evidence against Frederick. I want to make sure it aligns with your knowledge about his debts as well as mine, because at this point, there is no room for even the smallest error."

"Tell me."

"It has to do with tying in someone else Croker wants to get rid of. And if I'm honest, I am pretty sure Richard wants this guy out of the picture even more than Frederick."

"Well, hell!" Celeste cried, almost tickled by the news. "Who is this man? How is he connected to Croker?"

The Madame had a sip of wine. "It's a long, long story, darling, so I'll give you the shortened version as best I can. We are all very aware of Richard's past as a boxer, and that he has a special relationship with Edmund down in the Bowery to box whenever he likes."

"Yes."

"Well, I guess years ago, before he got seriously involved in politics and Richard was beating the shit out of anyone he could get his hands on in the ring, Edmund had a partner—well, a trainer, I should say. This was a man named Virgil."

Celeste held up a hand to stop her. "Virgil Archibald?"

"Yes, you met him the other night at the Rockefellers', am I right?"

"Right. He's married to Sydney Turlington..." Her voice trailed off. "Sydney's family owns Jackson Park and most of the land surrounding it, and they're the ones competing with New York to host the Columbian Exposition."

The Madame saluted her. "You've done your own digging, I can see. Well, Virgil used to run the boxing docks in his previous life. Until one day, when Edmund was thinking of quitting the ring for good and wanted an equal share with Virgil. At the time, that prick was taking seventy percent of their profits and handing off only thirty to Edmund, but the logistics aren't what's important. What's fucking important is that Virgil woke up one morning, took every penny the two of them were making, and ran. No one knew what had happened to him until a few years later, when his wedding was national news and Virgil had earned a nasty reputation around Chicago with his business tactics."

"So, what does he do now in Chicago?"

"Runs all the rings, and rumor has it he has been running one hell of a lot more than that. Either way, by the time he popped up, Edmund didn't give a shit and had rebuilt his entire business. Now, that greedy son of a bitch is here, wants to take over Edmund's position here and have Chicago and New York making him money, and is threatening to expose Croker's past if he doesn't help convince Edmund to do it."

Celeste was perplexed. "Expose Croker?"

The Madame downed more wine from her glass. "Richard had a nasty temper back in the day, worse than it is now. And he left a few bodies in his wake."

"And Fifth Avenue hates that sort of thing," Celeste furthered, understanding the Madame's insinuation. "He'd lose the votes for Grant."

"Precisely."

"Well, how do we fit Virgil into the hit?" she posed, setting her empty wine glass aside. "There is no real connection to be made between Frederick and Virgil."

"There is one way," the Madame confirmed. "Were you ever told exactly where Judge Frederick's debt stemmed from?"

Celeste thought it over. "No, no, I was not."

"To my knowledge, the only people who know where his debt

comes from are Judge Frederick, myself, and his collectors. And I met with his collectors yesterday to pay them off."

"How much did they want?"

The Madame shrugged. "I paid a third of what he owed…and may have added a night at The Palace free of charge. They were just happy to get anything at this point, mainly with the knowledge that he wouldn't be amongst us too much longer." She leaned forward and picked up the wine bottle to refresh their drinks. "For the safety of plausible deniability, I'll save you just what it was this man was spending all that fucking money on. But I've fixed the documents I am going to give Esther to make it seem as if Frederick owed Virgil Archibald on gambling debt, and that after months without pay, Virgil came into town with his wife under the premise of a visit, though in reality it was to kill Frederick."

"What are you using as evidence?"

The Madame smirked, almost happy she asked. "That's where this gets good. I had Judge Frederick sign a small contract that I vowed to burn at the termination of our agreement. I've been able to use that handwriting to forge together letters from Frederick to Virgil, as well as steal his signature. Virgil was more of a challenge. Croker had Walsh pilfer some documents from his desk, and I've used those with a similar purpose. In addition, your father has managed to put the idea in the Judge's wife's head that whoever it was the Judge owed, that person lived in Chicago."

"You do have some of the best forgery skills I've ever seen."

"Years of hard work, darling."

Celeste was visibly impressed. "Incredible. Frederick won't be able to deny it, and Virgil, being an outsider in town who killed a New York City judge, will be crucified for it. They won't care about the debt—New York will just want him to hang." She reached into her dress pocket and pulled out her smoking wand, followed by her lighter and a cigarette. "Even if for some reason Virgil wouldn't be charged, his reputation will be so tarnished here that nothing he says against Croker will be viable. Sydney Turlington will divorce him. He'll have nothing."

"Just like he left Edmond with nothing."

"Making even the worst case scenario a win for us." She took a long drag of her cigarette, and exhaled. "All right, you've made me feel better."

The pair had some more wine, and the Madame made sure Celeste had consumed just over two glasses when she chose to bring up the subject that had been bothering her all week. It was the same sickness she'd felt when she discovered Timothy had raped Esther, and that Esther had chosen not to tell her. Neither of the two girls shared anything about their assaults because they didn't want to appear weak in the Madame's eyes; rather, they wanted to try and handle these things on their own and not bother her with something the presumed to be trivial. The Madame, on the other hand, found this to be infuriating—not with Esther nor with Celeste, but with herself. She had a tendency to give off the type of impression that implied these kinds of incidents didn't matter to her, when really it was just the opposite. No, she did not respond well to weakness, however, she did respond strongly and vehemently when it came to protecting her girls—all of her girls. The only thing worse in her eyes than weakness were secrets—secrets were what caused mistakes, and not one of her people could afford a mistake at that moment.

"Darling," the Madame began, rotating to look at Celeste directly, "why didn't you tell me that Captain Bernhardt attacked you?"

The color in Celeste's cheeks vanished. "I…well, Madame at the time I just…" Then, she was very suddenly and very visibly irritated. "It was Ashleigh, wasn't it? He told you about that night?"

"Actually, no he didn't," the Madame clarified for her. "Ashleigh told Louis under the assumption that you had already told me. Although I am at least happy you were honest about what happened after." There was no response, and so she carried on, "You know I really don't give a damn about what you do with Ashleigh. What I do give a shit about is you telling me that some prick verbally and physically assaulted you and, I am going to assume, was thinking of taking it further. Especially when it's some son of a bitch who wants to marry you, Celeste!"

"I told him no."

Her response took a second to sink in.

"When?" the Madame entreated her with interest.

"Just last night," Celeste confessed, her head dropping slightly. "I wrote him a note. I couldn't bear to see him."

"How could you, after what he did to you?"

Celeste reached for another cigarette. "If Ashleigh hadn't been there, I don't know what would have happened. And I swore to myself after Timothy, I would never be with a man who had that type of potential. No matter what I…" Her voice trailed off, and she collected herself with a drag of tobacco. "No matter what damage I felt I did to him, or what I felt I owed him as a result."

"You don't owe that bastard anything," the Madame assured her. "What, because he helped you through the most devastating time of your life? He came home from the fucking frontier a different person, and in that time, you changed, too, and for the better." The Madame winked at her.

Celeste grinned. "Thank you," she said proudly. "I suppose I ought to talk with Ashleigh about what's been going on."

"I think, at the very least, you should let him know that you aren't marrying the Captain. But we need to get through this week before you two can start, well, whatever the hell is going on between the two of you."

Celeste finished her wine, changing their dialogue to the undertaking at hand: "Once I get them to the hotel, I'm going to house them in the attic above our residence. It's completely secluded and none of the staff have any access to it. Mrs. Ryder gave me the keys a few months after we moved in. She thought it would be a great place to store my old gowns that were out of season."

"You have it ready for them?"

"Three beds, table and chairs, the works. Whatever they need, all they have to do is ask."

"Perfect. Great work, darling."

"When should I expect Sally?"

The Madame eased back, resting against the couch. "I hope Friday. She'll get them out using her father's old Underground Railroad contacts from Concord and into Massachusetts. Once they're out of the city, they'll have safe passage to Boston, and from there, they're on their own." She gulped down wine, trying to mask her own anxiety at losing Louis and Esther at once.

"Do you think they'll leave the country?"

The Madame shook her head. "I can't be sure. They're under strict instructions not to tell anyone except each other where the fuck they plan on going."

Celeste became troubled. "But Madame, how…how will Thomas find her?"

"Apparently, Louis is taking care of that."

Her gaze went to her wine glass. "I won't see her again, will I?"

Sympathetic to Celeste's pain, the Madame bent toward her and grasped Celeste's hand. "It isn't going to be easy for either of us, but we both know it's the only shot she has."

A small tear trickled down Celeste's face. "I know."

"Once they're gone, your father and I will secure our standing with Croker by having this little 'peace talk' with Thomas. The three of us will be in the clear. Thomas will do the rest."

"What makes you so sure he is going to go along with your 'peace talk', Madame? He would rather get gunshot than be near Croker for more than five minutes, let alone pretend to make peace."

"Darling, I haven't gotten this far in life by being unprepared. Speaking of which, we have a busy night to get ready for." The Madame let go of her hand and got to her feet. "Are you sticking around for a while?"

Celeste also rose to stand. "I've got a dinner party in a few hours, but until then, I am at your service."

In the last few weeks, Celeste's presence at The Palace had become so frequent, the Madame was almost certain she spent more time with her than anyone else. This was no revelation to the Madame—in fact, it was what she hoped for. The Madame wasn't getting any younger, and with more and more of her time being occupied by tasks that didn't involve her girls and their clientele, she realized she needed someone she could rely on to help keep order, or better yet, keep the money rolling in without issue. Celeste was showing promise. Her interest in the business was beginning to outweigh her desire to spy for the Madame, and in the future, the Madame intended to bring a healthy balance to both sides of that coin. Now, the only worry was whether to squash whatever was going on between her and Ashleigh, or ensure that it thrived and blossomed into a working relationship, much like that of her and Samuel's relationship.

"Ashleigh!" the Madame hollered, and within seconds he burst into the office, looking eager.

"Yes, Madame?"

"I need you to grab Marcy, Paige, and Claire. And Dot. We'll need to cover the clientele list for the night."

"Of course, Madame," he replied. "What time ya think will Louis be here? He mentioned somethin' about a guy wantin' to pick on Claire couple days ago, but ain' heard 'bout it since then."

Celeste crossed her arms over her chest, as if getting a chill. "You think Marcus will show up here tonight, of all nights?"

The Madame shrugged. "I really don't fucking know, but my gut is telling me that something is coming. That son of a bitch has proven in the past to be all talk, and one lousy threat doesn't mean he has the balls to actually show up here when we have a full house on Saturday." She went to her desk and lowered down into her chair. Ashleigh still appeared confused, and the Madame rolled her eyes.

"Celeste, why don't you accompany Ashleigh and fill him in on Marcus's backstory so I don't have to repeat myself every time this bastard comes up in conversation."

Celeste gave the Madame a dismayed glance. "But Madame…"

"I don't want to fucking hear it. Go. Be back up in ten minutes with the girls, I don't have all damn day."

Ashleigh left first, followed closely by Celeste, whose steps out of the office were reluctant and moderately disconcerted.

When she was sure they had made it downstairs, the Madame went over to the decanter and grabbed the key from its neck, then returned to open the locked safe underneath. From inside, she withdrew the papers for Esther to plant on Judge Frederick the following Sunday, and carefully thumbed through them to double check that everything was in its place. Once she was satisfied, the Madame placed the papers back into the safe to wait. Esther planned to come by in the late hours of that night for one last meeting with the Madame just prior to completing the hit and then disappearing for good. The thought made the Madame melancholic, recalling the brutal years Esther endured and how close they'd become in the process.

In a strange way, Esther filled the void Mary left in the Madame's heart—she'd been a daughter to her, one she would do whatever was necessary to protect, and someone she personally had gone to great lengths to keep alive. If she could manage to give the people she loved an escape, a way out to a simpler life away from New York City and Richard Croker, the Madame would not let anything deter her from that design. What would happen once Esther, Will, and Louis were gone, the Madame couldn't foresee, yet she was about to grant freedom to the two people she cared for most aside from Thomas, and that notion was enough to keep her satisfied.

At least for the time being.

Her whiskey glass sat empty, and she stretched over for the bottle on her desk, popping the cork out to fill it. For over three decades, the

Madame and Louis had worked side by side, their strange friendship being the only constant in the Madame's life formed out of Louis's love for Thomas's father and the Madame's own daughter. No matter where life took them, Louis had made himself her kin. He'd spent years devoted to her as well, and the Madame had been devoted to him, to their survival, and most importantly, to their prosperity. They would all be gone in time, all of them but her. New York City was her home, and she was a warrior, a survivor, and would stand her ground up to the bitter end, knowing full and well that ultimately, it would cost the Madame her life. But until that day came, the Madame would hold her ground, and as always, she would be ready to flow with the ever-changing tide of her city's turbulent waters.

A minute or two passed before the sound of feet on the staircase grabbed her attention. She downed her whiskey and poured another just as the door to her office flew open, and in marched Dot, Claire, Paige, and Marcy. Ashleigh and Celeste accompanied them, Celeste seeming a little flushed and Ashleigh amused as he kept his air of professionalism. The Madame eyed Celeste, and in her gaze alone the Madame was able to ascertain that she'd told Ashleigh her relationship with the Captain had come to an end.

The Madame smirked. "Where's George?"

"Downstairs," Claire told her. "I left him at the bar to handle the restock."

"Fine. Go ahead and grab wine if you'd like, ladies, I left glasses and a bottle on the side table. Ashleigh, please go and see if Jeremiah has arrived for the night. Celeste, you can help the girls with arrangements of clientele."

Ashleigh threw a look at Celeste that promised he would find her later, and she smiled back ever so slightly.

"Madame," Marcy addressed her, pouring wine into her glass, "we need to discuss our stock of opium."

"What about it, darling?"

Marcy had a gulp of her drink. "The chink we buy our supply from in Chinatown said he's already out."

The Madame's jaw dropped. "Again? That's the third fucking time this month!"

"The Tong said they are getting less of it. I asked around, and..." she sighed, irritated, "the Whyos are trying to take over opium in the city. Lee is claiming he barely gets any in and it's gone in a blink."

"The Whyos?" Paige asked, sitting down in between Marcy and Claire.

"Main gang in the Points, Paige," Dot educated her, lingering by the drink cart. "Madame, mind if I have a whiskey instead?"

The Madame's left eyebrow rose. "You? Whiskey?"

Dot shrugged. "I've just taken a liking to it."

The Madame glanced toward the other three, and Claire spoke up, "Hardy had her try some the other night, and it stuck."

Claire gazed over at Dot and winked. Aside from being mildly embarrassed by Claire announcing this to the room, Dot didn't lose her cool, and the Madame was happy to see that after her last temper tantrum, Dot was attempting to get her mood swings under control.

"So, things are back to normal with Hardy?" the Madame questioned her, with an air of entertainment.

"More or less. Whiskey?"

"I suppose." The Madame then turned her attention back to Marcy: "Tell the chink I want to meet with him as soon as possible. There's no way in hell I am dealing with Whyos, so let's get this issue sorted out before it becomes a shit storm. Do we have enough to get through the week?"

Marcy was pensive a moment. "Barely."

"It'll have to do. Claire? We will take the hit on booze. Make cocktails stronger and pours heavier to compensate in the meantime. Got it?"

"Of course, Madame."

268

"You've also had a request for tonight. Do you want to take it?"

For a number of reasons, the Madame allowed Claire and Marcy to stay on at The Palace, notwithstanding being older than the girls she'd normally employ. Marcy, who was once the disciple of Hope, was a genius at curing any sort of malady that arose, and the Madame swore in another life she must have been an apothecary. Her concoctions were so incredible, even Jeremiah was amazed by her skills, and therefore Marcy made herself indispensable in spite of the fact that she hadn't had more than a handful of clients in months. In reference to Claire's situation, circumstances were a tad different. Claire had been her bartender since the tender age of fifteen, and on top of being gifted with people, Claire could use a gun almost as well as Ashleigh or Louis. If the time should ever arise when her guard dogs went down, Claire was the final line of defense, and she'd never disappointed the Madame. For the last two years, Claire and Marcy had only taken customers if requested and previously booked, and additionally, only if they personally approved. Marcy still sometimes enjoyed work when the right man came along. Claire, however, was happy to leave that part of her life at The Palace behind, and the Madame was quite sure she and George had been romantically tied for years without admitting it to her. Either way, Claire and Marcy made The Palace their permanent home, and the Madame couldn't imagine running her business without them.

Claire's eyes went to her wine glass. "If it's fine by you, Madame, I'd rather just stay behind the bar."

"Done. We'll give your request to Jasmine."

Dot was now sitting beside Celeste, and the two were reading through the scheduled list of customers for the night.

"I'd say at least a quarter of these are all from Tammany," Celeste remarked coolly. "Roughly coming in around the same time. Should we prepare one of the big rooms for them?"

"I could have the India Room prepared in a snap, Madame," Paige told her with self-assurance.

The Madame thought on it. "Are any of them new?"

Dot shook her head. "Only two that aren't regulars, but they have both been in before."

"Then let's save ourselves trouble and open up the India Room for business," the Madame concluded as she took a sip of whiskey. "How is Lena adjusting?"

Lena was the newest addition to The Palace, and she'd only been working for the Madame for a little over a month. She was a gorgeous Italian girl who turned to whoring after arriving in New York and discovering the extended relatives she'd planned to live with had been killed in a ferry crash, leaving her penniless. Nevertheless, Lena didn't just run to the nearest brothel—she sought the Madame out personally, knowing damn well how beautiful she was, and proposed a trial period. If things continued as they were, she'd be moved into The Palace in a few days. There was, however, one worry on the Madame's mind: with Lena's curves, long dark hair, and stunning smile, the Madame had an inclination there would be some jealousy in the air. Not to mention she'd taken to the life quicker than almost any other girl the Madame had ever hired.

Paige took a sip of her wine. "Uma has taken her under her wing. Rose is being a cunt, as usual, but that's to be expected."

"What the fuck is Rose's problem?" the Madame asked.

"She's just being Rose," Celeste chimed in, leaning back into the sofa. "Being a bitch is what she does to initiate everyone new."

The Madame looked to her two veterans. "Marcy? Claire? What's your take?"

"I think we need to get everyone in here and make it clear Lena is staying," Claire offered, finishing the wine in her glass.

Marcy nodded. "Seems like the best option."

Celeste was on her feet. "Should I go and gather the girls up here?"

With a shake of her head, the Madame waved her on, "Go. Have George bring up wine and put Ashleigh on the front door. I don't want any unwelcome visitors with us all corralled in here like a bunch of goddamned cattle."

Celeste smirked and left quickly.

Dot let out a tiny giggle and got up to pour herself a little more whiskey. "Celeste better act fast if she wants to keep her hands on Ashleigh."

"Oh Dot, drop it," Claire hushed her.

The Madame rolled her eyes. "Which one?"

"Rose," Dot informed her, picking up the decanter.

"She's been on and on about him for weeks," Paige clarified. "I wanted to tell Celeste but, well,. I wasn't sure how she'd react. We all see the way they look at each other. You know Rose, though. She can be a little…"

"Competitive," Marcy finished for her, though whether that was the word Paige was actually going to use was a different matter.

"Paige," the Madame addressed her directly, "keep an eye on the situation. I won't allow bickering over dicks in my establishment."

"I'll get Rose to back off," Paige said, straightening up slightly. "She could use a bit of an ego check, Madame, if you're up for it."

"Fine."

Seconds later, the other girls were filing into the Madame's office, George leading the way and opening wine from the cellar for them. First was Arabelle, by far the most intelligent of any of the girls the Madame had ever hired, with a vocabulary that crossed five different languages. In her previous life, she claimed to have been the mistress of a Germanic prince, and in spite of her relatively plain ensemble of dark blonde hair, light blue eyes, and rosy skin, Arabelle was sharp, funny, and boisterous, which, in turn, made the Madame believe her story. Second was Jasmine—originally from New Orleans, Jasmine was Creole and could speak French as well as any Parisian. She was extremely petite, dark in her complexion, and somewhat secretive about her past, but she worked hard and the Madame often enjoyed listening to her and Celeste go back in forth in French when they'd had too much wine.

After Jasmine came Uma—or, as the other girls referred to her, the "Crown Jewel." Every man who walked into The Palace had a hard time taking his eyes off of Uma. With almost white blonde hair, deep dark blue eyes, and perfect high cheekbones, Uma was stunning, and her physique made her all the more desirable. Along with being lean, Uma was a whole head taller than the rest of the girls, making her appear more like a goddess than a human, and while some men found this to be a little more than they could handle, there were equally as many on the other end who would kill to have a night alone with Uma. Arm in arm following Uma came Penelope and Rose, the best of friends since Penelope's arrival at The Palace and very, very different from one another. Penelope was the youngest of the group, quieter than most yet extremely observant, and what most men found so alluring about Penelope was her humor—she didn't have to be loud or overcompensating; on the contrary, Penelope could make anyone laugh at the drop of a hat from her witty and candid commentary, and it did help that she had enormous breasts and a wide smile. Rose was what the Madame considered a typical upper-class whore: she was a knockout, with full and shiny chestnut brown hair, light hazel eyes, and full red lips along with a body she loved to show off whenever the opportunity arose. On the other hand, though she wouldn't dare to do so in front of the Madame, Rose had a habit of picking on the other girls for any little thing she deemed was not up to par. Without Penelope or Razzy around to keep her in line, Rose would probably not have lasted at The Palace more than a month without incident.

Two steps behind Penelope and Rose was Razzy. Razzy was her enforcer. There was not one moment when Razzy had been unpredictable or erratic, and with zero toleration for bullshit and a heart of gold, it was hard for the Madame not to love her. Razzy was black, British, and had come to the States as a servant, only to abandon her post the moment her party arrived. By happenstance, it was Arabelle who had found Razzy when she was out in Midtown, and immediately convinced her to give The Palace a try. She decided to give it a go, and Razzy hadn't left since.

At last, Lena strolled in with Celeste; the Madame smiled. Being the new girl, Lena was a tad intimidated by the others, but the Madame had a sense Lena was holding her own—the expression on her face was contented and relaxed, not vexed in any capacity. Celeste had her arm around the girl's shoulders, not in a consoling way, but in a maternal and gracious fashion, a signal to the others to be warm and welcoming. Her contributions and effort to make business run smoothly and assist with the girls came easier than the Madame had anticipated. Instead of butting in to mediate, the Madame communicated to Celeste through a small gesture that she could take the lead and announce that Lena was a permanent member of The Palace.

When the girls all had a glass of wine in hand, Celeste moved and stood in front of the Madame's desk, and the room went still.

"The Madame and I thought it would be best to have a small meeting to discuss how Lena's time thus far has been, and also go over a few matters regarding The Palace's schedule tonight."

"Lena, darling, how was your first week?" the Madame asked, simultaneously refilling her whiskey.

"With your permission, I would like to sign on to stay at The Palace, Madame," Lena replied merrily, having a gulp of wine from her glass. "I really like it here, and I think I would be a good addition."

Celeste faced the rest of them. "Are we in agreement?"

That was the way things were at The Palace: the Madame forced them to make decisions together to prevent any problems from festering, and additionally, it was typically a time when unresolved issues would be fixed.

Everyone saluted in affirmation, and then Lena leaned over and whispered something into Celeste's ear. With a friendly signal, Celeste turned the floor back over to Lena, only this time, Lena addressed the girls, not the Madame.

In this case, one girl in particular.

"Rose," Lena initiated, and instantly Rose's cheeks went scarlet in both recognition and guilt, "I understand why you act the way you do, me being new to The Palace."

This unexpected confrontation sucked all the air out of the room, and the Madame found it hard to keep a straight face as she watched Rose finally get what had been coming for a while.

"But now that I am officially working here, this must stop. Are we good on that?"

No one moved, and Rose's countenance was completely bewildered. "I don't...I don't know what you mean..."

"Oh, don't you fucking dare," Razzy cut in, not aggressively, but in a tone that didn't offer any kind of retort. "You're a bitch to every new girl we get. Enough is enough, Rose. You were even that way to Penelope. Right, Pen?"

Rose glanced to Penelope, who shrugged. "It's true, Rose."

Unable to find a response, Rose's gaze shot to the Madame, as if expecting a defense from her. The Madame inclined forward, resting her forearms on her desk.

"Any objectors, other than Rose?"

There wasn't one.

"Then it's settled. Rose, get your fucking act together, and if this continues, I'll start by docking your pay. After that, it'll only get worse. Apologize to Lena, and let's move on."

Initially, Rose hesitated, and Celeste spoke up, "Rose, the Madame gave you a mandate."

Rose glared at Celeste. "The Madame did, not you."

"And if you don't follow that mandate right this second, I will beat the living hell out of your snooty ass," the Madame snapped, getting to her feet. "This is not a debate. You don't run The Palace,

I do, and you do not fucking second guess me or Celeste. This entire room has decided you've been a bitch, and so now, you'll be a good little darling and do as you're told."

The Madame couldn't tell if Penelope shoved Rose to her feet, or if the girl leapt up herself, but one threat from the Madame was all it took.

"I'm, I'm sorry, Lena. It won't happen anymore."

"Or at all," Arabelle elucidated, giving Rose an icy stare.

Rose didn't say another word and sank back down to her spot like a struck puppy as Penelope took her hand sympathetically.

"Thanks, Lena," Celeste stated, motioning for her to sit down. "Now, let's run through the clientele and talk about setting up the India Room for our Tammany customers."

A few short minutes later, the meeting ended and the girls started to disperse. With a quick wave of her hand, the Madame gestured for Razzy to stay back alone. The room cleared out, with Celeste needing to get to her own dinner party that night, and thus the Madame was able to bring up a subject she presumed would be uncomfortable—evidently she was in the mood for tackling secrets, and thought it best to get everyone's bullshit out on the table.

"Darling," the Madame said as she went to sit beside Razzy on the sofa, "you need to tell Celeste about Jeremiah."

In a similar way to Rose, Razzy was dumbfounded. "W-what about Jeremiah?"

"You need to tell her about you and Jeremiah."

Rather than seeming embarrassed, Razzy's eyes narrowed. "How did you find out about that?"

The Madame smirked. "I saw him leaving your room two nights ago."

Razzy let out a heavy exhale. "Christ. I thought we were being discreet."

"How long has this been going on?"

275

"Well, Madame, we started fucking about a month after he start-ed officially working at The Palace."

The Madame's jaw dropped. "Razzy, that was ages ago! How the fuck have you been hiding this so well?"

"Like I said," Razzy answered coyly, "we've been discreet."

"Well...Jesus..."

Within seconds, both of them were laughing, and the Madame downed the remainder of her whiskey. "You need to tell her before she finds out on her own."

"Why does that matter?"

"Because she likes you, Razzy, and she loves her brother. And I don't need more shit going on in this house than we already have."

Razzy reluctantly surrendered. "All right, I'll tell her first thing tomorrow."

"Not tomorrow," the Madame corrected. "Give it a few days, but by the end of next week."

"I'll take care of it." Razzy got up. "Thanks for not outing me in front of the others."

"Is this love?" the Madame inquired. "Or a distraction?"

As she anticipated, Razzy's face gave her away, and the Ma-dame went on: "You know the drill. If it gets to the point where you can't do your job, I need a month's notice and for you to find your own replacement."

Razzy set her empty wine glass down on the side table. "Don't worry, Madame. I'm not going anywhere, but I do have one thing I want to ask."

"What's that?"

"One night, after Jeremiah had been in my bed, I came up to see if you were still awake and have a drink. We all know you don't sleep."

"And?"

"And…there was someone else here. Someone I had never met before."

The Madame discerned instantaneously where this was going. "You saw her."

"I did," Razzy admitted with some reluctance. "I told Jeremiah, then he told me about the night he…met her."

Furious with herself, the Madame got to her feet to get more whiskey. They should have been more vigilant.

"Who is she, Madame?"

As she filled her glass, the Madame kept her back to Razzy. "She's someone I love very dearly, and for her sake and for her protection, that's all I can tell you."

Razzy seemed to accept this answer and stood up, walking casually over to the Madame.

"I've never heard you say that before."

"Say what?"

Razzy smiled at her forlornly. "That you love someone."

The Madame threw back her drink. "There's a reason for that, darling." She picked the decanter back up. "This stays between us. If it gets out amongst the other girls…"

"I know." Razzy made her way over to the door. "You're a cold bitch on the surface, Madame, but I'm happy to see the inside is different, for all our sakes."

The Madame picked up her whiskey and returned to her desk, throwing her feet up and relaxing back into her chair as she watched Razzy take her leave.

"Yeah," she mumbled softly to herself, "and it's going to be the fucking death of me."

Many hours later, it was another typical Saturday night at The Palace, and with a full house of customers, the Madame found it easy to let herself relax and do what she did best: entertain. She saw to it the girls got the India Room ready, and when the clients started to arrive, the Madame assumed her post near the bar, greeting the high-end customers and ensuring those guests had access to whatever it was they needed. Ashleigh and George were running security at the front door and around the main areas of The Palace, while Louis kept an eye on the girls in the India Room.

With Marcus's threat seeming to be another farce, the Madame was relieved—sure, she had three strong and capable men keeping a close eye on every single movement made, but in a time of crisis, that wouldn't make any damn difference. All it would take would be Marcus cornering Claire with just enough time to shoot her, and there would be nothing she could do to bring her back. As a precautionary measure, the Madame had Claire keep a pocket pistol in her dress pocket, and instead of one shotgun behind the bar, they'd stocked two. Not to mention that, just in case, the Madame was wearing her Colt revolver, four knives, and three extra cylinders for good measure.

She'd learned never to be unprepared.

"Madame?" came a voice to her left as she poured another whiskey for Secretary Bayard, and when she turned, she found George lingering nervously, his eyes on the ground.

"Excuse me a moment, Mr. Secretary," the Madame remarked with an enchanting smile.

He winked at her. "Don't be too long, Madame!"

The Madame moved a step closer to George. "Is everything all right, George?"

"I just…I need to talk to you about something…"

"Right fucking now?"

"Well…yeah."

The Madame peeked over her shoulder at the secretary of state, snapped her fingers, and immediately Arabelle picked up right where the Madame had left their flirtation. If it wasn't already almost the end of the night, she would have told George to fuck off.

"My office," she whispered to George, who followed right behind her the entire way up.

When they made it upstairs, George closed the doors of the office and took a seat while the Madame went to pour herself and George a drink.

"What is so goddamn important that you have to interrupt my night, George?" Her voice was annoyed, yet she was intrigued as she walked over to sit beside him. The Madame couldn't recall the last time they'd been alone together…or if they ever had, for that matter.

"It's the only time we could talk and not have anyone else here," he professed firmly as she handed over his glass to him, "and I don't want to cause a fuss."

"A fuss?"

George downed his whiskey. "About Claire." He paused. "And me."

"Well, it's not new information, but at least I've finally heard it confirmed." She had a sip from her glass and gazed at him. "What is the issue here, George? She hasn't seen a client in months, and I pay both of you pretty fucking well, if I do say so myself."

George reached into his pocket and pulled out a gold band sitting in the palm of his open hand. "I want to marry her, Madame."

Her eyes opened wide. "Well, damn you, George." She saluted him with her glass, and finished her whiskey. "When?"

George grinned. "I'm going to ask soon."

"How soon?"

"I was thinking one day this week. Could you…help me surprise her? I just want it to be…well, ya know…special."

It was hard not to feel her heart melting as she looked at how happy George was, but the Madame had to do her best to hide it. "I would be honored to help you, George. You two have been my most loyal employees other than Louis…and I am thrilled for both of you."

The clock in her office struck two at that moment, and the Madame rose to grab the whiskey decanter, wanting to pour George another celebratory drink. Instead, just as she made a grab for the bottle, a high-pitched shriek came from outside in the back alleyway. Whipping around, the Madame caught a quick glimpse of George's panic-stricken face, and instantly the two of them knew what was happening: Marcus had made it to The Palace.

They were leaping down the Madame's back staircase within seconds, the Madame leading, with George right on her heels. When they hit the first floor, the Madame pulled her revolver out from her thigh holster and cocked it, praying Louis had made it to the alley in time to catch Marcus and also, that whoever had screamed hadn't ruined the night for her high-paying clients. Rushing, they turned the corner at a full sprint down the hallway as a few of the girls' heads poked out of their rooms, wondering what was going on.

"Everything's fine!" the Madame bellowed as she ran past, aware that this probably didn't convince anyone that the coast was clear.

Nonetheless, Razzy appeared out of the India Room at the end of the row of doors, and the Madame took the opportunity to keep things calm.

"Razzy, make sure everything keeps rolling!" the Madame ordered, and with a nod, Razzy blew by them in the opposite direction.

The back door was already cracked slightly open, and the Madame burst through it, gun pointed at the dark figures she spotted just a few feet away. There was a spurt of frenzied movement upon their arrival; thankfully, Louis had reached the alley ahead of them, and currently stood with a gun outstretched, pointed directly at the man she assumed to be Marcus's forehead, who stood a few strides away from Louis. He wasn't what she had expected—he was just a little taller than Claire, thin and sinewy, with a round face and dark, unsettling eyes. The Madame could perceive the similarities between Claire and Marcus: the same button nose, same jutting cheekbones, though conversely, Marcus appeared much older than Claire described, more than likely a hazard of the life he'd led on the run for so long. The most distinguishable feature of this man was the panic in his countenance, and if the Madame had learned anything, it was that she didn't want Marcus to feel cornered. If you corner a wild animal, there's no telling the damage it can do, and she could really use a night without a fucking incident.

Ashleigh was there to restrain him, a miracle in the Madame's mind, because the scene in which she and Louis now both had their guns pointed at was somewhat of a catastrophe. In one way or another, Marcus had managed to get ahold of Dot and held her close against him with a knife at her throat while facing the Madame, Louis, Ashleigh, and George, who was furiously trying to break free of Ashleigh's grip. Simultaneously, in his other hand, Marcus had a gun pointed at Claire, who was standing just beyond an arm's length away from her brother, both hands held up in the air. The Madame's gaze found Louis's, and they communicated in just one glimpse that this was going to get ugly before it got better—there would be at least one casualty from this encounter, and the Madame sincerely hoped Claire had formulated her own plan for this in premeditation.

"Let the girl go," Louis demanded, his voice remaining calm.

Marcus didn't budge. "I will let her go as long as I get to take my sister."

"I'll fucking shoot you dead before you take Claire," the Madame hissed, cocking her revolver.

"Then you'll lose two girls in the process," Marcus countered, his eyes still eerily locked on Claire. "All you have to do is come with me, Claire, and this can all go away." He brought the knife closer to Dot's throat, causing her to whimper. "It took me a long time to get to you, and I'll be damned if you slip away again."

Claire peered at the Madame for a second, then her attention returned to Marcus. "You have killed innocent people, brother. For no reason—"

"For good reason!" he yelled, staggering a little on his feet yet managing to keep his gun aimed and Dot in his grasp. "I had to find you. You belong to me."

"Brother, you know that's not true," Claire said mildly. "You killed...you killed our entire family...do you not remember that?"

The Madame and Louis gaped at each other, trying to comprehend the interaction. George even ceased his struggle against Ashleigh, as he too appeared engrossed in the exchange between Marcus and Claire. Seeing George was collected, Ashleigh took a step to stand beside the Madame, and this caused Marcus to grew more anxious.

"Nobody move an inch!" he roared, retreating three paces with Dot.

Claire managed to move with him so that she lingered near, her gaze shifting from Dot to Marcus, and the Madame could recognize that Claire was making the choice every one of them was afraid of.

She swallowed. "Marcus, if you let Dot go, I'll come with you."

To the Madame's astonishment, this caused Dot to become furious. "Don't you dare go with him, Claire. He's a fucking bastard and he's just going to—"

"Shut up!" Marcus snapped, in a tone that caused Dot to rescind her argument. Marcus gawked at Claire. "You'll come with me?"

Claire nodded. "I will." She moved a little closer.

The Madame could only watch, in a futile attempt to understand just what in the fuck was happening. The others, too, were frozen in place, motionless.

"Does she got a fuckin' plan?" Ashleigh uttered almost inaudibly, his hands twitching not an inch from his pistols.

From behind them came George, so only the two of them could hear: "Yes."

282

The Madame's head whipped around, and George was patiently standing there, his eyes on Claire as if waiting for what was next.

The sound of Marcus speaking again caused the Madame to rotate back to the action, more confused than ever.

"And you'll marry me, Claire?"

This made Louis's jaw tighten, but Claire didn't seem startled. "You know we can't do that, Marcus. That's what Mama was trying to tell you before you killed them. We can't be together like that. It's against the law."

Marcus's brow furrowed. "Then we'll lie."

"Or we can just be together without being married."

Marcus's gaze filled with hope. "You'd do that?"

"I will. If you let Dot go first."

Louis aggressively started to move toward them.

"Louis!" the Madame called. "Stay where you are."

Anger swept over his face, yet Claire again pacified her brother, and glided to Marcus. Immediately, Marcus lowered and holstered the gun he had aimed at her and released Dot. Claire put her hand on his shoulder lovingly and Marcus sheathed the blade at his belt. Sweeping Claire up into his arms, Marcus kissed her—and not in a brotherly fashion. The Madame's repulsion almost caused her to drop her gun, aghast at what she saw.

Then, it happened.

The Madame barely caught it—despite the atrocity of deeply kissing her brother, one of Claire's eyes opened, and when she saw that Dot had made it to Louis, Claire made her move. In a flash, she drew Marcus's gun straight out of the holster, hit the hammer with her thumb, and shot Marcus directly in the chest. Marcus dangled in limbo for a moment, the perplexity on his face immeasurable. Then, he fell backward to the ground, holding his gaping and bleeding wound. Without a word, Claire cocked the gun again and fired again, and again, and again. The bullets had run out, and Marcus lay on the ground in a pool of his own blood, not the tiniest flicker of life left. Claire stared at her brother's body, without an ounce of remorse on her face.

"Holy fuckin' shit," Ashleigh breathed.

"Dot?" the Madame mouthed to Louis.

"Fine," Louis mouthed in return.

Claire remained where she was until Ashleigh spoke up again, "Girl, you drew that pistol faster than anybody I ever saw."

That brought Claire out of her concentration. She spat on Marcus's body, glided over to the Madame, and handed over Marcus's gun, not acknowledging the others just yet, only the Madame.

"You never told me that he tried to marry you," the Madame stated, "only that he abused you and killed your family."

Claire peeked with disdain over her shoulder at Marcus, then at the Madame once more. "When my parents found out he was raping me, they sent him away. I don't know where. He came back and tried to get me to run away with him, told me that we were meant to be together, and told my parents he was going to marry me whether they liked it or not. They refused, so he killed them and the rest of our siblings."

The Madame felt Ashleigh cringe beside her.

"Well, shit," he mumbled. "Where in the hell ya learn to shoot like that?"

"I managed to get away from Marcus. I was damned good on a horse, growing up on the frontier. Made it to Cheyenne and got taken in by a group of bandits. They taught me everything I know about shooting." She paused for a second. "And after a few months, we caught word that my brother was trying to find me. Killed a few people in an altercation. So, I got out of the Wild West and headed to New York."

Dot jogged up behind Claire and wrapped her arms around

her. "You are so brave, Claire. I thought for sure I was going to get my throat slit."

Claire pulled her in and embraced her. "You know I would never let that happen."

"And you were aware of all this, George?" the Madame asked, circling around.

He didn't respond, only nodded, observing Claire with trepidation and awe. The Madame appreciated that George must have known this was what she planned all along, to buddy up to Marcus only to have the opportunity to send him to his grave.

The Madame sighed, handing Marcus's gun to Ashleigh and holstering her own back onto her thigh. "Well, just one thing left to do. Louis?"

"Yeah, I've got it." Louis made his way over to Marcus's lifeless body and threw it over his shoulder as if it weighed next to nothing. As he neared the Madame, Louis halted.

"What do you want to do with this?"

"I can help ya with that," came Will's voice, approaching them from the darkness of the alley. When he got to Louis's side, he smiled, and the Madame rolled her eyes.

"Are you here to retrieve him?"

"Somethin' like that." Will nodded to Ashleigh. "Son."

Ashleigh's expression remained emotionless. "Daddy."

"Louis, just usual protocol. Get the wheelbarrow and take him to the river. Claire, get the mop and scrub brush for the blood," the Madame ordered.

Claire let go of Dot, and she and Dot proceeded to follow Ashleigh inside. George still stood there unmoving, his eyes lost somewhere else entirely.

"Hey Georgie, you all right there, brother?" Will beseeched him.

Will, of course, had no knowledge of George's relationship with Claire or that Claire had just murdered her incestuous brother in front of all of them, and the Madame wondered how he would react coming out of his state of shock.

Ultimately, George shook off whatever it was holding him and took a step closer to Louis.

"I'll take care of him," George said. "It's my burden, not yours."

"Really, George, I can handle it," Louis protested.

"Nah. You need to get out of here. I'll get rid of Marcus. Then it'll really feel like…like this whole nightmare is over…"

Will and Louis looked at each other, and eventually to the Madame. She had the last word, after all.

"Fine. George get rid of the body." She went on to address Will as Louis tossed Marcus's body over George's shoulder, "Is everything ready for…?"

"'Course it is," he replied smugly.

The three of them observed George as he shuffled into The Palace, and when the door closed behind him, they huddled together, voices hushed.

"Real reason I'm here early is 'cause Tommy struck again in the Points, and them fuckin' Whyos are losin' their shit 'bout it."

The Madame sneered. "Where did he hit?"

"That's the thing," Will continued, "it wasn' no place. He raided the goddamned opium supply comin' through. And not jus' one tiny little batch." Will stared right into the Madame's eyes. "Tommy took all o' it, and he killed the eight bastards runnin' it into town."

A chill ran down her spine. "He fucking knew about the opium increase to the Whyos," she thought aloud, "that's why he hit there next. He wanted to cripple Tammany and the Whyos while he had the opportunity."

"How long before Croker will hear about this?" Louis asked Will. "Soon 'nough."

Louis took a cigarette out of his pocket and lit it. "The alliance between Croker and the Whyos isn't going to last."

"Not much longer," the Madame agreed, "and when the split

happens, Croker being the son of a bitch he is will probably use his personal war against Walsh and the Whyos as fucking ammo in the election." With a shake of her head, the Madame sighed. "We need this hit to go perfectly, or Esther could find her ass in some serious trouble. You boys want a whiskey before you go?"

"I'll take ya up on that, Madame. Gonna be awhile 'fore we get to do that again."

Louis took a long drag of his cigarette. "In a matter of days, this is all over."

"After the hit, you're both free," the Madame added. "No matter what, Louis, you are not to come back here. Ever."

For a moment, Louis was taken aback and hurt by her words; however, that quickly transformed to understanding.

"I know," was all he managed to get out, and the Madame could see his departure from her was as painful for him as it was for the Madame; nonetheless, this was not the time for goodbyes. There was work to be done.

"Whiskey," she declared, and marched to the back door of The Palace. "We've got one fucking task ahead of us, boys. Let's hope we live through it."

The next week went by in a hurry, and soon, the Madame found their golden hour had arrived at long last.

She was hoping for a little sleep, but the Madame never could close her eyes when one of her plots was in motion, and this plot in particular had been years in the making. At long last, she was saving Esther, she was saving Louis, and she would do it without an ounce of suspicion from Croker and Tammany Hall.

Esther had been by around four that morning to discuss the angle of the hit and gather the evidence to plant, but more importantly, she took the time to say a personal goodbye to the Madame.

There was no way to predict whether or not they would see each other again, and frankly, neither the Madame nor Esther was eager to bring that subject up. Instead, the pair of them discussed the hit, the transition to the Hiltmores' room at St. Stephen, and the ostensible havoc wreaked by Thomas onto the Whyo opium trade. The exaltation in Esther's face made the Madame feel as if she hadn't completely fucked everything up for the pair, and she wondered how many times they'd secretly met since Thomas's arrival back in the city. A handful, perchance, or they'd draw notice—both Esther and Thomas were incredibly gifted at being invisible when necessary, but Croker still had Walsh and the Whyos, making everyone's life hell, and they couldn't risk being caught—not now.

As the tenth hour approached, the Madame had Paige run and grab her a Sunday coffee—liquid courage would be a good friend to have while she waited to hear of Frederick's demise. Louis, Will, and Esther would be arriving closer to eleven, and Douglas and Celeste should be bursting through the office doors at any second with the carriage prepped and ready in the back alleyway behind The Palace. To protect her people, Ellis would also have a role in smuggling Louis, Will, and Esther to safety, by escorting the three of them and Celeste to the hotel in case an issue should arise. The Madame, in her meticulous methods, covered every aspect of their escape to freedom, and thus far, nothing had gone awry.

A loud knock came to the door.

"What is it, Ashleigh?" she called.

He opened the door and walked inside, carrying her whiskey and coffee.

"Douglas and Celeste just got here," he told her, setting the mug on her desk. "Whatcha need me to do?"

The Madame glanced up at him from the newspaper she was reading, and noted the uncharacteristic level of sincerity in his tone. "You'll keep an eye out while we load the carriage. Follow them south and make sure no one has any fucking idea what we're up to. Once they're in the hotel, get your ass back up here to give me a full report. We have our talk with Thomas and Croker this afternoon, and we cannot fuck that up."

"Course, Madame." He paused. "What in the world do ya think Lord Turner did with all that opium? Seems mighty crazy, takin' from bastards like them Whyos."

"When Croker and Douglas leave tonight, you can ask him yourself," she said with a smirk. "I told you that I would allow you to be a part of this. Don't get a limp dick when I finally deal you into the game."

"Ya got nothin' to worry about there," he countered, sauntering towards the door of her office.

"Madame!" Celeste greeted, throwing Ashley a besotted grin as she passed. "We are ready. The carriage is in the alley."

The Madame took off her spectacles and had a sip of her coffee, then raised the mug in question. "You want one?"

"Yes, please," Celeste replied, turning to Ashley, who smiled and nodded.

"Where is your father?"

Celeste moved over to the love seat. "Downstairs. He's nervous and is trying to pull himself together. Samuel is with him."

"Good." The Madame eyed her closely. "You all right, darling?"

"Paige is still worried about George after last week."

"Well, it certainly seems like George is more shaken up than either of the girls," the Madame stated with an air of amusement. "Always happy to know how tough those bitches can be when they want to be."

Celeste sighed, "I should have been here. I could have helped."

"Don't be ridiculous, Celeste, you have our own role to keep playing."

She was pensive for a few determined seconds. "I want you to teach me how to handle knives, like you can."

The Madame was baffled by the request—this was certainly a new pursuit for her. "Celeste, I just…why?"

"Because I want to be ready to fight. You don't show it often, but I've never seen anyone who can handle knives like you can. I want to learn."

"Well, all right. We can start tomorrow, I suppose."

"Perfect."

It wasn't long before Douglas and Ellis joined them in the office, with Sunday coffees for themselves and an extra for Celeste.

"Ladies?" Douglas asked, looking from the Madame to Celeste. "Have we missed something?"

"Not at all!" Celeste pronounced, standing up and curtseying politely. "Samuel, it is always wonderful to see you."

"And you too, Miss Hiltmore," Samuel returned, then addressed the Madame. "How long do we have?"

"Another ten or fifteen. It's impossible to know anything until the three of them are here. Let's just hope nobody has fucking—"

The Madame was cut off mid-sentence by shouts from downstairs. A wave of alarm hit every person in the room, and in seconds, each one of them was dashing out of the Madame's office to hear the news.

"…gone, just fucking gone!" Louis was shouting, his expression filled with horror. "She slipped us after the hit and we have no goddamned idea how!"

He and Will were racing up the stairs toward her, with Ashleigh not two steps in their wake.

"What the hell happened?!" the Madame demanded, attempting to mask her own dismay. She'd known something was going to go wrong; she just prayed the damage wasn't irreversible.

"She did the hit," Will answered when they reached her, "everythin' was goin' just right. Then she didn' show to the meet point. I

290

don' get it, Madame, it don' make no sense. She knows what's goin' on, don' she?"

"Are you two sure she didn't just set out on her own to come to The Palace?" Samuel implored from the Madame's left. "Esther could easily have seen something that may have made her anxious and thought it better to venture solo."

Louis shook his head. "Not possible. Esther's good, but Will and I are much more advanced at spotting tails." Louis stared at the Madame. "Where did she go?"

They were appealing to her.

"There has to be a reason..." the Madame began, flustered by the combination of anger and confusion. "This was her way out. What possible reason would Esther have to not get the fuck out when she has the chance?"

"Thomas?" Douglas suggested.

"Nah, that ain' it."

"She and Thomas were never a part of this equation," Louis established, "and that's because, if anything, getting Esther out would only make their being together easier."

"And it's not like she has any loyalty to Richie," Ellis added. "There's something she was hiding from us, and I think..."

Abruptly, Celeste's cracked voice came from the Madame's right: "She's going to kill him."

All six of them whipped around to face her.

"What?" the Madame cried.

"Walsh?" Louis beseeched her. "She can't win that fight!"

The color drained from Will's cheeks. "Nah, brother. Girl didn' mean the lunatic." His tone was somber. "She went to fuckin' kill Richie."

Dread struck the Madame as she realized Celeste was right. "Oh...oh no..."

Louis gawked at Will, astonished. "Will, tell me you didn't know."

"'Course I didn' fuckin' know!" he hollered, the rage evident in his words. "Christ, I shoulda seen this. She's been talkin' like that lately, with me at least. Wants it to end. For everybody, not just us. And yesterday—Louis, you remember what she told us. She ain' ever been like that before, and you know it." Tears were forming in his eyes. "She thinks she's gonna die."

"What did she say?!" the Madame insisted.

Before he could answer, Louis interrupted, "I've got to get to Tommy."

Will nodded. "I'll get to Tammany and...and..."

Samuel had clued in. "Will, I am going with you in case I need to help cover this up. God knows what kind of damage Esther could do."

The Madame rotated to Celeste and Ashleigh. "Get to St. Stephen. Make sure everything is fucking ready in case we can salvage this situation, or in case we..." She couldn't think like that—it was that type of thinking that got people killed. "Louis, Will, Samuel, go!"

In a rush, the men were sprinting down the stairs and out the front door of The Palace; Ashleigh took Celeste by the hand and they pursued their commission, heading out the back to get the carriage to ride south.

Douglas gently touched the Madame's arm. "What do you need me to do?"

The Madame shook him off. She paced back into her office and to her desk, pulling open the top drawer to grab her Colt and extra cylinders.

"We are going to pray to fucking God that Esther isn't dead. In the meantime, Claire and George are locking The Palace down. Douglas, you are staying here in the case that Croker isn't dead and shows up for this fucking meeting." The Madame finished the now-cold Sunday coffee on her desk, so furious with Esther she could barely get ahold of herself. "Claire!"

In under a minute, Claire was up the back stairs, breathless. "What's going on? I heard Louis and Will yelling."

"Are most of the girls still asleep?"

"Yes, Madame."

"Get George. Lockdown."

Claire didn't dawdle. "Yes, Madame."

"Fuck!" she yelled aloud in frustration, slamming her fist down onto the desk.

The anger was so overwhelming, her hands had started to shake—she needed to steady herself. She couldn't control Esther. She could only use the tools at her disposal. The fury, however, wouldn't fade.

"How could she do this, Douglas—why? We'd worked so hard, every single one of us sacrificed our own asses for her."

"Do you think she'll kill Richard?" Douglas asked, pouring the Madame and himself a whiskey from the drink cart.

"I don't know," she confessed.

Douglas sauntered over to her and handed over her drink. "If she kills him, the war will be over. Isn't that what you want?"

"It's not that, Douglas. It's that there is no way she'll get out of there alive. With Sullivan and O'Reilly, the Whyos, Walsh...Walsh will hunt her down, fucking bastard, and he'll do it for fun. Without Croker keeping a leash on him, he'll be delighted to finally have the chance to kill Esther."

Douglas moved beside her, his gaze going to the outside world. "Well, I hope Louis can run fast, then."

She glanced at him blankly, taking a gulp of whiskey. "Why the fuck...oh..."

"Seeing it now, are you?" Douglas teased that for once he was ahead of her. "Louis, like the rest of us, is aware of the very scary reality that everyone faces at this point: that Thomas is probably the only one who can save Esther. Or..."

"Or he will die trying."

"Precisely."

"You cannot seriously be considering attending this bloody charade!"

It was nearing lunchtime, and William and Thomas had been debating one another for the last half hour about the Madame's invitation to The Palace later that afternoon. William was not exactly thrilled by the prospect of a peace meeting between Thomas and Richard Croker, although what William couldn't understand was that Thomas wasn't going to make peace. Peace was the last thing Thomas wanted with Richard Croker. Instead, he planned to do what Hiroaki trained and educated him to do—to keep his enemy close, so that every move Croker might make, Thomas would be able to swiftly counter.

"Can you just calm down for a moment, William? Really! You are not perceiving this in the right manner."

Athena was resting on Thomas's forearm, and from behind Thomas's desk, her ice cold gaze was locked on William. Athena and William had been making incremental improvements in their toleration of one another, and Thomas speculated as to whether she took a certain level of pleasure in torturing William with her random bating and screeches.

But as to his afternoon at The Palace, William wouldn't soften. "You are going to meet with a brothel owner, a convicted felon, and the leader of Tammany bloody Hall!"

"I am well aware of that."

"How on earth is that going to get you anything but trouble? And with Richard Croker, of all people, the man who imprisoned your mother for nearly a decade!"

"William, please try to hear me out."

"Fine! Tell me how you can justify this one, Tommy, because you could potentially undo everything we've been working so hard for!"

It was difficult to not tell William what was truly going on, and that Thomas's entire motivation behind Turner S & D and befriend-

294

ing Croker was a cover to cripple the Grand Sachem's empire. There was more at stake than the Turner family pride. The next few days were probably the most crucial in securing Thomas's future—Louis covertly left a note with Tony, which Thomas burned after reading, informing him of the plan to get Esther out of New York City. Thomas could not have been more ecstatic at the news. Nevertheless, Thomas had his own role to play to secure that the Madame, the Hiltmores, and he were not implicated in her disappearance: he had to make peace with Richard Croker the very afternoon she vanished, or at least, feign peace until Esther successfully made it outside city limits alive. Louis apologized profusely over and over again, understanding that this was by no means the way Thomas originally planned to take Croker down. In reality, Thomas had no objections—it was, instead, an opportunity for him to gain the upper hand.

He was about to commence coaxing William down with a bit of brandy when Tony surprised them both by violently bursting into Thomas's study.

Only it wasn't just Tony.

"Tommy!" Louis was red in the face, sweating profusely. "Tommy, you have to get to the Hall."

William stood up, gaping at Tony and Louis. "What in the hell is going on here?"

Both Tony and Louis ignored William.

"She went to kill him, Tommy," Louis gasped, leaning against the wall and clutching his chest as he tried to get his breath. "I couldn't stop her. Will couldn't either…we didn't know. But if you don't go now, it'll be too late. I don't know what brought this on…I don't—"

"Tony!" Thomas commanded, and in a flash, Tony was at his side to grab Athena, glove already on his arm.

As fast as he could, Thomas raced to the hidden closet in the corner and pulled out the key, unlocking it and swinging the door open wide to grab his tools; in seconds, Thomas threw on his own bowler hat, fetched the tin of soot for his eyes, and tucked the Griswold into his pocket. With a sharp whistle, Athena flew from Tony's glove to Thomas's shoulder, where he'd fastened a thick leather sling of his own design for her to perch.

"When did you lose her?"

"Not thirty minutes ago. Will is already running to Tammany. Ellis is with him."

Thomas cursed under his breath. "Louis, if I get there in time, it'll be a fucking miracle."

"I am not worried about saving Croker," Louis declared firmly. "I am worried about what happens when Walsh gets to her."

Thomas vainly tried to keep that notion out of his mind and clear his thoughts. "Tony, secure the household. William, you and Lucy are to stay inside until I return. Is that understood?"

William's mouth had fallen open, his eyes on Thomas. "I've read the...the papers..."

"I know, William."

"You're...you're the Vigilante?"

Tony grabbed lightly onto William's arm, ushering him aside. "Thomas, there are two extra cylinders and your dagger in the pack in the upstairs closet. And jesses."

Thomas rushed out of his study, down the hall, and directly for the front door, Athena gripping tightly onto him with her talons— she knew when a hunt was on, and she was ready. He reached the closet, grabbed the pack as Tony instructed, then whipped around to find Louis and Tony.

"Louis, get back to the Madame. Protect her. I'll find Esther."

Without another word, Thomas was outside, hurdling down the stoop.

"Fly, Athena!" he whispered, and instantly, she was airborne as Thomas hailed a carriage.

"I need to go forty blocks as fast as you can!" he barked to the driver. "I'll pay triple your fee!"

Thomas tossed a wad of bills from his pocket at the driver, and the second he was in the cab, the driver flicked his reins hard and the carriage took off, the horses nearly transitioning into a full canter.

Removing the Griswold from its holster, Thomas checked the loaded cylinder and opened his pack, sheathing Lawrence's blade against his hip and pocketing the two extra loaded cylinders. He ripped off the shoulder perch and his dress shirt to pull the basic, cotton-sewn shirt over his head. After, he tied the jesses from the pack to Athena's perch before reattaching it onto his shoulder. Reaching for the tin of soot, he darkened his eyes so he wouldn't be recognized, his nerves standing on end at the thought of losing Esther when he'd only just gotten her back. For a brief moment, he clenched his eyes shut tight, reminding himself not to let his emotions rule his actions. The mission was clear, and he understood what he had to do to save her.

"What were you thinking, Es…" he considered aloud, returning to his preparations. "What the fuck were you thinking? I hope Will gets there in time to intervene…Louis and Tony better lock everyone down…they…they…"

The realization hit Thomas in that moment. Apart, Thomas never might have guessed it, yet side by side, it was unmistakable. Louis and Tony had such similar features, and while Louis was much larger than Tony, their stature was…identical. Tony had an inside source, a connection to the Madame, Croker, and the gangs—and it was Louis. He reflected on his father's friendship with Louis, and how Louis had watched out for him throughout the majority of his childhood, being there for him and Mary whenever they needed him. And Tony, in an exactly mirrored fashion, had been employed by his father to protect William and Lucy, disguised as their reliable butler…while trained extensively by Edward in case any of his former enemies might go after them. Rapidly, every one of the pieces

297

that never previously made sense added up into one giant, convoluted connection of nearly everyone in Thomas's life.

"Holy shit."

CHAPTER XXXVII.

She knew the Madame would never forgive her.

Esther had done everything right—she'd played her part in this war of powers, and while her family had made the necessary arrangements to save her, she simply couldn't go along with bowing out when there was still so much to be done. Every nerve, every muscle, every fiber of her being had been in protest of abandoning her post, regardless of her initial agreement to leave New York with Louis and Will. For years, self-preservation was what had kept her alive, and instead of assenting to that strategy, Esther decided it was time to go a different direction, one that might end in sacrificing herself entirely for the chance of saving the people she cared about. The Madame's voice in her head couldn't fathom Esther's reasoning, and therefore, for the first time, Esther ignored her, stepping one foot firmly in front of the other as she neared the entrance to Tammany Hall. If there was one thing she'd learned from the Madame, from Louis and Will, or even from Thomas, it was that certain opportunities would only come once in a lifetime. The opportunity to end the reign of Richard Croker was in her grasp, and she was going to see it through, no matter what cost might fall upon her.

The hit on Frederick was easy. A quick cut to the throat after she slipped into his study, followed by a hasty plant of the forged letters between the judge and Croker's old nemesis, Virgil, and the evidence was perfectly set. Poor Virgil could never have anticipated the level of destruction an angered Richard Croker was capable of, and his biggest mistake was confronting Croker head-on, rather than slowly making his moves in the dark. To seal the deal, the Madame had gone to ridiculous lengths to track down the sleazy bastards Frederick owed and paid off the judge's debts; she'd managed to argue down the cost with the special addition of a night free at The Palace, and with the snap of her fingers, the deal was done. With that out of the way, as well as the notion that Croker had every judge and jury in New York City in his pocket, Virgil would have no defense to counter. He'd be hanged, his blue-blooded wife would return to Chicago, and Croker could tell Edmond that his worries were henceforth futile.

At the thought of Virgil, Esther felt a tinge of disgust in recollection, particularly in his recent manipulation of Captain Bernhardt, who, Esther noted, was not taking Celeste's rejection well in the slightest. She hated to admit it, but it hurt her to see how low Jonathan had fallen from where he'd once been. Esther's staged death seemed to be just the start of his troubles—the long years on the frontier fighting the natives made him cruel-hearted, and he'd placed every ounce of his hopes in marrying Celeste as his redemption. The Captain hadn't planned on Celeste changing with the times, and his hope turned to bitterness, anger, and violence. When Croker mentioned the Captain had been taken under Virgil's wing in the boxing ring, Esther's concern heightened, and she'd followed him a few nights when he'd gone to train. A tiny part of her hoped that perhaps she could find a way to help him, to get him out of whatever hole he'd fallen into, yet she saw that idea was pointless. His sessions with an old boxer named Casper proved to her that the only person who could save Jonathan was himself; it was obvious he placed the blame for Esther's demise and Celeste's rejection on Thomas, though whether he believed that deep down was another story. And he hit the bag hard—so hard that a lot of the other fighters were increasingly intimidated by him. Still, Esther could see through Jonathan's rage: it wasn't the result of him being a violent or savage person. Captain Berhardt was hurting, so much so that the only place he found consolation was in a physical release. That was a feeling Esther understood better than most, and she meant to discuss Jonathan with Thomas the next time they were able to meet.

Whether or not they did meet again would rely solely on if Esther could make it out of Tammany Hall alive.

Somehow, she and Thomas had managed to meet privately just once after Thomas made his introductions amongst the Whyos at The Dry Dollar, and for Esther, it had been the best night of her life. A few days following the attack, Thomas left her a note at the apartment above the barbershop, letting her know an upcoming day when Lucy and William would be out to dinner with old friends, and if she wanted to see him, to meet him in Central Park where they'd first seen each other years ago after being apart so long. While at first she was unsure of the invitation, Esther went nervously on the appointed day, and she was relieved to find Thomas there waiting for her. The moment she was within arm's reach, he pulled her in close and kissed her hard. Then, without a word, they'd made their way out of the park, out of sight, and out of the risk of being caught together by Walsh, Croker, or anyone, for that matter. Thomas stayed a few paces ahead of her, leading their way down Fifth Avenue, and Esther couldn't restrain from rolling her eyes upon noticing the enormous mansion Thomas was heading for.

Incredibly, Thomas managed to sneak Esther through the rear servant's door into his new residence without Tony's knowledge, and once they'd made it upstairs, they didn't waste any time. In the very few minutes they were physically able to untangle themselves—this being, of course, after making up for their respective sexual deprivations from one another—they were able to talk, to make promises, and to even make plans of what would come in the future. Thomas's objectives paralleled Esther's, though they differentiated on one point: his primary goal was to get Esther out of Croker's clutches before he struck Tammany Hall, whereas hers was simply to get rid of Richard Croker. This really did not surprise Esther—she'd been in the trenches for years, a witness to the manipulations Croker could pull off and the power he had as the Grand Sachem. She wanted to at least attempt to get rid of him before he got Grant elected mayor, because in her heart, Esther understood that if he got his candidate in office, Croker would be permanently out of their reach. Thomas fought her on this, swearing he could take Richard out, but not with her at risk in the crosshairs; in the end, she gave in, but her surrender was only a temporary bargain.

Later that night, as Thomas dozed next to her, Esther got out of bed to pour herself a whiskey from across the room, coveting nothing more than to enjoy every second of their reunion. It was strange to her; they had been apart for what seemed like an eternity, and yet, as she watched Thomas dreaming, Esther couldn't believe how right the world felt, or better yet, how much she truly loved him. Nonetheless, after silently collecting her drink from the whiskey decanter, Esther spotted something on Thomas's small bedroom desk, and what caught her eye was startling: it was the name Richard Croker. Written down on a small, torn-off piece of paper in what Esther recognized to be Mary's handwriting, were the words "Richard Croker's safe combination," and below it was a series of numbers...

Esther couldn't believe what she saw. Her gaze shot over to Thomas, who remained breathing deeply, lost in sleep, and once she was convinced he was unaware, she glanced back to the piece of paper. How in the world had Thomas been able to get the combination to Richard Croker's safe? There was no way to forget it now, no way to un-see the one thing they'd been desperately trying to discover for years. Instantly, Esther made the choice. She returned to bed with Thomas for another few hours, savoring her time with him while also being keenly aware that it might be their last.

The loud crack of thunder over her head nearly caused her to jump as a late June storm started to swell in the sky above her. The clouds were dark, building larger by the minute, and a shower would soon follow. Taking a quick left, Esther shot down her usual alley outside Tammany Hall to collect herself, the full weight of what she was about to do heavily resting on her shoulders. Was she crazy for making this attempt alone? Or was everyone so used to protecting her, they'd forgotten this was her fight, too?

Darling, you are being foolish.

The Madame had returned.

"I am not being foolish. This is my purpose and it's the right thing. For everyone."

Stick to the goddamn plan!

Esther hastily grabbed a cigarette from her vest pocket and lit it. "I am not going to let him win. I've been his slave for too long." She took a long drag—her time was precious, and she had to hurry. "It's time he got a taste of his own medicine."

We will get him. Your job is done.

"No, it isn't. I can do this."

You won't fucking make it out of there alive. You know you won't.

She let out a large exhale of smoke and shook her head. "Then so be it."

Little droplets of water fell from the sky, and Esther dropped the cigarette to the ground and put it out with the heel of her boot. With a quick tug of her newsboy cap over her eyes, Esther took off and out of the alley, walking into the street and marching up the front stairs of the Hall. Her plan was not complicated—she had to shoot Croker, get what she could out of the safe, and run, because her life really did depend on it. There was no way to guess what dirt she could uncover in Croker's infamous safe, though it was widely understood amongst his crew that if anything happened to Richard, the contents of that safe were to be destroyed without delay. Ledgers, names, blackmail, money...there were endless possibilities. Esther sought to cut the legs out from Tammany Hall in one swoop by killing the Grand Sachem and stealing Croker's longstanding stash of blackmail. The only downside was the unpredictability of her escape, and who, specifically, Esther would have to face to get out of the Hall in one piece.

Once inside, Esther continued through the lobby, saying hello to Shaughnessy at the front desk as she passed with a small wave. He motioned for her to pass, and she scaled up the staircase to the right of the lobby. Once up two flights and around the corner, she was greeted by the friendly face of Brian, and Esther casually said hello and asked if Richard was in. To her delight, Brian replied that he was, and that he was alone.

"Tread carefully," Brian warned her. "He is absolutely furious right now."

"Why? What is the issue?"

Brian gestured for her to come closer, and she complied.

"Opium raid went sideways," he said softly in her ear, as if afraid of being overheard. "Same Vigilante goon took the whole stash. Richie is losing his mind."

Esther pretended to be stunned by this. "Holy shit."

"I know," Brian sighed. "You're probably the only one that could get him out of this mood. Good luck."

"Thanks, Brian. Hey, actually, would you do me a favor?" A stroke of brilliance struck her, and Esther pulled a large wad of cash out of her pocket. "Let's try and help him forget about it. I don't suppose you could go out and grab us his special brandy? The absurdly expensive one he only drinks when he's had a win—it might lighten his mood."

For a brief second, Brian hesitated. "Well, I don't know if..."

"Don't worry," Esther assured him confidently with her most charming smile. "If I am here, he's in good hands."

Brian nodded, taking the money and his jacket from the stand beside his desk. "All right. Tell him I'll be back in a jiffy."

"Of course."

She watched as Brian turned the corner, lingered for a few seconds to self-consciously feel for the pistol loaded on her right leg, and took a deep breath.

You don't have to do this.

"Yes, yes, I do."

When she opened the door to Croker's office, he stood with his back to her, looking out the window behind his desk, cigar smoking in his hand. Rain had already started to pour, with drops hanging thick onto the slightly fogged glass.

"I don't want to be fucking bothered right now, Brian."

"It's just me, boss," Esther answered in a warm tone. "I wanted to check in after the hit. But Brian told me what happened."

He barely glanced her direction. "Ah. It's you."

"Well, I am your Assistant, sir."

Croker had a puff of his cigar, and Esther could sense he was considering telling her to come back later. Instead, he pointed at the two empty glasses on the side table to her left.

"Pour me one, too, would you?" he requested, sinking down into his chair. "And please, for God's sake, tell me you have some good news."

"Great news," Esther informed him, wandering over to grab the whiskey bottle. "The hit on the judge was clean. Everything is set. The letters were planted in his desk, I made it appear that there had been a tiny scuffle, and left him there to rot." She poured them each a generous amount and proceeded to bring Croker his beverage. "Virgil should be behind bars in days. I'd call that a big victory for you."

"Thank Christ," he declared, taking the glass from her and holding it up to salute. "Cheers to you, my Assistant. For killing two birds with one stone. Literally."

The two clinked glasses, drank, and Esther took a seat across from his desk. "So, what about this raid last night?"

Croker had another long inhale of his cigar. "The whole band of Whyos involved in the transport are dead."

"Dead?!"

"Dead," he reiterated. "Same fucking guy who has been blitzing us from day one. Took the whole damn loot, too. No idea where the opium is, and those Whyo bastards are blaming us for the loss."

Esther again feigned surprise. "He took...all of it? How is that even possible?"

"Hell if I know. It's gone. That was an entire month's supply for the Whyo saloons. This is not going to go over well."

"Has Walsh been in?"

"Of course he has. Son of a bitch had the nerve to threaten me about this happening again. He and Sullivan left to meet O'Reilly at The Dry Dollar about an hour ago. They were at least going to try and pacify Danny and Kitty while the other two boys were off with you. This is going to be a giant pain in my ass." Croker had a sip of whiskey. "Speaking of those two devils, where are Louis and Will?"

In that moment, Esther was very aware she needed to hurry this along. "Louis was heading by to tell the Madame the hit was a success," she lied.

"And Will?"

"Points. I have a feeling he'll be running into the boys at The Dry Dollar shortly."

"How have things been with the three of you?" Croker went on inquisitively.

Esther wasn't quite sure what he was implying. "What do you mean, Richie?"

"Since, well, since Walsh gave it away you were spying on the Madame for me. Are they still feeling betrayed?"

Was this a trap? Esther felt her anxieties standing on end, and she couldn't get a good read on Croker's disposition. She couldn't implicate Louis and Will—she had to make it appear, for their own safety, that Will and Louis were first and foremost working for Croker; otherwise, if Esther failed, Croker would be after them as well as her. However, something felt off about this encounter, like Croker was setting her up for something, and Esther finished her whiskey coolly, wanting to seem at ease.

"Will has gotten better," she fibbed again. "Louis won't discuss anything with me that isn't work related."

Croker's eyes closely considered her. "Walsh told me that he and Will moved into their own place. Is that correct?"

"Yes. Not far from me, but they told me they don't trust me with vital information that isn't known by everyone in our group. Will said they wanted space."

He looked at her for a few seconds before putting out his cigar. "Well, Esther, I apologize for you being outed in such a way. That was never my intention."

"I know. It's just a hazard of what we do, Richie."

"Yes, my dear, it is."

What happened next passed so quickly, Esther was beyond grateful her reflexes processed the situation faster than her brain did. In a flash, Croker opened his desk drawer and pulled out his revolver, pointing it directly at Esther; Croker, on the contrary, was naively heedless of how steadfast of a draw Esther was, and in the same instance he peered at her from behind the barrel of his gun, he found another aiming for him as well.

Esther cocked her pistol, her heart racing. "What the fuck is this, Richie?"

He smirked at her spitefully. "Oh please, Esther. You had to know this day would come. Put the gun down. Brian is outside with the shotgun. You have absolutely nowhere to run if you shoot me."

Her hand remained steady on the trigger. "So, you're going to kill me right after I secure Judge Frederick's fate and get rid of Virgil for you? That's a little fucking inconsiderate, don't you think?"

Croker shrugged. "This is the game. I can't have a loose end like you running around with what you know, particularly since the only two people you were tied to have now cut that cord. What's to stop you from moving against me? Especially with Lord Turner once again on the streets of this city…who is to say you won't go running back to him? I don't need the liability, Esther. Put the gun down, and I promise I'll make it painless."

A jolt of lightening flashed through the room, instantly followed by the boom of thunder.

"What about loyalty, for starters?"

"Esther, there is no loyalty on my part. It's the dog that's loyal. You've been a good mutt, but I cannot afford for you to bite the hand that's been feeding you. The purpose for your presence has been served. If you don't put your pistol down, I will shoot."

Esther reluctantly lowered the gun, yet she left it hot in her hand, evolving her strategy to take on a different angle. "Our deal was that I worked until the end of my sentence, and then I would go free," she hissed angrily. "Was that bullshit from the beginning?"

Croker was unperturbed. "To be honest, I never thought you'd make it through your training. Therefore, yes, you could say it was bullshit from the beginning. You astounded everyone, even Walsh. But this ends today."

Esther swallowed hard—she had to push him a little further. "And what is the Madame going to say?"

"The Madame?" Croker scoffed. "That stupid cunt won't have a connection left to flee if she betrays this organization, and if she does, well…there is a reason I keep Mr. Walsh around, after all."

"Douglas Hiltmore would back her."

Croker laughed aloud. "Hiltmore?!"

"He's devoted to her, and you know it."

Another crack of thunder.

"Douglas is ladder-climbing scum," Croker snapped, his grip on the revolver tightening. "He is still around because I allow it, and because he needs me to survive. If he sides with her, he'll find himself back in prison. Not to mention that bitch of a daughter of his has it coming, too."

Esther felt her hair stand on end, and involuntarily took a step forward. "If you do anything to harm Celeste—"

"Very shortly, my dear, you will no longer have an opinion on anything in this world. Celeste is on my short list of people in this city who need to be watched very carefully. Her behavior mirrors that of the Madame herself, and God knows we only need one of those fucking catastrophes on the loose in this town." Very slowly, Croker got to his feet, though Esther kept steady where she was. "There is nothing to stand in my way, Esther. You've been a vital part of Tammany for years; even before you were born, you were a part of this."

"It doesn't matter if you kill me, Richie, it won't change the fact that there will always be people who want you gone. One day, you'll go too far, and there will be no coming back from it, and this empire you built will crumble."

Croker then cocked his revolver. "Tweeds were meant to be the building blocks of this organization, yet like your father, my dear, your purpose has worn it's welcome." Esther stared at him blankly, and Croker, entertained, went on. "You want to know who you really are, little girl? You are Esther Tweed, the illegitimate daughter of Boss Tweed, the man who originally made this Hall a partner of the Irish and put us on the track where we find Tammany Hall today. If he hadn't pissed off the wrong people, he might still be alive. With your father gone, your mother couldn't support you without her allowance and dropped you at The Palace with the Madame. She died penniless of consumption within six months. You were never like your mother—you are your father's daughter. And now, like Tweed, you are being put down before you get ahead of yourself."

"You lie," Esther spat, trying to stay neutral.

"It's been a real pleasure, Esther. Truly. But it's time to say goodbye."

Suddenly, the words came pouring out of Esther before she could stop herself. "You never owned me, you fucking bastard. I played your pet, but I never gave a lick about you, the Hall, or any of it. I got what I wanted out of this, and if I die, I am taking your ass with me and finishing what I started. And guess what? Brian is not outside to protect you. I sent him to get brandy." She aimed her pistol once more.

"You—"

Esther didn't wait. She pulled the trigger, the bullet hitting Croker precisely over his heart, and for a split second he lingered in the air, his eyes wide in bewilderment. A moment later, he toppled over the leather armchair behind his desk and to the ground. Esther moved over to shoot again, first kicking the gun away from Croker's hand, but as she took aim, she was interrupted when she heard shouts from outside loud enough to cut through the downpour of the storm. Wiping her hand across the clouded glass for a clear view, Esther peeked out of Croker's back window to see a group of Whyos on the steps of Tammany Hall—maybe ten or fifteen of them—with Walsh, Sullivan, and O'Reilly running toward the entrance, presumably following her gunshot. What they were doing there, Esther couldn't be sure, and the need to save her bullets prevented her from unloading into Croker's head. Hastily, Esther holstered her gun and rushed toward the safe, yanking the painting off the wall and carelessly tossing it aside. She dialed the nob with the combination code she'd memorized from Thomas's desk, her fingers moving frantically to turn it.

"Come on…come on…" she said aloud to herself as she patched the last two numbers. "Please, please work…"

With the last rotation, the safe clicked to unlock, and Esther pulled the handle to open it. She had maybe another twenty seconds to grab what she could and leap out the window without being captured or killed on sight—

"Esther!"

Esther halted where she was upon hearing the double load of a shotgun, and she glanced around the open door of the safe to see Brian standing there, pointing the nose at her.

Thunder.

She held up her hands. "Brian, you have to let me go! Please!"

"You have five seconds to make it out the window before I shoot. On the condition you leave everything in the safe. Otherwise, you're dead."

"Brian, I can't—"

Brian fired a shot into the ceiling to let her know he wasn't kidding. "Go. You hear me? I—I always liked you…you were always so nice to me. I don't want to kill you, Esther…just—just go!"

Esther didn't wait to be told again as the echoing voices of Sullivan and O'Reilly came into earshot. Esther whipped around and fired her pistol through the window to break the glass, then leapt out onto the roof of Tammany Hall and into the heavy rainfall, leaving the open safe in her wake.

Within seconds, she was drenched. A chorus of profanity, shouts, and jeers clamored up the walls of the building as Esther scrambled over to the drain pipe in the corner, planning to climb to the top. She took a flying leap and hit the pipe halfway up to the next floor, and as she pulled herself higher, she slipped here and there from the slick wet of the metal. Esther could hear the Whyos shouting up to Walsh in the window where Esther was headed, causing her to move faster. Once she'd scaled her way up two floors and onto the roof, Esther raced to the fire escape and acrobatically swung down as fast as she possibly could, dropping from one set of stairs to the next until her feet hit the alleyway. In that second, Walsh came flying around the corner to her left, and Esther panicked—there was only one way to go, and she wasn't sure where this route would take her. She had no choice. Esther took off.

Her mind was racing as she ran, her lungs burning as she sucked in air. Croker had to be dead. Nothing had gone as expected, but that didn't matter anymore—there were a dozen gang members, Walsh, Sullivan, and O'Reilly on her tail, and they knew these streets just as well as Esther did. What was worse was the weight of her clothes and the puddles in the oversaturated streets, splashing with every stride and making it impossible for Esther to slip away. In a full-out sprint, Esther rapidly made her way north without any clue as to where she would run and hide, but if she didn't disappear soon, there was no way she'd get through the night alive. What were all those Whyos doing at Tammany Hall?!

They were there to try and scare Croker. They are furious about the opium raid. Walsh wanted to assert his power with the gang.

Of course. They'd all gotten drunk at The Dry Dollar and made Sullivan and O'Reilly take them back to the Hall to tell Croker something had to be done. And instead, Esther was in severe trouble.

Trekking up the alleyways of the Bowery, Esther didn't let up on her speed, dodging all sorts of garbage and rubbish covering the slick cobblestone road beneath her. Her clothes had become heavily weighted from the rainfall, exhausting her muscles faster than she would have liked. When Esther had a chance, she squinted over her left shoulder, and her stomach dropped. On her tail not more than a half block away, she could spot Walsh barreling closer and closer to her through the storm, and every few feet, he was yelling out the Whyo call to keep members in hot pursuit of Esther, managing to attract members who weren't initially on the chase to join. It meant only one thing: this chase was escalating, and the Whyos wouldn't stop until Esther was dead.

She pushed harder, leaping over a wagon here, knocking over a few barrels at another turn to delay Walsh and the others as she passed, yet nothing gave her the advantage of being out of view long enough to slip away. If she stopped to fight Walsh one on one, she would lose, that much was certain—he'd nearly killed her before, and this time, Louis and Will wouldn't be there to back her up as the offensive escalated. Esther had to keep running. On foot was the only possibility she had of surviving, and with Walsh unable to feel pain, she began to fret that her fate was already sealed.

Out of nowhere, the rain ceased, and Esther was blindsided by a blow that felt like an oncoming train. Whoever it was tackled her from the side and must have been waiting to hear them coming. Esther managed to remember her training, and despite hitting the ground with a thud and feeling two of her ribs crack, she managed to swiftly roll back onto her feet and stand. A few feet from her was Paulo, her assailant, who looked worse for wear than Esther, with his arm still wrapped up tight and his face healing from old bruises; nevertheless, it took just seconds for Esther to realize why he'd picked there. Paulo blocked one route of escape, Walsh the other, and Esther's third and final option was instantly eliminated as she spotted the familiar figures of Danny and Kitty walking her way, Kitty with a blade drawn and Danny with a club in his clutches. Sullivan and O'Reilly were nowhere to be seen, and Esther assumed they stayed back at Tammany Hall. Trying to remain composed, Esther slid her hands into her pockets and slipped on her brass knuckles—a gun at this range with so many incoming attackers would be pointless. Like a steady stream, Whyos started to appear behind the others, all calling out "Whyo!" every couple of seconds. Zayn, Lonny, Mac, Silver, Acker, Kit, Teeny, Mugs—in no time at all, Esther was cornered by just over twenty Whyos, every single one of them armed, and every single one there for one purpose and one purpose only.

Once they'd gathered, all eyes were on Esther, and Walsh motioned to the others to stay where they were and moved closer, halting when he and Esther were a few feet apart. He grinned that sinister grin that he wore in times like these, when he was about to enjoy killing someone he despised. There was a blade in his hand.

"Your day of reckoning is here, Esther," he uttered smugly.

She spat at his feet. "Fuck you, Walsh." With conviction, Esther pulled her hands out of her pockets, brass knuckles yearning for blood.

"You left just as the party started," he carried on. "Will and Samuel arrived just after we did, which is why Mr. O'Reilly and Mr. Sullivan are not present for this."

"Present for what? My lynching?" Esther barked at him.

Walsh's face grew threatening. "Teal and the others are dead, thanks to you, and our Whyo brothers are not going to take this lying down. They got killed in that opium raid last week...a delivery known only by two people other than us: yourself and Richard Croker. Now, I know Croker didn't tell a soul—his livelihood, like ours, depends on the opium trade coming in. You were the one that ratted the Whyos out, weren't you, Esther?"

The picture was clearer now. "That's why the Whyos went to the Hall. You wanted to try and convince Croker I'd snitched on the opium deal."

"We have a proposition for you, Esther." Danny took a step toward them, and Esther noticed a brief wave of repugnance cross Walsh's countenance at being interrupted.

"And what's that, Danny?"

"You tell us who this fuckin' son of a bitch is causin' all these problems, and we'll let you go free, as long as you leave the city and don't come back."

"You'll let me go free if I admit to ratting on you?"

"Sure as shit."

Esther gritted her teeth. "I may not be a Whyo, but I sure as hell am no rat."

"Fuckin' liar!" Kitty shouted at her.

Esther glowered at Kitty, then turned back to Danny. "You know he's going to kill you, Danny," she asserted firmly.

No one moved a muscle, and Walsh answered for him sardonically, "Now, why would I do a thing like that?"

Danny, however, continued to hold eye contact with Esther. "Won' happen."

"It will, and you know it," she retorted. "The first chance he gets, he's going to slit your fucking throat. And Kitty won't say a goddamned word to stop it. Now, how does that feel for betrayal?"

The color drained from Danny's cheeks, and he looked at Walsh, who was scowling at Esther. "I think the negotiation has come to a close."

Instantly, the order was known. Every Whyo prepared themselves to attack Esther on command, and Walsh, in his usual fashion, moved aside to survey the unfolding carnage—or rather, let Esther tire herself out before he came in to finish the job. Esther clenched her fists tight around the brass, ready to fight until she couldn't fight anymore, when overhead something caught her eye. Her eyes tracked toward the sky, where she saw a bird circling the spot where they stood in the breaking storm clouds, and in a hastened dive, the bird landed on the side of the building overhead as if surveying what was happening below.

Only it wasn't just any bird. It was a falcon.

"Last chance, Esther," Danny offered, this time in a more pleading tone.

"I tried to warn you, Danny." She rolled her shoulders back. "I would rather die than ever surrender to the lunatic."

"Who wants the first piece?" Walsh hollered, offering Esther up.

Rather than respond, Mac and Lonny moved to the front of the pack, Mac with a blade drawn and Lonny with a club twisting gleefully in his hand. Both were drunk fools who spent every dime of their hard-earned money at The Dry Dollar on booze and whores, making them slower than the rest. They blamed her for the Vigi-

315

lante breaking into their bar and killing Whyos on the streets, and Lonny, like Kitty, was never shy to tell the others how much he despised Esther's presence in the gang. Single-handedly, Esther could take these two buffoons out in about ten seconds, and more than likely without breaking a sweat. Her only predicament was if they swarmed, which Whyos were known to do once they'd made an attempt to let a few members earn more menacing reputations. For the first time, though, she happily realized she wouldn't have to take on the Whyos alone.

Esther sneered, waiting for it.

Glass shattered overhead, and every Whyos' gaze whipped above to see what had happened. Conversely, Esther merely covered her face and eyes from the falling glass with her forearm, then heard a loud thud beside her as Thomas leaped down from the broken window.

"You had to go alone, didn't you?" he murmured so only Esther could hear.

She peered over at him, expecting a look of annoyance; instead, she could sense he was fighting off an amused smile.

"Holy hell!" Danny yelled, eyes wide upon realizing that the Vigilante was now standing right in front of them.

"Well, isn't this a lovely surprise," Walsh spat. "Lonny, Mac, you've wanted your revenge—well, here's two for the price of one."

Uncertain at first, Walsh's words snapped Lonny and Mac to the present, and once again, they centered in on the gang.

"Well, this should be fun," Thomas quipped.

Esther's heart was pounding in her chest from the anticipation of the fight and also in having Thomas fighting by her side. They'd never sparred together, never shared training tactics, and by no means had any strategy to get through the next fifteen minutes, yet Esther's gut told her she didn't need to worry. She was well aware of what she was capable of, and in Thomas's case, she'd witnessed firsthand the carnage he left in his wake with the Whyos. It felt as if everything in her life had led to this moment, to her and Thomas unified in battle against the worst criminals in New York City. If they could kill Walsh and Croker in one afternoon, they would have managed to win the war they'd been fighting for too long. And that final thought kicked Esther's adrenaline into overdrive.

Lonny went for Esther, Mac for Thomas, and overhead, as if on cue, Athena let out a paralyzing screech. This gave Thomas and Esther the upper hand on the attack, and while Lonny wound up to take a swing at Esther with his club, she dropped low when they were only a few feet apart, spinning to kick Lonny's feet out from under him. Lonny hit the ground hard on his side as Esther rose from a stooped position and, with her left foot, cracked him across the face, sending him reeling onto his back. With her adversary completely defenseless, Esther went in to silence him and immediately crouched down, punching him once, twice, three times in the face until Lonny no longer twitched. Her brass knuckle was dripping with blood as she took a receding step, not caring whether or not Lonny still breathed.

To her right lay Mac, his own blade sticking in the side of his neck with blood pouring out and covering the street underneath him. Thomas was standing just a few feet away, barely ruffled from whatever had ensued between the two.

"Three moves?" she asked.

He sniggered. "Two."

"Dammit."

In a rush, three more Whyos ran to take on Thomas and Esther—Zayn, Silver, and Acker. Zayn and Silver went straight for Thomas, while Acker's target was Esther. Before she could make a move, Acker pulled a revolver from his front jacket pocket. She froze as he pulled the hammer back to fire, realizing too late he was beyond her reach, and out of the blue, she heard Athena's cry as the bird dove from her perch. In under a second, Athena plunged down and snatched the revolver clean out of Acker's hand, then returned to her post after a few circles overhead. She was taunting Acker with his own weapon. The distraction proved to be an advantage for Esther, who attacked Acker with an immense amount of ferocity. Her first hit, a hard jab across his jaw with her left brass knuckle, nearly knocked every one of his teeth clean out. Unlike Lonny, Acker didn't concede, and came back with a hook directly into Esther's stomach, something she should have counteracted but didn't anticipate; he was left-handed, and she'd forgotten. With speed, Esther clutched each of her hands onto Acker's shoulders tightly, and in turn, thrust her leg up to knee him directly into his groin. Stumbling back slightly, Acker was attempting to shake off the pain and keep a level head, yet those efforts were fruitless. Esther took two quick paces and leapt up into a roundhouse kick, her right foot connecting with Acker's right temple and sending him to the ground, unconscious.

Over her shoulder, Esther watched the last of Thomas silencing Zayn, whom Thomas quashed with a blow to the back of Zayn's head with the Griswold handle. A little off to their right lay Silver, unconscious or dead, blood coming out of his nose and leg broken horribly to the side. Stepping over Zayn, Thomas leisurely resumed his assault position on Esther's right while he flipped the Griswold in his hand and holstered it inside his jacket.

"Well, this has been extremely entertaining for me to witness," Walsh remarked sarcastically as the pack of remaining Whyos started to close in on Esther and Thomas. "But play time is over. Kitty? You and Danny put the Assistant down. The rest of you, you take care of the other one. Neither of them is leaving here alive."

Thomas glanced at Esther, and she nodded just as a group of six Whyos came after them. With Kitty leading the pack, Kitty and Danny headed for Esther, while Vonn, Marsh, Jackson, and Hal surrounded Thomas. Screaming crazily, Kitty made a move to tackle Esther. In turn, she made a quick grab for Kitty's hair with her left hand and Kitty's upper arm with her right, evading Kitty's clutches by throwing her directly into the brick building to Esther's left. Toppling to the ground, Kitty groaned, and she didn't get up. Esther was grateful—she'd kicked the shit out of Kitty more than enough times. Contrariwise, it was Danny she worried about—as far as hand to hand combat went, Esther was the better fighter, but Danny was relentless, and to Esther's chagrin, he was also damn good with a blade. Drawing near, Danny had his dagger out and ready.

"Danny, I don't want to kill you."

He hesitated. "If I don't take you out, someone else will."

"No, they won't. Look behind me."

Thomas was nearly done beating the hell out of Jackson and Vonn as Hal tried to drag himself away from the onslaught. The body of what used to be Marsh was discarded in their wake, with his own club decorated with rusty nails sticking into his skull.

"We are the ones walking away from this, not the Whyos," Esther whispered to Danny. "This isn't a battle you'll win, Danny."

"Danny!" Kitty bellowed from the ground through bloody teeth. "Fuckin' kill her!"

Esther saw she'd lost him, and Danny didn't say another word. With a hasty two steps, he made his first swipe left and then right with the knife directly at Esther's waist, cutting her shirt and missing her by less than an inch. Lunging, he pushed the blade in an attempt to make a stab at her, yet with his arm outstretched, Esther was able to clutch onto his right wrist and spin around, cracking Danny in the nose with her left elbow. The blade fell to the ground, but Danny held his composure and made an ill-advised endeavor at getting Esther in a chokehold. Esther grabbed onto the arm around her neck and leaned backwards into it briefly, her feet coming off the ground. Then, with all her strength and bodyweight leveraged, Esther thrust herself downward and returned to her feet, yanking Danny over her head and throwing him onto the ground like a sack of flour. This knocked the breath clean out of him, and Esther, not wanting to kill Danny, struck one hard blow across his cheek with her brass knuckles.

She squatted down, pretending to check his pulse, and said inaudibly just for Danny, "Stay the fuck down."

To her right, Kitty was trying to stand against the brick wall, and in an identical fashion to Danny, Esther delivered Kitty a blow just across the face, knocking her out completely and once more to the cobblestone street.

Before Esther and Thomas could unite in their front, another wave of Whyos hit, this time the six members trapping each of them on opposite sides.

"Friend!" Esther yelled out in warning, not wanting to give Thomas's identity away. Thomas had just snapped Jackson's neck as he rotated around to see the approaching assault. Instantaneously, the Griswold was drawn, and with exact precision, Thomas took down Andy, Kit, and Turtle with bullets right between the eyes. Prior to getting another shot off, Paulo was on Thomas, and he had to cease fire to deflect a hook aimed at his head—aside from her and Strat, Paulo was the best fighter the Whyos had, and she was certain he wanted nothing more than to kill Thomas after their encounter at The Dry Dollar. Barry and Zeke were rushing over to help Paulo, forgetting or choosing to ignore Esther for the time being in order to take Thomas down. Esther seized the opportunity happily. While Paulo and Thomas delivered blows to one another, Esther sprinted up behind Zeke and leapt up his back, landing on his shoulders with his head between her legs. She made a fist with her right hand and brought it down with such force, she heard Zeke's skull break, and he fell to his knees. With a release of her thighs, Zeke collapsed to the ground face first, a dribble of blood coming from his head.

Suddenly, Barry was on her, and Esther found she had been caught off guard. Tackling her to the ground, Barry, who had a good hundred pounds on Esther, began to beat her with his fists, and Esther struggled to get free or maneuver out of being pinned.

That's when she heard it.

Athena again shrieked, and in a flurry of feathers, Barry's fists stopped pummeling Esther and he screamed out in agony. Esther rolled out and away from under Barry, and her eyes grew wide when she saw the damage done by Athena: her talon had sliced perfectly across Barry's back and the wound was bleeding profusely, his arms flailing wildly in pain as he ran away as fast as his legs could carry him. In his place charged Sanders, Ned, Teeny, and Mugs, all again heading for Thomas, who was now down to finishing off Andy. Esther got to her feet and was about to go help when she heard a gasp from over her shoulder. Circling to make sure she wasn't caught off-guard again, Esther watched helplessly just as Walsh tore his knife across Danny's throat, staring at her with satisfaction while he did it.

"You son of a bitch," Esther snarled. She couldn't do anything other than be a bystander as Danny bled out, coughing violently for a few seconds while he clutched at his neck in a vain attempt to stop the bleeding.

"You were right," Walsh told her. "I was going to kill him. And now, for bringing that Vigilante here and killing so many of my men, I am going to kill you, too."

Esther's grip on her brass knuckles strengthened. "Fuck you."

She and Walsh shot at each other in a rage, Esther having the lead with being on her feet when they simultaneously charged. Striking first, Esther got a hit through and into Walsh's chest just before he got his own jab in with a solid hit to her right temple. The blow made Esther blink hard, but it also assisted her in winding up her left hook, and she pummeled Walsh in the ribs four times until Walsh seized her and ferociously launched her aside. The force with which he was able to handle Esther unnerved her, although it didn't deter her from her assault. She baited him in and batted away one punch, then another, and with his left arm fully extended after she barely dodged a jab to her jaw, Esther made her move.

Staying low, Esther tucked herself under Walsh's left arm and used his own half-bent leg as a mounting block, hoisting her body up onto his back. Similarly to how she'd trapped Zeke, Esther planned to lock Walsh's head between her legs and not stop hammering down on him until he was utterly lifeless. Right as she was getting her left leg onto Walsh's shoulder, Esther recognized he had grasped onto her left forearm with his free right hand, and his grip was like steel, digging his fingers down to her bones. She commenced beating his hand again and again, seriously hurting her own arm in the process, but Walsh did not let up. In one absurdly strong yank, Walsh managed to dislocate Esther's shoulder from the socket, and she let out a cry of pain. With her left arm rendered useless, Esther struggled to stay on top of Walsh, getting one blow in as he managed to pull her off of his shoulders and throw her down at his feet. He kicked her in her stomach over and over, and Esther could taste the blood leaking up into her mouth. To add insult to injury, Walsh saved his final kick for Esther's face; the impact broke her nose instantly, and it didn't stop there. Next came a barrage of punches and strikes, and Walsh's hits were done with such strength and viciousness, Esther felt as if she'd been trampled by an entire herd of horses, recoiling as best she could to protect herself. Then, with Esther incapacitated, Walsh yanked his dagger out from the scabbard on his hip as he stood over her.

"I've been looking forward to this for quite some time," he confessed.

Kneeling at Esther's side, he propped her up as she fought savagely with her right arm to get free of his clutches. Nevertheless, Walsh was able to bring her in just enough to get the knife held firmly at her jugular.

"Time to be executed, Esther."

"Put the knife down, Walsh!"

Esther's blurred gaze went to Thomas only five feet from them, Griswold drawn and aimed at Walsh.

Walsh smiled strangely at Thomas. "Do we know each other?"

"We do now. Put the knife down."

Walsh rose up to stand, somehow bringing Esther up with him as if she weighed nothing whatsoever. "You are familiar to me, sir, though sadly, I am not as heavily armed as you are. Do you want to wager whether I could slit Esther's throat before you could get to me? I'm not a gambling man, but I would bet I'd win. And let's face it, even if you are a dead shot, those Griswolds are so pesky and un-reliable. Would you ever forgive yourself if the gun misfired and it was you who killed this young woman? The fact that she matters so greatly to you is extremely interesting to me."

Esther's useless left arm was on fire from the shoulder down. "Walsh, you're not leaving here alive. We've got you."

"Wrong."

Kitty's voice took all three of them by surprise. She remained laying on the ground, yet now she held a pocket pistol aimed at Thomas.

Walsh grinned. "There's a new arrangement," Walsh informed Thomas. "We walk, and you walk, on to fight another day. You'll get your chance. I don't plan on leaving New York City anytime soon, and I take it you are by no means leaving either." An enlightened expression instantly struck Walsh's face. "It—it cannot be."

Thomas's eyes went to Esther's for a brief second, then returned to her captor. "No one will believe you, Walsh."

With a haunting glimmer in his eyes, Walsh let out a chortle. "Well, well, well. If it isn't Lord Thomas Turner of Amberleigh, all dressed up to join the circus!"

If Thomas had a tell of any kind, he didn't show it, and Esther was amazed at how poised he stayed. "I could still take you out, Walsh."

"And lose your long-lost love? No, I do not believe so, Lord Turner. You would shoot me, Kitty would shoot you, followed closely by Miss Tweed here, and then on my orders, she would have the Whyos destroy The Palace, kill the Madame, and perhaps after that your family up on Fifth Avenue."

Kitty loudly began to call aloud. "Whyo! Whyo! Whyo!"

"They're coming back now," Walsh went on. "You have only a few seconds to make this choice. I hope it is not the wrong one, Lord Turner."

Thomas's eyes were on Esther. "How good a shot is she?"

"She…she's…good," Esther admitted through a slight gasp of breath.

Thomas did not delay. "I'll lower if she does."

Walsh nodded to Kitty, and Esther watched her lower the pistol. Thomas, in turn, did the same, and Walsh tossed Esther out in front of him. She stumbled on the drenched cobblestone, tripping onto her knees, then scrambled up and to Thomas, who was rushing toward her to grab her. In the meantime, Kitty leapt up and clambered to Walsh just as two Whyos came running down the alley behind them.

Rapidly, Thomas threw Esther onto his back, ignoring her cries of pain as she wrapped her good arm around his neck, and Thomas sprinted the opposite direction of the incoming Whyos. Esther tried to stay present, watching their tail to be certain there were no followers.

"We are going to have to hide out until dark," Thomas huffed with heavy breath, running north and away from trouble. "I have a place I can take you until then, but then we need to come up with a plan." Thomas bolted out of the alleyway and into the street, crossing over the road and nearly being run over by a carriage. "It's only a few more blocks, so hang on."

Esther stayed quiet and focused all her energy on not falling off of Thomas's back. Her head bobbed along as she strained to hold onto consciousness, her abdomen and lungs screaming in pain along with her shoulder. It was then Esther grasped that her broken nose was bleeding so badly, the back of Thomas's shirt was completely soaked in her blood.

"Thomas," she murmured.

"What? What is it?" he panted through breaths.

"I killed him, Thomas. I actually did it…I killed…Croker…"

Everything went dark.

The smell of blood sausage and stale beer filled Esther's nostrils, so pungent she knew it must be her reason for waking. Esther's entire body was in excruciating pain, and with a long groan, her eyelids fluttered open. For a few seconds, her gaze had to adjust, but when everything at last started to focus, she was able to assess the bodily damage done, and it wasn't pretty. Her left arm was in a sling, and Esther was happy to feel she did have some control over it again, meaning while she was unconscious, Thomas must have gotten her arm back into the socket. Her torso was wrapped tightly in bandages, and with a shaking hand, Esther cautiously and softly touched her nose. To her relief, it had also been fixed and straightened, yet the moment her fingers came in contact with her septum, tears instantly commenced streaming down her face.

Taking in her surroundings, Esther realized she was laying in someone's bed, in a change of men's clothes that were far too large for her and stank of hops. There wasn't much to the little room: a small side table by the bed with a bowl of water to wash up, a rope rug on the wood floor, a small chair and desk in the corner, and a trunk at the end of the bed, full of more hop-smelling clothes, Esther supposed. She listened, unable to hear anything, and decided to sit up and investigate. Upon moving not so much as an inch, the brass bed frame let out an enormously loud squeak, and within seconds, Esther heard footsteps approaching the closed door in front of her.

When it swung open, Thomas stood there.

"Es? You awake?" he whispered gently, not wanting to wake her if she was still asleep.

"Yeah, barely."

Thomas strolled over to the bed and helped her sit upright. "You got the shit beat out of you. I couldn't believe more of your ribs weren't broken. Your nose should stop swelling in a few days."

Esther noticed he'd washed the soot from his eyes and changed his clothes, though he had taken some hits himself. There was a deep, bloody bruise under his left eye, a few tiny cuts here and there along his cheek, and as she grabbed for his upper right arm, he flinched ever so slightly.

"We both got a tad beat up, I think," she teased, and unable to stop herself, Esther leaned over and kissed Thomas. Her nose screamed in agony, but she ignored it.

After a time, Thomas pulled away. "Listen, we have to get a plan together here. We aren't out of the woods yet."

"I know, I'm sorry, I just had to."

Thomas managed to smile. "I didn't say it wasn't welcome. But…" His mood went from happy to solemn. "Es, there is a manhunt out for you right now. What the hell were you thinking?! The plan was set and we were all going to make it work!"

Esther felt her cheeks flush with frustration. "So what, I go free and stay on the run with Will and Louis and put everyone else here in danger? I saw the chance to end this charade, Thomas, and I took it. You would have done the same thing."

"We should have done it together!"

"No, we shouldn't have." Esther was defensive now. "You don't know the ins and outs of those people and that place like I do, Thomas. I wanted to save everyone and get the Madame what she needed to get rid of Croker, and the Whyos fucked it up."

"You didn't even tell me you took the combination, or hint that you were considering something like this!"

"Because you wouldn't have let me do it!" she argued hotly. "At the very least, I shot that son of a bitch and took down some Whyos with him. I was willing to die trying. I wasn't going to ask that of anybody else, especially you."

She could sense he was trying to pacify the situation and put his temper aside. "Fine. It's done, and we're here, and that's all there is to it. But I swear to God, Es, you don't pull shit like this again unless I am with you. This isn't a one-man show for you anymore, and it never should have been in the first place. You aren't fighting alone."

Like Thomas, Esther's anger swiftly dissipated, and she found herself overcome with gratitude at being with him, for finally having Thomas by her side.

With a sigh, she nodded. "I know."

Esther fell into him, and Thomas wrapped his arms around her tight.

He kissed the top of her head. "We have very few places we can hide you. Lawrence is already putting himself at risk having us stay here for a few hours."

Esther's jaw dropped, and she pushed back from him in surprise. "Lawrence, as in your old master, Lawrence?"

"Yes. You should have seen the look on his face when he saw you. He wanted to march down to Tammany Hall and start a riot."

"Jesus Christ," Esther muttered. "Okay, let me think. Celeste and the Madame originally made plans for me to hide out at Hotel St. Stephen. If we can get me to Celeste, I think I should be safe."

"Do you think they'll be at The Palace?"

"I have no doubt."

"Right. I will head to The Palace and get some backup to help me transport you."

"Get Ashleigh," Esther said. "He's the new Louis."

"Consider it done. I'll try to be back within the hour." Thomas paused, crestfallen. "There is something I need to tell you."

"What is it, Thomas?"

He didn't want to say, that much was evident. "Just promise me you won't do anything too rash, all right?"

Her eyes narrowed. "How bad is it?"

"Richard Croker is alive."

Esther's whole body tensed. "But that's...that's impossible... Thomas, I shot him!"

"I know you did," he sighed. "The bullet went clean through, and Brian managed to have Will get his surgeon there in time to stop him from bleeding to death."

"How in the hell did you find this out?"

"Because I'm good at being invisible."

Esther didn't want to despair, but very suddenly, her sacrifice felt incredibly foolish.

"Goddammit." She could feel her throat choking up and she swallowed it down, not letting emotion get the better of her. "I didn't shoot him a second time because I thought I would need the bullets with the fucking Whyos, and Brian ambushed me with the shotgun."

Thomas was sympathetic. "I knew you would be upset."

"Of course I'm fucking upset! Why aren't you more upset?!"

"Because it's done and we can't change it, that's why." Thomas reached up and caressed her cheek. "Es, the relationship between the Whyos and Tammany Hall is in tatters. This is something that will have serious consequences for their organizations if they end up on opposing sides. Plus, we got you out, and I don't really give a shit about much else."

Thomas's words did not put her at ease, and yet she recalled the one thing from the afternoon that could prove to be useful. "Tommy...wait."

"What?"

She clenched her eyes shut, remembering as clearly as she could. "I did get something, something from the safe."

Thomas was ecstatic. "What? Where? I searched your pockets—"

"No, not an object." Esther pointed towards her eyes. "I saw

328

something, and the reason why it stuck out was because it was a list of names, with every name crossed off except the bottom two."

"A list of names?" He thought on it. "Well, hell, Es, that could be for any kind of reason."

"I know. The catch is that the Judge Frederick was on that list." Esther looked into his eyes. "I think it was a hit list of people who know too much, and who Croker wants gone."

"Well, what were the names?"

"It was a long list, Thomas, with almost every name crossed out except the bottom two. The last name was Patrick McCann...I have absolutely no idea who he is or how he is relevant to Richie or the Hall. The other was a name I know all too well: Samwell Priestly. He's a reporter for *The New York Times*, and he wants to destroy Tammany Hall. His name was directly under Judge Frederick, and last was McCann. And Thomas, Mary's name was on that list, too."

His nostrils flared. "Was it crossed off?"

"Yes."

Relief fell over him. "Well, let me take this to the Madame for now, and see if she has any idea who McCann might be. I'll do some digging on Priestly and figure out just what he's been up to with the Hall."

"Right. I think that's a good place to start. But what am I going to do? I can't hide at St. Stephen's forever, and even if Sally could get me out of the city, there's going to be a fucking bounty on my head."

Thomas was pensive. "Let me work on that. For the time being, you'll stay at the hotel." Thomas then took her hands in his. "You have to listen to me, though. You cannot be seen outside, no matter what happens. The best thing we have going right now is that no one has any idea where you might be, or how bad your wounds are from Walsh. You could be dead, for all the Hall knows. But unless it is me, the Madame, or Louis, you do not take one step outside. Got it?"

Esther squeezed his hands. "Got it."

Thomas pulled her in and kissed her until a knock came from the door.

"Tommy? You guys all right?"

"Yeah, Lawrence!" Thomas responded, pulling away from Esther. "Hold on for just a moment."

Quickly, Thomas got to his feet. "I'll be back in an hour. We'll get you to Celeste's hotel. Just stay here with Lawrence. He's going to want to shove sausage and beer into you until you want to burst."

Esther was about to let out a small chuckle and caught herself, her abdomen aching. "Don't make me laugh—it hurts too much."

Thomas reached out and helped her to stand. "Whatever you do, do not go outside."

"Again, Thomas, I am not going outside. I can barely move around without wanting to scream. A beer and some food will do just fine."

"Good. Lawrence? Come in!"

Lawrence came bounding in, and Esther couldn't believe that Thomas's old blacksmithing master was standing in front of her.

"How are ya, Esther? Barely recognized you without your hair!" He winked. "Still pretty as ever, though." Without warning, he shoved a beer stein into her good hand. "Have a little of my homemade pilsner. That ought to help with the pain, and then we can get some food in ya!"

Esther took a large gulp. "I could use a drink after a day like today."

When Thomas had gone, and after a full German dinner with multiple steins of pilsner, Lawrence snored loudly from his armchair in the corner of his living room while Esther smoked a cigarette at the kitchen table. Everything hurt, and her body was mangled and bruised from the beating Walsh gave her, but the part that was unsettling to Esther was something she hadn't told Thomas—ot because she felt the impulse to lie to save her own skin or to try and protect him, but because for the first time, she understood just what she was to Richard Croker. And though she knew from her first day out of the Tombs what her purpose was in the war, Esther had never fully realized how right the Madame had been about him.

Because just underneath Judge Frederick's name on Croker's list, above Priestly's, was Esther Tweed's, and it had already been callously crossed out.

Samuel Ellis had been sitting in the Madame's office at The Palace for hours, praying that any minute, someone with answers might walk through the door. What they'd heard only came from the rumors Will managed to bring back after hanging around Tammany Hall for the afternoon and evening: Richard Croker had been shot by Esther and miraculously survived. She'd attempted to break into the safe at Tammany Hall but was apprehended, and then once cornered by Whyos, she and a man Samuel assumed had to be Thomas took out roughly twenty Whyos, disappearing in the aftermath. It was an incredible feat, but there was one more rumor he was hoping was false, and that was the rumor that Walsh had killed Esther.

In a flurry, Samuel and Will arrived at Tammany Hall just as Esther went on the lam with the Whyos close on her tail. Consequently, Will was sent to get his proven-to-be-reliable negro doctor from Chinatown while Samuel had to put together an official police report on the incident. For the duration of Samuel's stay at the Hall, Richard had been tamed by the loss of blood, and Sullivan ordered Ellis and Will to head to The Palace to see if Esther showed up there, with a report back sometime after midnight. Walsh hadn't come into Tammany either, and due to the lack of information at hand, Ellis had no choice except to do as he was told, and he and

Will made their way back north to see if the Madame had heard anything from Thomas.

She hadn't.

As they waited, they killed one glass of whiskey after the other, everyone silent in their impatience. The Madame sat behind her desk, feet propped up on the top, her mind somewhere else entirely. Louis and Will were by the vacant fireplace, every once in a while whispering urgently back and forth, then disintegrating once again into speechlessness. Ashleigh would pop in and out from time to time, patrolling the locked-down Palace like a loyal watchdog, and Celeste and her father sat across from each other on the Madame's loveseats, two bottles of wine deep. Samuel hadn't moved from the chair opposite the Madame's desk, worrying over her sanity if Esther had indeed been killed, or worse, what was to come in the repercussions of an attempted assassination of the Grand Sachem of Tammany Hall.

Footsteps on the main stair caused them all to perk up in the same moment, and as everyone's attention flew to the door to the Madame's office, Thomas hurriedly trooped inside, George and Ashleigh right behind him.

The Madame was already on her feet. "Is she alive?!"

Thomas glimpsed at George, who bolted the doors shut behind them.

"Yes, she's alive," Thomas primed them. "I need to get her to Celeste's hotel undetected. Can we do that?"

"I have the carriage out back!" Celeste cried. "Just tell me where to go."

"It is much too dangerous for you to go, darling," the Madame disallowed.

"Esther told me to bring Ashleigh with me," Thomas added, turning towards him.

Ashleigh was downright flabbergasted by this. "She said…to bring me?"

Samuel gazed at the Madame, who nodded.

"That's a solid plan. What about your lot across the park?" Ellis asked.

"They're fine for now," Louis jumped in. "Tony has them locked down."

Thomas and Louis exchanged a glance that Samuel couldn't read, though clearly there was something unspoken he was unaware of.

The Madame marched around her desk, whiskey still in hand. "Louis, Will, and Samuel will need to be heading back to Tammany sooner rather than later with news that Esther more than likely died of her wounds…or at least try and perpetuate that rumor as best you fucking can. George needs to stay here to keep an eye on The Palace. He, Claire, and I can keep it safe in case I am blamed for this. Douglas, you and Celeste need to head downtown to St Stephen to make sure everything is ready to go for Esther's arrival." Her attention went to Thomas. "The minute she is safe and off the goddamn streets, you get your ass back here to tell me what the fuck happened today."

"Yes, Madame," Thomas agreed, "but there's two things you need to know first. And probably for the best you and you alone know."

She studied him closely. "Everyone out, except Samuel and Thomas. Will and Louis, it's better you arrive separately from Detective Ellis anyhow. Ashleigh, you will wait downstairs for Thomas."

Without another word, everyone departed from the Madame's office. Thomas went over to the drink cart and poured himself a whiskey, while Samuel looked over at the Madame curiously.

"Why did you want me to stay?"

She didn't respond, and she didn't have to—he could read it in her face. He wasn't a middleman anymore; he was one of them.

"Thomas, what is it?" she pressed. "Time is of the essence here."

Thomas rotated around. "I think I earned a whiskey today." He took a gulp of the drink he held, then went on, "Do you know of a man named Patrick McCann?"

The Madame was pensive for a moment. "Not off the top of my head."

"We need to find him. He and Priestly are ostensibly on some kind of hit list Esther found in Croker's safe."

"How do you know it was a hit list?" Samuel asked him, throwing back the rest of his own whiskey.

"Because Judge Frederick's name was on that list, and crossed off. Mary's, too."

"Well, Priestly would make sense," Ellis observed. "Croker hates that bastard and how he's always trying to undermine the Hall."

"McCann...McCann...shit, I can't seem to remember. I'll get Louis on it." The Madame set her empty glass down on her desk and crossed her arms over her chest. "What is the other issue?"

"It's about Esther."

The Madame's countenance grew concerned. "Is she...?"

"She'll recover, Madame. It's not that. It's just something I overheard Walsh say today that caught my attention. Something I thought you should hear from me, considering your own...past."

Samuel glanced at the Madame, who was just as confused as he was.

"What is it, Thomas?" she queried.

Thomas swirled the lingering whiskey in his glass for a second, tentatively. "Walsh called her Miss Tweed."

For what felt like an eternity, no one said a word.

"It can't be possible," Samuel remarked at last, breaking the tension. "It would have been public if Tweed had surviving children outside of wedlock."

The Madame's expression was like that of stone. "I never asked who the father was," the Madame confessed. "So, yes, Samuel, it is possible."

"Madame, I know Tweed betrayed you, but Esther—"

"Esther is nothing like her father," the Madame interrupted brashly, "and that is if this does prove to be true. Either way, this only provides clarity regarding her origins. Or better yet, how in the hell her mother found me in the first place."

The Madame picked up her glass and glided over to Thomas, who obliged to give her drink a refill. "Get her to the hotel. Leave Ashleigh there to guard Celeste and Douglas. They'll be suspicious of the Hiltmores, yes, but I'll see to it that that suspicion dies. We will be prepared to put our masks on with Richard, and you need to do the same, Thomas."

Thomas put a hand on her shoulder. "I'll take care of it."

With a small salute to Ellis, Thomas left the Madame's office and closed the door behind him, leaving the Madame and Samuel alone.

"You need to tell him."

The Madame sauntered over near Ellis again. "Why?"

"Because he deserves to know. And because God knows how much longer any of us has."

She didn't speak, only half-nodded in acknowledgement, and so Samuel went on, "I've got to get going to Tammany Hall."

"Stop by the precinct on your way," she advised. "Find out if there is any news about Judge Frederick to distract Croker from this fucking debacle."

She had a point.

"I'll do that."

"Samuel?"

"Yeah?"

"I want you to consider something."

Detective Ellis got to his feet and moved closer to her. "What is it?"

"I want you to consider working for me and quitting the force."

"Is that why you let me be a part of this? As an incentive to be another one of your...your own gang of misfits?"

The Madame didn't baulk. "Yes."

Samuel let out a laugh and wiped the perspiration from his brow. For a few seconds, he stared at her, shaking his head, then he drew her in and kissed her before she could refuse him. He let her go, circled around, and headed for the door of her office.

"I'll think about it."

It was a quarter to five in the morning, and Richard Croker refused to wait any longer for Walsh to show his face at the Hall. The pain in his left shoulder and chest was so overwhelming, he'd put away almost an entire bottle of whiskey to keep it at bay. The negro doctor brought by Will didn't try to hide the fact that he had been one lucky son of a bitch; the bullet had gone straight through and missed Richard's heart by a quarter of an inch. If it had broken or lodged into his body, there would have been nothing the doctors could do, and he most certainly would have died within an hour or two. Instead, after losing an immense amount of blood, the doctor cauterized the wound internally before sewing him closed. Croker despised hospitals, and demanded the doctor fix him at Tammany Hall, which he did after a brief time of protestation. Thankfully, Elizabeth was up north in the country with the children, and he sent a wire to her immediately of his injuries but that he was recovering, so she need not worry. Now, Croker sat propped up on his sofa, arm wrapped up and in a sling; with a giant glass of whiskey in his hand and surrounded by his men, he was enraged. He wasn't sure if it was the adrenaline of surviving a murder attempt or the sheer hatred flowing through his veins, but either way, he was wide awake with one, sole purpose: find and kill Esther Tweed.

"I don't give a shit who you tell!" Croker bellowed, and his intensity caused a small bit of whiskey to spill onto the floor. "I want the word out now: 500 dollars to bring her to me, dead or alive. You got that?!"

"Yeah, Richie, course we do," Will assured him.

Will was sitting in the armchair next to the sofa, and standing a few feet to his left was Louis, chain smoking cigarettes and seemingly agitated. Sullivan and O'Reilly sat on the couches by the empty fireplace, nodding along as they joined Croker in his consumption of whiskey. Across from Richard, Samuel Ellis and Seamus Murphy were standing by Croker's desk, both with their arms crossed and baffled by how to deal with this situation.

Croker pointed to Louis. "You listen to me, Frog," he hissed angrily. "If I find out you, the Madame, or Will are any part of this, I will kill the three of you without a second fucking thought, and add Will's son to the body count just for good goddamn measure."

This did not please Will. "What the hell, Richie?! I ain' got no part o' this!"

"You think that really matters to me?" Richard snarled back. "The two of you don't operate without the other's consent, that much I fucking know, which means if one of you helped her, both of you bastards did."

Louis's expression contorted up indignantly. "If you think we would do anything to help that bitch after she betrayed us, you've got another think coming."

"Oh please, Louis!" Croker threw in his face. "You begged me to save her life when she was headed for the noose. You think I fucking forgot about that?"

"That was years ago, and a lot has changed since then."

Richard's huffed loudly. "You expect me to believe that?"

"You better goddamn believe it."

Louis took a step toward Richard, scowling down at him, and for a brief second, Croker found himself nervous and exposed in the giant Frenchman's shadow. There was no light in Louis's eyes, and his mien had taken on a form Croker had never witnessed previously—not just ferocity, but cold—cold, unwavering, and callous. Very rapidly, Croker saw in Louis's gaze exactly what he was to him: a bug to be squashed, a nuisance to be conquered. While he tried to shield it from the onlookers, Richard felt his hands tremble.

"Will and I kept things cordial with your Assistant only because you fucking asked us to. But we've been done with her since we found out she'd been leaking information—our information, that we bled and battled for, to the Madame." His pitch lowered, yet his voice was vicious. "I told you when I crossed over to the Hall I was yours, and if you don't believe me, you can go fuck yourself, Croker. You know what I used to do to bastards who falsely accused me of things?" He paused, a more aggressive scorn forming. "I would gut them in the street and watch those sons of bitches bleed to death, crying for mercy, mercy they never got. If you don't believe me, you can ask Mr. Sweeney." Louis threw back the last of his whiskey. "Don't push me, Croker, or you won't like what happens as a consequence."

There had been very few times in Croker's later life when he'd actually felt afraid: the fury and the power behind Louis's words was so overpowering, Richard had unknowingly receded down and away into his seat. He did believe Louis, and he was also very suddenly aware that Louis would have no contest to killing Richard then and there; that realization was something that would haunt Richard for years to come.

To save face, he pointed to Louis's empty whiskey glass. "Go pour yourself a big drink, and grab another for me." It was all Croker could manage, a tiny quaver in his tone he desperately tried to mask.

As Louis revisited the drink cart and the remainder of the room came into Richard's view once again, Croker saw that he was not the only one fearful Louis might take some kind of action. Will was gaping at Louis, hands on his pistols, and while Will was staring Louis down, Louis refused to return Will's gaze. Behind the sofa, Sullivan and O'Reilly were both on their feet, their own stunned eyes locked on Louis as he strolled over to the whiskey decanter. Croker glimpsed to his right, where Samuel was removing his hand from Seamus's wrist, and Seamus holstering his drawn revolver, glowering at Samuel. This was the side of Louis even Will dreaded, and for the first time, Croker had born witness to the ghost of the old Louis, the one he'd heard so many tall tales about: the young man who didn't have any woes with murder, who would steal just for a laugh, and who ran the Five Points when it was at its worst. No, regardless of those stories, Richard had never truly believed that version of Louis existed.

He certainly believed now.

At that exact moment, Walsh burst into Croker's office, and upon recognizing he wasn't the only man in the room, halted in his tracks

"I apologize that I couldn't get away sooner, Richard. I was trying to keep the Whyos from marching down here and demanding answers."

Croker rolled his eyes. "And just why in the hell would they want answers for?! It wasn't the Hall that did this! It was that little bitch!"

Walsh cleared his throat. "Yes, but, that little bitch worked for you, and she killed Danny Lyons."

"Shit." Croker hoisted himself to sit up straight right as Louis brought over a newly poured whiskey. "How the fuck did that happen?"

Slowly, Walsh made his way closer to Croker. "We cornered her and had her surrounded. Unfortunately for the almost twenty Whyos killed today, your old Assistant had some help."

"Help?" Seamus asked. "What the hell does that mean?"

"It means, Detective Murphy, that this Vigilante everyone is chasing showed up and helped dear Mr. Croker's Assistant murder my men in the street."

Will's eyes grew wide. "You gotta be shittin' me…"

"The Vigilante?!" Sullivan exclaimed. "Ya mean them two are workin' together now?!"

"They certainly seemed to know one another," Walsh stated candidly.

Croker couldn't believe what he was hearing. "What do you mean he just fucking showed up, Walsh?! It was two people! You had almost two dozen Whyos to take her out, and you couldn't get the goddamn job done?!"

"To my own credit, I was able to stop her by injuring her quite severely." Walsh remained unfazed by Croker's rage, almost appearing somewhat annoyed, which only caused Richard to become more irritated. Walsh picked up on this, and let out a loud exhale. "He literally dropped in from a building. I don't know what you expect of me, Richard, but I did what I could with my people. Your concern should be that Esther and this Vigilante have been working together all along, and that she is probably the one who has been tipping him off to the opium deliveries and who knows what else."

"Well, that shouldn't matter now," Louis cut in abruptly. "Everyone in this city is looking for her: Tammany Hall, the coppers, the Whyos, even the Madame, and no one can find her." He took a sip of his whiskey. "Maybe we should send a man to The Morgue. If you injured her badly enough, Walsh, the odds of her surviving are small at best."

"Fuck the odds!" Croker yelled. "I want her six feet under!"

"I'll take care of it," Walsh asserted. "If there is anything left of her, I will find her and get rid of her like we previously discussed."

Croker's heart was racing in his chest as he attempted to comprehend just what exactly had come to fruition that day. His plan to kill Esther personally backfired because he let his ego get in the way of simply shooting her dead in his office. By some twist of fate, she'd actually possessed the combination to his safe, and ironically, nothing was missing from it. From Brian's retelling of the events that unfolded, Esther escaped empty-handed. Regardless, Esther and this…vigilante accomplice took out an entire faction of the Whyo gang, and not the idiotic lower-tiered goons; Esther had killed Danny Lyons and his closest associates, the leaders of the Whyos for years and years. Not to mention, the Whyos were already furious with Croker and the Hall regarding the opium raid going sideways. Richard realized the time to make a decision was fast approaching—he would have to either permanently sign on with the Whyos as a backer, or let them disintegrate without the help of Tammany Hall. There was no one left to lead them, and he could use gang control as a pivotal aspect of Tammany Hall's promise in the election of Grant for mayor. No, he couldn't keep siding with the underworld of New York. Change was coming, and Croker had to change with the times.

"Richie," Samuel muttered, interrupting his deliberations, "there is some good news."

Everyone looked inquisitively at Detective Ellis, including Croker. "What is it, Samuel?"

"Judge Frederick's wife found the body of her husband a couple hours ago and called our boys in to investigate. It was ruled a homicide, and they're out now looking for Virgil to bring him in for questioning. The evidence is overwhelming, and Mrs. Frederick is in hysterics, saying Virgil was threatening her and her husband constantly, confirming they had been in debt to him for some time." Samuel smirked. "No matter what he says, he's the only suspect they have, and considering it is a New York City judge…well, let's just say it'll be a quick conviction."

A nasty smile came to Croker's lips. "That is good news, detective. Thank you."

"So, what now, Richie?" Will inquired, leaning forward towards his boss. "We got a search out for Esther, Judge is dead, Virgil's not gonna be a problem, so, what's next?"

Croker finished his whiskey. "Sullivan and O'Reilly, I want you to go see Edmund and let him know Virgil is out. Detective Ellis and Seamus will resume observing the arrest of Virgil and keeping an eye on the investigation into my shooting. Will, you and the Frog are going on a special mission for me. You are going to pay a man by the name of Priestly a little visit. It's time to muscle out the last of the opposition. Do what you must, but don't break his hands— he'll need those to type."

Walsh spoke up. "And what about me?"

"You, Mr. Walsh, are going to find Miss Esther Tweed, and when you do, you are going to give her to the Whyos as a peace offering. I don't give a fuck who you have to go through to find her, but when you do, you will make sure she suffers until her last breath."

Though his face was placid, Croker noted the delight in Walsh's gaze upon hearing this.

"Now, everyone out so I can get some damn rest! And send Brian in on your way out!"

Once they'd all left, Brian rushed in and straight to Croker. "What can I do for you, Mr. Croker? Can I get you anything?"

Croker shook his head. "Go home, Brian. I am going to sleep here tonight. But before you go, I want you to send a quick note to Mr. Grant uptown."

Brian adjusted the pillow behind Croker's back, and assisted him to a more horizontal position. "Of course, sir. What do you want me to send his way?"

"Tell him I have a new campaign idea, one that I think will at last get us the upper class votes we've been pining for." Croker shuffled around to get comfortable, wincing as he moved his arm unconsciously before grabbing it to refrain from crying out. "Tell him to come see me tomorrow," Croker continued through gritted teeth. "Sometime in the afternoon."

"Sure thing, Mr. Croker."

Seeing Croker was settled, Brian started off for the door, then stopped for a moment. "Sir, what happened to Esther?"

"She'll be dead soon," Croker said plainly. "Why do you ask, Brian?"

Brian was quiet for a few seconds. "I just always liked her, that's all. Guess I am a bad judge of character. She...she did send me out to get a gift for you today. I mean, it was to get rid of me, I think..."

Croker was already exhausted, fading into a hazy doze. "Hmm?"

Brian rapidly went outside to his desk, grabbed something, and returned to Croker on the sofa. On the coffee table in front of Richard, Brian opened and put down a bottle of Richard's favorite brandy, along with a glass.

"She, uh, said it was to celebrate."

Croker stared at the bottle, speechless for reasons he couldn't understand, and Brian took the hint. "All right, sir. Get some rest. I'll be back in a few hours."

Brian dimmed the gaslights on his way out, yet Croker couldn't break his gaze from the bottle.

When minutes had trickled by, he huffed and sat himself up once again, reaching out with his good arm. Richard poured himself a glass of brandy, a brandy he would only drink on the best of occasions, astonished at Esther's acuity on a subject he probably brought up with her once or twice.

Swirling the liquid in the glass, he was overcome with an odd sense of wistfulness. He wanted to drown this sentiment down, and Croker took a gulp of the brandy, letting out an exhale of delight as it washed down into his belly. He wouldn't miss her, no—it wasn't that. He would miss the control, and the level of power her muscle had given him. Losing Esther was like losing his favorite hunting dog. Still, hunting dogs could always be replaced with a new pup, and the old were forgotten like they never existed at all.

With another long and satisfied drink, Croker's eyes went to the window behind his desk as dawn crept over the city and the sky started to lighten. Sleep was needed. Croker finished the glass he'd poured, accepting that today had, in reality, been a win for himself and for the Hall, and he sank down onto the sofa, vindicated.

Just prior to letting his eyelids close at last, Croker peered one last time at the fading night outside the window, and nearly jumped out of his skin.

Glowering at him from the other side of the glass was the same Peregrine falcon he'd noticed there before. Only this time, she didn't fly away when he spotted her; instead, she stayed put, her piercing golden eyes more intimidating than an animal's ought to be. Then, Croker noticed something odd: striped diagonally across her belly and on the front of her beak was something dark, and he squinted to make out what it was.

It was blood.

CHAPTER XXXVIII.

Thunk.

"Dammit," Celeste muttered under her breath, her knife once again missing the aspired bullseye. The Madame had given her specific instructions on how to practice her throws, and once she perfected that undertaking, they would proceed onward; however, to Celeste's chagrin, she was struggling with her aim. It seemed that no matter how she chose to propel the blade from her grip, it would miss by barely an inch, and missing by an inch was not remotely what the Madame meant by "perfection."

With a heavy sigh, Celeste walked to the target hanging just to the left of the headboard in her bedroom. She would remove the knife and try once more with the hope that, with repetition, she would be able to master the necessary technique.

As she was about to pull the knife from the wood, she heard a voice from the doorway: "You aren't following through with your hand when you've completed the throw."

Celeste whipped around to see Esther standing there, arms crossed over her chest and smiling as she leaned against the doorframe.

"When you are releasing, you are retracting your hand. You

345

want to leave it out and steady, as if you are willing the blade where you want it to go with your fingertips."

With a yank, the knife was free, but instead of taking Esther's advice and attempting another throw, Celeste casually lifted the side of her skirt and sheathed the blade on her thigh.

"You shouldn't be down here, Esther. You could be seen," Celeste remarked coldly.

Since Esther's arrival at the hotel, Celeste found she was fairly bitter of her friend's presence. She and her father had gone to great lengths, alongside the Madame, to arrange for Esther, Will, and Louis to get out of the city safely, putting their own selves in danger as a result. Without a care, Esther had decided to take matters into her own hands, and therefore sent their whole plan off the rails, risking the lives of everyone involved. And what had it gotten them? Two names and an even angrier than normal Richard Croker—to Celeste, Esther's motives seemed purely selfish, a commission Esther did of her own volition with no regard as to what happened to the rest of them. There had been no apology nor any kind of explanation, and until Celeste got both of those accounts from Esther, her heart had hardened.

Esther's amused expression faded into consternation. "Are you upset with me about something, Celeste?"

Celeste dropped her gaze, pacing toward to the washing station to splash some water on her face. "I would say confused is a better term for how I feel." She dipped her hands in the bowl and let her palms fill with water. "You've been here two days, Es, and you haven't brought up the fact that you are the one who screwed this whole thing up."

About to rinse the sweat from her brow, Celeste nearly jumped out of her skin when she realized Esther was suddenly right beside her, having managed to move silently from the door to Celeste without making a sound.

"You're mad because I didn't abide by the plan."

Celeste let the water drop and stood, turning to Esther. "No. I am mad that you have so carelessly put us in jeopardy because of a goddamn whim. We spent weeks putting this together, Esther, and you have now sent us back to square one. And for what? Two names?! One of which we already had!"

"Celeste…"

"No, I don't want to hear excuses from you. I want to know why. Why did you go against everyone who cared about you? We did this for you!"

Esther shook her head. "I didn't go against anyone," she replied calmly. "I worked with Croker for a lot of years, Celeste. I didn't think we would have another shot." She paused for a second, intently staring into Celeste's eyes. "And honestly, I am not sure we will get another chance, either."

Again, Celeste looked away and went back to washing her face. "You can't possibly know that. Things are constantly changing at the drop of a hat!"

"It is an instinct, and even if you don't agree, that is what my gut tells me, but I do understand why you can't see it, and I am sorry for that."

Celeste felt a rage rise up in her chest, and she wiped her cheeks dry with a towel, hardly holding her composure. "You cannot know what I see or don't see. You want to know what I really think happened?"

Her friend moved to sit on the end of Celeste's made bed. "I already know what you think, Celeste. You think I did it because I was self-centered and wanted to kill Croker on my own, but that isn't why I did it."

"Then why did you? There is no other conceivable reason!" she exclaimed, throwing her hands in the air in frustration. "Not when we had everything ready!"

A lull came and went.

"For the same reason I killed Timothy," Esther murmured, her tone crestfallen, "because I wanted to save the people I love, even if it meant me dying as a consequence."

Celeste felt as if all the air had been sucked out of her lungs. Unconsciously, her gaze flickered to the exposed scar on Esther's neck, that horrible, deep, ugly scar reminding them both of a previous existence that felt lifetimes away; a life that much like this one, was filled with pain, suffering, and strife. She didn't know what to say or how to respond to such a statement, and while Celeste wanted to let the issue go, she couldn't manage to forgive the blame she'd placed on Esther for the turmoil they were up against. Celeste assumed Esther's perspective of the situation was delusional stemming from her belief in her own righteousness, and nothing Celeste said was going to change that.

The pair of them remained wordless for a minute while Celeste brooded over their divergence, until Esther again spoke up.

"I ought to have Jeremiah check my ribs. My breathing is more painful today than it was yesterday."

Celeste nodded, motioning for her to leave, and Esther got up, marching over to the exit. She halted with the door half closed, glancing back at Celeste with apprehension.

"I will share with you that Richard Croker is unsettled by you. He mentioned that right before he tried to shoot me in his office. You can take that however you like."

Quietly, Esther shut the door, and Celeste rotated back around to her washing station, peering at her reflection in the mirror—she couldn't recall a time when she'd been unable to absolve her oldest and best friend, and perhaps it was because, on this occasion, Celeste was one of the people in the line of fire. The hurt she felt was personal, as if Esther had done this to her and her alone, and Celeste couldn't ascertain why forgiveness seemed so far away.

Two nights before, when Esther had arrived in the early morning hours, Celeste felt no anger whatsoever. In truth, the only result Celeste needed was to have Esther mended and safe in the hotel, off the streets and as far away from Richard Croker as possible. The access to the attic was solely in the Hiltmores' hands due to Mrs. Ryder giving them her only keys, and just for good measure, Celeste had changed the locks and additionally installed a deadbolt on the inside of the door. The attic was originally arranged for Esther, Will, and Louis, and therefore Esther had more than enough room during her stay, the length of which was now undetermined. Celeste supplied the room with basic yet functional décor: three beds; a crate of wine; a small table and chairs; a few changes of clothing for each of them; some dried meat and crackers if they grew hungry between meals; and of course, a sufficient amount of tobacco and matchbooks. On the sly, Celeste additionally put together a small gift for Esther, one that had cost her a minute fortune, but the time for gifts was later. Esther reached St. Stephen's in a state Celeste would not forget, mangled and bloodied worse than she'd witnessed since the night Esther shot Timothy.

Douglas and Celeste had met Esther, Thomas, and Ashleigh expectantly in the alley behind St. Stephen, sneaking them up the servants' passage and to their rooms on the top floor of the hotel.

At Celeste's request, Jeremiah had been in the attic waiting for Esther with everything he might need to patch her up, and once Thomas helped Esther to the top of the staircase and into her new quarters, Jeremiah tended to Esther's injuries while Thomas joined Ashleigh and Celeste for a briefing on what exactly they ought to do next. Douglas, oddly enough, chose to stay upstairs with Esther, and Celeste had the inclination that her father's paternal constitution kicked into full gear—she was cognizant that her father wanted to mend old wounds with Esther, and allowed him the time and space to do so.

That had left Celeste with Thomas and Ashleigh, and she'd had very little idea of what to expect from either of them.

She'd poured both men whiskey, while she herself went for a

glass of wine, leaving the bottle empty on the side table to her right—
Celeste had the impression she might need more than just one glass.
Conscious of how tired Douglas already was, Celeste took Thomas
and Ashleigh to the sitting room in her section of the Hiltmores' living quarters and closed the doors, so that when her father came down
from the attic, he could either choose to join them or go to sleep.

Most of what was exchanged, Celeste had merely listened to,
and as she thought back on Thomas and Ashleigh's conversation,
she marveled at how the two appeared to be friendly with one another so fast.

Thomas sat across from Ashleigh on the sofas, whereas Celeste
took the armchair opposite the empty fireplace, each of them like
the point of a triangle. They took the first few seconds to drink down
quite a bit of their respective beverages, and Celeste waited for one
of them to commence whatever discussion might ensue following
the day they'd sustained.

Thomas spoke up, "This is not the day I planned on having."

Ashleigh broke into an ironic chortle, swishing the whiskey in his
glass around. "I don' think this was the day any o' us thought we'd
have, brother. It's a damn miracle ya got to her in time, if ya ask me."

"If Walsh hadn't been there," Thomas replied, "I think there
would have been less of a need for my interference. Esther is tough,
tougher than I realized. That son of a bitch, though, I can't figure
him out."

"Ya know, he's the one that came and found me, 'fore New York.
I can' tell ya how startlin' of a sight it is, seein' that man waitin' for
ya on the front porch."

This locked in Thomas's attention. "Christ, I didn't know that's
how you got here. Did Croker send him? Or Will?"

"Course not. Bastard wanted to cause problems for Will and
Louis. Didn' realize all that 'til I was already here, but yeah."

"And what happened when you showed up at Tammany Hall?"

Ashleigh sniggered. "Well, to be honest, I don' think even Walsh

350

was sure I'd make the trip. When I did, I met with Croker, and not two days later, I was at The Palace, bein' ordered by him to spy on all the shit the Madame did without Croker knowin'."

"What turned you?" Thomas asked, having a sip of whiskey.

There was momentary silence.

"Everyone always makes the assumption that cause I'm angry with my daddy, I wanna do him some kinda injustice." Ashleigh mirrored Thomas and took a drink from his glass. "Ain' ever been the case. I don' know if we'll ever make things right, but it never woulda been a possibility if I kept runnin' from it. So, I came to the city, found employment somewhere I can stand, and here we are." He winked at Celeste, and she tried not to blush. "Plus, I never liked nothin' about politics anyhow."

Thomas studied Ashleigh for a moment. "Goddammit," he mumbled, smirking.

"What?"

"Not sure I could tell the difference between you and your father after a few more of these whiskeys."

Celeste worried if Ashleigh might take offense to that, but he amazed her with his ease.

"If you saw him twenty-five years ago, wouldn' be able to, that's for damn sure."

"My father and I were like that, too."

"Whatcha mean?"

Thomas's expression was melancholic. "The same man. Different generations."

Ashleigh held up his glass, and the two of them saluted one another.

"It ain' easy, Tommy, but I s'pose that's the curse."

They each drank, and Celeste took the opportunity to press Thomas for information. "Thomas, I know you should probably go to The Palace and see the Madame, but I—"

"I can't go tonight," Thomas conveyed wearily, leaning back

against the sofa. "Honestly, Celeste, I am just too fucking tired. I'll go first thing. She'll be pissed as all hell, but if I don't get a little shut eye, I'll be delirious."

"You can crash right here, then."

"Thank you."

She took a sip of wine. "What happened? If you don't mind telling me."

"You are...certain...you want to know?"

"Yes, Thomas."

"Well," he opened with a heavy exhale of breath, "I was in a meeting with William when the madness commenced." He crossed his right leg over the other. "Louis and Tony burst in...I mean I knew immediately, whatever it was, it had to be Esther, and it had to be really fucking bad. There was no other reason Louis would show up and interrupt anything with my family—you know how he is. Athena and I took off and I spent the carriage ride down to Tammany getting...dressed." Thomas stopped his story and peered around, as if remembering something vital. "Actually, Celeste, do you mind opening that window? She should be returning soon."

Celeste was confused. "Who?"

"His falcon," Ashleigh informed her, with another wink.

As requested, Celeste politely nodded and went to the nearest window, unhinging the locks and opening it wide.

"Will that work?"

"Perfect. Don't worry, she'll let us know when she's here."

"We oughta chat 'bout them birds at some point, Tommy...I used to hunt with red tails when I was a kid, and I always wanted a Peregrine—"

"Hold on, Ashleigh," Celeste lightly interposed. "Thomas, what happened when you got to Tammany Hall?"

He sneered. "It was a disaster. I got there just as Samuel and Will were rolling in, along with Whyos coming in from every direction. It was pouring down rain, but I caught a glint of Esther scal-

352

ing down the fire escape. Athena tracked her and I got to the spot just as Walsh cornered her. So, I did what I do best."

Celeste studied him. "Which is?"

"Well, Celeste. Esther and I killed a couple of people. Though to be fair, it was a fight or die situation."

"An' Walsh got 'hold of her somehow?" Ashleigh inquired.

Thomas's face grew dark. "He would have killed her if I didn't have the Griswold."

"True what they say? Son of a bitch can' feel nothin'?"

"Either that, or he has an unbelievably high tolerance of pain," Thomas clarified. "I watched Esther hit him over and over again with those brass knuckles. Those things will put a damn hole in your skull if she strikes the right spot."

"How'd he get her?"

An aggrieved air came over Thomas. "He pulled her arm out of the socket."

Celeste felt the grip on her wine glass tighten. "Holy shit," she cried. "How do you do something like that?!"

"Lots of practice, Celeste. I got to them just as Walsh pulled a blade out to slit her throat. The only reason they got away was because his girlfriend pulled a pistol, or I would have killed him. Thankfully, I got Esther to Lawrence's, taped her ribs up, and popped her shoulder into place. She was coughing up blood for a time, but I think the internal damage is manageable, especially for a doc as good as your brother."

At that moment, a high-pitched shriek caused Celeste to gasp and nearly spill wine all over herself. Like a bullet, a bird came flying in through the window and directly to Thomas, who casually lifted his arm, a leather glove covering his hand and forearm—Thomas had ostensibly put the glove on as he recounted the afternoon to Celeste, though she hadn't remotely noticed him do so. The bird

landed with a graceful force, and Thomas reached into his pocket, pulling out something that made the room smell like old meat.

He caught her gaze and smiled. "It's chicken breast. Ashleigh,
can you grab my shoulder holster?"

"Right here."

Ashleigh got up and went for Thomas's jacket hanging on the
hat stand by the door. He removed what appeared to be another
wrap of leather, and as if he had a practiced hand, Ashleigh strolled
to Thomas and fashioned the leather onto Thomas's right shoulder
for Athena to perch. The bird noticed and acknowledged its existence, finishing her chicken and then bouncing up Thomas's arm.
After tying the falcon down, Thomas reached into his pocket and
grabbed something else, placing it carefully over the bird's head,
and she obligingly allowed him to do so, her movements becoming
less and less frequent.

"She'll be snoozing shortly with the sun on the horizon," Thomas told them. "Sorry for the interruption, Celeste. Where were we?"

Celeste was gaping at the Peregrine. "I've...I've seen this bird
before!"

"What? Really?"

"Yes, at The Palace...and here as well!"

"Athena is sharp," Thomas observed. "She likes to observe her
surroundings when the two of us are out on our...errands. Sometimes I feel like she knows more about what is happening in the city
than I do."

Ashleigh guffawed, lowering down to his spot. "Ain' that the
truth."

Detecting that Celeste remained discontented, Thomas cleared
his throat. "Listen, Celeste, I don't have much to tell you. The one
we need to be pressing for information is Esther, but we need to give
her a little time."

"Time?" Celeste could have laughed. "We don't have time, Thomas."

To Celeste's astonishment, Thomas frowned at her reaction. "We have all been through a lot. Please just be gentle with her. It's not the injuries we can see that I am worried about."

"Whatcha think about gettin' her outta New York?" Ashleigh went on. "That a viable option for us, or we too late?"

"I have a few ideas…nothing I can confirm without talking with the Madame first."

"All right," Celeste acquiesced. "Do I need to find a…a cage or something for…uh…"

"Athena," Thomas reminded her.

"Right. Athena."

"Do you have an old solitary music stand?"

"Actually…" Celeste thought for a moment. "Yes, I do!"

"If you could grab that, it will work perfectly as a perch, and she can just sleep right here with me."

Getting to her feet, Celeste walked over to the closet beside her pianoforte and opened the door, pulling out one of her older music stands. She carried it back over by the sofa near Thomas and proceeded to set it to the appropriate height. Shuffling a somewhat disgruntled Athena onto the wood frame, Thomas tied her leg to it with a small strap. The falcon, once comfortable, did not stir, and Celeste supposed she must have been resting after a long day of being out.

"Thomas, do you want me to get a rag for…her…?"

He was removing the strap from his shoulder. "Why would she need a rag?"

"I gather Miss Hiltmore wants to get some of that blood off your girl," Ashleigh enlightened him, pointing towards the peculiarly tranquil Athena's chest, which was spattered with dark red stains of blood.

"I'll clean her up in the morning," Thomas told them, picking his whiskey glass back up. "She hates to be disturbed once she's down for the night." He finished his whiskey. "You two mind if I catch a little shut-eye now that the sun is rising?"

Celeste took the hint and rose, Ashleigh doing the same. Propping his legs up, Thomas lay flat on the couch and dipped his hat down over his eyes. Within seconds, a gentle snore indicated to Ashleigh and Celeste he was asleep, and Celeste gestured for Ashleigh to join her in her bedroom.

Just because one part of the night hadn't gone the way Celeste envisaged, didn't mean it had to be a total loss.

Back in the present, there was a startling knock on Celeste's bedroom door, and her reminiscing was brought to a screeching halt.

"Who is it?" she called.

"You have a visitor, Miss Hiltmore!" her maid Becky answered. "It's the late Judge Frederick's wife." Her voice lowered ever so slightly. "She's pretty upset, ma'am."

"Christ. Okay. Sit her down for me, Becky, and get her a glass of wine and some lemon tarts. I will be right there."

Hastily, Celeste went to her wardrobe and grabbed a more formal day dress, slinking out of her current one and hopping into the other. Pulling the half sleeves up and her arms through and prudently positioning the skirt, Celeste pulled the corset strings tight, letting out a long breath of air as she did so. She glanced in the mirror, and her hair appeared to be decent enough, though she dabbed a bit of rouge on her lips and cheeks to brighten her complexion. It was last minute, yet it would have to do.

"Mrs. Frederick! How are you?" Celeste sang as she glided into her sitting room minutes later.

Becky had already seen to it that her guest was sufficiently provided wine and sweets, but the warning had been spot-on—Mrs. Frederick was an absolute disaster, her eyes red and nose swollen from crying, donned in a head-to-toe black ensemble that did the beautiful summer weather no justice.

The widow shook her head, tears forming. "You were supposed to help us! You and the Madame…" She sniffed, dabbing her eyes with her handkerchief. "Now my husband is dead! Who am I to blame?!"

Celeste had prepared herself for this, and she swiftly went to Mrs. Frederick's side, dipping down to her knees and taking the older woman's hands into hers.

"I am so incredibly sorry, Mrs. Frederick, truly I am. I promise you I did what I could, but please, the blame is not on any one of us! It is on that horrible man who killed your husband!"

The widow wouldn't have it. "You told me the…the Madame would fix this!"

Celeste firmed her sympathetic attitude. "Mrs. Frederick, I did everything in my power. I arranged for the meeting with the Madame, and she informed me that the issue had nothing whatsoever to do with your husband and her working together. The man he owed—Virgil was his name, right? He refused her intervention, and threatened the Madame if she interceded. The judge himself even told the Madame to back off, I think in the hopes Virgil might change his mind!"

This caused Mrs. Frederick to burst into sobs, which was precisely what Celeste had hoped for. She paused in her speech and squeezed the widow's hand, then released her and grabbed the widow's full wine glass. While Mrs. Frederick blubbered into her handkerchief, blowing her nose so loudly it sounded like a trumpet, Celeste discreetly pulled a tiny vial of liquid opium from her dress sleeve and put two drops into the wine, hoping it would mellow the widow's mood. As easily as she'd drawn the vial, she placed it once again in her sleeve, eyeing Mrs. Frederick for a few seconds to be certain she hadn't been caught.

When it was confirmed she was in the clear, Celeste nonchalantly put the drink in her guest's hand. "Please, have a little wine. It will help ease your nerves."

The widow complied, and took a nice, long sip. "I just didn't…I didn't realize this was a life or death bargain! I didn't…I didn't know…"

Celeste moved to sit beside her. "I don't think any of us did. The Madame wrote me a note just yesterday, horrified at the news, and—"

"But the debt, Celeste, we don't have any money to spare! Someone else will come for it, I know they will. I don't have anything to give them!"

"That is what I was just about to tell you, Mrs. Frederick," Celeste elucidated. "The Madame wanted me to tell you that she has reached out to the organization behind this 'Virgil' and has agreed to settle your debts as an apology for not having a better read on the situation. If either of us had known, or even you yourself! But alas, we did not."

Mrs. Frederick gawked at Celeste. "The Madame…she…she paid the debt?"

Celeste again took the widow's hand and patted it. "She didn't want you burdened with your husband's mistakes, Mrs. Frederick."

Mrs. Frederick was so shocked, it was hard for Celeste not to smile. "I don't…I don't know what to say, Miss Hiltmore…"

"You don't need to say a thing. Just remember this kindness when you do think back on this traumatic experience."

The widow nodded, drinking more of her wine, and Celeste poured herself a glass merrily to celebrate a job well done.

"Now, Mrs. Frederick, let's try and distract you. What are your thoughts on the upcoming election? It seems like it is all anybody is talking about these days!"

"Darling, what exactly seems to be the problem?"

Hours later, Celeste was at The Palace with the Madame, lost in her train of thought as the pair of them waited for Marcy, Dot, Paige, and Claire to discuss the clientele for the evening.

"I just…I mean, is she okay with this?"

"Okay with what, exactly? Leaving New York, or leaving us?"

"Well, both!"

The Madame threw her feet on top of her desk, leaning back into her chair as she took a sip of whiskey. "Celeste, there is no other way. She's going."

The reasoning didn't sit well with Celeste. "Esther is heading to England to…to stay at Amberleigh?"

"Yes."

"For how long?"

"As long as it takes," the Madame told her. "Your brother agreed that her physical condition is in such disrepair that she needs weeks, if not fucking months, to fully recover without risking an internal rupture. Esther has multiple broken ribs, bruised internal organs, and a nearly ruptured spleen. Her face looks like someone took a wrench to it. And her knuckles have their own goddamn fractures from those fucking brass knuckles. What do you want her to do, stay here and rot in your attic?"

That, of course, was not what Celeste wanted, but the Madame was trying to make her point, and Celeste heard her loud and clear.

She took a gulp of her wine, shaking her head. "Madame, I just…I am having a hard time trying to…to understand…"

"Oh, for fuck's sake, just spit it out."

The anger was rising in Celeste's throat. "Why am I the only one who seems to be frustrated that Esther abandoned the plan we spent so much time piecing together?! Why? Everyone else is acting like nothing happened! And it's making me furious. We all put ourselves at risk for her and…and…"

The look on the Madame's face made Celeste halt in her rant, and it was not a look she was used to getting from the Madame: it was one of pure abhorrence. The Madame's feet hit the floor, and she leaned onto her desk, as if she were about to lecture Celeste— instead, the Madame had a gulp of whiskey, pointing a long, accusing finger directly at her.

"You are so fucking out of line, I could strike you."

Celeste retracted backward in her chair. "W-what?"

Before Celeste even realized what was happening, the Madame was up from her chair, pacing around her desk.

"I want you to listen to me, and listen to me good, darling, because if we have to have this conversation one more time, I will not restrain myself. And we have already had this same talk way too many fucking times for my liking."

The Madame stood not two feet from her, and Celeste was momentarily terrified. "I didn't...I just don't understand..."

"What you don't understand is that sometimes your ungrateful upbringing brings that upper-class bitch out in you, the heartless one that never appreciated Esther from day one," the Madame snapped unrelentingly. "You think you've sacrificed for this cause? Ha!"

She consumed the remnants of her whiskey and slammed the glass down so hard on her desk, Celeste thought it might shatter. In a flash, the Madame pounced her way and threw both her hands on the armrests of Celeste's chair, invading her personal space so closely, their noses were almost touching.

"Esther fell on the sword. For you, for me, for every single fucking one of us, you insolent shit. Do you know how many people she had to kill to keep you safe at night? Do you know what she risked, visiting you at that goddamn hotel and leaving you pictures, just because she knew if she didn't, you'd be hanging from the rafters?! You don't, and you never will."

It was the most afraid Celeste had ever been of the Madame, and she felt as if someone had stabbed her in the chest. "No, Madame, please...that's not at all what I—"

"Yes, it fucking was," the Madame hissed. "You know why you're mad? You're mad because, for the first time in years, you aren't the goddamn center of attention. You realize the people here love her as much as they love you, and you feel threatened. I thought I was raising you better than that. Clearly, there is still much more work to be done."

A tear trickled down Celeste's cheek. "Madame…I…"

Unexpectedly, a knock came to the door, and the Madame pulled away from Celeste.

"Yes?"

Ashleigh came into the room, and stopped in his tracks upon feeling the negative tension. "You ladies all right in here?"

"A lesson was needed, Mr. Sweeney. What is it?"

"Just wanted to pass along that the girls will be up shortly." Ashleigh glimpsed at Celeste, his face full of concern, and the Madame ignored it.

"Thank you, Mr. Sweeney. Now, if you'd be so kind?" She gestured toward the door.

"Yeah. Of course, Madame."

Ashleigh departed, and the moment he was gone, the Madame's attentions returned to Celeste. Resting against her desk, arms crossed, she glared at Celeste for a minute or so, and Celeste wasn't sure if the Madame would go on berating her, or possibly throw her out of The Palace altogether. When she couldn't sit stagnant any longer, Celeste wiped her cheeks, embarrassed that she'd shed tears in front of the Madame. The previous two days, her emotions had gotten the better of her, and Celeste chastised herself for not buckling down and getting a grip over herself. How was it that, out of everything that had occurred that summer, Celeste's biggest trigger was evidently Esther's escape from Richard Croker? Why was that suddenly the cause of her mental strife?

An odd, amused snort came from the Madame, and Celeste stared at her, confused. The vehemence had retreated, and instead, the Madame had a hand over her mouth, shaking her head, a glimmer of laughter in her eyes.

"Darling, when you wiped your cheeks…you…well, Christ. You've got rouge all over your face."

If it was possible, Celeste was more mortified. "Goddammit," she uttered. "Do you have a rag?"

The Madame took off toward the southern corner of her room, where a door led to her private quarters.

"Coming?" she called.

Celeste leapt to her feet and followed. The Madame pulled out a key and unlocked the door, pushing it open and dragging Celeste inside with her. This room was one of the most magical Celeste ever remembered setting foot in, and each time she was granted access, it was like stepping inside a dream. To the left against the wall were four giant oak wardrobes, three of them stuffed full of gowns, jewelry, shawls, head pieces, and shoes, and the last holding the Madame's knife collection, something Celeste had only become privy to recently. Straight ahead lay an enormous canopy bed, with a hand-carved wooden frame depicting various versions of the Greek gods and goddesses—a piece that surely had taken years to create. All down the right wall were nothing but bookshelves, each case stuffed with more books than Celeste could admit she'd read in her lifetime, their spines bound in a colorful array of leather and gold foil. To the left side of the bed was a small lounging area, including an enormous chaise, dividers for the Madame to change behind, a side table, and of course, a drink cart with wine and whiskey. Between the dividers and the bed rested the vanity, with five candles already lit around it, a washing station, rouge and charcoal laid out on the surface, with pins for styling hair scattered about.

The Madame pointed to the washing stand. "Rinse it off, then you can use my vanity to touch yourself up."

Celeste did as she was instructed, practically jogging toward the bowl of water to rinse the humiliation off of her cheeks. Once her face was clean, she moved on to sit at the vanity, gently drying before reaching for the rouge to add some much-needed color.

"Add some liner, too," the Madame ordered. "Just the top of your lids."

"But I never wear liner," Celeste protested.

"Just do as I ask."

As Celeste picked up the lining wand, the Madame went to her personal drink cart and made them each a whiskey. Celeste rarely drank hard liquor, but she politely accepted her drink from the Madame when it was handed to her, not wanting to engage the Madame's anger into another quarrel.

"You know I don't usually drink this stuff," she remarked, taking a gulp and trying not to scowl as the liquid burned down her throat.

"That will change, darling," the Madame replied, observing the work she'd done on her makeup. "Good. You need the charcoal slightly thicker on your left eye."

"Okay."

Celeste spun around on the stool, set down her whiskey, and made sure her eyes were more even. When she was done, Celeste peered at the Madame in the reflection of the mirror, and received an accepting nod. The Madame then started to march in the direction of her office, and when she was about halfway there, she paused, talking with her back to Celeste.

"I am hard on you," she began, "because you can take it. You have earned your spot here with us, Celeste, you are well aware of that. However, I say this with no intention of ranking either of you. What Esther has done to survive in this world is such an extreme it goes beyond even what I am capable of as a human being. Do you understand that?"

As she observed the Madame, Celeste finished her whiskey, a buzz coming on strong. She bit her lip, trying to find the words she wanted to speak. "Madame, I don't know why I feel like this, or why

I even blame her. I don't like it any more than you do, but I cannot just pretend it's not there. And it's not that I'm jealous…honestly, I wish it was."

An audible sigh. "Then what is it?"

A few seconds trickled past while Celeste endeavored to put into words what she herself wanted to decrypt from her feelings, though the words never came out. Just as she was about to speak, another knock came from outside the office to announce that the girls had arrived and were ready to discuss the clientele for the evening.

Rapidly, Celeste clambered to her feet and out of the Madame's private room, moving to sit on the sofa in preparation for company. There was no time to transition for either of them, and while Celeste got settled, the Madame went to grab a tray of wine and wine glasses for her girls, as well as two more whiskies for them. In marched Claire, Paige, and Marcy, merrily making their way over toward Celeste. The three girls took their place opposite Celeste, and the Madame, after setting down their giant tray of beverages, took her place beside Celeste. It took Celeste a moment to notice, but both Paige and Marcy were grinning, apparently tickled by something regarding Celeste.

"What?" she cried at last.

If it was possible, Marcy's smile grew. "You know, this should become a new look for you."

Celeste rolled her eyes, having a sip of whiskey. "You know I hate being this painted."

"The only thing missing is a cigar and—"

"All right, can we get to the fucking guests tonight, please?" the Madame interrupted her. "We are already almost an hour behind schedule, for Christ's sake."

Claire handed over a piece of paper. "It's pretty much all the usual clients, and Dot has put the list together for everyone."

"Where is that girl, anyway?" the Madame beseeched her.

"Hardy showed up early," Claire primed her. "She was taking care of him. She should be up any second."

While at first Celeste thought this might frustrate the Madame, it was the opposite. "Glad she's making more time for customers. Anything else? Or can we just get right to it?"

The glanced at each other, shrugging.

"The only new customer will be seeing Penny at ten," Marcy declared, "but he's Commissioner Porter's son."

The Madame's left eyebrow rose. "With Penny?"

"He requested her," Claire mentioned. "Why? Should we switch him?"

"No, darling, I think it will work fine. Celeste?"

She was mid-sip of whiskey. "Mmm?"

"I want you to take the floor tonight."

"Sure thing, Madame," Celeste rejoined. "Do you want me in the bar?"

"Of course. Grant may be in tonight, and Christ knows he fucking loves to ogle over you once he's downed a few bourbons."

Celeste couldn't fight her on that one—Mr. Grant had taken quite a liking to her at his last fundraiser, and found it intriguing that Celeste spent her non-social hours helping to run a whorehouse. There had been no sexual advances…yet, and Celeste was doing her best to keep it that way. On her part, she had zero interest in a man like Hugh Grant, no matter if he was to be the next mayor of New York City or not.

"Oh, Madame, one more thing," Claire spoke up. "We are supposed to get a delivery from the Tong tonight, and Lee wanted to put in a special request to meet with you."

"When?"

"Before midnight. He was adamant."

The Madame scoffed. "Fine. Have him here at eleven, and make

sure George is up in my office in case that chink gets out of hand…
fucking Whyos are ruining everyone's lives…"

At ten minutes after eleven, Celeste had just gotten Grant's
hands off of her and sent him scampering down the hallway with
Rose when something strange happened. Celeste was sitting at the
bar, quite a few whiskies deep and waiting on their last few appointments to show, whereas Claire was halfway through telling her a story about the Tong from Chinatown, who had only just arrived and
were upstairs with the Madame and George. Although she loved
Claire, Celeste was exhausted and only half listening, wanting nothing more than to get home and into bed for the night. There were
only two men left on the schedule, and right as Celeste was about
to ask Claire to add a bit more whiskey to her glass, a scream rang
out through the first floor of The Palace.

Claire's eyes instantly met Celeste's. "What the fuck could possibly be happening now?" she cried, reaching under the bar for the
shotgun. "I swear, we can never have just one normal night in this
goddamn place."

Checking to be sure the cartridges were loaded, Claire swung
the gun shut, and Celeste slid off her barstool and onto her feet.

"You stay here," Clair commanded. "I'll go—"

But before Claire could finish her sentence, a young man sprinted by the bar, his shoes in one hand and a wad of paper money in
the other. He was heading straight for the front door, apparently
wanting to make a break for it with whatever he'd taken, and Claire
stepped lively, leveling the shotgun up to fire.

In the same few seconds, however, Celeste had drawn the
blade she kept strapped to her thigh, and with incredible speed, she
launched it at the thief trying to make a break for it. The tip of the

dagger struck him directly in the back of the thigh, and in a heap, he toppled to the ground, his shoes flying one way and a cloud of paper bills floating through the air like butterflies. His bellows echoed through the lobby of The Palace as George sprinted down the staircase from the Madame's office, Claire already beside the man in agony on the floor with the shotgun aimed precisely at his head. Celeste stood frozen, unable to believe what she'd just done.

"How much did you take?" Claire pressed, jamming the nose of the gun into the back of Commissioner Porter's son's head.

"Ahhh! Please! My leg!"

To her right, Celeste saw Razzy appear in the doorway to the bar.

"Go get my brother," she commanded her, and Razzy disappeared in search of Jeremiah. Then again, without realizing it, Celeste was marching over to the man on the ground, where she yanked her blade clean out of his leg, causing him to scream louder.

George had positioned himself at the front door so no breakaway would be possible, and when Celeste looked over at him, he nodded to her, as if in encouragement to go on.

"My leg…please…it hurts so much…"

Using her own might, Celeste dropped to her knees and flipped the man over. "Your leg will be tended to when you tell me how much money you tried to steal."

"I can't…" He was gripping at his thigh, his hands covered in blood. "I can't concentrate with…with the pain…"

In her mind, Celeste entertained the idea of halting the interrogation until after Arnold Porter had been mended by Jeremiah; instead, another small portion of her understood that all the eyes of The Palace were on her. She knew protocol, and though she personally had never had to carry out justice, her time had come to prove herself.

Celeste slapped him hard across the face. "Like I said, you will be tended to when you tell me how much goddamn money you took!"

The hit to his face seemed to snap Arnold into the present. "I only took a little. Penny knew I had gambling debts...I thought..."

"You thought what?!"

"I could...pay her back...." He was gasping now. "Ahhh... please, just help me with my leg!"

Her eyes narrowed. "How fucking much?"

"Twenty—just twenty!"

Pausing, Celeste glanced up to the top of the staircase, where the Madame stood, arms crossed over her chest, a giant smirk on her face.

"George!" she called. "Go to the commissioner's house at once. It's only six blocks away. Tell him his bastard son is here and tried to steal from his whore."

"No—no please!" Arnold was frantic. "You can't...don't tell my father..." The blood loss was showing in his face, which was turning a ghastly shade of white.

"Jeremiah?" Celeste yelled to her brother, who was promptly kneeling beside her, examining the wound in his leg.

"It's not too deep, but it could easily get infected," he perceived, talking over Arnold's groans and persistent squirming. "George? Help me get him to the back. I can stitch him up easier, and we can get this mess cleaned up for the existing customers."

For one reason or another, Arnold seemed to grasp that there was no fighting his circumstances, and that he was additionally at the mercy of the people he'd just tried to steal from. As George wrapped his arms under Arnold's shoulders, he weakly thrashed to evade him.

"Where...where are you...taking me?"

He was struggling against an increasingly annoyed George, who audibly sighed and punched Arnold across the face. The groans temporarily died down, though somehow Arnold managed to hold onto consciousness, and Celeste therefore stood up as George and her brother lifted Arnold from the floor.

"You listen to me," she barked at the commissioner's son. "You have a week to pay The Palace in return for this inconvenience. Due to your…injuries, rather than making it an additional twenty, I'll cut it down to fifteen. However, if you don't pay, I'll be stopping by for a visit with Commissioner Porter. Do you understand me?"

He didn't answer, but the fear in his eyes told Celeste they had nothing to worry about.

Once George and Jeremiah disappeared down the hallway with the injured party, Celeste peered up to the second story; the Madame was already back in her office, undoubtedly explaining to her guests that everything was under control. Claire, on the other hand, beamed at Celeste as she threw the shotgun over her shoulder, nudging her towards the bar.

"Jesus, woman. That was one hell of a throw! Let's celebrate!"

A little shocked with herself, Celeste played along, and the pair of them made their way over to the bar. Restocking the shotgun where it belonged, Claire reached up for their best bottle of Casper's on the top shelf and grabbed three glasses.

"Who is the third for?" Celeste asked.

"Me," came Ashleigh's voice from behind her.

Celeste wasn't sure if it was the adrenaline or the unfamiliar buzz of the liquor she'd been subjected to all night, but for a second, she no longer cared who knew about her and Ashleigh. Reaching out and grabbing onto his shirt, she pulled him in and kissed him, the whole room around her melting away like candlewax.

"Oh, for fuck's sake," the Madame interposed, and as Celeste and Ashleigh broke apart, rather than recoiling in embarrassment, Celeste turned and grinned at her, shrugging.

"Sorry, Madame. I couldn't help myself."

Claire stood behind the bar, trying not to burst into laughter, and the two lingering clients with Razzy and Jasmine at a nearby table were so engrossed with the girls they hadn't taken notice. Conversely, the Madame leaned against the doorframe to the lobby, a whiskey in one hand and a cigar in the other, pretending to be repulsed.

"Do that on your own goddamn time. I don't want to bear witness to you two chasing after each other in my establishment, understood?"

Hastily, Celeste peeked to a pleased Ashleigh, then again to the Madame. "Not again at The Palace, Madame. Understood."

"Psh, it can happen at The Palace," Claire added with a wink at Celeste. "Just don't let the Madame catch you."

The Madame rolled her eyes. "Ashleigh? Get the carriage ready for Celeste."

"Sure thing, Madame."

When he left, the Madame sauntered over and sat down next to Celeste at the bar, picking up Ashleigh's whiskey glass and dumping the contents into hers.

"Did you pacify the guys from Chinatown?" Celeste asked her, grabbing her own drink and having a sip.

"Pacify?"

"After the…well…the incident in the lobby."

"Hah!" the Madame cried. "Don't be ridiculous, Celeste. They are so used to that kind of shit in Chinatown, they were only surprised we didn't kill him." She had a drag of her cigar. "Brilliant throw, darling. You mastered your follow-through quite nicely."

"Thank you, Madame."

"And you handled the thief better than I'd hoped. Stupid son of a bitch. Don't worry, he'll pay. The commissioner, as you know, is here at least two nights a week. How was Grant?"

"He went off with Rose."

"Perfect."

George came into the bar area, directly addressing the Madame. "He's fine. Jeremiah is patching him, then we'll throw him in a carriage. I roughed him up a bit more. Poor bastard is only nineteen and can't seem to stop making bad bets on cock fighting."

"Well, hopefully this teaches him a lesson," the Madame remarked candidly.

George and Claire fell into their own brief conversation, and as they did, the Madame set down her whiskey glass, staring at Celeste.

"I am very proud of you, darling."

Celeste didn't know what to say, overcome with an immense feeling of adoration and gratitude.

Just as she was about to thank her, Ashleigh resurfaced to escort her home.

"Carriage is ready."

The Madame wasn't quite done with her yet. "Celeste?"

"Yes, Madame?"

"Think on what we talked about earlier. Don't make the same mistake I did."

"What mistake, Madame?"

Her jaw twitched. "Letting yourself get in the way of finding resolutions." She lowered her tone so only Celeste could hear. "Fix whatever this is with Esther, or you will regret it."

"I will."

Satisfied, the Madame spun around and hopped off her bar stool, floating out of the bar as she continued smoking her cigar. Biting her lip, Celeste understood the Madame was correct, and she gulped down the last of her whiskey and made her way over to Ashleigh.

Ashleigh put her arm through his. "Ya know what I wonder sometimes?"

"What?"

They walked down the hallway toward the back alley of The Palace. "Sometimes I wonder if there is any one person that knows every one of the Madame's secrets. Because she sure as shit has a lot o' 'em. There is some history there…somethin' we all is missin.'"

"She likes it better that way," Celeste suggested. "But I'd bet if anyone knew her secrets, it would be Louis."

"Why ya say that?"

He opened the door and together, they stepped down and over to the carriage.

"They've been a team since the beginning."

Ashleigh opened the door of the coach and held out his hand for her to take. "Nah, I think it's the detective."

"Ellis?" Celeste inquired, climbing up and inside. "Why?"

Ashleigh shrugged, hopping in behind her. "Just a hunch."

At first, Celeste dismissed Ashleigh's opinion, thinking that because he hadn't been around The Palace long enough, Ashleigh couldn't possibly have that much insight into the Madame's character. But the longer it marinated in her mind, the more she started to believe he was right, and that Ashleigh, out of every one of them, might be the best reader of people she'd ever met.

Celeste and Ashleigh shared a cigarette on their carriage ride to the hotel, and while he wanted to come upstairs, Celeste promised the next night he could. Tonight, she was just too damn tired, not to mention she had some personal demons to sift through with the hope of understanding just where her animosity towards Esther had blossomed.

After a long, passionate few minutes of saying goodbye, Celeste slipped out of the carriage and adjusted her dress before strolling to the front door. Inside, Mrs. Ryder was snoring in her chair, an empty sherry glass beside her on the small table and her latest book of Byron poetry resting on her chest. She had clearly decided to take a small snooze as she read, and Celeste softly unlocked the outside door, not wanting to startle her.

Once in the lobby, Celeste went to her.

"Mrs. Ryder?" she whispered, gently squeezing her shoulder.

Within seconds, she was awake. "What! What is it?! Oh, Celeste, dear. Did I fall asleep in front again?"

"You did," Celeste responded with a kind smile. "Can I help you up to your room?"

"Thank you, dear, I would appreciate that."

Celeste picked up the empty glass and held her arm out for Mrs. Ryder to take, which she did obligingly, and the two of them sauntered just a few feet away to Mrs. Ryder's door. The landlady lived on the first floor due to her arthritic knees and love of being present in the lobby, observing her guests and there to answer any questions at whatever moment necessary. Mrs. Ryder reached out and opened the door, and Celeste released her, handing over the sherry-stained glass.

"Have a good night, Mrs. Ryder."

"You too, dearest. Oh! You did have a guest that went upstairs to wait. Becky knew him, and so she let him in. Arrived about an hour ago and hasn't left."

It must be Louis visiting Esther. "Not a worry. He is probably drinking brandy with Father and smoking my tobacco."

Mrs. Ryder laughed. "Tell your father good evening for me, and also mention that I have the wine he ordered!"

"Of course. Good night, Mrs. Ryder."

Celeste climbed the stairs, the weight of the day hitting her. Yanking her skirts up so it was easier to move, she trudged step by step, hoping that she wouldn't have to deal with some kind of confrontation from Louis and Esther together. Maybe the Madame was right—was it jealousy? Was it frustration that Esther was no longer in the shadows and attracting more attention than herself?

She froze mid-stride. No, that wasn't it. It had killed her, witnessing her best friend in such a fragile state, and it made Celeste want to go after anyone who had ever hurt Esther in whatever manner she possibly could. So, what was it that then gave birth to this grudge? What was it that was causing Celeste to be such a stubborn bitch?

A large glass of wine, a good night of sleep, and perhaps she would wake up with a clear head to figure out this predicament.

At last, Celeste made it up to her rooms, and she opened the door with her key. When she walked in, a voice carried over as the door swung shut behind her.

"Hello, Celeste."

Captain Jonathan Bernhardt was seated on her sofa, a bottle of wine open and a full glass in hand, and he was looking at her right in the eyes. Oddly enough, it wasn't Jonathan's company that was sending her into agitation; instead, it was the notion that upstairs, only floorboards away, was Esther. The woman Jonathan had loved, and whom he believed to be long dead.

He noticed her reluctance and set his wine glass down, making an attempt to appear docile. "Please, come sit. I swear to you, this is not...I just want to end this. Civilly."

"Jonathan, the last time I saw you, you assaulted me. Then I told you I wouldn't marry you. Do you really expect me to be all right, coming home with you sitting comfortably in my rooms uninvited?" Celeste noted how strong he had become, spending time in the boxing ring. His arms had filled out, his shoulders broadened—if a physical altercation did ensue, she would have no chance.

But the expression on his face told her different. "It was a bad thing I did, and I want to apologize to you because you deserve so much better than that. But please—please sit down. I don't want the...I really don't want to leave things like this."

Reluctantly, Celeste went to grab herself a fresh wine glass, and then went and sat opposite of Jonathan. He poured her a share and leaned back onto the sofa, taking a gulp of his own drink. It was at that moment Celeste saw that on the side table beside Jonathan were a bunch of letters, and she grasped that the letters were the ones she'd written to him while he'd been on the frontier years ago.

"I wanted to return your letters," he confessed quietly. "Not out of malice or anger, but because…I was never fair to you. I expected you to be someone you were not. You changed just as much as I did in our time apart, for the better, might I add, whereas I became a raging drunken asshole."

"You went off the deep end, Jonathan."

"I did," he conceded. "I am very ashamed of how I acted. Celeste, I wish I could convey to you how much those memories haunt me. How I was with you…that is not who I am. That was a version of me no one will ever meet again, I will make sure of that."

"How do you suppose that?" she entreated him.

"Because it wasn't until I found an outlet for my frustrations that I grasped where the problems truly were, and I am finally processing my past in a way I never really have before."

Celeste had more wine. "Where were the problems, then?"

"I'd been running, running from things for a long time. Originally when I signed up for the frontier, it was just days after…well…"

"After the Tombs," she finished for him.

"Yes. In the end, the anger I felt didn't come from the frontier, although the nightmares I am grappling with definitely do. That time made a cynic of me, but the difficulty from the start has been—something else."

It hit Celeste straightaway. "You never got over Esther, did you, Jonathan?"

Captain Bernhardt no longer held eye contact with her; his gaze was on his wine glass, fixed, like he didn't want to admit to it out loud. "No, no, I didn't."

An emotion came over Celeste, one so strong it was overwhelming. "I am so, so sorry, Jonathan." It was the guilt—the guilt of knowing and not telling him the truth, and understanding that he would be miserable for the rest of his life as a result.

"Don't be sorry, Celeste. We have our demons. I should have handled mine with as much grace as you did, yet unfortunately, I did not."

"It doesn't mean that I am not sorry—if there is"

A loud knock came from the door adjoining her father's rooms to hers, and suddenly, Douglas burst through, grinning, with two glasses of brandy in his hands.

"Celeste, I saw your light still on, and I thought…"

His voice trailed off when he caught a glimpse of Captain Berhardt seated across from her, and immediately, his enthusiasm faded and was replaced with ferocity.

Douglas let both glasses of brandy drop to the floor, marching towards the Captain. "How dare you have the audacity to show your face in front of my daughter?!"

The Captain leapt to his feet, his hands raised up in surrender. "Please, Mr. Hiltmore, we are making amends, I assure you!"

"You bastard, I cannot believe you broke in here."

Celeste had never seen her father like this, and it took her by complete surprise. Douglas was cursing at Jonathan, pushing his chest, and she worried what might happen as a result.

"Father! Please! Contain yourself!"

"You know what that son of a bitch did to her all those years," Douglas went on ranting, "and yet you still tried yourself?! What kind of a man does that to the woman he loves?! She trusted you, and so did I, Captain!"

"Mr. Hiltmore." Jonathan was trying to stay composed, but Celeste could see he was becoming agitated by the onslaught. He fixed his hands on Douglas's shoulders to try and keep him at bay. "I am here to be a gentleman and apologize to your daughter for what I have done. She and I are fine for the time being, and are working through—"

Douglas shook off his grip, a finger pointed directly at his nose. "I don't care what she says, I am her father!"

Unwisely, Douglas shoved the Captain, who retreated a few paces. "I'll show you what happens to the man who attacks my daughter!"

"Father! Stop!"

Celeste lurched their way to try and get ahold of Douglas as he wound up to punch Jonathan; before his fist was able to make contact with the Captain's face, it was caught mid-swing by Esther. Somehow, Esther managed to insert herself in the very small amount of space between Jonathan and Douglas in the blink of an eye. Where she'd come from, Celeste couldn't tell, but it was as if she'd appeared out of thin air.

"Mr. Hiltmore," Esther stated mildly, "I am going to let you go now, as long as you swear not to hit Jonathan. Or me, for that matter."

Douglas was petrified, unable to move. "Esther…you cannot be out…you can't be seen or…or…"

"It will be okay, Mr. Hiltmore."

She let go of his hand, and he let it fall at his side. Douglas, in disbelief, went to the armchair and lowered down, his stare fixed on Esther and Jonathan.

"Es, how did you…?" Celeste initiated, and her friend twisted to her and smiled.

"Maid's stair. I've been there since the Captain arrived, wanting to make sure everything was all right. I was halfway up the stairs when I heard Douglas drop the brandy glasses, and honestly, nothing good is happening this late if glass is breaking. So, I came down to find Douglas going after Jonathan."

Captain Bernhardt's eyes were wide. "No, no, it can't be…"

Not sure what to do, Celeste tried to appeal to him. "Jonathan, I'm so sorry."

Esther's eyes went to the ground, and Celeste sensed what she was trying to hide: shame.

"Please, don't be angry with anyone but me," she emitted quietly.

"Esther?" Jonathan uttered in a shaky tone, gaping at her. "But it...it can't be."

To be fair, Esther looked nothing like her former self: her body was muscular, toned, and took on a somewhat intimidating charisma it hadn't previously. There was no trace of makeup or perfume, only a small amount of hair on her head, and rather than a dress, Esther was sporting her usual pair of brown slacks, lace-up boots, and a loose, white cotton shirt. At her waist was a blade, and on her other hip, a pistol. No, this was not the Esther Jonathan remembered. That Esther had died with Danny.

Though she wavered, Esther faced Captain Bernhardt. "It's me, Jonathan."

Tears welled up in Jonathan's eyes, and his right hand trembled as it moved to touch Esther's cheek. "But I watched you die... in the Tombs..."

"That was a decoy," she granted. "It was someone—a friend— who took the fall for me because she wanted to. I didn't know until right before they brought me out." Both her hands went up and pressed onto Jonathan's hand on her cheek. "I am so sorry."

"Esther," Celeste interrupted, "I think that, well, now it is unavoidable. You should tell Captain Bernhardt what happened." She took a deep breath. "I am going to join my father next door. When you are done, please come over."

Earlier than Esther could reply, Jonathan burst into sobs, pulling Esther into his arms and holding her tight. "Esther...Jesus Christ... what happened?! Tell me what happened?!"

Celeste felt a catch in her throat when she observed that Esther's eyes were also welling with tears. "I had to…to go away for a while," she mumbled.

He pulled away from her in suspicion. "But why?!"

Celeste could see Esther was disinclined—she didn't want to tell Jonathan anything that might sacrifice everything they'd done. Without thinking, Celeste went over to them, and gently touched Esther's back.

"Tell him. I'll be next door."

Esther glanced at her, her eyes red and swelling with tears, and she nodded.

Celeste rotated to Douglas. "Father? Brandy?"

He was already on his feet. "Of course, daughter."

They slowly walked to the door and Douglas led the way, taking off his jacket and dropping it over the glass for Celeste to walk over safely. After cautiously shadowing him, Celeste took one last look back at Esther and Jonathan: they had sat on the couch, both of them weeping and holding each other's hands. Celeste closed the door.

Three hours had come and gone, and finally, Esther peeked her head through the doorway to Douglas's rooms. Douglas had already gone to bed, and Celeste, unable to even think of sleep, was awake, on her fifth glass of wine, chain smoking as if it were the end of the world.

"Celeste?" Esther asked. "Would you mind taking Jonathan out?"

"No, of course not," she answered, putting her cigarette out. "Will you hang around so we can…well…talk when I get back?"

"As long as I can smoke about five of those cigarettes," Esther bargained.

This caused Celeste to grin. "Go for it. Pour us a round of wine as well, would you?"

Celeste showed the Captain out, and while they descended to the lobby side by side, Jonathan didn't say a word. When they got to the front doors of the hotel, Celeste took the Captain outside and paused, her defensive instincts kicking in.

"If you give her away, I will kill you, Jonathan."

Jonathan immediately stopped walking, confounded at what she'd just said. "Are you crazy? Why on earth would I do something like that?!"

"Because I trusted you once, Jonathan," she snapped, unrelentingly. "Trusted you beyond measure, and you broke that trust. That is my sister, and I will go after any bastard who tries to hurt her again!"

Captain Bernhardt did not hesitate to get straight into Celeste's face.

"How...dare...you..."

"Don't you start that bullshit with me."

"With you?!" he exclaimed. "You knew all along she was alive, and you didn't fucking tell me! Do you realize how horrible you are?! We agonized over her—together! And the whole time, it was just a ploy for you!"

"It was not a ploy! I didn't know for sure she was alive until after you'd left for the goddamn frontier, Jonathan!"

He retracted, managing to control his anger. "You could have told me at any time, Celeste, and you chose not to."

"You're right," she declared, "and I did it because my best friend and her life—and her safety—meant more to me than you did."

While she thought this might upset him further, instead, it mollified the Captain.

"Jesus Christ," he uttered quietly, shaking his head. "I just...I just can't believe it."

Celeste eyed him closely. "Did she tell you all of it?"

"Yes, I believe she did. I am having a hard enough time wrapping my fucking head around Esther hurting anyone, let alone murdering gang members, and this is coming from a frontier soldier. So, can you please stop acting like I don't know the gravity of the situation? I love her, Celeste. I'd rather die than have anything happen to her."

That was all it took to cause Celeste's claws retract. "I apologize. I am just…I am trying to diligently protect Esther because it's…it's what she's always done for me…and…"

Involuntary tears were welling in Celeste's eyes, and in that moment, she decisively grasped why she was furious with Esther. She wiped her eyes.

"It has just been a long few days, Jonathan."

He nodded. "I, too, am sorry I took my anger out on you. I know I shouldn't feel cheated, but I do, and that'll take time for me to get over."

"Well, I hope you can at some point."

"I'll do my best."

For a few seconds, she thought he might leave, but the Captain hadn't concluded just yet.

"Celeste, I know she is leaving, but you are not, and I want to say something."

"All right."

"I know Virgil was a complete bastard, and he deserves what he got, but even Edmund has confirmed some stories Virgil told me about Richard Croker, and I…" Suddenly, Jonathan was distressed. "Please, just be careful."

There wasn't even a touch of patronization in his tone—Captain Bernhardt was worried about her, and after the display she'd caught between him and Esther, Celeste felt her resentment toward him melting away.

"I will be careful, Jonathan," she promised. "Where are you going from here?"

"Home to Vermont," he told her. "Esther asked that I go home for a few months until the election is through, and I will respect that wish. I wanted her to come with me. I just want her to be safe." Captain Berhardt took a deep breath. "People—we do things some-

381

times, to try and heal. There was a void for Esther, when Thomas was gone, and I was the one who filled that for her. I did that same thing to you, and I am so grateful that, unlike me, you are not…"

Celeste moved forward and, though it was somewhat uncomfortable, she hugged Captain Bernhardt. "Are you going to be all right, Jonathan?"

He embraced Celeste in return. "Knowing Esther is alive, strangely enough, makes this whole ordeal easier to cope with." Captain Bernhardt let her go, smiling down at her. "Will you do me a favor, Celeste?"

"Sure."

"Will you please write to me, and keep me informed on how she is?"

"Of course I will, Jonathan."

With a nod, he left her there, heading toward the street to find a carriage.

Once Jonathan got picked up, Celeste made her way upstairs with the knowledge that she and Esther were about to have a conversation that would bring to light what had been haunting Celeste.

Esther, as requested, had filled their wine glasses with about two portions worth, and was halfway through a cigarette when Celeste returned. She took a long drag and glanced over at Celeste.

"He made it out?"

"Yes, he did." Celeste went and sat beside Esther on the sofa, grabbing her glass of wine. "Es, you shouldn't have interfered. What if he hadn't been so understanding?"

"I was going to tell him, Celeste," Esther affirmed. "Whether I went and found him or it happened tonight, it's no matter. He needed to know. And as we both discovered, he needed a reason to move on with his life."

Her friend's voice caught at the end, and Celeste touched Esther's arm. "Why don't you tell me what happened after we left you two alone?"

Esther picked up her wine glass, trying to mask that she was hurting. "I told him everything—about the deal with Croker, about the Whyos, about the people I killed, everything I did in the time I've been gone." She had a large drink from the glass. "He wanted to take me to Vermont, and I told him it was impossible. I'm going to England."

Celeste appreciated that what Esther really meant to say was she had picked Thomas over the Captain, and there was no changing that. "Love is a bitch," Celeste blurted out.

Remarkably, Esther let out a little, biting laugh of relief. "Yeah, yeah, it is." She took another inhale of her tobacco. "I will only ever admit this to you, because you understand. I...I told Jonathan that I loved him, because, well, I do. But I also told him that I love Thomas more, and that Thomas is the love of my life. And then, that was it, really."

"How did he react?"

"Terribly. It was fucking awful. But it's more than that."

Celeste was puzzled. "More than that?"

What Esther was about to say pained her: "It's tough to try and put into words...in comparison from what Jonathan and I used to be, so many years ago, when we first met...I mean, we are both... kind of ruined. I firmly believe Jonathan can recover from that, and I told him as much. But I...I probably will not be as lucky. And for me, the reality is, there is no going back to the way I once was. I am fortunate that Thomas is on a similar path, and that our stars have aligned in the best and worst possible ways."

This response left Celeste speechless. The two of them sat in silence, drinking and smoking for nearly ten minutes, until Celeste was able to speak up.

"I couldn't figure out what it was until I said goodbye to Jonathan."

"What what was?"

"Why I've been so upset with you."

383

"Oh," Esther said. "That."

They each took a sip of wine.

"I am not mad at you, Es. I'm mad because…because so many times, you have kept me safe. So many times, you have had my back, and what have I done? Nothing!" She could feel the heartache in her chest. "I wanted to help save you. For once, I wanted to be the better friend and save you from your despair, to get you free of Croker, of Tammany Hall, of everything that has been enslaving you to this, and I…I didn't get to. Why didn't you let me save you? Why? Just this one time!"

Celeste couldn't hear the anguish in her voice, and by the time she was done, Esther was almost tilting back in her chair, astounded.

"Celeste," Esther started, "why in the hell would you ever think such things?" She scooted closer to her, putting her cigarette and wine glass aside. "You being here has saved me from day one. If you hadn't been involved with the Madame, The Palace…if I wasn't able to paint those paintings for you, to know you were on the other side of this, I am not sure I would have survived! You did save me, Celeste. More than any of the others!"

"How? I didn't do anything!"

"Yes, you did. You signed onto The Palace. I am not sure I would have kept fighting if you hadn't done that."

In a flurry, they wrapped their arms around each other, holding each other close. When Celeste was able to calm her nerves, they moved apart, and Esther got up.

"One more glass, then to bed."

Celeste released a shaky exhale. "Agreed." She settled back. "God, I've missed you, Esther. And, hell, now you have to leave, just when I got you back."

Esther brought the bottle over with her. "Celeste, if I share something with you, you have to promise me this stays between us."

Celeste rolled her eyes. "Really? Now you question my loyalty?"

Her friend chuckled. "Fine." She poured their glasses of wine. "I am not going to stay at Amberleigh for long."

"I didn't think you would."

Esther held up her wine, and the two clinked glasses.

"I want to see Mary. I need to heal my body, because let's face it, I am a fucking wreck. But most importantly, that Samurai is going to help me prepare to end this."

"End what? The war?"

"Yes," Esther confirmed. "Whatever happens with this election, we have all become names marked on a list. And before I can quit, we are going to end this thing, and I will put Walsh in his fucking grave. So, yes, I am going to end the war."

Though Louis swore they wouldn't be waking her, Will had different feelings at the idea of stopping by The Palace at six in the morning. They had news, of course, and there was no other reason not to wait until morning; and yet, the two of them had a busy day tomorrow, one that would be carefully watched by the others, thus why Louis was able to convince Will that this would be the right move.

It wasn't that Will didn't like The Palace—or the Madame, for that matter—conversely, it was that he still had to come to grips with the fact that his son had become a somewhat altered version of himself, a life he hadn't wanted for Ashleigh. He didn't have any right to tell him otherwise, that much Will knew, but it didn't change how he felt in his heart. Will had never wanted his son to become a hitman—he wanted him to be happy, and happiness was not something a hit really ever found. But there was no denying that ship had sailed, and Will's opinion on Ashleigh's choices was utterly irrelevant.

Louis knocked on the door, and within seconds, Ashleigh pulled it open, a respectable glance to Louis, and a somewhat ambivalent squint at Will. Without a word, he let them through, and quickly shut the door after them.

"Is she in her office?" Louis asked, already heading for the staircase.

"Yessir," Ashleigh responded. "Daddy."

"Son," Will countered, passing him by, two paces behind Louis.

Once on the second floor, Louis and Will paced into the Madame's office, finding her in a state very different than either of them would have guessed. She was in her corset, garter belt, and stockings, with a very thin robe wrapped around her waist. The rouge had been washed from her face, which was now bare, and she sat with her feet up on her desk top, drinking whiskey and smoking a cigar.

Louis pretended not to notice and went directly to pour himself and Will whiskeys. Will, on the other hand, couldn't help himself.

"Might I just say, I prefer ya like this?" he avowed with a huge grin, taking a seat. "I think ya look better with less, Madame."

"I appreciate your flattery, Mr. Sweeney," she remarked, also smiling. "What have you got for me?"

"Just saw Croker," Louis informed her. "Samuel and Seamus are going to make sure that Danny Lyons's death is state-ruled. They're going to claim it needed to be a private execution to prevent riots amongst the gangs."

"Whyos agreed to this?" the Madame asked.

"Wholeheartedly." Will shrugged. "Croker's promised a bounty on Esther. They wanna keep this hushed anyhow—makes them look less dangerous and all."

"Right." She set her whiskey glass down, puffing smoke from her cigar. "How is Croker trying to play this, though, I wonder."

Louis ambled over to Will, handing over his drink as he sat beside him. "What do you mean?"

"I mean, darling, that Croker is probably going to try and fucking play this as Tammany Hall coming together with the law to take a stand against gang activity after Croker's attempted assassination."

"Richie'll deny that to Walsh, to the Whyos, prolly allow the press to assume that's the case," Will sustained. "He's gonna pretend it ain' him…it's the press."

"When really, it's him," added Louis.

"Correct," the Madame finished. "And that will certainly turn into a fucking disaster fast. Now, how is Esther?"

"We are headin' to see her day after next," Will said. "We are gonna get her to the Turners' from the hotel, then…"

Louis picked up for him, "Then she'll go to Amberleigh."

Will hated this part—he hated the idea of Esther being so far from them, away from the only things she'd ever known. On multiple occasions, he'd fought Louis on this. He firmly believed they could still run and make it out just fine; Louis, on the other hand, was resolute in his standing that they needed to remain here, and Esther would return. That was a subject not one of their group was bold enough to breach, and yet every one of them understood Esther was not going to linger in England longer than necessary. It wasn't in her makeup. And without Will and Louis there to restrain that particular drive, no one could stop her, not even the Chinaman.

Unconsciously, Will finished his whiskey, and Louis threw him a sideways glance.

"What?" Will asked.

"The Madame asked about Virgil."

"Ah." Will realized he must have tuned out their conversation. "Trial is next week. Richie got his judge. Everythin' is set for him to hang, and that little socialite wife o' his has already put a statement in the paper, sayin' she's disownin' him."

"That isn't a fucking surprise."

"Now the worry is Priestly, and just when and how Croker is going to take him out," Louis added.

Will peered over and saw Louis, too, needed another round of whiskey, so he rose to get the decanter.

The Madame held her empty glass up as well, and Will acknowledged her with a nod.

"You think it'll be you two? Or Walsh?"

"We did our part," Will emphasized, walking first to the Madame to pour, then Louis. "Roughed him up a bit. Threatened. Ain' enough with a do-gooder like him. I honestly reckon it'll be the lunatic, and with Priestly gone and the election won, Richie'll cut ties with Walsh and let the Whyos fall apart."

"There is one thing that worries me," the Madame confessed, sliding her legs down from her desktop. "And that is, what happens if the Whyos don't fall apart, Mr. Sweeney?"

Will scoffed. "The Dannys is gone. Only person holdin' it together is Walsh, and pretty sure Richie will cut him a deal to leave the organization quietly. He ain' gonna fuck with Walsh. He's as scared of him as we all is."

Louis shifted in his seat. "She is right, Will. What if he doesn't go quietly?"

No one could answer the undeniably haunting question, and then abruptly, Ashleigh let himself into the Madame's office.

"Sorry to bother ya, Madame, but we're havin' a bit of an issue downstairs."

"What is it, Ashleigh?"

"Apparently Uma and Jasmine were due to see the doc, and they...uh...found out about him and Razzy."

The Madame gaped at him. "How did you know about Razzy and Jeremiah?!"

"Celeste."

"Celeste knows?!"

"Course she does. She figured it out ages ago."

With a shake of her head, the Madame downed her drink and got up. "Keep watching the front, Ashleigh. Louis?"

"Yeah."

Before Will recognized what exactly was happening, he and Ashleigh were alone in the Madame's office.

"I…uh…gotta head downstairs," Ashleigh began. "You wanna have a whiskey down there while we wait?"

If he said no, he would basically be telling his son to fuck off. "Yeah, I'm comin'."

Will got up and trailed Ashleigh down the main staircase, where he checked the locked and bolted front door before leading Will to the bar area.

Due to the hour, Claire was not on duty, but Ashleigh made himself at home and went to fetch a bottle of whiskey and two glasses. He pointed toward a vacant table, already cleaned for the night, and the two of them lowered into their chairs. Will recognized it was the first time since his son was a boy that they'd been alone together, and strangely, he actually found he was nervous.

Ashleigh set the bottle between them after pouring them each a full glass. "How has everythin' been with Croker?"

"Ah, just a shit storm—cleanin' up messes, tryin' to keep the press at bay. Everyone wants to make this into some kind of political thing, and Louis and I are runnin' our asses off to muscle the story our direction."

"How's he handlin' Esther disappearin'?"

Will chuckled. "'Bout as well as you can imagine. It won't matter long. She'll be outta here, he'll win his election, and her importance will fade, like everythin' else."

A small pinch of pain hit from his knee, a sharp stab that surfaced from time to time, and Will flinched in response. He bent and straightened his leg a few times to loosen it up. "Damn knee. Never was the same after Georgia."

"Ya gonna try and get out? Or ya stayin'?"

"Stayin' til the end, I'm 'fraid."

This answer disappointed Ashleigh. "Daddy, ya ain' gettin' younger, I just—"

Will held up a hand to stop him. "This is all I know, boy. And I'm gonna die with my goddamn boots on."

"Well, I assumed. And I can' say I'm any different," Ashleigh agreed. "I just wish I knew what was comin', or how ugly it was gonna get before it's over."

The hair stood up on Will's neck. He'd forgotten Ashleigh was a part of this, just as much as any of them were. Will had an idea of what was next, of what it would take to at least attempt to accomplish what they felt obligated to do, and rather than say it aloud, Will bit his tongue. It wasn't because he was in denial, but rather, in that moment, Will felt the need, above every other emotion, to protect his son from the hard reality on the horizon.

"Lord knows," he lied quietly, finishing his whiskey. "We can only wait and see, I suppose."

CHAPTER XXXIX.

It was a warm July morning, with the sky above giving only the faintest hint that dawn was on the horizon, its hue taking on a shadowy sapphire without a cloud in sight. Because the summer heat was increasingly unbearable in the afternoons, Thomas had grown used to this shade of sky, setting out early each morning with Athena on his arm and heading for the northern segment of Central Park to allow his Peregrine to hunt and stretch her wings. He could already feel the sweat on his brow, gravel crunching loudly under his feet while he battled the haze of sleepiness, wishing he'd been smart enough to consume a cup of coffee before leaving the house. Athena, too, was waking sluggishly, but she was well-aware that morning was her time to get out of the house, eat a big, fresh meal, and find the freedom of flight. By the time the pair of them reached their designated spot, the birds around them chirped merrily and the first beams of light trickled over the ocean in the east.

"You ready, girl?" Thomas asked, steadily raising his arm and moving to untie Athena's jesses.

With a quick tug, she was free, and in a flurry of feathers, Athena was tracking high above Thomas's head.

He grinned. "Happy hunting!"

Athena danced around the sky, hovering hundreds of feet overhead one moment, then diving like a bullet the next. No matter the
circumstances, Thomas was eternally in awe as he observed Athena
in her element: she was a predator, well-trained and eager to earn
her reward. Ever the worrier, though, this did not change the fact
that things could go awry, and Thomas scanned the skies diligently for other predatory birds. One of his greatest fears was having to
look on as Athena found herself hunted by another raptor of the
sky. They had trained for that kind of an emergency, and Thomas.
prayed whenever he set her loose to fly it was an unnecessary, if not
paranoid, protocol to rehearse.

Once her wings were liberated from the cobwebs and she felt
adequately ready to hunt, Athena found a high branch on a nearby tree, her eyes sharp and focused with one goal in mind: food.
Though he continued to monitor her closely, Thomas couldn't help
but think about the upcoming days, and how in a very short period
of time, his currently full house would feel quite empty.

Moving Esther out of the Hotel St. Stephen had occurred without incident. About a week prior, Esther had been transported by
carriage in the early hours of the morning by Will and Louis, first
to The Palace to be assured they weren't tailed, and then later in the
afternoon, Esther was taken to the Turners'. In preparation for her
arrival, Thomas sat William and Lucy down, forced them each to
have at least two drinks, and proceeded to wait in the great room,
explaining that they would be hosting a guest shortly. There were
a few minutes of Lucy's expected interrogations, yet Thomas remained infallible, and when she recognized this, she relented with a
pout. William, on the other hand, seemed to understand that whoever was coming was by no means going to be someone they could
guess, and he was silent, diligently downing two glasses of brandy,
sporting a guarded countenance.

When the fated hour came, Tony went to meet Esther at the
door while Thomas stayed in the sitting area with William and Lucy.

These seconds felt like hours, and Thomas actually recognized himself growing nervous, unable to gauge what type of reaction William and Lucy might have at beholding Esther alive, and additionally, in a much different manifestation.

Esther entered the room cautiously, and to Thomas's delight, wore her usual ensemble rather than trying to pretend donning a dress would make this encounter easier. The scabs on Esther's face were beginning to heal and the swelling had receded immensely, though the wrapping around her torso was noticeable, as was the dark blue bruising on her hands and wrists.

As Esther gradually came forward, Thomas stood up, gesturing for her to come and sit on the couch beside him. William and Lucy sat on the sofa opposite Thomas, their backs to Esther, and the two of them turned in unison, peering toward the doorway to see who their mystery guest was.

Thomas watched as William's eyes almost popped out of his head, an audible gasp coming from his lips once he realized that the woman in front of him was Esther.

Lucy, ever so calmly, set her drink down on the side table and fainted.

As they all became absorbed in helping Lucy, Mrs. Shannon burst into the great room from the hallway, a special mixed tonic in hand. It was then Thomas remembered he had completely forgotten not only to tell Esther that Mrs. Shannon was the head of the Turner household, but he also had forgotten to tell Mrs. Shannon that Esther would be the Turners' guest. Their gaze met from across the room, and Mrs. Shannon halted, the color draining from her cheeks as if she'd spotted a ghost. Then, large, heavy tears welled up in Mrs. Shannon's eyes, whereas Esther simply gaped at her, unable to speak. Taking a bounding stride forward, Mrs. Shannon thrust the tonic into Tony's hands and paced straight for Esther, who she wrapped up tightly into her arms, her focus shifting instantly from Lucy to the girl she'd helped raise. They stayed that way for some time, and when Mrs. Shannon finally let Esther go, she gently stroked her cheek before disappearing the way she'd come, leaving Esther mystified.

Once she'd been revived, which took only a few sips of the tonic from Mrs. Shannon, Lucy was so deliriously happy that Thomas had to move to sit by William to allow her to take his original spot on the sofa beside Esther. William, too, was thrilled, that much Thomas could tell, but he was clearly shocked at this revelation and needed to understand the full scope of just what had happened.

At the point when Lucy finished doting over Esther, Thomas interrupted them to commence the much more difficult portion of the evening.

Ahead of Esther's debut at the Turners', she and Thomas made the decision that Esther should be the one to do the talking—she was, as far as Thomas was concerned, the one with a bigger story to tell. Once she started, it became a series of painful flashbacks for Thomas, recalling everything from Esther's faked execution at the Tombs to watching Walsh nearly slay her directly in front of him. Years of their lives were reduced to mere minutes, minutes that deeply affected William and Lucy, who, at various times, were both in tears.

It took Esther nearly two hours to cover what had happened over the time they'd been apart, and William and Lucy were stunned and horrified to hear the life Esther had been forced to endure; that horror only amplified when the pair grasped that Thomas was a part of this violent underworld as well. Esther did him that favor, describing as best she could Thomas's role in helping her escape, and what he was trying to do to get the Whyos under control and put a stop to Richard Croker. Her words were spoken with pride, but unfortunately, they were received with fear and apprehension; not because William and Lucy were scared for themselves, but because they were appropriately nervous that Thomas was in over his head. It was difficult to wave off their insistence he go with Esther to England and get out of New York City; yet, right on cue, Tony came in to let Thomas know that William and Lucy's railroad tickets to San Francisco were successfully booked for the same day Esther was setting sail for England on the White Star Line.

Wanting to protect his family, Thomas had sent a wire to Bernard in San Francisco, informing him that William wanted to visit to make sure Turner S & D was adequately organized and running on the West Coast. Francis could not have been more excited to have them as guests, and Cornelius Vanderbilt graciously booked them in his own personal cars for the railroad journey across the country on the transcontinental express. Both wholeheartedly protested, but Thomas dismissed their objections, insisting this was the way it was going to be. In spite of the grumbling from William and a little more pouting from Lucy, when Thomas's mind was made up, there was no changing it. For the rest of the night, the four of them got ridiculously drunk and celebrated having Esther back in their family, and in the week that followed, it was like no time had passed between any of them. Those days had come and gone faster than Thomas cared to admit, and irrespective of the happiness Thomas took in their reunion, the moment had arrived to send them on their way to safety.

The morning sun was at last glaring light out and over the cityscape. Athena was circling overhead, having spotted her meal somewhere in the vast expanse of land beneath her. As the sun's rays grew stronger, a tiny shadow approaching him from the southwest corner caught Thomas's eye, and though he didn't turn, he could spot that gait from two miles away. It was Louis. He, in turn, was conscious that Thomas spotted him from afar, and didn't make any attempt to surprise him; on the contrary, Louis ceased walking some twenty yards away, bowing in his typical mock salute, and Thomas returned it, elaborately taking a deep curtsy.

Smiling wide, Louis advanced again, and when he was close enough, pulled Thomas into a huge hug. Thomas realized the two of them hadn't been alone together since that awful day years ago—

the day after Edward was murdered on the street by Walsh—and the thought overwhelmed him with guilt. There was no excuse. He should have done this sooner, rather than let it linger in Louis's mind that anything between them was wrong.

Louis let him go, still smiling. "Will told me you'd be here."

"He did, did he?" Thomas chortled.

"I figured we needed to meet...discreetly."

"Yes," Thomas agreed. "You know, Will has been out here a few times to fill me in on all of the Hall happenings."

Louis glanced to Athena, where Thomas's regard laid. "I gathered as much."

"But he didn't really need to," Thomas carried on. "Not with you passing everything along to Tony. And then I met Ashleigh, and it was pretty clear that he was coming out here with me because he missed his son."

Louis was quiet, and once Thomas spotted Athena close by, munching on the last of her catch, he twisted to face his friend.

"Louis, why didn't you tell me?"

His countenance was unreadable. "Tell you what?"

Thomas rolled his eyes. "That Tony was your brother, and that you have been his contact here all along, giving him the information that has been keeping me up so late at night."

"He told you, did he?"

"No. I figured it out when you both burst in on me and William. I couldn't believe I hadn't seen the similarities before." Another epiphany hit him. "Is that why you shave your head?!"

When Louis again didn't respond promptly, Thomas realized he had guessed correctly.

"Your father was worried that if it came out, it would ruin my original cover with the Madame."

"Your cover?"

"I didn't join with The Palace to become the Madame's bodyguard, Thomas. Though, of course, that is what we try to tell everyone now."

A little confused, Thomas pressed him for more. "Well, why did you start to work at The Palace, then?"

"I joined because your father asked me to."

Thomas gazed over to Athena, then back at Louis, contemplating this new intelligence. "Why would my father…" His voice trailed off. "He wanted you to protect Mary."

Louis grabbed two cigarettes out of his vest pocket, lit them both in his mouth, and handed one over to Thomas. "The false news came that your father had died, and so I did what I thought Edward would want me to do: protect you and your mother at all costs. That meant staying at The Palace until you two decided to go elsewhere. Mary may never have told you this, but you two were not going to go to the frontier alone." He took a long drag of his cigarette. "I was planning to go with the two of you. She and I just weren't going to tell the Madame."

Thomas ran his hands through his hair. "Is the Madame aware of how connected we are? I mean, almost everyone around her is…"

A strange look crossed Louis face. "She is aware now, yes."

Suddenly, a tiny squawk came from Athena, and she flapped her wings from her spot on the ground.

"Athena?" Thomas called, holding up his arm. Within seconds, she was perched on the holster, and Thomas commenced tying her jesses.

"Louis, I want to apologize for not seeing you sooner. It had nothing to do with my being upset with you about the past, I want to assure you of that." He had a long drag of his tobacco. "I just couldn't find an opportunity."

"That was never it, Tommy."

"It wasn't?"

Louis's eyes were on the ground as he exhaled a cloud of smoke. "I should have never yelled at you the way I did. We were all upset about your father. In that moment, I nearly confessed it to you...what really happened, because I was so angry that you didn't understand. But if I had, it would have been a grave mistake. I am only glad to have you here now." Louis glanced up at Thomas. "He would be so furious with me, and with Tony, for allowing you to become what you are. And yet, I can feel how proud he is of you. You are doing what he never could—you are righting the wrongs of society, not just of those who will pay you to do so. It is a noble cause, Thomas."

"I can't say noble is how I would describe what I am doing," Thomas acknowledged reluctantly. "My initial goals were purely selfish, and they morphed into this."

"Don't be ridiculous, Thomas. You are ridding this city of its scum and pushing back against the corrupt. What more noble cause is there?"

Thomas took another drag of his own cigarette. "Even if, at first, my only intention was to free Esther?"

"Esther is freed, and you are staying to fight. She will be back to join you, do not doubt it. This battle is as much hers as it is yours. As long as you fight it together, you will be able to invoke the change you want, and we will help you every step of the way."

Thomas hooded Athena, and a curious thought struck him: "Have you and Hiro been writing to each other?"

Louis attempted to hide a smirk. "We are in touch from time to time." Dropping his cigarette, he put the smoke out with his foot. "Come on, I'll walk back toward Fifth with you."

"Is that sanctioned?"

"Fuck it."

Thomas chuckled, and they set out, taking a leisurely pace toward the gravel path that led southeast.

Feeling the burn at the end of his tobacco, Thomas discarded his cigarette. "Louis?"

"Hmm?"

"You know about the 'peace talk' arranged by the Madame and Douglas, I presume?"

"Yes," he replied, somewhat halfheartedly. "The day after tomorrow, if my memory serves me correct."

Thomas swallowed. "I am not going to yield."

If this shocked Louis, he didn't show it. "I would be disappointed if you did, Thomas."

"You disagree with her, then?"

"I do, for lots of reasons." Louis got out another round of cigarettes for them. "The first is that you have no reason to. You are one of the wealthiest men in this city, and you've become close friends with two of the biggest industry tycoons New York has ever seen. Second, what will it gain you, other than a tie to Tammany Hall, an organization that so many of the wealthy already turn up their noses at? It doesn't matter that Grant is a choice pick, Tommy. Everyone knows it'll be Croker running this city, not him. Third, of course, is his affiliation with the Whyos and the lunatic."

He took his second lit cigarette from Louis. "Is there a fourth?"

Louis inhaled. "Fourth is that, no matter what sort of deal you could get from it, if I were you, I would never forgive or condone what that son of a bitch did to your mother, not for anything on this earth."

It was the exact sentiment Thomas had been experiencing the last three days. When the Madame and Douglas formerly sought a peace meeting between Croker and Thomas, it was to ensure the safety of Esther, Will, and Louis, and to be certain that the Madame and the Hiltmores were not suspected in their joint escape from Croker's grasp. Now? What truly was the point? Thomas could feel his fist clench just at the mention of Croker's incarceration of Mary at the asylum, and appreciated that without comprehending what he'd done, Louis gave Thomas permission to take this chance to stand against Croker. What would the compliance of Lord Turner do other than give Croker a bigger ego, building his self-assurance that he was utterly unbeatable? There were no benefits Thomas could gather, other than one.

"He might guess that I am the Vigilante," Thomas added.

"So what if he does?" Louis countered. "He's going to find out at some point anyhow."

"He could arrest me."

"For what? Cleaning up the streets?!" Louis laughed aloud. "Don't be ridiculous, Tommy. Even if he could, you're forgetting that in the end, he needs you, not the other way around, and if you don't pardon Richard and Tammany Hall, the only one who loses is Richard."

Thomas and Louis reached the end of the park only a few blocks from the Turner residence. To keep Louis out of trouble, Thomas stopped and held out his hand, which Louis shook.

"With the secret out, I expect you to be around more," Thomas remarked warmly.

"You can bet on it," Louis replied with a sly grin.

Thomas continued to lean close to Louis, keeping his voice as low as possible. "I want in on Priestly. I want to help keep him protected. It's a loose end for Croker, and we can do it as a team."

"What about Walsh?" Louis uttered softly.

Thomas straightened back up. "I haven't formulated a strategy for him yet, but I'll tell you one thing, Louis: I am not leaving this city until he's dead."

"That is music to my ears, Tommy. See you in a few days?"

"I'll be doing horseshoes with Lawrence on Saturday morning."

"I could always go for a pint of German beer."

Thomas saluted him, and the two parted ways.

On the rest of their walk home, Thomas was amused by the usual stares Athena brought upon them from pedestrians. She was completely oblivious to the attention and practically unconscious as she dozed comfortably on his arm after feasting on whatever pheasant she'd picked off in the brush of Central Park.

It was a pretty mild Thursday morning, and Thomas saw only four carriages rolling down Fifth before they reached his residence. He hopped up the steps two at a time, much to Athena's vexation, and once inside, went straight to his study and tied the Peregrine to her perch to rest. Next, Thomas moved to his desk, expecting that Esther, William, and Lucy would be sleeping for another few hours, which allowed plenty of time for him to catch up on business.

Tony, as usual, had perfect timing, hustling into Thomas's study with a tray of breakfast sausage, toast, and coffee.

"Good morning, Lord Turner, I have your breakfast and the paper as well."

"Thank you, Tony," Thomas remarked, sinking down into his chair. "I will definitely be needing a bit of extra coffee this morning, if you don't mind."

"Not at all, sir. How was Athena's hunting?"

Thomas reached for his cup of coffee and a piece of toast. "She did quite well, I'd say. Huge pheasant." He took a large gulp of his drink, grateful he didn't burn his tongue. "Louis showed up to say hello."

Tony handed him the paper. "And did you tell him you are aware that we are brothers?"

"I did. He seemed to think it was you spilling the beans."

With a scoff, Tony shook his head. "Bastard."

At this, Thomas laughed heartily. "Anything interesting in the paper?"

"Priestly wrote another scathing article about the Hall," Tony informed him. "He really has become relentless, though I can see why. He is one of the few reporters who refuses to let Croker intimidate him."

"He didn't identify Louis or Will, did he?"

"No, thank Christ," Tony stated with relief. "But he doesn't hesitate to establish that Croker is out to get him."

Thomas flipped the article open. "Well, that is smart of him, I would say."

"Why, sir?"

"Because if he wasn't pointing that fact out publicly, Croker would have already killed him. It gives him a nice layer of protection, at least for a few months, until Grant is in office."

"Too true, Thomas. Too true." He went to the door. "More coffee? Anything else?"

"Coffee will do for now, Tony. Thank you."

"Of course, sir."

When Tony left, Thomas went straight to the pile of letters and wires sitting on his desk that had been accumulated over the last three days. First was Cornelius Vanderbilt II, again putting forward the offer to Thomas of buying Turner S & D. It had come as a complete surprise to Thomas—he and Vanderbilt vigorously discussed a collaboration, and eventually a partnership between the two companies. Out of the blue, Cornelius had made the proposition, adding that Thomas would still be granted an enormous stake in their enterprise as well as a seat on the board. The offer was tempting— so tempting that Thomas was considering taking it. Edward would probably roll over in his grave, but Thomas had made his family an exorbitant amount of money over the years. Even without taking shares from Cornelius, the Turners would only need to manage their investments responsibly, and for generations, their source of income would be purely sustained by that. This also allowed Thomas the chance to put the business aside and focus solely on Richard Croker and the Whyos, yet he wasn't sure how healthy that was, either. He wrote a quick yet polite wire to Cornelius, telling him he'd need a little more time, and hopefully might have a final answer for him.

Next came letters from Hiroaki and Mary with updates from Amberleigh, and while Thomas had sent word to them both that Esther would soon be joining the family in England, the delay of time between letters meant he wouldn't hear their reactions until after Esther was already on her way. He wished he could be there to see Mary and Esther reunited, especially since Mary was finally back to her old self and Esther and Thomas were again engaged to one another. The night Will and Louis brought Esther to the Turners', Thomas presented the same ring he'd initially proposed with, and before he could finish the speech he'd spent hours rehearsing, she'd accepted. Once their burdens were resolved in New York, Thomas would marry her at Amberleigh. Until then, planning would stay on hold, though his primary purpose had been achieved: Thomas didn't want Esther to have a single doubt in her mind that she had a future with Thomas when their time in New York was done. As far as he could surmise, that was the precise result he'd gotten.

He worked diligently in the hours leading up to lunch, and when Tony appeared with his fifth cup of coffee, he shared that Thomas had an unexpected guest.

"Miss Hiltmore is here to visit with Esther and Lucy; however, she has requested a quick meeting with you if you are not too busy, sir." Tony brought the coffee over and sat it down on Thomas's desktop. "I think a break from correspondence would be healthy. You've written almost twenty posts, Thomas."

Thomas set down his pen and wiped his eyes with his hands. "You're right. I've been at it for too long. Send her in."

With a small bow, Tony went to fetch Celeste, and not a minute later, she knocked on the door to his study. "Thomas?"

"Come in, Celeste."

She entered, smiling when she saw him; in her hands she carried a huge leather bag, clearly struggling with the awkwardness of the weight.

"What do you have there?" Thomas asked, rising to his feet and going to her. "Let me take that for you."

"I brought it for Esther," she told him, wiping the sweat from her brow and taking a seat across from his desk. "I told Tony to bring us each a glass of wine. Is that all right?"

Thomas lowered down into his chair, setting the heavy bag on his desk. "I never have an objection to wine." He examined the duffel. "So, are you going to tell me what this is, or do I have to guess?"

Celeste excitedly clapped her hands together. "Look inside!"

He obliged and unfastened the top toggles of the bag, and his mouth fell open.

"It's a present for Esther," she announced animatedly. "I went to this incredible Italian artisan in Midtown. He is a wood-working genius who kindly helped me design one of my piano benches last year. And with our original plan for Esther, I thought she would be so bored in the attic hiding out, so I had this gentleman make her a hand-constructed paint set. It is completely unique. He even consulted with a fellow trader on how to get the best hair for the paint brushes. What do you think?"

Thomas was touched. "I think she is going to absolutely love it."

If it was possible, she smiled wider. "It has everything: brushes, canvases, easel, wood palate, and a few jars of the prime colors."

"Why don't you give this to her yourself?" Thomas beseeched her. "She would be so ecstatic to get this from you."

"Well, I want you to give it to her right before she leaves."

He was confused. "Why then? Why not now? She'll be delighted!"

"Because, I just…" Celeste wavered for a moment, biting her lip. "I just wanted it to be special, and I don't want Esther to think of this place in a…a purely negative way. I want her to want to come back. There are people who love her here, Thomas, me being one of them, and the idea of never seeing her again is not something I want to consider right now. I am providing her a sentimental connection so that—"

This he understood. "You want her to miss you."

"Of course I do!" She shifted in her chair.

Thomas closed the bag up and put it carefully on the floor. "Consider it done."

Another knock came, and Tony brought wine for the pair of them. At Thomas's request, he took the leather duffel to place with Esther's already packed trunk for her journey the following morning.

"Was that the only thing you wanted to discuss?" Thomas pressed her, having a sip of wine.

She did the same and yielded. "No, of course not. I wanted to ask about the peace meeting in two days."

He'd assumed this was her real aim. "What about it?"

"Well, you've already confirmed your attendance. I think I am just curious what you're going to say to Croker. I mean, the situation is much different than it was a few weeks ago. The Madame is convinced you are going to pull a stunt. My father thinks you will play nice, at least to a certain degree."

"And what do you think?"

Celeste took another drink of wine. "I really can't make up my mind. I can imagine it going either way."

"Sorry, I should rephrase," Thomas corrected himself. "What do you think I should do, Celeste? I can tell you want to give me your input."

Her countenance altered, as if she were a tad troubled. "I think you should go along with it and make him think you've crossed over."

"I say this from a place of friendship and respect, Celeste—no hostility whatsoever. But how can you expect me to want to concede my alliance to a man who has enslaved the two women I love most in this world? For years, might I add."

"And I would say, aren't we all slaves to survival, Thomas?"

This comment gave Thomas pause, and when he didn't respond, Celeste went on.

"We are all slaves to the trials of our lives. Think of what you've been through, what I've been through, what Esther has been

405

through…the Madame, my father, Louis and Will…every damn one of us has and still is suffering in one way or another. And yes, I can appreciate that this has been years of our lives trying to fight Tammany Hall and Croker from the shadows. However, we are so close. We have Priestly, and Louis is working day and night to track down whoever this McCann character is. You are keeping the Whyos below Midtown and hurting their relationship with Tammany. The only thing we have to do is bide our time, and we will have evidence—real evidence that will stick. Isn't that our goal here? To bring the whole organization down? The best way to do that is by befriending our enemy, because he will not suspect the hit when it comes."

"Shouldn't I send a message that he doesn't have everyone in his pocket? If no one stands up to him, he will think he is the king of this city. I want Croker to know that as long as I breathe air, I will never disregard the atrocities he's committed to get there, and that they will come back to haunt him."

She contemplated Thomas's testimony, swirling the wine in her glass. "I think you ought to look at it from this perspective. It will keep us protected for another few months. Once the election is over, he'll go after Priestly, and that's when we strike. It gives us enough time to track down McCann and figure out who he is, and it gives you the opportunity to finally shatter the relationship between the gangs and the Hall."

There was no denying Celeste had a point, and Thomas could feel his determination waver after listening to the rationality behind her argument.

"Right. You are right, Celeste."

"Does that mean you are going to go along with it?"

He sighed. "I don't know yet," Thomas admitted. "What I do know is that there is more to consider than I previously thought."

"Well, that is a start." Celeste finished her wine and set her glass aside. "I had better get to lunch. The girls will be wondering where I am."

"Tell Esther and Lucy I'll be seeing them in a few hours," Thomas entreated her.

Getting to her feet, Celeste gave him a small curtsy. "I will."

"I have to ask…did you come up with that on your own?"

"Come up with what?"

"Your reasoning. Not one person presented that perception to me on this whole ordeal. It was…strangely convincing."

She just shrugged and made her way toward the door. "It is how I am able to justify not tearing Richard Croker's eyes out every time I see him. Have a good afternoon, Thomas."

"You as well, Celeste."

As the door shut behind her, Thomas released a small huff, resting back into his chair. He'd never dreamed there would be a circumstance wherein Celeste Hiltmore might challenge him in a way that might make him reconsider his choices.

This new order of things was certainly getting interesting.

The hours went by in a blur, and when Thomas hadn't come up for air, William was sent down by Esther and Lucy to fetch him for their final happy hour. Shocked that it was already nearing four o'clock in the afternoon, Thomas consented to join them in thirty minutes, once he'd wrapped up running numbers and was able to get himself cleaned up. He rang for Tony, passing over the dozen or so letters left to be sent out, at last wrapping up what had been a grueling day of expense reports for Turner S & D. His short talk with Celeste was fresh on his mind, and Thomas was unable to stop thinking about what she'd said regarding Croker.

"Sir?" Tony's voice disturbed his train of thought.

"What?"

"I asked if you wanted me to get out your dinner jacket for tonight, sir."

Thomas had completely missed that Tony was addressing him. "Yes, that would be great, thank you." He hesitated. "Tony, I can't seem to make up my mind about Richard Croker."

Tony set the letters aside and lowered down into the chair across from Thomas's desk. "In what manner, Thomas?"

"Miss Hiltmore believes challenging him will do no good. She is concerned that it will endanger the others and with the order for a hit on Priestly coming, as well as the prospect of a lead on Mc-Cann, she is convinced we will have no issue pulling a committee together to form an investigation."

Tony deliberated, "And what do you feel in your gut?"

"You mean aside from the fact that I want to kill him?"

"Yes."

Thomas let out an exhale of irritation. "My gut tells me that something will go amiss with this Priestly endeavor. However, it also tells me that this McCann character, whoever he might be, is the break we've all been searching for."

"That isn't what I meant," Tony went on. "I meant about meeting with Croker and alluding to the notion that you are on good terms."

"Not a single fiber of my person thinks it is a good idea."

Tony grinned expectantly. "Then that is your answer, Thomas."

"He's going to find out it's me eventually, Tony," Thomas reiterated, concerned. "What do we do when he grasps that I am the one being a pain in his ass?"

"Well," Tony began, "you are missing the bigger point. What will Croker do, is the better question. And therein lies the answer to both. He will do nothing, because he can do nothing. You are English nobility, Thomas, and on top of that, you are one of the richest men in New York City and all of England. You're a more prominent social figure, definitely a more popular dinner guest, and you do not have the salacious rumors encircling you that Richard Croker and Tammany Hall fight on a constant basis to discredit. Even if he did bring about accusations, there is no proof. The only thing you would have to do is publicly laugh in his face, and the rest of this city will do the same."

Thomas was honored by Tony's words. "But the others—will it affect the others? That is what I cannot determine."

"I doubt it. Especially if the Madame and Douglas are the two planning this from the start. If anything, in Croker's eyes, it will make it seem that your relationship with them will be strained as a result. Probably better for the others, if you ask me."

Thomas reached over to his top desk drawer, opened it, and pulled out a cigarette and matches. "I don't know, Tony."

"You should kick him while he's down, Thomas," Tony said mildly. "That is my opinion on the matter."

Tony got to his feet, and with a small bow, left carrying Thomas's outgoing business letters.

With an exhale, Thomas lit a cigarette and took a long drag, considering the very different angles painted for him by a group all working toward the same goal. There was merit in what Celeste contended, Thomas could give her that, but Tony and Louis were both firmly in accordance with Thomas's intentions to tell Croker to go to hell, and Thomas would rather shoot himself in the foot than play nice with that bastard. If his hunch was correct, and it typically was these days, Celeste and the Madame were aligned, and Louis and Tony had their own motives to object, so there would be no right choice; it simply had to be a choice Thomas was capable of living with. And with William, Lucy, and Esther all soon beyond Croker's reach, why on earth would Thomas pander to the man responsible for so much pain and destruction amongst the people he loved?

In the corner, Athena stirred restlessly on her perch, and Thomas put out his cigarette before going to tend to her. Cautiously, he removed her hood to reveal her sharp, piercing eyes, staring at Thomas with their usual disquieting intensity, an intensity Thomas admired for a multitude of reasons. He gave her head a few strokes, went to the cabinet that stored her tackle, and picked out a small snack for her, supplied by Maximus, their head of the kitchen. After pocketing the tiny piece of meat, Thomas untied her jesses and went to the other side of the room—Athena was more than ready to exercise. Once he was about twenty feet away, Thomas gave the signal. In an instant, she took off and was on his arm, and he rewarded her with a little sliver of meat for cooperating in the drill. A few rounds of this later, Thomas knew if he didn't get moving, Lucy would murder him for being so late, so he put Athena back onto her perch with the promise of a visit later and went to his room to dress.

The three of them were eagerly awaiting Thomas in the great room. Lucy and William were seated across from Esther, who was laughing so hard when Thomas walked in there were tears in her eyes, and in anticipation of Thomas joining, William was cutting the pair of them cigars. A flute of champagne was resting on the side table for Thomas, and the three of them waved him over, Esther trying to get ahold of herself and failing while Lucy's eyes narrowed.

"Thomas, it has been an hour when William swore you'd only be twenty minutes!" she exclaimed. "What kept you?!"

Hastily, Thomas had thrown on his dinner jacket and splashed some water on his face prior to joining William, Lucy, and Esther, though clearly, they hadn't waited to start the party, and had already made it through a bottle of champagne. Thomas noticed that Esther had taken great pains with her appearance: she donned a beautiful, cream-colored dress with gold trim that sparkled in the light, and while she refused to wear a wig to hide her short hair, Esther put on rouge and made herself up, more than likely with the help of Lucy. Esther was having a tough time readjusting to what society life was like, but William and Lucy did not mind in the slightest when Esther chose to wear trousers instead of dresses. William had even gone so far as to compliment Esther on this, not wishing her to feel she had to be anyone other than herself in their household. He did, however, with the assistance of Mrs. Shannon, confiscate her brass knuckles for the time being, on both Jeremiah's orders and because after hearing stories of the damage Esther could do with them, they terrified William.

"I got caught up with work, Lucy, I apologize," Thomas confessed, flopping down onto the sofa beside Esther and grabbing his flute of champagne. "I want to know what you said to cause Esther to lose her mind. Was it you or William?"

Esther was clutching her side, gasping for breath. "It was...was..."

"I caught William trying to befriend Athena," Lucy declared, giggling herself. "That poor bird went crazy and dove at him. William fell down in a heap, and then ran out of there so fast, I could have sworn he was being chased by a lion."

William handed Thomas one of the cigars. "Not one of my prouder moments. Thanks for sharing that with anyone who will listen, dear."

"Anytime, husband."

Thomas had a gulp of his drink and reached for the timber on the coffee table, chuckling. "Well, I appreciate the effort, William. It will be good to let your ongoing feud with Athena cool off for a few weeks." With a couple of puffs, his cigar lit beautifully. "Has everyone gotten packed?"

There were nods all around, and at last, Esther was composed. "Selfishly, I still think you should consider coming to England with me, just until the end of the summer."

"Trust me, if I could justify it to myself, I would," Thomas conceded to her. "But I feel like if I leave now, the ground we've made up would be lost."

Lucy and William exchanged a fretful glance.

"Dare I ask what is coming next?" Lucy inquired.

"If you want to know, I will happily share that with you."

"Well, now that we are in the loop, I would at least like to know what sort of trouble you're getting into," William stated, taking a drag of his cigar. "I never pressed Eddie when I should have, so don't think you're getting off that easy."

"I wouldn't dream of it," Thomas replied with a smile. He took Esther's hand and kissed it. "I think the next order of business for me is to break the affiliation up between Tammany and the Whyos. Croker is more than likely aiming for that on his own, but what he doesn't realize is that once they are two separate entities, it'll be much easier for me to break them apart. And while we work on digging in Croker's closet of skeletons, I can handle the Whyos."

"But, how many Whyos are there?" Lucy asked.

Thomas peered at Esther, who answered for him, "Hundreds, if not thousands."

Lucy's mouth fell open, and William nearly dropped his cigar. "How on earth can that be done?" he queried.

"Well, it's not about getting rid of each member," Esther continued, taking out a cigarette and allowing Thomas to light it for her. "It is about destroying the top tier of leadership. There will always be gangs. This is about destroying the interconnected network of the last twenty years—a network that progressively has become more unstable and more violent." She had a sip of champagne. "Without Tammany, the Whyos will already be struggling, and they'll have to partner with the Celestials to get their opium, which is something they won't like in the least. If Thomas could get rid of Walsh and Kitty, there will be very few people smart enough to stand up and run that kind of an enterprise. It'll crumble in months, and the gangs will splinter off into warring factions, like they used to be."

"That's fascinating and...and so chilling!" Lucy cried.

William, too, was mystified. "How can you know that?"

Esther smirked. "I spent the better part of the last few years working with these people, in their bars, brothels, saloons...once the masterminds are gone, it's like cutting the head off a chicken.

If they don't have someone telling them what to do, they run wild, and without Tammany protecting them anymore, the police won't let every little thing slip by."

"The police have to be outnumbered though, to be sure."

"Of course they are, William. That's why everything south of Midtown is, frankly, lawless. But the Whyos will get theirs— Tammany and the police force will team up, and there will be an increasing pressure to crack down on the Whyos. Croker can't just shrug it off anymore, not to mention that Croker himself wants to rule the city independently, rather than use a third party."

"Bloody hell," William mumbled.

"That is a lot to take in," Lucy remarked, her mien that of someone who'd just received more information than they'd bargained for.

"The important thing is that you both will be safe in California," Esther settled. "And far, far away from this."

"That's reassuring," William chortled sarcastically.

Thomas looked at Esther, beaming. "You are brilliant. You know that?"

"I sure do," she said with a wink, leaning in to kiss him.

"Oh Christ, don't get sappy on us now," Lucy interjected. "Tony, can we get another round of champagne?"

Tony appeared and refilled their glasses, while Lucy held up her flute to salute them. "Now, it is at last time for me to give my toast."

Merrily, she hopped up to her feet, spilling a little champagne as she did so and ignoring her fumble diligently.

"I am so thrilled that Esther is home at last, where she belongs. It was a…a shock to hear what both of you have been enduring these last few years. We did have our suspicions, Thomas, but didn't want to interfere. I am just delighted that you found each other again. So, let's toast to when we are reunited in a few months!"

"Cheers!" Thomas professed, and the four of them clinked glasses.

"Thank you, Lucy," Esther said, beaming.

"Are you sure you don't want me to send Athena with you, William?" Thomas teased. "It could be a good bonding experience for the two of you."

William scowled at him. "I would rather face Esther with those brass knuckles, thank you very much."

Dinner went by too fast, as did Thomas and Esther's last night together, neither of them getting any sleep for fear of wasting the precious bit of time they had left. Naked and tangled up under the covers, they watched the sun lighten the room around them in dismay, wanting nothing more than another hour or so just the two of them, but there was no way around it. The dreaded day of departure had arrived, and reluctantly, the pair got up and got dressed. They would breakfast with William and Lucy, send them on their way to the train station, and then Thomas would take Esther to the harbor himself to say goodbye. He hated the thought of sending her off alone, despite being conscious that Esther could take care of herself; more than that, Thomas was disinclined to let her out of his sight, the anxious fear creeping in that any time could be the last time. Taking some deep breaths, Thomas tried to not let it sway him. The safest place in the world for Esther would be at Amberleigh, and he appreciated it was his own safety that he ought to prioritize. His undertakings would not be easy these next few months, and if he lost focus, it could bring about dangerous repercussions.

It was the mistake Edward had made, and not one Thomas wished to repeat.

Once coffee and tea were consumed as well as a hearty breakfast, they said their farewells to William and Lucy, who were escorted to the train station by Tony, and Thomas and Esther got into their own carriage heading to the harbor. Esther smoked a cigarette while Thomas held her hand, the windows drawn to ensure Esther was not spotted. In the previous week, Thomas had made arrangements with the harbor master to have Esther privately board the White Star steam ship, an incentive that cost much less than Thomas had anticipated. While general boarding would begin at one o'clock in the afternoon, Esther would board at nine in the morning, when the crowd was only beginning to line up for inspections. To further add to her disguise, Esther agreed to travel under Lucy's name and borrow an assortment of gowns from Lucy for the trip over the Atlantic. Not to mention, Esther wore a chestnut brown wig, one that she refused to put on until they arrived at the harbor because it made her head itch, and this excuse caused Thomas to laugh. Her stubbornness had never changed. So much of Esther was different, but in her heart, Esther was the same girl he grew up with lifetimes ago, and he loved her all the more for it.

The harbor master and two White Star employees, both of whom Thomas had personally vetted, were ready for Thomas and Esther when the carriage pulled up. They signaled for the driver to park right next to the vacant dock, and in a flurry, the two White Star sailors commenced unloading Esther's limited amount of luggage and taking it aboard. Thomas assisted Esther in securing the wig on top of her head, then climbed out of the carriage, holding a hand back to help Esther down. Daintily, she descended, keeping her head low as she did so.

"Good morning, Lord Turner," the harbor master, a man named Leo, greeted. "We have everything ready for Miss Lucy Turner: one of the finest suites prepared on the ship, and she will be the first passenger aboard, sir."

"Wonderful. Thank you, Leo. And like we discussed, you get half now, half when she arrives safely in England."

He nodded. "Of course, Lord Turner." With a courteous smile, his gaze went to Esther. "Whenever you are ready, Miss Turner, you can follow me."

Esther peered up at Thomas and quickly mouthed an "I love you." Though they'd agreed it would be better not to embrace in public, Thomas no longer cared. A kiss was out of the question, yet he hugged her tight, whispering that he loved her too, and let her go.

He watched Esther be led away by Leo towards the ship, and nervously, Thomas searched the surrounding area with his eyes to make sure they were not being followed. It was abandoned—there was no one nearby, and the only people close were the White Star employees setting up the inspection booths. With a wave of reprieve hitting, Thomas felt his nerves settle: he'd done it. Esther was out, going to their future home to recover and hide out for as long as she needed, and what happened beyond that, Thomas couldn't say. As Esther marched up the plank and onto the ship, Leo still in the lead, Esther halted and blew Thomas a kiss before disappearing inside.

Thomas pulled out a cigarette and lit it, inhaling deeply. He would pay Leo upon his return to the dock, and after, he would venture to have a long-awaited visit on the Upper West Side of town.

"How is it fucking possible that you get more handsome with age, and I just get old?" the Madame bellowed as Thomas moseyed into her office.

Before Thomas could say anything, the Madame was on her feet, walking to the drink cart. "How are you, darling? I am assuming whiskey is where your heart is at."

Thomas needed this—he needed time with her, no matter how insane it made him later. "You read my mind, Madame."

He took a seat on the sofa by the empty fireplace, where she joined him with their drinks. Thomas happily scoffed as, to his surprise, she produced two cigars for them, already cut and ready to light. Handing his over, Thomas produced matches for them, and she set his whiskey down on the small side table.

"The drop went as planned, I assume?"

"Would I be here if it didn't?" he bantered playfully, letting out a cloud of smoke and reaching for his drink.

She took the bait. "No need to be a smartass, darling. It is not very becoming on you."

He laughed. "Yes, the drop went smoothly. She should be out of New York shortly."

"And my contact, Leo, proved sufficient?"

"He got half now, gets the next half as soon as Esther wires me from Liverpool."

"Good." The Madame had a long inhale of her cigar. "How was she?"

"She didn't want to leave me here," Thomas confessed with a shrug, "and it was difficult to watch her go, but this is the deal."

The Madame eyed him closely. "You could have gone with her, darling."

"See, that is where you are wrong," Thomas stated in a mischievous tone. "Getting Esther out of Croker's grasp was a gift I am forever grateful for. That wasn't my main mission, though, or else yes, I absolutely would be leaving with her."

"So, it is about revenge."

"I would be lying if I said no, but it's not just about revenge. This is about changing the tide. I may not be able to get rid of the corruption entirely; that would be impossible from any standpoint. I can, however, even the playing field to try and do some good."

"You know," the Madame said, taking a sip of whiskey, "you sound just like your father when you say shit like that."

Thomas was intrigued. "What do you mean?"

"Well, I only know a little about his...missions...but that was always what he would say. He wanted to do some good. You two are so fucking similar it is...remarkable. And I have to say, I respect the hell out of the fact that you want to clean this city up. Edward said once, when he'd been here drinking with Louis, that just saving one life was better than not saving one at all. It's a drive I wish I had. That fucking chink did a number on both of you with his bizarre vendetta philosophy. I'm surprised he's not here trying to be your goddamned sidekick. He was your father's, after all. Refill?"

"I've got nowhere else to be."

This time, she brought the decanter back with her and poured another round. "Thomas?"

"Hmm?"

"I want to say I am sorry."

"Should I ask what for? The list is long…"

"I wanted to say I am sorry about…Mary."

Thomas was quiet for a few seconds. "If you hadn't gone along with it, we would both be dead, Madame. So, I do not think there is anything you need to apologize for."

"But your father—"

"Edward didn't understand the scope of this thing. I do. You tried to tell him and he didn't fucking listen when he should have. I listened, Madame. And rather than trying to fix it on my own and make the same damn mistake my father did, I have others to help me. Edward was smart, but you can't fight a war by yourself." He threw back his whiskey. "Don't apologize to me for wanting to keep you and me alive. We got Mary out. We got Esther out. Now, we can really focus on putting an end to this bullshit."

The Madame finished her drink as well. "What type of end do you have in mind?"

"Croker out of power—humiliated and with nothing left."

"And Walsh?"

Thomas had a drag of his cigar. "Dead."

"Does that mean you're going to be Croker's best fucking buddy tomorrow, or are you going to throw a wrench into the engine?"

"I don't know yet. There is a fair argument for either." He paused. "Did you send Celeste?"

She grinned. "I don't know what you're talking about."

"Right." Thomas gulped down some more whiskey. "She's gotten really fucking good at that. I was impressed. She's clever. You've worked your magic there."

The Madame pretended to blush. "I'll take that as a compliment."

"You're welcome."

They sat in contented silence for a minute or so, and then the Madame asked what Thomas hoped she would: "Do you have dinner plans?"

"Not that I am aware of."

"Good. Then you can eat and drink with me here. Louis will be by, and I am sure he will be fucking thrilled to see you."

By the time midnight rolled around, Thomas had to get home. The Madame refused to let Thomas wander to Fifth alone and sent Ashleigh as his escort; Thomas didn't complain. For reasons he couldn't quite put a finger on, Thomas found he really enjoyed Ashleigh's company—perhaps because the two of them had a strange understanding of one another. He'd never befriended a man so quickly, a man who he felt he could trust regardless of the short time they'd been acquainted. Ashleigh fit into the world of The Palace as easily as the rest of them, almost like he'd been there all along. The only thing that bothered Thomas was the somewhat mangled relationship between Ashleigh and Will, particularly since Thomas had been so close with Edward and missed him more than he could ever put into words. He hoped that before it was too late, father and son could find a way to make things right.

They were a quarter of the way across the park, smoking cigarettes and bantering back and forth about falconry, when Ashleigh became more sober in his tone.

"So, we all got different ideas 'bout how you're gonna handle that son of a bitch tomorrow, Tommy. Louis and Daddy and I match up, Celeste and the Madame got their own opinions…I reckoned I just oughta ask ya."

The whiskey was going to Thomas's head, making him just drunk enough to be blatantly honest with Ashleigh. "Well, I can't really decide how to deal with that bastard. I don't want to bow down, but I don't want to put anyone in any more fucking danger than we already are."

Ashleigh nodded. "I know you've had everybody tellin' ya which way to go and why, so I'm just gonna add my two cents and shut up 'bout it."

"Oh yeah? What do you think, then?"

"Men like Croker…they don' respond to passivity, Tommy. Richie is a damn tyrant. And tyrants don' hold themselves accountable for nothin'."

Thomas expected that this would be Ashleigh's input. "So, you want me to tell him to fuck off?"

"Not just to fuck off, Tommy." He tossed his cigarette away. "You tell him you're comin' for his ass. You didn' do this just to play along, you did this to put Richie in check. So, fuckin' put his ass in check! The only thing that's gonna do it is by sayin' to his face that ya have the better hand than him, and if he don' be careful, you'll be the one throwin' down."

"Yeah, but if it backfires——"

"Then what? Madame and the Hiltmores is fine. Louis and Will work for the guy. Your people are all outta here." Abruptly, Ashleigh halted and took both of Thomas's shoulders. "I've been waitin' weeks to see the tables turned on this prick. Esther was the beginnin'. Keep the momentum, or he'll forget he oughta be scared."

"Scared of what?"

"Of you. Of all o' us."

It was three hours of horseshoes before Thomas's mild hangover finally dissipated, a result, no doubt, of the relentless heat of the flames and the sweat pouring out of him on such a hot summer morning. Lawrence wasted no time teasing Thomas about it either, and the two of them spent the morning trading jibes in jest. At a certain point, Lawrence was able to convince Thomas to have a small pint of his new pilsner with the promise of it being a necessary cure for his headache; remarkably, it worked, though Thomas chased it with copious amounts of water from the pump in the back alley. He only had one hour left to spare, not wanting to be late for his meeting at The Palace, though also wondering if Louis would show up. That hour came and went, and after changing out of his soaked and dirtied shirt, Thomas said goodbye to Lawrence and left to catch a coach uptown.

Not two steps outside of his old master's house did Thomas spot Louis in his usual cloud of smoke, and they grinned at each other.

"Split a hackney?" Louis called, walking his direction. "I've got to make a stop at The Palace anyhow."

Thomas nodded. "If you don't mind sitting next to a smelly bastard."

Louis laughed aloud. "You've smelled worse. Believe me."

After a minute or two, they were able to wave down a driver, and once they'd given the driver their destination, they hopped into the cab together. Louis produced a cigarette for Thomas, a smile still planted on his face.

"What?" Thomas asked, striking a match.

"Nothing," Louis replied, though clearly amused. "Just feels like old times."

Thomas had a drag of his cigarette and the coach took off at a relaxed pace. "Some things will never change, Louis, no matter how much time goes by."

"That's true. Did you ever think you'd actually enjoy shoeing horses when you were seventeen years old?"

A deep chuckle came out of Thomas's belly. "Nah. Not ever. Now I can't get enough of it."

Louis let out a cloud of smoke. "I've got something for you."

"Talk to me."

"Richie has put Will and me back on with Walsh, and the Whyos know that his Assistant has evaporated into thin air," Louis disclosed. "And don't worry. No one has any idea about Esther heading to England. Croker is convinced she's still in the city, holed up in a negro hospital for cover. He's losing his mind—making random accusations against everyone about why we can't find her, even against Seamus, like it's all some conspiracy against him. He's gone off the rails when it comes to Esther."

"That is the best thing I've heard in months," Thomas responded, overcome with relief. "She's out of his reach as of yesterday morning."

"There is more."

"More is good."

"There is a new delivery of opium coming in. This time, in Chinatown."

Thomas took a deep inhale of tobacco. "So, they're finally working with the Orientals?"

"They don't have a choice, it seems," Louis asserted. "Chinks aren't happy about it either, but it's money, and they're worse off than the colored folks."

"Where at?"

"Zhìmìng de lóng. Just off Canal."

Thomas's eyes grew wide. "Isn't that where…"

"Yeah. It's the Tong headquarters."

"Louis, if Lee catches me there, he'll hand me directly over to the Hall."

"See, that's where you're wrong." A haughty look crossed Louis's face. "What you are unaware of, Tommy, is that Lee is not on great terms with the Hall. Richie's prices for protection are skyrocketing, and they are getting nothing in return. Don't forget that the Tong have been The Palace's suppliers of opium since the Madame opened The Palace decades ago. The Madame and I have made an arrangement with Lee."

It was like Christmas morning. "What kind of an arrangement?"

"The Madame paid him extra this month, and consequently, they are very aware that the New York City Vigilante will be showing up tonight. I am giving this to you as a gift. You can take out as many goddamn Whyos as you want, but you don't touch any of the Tong, and the opium stays. Trust me, they will not get in your way. They hate the Whyos as much as we do."

"But Louis—"

He held up a hand to stop him. "No. You can't get on that fucking high horse right now. We need this."

"Fine. Can you give me a time?"

"I am going to meet with the Madame and Lee at The Palace now. I'll drop the exact time off with Tony once we are done."

Thomas leaned back against the carriage bench, finishing the last of his tobacco. "Jesus fucking Christ, Louis. How did you get an in with the Tong? They don't associate with anyone outside of Chinatown."

"Will," Louis confessed. "Will has had contacts in Chinatown since he came back to New York to work for Richie. The doc that sewed Richie up after Es shot him? He's the one patching up the Tongs when they have their battles with the Hip Sing. Their own version of Jeremiah. You know how it is for negro doctors. They barely make more than the factory workers."

"How did Will get connected with him?"

Louis smiled. "Will saved that doc's life during one of the riots. He lived there until we moved into the apartment above the barbershop with Esther."

"Blood brothers," Thomas uttered.

"Exactly. It was where we used to meet to swap information."

Noticing Thomas had finished his tobacco, Louis got a second for Thomas out of his vest pocket as well and handed it over.

"Thanks," Thomas remarked, astonished. "Fuck. You realize that this has completely changed everything, don't you, Louis?"

"Of course I do."

"Why did the Madame not tell me about this last night?"

Louis shrugged. "You know her. She plays everything close to the chest. I, on the other hand, am happy to use any help we have to push the agenda."

"Right."

The carriage was taciturn as it rocked to and fro.

"Well, I believe I have made my decision about how to handle this meeting."

"Oh, have you?"

"Yeah," Thomas replied, inhaling and exhaling a large cloud of smoke. "Fuck that son of a bitch. I want him to know that a storm is coming."

Louis sniggered. "Good. I'll let her know when I see her."

Tony anxiously waited at the Turners' residence off Fifth Avenue. The hour was nearing nine, and there was no word from Thomas or any sign of his approach, worrying Tony as to how Thomas's rejection of Croker's want of peace had gone over. In his usual routine, he'd seen Athena eat enough to get her through a late-night adventure, he tended to the upkeep of Thomas's gear in preparation for assailing the opium den at midnight, and later dismissed the household staff for the evening. What could possibly be detaining Thomas for so long? He couldn't miss this chance to strike at the Whyos, not with the Tong readily stepping aside. It was an opportunity to designate a future alliance, one that they desperately needed to stand up against the Whyos.

The sound of horses outside caused Tony to leap to his feet. Nearly running to the front door, he yanked it open to find Thomas at last making his way toward the front stoop, his countenance both determined and angry at the same time. Tony wanted to press him for the details, but knew his place and thought it better to let Thomas tell him everything once they were safely inside the house and out of earshot.

"Good evening, sir," Tony welcomed him with a small bow. "How was the meeting?"

Thomas marched inside and allowed Tony to close the door before he spoke: "Did Louis come by with the time for tonight?"

"Yes, Thomas. Midnight. They're expecting you."

"Perfect. Grab us each a whiskey and let's talk it over in the great room."

"Right away."

Tony went straight to the drink cart, fetched them a pair of clean crystal glasses, and poured a generous portion into each. Grabbing the drinks, he hastily went to sit with Thomas, eager to hear about what had ensued.

Thomas had a gulp of whiskey. "You want to hear it from start to finish, or should I just give you the highlights?"

Though Tony wanted to hear everything, their time was short. "With midnight so close, I think it's better that you just hit the highlights, sir."

"True. Very true." He had another gulp, and Tony mirrored him. "Well, Croker, Douglas, the Madame and I met in her office. Louis let the Madame and Douglas know what was coming from me, but then something interesting happened."

"What?"

"Croker attacked me first," Thomas reported, a small laugh en-

425

suing. "He demanded to know whether or not I had any inclination of Esther's whereabouts. Rattled and flustered to an uncontrollable degree. Louis mentioned to me earlier today that he was losing it about not finding her, but I didn't grasp how bad it really was."

Tony nearly dropped his glass. "Christ. He…he set you up perfectly."

Thomas agreed, "Perfectly. And at first, I considered throwing it entirely in his face—that I had rescued her, knew it all along, that he thought he was smarter than us and he wasn't, but I understood that this would throw everything off course."

"So, what did you do?"

"I don't think I could have had a better performance. He completely bought it. Croker was so furious he basically confessed that Esther had been alive and hadn't been executed, I became so enraged that I went berserk. I cursed him and shed a few tears. I told him he had picked the wrong family to fuck with, and from the look on his face, he certainly believed me."

"How did the others react?"

"They read the situation precisely how I had. Douglas and the Madame hopped right on board, Douglas at one point tried to restrain me as I 'attempted' to attack Croker, with the Madame standing between us. When he…well…when Croker believed that he had completely ruined his chances, it was as if he'd been struck by his own mother across the face. There were apologies, a few disheartened speeches trying to convince me that this had been for a greater good, and when I refused, he and the Madame disappeared for an hour downstairs while Douglas and I drank whiskey in her office. She returned to inform us he'd left, defeated, and under the impression it was his own doing."

"Holy shit. Which means…"

"Which means any crusade I go on against Croker on a public or private front will be a sore spot for him, because in his own mind,

I am justified in hating him. Justified to such an astounding degree, he wouldn't dare try to fucking challenge me."

"All because he couldn't track down Esther," Tony thought aloud. "He's literally gone a little mad, not able to tie up that loose end. That's knowledge we can work with."

"With Priestly?"

"Yes, and with whoever McCann is. It seems, Tommy, that this list in Croker's safe is proving to be quite valuable. These people, they aren't just loose ends. They are all, each one of them, the straw that could break the camel's back. If one is left alive, it presents a serious problem for Croker and for Tammany Hall."

Thomas finished his whiskey, pensive. "Who in the hell do you think this Patrick McCann character is?"

"I have no idea," Tony admitted. "But I do know that my brother can find anybody, and if he's having this difficult of a time, it's for a reason."

"What reason do you think that is?" Thomas pressed.

"It's that Patrick McCann doesn't want to be found, Thomas."

"Do you think Louis will find him?"

Tony threw back the last of his drink. "I think he will find us."

PART V
NEW YORK CITY, NOVEMBER 1888

CHAPTER XL.

Croker didn't give two shits about Harrison beating Cleveland. No, that didn't come as a surprise to him in the slight-est. November 6 had come and gone, and with the passing election day, Richard finally accomplished the one thing he'd spent his en-tire career aiming for: he'd gotten a mayor in office, and not just any candidate, either. This mayor owed him for the entirety of his own political gains; therefore, Grant had promised Richard that if he was elected New York City's mayor, thus promoting Hugh from his current position as sheriff, Croker would have free reign to do as he pleased. It was a promise Grant had reiterated time and time again whenever the two of them spoke privately regarding the elec-tion, and Richard hoped for Hugh's own sake that he kept his word, or he would find himself in more trouble than he could manage.

When the results were final, every soul at Tammany was ecstatic and the Hall erupted into celebration. All parties involved had been out late celebrating, and until only a few hours ago, they were arm in arm, drinking champagne in one of the great Tammany ballrooms on the main floor. When the night wrapped, Croker succeeded in placing his exhausted wife Elizabeth into a coach headed uptown toward their residence, whereas he stayed at the Hall, catching a bit of shut-eye prior to meeting with Grant at noon.

This was Richard Croker's day of reckoning—this was, at last, the reward that had cost him more blood, sweat, and money than he'd ever admit to anyone.

His head was pounding, the consequences of a night of too many glasses of champagne and probably one cigar more than his body could handle, and the temptation of a whiskey purely to level out his bloodstream was seeming like a better and better idea with the passing minutes. What did the Madame call it? Sunday coffee?

"Brian!" Croker bellowed, and within seconds, his assistant came barreling into his office.

"Yes, sir?" he asked, stopping once he was close enough not to raise his voice.

Croker leaned back into his desk chair. "Grab me a coffee from downstairs, would you? And when you bring it in, throw some Casper's in it."

"Of course, Mr. Croker. How much Casper's?"

"As much as you think I need to get rid of this goddamned headache, Brian." He chuckled at his own misery as he pressed his temples to alleviate the pressure. "I should have known better than to let Elizabeth talk me into drinking champagne with the group."

"She had good reason, sir," Brian mentioned. "It was a night to celebrate."

"You're right. Thanks, Brian."

As Brian reached the door, Croker called out again, "One moment!"

"Yes, sir?"

"From now on, let's just call this Sunday coffee. Got it?"

Brian smiled. "Got it, Mr. Croker."

"Oh, and bring one for Mr. Grant as well."

Within minutes, Brian returned with two Sunday coffees, one for

Richard and one for Hugh, and Croker was delighted to put his nausea to rest with the familiar burn of whiskey in his stomach. Grant would be arriving any minute now, and once Croker dismissed Brian, he got out a fountain pen and a few pieces of paper, wanting to quickly note each point he wished to discuss with Hugh before their meeting came to a close. Unlike the last time, when he'd tried and failed to get Tammany's candidate elected into the mayoral office, Richard went directly to the Madame the weekend prior to the election and not only asked for her opinions on how to keep Grant under his thumb, but also requested the dirt she'd collected on him at The Palace over the last few years. Grant had always been a regular there, and the Madame proved herself invaluable yet again, though she'd hesitated, offering one piece of information Richard by no means expected.

"There are certain items about Grant that are not in this envelope," she'd declared. "And those are things you ought to ask Celeste about if that bastard decides to negate your deal."

When Croker pressed her on it, the Madame merely shrugged him off, saying he'd been relatively infatuated with her for the last year, and while they'd never slept together, the Madame was certain Celeste had acquired more intelligence on Hugh Grant during their flirtations than any one of her whores could fuck out of him. Not wanting to argue, Croker had gone through what he'd been gifted with a hint of amusement and stored it in the safe. At some point, he'd find the time to try and solicit a conversation with Miss Hiltmore about the newly elected mayor, but for now, what The Palace had provided would suffice if his loyalty was not up to par.

Just as he managed to scribble down his objectives, a knock came at the door, and in strolled a much more enigmatic Hugh Grant than Croker had anticipated; he assumed the adrenaline of his win had yet to fade away.

"Morning, Richie," Grant greeted with a smile, heading straight for the chair across from Croker's desk. "You hanging in there?

If I wasn't so goddamned thrilled about the results, I probably never would have made it today." He sank into his chair, eyes falling on the coffee cup on the side table. "What's this?"

Croker took a sip of his own drink. "A little something for you called Sunday coffee. It ought to help after last night."

"This is what you have?"

"Brian just made them for us."

Grant nodded and picked up the mug, helping himself. "Ahh. Whiskey. A nice and very necessary touch after last night's celebration." Another big gulp, and he leaned back into his chair casually, crossing his right leg over his left. "So, talk to me. What couldn't wait until Monday?"

"From this moment forward," Croker began, "nothing will ever wait until Monday, Hugh. Nothing."

He seemed to accept this without surprise. "Of course, Richard." Grant momentarily set down his Sunday coffee. "Well, let's get started then."

This was why Richard had picked Grant: he was young, ambitious, and after battling to get ahead in the real estate world of New York City for roughly a decade, Hugh knew what hard work was. No matter what sort of issues arose, for the next two years, the pair of them would be spending countless hours together talking strategy.

Still, before they could get to the inevitable of what lay ahead for the Hall, for the newly-elected Mayor Grant, or even for Richard Croker, their agreement needed to be set in stone, and Richard did not plan to concede anything that had been previously promised. In the months leading to October, Richard had been uncharacteristically forthright with Hugh that if Grant tried to force a compromise, he would lose Tammany's support outright. That was why he kept the Madame around to assist in providing an incentive for Grant to cooperate if necessary—she was well worth her weight in gold, literally.

"There are a few points I want to make about where I want your campaign to go, Hugh, but first thing is first." Croker had a drink of his Sunday coffee. "I want your word that I get free rein to do what needs to be done behind closed doors. I didn't get you elected mayor to have the opportunity wasted, and I'll be damned if—"

"Richie, please," Grant interrupted him, holding up a hand to stop him. "I don't give a shit what you do. I told you that from day one. Keep me on a need to know basis, keep me in the loop about where things are at when the time calls for it, and as long as you stay honest with me, we are good."

"You're not going to give a damn about me telling you what policies to invoke?"

"Nope."

"Or what stance to take on certain...social issues?"

"As long as we stay aligned, no. I don't pretend to thrive on idealism, Richard. I am a Tammany man to my very core. My allegiance is to you and to the Hall first. New York City and its people are second."

Clearly, his belief that Grant might prove argumentative was wrong. "Well, Hugh, this was much easier than I anticipated. To be upfront, I thought you'd be way more of a bastard about it, and I am pleased I don't have to threaten you into submission like I have to with the others."

Hugh scoffed. "Richie, you got me elected sheriff in the first place. What stupid son of a bitch would ruin the foundation he stands on?"

"More than you know, Hugh. Well, to hell with that, then! How are your last days as sheriff looking?"

"Like a joke, as you can probably imagine." Hugh threw down his Sunday coffee and set the mug aside. "You going to the fight tonight?"

"I haven't seen Edmund in a few weeks, so yeah, I am pretty damn overdue. Plus, at this rate, I've had enough coffee to stay up

435

for two fucking days, so I might as well make the most of it. Are you thinking of making an appearance?"

"Nah. I am going to go sleep last night off and perhaps venture to the Madame's." He paused for a moment. "How have things been with Edmund?"

Croker straightened up. "You are asking how he is since I got rid of that son of a bitch from Chicago trying to steal his business?"

Hugh chortled. "You read my mind."

"Couldn't be better. And the Turlingtons are now so caught up in the Columbian Exhibition, they could give two shits about Sydney's mess. So, we are in the clear."

A sigh escaped Grant's lips. "I still can't fucking believe we lost out to Chicago."

"Save it, Mr. Mayor," Croker rebuked him. "We've got bigger fucking problems than some summer fair."

"What's on your mind?"

Richard smirked. "Well, let me get out the goddamn list…"

An hour later, Grant went home to sleep off his residual buzz, whilst Croker took a card from the Madame's deck and kept the Sunday coffees rolling. There were many ideas and thoughts he needed to reflect on, the most significant of those being the Whyos, Walsh, and the perpetual thorn in his side, Samwell Priestly. He and Grant agreed—the police needed a morale boost in the city, and that went hand in hand with Croker's idea of not wanting to directly interfere with the gang violence, thus openly breaking the longstanding contract he'd upheld with the Whyos for over a decade. It was obvious that Walsh was becoming more and more of a problem for the Hall, and throughout his hour with Grant, Croker had an epiphany regarding how to at last rid them of Walsh for good. Initially, Richard wanted to give the Priestly hit to Will and Louis due to their impeccable and, to that day, unconditionally reliable skillset with hits; on the other hand, Croker was able to grasp that this could be an opportunity to make Walsh, along with the Whyos, the scapegoat for the state of gang violence running rampant. Without batting an eyelash, Richard could pin Priestly's murder on Walsh and the Whyos, and the police would have no choice but to crack down hard on crime.

Nevertheless, if Richard was fair, the Whyos were already being served their own form of justice these last six months.

The Vigilante, still loose on the streets of New York, had cut drug crime in half by somehow ensuring that the only opium coming in and out of the city was through Chinatown. Not that Richard minded in the slightest—Lee and the Tong were friends of Tammany Hall, after all, and like so many of the other brothels and saloons, the Tong paid their share in votes for Hall protection. The fascinating result of the Vigilante's constant barrage of every Whyo entity was that while it had Walsh hiding in the shadows, the Whyo number was growing every day, as if Walsh were constantly recruiting young, fresh off the boat adolescent men to his side. Croker wasn't sure how he did it, but their devotion to Walsh, to the Whyos, and to the street life was unlike anything Richard had ever witnessed. It was as if they'd been brainwashed into thinking there was no other way to survive.

He shook his head, taking a sip of his Sunday coffee and a drag of his just-lit cigar. The Walsh and Whyo predicament would be taken care of in due course; what kept Richard awake at night, no matter the hour, was the mistake he'd made last July, a mistake that haunted him to nearly the same degree as the notion that Esther had not been seen since the day she shot Croker in his office. Predictably, it was the immense error he'd made with Lord Turner during a time when he was by no means healthy, mentally or physically, and grasping at straws with the sole purpose of trying to find someone to blame for his own missteps. Rather than cleverly assessing Lord Turner's possible involvement in Esther Tweed's disappearance, Croker instead went right ahead and pointed the finger at him in a rage, unable to control his temper. By the time Croker grasped that he had just admitted firsthand to Lord Turner that his late fiancée was actually not dead, and more or less served as Richard's indentured servant to pay off the debt of her life for five years, the damage was done. It would be impossible to forget, and seeing Lord Turner's reaction had brought about an emotion Richard very rarely felt: disappointment in himself.

There had been no communication between them since: every party, ball, gala, event, fundraiser, or the like, Lord Turner evaded him like the plague, and in turn, Richard avoided him as well. When a man is aware he has perpetually ruined the happiness of another on almost every front, no words are left to be said. The sole reason Richard wanted to mend the hurt he'd caused was purely a selfish one, and it was that he knew Lord Turner was using every avenue at his disposal to try and find Esther Tweed. Her knowledge of the depth of Richard's involvement with the Whyos stretched further than any of the others, save for Walsh, and the thought of what that information could do to him in the years to come was unsettling. Yes, Brian had stopped Esther from taking anything from Richard's safe, yet there were items she could have spotted and memorized, items that were extremely damning for Croker and the Hall. Walsh had been closely watching Lord Turner when he was away from the Whyos and had not detected any progress in Lord Turner's search for Esther, although Richard was convinced it was only a matter of time. He only hoped Walsh could get to her before Lord Turner did, because with the wealth and resources at his disposal, Lord Turner would be virtually untouchable, regardless of who Richard had in office to cover his ass. Not to mention, with Walsh's fate nearly sealed, Croker needed him to complete this last task of putting his Assistant into the ground, because if he was honest, Richard was very nearly certain that Walsh was the only one of his men who could actually kill Esther Tweed.

Thankfully, the incident with Lord Turner at The Palace had not impacted the Hiltmores or the Madame in their progress of winning Grant and Tammany Hall the upper class votes Croker so desired. In his pettiness, Richard had feared the worst, expecting that Lord Turner would unleash a vendetta against him amongst the rich uptown. Miraculously, this fear never materialized, and while Croker had no doubt that Lord Turner despised him privately, he publicly kept those thoughts to himself and merely retracted his participation in supporting Grant and the Hall on their social platforms. It was a loss, but not one Croker couldn't overcome, and aside from the search for Esther, the only lingering emotion Richard had toward Lord Turner was pity for him and his family. They simply could not keep their noses out of Croker's business, and therefore, sustained heavy losses in the aftermath; the righteousness they felt was hastily squashed by reality, and the reality was that Richard Croker was, as of that very day, untouchable.

"Excuse me, Mr. Croker?" Brian broke his train of thought, peeking his head into Croker's office.

"What is it, Brian?"

"Sullivan and O'Reilly are here to see you, boss."

Right on time. "Send them in, Brian."

Brian opened the door and in marched Sullivan and O'Reilly, both of them appearing a little worse for wear after their own celebrations the night prior.

"Afternoon, Richie," O'Reilly addressed him. "You're lookin' mighty chipper, considering you were up late."

"Coffee and whiskey, boys," Croker confessed, "and a little bit of tobacco. Grab a drink and sit down. What have you got for me?"

Sullivan went to the drink cart and grabbed them each a glass of whiskey, whereas O'Reilly made his way over to sit across from Richard, plopping a sealed envelope down on the top of his desk.

"From the Madame," O'Reilly told him. "Wants you to come by later for a drink."

Croker reached for the parcel and opened it, scanning the page. "I see. Anything else happen in the last twelve hours I should know about?"

Sullivan walked to them and handed O'Reilly his beverage, collapsing down in the other vacant chair. "Three Whyos dead."

Croker grabbed his mug, needing more of his whiskey. "What the fuck happened this time?"

The two men opposite him eyed each other, and Sullivan spoke first, "Kind of an odd one, to be honest, boss."

"Talk."

"Well," O'Reilly began, "I guess a few Whyo boys was tryin' to have some fun with one of the whores at The Dry Dollar after her shift. Didn't take long for that to go sideways. Girl said it was the Vigilante, no fuckin' question. He killed all three of 'em, and he...uh..."

"He what?"

"He did that same thing he's been doin' lately," Sullivan cut in. "Slicing through the damn W's marked on their arms so the coppers can't tell if they Whyos or not."

Croker was mildly appalled. "When did he start doing that shit?"

O'Reilly shrugged. "Can't be sure. Maybe three weeks ago?"

"And Seamus and Samuel are aware?"

"Yeah, and they can't do much. Word is getting out about this bastard, and people..."

"What? What are those assholes saying in the pubs?" Croker demanded, annoyed.

"They like him, boss," Sullivan replied bluntly. "They hate the Whyos, and they like that some son of a bitch is takin' 'em out."

Croker finished the last of his Sunday coffee. "Well, shit."

Not a second later, another knock came at the door, and Louis and Will joined the already tense conversation, both of them halting a few feet shy of where O'Reilly and Sullivan sat.

Will's brow furrowed. "Somebody die or somethin'?"

Setting the empty mug aside and grabbing for another cigar, Richard let out a heavy sigh. "No, unless you two have other news to report."

Louis remained expressionless. "No deaths, if that is what you mean."

From his tone, Richard could sense that the two of them wanted his undivided attention, and that Sullivan and O'Reilly ought to be on their way.

"Boys, thank you for the updates," Croker addressed the men sitting in front of him. "If you could run down to the Bowery and tell Edmund to expect me for the fight tonight, it would be appreciated. I'll put fifty on the boy from the Points."

With the understanding their time was up, Sullivan and O'Reilly downed the rest of their whiskey and set their glasses aside.

"You got it, Richie," O'Reilly said firmly, and he and Sullivan rose to their feet and left Croker's office.

The moment the door closed behind them, Will and Louis proceeded to grab themselves each a drink, and took the places of Sullivan and O'Reilly across from Croker.

"We have a problem, Richie," Louis shared, also grabbing for a cigarette. "With Grant getting elected, a few state representatives have gotten bold and want to try and stir up some fucking trouble with the Hall."

This had been coming. "Who?" Richard asked. "And Will, can you top me off with a bit of whiskey?"

"Sure thing, boss," Will obliged and went to the drink cart, grabbing the decanter. "And they ain' sayin'. Nobody is at the helm just yet, but I gotta feelin' that this ain' gonna fade away, either."

Croker wasn't worried. "Louis?"

"My money is on Fassett. He is a crony of Parkhurst, that Protestant prick who wanted to team with Frederick for an investigation last summer. We should keep an eye on it."

Will returned Croker's mug half full of whiskey, and as Croker took it, he saluted Will in thanks. "Do they have anything?"

"Nothin' other than that bribery shit Priestly keeps rollin' with," Will stated, lowering down into his own chair. "Louis is all concerned. I think it'll pass. Your call, boss."

"I'm going to side with Sweeney on this one, Louis. Unless they come after us with something legitimate, in writing or with Grant's blood all over it, I don't give a damn. We just won the mayoral seat of New York City, so those Swallowtail pricks know they're dead in the water. It was a predictable play, to be sure, and not one we are going to even address, because those bastards don't deserve our attention."

Will was satisfied, but Louis wouldn't let up: "Richie, just let me keep an eye on it. Right now, it doesn't matter. That doesn't mean that in two years, four years, or even ten that it won't. You never know with some of these politicians—they are real sons of bitches. One slip, and it could be a crisis for the Hall."

Leaning backward into his chair, Croker saw his point. "All right. Keep an eye on it for now, but don't make this bullshit the center of your goddamn attention, you got me? We got bigger problems to deal with."

"What did we miss?" Will asked him.

"Three more Whyos dead."

Louis had a gulp of whiskey. "Let me guess…"

"You got it."

"Whatcha need us to do, boss?"

"For now, nothing," Croker declared, finishing his drink. "I am headed to the Madame's in a short while. Anything I should be privy to, Louis?"

"She wants to talk about Frederick's widow."

Richard could sense Louis had more to say. "And?"

"And Lord Turner."

"What about Lord Turner?"

Will spoke for him. "That Lord Turner found Esther," he asserted. "And she's dead."

"With that bastard's hanging finally over with," the Madame stated blandly, "I think we should just send Frederick's widow out of the city so that the fucking drama can end. Seriously, Richard. I paid her debt and at the same time eliminated a goddamn liability by killing her husband off! Celeste has more important things to do than babysit that woman and listen to her whining and bullshit every week."

Both Celeste and Richard sat across from the Madame on the sofas next to a roaring fireplace, with just-poured drinks in hand. Croker recalled Virgil's hanging three weeks prior, and the spectacle that had ensued as a result.

With no reason to remain discreet, Virgil consistently tried to proclaim his innocence, blaming the entire thing on the corrupted Tammany Hall and Richard Croker; for a time, Priestly and the New York Times hit the ground running with Virgil's story in a last-ditch effort to try and sway the upcoming mayoral election. However, what Virgil hadn't seen coming was his wife's utter contempt for the mess Virgil found himself in; following an initial public statement in support of her husband, the pressure the Turlington family put on Sydney caused her knees to buckle, and she filed for divorce. Sydney was the one with the inheritance, after all, and Virgil's Chicago empire, regardless of how substantial it might have seemed, was fleeting. The divorce was covered on the front page of every paper, and Virgil was deemed guilty before the trial even commenced. It didn't last long—with a New York City judge murdered and Croker paying off both the judge and certain jury members to seal the deal, Virgil was sentenced to death. In one swoop, Croker won his election, helped Edmund at last get his revenge, got rid of Judge Frederick, and felt not one ounce of remorse.

"What do you want to do about her, then?" Croker asked.

Judge Frederick's widow had been a giant pain in the Madame's ass since Virgil's arrest, and while he really didn't give a shit what happened to her, Richard was frankly just tired of hearing the Madame complain about her.

Rather than the Madame, Celeste spoke up. "Boston. She has family there."

Croker turned Celeste's direction. "And how do you suppose I will be able to assist in getting rid of her?"

The Madame and Celeste locked eyes for a second. "Elizabeth," they said in unison.

"What? No, that's simply out of the question."

"Richard, Elizabeth has her ear, Celeste as well. The two of them can go for a visit to the widow together, say for the sake of her health they think she ought to go to Boston for a while and see if she improves."

"Why the hell don't you just send Celeste then?"

"Because," Celeste declared, "if Elizabeth and I go together, it will seem natural. And then the widow won't refuse, either."

Croker reached into his jacket to grab a cigar. "What in the world makes you think Lizzie would be on board with something like this?"

He put the cut cigar in his mouth, struggling to find matches in one of his pockets, while Celeste coolly grabbed a box of timber from her own dress pocket and handed it over to him with a smile.

"I have already put the thought into her head, Mr. Croker. I have mentioned to her that the widow seems a little off, in need of rest and perhaps some respite from the city after such a traumatic ordeal. If I appeal to her to go by my side, I have no doubt Elizabeth will accompany me. We are becoming good friends."

The thought of Celeste Hiltmore and his wife becoming friends made Croker somewhat uneasy, yet there was no getting around it.

"Fine, as long as she is unaware of what is really going on with the widow."

With a content nod, Celeste saluted him with her glass of wine. He reciprocated, though not without feeling somewhat puzzled by Celeste and her role in all this. It was impossible not to notice that most of Celeste's waking hours were spent either at The Palace or in some errand or pursuit for the Madame, not to mention she'd taken to carrying blades rather than a pocket pistol in a fashion that mirrored the Madame's. She'd never given him a cause to be skeptical of her other than her previous connections to Esther and her very close friendship with Lord Turner, a friendship that on numerous occasions saw Celeste taking Lord Turner's side as he faced off with Croker. Still, once the summer months came to an end, Celeste changed her tune, and with Lord Turner's absence, Croker found she was endeavoring to forge a professional rapport between them. The attempts were gradually softening Richard—the two of them couldn't operate a successful enterprise with the Madame if they were at odds, especially when Croker was now attending almost every event alongside the Hiltmores; with Croker's blossoming wealth and heightened status as GS, he was, unofficially, king of New York. He would make the necessary efforts in complementation, yet internally, until Richard could figure out her own purpose and drive, Celeste Hiltmore was an untrustworthy danger, one he would not remotely be afraid to squash if necessary.

He'd done that before, after all, and mad houses ran in plenty.

The Madame cleared her throat and had a sip of her whiskey. "Now, Richard, we need to talk about something that is a little more…sensitive."

"Louis mentioned something about Lord Turner finding Esther."

Her left eyebrow rose. "I was hoping to tell you myself, but clearly, Louis saw to use his own means of fucking discretion."

"It doesn't matter, Madame. I don't buy it."

"You don't buy what, Richard? That Lord Turner found Esther, or that she is dead?"

"Both." He finally lit his cigar.

Celeste shifted and straightened up. "Mr. Croker, I've personally talked with Lord Turner, as has the Madame. He hired a team of Pinkertons—some of the best in the business—and they tracked her down to Baltimore."

Croker took a few puffs of his tobacco. "How in the fuck did she end up there?"

"She hopped a ship out of the harbor," the Madame informed him. "Unfortunately, her wounds festered and she was hospitalized. The girl died only four days after arriving. The hospital has it on record, if you'd like to wire them."

"What's the name?"

"Hopkins…something Hopkins. It's the university hospital." Celeste was suddenly overcome with a stricken look, and her confident gaze moved from Croker to her wine glass. "Esther's death records are on file. She was buried in August in an unmarked grave outside one of the railroad yards."

"You really buy it?" Croker queried the Madame inquisitively.

"I personally know the Pinkerton agent," she told him. "He's the best there is. So yes, Richard. I think she's…gone."

"Official cause of death?"

The Madame's jaw tightened. "Her spleen ruptured. The wound later became infected and she never recovered."

Croker took a drag of his cigar. "Send Louis. I want personal confirmation from one of my own, understand?"

"Done."

"And just how is Lord Turner handling this news?"

"Horribly," Celeste answered, having a drink of wine. "He hasn't been seen all week, trying to pass off that he simply is under the weather with a slight fever."

An idea struck Richard. "Celeste, how would you feel about checking on Lord Turner for me?"

This surprised her. "Check on Lord Turner...for you?"

He expected the Madame to interject, but when she didn't, Croker went on, "Yes. Stop by. Get a read on his mind. Bastard is probably a wreck, and I want to make sure this intel is solid, Louis or no Louis."

Celeste was very aware that this was a test, and Croker watched her closely. Rather than shy away, an expression of amusement crossed her face, followed by a small smirk.

"I'll go tomorrow afternoon, Mr. Croker, and immediately take a carriage down to the Hall afterward. Expect me around four?"

"Fine."

"And you'll bring Ashleigh," the Madame declared, her eyes narrowing at Richard. "Fucking Whyos are out of line, and I am not having you put yourself at risk, considering the company Tammany Hall keeps these days."

Croker scoffed. "Please. Like any of the bastards around here are better."

"Not one of them is Walsh," the Madame snapped. "Forgive me for not giving a shit about your parameters, Richard, and wanting to protect my own."

He was about to retort and put the Madame in her place before Celeste interrupted. "It's not meant to be an imposition, Mr. Croker. My father would be furious if he knew I was traveling downtown alone, and the Madame is trying to adhere to his wishes."

"I see," he declared, downing the rest of his whiskey. "Well, moving on. The Vigilante has struck again, taking out more of the Whyos and causing even more goddamn tension with the police." Croker set his glass on the side table and inhaled smoke. "My alliance with Walsh is becoming more of a fucking burden than an asset, so you can expect a plan to deal with that shortly."

Croker felt the energy of the room shift as the Madame stared at him. "You're going to cut that motherfucker loose?! Are you insane, Richard?!"

"Don't be ridiculous!" Croker barked in response. "I am not cutting that bastard loose and risking my own neck in the process. Jesus Christ, Madame, a little more respect!"

"Oh, thank Christ," Celeste gasped, taking a large gulp of wine.

The Madame was suspicious. "Then what are you doing, Richard?"

"I'll keep you up to speed as soon as I've worked out the more minute details, and who is playing which part." His focus transferred to Celeste, wanting to push her further, "And if you can prove yourself, Miss Hiltmore, perhaps you'll have a role in it, too. Walsh is a name I know is used with contempt in this establishment for what he's done over the years in the name of Tammany Hall. I'll give you a chance to avenge your…" His voice trailed off as his jaw tightened in rage, and Croker took a deep breath to let it pass. "To avenge your…friend…along with the others."

"My…friend?" Celeste asked.

"Yes."

"You mean Esther."

When Croker didn't acknowledge her outspokenness with a response, Celeste continued, "Mr. Croker, the Esther that worked for Tammany Hall was a far different woman than the girl I grew up with. I would only be interested in pursuing Walsh because of his actions against the Madame and The Palace."

"Happy to hear it, Miss Hiltmore. I can promise we will have a solidified plan shortly."

The two women glanced at each other perceptively.

"Is this going to tie in with Priestly?" the Madame inquired, finishing her own drink.

"You know I like to kill two birds with one stone."

"We are all aware, yes," Celeste remarked under her breath, and when he threw her a cautioning look, Celeste didn't seem remotely fazed by the reprimand. "No offense, Mr. Croker, but you really expect us to just comply without offering any more intelligence? Every one of us works together to assist you and the Hall, and there are times like this when you think you are privy to things we are not. You can pretend with your men and the Hall that you have a face of grandeur—that you are more informed and better prepared than we are. You've made this mistake with the Madame previously, so do both of us a favor and get off your fucking high horse when you're here."

For a brief moment, Richard was speechless as he watched Celeste then gracefully pull a cigarette from her dress pocket, place it in her smoking wand, and light it.

He peered over to the Madame, who was grinning from ear to ear.

"We call it like we see it, Richard," she replied to his glower. "Maybe it's about goddamn time you gave us the same courtesy."

With barely a second to spare, Croker made it down to the Bottleneck Saloon in the Bowery at ten minutes to ten, just enough time to find Edmund and confirm his bet. Taking the descent down to the basement three steps at a time, the underground arena was packed to the brim for one of the biggest fights of the year, and Croker scanned the mass hoard to find Sullivan and O'Reilly pushing their way through the crowd to meet him at the bottom of the staircase. When they reached him, Sullivan took the lead with O'Reilly behind Richard, and upon hearing Richard Croker's name being bellowed out by his associates, the mob parted to let him through without hesitation, many with a tipped cap and others calling out in greeting from every direction. It was a gesture Croker had gotten accustomed to at fights, but one that filled him with a sense of pride and invincibility amongst his people. He wouldn't be there without

449

them, that much he could grasp, and still, they wouldn't have made it this far without him either. The Irish were loyal to their very core, and if Croker had done one thing right in his career, staying true to his roots was definitively that.

Edmund was waiting for him ringside with a shit-eating grin on his face. "Richie!" he shouted, waving them over. "Get your ass over here, boy-o!"

Over the years, Edmund certainly had aged, but his attitude, particularly after seeing Virgil put into his grave, seemed to give Edmund a second wind, and he'd scheduled this fight by the skin of his teeth as a celebration of putting to rest his old demons.

"Edmund, you son of a bitch!" Croker pulled him in for a hug.

After releasing Richard, Edmund produced a clean glass for Richard and a bottle of whiskey. "Your drinks are on me," Edmund assured him, filling Croker's cup. "You ready for one hell of a fight tonight?"

"You know I am," Croker replied, clinking glasses with Edmund. "Who's calling it?"

"Wooley," Edmund primed him. "Kavanagh has a hairline fracture in his left pinky, a real shitter for the fight, but bastard is ready to tear Nagie's head off with all the trashin' these last few weeks."

Croker chortled, shaking his head, "Fucking hotheads. Secondaries?"

"Nah, we are gonna go big with one solid fight. Ain't no use for secondaries when it ain't about a turf war."

"I like the sound of that. I threw mine on Kavanagh."

Edmund winked at him and threw back his whiskey. "Me too, boss." Leaning in close, Edmund whispered so only Croker could hear, "Fourth round. Let's grab whiskey when it's over."

"You can count on it."

Letting Edmund go, his old friend took off in the direction of Joe Wooley, who would be calling the fight, and Croker rotated around to find Sullivan and O'Reilly lingering with a bottle of whiskey.

450

"Another one, boss?" Sullivan asked, holding the bottle up.

"You bet your ass. Either of you boys have a cigar handy?"

"I've got one right here, Richie," came Seamus's voice from Croker's right.

Pushing through the swarm of sweaty bodies, Seamus appeared with a wide smile and his own glass of whiskey, thankfully out of uniform and with a cigar outstretched toward Richard.

"You're the man, Seamus," Croker welcomed his friend, taking the cigar. "No work for the precinct tonight?"

"Nothing I couldn't get out of," Seamus clarified, nodding a hello to O'Reilly and Sullivan. "How is the fight lookin'?"

Richard lowered his tone to an almost inaudible level. "Nagie will go down in the fourth."

"Figured as much. Edmund says he's one hell of a fighter."

"Sure as shit." Croker lit his cigar. "Seamus…"

"Don't fuckin' start with me, Richie."

His temper rose. "I am going to fucking start with you, Seamus. You know damn well there are Whyos here, and you know damn well they know who you are."

Seamus rolled his eyes and held his glass up for Sullivan to fill. "We haven't had a problem with this before."

"You weren't a goddamn detective before, Seamus."

"No one will spot me out of uniform, Richie."

"Boss," O'Reilly interrupted them, pointing to the other side of the ring.

There, arms crossed across his chest with Kitty McGowan beside him, stood Walsh, and he was staring directly at Richard. Behind the pair of them was a group of Whyos, most of them drunk, though the majority of them were armed and ostensibly irritated. Emphatically, Walsh's eyes shifted over to concentrate on Seamus for a few seconds, and then immediately his glare returned to Richard. He didn't say the words aloud, only mouthed them to Croker: "He has to go."

It was like Croker's blood had gone cold. With a hoard of intoxicated and heavily armed Whyos behind him, Walsh was the one
giving orders here, and Croker had no choice but to oblige. If he
caused a scene, it could also cost Seamus his life and perhaps make
an even greater spectacle of how much power the Whyos had in the
underground. Richard's teeth gnashed together in angered frustration, caught in yet another one of Walsh's bullshit schemes to make
the Whyos believe it was in fact he who was running the show, not
Croker. Reluctantly, he turned to Seamus, and Richard perceived
the color had drained from his friend's cheeks as he, too, observed
the Whyos threatening him from the other side of the ring.

"I told you, Seamus," Croker muttered softly. "Now, get the hell
out of here before this gets ugly."

Seamus finished his whiskey and leaned in while he handed the
glass to Richard. "You need to put the dog down, Richie. This is a
fucking menace."

Without waiting for a retort, Seamus stormed out the way he'd
come, and Croker watched him leave with both a hint of resentment
at Seamus for putting him in such a predicament as well as a bub-
bling hatred of Walsh. Still, the notion lingered that, if he was honest, Richard understood this was completely his own fault. For too
long, he'd allowed Walsh a loose leash…for too long, he'd let things
slide out of wanting to pacify the monster and keep him on at the
Hall. Not anymore—Walsh had to go, there was no question about it.

For the remainder of the fight, Richard didn't spot Walsh once,
almost as if he'd simply shown up to make a point with Croker and
then evaporated into thin air. His rowdy cohorts, on the other hand,
stayed, nearly causing a riot when Nagie lost, proving as usual that
they were a band of drunken mongrels willing to kill anyone that
pissed them off. Their outrage brought Richard more personal satisfaction than he cared to admit, and while he collected a handsome
amount of winnings from his bet, Croker found he was laughing to

himself as the Whyos grew increasingly more belligerent in their losses. At least in that, he could relish.

Sullivan and O'Reilly escorted Croker out of the basement of the Bottleneck cautiously, but the three of them stuck around to drink for another couple of hours with Edmund at the Bottleneck Saloon's bar once the ring and the arena were cleared. The four of them had a grand rest of their evening, and Croker had almost as much to drink as he'd had celebrating his mayoral win the night prior, with the intention of numbing away the irritation of his encounter with Walsh at the fight.

Sullivan was the first to stumble out drunk in search of a cab, closely followed by O'Reilly, whose wife would certainly be awake and waiting for him in a fit. Edmund and Richard lingered for one more round before Croker had the barman cut them off, and they stumbled out to the street in search of their own coaches. Being just a hair more sober, Richard threw Edmund into the back seat of a carriage and paid the driver, giving him Edmund's address and also adding a little extra to wake up the snoring Edmund upon their arrival at his apartment. The driver agreed and took off in a hurry, leaving Croker alone on the side of the road.

He considered hailing a ride for himself, but refrained—Richard realized he was only a few blocks from Tammany, and rather than suffer through a nauseating forty minute drive to the Upper West, he could be asleep at the Hall in fifteen.

Setting out, Richard cracked his neck from side to side, pleased that he wasn't nearly as drunk as he'd originally presumed. A splash of water to the face along with a quick mixed tonic, and he'd wake up as if he'd had a full night of sleep at home in his own bed. It was a crisp November night, and a crescent moon hung overhead, lighting up the cobblestone under Croker's feet where the gaslights failed.

He'd certainly made some money on the fight, and he was even more thrilled to see Edmund in such good spirits with the Virgil difficulties finally sorted out; conversely, Richard couldn't stop seething about Walsh, and the embarrassment his presence caused on a night when Croker should have felt indestructible. Seamus was correct—Richard had to get rid of him, for the sake of Tammany Hall, as well as for the sake of everyone around him. He was a plague that would only spread further if it wasn't contained, and Croker would be damned if he let that bastard get the better of him again.

In a flash, Croker had reached Tenth Street, yet just as he began to eagerly anticipate a couple hours of sleep, he heard footsteps from behind him, and not just one set. Multiple people were about to flank him, and straightaway, Richard had a dreaded hunch as to who they might be. He took a deep breath and spun around to discover a group of five Whyos, two of whom Richard recognized from the fight earlier that night; the rest he assumed were members based on their haggard appearances, as well as the fact that every one of them was carrying some kind of weapon, though thankfully, Croker didn't spot the glint of a gun. When the group saw Richard turn to face them, the pack slowed their pace and continued their approach until the Whyos and Croker were only feet apart.

"What the fuck do you want?" Richard spat, trying to keep his confidence intact.

"You brought a copper to the fight," said the one at the front, and Croker was disgusted to note he could smell the stench of the bastard from where he stood. "We don't allow that in the Bowery no more."

"You'd better take that up with the city, then," Croker hissed. "And I didn't invite him. He came on his own accord."

Another one stepped forward with a knife in his hand, his rotting teeth and pocked face his most prominent features. "He was with you. We all saw."

Croker's fists clenched in his jacket pockets. "Do you stupid bastards have any idea who the fuck it is you are talking to right now?"

"Yeah, Croker," the first one resumed, pulling a life preserver from his jacket and pointing it at Richard as he spoke. "We don't give a shit. Walsh runs this city, not you."

"He'd like you to think that," Croker retorted, assessing his surroundings. There was no one in immediate sight of them—Richard was on his own, and he had to figure out a way to talk himself out of getting his ass kicked or worse. "Look, gentlemen, what is it I can do for you? Clearly you have something in mind."

"Nothin'!" shouted a third, who Croker was barely able to see from behind the other two. "We just gonna do Walsh a favor and put you in the ground."

Richard sized up the group of Whyos. Undoubtedly, he could take down three, maybe four of them, but his best chance was to get to the Hall and pray the night watch was ready for intruders. If he could concentrate his punches and remember his training, Croker believed he had a shot at getting away; unfortunately, it was then that Croker heard a rustle of movement over his shoulder. Glaring behind him, he saw two more Whyos come jogging around the corner with menacing grins, each of them carrying a bludgeon out and ready to use. The pair of them closed in, and the Whyos completely surrounded Richard, leaving no place to run.

This was familiar to him, in such a daunting way that Croker felt chills shoot down his spine. A horrifying thought struck him in that instant, one that was far more profound than could be expected from Croker realizing he was about to be murdered in the street: this was Richard's comeuppance for Edward Turner—to die just as Edward had.

Sucking in air to try and fuel his muscles, Croker prepared himself to fight until he had nothing left to give. He took off his coat, folded it neatly, and then placed it on the ground by his side. His top hat followed, and as he eyed the group of Whyos preparing to kill him, Richard made a mental note of the details of every face: the lines of every sinister grin, their heights, their weights, their gaits, all things he was used to assessing as a boxer before taking on his opponents.

455

Rolling up his sleeves and unbuttoning his collar, Croker rolled his shoulders back and held up his hands in perfect match stance, because if he was going to die, he was going to kill as many as these piece of shit Whyos as he could lay his hands on.

The five Whyos at his front formed a circle as the two from Richard's back drew closer with their bludgeons, smacking them into their hands in a kind of tribal reckoning of what was to come next. With his back against the brick wall of the building behind him, the seven armed Whyos closed in, and Croker readied himself for battle.

The two facing him first were young, maybe in their early twenties, one heavy and one lanky, each carrying the expressions of men who had seen too much death already and no longer carried any empathy for their fellow man. Boldly, the heavier one lunged first, taking a hard swing like he might be able to take Richard's head off if he was lucky. With an easy duck, the club cleared Croker by a foot, and he made two quick jabs, first right and then left, directly into the goon's right ribcage as his body carried with the follow through of the swing.

Up next, the lankier asshole came in running with the bludgeon held over his head with both hands, and he brought it down with such ferocity, the hit nearly caught Croker even while he tucked under and out of the way. The bat struck the ground with such force Richard heard the bludgeon crack, and the gangly one ducked while another sprung over his back for another attempt at Croker.

Mid-swing, Croker clasped the bat, pain shooting from the tips of his fingers up through his arms and to his shoulders, but the fear in the fat goon's eyes gave Croker the rush of adrenaline he needed. He tugged hard, sending the unstable Whyo to stumble forward his direction, and using every ounce of the might in his neck, Richard head-butted the fiend and sent him writhing to the ground. It took a few hard blinks for Croker to stop seeing stars, and right as he came to, the skinny bastard came into focus, unarmed, and Croker's confidence swelled. The man rapidly covered the few paces he had left to Richard, and Croker hit him hard directly in the jaw with a left hook, sending the man airborne before he hit the ground in a heap.

To his disdain, Croker understood too late that he was going to be overrun by the remaining five Whyos. Before he could reassess his surroundings, there was a Whyo on his back with his forearm on Richard's windpipe, and another beating the hell out of his abdomen. There was no way out for Croker, that much he could understand, and regardless of his best attempts to wriggle free, he was only struck harder and harder until he submitted. On the ground in a bloody pile, Richard felt the hits continue to come and waited for the blade as he covered his head and neck, the muscle memory of past fights kicking in, when suddenly, it was as if the air stood still.

Shots rang out like rapid fire, and the sharp cracks through the air fueled Croker's consciousness into the present. There was blood in his mouth and blood on his hands. His muscles screamed and his body ached in a way he hadn't experienced in well over a decade. When he was aware that he was no longer being attacked, Richard managed to prop himself up with his arms, and what he saw nearly made him collapse back down.

There were three—no four—Whyos dead on the ground already, and amongst the remaining three was a figure moving so quickly Croker could barely keep track of him with his naked eye. A round house kick to one. A one, two, three-fold punch and then a breezy neck snap to another. He went back to the first, attacking with a knee to the diaphragm, which sent that Whyo to the ground, and just when the last prick thought he might have a chance at escape, a screech rang out that made Croker's hair stand on end.

A blur of grey flashed and disappeared. The man screamed, and Richard saw that his back had been sliced by something he had not been able to witness. Another squawk rang out from overhead, this one a different tone, and the shadowed man put a gun to the cut Whyo's temple and pulled the trigger, sending him to meet his maker. Groaning came from the last man alive, followed by a final shot, then silence. In the meantime, Richard's stupefied gaze went toward the heavens, and it was there he spotted a Peregrine, blood on her chest, her ferocious gaze locked on him as if waiting to be beckoned to strike.

"Holy…fucking…shit…" he mumbled, gaping up at her, and then abruptly, there was a hand around his neck that forced him to sit up against the brick wall, and an old Civil War Griswold being held at his forehead.

"Give me one good reason why I shouldn't fucking end you, Croker," the Vigilante spat. "You know you've earned a Whyo death. Why shouldn't I grant that to you?"

At last, Richard's eyes could focus on the man in front of him. "You…how did you…"

"Doesn't matter," the Vigilante interjected, "you earned this fate. Rest in peace, Ri—"

"No!" Croker bellowed. "Wait, please." He held his shaking hands up beside him. "I don't know who you are, though you clearly know me and my business ventures. I beg of you. Don't kill me. We can work out a deal of some sort…money…anything your heart desires!"

To Richard's horror, a smirk formed on the Vigilante's face. "I don't want money. You can't buy me like the others." He cocked the Griswold. "Goodbye, Richard."

"Wait!" Richard screamed, wracking his brain to find a solution. "Wait—I've got something I can give you…I…"

"You have nothing you can give me that would satisfy me more than your death."

Croker paused, looking directly into the Vigilante's eyes. "What about Walsh?"

"What about him?" the Vigilante jeered.

"I know you want to kill him."

"And? I want to kill you, too, Croker."

"You should get in line then," Croker quipped, attempting to keep things lighthearted. "I mean this. I can give you Walsh. The time, place—he'll be at a disadvantage trying to perform a hit for the Hall. You can kill him as soon as he completes the task, and I honestly could give a fuck what you do afterwards. I give you him, we call it even."

For a few seconds, the Vigilante only glared at Richard through his smutted regard. "If you make this promise, you can't unmake it, Croker."

"I know."

"And if you lie—"

"I am not goddamn lying!"

"If you lie," the Vigilante roared, "the repercussions will not just be on you. Your family is at risk. I know where you summer home. I know about the children, Lizzie, and the like. And don't think that the Madame can protect you—I have jurisdiction even where she does not."

Croker took a couple of breaths. "Can you take the gun away from my fucking forehead, for Christ's sake?"

Seemingly irritated, the Vigilante removed the gun. "You will disclose to me when and where I will find Walsh."

"Yes."

"You'll get a visit from me at Tammany Hall, one week from tonight, and you had better be alone in your office."

"Consider it done."

"And if you try to fuck me over, your family dies."

The Vigilante let out a loud whistle, and the Peregrine descended swiftly, perching happily on his shoulder. "Goodnight, Mr. Croker. Until next time."

Without another word, the man circled around and disappeared into the gaslight smog of the city streets, his shadow fading from view faster than what seemed possible.

Using what little vigor he had left in his quadriceps, Croker hoisted himself upright to stand, scanning the dead Whyos scattered around him. All seven of them were completely lifeless, and the shock of Richard's fight with the gang followed closely by his encounter with the Vigilante was tremendously heavy. The carnage was almost like a work of art. Croker walked from body to body, gawking down at their battle wounds, and recalling as best he could the very few marks that he could surmise on the Vigilante, despite having had a gun held to his forehead. Was he even bleeding? And that Peregrine…it was the same goddamn Peregrine that spooked him at his office that night, wasn't it?

The echo of jogging footsteps soon approached, and Croker looked up, thankful to spot Seamus with two of his patrol officers heading right to him.

"Richie!" Seamus shouted. "You all right?!"

Croker spat blood onto the cobblestone. "Best I can be."

One of the two officers behind Seamus was horrified as they drew close to the scene. "What in the fuck happened here?!"

His voice was so weak, Richard barely heard him, but he chose to elaborate anyhow, "It was the Vigilante," he told them. "I got jumped by this group of Whyos, and that son of a bitch showed up and saved my ass. How'd you find me?"

"I was at the Hall," Seamus admitted. "I heard gunshots, so I grabbed these two from the corner and we got here as fast as we could."

He marched over to Croker's top hat and jacket, picking them up off the ground for him and dusting them off. "You might want these back. It's damn near freezing out here."

"Detective," the other officer shouted, "get a load of this!"

The patrolman was leaning over one of the Whyo corpses. "Put a gash through the W on the arm, like last time…"

"Check the rest of them," Seamus ordered. "Let's see if he did that to each member."

As the two officers ambled from one body to the next, Croker threw his jacket and top hat back on.

"I need to get bandaged up," Croker said to Seamus. "You got this from here?"

"'Course, Richie. You need me to get you a coach?"

"Nah, there's one sitting just up the block there. But I want you and Samuel by tomorrow to discuss this."

Looking from side to side to make sure the patrolmen didn't overhear him, Seamus moved closer to Croker. "Are you serious that he...saved you?"

"I don't fucking get it either, Seamus."

"Christ. Well, did he say anything?"

Croker shook his head. "Killed them and was gone," he lied. "That's all."

"All right. Get home, Richie. I'll see ya tomorrow. Give Lizzie my best. And call a doctor."

Stumbling toward his ride home, Richard knew just the doctor he was going to call. A pang of self-reproach hit him for not sharing his conversation with the Vigilante with Seamus. It wasn't that Croker didn't trust Seamus, if anything, Seamus was one of the only men alive that Richard could rely on no matter what the stakes were. The real reason was his desire to protect his oldest friend from Walsh, because it was evident more than ever at the boxing match that confrontations between the police and the gangs were going to get worse before they got better. If the Whyos were growing to the degree Walsh claimed they were, New York City could by no means afford a riot on its hands. The Whyos outnumbered the police, that much Richard could be certain, and if they wanted to, the gang could tear New York apart in a matter of days. Richard needed to get rid of Walsh and put this problem to bed, and with the Vigilante taking him out, Croker could wipe his hands clean of it without breaking a sweat.

He reached the coach and gave the driver his address, then hobbled into the cab. As the carriage set out for uptown, Croker began to wonder if he could find a way to permanently get the Vigilante on his side. If he could get a man of that caliber working for the Hall, there was nothing Richard couldn't do. On the other hand, the more chilling aspect of that notion was the possibility of making an enemy out of the Vigilante; if that became the case, Croker knew there was nowhere he could hide.

He had to think fast.

"There is no fucking way on God's green earth that that will ever happen, Richard."

The Madame was more than a little irritated. She'd been in a serious discussion with Will and Louis at The Palace, who'd received a letter from Esther about her prospective return in a few weeks' time, when they were interrupted by a late-night message from Croker demanding their presence at his home. Initially, the Madame had been surprised, given that the Crokers lived only a few blocks from her and she'd never anticipated receiving a personal invite to their residence; yet, on the other hand, his insistence that they show up immediately and bring Jeremiah made her blood boil. There were moments when she regretted ever having bargained with such a narcissistic prick like Richard Croker, especially at times when she had more than enough bullshit to deal with on her own plate, but the addition of bringing Jeremiah with them gave her pause.

Hastily, the Madame grabbed a snoozing Jeremiah from Razzy's quarters, along with Will and Louis, and the four of them made their way north on foot due to the lack of carriages at that hour, and also because it was only about six blocks uptown.

A somewhat panicked Elizabeth was waiting for Jeremiah in the entrance lobby, and the Madame had to hide a smirk when she observed that Elizabeth was not expecting the group of visitors that arrived. First was the negro doctor, followed by the obscenely large Frenchman, the handsome and ragged cowboy, and best of all, her.

Courtesies, apologies, and thanks were quickly exchanged as Elizabeth and their butler escorted the rag tag group upstairs, nervously eyeing them and then one another, not sure of what exactly was happening. Upon reaching the second floor, Lizzie led the way to what the Madame assumed was Croker's study, and halted outside the door to knock.

"Richard!" she called. "The…um…doctor is here with his… friends…"

"About damn time!" he shouted. "Send them in and have Frank get us more brandy, Lizzie!"

Elizabeth stepped aside from the still closed door, signaling for them to enter in without her. "Go right ahead."

The Madame paced forward, nodded at Elizabeth in gratitude, and pushed the door open. Croker's home office was an exact replica of his office at the Hall, filled with stacked bookshelves, artwork on the walls, and glass cases filled with decorated antiquities, though the Madame noted that where his Civil War painting hung to cover his safe at Tammany Hall was not present on the Upper West Side. A fully loaded drink cart was to her left, a roaring fireplace to their right, and in the middle, stretched out on one of his leather sofas, was Richard with an empty brandy glass in hand, looking like he'd had the absolute shit beaten out of him.

"Richie, you didn' tell me you was boxin' tonight," Will remarked from her left, a hint of sarcasm in his tone.

Jeremiah stood to the Madame's right. "Madame?" he whispered softly. "This is the man I am tending, correct?"

"Do you see anyone else beaten to a fucking pulp in here, Jeremiah?"

Jeremiah rolled his eyes at her and went to Richard, kneeling in front of him while the others gathered around, Louis headed for the drink cart.

"Walk me through your injuries," Jeremiah requested, earnestly skimming Croker's beaten-up frame.

"Broken ribs. Bruised windpipe. A few facial contusions—"

"More than a few, Richard," Louis corrected, going to pour himself a whiskey. "Have you looked in a mirror?"

Croker ignored him. "Sprained wrist. Possible fractures in three fingers. Everything else is just bruises that will heal."

"Louis? Get me a whiskey," the Madame ordered, and he obliged, reaching for another empty glass on one of the cart shelves.

Marching around to the couch opposite of where Croker lay, the Madame sat, studying him closely. "Richard, what happened to you?"

"I got jumped by a band of Whyos, Madame," he confessed, holding his hand out for Jeremiah to assess and wincing a little in pain as he did. "I really thought I was going to die. And then that goddamn Vigilante showed up."

The Madame and Louis instantly locked eyes in bewilderment, and while trying to appear unruffled, Louis casually brought the Madame's whiskey to her and lowered down at her side. Will was just as astonished as they were, and he went to sit in the remaining vacant armchair as Jeremiah moved on to Richard's trunk.

"You mean to tell me," Will started, "that the bastard who has been runnin' 'round fuckin' things up for everybody just showed up while you was gettin' beat?"

"Yes, Will. That's what happened. Him and that goddamn bird of his."

It was the most sober the Madame had felt in over a decade, and she downed her whiskey in one gulp.

A loud knock came at the door, and Frank entered with another bottle of brandy and four extra glasses. Once he'd set down the contents of his tray on the side table by Richard, Frank poured a generous share of brandy in each glass and took his leave, bowing slightly and closing the door behind him.

Hopping up, Will went over and grabbed a glass of brandy, handing it over to Richard, who took it obligingly with his unhurt hand. Will then went back, procured two for himself, and returned to the armchair, glancing first at Louis, and then back to Richard in expectation.

"You want to tell us the story?" Louis finally beseeched Croker. "Or do we have to guess?"

"Jesus Christ!" Richard yelled out as Jeremiah felt his ribs. "I told you a few of them were fucking broken!"

Jeremiah exhaled in annoyance. "It's one of your floating ribs, which means we are going to have to keep an eye on your spleen and liver to make sure they aren't damaged as well. That means you have a little over a month before you'll be healed, and no vigorous activity for at least three weeks."

"Fine," Croker spluttered in return, cringing. He looked over to the Madame and Louis, his countenance exasperated. "I was in a heap on the road, just a few blocks from the Hall. I don't know how that son of a bitch found me, but I was done for, just waiting for the blade. Shots rang out, and by the time I got up, he'd killed all of them."

The Madame's grip on her whiskey glass tightened, and from the corner of her periphery, she perceived Will finish one of his brandies.

"He must have said something to you," the Madame interposed. "You don't just kill seven fucking Whyos to save someone and walk away like nothing happened."

For a few seconds, Croker hesitated, and he pretended to be temporarily preoccupied with whatever it was that Jeremiah was doing. The Madame recognized he was deciding whether to share whatever the exact details of what happened next because it was what Richard assumed to be the most important, and she pounced.

"Enough with the games, Richard. You brought me out of my place of business in the middle of the fucking night, you make me drag my doc along for your personal at-home exam, and think that I won't expect you to tell me every goddamn detail I want to hear?"

465

She got to her feet. "I will walk out of your fucking house and take these three with me unless you start talking."

Dutifully, Jeremiah backed away from Croker and stood up, crossing his arms over his chest. "I am her employee, sir. Not yours. So, if you want me to keep treating you, I suggest you do as the Madame asks. And to be honest, you will get sub-par care at a hospital at this hour, and your ribs could be a serious problem."

"Oh, please. Louis and Will aren't going anywhere. They work for me, Madame, not for you, or did you forget that?"

Louis nervously glimpsed to the Madame, but Will was markedly just buzzed enough not to keep his mouth shut.

"Oh, for God's sake, Richie, just fuckin' tell us. Ya ain' got nobody else, and no offense, but you're the one beat to shit needin' our help right now, not the other way 'round."

It was as if Will had slapped Croker right across the face. His expression contorted from ambivalence to rage, and the Madame feared he was going to lunge at Will for speaking to him in such respects. Yet before Croker could make any sudden movements, Jeremiah had Richard's broken hand in his clutches, and he held it threateningly.

"If you make quick movements right now," Jeremiah asserted with authority, glaring down at Croker, "you will have internal bleeding that I am not certain I can stop. And if I can't stop it, no doc can. You hear me?"

The two of them glowered at one another, Croker's gaze burning with anger, though Jeremiah was resolute, "I'm not fucking around. I will break this hand again if you try anything. You think because I'm a negro doctor I won't stand up to a white prick like you when it comes to my professional integrity? You're damn wrong, so keep your ass on the couch, sir."

In a flash, the entire ambiance of the room shifted, and Croker at last began to realize that he was essentially at their mercy.

"Insolence," he uttered, trying to steady his voice, "is something that I do not tolerate."

"We aren't being insolent, Richie," Louis declared. "We want to figure out what happened and what to do next. The only way we can do our jobs well is if we have all the facts. You didn't call us here just for Jeremiah. You can't trust anyone else. So, trust us."

To the Madame's relief, their appeals seemed to be working, so she pressed a little further, "You can't count on Sullivan and O'Reilly for this, Richard. Not Seamus. Not Walsh. And Esther is fucking gone. You've got us, or you've got nobody."

It seemed that upon hearing the Madame's words, Croker appreciated she was right. The room remained silent as Croker stared at her, then Louis, and at last Will.

"I...I really am stuck with you lot, aren't I?"

"Looks that way, boss," Will affirmed.

The Madame glanced to Jeremiah, nodding that he could go on with treatment, and he did just that, releasing Richard's mangled hand to resume wrapping his ribs.

"He...the Vigilante..." Croker returned to the subject. "The bastard would have killed me, too."

Louis finished his whiskey. "Why didn't he?"

"I offered him Walsh as a counter option."

"Ya offered him Walsh?!" Will cried aloud.

"He wants to kill Walsh more than me, that much he's made clear," Croker responded with a shrug. "Plus, I have an idea."

The Madame was astounded. "An...idea..."

"An idea for what?" Louis pressed.

"I want to hire the Vigilante to work for me and the Hall."

"There is no fucking way on God's green earth that that will ever happen, Richard," the Madame replied, peeved with his stupidity. "He wants to kill you. You just aren't number one on the damn list yet."

He scowled at her. "I could—no, we could turn him. We've done it before. And with his hatred of the Whyos, once the Whyos are no longer aligned with Tammany, we could negotiate an alliance. Think of what we could do with that man working with us!"

"I wanna get back to this whole, 'givin' him Walsh' idea. How in the hell ya gonna pull that one off?"

"I'm going to give Walsh the Priestly hit. I'll pass on to the Vigilante the time and place. We blame Priestly's murder on the Whyos, we get rid of Walsh, and it's done."

Handing her empty whiskey glass to Louis, the Madame's eyes darted to the drink cart, and Louis rose and went to get her a refill.

"Richard, it is a wonder you are alive. I think this plot for Walsh might be plausible. But don't get your hopes up about turning the Vigilante. Men like him, they don't switch sides, no matter how much they are bribed."

Croker scoffed. "Everybody has a price, Madame. I think you know that quite well. Or do I need to reminisce on our first meeting?"

The Madame felt her chest swell with such an intense fury, she nearly pulled the pocket pistol from her skirt and shot him directly between the eyes. Thankfully, Louis put the glass in front of her, breaking that train of thought, and she grabbed it, taking a big swig.

"There ain' no need for that, I don' think," Will added, wanting to shift the topic. "So, then, what went down? He just leave?"

"That was it. He said he would be by a week from tonight at the Hall to meet about Walsh. And he disappeared."

"What about the bird?" Louis asked.

"I watched that beast shred a man nearly to pieces. I've never seen a falcon do a thing like that…" Croker's voice trailed off, and he was pensive. "When it was done, the damn thing just flew down, held onto his shoulder, and they were gone. Will, you trained hawks. Can they do shit like that?"

"No, Richie. No, they can'."

"Well, fuck me."

Jeremiah finished patching Croker up and grabbed the fourth

and final full brandy glass from the side table. He had a sip, smiled, and proceeded to the vacant spot by the Madame on the couch.

The Madame had the last of her drink. "Do you remember anything else, Richard?"

He shook his head. "It was odd. I felt like he was familiar somehow."

She could feel Louis tense beside her. "Familiar in what type of way?"

"I can't really put a finger on it. His eyes just were...familiar."

"Hah!" the Madame bellowed, purposefully emphasizing her disbelief. "Familiar from your nightmares, Richard. If there is one thing I can ascertain from what I know about this Vigilante, particularly after your more recent encounter, it's that if he'd ever run into you before, you would have had a fucking gun pointed at your head just as you had tonight. So, enough with the bullshit semantics and let's talk about the change of plan on Priestly, because that is going to take some goddamn maneuvering."

Reluctantly, Croker took the bait as the Madame hoped, and for the next half hour, they went on to plot just how the Priestly hit would take place with Walsh at the helm instead of Will and Louis. While Croker, Will, and Louis discussed details which didn't require her input, the Madame comprehended the beauty of Thomas's move in saving Croker. Not only would that give them Walsh's head on a platter, but it additionally put a deep fear into Richard of the Vigilante by demonstrating just what Thomas was capable of. It would give her more time to put their vault together, and they could take Richard Croker down the way they'd planned all along: by taking away his kingdom.

Out of the blue, there was suddenly a light at the end of the tunnel, and the Madame could not wait to get back to The Palace and write a return letter to Esther.

Because the war was coming to an end.

CHAPTER XLI.

"Again!"

Esther's knees were buckling beneath her. Her mouth had gone completely dry as she gasped for air, carrying two outrageously hefty packs of sand on her back as Hiroaki bellowed at her to jump up and onto the platform in front of her once more. Still, regardless of how determined she was or how much Esther loved training as hard as she could, her muscles were aching, and the only thing that kept her standing was sheer determination.

"Hiro," she panted, "I...my legs..."

Hiroaki's eyes narrowed as he stood watch ten yards away, arms crossed over his chest. "You will jump one last time, as if your life depends on it."

In Esther's mind, she directed a thousand curses at that tenacious bastard, sweat pouring from her temples and streaming down her face. It didn't matter that it was November, nor that it was below freezing with a hint of rain every few minutes; her arms, legs, and torso were coated in perspiration from the struggle of her efforts, and Esther endeavored to concentrate with the knowledge that this was her last training session with Hiro before she made her way back to New York City. She sucked in air and sat into the squat using her legs, the heavy bags strapped tight to her back pulling Esther down towards the ground, as if beckoning her to it. Gritting her teeth, Esther resisted the temptation to quit. All she had to do was leap up onto the platform right in front of her one last time. There had been numerous occasions in the past where Esther had missed the platform during this drill, and the thought of those painful occasions nearly caused her to grimace.

"Concentrate!" Hiroaki bellowed. "You must make the jump!"

"I must make the jump," Esther repeated to herself, psyching her brain and body into the task.

The platform was a few feet off the ground, and Hiro explained to her that if he could improve the distance and height of her jumping, she would be able to keep up with Thomas as he traveled from rooftop to rooftop. Initially, Esther waved him off, not believing her body to be capable of such undertakings. In time, however, Hiroaki's training tactics proved true, and when Esther realized this, she commenced putting every ounce of energy she had into their daily sessions. Esther had no intention of being left in Thomas's wake— she wanted to be able to match him stride for stride, not out of competitiveness or pride, but rather, because, like Hiro said, her life, or Thomas's, might depend on it.

She tightened her core, stretched her arms down and diagonally at her sides, and lifted her gaze up and to the platform. The weight was evenly balanced between both of her feet, and with a few adjustments, Esther shifted the heaviness more towards her heels to gain significant momentum in her leap. Inhaling, every one of her muscles tensed in preparation. With the forward drive of her arms, Esther exploded from the ground using as much power as she could muster, letting out a roar in her battle to put her mind over her body, and the exertion was just enough to propel Esther high enough to pull her feet underneath her and onto the platform. She barely stuck her landing, and the load of the bags very nearly kept thrusting forward, though Esther managed to resist against the force of the weight. Wobbling to and fro, she nearly toppled over, yet she was able to stabilize her spasming muscles and stand upright triumphantly, looking to Hiroaki for approval. Though his expression stayed firm, Hiro's eyes were smiling, and with a nod, Esther's trembling hands went to release the straps crossed over her chest and liberate her body from the weighted bags. She undid the buckles, and with a loud thud, the bags hit the platform. Feeling relieved and far lighter, Esther lowered down to sit, dangling her legs over the side as Hiroaki drew near.

Now, he was fully grinning.

Her first day at Amberleigh, Esther had to hide the perpetual state of shock she was in, never having seen as many trees, green rolling hills, or such open and vacant land in her entire life. On the train transporting her from Liverpool to Southampton, she spent the majority of the ride with her face pressed to the window of the first class carriage car she had wholly to herself, with a staff that fed, bathed, and dressed her while providing some of the best wine and cuisine Esther had ever tasted. The only aspect Esther had to be particularly cautious about was her wig, as she'd sworn to Thomas that until she reached Amberleigh, she would not take it off in front of anyone; thankfully, Esther made the journey without a mishap. Upon exiting the train, she was immediately taken to a waiting carriage, where for the first time, Esther met the ridiculously delightful Connor O'Brian. He stood tall beside her coach, waving her and her valet over, and the moment Esther spotted him, she halted where she stood, unable to suppress a huge smirk. Connor was exactly like she'd imagined him: big, burly, with a wild mane of red, blonde, and grey hair tied back into a ponytail and a long, coarse beard to match. When his gaze found hers, Connor's eyes lit up and sparkled, and he opened his arms wide.

"There's me girl!" he bellowed merrily.

It was like being introduced to the Irish version of Louis, and without thinking, Esther trotted over to Connor and threw herself right into his arms for a bear hug. She could give a damn what people thought—Connor was her family, even if they'd never met before.

"I am so happy to be here," Esther uttered into Connor's chest. "Thank you for coming to retrieve me from the station."

"Are ya kiddin'? I wouldn' let these boy-os come and have ya all to themselves!"

Letting her go, Connor set his sights on the valet with Esther's luggage. "Ay! Right here, brother. You can set 'em down, eh? Driver had to take a piss."

The valet did as he was told, and Esther tipped him more than she should, because apparently that was the Turner way of doing things.

When the driver returned, he and Connor loaded Esther's luggage up and onto the top of the carriage in a flash, and within minutes, Esther found she was hurdling toward Amberleigh, laughing with Connor in the cab for most of the ride. At one point, Connor produced a flask to ease Esther's nerves about meeting Hiroaki and Akemi; but what was causing her the most anxiety was that after so many years apart, Esther was going to see Mary Dougherty. For the longest time, Esther had believed her to be dead, and the memories of their brief but happy time together faded into the darkness of what felt like a previous life she'd lived, one wholly separate from the present.

It took roughly two hours before Esther and Connor arrived at the estate, thus giving Esther enough time to smoke a few cigarettes and down some of Connor's whiskey while updating him on what was happening in New York. She realized that Thomas shared everything with Connor, and therefore did not feel obliged to hold back.

Their trip went fast, and as the carriage made a turn down the long driveway of Amberleigh Manor, Esther could barely believe what she was witnessing. The mansion-house, the gardens, the property that seemed endless in the distance—it was so stunning, Esther was speechless, her mouth agape in awe.

As the coach came to a stop in front of the house, Connor went barreling out first, and Esther slowly followed second. She kept her head lowered while she stepped down and out of the coach, and when she did glance around, Esther immediately recognized the people in front of her. To her right was, unmistakably, Hiroaki, with his wife Akemi at his side, her arm wrapped comfortably through his. Directly in front was their driver, who had taken his hat off and stood respectfully smiling at Esther, offering a small bow of his head in salutation when their gazes met. Last, to the far left, was Mary, Connor now loitering beside her, and Esther felt tears forming in her eyes. In their years apart, Esther had forgotten how incredibly beautiful Mary was, with her gorgeous long red hair, glowing fair skin, and those mesmerizing honey-grey eyes that were locked on her with a combination of amazement and, if Esther guessed correctly, immense relief. Suddenly, a strange feeling came over her, and for reasons Esther couldn't quite comprehend, she reached up on top of her head and pulled the wig off, revealing her nearly hairless head as she tossed the wig aside.

For a few seconds, it was silent.

"Well," said the driver, chuckling under his breath and simultaneously breaking the tension, "ain't that somethin'!"

Connor rolled his eyes. "Esther, that bastard is Sal, the family driver."

Esther gave a small curtsy. "Pleasure to meet you, Sal."

Still staring at Esther, Mary started to cry, tears streaming down her cheeks. To quell a sob, her hand went to cover her mouth while she took a long, shaky few breaths.

"You are so much more than I ever could have dreamed," Mary articulated, shaking her head in disbelief.

"You dreamed one day I'd be bald?" Esther jested.

Connor snorted, and with a laugh, Mary strolled over to Esther. Wrapping her arms around her once-adopted mother, Esther held Mary as she cried, feeling overrun herself by intense emotions. The two of them stayed that way for a few minutes, Mary attempting to cease her tears, though without much success.

When the moment passed, Mary pulled back and touched Esther's cheek. "I am so happy you are here."

Esther smiled down at her. "I am so happy to be here." She kissed the top of Mary's head, letting her go and turning to Hiroaki and Akemi, who were both beaming at her.

"We have waited many years to meet you," Akemi greeted with a low bow.

Esther did the same in return, as instructed by Thomas. "I am beyond honored to meet both of you." Her regard went to Hiroaki, and she bowed this time to him. "Sir."

Leaving Akemi's side, Hiroaki ambled toward Esther, halted, and bowed to her as well. "I hope your journey was an easy one."

"A good night of rest and I'll be brand new again," Esther declared wholeheartedly. "When is a good time for us to begin tomorrow?"

A little astonished, yet understanding her implication, Hiroaki was quiet for a second or two, then smirked. "I like an early start."

"Good thing I am an early riser."

"Hiro," Mary interceded, "take it easy on her while she recovers."

"I do not think, Mary, that it is Esther you should be worried about." Hiro winked at her. "Dawn, then."

"Dawn," Esther reiterated, the pulse of excitement running through her veins.

Months had come and gone since then, and Esther felt like a spectator as she watched her abilities transform, her muscles and her mind stronger than they were even in her prime in New York with Will and Louis. Her last day in England had finally arrived, and Hiroaki challenged her in his relentless pursuit of preparing Esther for what was to come. Her return across the Atlantic had hung like a cloud over Amberleigh for the previous week, with every member of her new family pressuring Esther to stay another week, or just another day, for that matter, but Esther knew this was not the time to delay. The election had just been won by Croker, and Esther's presence was needed to end this war, particularly now that she had become a new and improved form of her prior self.

Hiroaki gradually made his way to the platform. "How do you feel?"

"Fucking exhausted," Esther admitted, still trying to catch her breath, "but I'm stronger now than I ever have been, thanks to you."

He nodded graciously. "The others won't expect you until Christmas. Are you certain that now is the right time?"

"I think the mission needs me now. Grant isn't in office yet. If we could strike hard...if we could knock Croker off his throne before all that even begins, we can count it as a win."

"And Mr. Walsh?"

"From what I can gather, his alliance with Croker has about worn through," Esther declared, wiping sweat from her forehead. "I don't think it's going to be as easy as the Madame or Thomas believe to put him down. I really don't."

Hiroaki went to sit beside her on the platform. "I agree with you, not because I have any doubt in Thomas or his capabilities. It is because the environment and the circumstances in that vile city are volatile, constantly changing, and increasingly lethal. He will need you as much as you need him, and one or both of you might die in your attempts to kill Walsh. It is a hard truth to accept, and a necessary one."

The mention of anything happening to Thomas made Esther's hair stand on end. "We can't afford to think that way, Hiro. One step at a time. First step is getting to New York."

"Are you referring to your insistence that I go with you?"

"Yes. I have the details worked out, Hiro. We both need you. Tony needs you, too. And let's be honest, the Madame would absolutely kill for the chance to meet you." She paused, peering over at him. "I can't seem to understand your reluctance."

"It is a very long story, Esther."

"I've got time."

Tentatively, Hiroaki took a deep breath. "When I was a young man training in Bushido, a group of performers came to our town—gypsies, as you call them here. A woman amongst the group claimed to be connected to the spirits of the afterlife, and for a hefty price, swore she could predict how one might meet their end. Everyone wanted to visit with her, though only the wealthiest in the village could."

"Really?" Esther remarked snidely. "Death predictions?"

"At first, I had no interest in such knowledge, and waved it off just as you did, but it was as if a seed had been planted in my mind, growing at such an exponential rate, I couldn't resist."

"How did you find the money?"

"That is another story," Hiroaki said, and Esther could tell by his tone he wouldn't budge.

"So, what did this woman foretell?" she asked.

Again, he sighed. "She told me I would lead a life of trials, yet that I would find peace in a new land. In the end, however, she declared that I would die on my feet in battle, just the way I, as a Samurai, would find most honorable and fulfilling."

Esther shrugged. "It sounds to me like almost everything has aligned, Hiro, except the grand finale."

Reaching into the pockets of his robe, Hiroaki removed something she could not initially see, and then Hiroaki held Esther's brass knuckles out to her.

"When I asked her for a sign of when that time was to come, she told me a beautiful woman who had no hair, with eyes like daggers and hands of metal, would be my guide to reach my death and destiny." He put the brass into Esther's palms and closed her fingers around them. "You are to be my guide, Esther. My hesitancy is only that I am aware this will be my final night in this magnificent place. I will have to say my goodbyes to Mary and Connor, to my wife, and also to Edward."

Esther was speechless as she squeezed the brass in her grip. "Hiro, not all prophecies are fulfilled. You can stay here. I feel... Christ, I feel like shit. I had no idea this was your reason for not wishing to go."

Hiroaki gently touched her shoulder. "Esther, I never said I did not want to go. I am an old man. I have trained three of the greatest warriors I've ever seen. My life has been simple, yet contained so much true purpose. There is no greater way to leave this life than fighting for honor and for those you love."

"You really think I am right, then? About what is going to happen?"

"I do, which is why I would never argue that you and I are needed as soon as possible."

In practiced fashion, Esther slipped her hands into her blunt instruments, wrapping her fingers around the center weights of the brass one by one, unable to suppress the sensation of exhilaration. "I missed these."

Hiroaki smirked. "You have earned them, and there will be much use for them in the upcoming weeks."

"Is Akemi going to be furious with me for requesting you go to New York?" she pressed, worried that Hiroaki's wife might place blame on Esther if anything happened to him.

"She already knows I intend to go. In fact, I am already packed."

Esther gawked at him. "Already packed?"

"I was planning to go before you even asked."

Her shock did not recede. "Why...why didn't you just tell me?"

"Because, Esther," he started, his tone almost somber, "we are about to willingly travel into the hornets' nest, and I wanted you to be as prepared mentally as you are physically. Walsh and his gang are not going anywhere without a fight, which, additionally, means not all of us will be there to witness the victory."

Whenever Hiro brought up the undeniable consequences of the future, Esther would have second thoughts—today was no exception. "Why do we do this, Hiro? If that is the cost? I am fine sacrificing my own life, but the thought of losing, well, any one of us, and suddenly I am reluctant to go."

"Well, Miss Tweed, if we do not go, then who else will? Are you willing to live with the cost of doing nothing? Of watching New York tear itself apart? Your friends and family dying in your absence?"

She bit her lip. "No fucking way."

"Good." Hiroaki got to his feet, looking directly into Esther's eyes. "We do this because we can. It's the right thing to do, and not one of us will sleep soundly until Mr. Walsh is dead. Now, you have a lunch to attend, and I have horses to feed. I'll send Akemi over later this evening. And tell Connor to meet me when you all are done— he's got large shoes to fill here."

Once she'd sprinted the short distance through the land of Amberleigh and reached the main house, Esther dashed through the kitchen and up the back stairs, already running late for her lunch with Connor and Mary. She took the stairs three at a time, racing down the hallway and through her bedroom door, bellowing for Cassandra to assist her in dressing for the afternoon. Thankfully, the maid already had two large bowls of water ready, along with rags and perfume for Esther to clean herself up in a hurry after sweating the entire morning. Without hair on her head to worry over, the whole process of primping proved to be much simpler for Esther, and she only hoped that by the time she got downstairs, she had at the very least stopped sweating, though it was highly unlikely.

Cassandra was a professional at their last-minute routine, and she had Esther in a beautiful new wool walking skirt, corset, and blouse in under ten minutes. Not to mention the addition of rouge to her cheeks and lips, as well as a little ash and elderberry to her lashes. After scolding Esther regarding the state of her hair, or lack thereof, and repeating her absurdly frequent lecture that Esther really ought to initiate growing it long again, Cassandra dismissed her in a huff, waving Esther's protests off in irritation. Esther stifled a small laugh—Cassandra's presence was a welcome one, almost as if she had Celeste there critiquing her appearance and fashion like the old days, when beauty seemed to matter so much to them. Esther rolled her shoulders back and glanced hastily into her looking glass, checking that nothing was smeared or out of place and dabbing the sweat still escaping from her brow. Satisfied with herself, Esther rushed out of her rooms and down the hall, noticing from the grandfather clock in the hallway that she was a quarter of an hour late.

"Sorry!" Esther greeted emphatically as she burst into the dining room. "I got caught up with training and just completely lost... track of..."

Sitting at the table were not just Connor and Mary; to Esther's amazement, Lucy and William beamed back at her.

"What are you doing here?!" she shouted happily. "You were supposed to stay in Bath for another month!"

"Well, when you decided to return to New York early, I wrote to them," Mary confessed, her face full of guilt. "They were looking forward to seeing you just before you left, and I swear to you I only just wrote a few days ago. They got in this morning."

Lucy clapped her hands together. "Esther, you look positively radiant!"

"We were thrilled to leave Bath," William professed with a slight grimace. "Goddamn people and that sulfur water. It doesn't do a bloody thing!"

The lot of them chose to ignore William.

"Well, I am certainly glad you came all this way for the day!"

Esther went to sit beside Connor on the nearest side of the table. Mary sat at the head, with William on her left and Lucy across from Esther. Within seconds, Alexander had a full glass of wine in front of Esther, and the group was served their initial course of a lobster bisque.

"Did ya get a good mornin' in?" Connor whispered into Esther's ear while the other three discussed the social scene at Bath.

"You know I did." Esther winked at him. "An hour of running and platforms, another of hand to hand, and of course, a quiz on Athena and how she flies."

"Ya packed?"

"Not even a little. But it's not like I'm bringing much."

"Ya got your brass back though, eh?"

"I did." Esther made sure the other three were engaged before she grabbed them out of her skirt pocket to quickly show Connor. "They feel like heaven."

He gave her a big grin. "That's me girl."

Lucy glanced at Esther for a moment, then returned her focus to Mary. "Should we talk about...uh...the days ahead?"

"Yes!" Esther replied. "I apologize for being quiet, I was telling Connor about the morning. How long are you two staying at Amberleigh?"

"Esther, darling," Mary uttered after taking a gulp of wine, "William and Lucy are...well...they are..."

She was confused. "Are what?"

William scoffed. "Oh fine, I'll bloody say it. We are coming with you, Esther."

"To New York?!" she exclaimed. "You cannot be serious."

The entire table became apprehensive, even Connor.

"We were planning on it anyhow, around Christmas," Lucy told her. "We just moved dates up a little, that's all."

"But you have only been back in England for three weeks!"

In practiced fashion, Connor placed his hand on Esther's left forearm, signaling for her to pull her wits together. "Take it easy," he said under his breath.

Esther conceded, "I only meant that it seems rushed."

William finished his soup. "Esther, you don't have to pander here. Lucy and I understand your concern with the way things are in the city." His eyes went to Mary and returned to Esther. "What you do not comprehend is something that the four of us deliberated over prior to your arrival."

"Which is?"

He picked up his wine glass and took a sip. "Mary cannot go to New York, no matter what happens. This, we are all privy to. But Esther, dear, Lucy and I consider you and Thomas to be our children, and I'll be damned if I am not there to keep an eye on both of you, regardless of whatever turmoil awaits."

Esther, too, had another drink of wine, wanting to compose herself. "William, please listen to me. There could not be a more dangerous time for either of you to be in that city. If anything were to happen to the two of you because of the...the life Thomas and I have chosen to pursue, I would never forgive myself."

William was unrelenting. "I think between the two of you, Tony, and the others, we will be just about as safe there as we will be anywhere else."

"You don't understand," Esther asserted, not giving up either, "Walsh wouldn't give a second thought to using either of you against us if he finds out how connected we are. He would hurt you, torture you, kill you, anything to settle the score. I have established I am fine putting my neck on the line, but I am not for a minute going to agree to putting either of you in that kind of danger."

"We don't care about the danger, Esther," Lucy stated with warmth and firmness. "We are going. Not to mention, William is needed to negotiate some deal with Vanderbilt that Thomas keeps going on and on about."

483

She couldn't believe what she was hearing. "But Lucy—"

"No, Esther. We aren't changing our minds."

Esther rotated toward her last hope. "Mary?"

Her gaze held Esther's. "I support their choice. It is theirs to make, not ours."

"Thomas knows," William added. "We wired him to expect us around Christmas along with you, though a few weeks early shouldn't make that large of a difference."

She was utterly astonished. "Well," Esther yielded, "I suppose I ought to tell you that Hiroaki is coming as well."

No one appeared to be as surprised as Esther had anticipated.

"I think we had a feelin' he was gonna go wit' ya, Es," Connor said, chewing a mouthful of salad. "He wants to be at Tommy's side, not stuck here waitin' 'round to hear about what's happenin' next."

Dialogue in the dining room faded until the main course was brought out and served, and Alexander refilled everyone's wine glasses, his gaze searching the room, undeniably curious as to what the problem was amongst the group. When the servants disappeared, Mary and Lucy resumed their discussion of Bath, and after eavesdropping for a few seconds, Esther found she couldn't keep her mouth shut. Fruitless or not, she pursued her argument, not grasping how the decision was allowed to be made without her input.

"I'm not okay with this," Esther declared.

"Esther, you will get ahold of yourself," William said harshly.

"Don't badger me, William. I am upset because I care about you and Lucy. How can Thomas be fine with it?!"

Again, Connor tried to appease her, "It ain' like that, Es. Really. Tommy…he just…" His voice trailed off.

"Just what, Connor?"

"Darling," Mary said tenderly, setting down her napkin and getting up from her chair, "grab your drink and let's take a walk. I can see the sun peeking out from behind the clouds as we speak."

It was a polite way of pulling Esther away from the situation before she grew even angrier, and it was useless to quarrel with Mary, that much Esther knew. With a nod, she pushed her own chair back and stood, her appetite lost anyhow.

A few minutes later, Mary and Esther were bundled in jackets, scarves, and gloves, sauntering through the bare rose garden on that mild fall afternoon, Esther's mind trapped in a loop of just what in the hell had gotten into everyone. Leaves blew serenely in the unusually warm November breeze while Esther and Mary walked arm in arm, carrying their wine glasses along for their stroll under a bright and shining sun. Esther waited patiently for Mary to commence whatever it was she had on her mind, while Esther, in turn, continued fuming over how Thomas would allow his cousins to put themselves into peril for the sake of family closeness. Were they absolutely insane?

Wandering down the winding path, they reached Mary's favorite bench across from the waterless fountain in the garden, and the two of them sat down side by side. Mary held up her glass to salute Esther, and they clinked their glasses together, each having a large gulp of wine.

"I am going to tell you some things, Esther," Mary declared, staring out over the flowerless garden. "A few of these histories you already do know; however, there are some which Thomas was hoping to tell you upon your return to New York, and, well, one very sensitive story that he is unaware of."

Esther wasn't sure where this was leading. "All right…"

"You have to promise me that when you hear this final story, you will not tell Thomas. That is my only condition."

"Mary, you know I cannot do that—"

"Yes, Esther, you can." She revolved towards her. "This is not your secret to tell. But it will help you understand this family a little bit better."

When Esther remained quiet and had another drink of wine,

Mary accepted this as an answer of yes, and her eyes went back to the garden, her mind somewhere else.

"I was very young when I met Edward, and I realize Thomas has told you the details of our time together; nonetheless, there is a much greater story behind what happened prior to our meeting, which I wish to tell you now." Mary cleared her throat, and again, had a sip of wine, growing nervous as she spoke. "When I was a young girl, I was taken in by a family under the guise that I was orphaned on the streets. I was handed to this family by the Madame herself, who'd found me living in a doorway in the Points. The Madame would visit me whenever she could, and as I learned arithmetic and letters in school, I taught her as well. She was not much older than me, you see. It was like having an older sister."

Another pause, and Esther noticed Mary's hand move upward from her lap to her neck, clutching habitually onto the silver locket she wore every day.

"In time, the family wanted out of the city—so many did, with the knowledge that the war between North and South was definitively on the horizon—and they offered to take me with them. But I just...I couldn't abandon her, and instead, chose to work for the Madame. There are few professions for a young woman such as myself, without any money or status, and at The Palace, I lived like a queen in comparison to my earlier years."

Esther reached over and touched Mary's arm affectionately. "You don't need to defend anything to me, Mary. I know how the girls live at The Palace."

She smiled, her expression somewhat pained. "I will have to skip forward here for a moment, though I promise you'll see why. When I was made to believe Edward was never returning to New York, something very strange happened."

"What?" Esther asked.

"It was very late one night at the apartment, and I had been up crying over a bottle of wine, trying to comprehend just what losing Edward meant. Thomas was already asleep, and who should come knocking at the door but none other than Louis. I was aware that he and Edward were friends before Louis signed on with the Madame—that is why, by Edward's request, he was the only witness at our wedding—but the depth of their connection was never explained to me until that very night. I do not want to get into too many details, for those are for Louis to share and not me."

"I understand."

With a deep breath, Mary turned so they were face to face once more. "Louis was raised at Amberleigh. He and Tony both were— they are, in fact, brothers, and their father tended to the general landscaping and upkeep of Amberleigh. In a tragic village fire, their parents perished, and Louis was barely able to save Tony and himself from being burned alive. Louis couldn't live with the guilt of not saving his father and mother. He punished himself and abandoned the Turners and Tony, running to America in the hopes of starting new. Sadly, the anger didn't leave him for years."

Esther's jaw dropped, but before she could respond, Mary went on with her story.

"He's very discreet, that one. On that night, he told me he had promised Edward he would protect me no matter what future lay ahead, and that from that day forward, wherever Thomas and I went, he would go with us. And it was then he relayed to me what had happened to him in America." With a long swig, Mary finished her wine. "I am going to tell you about the Louis we never knew, because you are the daughter he always wished he'd had, and someone other than Will needs to understand just how much this man has been through."

Mirroring Mary, Esther downed the wine in her glass with eager anticipation. "I asked Louis, and on a handful of occasions I even got Will drunk with the intention of trying to hear about their early lives. Neither of them would tell me anything."

A gust of wind blew the leaves around them up and into the air, providing a spiraling backdrop of dark hues that was very fitting for such a conversation.

"I do not believe the Madame knows either, Esther. Louis swore me to absolute secrecy, and I am breaking his confidence because you deserve to hear the truth.

"Louis made it to America and spent his first few weeks starving. The only work he could find was in manual labor because of his size, and those jobs were waning with all the new factory work taking over the city. One night, Louis was wandering through the Points to some boarding house he'd found when he came across a fight and broke it up. Louis was already massive, as you can imagine, and strong, regardless of his lack of sustenance. It was, of course, some sort of gang fight. I think it may have been a scuffle over turf, and rather than pick a side, Louis beat both of the men so badly, one of them couldn't walk again in the aftermath. The other, well, I can't say I know for certain. Every one of the onlookers ran off and reported to their respective leaders what they'd seen, and that very night, a man by the name of Chichester found Louis and recruited him to join his gang. Young Will Sweeney at the time was John Chichester's right hand man and aided him in getting Louis on board. Chichester offered a bed, money, and food if Louis did as he was asked, and as you can probably guess, Louis took the job willingly."

"Chichester...are you talking about the Chichester gang?" Esther beseeched her. "I thought they were strictly Irish!"

Shaking her head, Mary set aside her empty wine glass. "If you could have someone like Louis on your side, would you really be that picky?"

"Touché."

"The particulars of what came next, well, they are relatively scarce," Mary admitted. "There were dozens of men he killed: for turf, for money, for anything that was requested. And let's also add robberies—that's how he became so incredibly talented at hopping from one building to another. Louis was the muscle and force behind John's gang, and no one other than Will was ever able to keep him level. It started as a friendship until one day it was something more, and the pair kept their relationship a secret and got away with it for a number of years. The Chichesters joined forces with the Dead Rabbits and the Shirt Tails, and their numbers grew substantially; still, slowly, John began to perceive the Chichester loyalty was no longer to him, but to Louis and especially to Will. They were treated as the true leaders, both feared and respected for the hell they'd raised. Somehow, John managed to uncover the true nature of Will and Louis's relationship, and he stupidly used that knowledge to threaten them. If that ever got out, the two of them would have...well..."

"The gang would have fucking torn them apart," Esther finished for her.

"Precisely, and on John's order."

There was silence.

"So, what happened, Mary?"

Mary looked away. "Louis saw red and killed John right then and there. Brutally."

"Jesus Christ."

"That's not the worst of it," Mary illuminated, her countenance exacerbated. "The worst of it is that they got caught."

Regardless of it being in the past, Esther felt her heart sink. "Will took the fall."

"He did," Mary affirmed, "and due to the ruthlessness of the crime, the gang gave him over to the police—something that does not happen very often, as you know. Louis was banned from the Points for life, and after the war, the gangs came together as the one unified group that, today, are the Whyos."

Esther struggled to find a train of thought. "What did he do after?"

"Louis?"

"Yes."

"He was a gun for hire. Little jobs here and there, mainly helping Sally with the Underground Railroad and transporting negroes in and out of the city undetected. There was the occasional contract to keep his skillset fresh, though I think Louis was haunted by losing Will. It impacted him deeply, scarred him in the worst of ways. Eventually, he saw the light, but for a moment, it was all darkness."

Esther could sense Mary was insinuating something. "What do you mean?"

"I mean," she resolved, "once the trial was over, and Will was believed to be dead, Louis hunted down every one of the boys who turned Will over to the coppers. It became his...obsession."

"He killed them."

"In the most unpleasant of ways. Slowly, was what Louis alleged, and then I told him I didn't want to hear any more. There were fourteen of them, and within a month, not one of them breathed again." Mary extended over and patted Esther's skirt pocket, where the brass knuckles rested underneath the fabric. "He never used brass again, but that is why he trained you with them. They were his original weapon of choice."

This was yet another colossal shock to Esther. "Louis used these?"

"He did. I think Edward was the one who convinced him never to use those things again."

"So...how did Edward find him?"

"The Underground. Not a week after meeting me, Edward was approaching The Palace and saw Louis leaving with Sally and her father. The Madame would always extend an offer to any negro women that if they wanted to work for her, she would house them, feed them, and give them a roof over their heads, as well as offer protection. The rest, I am sure you can fill in on your own."

"So, along with Louis's origin story, you're telling me every one of you is connected," Esther exhaled, rubbing her temples with her fingers in consternation. "Well, everyone except the Madame."

Mary's jaw tightened. "When this conversation commenced, you made me a promise. Please remember that."

Esther squinted at her, confused. "What is it, Mary?"

"Esther, the Madame is my mother."

It was like being hit in the face with a bludgeon. "W-w-what?!"

"I realize this might come as a shock to you—"

It was far more than shock—Esther's entire body went cold. "This is what you want me to keep from your son?!" She was enraged. "You cannot be serious! How long have you been keeping this from Thomas?!"

"I only found out a short time ago," Mary tried to console her, taking up Esther's hands. "Please, Esther, you have to understand. She made me promise. This was not up to me, and it's not up to you. It is for her to tell Thomas when she is ready."

"This is fucking ridiculous," Esther hissed, yanking her hands from Mary and leaping to her feet. She commenced pacing to and fro, fuming. "Do you know what this would do to him? To find this out now?! That she's been lying to him?!"

"She hasn't been lying to him."

"Don't you dare take her side! She left you in a goddamn mental institution to rot!"

Mary, too, got up, and her eyes narrowed. "She left me there so that Thomas would survive the wrath of Tammany Hall. I made those mistakes. I got myself locked away. She protected the only family she had left, and you have no fucking right to cast a shadow over her actions, do you understand me?"

Esther took two bounding steps towards her, their faces inches apart. "You do not get to scold me like a child any longer. I am not your daughter. What you are doing to your son is deceitful, and he will never forgive you for it."

To Esther's surprise, Mary did not back down. "You are my daughter, whether you want to accept that or not. You love my son, you'll marry my son, and I took you in when you had nowhere else to go. And what's more, you're Louis's daughter, and Will's, and even the Madame's. You are a part of this family, and we do what is best for each other. Thomas will know the Madame is his flesh and blood soon enough, yet until the correct moment strikes, you will keep your goddamn mouth shut because you made me a promise."

"How is this doing what is best for Thomas? Just tell me that much."

The hardness in Mary's gaze softened, and she put her hand on Esther's cheek. "She would become a liability to him, a distracting disadvantage that did not previously exist. There is much to be done, and she does not want him to make protecting her a priority. Ever."

"Protecting her?!"

Mary sighed. "She'd rather die than have Thomas risk his own life to save hers."

For the first time in ages, Esther felt tears forming in her eyes, grasping what Mary was trying to explain so delicately. "But…it's so…unfair."

"She loves him, Esther. Love isn't fair." Mary pulled out a handkerchief and wiped away the tears from Esther's face.

"Mary, he needs to know."

"He will, Esther."

"When?"

"When she thinks it's time."

There was no way she would win this round, and so Esther conceded, "Well, I guess there isn't much I can do about that."

Putting the handkerchief away, Mary didn't react to her final comment. "Come and let's walk back to the house. I have a small favor to ask of you."

Without waiting for a reply, Mary locked her arm in Esther's and led them along the walkway returning to the house.

As they neared the manor, Esther's emotions seemed to subside enough to speak. "I can do favors, but please, no more secrets to keep," Esther pleaded with a small chuckle. "This one might just kill me, and I am already a terrible liar."

"No more secrets," Mary agreed, squeezing her arm. "It is an inquiry, one I cannot figure out from this side of the Atlantic. There was a woman who was in that dungeon with me—one that Hiro believed was still alive. Her name was Grace. I do not know if she survived, but I would like to."

"I'll take care of it," Esther assured her.

It was a minute before Esther spoke again, "So, this is why Lucy and William want to come with me. Because we are all family."

Mary nodded. "They're going for you, for Thomas, and for me. They will not be a burden, I can promise you. Yet, they will do the justice of keeping you and Thomas grounded when you need it most."

"All right, I can get beyond that. There is just one last thing I need to say."

"What's that?"

Esther halted, and the two women looked at one another.

"I need you to understand the very real possibility that I may not make it home again."

Mary pulled Esther into an embrace and held her close. "You do what you need to do, my darling. It's all in God's way. We are in this together, every one of us." She released her. "I think if you keep one thing in mind, you'll find yourself home again in no time at all."

"What one thing is that?"

Mary smiled at her. "That you are no longer alone."

In the hours she had prior to dinner, Esther packed only her necessities for New York, and while it went against her instincts, she chose not to carry her brass knuckles with her. Esther had to be extremely careful, not just for her own safety, but for that of William and Lucy: as far as Richard Croker and the Whyos were concerned, Esther was dead, and for no reason was her cover to be jeopardized. That included dressing in the latest stylings from London, sporting her horrible itchy wig, and keeping her head down around absolutely everyone who was a stranger to her. To be discreet, Esther had dismissed Cassandra for the afternoon, wanting to be able to hide her alternate identity from her maid, who would also be traveling with them to New York. Cassandra certainly had her own suspicions about Esther, given her consistently shaved head and clandestine training sessions with Hiroaki, though if it was a problem, the maid certainly hadn't brought it up with her. To the extent that Esther was concerned, the less Cassandra knew, the less danger she was in—and Esther already had enough people in her life she had to worry about protecting.

A handful of letters were waiting for Esther at her writing desk. There was one from Thomas in code, relaying his excitement at Esther's return to the city in December. She had not yet informed Thomas of her early arrival, as the choice had been made just a few days prior, and that was partly due to the fact that Esther wanted to be unexpected. Without anticipation, there would be no room for anyone to conceal the reality of what was going on, as many often had with Esther in the past. This included giving her the advantage while sneaking Hiroaki across the ocean into America—Orientals were still banned from migrating over to the United States, and Esther had to pay an exorbitant number of people off to make sure Hiroaki could cross the pond without being tossed off the ship. Thomas swore by the White Star Line, but Esther booked their passage on one of the new Cunard steamers through Connor's former contacts at P & O, and they'd assisted in arranging the details. In just under two weeks, she would be standing on Thomas's doorstep, and the thought of finally seeing him again made Esther's stomach fill with butterflies.

Next to Thomas's letter was a customary, weekly letter from Celeste, also in code and addressed to Lucy, as per Esther's request, keeping Esther up to date on the happenings of The Palace. As Esther reached to pick up the two letters, it was then she realized there was a third underneath Celeste's, and she grasped the bottom envelope. The handwriting was unmistakable: it was from none other than the Madame, and it was the first time in her months away that Esther heard any word from her whatsoever. She held no grudge as to why—Esther was not naïve enough to think that just because the Madame and Croker had an understanding, Walsh wasn't watching every single move she made. Conversely, after Mary's confession earlier that day, and upon learning of the Madame's ties to Mary, Thomas, and Louis, Esther was longing to see her, to sit down with her, and to at least attempt to appreciate the Madame's rationale for hiding such a monumental secret for so long. Initially, she had been furious, and that fury subsided into something Esther could grasp better than anyone—the Madame would do anything to guard and shelter the people she loved, even if it meant removing herself from the picture. At ten years old, she'd perceived their likeness, and again, Esther was reminded she and the Madame were cut from the same cloth.

Reaching for her letter opener, Esther broke the Madame's seal on the envelope, opening the parcel and seizing the letter.

My beautiful Esther,

I hope this note finds you well, and most importantly, healed after your time away from us. My apologies for not writing to you until the end of your stay. To be frank, I had no intention of writing this letter, and thought we would catch up upon you return in December, but I am wary, and time is of the essence in these next few crucial months.

Louis is currently on his way to Baltimore, where we have declared your demise to have taken place after escaping the city. The necessary documents have been created to mislead Croker or anyone amongst the Hall who might assume otherwise, and with this news, I wanted to caution you to disguise yourself thoroughly. Croker may believe us, yet Mr. Walsh certainly will continue to have his own opinions, which leads to my very next point.

Last evening, Richard was attacked by Whyos, angry over Seamus Murphy attending a boxing match. They would have killed him, darling, yet Thomas saved him, for reasons I will ascertain as quickly as I can. I do believe that Thomas is trying to find a way to take out Walsh, and views Richard as the way to do that through the hit Richard is planning on Priestly. My concern, as usual, lies with Walsh. He has a substantial number of horrendous bastards at his disposal, and Richard is scared—more scared than I have ever witnessed previously. He has begun to comprehend that we are his only chance. I only wish you had been there to see him cower.

Esther, I know Thomas would murder me for asking, however I want you to come to the city as soon as you can, earlier than December if you can manage. We need all the help we can get, and something tells me that the stars are not currently aligned in our favor. If you are ready, please come home. We need you.

I need you.

See you soon, darling.
M

It was the confirmation that Esther's instincts had been correct: they needed her, and it was time to go home.

Setting her three letters aside, Esther went to the easel beside the western-facing window and sat in front of her nearly finished painting just as the sun started to sink below the faraway hills. It was not a large painting, definitively smaller than her usual style, yet this vibrant splash of color was something that meant more to her than any other painting Esther had created. She wanted to remember Amberleigh, to remember what it felt like to be in such a special, magnificent place. The paint needed to dry by morning, since the picture would be going with her to New York, and it required just a few more brush strokes of the most effervescent red she could create, with a subtle fade into the deep purple of the heightened sky. There wasn't a second to spare, and when the moment came that she set the paintbrush down, Esther was almost overdue for her farewell dinner.

The hours came and went hastily, and with a merry buzz and a full glass of wine, Esther dismissed herself from the dinner party, wanting to finish packing and prepare for a visit from Akemi with the last of her treatment. Throughout her stay at Amberleigh, Akemi had been closely monitoring Esther's progress, giving her herbs and tonics to consume which assisted in healing the internal damage done to her organs. She insisted on sending Esther with a batch of tea that would continue to keep improving her health in more ways than one, and while Akemi was not specific in just what these improvements might be, Esther had an inclination Akemi was pumping her body full of whatever she could think of to keep Esther in her prime.

She opened the door that went into her rooms and found Akemi was already waiting there for her, resting across from the fireplace with a small glass of wine for herself. Peering up, Akemi smiled kindly at her, motioning for Esther to join her on the sofa. Making her way over, Akemi held up a small bag and set it on the coffee table.

"Enough to get you through the next six months. If you are there longer, I will send more."

"Thank you, Akemi," Esther replied gratefully, lowering down beside her. "I hope you haven't been waiting long."

"Just long enough to enjoy a bit of wine. I am glad you were taking the time with your family. It is the most important thing of all."

"I couldn't agree more," Esther matched, leaning backward against the sofa and temporarily setting her wine glass on the side table. "Do you mind if I smoke, Akemi?"

"Not at all."

Reaching into her skirt pocket for a cigarette and matches, Esther removed both and struck the timber, taking a deep inhale to light her tobacco. She then put the matchbox into her pocket once again and picked up her wine, rotating between drags and sips of her drink.

"I am anxious to go back to the city," Esther conveyed. "I am worried of what could happen, and at the same time, I cannot deny that…that some of us…well, we won't make it."

"Loss is a part of every revolution," Akemi observed. "You are ready for death, Esther, this I can sense in you. What you are not prepared for is the loss of others. This is something Hiro and I have discussed, and he will work with you to accept the inevitability of death."

"I cannot lose Thomas," Esther blurted out before she could stop herself. "I will do anything, including sacrificing myself, to keep him alive."

Akemi's head tilted a little to the side, studying her. "What makes you think he has not made a similar bargain with himself?"

"What do you mean?"

"You love each other, Esther. You have both fought to get back to one another. Do you not see that he, too, has made this oath? If anything, such a vow will make you both more inclined to win, to protect one another. But you must not forget that there is work to be done, work you and Thomas have spent most of your lives dedicated to. And you…you are the most important."

This caught Esther off guard. "Why on earth am I the most important?"

For a moment, Akemi became markedly uncomfortable and quiet, and Esther did not relent. "Akemi?"

She closed her eyes and breathed in deeply. "You, Esther, are the one that must vanquish the dragon."

"Walsh?"

"Yes."

Esther was perplexed. "How do you…how could you know such a thing?"

Scooting closer to her, Akemi's expression was melancholic. "Hiro mentioned to me after your training this morning that he told you of his encounter with the gypsy woman."

"Yes, he did."

"Well, he did not tell you all of it, for fear that it might shake your resolve."

It took a moment for Akemi's words to sink in.

"How would that change anything? I mean, I love Hiro, Akemi, but I don't even know if I buy into this woman's, uh, prediction."

Akemi finished her wine. "Before today, I was the only one who knew of the gypsy, and what she told Hiroaki about his death. Not even Edward was aware of this."

"Nor Thomas?"

Akemi shook her head. "Is there more wine, before I begin?"

"Of course!" Esther hopped to her feet and paced to the drink cart, resuming her previous spot with a bottle of wine and a bottle opener. "Hold on, I have a feeling we both will need a bit of this."

"Yes, we will," Akemi stated cryptically.

Esther hurried in uncorking the bottle. Once popped, she filled their glasses, and the two women clinked them together in salute.

"To you, Esther."

"And to you, Akemi."

Once they'd taken their fill, Akemi resumed their discussion: "Hiroaki had been there to talk with her, and it wasn't until the gypsies were gone that he divulged what occurred between them. And yes, the first part of you being Hiro's guide is accurate. Yet the portion he left out was what exactly his destiny was."

"Well…what is it?!"

"That he would die in battle, aiding his guide so that she could slay the dragon."

"Which therefore makes you assume Walsh is the dragon."

"He is, Esther," Akemi asserted earnestly. "What Hiro feared was that the gypsy woman claimed his guide would have to be the one to complete the task."

Esther straightened up. "Why does that matter?"

Akemi's eyes went to the ground. "Because she would be the only one left."

It was hard not to scoff at these superstitions, but Esther restrained her disbelief out of respect. "Without meaning any offense to you," Esther began, "I don't really believe in this kind of prophecy bullshit, Akemi. I never have. Fate has changed its plans for me on many separate occasions."

"You must heed the warning at least. Please. For your own sanity, Esther." The woman looked at her with pleading eyes.

"All right, I will," she promised. "I already plan to kill Walsh, Akemi. If anything, this strengthens my resolve rather than heightens my trepidations. You can tell Hiro I said that."

The pair of them had another gulp of their drinks.

"You really believe that Hiro won't come home, don't you?" Esther asked.

"It's not a belief. I know he will not return alive."

"And what about me?"

Akemi gave Esther the up and down. "We will see each other again, you and I."

"How can you be sure?"

"It is a feeling," Akemi professed, exhausting the contents in her glass. "You need to rest before your journey. Continue your herbs, and if you need more, I will happily send as much as I can to you in the city."

Rising, Akemi bowed, and Esther did so in reciprocation.

"My story, or rather, my choice to inform you of the entirety of Hiroaki's visit with the gypsy woman, ties in with Hiro's wishing to prepare you for the inevitable loss that you will endure in the future. Safe travels, Esther."

"Thank you, Akemi."

When her friend was gone, Esther again filled the wine in her glass, reliving the very strange conversation she'd just had with Akemi. While she found it fascinating that somehow a gypsy woman was able to so accurately envision Hiroaki's future, a large part of her did not trust that this story was real. Instead, Esther deemed it to be a ploy by Hiroaki and Akemi, a ploy meant to strengthen her fortitude and prepare her for what would undoubtedly be blood—and death—for some of her family. There were evidently no doubts in Akemi's mind that Hiroaki would die in New York City, yet when it came to Esther, this resolution was the opposite: that Esther would survive what was to come. In the end, Esther took away from the encounter what she supposed the purpose of the gypsy woman was: Hiroaki and Akemi were worried of what she might do if Thomas did not live. What they did not recognize was that Esther, in her own stubbornness, would not let anything happen to Thomas. Not while she still had air in her lungs.

With her glass of wine, Esther went to her desk, seating herself in the chair and grabbing for ink and a pen. On a blank piece of paper, she began:

My beloved Mary...

Louis was exhausted.

Three days in Baltimore had worn on him in a way he never could have anticipated, and as he was rocked back and forth in his coach on the way to the train station, he was at least relieved that his commission of forging Esther's death was fulfilled. The paperwork had been manufactured by the Madame, whose skillset when it came to falsifying documents was much more advanced than Louis's, and the only thing required of him was to make sure her death certificate was on file at Johns Hopkins Hospital. From that point forward, it didn't matter who went searching for her. Esther was noted to have died from internal injuries and tossed in an unmarked grave behind the hospital due to lack of funds for a proper burial. The task had taken Louis the entire afternoon to accomplish. His more difficult aspect of this trip was to chase a new lead Samuel unearthed on Walsh in the city of Baltimore, one that might at last give The Palace some of the answers they'd been trying to unearth.

In 1873, there'd been a fire in downtown Baltimore, a large fire that consumed five square blocks of the city, destroying apartments, shops, and a small children's hospital that housed about thirty patients, taking victims from the age of two and older. For Louis, fire brought about a strange emotion, given his own experience. When Ellis first announced his suspicions to Louis about the fire, Louis cast the detective's theories aside and voiced his reservations about going all the way to Baltimore on a hunch. Never one to give up on a cause, Samuel kept to his pursuit, and another week later, acquired more information from the police department in Baltimore: the Clay Street fire's source had been an utter mystery, though the flames originated from the children's hospital. What was so strange about the case was that when the charred remains from the hospital were collected, nobody was missing. The one survivor, a nurse, only made it out because she threw herself out of a third-story window and landed in a manure cart in the middle of the street—she was in a coma for two days as a result. The fire department added that the hospital was fully engulfed by the flames within minutes, a very rare and unique occurrence unless the fire was intentionally set by an individual who knew what they were doing. Additionally, Samuel produced a telegram from his contact at the Baltimore P.D., a telegram which confirmed that two months prior to the Clay Street fire, a sixteen-year-old boy with the last name of Walsh ran away from a state-sponsored reform school just outside Baltimore, and for years was on the missing persons registry of the city.

He'd never been found. Louis went to Baltimore.

A few hours after planting the forgeries proving Esther to be deceased, Louis made some inquiries around town with very little luck, thus making his options in how to proceed challenging. Rather than waste time, Louis took a gamble and showed up to the police department pretending to be Detective Ellis from New York, and without breaking a sweat, was given the address of the nurse who survived the fire by Ellis's contact, a Detective Larry Sherman. The two chatted like old friends, and Louis left the station both amused and concerned by how easy it had been to impersonate a police officer.

Liv Killgard owned a home outside of the city with her daughter, and rather than call on her, Louis waited and chose to visit the following morning. The address took him to a small house with about a quarter of an acre of land, and as Louis approached, he could hear chickens clucking in the backyard and a dog barking somewhere inside the house. A light layer of snow lay on the ground and on the roof, and when he reached the front door, Louis could smell coffee brewing inside. He knocked.

"Who is it?!" came a younger woman's voice.

"My, uh…my name is Detective Samuel Ellis, ma'am!" Louis shouted in his best feigned American accent.

"Detective?"

"Yes, ma'am!" he responded kindly. "There is no problem here.

503

I was wondering if I could ask Liv Killgard a few questions! It's about an old cold case."

No response came, and just as Louis was about to knock again, he heard footsteps approaching the door, and it swung open.

"What do you want with my mother?" the woman pressed, her stance unwelcoming. She was very plain and somewhat rotund in appearance, and the wrinkles on her face gave her age to be much older than the sound of her voice.

"Like I said, I am a detective from New York."

"I asked what you wanted, Detective."

Louis managed to hide his annoyance. "I wanted to ask her about the fire."

"She already talked to detectives about the fire."

"Not to me," Louis asserted. "What is your name?"

She crossed her arms over her chest. "Allison."

"Allison, I am Detective Ellis." He held out his hand to shake hers, and after a second or two of hesitation, she took it. "Look, I am not here to be a bother. This is a cold case and we just got a lead on it. I am here simply to confirm some of the details that have come to light. That is all, I can assure you."

Her eyes were filled with scrutiny, but she conceded, "If you upset her, Detective, you're gone. Is that understood?"

"Of course, Allison."

Louis stepped inside and Allison closed the door behind him before leading him down a dark hallway. They came to the light in the kitchen, where two cups of coffee were poured hot and waiting at the table; Allison went directly over to the stove to pour another for Louis. In a chair facing Louis sat a much older woman Louis assumed to be Liv, only there was one tiny surprise: she was blind.

"Who is it, dear? I can smell him from over here," Liv remarked, sniffing the air around her.

"It's a detective, Ma. He wants to ask you some questions about the fire."

"The fire?"

"At the hospital," Louis added. "Hello, Liv, my name is Detective Ellis. I am from New York. Do you mind if I sit down?"

"Not at all! Please, Detective. Allie? Coffee?"

Allison set a cup of coffee down in front of Louis and joined the two of them. "Already done, Ma."

"Right. Well. Go ahead, Detective," Liv instructed, having a sip from her mug. "How can I offer my help?"

Louis did the same, then went on, "The fire I am referring to is the Clay Street fire. You were the only survivor from the children's hospital."

Her countenance became somber. "Yes, I was the only one. I lost my sight, the use of my left leg, and many friends that day."

"Can you tell me anything you recall from that day? Anything out of the ordinary?"

"No, not a thing. I was a few floors up, treating one of the children, when I heard screams. The boy I was assisting was perhaps thirteen or fourteen, and in a wheelchair. We made it to the hallway in an attempt to get to the stairs, but the flames were already everywhere—it seemed like the walls and the floor and the ceilings were all ablaze around us. Then came an explosion, and I don't remember anything after that. I do not remember jumping from the window. I've even told Allison—"

"Ma, there's no way."

Liv waved her off. "There is too a way."

"What is it?" Louis queried.

"She thinks someone threw her out the window," Allison told him.

Needing more, Louis carried forward with his questions: "How long had you been at the hospital, Liv?"

"Six years," she answered, having another gulp of coffee. "It was my life, that hospital. We took care of every child we could."

"Did you have special cases you treated? Cases with symptoms you couldn't quite identify?"

"All the time," Liv remarked candidly. "We saw children of all ages, including immigrant children who would pour in...so many orphans, too, just looking for a place to sleep."

"There is a name I would like to see if you might recognize."

"Whatever you need, Detective."

"Walsh."

This was not a name Liv Killgard expected to hear, and Louis was intrigued to witness the old, blind woman nearly shudder at the sound of it. The color drained from her cheeks, and her daughter, noticing the transformation from content to horrified, suddenly became startled.

"Ma, you all right?" She scooted her chair closer to Liv and took her mother's hand. "You know who this guy is the Detective is asking about?"

"I haven't...I haven't heard that name in...in..."

"It has been a long time, I am sure," Louis made an effort to comfort her. "Was he ever a patient at the children's hospital?"

Shame came to her countenance. "He...he was..."

"When?"

"My first two years as a nurse. My...my first year...I had no idea what was happening. He wasn't one of my kids, you see. In a different wing. I was only treating basic cases of infections and things of that nature..."

Allison was worried, clearly not having seen this side of her mother too often. "Ma, do you need some water?"

"Yes, dear."

"I'll go to the well. Detective?"

"Yes, please. Thank you, Allison."

Getting to her feet, Allison left the kitchen, leaving Louis with Liv. "Do you want to tell me about him?"

"You have to understand," she said hastily. "I was new. I needed the money I...I just had Allison, and her father left me with nothing..."

"Please, please, there's nothing to defend!" Louis consoled her. "I only want to know what you know, Liv. Just tell me what you remember."

She was stricken, yet she took a deep breath and steadied herself. While she couldn't see Louis, she reached out for him, and Louis went to her, grabbing her hand. "We must not tell Allie. She can't know what I...what I..."

"She has only just gotten to the pump," Louis uttered softly, glancing out the kitchen window to the backyard. "We have a few minutes."

"All right, all right." Another long inhale and exhale. "The boy had been there years. Orphan, I think, though I never asked. Like I said, he was kept in a separate wing of the hospital for the incurable cases, mainly ailments that handicapped children in such a manner they could not live by themselves. It was the top floor of the building."

"How many stories was the building?"

"Four. A few months into my second year, I was working on call, and one of the doctors was...well, a nurse came down to get me in a panic. Said a patient had attacked the doctor. I went with her to the boy's room, and the boy had beaten the doctor very, very badly. He was nearly twelve at that time, I believe. But when I saw the boy, he was cowered in the corner, shaking, scars all over his body... fresh scars..."

Louis took a deep swallow. "Tell me about the scars."

A tiny tremor was in her breath now. "They experimented on him. Originally, he'd gone to the hospital for a broken arm, and the doctors thought there might have been nerve damage, because the boy didn't feel a thing. A neurological dysfunction of the brain, they eventually discovered."

"Who is 'they,' Liv? Which doctors?"

"A doctor by the name of Harvey was running the operation. There were two other doctors…I cannot remember their names. The last was the physician I found beaten that night. He was a medical student studying under Harvey. Halsted…that was his name."

"Why does that name sound familiar?" Louis thought aloud.

One of Liv's blind eyes twitched. "He is now running Hopkins."

"Holy shit," Louis uttered before he could stop himself, and he retracted in pretended horror at his words. "Goodness, Liv. Forgive me, I was shocked. Please continue."

"Harvey kept the boy locked away, running repeated experiments on the poor soul, all to no avail. Ugly, nasty experiments that really didn't make much progress." She took a breath, considering her words. "Harvey was very stubborn, ambitious…He was mentoring Halsted, who was still studying at Columbia in New York."

"Jesus," Louis whispered, noticing that Allison was wrapping up with her pumping. "Liv, why didn't the boy run away when he'd beaten Halsted to a pulp?"

"His glasses. He didn't have his glasses. The poor boy was legally blind without them; couldn't see a damn thing in front of his face."

"I see. And what kind of experiments?"

This time, a small whimper. "They cut him, burned him, broke…broke bones…oh Detective, it was simply awful. They tortured him, and when I went to try and comfort him, the boy tried to attack me! He had managed to snag a scalpel and nearly sliced me!"

Allison was nearly done. "So, then what happened?"

"Harvey sat me down along with the other nurse and asked us not to report it, because the boy was being transferred out anyhow. Halsted left the very next day after resigning his post. We complied with his request, and five days later, the boy was gone."

"Any idea where?" Louis pressed.

"A reform school just outside Baltimore."

"Liv, there is something I am going to tell you that will frighten you very much, but I need you to listen."

"Yes, Detective?"

"As a boy, Walsh escaped from that reform school a short time before the fire. And I believe it was he who started it, in order to kill everyone at the hospital who'd hurt him."

Her expression was one of pure horror. "Good God."

"Do you have any idea why he would save you? Why he threw you out that window?"

Rapidly, Liv's eyes filled with tears. "Those last few days...before they took him...God forgive me, I should have done more. I brought the boy food. Extra food, bread, water, a little beer, a bit of chocolate...I was so, so devastated by what I'd witnessed..."

The back door opened, and Allison appeared with water. She halted in the doorway, observing the two of them closely, specifically Louis. "Everything all right in here?"

"Your mother has been a significant help in this case, Allison. Thank you both for your time, I do very much appreciate it."

As Louis stood up, Liv touched his arm gently. "Is he...is he still alive, Detective?"

Louis's gaze went over to Allison, and then once more to Liv. "I am afraid he is."

"Has he...has he hurt others?"

"Many. I will be honest, Liv. You are the only living person he has ever shown mercy without some sort of gain for himself." Louis paused for a few seconds. "What happened to the rest of the doctors who experimented on Walsh? Were they in the hospital when it burned down?"

An odd look came over her. "Two of them were there. Halsted...well, like I mentioned, he's at Hopkins...and I am honestly not quite sure how much he had to do with it at all. As a student, you cannot be liable…"

"But Harvey?"

Liv didn't say anything, but Allison did. "Dr. Harvey wrote to my mother upon hearing about the hospital—nothing out of the ordinary, purely out of politeness. My mother wrote him back the following week and did not receive a response until perhaps a month later. Dr. Harvey was dead…"

It all made sense to Louis now. "Was it a suicide?"

"Why, yes it was!"

Louis nodded. "All right, that is all I will be needing, ladies. Thank you again for your time. I will let myself out."

The very next day, Louis returned to Hopkins, with one person in particular he needed to see. After at last convincing a very suspicious nurse he was the brother of a patient of Dr. Halsted's, she showed Louis to Halsted's office and sat him down, telling him it would be a few minutes, as the doctor was currently wrapping up his morning shift with resident students.

Curious, Louis asked her what a resident student was, and she replied that it was a brand-new method of education introduced by Dr. Halsted, wherein he took on still-learning students and immersed them into the medical field firsthand, thus drastically improving their skillsets and experience with medicine. As she left, Louis wondered to himself if this was the result of spending a vague amount of time experimenting on Walsh with Dr. Harvey, but he didn't really care. There was one subject he needed answers on, and that was how in the hell Dr. Halsted was still alive after the atrocities he'd committed in his youth on the lunatic.

Footsteps came echoing from the hallway, and abruptly, the office door swung open behind where Louis sat. Halsted didn't even glance up from the clipboard he was reading from, only let the door shut as he marched around his desk and sat down opposite Louis.

His eyes lingered on the paper, ignoring Louis's physical presence. "You have a brother here, sir?"

"Actually, no, I don't. I am here for you, Doctor."

Instantly, Halsted peered at Louis, and his reaction upon beholding the giant Frenchman was priceless.

"I...uh...how can I help you then, sir?" Hastily, he pulled his pocket watch out from his lab coat. "I am needed in surgery in fifteen minutes, you see."

"I only need five of those, Dr. Halsted," Louis remarked bluntly, "and you will be honest with me, because your life depends on it." Without hesitation, Louis pulled the revolver from his jacket pocket and laid it gently across his lap. "Are we clear?"

"Crystal," Dr. Halsted whispered, his stare moving toward the gun.

"You know the name Walsh, I presume."

The sound of his name caused Dr. Halsted to twitch. "I am familiar, yes."

"Lovely. And in that case, you probably can assume what my next question probably is."

"I am afraid I cannot."

Louis rolled his eyes. "Why the hell didn't he kill you, Halsted? Why are you the only one left?"

Initially, Halsted didn't utter a single word, only gaped at Louis, perplexed. Grasping his time was limited, Louis put his hand onto the revolver.

"Doctor? Don't make me force you. You will not like it."

Halsted gulped, then took a deep, shaky breath. "He came to kill me, and we made a bargain."

"When?"

"Years ago, when I was living in New York. He just showed up...out of nowhere."

Moving frantically, Halsted went for his top right desk drawer and opened it, rustling around inside, searching for something he could not find.

Louis held up the needle and vial. "You can have your morphine after you've talked to me, Dr. Halsted."

He was appalled. "You don't understand…I need that…"

"Yes, you do. And you can have it as soon as you tell me what the fuck happened."

With spite and reluctance, he complied: "Walsh came to me and told me I could choose how I wanted to die. I made him a counter offer. We shook on it, and…and that was it."

Halsted reached across his desk for the morphine, but Louis didn't move. "What was the counter offer?"

"If I told you, I would be violating my medical code of ethics—"

"Pretty sure you violated your code of ethics when you experimented on an imprisoned, orphaned child for your own professional gains, Doctor."

"That research was going to change medicine!" Halsted spat.

"And then you were attacked," Louis reminded him. "He would have killed you then if you hadn't hid his glasses."

A look of shame came over his face. "It was…I…I never…"

"What was the deal, Halsted?"

The doctor leaned back into his chair, defeated. "For a time, when I was still working in New York, Walsh would allow me to… to use his blood for experimentation on local anesthetics. As a result, he made an incredible amount of money. He was handsomely paid each time. This is how I was able to discover the beauty of cocaine with local anesthetics—something that has revolutionized anesthesia medicine."

Louis's gaze narrowed. "What else?"

He bit his lip, clearly having believed Louis would rescind with that explanation alone. "I told him how to find Harvey. He'd been hunting for him with no luck. He would have burned all of America down to find him, I would think. I was one of the few who knew

Harvey had some gambling debts and was trying to outrun creditors. He was very careful about where he went, and he'd made his way west to cover his tracks."

"So, you gave Walsh Harvey for your own life."

"That is correct."

Disgusted, Louis got to his feet, holstered his revolver, and held the morphine out to Halsted. "One more thing, Doctor."

Halsted glared at him expectantly. "What?"

"Within a matter of days, Walsh will show up here, asking about a girl. You will tell him she died here, on your table. Her death certificate is on file, along with forged medical records, in case you want to be prepared with details."

Halsted's head tilted to the side. "And what if I don't?"

"Then I'll be back here to kill you and expose everything you've done."

Halsted gulped and nodded reluctantly, reaching for the morphine, yet Louis pulled it just out of his grasp. He needed confirmation at last. "Is it true, Doctor, that he cannot feel anything?"

"He cannot feel physical pain, no. It is a neurological disorder, one I have never seen previously, and one that I doubt I will ever witness again in my lifetime."

"And do you realize that you helped build this monster into what he is?" Louis snapped. "By torturing him as a child, turning him into a complete psychopath, and providing him with compensation to thrive in his own malicious existence? You are responsible for him. You made him into the murdering lunatic he is."

Snatching the morphine from Louis, the doctor immediately put the needle into the vial and drew the plunger away from the barrel, filling the syringe with fluid. Louis watched as, openly in front of him, Halsted tossed his foot onto his desktop, took off his shoe and sock, stuck the needle between his first and second toes, and shot up with the drug. Exhaling a giant sigh of relief as the morphine hit his body, Halsted's tension relaxed, and in an oddly clarified haze, the man glanced at Louis, quite serious.

"Why do you think I left New York?"

CHAPTER XLII.

The hour was just beyond two in the morning as Thomas set aside his brandy glass and went in search of his coat, not wanting to be too late in meeting the Madame at The Palace for what she called an overdue "circling of the fucking wagons." Initially, Thomas had been against having every one of them all in one place—it made their faction an obscenely easy target, and would give away the covers each had carefully been building over years of blood, sweat, and loss. Conversely, the Madame was unrelenting in her contention that this gathering was a necessity for progress, and with Esther safely at Amberleigh and Louis traveling back from Baltimore, Thomas acquiesced. They'd agreed to arrive at different times between the hours of two and three to not draw attention to The Palace, and thankfully, Ashleigh and Celeste would already be present to assist the Madame with her typical Friday night crowd.

Between Croker being attacked by a disgruntled band of Whyos to the upcoming presumptive hit on Priestly, Thomas and the rest of the Madame's renegades had their hands full, to say the least. In a strange turn of events, Richard Croker chose to rely heavily on the Madame for reprieve and advice on what he and Tammany Hall ought to do next, something that not one of them would have guessed. Most originally assumed that the moment Grant was elected to office, Croker would distance himself from the Madame and her affiliates; instead, with the growing gang violence and Walsh more unpredictable than ever, Croker saw the Madame as the key to his survival, and additionally had cast his sights on turning Thomas's Vigilante alter ego into Walsh's replacement. Thomas played Croker, manipulating him just enough to give the man hope—hope that, perhaps, Thomas could be brought over to the Tammany Hall side in the end. Using Croker was easy for Thomas, and he believed if he could strategize the hit on Priestly right, Walsh, the Whyos, and Croker could be taken care of before the start of the new year. His only concern was the suspicious notion of just what Walsh might be planning himself: if there was one thing Thomas understood about Walsh, it's that he was one clever son of a bitch, and he was very good at not showing his hand until he was called.

Tony was waiting for Thomas in the front entryway, holding his long coat. "She will be happy you decided to show." He held the jacket by the shoulders for Thomas to slip in. "I am assuming you've armed yourself in case of an incursion?"

"Lawrence's blade, just sharpened, and the Griswold," Thomas replied, putting his arms through the sleeves.

"No Athena?"

"I want her to rest before tomorrow night. In case my drop-in on Croker should go awry."

Tony nodded and went to the door. "When should I expect you?"

"Two hours at the most. I need to get a little goddamn sleep for once." Thomas smiled good-humoredly at Tony. "Keep the house in one piece while I am gone, would you?"

"Of course, sir. Send my regards."

Thomas took off in the brisk early morning air, his breath sending a cloud of steam into the darkness while the chill pricked like needles at his ears, neck, and nose. The night sky was completely clear, with an array of stars twinkling in the absence of the moon, and Thomas followed the walking path north towards Central Park, where he could make his way to The Palace without being spotted. To Thomas's relief, the streets were practically deserted, and he made it to the park without incident. He halted once he neared a tree and quickly pulled a cigarette and matches out of his jacket pocket, lighting his tobacco and inhaling deeply.

"Hey, Tommy."

"Hey, Will," Thomas turned around to greet the Cat firsthand.

Will gave Thomas a crooked grin. "How close did I get 'fore ya saw my ass comin'?"

"I saw you when I left the house."

"You're shittin' me."

It was impossible to suppress a laugh. "To be fair, Will, I spent months with Hiro trying to learn how to spot shadows. Not to mention, I had an inclination you'd want to walk and talk before we made it to The Palace."

The two men commenced forward again.

"How's Es?" Will asked, spitting tobacco.

"She's been training with Hiro, and Akemi healed the last of her injuries. I think she is chomping at the bit to get back to New York." Thomas peered behind them. "You got the whereabouts on the lunatic?"

Will mimicked his surveying of the park, though his air was relaxed. "He's on a train to Baltimore as we speak."

"Croker is sending him to make sure Esther's paperwork lines up."

"I would assume so, yeah. Fuckin' Richie, brother. He don' trust nobody."

This eased Thomas's nerves. "Well, that's one less pain in the ass to worry about tonight. Louis is on his way back?"

"Should be arrivin' around lunchtime later today."

"Will, there is something I want your help with."

"Sure thing, Tommy."

"I want to try and turn a Whyo."

Will halted in his tracks, startled. "You gotta be fuckin' kiddin' me."

"No, I am not. Tony and I both think it would be a huge asset to finally squashing Walsh and his hold over the gang. I've already gotten their drug trade fucked up so that they have to buy from Chinatown. If I can get rid of Walsh, we could disintegrate the gang into smaller groups. We just need someone to give us the inside hierarchy—we don't have Es to do that for us anymore, Will."

With a sigh, Will continued on with Thomas at his side. "What do ya need me for, then?"

"You need to be the middleman. I can't get anywhere near the Whyos. You can at least be in the same room as them."

"Hell, Tommy...I don' know..."

"Just think about it, all right?"

The pair was silent for a few strides.

"Tommy, I need to tell ya somethin'."

"What is it?"

"Louis and I...once ya kill Walsh, we are runnin'."

This came as no surprise to Thomas. "I think it's the right thing to do. Walsh won't be alive to track you down. Richard will have so many fires to put out, he won't give a shit after a week or so. The Madame can diffuse that situation without breaking a sweat." Thomas paused. "You haven't told her, have you?"

"Louis thinks it's better if only you know 'til the time approaches. He already met with Sally—we are gonna do what we planned on with Es. There ain' nothin' here for us. And we are gettin' too old to be playin' cowboys and Indians."

"Am I the only one who is going to know?" he pressed. "What about Ashleigh?"

"The boy…" Will uttered under his breath, looking grave.

"He's your boy, Will."

"He ain' gonna give a damn. Prolly'll be glad to see his daddy finally gone for good."

Thomas wasn't going to let Will keep deluding himself. "The only reason your son is here is because of you. Have you even looked at him? Ashleigh turned himself into you, just like I turned myself into my father. He's not going to be glad to see you go. He's going to be devastated that he's losing you, again. If he didn't give a damn, he wouldn't have stuck around."

"Tommy, ya don' get it. Things jus' ain' like that."

"No, Will. You don't seem to get it. You know what I did when I found out my father was still alive? I went and found him because I wanted to be near him." Thomas stopped and put a hand on Will's shoulder. "Look, I don't know why you keep punishing yourself. Let it go. What's done is done, and there's not a damn thing you can do about it. But you can make tomorrow different if you just fucking try. Ashleigh deserves a father."

Will's gaze went to the ground. "I don' know how to be that."

"I think Esther might disagree with you."

At that, Will's eyes rose and met Thomas's. "All right. I'll talk to him."

Thomas finished his cigarette and they made their way out of the park.

"I lied," Thomas admitted as he flicked his tobacco from his fingers.

"'Bout what?"

"I didn't spot you at the residence. I was grabbing the timber from my jacket pocket when I spotted you."

Will let out an amused snort. "You was gonna make me think I was losin' my edge, eh? Sneaky bastard."

"If it keeps my ass alive, you bet I would."

They were the last to arrive, and Ashleigh was impatiently waiting for them in the lobby of The Palace.

"What, y'all been braidin' each other's hair or somethin'?" he quipped as they came through the door.

"Sounds like somebody's got them corset strings a lil' too tight," Will said snidely, winking at Thomas. "Gang all here?"

"Upstairs," Ashleigh declared. "Got a cable from Louis."

"And?"

"It ain' good, that's for sure."

Every head turned as the final three strolled into the Madame's office. The Madame herself was, of course, seated behind her desk on her throne, a glass of whiskey nearly drunk and in need of being refilled. At the drink cart were Samuel and Douglas, who saluted Thomas, Will, and Ashleigh as they strolled inside. Across from the Madame was Celeste taking a sip of her wine, with a vacant chair beside her that Thomas could sense was meant for him. Claire and George were side by side on the loveseat, staying warm by the fire and each with a whiskey in hand. To Thomas's surprise, Jeremiah was also there, leaning back into the armchair next to where Claire and George were, and like his sister, he was holding a very full glass of wine.

"Well, it's about goddamn time!" the Madame accosted them.

Thomas ignored her and went straight to the drink cart. "Louis has sent a wire?"

"Yes, and it's even more fucking insane than we thought."

Reaching for three empty glasses, Thomas poured himself, Will, and Ashleigh each a strong drink. "How bad is it?"

The Madame finished the last of her whiskey and held her glass up to Thomas to signal her need of more. "Well, we finally have some idea of who Walsh is."

"You're shittin' me," Will stated, moving over to sit opposite Claire and George. Ashleigh did the same, and Thomas went to provide the Madame with replenishment.

"So, Louis was able to dig up Walsh's past?" Thomas queried, leaving the decanter on the Madame's desk and taking his presumed spot beside Celeste.

"The rumor that this bastard can't feel pain is true. He was experimented on for years, and finally, when the doctors gave up, they sent him to a fucking reform school. He escaped a few years later, burned the hospital to the ground, and hunted the rest of the doctors down who weren't there to die in the damn fire."

"Jesus Christ," Douglas uttered under his breath.

"I've got a contact with Baltimore P.D.," Samuel added. "Walsh has been listed as a missing person since his break out of that school. He did save one woman from the fire—"

Thomas nearly spat out his whiskey. "Saved?!"

"Well, saved is a fucking pejorative term," the Madame informed him. "He threw her out the third story window."

"She seemed to think it was an act of mercy," Samuel went on. "I must say, I am not so sure. Either way, she led us to the truth of Walsh's origins."

"Anything else?" Claire asked, her own mien a little aghast.

"That's all Louis could send," the Madame replied. "Will? What is the latest with Walsh?"

"I was just tellin' Tommy here, the lunatic is on his way to Baltimore to confirm for Richie that Esther is long dead."

"So, who is runnin' them Whyos while that bastard is outta town?" Ashleigh asked him from the fireplace.

Will shook his head. "That's one of the issues we is havin'. Es was our inside gal with the gang. I don' got eyes in there no more. And we gotta figure out a way to know who else we up against other than the lunatic."

"He's right," Thomas agreed, having a gulp of whiskey. "And I think I have a solution."

The group stared at him, and Thomas locked eyes with the Madame, who smirked. "Go on then, Thomas."

"I am going to turn one of them."

A scoff came from Samuel. "It cannot be done."

"Tommy, ya can' be serious," Ashleigh remarked.

"Hold your horses there," Will interjected. "I wanna hear this."

"Thomas, how could you ever know you weren't being played?" Celeste entreated. "We play both sides. We could never trust one of them."

"I understand it sounds completely ridiculous," Thomas told them. "But I ran this by Esther, and she thinks there is really only one person we could turn."

"Who?" the Madame asked.

Thomas glimpsed over at Will. "Strat."

As he had hoped, Will's face lit up. "He was always friendly to her—she was the one who recruited him in the beginnin'."

"So, if you think this is possible, Thomas," the Madame said, "I am wondering how the fuck you plan to find Strat without setting off alarm bells."

"One thing I do know is that Strat is moving up the power ladder. He will be easier to find—"

"No," she articulated firmly, "I know how we can do it."

Samuel was still doubtful. "How?"

Again, the Madame's eyes met Thomas's. "Your meeting with Croker about the Priestly hit is tomorrow, correct?"

"Yes, it is."

"Perfect. Before you go to Tammany Hall, you and Ashleigh

are going to assist a little operation in Chinatown. The Whyos are meeting the Tong for a shipment of opium and have been trying to skimp on payment. The Tong have enough of their own shit going on to be preoccupied with killing off Whyos right now."

Nodding along, Ashleigh got to his feet and approached her desk. "Strat would be there if he's movin' up ranks, 'specially without Walsh bein' there to run the show."

"We will only have seconds to make it work," Thomas determined. "Otherwise, Strat's absence would be noticed. But if he's willing, we can at least set it up."

"Where could he meet us?" Ashleigh thought aloud.

"I got a place," Will announced. "My doc's house in Chinatown. Have him meet ya when the coast is clear. I'll get word over to him to expect visitors. No one would suspect nothin'."

"That would give me plenty of time to meet with Croker and then make it back to Chinatown within a few hours," Thomas concluded, liking the sound of this more and more. "We need an inside guy. There is no other way to have any idea what the Whyos are plotting."

"There is another aspect we need to discuss here about the Whyos," Samuel jumped in. "And that's the fact that they are, well, purposefully seeking out coppers. We can't link any killings to them directly as of yet, but everyone at the station knows what's going on."

"It's because of Grant promising a crackdown on their fucking antics," the Madame asserted, her tone grim. "Which is why we need to get the goddamn lunatic in his grave before January, or I can fucking guarantee the Whyos will start a riot."

Celeste cleared her throat to get everyone's attention. "While I do have faith that we will get Walsh six feet under in the next few weeks, I would like to also point out that during that time, we need to remember one thing."

The Madame glanced at her curiously. "Which is?"

"That Walsh has a very strange obsession with you, Madame, and you are a target of his for reasons not one of us can really fathom. If he somehow manages to escape Thomas at the Priestly hit, you're the first one he's going to come for."

For a moment, this seemed to render the Madame speechless.

Thomas spoke up, "Celeste is absolutely right. Which is why Louis, Will, and I will need to meticulously map out how the hit will go once I get the information from Croker." He paused for a second or two. "We cannot let Walsh get away. He might go for the Madame first, but every one of the people we care about would be in danger if he escaped."

"Which is why we won' let him," Will professed confidently. "Louis and I are ready to die to get rid of this bastard. If it comes to that, so be it."

Ashleigh's gaze shot to his father in alarm, then immediately dropped to the floor. No one except Thomas caught it, and he observed Ashleigh's cheeks reddening ever so slightly, his jaw clenched in frustration.

"We can get around to that when Louis arrives home and Thomas gets what he needs from Croker," the Madame responded. "In the meantime, here is how this will go. Douglas, I expect you and Celeste to have dinner with Croker and his wife sometime this week to keep an eye on that son of a bitch. When Louis is in the city, he and Will can sit down with Thomas to formulate how to proceed with Priestly. Claire, when Grant is here next, we are getting him as drunk as possible and assessing just how much of an anti-gang push he and the Hall are aiming for. Samuel, your job is to stay alive with all this bullshit happening on the streets. And Thomas and Ashleigh, you will stay and talk over this presumed Whyo drug deal. Last, Jeremiah, I need you to send a letter of inquiry to a Dr. Halsted at Johns Hopkins. At lunch tomorrow, you will join me to discuss what to write." The Madame drank some of her whiskey. "I want to make one thing clear. Unless you are either at The Palace, or at Thomas's residence on Fifth, you are no longer to converse about anything we are doing. Is that understood? These are the only two safe places for us in this city, and we all need to watch our asses."

"Not St. Stephen?" Celeste asked.

The Madame shook her head. "Not anymore, darling."

Celeste nodded, and the group finished their beverages before filing out one by one until only Thomas and Ashleigh were left.

"So, we workin' with the Tong tomorrow?" Ashleigh queried, lowering down into the seat where Celeste had once been.

"You'll meet them there tomorrow at eleven. Thomas knows where. The Tong are nervous…the Whyos are buying their opium, but they are indignant and always trying to cheat out of paying full price. They've made threats the last few days and are accusing the Tong of sabotaging their prior shipments. It could get pretty fucking ugly."

Thomas's left eyebrow rose. "Nothing we can't handle, Madame."

With a chortle, Ashleigh leaned over to the Madame's desk and refilled his whiskey. "I'll pack some extra cylinders, then."

Thomas reached his own glass towards Ashleigh, and his friend obliged. "I will point out who Strat is as soon as I spot him. I'll tell him to meet us just before dawn. Can you spare Ashleigh until morning?"

She let out an entertained snort. "With George and Claire here, and Walsh in Baltimore? Fucking piece of cake."

"Then I think we are all done for tonight," Thomas settled. "Ashleigh, I'll meet you here at eight sharp tomorrow evening."

"I'll be here, brother."

As Thomas made his way down the staircase, he could see Will quietly lingering in the lobby. "How'd it go?"

"I want you to be there tomorrow when we try and cross Strat."

This was a request Will was not expecting. "I mean…if ya want me to be there, I sure as hell will be. What's your reasonin'?"

They passed by George on the way out and the two of them said goodbye, then descended The Palace's stoop out into the brisk early morning air.

"Strat needs a familiar face. And I need backup when I tell him how Esther is still alive."

"Whoa, Tommy. We can' put her at risk like that."

Thomas reached in and grabbed a cigarette from his pocket. "We have to, Will."

The Cat handed over a box of timber to Thomas. "Why?"

He lit his cigarette and took a drag. "Because Esther swears it is the only way he'll do it. And I'll be damned if Esther hasn't been right about almost everything all along."

"An' just how are we gonna cover ourselves on this one? What if Strat decides he's gonna betray us to the Whyos anyhow?"

"Then we use that to our advantage and manipulate the information we give him."

"And how in the hell we gonna know?"

For a moment, as he exhaled smoke, Thomas was contemplative. "I can almost guarantee that we are going to do some fucking damage to the Whyos tomorrow. I have an idea, but it's a gamble depending on the outcome of Chinatown."

"Talk to me."

"That doc of yours still patches up the Whyos, correct?"

"He does. That's why we had to use Jeremiah to keep Esther breathin'. They still think I am Croker's, ya know."

Suddenly, his idea didn't seem so crazy after all. "I know how we can do this."

"Lord Turner?!"

A very loud banging was coming from outside the door to Thomas's rooms. Through hazy eyes, Thomas peered over at the clock on his nightstand. It was just after nine in the morning.

"Excuse me, Lord Turner, but you have a guest downstairs!" It was the voice of Mrs. Shannon.

Once Thomas had arrived home from The Palace, he and Tony stayed awake until the sun came up, strategizing until Thomas could no longer keep his eyes open. After a quick two hours of sleep, the last thing Thomas wanted to do was deal with an unexpected social call.

"Lord Turner!"

"All right, Mrs. Shannon! Jesus fucking Christ." Drawing the covers back, Thomas grabbed his robe from the foot of the bed and went to his bedroom door, opening it.

"You are not to use that language in the presence of guests, sir," Mrs. Shannon commanded, her countenance firm.

"Who is it?" he asked, choosing not to address her comment he wasn't in the mood for a three-hour lecture on etiquette.

"Captain Jonathan Bernhardt, Lord Turner. He apologizes for the early hour, which I told him was nonsense. I already have breakfast for the two of you being prepared."

This visit was so unprecedented, Thomas was having a difficult time processing it. "Right. Well, can you make us each a Sunday coffee, Mrs. Shannon? Tell him I will be down in just a few minutes."

"I don't think—"

"Just do what I ask, Mrs. Shannon. Thank you."

With a curt bow, she left, and Thomas knew he would pay for that later. As he closed the door and went to throw on some slacks and a simple cotton shirt, he was perplexed, though not nearly as angry as he probably ought to be. His quarrel with Jonathan had never been on a personal level—they had both loved Esther, and because of that, friendship was a concept out of reach. The last time he'd been in the Captain's presence, Jonathan had been a drunken moron, causing a scene and behaving like a complete asshole. However, Thomas understood the Captain to be a good man beneath the surface. He had gone out of his way to make amends with Celeste, and from what Celeste shared with Thomas, was suffering greatly from the horrors he'd witnessed out west, as well as what appeared to be a broken heart following rejections from both Esther and Celeste in marriage. Curiosity was certainly getting the better of him, and as he laced his boots to go downstairs, Thomas couldn't help but wonder why, of all moments, the Captain chose to show his face now.

The Captain was seated by the fire, a Sunday coffee in his hand and another coffee concoction waiting for Thomas on the side table by his armchair. These last few months, Jonathan had been in Vermont, and he looked infinitely healthier than he had that last summer. His handsome face was less jagged, fuller, and his eyes were bright rather than dark. On top of that, his figure had filled out once again, and with his hair tied back and a smile upon spotting Lord Turner enter the room, Thomas strangely recalled why he'd liked this man so much when they'd first met.

"Captain Bernhardt, it's a pleasure," Thomas greeted, walking over and shaking his hand. "I am sorry I was still asleep when you called. I am working on a new business merger and have been keeping terrible hours with my family home in England."

"Lord Turner, it's an honor."

The two men sat down.

"Your housekeeper, Mrs. Shannon, begrudgingly left these and announced breakfast would be served shortly. I must admit, I am happy to have a little liquid courage."

Thomas smiled at him and picked up his coffee. "What is it I can do for you, Captain?"

Jonathan became thoughtful. "My behavior this last summer was absolutely and outrageously inappropriate, towards you and

528

Miss Hiltmore and many others. I wanted to personally apologize to you. I made false assumptions about who you are, about your motivations, and I let my imagination get the better of me, as well as the strong influence of too much alcohol to try and ease my pain. I wanted to ask your forgiveness."

Thomas nodded. "You unequivocally have it, Captain. I can grasp what grief does to a person, and how it tears you apart inside. I am happy to see firsthand how improved you are in such a short amount of time. Have you been in Vermont?"

"Yes." He had a sip from his mug. "I spent some much-needed time with my family there, healing after so many years of ignoring my condition..." Jonathan's voice trailed off. "There is something you do not know, something that assisted in helping me to finally move on."

When he paused, Thomas pressed him to share. "What is it, Jonathan?"

"I...well...I know Esther is alive."

Instantly, Thomas could feel his cheeks get hot. "How?"

The Captain held his gaze, his eyes pleading. "She told me herself. The night I went to make peace with Celeste, Douglas attacked me. Esther appeared out of thin air to put a stop to it. It would have ended poorly, and she could sense that. I was still trying to get ahold of my anger, and Douglas was out for blood."

Thomas's irritation marginally eased. "What did she tell you?"

"Everything."

He could feel his anger mounting. "Goddammit, Esther," Thomas hissed under his breath, taking a gulp of his drink. "I should have known that—"

"Known what? That she did this for you?" Jonathan interrupted him abruptly, his tone resolute. "For God's sake, Thomas, she picked you. There is no me and Esther, there never was. It was only you from the beginning. She told me because she saw what was happening to me, and her decision to tell me the truth is what has saved my life. That was what I needed. I am a better man for knowing. She did the right thing."

Thomas was silent, with the words "she picked you" echoing in his ears. For what felt like their entire attachment to one another, Esther and Thomas's only sore spot had been Jonathan; conversely, the message Jonathan relayed was one Thomas realized he'd been too thick-headed to ever really process. Like he'd only just told Will the night prior, they needed to trust Esther, because she saw the bigger picture better than most. Perhaps he should take his own advice and understand Esther had only done what Thomas figured he would have done in her shoes. The Captain had been on a destructive path, and she chose to make it right after years of leaving him to live in the dark when she by no means had to. Jonathan was right—Esther had picked Thomas, she had picked him time and time again, and spent years of her life working for Richard Croker so that she and Thomas could be together in the end. There was no arguing with the Captain on this one. Thomas's own stubbornness faded away, and oddly enough, he felt he loved Esther all the more because of it.

He sank back into his armchair. "Well, I am glad she told you," Thomas admitted at last. "You deserve to know." Holding up his mug, he and Jonathan saluted one another, and had a drink. "This must also mean that you know about me."

A smirk came to Jonathan's face. "I've been cheering you on from Vermont. The papers call you a Vigilante. I tend to think of you as more of an...an equalizer."

This made Thomas laugh aloud. "An equalizer. I like that."

"I just can't put it together. How did you...how did you become this?"

"My father walked a similar path," Thomas divulged, setting his empty mug aside. "I only kept the tradition alive."

"Edward?"

"Yes. Although, Edward was a little different. He would take cases throughout Europe and help people who were facing violence and death or those who could not help themselves. I, well, I trained to take down the criminal underworld of Manhattan."

"Well, shit." The Captain was astonished. "That's one hell of an undertaking, Thomas."

"Yeah, tell me about it."

"It's not just you. There's more of you."

"There are, but I cannot give you specifics for their own safety."

"Is your aunt one of them?"

It had been years since he'd thought of her as an aunt, and it made him grin. "The Madame is involved, yes."

"That's no news. If you and Esther are involved in anything, I had a feeling she'd be right there with you."

"What do you mean?"

"Well, she's been a guardian to both of you," he remarked with a shrug. "I always thought of you all as being an unusual sort of family."

"Well, that I can agree with."

"Thomas, there is one other reason I came here today."

"All right, let's hear it."

Jonathan let out a small sigh. "I want to help."

"You want to help?"

"I want to help you. I want to…to be a part of something bigger. I have a place in society. I am a war hero, I am incredibly wealthy, and I am a bachelor. There has got to be a way in which I can put myself to good use, even if it's just eavesdropping in on conversations."

His offer humbled Thomas. "Jonathan, if you get involved, you are accepting a certain amount of danger to follow you wherever you go. I won't be able to protect you."

"Do you really think I give a damn about that?"

Again, Thomas chuckled. "If you are really sure…"

"I've already rented a place across from the park," he informed Thomas. "I am not going anywhere."

Suddenly, Mrs. Shannon appeared by the fireplace. "Gentlemen, if you are ready, breakfast has been set out in the dining room."

Thomas peered over at the Captain. "Hungry?"

"Starving."

The two men got to their feet, and an idea struck Thomas as he led Jonathan out of the great room and into the dining room— sure, they were trying to find someone to cross from the Whyos, but there was one other realm they could use some ears and eyes into. Somewhere not one of them would have an easy time gaining entry to, yet one that Jonathan could access in the blink of an eye if he so wished.

"Well, Captain," Thomas said as they grabbed chairs at the table, "I just have one final question for you, then."

Coffee was poured, and Jonathan reached for some salted bacon. "What's that, Thomas?"

"How do you feel about becoming a Tammany Hall man?"

As Thomas's request materialized, the Captain smiled. "Well, to be frank, I've always wanted to wear a top hat."

The Madame was gaping at Thomas.

"You told him to what?!" she exclaimed, spilling whiskey from her glass in disbelief.

"We were pining for one insider yesterday, why not two?" Thomas beseeched her, finishing his drink and setting his glass down on the drink cart. He and Ashleigh needed to get down to Chinatown sooner rather than later, though he thought sharing his new recruit with the Madame would be a good idea before they left. "He and

I will both be attending the Vanderbilts' dinner in two days, along with Celeste and Douglas, and both Grant and Croker will be in attendance as well. Celeste has done a brilliant job befriending Elizabeth, which will give us access to Croker at almost every social event the Captain and I might attend. He and Croker already both love boxing. It would barely take the smallest suggestion to have Croker want him associated with the Hall."

"What you are managing to forget, Thomas, is that if Croker were to find out I have a fucking spy at Tammany——"

"Whoa! You have a spy? As far as you are concerned, you don't know a damn thing about it. The Captain will only share what he learns with me. He knows he cannot ever be spotted at The Palace unless it is something scheduled by the Hall or Croker."

Ashleigh and George shared a glance, the two of them seated in front of the Madame.

"I mean, I think it's worth a shot," George declared.

"I'm with Georgie," Ashleigh granted.

The Madame's gaze narrowed. "He is aware that he is on his own? If he gets found out, it's on him?"

"Yes."

With the three of them staring at her, the Madame let out a heavy, irritated exhale. "Fine! For now, the Captain can assist. But I swear to God, if that son of a bitch leaks anything, I'll cut his balls off myself. Got it?"

Thomas rolled his eyes. "Give him some credit. The Captain has witnessed a lot of bad shit on the frontier. He's smart. This could be a huge asset to us."

"Let's see if he can get in first." She finished the whiskey left in her glass. "In the meantime, you and Ashleigh will be late if you don't take off now, and we don't want to piss off the fucking chinks right now. They're more on edge than ever."

"Why is that?" Thomas asked.

"Some fucking rivalry gone wrong. Lee has been up in arms for weeks. Just watch yourselves."

"All right."

Ashleigh popped out of his chair. "Tommy?"

"Yep, let's go."

"I expect you in the morning!" the Madame reiterated as they left.

When he reached the door, Thomas turned around and gave her a mischievous glance. "You better have coffee."

Both Ashleigh and Thomas were quiet on the ride down to Chinatown as Thomas rubbed soot around his eyes and prepared jesses for Athena. Neither of them was fully certain of what sort of encounter they might have with the Tong, or Whyos, for that matter. Wanting to be prepared, Thomas had armed himself with his Griswold, Lawrence's blade, and Athena, who at that moment was closely following the carriage overhead. It was late in the season for her to be out, yet if Thomas had come to learn anything about his Peregrine, it was that she was anything but ordinary. For his own part, Thomas could assume from Athena's body language that if he left her at home, she would torture him for it later, and therefore, he had Tony get her ready for what he hoped would be no more than a skirmish. Nevertheless, if the Madame was sending Ashleigh to be his cover, Thomas had the feeling this was going to be more than just a mere skirmish— it was going to get ugly.

The driver stopped on the outskirts of Chinatown. "Out here!" he bellowed to Thomas and Ashleigh. "I ain't goin' into the fuckin' chink town!"

Thomas and Ashleigh exchanged a scowl.

"Fine!" Ashleigh shouted in return.

Heading out first, Ashleigh stepped down, followed closely by Thomas, and once they'd paid the driver, the duo set out on foot toward Mott Street, where the giant pagoda and the mayor of Chinatown were expecting them.

When they'd made it a block, Ashleigh spoke at last, "You think this is gonna be a fight?"

Thomas grabbed for a cigarette and lit it. "I don't know, but she sent both of us for a reason, and you heard what she said about the Tong."

"Yeah. I was worried 'bout that." Ashleigh bummed a cigarette and matches from Thomas. "I ain' ever met this fella on his home turf. He's nasty enough at The Palace. Gonna be real interesin' to see him fluffin' his feathers when we roll up."

Thomas had to suppress a grin. "I'm sure it'll be a show. Just watch your ass. If something goes awry—"

"I know the drill: one whistle to get out, two if ya think somethin' ain' right." He took a drag of his cigarette. "Been workin' with your girl and my daddy long enough to know the drill, ya know?"

"I do."

They made it to Mott Street.

"Stop here," Thomas ordered.

The two of them halted just in front of a closed butcher and grocer, watching the people of Chinatown pass them by, not one of the pedestrians endeavoring to look the direction of the tall white men who were completely out of place. Every person that passed knew why they were there, and Thomas had a sneaking inclination Lee had put the word out he and Ashleigh were not to be touched. With a few puffs, Thomas finished his cigarette, and motioned for Ashleigh to do the same.

"You ready, brother?"

"Let's just get this fucking over with."

The pagoda could be spotted for blocks—it rested on top of an older brick warehouse, a beacon for Chinatown to behold in wonder, awe, and fear. It was lit up brilliantly, torches flickering underneath each roof gutter, and the light outshone every other structure as far as Thomas could see. Underneath the pagoda, Thomas was aware there were an assortment of commodities for Lee and the On Leong: an opium den, a brothel, a bar, a restaurant, yet on the first floor, he'd heard Lee invested in a giant market, filled with everything the people of Chinatown could desire. The Tong were not just interested in running their own brothels and opium dens—their people were shunned by the rest of New York City, and as a result, Lee went above and beyond to show he took care of his own, dumping as much money as he thought gallant into Chinatown and providing protection for those who lived on their turf.

That is, if they earned it.

At the point in time when they were across Mott Street from the entrance, Ashleigh and Thomas gave each other one last look.

"You brought extra cylinders, right?"

"Course I did."

A sharp cry came from the sky, and Thomas happily peered above to see Athena perched on one of the edges of the pagoda, lingering patiently for instruction from Thomas. He took the lead, striding ahead and moving straight for the double doors that opened into Tom Lee's headquarters; it was a place Thomas hated walking into blind, but the objective of getting Strat on their side was worth the risk of dealing with Tom Lee, the man held out as the unofficial mayor of his people, whether they liked it or not.

There were two guards outside, one on the left side of the sliding door and one on the right. The one on the left was a whole head shorter and vaguely round at the waist, though Thomas had a feeling out of the two guards, he should not underestimate this one. The second was tall for a Chinaman, lean, and probably a decade younger, more than likely still learning what it meant to work for the most notorious oriental gang in New York City. They sported matching black suits, their hair tied back behind their heads, staring at Thomas during his and Ashleigh's approach like two insects that must be immediately squashed. As Thomas and Ashleigh drew near the guards, Thomas stopped and motioned for Ashleigh to do the same. He bowed low.

"We are here at the request of Mr. Lee," he announced, staying in his passive, bowed stance. "Would you be so kind to inform him his guests from The Palace are present?"

The short one whispered something to the tall one in a curt, harsh tone, and the lanky one disappeared between the doors while the other went on to position himself front and center, his countenance stern.

"You wait," was all he said, his glare growing more intense with every passing second.

"Ain' he s'pose to be expectin' us?" Ashleigh muttered just loud enough for Thomas to hear.

Slowly rotating to Ashleigh, Thomas winked and mouthed delicately, "It's just for show, Ashleigh."

"Gotcha."

Thomas rolled his shoulders back, and Ashleigh paced forward so the two were side by side. It took Thomas about a half minute to notice that Mott Street was completely deserted. The scene was eerie—Thomas could not make out a single human being as his eyes searched, looking suspiciously to the left and to the right.

"Ashleigh," he spoke softly, "can you see anyone?"

Ashleigh's gaze grew wide, realizing he couldn't. "I can' see shit."

"Where the fuck did everyone go?"

"Lee," Ashleigh answered, "he must have not wanted witnesses."

On edge, they resided patiently outside of the entrance for what felt like nearly a quarter of an hour before the lanky one returned and nodded to the short one; in unison, the guards opened the doors, gesturing for Ashleigh and Thomas to enter.

"Is this what happened last time you was here?" Ashleigh murmured in a low tone, somewhat sarcastically.

They strolled to the door.

"I only met them at the opium dens before. This is the…uh…
first time I'll be meeting Lee."

"Well…shit."

The light was dim on the first floor, and once the pair crossed over the threshold, Thomas and Ashleigh were welcomed by another two guards, these two dressed in the exact same suits as the duo outside, and each of them took a low bow. Thomas and Ashleigh reciprocated, and then, without a word, their greeters spun around and commenced a march toward the rear of the room. Observing his surroundings, Thomas could tell the ground floor was not used for anything related to the Tong; on the contrary, this floor was a giant marketplace as he'd been informed, with empty booths and tables scattered about, every one of which would undoubtedly be full by dawn with vendors and whatever it was they wished to sell. Tonight, however, it was utterly abandoned to the darkness and the rats, who feasted on any scraps they could manage to uncover, their squeaks and chattering distinct beyond the sound of their group's footsteps.

A spiral staircase emerged from the shadows, where yet another two guards were stationed at the bottom. Silently, their previous guides motioned for Thomas and Ashleigh to go on without them, and in the wake of the two new guards now climbing the staircase, they ascended upward until they reached the third floor, at which time, again, they were passed on to another two guards. Growing increasingly annoyed, Thomas wondered how long this relay would last, until he recognized as he looked to and fro that they were no longer in the mere gathering area of this premises—no, they were heading to wherever it was Lee operated out of.

Quite abruptly, the surrounding décor went from the standard, basic brothel ornamentation to bold, beautiful colors of red and black on the walls, which were the Chinese colors of honor, along with magnificent gold sconces as ornamentation; the smell of cherry blossoms, opium, and jasmine filled Thomas's nostrils. They took a right-hand turn at the top of the staircase, pacing down a narrow hallway that was so faintly lit, Thomas could barely see his boots on the ground. Without speaking, he could sense that Ashleigh was having certain reservations about just what they were getting themselves involved in with Lee and the Tong, and while he hated to admit it, Thomas felt the same way. No matter what, he and Ashleigh were stuck riding this one out, and he was thankful the two of them were armed to take down an army if necessary.

At the end of the hall there was a sharp left, where they found a door with one final sentinel established out front, his arms crossed over his chest and a sword dangling from his belt. The two leading Ashleigh and Thomas stopped abruptly and said something in Chinese, to which the sentinel nodded and whipped around, unbolting the door and sliding it open. One final time, Thomas peeked at Ashleigh out of his peripheral vision, and with a small exhale of compliance, the two of them went inside Lee's office.

The room was minimally decorated, with a few pieces of calligraphy on the walls and a small cart of glasses and sake; straight ahead sat Lee behind his desk, gesturing towards the two vacant chairs for Thomas and Ashleigh to join. There was a guard in each corner, heavily armed with sword and pistol, and a hidden door on the wall to Lee's left, which Thomas presumed was for emergency situations, much like the back door in the Madame's office at The Palace. A servant loitered just behind Lee on his right, seemingly to wait on him hand and foot. Thomas chose not to sit, not liking the idea of putting himself at a disadvantage in a foreign environment, and instead, he stood behind the chair and stared at Lee. Ashleigh mirrored him.

"At last, we finally meet," Lee welcomed him, snapping his fingers.

His servant leapt over to grab the bottle of sake and poured two glasses for Thomas and Ashleigh, bringing them over on a tray and keeping his head down as he did so.

Thomas picked up the sake, saluted Lee, and downed it. "Thank you, Mr. Lee." He set the glass onto the tray in unison with Ashleigh. "Now, what is it you require of us? The Madame believed this to be an urgent matter."

In spite of his reputation, Lee did not look to be a particularly menacing man. He was small, two heads shorter than Thomas, with a narrow, sharp gaze and a wide nose, a somewhat scraggly beard hanging to just a few inches below his chin. Lee's ears were noticeable as well, standing out on the sides of his head, and regardless of the bowler hat he wore, Thomas noted he had a very tall forehead. Instead of a simple suit like his guards, Lee sported a three-piece black suit, crisp white shirt, and a deep red cravat, a gold pocketwatch chain dangling from his vest. There was a walking stick leaning against the wall nearby, and a slightly larger glass with very little sake left resting on Lee's desk.

"It is not just Whyos that are my problem," Lee declared somewhat quietly. "There is a rival who has recently arrived in New York, and he is eagerly trying to undermine my business."

"A rival, sir?" Ashleigh questioned.

Visibly irritated at being addressed by Ashleigh, Lee practically sneered at him. "He is from California."

Ever the professional, Ashleigh ignored his disrespect. "Is this fella Chinese, like yourself? Or somethin' else?"

"Chinese, yes. His numbers are small but their…contingent is growing rapidly."

"You think he will also be an issue with the opium delivery?" Thomas asked.

"I have my doubts, though it is a possibility." Lee took a moment and had a sip of sake. "I would prefer you to stay in the shadows, unless my suspicions prove correct and these mongrels try to cheat me once again."

"And if they try to cheat ya?"

"You have my permission to do what is necessary to protect my shipment without any retaliation from Chinatown."

"Shipment first," Thomas reiterated, wanting to solidify terms. "Which means if some of your men get caught in the crossfire, we will not have an issue."

He didn't like it, but Lee nodded. "Fair."

"All right, we are in," Thomas confirmed.

"You will meet at the opium den on Pell Street—it has been emptied for the night. Lee Toy, my nephew standing back here, will take you through the tunnels so you are not spotted." He cleared his throat and added reluctantly, "Thank you for your assistance."

One of the guards in the corner stepped closer to them, and Thomas presumed it was the nephew Lee had spoken of. "One last clarification, Mr. Lee."

"Yes?"

"Who is this rival of yours? From California?"

Again, Lee was aggravated. "His name is Mock Duck. He was the leader of the Hip Sing in San Francisco, and has recently relocated to New York."

"Do you have any thoughts on why?"

"Because," Lee said, leaning back into his chair, "what white men do not understand is that there is a war between the Tong, no matter what city you are in. I am On Leong, they are Hip Sing. We have very different philosophies on how to rule our people."

"Sounds like a damn shame," Ashleigh retorted.

Lee studied him. "A shame, Mr. Sweeney?"

"To come all the way to America hopin' for a new life, only to be subjugated by your own people's greed and hubris."

"How dare you!" Lee bellowed, jumping to his feet.

Thomas was dumbfounded by Ashleigh, and before he could say anything to recover the situation, the two guards in the corners by the door lunged for Ashleigh. Thomas hurriedly yanked the Griswold from its holster, yet he saw there was no need. In a split second, Ashleigh whirled around, drew his guns, and cocked both pistols, which were aimed at the foreheads of his two assailants. Assuming command of the room, Thomas turned his Griswold on Lee, and motioned for him to sit back down with the barrel.

"If not for my history with the Madame," Lee hissed, lowering down, "I would have you both skinned alive for your impertinence."

"You forget, Lee, that the only reason we here is 'cause you need our fuckin' help," Ashleigh countered, unwavering in his stance. "If ya don' want what ya ordered, we will take our asses back up to Midtown and wish you a nice evenin'."

Thomas, too, remained unflinching. "Call back your guards, Lee, and let's just get this over with."

With reluctance, Lee yelled something to his men, and glared at Thomas as they retreated. "The Madame promised me professionals."

"I don't work for the Madame," Thomas asserted.

"Yes, and who does the infamous Vigilante work for?" Lee carried on. "Maybe I will put a bounty on your head to see what information I can uncover."

Holstering the Griswold, Thomas smirked at him. "If that helps you sleep better, by all means. I like a challenge."

With a red face, Lee uttered another phrase in Chinese, and Lee Toy marched over to the door on Lee's left. "You will follow Toy through the tunnel. I will pay the Madame once I have my delivery safe."

With a heave, Toy had the door open and went through it, and Thomas and Ashleigh squinted at each other.

"Ready?" Ashleigh queried.

542

"Sure." Thomas turned to Lee. "You'll get your money in a few hours."

Lee gave a curt nod of goodbye, and they shuffled around the desk to follow in Toy's wake. The doorway led to nowhere but darkness, and Ashleigh went through first with Thomas behind, making sure the door closed once they were over the threshold.

"Ashleigh, what the fuck was that?!"

Though Thomas couldn't make him out, he knew Ashleigh had a grin on his face.

"Bastard is a piece of shit. Just thought someone oughta tell him so."

Without warning, Thomas let out a small laugh. "Well, I guess we just...keep going..."

"What're the odds the nephew tries to slit our throats?" Ashleigh quipped, walking slowly into nothingness.

"Fifty-fifty."

"I figured as much." Ashleigh halted brusquely, keeping his voice nearly inaudible. "What the hell does the Madame have us comin' down here for? Somethin' ain' right."

"I don't know, but I suspect we are going to find out."

"Vigilante!" Toy shouted, lighting a torch up ahead with timber. "Follow!"

As the area surrounding them lit up, Thomas could see they were headed down a dark hall towards another spiral staircase, this one made of sparsely minimal metal parts, though where they were descending into, Thomas couldn't say. Keeping an eye out for tails, Thomas shadowed Ashleigh and Toy, who did not look over his shoulder once on their entire journey to be certain Thomas and Ashleigh were in his wake. The upcoming staircase was narrow, and once they reached its end, the tunnel continued on underground, and Thomas noted that whoever had dug these passageways must have done so years prior, perhaps even before the Civil War. There wasn't much to know about these tunnels other than the fact that they connected each of the On Leong's business establishments, whether that be brothels or opium dens, and if any person not of the On Leong was caught in them, they were executed on the spot.

At last, they reached the bottom of the staircase, and as Thomas observed the path Toy was taking them down, he marveled that the tunnels must have been hand carved: they were so low, all three of them had to slightly duck to move around, tapered from side to side, and the ground beneath their feet was basically wet gravel. Thomas could hear the thunder of horses, carts, and carriages above, and every few feet, a bit of dust and rock would shake loose and fall onto his head from the vibrations. Toy kept a fast pace as they wandered along the underground passages of Chinatown, wandering by a staircase here, another doorway there; for nearly a half hour, they silently kept up with Lee's nephew until ahead, Thomas spotted Toy come to a stop.

"Here!" He pointed to a door. "We go here."

Pulling a set of keys from his pocket, Toy unlocked the door. Inside was a ladder upward, and the three of them ascended upward into a back room of the Pell Street opium den; waiting to greet them at the top were four other members of the On Leong Tong. For about thirty seconds, the five Tong conversed with one another in Chinese with occasional emphatic pointing toward Ashleigh and Thomas as they spoke, and then Toy revolved toward them.

"Alley. Whyos here in ten minutes."

"Per Lee's orders, we will be hidden," Thomas reminded him, "unless things get out of hand. In that case, we will intervene to protect the shipment and, well…you. But that is only if absolutely necessary."

Toy grunted something Thomas didn't understand, sauntered out of the room, and took an immediate left, which Thomas noticed led straight to the alley. A small cart holding two barrels of opium was rounding the corner of the adjacent building, and there was only one gas lamp lit for the exchange. The alley layout was wider than Thomas initially presumed, perhaps twenty feet from the building he was currently in to the opposing one; however, the alley hit a dead end a few feet to the rear of the opium den, which meant the shipment and Tongs protecting it would essentially be backed into a corner. Whether or not they found this to be an advantage, Thomas couldn't say, but he wasn't in the mood to try and play charades with Toy about battle tactics. Conversely, he and Ashleigh moved themselves out of the way as the Tong prepared for the Whyo arrival so the pair could assess and strategize.

"We oughta flank 'em, if we can," Ashleigh considered. "Think it would be our best shot at surprisin' them and havin' the upper hand on 'em."

"I agree. Walsh won't be with them, so that's half our worry gone." Thomas pensively rubbed his chin with his hand. "All right, the opium cart will be basically sitting at the dead end. I want us both in the same corner, we should have enough cover of darkness there behind those old beer barrels, and if everything goes to hell, you bank over and to the rear of the cart to the right and I'll stay left to charge right into them. The Tong typically line themselves up in a triangle—one man to do the business, two on either side of him, and another two to back them up."

"Which means them Whyos will be headin' into the center of the Tong and not catch us sneakin' 'round the sides."

"Exactly."

Ashleigh reached into his pocket and pulled out two cigarettes. "Want one before this fuckin' thing starts?"

"You read my mind."

With the opium cart behind them, the Tong lined up in their usual manner, with Toy at the front mimicking a sharp point at the incoming Whyos. Toy crossed his arms over his chest, the whole alley becoming dead silent, and the others mirrored his stance in preparation, each of them armed with a sword and Toy with a gun.

Ashleigh tossed his cigarette aside. "Guess we oughta get in our spot, eh?"

Thomas nodded, doing the same. "Hopefully, this is over quickly."

"Wishful thinkin', brother."

They made their way over to the pungent and rotting beer barrels sitting innocently in the darkness, hiding themselves enough to not be remotely noticed by the onlookers. While Ashleigh readied his extra cylinders and unholstered his pistols, Thomas let out a loud whistle to signal Athena, which both startled and angered Toy and the Tong. As Toy shot him a glare and resumed his post, Thomas pulled the Griswold from its holster and made certain Lawrence's blade could be easily unsheathed from his ankle.

"Tommy," Ashleigh whispered a few seconds later, "look up."

At the corner of the brick building overhead sat Athena, eyeing Thomas closely from above. It made him smile.

The sound of footsteps approaching caught Thomas's attention, and he and Ashleigh sunk even lower behind the barrels, observing as best they could from their hiding spot. Front and center of the Whyos was Kitty, her bad temper seemingly manifested into her disposition, with a snarl on her face and her jaw clenched in irascibility. To her right was a relatively calm looking Strat, who Thomas pointed out to Ashleigh, and on Kitty's left was a Whyo Thomas had not seen before. Behind those three were three more Whyos, each unrecognizable to Thomas, followed by five more. Throwing a quick glance at Ashleigh, Thomas cocked his Griswold—the Whyos were out for blood, that much was obvious in their numbers, and again, Thomas was very aware that he did not truly know the depths of his enemy's resources. He had to get Strat—had to cross him—or they'd be fighting blind.

Toy's head gave a tiny bow. "Your share of opium is ready."

With the snap of his fingers, the two Tong at the back hustled over to the cart and grabbed the two small barrels. The duo then went beside Toy and set the barrels down and withdrew.

"Right," Kitty uttered, and gestured for two of the Whyos Thomas didn't recognize to collect the barrels.

Instantly, Toy held up a hand. "Not until payment."

Kitty rolled her eyes and reached into her vest, removing a wad of cash. "Here, ya fuckin' greedy chink," she jeered, tossing it over to him.

Toy caught it and counted it, not pleased. "You are short."

Her eyes narrowed. "That is the agreed upon amount."

Without responding, Toy snapped his fingers once more, and the two Tong went to the front to collect the barrels in retraction. Out of the blue, Kitty, Strat, and the third all drew pistols in retaliation, aiming them at the Tong, who halted in their tracks and raised their hands into the air. The hoard of Whyos moved in closer to their leaders, drawing weapons of their own, waiting to hear what Kitty ordered next.

Toy was unfazed. "You break our deal, you will find no opium."

"Walsh already found a new fuckin' dealer," she said matter-of-factly. "We don't need your bullshit anymore, chink. Give us the opium, and we won't have to kill you."

"No money, no opium. Randall knows."

"Well, Randall isn't fuckin' here," the Whyo at Kitty's left snapped.

"Give us the goddamn opium!" Kitty bellowed, the hand holding her pistol beginning to tremble.

Taking two steps forward so they were barely arms-length apart, Toy spat at Kitty's feet. "Shoot me. You won't make it out of Chinatown alive."

Thomas knew he had to act. In haste, he let out a screeching whistle, causing everyone in the alley to jump in surprise, but before a Whyo could fire their weapon as they sought frantically to find the whistle's source, a flash of feathers tore through the triad at the lead of the gang. There was the clinking of metal, a handful of curses, and one shot to the ground that ricochet off the brick walls and disappeared into the abyss of the sky. It had taken years to train Athena how to disarm multiple enemies with guns in one dive, yet those years were well worth their weight in gold. All three pistols were on the ground and beyond reach of Kitty, Strat, and the other unknown Whyo, and for the briefest moment, they looked at each other, stunned. And that was right when Toy drew a revolver of his own from his waistband, pointing it straight at Kitty.

"Money. Or leave."

Pure rage filled Kitty's face, and within seconds, her rage went off the rails. Letting out a guttural scream, she drew a blade from her belt and charged at Toy with every Whyo rushing into the Tong with her, and Thomas heard Ashleigh utter a "fuckin' hell" under his breath as they both hurdled into action.

As Ashleigh sprinted around the rear of the opium cart to flank the gang, Thomas vaulted himself over the empty barrels and without hesitation, leapt into the brawl with his Griswold drawn. Two Whyos from the rear of the group were heading directly for Thomas, and with his left hand slamming down on the hammer of the Griswold, his rapid fire took each of them down with hits right between the eyes. From a quick glimpse, Thomas saw that Toy was busy with Kitty and another Whyo, and Ashleigh was on his opposite side beating the hell out of some bastard with a black jack, with everywhere in between scattered by battle.

"He's here!" another Whyo screamed. "The Vigilante is here!"

Thomas heard Ashleigh's gun fire twice, a most welcome sound to his ears; meanwhile, Kitty seemed to at last have spotted Thomas in the tussle.

"Kill the Vigilante!" she yelled maniacally, just as Toy struck her hard with a punch to the gut, sending her to the ground in agony.

The unknown Whyo who had been on Kitty's left and another came for Thomas from both sides, and he assumed their hope was to throw him off with misdirection. He took off toward the one on the right, holstering the Griswold, and as he dropped in to slide tackle, he grabbed Lawrence's blade from his calf and launched it toward his opponent on the left. The blade hit the assailant with such force it threw him against the brick wall and pinned him there, stuck through his left shoulder firmly into the brick. Meanwhile, Thomas tackled the other attacker to the earth, and as his opponent slammed to the ground, Thomas was already back on his feet. Using the momentum of his bodyweight as force, Thomas leaned into a punch to the bastard's left temple, knocking him unconscious instantaneously. Then came another Whyo running his direction, bludgeon in hand; rather than rise, Thomas stayed low and charged, taking a hard yet measly hit from the bludgeon to his back as he picked the man up by the waist, raised him into the air, and threw him to the ground with as much might as he could muster. Rather than wait to see if he was still cognizant, Thomas gave him a kick to the head to make certain this one wouldn't get onto his feet again.

While the Whyo pinned against the wall with Lawrence's blade screamed in pain and frustration at being immobilized, again, a Whyo made a go at Thomas. This attacker was already within close range, a blade drawn and taking swipes at Thomas, which proved to be experienced. Reading his enemy, Thomas stepped back right to avoid one slash, then left, and as his left foot planted, Thomas brought both hands around and clamped down on the man's wrist. He took control of the weapon, and with the rotation of his hands, broke the man's wrist and sent the blade to the ground. Distracted by his own injuries, the man lost his motivations and went limp as Thomas twisted the goon's right arm behind his attacker's back and proceeded then to bend his torso at the waist as if it were no heavier than a rag doll, the attacker's skull being struck once, twice, three times by Thomas's right knee. The damage had been done—Thomas released the Whyo, who lingered for all of a second or two, then toppled into a heap on the ground.

Suddenly, Thomas was pelted hard across the head, sending him in retreat a few paces, and when he got his bearings, he realized that he now stood face to face with Strat, who had just hit him with one of the hardest punches Thomas had taken in ages.

He gave himself a shake and readied for his assailant, though he wanted to keep Strat in one piece if possible, and Strat came after him in a fury. Blocking one punch after another, Thomas took a kick to his flank and a jab to his stomach as Strat pursued, until Thomas landed a hard hit to Strat's nose; the echo of the crack nearly made him smile. With Strat distracted temporarily, Thomas switched to offense and struck Strat hard in his solar plexus, which oddly appeared to wake Strat up that the fight was still going on. He went after Thomas with a jab; however, his next kick was too low, and Thomas saw his opportunity. Bringing his heel up rapidly, Thomas caught Strat in the shin, and the radiation of the blow went from the tip of Strat's toes to the top of his head, disorienting him for just the right amount of time. Strat took one step back in rattled confusion, and switching legs, Thomas front-kicked with every ounce of his power, sending his sole into Strat's chest, who launched backwards. This winded his opponent and gave Thomas a few extra feet; therefore, Thomas drove into a sideways flip-kick, bringing his right foot down across Strat's face, sending him to the street.

The whole alley was immediately still, other than the man still pinned against the brick wall with Lawrence's blade, whose eyes were locked on Thomas.

"Holy shit," he uttered, ceasing his wails of pain, "It is...it is you...holy shit..."

Thomas leaned down, pretending to check Strat's pulse, and instead whispered inaudibly in his ear, "Stay the fuck down and don't move, or I will kill you."

Standing tall, Thomas went directly over to the man, who was squirming and yanking anxiously at the blade, only making the cut deeper and bleed more heavily.

"Tell Walsh I'm coming for him," Thomas snarled, not breaking eye contact and yanking the blade from the brick.

The Whyo fell forward, desperately grabbing his gushing shoulder and hobbling away from Thomas down the alley to escape.

Thomas called after him, "If you don't see a doctor within the hour, you'll bleed to death."

The Whyo didn't respond, only turned left and disappeared from sight.

His concentration now centered on Strat, who continued to lay motionless on the cobblestone road. Toy and two of the Tong stood by the cart, with both the opium and the money from Kitty, while Ashleigh marched in Thomas's direction. There were four dead Whyos on the ground, excluding Strat, and two of the Tong guards butchered by clubs and blades.

When Ashleigh reached him, he kept his tone low, "We need to get rid of them Tongs and get the fuck outta here."

"They can't know Strat is still breathing."

"And they got the money and the drugs. Whyos will be back, but not without Walsh, and that ain' our problem no more."

Thomas observed Toy, who appeared to be completely unfazed by the situation and waiting on the two of them. "He doesn't want us here. Something is amiss with Lee and the Tong."

"You think after all these years, Lee would cross the Madame?"

"No doubt in my mind. If the price was right, I think that motherfucker would be rid of her without batting an eyelash. Loyalties don't matter to him, but the money and the power do."

"So, let's give him his money and get the hell outta here."

Thomas walked over to Toy, Ashleigh by his side. "We are sorry for the loss of your men. You have both the money and the drugs. I would say that is a better ending than expected."

Toy grunted and pulled some bills out of the bundle from Kitty. "You take."

Confused, Thomas waved him off. "Lee said he would pay us through the Madame."

"More would have died, if not for you." Toy shoved the money into Thomas's hand. "You take."

"Toy, I cannot take this. It would be like stealing from Lee."

For a moment, it almost looked as if Toy grinned sheepishly. "You not fear him. He fear you." Toy gave him a small bow of his head. "You will be safe on way out of Chinatown."

With that, Toy snapped his fingers, and the two remaining Tong guards grabbed the opium from the cart, strapping it onto their persons with leather straps to help bear the weight on their shoulders. Once they were loaded like mules, they followed in Toy's wake back into the opium den and vanished, leaving Ashleigh, Thomas, and Strat alone in the alley. Lawrence's blade was gripped between Thomas's fingers, and he marched over to Strat, who was on his hands and knees. Grabbing onto Strat's shoulder, he threw him onto his back and squatted down over him, the edge of the blade held tight against his jugular.

"You have three options," Thomas declared, glaring at Strat, who was wide-eyed in fear. "First, you can go back to the Whyos and expect to die like one of your brothers right here in some ridiculous spat over opium. Second, you can meet us in three hours at the location written down on this piece of paper Mr. Sweeney is about to give you."

"T-t-third?"

"I can slit your throat right now."

552

Strat's breathing became somewhat hysterical. "I…I just…
I can't…"

"You can't what?"

"They'll know…"

"Walsh is in Baltimore," Ashleigh reminded him. "That's why
we picked tonight."

He swallowed. "It's a farce…he's…he will be back any minute
now. You don't understand what they'd do to me…I just…I can't
take the ris—"

"Strat," Thomas interrupted him, "we picked you because she
told us to."

"W—who?"

"Esther."

The color vanished from his cheeks. "Esther is dead."

"Nah, brother," Ashleigh cut in, "she ain'."

There was the sudden sound of voices from inside the building.

"Listen, Strat, you either meet us and help us bring down Walsh,
or you die with him. Three hours." Thomas removed Lawrence's
blade and Ashleigh handed over the address. "It's up to you."

Without another word, Thomas and Ashleigh took off and out
of the alley while Thomas let out a loud whistle to signal Athena
to follow him. They went for one of the main streets to hail a carriage out of Chinatown, and it took a few blocks to find one. When
they did, Thomas instructed the driver up toward Tammany Hall
on Fourteenth Street, hastily slinking into the coach car.

They each grabbed for a cigarette, and just after Thomas lit
and took a drag of his tobacco, a shadowed, dark figure leapt into
the coach car through the barely open window to his right. In an
instant, Ashleigh had his pistols drawn and pointed at the shrouded
man sitting beside Thomas, his face low and hidden just enough by
the shadows. Thomas, on the other hand, took another drag of his
cigarette, and rotated toward their visitor.

553

"You must be Mock Duck."

Without lifting his head, the man gave a small nod. "You are the men who work for the Madame, I presume?"

"Well, I sure as shit am. This bastard runs his own game. What the hell you playin' at here, prick?" Ashleigh countered.

The clinking of metal caught Thomas's attention, and he noticed beneath Mock Duck's suit jacket was a thin layer of chain mail.

"You getting into a medieval battle sometime in the near future?" he quipped, gesturing towards the armor.

"In California, it saved my life more than three dozen times," he asserted firmly. "I would like a chance to meet with your Madame. I can get her opium at a cheaper rate, and a promise of firm alliance I do not plan on breaking."

Ashleigh's pistols did not falter. "Are you suggestin' Lee ain' reliable?"

"Of course he is not. He is in talks with Richard Croker, and has been for two weeks. Lee wants to become the official sheriff of Chinatown, and Croker has promised that if he begins to work with Tammany Hall again."

Thomas let out a cloud of smoke casually. "Why on earth should I listen to a goddamn word you say?"

"Because Lee is a disgrace to our people. We have an honor code he breaks for his own gains, one that so many of the Tong are not in agreement with. The Hip Sing have cleaned up San Francisco and Chicago. New York is next."

"Honor code?" Ashleigh pushed mockingly.

"The Flying Dragons do not abide by customs you would recognize, Mr. Sweeney."

Ashleigh cocked his pistol. "How the fuck do ya know my name?"

"The same way I know that this Vigilante is actually Lord Thomas Turner," Mock Duck responded, frowning at him. "I have done my own investigating."

Thomas and Ashleigh gaped at each other for a second, though surprisingly, Thomas was not apprehensive about this man unearthing his true identity. On the other hand, he was intrigued, because the Hip Sing this stranger spoke of seemed to parallel that of the Samurai, and Thomas was all too familiar with their culture after years of training with Hiroaki.

"I will arrange a meeting at The Palace," Thomas declared, having another inhale of his cigarette. "I presume you know where I live?"

"I do."

"Lovely. Visit me in three nights at midnight, and I will have a meeting scheduled by then."

Finally, upon hearing those words, Mock Duck lifted his chin and looked at both Thomas and Ashleigh. "I will see you in three nights, Lord Turner."

Despite the moving carriage, Mock Duck got to his feet and bowed low, as if the swaying did not affect his balance, and left the way he had come, out the coach window.

Ashleigh was in disbelief while he holstered his guns. "What the fuck was that?"

"I have no idea," Thomas admitted, a strange smile coming to his lips. "But whoever Mock Duck is, I am happy to know he is on our side."

"Why ya say that?" Ashleigh asked, reaching for another cigarette.

"Because he reminds me of Hiroaki, and if that resemblance proves true, he is probably one of the most dangerous men in New York City. And we could use all the friends we can get."

"The hit will be two weeks from tonight," Croker told Thomas while the two men sat awkwardly across from each other, Croker at his desk and Thomas in one of the opposing chairs. They each had a whiskey, and though he was trying not to show it, Thomas could sense that Croker was nervous in his presence by the minor tremor of his hands. "It will be at Priestly's residence just after dusk. If you want Walsh, you can have him. But none of this ties back to me, understand? And Priestly dies."

Thomas didn't address the second condition. "Will Walsh be alone?"

Croker shifted uncomfortably in his chair, taking a sip of whiskey. "I will ask he brings as few as possible, but I would assume you can count on three or four others keeping a lookout."

"That shouldn't be a problem. I assume Walsh will be back from Baltimore tomorrow?"

A startled expression came to Croker's face. "How do you know he is in Baltimore?"

"Answer my question."

"Yes, he is in the city tomorrow. He was there on a bit of business for me."

"You mean confirming Esther Tweed's death." Thomas had a gulp of whiskey from his glass, a tiny pang of amusement on his face as again, he markedly surprised Croker. "You think I was unaware of your motives? It was killing two birds with one stone—you get the truth about your old Assistant and also get to meet with me while Walsh is out of the picture."

There was nothing Richard could say to counter him. "Yes, that's precisely it."

"And you didn't share that information because you want to play this close to the chest. And trust me, I don't blame you. Your beloved Assistant was never going to make it in this game anyhow."

Croker finished his whiskey. "Then why did you help her?"

556

"Because she had value," Thomas answered smartly. "My intention is to bring down Walsh, and the Whyos, and I align myself with any person willing to aid me in that endeavor."

"I have to ask you, why? Why are you on this vendetta? What gain is it to you?"

Thomas gave Croker a glance that increased his uneasiness. "The gain, Mr. Croker, is something a man such as yourself would never understand. You crave power, not wealth, not a body count—power. I am here to rid the earth of demons, and Walsh is one of them."

"Can I have your word you won't turn on me?"

"Absolutely not."

"And why the hell not?!"

"Like I said," Thomas enunciated, short of patience, "I do not work for you. I do not work for anyone other than myself."

Rising, Thomas went and grabbed the whiskey decanter from the drink cart, brought it back over to Richard's desk, and filled his enemy's glass along with his own. He plunked the bottle down and resumed his chair.

"I am doing you a favor, Richard. We will leave it at that."

Croker could not believe what was happening in front of him. "What will you do after you kill Walsh?"

"Clean out the Whyos and move on."

"Move on?"

Thomas didn't respond, only nodded, so Croker carried on, "Well…then, I assume we have an accord? I give you Walsh, and we pretend this conversation never happened."

"I can agree to that."

Croker was pensive for a moment, twirling the whiskey around in his glass. "Do you have any ties to The Palace?"

"You mean the Madame?"

"Yes."

"She has hired me for an odd job or two, yes."

His eyebrow furrowed. "How did she find you?"

"She didn't. I found her. Crazy bitch hates the Whyos, and I figured I could cover more ground seeking her out." Thomas narrowed his eyes. "Why the hell do you care about some brothel uptown?"

Croker let out a sigh. "The Madame and I have a very turbulent history. I admire her, I really do. We started at war and have mercifully come to peaceful terms."

Thomas realized where this conversation could go if he steered it the right direction. "You started at war?" he pushed delicately.

"It was…a misunderstanding," Croker stated, downing some of his whiskey. "A girl who used to work for her, a very intelligent young woman the Madame had taken under her wing, had a young son she was raising alone. I hired the woman to do the books for the Hall. She was loyal at first, until she saw what this enterprise really runs on, so she…" His voice trailed off.

"So she what?"

"We caught her stealing evidence to give to the police."

"You kill her?"

Taking a deep breath, Croker strangely relaxed, as if this confession was reducing his burden. "I couldn't kill her. I didn't want to. I locked her up, you know, in a mental institution, with the hopes that she'd break and I could let her out. Turns out, I fucking couldn't."

"What happened then?"

"Well, the Madame was very fond of this woman's son. We made a deal, that if I could keep her friend locked up, I wouldn't kill the boy for her betrayal of Tammany. His luck changed over the years. He's one of the richest bastards on Fifth Avenue now."

"The woman die?"

Unexpectedly, Croker chuckled. "No, no, she didn't. That son of hers…he hired some guy to break her out. A chink, of all fucking things! I spent months trying to figure out how it was possible…

I even made an alliance with that son of a bitch Lee in Chinatown—paid that motherfucker more than enough money to try and find that son of a bitch, but we never managed to."

"So, has the son confronted you?"

"Yes. Mild threats, mainly just with the intention of keeping me in my place. I have no idea where his mother is, I would assume she's hidden away." He had a big drink. "The hatred that man has for me…I wish I could say it's unwarranted. But it isn't. I fucking deserve it."

Thomas tried to play it off with a shrug. "Well, he got his fucking mother back."

"It's not just that."

"Then what is it?"

Another heavy exhale—Croker was just drunk enough to keep rambling, perhaps thinking that this Vigilante would keep his secrets. "The boy had an estranged father. When he discovered the woman was locked up, the father went looking into things, and it got out of hand. I only meant to scare the shit out of him, just give him a beating and send his ass back to England…" Croker's jaw twitched in anger. "That was the first time Walsh went rogue, and when I could grasp what a fucking mistake I'd made with him. That bastard killed the father without my say-so. And I've let him have too many similar incidents over the years of a similar fashion because I can't fucking control him. He has to go."

With his right hand relaxed around his glass of whiskey, Thomas's left fist squeezed so tight he could feel his fingernails cutting into the skin of his palm, blood releasing into his hand. He had to be steady, or he would give himself away to Richard Croker.

"Well, this problem will be over for you in a fortnight." Thomas drank the rest of his whiskey. "I must be going, Mr. Croker. It's been a pleasure."

As he set the empty glass down on Richard's desk, Croker

stopped him. "If you change your mind and want to make a decent living, consider working for the Hall. I'll pay you a high wage, and you can pick and choose your assignments as you please."

Thomas shook his head. "You have more than enough men, Richard."

"I need you. Together, we would be invincible, can't you see that?"

"I can. And that is exactly why you will never win me over. Goodnight, Richard."

Thomas spun around and strutted out of Richard Croker's office, his heart pounding in his chest, a confirmation of the horrible deeds on Croker's conscience and the injustices he'd wreaked upon the Turner family; nevertheless, what struck Thomas most was the reverence and adoration he had in that moment for the Madame. She truly had fought tooth and nail to keep Thomas alive, and deep down, he understood that one of the main reasons her relationship with Croker carried on was for him, and him alone. As he marched out of the Hall and into the night, Athena dutifully expecting him, Thomas slipped on his leather glove and called to her—she'd earned a break after flying through the city to keep up with Thomas and Ashleigh. Athena landed merrily on his forearm, munching on the dried chicken breast Thomas held out to her. On to Chinatown they would go, where Will, Ashleigh, and the doc awaited him in what was certainly to be a memorable encounter with Strat.

For the briefest second, Thomas wondered if this war might be coming to an end at last. With Walsh dead and the Whyos gone, perhaps this conflict would conclude sooner rather than later.

Either that, or all hell was about to break loose. But no matter. Thomas was already on the train, and jumping off was no longer an option.

The incredible rage Walsh felt only escalated when Strat walked into The Morgue, beaten, bloodied, and late.

"Where the fuck have you been?!" he roared as the door slammed behind Strat.

To his right sat Kitty, bloodied, bruised, and beaten senseless… not that she had any fucking sense to begin with. Auggie was in the corner with some negro doc trying to patch his shoulder up, the gash and laceration so deep it was a miracle he hadn't died yet from blood loss. Two chairs to the left was Berlin, with a completely swollen eye, broken hand, and a gash across his flank the doc had already stitched together. Nash was across the table, spitting up blood in his whiskey, a shiner on his left cheek, but still breathing. Behind the bar, Zeke was grabbing an empty whiskey glass for Strat, limping from a nearly broken leg and a punch to the head that Walsh knew still had his ears ringing.

If you want something done, you have to fucking do it yourself.

Strat limped over to a vacant chair at the table, dropping down into it and consequently wincing in pain. Zeke slid the glass across the table to Strat, and reaching over, Strat clutched onto the whiskey bottle a few feet from him and poured his glass full. Though he initially wanted to bash Strat's face in, Walsh's rage subsided, appreciating the expression Strat wore was one of conquest—he had something…something big.

This better be fucking good.

"Well?!" Walsh pressed, scrutinizing him carefully.

Strat threw down his whiskey and poured another, reaching into his pocket and pulling out a small slip of paper.

"The Vigilante and that bastard who works for The Palace want to meet me in an hour. At this location."

"What the fuck?!" Kitty exclaimed.

"Why?" Nash managed to spit out between coughs of blood.

Leaning forward onto the table, Strat peered up at Walsh.

"I think they want to cross me, Walsh. This might be the way in we've been searching for."

Something is missing. "What did they offer you?"

"Nothing yet. A chance not to die as a Whyo. But they did share a piece of information I thought you might find interesting."

Walsh's annoyance was rising. "What?"

"The Assistant is still alive."

It was as if all the air had been sucked out of the room.

"But that's impossible," Berlin declared, aghast. "Walsh just got confirmation from Baltimore…from the goddamn doc! The girl is fucking dead."

"It could be false intel to try and win Strat over," Auggie called from the corner. "They may just be bullshittin' Strat to get him to cross."

Kitty was intently staring at Walsh. "You think she's alive, don't you?"

I would burn this city to the ground to find her.

"If she is," he uttered guardedly, "then this proves to be another problem altogether. And I will be making a return trip to Baltimore as soon as I cut her fucking throat."

"Walsh," Zeke said softly, "even if that bitch is alive, it doesn't change anything. She ain't with Croker no more. We all want this to work. We can't let a few rumors from that Vigilante prick sway us to change course."

"Actually, Zeke, that is precisely what we are going to do."

He was baffled. "What?"

"What are you saying?" Kitty pleaded.

"I am saying that we are moving plans ahead of schedule," Walsh professed loudly. "I am going to initiate the break with Tammany in two days."

"Two days?!" Berlin cried.

"Don't you think a week or two would be wise…to recover…" Nash spat out.

"Randall and Marley will pick up your slack," Walsh hissed at him. "I need a brawl tomorrow. Borderline riot. We are going to fucking push this rift with the police to the edge and then I will send the message to Croker myself."

The time for retribution is finally here.

"You're going to kill the copper?" Kitty asked.

"I am," Walsh told her, "and then we are going to do what we should have done months ago."

Slowly, the Whyos around the table began to smile darkly, glancing at one another.

War," Zeke stated with eagerness.

"War," Kitty repeated.

"War," Walsh confirmed. "We've discussed our plans thousands of times. We all know our parts."

We are going to kill them all.

Hobbling over, Auggie sat down in another empty chair, paying the doc with a few dollar bills from his pants pocket and grabbing the whiskey bottle to take a swig. When the doctor had gone, Auggie too grinned wide.

"We want Strat to play both sides, 'ay boss?"

"Sure as shit," Walsh countered. "Strat, you play the snitch. Your task is to gain as much knowledge as you can about the Madame's renegades and figure out when and how they plan to strike against us."

They are too proud to see their mistake.

Strat held up his glass in salute. "Consider it done."

"Auggie, you need to keep the saloons rolling. We need young, dumb recruits. I don't care how fucking drunk they are. I just need bodies."

"You can count on me, Walsh."

"Berlin, Nash—I need the girls loyal."

"How?" Nash inquired, Berlin nodding along.

Walsh glimpsed at Kitty. "Brands."

"The W?"

Walsh nodded. "Increase their pay, too. Bonuses for dependability. Zeke, we good on booze?"

"Shipments still consistent, Walsh."

"Good."

"What about the opium?" Kitty asked. "Without the fuckin' chinks, we ain't got nothin'."

His eyes narrowed, glaring at her. "You will go to Lee tomorrow, with Randall, and fix the fucking mess you made. He can keep the cash from tonight and you will pay him in full anyhow."

How did I ever fuck you?

"But…but I thought you said…"

"You thought wrong!" Walsh bellowed, and Kitty retracted like a struck puppy. Cracking his neck from side to side, Walsh added, "Make sure Marley keeps the rings active. Try and get him to bring on a few from Edmond's side of town. We need some heavy hitters on our side."

Auggie had another shot of whiskey. "We want to make 'em Whyos?"

"We need as many as possible. So, I think that would be a yes, August."

"So, first the detective," Strat began, "then we get the Madame's girl. What's her name again, Walsh?"

"Celeste Hiltmore."

"What then?" Nash pressed.

"With the rug ripped out from beneath Croker and the Madame's feet, we commence our final play. We lure them out, one by one, and once enough of them are gone, we can finally take the city."

Berlin chortled. "And New York fuckin' City will be ours."

A loud Whyo call rang out at The Morgue, and glasses of whiskey were had in celebration of the ominous future on the horizon.

Walsh sunk back into his chair, watching this band of imbeciles he'd assembled, imbeciles that would bring him what he'd wanted all these years: anarchy. The hierarchy would be gone, the law disassembled—there would never be shackles to bind him, there would never be men to imprison him, and he would punish those who had hurt him. He would punish the system that made him what he was, he would kill the people who perpetuated the cycle of oppression, and most importantly, he would purge New York City of those who unrightfully had their power. The rich would die first, then the politicians, and last, anyone who did not wish to stand beside them, because what Walsh appreciated quite early on in his formation of a different vision of New York City, was that every immigrant, every negro, and every poor man struggling to make a meal would pay to watch the rich burn alive in their homes for a chance at taking it for themselves.

All they needed was the element of surprise. And once the fire reached Midtown, there wouldn't be any more fighting, no more bloodshed. It would be a revolution all on its own.

And I won't feel a goddamn thing.

CHAPTER XLIII.

"I am assuming Will gave you the rundown on Thomas and Ashleigh's conversation with that bastard from the Whyos?"

Louis nodded. "He did, Madame. The doc was your idea?"

"Thomas's idea."

"How the hell did Thomas know he would be at The Morgue that night?"

The Madame smirked. "Well, he fucking didn't, but we took a chance and got it right."

Leaning back into his chair, Louis took a sip of whiskey. "So, we are feeding the Whyos false information and trying to extract as much truth from this son of a bitch as we can?"

"That's the idea. The plan is that we will control what the Whyos know, and because Walsh is over-eager to kill every one of us, he's allowing Strat to share quite a bit to earn trust and do this fast. I hate to say it, but we may finally have the upper hand."

"So, we've gotten their leadership." Louis let out a small chortle. "It's about damn time."

"At fucking last!" the Madame exclaimed merrily, throwing her feet up on top of her desk. "We have a few more we are trying to track down, but I already have the top tier down."

"Enlighten me."

She had a gulp of her drink. "Walsh is calling the shots, as you very well know at this point. He has three immediate underlings who take care of his shit and report directly to him. That's Kitty, of course, Strat, as we have learned, and some other prick named Auggie."

"Kitty is vicious and relentless—"

"And would do any fucking thing Walsh asked of her."

"Right," Louis approved. "And we have become more than aware that Strat is one hell of a fighter."

"Thomas was adamant he was the toughest Whyo he's faced thus far, but let's be honest—Thomas hasn't gone head-to-head with the lunatic yet. The only one who has is Esther, and we remember how that fucking turned out."

"It's only a matter of time before Thomas corners Walsh, Madame. What about this new one? Auggie?"

"He manages the Whyo saloons," the Madame informed him. "Apparently, his father used to be McGloin's best friend, which means—"

"He is unshakably a Whyo for life," Louis finished her sentence for her. "Will mentioned Thomas put a hole in his shoulder?"

"A bad one—the doc said the damage was pretty substantial. So, he will be a weak link for the time being."

"I'll take it." Louis got to his feet and went for the drink cart, noticing both he and the Madame needed a refill. "Who is next?"

"Two brothers named Berlin and Nash."

He grabbed the decanter and made his way back toward the Madame. "Twins?"

"Nah, a few years apart," she replied, holding up her glass for Louis to fill. "Nash is older. They were orphaned, ran with the Bowery Boys for a while, then Walsh lured them in with his bullshit semantics. But we need to be wary of these two."

Setting the decanter on her desk after pouring their shares of whiskey, Louis resumed his seat. "In what way?"

"Apart, they aren't much. Together, they are a fucking nightmare. They run the brothels and are used to one hell of a lot of violence. Nash always has a pistol, and Berlin carries a black jack."

"Jesus. I haven't seen those in years."

"They're getting creative, apparently."

"And who is left?"

"You've got Zeke, who runs their booze. He's got a limp from a sprained knee, so he'll be easy to spot. Will knows Zeke, and Esther does too. Zeke used to be lower level, but proved himself to Walsh by slicing the throats of two of their own for stealing, and he's smart. He's not a fucking hothead like so many of the others. He picks his battles carefully and is stone-cold sober at all times."

"Probably why Walsh has him running the booze."

She smiled. "You fucking nailed it. The last two we are familiar with: Randall, who deals their opium, and Marley, who arranges the fights."

Louis's eyes grew wide. "Wait a minute. Marley...Marley used to work for Edmund."

"Technically, he still does," the Madame declared. "He is not only stealing Edmund's fucking money for Whyo gains, but he is also taking boxers."

"Does Croker know?!"

"Not yet. We are keen to see what Edmund would do to that bastard if he found out."

Amazed, Louis threw back his whiskey. "So, we have nine we need to watch."

The Madame's feet went back to the floor, and she straightened up in her chair. "It's not just the gang shit, Louis. This is fucking organized—more organized than any Five Points gang of its time. Even the Tong wouldn't dare underestimate them. Walsh has done a brilliant job making his people believe they can run the city if they so choose. We cannot let that happen."

"I agree." Louis stopped, letting the information sink in. "What has Thomas said...about that night, the encounter...all of it?"

"We will know more about the Chinatown situation in a few days. As far as the Whyos go, Ashleigh and Thomas will meet with Strat again later this week. Strat mentioned that Walsh said something big was about to happen, but did not have specifics. Obviously, we know that's a load of shit, and that little son of a bitch knows exactly what's going to happen, yet the one thing Thomas swore was it must be some kind of strike against Croker."

This struck Louis. "Why do you say that?"

"Because Strat told him that their ties with Tammany Hall were coming to a close, and there were no questions on his end regarding us, me, or The Palace, though I would fucking bet it's coming."

"If they were striking against us, he would have pried Thomas and Ashleigh for whatever he could get," Louis thought aloud. "What did he ask?"

"Strat's inquiries were meticulously calculated. He repeatedly asked Thomas to identify who he was, which Thomas refused on every attempt, and Strat used that against him, as if he needed that to establish trust. Fucking insanity. The interest then turned to Ashleigh and Will. Will, as you know, did not show his face, but Strat was particularly interested in whether or not Will was tied to The Palace, which Ashleigh vehemently denied. You can probably guess that your loyalty to Croker was called into question. However, the last ask was the most puzzling."

"What was it?"

Her countenance was oddly anxious. "He wanted to know what Celeste's role was."

A deep pit formed in Louis's stomach. "How the fuck do they even know about Celeste?"

"I don't have a goddamn clue. Thomas and I both think they are trying to size up our numbers similar to how we are the Whyos, but I am pretty fucking unsettled by it."

"Shit." He rose and poured more whiskey in his glass. Just as he put the decanter back down, a knock came to the door, and in walked Thomas, dressed in a handsomely cut tuxedo with Ashleigh right beside him.

"Shouldn't you be at the Vanderbilts'?" the Madame questioned him, staying seated.

"The party is in an hour," Thomas assured her, going for the drink cart and picking up clean glasses for him and Ashleigh.

Heading to the Madame's desk, Thomas fetched the decanter to pour them each a round, and once he'd done so, marched over and handed the glass to Ashleigh. The two of them looked exhausted, particularly Ashleigh, who had dark circles underneath his eyes and a hardened expression that held no humor. Thomas, on the other hand, appeared tired but determined, and was the spitting image of Edward during his father's glory days, especially in such a fine suit. While Ashleigh remained standing, Thomas went and sat in the chair by Louis, glancing from him to the Madame to get a read on the situation.

It was clear he could sense the tension in the room. "All right. What's going on?"

Louis reached for a cigarette and matches in his pocket. "The Madame just informed me of the details Strat asked of you," he divulged. "I am mildly concerned regarding Celeste's name being thrown around."

"Yeah, well, join the fuckin' club, Louis," Ashleigh chimed in, taking a swig of his drink, his air inflamed and tense.

Thomas did the same. "I understand the worry, Louis. The Madame and I don't think there is reason to get in arms yet. I really believe he and the Whyos are doing just what we are: wanting to uncover who exactly is their enemy."

"Not to mention," the Madame chimed in, "that it was only a matter of time before Celeste was linked to The Palace and to me by the Whyos. She is here every fucking day, for Christ's sake, so let's not jump to any conclusions."

"An' what are we 'spose to do if she becomes a target?" Ashleigh pressed.

"We are all targets," Thomas countered steadily. "Risk is a part of this, and it's something each one of us has accepted, Ashleigh. You know that."

Ashleigh went silent, and Louis took a drag of his cigarette. "Let's just be careful with how much we are giving Strat—"

There was shouting on the stairwell, and instantly, Louis stopped talking, his eyes locking with the Madame's. "That's Will," he uttered, his heart rate increasing.

In unison, everyone stood and turned to face the door, an odd sense of dread creeping amongst them. Louis identified it—he could feel it in Will's voice, even if he couldn't hear the words. Something was wrong…terribly wrong.

Bursting into the Madame's office with Claire behind him, Will was a ghastly shade of white, and he peered around at the group in attendance with trepidation.

"Samuel and Seamus is missin'."

"What?!" Thomas cried.

Louis again looked at the Madame, whose composure was barely held together. "Both of them are fucking missing?" she entreated him.

"Yeah, Madame." Will was shaking his head in utter disbelief. "It started last night. There was some kinda shootout outside the fuckin' Dry Dollar…drunk Whyos always startin' shit with each other…but they happened to be causin' problems just as two patrol coppers were saunterin' past." Taking off his Pendleton hat, Will aggressively ran his hands through his hair. "Someone get me a whiskey, goddammit!"

Hastily, Ashleigh went for the drink cart, grabbing his father an empty glass. Louis was having a hard time processing what he was hearing, as was the entire faction present.

"What happened next?" Louis urged Will.

Will walked to Louis, who stood and offered Will his chair, and Will took it obligingly just as Ashleigh shoved a full whiskey glass into his hand.

"Whyos killed both of 'em."

"You're fucking serious?" the Madame exclaimed. "They deliberately murdered two coppers in the open street?"

"Sure did."

Thomas motioned for Louis to grab him a cigarette just as Louis reached into his pocket for another. "Was that the end of it?" Thomas queried.

"Course it ain'. 'Round the city, they found four other coppers dead, eight more beaten to a goddamn pulp, all patrollin' Whyo territory." Will threw back his drink in one gulp. "Croker and I found out 'bout the brawlin' together from Sullivan, so I went down to the precinct to find Samuel, or hell, even Seamus, to have 'em come back to the Hall and decide what to do next…" Will's voice trailed off.

The Madame's patience was nonexistent with Samuel's life on the line. "And?!"

"Pair of 'em never checked back in last night after bein' on the streets with a case. Nobody saw their asses the whole day. I went to Samuel's apartment, went to see Seamus's family, ain' a fuckin' trace o' nobody."

Louis put his hand on Will's shoulder, and uncharacteristically, Will put his hand onto Louis's and held it, needing his partner's support. He looked to the Madame, his eyes desperate. "Madame, I don' know what to say, other than you just tell me what to do, and I'll fuckin' do it."

She was in shock, but Louis saw the wheels of her mind turning. "Does Croker know yet?"

"Nah. I came here first."

"Good."

It was evident that Thomas was studying the Madame as diligently as Louis. "What are you plotting?"

Waving him off, the Madame had a sip of whiskey, taking a deep breath in and out while the rest of the room waited for her orders.

"Will, Louis, Ashleigh—the three of you are going to Croker's residence uptown and immediately telling him before this fucking party that his best friend is gone, and you assure him I am taking care of it."

"Like hell they are," Thomas cut in. "Fuck this party. I am going with them."

The Madame turned on him. "You will do no such thing. You are going to that goddamn party because you have a goddamn cover to uphold, do you understand me?!"

"Do you think I give a shit about that with Samuel's life on the line?!" Thomas fired back. "He is just as important in this as I am and I'll be damned if—"

"You are going!" she bellowed, not backing down. "If you give yourself away now, we are all fucking dead! You do your part, just like everyone else does, so we stay alive, or so help me God, I will take you out of this equation without a second thought!"

Louis was taken aback by their clash, as were Will and Ashleigh, but in that moment, Louis realized while he observed the faces of Will and Ashleigh that both men caught the Madame and Thomas's uncanny resemblance—their tempers, their eyes, their overall demeanor and stubbornness were too matched not to be blood. As their back and forth went on, Ashleigh peeked over to his father with astonished eyes, and Will returned a sideways, knowing glance, equally as stunned as his son. If they hadn't known before, the Sweeneys certainly recognized now that Thomas and the Madame were kin, though to Louis's relief, neither of them said a word, and kept their newfound realization to themselves.

Louis could sense it was time for him to play mediator. "She's right, Thomas," he chimed in, stepping over toward him and handing Thomas a cigarette. "I know you want to come with us, but there is only so much to be done tonight. You know as well as I do the Whyos are going to try and send a message. We just don't know what that message is yet."

Thomas's cheeks were flushed red in frustration, however, he conceded and turned to Louis, taking his cigarette. "You will find me if this escalates."

It wasn't a question. "In a heartbeat," Louis promised.

With a nod, Thomas rotated to the Madame, pulling timber from his jacket pocket to light the cigarette. "I will be here after the party."

The two of them exchanged a look, one that Louis couldn't quite comprehend, yet the Madame and Thomas appeared to have come to some sort of an agreement.

"After the party," she replied.

Taking an inhale of smoke, Thomas was temporarily pacified. "Louis, Will, Ashleigh—best of luck. I believe Celeste is at the Crokers' residence with Elizabeth as we speak, so don't be shocked when you spot a friendly face."

With that, Thomas spun on his heels and marched out of the Madame's office; it was only then that Louis remembered Claire was lingering by the door.

He wasn't the only one who'd forgotten. "Claire, darling?" the Madame began. "You haven't left the doorway."

"I have an idea, Madame, but I want privacy."

When Claire asked for something, as it very rarely if ever happened, she got it.

"Boys, out," the Madame commanded. "Get to Croker's. Fill him in on what's going on, and then we will figure out what the fuck to do next."

Louis didn't need to be told twice. Taking the lead, Will and Ashleigh filed in behind him, and the three men left the Madame's office with the intention of heading the direction of Richard Croker's, just a few blocks north. Once they were out of The Palace and in the damp, cold winter air, Louis took a hard left and followed the line of gaslights toward Richard's residence on the Upper West Side.

"He ain' exactly gonna be happy to see us," Will brought up when they were about a block shy of the building.

"We don't have another option, and if this is as bad as I think it is, it will be a miracle to find Seamus or Samuel alive. Croker has to at least smell that something has run foul with the Whyos in the last few days."

"Well," Will returned, "I do know that the lunatic ain' had the motivation to see Richie after gettin' home from Baltimore."

"Smells to me like Walsh is ready to be his own man," Ashleigh perceived, pulling a cigarette from his pocket.

"Ya think he'd really kill Seamus?" Will directed to Louis. "I mean, hell, this ain' just no-names no more."

Louis could sense Will's apprehension. "We knew this day was coming, Will."

The front door of the Crokers' came into view, and Louis paced right to it, ringing the doorbell and eagerly waiting to be let in.

It was Frank, the butler, who answered the door; upon seeing Louis, his eyes nearly popped out of his skull in horror.

"You again! No! Not at this hour!"

576

"We are here to see Mr. Croker," Louis announced firmly, holding his ground.

"This is outrageous, sir. The Crokers currently have guests in the parlor! I absolutely cannot allow you to—"

Before Frank could finish, Will was beside Louis. "You get your ass in there and tell Richie this is a real fuckin' emergency. Ya here me, Frank?" Will calmly pulled his jacket aside to reveal both guns holstered on his hips, and with a tiny squeal of fright, Frank disappeared, closing the door.

"Daddy, ya didn' have to make the poor bastard piss himself," Ashleigh chuckled, grinning from ear to ear.

"Nah. But it was fun."

Louis was suppressing his amused smile, wishing to remain serious. "It's probably to our advantage Celeste and Douglas are here. They will keep Elizabeth distracted and not fretting over a bunch of thugs being in her house."

"Don' fall for that shit," Will commented sourly.

"What do you mean?"

"Lizzie's Croker's wife. Sure, them two live uptown now, but she ain' dumb, brother. She's been there for it all, and she's good at playin' her part."

"You sayin' she's as bad as Croker?" Ashleigh asked.

"I'm sayin' don' underestimate her."

Minutes came and went, and Ashleigh finished his cigarette just as Frank reappeared.

"Upstairs," he ordered in a hushed tone. "You are not to utter a word and disturb the guests!"

"Fine," Louis agreed.

After he pushed past Frank, the three of them moved through the entryway and to the main staircase; all the while, Louis sincerely hoped Croker was already up in his home office with a whiskey.

He was.

Croker was standing with a glass full, hands crossed over his chest, with an irritated countenance at being interrupted on a social night at his residence.

"Just what in the hell do you three think you are doing in my goddamn house?!" he berated them as soon as Frank left the office, his face turning red.

There was no welcome—Croker stood in front of his desk as if to signify not one of them would be staying for very long, and if they did, it wouldn't be with his permission.

"I have to be at the Vanderbilts' within the fucking hour and you decide that there is something you cannot sit on for four damn—"

"Richie, Seamus is missin'," Will interjected.

Croker stopped dead, speechless for a few seconds. "Seamus is...what?!"

"Ashleigh, could you pour us a drink as well?" Louis asked him courteously, and Ashleigh did not hesitate to oblige. "Richard, I understand you already know some coppers were deliberately killed last night by Whyos. Last night, Seamus and Samuel were out on a case, but neither of them came home, and they haven't been seen since."

Croker glanced to Will, who nodded. "It don' look good, boss."

Frozen with the news, Croker was struggling to put words together. "How the...how did this happen? Do we know who the fuck has them?!"

"Course not," Ashleigh piped up, bringing whiskies to Louis and Will before returning to make a drink for himself. "But we sure as shit can guess, Mr. Croker. And I would put money on the lunatic wantin' to make a statement with them detectives, 'specially if he ain' been to see ya since Baltimore."

Louis couldn't tell if Croker was more astonished at being so directly confronted by Will's son or by the news that Seamus was at the mercy of the Whyos; regardless, Seamus and Samuel's absence at the hands of Walsh was something they needed to strategize sooner rather than later, irrespective of the Vanderbilt party.

"No one has heard anything from them?" Croker endeavored to ask, taking a mighty gulp of his whiskey and resting back on top of his desk.

"Not as far as we can tell," Louis replied, having a sip from his glass and lowering down into one of the empty chairs across from Croker. "Look, Richard, there isn't anything we can really do right now. We came here as a courtesy to fill you in on everything we know, as promised. They could be anywhere, and there is no way to truly know how to find them until we hear something from the Whyos or from Walsh. Sadly, I do agree with young Sweeney. A statement is about to be made, and I think…" His voice trailed off.

Croker stared at him. "What is it, Louis?"

"I think we are about to see the side of Walsh we hoped we never would."

In silence, each one of the four men in Croker's office finished their whiskey, because what no one wanted to say aloud was the bitter truth—that life, as they knew it, was about to come to an end.

"Well," Croker began, almost half-heartedly, "what the fuck does the Madame propose we do next?"

It was a phrase Louis never thought would come from Croker, and a moment he could not wait to share with her later.

"You go to the party with the Hiltmores. When we get our bearings, you're our first stop, and we will figure out how to deal with the lunatic and the Whyos."

Croker approved, pondering the situation. "Is there…fucking Christ, I will sound like an imbecile asking…"

"What, Richie?" Will pressed.

He bit his lip, reluctant. "Has the Madame reached out to the Vigilante? He told me himself he…he is out for Whyos and Walsh. I know he's worked with the Madame previously…I just…we need all the goddamn ammunition we've got, you know what I'm saying? He could…he could help us find them."

Louis chose to use this to his advantage. "He was the one who gave us the gory details of what occurred last night, and also the information that both Seamus and Samuel were missing."

This appeared to brighten Croker's spirits, so Louis added, "He isn't on our side, Richie. You won't cross him. But he has the same goal in mind that we do, at least for the time being."

The spark of hope faded from his eyes, and Croker accepted his words. "Better than nothing, I suppose," he uttered. "Will, you head down to the Fat Sow and find Sullivan—I am sure he is there, racking up a bar tab. Fill him in and find O'Reilly. I want everyone in the know, understood?"

"You got it, Richie."

"Louis, once the Madame and her cohorts get this put together, I want you to immediately find me. Even if I am still at the Vanderbilts'."

"Absolutely, Richie."

Croker's eyes shifted onto Ashleigh. "As for you—"

Without hesitation, Ashleigh confidently stood his ground. "With all due respect, Mr. Croker, I took my leave from the Hall. Far as I'm concerned, I'll work with my daddy and Louis here, but you ain' gonna expect nothin' from me."

Richard's gaze hardened. "So, The Palace it is for you, then?"

"Yes, sir, The Palace it is." Ashleigh stood up straight, not shy about the fact that he was happy about his choice, and that he had two pistols on his hips.

For a few seconds, it seemed like Croker might snap; instead, he let out a low chortle, shaking his head.

"Tell the Madame I'll be waiting."

They were a block away from The Palace when Ashleigh stopped walking, and Louis had an inclination of what was about to be asked of him. Ashleigh reached into his pocket and grabbed another cigarette, and as he lit it, his courage prevailed.

"Tommy don' know, does he?"

Louis reached into his jacket for his own cigarette and matches. "No, he doesn't."

Letting out a long exhale of smoke, a flicker of anger crossed Ashleigh's face. "How in the fuck has nobody told him?!"

"It's not that simple, Ashleigh." Louis sparked his tobacco. "If it was, we would have told him a long time ago."

"We?!" Ashleigh shook his head. "You tellin' me that Tommy's the only one of y'all that don' know?!"

"It's not like she is his mother, Ashleigh," Louis hissed. "Get ahold of yourself before someone hears you."

Ashleigh glared at him. "Yeah, well, from what I hear, she might as well be, brother. What possible reason could ya have for hidin' somethin' like this for so long?"

"Because if it came down to it, she doesn't want to be a liability to him."

"A...a liability?"

Taking a long drag, Louis shook his head. "Thomas has enough people in this city he's trying to fucking protect. If he found out, you know as well as I do he wouldn't let her take the kind of risks she wants to."

This caused Ashleigh pause. "He'd coddle her. And she don' want that."

Louis nodded, and the two of them delayed another few seconds.

"His mama know? Or she in the dark too?"

"She is aware, yes."

"And she didn' come back?"

The thought saddened Louis. "If she came back, Ashleigh, it would be her death. That's why she's stuck in England."

"I see." Finishing his cigarette, Ashleigh tossed it to the ground. "Listen here. I'm gonna keep your secret for now. But if she don' tell him soon, I will, ya hear me?"

"You realize she would skin you alive, don't you?"

"On the contrary, Louis, I think she'd fuckin' thank me."

Louis let out a loud scoff. "Thank you?!"

"Yeah."

"What in the hell makes you think that?"

"Because for the first time, he would know who he was. And I think you're wrong about Tommy."

"How so?"

"He wouldn' coddle her. He ain' like that, ain' got a bone like that in his body. He'd fight harder, brother, and ya know why? Cause he'd be fightin' for her, too. Haven' any of y'all learned yet that keepin' secrets ain' gonna win this war?"

Louis tried to keep a level head. "We built our lives around keeping secrets, Little Sweeney," he responded candidly.

"And how far has that gotten you, Louis? How did ya feel seein' my daddy alive, or Edward, for that matter?"

"Edward," Louis whispered aloud. He hadn't truly thought about Edward in some time, and deep in his chest, he felt a tinge of remorse for his oldest friend.

"Do ya really think Edward woulda waited so long to tell Tommy?"

"No, I don't," Louis said honestly. "But it's because of Edward's tenacity that he's not here, because sometimes the truth does get you killed."

He flicked his cigarette aside and looked Ashleigh square in the eyes, an anger rising. Taking a menacing step his direction, Louis backed Ashleigh up against a lamppost; it was then that young Sweeney realized he had gone too far with the Frenchman. Louis got right in his face so that they were just inches apart.

"There are many things about me you will never understand, but one thing you do need to understand is that if you decide you know better than the rest of us, I won't hesitate to silence you. I love your father. I don't love you. And if you proceed to threaten any one of my family with your own personal vendetta that only comes from the fact that your father kept secrets from you, you'll find a fucking bullet in your mouth. You can have your fun rattling Croker with your bravado, but I have five decades of killing under my belt, and one more soul to my roster won't make me lose any sleep at night, no matter whose bastard son you are. So, you keep your fucking mouth shut, Ashleigh, or you'll find this life you love so much gone before you can even see it coming. Are we clear?"

Without getting a reply, Louis spun and paced away from Ashleigh, who stood motionless on the roadside, the color gone from his cheeks.

It wasn't that Louis liked the idea of frightening the boy, but there was one big lesson here Ashleigh Sweeney needed to learn, one his ego hadn't quite figured out yet.

He, like the rest of them, was dispensable. And the sooner he learned that, the better chance he had at surviving the war.

Hours later, after leaving a somewhat rattled Ashleigh at The Palace and letting the Madame know what had taken place at Croker's, Louis hopped in a carriage downtown, hoping that Sally had made herself comfortable in the apartment above the barbershop. In a very short amount of time, Will and Louis would finally have their chance to leave New York City in the dust, and find a new start somewhere far away from the East Coast. Sally had diligently commenced the planning of their evacuation just after the hit on Priestly was to occur, though what increasingly worried Louis was that this hit would go awry. If it did, and if Walsh lived on, he and Will would have to make the decision together to either stay and fight with the others or follow through on their plans to run. He'd called the meeting tonight at their apartment to keep Sally in the loop of what was happening with the Whyos, and to make her aware that their plans had changed from definitive to tentative.

When he arrived, Louis hastily jogged up the back staircase and was thrilled to hear Sally and Will laughing inside. He opened the door, where they greeted him with smiles and salutations, a wave of warm air from the fire hitting his body. Louis bolted the door shut and took a seat at the kitchen table, pouring a glass of wine and cutting himself a slice of bread and cheese from the board in front of him.

"What have I missed?"

"Oh, nothing, I only just got here," Sally confessed. "We were just laughing about how the barber still asks me if I am married." She rolled her eyes. "After over twenty years of this shit, you'd think he'd drop it!"

Louis chuckled. "He is a relentless son of a bitch, that's for certain."

Will had a sip of wine. "How was The Palace?"

"Didn't stay too long. The Madame and Claire were in some kind of deep discussion about brothel connections with the Whyos, and I didn't stick around."

Sally's head tilted to the side in confusion. "That's not like you."

"Well…" Louis sighed and peered guiltily at Will. "I had to lay into Ashleigh."

"Boy needs an ass whoopin' every once in a while."

"He confronted me."

"'Bout what?"

Louis's gaze went to Sally, and she immediately stood. "I'll be back in five minutes. We need more wine anyway." With that, she disappeared out the back door and down the staircase.

"About the Madame and Thomas."

Will held up a hand to stop him. "You listen here, brother. I ain' sayin' anythin'. If Ashleigh got all high and mighty on you, I hope you put his ass in check."

"I did."

"Then, that's all there is to say about it."

The two carried on discussing the day until Sally returned, and more wine was poured as the conversation turned to current events.

"Well, shit," she declared, sinking back into her chair after hearing the news about Samuel. "I hope to God he's alive."

"Us too," Louis agreed. "If this goes sideways, Sal, we may have to delay…again."

"I can understand that. Look, boys, I can get you out of here any time you want. I just need a day's notice to send word out. I'll get you to Boston, and then you're on your own as previously planned. Where you go from there is up to you. But until then, just keep me up to date."

"Yes ma'am," Will granted, saluting her with his glass, and they all drank.

"So, Sally," Louis went on, "do you have anything for us?"

This time, the "us" wasn't referring to him and Will, and Sally smirked. "I do."

"McCann?"

"Not McCann, but almost as good."

Will's ears perked up. "What is it?"

Her voice lowered, "This stays only with you two and the Madame. If word gets out, it'll be over before it begins."

"Done," Louis promised.

"Done," Will added.

"There are two men who are trying to find recruits within the Pinkertons to go undercover at the Hall."

"To what end?" Louis asked.

"Well, there is an underground effort that sprouted following Grant winning the mayoral race. Some social reformer and a couple of state senators want to get rid of Croker sooner rather than later."

"An' just how did ya find out 'bout all this?"

"Well," Sally started, "one of the men pursuing the onslaught is a close friend of a man you might recall, Louis."

Louis couldn't believe it. "John?"

"The very same," she confirmed with a grin. "They are starting small, wanting to get as much input from civilians as possible, because the hard evidence just isn't there. Which is why—"

"Which is why we need McCann. If we can find him, he could be the hard evidence we need to bring on an investigation."

"And why Tommy should prolly be brought on as this thing escalates," Will remarked. "If he knows somethin' like this is comin' Croker's way, he'd do anythin' to demolish that bastard for what he did to Mary."

The mention of Mary's name caused Sally to noticeably react and sip down some wine. "How is she?"

"Tommy says she's better," Louis told her. "That's how Esther got the combination to the safe. Mary remembered it. In her letters, Esther says you would never know Mary had been locked away, other than the large scar from her suicide attempt."

Sally shook her head. "Fucking son of a bitch." She finished her drink and set the empty glass on the table. "All right, boys. We will hold firm on the plan for now. I do think the sooner you both get out of here, the better. None of us are getting younger, and this game is getting more ruthless."

Will nodded. "Ruthless and gutless."

"Thank you, Sally," Louis declared with a smile. "We owe you."

"I'd do anything for you, Louis. You know that." Rising to her feet, Sally went to the hat stand to put on her coat and gloves. "Another few days, and this is over."

Louis and Will held their glasses up to salute her.

"'Night, Sal," Will called after her as she exited the apartment.

Reaching over, Louis put his hand on top of Will's, which was resting on the table. "She's right, you know."

"What are the odds we make it this time? With all this Walsh shit blowin' up, I ain' sure we gonna get out."

"I think we need to heed Sally's advice and leave, regardless of what happens."

This surprised Will. "Ya wanna leave even if it ain' over?"

"Let's face it—when will it ever be over, Will? I think as soon as this whole Priestly debacle is done, we still go."

"And what are we gonna do 'bout Es when she shows up and we ain' here?"

"She knows how to find us," Louis reminded him.

He seemed to be accepting Louis's proposal. "All right. Final question." He looked Louis square in the eyes. "What if Tommy asks ya to stay? For us to stay?"

"How would he know we are..." Louis's voice trailed off, and he leaned back into his chair. "You told him."

"I did."

"Why?"

"Because, brother. I think ya need to take a step back here and see the big picture."

"What big picture, Will? That we die and don't get a chance to be free of this?"

"No," Will stated diligently. "I mean the guilt that's gonna eat both o' us alive if we leave and this whole thing goes south. How ya gonna feel if Tommy, Es, the Madame, Celeste...what if they all go down fightin' and we ain' here? What if New York burns to the fuckin' ground? We was here durin' the draft riots, brother, and with them Whyos, it'll be worse. The only thing standin' in the way o' them is Tommy and The Palace. Ya wanna tell me how it would feel if we abandoned them to die?"

This wasn't a new thought for Louis. It was one that haunted him to his very core, like a recurring, ominous nightmare of what would transpire if he and Will decided to run while they still could. Louis was approaching a fork in the road, and he grasped whichever way he chose, Will would follow, essentially making him the one to seal their fate. He wanted to escape Croker and New York City, yet what he wanted more was to put Walsh in his grave and assist in formulating Richard Croker's destruction. There were certain things Louis would never forget: the Madame's battered frame after meeting Richard for the first time in the Points, Mary's incarceration for nearly a decade of her son's life, Esther's perpetual enslavement to a man who then turned on her to keep his corruption a secret, but the worst of them all...the worst was Croker unleashing Walsh upon them with the ego to imagine he could control the lunatic. The concept Louis kept returning to was the very simple question of whether or not he still wanted to give his life for the cause; that answer was an unwavering yes. If they needed him, he and Will would stay.

But did they need them?

"We won't desert them," Louis concluded. "But the second this is done and we have an opportunity, we are fucking taking it."

Relief hit Will's face. "Agreed."

Louis grabbed the wine bottle and filled their glasses. "I just wonder sometimes, Will. I wonder what life could be like on the other side."

"Louis, that ain' what's important."

"What is important, then?"

Will smiled at him. "That we're together. And we gon' do this together. Ain' nothin' gonna top that, ya hear me?"

588

Louis smiled too, and scooted his chair closer to Will's, wrapping his arm around Will's shoulders and kissing his temple.

"I couldn't do this without you, you know."

"Me either." Will took a large gulp of wine and winked at Louis, flicking his head the direction of the bedroom. "What do ya say we take our wine in there? Might be the last time we is alone for a while."

This time, Louis kissed him on the mouth. "You read my mind."

"Louis, wake up!"

Will was shaking him while simultaneously fumbling for his pistol on the side table in the pitch-black bedroom. Sitting up, Louis leapt out of bed and went to light a candlestick, unable to make out anything that wasn't directly in front of his eyes. Someone was pounding on the door to the apartment, hollering for Louis or Will to let him in. Feeling around on his dresser for matches, his fingers stumbled across a box, and in haste, Louis sparked the timber, dimly illuminating the room around them.

Will tossed Louis his revolver from the other side of the bed, which he caught with his free hand, candle in the other.

"Who the fuck is that?!" Will whispered, trying to stay quiet.

"I have no damn idea," Louis mouthed.

The pair of them slowly crept out of their bedroom, guns cocked, and when they were a few feet from the back door, Louis was at last able to make out their visitor's voice.

It was Ashleigh.

"Louis! Daddy!" he yelled, banging desperately now. "Ya gotta let me in! Now!"

Will lunged for the door, unbolting the locks and yanking it open. "What in the fuck are ya doin' boy?! It's gotta be two in the mornin'!"

It was hard to make Ashleigh out, but as he stepped inside the apartment, Louis caught the sight of blood smeared on his cheek down to his neckline, and his stomach dropped.

"We gotta get to The Palace," he panted. "It's bad. Real fuckin' bad."

"Talk while we dress," Louis commanded, shoving the candle into Ashleigh's hands and taking off toward his and Will's room.

"Follow, son," Ashleigh ordered after bolting the door shut, trailing Louis to find clothes.

Ashleigh did as he was told, hustling in their wake. "It's worse than we thought," he went on. "I don' know how we got so fuckin' lucky, but it was Claire. She had this whole damn thing figured out from the start!"

"Is Samuel alive?" Louis asked, pulling his shirt over his head.

"Barely," Ashleigh declared. "It happened so fast. Claire had a hunch that they would leave Ellis breathing. Seamus, on the other hand…"

Will stopped. "Is he…?"

"Yeah, Daddy. He dead."

This gave Louis pause as well. "Fucking Christ."

"They didn't do it quick, either. Poor son of a bitch was tortured for hours. Days, even. So was Ellis."

"How did you find them?" Louis pressed, resuming his dressing as he searched for his shoulder holsters.

"That's the thing. We didn'. Claire thought they would dump the bodies at Tammany…on the front stoop, ya know…to make a statement. Girl was right on the money." Ashleigh took a breath. "She and I got there and…and sure as shit, both of 'em were sprawled out. Couldn' have been there long—"

"Where is everybody now?" Will interrupted.

"Claire and I got Samuel into the carriage. Seamus, well, we couldn' take him. It'd look like we had somethin' to do with it, ya know?"

590

Fully dressed, Louis peeked over at Will, who was only a few seconds behind him. "All right, Ashleigh, what did the Madame say our orders are?"

His gaze went to his father, and then to Louis. "That's the thing, Louis. I have no fuckin' idea."

Louis stared at him. "What?!"

"Boy, what you on about?" Will demanded.

"The minute we got Samuel into The Palace and with Jeremiah, she and Claire were gone. She told me to find you two and get back to The Palace. George stayed to lock shit down, and I got here as fast as I could."

Will's head slowly turned, gaping at Louis. "She...she didn'..."

"I think she fucking did, Will."

"Did what?!" Ashleigh entreated them.

Louis paced out of the bedroom, passing Ashleigh and heading for the back door. "We need to get moving, right now. Will? Extra cylinders in case they come."

On his heels, Ashleigh was not to be ignored. "Tell me what the fuck is goin' on, Frog."

"Two things are about to happen, Ashleigh. First is that the war is officially on. Second is that you are going to find out if you are really meant to be a part of this."

"What the hell are ya talkin' about?"

"She went to get Tommy, son," Will said, putting on his Pendleton hat.

"And they went to get a victim," Louis finished.

Ashleigh was confused. "A victim?"

"A victim," Louis elucidated, "because in this game, it's one for one. And she needs Tommy to get her."

"Her?"

"Kitty," Will declared.

"Why her?" Ashleigh asked.

591

"Because once upon a time, Kitty was a whore at The Palace," Louis told him reluctantly. "The Madame had to throw her out for stealing and abusing the other girls. We kept an eye on her, which is why the Madame knows where to find her." Louis rotated toward Will. "You are to go get Croker from the party."

Will nodded. "I'll get his ass to The Palace just a few minutes behind y'all. Make sure Tommy is disguised so it ain' a fuckin' disaster."

The three of them left the apartment in a hurry, with Will grabbing a separate carriage to the Vanderbilt residence, and Louis and Ashleigh catching a coach to the Upper West. As the car rocked to and fro, Ashleigh reached into his pocket for a cigarette, and Louis did the same. They each took a few drags before Ashleigh finally spoke.

"Are we gon' kill Kitty, Louis?"

"We aren't," Louis responded truthfully.

"But…but I thought you said…"

Louis took in a deep inhale of smoke and let it go. "We have Samuel. Croker lost his man. He gets to decide what's to be done. Those are the rules."

"An' you said she worked for The Palace?" he continued. "How is that possible? Ain' a soul know 'bout her bein' linked to us before."

A feeling of disdain struck Louis, a foul taste in his mouth. "Kitty used to go by the name Katie, or at least she did at The Palace. It was over ten years ago, maybe fifteen, I can't be sure, but it was just before Thomas's mother was kidnapped. Katie was stealing from some of the girls, hurting them to keep their mouths shut, and then two girls you never met showed up. Their names were Danny and Hope. They discovered what was going on, and after Katie threatened Hope, Danny nearly killed her."

"Well, fuck me."

"As you can imagine, the Madame interrogated all three, then the rest of her girls. Katie's secret was out, and this wasn't her first warning either. The Madame tossed her, something she has very rarely ever done in my experience, and a few years later, she resurfaced as a Whyo."

Ashleigh stared at him. "Is that the reason ya think Walsh has some kinda affinity for the Madame? Some sorta vengeance for Kitty?"

"Nah," Louis replied plainly, having a long drag of his cigarette, "Walsh's affinity for the Madame is due to her status in the city. He wants to get rid of anyone with power, and the Madame...well... her power extends further than any of us could probably guess."

It went quiet again.

"The Madame..." Ashleigh started, deep in thought. "I know I ain' been here long. But she don' go on these errands, Louis. It's too risky. What in the hell is she doin' out with Claire?"

"There is something you should know about the Madame," Louis stated, "something that might change the way you perceive her."

"What's that?"

"The Madame doesn't sit out when it comes to the very few people in this world she cares about. If Samuel is in as bad of shape as you described, I can honestly say I am more shocked that she didn't load an arsenal into a carriage and head down to The Morgue to start shooting whoever she could take out. She doesn't give a shit if she dies. But if you hurt someone she loves, well, you won't be long for this earth."

Ashleigh had another drag. "An' just who are these select few?"

Louis hesitated. This would be a moment of absolute honesty with Ashleigh, a kid who, earlier that day, Louis scolded like a child for his misinterpretations regarding The Palace and the Madame herself. A real doubt lingered of whether or not honesty was appropriate, considering the context of the situation they currently found themselves in; yet, Louis submitted.

"Samuel; myself; Thomas, of course; Mary Daugherty, Thomas's mother; Esther; Celeste; George; Claire; every one of her girls; and you."

Letting out a scoff, Ashleigh rolled his eyes. "Don' patronize me, Louis."

"Do I look like the pandering kind?"

With a heavy sigh, Ashleigh let it go. "Nah. I just don' see how she'd give a damn about a hired gun."

"I used to be that man," Louis declared. "And like me, you were tested."

"Tested?"

Louis grinned, taking a long inhale of smoke. "The Madame was not exactly keen on having a bodyguard, until I saved her life. Some crazed woman nearly gutted her in the middle of the street for her husband's antics. You, on the other hand, were a little luckier than I."

"How's that?"

"You had Celeste to push you the right direction. The minute you told Croker you were done and signed onto The Palace...you earned your spot. And her respect."

This didn't appease Ashleigh. "Yeah, but I ain' you, Louis."

"You must be pretty damn close, because she doesn't ask me to tail you anymore."

His head whipped around. "She...she did what?!"

"Oh, calm the fuck down, I spy on everyone for her," Louis said nonchalantly, tossing his cigarette butt out the window. "Listen, Ashleigh. Tonight is going to be hard to stomach, but it's only a brief foreshadowing of what's to come."

"I understand."

"I'm going to give you a piece of advice, and you can take it or leave it. But hear me out."

"All right."

He reached for another cigarette. "Protect the ones you love most, and fight for what you have. As your father would say, the only thing that matters is we are together." Louis struck a match and lit his tobacco.

There was a lengthy silence before a response came: "This comin' from the man who threatened to kill me earlier?"

Louis smirked. "Oh, I'll still kill you, Ashleigh. But I'd rather not."

George could not have been happier to see Louis at the front door of The Palace. "Thank fucking Christ you're here, Louis. I have the upstairs ready for them. Sent some of the girls out for the night, the rest are all under strict orders to stay in their quarters or in the India Room. Jeremiah is in the back with Samuel—"

"How is he?" Louis asked, pushing past George and heading up the front staircase, both George and Ashleigh a few steps behind.

"He's alive," George granted. "Poor bastard is lucky. If Jeremiah hadn't been here, I'm not sure he would have made it."

Louis shook his head, pacing into the Madame's office. "George, keep an eye on the front door for the others. Are you armed?"

George pulled a pistol from his hip holster. "Shotgun is down by the door for back up."

"You don't let anyone in that isn't with us. Understand?"

"Loud and clear."

As George disappeared to man the front door, Louis noticed the chair and rope ready just in front of the Madame's desk.

"Ashleigh, go arm yourself with extra cylinders in case the Whyos show up and want a shootout to get her back."

"Ya really think they'd come here?"

"I honestly don't know."

Heading to arm himself further, Ashleigh left the Madame's

office, and Louis poured himself a whiskey in an attempt to focus himself in what seemed like the eye of the hurricane. There would be far more blood spilled than just tonight, and Louis wondered if Croker truly did have the balls to kill Kitty in retaliation for Seamus's murder—not because he believed Croker to be inept, but instead, because of one small fact he knew to be true. Croker did not want the weight of murdering a woman with his own hands on his conscience. He'd never been able to kill Mary; while he'd certainly left the other two to die, presumptively, Croker had not been the one to carry out the task, just the one to give the order. The worry Louis couldn't suppress was what they would do if Croker recoiled. With Kitty in their possession, would they really let her go after all the horrible things she'd done?

If they did, Louis would take it upon himself to end it. Not for The Palace or Seamus, but for Esther.

Without thinking, Louis went to the door to the back stairway and opened it up, descending down to the first floor and searching for Jeremiah and Samuel. He found them in Jeremiah's quarters, with Samuel lying flat on the surgeon's table in a bloodied and bandaged heap. His clothes were torn and covered with the red and brown color of blood. There was an enormous gash from his temple to his jaw line on the left side of his face, and cuts covering his arms, not deep enough to kill him, yet prominent enough to scar him permanently. His right knee was splinted. A shiner on his right cheek was swelling his eye shut, and his lips were cracked. Still, as Louis entered Jeremiah's room, Samuel's gaze met his, and he waved Louis over.

"Louis," he uttered softly.

Jeremiah, who was facing the opposite direction of the door, spun around and nodded. "Hello, Louis. Could you watch him while I take a piss?"

"Of course." Louis grabbed a vacant chair sitting by the door and pulled it over beside Ellis. When the doctor had gone, Louis sat down. "How bad was it?"

"Well, I didn't think I would see this place again."

This caused Louis's anger to swell. "What did they do to you, Samuel?"

He let out a heavy exhale. "They grabbed me and Seamus off the street, just a block from the precinct. We'd spent most of the night trying to track some fucking lead down…I can't even remember what it was now. We were beaten until we didn't fight any longer, then tied up and tossed in the back of a mule cart. Next thing I know, we are in a vacant building somewhere, each sitting on the ground, arms tied up behind us around a wood post, facing each other."

Suddenly, Samuel began to cough violently, and Louis leapt to his feet, pulling a handkerchief out of his pocket. He held it to Samuel's lips, tilting his head gently to the side, and when the fit passed, Louis saw his handkerchief was bright red. Louis spotted a cup of water resting on the table beside Samuel, and he moved around to grab it and provide Samuel a few drinks of water to ease the cough.

"Doc says it'll be like that for a few weeks," Samuel reassured him. "Got a lot of damage done to my body."

Setting the empty cup down, Louis resumed his seat. "I can see that whoever got to you thought knives were the way to go."

This pained Samuel. "Walsh. And the girl. The rest just…stuck around."

"What did he want?"

"There was never a demand. Seamus fought it at first, cursing him, saying Croker would kill him for it. I don't know which was worse, Louis: witnessing another man getting tortured beside me, or watching as Seamus finally understood he was going to die."

Louis had a drink of his whiskey, which had been sitting on the ground beside his chair. "How'd they do it?"

Samuel's eyes came to his. "Give me a sip of that."

Louis did as he was asked, and Samuel gulped down the rest with Louis's assistance.

"It started with the cuts. Walsh has them covering his entire body...son of a bitch showed us...then he would just keep on...on going. When he was gone, the others would beat us. At sun down the next day, Walsh returned with Kitty, and they cut Seamus's throat. They said they had to leave me alive to tell you what happened, and to tell Richard that Walsh and the Whyos no longer want anything to do with Tammany Hall. The girl and three others took us to the Hall and dropped us on the stoop. They thought they broke my leg, which, thankfully, the Doc has told me is just a dislocation, and then beat me senseless. Not an hour went by, and Claire and Ashleigh were there grabbing me off the stairs."

Louis's temper was becoming harder to control, and he tried to swallow it down. "I am sorry, Samuel."

"Be sorry for Seamus's family, Louis. I'm still here, ain't I?"

"The Madame, Claire, and Thomas caught Kitty. They're bringing her back here."

His eyes were up on the ceiling, but Louis could sense Samuel was just as enraged as he was. "I am glad," was all he managed to get out before Louis heard the sound of voices in the distance and took his leave of Samuel, heading the direction of the Madame's office.

An unconscious Kitty was being tied to the chair in front of the Madame's desk by Claire. George restrained Kitty's arms in case she managed to wake and struggle against them. The Madame was sitting at her desk, a glass of whiskey in her hand and her feet propped up, while Thomas stood close to the fire with a whiskey and a cigarette. Hearing Louis approach, everyone's attention was on him as he came up the back stair and shut the door behind him.

The Madame motioned to the drink cart for Louis to fill his glass. "Ashleigh has filled you in, I presume?"

"Yes, Madame," Louis replied, heading for another drink. "Will has not arrived yet?"

"Not yet," Thomas told him, making his way over. "Ashleigh is at the front waiting."

In disguise, Thomas was something to behold: he was unrecognizable in a bowler hat, dark soot smothered around his eyes and across his face, in a common man's clothes and with Athena resting on his shoulder, her eyes locked on Louis as if he would be her next victim. It was a far cry from his mask as Lord Thomas Turner, because in reality, the man who stood in the Madame's office was the true Thomas Turner, the boy that Louis had helped raise, the man who would stop at nothing to make things right, and the one who was Edward's son and the Madame's grandson.

George and Claire finalized Kitty's bindings, and she remained unconscious. "What do you need us to do now, Madame?" Claire inquired.

"Guard the fortress," she commanded. "Grab the guns from behind the bar and keep The Palace locked down. I doubt they will come for her, but I want to be prepared if they do."

Obligingly, the pair dutifully marched out of the Madame's office, leaving her, Louis, Thomas, and Kitty.

Louis had a sip of whiskey. "You think he'll do it?"

The Madame and Thomas exchanged a glance that was undecided. "We will find out, that's for damn sure," Thomas stated, circling Kitty. "For all the shit this bitch put Esther through, I ought to kill her right now."

"She's put more than just Esther through hell," Louis commented, walking over to stand beside Thomas and closer to the fire.

Kitty was by no means badly beaten—there was a small trickle of blood dripping from her hairline, a consequence of the blow that had knocked her out, yet the one aspect to catch Louis's attention were her arms. He handed his whiskey to Thomas and went to her, kneeling at Kitty's side and examining from her forearms to her shoulders. There weren't nearly as many as Samuel withstood, yet Kitty's arms had over a dozen deep cuts into her skin.

"Fucking hell," Louis muttered, "he's done it to her, too."

Instantly, Thomas was kneeling beside him. "What?"

"See these cuts? They're all over Samuel. He said it was how they tortured him and Seamus, and that Walsh…well…Walsh's entire body was covered in cuts like these." He peered to the Madame. "This must have been what they did to him at that hospital."

She nodded. "Deep enough to cause pain, not deep enough to permanently damage his muscles or his nerves. Or kill him."

Thomas's eyes narrowed. "Why do I feel like she seems so familiar?"

"Familiar?" Louis repeated.

"I've fought her, yes. Met her along with other Whyos in the streets. But…I just feel like there is something so…familiar…"

The Madame got up from her throne and paced to the drink cart. "That's because before this little bitch went by the alias Kitty, her name was Kristina. We called her Katie. And she worked at The Palace."

The realization hit Thomas, and he stood abruptly. "Oh…oh my God…"

A loud knock came to the door, and without warrant, it swung open. In came Richard Croker, followed closely by Ashleigh and Will Sweeney, and the moment he spotted Kitty bound to a chair in the middle of the office, Croker stopped dead, gaping at her.

The Madame was ready. "Here is the deal, Richard. You can do whatever you'd like with her. Interrogate her, hurt her, kill her. That's the way this game works. They took one of yours, you take one of theirs."

Croker's gaze did not leave Kitty. "Samuel?"

"He's barely alive and downstairs with Jeremiah."

"Why didn't he kill both of them?"

"Because," Louis cut in, straightening up and stepping toward Richard, "Walsh wanted to deliver the message that he was done with Tammany Hall. And to do so, he left Samuel alive and killed your oldest friend."

"Where is Seamus?"

This time, Ashleigh spoke up. "He is at the Hall, Mr. Croker. We couldn't bring his body with us, otherwise the murder could have easily been blamed on The Palace."

Croker circled toward the Sweeneys. "Will, take care of it."

With a nod, Will was gone, and Croker's attention went to Thomas. "What the fuck are you doing here?"

"He's the one who fucking got us a Whyo," the Madame snapped. "Show some goddamn respect, Richard."

It was in that moment Kitty started to stir, and everyone froze. Realizing Croker was cowering, the Madame gave Louis the signal, and he shuffled Croker and Ashleigh closer to the drink cart to give her and Thomas space. Thomas stood directly in front of Kitty's line of sight, the Madame on his right, their arms crossed over their chests as they watched her wake slowly. Her eyelids fluttered open and she groaned, attempting to reach for her bruised head. It took a few seconds for Kitty to realize she was bound and could not move her limbs; when that recognition struck, she desperately thrashed in a vain attempt to break free of her ropes, sadly, to no avail. She let out a raucous, panicked scream, her breath quickening, and slowly, her eyes found the Madame and Thomas glowering down at her.

"Hello, Kristina," the Madame sneered. "It's been quite a while, hasn't it?"

"Where am I?!" she demanded.

"You're at the fucking Palace."

Kitty's breath became hysterical. "No!" she yelled, fighting her restraints. "No! No! No!"

"You can scream as loud as you want," Thomas said blandly. "I can promise, no one is coming to save you."

Lifting her skirt, the Madame drew a blade, and Kitty's body trembled. "Ahh, so I see you remember?"

In a flash, Kitty transformed. "Madame, please!" she begged. "I only did this to survive. You don't understand what it's fucking like out there!"

The Madame's face contorted into a foreboding, broad sneer, and she let out a loud, subterranean laugh.

"I don't know what it's like out there, do I? Because I wasn't born on the fucking streets and abandoned at the age of three. I didn't become a whore at the age of ten to eat. And I didn't kill just so I could fucking stay alive and see another sunrise." The smile vanished and converted into a threatening scowl. "You, darling, have been dead to me. Kristina has been dead since she decided to put herself ahead of everyone else. You are just another Whyo, another one of the bastards who has been ruining my opium deliveries and hurting my fucking people. Watching you die will be a pleasure, darling."

As quickly as Kitty had put on her previous mask, that mask vanished, and she glared at the Madame. "Your time is coming, whore. He'll be here to kill you and the others. Even him," she hissed, spitting at Thomas's feet.

"Let him try," the Madame murmured.

In a blur, the Madame struck, sending a blade through Kitty's hand and through the arm of the chair beneath her. The girl bellowed in agony, writhing to try and get free of the blade, and the Madame looked over to Richard, Louis, and Ashleigh expectantly.

"Richard?"

Louis knew Croker wouldn't...knew he couldn't. Though consequently, none of it mattered. Brusquely, the back door of the Madame's office was thrust open, and there stood Samuel, barely able to stand and more maddened than Louis had ever seen him.

"One for one," he wheezed, limping over to the agonized Kitty. "Seamus...was my partner..."

No one stopped him, not even the Madame, who appeared dumbstruck at Samuel's sudden appearance. In horror, Kitty peered over her shoulder and saw Samuel hobbling closer, and her dread increased exponentially.

Samuel halted beside Thomas and held out his hand, not even looking at him. "This is for Seamus," he pronounced, "and for Esther."

Thomas drew the Griswold from its holster and handed it to Samuel. "One for one."

Without hesitation, Samuel cocked the pistol, pointed it, and fired. Kitty's head fell to her chest, her breathing ceased, and blood poured out from her chest.

Pretty Kitty McGowan was no more.

On the cover of every paper the following morning were the grisly details of Seamus's murder, the Whyo gang killings of coppers throughout downtown Manhattan, and the promise of retribution by newly elected Mayor Hugh Grant alongside the police department. Louis escorted Croker down to the Hall shortly after Ellis shot and killed Kitty, where Will, Sullivan, and O'Reilly met them; the five of them stayed there the entire rest of the night with Richard, drinking mainly in silence with a few occasional toasts about Seamus's dedication to Croker and Tammany.

As the sun rose and light reached the sky, Croker finally spoke: "We have to kill him."

Sullivan was dozing on one of the couches by the fireplace,

and on the other sat Louis and O'Reilly, smoking. Will sat opposite Croker, who was at his desk, on his third cigar and second bottle of whiskey.

"Richie," Will began, "I think we need to figure out this whole Priestly hit first. How we gonna handle that with Walsh bein' out?"

"You and Louis will handle it with the presumption that Walsh will be there to try and fuck it up. You will kill him and Priestly, and then this will end."

"What if he don' show?"

"Then after you kill Priestly, you will find and kill Walsh."

"What makes you so sure he will show?" Louis questioned.

Croker had a long drink of his whiskey. "Because he knows if Priestly sticks around, he gets what he fucking wants. And…" he let out a heavy sigh, "let's be honest. He will want to kill both of you."

Will was none too pleased. "So, you is usin' us as bait, that right?"

"I am having you complete a task I need done. And yes, you are bait."

Putting out his cigarette, Louis got to his feet. "And if we refuse?"

"I will kill the Madame and Ashleigh at my earliest convenience."

"With who?" Will jeered. "Sullivan and O'Reilly?"

"No," he hissed, "I'll send the Tong. They wouldn't mind finally putting you two in a grave, I think?"

Will glanced at Louis nervously, because what Croker said was absolutely correct.

"Fuck you, Richard," Louis declared.

"So, we have an understanding?"

Louis wasn't done yet. He marched right to Croker's desk and slammed both his palms down onto it, causing Croker to jump and Sullivan to wake.

"If you think Walsh is your worst nightmare, I can fucking assure you, Richard, you've never met the worst of me before." He leaned in close, so his and Croker's noses were only inches apart. "I do this job and we are both fucking done, you hear me? Or I will not hesitate to kill you, you son of a bitch, slowly ripping you apart piece by piece until there's nothing left to find. Your family will not be safe, either, I will see to that. And if you think I'm bullshitting you, I dare you to fucking test me."

There was no response from Croker, whose eyes were wide, his drunken haze lifted with the fear of the man before him, a primal fear of that part of Louis lying dormant within—the man who killed without remorse. Furious, Louis spun on his heels and walked out of Croker's office, hoping with every ounce of his being Richard would retaliate.

Because deep down, Louis knew he would enjoy killing Richard Croker, even if it meant he went down with him.

As arranged, Mock Duck made an appearance at the Turner residence the following night, and he did not disappoint.

Thomas was sitting across from a blazing fireplace in the great room waiting for him, swirling a bit of brandy around in his glass, when very suddenly, the man was merely sitting across from him, a small grin of satisfaction on his face. On this night, he wore a bowler hat with a long, dark overcoat, and Thomas noted that Mock Duck was at ease in his presence. His face gave off the impression of boyish naivety, though in reality, he was far from innocent. Like Thomas and all the rest of them, he had a purpose, and he needed to grasp just how far Mock Duck was willing to go to see it through.

Thomas nodded in salutation. "Would you like a brandy?"

"Please."

Rising, Thomas went to grab his guest a fresh glass. "I am assuming you are somewhat well-versed on what is happening here."

"I have not been here long; however, I sent men ahead of me to gain perspective, and they have proven to be invaluable."

"Invaluable how?" Thomas asked, pouring Mock Duck's drink.

"Well, for starters, Lord Turner, figuring out who this Vigilante was, and what his purpose was in picking a fight with Mr. Walsh and his gang."

"I am by no means the only man fighting the Whyos."

"You are certainly the only one winning."

He returned to hand Mock Duck his brandy and resumed his seat. "So. The Hip Sing are the most notorious Chinese gang in San Francisco. What is it you want with New York?"

Mock Duck gazed at Thomas intently. "Lee has been corrupted. Like I mentioned to you three evenings ago, we have a code he has broken. I am here to put an end to his reign."

"My master was a Samurai," Thomas told him. "A moral code is something I understand all too well."

"Ah, I wondered where you received your training. You move as we do. Quiet, like a ghost in the shadows."

"That's the idea."

"And what is it Lord Thomas Turner seeks to gain from harming the Whyos?"

Thomas had a gulp of brandy. "The Whyos and Walsh have hurt people I love. I will be doing this city a service by disbanding them, not to mention the personal retribution I would feel by killing Walsh."

"The Whyos have started a battle with the police already."

"Yes, they most certainly have."

"And which side is it you stand upon, Lord Turner? Because from my perspective, there are more than two sides."

"Enlighten me."

Relaxing back onto the sofa, Mock Duck had a sip of his brandy. "You have an army of Whyos, scattered throughout this city, their numbers rising on an almost daily basis. There is Richard Croker, Tammany Hall, and the police. And then, there is you."

Thomas smirked. "What about the Madame?"

"I honestly will admit, I cannot determine where she stands, and this is one of the many reasons I wish to meet with her."

"She is on the side that ensures her survival."

"Then, I believe we will have a lot to discuss." He paused. "Were you able to find a time for her and me to meet?"

"One week from tonight," Thomas declared. "Plan on being at The Palace between seven and eight."

"Will you be present as well?" Mock Duck inquired.

"Your business with the Madame has nothing to do with me."

"On the contrary, Lord Turner, it has everything to do with you." He set his drink aside. "Lee wants Richard Croker to make him sheriff of Chinatown, a position he wishes for his candidate Mr. Grant to implement once in office."

Thomas shrugged. "What you are failing to see is that the Madame is in alliance with Croker and has been in business with Lee for years. Why would she turn her back on them to associate with you?"

"Do you truly believe that the Madame will not be disposed of if Richard Croker deems it necessary?" Mock Duck posed. "Lee would do anything for more power, even cross the Madame. I am offering her cheaper opium, a loyal ally, and an opportunity to join with us before Lee goes down in flames. Because, I can assure you, Lord Turner, if you have heard anything about my time in San Francisco, you are aware that I do not commence a task I do not intend to finish."

This Thomas knew. His research into Mock Duck's history in San Francisco spoke of a gang leader with a reputation for brutality and cunning. The Hip Sing defeated every other faction of the Tong in a bloody onslaught that cost many lives, and Thomas did believe Mock Duck intended to have his Flying Dragons put an end to Lee's reign.

Thomas's eyes narrowed. "How?"

"How what, Lord Turner?"

"How do you plan on dethroning Lee when he has decades of resources at his disposal, and you are a merely a small faction from the West, running purely on your reputation as a merciless bastard?"

"I have a friend who wishes to take on Mr. Croker. We are helping one another to see it through."

This got Thomas's attention. "And who is this friend?"

"For now, I cannot say, to protect his interests."

"Please do me a small favor, as a means of thanks for my assistance in bringing you and the Madame together."

"Of course," he complied, grabbing his glass.

He cleared his throat. "Please tell whoever this man is that my services can be extended in aiding that endeavor if needed."

A large grin came to Mock Duck's lips. "I certainly will." He had more brandy. "This Walsh…he is a devil if there ever was one."

"A word of advice," Thomas passed on, "leave the lunatic alone. Any men you send his way will not survive."

"I have heard many rumors."

"They are probably true. He has broken from the Hall and plans on causing mayhem. I don't know what exactly he is planning, but whatever it is, it's going to happen soon, and it's not going to be good."

Mock Duck was pensive. "You are trained in the ways of Samurai?"

"Yes."

"Have you faced him?"

"Not head to head."

"Well, Lord Turner, if you cannot defeat him, I would imagine the city will be in quite a bit of trouble. But I would like to extend a hand of friendship to you. If there comes a moment when you are in need of me, you know where to find me."

Thomas studied him. "Are you so sure you want to offer yourself up for slaughter?"

Mock Duck chuckled. "Slaughter, Lord Turner? No, it is not slaughter. Like your Samurai, it is our greatest honor to die in battle, and it is an even greater honor to die eliminating an evil such as that man."

Getting to his feet, Mock Duck left his empty brandy glass on the side table and bowed to Thomas. "I will be in touch."

"Lovely."

For a few seconds, he lingered. "Can I make an observation?"

"I don't see how I could stop you."

"You will never defeat this Walsh if you do it alone."

This time, Thomas genuinely smiled. "Who said I was alone?"

CHAPTER XLIV.

It wasn't worry that consumed the Madame. No, worry was an emotion that was long forgotten—this was instinct, an instinct telling her whatever might happen next would be quite similar to inching along on cracked ice. One wrong move, and they were all dead. Chinatown was at war. The Whyos and Tammany Hall were no longer allies. Croker still wanted Priestly dead, and The Palace was scrambling to get its bearings. They had a vague knowledge of their enemy, and Thomas's weekly meeting with Strat would be in just a few days' time for an information swap, but what the Madame hated more than anything was being blind. There was no time to waste with their lives on the line. She needed to know what the Whyos planned next, whether or not Walsh would attempt to ambush the Priestly hit, or more importantly, how her next opium shipment was going to be delivered. Her establishment had a reputation to uphold, and with the Tong bickering over who was in power, the Madame's patience was running thin.

She had customers, after all.

Thomas sat in front of her with Douglas in the chair beside his. Near the drink cart lingered Ashleigh, and Celeste was propped up on the left side of the Madame's desk, gulping down wine as the others had their fill of whiskey.

"Please tell me you didn't fucking say who we were," the Madame said with an air of provocation.

Letting out a slight chuckle, Thomas shook his head. "Don't insult me."

"So, them chinks are in a power struggle," Ashleigh remarked, having a sip of his drink. "How in the hell are we s'pose to get our opium?"

"We have enough to get us through the weekend," Celeste insisted. "The Madame will meet with Mock Duck tomorrow and we will figure out our next step from there."

"Not to mention," Douglas interrupted, "you have a meeting with Edison about Westinghouse tomorrow."

The Madame scoffed. "What the fuck does that crazy son of a bitch want now?"

"Well, he would like for us to kill Nikola, but I told him that was not a viable option."

"Nikola has done nothing wrong," the Madame replied candidly, her secret hope being that Tesla would bury Edison. "So, tell Edison I'll meet with him and strategize for this war of currents, but if he wants to murder Tesla, that bastard can do it on his own time."

"I couldn't agree more," Douglas agreed, saluting her. "He is one step away from becoming completely deranged. If he didn't pay us so much money, Madame, I would never have initiated the connection."

She waved him off. "Let's just hope he fucking electrocutes himself and does the world a favor to rid us of him."

Thomas cleared his throat, shifting in his seat. "Well, as long as you have what you need for the next few days, our biggest issue is what to do about the Whyos."

"Louis and Will have been given the Priestly hit, I assume?" the Madame queried.

"They have. I will be visiting Richard this evening to offer Croker my services as a tertiary aide, especially if the fucking lunatic shows up."

"And if he says no?"

Thomas shrugged, having a gulp of whiskey. "It's not like Croker will actually be at the hit, and I'll be damned if I let anything happen to Will and Louis."

"And then what's the plan?" Celeste pressed.

"I'll get Priestly to Samuel. We will get Will and Louis out of New York. And we will continue to keep putting an array of evidence together. Louis is certain that this push for an investigation into Tammany Hall could use my assistance, and with him and Will on the run, I am the only one who knows the streets and the ins and outs of downtown as well as they do."

"Well..." Celeste started, then paused.

"Well what?" Thomas asked.

"Esther knows them better."

For a brief moment, the Madame saw irritation flash in Thomas's eyes, yet after a second or two, he conceded, adding quietly, "I am also the one who is in the least amount of danger being there."

With a nod, Celeste retracted her point, "You are right, of course."

Her face was crestfallen, and it was easy for the Madame to recognize the true problem: Celeste missed Esther.

"She will be here soon, darling," the Madame remarked, putting her hand on Celeste.

"What do you think will happen," Douglas uttered, "when he finds out she's alive?"

"Croker?" the Madame asked him. "Or Walsh?"

"To be fair, both."

"Walsh will want to kill her," Thomas interjected.

Grinning, the Madame supplemented, "Croker will be... astonished."

"We cannot keep her a secret, can we?" Celeste asked.

"I'm afraid not," Thomas told her, clearly bothered by that.

"This is her fight too," the Madame asserted firmly. "And she fucking wants to be here more than most of us."

The room went silent—no one could argue that element with the Madame. Nor did they really want to.

"Tommy," Ashleigh said at last, "ya want me with ya, seein' Strat in a few days?"

"No need. I'd rather have you here, keeping an eye on The Palace, until we can figure out what the fuck Walsh is up to."

"Agreed," the Madame chimed in.

A knock came to the Madame's door, and Claire poked her head inside the office. "Madame, are we ready to go over the night?"

"Ah shit, darling, I didn't realize it had gotten so late. Boys? Out. Thomas, you'll be by to visit in the morning with Will and Louis?"

"Of course."

With a raise of her glass, the Madame addressed the room: "Stay determined."

"Stay determined," they replied in salutation, and they finished the contents of their glasses.

Once everyone save the Madame and Celeste had evacuated the office, in paraded Claire with Paige, Dot, and Razzy in her wake, and the group sat down, though it was obvious they had more than purely the night ahead on their minds. In her usual manner, Celeste remained by the Madame, whereas Marcy and Claire took the empty armchairs opposite the Madame's desk, and Razzy, Dot, and Paige sat just behind them on the loveseats. Every eye was focused on her, and after a brief, wary glance toward Celeste, the Madame centered in on Claire.

"What is it?"

It was Razzy who proceeded to get to her feet. "Promise us we are safe."

Before the Madame could respond, Celeste stood from her perch. "Excuse me?"

This startled the five of them, including Razzy, which was a rare sight to behold. "I just...I mean...we are nervous, Celeste..."

"Nervous?" Celeste carried on. "Do you understand the lengths we go to on a daily basis to keep you sleeping soundly in your beds?"

The Madame rose and moved beside Celeste, throwing her a calming glance. "Darling, it's all right."

After a breath, Celeste eased, and the Madame turned to Razzy. "You are worried because the threat has become a little too close to home, I presume?"

"That's not it, Madame," Paige spoke next. "It's about, well, it's about Kitty."

"What about Kitty?"

"That she was one of us," Dot said.

"And that she was...eliminated..." Paige finished apprehensively.

Straightaway, the Madame peered toward Claire and Marcy. "Would either of you like to tell them firsthand?"

Marcy shrugged. "It would be better if you did, Madame."

The Madame gallantly reclined onto the front of her desk, finishing her whiskey and setting her vacant glass aside.

"Another lifetime ago, Kitty was formerly Kristina, though she went by Katie with her friends and regulars. She was quite beautiful. Too fucking smart. Charismatic in the best and worst ways. She was our highest earner for two straight years. Very suddenly, her true colors began to show. She was pushy, she was a cunt to Louis, and then she began stealing from other girls, hurting the other girls, threatening them to keep them quiet and taking their clients when she could. Kristina was manipulative, driven by money and her power over men, and then it became clear what she truly desired. She wanted to take my place."

"What did you do?" Paige pressed eagerly.

"We tried to mediate her for a time, and it didn't fucking work. So, we kicked her out." The Madame stopped, a tinge of anger hitting her heart. "I will share something with the five of you, something no one else knows other than Louis."

"What's that?" Dot entreated her.

"She was the only one I've ever made leave The Palace."

The girls exchanged glances, as if this was what they had been expecting.

"Madame," Dot mumbled quietly, "did you…were you the one…to…"

"The one to what?"

"Kill her?" Razzy finished.

"No, darling, I wasn't. It was Samuel."

"Samuel?!" Razzy exclaimed in disbelief.

"Why Samuel?" Paige inquired. "What possible motive could he have?"

"Because," the Madame told her, "Seamus was Detective Ellis's partner. Reluctant partner, yes. But partner."

"And that means he gets the hit," Claire confirmed.

"So, that's why you got to kill Ralph," Paige addressed Claire softly. "Because of what he'd done."

Completely unruffled, Claire nodded. "Spot on, Paige."

"Marcy," the Madame initiated, "you have been discreet in our discussion. And your input would be valuable when it comes to Kristina."

Letting out a breath, Marcy shifted in her seat, her expression hard to read. "I think she got what she deserved. Kristina was never one of us—she only ever worked for herself."

"You knew her?" Dot asked.

Standing from her chair, Marcy rotated around towards the girls behind her, and pulled the right sleeve of her dress up high, pointing to three thin, long scars tracing from bicep to elbow.

"For months, she took half my earnings. I was very young, brand new to The Palace. Kristina would hurt me to keep me from telling anyone, but eventually, Danny, a veteran, figured out what was going on and took care of it. These nail marks were from the final time she attacked me, and they left a lasting impression. So, no. I don't give a damn that she's dead."

Paige was baffled. "Why didn't you tell us before?"

Resuming her spot, the Madame could tell Marcy was trying to keep those horrible memories at bay. "It's not an experience I like reliving. Like I said, she deserved what she got."

These final words from Marcy left an oddly settled sense of resolution, and the Madame knew what they needed to move forward.

"George!" the Madame bellowed. "Wine!"

With the girls preparing The Palace for the night, the Madame was left to her own devices until an unforeseen guest arrived. She was about halfway through reading the more recent *New York Times* article about Edison's theatrics regarding Westinghouse to prepare for her meeting the following day when Ashleigh knocked at the door, announcing Croker was there to visit with her. For over a week, he'd been absent, burying Seamus with a hero's funeral and simultaneously campaigning hard alongside Grant for reform in downtown Manhattan, with a firm backing of the police department to take on gang violence. The Priestly hit was temporarily on hold, yet the Madame had a feeling it would be one of the various topics he wished to discuss following his insistence that Louis and Will be the ones to carry it out.

Croker came into her office and went directly to the drink cart to pour himself a whiskey. The Madame didn't say anything, only allowed him to pour what he needed and find a seat across from her desk.

"How are you, Richard?"

"I've been better, Madame."

"You have had success with Grant. The people of the city are unifying under you to crack down on the fucking Whyos."

"Yeah. And it came at the cost of my goddamn best friend." He had a sip of his whiskey. "I should have fucking killed her," Croker uttered. "I should have done it for Seamus, for his family…"

"And why didn't you?" she asked interestedly, setting her paper aside and reaching for her own glass of Casper's.

He was reluctant to open up. "I made a promise I intend to keep."

"To who?"

"To Mary Daugherty."

The Madame felt her hair stand on end. "What sort of promise did you make, Richard?"

"That I wouldn't kill a woman. Under any circumstance."

"Why the fuck would a promise like that matter now?" she managed to communicate steadily.

There was a small halt in conversation before Croker spoke: "I felt I owed that family something, so I've chosen to honor that."

"You mean you felt you owed Lord Turner after Esther, after Mary, and after Edward?"

His jaw clenched. "Yes."

"I see."

Croker grabbed a cut cigar out of his jacket pocket and lit it, taking a long drag. "I've got to get this Priestly hit over with," he mentioned, changing the subject.

The Madame was in agreement. "You most certainly do."

With an exhale of smoke, Croker finally seemed to relax. "Do you think the Vigilante would assist in this?"

It amazed her, sometimes, how perfectly her schemes aligned. "I can send him by tonight if you'd like."

"You can do that?! How can you find him?!"

"We've become...close."

The look on Richard Croker's face was one the Madame would never forget. "Well...I'll expect him at the Hall?"

"I'll send him to your residence office."

"That lunatic will not be allowed into my house."

She tilted her head to the side, amused. "I don't think he's the lunatic you need to be worrying about here, Richard."

Her point was taken. "We need to get rid of that sick son of a bitch before he does something else."

Having a gulp of whiskey, she threw her feet up on her desk. "What do you think Walsh would do?"

"Other than kill us and everyone else that matters to us?"

"Correct."

"I don't know. Start a fucking riot, or a war, for that matter. We don't have enough police or reserve here to take on the numbers that gang of bastards has."

The Madame rolled her eyes. "A war, Richard? Don't be dramatic."

"Madame, you have no idea what that son of a bitch is like on a personal level," Croker declared firmly. "You know how I was able to recruit him?"

"Truth be told, no, I do not."

"He already had a reputation amongst the Whyos and was a part of the gang in his own fashion. Aligned is perhaps a better word. Walsh was young, and a lone wolf for a reason. Sullivan met him at The Morgue one night and got him to meet with me, and I then proceeded to convince him we were, well, a vehicle of dissent. That we did what we wanted and did not give a damn about rules, regulation, or law. He was eager, eager to cause mayhem, and initially, he was loyal. The more Tammany expanded and grew in power within the city, the fiercer Walsh became, but our conflict arose when he rejoined the Whyos."

"What happened?"

Croker exhaled a cloud of smoke. "He realized he could build his own empire of dissonance. And has proceeded to do just that. The time finally came when he didn't need me or the Hall any longer, and that is where we stand."

"Which is why you want to make Lee sheriff of Chinatown," the Madame stated boldly. "You want the Tong on your side."

"I plan on doing just that," Croker admitted. "But it's not even me I worry about, Madame. It's my children. It's Lizzie. Who can say whether that bastard can break into my house and kill them whenever he wants?"

"I think the difficult reality to accept here, Richard, is that we both know deep down he can do just that right now, or at any moment he fucking chooses."

Running his fingers through his beard, Croker was bothered. "I'll send them away to the country the first of the year, before Grant is officially in office."

She nearly finished her whiskey. "A wise decision."

Croker, too, downed his, and got to his feet. "I'll expect your Vigilante friend sometime after one."

"I'll pass the message along."

Walking to the drink cart, Croker sat his used glass down, and paced to the door of the Madame's office, where he halted and gazed over at her.

"I am losing my reliable friends, Madame."

She gave him a convincing smile. "Not all of them."

With a bow of his head, Croker slipped out the door, and the Madame sat for a moment, her own determination mounting.

"But I am not one of them," she whispered to herself. "Because I will never be a fucking friend to any man who has hurt my family."

The Madame dumped the last of her drink down her throat. "Retribution will come, Richard. And she's a bitch."

The grandfather clock at The Palace struck two in the morning, and the Madame was seated at the bar beside Marcy, enjoying a nostalgic conversation about years prior, when Danny and Hope roamed the halls and each one of their lives seemed far, far simpler. From time to time, Claire would chime in from behind the bar, keeping their glasses full as they laughed loudly about one incident in particular, when Marcy confused ground anis and powdered arsenic, nearly killing one of their top-tier clients. There were only two customers left at The Palace, one back with Uma and the other with Lena, and most of the other girls were asleep already after a surprisingly busy evening. Celeste and Ashleigh had disappeared about a half hour before, and the Madame had an inclination as to where they'd gone. In his usual spot, George was guarding the front of house, and in the back, Jeremiah was doing a check on Ellis, who had stayed at The Palace since they'd found him on the steps of Tammany Hall. She knew he would go home sooner or later, but having him there with her kept the Madame in good spirits, and she couldn't decide whether it was because she relished his company or that they were having sex on average about three times a day.

Either way, it was a bit of light in the darkness surrounding them.

"Madame," Claire interrupted her thoughts, "why don't you go grab a cigar? We've got something to celebrate tonight."

Her left eyebrow rose. "Oh? And what might that be?"

With a grin, Claire held up her left hand where, on her ring finger, rested a brand new, beautiful engagement ring.

"Georgie and I are getting married."

Marcy let out a loud squeal. "Fucking finally!" she cried out in delight.

The Madame clapped her hands together. "Ah, darling, I am so happy for you!"

"When?!" Marcy bellowed.

"Just a few nights ago. I had no idea, it was such a surprise!"

"Well, you are right, darling. I think it is time to celebrate," the Madame announced with a toast. "Get us another round of whiskey and I'll be back with a cigar shortly. I'll have George lock up on my way back down to you."

The Madame stood up as Marcy stretched over the bar to grab Claire's hand, demanding to see the ring, and the Madame marched out to the lobby and up the stairs, nodding to George as she passed. She, of course, had already known—the Madame had helped George plan the whole thing, and was only waiting for Claire to be ready to tell the rest of The Palace their engagement was official.

When she reached the top of the stairs, the Madame saw the door to her office open ever so slightly, and with a scoff, she prayed she didn't catch Ashleigh and Celeste fucking in her office, or she'd have to skin them alive. She made her way to the door and thrust it open, expecting to witness something she would really rather not. Instead, the Madame was greeted by another sight: a revolver barrel pointing directly between her eyes. And the face behind it was one that made her stomach drop.

Walsh.

"Do not make a sound," he ordered unobtrusively, cocking the hammer. "Close the door behind you."

She was keen enough to notice he was alone, anxious that it was only Walsh rather than him and a group of Whyos. Walsh was intelligent enough to understand that coming alone would make his entrance and getaway easy, whereas a group of Whyos would draw attention from her staff at one point or another.

"Madame," Walsh hissed, "now."

Slowly, the Madame twisted around to close her office doors, then returned to Walsh.

"If you're going to kill me, just fucking get it over with," she said, her fear subsiding as adrenaline fueled her veins. "Nevertheless, that can't be why you are here."

He was pleased. "And why do you think I'm here?"

"You want to know how she died."

A smirk of malevolence came to his lips. "I assume you are the one who had the honor. She was, I believe, formerly an employee of yours."

"You fucking know she was."

Walsh gave a flick to the gun, gesturing toward her desk. "Come. Let's have a chat, you and I, and you can tell me about how Kristina met her end."

Glaring at him, the Madame stepped around to her throne, lowering down into her chair as her mind raced with how to signal to someone, anyone, that Walsh was at The Palace. With the Madame seated, Walsh placed himself across from her, revolver still aimed at her forehead, and he made himself comfortable.

"You were saying?" he insisted, almost with an air of impatience.

"I wasn't the one who killed her."

"Oh? And which of yours was it, then?"

"Ellis."

Walsh settled into his chair. "Not Richard, then? Or your grandson?"

Her eyes narrowed sharply. "I certainly don't know who you mean."

Letting out a nasty chortle, Walsh shook his head. "No...no I suppose you don't, Madame. Because as Miss Tweed herself pointed out, who would ever believe such a far-fetched tale that the beloved Lord Thomas Turner was also the New York City Vigilante?"

"Are you going to tell me what the fuck you want, or just point that gun at me?" the Madame strove to ask, praying at any moment someone would walk into her office.

"Ah, yes. Why did I make the trip here for a visit if not to finally kill you, as I've long promised to do? Well, I wanted to issue a warning."

"...A warning..."

He grinned. "Just that you ought to be ready. We are coming for you, Madame."

"And we is your gang of murderers?"

"Yes, a gang not much different than your own."

"My gang? Hah! Don't be ridiculous."

He studied her maliciously. "You might be able to fool Richard Croker, Madame, but if you think I am ignorant to the fact that you have your fingers in almost every pot, you are quite mistaken."

"Go fuck yourself, Walsh," she snapped, "and get the hell out of my fucking office."

Walsh's countenance altered, and he un-cocked the gun, holstering it in his belt. "You know, I think I will actually kill you. It'll save me the trip back."

It was too late to recant her mistake. She couldn't retreat from him. It was only her and Walsh, and the Madame had no way to escape.

Casually, Walsh hopped to his feet and unsheathed a long, silver dagger, sauntering around the Madame's desk toward her. "I'll just cut your throat, as a means of respect for a battle well-fought."

Scrambling out of her chair, the Madame appreciated she couldn't outrun him. She could scream, but they wouldn't get there in time. There was only one way she could outwit him, and that was if she could manage to reach and throw the blade on her thigh faster than Walsh could get to her. Then, as she was in withdrawal from her desk, the Madame felt it in her dress pocket—Claire had handed it to her earlier that evening, and by chance, the Madame understood she had the upper hand. With haste, she plunged her hand into the pocket and grabbed the small pistol as she hustled away in refuge around her office, then drew the gun on Walsh, who was not five feet from her. The Madame stood on one side of the loveseat, Walsh on the other, and he ceased in his pursuit, knife ready.

"Are we so sure it's loaded?"

Her thumb yanked the hammer. "Let's find out."

The Madame knew in foresight that it wasn't, however, the point was to give her an extra minute to yell. The trigger was pulled, and when no shot fired, the Madame was about to scream at the top of her lungs when a shadow emerged from the windows, leaping out and down onto Walsh, who was completely unaware of the sudden emergence of a third party. The two of them landed in a heap on the floor, with Walsh's dagger flying across the room as he struggled to get on all fours. Their visitor rolled instinctively away from him and stood confidently braced to fight on her feet, a thunderous look in her eyes.

Esther was home.

Fury erupted from Walsh: "You!"

Esther rolled her shoulders back, fists raised. "Your mistake for coming here." She smiled darkly. "Time to die, you fucking bastard."

She didn't wait for Walsh; instead, Esther barreled toward him, and she and Walsh ensued in a fight that the Madame could barely comprehend. First, Esther was pummeling Walsh with punches, his own swings empty misses, and her hits with those brass knuckles were debilitating him, regardless of his numbness. Then, Walsh was in the frontrunning, viciously attacking Esther in return with

625

a blow to her ribs and jaw; it was as the tide turned that the Madame snapped to reality and grasped she needed to act quickly. The brawl was moving so rapidly back and forth that the Madame had no opportunity to get to her desk without being ensnared in it, and out of the blue, an opening came. Knowingly, Esther pinned Walsh near the back-stair door, giving the Madame a chance to run and yell for help. Just as she was about to reach the front doors to her office, the Madame was struck hard across the back of her head, and she toppled to the ground just inches shy of the handle, temporarily unable to see anything but stars. Another hit came to her shoulder, and in a blur, the Madame watched Esther wrench Walsh off her and launch the back of her hand straight into his face, blood squirting everywhere from Walsh's nose. Unfazed by the strike, Walsh grabbed Esther's outstretched arm and yanked it in external rotation, and she let out a small whimper, attempting another blow from her free hand. Walsh took it in his ear, a gash splitting through the cartilage, and with the momentum from Esther's bodyweight, he threw her up against the wall, hands around her throat as her legs dangled beneath her.

A creak echoed through the office, and as the three of them spun around, there stood Celeste in the doorway of the back stair, aghast.

Thankfully, she used her brain.

"Ashleigh!" she shrieked, so loud it nearly made the Madame cringe.

Trying to get upright, the Madame glanced to where Walsh kept his grip on Esther, and her cheeks were turning purple as her strength waned. She couldn't stand, but the Madame found the blade on her thigh at last, and she drew it and threw, hitting Walsh in the left hip, weakening his hold on Esther. But it wasn't enough, and he straightened up again almost instantly.

"Celeste!" the Madame shouted, though, to her amazement, Celeste was already in motion.

Lifting her own skirt, Celeste acutely pulled and propelled the two blades from her own thigh, both penetrating Walsh's left arm and causing him to release Esther to the floor. The next second, Ashleigh was in the doorway, pistols drawn, and with an extraordinary roar of wind from nowhere, the Madame's office went dark.

"Someone light a fucking candle!" the Madame demanded, and with the hiss of a match, Celeste was kneeling down beside her.

"You all right?"

"I'm fucking fine. Check Esther."

"I'm fine, Madame," came the beautiful sound of Esther's voice, raspy from Walsh's onslaught.

Ashleigh got another candle lit, and within a few minutes, the entire office was illuminated once more. In haste, Celeste ran to fetch her brother and Ellis, whereas Ashleigh went outside, prowling the premises in case Walsh was anywhere near The Palace. Sitting on the floor against the wall was Esther, with her shaved head and sparkling green eyes, a little worse for wear, yet grinning at the Madame while she rolled out her shoulder.

"I fucking missed you," she said warmly.

"And I fucking missed you," the Madame proclaimed, beaming. "You saved my ass."

"Just like you've saved mine a hundred times."

The Madame chuckled. "You hurt?"

"All minor injuries," Esther guaranteed. "Nothing I can't handle." She slipped her hands out of her brass, letting them fall to the ground.

"Does Thomas know you are here so soon?"

"No," she confessed. "Tony and I quickly caught up, and with Thomas at Croker's, I figured I'd stop in to check on you. I didn't realize that son of a bitch would be here. I arrived right as he drew his blade and thought I should break up the party." She let out a long exhale. "Hiro came with me."

"The chink?!"

"Yeah."

She let out a small snort. "Thomas will be thrilled."

Esther scooted closer to her. "Madame, before Celeste gets here, I need to tell you something."

The Madame considered her tone. "Mary told you, didn't she?"

There were a few seconds of silence.

"You need to tell him. If he knew, Madame...if he had any idea who you actually were—"

"Stop it, Esther. Not now. We can't now."

"Why can't we tell him?! You are not a liability—you are his flesh and blood!"

"If I wanted him to know, if I thought there was anything fucking positive about telling him, I would have!" the Madame barked.

Esther's emotions were taking hold of her. "He is the only one who doesn't know," she asserted angrily. "How can you do that to him?"

The Madame sighed. "Esther, darling, it's the one and only way I can protect him. One less person to worry about means one less distraction when all hell is breaking loose. The only reason I told Mary was because she is safe from this. Thomas is not. And until he is, you will keep my secret."

"But Madame—"

"No. You will do this for me. Understood?"

She bit her lip furiously. "Understood."

Slowly, Esther pushed herself up to stand, and stepped to the Madame, taking her hands and gently pulling the Madame to her feet as well.

"Not that it makes any kind of difference," the Madame told her, "but you do realize what this means."

"What?" Esther inquired.

The Madame smiled genuinely. "You are officially my family now too, darling."

As her words sank in, Esther's frustration melted away, and her eyes glistened. "Does that mean you'll listen to me more often?" she teased.

The Madame laughed. "We'll fucking see."

Esther helped the Madame over to her desk; as she sat, Jeremiah and Celeste returned, with Jeremiah heading first to tend to the Madame, whose head and neck were throbbing in pain as a consequence of the hits from Walsh. As she leaned forward over her desk, Jeremiah inspected just where he had struck her to cause her fall, and the Madame replayed the scene over and over in her mind.

"How the fuck did he do that…" she whispered.

"Do what?!" came Celeste's voice.

Squinting ahead, the Madame saw both Esther and Celeste were seated in the two arm chairs opposite her, with Esther holding a cold piece of meat to her jaw and Celeste staring at her pensively.

Esther looked at her. "Walsh has a…a method, I guess, of withdrawing we cannot seem to figure out yet."

"What is it?"

"He fucking makes all the candles go out," the Madame stated irascibly, her words a little muffled from her tucked chin. "Every goddamn time he's in a fucking bind, he manages to get out with that trick. What is that?!"

"I have no idea," Esther shared, frustrated. "He is able to do that on command. I've seen him do it to the Whyos, too. Will has been trying to figure it out for years, and the conclusion is that it isn't fucking possible."

"But he…he must have a device of some kind…perhaps from an illusionist?" Celeste inquired, astounded.

"Asked everyone we could find, Celeste," Esther told her, "and we got nothing."

629

Jeremiah hit a sensitive spot on her head, and the Madame let out a tiny gasp of pain. "For Christ's sake, Jeremiah, I was just stuck by a man who can't fucking feel. Be gentle!"

"Jer," Celeste directed her attention to her brother, "how's it look?"

Jeremiah's concentration lingered on the Madame's skull. "No bleeding under the skull bone that I can tell."

With an audible exhale, the Madame rotated to Jeremiah. "So, I'll fucking live, then?"

"For now," Jeremiah remarked sarcastically. "You've got a secondary blow to your shoulder here. I need to examine it."

"All right, can we do that—ahhh!" the Madame exclaimed with a large wince as Jeremiah softly put pressure on her right shoulder blade. "Jeremiah! You fucking bastard!"

Ignoring her in his usual, tickled manner, Jeremiah didn't balk. "I am going to have to consult with Marcy on this. There is no fracture to your scapula, thank God; however, I am concerned with the deep tissue bruising, and we'll have to administer topicals to keep your pain levels as low as we can."

"Fine," the Madame snapped through gritted teeth. "Now, as I was saying—"

In that moment, Ashleigh burst through the doors to the Madame's office, put off. "Son of a bitch is gone, Madame," he confirmed, going to make himself a whiskey. "The Palace is up to speed, and Claire and Georgie got downstairs covered. You girls all right? That was one hell o' a round, I can tell." He nodded toward Esther. "Es, good to see ya."

She smiled at him. "Good to see you too, Ashleigh. Can you, ah, make me one of those? And a damn big one?"

"Course."

"Make that four, Little Sweeney. Celeste, darling, you'll be drinking with us tonight, so whiskey it is."

This didn't seem to bother Celeste. "Of course, Madame."

The Madame sank into her chair as Jeremiah packed his bag. "Jeremiah, have Marcy bring me whatever it is you two come up with when it's ready, and you can go home and rest."

Marching over, Ashleigh placed the Madame's whiskey into her hand, then dispersed two more to Esther and Celeste before he found a spot on the upright loveseat just behind them. Jeremiah agreed and took his leave, giving Celeste a squeeze on her shoulder as he walked by her and to the back-stair door.

"So," the Madame commenced, taking a big sip of her whiskey, "Walsh came to The Palace, first to threaten us as predicted, then decided, as I told him to get the fuck out, to kill me then and there."

"An' just how did he take to seein' Es back?" Ashleigh asked.

"About as expected," Esther said. "Prick wanted to rip my head off."

She reached into her pocket and pulled out two cigarettes, one for herself and one for Celeste, who was reaching into her dress pocket for her smoking wand.

"I'm just glad I got here when I did, or the four of us might not be having this conversation."

"Damn right you would," the Madame asserted, "there would just be three of you. But the one thing I would like to mention, Esther darling, is that you are...well...to be forthright, you are a spectacle to behold."

Esther straightened up, touching various parts of her face while she glanced around at them, troubled. "What? Do I really look that horrendous?! I thought I'd only taken a couple of bad hits!"

Ashleigh chortled. "She don' mean that, Es. She means your fightin'."

With her eyes lighting up, Celeste enthusiastically peered at the Madame. "Oh! Tell me all of it, please!"

The Madame proudly regarded Esther. "Darling?"

"I mean, he won," Esther stated frankly.

"No," Celeste countered, "if he'd won, you wouldn't be here!"

"He got the upper hand on her only because she was saving me," the Madame specified, having a sip of her drink. "Otherwise, that son of a bitch never would have gotten you in that choke, and you know it."

Taking a moment, Esther had a sip of whiskey. "Hiro. It's all Hiro."

"Who is Hiro?" Celeste asked. "Is he the Samurai?"

"Yes, and he's come to New York with me."

Celeste's gaze shot to the Madame. "How…how did you get him…well, into the country?"

"We were careful," was the only answer Esther gave.

"Tommy should nearly be done at Croker's," Ashleigh interjected. "Es, ya wanna stick 'round and see him?"

"At this hour, I suppose I will."

The Madame, with her head and shoulder still aching, managed to lean back into her chair with a cringe. "Esther, we need to fill you in on the fucking disaster that's been ensuing."

"I saw the papers. Seamus Murphy was murdered."

"It's not just that," the Madame continued on. "Chinks are at war in Chinatown. Whyos have split from the Hall. Croker is planning on murdering Priestly shortly. And we finally figured out the truth behind the lunatic."

Immediately, she had Esther's unbridled attention. "Tell me everything."

Before the Madame could begin, Celeste cleared her throat. "Madame, perhaps you should tell her about, well, other people joining our…party?"

The Madame nearly scoffed. "You mean Captain Bernhardt?"

Esther nearly dropped her whiskey glass. "What?!"

"The Captain returned from Vermont a few weeks ago and went

632

to see Thomas. He offered himself up to be a part of this and...
Thomas accepted." Celeste had a large gulp from her glass, the uncertainty of Esther's reaction looming.

"Darling," the Madame remarked carefully, "it was entirely of
his own volition."

Flustered, Esther finished her whiskey. "The more help we can
have, the better." Esther held her glass up high, and Ashleigh, ever
the gentleman, hopped up and grabbed it from her to refill. "Where
is he assisting?"

"The Hall," the Madame told her. "Thomas has him buddy-
ing up to Tammany—he's hoping between Jonathan's new affiliation there and his boxing with Edmund, Jonathan will have Croker
warming to him in no time."

A mien of support came to Esther's face. "Brilliant. It won't
take long. Croker is grasping for new allies now that Seamus and
Walsh are gone."

Ashleigh returned with her whiskey and resumed his spot.

"I want to hear about Walsh."

"Well, it's a fucking nightmare," the Madame admitted to her,
"and the theory has proven true. He was orphaned, a handful of
doctors got ahold of him and discovered he couldn't feel pain, and
abused the fucking system. Experimented on him for years until those
bastards finally sent him to a reform school when the results weren't
adding up. Short time later, Walsh broke out, burned the hospital
down where they'd kept him, then tracked down and murdered one
of the two doctors running their goddamn medical trials on him."

"Wait," Esther demanded, "why only one of the doctors?"

"He left one alive only because they made a deal. Walsh gave
him his blood to continue running tests, and the doc paid Walsh copious amounts of money for it."

This puzzled Esther. "If Walsh has money, why the fuck would
he run with the Whyos? Why look and live and present himself the

way he does?" She halted mid-thought. "What is he going to do with that money, Madame?"

She let out a heavy sigh. "That, Esther, is yet another question we want to fucking solve, because I can't figure it out."

"Well, shit."

A knock came to the office door, and Marcy peeked inside. "Madame, I'll have your topical ready in no time."

"Thank you, Marcy."

"George and Claire have The Palace locked up. We are going to have some whiskey at the bar, if that is all right with you?"

"Of course, darling."

Marcy glanced at Esther, beaming. "Happy you're home, beautiful."

"Me too, Marce. I'll meet you down there."

When Marcy withdrew, the room was quiet for a moment.

"Celeste, Ashleigh?" Esther spoke up. "Can you two give the Madame and me a minute?"

"Sure thing, Es," Ashleigh replied, hopping to his feet.

Celeste, on the other hand, hesitated, and the Madame immediately recognized she felt snubbed.

"Celeste, darling, I believe this is in reference to a matter regarding Esther's own past. Something she probably wants to hear with her own ears, and not in the presence of others."

Throwing the Madame a grateful glimpse, Esther then turned to her friend. "I'll meet you down at the bar. Tell Claire and Georgie I'm here."

Though hurt, Celeste nodded, following Ashleigh out of the Madame's office. When the door shut behind them, Esther spun back to the Madame.

"Thank you."

"You'd better make sure you fucking tell her later."

"I will." Esther had a sip of her drink. "Mary asked something

of me. A task that I swore I would see through for her, and I just…
I don't really know where to fucking start."

The Madame had an inclination. "What is it, darling?"

Letting out a heavy exhale, Esther's gaze went to her whiskey glass. "When Croker put her in the dungeon after his sister-in-law died, she…Mary told me one of the women locked in there with her…Bethany…died. But she swore Grace was still alive."

"And her conscience is guilt-ridden because the chink did the right thing and left her goddamn dying friend to die, only due to the fact that he couldn't fucking carry both of them."

She swirled the whiskey. "Yes."

A small chortle escaped the Madame's throat. "Well, it's a good thing I know where the fuck she is, then."

Esther's head snapped up. "What?!" she cried in disbelief.

The Madame's left eyebrow rose. "Esther, do you really think that after Thomas and the chink broke Mary out of Blackwell, I wouldn't immediately send Louis in to follow up on the raid? To see what The Palace could uncover about just what the hell happened?"

"So…what did you find, Madame?"

"A nurse. A nurse who adored Mary, and who rescued Grace after Hiroaki's assault on Blackwell. I paid her handsomely, and the moment Grace was healthy enough to be transported, I shipped that nurse off to Chicago, and Grace came here until Marcy and the old doc, God rest him, could get her well."

Her jaw hung wide open, flabbergasted. "But…how did you… how did nobody…"

"Because we are careful as shit, that's why."

Esther was stunned. "So, where did she go?"

"The amazing Grace found an apartment in Midtown—somewhere I believe you know quite well. She runs a bakery now. Still doesn't talk much, but makes a damn fine sourdough loaf, if I do say so myself."

"So, that's it," Esther articulated slowly. "I just…go to the old apartment. Introduce myself. And tell her…give her…Mary's message."

"Easier than you thought?" the Madame asked her with a wink.

"You are…astounding at times, Madame," Esther told her, staring straight into her eyes. "There are so many strings in your spider web I think I'll never uncover…so many loose ends you've tied without mentioning it to anyone other than those who need to know. I think of all these things you've done, both wonderful and ugly, and I just am in awe that I never was able to notice it before."

"Never noticed what before?"

"That you…you, Thomas, Mary…I mean, you are so alike. It's fucking ridiculous."

"It is fucking ridiculous," the Madame concurred. "And Esther, I understand you want Thomas to know. But it just cannot happen yet."

Esther's expression became lamenting. "Do you know what Mary said to me after she told me you were her mother?"

The Madame's ears perked up. "What?"

"That she wished she'd known. That it would have changed so much for her, and for Thomas. I do understand you, Madame, yet I have to say, I think you need to listen to your daughter on this one."

"It won't change our course, Esther."

"No, it won't." She bit her lip again. "He loves you so much. If he knew, it would give him more fire, not less. It would make him want to fight, not just for me, for Mary, or for Edward, but for you. For all of us."

She realized it then. They were telling her. They were all telling her, over and over, and the Madame had held her ground for as long as she could.

"Fine," she whispered, almost inaudibly.

Esther's eyes grew wide. "W-what?!"

"Let's tell him." The Madame took a swig of the last of her whiskey. "I don't want you having secrets from Thomas, even when the secret is mine."

Gaping at her, Esther nodded. "Well, let's tell him."

An urgent pounding came to the door not a second later; before the Madame could shout out for Ashleigh to come in, the door flew open and Thomas stood in the doorway, Athena squawking loudly from his shoulder.

"Walsh was here?!" Thomas exclaimed, glancing from the Madame to Esther.

The Madame reached into the second drawer of her desk and pulled out her heavy leather glove, placing it on her arm, and then whistled for Athena. Without hesitation, the falcon darted from Thomas's shoulder to her forearm, and the Madame had a sliver of hen breast waiting for her.

"Darling," the Madame greeted with a smile, "that is fucking irrelevant at this point. Say hello to your fiancée. I know you've missed her terribly."

They didn't waste time—the two ran to each other and Esther leapt into Thomas's arms, pulling him close. The Madame looked away for a moment or two to give the pair a little privacy, her attention shifting to the stunning Peregrine on her arm, munching happily on her snack. Months prior, they'd made a perch for Athena in the Madame's office just to the right of her desk, and as Athena downed the last bits of protein, the Madame moved her arm towards the wooden post, which the falcon hopped onto readily. She tied the jesses and gently hooded Athena, and just as she finished her task, the Madame heard Esther clear her throat.

The Madame's gaze returned to Esther and Thomas, and for the first time in decades, she had butterflies in her stomach.

"What is it?" Thomas queried, peering from Esther over to the Madame.

Esther smiled warmly at the Madame. "We have something to tell you. Or rather, the Madame has something she would like to tell you."

"Please tell me no one else has fucking died."

"Well, nearly both of us, darling, but we'll get to that," the Madame remarked slyly. "Take a seat, if you don't mind. Esther, whiskey?"

Complying, Esther went to the drink cart and grabbed Thomas a glass, returning with the decanter and pouring them each a large share. Thomas and Esther took seats opposite the Madame's desk, and she straightened up on her throne.

"Thomas," she began, stifling the quaver in her voice, "there is something you need to know, something I wish I had told you a long, long time ago."

He had a sip of whiskey, and she could sense his nerves on edge. "All right…"

"Before I tell you, I want to say I am sorry. Sorry for keeping this hidden, and sorry I didn't have the fucking courage to…to…"

"Seriously," he declared, rotating to Esther, "what the hell is going on? Is it Mary?"

"No, Thomas, it's not."

"Then what?"

She took a deep breath, and let it go. "I am your grandmother."

It was nearing dawn when Thomas and Esther left The Palace. The Madame rested back in her chair, finishing the last of her cigar, an almost empty glass of whiskey in her hand as the beams of the morning sun lightened the room around her. In a sudden turn of events, the Madame chose to confess the truth to Thomas about their connection, about the fact that he was hers, her flesh and blood, her family, with no expectation other than the hope of release and relief from the secret she'd been hiding from him for so many years. Her desire to save Esther the burden of carrying it, too, was the sole reason the Madame's resolve broke at last, and when she'd spoken the words, she had no idea what sort of reaction Thomas might have. Anger, she thought, or even rage at being kept in the dark.

But Thomas wasn't angry.

Her revelation had hung in the air like the smoke of her cigar, lingering, waiting to be addressed, his gaze not drifting away from her. And then, he spoke.

"You must have been so, so young."

There was an immense amount of empathy in his tone, the Madame felt a catch in her throat. "I was."

"I just..." Thomas ran his hands through his hair, wiping the soot away from his eyes with a handkerchief from his jacket. "Mary knows?"

"She does now," Esther answered for her.

"When did you find out, Es?"

"In England, just days before I left. Mary was the one who told me."

The room was quiet, with Thomas again unable to take his eyes away from the Madame, as if he was finally seeing her for the first time.

"You didn't want to tell me because you thought you'd be a weight."

It was an intelligent observation. "Yes," she conceded.

Something pained him, and he frowned. "You were what? Twelve? Thirteen?"

"Almost eleven."

That was when the anger came. "Fucking Christ," he hissed under his breath, his brow furrowing. "What the hell is wrong with the world!"

"Too many things, darling."

"So, you did the best you could," he went on. "Got her to a family, stayed close. That part I already know."

"Yes."

"And then you raised me while she worked."

"That's correct."

Thomas held out his glass for Esther to refill. "You really didn't think Edward would come back for her. You were just trying to be a good mother."

Another statement. "I should never have done what I did. But that is water under the fucking bridge at this point."

Getting to his feet, Thomas stood and walked over to the fireplace, pacing. Athena stirred, curious as to what her master was doing.

"Thomas?" Esther called, worried.

He didn't respond, only drank his whiskey and muttered to himself under his breath for a few minutes, leaving Esther and the Madame shrugging and throwing each other unknowing peeks as they sat patiently.

Decisively, the Madame rose, grabbing her glass, and she went to him. She didn't speak, and when they were face to face, she reached out and touched his arm gently.

"You see it, don't you? Why I did this? I wanted to protect you, to keep you safe."

"Yes, I understand. I just…how did I not see this before?!"

"Because I wouldn't let you," she divulged gently. "Thomas, the time for secrets amongst us has long passed. You needed to know."

A genuine smile came to Thomas's lips, and he took her hand in his, knelt down, and kissed the top of it courteously.

"I am pleased to make your acquaintance, Grandmother."

Her eyes narrowed. "If you ever call me that again, I'll fucking skin you alive."

A deep belly laugh escaped from Thomas. "As you wish, Madame."

They'd turned to find Esther standing just a few feet away, tears in her eyes.

The Madame snorted. "Esther, really. Don't be so dramatic. Come, let's sit."

"So...I guess what I want to know is, what the hell happened with Walsh?" Thomas threw out, as they sank down into the sofas by the fire. "Ashleigh mentioned he was here?"

"Your little Esther saved my ass," the Madame divulged. "He would have killed me if she hadn't fucking leapt down from the windows."

Another knock at the door, and Celeste's head peeked inside. "Pardon the intrusion, but there is one hell of a celebration going on downstairs, and I thought you'd like to join."

Thomas was puzzled. "Celebration?"

Beaming, the Madame stood. "Claire and George are engaged Celeste, we are right behind you!"

With a beckoning smile, Celeste led them downstairs, where the merriment truly started, and the Madame found she was happier than she'd ever been in her entire life.

As the festivities came to a close, she saw Esther and Thomas safely put into a carriage in the back alley to prevent being spotted, and the Madame had wandered to her office with an enlivened sense of purpose. He knew, and just as Esther predicted, Thomas appeared to love her all the more as a result. The hours they'd spent toasting Claire and George, he did not once leave her side, and on a handful of occasions, the Madame caught him simply staring at her, making her maternal instincts course wildly through her body. Thomas was not her son, though he undoubtedly felt like hers, and while he was the spitting image of Edward, he had her instincts, her ferocity, and her determination. They were connected in a way she could never describe, and now, now that the truth was in the open, the Madame grasped that their relationship would only be stronger, more resolute, and unbreakable.

Taking a drag of her cigar, she noticed the ache was gone. In a strange way, the Madame had rid herself of her last regret. That was better than any victory cigar she'd ever smoked, or any sunrise over the city she loved.

Sound crept up from the lobby, the hushed vibration of urgent voices and rushing feet. Her ears perking, the Madame spun away from the windows and set her cigar on the ashtray just as Ashleigh burst into her office.

He was covered in blood.

"Send Claire to the Turners'!" he yelled. "I need Esther at St. Stephen fast as she can!"

The Madame was on her feet, running to him. "What the fuck happened?! Is Celeste hurt?!"

"Nah, Madame," Ashleigh's head hung low, "Douglas."

"Is he...?"

"Madame, we got there, and that son of a bitch was...at the hotel."

Her stomach dropped. "Walsh?!"

"Listen, we have to get you there, fast as possible. I left her with her brother, but she's in hysterics."

Within a quarter of an hour, The Palace was under lock and key, with George and Samuel manning the property while Claire took a carriage straight to the Turners' to fetch Esther. Ashleigh and the Madame caught their own coach, paying him extra to drive as fast as he could through the early morning streets of the city. When they reached the hotel, the lobby was empty, and they sprinted inside, hustling up the stairs and to the Hiltmores' rooms. Ashleigh hastily knocked using a pattern pre-ordained by The Palace and proceeded to unlock the door. They walked inside, and the Madame was utterly aghast.

On the floor, covered in a bloodied sheet, lay the body of Douglas. Distraught cries of grief came from Celeste, who was sobbing on the loveseat in the sitting area of Douglas's rooms, with Jeremiah's arms around her. Blood covered the floor, and reluctantly, the Madame stepped over to Douglas's side and lifted the sheet, grimacing at what she beheld. He'd been brutally slaughtered, cut savagely and mercilessly in what the Madame recognized was a slow and painful death. The final blow had been the slice of his throat, and his pale, lifeless body sent chills down the Madame's spine.

"Ashleigh," she whispered.

"Yeah, Madame?"

"Tell me what happened."

"We got to the hotel, didn' even worry 'bout Douglas with it bein' late and all. Went to bed. Celeste woke up an hour later…said she thought she heard someone snoopin' around and thought it was that maid Molly always tryin' to peek in on her. Next thing I know, I hear Celeste scream, and I leap out of bed, grab my pistol, and run to her. Got to the doorway where she was pleadin' with him… beggin' him not to do it…but he slit Douglas's throat right in front o' her. And me. I shot, but motherfucker was fast. Grazed Walsh's arm, then the candles went out, and the bastard was gone. I tried to…to plug Douglas's neck up, but he was already passed. Jeremiah stumbled out in the darkness and helped me light the room back up, and she was just…just holdin' him on the ground…cryin'…"

The Madame's eyes fluttered shut, and she said a silent prayer for Douglas. "You did all you could, Ashleigh."

"I shoulda checked his rooms when we got in. I fuckin' know better."

She turned to him. "You do not blame yourself, you hear me? This is the goddamn lunatic, not you. And not your fucking fault."

Her focus went to Celeste and Jeremiah, and she gently glided toward them. "Darling?"

Through angry tears, Celeste glimpsed up at her. "He...he did this..."

The Madame sat beside her. "I know, darling. I am...I am so infinitely sorry. This should never have happened to your father."

"Madame," Jeremiah interrupted courteously, "should I run to The Palace? Send Samuel to the precinct?"

"That's a perfect idea, Jeremiah," she declared. "Take the coach sitting downstairs. He's under strict instructions to wait for either me or one of my fucking people. And if he's a prick," she shoved five dollars in his hand, "give him that."

Taking the money, Jeremiah kissed the top of Celeste's head and got up. "Thank you, Mr. Sweeney," he said to Ashleigh as he passed, then rushed onward and out of the room in a hurry to get Ellis.

Tears continued to flow from Celeste's eyes, though her weeping ceased, and she sat upright. "I need a drink."

"Got it," Ashleigh announced, hastening toward the drink cart and pouring each of them whiskey. He returned with three glasses and sat across from Celeste and the Madame, the worry in his eyes prevalent.

Celeste took a large swig. "He came here after he failed to kill you...Esther...me, even," she murmured furiously. "That bastard wanted to hurt us."

"He fuckin' wanted somebody," Ashleigh added. "Didn' matter who, in the end, long as it was one o' us."

An odd look came to Celeste's face. "You know what I think?"

"What?" the Madame asked.

"I think he wanted to kill me. But when he got here, I was still at The Palace, and so he took my father instead."

This astounded the Madame. "What the hell would make you think that?"

"Cause it makes the most sense, Madame," Ashleigh granted. "And he wants to hurt you most of all. He can' get Tommy. But
Celeste? Shit, if I hadn' been here with ya Celeste, it mighta been
both of ya."

Very swiftly, the tears stopped, and Celeste's jaw clenched in a
rage the Madame had yet to witness in her.

"Darling?"

Still nothing. "Celeste…" Ashleigh moved beside her, his eyes
vexed.

Celeste didn't respond directly. Instead, she threw back her
whiskey, and rotated to face the Madame. "I want to see Thomas."

It was a complicated task, playing the middleman, and yet Strat
was sure he'd started to get the hang of it.

He was on his way to meet the Vigilante at their given spot,
some old negro doctor's home in Chinatown, a place Strat understood he was an unwelcome trespasser. Still, the Vigilante had giv-
en him convincing assurances that the chinks knew he was here,
and that as long as he was gone within the hour, they didn't give a
damn. In his usual way, Walsh gave strict instructions on what to
share and what not to share as the Whyos primed their next move,
a strike that no one would imagine was possible; the scale of it was
beyond anything Strat could have believed. Walsh not only had recruited well, but also had deep pockets, pockets he was using to build
his "grand finale," as he called it, a plan every Whyo greatly anticipated on the horizon.

Everyone but Strat.

His original charge as the "snitch" to the Vigilante was procured
by himself, Walsh, and the rest of the head table, but with Kitty gone
and Walsh ready to unleash hell wherever he could, Strat was grow-

ing nervous. This enterprise he'd signed onto was evolving, evolving from a hoard of street gangs into a cause, with the sole purpose of unleashing anarchy on New York. Sure, they owned the majority of brothels, saloons, and opium dens south of Midtown, and no copper would dare cross a Whyo, yet that was not their purpose, according to Walsh. In Walsh's eyes, the Whyos had a bigger purpose, a calling…and that calling was destruction.

Up ahead, Strat saw the Vigilante on the porch of the house, seated at the rickety, small table, a chair vacant and a whiskey glass full and ready for him. Strat approached, saluting him with a quick nod, then hopped up the steps to join him. Before he sat, the Vigilante stood up, motioning for Strat to head inside the house.

"Better I'm inside," he said firmly.

Grabbing his whiskey from the table, Strat did as requested, walking through the open door and over the threshold of the house. As the door swung shut behind the Vigilante, Strat realized he'd made an enormous mistake.

Sitting in a chair just ten feet from him was the most beautiful woman he'd ever seen. She wore a beautiful, deep purple gown, a glittering black shawl, and her shining blonde hair was piled up on top of her head. Her blue eyes were darkened with liner, and her lips were a deep red. In her hands was a full glass of whiskey, and she had one leg crossed over the other, staring at him as if he were an inconvenience.

"Hello, Strat."

The Vigilante thrust a chair behind Strat, and placing both hands on Strat's shoulders, the Vigilante sat him down brusquely.

"What the hell is this?" Strat asked, revolving to the Vigilante. "We are supposed to be meeting in private!"

"This is private," she answered, her voice cold. "We are going to have a conversation, you and I, and you will either leave this house and do as I say, or I will kill you."

Strat let out a sneer. "You will kill me?"

Her head tilted to the side. "Is that so difficult for you to understand?"

"Look, I don't know what the fuck is—"

In a flash, her skirt lifted, her movements like a blur. She drew. She threw. And for the briefest instant, Strat thoroughly believed he was about to die.

The Vigilante caught the handle of the blade, the point of it not two inches from Strat's forehead, and Strat was frozen in terror as he stared at the tip of the dagger.

Her eyes went to the Vigilante, amused. "Evidently, Strat, your friend would like to keep you alive."

"W-w-what do you w-want?" was all he could manage to spit out.

She eyed him maliciously, downed her entire whiskey, and set her empty glass aside.

"What do I want?" she pondered aloud, floating dangerously his direction, halting when she was within an arm's reach. "You will do exactly as I ask, or like I mentioned, you will die."

Holding her hand out and to the side toward the Vigilante, he replaced the blade back into her hand, much to Strat's horror.

"You will turn to our side, you will stop giving information to Walsh, and you'll tell us the fucking truth about what the Whyos are up to."

"And what if I…what if I don't?"

Taking one step forward, and then another, she sat down on Strat's lap, straddling him. Gradually, she moved the blade up to his jugular and held it there, pressing just enough to nick the skin as an ominous grin came to her face.

"Then I'll kill you the way he killed my father. Horribly. Painfully. And without an ounce of pity. Because, my dear Strat, if you work for a man like Walsh, you don't deserve mercy. And I am certainly not going to fucking show you any." She pressed the knife just a touch harder, her eyes emotionless.

"Care to test me?"

CHAPTER XLV.

There were very few circumstances that made Esther nervous. This, however, was giving her more trepidation than she'd bargained for.

She'd spent nearly a quarter of an hour smoking cigarettes in front of her old apartment building in Midtown, a place that, while familiar, seemed like the distant memory of a dream rather than somewhere she'd called home for a short time. When the Madame confessed she not only knew where Grace was but also that the Madame had essentially nursed Grace back to health and then got her situated with a decent living, Esther was dumbfounded. Without thinking, Esther had sworn to Mary she would find Grace, believing the task would be a long, drawn-out escapade taking months of research, digging, and chasing a ghost. Instead, within days of returning to New York, Esther was now standing next to her old stoop, taking a last drag of her tobacco as she shook her head, still unable to believe the lengths to which the Madame would go to take care of her own.

Esther had tailed Grace for two days, getting an idea of her schedule and her whereabouts, and as usual, the Madame had been correct when it came to Grace's profession: she owned her own bakery and made a damn good sourdough loaf. So good, Esther took three loaves home for the Turners and Hiro. In the afternoons, Grace would take a walk through the city streets, buying ingredients for dinner, and return to her apartment for wine and a meal. Her day would end with a half hour or so on her violin. Esther saw that when she played, Grace would always have tears streaming down her face, and Esther couldn't help but wonder why Grace would play if it caused her so much pain.

The densely clouded sky was growing darker as the afternoon hour grew late, and Esther decided one more cigarette and she would at last have the courage to deliver Mary's letter. Reaching into her pocket, she grabbed one along with her timber, her hands numb from the cold, and with one strike her tobacco was lit. With a long exhale of smoke, Esther's nerves started to subside when she heard the window two floors above her open. She glanced up to see a woman around Mary's age staring down at her, smiling; she had dark blonde hair that fell long past her shoulders, a soft, warm face, and a shawl wrapped over her shoulders. In that moment, Esther realized she was looking directly at Grace, who apparently recognized Esther was there to see her, and as her smile widened, Grace waved at her to come upstairs.

"Well, shit," Esther uttered under her breath. "So much for staying fucking hidden."

She dropped her cigarette to the ground and put it out with the toe of her laced boot. When she peered up again, Grace had disappeared back inside with the window closed, and as a rush of ice-cold winter wind hit her cheeks, Esther shuffled her way up the stoop and through the door of the building. She took her time climbing the main stairs, grinning to herself as she noticed the all too familiar candlewax coating the bannister from the rickety and aged candle chandelier overhead. Anxiously, Esther's hand slipped into her pocket to feel for Mary's letter, the envelope softened after traveling over an ocean in Esther's possession, and she wondered just what sort of reaction Grace might have upon reading the contents. It was sealed—Mary knew Esther all too well, and therefore Esther assumed whatever it was she wanted to say to her friend was incredibly personal, and more than likely extremely difficult to articulate on paper.

The door to her old apartment was cracked open as Esther reached the top of the stairs, and walking forward, she halted in front of the doorway and knocked on the frame gently.

"Hi...uh...Grace? Is that you?"

There was a trudge of footsteps, a slight pause, and then the door flew open.

"Hi," Grace greeted quietly. "P-please, come in."

She took a large step back and gestured for Esther to step inside, and as she complied, Esther felt her entire mouth fill with saliva when she smelled the roast cooking in Grace's tiny stove. The apartment was completely redecorated, resembling a small family home, and while sparsely adorned, still managed to uphold the sensation of welcome, warmth, and comfort Esther recalled Mary provided for her and Thomas when they were young. There was a decently sized, round wooden table with four chairs, dinner set for two on the table with wine already poured, and an old tabby cat lingering near the far window where she sipped on a small bowl of milk. The stove was in the far left corner, with a small sitting area by the fireplace, and on a small set of shelves to her right, Esther spotted Grace's violin and sheet music, the sight of it causing her to bite her lip in sorrow.

"May I...I...take your jacket?" Grace asked politely.

Esther nodded. "Thank you, Grace." She pulled her arms out of her sleeves and allowed her hostess to hang her coat on the hat rack. "Did you know I was coming?"

Grace hung Esther's duster, then turned back around. "The Madame...she sent word...to expect you." Clearing her throat, Grace went to one of the chairs at the table and pulled it out for Esther. "I made a...a lamb roast."

Jaw dropping, Esther gaped at her. "Grace, no! Lamb?! That is far too expensive of a treat, I could never—"

She scoffed, spinning around and pacing toward the stove. "I don't...don't get guests. And I wanted lamb." Checking the oven, Grace peered to Esther over her shoulder. "Wine is...is quite good, I think."

Lowering down into her chair, Esther grabbed her glass of wine and took a sip. "Oh Grace, it's brilliant." She had another gulp. "Probably the best wine I've had in ages!"

"Good." Closing the stove, Grace walked to the table and sat beside Esther. "The lamb needs...just a bit longer. But I've got a great loaf, right here." She pushed a bowl toward Esther filled with buttered, sliced bread, and after a brief moment of hesitation, Esther grabbed a slice. The pair of them ate and finished their first glasses of wine before Esther brought out Mary's letter, and as she did so, Esther saw Grace's eyes grow wide.

"Mary wanted me to give you this." Placing the letter on the table, Esther slid it to Grace, whose stare was locked on the envelope.

"From Mary?"

"Yes."

Grace's fingertips went to the letter, but they didn't pull it out of Esther's grip just yet. "What...what does it...say, Esther?"

"I do not know," with a small chuckle, Esther gazed into Grace's eyes. "Mary knows I'm a little snoop. She sealed it."

This caused Grace's countenance to light up. "She always talked about how...how clever...you were. And how...how beautiful you were. A shooting star in her life. She...she always wanted a...a daughter. I am...am so happy she got one."

Esther felt her heart ache. "She talked about me? When you two were together?"

"Of course she...she did. She was so...Mary worried all the time...hated that woman. What was her name?"

"Catherine?"

"Yes. Hated her."

"We all did."

The room went silent for a few seconds, the letter unmoving. "Is...is Tommy...did he..."

"Thomas is now Lord Thomas Turner of Amberleigh," Esther declared proudly, filling their wine glasses. "He is everything Mary could have ever hoped for, and so much like his gr—" Esther caught herself and cleared her throat. "So much like his father, it's incredible."

A knowing expression came to Grace's face. "Grandmother," she said softly.

"What?"

"You can say...you can say grandmother. I know she...she is... Mary's mother."

"How in the hell did you know that?" Esther asked.

Grace smirked. "The left...left eyebrow. Mary's would always... raise when she was deep in...in thought. The Madame is no...no different."

Esther tried to disguise the fact that she had never noticed that trait, and the realization hit her like a train. "It's strange. To know their secret after all this time, and to suddenly grasp the similarities both big and small." She had a sip of wine. "Are you going to take the letter?"

"Perhaps." Grace mirrored Esther with a drink of her own wine. "I've been working hard to...to learn to speak again. It's taken... taken time, but I'm improving all the...the time."

"Did you stop speaking at Blackwell?" Esther inquired earnestly.

"No, it was before…when I…I saw what happened to my children…it was as if my whole…brain reset. I could understand what was said to…to me but couldn't…couldn't answer."

This struck Esther. "Is that why you were sent to Blackwell?"

"Yes, yes it was." Grace had a large gulp of her drink. "Do you want to…to know the truth?"

She hesitated. "Only if you want to tell me."

For a few seconds, Grace didn't speak. Then she went on. "In any other…circumstance…I would refrain. But I feel that I…I owe Mary an explanation. If you would be so…so kind to relay it to her."

"I absolutely will."

Another gulp of wine. "When the war happened, my…my former husband and…and I were…very much in love. I was…devoted to him. He came home and he…he was suffering. Wounded…not on his body but…but in his mind. There were good days and bad days. On the good days, we…we made the most of it, and he…he would always be so…so sorry he couldn't control it. Wanted to. And I…I believed it. I do think he…he really wanted to be his…his old self he…he just couldn't."

When her story ceased, Esther could see the pain in Grace's face. "I think I heard you had three children?"

"We did. There were…three boys. We…we loved them so much. But then the…the rage came, and I took it. I thought…thought if he just went…after me he would…would leave the boys alone. And for some time…he did."

Esther could feel her stomach knotting. "When did it happen?"

"I was at work. I…I came home and…all three of the boys… Jack was seven, Teddy four, and Harrington two. I walked into the… the kitchen and he as at the table crying. Said everything went black he…he just got so angry…and when he finally spit it out, I just… I snapped." Grace took a deep inhale, then let it go. "He'd drowned them. Son of a bitch was…was sitting at the table with his gun…

654

he was…was going to kill himself. So I did it…for him. He ran from me…can you believe that? It didn't matter to…to me anymore. I gunned him down…in front of the house. And then I…I sat down and waited for the coppers. I couldn't…couldn't make myself go and see…I think I…I would have shot myself if…if I…if I had."

"Grace I'm…I am so, so sorry."

"There is nothing to…to be sorry for, Esther," Grace replied sincerely. "This was…a lifetime ago. And their murder was…was just the beginning of the…real nightmare."

"Blackwell?"

"Blackwell."

They needed more wine, and Esther poured it. "I am privy to the horrors of day-to-day life from Mary, but it would be interesting to hear your perspective on those final weeks when you nearly died?"

"Well, the…the nurse…Nurse Montell. She'd gone off the… the rails—almost killed Mary. Nurse Finley and…and the doctor… Christ, they were sure she—she wouldn't make it through…the night. Bethany was devastated…and I…well…I had a habit of… of sneaking out. You and I are…two peas in a pod, honey. I was… I was irate. Mary was the…the best of us. I wasn't going to let that… that horrible woman win. So she…she fell down some stairs. And I…I made sure she…she didn't get back up."

"I would have done the same thing," Esther admitted honestly. "And then? Mary said somehow Croker found out and put the three of you in the dungeon?"

"Nurse Finley was…was put on leave. We were…were put in isolation…I didn't…didn't crack. Neither did Mary…I think Bethany…Bethany was scared. Out of the blue we…we were in the dungeon for…for weeks. They wanted us to…to die. Barely fed us. Kept us…heavily drugged. Poor Bethany, she…she had a fever and we… we couldn't help. Mary would have been…next. The celestial… he was like an angel. He kept trying to…to find a way to take me.

655

He was…distraught to leave. I made him go…I told him he…he had to save her. And I am…am so glad he did."

"The Madame told me she got you and Nurse Finley out a short time later?" Esther pressed.

"Within days, I was…was being picked up by a…very large Frenchman…and taken into the Madame's care. I think Nurse Finley is…is in Chicago."

Their conversation lulled, and Esther studied Grace closely. "What is it about Mary's letter that you are afraid of?"

A small, sad grin came to Grace's lips. "It is not fear. It is…sadness. A sadness I…I wish I could explain better."

"Believe me, Grace, with what you have endured, sadness seems appropriate." Esther finished her wine. "You really should read it. Mary was so adamant I find you, and I was under the impression I had a long journey ahead to make that a reality. She will be so thrilled when I write to her tomorrow, really. It was the only thing she's ever asked of me."

Grace sighed, her fingers seizing the letter from the table and then opening the envelope. The tabby cat reappeared, hopping into Grace's lap as she pulled out the note, and proceeded to hand it over to Esther.

"Could you…read it for me, honey? I can't…can't remember…since it happened."

Immediately, Esther was embarrassed. "Oh shit! Of course! Yes, here, I'll read it aloud now.

My Amazing Grace,

I hope that this letter and Esther find you well.

I want to apologize to you, Grace, because I never had the chance to tell you from the bottom of my heart how much you meant to me, and how your friendship kept me alive during our time together at Blackwell. Literally. I was haunted for many years by Blackwell, by the

horrible things done to us, and suffered immense guilt knowing I was
saved and you and Bethany were not spared. I am hoping with every
ounce of my being you have overcome the tragedies of your life and
have found some kind of contentment.

I would like to ask you, Grace, if you would have any interest in
a venture to England, and if so, I will happily wire the money to you
as quickly as I can. Only ask and you shall receive.

Please send along with Esther an account of your life and, again,
perhaps an answer to my request to have you as my guest at Amberleigh.

I send you all the love I have.

Yours & etc.,
Mary

Esther glanced up from the page to see tears streaming down Grace's cheeks.

"Amberleigh?"

"Yes. That is our home."

Giving the cat a few scratches on his head, Grace nodded. "What is it like?"

"It is beautiful," Esther said. "Unlike any place I've ever seen."

"I imagine it is." She placed the purring cat on the floor and got to her feet. "I can smell that the…lamb is done. Dinner, and then we…we will talk about what you're going to…write to Mary."

"You mean that you're coming to Amberleigh?" Esther pushed on her.

She let out a small scoff. "Amberleigh."

There were pot holders on her hands, and then Grace pulled the lamb out of the oven. "What would I…do about…work?"

"Grace, there are over twenty rooms you could stay in. I think Mary would see to it you didn't need to worry about that."

"I see."

When Grace returned, she had the roast lamb with her on a wooden pallet along with a giant carving knife as well as a giant bowl of rosemary russet potatoes. "I will make you a...a deal, honey."

"All right."

The food was set on the table. "I will go, but I want to...to meet Mary's son. I heard so...so much about him...I feel as if he...he is my own boy, too."

Esther's throat tightened. "He would be honored to meet you, Grace."

"Good," she replied with a smile. "Now, eat up. You need a little...little more meat on those bones if...you're going to keep...taking on Richard."

Alarmed, Esther froze. "Who told you such a thing?"

Another smile. "Doesn't matter. Eat. I'll go grab us a...another bottle of wine."

By the time Esther was back at the Turners', dinner had only just passed, and she hoped she would find Thomas, Lucy, and William either wrapping up dessert or in the great room downing brandy. The latter seemed to be the case, and she was welcomed to join the party with open arms and salutations as Tony trotted off to grab her a brandy glass. They were seated by the fire, Lucy and William on one sofa, Thomas on the other, and as Esther sank down beside Thomas, she noticed an odd expression on William's face.

"Did I miss something?" she asked, her eyes finding Lucy's.

"You most certainly did, Esther dear," Lucy told her. "William and I were finally told about Tony's connection to the Madame's bodyguard! And I must say, it gave William quite the shock."

He glared at her. "I did not...I was not bloody shocked, woman. I was surprised, just as you were."

Esther whipped around to Thomas. "You told them?!"

Laughing aloud, Thomas shook his head. "Hiroaki let it slip. He was at it with Mrs. Shannon again and complaining to Tony. Said something about sticking his brother on her. Then he had to explain to everyone what in the hell he was talking about, and now Lucy is tickled at the fact that she didn't spot it earlier."

"They look identical!" she exclaimed, her arms reaching out wide as a little brandy spilled out of her glass. "For God's sake, if Louis wasn't bald, I would have known ages ago!"

"Bullshit!" William retorted playfully. "How would we ever have guessed? Esther, I swear Eddie told me Louis died in that goddamn fire. How was I to know Tony's brother lived and breathed?!"

"No wonder Tony ran off so quickly to find me a brandy," Esther quipped with a smirk. "What was happening with Mrs. Shannon and Hiroaki?"

Lucy rolled her eyes. "He was on a covert mission to find William's whiskey."

This caused Esther to chuckle and peer at Thomas. "He wanted to get caught, eh?"

"Of course," Thomas responded, smiling at her and taking her hand.

"Bloody wait a moment," William interjected. "He wanted to be caught?"

Thomas gave Esther's hand a squeeze and then turned his attention to William. "William, do you really think the man who has trained me and Esther would ever be caught by Mrs. Shannon if he didn't want to be?"

"Well...she is a...a hawk, that one."

Lucy snorted. "William, don't be ridiculous." She took a gulp of brandy. "Esther, how was your visit?"

659

All three of them stared at her eagerly.

"I am not sure it could have gone better," Esther admitted, just as Tony returned and handed her a full brandy glass. She thanked him with a salute and took a large sip. "Strangely, I found I was nervous before I finally got to meet her face-to-face."

"Nervous?" William questioned her.

"Why on earth would you be nervous?" Lucy asked.

"Because I..." she paused, "I really can't be sure. I think a multitude of reasons, most notably that it is the one and only thing Mary has ever asked of me, and I didn't want to fuck it up."

Thomas lifted up her hand and kissed it. "You never would have."

"Did she read the letter?" Lucy went on.

"She did."

"And?"

"And," Esther declared, "I believe Mary's message was delivered. There is one hang-up. Thomas, she wants to meet you."

From his countenance, Esther could tell he was delighted. "Just tell me when, and I will be there."

Out of the blue, the bell rang at the house, and Tony took off from his post in the corner toward the front lobby. The four of them glimpsed at one another, wondering who might be calling at such an hour, with both Thomas and Esther on high alert, listening intently for any noises from the front door. Instead, within seconds, Ashleigh appeared in the doorway, weary.

Esther instantly knew. "Is she all right?"

His answer was not comforting: "I need ya to come with me, Es."

After setting his brandy glass down, Thomas was on his feet. "Ash, what is it? Celeste? The Madame?"

"Celeste," he said. "She ain' doin' so good."

"How bad is it?" Esther pressed.

"We oughta get goin'."

"Fuck," Esther hissed, turning to Thomas. "I could tell she's been in bad shape. I should have known better."

"Give me three minutes and I'll come with you," Thomas declared. "Tony? Can you please lock—"

"I will help lock the house, Thomas," came Hiroaki's voice from their right. In the doorway to the servant's passage stood Hiro, a small glass of whiskey in his hand and a smile once his eyes found Esther's. "She was alive?"

"Alive, and told me you tried to save her, too."

"I am happy to hear her fate took a turn for the better." Hiro then gazed to Ashleigh. "Young man, you are Mr. Sweeney's son?"

"Ah...yeah. Sure thing, sir." He studied Hiroaki. "You the bastard that trained these two?"

"Yes," Hiro answered. "And Thomas's father before him."

"Well...shit..."

"Thomas?" Esther whispered.

"On it." Within seconds, he and Tony disappeared past Hiroaki and down the back hallway.

"Already got brass in case we hit trouble?" Ashleigh questioned.

"Of course," she replied, marching to him. "What did she take?"

"Whatever the hell she keeps on hand...ya know, for calmin' nerves of the people she's meetin' and shit."

Esther whipped towards Hiroaki. "Opium, Hiro."

A pained appearance, then Hiro looked beyond Esther at Ashleigh. "How many days?"

"Three, sir. I told her I could understand one, ya know, dealin' with the pain, but she's not herself and I...I can' be the one to..."

But Hiroaki was already peering back to Esther. "Water. Tea. Lemon. To knock her out of her high, you will plunge her into an ice bath. Her withdrawal will be a lot on her body. Fever, shaking, the sort. I do not have Akemi's remedies with me, however, I do know the Madame has knowledge of this as we do."

"Ashleigh, we'll head straight to the hotel," Esther directed, spinning toward William and Lucy. "I am so, so sorry. Can we continue tomorrow?"

Lucy beamed at her. "Go take care of Celeste. She needs you, and we have all the brandy we could ask for!"

With a wink from William, Esther paced to the front lobby, finding her coat hanging by the door, Ashleigh at her heels.

"How bad is it, Ashleigh?" she asked. "We had plans to see each other tomorrow, for God's sake. I was trying to give her some space to grieve."

"Ain' nobody's fault, Es. She is just hurtin' and don' know what to do. It could be worse, I just…well…to be honest with ya, I just don' want her gettin' addicted, ya know? Them drugs is a slippery slope, I saw it with my momma. They don' solve no problems."

"No, no they don't." She pulled her jacket on and put her hand on Ashleigh's shoulder. "Look, Ashleigh, I know you love her. Thank you for coming to me and telling me."

"Well, she don' exactly know I'm here."

"What?"

"Yeah."

"I mean, I am flattered Ashleigh, but why me?" Esther pressed. "Why not Jeremiah? He could at least help her and get her some medicine!"

"Pretty sure girl don' need more medicine," Ashleigh replied. "And I came to get ya 'cause you're her fuckin' sister, that's why."

Because she trusts you, darling, that's why. And she doesn't trust anyone else.

Suddenly, Thomas was beside them, dressed far more casually than he'd been a few minutes prior. "Ready?"

"No soot, eh?" Ashleigh inquired.

"Not on house calls. Esther?"

"Let's go."

The three of them found a cab in no time and, once inside,

Esther was lost in thought, deliberating over how on earth she'd missed the signs Celeste was in such a state. She'd been home a matter of days, only to have her best friend's father murdered the very night of her return, and somehow, Celeste managed to convince Esther what she needed was to mourn the loss of Douglas. Diligently, Esther gave Celeste that to her, making plans for four days later to spend an afternoon catching up. While she hated to admit it, Douglas wouldn't be the last of Walsh's victims from their syndicate, especially when it came to the people they loved who were only secondarily involved in the war. They needed to be more cautious—the stakes were getting higher with every passing second.

Be careful. He is out looking for you. I know you can feel it.

Esther reached into her jacket pocket and pulled out a cigarette and matches. Upon lighting her tobacco and taking a long drag, she looked over to Thomas and Ashleigh, both of whom were watching her intently.

She exhaled smoke, "What is it?"

"Ya look like ya might murder one o' us if we get too close to ya," Ashleigh remarked, studying her.

"You okay, Es?" Thomas asked.

Taking another drag, she shook her head. "Of course I am not fucking okay. My best friend has been drugging the shit out of herself for the last three days and I had no idea."

"Like I said, she don' know I went to get ya. I think she was under the impression she just needed a day or two to relax, and instead, she's takin' more and more."

"Is she conscious?" Thomas inquired, motioning for one of Esther's cigarettes, and she obliged with a smile.

"Coherent, yeah."

As Hiro suspected. "Right. Well, I can promise you it won't be pretty. You two will follow my lead, all right?"

It wasn't exactly a request, yet they agreed. They rode the

carriage the rest of the way in silence, Esther smoking another two cigarettes while Thomas and Ashleigh joined her, their cab filling with smoke, and still not one of them cared, distracted by their stress. By the time they reached St. Stephen, the hour was late, and Esther was almost nauseated by inhaling so much secondhand tobacco. The fresh, freezing air of the night was a welcome reprieve as they paid and abandoned the coach, heading straight through the lobby with a polite hello to Mrs. Ryder.

You need more hands on deck.

At the door to the Hiltmores' rooms, Esther halted and took a breath. "Ashleigh, go find Molly and have her make some tea—a lot of it. Thomas, you will see to it a bath is drawn and filled with cold water as fast as they can."

"How cold?"

Ice cold.

"Put ice in it."

"Fuck. All right."

Esther reached up and grabbed the handle, then thrust the door open. Inside Celeste's rooms, everything seemed perfectly normal at first glance, and therefore Esther went straight for her bedroom and discovered Celeste seated at her vanity, a glass of water in one hand and a dropper completely filled in the other. Peeking over her shoulder, she watched as Ashleigh and Thomas went straight for the maid's passage, and once gone, Esther focused on Celeste, who had yet to perceive her presence. When at last Celeste spotted Esther in her doorway, she grinned, her eyes completely glazed over and pupils dilated large from ingesting opium.

"Esther!" she cried happily. "I am so delighted you are here." Celeste slowly peered back to her water and dropper, recalling what it was she was about to do. "Give me just…one moment! I need to take my medicine, and then we can have our afternoon together!"

"Celeste, that is not until tomorrow."

Her friend squeezed the dropper's contents into the water glass. "Oh, I am so sorry! I have been occupied so much lately I must have lost track of time…" Celeste's voice trailed off as she placed the dropper back into her large, glass vial of liquid opium. Once secured, Celeste moved the vial aside and grabbed onto the water glass, about to down the contents.

Esther, however, had another plan, and took three lurching steps forward, snatching the glass out of Celeste's hand.

"What are you doing?!" Celeste exclaimed in surprise.

"Getting you fucking sober," Esther hissed, marching to the window and unlocking it.

Before Celeste could actually comprehend what was happening, Esther had the window open and tossed the glass of water out, dumping the contents. She then proceeded to return and grasp onto the vial, which Celeste reached for and missed, too high to be accurate in anything she was doing. Back to the window she went, and out of anger, Esther cracked the bottom of the vial open against the side of the brick building, sending the opium and a few shards of glass down to the back alley below.

"Esther!" Celeste bellowed. "What are you doing?!"

The sound of shuffling emerged from the other room, signaling that Ashleigh and Thomas had returned with reinforcements.

"You've been high for three fucking days," Esther spat, tossing the remainder of the vial out the window before locking it shut. "I am not allowing you to get addicted to opium, and neither is Ashleigh. So, we're having a goddamn intervention."

Celeste made an attempt to appear offended. "Addicted?! For God's sake, Esther I just…lost my father! Can't you let me mourn in my own way?"

She's not fucking healing and she knows it. It's a goddamn distraction.

"Numbing yourself isn't healing, Celeste! The minute you come back to having a clear head, the pain will hit all over again, and no amount of opium will fix that!" She crossed her arms over her chest while Celeste sat pitifully at her vanity. A thought occurred to her: "What would she say, if she saw you right now?"

A wave of shame hit Celeste, though she tried to mask it. "Who are you referring to?"

Esther took a few steps to her. "You know who the fuck I am talking about."

Instantly, Celeste's face fell. "Please, please don't tell her…I was doing so well…"

"Celeste," Esther eased, dropping to her knees and taking her friend's hands in hers, "no one is telling the Madame anything. Unless you start taking opium again."

"But I…I need it…" Her eyes were far away.

"No, darling, you don't," Esther told her.

Get her in the fucking bath.

Releasing Celeste's hands, Esther made her way to the doorway and peeked out into the living room to spot Ashleigh and Molly, each carrying a tray of tea and lemon tarts.

"Where is Thomas?" Esther asked hurriedly.

"Bath is nearly ready, Miss Esther," Molly answered for him, a sympathetic smile on her face. "Please let me know if I can do anything, really."

Esther could tell she meant it. "I am grateful for you, Molly, and so is Celeste. We are good for now, but thank you."

In the next second, Thomas appeared from the adjacent rooms. "Her…uh…wake-up has been prepared."

Send them north. This is going to be rough.

"Molly, head home for the night. Ashleigh, Thomas, take the bottle of whiskey on the drink cart and go straight to The Palace. Send Marcy down immediately and wait for me there."

Thomas was concerned. "You don't want me to stay?"

Esther glanced to the comatose Celeste, who had yet to move

from where she was and was swaying faintly from side to side. Esther's eyes again went back to Thomas.

"To be fair, I don't think she wants you to be here for this."

"You can handle her?"

There was no condescension in his question, only trepidation. It was sometimes so elevating to feel how much he loved her, even in a time like this.

"I've got it, Thomas."

With a nod, he grabbed the whiskey bottle and took Ashleigh by the arm, who initially protested and quickly conceded, not daring to try to pick a fight with Thomas when he'd made his mind up. *Just like me.* When they reached the door, Thomas shoved Ashleigh through it and spun back, mouthed an "I love you" to Esther, then shut the door behind him. In the meantime, Molly disappeared down the maid's stair, leaving Esther and Celeste alone.

"Fuck," she said to herself, and took a deep breath.

Bath. Hydrate. Food. Wine.

"She is so dazed, I don't even know if this will work."

Marcy will send something. You just caught her before another fucking dose and cut her supply. Get her ass in the bath, Esther.

"And what if she fights me?"

We both know how that will fucking go.

Letting out a heavy exhale, Esther focused on Celeste, who continued to sit while facing the opposite direction of Esther, softly humming to herself, higher than Esther had ever seen her previously.

"Celeste?" Esther initiated, lightly stepping toward her and kneeling at her friend's side. "Celeste, I am going to help make you feel better!"

Her mien brightened. "You got more?"

Well, for Christ's sake, you set yourself up for that one.

"No, Celeste, no more opium. Why don't you come with—"

The delight rapidly became irritation. "I want my...my vial. What have you done with it?!"

"There is no more opium, Celeste," Esther vainly attempted to smooth over. "Come with me and take my hand, I am going to make it all feel better."

"No!" Celeste cried, pulling herself upright and away from Esther. "Give me my vial!"

Grab her.

Esther straightened up. "Goddammit, Celeste, just trust me!"

"No!"

Esther, do you really want to negotiate with a toddler all fucking night? Throw her ass in the bath!

"Fine," Esther hissed under her breath.

With determination, Esther paced to Celeste and crouched down, grabbing her around the waist and throwing Celeste over her shoulder. Esther stood, Celeste's writhing and efforts to break free almost humorous to Esther as she spun around and left Celeste's bedroom, taking her directly to the ice bath. As Celeste struggled, striking Esther's back with very little force and kicking her legs about, Esther hoped with every ounce of her being that Celeste would forgive her for this. Upon reaching her bathing suite, Esther flipped Celeste around to hold her in her arms, and before Celeste could even realize what was about to happen, Esther simply released her, dropping Celeste directly into the bath of cold water fully clothed.

That's better.

Celeste's entire body dunked into the freezing water, her head plunging below the surface. When she breached, she let out a shriek of shock, though as she made to leave the bath, Esther was there to stop her, placing her hands on Celeste's arms and holding her in the tub.

"Let me out!" Celeste screamed. "It hurts!"

"Well, at least now you can fucking feel something!" Esther yelled back.

"I want out! Let me out!"

"You will swear to me on the life of Jeremiah you will never do fucking opium again!" Esther shouted menacingly. "You are not getting out of this goddamn tub until you do!"

It was faint, but Esther could see the life returning to her friend's eyes. "Esther, let go of me this fucking instant!"

"Swear to me, Céleste!"

The blue was starting to sparkle once more. "I…I can't think… it's so fucking cold…"

Do it.

"No," Esther uttered.

Do it!

Reluctantly, Esther bit her lip, and then slapped Celeste hard across the cheek. "Snap out of it, Celeste! Swear to me on Jeremiah you won't do fucking opium again!"

The surprise of Esther's blow seemed to snap Celeste's wits about her. "Yes! I swear it! On Jeremiah!"

"That you'll never do opium again?"

"That I'll never do opium again!"

"And if you do, I will actually beat the hell out of you, even if you are my sister?"

"Esther, just let me out of the fucking bath!"

I think that's good.

Thrusting her forearms beneath Celeste's armpits, Esther hoisted Celeste up and out of the tub, dragging her to the floor, where an abundance of towels awaited them. Her actions fast, Esther got Celeste out of her soaking wet clothes and wrapped her tightly in towels. Celeste's entire body was trembling, and so Esther proceeded to wrap herself around her friend, hoping the heat from her own body would help to warm Celeste's. They sat on the floor of the

669

bathing suite for some time, Celeste's naked, shivering body enveloped with towels and Esther holding her tight, not sure of what to say next. When the shaking ceased, Esther didn't let go, only waited to hear if Celeste had anything she wanted to contribute.

"Es?"

Her tone was clear, and Esther hugged her tighter. "There you are."

"Jesus fucking Christ. I need some water."

"Well, I've got a shit ton of tea in the other room waiting, and lemon tarts. Have you eaten at all the last three days?"

"Barely."

Ask again.

She knew she had to. "Celeste, do you swear to me you won't do this again?"

"Why? So you can toss me into another fucking ice bath? No way in hell."

Fucking miracle.

This caused Esther to smile. "Good."

"Es, can you go grab me some…um…"

"Clothes. Right. On it."

A half an hour later, both women were seated by the fire, Celeste wrapped up in multiple layers, still chilled to the bone, and Esther beside her on the couch. They were each having a glass of wine as Esther force-fed Celeste as much tea as she could stand, although convincing her to consume half a dozen lemon tarts took no work whatsoever. The conversation stayed light-hearted until Celeste's color returned to her cheeks, at which point Esther turned the discussion to the issue at hand.

"Why didn't you tell me you were using?"

Celeste averted her gaze. "I don't…use. I've kept it to…well, in case of emergencies. With clients."

"And so you just decided to take opium nonstop for three days out of nowhere?" Esther pressed, unconvinced. "I don't believe it."

"No, no." Celeste finished her wine. "I've been using it to sleep. It helps me calm down. And when you left after the funeral I...I felt like I was...sinking. I was in so much pain and I couldn't control it..." Tears began to stream from Celeste's eyes. "I saw that bastard kill my father! I can't ever unsee that!"

Esther clutched Celeste's hand. "I know, Celeste. I am so, so sorry."

"I know you are," she sobbed. "I thought if I could just have a day, a day or two, and recover and sleep, I would be fine! I hadn't slept since the night he was murdered. And then I just—I didn't feel anything anymore, and I didn't want to hurt. So I kept dosing."

"Ashleigh came to find me," Esther confessed to her. "Something to remember, I believe his own mother went through a similar... uh...situation. She did not recover, as you are aware."

News of this appeared to distress Celeste more. "Oh shit," she replied faintly.

"He didn't want you to fall into it like she did," Esther assured her. "It can be a slippery slope, Celeste." She squeezed her hand. "He loves you so much, I can tell."

"Well," Celeste retorted, "he is just going to have to understand he is second."

"Second?!" Esther exclaimed in surprise.

Laughing, Celeste shook her head. "Esther, you will always be first."

Her cheeks grew hot. "Oh...I...well, I didn't mean..."

"Don't be ridiculous. Pour us some wine."

A few minutes later, a knock came to the door, and Marcy arrived with three bottles of some sort of concoction wrapped up in her arms, her expression stern.

"It's going to be that bad?" Celeste asked reluctantly.

"Let's just put it this way," Marcy remarked, flopping down on the sofa opposite Celeste and Esther, "I am on orders not to leave for at least four days. Tomorrow will be pain. The next will be agony. The third? Fever. Fourth? Everything will hurt. But on the fifth, you'll wake up, and the sun will shine."

Esther motioned for Marcy to grab a clean wine glass from the drink cart, and she did just that.

"Is there any way to expedite the process?" Esther beseeched her.

"Celeste, if you listen to me, I can have you healthy in three, maybe two days," Marcy asserted, resuming her seat and pouring herself a very full glass of wine. "Can you do that?"

"Of course I can!"

"Perfect." Marcy took a sip from her glass. "Esther, she already looks better than I would have expected."

"Ice bath," Esther stated. "It was not pleasant for either of us."

Marcy was horrified. "Well, fuck me!"

Celeste chuckled, a smirk forming. "Esther, you need to get to The Palace."

"You're probably right."

"Just do me a favor?"

"Anything."

She pulled a cigarette out. "Tell Ashleigh to give me a few days."

"I can do that."

When Esther reached the door, Celeste stopped her. "Wait, Es—one more thing!"

"Yes?"

"Tell him...tell him I love him."

Grinning, Esther nodded and left the apartment.

"Well, it's about goddamn time."

By Thirty-eighth Street, Esther was certain she had made a grave error in not taking a coach.

Between the freezing temperatures, snow on the ground, and wearing multiple layers, including a scarf and one of Thomas's old bowler hats, Esther firmly believed she would pass as any young New York man, sporting her usual masculine ensemble beneath her winter duster. There were very few carriages about at such a late hour and even fewer people, making the four men tailing her easier to spot as she coasted up Second Avenue toward The Palace. To her annoyance, four became five, and five became six, meaning the moment to make a decision was closing in swiftly. Either Esther needed to hop in a coach within the next block, or she would have to turn and confront her stalkers head-on, in the hopes that the six didn't become ten or twelve.

Without a single carriage in sight, Esther thanked her lucky stars she'd brought her brass, and cursed herself in the same breath for being so naïve. Of course Walsh was watching her. He knew Thomas was the Vigilante, where they lived, that the Madame was his grandmother...he was absurdly well-versed in every single one of their secrets. He more than likely had eyes at every one of their residences, just waiting for her to show, with a handsome reward for bringing her to him alive, and probably a little less if she were brought to him dead.

Her eyes went to the crisp, clear winter sky, with the tiniest hope she might spot Athena overhead. Nothing. Nothing except the bright twinkling of stars on a moonless night. Esther took off her gloves, slipped her hands into her pockets, and wiggled the cold brass around her knuckles.

Just a few paces away, they started jeering at her: Whyos, as she anticipated. She rolled her shoulders back and turned around, cracking her neck from side to side.

"What the fuck do you want?" she hissed through her teeth, glaring at the now eight Whyos in front of her.

Marley, Berlin, Nash, and five Whyos she didn't know approached, each armed and ready to strike.

"The Assistant is alive after all!" Marley sneered, his pistol visible on his belt. "What do ya think, boys? Should we take her to Walsh in one piece?"

"Or take her apart piece by piece," Nash suggested darkly.

Berlin licked his lips. "Maybe we ought to fight her down and teach her a lesson—we could take turns, couldn't we boys? Walsh wouldn't mind if we took a little somethin' extra for catching her, and I bet she's ripe as a peach."

Her jaw clenched, burying the tinge of fear in her gut. "Fucking try, and see what happens, you sick son of a bitch."

Glancing from Nash to Berlin, Marley shrugged, unfazed. "Meh. You boys can have some fun with her if you'd like. Let's just get this over with and get her to the Bowery."

As the Whyos formed a half circle around her, Esther yanked her hands out of her pockets, her breath steaming through the air. If she could take out Nash and Berlin, then without the brothers at his side, Marley and the rest could be run off. The issue was taking on Nash and Berlin; they ran the brothels and were very used to raping and beating the hell out of their whores. No matter what happened, she couldn't get ambushed.

Drawing closer, suddenly the Whyos paused, staring beyond where Esther stood, their expressions confused. Esther peered over her shoulder and tried not to gasp in shock when she spotted Hiroaki, with Athena on his shoulder, standing not five paces behind her. He was dressed in a plain black suit and heavy winter coat, and his long black hair was pulled into a tight bun at the nape of his head.

"Aren't you a little lost there, chink?!" Nash called, pointing southeast. "Chinatown is, uh, that way!"

674

Hiroaki reached Esther's right side, and without acknowledging each other, Esther whispered, "How the hell did you find me?"

"I've been following you the entire night."

"What? Why?"

"The three of you left, and I stayed to spot a few men in pursuit. I knew you in particular would not be safe. And Athena was restless."

"What the fuck is this?!" Berlin bellowed, grabbing for his blade.

"No matter," Marley answered. "Kill the chink and grab the girl. Now."

Esther became nervous for Hiro. "You shouldn't be here."

"You should have taken a cab."

The Whyos steadily closed in, and at last, Hiroaki let Athena fly, pulling from the scabbard beneath his jacket a sword which Esther had never seen before—it was his Samurai blade, glistening in the starlight.

"Kill him!" Marley yelled, treading to the back as Nash and Berlin led the other five in their charge, blades, bludgeons, and hatchets

"Like we practiced?" Esther asked hurriedly.

"Like we practiced."

With a mutual nod at each other, Hiro and Esther glanced in the direction of their assailants, and when they were roughly two paces away, Athena let out a shriek.

The Samurai sword went high over Hiroaki's head as he lunged to the left towards Nash, and Esther tucked and rolled, somersaulting just behind his heels as he passed her by. The moment she felt the grip of her toes find the earth, Esther propelled herself upward from a crouch, brass on her knuckles, leaping up through the air toward Berlin. She pulled her right fist back, and as the momentum of her bodyweight began to meet gravity once again, Esther brought the power of her fist down onto Berlin, who haphazardly attempted to make a block. Instead, the force behind Esther's bodyweight diverted into her brass, and consequently completely shattered Berlin's left wrist as a bellow of agony echoed off of the brick walls surrounding them. Berlin collapsed down onto his hand and knees, cowering over his arm as Esther's feet met the ground. Sending a hideous scowl up at her, Esther nonchalantly kneed him in the face, knocking Berlin unconscious and onto the ground. To her left, Esther caught out of the corner of her eye Hiroaki man-handling Nash like he was bored, allowing Nash to defend two solid strikes before Hiroaki actually made his move, and seemingly without effort, Hiroaki sliced Nash's face from the corner of his eye to the nape of his neck, just shallow enough not to kill him, yet deep enough to eliminate him from battle.

While Hiro charged two more Whyos, both of whom were cowering from his sword upon seeing the profusely bleeding Nash wandering about, Esther turned to find herself being flanked by the three remaining thugs. She smirked, amused. There were two to her right, one to her left, and their eyes bounced back and forth from Esther to Hiroaki, who had just cut off the arm of one of the fleeing Whyos. It was clear the Whyos were each recognizing that this was a fight they were going to lose, and lose badly. Esther went for the two on her right first, ducking the swing of a nail-covered bludgeon from the one with an eyepatch. As he missed, Esther simultaneously sent her brass directly up under his chin with such strength Esther swore she heard the crunch of his teeth splintering, his body going airborne before slamming into the brick building behind him. The next one, who looked like he'd barely hit puberty, held a knife outward in his hand, taking a few mangled and shaky swipes at Esther. Almost rolling her eyes, Esther kicked the bottom of his hand with her right foot, disarming him instantaneously, and before he could make another move, Esther sent a roundhouse kick to his jaw with the back of her left foot. He hit the ground with a loud thud, motionless.

The final assailant saw the carnage and spun on his heels to run, but Esther wouldn't allow him an escape. She sprinted up behind him and ran him down, managing to hop up his back and wrap her thighs tight around his head, pounding her fist down just once to send the man to his knees, and two more times to break his skull. With her feet planted on the earth, Esther released his head from her legs, and he fell forward into a pool of his own blood, lifeless. Then, surprised, Esther felt the grip of two strong hands on her shoulders, and she was yanked to the ground. Nash, in spite of the gaping wound on the side of his head, managed to tackle Esther to the ground, pinning her arms out wide with his knees to restrain her brass while he wrapped his fingers tight around her throat.

"Fuck...you..." he spat through the blood covering his face.

She spotted a flash of silver as her lungs began to burn, and Hiro plunged his blade through the back of Nash, the tip sticking out through his stomach. His hands released Esther's throat, the blood escaping his lips dripping down onto Esther, and with a grimace of repulsion, she hastily slid out from under him.

"No," she uttered, watching the life leave his eyes, "fuck you, you bastard."

Nash's eyes stopped blinking, and with a nod from Esther to Hiro, he placed his foot between Nash's shoulder blades and thrust him off his sword, his body falling face down onto the street.

Suddenly, both Hiroaki and Esther heard the cock of a pistol behind them.

"I'm going to tell Walsh you pleaded for your lives," came Marley's voice. "Begged, like a fucking woman and a chink would."

"I am a woman," Esther hissed, circling around and getting to her feet, "and he is a chink."

Marley had his pistol aimed directly at them, with a battered and bloodied Berlin by his side. The barely adolescent Whyo was in their wake, retreating glacially.

Esther was enraged. "You're a goddamn coward, Marley. Shooting us when you have no one left to fucking die for you. You're as bad as he is, you son of a bitch."

"You killed Nash!" Berlin yelled at Hiro. "You don't fucking deserve to live!"

"On the contrary," Hiroaki declared, sheathing his blade, much to Esther's chagrin, "your brother did not deserve to live, and I hope his life of dishonor comes full circle."

A loud shriek rang out, and in a flash, Athena snatched the pistol out of Marley's hands and was circling overhead, the gun dangling down from her talons as if taunting him.

Esther's fingers tightened around her brass as she threateningly smiled at Marley. "I'd run, if I were you."

Marley didn't need to be told twice. He gaped at Esther for no more than a second and then whipped around, hustling as fast as his legs would take him, with Berlin and the only other living Whyo right on his heels, disappearing into the darkness.

Letting out a whistle, Hiro signaled to Athena, and within seconds, she was perched on his shoulder, releasing the gun into his hands while he rewarded her with a bit of hen breast.

"She is most valuable."

"She is a fucking life-saver," Esther concurred, putting her brass into her jacket pockets. "I honestly wasn't sure what we would do."

"It is why having a secondary is so important," he reminded her. "Next time, you will take her with you. You should ask Thomas to fly her. You know the commands."

"I'll get there," Esther replied, letting out a heavy exhale. "Why do they always go for my fucking neck?"

"It is your only weak point."

This caused Esther to grin. "I guess you are right."

"We are heading to The Palace?"

"We?" Esther exclaimed.

"I believe it is time I met this illustrious Madame."

She chuckled, shaking her head. "Well, this ought to be one hell of a night cap."

"Next time, you come in the fucking back door!" the Madame chided Esther, her eyes furious. "I don't give a shit that he is a part of the fucking Turner family, not everyone is so goddamn open minded, and I cannot have chinks just waltzing through the front door like they fucking own The Palace! And with Athena?!"

It wasn't that Esther wasn't aware of this protocol—it was just that she wanted to stir the pot and observe what would happen when Hiroaki at long last made his way into the Madame's office. Esther sat opposite her enormous desk with Hiroaki sitting by her side in the other armchair; Thomas and Ashleigh stood over by the fireplace, each fighting to keep a straight face while the Madame laid into Esther. While she knew it was impossible, Esther could swear that Athena was giving her a smug stare from her perch to the right of the Madame's throne, chomping merrily on a dehydrated hen breast as the rest of them downed their usual glass of whiskey.

Hiroaki had yet to say a word, and instead only observed the Madame with a charmed expression, his countenance calm and serene.

"Madame," Thomas cut in, walking to the drink cart for a refill, "I think the more important thing here is that Esther was ambushed, and we are lucky Hiro was there to assist in the ensuing battle." His eyes found Esther's. "You can't be out and about alone, even if Walsh does know you're alive. Croker doesn't."

"I made a mistake," Esther acknowledged, having a sip of her drink. "I won't make it again. Blame it on my thoughts being distracted elsewhere and being out of the fucking game for six months in England."

"Well, now that you've had a lesson in just how fucking volatile our little city has become," the Madame snapped, "you better be more goddamn smart. Mistakes will get us killed." She let out a heavy sigh, tossing her feet up onto her desk. "How is she?"

"It'll be a few days of hell, but she's already coming around."

"Marcy is there," Ashleigh added, moving closer to them. "Esther dumped all that shit she had. I reckon she'll dry out faster than ya think."

"You will be surprised, young Mr. Sweeney," Hiroaki spoke up. "Her mind may move beyond it, yet her body will not, and it will take at least four or five days for the fever and illness to pass, and from there, if she does not fall to temptation, Celeste will find more improvement each day. I will bring her a few herbs in the morning as well. I have already let Tony know to dispatch one of our household staff to go to the marketplace in the morning."

The room was completely silent in the aftermath of Hiroaki's words, and Esther glanced at the Madame, waiting for a response.

She did not disappoint.

"Oh, so he does fucking speak?" she jeered, her gaze fixating on Hiro. "You will apologize to my staff when you leave The Palace for causing such a ruckus on your entrance. It's a goddamn miracle I didn't have any customers in the lobby!" The Madame finished her whiskey and casually set the glass aside, reaching into the top drawer of her desk. It was a small wad of paper money, and she tossed it over to Hiro. "You will not endanger the life of some poor servant at the Turner household to run errands in Chinatown. Walsh and the Whyos have eyes on us at ever fucking turn. George and Claire will be by in the morning, and the three of you will go. George is the man from the front door who nearly shot you ten minutes ago, or do you recall?"

"I do recall, Madame."

"Good. You will also be meeting a mutual friend of ours who has insisted the two of you become acquainted."

This was news to Esther. "Who?!"

"Mock Duck," Thomas answered for the Madame. "He caught up with the Madame earlier this evening before Ashleigh and I arrived."

"I have no interest in the wars of the Chinese," Hiroaki said steadily. "They murdered my child and I was forced to fight in their war of drugs and power against the West. I will not do so a second time."

"This isn't about the fucking power struggle in Chinatown," the Madame retorted. "It is a favor I am granting because that son of a bitch is going to help us take down Croker."

"Take down Croker?" Esther asked eagerly. "How would a Chinese gangster from San Francisco know anything about the Hall?"

"Last year, Celeste encountered a man at the Admiral's Ball named Parkhurst meeting with Judge Frederick," Thomas recounted for her.

Esther was confused. "The reformer?"

"Yes," the Madame replied. "Thomas? Whiskey, if you please. Parkhurst wants to take down Tammany. Rumor has been spreading about Mock Duck's assault on Lee in Chinatown, and apparently Parkhurst is putting some kind of team together."

"A team?" Hiroaki's attention was apparently grabbed.

"They need evidence," Thomas revealed, pouring the Madame a fresh round from the decanter and then handing her glass to her. "Mock Duck could be a huge component of that if Lee does become sheriff. But he also wants us, and most particularly, you, Es."

"What could he possibly want with me?"

"You know the Whyos, and Croker's previous connection to them," the Madame divulged. "And you also know all the fucking back door businesses Croker has under his belt and could expose those."

"Yeah, and it would be my word against his. That wouldn't get us very far."

"It's not about that," Thomas continued. "It's about how Parkhurst wants to present the case. He wants to show how corrupt Tammany still is, how it is toxic to the city in so many ways. You could show him how deep the depravity runs, and from there, he will decide how to present that to an investigatory committee. There's some senator that's backing him—used to be a Swallowtail."

"But first," the Madame interrupted, "we need Priestly. Alive. He will be an additional character witness. We'll get Will and Louis out of New York, and keep our hopes we can find this McCann bastard as the final missing piece."

"We have five days until the hit, correct?" Esther inquired.

"Right. Croker was adamant it be before Christmas," Thomas informed her.

The Madame and Esther simultaneously scoffed, then laughed together.

"He's such a fucking bastard," the Madame asserted. "I just cannot wait to see the look on his face when Priestly survives and Walsh is dead."

Thomas saluted them in agreement. "I'm going to tell Strat in two days and bait Walsh into sabotaging the hit so we can kill him."

"What if he brings back up?" Ashleigh pressed.

"Well, between Louis, Will, Esther, and myself, I think we will have it covered."

Esther and Thomas peered at each other, and he threw a wink her direction.

"It's a risk telling him ahead of the hit," Hiro stated.

"How so?" Ashleigh asked.

"In three days, Mr. Sweeney, he could make plans of his own." Hiro then addressed Thomas, "I would be cautious in how much information you share."

"The day is all. Nothing about Louis, Will, or Esther. Or even the location. He can do his own fucking work to figure that out."

Hiroaki seemed unsettled. "It seems foolish, to let this man have an advantage."

"It's the only way we can find him, Hiro," Esther interjected. "We have to pull him out of hiding…it's our one shot to have this be on our terms."

"And what if he surprises you?"

She smiled. "Isn't that what you trained me for, Hiro? Surprises?"

Regardless of it being almost two in the morning, neither Will nor Louis were asleep. Will could sense how nervous Louis was becoming in the days leading up to the Priestly hit—he very rarely slept, and when he did, Louis was restless, the lines in his face growing deeper in his stress. It was hard to articulate the feeling they both felt deep down in their bones, a feeling Will couldn't shake, no matter how hard he tried.

Something was about to happen.

It was an imminent awareness of destiny on the horizon, and Will couldn't be certain if this applied to him, to Louis, the pair of them, or their family. As they sat at the table in their apartment above the barbershop, Will studied Louis closely, recalling the years they'd spent together and apart, wishing even at their age that they'd had more time to be together. Complications had torn them apart, yet they always found their way back to one another, and how it was in the beginning would be how it ended. No matter how the hit on Priestly went, they would live or die together, and for Will, that was the only thing that mattered.

"Will?" Louis asked, gazing at him intently.

"What?"

"I asked if you wanted another whiskey."

"Yeah, 'course."

Louis got to his feet and went to grab the bottle. "Christmas is two weeks away."

"Sure is."

He returned with the Casper's. "Do you…do you think…"

"We been over this, brother," Will declared, sliding his glass over to Louis. "We gotta get outta here now, or we ain' ever gonna."

When both glasses were full, Louis slipped Will's to him and took a gulp from his own. "I am worried about leaving her."

"Who? Es? She is the only one we ain' gotta worry 'bout at this point."

"No, Will. The Madame."

Will paused. "You're worried about leavin' her? She's got Tommy, Es, Ashleigh…hell, she's better guarded than ever. Why in the hell are ya worried about her?"

Louis's hand went to his temple. "Three decades I've given her," he said softly. "Over half my life. No one knows her like I do…" His voice trailed off, and Will spotted the pain in his eyes.

"She's gonna be fine. Ashleigh will take care o' her."

"How can you be sure?"

"Because he's my fuckin' son," Will professed. "That boy would rather have his legs cut off than let anyone down."

"Just like his father," Louis quipped with a grin.

"Yeah, just like his daddy. To his own detriment."

Scooting his chair close to Will, Louis took his free hand. "You need to talk to him before the hit."

"And you need to find McCann," he teased, squeezing Louis's hand in return. "We both got our work to do."

A loud knock came to the back door, and the two of them locked eyes.

"Who in the hell could that be?" Louis thought aloud.

Will grabbed the pistol on his belt, yanking it from the holster and pulling the hammer back as he rose. "You got your blade?"

The dagger was already drawn. "I'll answer, you aim," Louis instructed, tiptoeing to the front door. His hand went to the deadbolt, and as he pulled the lock aside, Louis flung the door open as Will pointed his pistol at whoever stood on the other side of the threshold.

"Well, I expected a bit warmer of a welcome home."

There, in the doorway, stood Esther beaming at them, with Thomas right behind her. She held up a full bottle of Casper's. "Shall we continue the party?"

Will felt his throat choke. "Es…"

But Louis beat him to it. In the blink of an eye, Louis had his dagger sheathed and scooped Esther up into his arms, hugging her close. Will holstered his gun and ran to them, wrapping his arms around Louis and Esther in their embrace. Another few seconds later, Will felt Thomas then join their circle, his arms engulfing them.

The night was one of the happiest Will could remember in years: Esther, Thomas, Louis, and Will proceeded to get rip roaring drunk, just the four of them, reliving the last year and recalling how much their world had changed in such a short period of time. No plans were made, no talk of the future, only the absolute joy of spending time with the people Will loved most, other than his own son. And it was upon the realization that Ashleigh was absent that Will felt a pang of hurt and nostalgia, the guilt of his own mistakes with Ashleigh hitting him like a tidal wave.

"Will," Thomas addressed, pulling him from his contemplations, "we ought to go fly birds one day, you and I. In a few years, when all this is passed, I'll expect you at Amberleigh. I'll have some red tails waiting for you, if that is what you prefer."

"And you'll stay," Esther asserted, raising up her whiskey glass, "because once you are there, I don't ever want you to leave."

"You won't want to leave, either," Louis added. "To this day, it is the most beautiful place I've ever seen."

Will smirked, somewhat forlorn. "When enough time has gone by, Tommy, I promise I'll take ya up on that offer."

"Will," Esther said, her eyebrows furrowing as she leaned forward with apprehension, "what is it?"

He shrugged. "I dunno, Es. Ya gotta understand. Louis and I were just talkin' before you two hooligans busted in here. We ain' exactly thrilled to be leavin' ya in this kind of a state. It's the only out we got, but now that it's here, we both, well, our feet are draggin'."

"Please don't," Thomas assured him. "We want you both to get the fuck out of here. Don't you understand that?"

"He's right, Will," Esther agreed. "We want you and Louis to get out. We'll take it from here. You two have done your part! Let us finish what you started."

"Ya know, Es, I wanted to tell ya somethin' before we left."

She smiled wide. "What is it?"

"I love my son, I love him so much it don' make sense," he announced, taking a sip of his drink. "But I always wanted a daughter. And I feel so goddamn lucky I got one." Will looked at her, tears forming in his eyes. "That first day when you got in the coach and I had to cut your...your beautiful hair off your head, I didn' think you'd make it. I told myself to try not to get attached to ya, to keep my distance in case shit went sideways and Louis and I couldn' make ya a place with the Hall. Lord Almighty, you proved my ass wrong. Over and over ya have. And I'm so fuckin' proud of what ya are. Of who ya are. And I just..." Sniffing back tears, Will shook his head. "I just wanted ya to know I love ya, is all. You mean so much to me...to us," he reiterated, glancing at Louis, whose eyes were red and swollen. "Louis is scared of leavin' the Madame, and I'm just scared of leavin' you, 'cause if anything happens to ya, I just...I don' know what I'd do, I really don'."

Esther leapt out of her chair and went to Will, sitting on his lap and hugging him close. "I love you too, Will." He could feel the hot tears falling off her cheeks and onto his shoulder. "You and Louis have been the fathers I always wanted. I wouldn't be here without you."

Pulling her in close, Will didn't want to let her go. "Promise me you'll watch yourself. Promise both of us."

A small sob left Esther. "I promise."

CHAPTER XLVI.

Thomas did not try to mask the concern on his face as he stared at Celeste, and in return, she shot him an ice-cold gaze.

"What?!" she demanded, crossing her arms over her chest, chilled to the bone and trembling with fever, yet refusing to stay behind

"Strat's gonna know, darlin'," Ashleigh predicted, reaching for a cigarette and throwing Thomas a wary glance.

"I don't give a damn about Strat," Thomas declared, gesturing for Ashleigh to grab him tobacco as well. "Celeste, your body is in withdrawal. You can barely stand. How in the hell do you expect to hold a straight face with Strat?"

Her hand went into her inside jacket pocket, and Celeste drew out a vial of violet liquid, a cork holding the contents inside. "Marcy said to consume this ten minutes prior to the meeting. It'll hold me together for an hour or so, which is enough time to scare the shit out of Strat and get back in a carriage uptown."

Thomas nearly scoffed. "You really think some, some potion Marcy put together for you is going to completely change your physical disposition?"

"You don't?" she challenged firmly.

"Brother," Ashleigh said, handing over a cigarette and box of timber, "don'."

"He's right, Tommy," Celeste added. "Don't."

Putting the cigarette between his lips, Thomas struck a match and lit it. "Fine. But you better drink it soon. We are just over ten blocks out, and the carriage is moving fast."

In an instant, Celeste had pulled the tiny cork and consumed Marcy's tonic, and Thomas watched her closely, fascinated and nervous that it wouldn't have the effects promised.

Noticing Thomas's worry, Ashleigh changed the subject: "Chinatown's gonna be a tough meetin' place soon. We got a new spot we can scout?"

"I'm working on it," Thomas told him. "It's harder than you think to find middle ground with the city as it is."

"Es mentioned…" Celeste cited, her eyes closed and her jaw clenched as she endured whatever it was Marcy's concoction was doing to her, "Es mentioned Lawrence was up to…to help. Agh!" she exclaimed, rounding over and rocking forward and back a few times. "God…damn…Marcy…"

"Celeste?" Ashleigh was mildly exasperated, placing a hand on her shoulder. "What do ya need?"

"Time. Give me a fucking minute."

Ashleigh peered at Thomas, who shrugged, and the two of them resumed smoking their cigarettes in the coach as if nothing were the matter.

"We will give him the day," Thomas instructed, "the day of the hit and nothing else. Nothing about Es, The Palace, or any of it. Walsh's spies are fucking everywhere and we cannot afford to give him any more than he already has."

"That'll be 'nough for him. But I'm with the Samurai. I'm worried we might even be givin' him too much. Son of a bitch's got eyes on us as is."

"We gotta do it, Ashleigh. It's the only way."

"Esther sparrin' with Daddy?"

"Yeah, she's training with Will and Louis. Thought it would be best for her to stay behind and not to add fuel to the fire following the eh...encounter she had with Hiro and the Whyos on their way to The Palace."

This sparked a sudden laughter from Celeste, and when Thomas looked, she was beaming from ear to ear.

"No, we are going to use that against them."

"Against them?" Thomas queried. "In what way?"

"Rumors, Tommy, are more powerful than facts. Remember when we were all terrified of discovering what it was about Walsh that made him special? That the bastard couldn't feel pain and therefore was seemingly unstoppable?" She grabbed the cigarette from between Ashleigh's lips, took a drag, then placed it back there once again. "We are going to fuck with them just like Walsh let his table fuck with us."

Thomas could see where she was going with this. "We say Esther has gone rogue. Working with Chinatown. Wanting vengeance on the Hall and the Whyos and Walsh most of all."

Celeste nodded. "Why not?"

"And what 'bout Tommy?" Ashleigh asked, amused.

"Like he said," Celeste reiterated, "Esther went rogue."

Without truly being able to believe it, Thomas could recognize how, in three or four minutes, Celeste had color return to her cheeks, her confidence was overflowing, and her smarts were as sharp as Lawrence's blade wrapped around his calf.

"Marcy is a fucking genius," he uttered under his breath, exhaling a cloud of smoke. "I would swear on William and Lucy, Celeste, you are..."

"Normal?" she countered cheerily.

"No," Thomas conceded, "even better. You're yourself."

The coach came to an abrupt halt, the driver hollering for them to get out of his cab so he could be out of Chinatown as fast as humanly possible. Without argument, Thomas paid him handsomely while Ashleigh and Celeste made their way toward the steps of the doctor's house. Thomas was right behind them, aware that they had only a matter of minutes to get everything ready before Strat was set to arrive.

The doc was leaning against the doorway. "How y'all doin', Tommy?"

"Good, Jimmy," Thomas replied, and they shook hands. "How are you?"

"Good. Grandson was born. Thinkin' of headin' to Philadelphia and movin' in with my boy and his family. We ain' gettin' any younger."

"Might be for the best. Shit is about to get real."

Chuckling, Jimmy playfully hit Thomas on the shoulder. "Get to work. Your boy will be here soon."

"Right," he granted, "no more than an hour."

"We'll be in the kitchen."

With Jimmy and his wife safely tucked away in the back of the house, Thomas joined Celeste and Ashleigh in the front sitting room by the fireplace. There were four chairs and a small table in the middle where a whiskey bottle and glasses waited for them.

"Guns loaded?" Ashleigh checked, clarifying his own cylinders.

"Griswold is full and I have six full backups."

Ashleigh smirked. "Good. Me too. And Lawrence's blade?"

"Ready for blood." Thomas flopped down in his chair and grasped the whiskey bottle, pouring them each a round. "Celeste?"

But Celeste was already ahead of him. Bringing her foot up onto the seat of her chair, Celeste hiked her skirt up to the top of her thigh without an ounce of timidity, unsheathing both of her throwing knives as she examined them with scrutiny.

"Couldn't be sharper," she confirmed, returning them to her thigh and letting her skirt fall.

"I think we oughta ask Miss Marcy just what in the fuck she put in that potion," Ashleigh teased, grinning, "because Lord Almighty, I want some o' that."

"You'll get some of this later," Celeste returned, a coy look on her face.

"All right," Thomas held up a hand to stop them. "Let's focus on the fact that Strat will be here any moment."

"Already here," came Strat's voice as he entered the room. "We have whiskey?"

"Course," Ashleigh answered, waving him over.

Thomas's friendly demeanor evaporated. "Strat, good to have you," he remarked coldly.

"Yeah, well, we got a lot to cover in a very fuckin' short amount of time," Strat announced, taking a seat and reaching for his whiskey. "How's The Palace?"

Thomas turned to Celeste, who took charge instantaneously. "The Palace is thriving, as always, yet that is not the purpose of this meeting," Celeste sang, crossing one leg over the other and leaning back casually into her chair. In an odd way, Thomas had to admit he loved the way Celeste worked: in her hand was her smoking wand and a lit cigarette, glass of whiskey in the other, and she was glaring at Strat without an ounce of emotion in a dress that more than accentuated her gorgeous figure.

"You told me you'd give me the hit to slip to Walsh," Strat responded, throwing his drink down his throat. "But we've got bigger fucking problems."

"Like what?" Ashleigh pressed contemptuously.

Strat held his glass Thomas's direction, and Thomas filled it for him. "I want out."

Letting out a loud cackle, Celeste took a drag of her cigarette.

"Bull fucking shit," she pronounced, exhaling smoke. "You are going to uphold your end, just like we will uphold ours until this hit is fucking over."

Her callousness caused Strat to become upset. "You don't understand, Celeste," he stated, taking a sip of whiskey. "He already has accused me of playing both sides. I'm going to get fucking cornered and gutted if even the tiniest thing goes wrong."

"Nothing is going to go wrong, Strat," Celeste assured him, her tune completely changing from self-assured to compassionate. "It only feels that way because the pressure is mounting."

"She's right," Thomas concurred, jumping into the conversation. "Now is not the time to abandon ship. If you did, Walsh would assume you were a guilty party. The safest thing you can do for yourself and for us is to stay put and deal with all the shit he throws your way. It's a matter of days, Strat. Days."

Strat let out a heavy sigh, having another drink of whiskey. "When is it?"

"Three days," Thomas responded.

"Where?"

"His residence."

"Time?"

"We don' have a time," Ashleigh disclosed. "Walsh can get that for himself. If ya gotta tell him somethin', I'd recommend afternoon. But he'd already know that, bein' that he's got some o' his boys tailin' Priestly anyhow."

These comments baffled Strat. "How could you know that?"

"Because, Strat, we aren't fucking blind," Celeste asserted, displeased. "He's got eyes on every one of us. So cut this act of innocence and let's be real." She had another inhale from her smoking wand. "What did you bring us?"

When only silence followed, Celeste glanced at Thomas, who was skeptical. "He sent you here with nothing?" Thomas asked him.

Strat was uncertain. "He thought I'd given you too much without getting enough. I was told to…to get the day of the hit and…"

"And give us nothin'," Ashleigh finished for him.

"Yeah," Strat replied, visibly not thrilled. "Basically."

Ashleigh, Celeste, and Thomas exchanged wary gazes until Thomas spoke up: "Well, you can tell me one thing."

"What's that?"

"How bad is it?"

Strat studied him. "How bad is what?"

"How many people does he have?"

Any humor in Strat's expression faded. "An army."

"How?!" Celeste demanded, consuming a large gulp of her whiskey. "How is that possible?!"

"He's pulling in everyone," Strat explained. "Orphans, immigrants, the poor and desperate. He turns them bloodthirsty and then convinces them the Whyos are going to rise and take over New York and I can't—"

"When?" Thomas interrupted him.

"When what?"

"When does Walsh promise to take over, you fucking imbecile?" Celeste snapped.

Again, Strat finished his whiskey. "You aren't going to enjoy my answer."

"Does it look like we enjoy talking to you when you don't hold up your end?" Celeste retorted mercilessly.

"Celeste, please," Thomas reproached her softly, and she withdrew. "When does Walsh say this…this takeover is going to happen?"

"Weeks."

"W-w-what?!" Celeste exclaimed.

Ashleigh nearly dropped his glass. "What do ya mean, weeks?"

"I mean by spring, Walsh wants the Whyos running New York."

This was not what Thomas wanted to hear. "Fucking Christ,"

he mumbled under his breath, his attention on Celeste. "It's worse than we thought."

She didn't have to say a word—her countenance said everything.

"Guess I didn't have nothing after all," Strat stated morbidly. "This may make me sound like a prick, but I honestly thought you knew."

Thomas didn't want to answer that question, because deep down, he still did not trust Strat. "I want an estimate."

"Hundreds. If not thousands."

As if they'd practiced, Celeste slammed her glass on the table and then thrust it over to Thomas for a refill.

"Well, I guess we're going to have to fucking do what you wanted anyhow."

"I told you," he said smugly, trying to follow her lead without any idea where she was heading with it.

To occupy himself and observe Celeste's direction, Ashleigh took out a cigarette and lit it slowly. She had the floor.

When he handed a full glass back to her, Celeste was feigning irritation. "I'll send word to her as soon as we're back."

"Her?" Strat asked. "So, it's true?!"

"Yeah," Ashleigh nodded, "Es is alive and kickin'."

"The attack…she and that chink took out more than their fair share of Whyos. Is it true? She's working with Chinatown?"

"She went rogue," Celeste confessed, snapping her fingers for Ashleigh to grab her another cigarette. "In a very similar fashion to our dear friend Walsh, she is…someone that finds you. You cannot find her."

"Why Chinatown?" Strat thought pensively. "Why there?"

"Because they are having their own fucking war," Celeste reminded him. "And if she helps them, they'll help her and get rid of Walsh, the Whyos…even Croker."

He seemed flabbergasted. "I just…how…?"

"She's a fucking Tweed," Thomas prompted him. "Convincing people to do her bidding is in her blood."

Diligently, Thomas observed Strat, hoping with every ounce of his being that Strat would be convinced.

When the sound of rushed footsteps caught Thomas's ears, his head whipped sideways just in time to spot Mock Duck striding into the sitting area of Jimmy's house, his chest cut through his chainmail, and his own hands covered in blood.

"I need you," was all he said, his eyes locked directly on Thomas.

Thomas was already on his feet. "What the hell are you doing here?" he hissed.

"You don't understand," Mock Duck pleaded urgently, "they are just behind me." His tone was frantic.

"Who is?" Thomas asked

"Lee's men," he replied, his gaze scanning the room, as if in anticipation. "We were ambushed, me and two others, and I was the only survivor. It's only a matter of moments before—"

Glass broke behind Thomas, and he circled around to see three of Lee's men leap through the windows as if they could fly through the air like birds. Pounding came from the front door, once, twice, three times, at which time the door was promptly broken down to the floor, and in filed eight more of Lee's goons, heavily armed with swords, pistols, and daggers.

"What in the fuck is goin' on?" Ashleigh called out to Thomas, grabbing Celeste's arm and thrusting her behind him, guns drawn and cocked.

"Esther?" Strat cried. "Did she do this?"

Mock Duck's eyes found Thomas's, and with a raise of Thomas's left eyebrow, Mock Duck got the message. "They are killing everyone they can to find her," he lied loudly enough for Strat to hear, pulling his blade in one hand and drawing out a revolver in the other, then leaned close to Thomas. "You will clarify later."

697

"Yeah, I know."

One of Lee's men from the front door began to yell aloud in Chinese, to which Mock Duck angrily spat back a multitude of responses as he unhurriedly retreated alongside Thomas. The pair of them took slow steps backward until they met the backside of Ashleigh and Celeste, who were face to face with the two thugs from the windows.

"I guess I should thank my lucky stars I brought extra knives," Celeste whispered, her blades in hand, ready to throw. "What the fuck are they doing here?"

"I am sure we'll get an explanation later," Thomas uttered, drawing the Griswold. "For now, let's just try and get out of this alive. Where's Strat?"

"Cowerin' in the corner like a fuckin' child, claimin' it ain' his fight," Ashleigh murmured, his tone irate, while Mock Duck continued roaring in retaliation at the enclosing members of Lee's Tong faction.

Out of the corner of his eye, Thomas could spot Strat recoiling by the fire. "Goddamn fucking bastard." He cocked the Griswold hot. "All right. Ashleigh, Celeste, the two ahead of you. Mock Duck and I will do the best we can with these pricks, and when you're done with those two, you come to our aid."

"Got it," Celeste declared, her grip tightening around her blades.

"What are they saying?" Thomas pressed Mock Duck, wondering why bullets had yet to fly.

"Apparently," he uttered, amazed, "they will let me go if we give them the man by the fire. I can only assume he is with the Whyos?"

"Yeah, he is," Ashleigh disclosed, "but we need his ass to get Walsh."

It was the answer Mock Duck was looking for. "So we protect him?"

Thomas let out a heavy sigh, rolling his eyes. "I fucking guess so."

"They will attack upon my announcement. Are you ready?"

"Just do it," Celeste commanded, and Mock Duck complied.

Within seconds, bullets were flying as the Tong rushed. Thomas could hear Ashleigh firing over his shoulder, and therefore, without hesitation, Thomas pointed the Griswold's barrel straight for the leader of Lee's group and shot him right between the eyes, the surprise of his accurate aim evident by the final expression on the man's face. To his left, another came barreling towards Thomas, too close for a bullet, so he bent his knees into a crouch, spinning counterclockwise while he pulled the Griswold down toward his left hip and simultaneously drew Lawrence's blade from his right calf with his left hand. He came full circle just in time to defend himself from his assailant's sword coming down from overhead for a high blow; the impact of the blades hitting sent a pulse through the room Thomas felt down to his bones. Holding his opponent's gaze, Thomas merely pulled the Griswold back to the midline and sent a shot through the thug's chest, killing him immediately.

Suddenly, Thomas was on the ground, tackled by a man to his right with a dagger aimed at Thomas's jugular. The Griswold was knocked clean out of his right hand, though he still had Lawrence's blade in his left. As he clutched the man's dagger-wielding hand tight around his wrist, Thomas plunged his knife between the man's ribs, holding and then twisting the blade, only to see Mock Duck's sword plunge through the man's chest.

"All right down there?"

"Yeah, mind pulling him off me?"

With a heave, Mock Duck yanked Thomas's attacker off him and withdrew his blade, turning back to the fight. Thomas reached and grabbed the Griswold beside him on the hardwood floor, standing tall just in time to take a bullet graze to his right upper arm. Again, the gun fell to the floor as a surge of pain shot through Thomas's body. Reading where the bullet came from out of his peripheral

699

sight, Thomas used all the strength in his left arm to launch Lawrence's blade the gunman's direction; to his delight, it went straight through the man's left eye and exited the back of his skull. The already lifeless body teetered for a second or two, then toppled to the floor. Feeling a presence approaching at his rear, Thomas spotted the Griswold and managed to fall onto it, rapidly roll over, and draw the hammer towards him, firing three shots in a row at one of Lee's men about to strike him with a bludgeon. Each one pierced his chest, and as blood poured out of his lips, the man fell to his knees, then fell face down onto the ground.

Peering over, Thomas observed Mock Duck in a hand-to-hand battle with one of his mortal enemies, and due to the injuries he'd sustained earlier in the day, Thomas wasn't sure that Mock Duck was winning. In haste, Thomas sprung up to assist in the onslaught, only to hear the slightest hint of a whistle and then be sprayed with blood. A throwing knife stuck out of the side of Mock Duck's assailant's head, and the man slipped in his steps from side to side as his right hand reached up, merely touched the blade, and he collapsed into a heap on the ground, dead. Thomas glanced over his shoulder toward Celeste at the opposite side of the room, who was sluggishly straightening up.

"Celeste?!" Thomas shouted out, panicked.

"Ain' hurt, that magic potion just be wearin' off!" Ashleigh called in return as Celeste crumpled into his arms. "I gotta get her ass outta here."

"The last man," Mock Duck panted, "he fled. There will be more."

"More?!" Celeste yelled, obviously in pain.

"If the word gets to Lee that there is a Whyo cornered," Mock Duck went on, "Lee will stop at nothing to get to him."

Strat didn't say a word, only stayed where he was, tucked up against the wall by the fireplace.

There were shouts echoing from the street, and Thomas thought for a moment. "Ash, get Celeste, Jimmy, and his wife out the back door. We'll hold them off as long as we can."

"We could just give them the Whyo," Mock Duck reiterated under his breath.

Suddenly, Thomas recognized the voices in the street. "Wait."

In a flash, Esther, Louis, and Will came sprinting in through the demolished front door, their expressions agitated and then relieved the moment they spotted their cohorts alive.

Esther sprinted to Thomas and leapt into his arms. "You okay?" she murmured in his ear.

"What are you doing here?" he questioned almost silently into her ear.

Her voice volume matched his: "The three of us were worried—we had a feeling something might go wrong with how high tensions are down in Chinatown." She glanced over his shoulder. "From the looks of it, we were pretty fucking spot on."

"Es, we have to get Celeste out of here, and Strat before he realizes you actually aren't working with Chinatown."

"Jesus fuckin' Christ," Will said, absorbing the aftermath of the onslaught. "What the hell happened?"

"Lee's men?" Louis asked Thomas.

"Yeah," Thomas replied, releasing Esther and sending her towards Celeste. "More are coming. We need to get Jimmy, his wife, and Celeste out of here."

"And Strat," Ashleigh added. "Fuckin' Chinatown wants his ass, and we ain' givin' him up."

"What the fuck is he doing in the corner?" Louis asked.

"Honestly, I haven't had enough time to think about it," Thomas retorted. "Will, you have a way you can get everyone to safety?"

"'Course, I'll get to Jimmy and the wife. Ash knows the way. Send him and Celeste."

With that, Will ran out of the room, and Thomas looked to Esther, Ashleigh, and Celeste. "Time to go." His attention then went to Strat. "You need to get the fuck out of here."

"Can't Esther convince them?" Strat pressed. "She's one of them now!"

"She ain' one o' Lee's. She's one o' Mock Duck's," Ashleigh shot back. "Get your ass up and let's go."

He was already up, walking towards them. "Esther, I can't believe you're really alive."

"And I'm wondering what the fuck happened to the Strat I knew," she countered as Thomas tried to mask a sneer. "Because he would never sit out of a goddamn fight and hide like a coward in the corner."

Strat didn't blink. "Walsh's orders—get back alive, no matter what happens. I'm not getting killed sparring with chinks."

Her eyes rolled. "You're an asshole."

Footsteps echoed in from outside.

"They're here," Mock Duck mumbled with anticipation. "If you wish to get them out, they must sneak out the back windows. We can hold them off and keep Lee's men occupied."

Ashleigh ducked under Celeste's arm to support her, retreating toward the shattered windows as he ushered her along. "Strat, you can either come with us, or stay and die, brother."

Not needing to be told twice, Strat followed. Within seconds, Lee's men came barreling in through the front entrance of Jimmy's home. Just as Thomas prepared to fire his Griswold at the primary target, there was the small whistle of movement; the assailant suddenly had a knife between his eyebrows, then toppled to the ground. Thomas peeked to their rear to see Celeste sporting a smile on her face after hitting her target. With an order from Ashleigh, who was already outside, she clambered out the window behind him and Strat, disappearing from view.

"Thomas!" Esther yelled, snapping him back to the attack.

702

She stood to his right, Mock Duck and Louis on his left, and with the lead man's corpse lying on the floor, eight more of Lee's men were ready to fight to the death.

"We can each handle two, right?" Thomas quipped, cocking the Griswold.

"In my sleep," Louis responded from Mock Duck's left. "Let's just get this over with so we can get back to work."

The man closest to Mock Duck uttered something in Chinese, and whatever it was, it absolutely enraged him. His response had a similar effect on Lee's goon, who proceeded to draw the blade on his belt from its scabbard.

"You and your friends will die," one of them spat.

"Meh. No, we won't," Thomas declared nonchalantly, aiming the Griswold and firing a shot through his temple, sending blood spraying over the men standing behind him.

A second round of battle commenced, though this was a fight in which Thomas was more than confident his team would conquer without breaking a bead of sweat. Mock Duck found himself engulfed in a thrashing of swords from two separate opponents, whereas Louis had already slit the throat of the first of Lee's thugs to come his way, and was more than man-handling the second, clearly enjoying the sport of it. A few teeth flew passed Thomas's gaze, signaling to him that Esther had her side of things under control, bringing Thomas head to head with a celestial, revolver drawn and barrel aimed right at Thomas. He fired a shot, then two, which Thomas managed to dodge by tucking forward and rolling into a somersault, bridging the gap between himself and the shooter. When his feet hit the floor, Thomas launched himself and tackled the man at his waist, losing the Griswold in the process, but also knocking the revolver from his attacker's hand when they hit the ground, with Thomas having the upper hand by being on top.

Immediately, the man struck down hard on Thomas's open

wound near his shoulder, sending a searing shot of pain through Thomas's body. In agony and furious, Thomas rocketed an upper cut to his foe's jaw with his left fist and promptly added to that by sending his right elbow down into the man's face using the entire force of his bodyweight. The result wasn't pretty, and Thomas's aggressor went limp in unconsciousness. Peering to his right, Thomas saw Esther locking her own opponent into a bind, realizing that while she absolutely did not need assistance, he could at the very least bring about their progressive win a tad faster. He hopped to his feet and received a series of attempted jabs, punches, and kicks from another celestial. It was easy to defend and duck each one, until Thomas decided to end it, grabbing the man's outreached right arm and twisting it up behind his back. Quickly looping his left arm over his attacker's left shoulder, Thomas grasped the right side of his jaw and the top left side of his head, and with a massive yank, one of Lee's last men fell to the earth in a heap, neck snapped.

"Ready!" came Esther's voice as she yelled to Thomas, and in one swift motion, Thomas drew Lawrence's blade, threw the blade underhand from its scabbard around his ankle, and was pleased to witness it stab the man Esther was holding directly through his chest. Within seconds, he was dead, and Esther let go of her bind, tossing his body onto the ground.

"Took you two long enough," Louis teased from the other side of the room. Thomas noticed him wiping blood off his hands, grinning at him and Esther. Mock Duck stood, sword still drawn and bloodied, taking in the damage that had been done.

"We did what we had to do," Thomas remarked, his own eyes examining the carnage. "Es?"

"A nice way to end a day of sparring," she remarked, yanking Lawrence's dagger out of the man's thorax, cleaning the blade on her shirt tail, then stepping over the deceased body and returning it to Thomas. "Think Ash, Celeste, and Strat made it out okay?"

"I have no doubt," Mock Duck added, sheathing his sword. "We took on a very powerful portion of Lee's army."

"Took on and slaughtered," Louis reminded him, moving closer to the group and addressing Thomas and Esther. "Lee will break from The Palace the minute he discovers we assisted Mock Duck." Louis turned to Mock Duck. "You can have opium by next week?"

"Absolutely."

"Well, then at least we won't deal with the wrath of the Madame," Thomas observed, leaning over to pick up his Griswold. "Duck, you good?"

His friend nodded. "Good, Lord Turner. Thank you for keeping me alive."

"Just promise me, if a time ever comes for it, you will fight at my side as I have done for you."

A tiny smile came to Mock Duck's lips. "I am insulted you asked."

"I'll get to The Palace," Louis inserted, casually stepping over the bodies to the exit. "I'll see you both tomorrow?"

"You can count on it," Esther answered with a wave goodbye.

"Es? Let's head uptown."

"I could use a hot bath and a glass of wine."

Thomas looked to Mock Duck. "I am not sure how you handle these types of things in Chinatown. There is one hell of a lot of clean up."

"We can manage," he replied with a shrug. "Please apologize to the doctor for me."

"I think he'll be grateful. Now, he can move to Philadelphia and not worry about leaving New York behind him." Thomas held his hand out to Esther. "Shall we?"

When Thomas and Esther reached their residence, Tony was at the door waiting for them, a guise of warning on his face.

"There is a…er…Captain Bernhardt here for you, Lord Turner. A small sigh came from Esther. "Really? Now, of all moments?"

"He's probably just here to report on the Hall and Croker," Thomas assured her. "I don't think he has any idea you're back in New York yet."

"Would you like me to assist you in sneaking up the stairs unnoticed?" Tony offered politely.

"Actually, Tony, that might be for the best, if you don't—" Esther stopped mid-sentence, and Thomas instantly saw why. There, over Tony's shoulder, stood Captain Bernhardt in the front lobby of the residence, mildly embarrassed, his gaze falling.

"I…uh…I apologize, I didn't…I wasn't expecting…"

"Lord Turner and Miss Esther only just arrived home from an errand," Tony pronounced over his shoulder.

"Right," Jonathan uttered. "I will…uh…wait for you in the…uh…"

"Unfortunately, Jonathan, I will have to excuse myself due to another social obligation," Esther said smoothly. "But we'll catch up another time. It's great to see you."

"Lovely to see you too, Esther."

Without glancing at Thomas, Esther marched in the direction of the stairs, and Thomas watched her go, respecting her decision and truthfully, grateful he wouldn't have to sit through what he presumed would be an awkward reunion for each of them.

"Thanks, Tony," Thomas declared, in a tone that was courteous but dismissive enough to allow Tony to check on Esther for him. "Captain? To the great room?"

"Certainly, Tommy."

Spinning on his heels, Jonathan turned around and made his way out of the lobby and into the Turners' entertaining area, re-

706

suming his seat on the sofa by the fire, where a whiskey was already poured. Thomas veered off to grab a drink for himself, then proceeded to join Captain Bernhardt, sitting opposite him.

"I've never seen you in your full, well, outfit."

Thomas had a sip of his whiskey. "I apologize for being caught in my disguise, but since you know the reality of what's going on here, I assumed you wouldn't mind."

The Captain let out a small chortle. "What kind of errand was it? You both have blood all over you."

"Trouble in Chinatown," Thomas revealed. "If Esther and some of the others hadn't shown up, it would have been far worse. We managed to kick the shit out of them and get out of there in one piece, thank Christ."

"I would pay one hell of a lot of money to see her fight," Jonathan said, shaking his head. "When she stepped between me and Douglas, God rest him, I don't think I've ever witnessed a human being move that fucking fast."

This made Thomas beam. "She's better than me, you know."

Jonathan's eyes grew wide. "No shit."

"She's more efficient, more careful, but also more relentless. And like you said, she's fucking fast."

With a gulp of whiskey, the Captain also smiled. "Well, I'm glad she's watching your back," he bantered, saluting Thomas, who returned it.

"You and me both, Jonathan."

They drank, and the Captain spoke first: "Please tell her I am so, so sorry to show up here unannounced. If I'd known she was back from England, I would never have just dropped by without calling."

"Really, don't be ridiculous," Thomas coaxed him. "It's not your presence or anything that has to do with you. Give it some time. She's adjusting to the idea that you are a part of this and that you and I are…well…"

"Friends."

"Yes."

He had another drink. "I would have thought that would make her happy."

"I think it does," Thomas responded, though he wasn't certain he believed that. "Look, it's not your fault. A few weeks, and everything will normalize."

"I know, I know you're right."

"So, what have you got for me?" Thomas asked, changing the subject.

Jonathan smirked. "I've got a date with Croker tonight."

"No shit!" Thomas exclaimed. "Fantastic. Where?"

"His residence, just north of The Palace. Not until late, I assume once his children and wife have retired for the evening. Is it all right if I return at lunch tomorrow with a full report?"

"I would encourage it. We need to know as much as we can about what Croker is up to, with Grant assuming office in just a few weeks' time."

"I'll get as much out of him as I can." The Captain finished his whiskey and rose. "Thank you, Thomas. I don't think I could ever express how much being a part of this means to me."

"You're invaluable, Jonathan. You are the inside eyes we no longer have at Tammany. I don't think I could ever express how grateful I am for you, either." Setting his whiskey glass aside, Thomas stood up and held out his hand. "A pleasure, as always."

"Likewise."

Esther was waiting for Thomas, a second round of whiskey already poured for him. "How was Jonathan?"

The two of them moved into the sitting area of their bedroom, flopping down side by side on one of the sofas, a fire roaring in the fireplace.

"He's meeting with Richard tonight."

"No fucking way."

"Exactly what I said. He will be by tomorrow around lunch in case you are...er...wanting to not be here."

Esther scooted back to the corner of the sofa, propping her legs up and onto Thomas's lap as she leaned against the armrest, swirling the whiskey around in the glass.

"What is it?" Thomas beseeched her inquisitively. "You only look at me like that when you have some kind of proposition."

"When I see Jonathan, it just has a tendency to remind me of the time we split, when we both made huge mistakes that cost us too much time."

"You mean when I was a giant asshole?"

She playfully hit his arm with her palm. "Stop it. I'm being serious. It just reminds me that we had all these ideas of being together, and none of them came to be."

He could predict where this was going. "You want to get married."

Gaping at him, Esther couldn't believe she was had. "How... how did you..."

"Because even though you hate to admit it, you can't hide anything from me," Thomas stated frankly, grabbing her free hand. "What if I told you I had an idea?"

"An idea?"

The priest wasn't thrilled about the hour, yet considering the history of the church in the Turner family and the exorbitant amount of money Thomas paid him for compensation, the complaints ceased after about a quarter of an hour. It had been a last-minute hustle, and Thomas was surprised that his plan so magically came together, as well as the fact that the church, after so many years, still happened to exist. Tony had gone to fetch Louis, Will, and the Madame; the four of them sat together in the tiny front two pews, candles lit on every stretch of surface Thomas could find to illuminate the small yet stunningly beautiful chapel. Standing beside the priest, Thomas chose not to wear a suit—instead, he wore casual black trousers, a loose white cotton shirt, and polished boots, wanting to be as much himself as he could on the day he got to marry the woman he loved. Ashleigh was diligently standing guard at the door, and after refusing to stay confined, Celeste shakily commenced playing a beautiful melody on the extremely out-of-tune pianoforte in the corner.

That was the moment Esther appeared at the end of the aisle, and Thomas felt his heart stop. His gaze shot to the Madame, who only grinned.

"I thought I would hold onto it for safe keeping."

Thomas was stunned to behold Esther gracefully floating down the aisle his direction while wearing Mary's old wedding gown, still a striking shade of white paired with a decadent navy-blue sash at the waist. Clearly, Celeste had done her best to try and put a little paint on Esther's face, and the little effort she did put forth made Esther look more handsome than Thomas could remember. Her green eyes glittered in the candlelight, and the closer she came, Thomas recognized she was crying happy tears of joy, and it made his heart soar. She reached the pew where Louis sat and, hastening to their feet, Will and Louis each kissed her cheeks before gesturing for Esther to stand facing Thomas in front of the priest. Taking each other's hands, Thomas smiled at her. Esther smiled in return, and the only regret he felt was that this moment hadn't come earlier.

The next thirty minutes or so were a complete blur to Thomas, with everything around them fading away as he became lost in his own ruminations. They had planned on wedding at Amberleigh the following year, but for reasons Thomas would never share with Esther, he was relieved that they would be legally bound to one another sooner rather than later. Of course, Thomas loved her more than he'd ever loved another person in the entirety of his life, and that was reason enough; however, there was a very real, and very dark cloud hanging over their prospective future, and if anything happened to him, he was going to be damn sure that she was provided for with a home and a future far away from New York City.

Husband, wife, and their wedding party made their way to The Palace for a celebratory drink when the service concluded, the Madame insisting that they open some of her best bottles of wine. The group was in high spirits, ecstatic to witness Thomas and Esther at last marry following years of separation and turmoil, providing a little spark of light in the seemingly dark world around them. And though Thomas put on a good show of portraying the enthusiastic new groom, internally, his mind wandered elsewhere, a strong feeling emerging deep in his gut that before things would get better, they would become much, much worse. His focus went from Esther, to Will and Louis, then onto Tony, to Ashleigh and Celeste, and at last to the Madame, at which point she returned his gaze. It was as if they could read each other's minds: she, too, felt it, and as they stared, a strange, silent communication passed between them.

Death was coming.

"What did you think of Edmund's latest prospect?"

Jonathan thought about it for a moment while he had a sip of bourbon. "He was slow. A lot of room for improvement, but Jesus Christ, can he throw a punch."

This made Croker chuckle. "That right hook, eh? Fucking diabolical! It's been a long time since I've seen a man hit that hard, Captain. We'll have some fun at the ring this weekend, that much is certain."

Captain Bernhardt had only been at Richard Croker's Upper West residence for a half hour, discussing the latest round of matches Edmund put together the previous week. When he'd arrived, Lizzie and the children were already asleep; once the butler showed him up to Richard's study, he and Jonathan skipped over the formalities and went straight to boxing, common ground for both of them, to break the ice. The moment would eventually arise when Jonathan could broach the subject he intended to upon aligning himself with Tammany Hall, but until then, he would banter with Croker in the hopes that this visit would not be a complete waste of time and effort.

The two of them clinked glasses in salutation and had a drink.

"It's nice to see Edmund in such good spirits now that that prick Virgil is gone." Jonathan shook his head. "What a goddamn catastrophe that was!"

"You want to know something? This will just stay between you and I."

"Of course, Richard."

Croker leaned back into his chair, smug. "I was the one who made it happen."

He tried to appear shocked. "What do you mean?"

"I set it up," Richard confirmed. "It's how Tammany Hall takes care of its opposition. We find ways of eliminating our antagonizers in one fell swoop. Virgil would have caused me an enormous amount of problems; Edmund, too. Let's face it: we don't need these fucking Chicago aristocrats coming into New York and thinking they can run this show. He needed to be taken care of, and he was."

"And Tammany has the power to do that?"

"The Hall rules this city," Croker declared boldly. "We can do whatever the fuck we want because we've paid our dues."

Jonathan nodded. "That you have."

"How is your family doing in Vermont? Are they missing you, now that you're back in the city again?"

712

"I promised to make it home in the spring," Jonathan told him. "The winter is so bleak and dark up north, I can barely stand it after October."

Croker was in agreement. "I can't even imagine. Lizzie and the children will head north in the New Year, but that's purely upstate, and I don't venture that direction until well after Easter. There will be no time to spare once Grant is in office."

The Captain held up his glass to Richard. "Ah yes! Congratulations are in order. That is one hell of a feat, Richard."

"A feat that will finally give us the space to do what needs to be done. This city will be all the better for it." Croker had some of his bourbon. "I have been meaning to ask, and this is a question I hope does not bother you..."

"Very few things do."

"How is Miss Hiltmore? It has been weeks since I have seen her at an event, which is quite unlike her, though she still is donating quite a bit to the Hall."

"The loss of her father has impacted her significantly, and prior to that, I do believe she has been spending more and more time at The Palace."

Richard snorted. "Lord Almighty. That's a hard-left turn from the society woman she was not a year ago."

"It is one of the many reasons we are no longer engaged. She is taking after the Madame in more ways than one."

"How the mighty fall," Croker remarked, shaking his head.

Jonathan finished his bourbon. "It's strange how things change."

A few seconds of silence followed, each of the men reflecting on what was discussed, before Croker broke the quiet with the question Jonathan had been waiting for:

"So, Captain, what is it you seek from Tammany Hall?"

"Well, Richard," he began, shifting in his seat to become more comfortable, "a multitude of things: power, comradery, a sense of purpose…"

"Basically being in the fucking army without being in the army?" Croker asked bluntly.

"Precisely," Jonathan replied, his grip on his glass tightening ever so slightly. "I have no political aspirations. I do, however, have an olive branch to offer."

"An olive branch is hardly necessary at this point, Captain. With your prestige, your experience out West, your family's legacy up in Vermont…hell, it's like you were born to be one of us. We feel lucky to have you."

Jonathan smiled. "Thank you, Richard. I appreciate that. Well, if we aren't looking at this as a prospective olive branch, how about a…a project of mutual interest."

"I'm listening."

"Lord Turner," Jonathan named, "he is no friend of the Hall, if I am not mistaken?"

The expression on Croker's face was a pained one. "He was. Our tie was severed. He is not an outspoken enemy of Tammany Hall, yet he is someone I, well, I do not trust. His family's history with the Hall is…appalling, to say the least. I've endeavored to make it right, and he will not accept."

"I see."

Croker paused, studying Jonathan. "Why is it you bring up Lord Turner? I presumed you two had made peace ages ago."

Letting out a sarcastic laugh, Jonathan took a drink of his bourbon. "Ah, Richard, no, you are mistaken. I have made Lord Turner, Miss Hiltmore, and their inner circle all believe I am their friend once again. I've positioned myself perfectly to seek the revenge I have wanted for so many years."

"And that revenge would be for…?"

"For Esther."

"Ahh. Yes." Croker reached for the decanter on the table between them and filled both of their glasses. "And what sort of revenge are you seeking?"

"What happened to her is entirely Lord Turner's fault. I want him to pay for it."

"Pay for it how?"

Setting his bourbon glass on the side table, Jonathan locked eyes with Richard. "He's helping that Vigilante. I can't prove it, but I know he is. He believes us to be fast friends, and after learning I was a new member at the Hall, propositioned me into keeping him in the know of what Tammany is up to. I, however, plan to do just the opposite."

This grabbed Croker's attention. "You'd spy on Lord Turner for me?"

"I absolutely would."

"And your motivation is strictly gaining the revenge for Esther?"

"Esther would still be alive if it wasn't for him," Jonathan answered heatedly. "I want that bastard to burn, and I am willing to do whatever it takes to make that happen."

It was evident Croker would say yes, and yet he took time to consider the offer. "You would be doing this at your own risk, Captain."

"Risk?"

Richard let out a sigh. "If Lord Turner is indeed working alongside the Vigilante, then I can tell you firsthand to watch your ass. That Vigilante is…inhuman. It's like he fucking lives in the shadows, doing only that which he wishes, and cannot seem to be bought or bribed to this very day. Oddly enough, that is similarly the sort of man Lord Turner has become. That makes them…exceptionally dangerous."

"The guilt he feels regarding Esther is a weak spot," Jonathan pointed out. "It is why he has gone out of his way to befriend me, to demonstrate that he has confidence in me." He shrugged. "That is a very easy thing to take advantage of. And I will be careful. I will be sure that most of my visits with Lord Turner will be when I know there are others present, and we will keep our discussions of progress limited to nights like these. Out of these walls, I'll pretend we have no knowledge of such a scheme."

"Now that," Croker replied, "is the kind of plan I can get behind."

"It is double pleasure to deceive the deceiver," Jonathan pronounced, quoting Machiavelli.

Mary's night terrors were worsening.

Connor was troubled, wondering if perhaps the trauma of Mary's experience at Blackwell was returning to her, but Mary could sense that was not the case, because every night it was the same horror. In her dream, there was no prison or asylum, no opium-laced potion being shoved down her throat or women's shrieks echoing through cold hallways. Instead, she stood in an open field with snow falling from an overcast sky, the bitter bite of winter on her fingertips and the smell of smoke filling her nostrils. There were bodies everywhere, bodies of men she had never met before, each corpse shot, stabbed, or beaten until the life left their eyes. Blood soaked the earth beneath her feet. She was unable to move, frozen in place by what she saw, until a screech would ring out from overhead. Lifting her gaze, Mary would spot Athena circling overhead, and then suddenly, her wings would cease, and the Peregrine fell down to the ground, disappearing from Mary's sight.

A small sob, somewhere far off in the distance, would find her ears on the wind, and frantically, Mary would turn, searching, until Esther would appear not ten feet from her, her back to Mary and breathing hard with her brass knuckles still on. Her skin and clothes were stained a deep, brownish red, and the grip around her brass was loose, as if to symbolize the fighting was done, though she did not turn—or as Mary intuited, Esther was reluctant to turn around.

"Esther?" Mary asked each time. "Esther, what is it?"

"I'm sorry, Mary," was all she would say through muffled cries, refusing to rotate around and meet Mary's gaze.

"Sorry for what?" Mary would press, only to be greeted with nothing in return. Peering from side to side, it was about that point Mary realized where she was, and every time, it was as if she were being kicked right in her stomach. Around her, the trees burned, smoke surrounded them, and Mary realized there were no other living souls. It was carnage, pure carnage, and as she observed the bodies strewn as far as she could see, Mary would feel something, something she hadn't felt in many years.

Fear.

She would wake up screaming, shaking, and in tears, unable to explain any of it, even to herself, wanting to wash the blood off only to discover there wasn't a drop on her person. Mary's mind would race...did Esther kill all those men? Why? Why was everything burning to the ground? Where was Thomas? Where was...where was everyone else? And the worst question of all: why was Esther sorry?

From a young age, Mary had a gift. Her dreams were a gateway of premonitions, yet rather than predicting the future, they served as a warning—a warning of what could be. Often, her dreams would center on the topic of death. When her adopted father died of a heart attack, Mary dreamed of it weeks before and desperately tried to plead with her adopted mother to discuss it with him. She waved Mary off as an imaginative child, and when Mary persisted, she was punished with going to confession every day she would bring it up.

Mary never told a soul what really happened in the aftermath. For years, she'd let the Madame, her real mother, and Thomas, her son, believe she chose a life at The Palace because of her adoration of the Madame. The truth was, Mary had no place to go. Her

717

adopted mother cast her out upon the death of her husband, by a heart attack, just as Mary mentioned to her, with the decree that no witch would be living under her roof. That was why the family moved north a short time later. With no husband to provide for them, Mary's adopted mother took her children to be with their grandparents, leaving Mary with nothing but a few items of clothing and two apples to keep her from going hungry that day. She'd gone to The Palace because it was all Mary had left, and no prospect of surviving on her own. In her later recollections, Mary understood why the Madame fought her so hard on "earning her keep." The Madame did not want Mary to work for her, and offered her housing and to find her a job as a maid in one of the wealthier residences on Fifth, and this intrigued Mary initially, up to the moment she saw the difference in what she would make being a whore versus being a maid.

She could hear the Madame's exact words when Mary finally broke her down: "I'd rather you be whoring here than anyplace else." If only Mary had been aware then of what that phrase really meant coming from the Madame, perhaps things may have been different.

After another morning of waking up in tears, Connor made her promise to talk with Akemi, and as Mary trudged down the snow-covered path to Akemi's guest home on the property that same afternoon, she was skeptical as to just what Connor made her agree to. Mary adored Akemi, yet she was certain that if she herself could not decipher these nightmares, there was no way in hell Akemi would be able to either. In most circumstances, they had a very apparent message to send, and that proved true over and over again, most notably in her dream of Edward being murdered in New York City. But in this vision, there was only death to Athena, and whether or not the falcon truly met her end was up for debate. Pulling her coat tighter around her waist as the English wind roared by her ears, Mary made it to the gate that led to the house and pushed through, happy to see smoke billowing out of the chimney and praying Akemi warmed some sake up for the two of them.

Just as Mary was about to knock, Akemi opened the door, grinning. "How are you, Lady Turner?"

"Well, Akemi," Mary greeted, smiling. "Please tell me you have something hot for us to drink? I think a blizzard is coming with that wind!"

"I prepared your favorite sake."

"You are wonderful."

Mary stepped inside and shimmied out of her winter fur, hat, and gloves, unlacing her boots and leaving them beside the door politely. There were two small ceramic cups and a carafe steaming on the kitchen table, and Mary took a seat. Akemi poured them each a bit of sake and lowered down in the chair beside Mary's.

"Tell me about the dream."

Mary smirked. "You waste no time, do you?"

"I am often too direct, I apologize."

"No, I have a great amount of respect for that," Mary stated, having a sip of sake and enjoying the warmth in her stomach. "I have a very odd kind of curse, Akemi. For as long as I can remember, I have been able to see death in my dreams before it happens, and it is not always people I know personally. It tends to have a mind of its own."

"I see," Akemi responded. "You do know what that makes you?"

"What?"

Akemi's gaze found hers. "That makes you an angel of death, Mary. You cannot stop a person from meeting the end, yet you see it, and try to warn that the horizon of life is by no means an infinite one."

"But Akemi, that is what makes this dream so, so challenging."

"Challenging?"

From start to finish, Mary recounted her nightmare to Akemi, sparing no detail and emphasizing that each time, there were no variations in sequence. They were identical, and it was a message Mary couldn't seem to crack. When she finished, Akemi was quiet, sipping on her third round of sake, her countenance crestfallen.

"You know the answer, don't you?" Mary pleaded with her.

"I only know my interpretation of your vision, and additionally, my own visions of what will befall New York City."

Mary's jaw dropped. "You—you have visions?"

"Yes, I do."

"Of what? The future? The past? What do you see?"

Letting out a sigh, Akemi filled her sake cup. "Like you, I cannot choose what I see. Mine is a projection of potential, not fate itself, but a possibility of what might come."

"Akemi—what is it?"

Another gulp of rice wine. "There will be a war. A war between the forces of good writhing in the veins of our family and friends in America, and the evil of this man Walsh," Akemi halted, taking a hard swallow. "We will lose many. They will lose many. I do not know who will win, and that is something I cannot change. But I do have my ideas."

Mary sat eagerly listening. "Tell me."

"If she does what I tell her, and abides by her training, Esther will either kill this man Walsh, or she will perish in trying."

"If she fails, Thomas will be there to save her. To kill Walsh. He would never abandon her, I know my son."

"Sadly, no, Mary, that is not the case. It is either that Esther will kill him and end it all, or she will die and Walsh lives."

Her heart sank. "And if Esther dies, Thomas dies with her."

"And all of the others. New York will be lost, and America will see its history swiftly rewritten."

This was a reality Mary could barely comprehend. "What about Thomas?"

"That, I really cannot say. My hope is that your dream is telling us Esther will succeed. At what cost, we cannot be sure until this battle has unfolded. But it seems to me the cost will be…" a slight crack in Akemi's voice cut her off. "…the cost will be…devastating."

The two of them sat, drinking sake for what felt like hours without speaking. When she was just drunk enough to accept what Akemi was telling her, Mary felt tears welling up in her eyes.

"At least our daughter will come home," she wept. "At least we will get her home where she belongs."

Akemi reached over and grasped onto Mary's hand. There was nothing left to be said.

Death was coming.

CHAPTER XLVII.

Celeste felt like her head was about to explode.

It had only been a few days since she awoke from her opium-induced fog, and since then, Celeste went back and forth between feeling somewhat normal to contemplating whether she would survive another day in such a state. Fevers came and went, along with chills, aches in every muscle of her body, nausea, dizzy spells, and emotional highs and lows that challenged her sanity. Just when she thought she'd pulled through, Celeste would be overwhelmed by physical and mental symptoms so horrendous it made her swear on her father's grave she would never touch opium again. She would take note from the Madame and stick with alcohol and tobacco, because even with those two vices, Celeste at the very least could remain a functioning member of society.

As Celeste laid pitifully on Marcy's chaise in her room, Marcy mixed together a tonic to help equalize the sensations coursing through her body while Celeste recalled the previous few days, and most notably, that she'd finally faced the one experience she'd been dreading: killing another person. There were expectations she'd put together in her mind of how she would feel as a consequence;

strangely, the emotions, remorse, and possible regret Celeste had assumed she would endure did not exist. The occurrence in China-town proved to be a kill or be killed scenario, and rather than hide away in the corner like that bastard Strat from the Whyos, Celeste was on the front line with Thomas and Ashleigh, protecting their own, and that high was better than any other drug she could imagine.

With the sound of a spoon clinking as it stirred, Celeste grasped her tonic was ready and sat upright. Marcy brought the glass of liquid over to her, it's hue an almost electrifying shade of pink, and when Celeste spotted it, she stared at Marcy in confusion.

"Trust me, you don't want to know," was the answer she received.

Grinning, Celeste took the glass from Marcy's hand and had a sip, the taste of it more than a little unpleasant, a combination of ingredients she was happy to not distinguish.

"Ugh, I've had better cocktails, Marcy, I can tell you that much."

Marcy let out a loud laugh and turned around toward the counter while Celeste had another sip. "Jesus Lord Almighty. Please tell me we are getting close."

Marcy peeked over her shoulder and winked. "By tomorrow, you'll be nearly yourself."

"I just need to get this down?"

"That, and not touch opium again."

This caused Celeste to laugh aloud. "We have a deal, Marcy."

Grabbing onto her nose, Celeste managed to chug down the rest of the tonic, trying not to make too many disgruntled expressions in the process.

A knock came at the open door to Marcy's room, and there stood George. "Almost got all your things unloaded, Celeste. Your new room will be upstairs, just two doors down from the Madame's."

Celeste sat the empty glass aside, a nasty taste left in her mouth. "Thank you, Georgie, you are amazing. What time is it?"

"About lunch."

Marcy circled around, wiping a glass clean with a towel. "You ought to get up there. I think Sally will be by shortly, and we've got a roaring night ahead of us."

"Dot said we were a full house, correct?" Celeste asked.

"Packed to the brim," Marcy said, smiling.

Shuffling to her feet, Celeste stood up, seeing a few stars, yet feeling lighter than she had just a few minutes before. "Marcy, I already can sense the change. Can I drink any wine?"

"If anything, it might ease the transition."

"Music to my ears. Georgie? I'll follow you up the back stair."

She trailed George out and into the hallway, making a left in the direction of the staircase, which led up to the Madame's office. After Chinatown, Celeste had made a resolute decision, and that was to at long last leave her world of New York City's high society behind her to take her place where she belonged, at The Palace. Jeremiah would stay for the time being, since the Hotel St. Stephen seemed to perfectly fall between The Palace and St. George's, the negro hospital he worked at on most weekdays. Georgie and Ashleigh spent the better part of the morning and afternoon hauling Celeste's trunks up from the five carts carrying them, most of the trunks filled with gowns of every color and cut fit for any occasion. When the moment arrived to dispose of Douglas's belongings, Jeremiah and Celeste together chose to bring his clothing to St. George's to give to those in need, though the rest of it, Celeste left up to her brother. Douglas left them with a generous library, vast cellar of wine, crystal and china that were fit for royalty, not to mention décor from the Madame's own importer in Paris and a vast assortment of men's accessories Celeste knew Jeremiah would love to possess, and so she did what any good sister should and left the musings of what to keep to him. Instead, the only décor she took were Esther's paintings, and she made Ashleigh promise to hang them on every inch of wall space around her room.

They arrived up in the Madame's office to find Sally already present with a glass of wine in hand, deep in conversation with the Madame about the next day. The following morning would be a pivotal moment for them: it was the morning of the Priestly hit, and each one of them hoped with every ounce of their being that they could save Priestly and kill Walsh in one fell swoop. In a matter of hours, Will and Louis would be out of the city with Sally, and Priestly would be in protective custody at the Turners' until they could get Senator Fassett and his allies to conduct an interview, and from there, Richard Croker would find himself in the middle of a government investigation for corruption. Though what Celeste didn't want to admit, even to herself, was that she worried something was going to go terribly wrong. Despite the fact that she grew up extremely wealthy and privileged, Celeste had certainly confronted hardships in her adult life, and with those experiences, she was cognizant that this win felt a little too easy. After so many years of pain, blood and loss, years of little to no sleep, of being consumed with worry and anxiety and losing people she loved, were they finally going to end this on one random December morning?

Only time would tell.

"Celeste, darling!" the Madame sang as Celeste walked into the office. "Come on in and join us! Ashleigh just popped in to say your room is nearly prepared."

Celeste saw a glass of wine waiting for her on the side table between the two armchairs across from the Madame's desk, and she went to sit beside Sally contentedly.

"Did he hang the paintings?" she inquired eagerly, reaching for a wine glass.

A glint of merriment flashed through the Madame's eyes. "Perhaps."

"What prompted the move, Celeste?" Sally asked. "By the way, you look ridiculously stunning, I might add."

"Probably the tonic Marcy just force fed me," Celeste remarked with a smirk. "But thank you, Sally, you are so kind. I think I just finally realized after losing my father that this—this is my family. And when he was still with us, I had every reason to be there with him, working alongside him and assisting the Madame with society, but my connection to that has withered. I will uphold the connections I've already made and utilize those as best I can. Otherwise, my skills are best put to use here for the foreseeable future."

"Well, seems to me you made the right decision," Sally declared, impressed. "How are you feeling about tomorrow? As apprehensive as the Madame and I are?"

"A lot is riding on this," Celeste observed, having a sip of her drink. "My only worry is that if one thread comes untangled, the whole quilt will unravel."

The Madame was eyeing her. "What worries you, darling? Thomas taking on Walsh? Priestly? Esther?"

"If I am honest..." her voice trailed off as she considered her words, "I am most concerned about Louis and Will."

"Oh!" Sally exclaimed. "Well, I can tell you right now, Celeste, from the minute I have them, they will be safe. No one knows the tunnels, not even that son of a bitch Walsh."

Celeste attempted to recover her resoluteness. "I think it might just be nerves. Or possibly that I am still recovering from nearly killing myself on opium."

This caused both the Madame and Sally to laugh aloud.

"To be fair, Celeste," the Madame interjected, "we all should be worried. We have to each tie up our ends to make this happen. And if it doesn't, well, let's be honest, we are fucked. But we do the best we can with what we have, and I would say, this is one of the best shots we've ever had at killing that bastard and taking Croker down in the process."

"Once Louis and Will are out of here," Sally added, having a gulp of wine, "there will be a lot more pressure on the rest of you to close the deal. At the point the smoke clears, I'll keep you informed of where I believe them to be. Otherwise, it's very much up to them whether or not they'll be found."

The Madame let out a somewhat defeated sigh. "It will be the first time in decades that Louis and I go separate ways." She grabbed her glass. "I have more than enough help, that much is fucking sure. But not having him here seems..."

"It seems unnatural," Celeste completed for her.

"Quite."

"To the future, and may God have mercy on us," Sally saluted, holding her wine glass in the air.

Celeste and the Madame mirrored her cheers, and they each took a long gulp.

After a moment, Sally turned to Celeste. "May I...can I share something with you?"

"Absolutely, Sally. Anything!"

Her eyes flew towards the Madame, who nodded her approval, and then Sally nervously gazed back to Celeste. "I knew your father... before. I knew the...the things that went on with his cotton trade. And in those years, I hated him. I was raised a staunch abolition-ist with Ralph and Bronson and Louisa, existing in this surreal little reality in Massachusetts, but when the railroad became real, I helped my father in every way I could, which was why, for so many years, your family was my enemy." She paused, taking another sip of wine for confidence. "When your father walked out of prison, he was a changed man. You brought him and his son together. You made him repent for the wrongs he'd done. And while he was a bastard, and I'll never forgive him for the atrocities he committed, it became clear what his one redeeming quality was."

"What was it?" Celeste asked.

Sally smiled. "You."

Celeste scoffed, "Me? Don't be ridiculous. I merely got my father out of prison."

"Well, theoretically, darling," the Madame interjected, "I got your father out of prison. But you gave him another chance."

"She's right," Sally agreed. "And my point, Celeste, is that with Walsh gone and Croker on his heels...well. The time has come for Celeste to decide who she wants to be. And the options seem infinite. You have a very unique way with people, and when you put your mind to it, you make them want to be better for you. That... that is something many people wish they could master, and for you, it is easy."

Initially, Celeste believed she could stomach discussing her father in the past tense; on the contrary, as the thought of his absence truly sank in, Celeste felt herself growing emotional at the idea of Douglas being gone. Quite rapidly, she set her wine glass aside, apologized profusely to Sally and the Madame, then hastened out of the Madame's office toward her new room at The Palace. Stepping quickly down the hallway, Celeste could feel her throat choking, the pain of the loss striking her deep down in her chest, and she bit down hard on her lip as she swallowed down a sob. Celeste reached the doors of her room and threw them open, relieved to see Ashleigh was no longer inside, and she circled around, closing the doors behind her before she finally let the tears start to fall. Leaning against the doors, the weight of grief came down hard, and Celeste sobbed, her face dropping into her hands.

She slid down to the floor, pulling her knees into her chest for comfort. "Father," Celeste whispered to no one, "Father, I am so, so sorry." It didn't matter how many times she wiped the tears away from her cheeks, they just kept coming. "I didn't know he would... I never thought..."

Suddenly, and very swiftly, her anguish shifted to outrage, and with a big inhale, Celeste let the anger wash over her. "I am...I am going to kill him, Father. One way or another, I'll see to it that it's done. By my hand or someone else's."

Her memories flashed to that night, to the discovery of what Walsh had done to Douglas as a retaliation for not being able to kill the Madame or her or Esther, and Celeste had no doubt Walsh originally hoped for his victim to be her. With Celeste dead, it would have been a blow to their faction that would have derailed so many aspects of their plans, and more than likely sent the Madame and Esther on a much darker path of retribution. In an odd twist of fate, Celeste was thankful her father had been the one and not one of the others, because in the case of Douglas, it was really only Celeste and her brother who would be devastated by his murder. They could go on without him, and the giant hole left in Celeste's heart was hastily transitioning into an absolute necessity to avenge him.

Taking another deep breath in and then letting it go, Celeste used the sleeve of her dress to wipe the last of her tears away, then pushed herself upright to stand.

"You can be angry," she told herself. "Use it. Don't let it be an imposition. Let it be a tool, Celeste." Another breath, followed by a long exhale. "You've been through worse than this, and you know it. Sally is right. It's time to decide which direction we are going. The time to be timid has long passed—the time to act is now."

Lifting her gaze, her mood of vengeance waned, and Celeste's eyes grew wide as she took in the beautiful room she was standing in. Her room, to be exact. Every wall was floor to ceiling covered in Esther's paintings, some big, some small, each of them exquisitely vibrant in color. Analogous to the Madame, Celeste had multiple wardrobes against the wall to her left, and in the far-left corner, room dividers for her to change as well as an enormous, gold-flake framed mirror. To her right, a few feet from the doors sat her vanity, and on the surface was every tool she could possibly imagine to paint herself to perfection. There was also perfume, a bowl of fresh rosewater to wash her face, an exorbitant amount of hair pins, and, to her delight, a beautiful ashtray and stand for her smoking wand. On the other side of her vanity in the far-right corner was a drink cart stocked with wine, fresh glasses, and her own crystal decanter she assumed was filled with Casper's. There was a small sitting area with two armchairs, a small loveseat, and a coffee table, and then there was her bed, an elaborate Santiago frame with a crown-shaped headboard, her linens all a crisp white and embroidered with flowers to match Esther's paintings.

It wouldn't have been better if Celeste dreamed it.

She went to the bowl and splashed rosewater on her face, washing away the tears and smudged rouge. Just as Celeste finished drying her skin, a knock came to the door.

"Yes?" she called, speedily piecing together an apology for the Madame and Sally.

"It's me!" came the sound of her best friend's voice.

"Es! Come in!"

In her usual way, Celeste pinched her cheeks and rolled her shoulders back, wanting to at least give the impression of being composed, despite knowing the minute Esther saw her, her friend would recognize she'd been crying. Esther sauntered in with a smile, though as predicted, she spotted something was the matter almost instantaneously.

"What?" she asked empathetically. "Tell me."

"Let's go sit," Celeste suggested, gesturing Esther toward her sitting area. "What do you think about it?"

Esther went to sit down. "About your new living situation? Well, the Madame certainly knows how to house her own. Everything is beautiful and also very…"

"Very me," Celeste proposed, opening a bottle of wine.

"Yes. And I have to say, all of my paintings side by side are… overwhelming. I really cannot believe you kept every single one."

"I wouldn't dream of getting rid of them!"

With the wine poured, Celeste went to join her friend. "What brings you to The Palace? Just here to visit?"

A big smile came to Esther's face. "Actually, I brought you something."

While she hated to admit it, Celeste loved presents. "Oh!?"

"It's downstairs waiting for you. I am not sure where the Madame will want to put it yet, but...I thought you could use a little less...darkness right now."

"Es...you didn't..."

Her grin grew wider. "Yes. You have a brand-new pianoforte downstairs."

Celeste was beyond moved by her friend's generosity. "Esther, I just...I don't know what to say."

"Don't say anything. I don't even want to hear a thank you. You just start playing again, and we'll call it even." She had a gulp of wine. "Now, what was it you were upset about right before I walked through the door?"

Swallowing her pride, Celeste had a sip of her drink as well. "My father," she sighed. "I was with Sally and the Madame discussing tomorrow and I...I really felt at first I could handle hearing him being spoken of, but I...I broke down. And it's really not because he is gone, it's more because of how...how he was taken..." A single tear escaped her eye, and Celeste swiftly wiped it away, the wrath once again blossoming in her chest. "I cannot put into words how angry I am, and in the end, I don't even give a shit what happens to Croker or the Hall. What I want is that Walsh bastard to die."

"I understand," Esther replied. "Celeste, I...I don't know how to make this better. But I am going to try. Tomorrow is it. It's the end. Thomas and I will both be there to make sure Walsh doesn't see another sunrise."

"What if something goes wrong?" she pressed. "What if we don't get him? What if he decides not to show?"

"Strat's intel says he wants to ambush the hit and keep Priestly alive to hit back at Croker. I really don't think he would miss this chance."

"And what if he does?"

"Is there something you aren't telling me?"

"No," Celeste recanted, sinking back into her armchair. "No, it's not information. I just have a...a..."

"A what?"

"It's too easy. Just out of nowhere, we have him and we get a huge strike against Croker? It seems like at any second, something will go amiss."

Esther gazed at her with conviction. "If something goes wrong, then we'll figure out another way."

Celeste nodded, though she wasn't persuaded. "I just want him gone. For my father. And for all of us."

"I am going to kill him, Celeste."

"You?" she questioned. "But I thought Thomas—"

"Thomas will be there to see it through if I do not."

The certainty behind those words struck Celeste hard. "Es, I can't lose you too. I couldn't bear it."

"Listen, this is just how it has to be. I don't like it any more than you do. It's just something I have to do. Just promise me something."

"Anything."

"If we cannot end it, you'll have to."

Celeste looked at Esther with poise. "If you cannot end it, I will."

The two friends saluted each other.

"Thank you," Esther said softly.

They sat for a moment in silence, alone with their burdens.

"Esther?"

"Yeah, Celeste?"

"Do you think we are going to die?"

Their eyes met again, and in Esther's, Celeste understood in her heart what her sister was about to say.

"Either we both will die, or neither of us will."

Celeste took another sip of wine. "Well, I suppose I'd rather have it that way than any other."

Esther smiled at her. "Me too."

It was nearing time for a night of festivities at The Palace to begin, and in preparation for what Celeste assumed would be an eventful evening packed to capacity with customers, she chose to venture to the Madame's office early for their usual meeting with the girls. She was well-aware Sally was gone by then, undoubtedly to prepare for shuffling Will and Louis out of the city undetected the next afternoon, and Celeste was grateful she would only have to apologize to one of them. Sally and the Madame were two of the strongest women Celeste had ever met, and Celeste was mortified she couldn't hold her composure in front of them. Thankfully, Esther stuck around for an hour or two, showing Celeste her pianoforte and simultaneously getting her best friend to drink enough wine to find the nerve to apologize to the Madame.

That day wasn't the only thing causing Celeste to feel shame. She was mortified that her friends and family had to come together to wean her off an opium bender, one she was using to numb the pain of her father's murder. Celeste had been punishing herself ever since for being so weak as to allowing it to occur in the first place. In her heart, Celeste felt she was stronger than that—smarter than that—and succumbing to those baser impulses haunted every step, every breath, every second of her days since. With Esther, her peace had been made, yet when it came to the Madame, Celeste was constantly in fear of disappointing her, and her want of approval was beginning to cause an anxiety she needed to coax.

Taking a moment, Celeste checked her perfected appearance in her vanity with a quick twirl to be certain her dress was stunning, then set out for the Madame's office, her rehearsed and thought-out speech ready to go. When she entered the Madame's office, it was as if she had been expecting Celeste to show up: the Madame sat over to the left by the fireplace on one of her sofas, a bottle of wine already corked, with one glass in her hand and another full on the side table, waiting for Celeste.

The Madame looked over and smiled. "Hello, darling. Come sit."

A little intimidated, Celeste did as she was told, walking gracefully over and sitting down beside the Madame. "You knew I would want to say sorry."

"I knew you would, and I wanted to be here to tell you to never fucking apologize when it comes to what happened to your father," the Madame asserted, pointing over her shoulder. "Grab your wine. I have a story I want to tell you."

Celeste reached over and grabbed her wine. "A story, you said?"

"Yes. One that, I think, you will find extremely relatable."

She had a drink from her glass. "I'm assuming this still has to do with my father?"

"In a...a matter of perspective, yes." The Madame had a gulp of wine. "There is one condition to our having this conversation."

"All right."

The Madame stared right into her eyes. "You will never tell a soul."

This surprised Celeste. "Not even Esther?"

"Not even Esther."

Celeste nodded, an almost thrilling sensation of privilege filling her at the thought of sharing a secret with the Madame. "You have my word."

With a deep breath, the Madame nodded in return. "I was a prostitute at age ten. Not by choice, but because on the ship over, my father died of fever and my mother…well…"

"What happened to her?" Celeste pressed.

"She was raped and murdered right in front of me," the Madame said forthrightly. "I was too fucking young to really…really grasp what happened, and those bastards got away. The coppers found me huddling over her, and I remember they tried to take me to a goddamn orphanage. It didn't fucking stick. Within days, I ran away, and within another few weeks, I was forced to whore myself to perverted creeps just to eat and have a place to sleep."

"Jesus fucking Christ," Celeste uttered, her eyes wide in horror.

"Don't get soft on me now, darling," the Madame chastised her, "the worst is yet to come." With another drink, she continued, "I was made pregnant by a regular, Mary's father. At the time, I was working for an Irish brothel owner—Johnny McCreery, fucking crazy son of a bitch, and Johnny was young. He was one of Tweed's. He didn't want to be in charge, and was especially fucking hostile about children selling themselves to the fucking assholes on the street, but he didn't have a choice. I was the only young girl he had. He took care of me, kept me fed, let me sleep in his quarters so I wouldn't have to deal with the other girls and their bullshit, never struck me, but would always threaten the way johns have to, similar to how I am with my girls now. I had Mary, and he helped me find her a family, and then my life went on as you already well know."

"You went on to work as a whore until you took over The Palace."

"Correct," she replied. "What you don't know is what happened in between, and why I…I understand what you are fucking going through right now.

"While I was still working as a whore, Tweed put me to work for him—apparently, I had fucking aptitude for leadership. I learned all about what I do now from him: bribery, extortion, blackmail, murder, and my counterfeiting skills. Those are things I learned from the masters behind Boss Tweed. Tweed himself was the fucking one who forced me to throw knives, and I had no choice but to comply."

"Of course you didn't," Celeste chimed in. "He fucking ran the city!"

"Yes, darling, he did. The...the first time he bedded me, I was fifteen. It continued for years, though I made sure to never get pregnant, and all the while, Johnny housed me. We became increasingly close, and he slowly became more than just a friend, standing up for me when Tweed demanded more. He even offered to get me out of New York to start over, away from Tweed and away from the goddamn disaster the Hall was becoming, but I was too scared to try. He was the first decent human being I'd ever met, and I think probably the first man I ever loved. We made the original Palace together, him and I, and very shortly thereafter, Louis was our right-hand man, though his intentions behind joining us I wouldn't realize until far, far later in our lives.

"The downhill spiral didn't commence until long after the war; however, the first cracks broke through just after the draft riots. Tammany was able to hide behind the war for a time, but Johnny and I both saw the worst side of Tweed. He was...well, rather, he fucking believed he was a god, that nothing and no one could bring a stop to his empire. The end of days for me came in '68, when I told Tweed I was fucking done with his bullshit and The Palace would no longer be affiliated with the Hall."

"Oh no," Celeste remarked. "What happened?"

The Madame let out a heavy sigh. "Johnny and I were...together, at this point. He wanted to leave the city, I wanted to stay, and so of course, we fucking stayed. I wouldn't leave Mary and Thomas... I refused."

She paused, visibly pained by the memory, and Celeste realized the Madame was sharing with her a side of herself she'd never shown another living person.

Reaching over, Celeste touched her arm. "It's not your fault."

"It was," she declared stubbornly. "But I've accepted it." The Madame drank some wine. "Tweed sent six of his best to the old Palace that night. It was ghastly, to say the least..." Again, her voice trailed off while the Madame collected her composure. "They snuck in undetected, beat me to a pulp. Raped me. Murdered Johnny right in front of me and told me if I wasn't at work for Tweed in the morning, they'd be back to fucking finish me off and burn The Palace to the ground."

"Where was Louis?"

"He'd drunk himself into a coma that night, missing Will, I assume, as well as Edward, and didn't wake up until I fucking burst into his room covered in blood, ready to kill him. All because I didn't want to be Tweed's puppet any longer."

The last of her words were said through gritted teeth, and immediately, Celeste knew where this story was going.

"What did you do?"

"I took my girls and we moved uptown."

"But...but where?!"

"Louis and I found a safe haven for a short period of time to run operations. Tweed put a bounty on both of us with the Whyos, and so those motherfuckers ran us out, swore if we came below Midtown, we would be gutted in the street. I took every dime I'd ever saved, used every contact I had, and bought and furnished The Palace we now sit in all in a matter of days. I promised every fucking thing you can imagine to get this place decorated enough to open, and within weeks, we had already paid every debt off; in half a year, we'd made more than I had in my entire life as a whore or madame."

"But...but Tweed..."

A very odd look came to the Madame's face. "Do you really want to know?"

Celeste rolled her eyes. "Of course I fucking do."

The Madame grew deadly serious. "You will not ever repeat what I tell you."

"Yes, Madame."

There was a smirk. "I gave the Committee of Seventy everything I had on him. He was arrested, imprisoned, and sat there for five years."

This much, Celeste understood. "But then he escaped."

"For a time," the Madame added. "It was the perfect opportunity to exact the revenge I'd been seeking for years. And he played right into my trap.

"Tweed thought he'd escaped. He thought he'd made it to Spain and would never be caught, but he didn't plan on my sending Louis to find him and bring him home to face justice."

Celeste nearly dropped her wine glass. "You...you sent Louis? But I thought—"

"You thought, like everyone else, and like history, that Tweed was caught at a border and thrown onto an American warship, sent home to rot in prison. When, in reality, it took Louis fucking months to track his ass down, and when he did, he handed him over to the government, because if there is one thing America hates more than foreigners, it's traitors. And to them, Tweed was a traitor."

"So, you gave him to the army," Celeste remarked aloud. "You... Jesus, Madame, you were the one that brought him home to die."

"Yes, I did," the Madame admitted.

"But how did you hide it?"

"No one needed to know, no one wanted to know, and I couldn't give a damn whose name eventually got credit for it. He got what he fucking deserved." The Madame set her empty wine glass aside and rotated toward Celeste. "I know what it feels like. To watch the person you love most be murdered in front of you. To hurt in places you didn't know you could. To want to kill another being with every ounce of your person. When I lost Johnny, I was enraged in a way I have scarcely been since. He'd been a part of me, and he was the man I truly considered Mary's father. I had to witness him be butchered by a man I despised, a man who did not feel, and who was only there to exert power." With a heavy exhale, the Madame shook her head. "The time will come and Walsh will meet his end, and I can promise you not one of us will rest until that son of a bitch ceases to fucking breathe. You, however, will stop fucking tormenting yourself about being affected by your father's end. You have every right to be devastated, and I want you to be. It means you're fucking human."

Fighting back a sob, Celeste's gaze fell. "I just keep wishing I could have done something different. I feel like I could have changed his fate, rather than leave him to the fucking butchery of that horrible, horrible bastard."

"Celeste," the Madame interjected, bringing her hand to Celeste's knee, "he wanted to kill you. He got your father instead, and I can promise you, Douglas is grateful for it. If you had been the one on the other side of that blade, this whole enterprise would have come crumbling down. And you fucking know it."

"Just like Johnny sacrificed himself for you," she uttered quietly.

For a moment, the Madame didn't speak. "Yes," she whispered at last in return.

Celeste didn't care if the Madame retracted. Without a second thought, she slipped her fingers through the Madame's and clasped her hand.

"Thank you."

The Madame squeezed her fingers lovingly. "You are welcome, darling."

With a sniff, Celeste let out a small, ironic laugh. "Well, now what?"

The Madame grinned, her grasp withdrawing as she poured

them each more wine. "Now, we have an entire fucking night of clients to prepare for."

"Good. I'm looking forward to it."

A knock came to the door, and Celeste and the Madame glanced at one another.

"The girls, perhaps?" Celeste asked.

The Madame's brow furrowed. "I hadn't sent for them yet... unless they've become fucking mind readers. Come in!"

Rather than Paige, Marcy, Claire, or Dot, much to the Madame and Celeste's surprise, in walked Samuel.

"Evening, ladies," he greeted them, his demeanor much softer than Celeste was used to.

"Ellis?" the Madame inquired, rising to stand.

"I am assuming I'm allowed to pour myself a drink first."

With confusion, the Madame peered at Celeste, then back to him. "Certainly."

"What is going on?" Celeste mouthed inaudibly.

The Madame shook her head in response, suspicious and without any leads. "Samuel, is everything all right?"

He had just finished pouring his drink and turned to them, walking to join them by the fire collectedly.

"I have a proposition for you," he informed them, motioning to the Madame, then pointedly looking at Celeste. "Actually, for both of you."

"Both of us?" Celeste entreated. "That sounds promising," she teased, taking a sip of wine.

Shifting in her seat beside Celeste and eyeing Samuel carefully as he lowered down opposite them, the Madame appeared to be playfully interested in what could be up Ellis's sleeve.

"Quit dancing around the fucking subject and tell us what's going on," she demanded, and while her tone was firm, a small smile was on her face.

In that moment, Celeste understood she was privy to something very few living souls on this planet were, which was a glimpse into the relationship between Ellis and the Madame. It was one they carefully kept concealed from those closest to them, cloaking their relationship of decades behind professional courtesy and work. This time, however, when the pair of them addressed one another, their energy was good-natured and mischievous, as if they enjoyed making each other guess in the best possible way.

Ellis had some of his whiskey. "I quit the force today."

In complete shock, Celeste's mouth fell open, and she felt the Madame instantly tense at the news.

"W-what?!" Celeste exclaimed. "Why? What happened?!"

His countenance became serious. "It was a wake-up call, what happened to me and Seamus with those goddamn Whyos. I guess I finally saw what could happen...or rather, the worst of what might happen to any of us. I laid in bed healing, wondering what the fuck I was doing. This isn't a fight for coppers or detectives or any of that. This is one that we have to win—we, as in it's us or no one else. When the Madame told me you were moving in, Celeste, and forgive me for saying so, but after what happened to your father, I decided to finally take you up on your offer, Madame."

"You want to come on at The Palace," she stated, as if not truly believing the words herself.

"I want to join The Palace," Samuel confirmed. "As one of you, not as a contact or a secondary. I want to be here to protect you, both of you, and to protect this place, because Lord knows the worst of it ain't over yet.

Celeste revolved to the Madame, delighted. "You didn't tell me this was even in the cards! When did this happen?"

"I've been making the offer for months," the Madame elucidated, taking a sip of wine to hide her enthusiasm. "I never fucking dreamed you would actually do it, Samuel."

"The department doesn't need me," Samuel addressed with annoyance. "I have been a royal pain in their ass for years, trying to be a decent detective and get this Whyo shit under control. I can't do it any longer. It's over. So, the façade has finally died, and here I am, where I've probably belonged all along."

"You already belonged here, whether you would admit it or not," Celeste spoke strongly. "You have been instrumental in keeping us out of trouble and in helping us to stay alive." She grinned at him. "We are lucky to have you."

"I am absolutely not fucking sold," the Madame asserted, relaxing into the sofa. "What sort of credentials are you bringing to the table? You can't just waltz in here and expect—"

"Oh, will you just shut the fuck up already," Samuel shot at her. "I'm here, aren't I?"

The only occasion Celeste recalled seeing the Madame happier was the night she told Thomas he was her grandson.

"Fine," she replied, maintaining her edge. "There are certain parameters we will be implementing now that you are here, and you will have George and Ashleigh run you through the ropes. Understood?"

He smirked. "Yes, Madame."

"Your number one priority will be Celeste's protection. I already have two fucking bodyguards, and that way, all of our personal attachments will not conflict."

"Touché," Celeste agreed, saluting the Madame with her wine glass.

"So, what kind of money do I make here?" Samuel teased, winking at Celeste.

"You know, if she decides to throw a knife your way, I won't be able to stop her," Celeste bantered.

"She'd miss me too much."

"Sadly," the Madame replied with a genuine smile, "yes."

Clients, more than Celeste could remember in recent memory, filtered in and out of The Palace that night, and while the vibe of girls with customers was full of charm, sexuality, and intrigue, the atmosphere amongst everyone else was almost a melancholic dream. Amongst the Madame, Samuel, Celeste, Ashleigh, Marcy, George, and Claire, their sideways glances or corner-of-eye peeks were almost entirely of a comprehension that this night might be the last night. It was a growing sentiment within the Madame's renegades: this idea that any night, any moment, could be one of the last, and as a result, each one of them found they relished the normalcy of what life was outside of the war with the Whyos and Tammany Hall. Celeste in particular felt a premonition deep within that she ought to enjoy herself, to really live in those hours with the people she loved and cared for. There would never be a way to know what tomorrow would bring, and at the very least, Celeste found comfort in the present—in the beauty that was The Palace, the Madame, and the enormous kingdom she had built into grandeur from nothing but rubble.

"Where did you go?" Hugh Grant asked, sliding over beside Celeste at the bar as Claire poured him a generous share of bourbon. The night wasn't quite through, and while Celeste wanted nothing more than to drink at the bar and hang out with the crowd, like the Madame would say, she had work to do.

"Hugh!" she cried in feigned delight. "Such a pleasure to see you, I wasn't expecting you to drop in tonight." Celeste wore a false grin from ear to ear, in a fashion that she knew made the future mayor feel like he was the only man in the room she cared about.

"Well, I wasn't anticipating an entire night here either, but everyone seems to be in such high spirits, I find it impossible to leave!" His eyes met hers. "So, tell me," he began, trying to entice her into a flirtation, "is that new pianoforte for you? I heard you used to be one hell of a beautiful pianist."

"I hope to one day again be as proficient as I used to be," she declared, reaching for her smoking wand and a cigarette.

Dutifully, Grant lit the tobacco for her with a lighter from his jacket pocket, and slowly, Celeste shifted the conversation: "So, how has the evening been? A visit with Uma?"

"Yes, she really is something to behold."

"That she is. Smart, too. I think she has taken a liking to you."

A tiny blush came to his cheeks. "It's her job, and she is quite gifted at it," he said, trying to be matter of fact, his gaze not leaving her. "My question is, have you finally taken a liking to me, Miss Hiltmore?"

Celeste pretended to giggle and rolled her eyes. "Hugh, please, you know I absolutely adore you!"

His countenance became more thoughtful. "I mean it. I am, of course, here for the entertainment and the pleasure, like almost every other man here. But I come back, Celeste, to spend time with you. To see you in your element. I find you just...intoxicating to be around."

She was careful to keep her lighthearted air. "Why, thank you, Hugh. I accept your compliment with gratitude, and you know you are welcome here whenever you like."

"Would you...well, I suppose I should just ask. Would you be willing to get dinner with me? Tomorrow?"

This had been a long time coming. "Well, to be fair, I am not sure. I would have to check with the Madame about our schedule, if that's all right with you?"

"I can wait on a calling card," he commented with a smile. "So, are the rumors true? Did you really move into The Palace today? Leaving behind the ways of the elite to do their dirty work alongside the Madame?"

Hearing her position phrased that way almost gave Celeste a thrill. "Someone has to do it," she jested, taking a long drag of her cigarette.

"The women I am around," Hugh went on, leaning his back against the bar, "they are so predictable. They don't have minds of their own, almost like they aren't…they aren't real—only there to fill a void of necessity."

"I think the question, Hugh, is that even if you were to have a woman with a mind of her own, could you, being the mayor of this city? There are certain societal obligations you have to uphold as a man of power."

"Obligations you are familiar with as well, Miss Hiltmore."

"True."

He sighed, "Couldn't we find a compromise?"

"A compromise?"

Hugh peered at her, his handsome eyes sparkling. "I will make you fall in love with me, Miss Hiltmore, one way or another. And when that day comes, I won't shackle you."

Without being able to restrain herself, Celeste let out a small snort. "Hugh, you have no idea what that would entail. I am a very different woman than you imagine. And I have no interest in ever being a wife again."

"Then we wouldn't marry," he assured her, drinking his bourbon. "Do you really think, with Richard Croker and the Hall behind me, that I give a damn how the papers portray me? In a few days, our last remaining thorn in the side will be eliminated, and we can make the *Times* write whatever the hell we want."

Hugh moved closer to her, so close Celeste felt herself immediately become uncomfortable, not because he made her nervous, but ashamedly, because she was trying to pull at the thread and prayed Ashleigh wasn't anywhere nearby.

"When I say I won't shackle you, I mean it." His hand moved to grab her free one. "You could live here half the week, the other half with me. I'm only just across the park. We could forge a permanent alliance…with you and me together, Richard and the Madame would find a lasting commitment to each other that could change this city. Think about what we could do together!"

Celeste had to admit it wasn't the worst idea he'd ever had. "Hugh, I think you are just…in lust from another night of passion at The Palace."

"No, no, Celeste, I am not." He stared at her intently. "I've already told Richard about my intentions, and while he's not exactly joyful, he does grasp that I am not changing my mind."

"Changing your mind about what?"

"That one way or another, we—you and I—will be together in the end." Hugh had another large gulp of bourbon for courage. "Think of what I could give you, and I swear on the city of New York, I would worship the ground you walk on every goddamn day, just like I already do."

Grant's affections for her had escalated much faster than Celeste or the Madame predicted they would, and she needed to consult with her superior sooner rather than later.

With a slight tilt of her head, Celeste smiled. "Dinner tomorrow, then?"

His face lit up in happiness. "Dinner tomorrow."

Throwing back his bourbon, Hugh stood up to leave, kissing Celeste's hand before he released it. "How about we hit the Grand? Champagne and a five-course dinner?"

Celeste beamed back at him. "I cannot wait."

Hugh slid off his barstool. "Oh! One last thing. I can be such a forgetful bastard sometimes."

"What is it?" Celeste asked.

"That friend of your father's you asked me about…McCann was his name, right?"

Her stomach dropped what felt like over a thousand feet. "Y-yes that's him."

"He's a family friend! Runs the Mount St. Vincent's Hotel in

Central Park. He's a quiet man, really keeps to himself, but a damn good manager and always has a full bar with some of the best brandy I've ever tasted. Should I send word along to him from you?"

Barely able to find her breath, Celeste managed to speak: "No! No, completely unnecessary. I'll drop by sometime in the next few days to meet with him. Brandy, you said?"

"Yes. A damn fine selection." For a moment, Hugh stopped where he was, hesitant. Then, without warning, he swooped in and kissed Celeste on the cheek, lingering for a second or two. "I am very much looking forward to tomorrow, Miss Hiltmore."

She watched him go, in a haze of wanting to make sense of the crucial information Hugh Grant had just given her in addition to some kind of romantic proposition, and when she rotated around towards Claire to ask for a glass of wine, it was Ashleigh who was standing there. Neither of them spoke, and rather than anger in his face, which Celeste would have preferred, it was only dejection.

"Ashleigh," she pleaded, "it's not like that."

He crossed his arms over his chest. "So, what was this then?" he asserted quietly enough to not disturb the customers behind her. "Was I just the guy you was fuckin' 'til the next best thing came along?"

"I am doing my job," she hissed, glancing from side to side to make sure she wasn't overheard. "Grant just gave me McCann."

"You think I give a damn about that right now?"

"Well, you fucking should!"

"You know what I give a damn about, Celeste," he continued. "You. And ya wanna know why I'm upset? Cause it's written all over ya. Ya tempted."

She let out an exhale of smoke and leapt up to her feet. "You do not get to tell me what I feel," Celeste shot back. "I have spent years being subjected to the bullshit of men, their judgments, and their assumptions of 'what I am' and 'what I ought to feel.' You of all fucking people know better, Ashleigh."

"Then why did ya agree to dinner?"

"Because when Priestly survives, I want a goddamn cover. Now, if you'll excuse me, I have work to do."

Whipping around, cigarette wand gracefully dangling from her fingertips, Celeste left the bar room, heading directly up to the Madame's office. Ashleigh had every right to be irritated with her, of course, allowing another man to swoon over her and more or less present her with an alternative offer of marriage; however, what frustrated Celeste in turn was that he honestly believed she considered the suggestion. How many conversations had they had where she repeatedly told him she didn't want that kind of life? After narrowly escaping the patriarchy of their society, why on earth would he think she would invite that in to toxify the existence she'd created in the aftermath? That, for Celeste, was utterly infuriating.

When she burst into the Madame's office, she found that the Madame already had a guest, and it brought a smile to her lips. There, in one of the armchairs across from her desk, was Louis, beaming at her and beckoning her to join them.

"Darling," the Madame called, "we were just discussing tomorrow. Grab some wine and we'll keep you out of Grant's clutches until he leaves."

"He's already left," Celeste sighed, heading for the drink cart. "We'll talk about it later. But first, I have something far more pressing to tell both of you. Something we have been waiting to hear for months."

She poured wine into a fresh glass, ambled over, and sat beside Louis.

"I found Patrick McCann."

Walsh was getting to the point where he wished both Berlin and Nash had been killed together in their attack on the Assistant and the chink, because Berlin was becoming almost as unbearable as Kitty had been.

He'll die soon enough.

Sitting at The Morgue with his crew of incompetent miscreants, Walsh only hoped that he'd built his base so dense that disappointment wasn't on the horizon. Years he'd been planning, and at last, he was about to cast the first stone down the mountain, one that would become an avalanche that swallowed New York City and destroyed absolutely anything and everything that came to stand in its path. Walsh had been smart—the Vigilante thought the Whyos were purely seeking to grow their influence on the city, rising in the opium trade ranks and taking over every saloon, brothel, and casino south of Midtown; what he didn't realize was this was by no means the primary objective for Walsh and the Whyos. While Lord Turner was running down opium rings and disciplining bad behavior, Walsh was smuggling in guns, weapons, and supplies for his gang, using the money he'd made for decades selling his blood in the name of science. There was something larger at work, far larger than the Vigilante, the Madame, or even Richard Croker could imagine, and Walsh was giddy with excitement picturing just what would happen as a result.

You will burn along with your city.

Strat had been playing both sides, of course, which Walsh was immensely grateful for. It was the perfect way to control the information trade, and with Strat in the dark about Walsh's true intentions, his plans would go almost unknown even to the highest tier of Whyo.

Until that very night.

Berlin was ranting once again, on and on about how they needed to find and end Esther as quickly as possible. The escalation was winding everyone around him up to a degree that Walsh was certain any moment they would leap to their feet and set off to Fifth Avenue to lynch her. It was time to end it and announce at last what their purpose was.

Holding a hand up to silence the jeers, The Morgue fell silent, and Berlin, Auggie, Zeke, Strat, Randall, and Marley each took their spots around the table by Walsh as the rest continued to stand back and hear their marching orders.

Walsh glared at them for a moment, then began, "The action you all think we are executing tomorrow is in fact, false."

Everyone at the table glanced at one another, confused.

"Ya mean there's been a change of plan?" Marley asked.

"We ain' grabbin' the reporter?" came Zeke, befuddled.

"No, we are not."

Auggie ran his fingers through his goatee. "Well, what's the plan, then?"

Walsh gave them a sinister grin. "We are going to murder the Cat and the Frog instead."

The color drained from Strat's face. "Will and Louis?"

"Yes, Strat. I can perceive that you are frustrated you didn't get a chance to pass this intelligence along to your new friends."

You've turned.

This comment offended him. "Fuck you, Walsh. I've been doing this for you to find out what the hell is going on at The Palace. My disappointment is that I think we are making a big goddamn mistake not fucking over the Hall while we have a chance."

"I have to admit," Randall cut in, "I agree with Strat. We need Tammany on their asses, not competing with us for control."

Berlin nodded along. "Agreed."

Walsh sighed heavily, "Well, there is something I do think I should tell you all, perhaps to give you a better perspective of who and what we are dealing with."

Imbeciles.

"Yeah? And what's that?"

"The Vigilante is not just any man," Walsh went on. "He is Lord Thomas Turner."

If it was possible, the room became quieter, and every gaze locked on Walsh.

That's right. Take it in, you idiotic bastards.

"You are shittin' me," Auggie uttered, in complete shock.

Strat looked like he'd been struck hard across the face. "You are telling me that some snooty rich bastard is actually the one down here givin' us hell all this time?"

Berlin was speechless, his mouth agape, and Randall was no different.

"Yes," Walsh declared, "it is him. It's why he helped the Assistant in the past, and continues to do so today."

An odd sort of reverence for Walsh spread around the room.

"That's...unbelievable!" Marley cried. "So, talk us through this. No reporter, but we're killin' the Cat and the Frog?"

"I'm happy as anybody we're finally killin' them two bastards," Auggie added, "but what's the angle?"

"The angle is we are attacking on every front," Walsh informed them smugly. "We will kill the Cat and Frog, while simultaneously leading an assault on The Palace, killing everyone of value inside, as well as the Turner residence, which we will burn to the ground if necessary." He paused for effect. "Three different locations, one goal. We are going to end the Vigilante, the Assistant, and the Madame's pursuit of us, so that when the strike happens, there are few standing in the way."

They'll all be dead.

"How will we know when to attack?" Strat pressed anxiously.

Walsh's minor concern regarding Strat's true allegiance was becoming a larger one. "The hit on the reporter was set for late morning. We will, at once, attack the three locations at nine o'clock on the mark, zero exceptions. Auggie, Zeke, and Randall, you will take your men with you to the Turners' residence. Berlin and Marley, you will have double your forces for The Palace. Strat and I will linger near the Points to take on the Cat and the Frog. That way…" Walsh's voice trailed off, his gaze narrowing at Strat, "no one will be confused about where they are supposed to be."

And you won't escape.

Strat huffed, "You want to babysit me."

Walsh could feel his rage rising, and he did his best to temper it. "No, Strat. I am giving you a chance to prove where your real loyalties lie, to put my questions to rest. Because if for any reason something goes wrong with our incursion tomorrow on the Cat and the Frog, you will be banned everywhere south of Midtown, and you will have a bounty on your head as a traitor to this gang and all we stand for. There will not be a place you can run or hide from me, I assure you of that."

I will hunt you down and enjoy slitting your throat.

"Are you calling me a traitor?" he demanded, aggravated.

"I am telling you that I do not trust you in our current climate, and you must earn that trust back or die." Walsh looked out amongst the group of Whyos listening in. "Let this be a lesson. I do not mind mingling with our enemy if it proves to be fruitful. But you will have to consistently demonstrate your allegiance, or death awaits."

You are a traitor, I can smell it.

"I have bled for this gang," Strat avowed. "Killed for this gang. Done everything I can to further our cause."

"I am only asking, Strat, that you continue to do those things," Walsh concluded, moving onto the next piece. "The strike is imminent. In the days following Christmas, we will at last have everything we need to see it through. Every one of you will be armed, and you should all be ready for blood."

Blood. Death. And fire.

A loud cheer rang out, along with a rant of Whyo calls echoing through The Morgue, and for a few minutes, Walsh let it carry on. He held up his hands, and instantly, the noise ceased.

"You have your orders, and you understand what is at stake. If you fail me, the consequences will not be pleasant, but we will not fail. We have been preparing for this for years. All you must do is execute the plan. Then…" he sneered, "then, by the new year, New York City will be ours."

Again, the cheers roared out, and Walsh leaned back into his chair, pleased.

Actually, it will be mine.

CHAPTER XLVIII.

The grandfather clock hit a quarter to nine in the Madame's office the following morning, and her trepidation regarding what was to come in the ensuing hours started to escalate. After an immensely successful night at The Palace, the day of their reckoning had arrived, and the only thing the Madame could do was bide her time in the hopes that good news came later. Good news— it was an expectation she felt was never quite fulfilled. With so much riding on these moments, the Madame kept her optimism in check with a healthy dose of anticipation that something was bound to go poorly; anticipation, and a shit ton of whiskey, of course. There had never been a better chance for them to succeed, and even if they lost a man or two in the process, it wouldn't matter in the grand scheme of the plan. Every one of them accepted the consequences of this life, and with the prospect of a dead Walsh and an ousted Richard Croker, no one gave a damn about the risk any longer, regardless of the cost.

Though it was earlier than she normally took meetings, Mock Duck sat in front of her, and to the Madame's left in the opposite armchair was Celeste, trying to assess what it was their visitor from

Chinatown was after. According to Mock Duck, it seemed that the circumstances in Chinatown were beginning to spiral out of control, and as a result, Croker wanted to make Lee sheriff as soon as the opportunity struck. The leader of the Flying Dragons, however, had other plans for Chinatown, and was desperately seeking a partnership with the Madame to strike back at Lee and gain some ground for his faction of the Hip Sing. Celeste had previously witnessed Lee's men and the damage they caused, and to the Madame's amusement, Mock Duck insisted Celeste join him and the Madame, having earned his respect and his loyalty by protecting him alongside the rest. The Madame couldn't help but be tickled— a beautiful woman could capture the attention of any room, but strap blades to her thighs along with a thirst for vengeance, and suddenly, every man is eating out of her hand.

It made the Madame smile.

"Madame," Mock Duck went on, his voice urgent, "I do not think you grasp just how terrible this battle will be in Chinatown."

"Terrible in what sort of way?" Celeste asked, peering toward the Madame, who shrugged in response.

"Terrible in that many men will die, and not just my people." He paused, having a sip of his Sunday coffee. "If you think this war will only be fought in Chinatown's streets, that is a blatant misconception. It is already seeping into the other neighborhoods, slowly yet steadily taking its toll."

"How far is it spreading?" the Madame pressed.

"It's moving northwest. Inching toward Midtown. It will only be a matter of time before New York realizes there is another battle ensuing. Other than yours, that is."

The Madame leaned back into her chair. "Lee has been a nasty son of a bitch for as long as I've known him. Truthfully, I wouldn't mind severing that cord, especially given the fact that he's fucking corrupt."

His eyes lit up. "Thank you, Madame, I don't know——"

"I am not finished," she interjected swiftly, her left eyebrow raising. "I can see this becoming a fucking slaughter, and that is not what I want. What I need to know is what exactly you want from The Palace."

"What I want?"

"You're saying there is a battle within the Hip Sing," Celeste recalled, "that you are purging Lee and his reign because they no longer follow the moral compass of your people. That is correct, right?"

Mock Duck nodded. "Yes, Miss Hiltmore."

"And so, what is it you need us to do?" the Madame carried on. "Fight alongside the fucking celestials? I will say, sir, if that is the case, you are pretty goddamn lucky to have such an open-minded ally."

"If it comes to that, perhaps," Mock Duck admitted honestly. "For now, what I want from you, Madame, as well as The Palace, is your loyalty with our opium distribution. We will be your supplier, and us alone. Because of your reputation and for the esteem with which this institution operates, others will follow in your wake. It would be an enormous win for the Flying Dragons, and it would immediately start to wean away Lee's hold on our people."

A smirk came to her lips. "All right, Mock Duck. I will make you a deal."

"I would expect nothing less."

"I will cut my ties with Lee, and you can become our brand new opium supplier, but I swear to fucking God, if your price increases within the year, if you get your ass murdered, or I get any fucking insubordination from your people, we are done, no questions asked. Do you understand that?"

A small bow of his head followed, "Yes, Madame, I do."

"Good. Now, as far as fucking manpower goes, I will offer assistance to you only in scenarios when it is feasible for my people. Yes?"

"Yes."

"And…" the Madame had a gulp of her own Sunday coffee, "and in return, I would like to ask you for loyalty with our own battles."

He was confused. "Madame?"

"There may come a day when you and your Flying Dragons would be needed to assist us, and if the time ever presents itself, I expect full and immediate cooperation."

"Against Croker?"

"Against them all."

From the expression on Celeste's face, she was utterly shocked at the Madame's request of Mock Duck; however, Mock Duck himself again bowed his head.

"Your people have already saved my skin once. I have no doubt it will happen again, and as a result, yes. You have our loyalty, and our force when needed. Especially when it comes to the Whyos and the dragon of the Bowery."

She held up her mug in salutation. "Then we have an accord."

Mock Duck mirrored her. "We have a deal."

"I assume the dragon of the Bowery is Walsh?" Celeste inquired while the three of them had a gulp of their drinks.

"He most certainly is," Mock Duck assured her. "In retaliation for Lee and the Whyos going separate ways, he has shown no mercy on Chinatown, allowing his men to attack our people on the outskirts of our neighborhood." The Madame observed the slight tremor of fury in Mock Duck's voice. "I will do anything to send that man to his death."

"We are hoping," the Madame told him, "that you will not have to."

"The hour is approaching, am I correct?" he asked her.

"An hour of reckoning for Walsh, for Croker, and even for your Mr. Lee," the Madame declared, having another sip of Sunday coffee. "What worries me, Mock Duck, is that Whyo numbers are growing, and no one can figure out what the fuck their endgame is. That is what I need to know."

"There are whispers in Chinatown," Mock Duck said, his countenance shifting to one of uneasiness. "Whispers that there is something far more sinister planned."

"Planned?" Celeste stared at him. "Like an attack of some sort? We definitely are privy to those rumors."

"A few of my men have been tracking Walsh and his Whyos, particularly around the harbor, and within these last few weeks of winter, he has received an exorbitant amount of wooden crates, more than would be expected in November and December."

A small pit formed in the Madame's stomach. "Crates from where?" She locked eyes with Mock Duck.

"From what we can gather, crates from the deep South, Madame."

"The South?" Celeste asked. "What could they possibly be… be…" The realization of Mock Duck's words hit Celeste like a train. "Oh. Oh no."

"So, your theory is that Walsh has been buying crates of weapons from the Confederacy?" the Madame surged.

"I think he has been able to convince those still loyal to that ghastly flag that he wants to restart the war," Mock Duck explained. "Giving the Confederacy New York would, well, change the world and the future of this country."

Celeste was horrified. "The war would be—well, for fuck's sake, there wouldn't even be a war at that point!"

"Yes, Miss Hiltmore, you are correct."

Oddly enough, this news didn't surprise the Madame. "He would never give New York to the Confederacy."

Both Mock Duck and Celeste looked at her.

"He wouldn't?" Celeste asked. "Even if it meant he could conquer you, Esther, Richard…all of us?"

"Darling," the Madame remarked, "you must understand. He does not think like us. He does not want to have power, he does not want to conquer, and he certainly does not give a fuck about notoriety."

"He is a dragon," Mock Duck inserted.

Celeste was perplexed. "A...dragon?"

"He wants to watch the whole world fucking burn," the Madame said, letting out a heavy, exhaustive exhale. "Walsh does not trust. He does not like the system. He wants anarchy—pure, unadulterated anarchy. It's the system that made that bastard what he is, and he wants that fucking system to be torn to shreds."

"He has, more than likely, been purchasing artillery," Mock Duck added thoughtfully, his brow furrowing. "Although with what money, I cannot be sure. It is not as if the life of a gang leader is highly fruitful."

The Madame glanced at Celeste. "Holy shit."

"What?!"

"The money from the doctor...from his blood...."

"Oh...oh my God..."

Mock Duck shifted in his seat. "Money from a doctor?"

"To cut a long story fucking short, Walsh made some money off of his own blood," the Madame divulged. "And not just money—a hell of a lot of money. Over years, to assist in this psycho's research, Walsh would give this doc his blood for compensation, and I think we just learned how he plans to spend it."

"You believe he will attack the city?"

She had to answer frankly: "I cannot really say, and we all know I don't keep my opinions to myself. All I fucking know is that son of a bitch wants a spectacle, and with that spectacle, who knows what the fuck he would unleash on us—Whyos, Confederates, an apocalypse. The only thing that is certain is fucking uncertainty."

"But the police!" Celeste inserted firmly. "The National Guard!

We could even get the goddamn Pinkertons! If it was a national threat, wouldn't they send the army?!"

"Do you really think," Mock Duck posed to her, "that the American army would listen to two women and a chink?"

Holding her ground, Celeste stood firm. "We have Thomas. They would listen to him if he sent word."

"One man," the Madame added, "with a conspiracy theory that no one would trust in a million fucking years. No one can value the notion that men like Walsh exist, darling. No one wants to believe it."

"So, what do we do?"

For a few seconds, the Madame and Mock Duck gazed at one another, communicating an entire conversation in a handful of heartbeats.

She is not aware of how bad things are, thought the Madame.

She lost her father to him, how could she not grasp the danger? Mock Duck posed with a look.

It's not the danger, it's the magnitude. Thomas and I are both aware that the target is bigger than we ever could have imagined, yet convincing everyone else of that will be a bit fucking challenging.

My people already fear him. Do yours?

I think hate is a better word, the Madame thought.

Hatred can be channeled, fear is far more toxic.

Yes, it most certainly is, and you should make sure before the end, your people are not afraid but angry.

Angry how?

Angry that some evil bastard has come to take away the life they've sacrificed everything to find here. I think that should be enough.

What about her? Mock Duck questioned.

She bit her lip. "Celeste, darling, could you give us a moment?"

Without hesitation, Celeste nodded and got to her feet, leaving the Madame's office.

"What about her?" Mock Duck asked again.

"She will only understand when the fire is ablaze around her," the Madame heartily acknowledged. "Celeste has endured a great many sufferings, while conversely being granted a life some of us would fucking dream of. She is a walking contradiction. Celeste has killed, yes, and will undoubtedly kill again when needed. She is strong, ruthless, I might say, and determined—determined to do something to change her destiny. And in time, she will know the path, but it will take one end to birth her beginning."

At last, he appeared to comprehend her words. "She will do you proud, Madame. And I will see to that personally."

"Thank you."

"Can I ask you something?"

She rolled her eyes. "One last thing, I fucking suppose."

Mock Duck rose, finishing his Sunday coffee. "You seem so certain of your future. How can you know?"

"I know," was all she asserted, and rather than push her any further on the subject, Mock Duck left it at that.

"Madame, I will bid you good day," he said with a small bow of his head, standing. "Shall I send Miss Hiltmore back in?"

"That would be lovely, thank you."

Within seconds of Mock Duck exiting the office, Celeste appeared, evidently having waited outside on the balcony rather than head downstairs as the Madame presumed she would. She must be avoiding Ashleigh after their tense interaction the night prior, one that the Madame assumed had yet to be forgiven on their behalf.

"You could have gone downstairs," the Madame stated, finishing her Sunday coffee and setting the mug aside. "Ashleigh is running to the Turners' to check on Esther and Thomas before they head south to join Louis and Will."

Celeste flopped down into her chair once again. "What about McCann?"

"Louis went by this morning to drop a calling card. I would imagine it's just a matter of time, but who fucking knows. Now, how do we…" Her voice trailed off at the sound of George and Claire's elevated voices in the lobby echoing toward the office.

The two women locked eyes.

"Do you think Mock Duck did something to offend them?" Celeste questioned, puzzled as she turned away from the Madame to face the door and their incoming visitors.

There was the distinct tremor of Claire racking the shotgun, and with her instincts awakening, the Madame moved fast.

"Darling," she hissed under her breath, "here!" The Madame reached into her top drawer and snatched two pocket pistols and an extra set of throwing knives. "Take these. Hurry!"

Sliding them across her desk, Celeste lurched forward and snatched them, cocking the pistol and shoving the blades into her dress pocket. Without speaking, the Madame and Celeste spun to the door, guns hot and aimed at whoever it was marching toward the Madame's office.

The door burst open, and a man nearly ran in and collapsed; a man the Madame saw Celeste recognized, though to the Madame, he was a stranger.

"Who the fuck are you?!" the Madame demanded, pacing around her desk and ahead of Celeste in case things got ugly. Behind the mystery man, Claire had the shotgun pointed at his back and George had his revolver out and ready, his face red in anger. Then, to the Madame's surprise, she caught sight of Mock Duck lingering over George's shoulder, his hand on the hilt of his sword, ready to draw it from the scabbard if necessary.

"Please," the man huffed, out of breath. He'd been dreadfully beaten, sliced on his arms and torso, and was struggling to stay on his feet. "I couldn't get here sooner. I had to get away from…from him."

The Madame turned. "Celeste? Do you know him?!"

"Madame, this is Strat, our connection to the Whyos," Celeste announced, though her pistol did not lower. "Strat, what the fuck is going on?"

"Darling," the Madame uttered, lowering her gun, "look at him."

Strat was barely able to stand. His breath was wet and heavy from serious internal damage, and he swayed his weight from one foot to the other.

"It was him…Walsh…I'll be…I'll be fine. Listen, as much as I…I need help, we don't have any goddamn time…"

Celeste and the Madame shot each other a glance.

"What do you mean we don't have any goddamn time?" the Madame spat.

"They're…they're coming, Madame," he asserted, "and not just a…a few of them. Twenty, maybe thirty, and what's worse is… they…they're not just coming here."

Strat coughed violently, blood splattering the Madame's beautiful carpet, and after, he managed to straighten up as every one of them heeded the messenger.

"They're going to the Turners'. They're going to the barbershop. They want to…to kill all of you in one fucking swoop. We have to get ready…we have…"

In haste, his eyes scanned the room until they found the grandfather clock, and the Madame saw his apprehension.

"We have less than three minutes until they…until they…invade…"

"We can send runners," the Madame insisted, pocketing her pistol and hastening to the back stair. "I can send the girls in pairs to warn them!"

"You don't have time!" Strat bellowed. "Madame, they are already there. The strike time is at nine o'clock on every…every single front…everyone. If you want your girls to survive…if we want to survive…we need to get armed immediately! And we will need every last one of us to hold this fucking place."

"Madame," Celeste cut in, "we have less than two minutes."

There wasn't a second to spare.

"Lock it down!" she yelled as loud as she could, and in a flurry, George and Claire were rushing out of the Madame's office, with Celeste, Mock Duck, and Strat eyeing her for instruction. "Well, aren't we a fucking rag tag group of renegades," she jeered. "Celeste, more blades are in my second drawer. Stack as many as you can and grab an extra five cylinders for your pistol. Mock Duck, Strat—lobby. Strat, I know you're beaten to shit, but you're going to have to suck it up for twenty minutes. I'll hold the stairs, Claire will hold the bar, and I'll send George to scout shoot from the balcony. Now, fucking go!"

Strat and Mock Duck bolted, leaving Celeste and the Madame to arm themselves. Peeking over her shoulder, the Madame spotted the clock. One minute. Forty-five seconds. Thirty seconds…thirty seconds and they would be fighting for their very lives. Strapped with as many knives as they could find, Celeste and the Madame then hurried to the office door just as George burst through the back, right on schedule.

"George!" the Madame bellowed. "Grab the twenty-two from under my desk and position on the balcony. We need a scout shooter. Pick off as many of those fuckers as you can, you hear me?! Extra cylinders are loaded!"

Without waiting for a reply, the Madame and Celeste sprinted toward the stairs right as the front door of The Palace exploded open and nearly off its hinges, the sound of bullets echoing off the walls and through the air, vibrating through the Madame's entire body.

It was a fucking nightmare. In a rush, Whyos flooded inside, some with guns drawn, already firing useless, drifting shots, others with bludgeons, black jacks, and blades, ready to take down whoever might cross their path. Celeste was up two stairs and to the right of the Madame, with Mock Duck directly ahead and Strat down beside him. The flicker of the shotgun caught her eye, signaling Claire had taken her post at the entrance to the bar, armed and ready; and to her left on the balcony with the twenty-two was George, the nose of the gun poking out between the newel posts. They were in place, as ready as they could possibly be.

The Madame knelt and swooped her skirt aside, grasping two blades tied to her thigh, throwing the first overhand and the second a sideways pull from her left shoulder, striking one Whyo in the chest and the other directly through his forehead, killing him. From behind her, the Madame saw blades flying past from Celeste's hand, and again the Madame drew two more, these aimed at her targets underhand, and one caught an assailant's quadricep while the other pierced a bicep; not the lethal throws the Madame desired, yet enough damage would be done to impede their fighting capabilities. On the floor, Strat was being manhandled by four Whyos. The poor bastard was obviously extremely weak from escaping Walsh, not to mention he'd undoubtedly run as fast as his legs would carry him from the Bowery to The Palace. He was barely holding his own, and as one of his attackers drew a bludgeon overhead to strike, the Madame drew the blade at her waist and sent it with as much force as she could. While it didn't kill her target, it knocked the baton right out of his hands, piercing his hand, blood spewing. One of Strat's other attackers circled around, though rather than making the Madame his objective, his eyes focused in on Celeste, and he pulled a gun from the holster at his waist, the barrel pointing at the center of Celeste's chest.

"Celeste!" the Madame screamed, fear striking every pore of her body as she watched in dismay, conscious that there was no way she could draw in time.

Thankfully, there was a slice, a scream, and before a shot could be fired, the man was bellowing in pain, his arm cut through the bone at his elbow. His forearm, hand, and pistol fell down in unison to

766

the ground, leaving the man without one of his limbs. With a smirk, Mock Duck peered the Madame's way, then went back to his own defenses against the never-ending stream of Whyos that seemed to be cascading through The Palace's front door. Still, Mock Duck's save of Celeste was quickly overshadowed by Strat being pummeled in the head with the butt of a gun, then falling senseless to the ground. This was then shortly followed by George letting out a screech of anguish from the balcony, and the Madame whipped around to see him in retreat, shot through his right shoulder, though thankfully, from what she could discern, the wound was by no means fatal.

That was when one came through the door, one Whyo who walked as if he owned all the others, and he went straight for Strat, gun raised.

"Marley!" he shouted to one of the men fighting Mock Duck. "We've got more comin'! I will execute this motherfuckin' traitor, so help me God!"

"Kill him, Berlin!" Marley screeched in return, battling yet losing to Mock Duck.

The pocket pistol wouldn't be enough to end him, and therefore, the Madame began to descend to the bottom of the staircase.

"George!" the Madame screamed, spinning toward the balcony.

He, too, was observing. "Coming down!"

With a toss, the twenty-two was launched up and over the balcony, and when the Madame snatched it from the air, she yanked the bolt back, locked the stock into her shoulder, and twirled, taking aim.

To her dismay, Berlin was standing over Strat, hammer cocked, with the nose pointed down at the back of Strat's head, an enormous grin on his face.

"Stalemate!" he huffed at her, amused.

"I could still fucking shoot you."

"And lose Strat? Bullet from a twenty-two ain' gonna do much, Madame."

"It will if I hit my mark."

"Wanna chance it?"

"You're a goddamn disgrace to this fucking city," she snarled. "One less of you, and I'll sleep better tonight."

"The traitors are always the first to go," he spat. "You of all people oughta know that shit by now, Madame."

It was in that moment the Madame realized Celeste had evaporated from her sights, and she prayed the girl had her flank.

"Walsh is the traitor," the Madame mocked, "and I hope every fucking one of you bastards burns alive with him when we take you down."

The man shrugged. "You'll be gone before then, I'm afraid."

"No, you will, you asshole," came Celeste's voice from the opposite side of the staircase, and before he could remotely perceive what was happening, a blade was hurled from the shadows, striking Berlin in the chest.

It hit him hard, causing him to retreat two steps, though to the Madame's horror, he did not cower or fall. Slowly, his left hand reached up, grasping onto the handle to take hold of the knife, and with a tug, he pulled it from his chest. Blood trickled out of his lips, dripping down his chin, and as he let the blade drop to the floor, his gaze found the Madame's.

He smiled. "Time to die, bitch."

His right arm extended, gun leveled straight at her, and in unison, they fired at each other.

The Madame didn't flinch—she took the shot without recoil, fully expecting to be hit herself, and conversely not giving a damn if it meant killing another Whyo. There was a brief moment when he looked surprised, and Berlin dropped his gun, right hand clutching at his throat as blood began to spew from his carotid artery. His legs shook, and he fell to his knees, unable to stop from bleeding out. Throwing his glance to the Madame, she glared back at the man mercilessly, noting the fear in Berlin's eyes that everyone had when they understood death was taking them. And yet, she was relentless—with one last shudder, he collapsed facedown onto the ground beside Strat, never to harm again.

Celeste ran and grabbed Berlin's revolver from the floor, then bolted to the Madame, shielding her as she cocked the revolver. "Madame, you've been shot."

The Madame lowered down to take a seat on the step behind Celeste. "So, that's why my fucking shoulder hurts," she perceived with sarcasm.

Celeste's head whipped around for just a second, discerning the Madame's left arm. "Just a graze. A deep graze, though."

A bullet zinged by the Madame's ear, and Celeste's attention went back to protecting the Madame from the last few Whyos. Mock Duck was slaughtering them, and Claire had done a decent amount of damage with the shotgun, which she was currently using as a bludgeon to beat the head in of a presumably unconscious Whyo. Firing left and right, Celeste was attempting to pick off anyone Mock Duck hadn't made his way to, when abruptly, Celeste ran out of bullets, and the entire energy of the room shifted. Every Whyo ear heard the empty pull of the trigger, and in unison, their attack became increasingly and monstrously vicious. ·

The Madame was still clutching onto the twenty-two, and in haste, she grabbed the pocket pistol from her skirt. Rising to her feet, the Madame shoved the pocket pistol into Celeste's hand, moving beside her.

"I appreciate you wanting to save me, darling," she remarked, the stock of the rifle back to her right shoulder as Whyos charged them, "but it looks like we are going to have to fucking do this together."

With a nod, Celeste seized the pistol to take aim, and as a wall of Whyos stampeded towards them, the Madame and Celeste commenced their fire, retreating up the staircase deliberately, first one step, then another, hoping higher ground could give them an advantage as they fired shot after shot after shot. When Celeste reloaded, the Madame kept firing, being careful as she counted down her bullets and thanking Christ George reloaded the cylinder before he tossed it to her. Her fourth shot struck a Whyo between the eyes, killing him instantly. The fifth hit one in another's gut, sending him to the ground, a slow and painful death undoubtedly earned. With two bullets, the Madame caught their final assailant in the shoulder, though he kept pummeling forward, and with her final shot, Celeste nailed him through the eye, ending the onslaught. The few remaining Whyos were cutting their losses and bolting as fast as their legs would carry them, yet in the corner over by the bar entrance, something caught the Madame's attention.

Claire was on her knees, arms stretched overhead in surrender, with a Whyo pointing a pistol at her chest; not far off, Mock Duck was being held hostage by Marley with a blade at his throat, the edge piercing his neck.

"Madame," Marley called, spinning with Mock Duck to face her. "You can pick, if ya like: the girl, or the oriental. Then, we will be on our way. You like this game, or so Walsh has told us."

The Madame locked eyes with Claire.

"You need him," Claire mouthed. "Not me."

Out of the corner of her eye, the Madame saw a glint of metal in Celeste's hand.

"I'm so glad Walsh has been sharing our history with you," the Madame shot back, trying to stall. "Maybe he also shared that I don't take kindly to people threatening my fucking family, you asshole." Her gaze flashed to Mock Duck.

Get ready to drop.

"Well, that's just too damn bad," Marley taunted. "Hal, would you do the honors?"

Hal's arm lengthened, the nose of the pistol extending the

direction of Claire's forehead to fire, when out of nowhere, Marcy leapt from behind the doorway to the bar, startling Hal into pulling the trigger and shooting Marcy in the chest.

"Marcy!" Claire shrieked.

The Madame took aim with the twenty-two, shooting Hal in the back before he could fire again, killing him with her final bullet. Scrambling on her hands and knees, Claire grabbed the shotgun taken from her by Hal, racked it, and shot Hal in the head, causing an explosion of human fragments the Madame hoped she never had to witness again. To her right, Celeste was frozen in place, blade static in her hand, her whole body shaking in rage. On the lobby floor, Mock Duck and Marley were in fisticuffs, though Marley managed to get the better of a badly beaten Mock Duck, knocking him to the earth with a leveling jab to his left cheek.

Marley then sprinted for the door.

"Celeste!" the Madame exclaimed.

Snapping back, Celeste pulled and threw the blade, but Marley was too fast. It missed him by less than an inch and struck the wooden frame of the front door, and Marley disappeared out into the street.

The Madame threw the twenty-two aside and hurried to Marcy, running down the steps in a panic. It was difficult to keep a level head as the Madame lowered down beside her, assessing that there was very little to be done. Claire already had Marcy wrapped in her arms, holding her tightly as tears streamed down her face, shaking her head.

"It's...it's fatal..." was all Claire could say, biting her lip to repress a sob.

One look at Marcy's wound confirmed to the Madame that Claire was right, and the Madame reached out, taking Marcy's hand in hers.

"Darling," she whispered, "darling, why?"

The color in Marcy's skin was completely gone. "Because you… you need Claire, Madame. I don't…matter…"

Claire let out a tiny howl, squeezing Marcy tighter, unable to articulate words as she cried.

Suddenly, Jeremiah was at their side with Celeste, kneeling to analyze the wound, and the Madame held up her free hand, touching his shoulder gently.

"Jer…leave it."

"But Madame, if you just let me—"

"Jer. Leave it."

He was stricken with grief. "I…I wish I could help…"

The Madame's attention returned to Marcy, who had very little time left. "You're going to a better place, darling," the Madame whispered. "Don't hold on. You can go."

"I…know…I just…"

"Just what, darling?"

A smile twitched at the corner of Marcy's mouth. "I'm just… going…to miss…you."

Her head gently dipped forward, and the light left her eyes.

Rocking Marcy back and forth, Claire couldn't hold it in any longer. She released a guttural, deep howl of anguish that the Madame felt in the deepest part of her soul, and the Madame sat back onto the floor, releasing Marcy's hand to wipe the tears from her own eyes. In no time whatsoever, Marcy was gone…taken from them without warning. There was no way to bring her back, no way to undo the bullet, no way to cure the pain that flooded every one of them.

"Jer," the Madame uttered, masking her own sobs, "bolt the back door. Check on the girls. Please."

"Yes, Madame," he replied with a catch in his throat, quickly shuffling to his feet to do what she asked.

The Madame managed to push herself up to stand, and she spotted Mock Duck leaning against the wall, defeated and bloodied, while Celeste was slumped over, seated on the staircase, crying with her head in her hands. Above, George was attempting to get up, grunting in pain as he ambled around. Strat was just beginning to stir, still down on the floor, and therefore, the Madame shuffled over to the front door of The Palace, slamming the open door shut and pulling the bolt down to keep the world out.

"Mock Duck," she said, circling around, "go see Jeremiah, then get out of here. You can consider The Palace your friend with anything you might need." Taking a deep breath, the Madame paused. "We would not have survived today if you weren't here. I mean what I fucking say—whatever you need, you have a friend in us."

His mien was downcast. "I only wish we could have saved everyone."

"We...did our best to..." she managed to respond.

Mock Duck bowed his head. "I am so very sorry for your loss, Madame. For all of your loss. Good day, Madame."

With that, Mock Duck limped down the hallway, following in Jeremiah's wake.

Next, the Madame went to Strat's side and crouched down, assessing his injuries. "Strat?" she solicited, her hand coming to his back. "Can you hear me?"

"Mmmuhhh."

"Good. I'm going to turn you over now and see how much fucking damage has been done. All right?"

"Muhh."

With her left hand on his shoulder and her right hand on his torso, the Madame drew Strat to face up, and the picture wasn't pretty. A grossly already swollen black eye, dislocated jaw, and the previous gashes from Walsh were oozing from various spots covering Strat's body. There was a deep gash in his thigh which he must have acquired during the attack at The Palace, and in addition, she found unquestionably ruthless bruising to his abdomen and internal organs. On further inspection, the Madame spotted that his right ring finger was dislocated, and she drew his hand into her lap, braced his wrist, and snapped the finger back into place.

"Fuck!" he yelled, launching upright to a seat and yanking his hand way from the Madame in shock. "What the fuck just happened?"

"I thought you would want to keep your finger, so I set it for you," she stated bluntly.

Strat blinked his eyes hard a few times, taking in the room around him as he glanced from left to right. "We made it?"

"Not...not all of us..." the Madame said quietly.

"Who?"

"One of my girls."

"But they...they were locked in?!"

The Madame shook her head. "She saved Claire and sacrificed herself as a result."

Rubbing his hand, Strat let out a sigh, "Madame, you realize that if Mock Duck wasn't here, we would be dead."

"It's absolutely fucking true." The Madame gazed at Strat. "But if you hadn't warned us, we also would be dead. I owe you my life, and the lives of my people you saved by crossing over from Walsh and the Whyos. I didn't think you had it in you to switch sides. In fact, I recall just telling Thomas I thought you were full of shit."

"I didn't think I would cross either," he told her openly, "until she showed up." Strat pointed up at Celeste, who was in a fog, gaping at Claire holding Marcy. "We got big things to talk about, Madame, things we need to address. First, though, we gotta circle the goddamn wagons and see who is left."

"The other attacks were at the Turners' and the barbershop?"

"Yeah, nine o'clock on the fucking mark."

"To prevent us from helping each other."

774

"Exactly," Strat agreed. "It was a time when he knew everyone would be in their respective homes, preparing for today."

She was furious with herself for not seeing this coming. "So, the Priestly interference was just a fucking game to get us where he wanted us."

"Yeah, it was. He fed me false intel. I think he knew I would turn. I...when Esther was one of us, I trusted her, Danny trusted her...and when I found out she was still alive, I knew it was a matter of time. Walsh would kill me eventually, and hell, I don't know if this is a winning side or not. But if I'm gonna die, I'd rather be on the right side of things."

"Well, you're fucking stuck with us now."

Strat let out a small chortle. "Yeah, guess I am."

"We need to find out if...if anyone else...made it."

"I've got money on Es and Thomas."

The Madame eyed him closely. "Walsh told you."

"I mean, I didn't believe it at first. Makes sense in the grand scheme of things."

"It's not just the two of them there," the Madame countered. "We still need to send someone to check. Ashleigh was supposed to be there, and I can only hope..."

"Madame," Strat interrupted politely, "it ain't the Turners' place you gotta be worried about."

Her heart skipped a beat. "Goddammit. Will and Louis. Walsh fucking went there himself, didn't he?"

"Yeah, yeah, he did."

"Well, whatever happened already happened," she verbalized, a deep pit of anxiety forming in her gut. "Let's put some of these pieces together and regroup. First, go to the back and see Jeremiah. He'll tend to you. Then, whiskey in my office and you can tell me what the fuck is really going on."

"What about your own injuries? Graze is a tad deep, I think."

775

"Just do what I fucking ask."

"Yes, Madame."

"Celeste?" she called. "Come and help Strat walk to Jeremiah, will you?"

Celeste was already headed towards them. "Yes, Madame," she uttered, assisting Strat up from the ground and wrapping his arm over her shoulders.

The two of them moseyed away, and the Madame at last brought her focus to Claire, who still refused to let Marcy go.

The Madame returned to Claire and crouched beside her. "Claire, darling…"

Claire shook her head, sobbing, "I can't."

"You have to. She's gone, darling."

Squeezing her eyes shut as tears kept pouring out, Claire's breath shook. "She…she shouldn't have…why…why did she do this?!"

The Madame stroked Claire's hair softly, swallowing down her agony. "Because she loved you, Claire."

Claire peered down at Marcy's body in her arms, and lowered her friend to the ground carefully and gently, taking the time to fold Marcy's hands over her chest. With a loud sob, Claire fell into the Madame, holding onto her waist as she cried into the Madame's shoulder in a complete sense of despair. As Claire's tears soaked through her dress, the Madame remained steadfast, gripping Claire tight, the anger swelling so strong in her chest, she could feel her teeth gnashing against one another, her breath shaking.

"We are going to end this, Claire. No matter what it takes. We are going to fucking end this. For her."

Thirty minutes later, a sparsely patched-up Strat and a relatively distraught Celeste sat across from the Madame's desk in her office, each of them about three whiskeys deep, silent as they absorbed the horror that had been The Palace's incursion. Jeremiah had just finished patching up the Madame's wound from battle, and the mood was more than a little despondent. Until word came from the Turners or from Will and Louis, the Madame had her establishment on complete and total lockdown, not wanting to risk further attack and put more lives at risk. Claire was inconsolable, though George was trying his best, and the rest of the girls were both terrified and confused as to what in the hell happened. The Madame was thankful Razzy and Jeremiah were able to keep the girls calm until the Madame could explain everything herself. Once given a quick check-up from Jeremiah, Mock Duck trekked south to be certain there was no Whyo assault on his own people, and thus left the Madame with Strat, for whom she had one hell of a lot of questions.

Taking a swig of whiskey, the Madame let out a sigh as she swallowed. "Strat..."

"Yes, Madame?"

"Tell me what happened this morning."

"With Walsh?"

"An explanation of how the fuck you got away and what the fuck is going to happen next, if you'd be so kind."

He relaxed back in his chair, having a sip of his own drink. "I was due, with another twenty or so, to raid the barbershop with Walsh. We had teams, each headed by leadership—the bastards in the Whyos no one wants to piss off, myself included—and Walsh's prediction that I would turn is what kept me in the Bowery with him, or I would have fucking been here sooner. We got to the meet point, just the two of us first, and it finally just started to...to sink in. What would happen if you—if you all—weren't around to stop him."

The Madame eyed him closely. "So, what happened?"

"The moment his attention was on something else, I took off."

"He obviously caught up to you," Celeste noted, scanning his bodily harm with a shake of her head. "I mean, Strat, you're still bleeding, even now."

She wasn't wrong.

"I got two blocks before he caught me," Strat divulged. "He and a few other boys, but unlike Walsh's usual tactic of letting the lesser men wear our target out first, he...well...he went after me. Savagely. I can fight, Esther can attest to that, but Walsh is...something else. Before I could get a hit in edgewise, he was on top of me, blade drawn. I fought him as hard as I could and only managed to get away because...well...because..."

Celeste's head whipped his direction. "Because what?"

"I broke his glasses. Even then, he did the most damage, like a fucking wild dog coming after me, blinded."

With wide eyes, Celeste glimpsed at the Madame. "Because he can't see without those goddamn glasses."

"Getting close enough to dismantle his spectacles is a fucking task altogether," the Madame declared, not wanting Celeste to get too optimistic. "Look at Strat!"

"She's right," he added. "To get close enough to knock those things off, you have to be willing to die."

"We are all willing to fucking die if we can kill him," Celeste remarked rather harshly. "We all signed on for it."

Strat turned to face her head on. "You say that now, Celeste, but until you face that son of a bitch head-on, you have no idea what you are in for."

"In what way?"

"It is like taking on the fucking devil himself. There is no mercy, no humanity. The only thing he wants is to end your existence, and he will fucking smile as he does it." Strat swallowed, fury in his words, yet he softened. "You deserve better than that."

In return, Celeste did not flinch, her gaze fixed on Strat. "You want a hard reality, Strat?" she went on, straightening up. "I was married to a serial murderer who raped me every day and beat me within an inch of my life on innumerable occasions. He also raped Esther, then tried to have her murdered before she could tell anyone. I then watched my best friend kill him to protect me as well as to avenge someone she considered family, and then be sacrificed as a result." Celeste took a deep breath, and the Madame noticed her hands tremoring slightly. "Do not tell me I have no idea what I am in for, Strat. I have endured more than you could ever fucking imagine, and I have no doubt there is more to come."

Celeste's monologue deeply affected Strat, and the color drained from his cheeks.

"I...I apologize...I had no idea..."

The hard stare in Celeste's eyes faded. "It's not something to be sorry for, Strat. How could you know?"

"Well...I, uh...won't second guess you again."

A silence temporarily filled the room as Celeste's story sank in, yet the Madame wasn't done with her inquiry.

"Strat, I need to know about the shipments."

His attentiveness shifted back to her. "Shipments?"

The Madame tried not to scoff. "The crates full of weapons. From the South. We fucking know about them and that they're coming from the Confederacy."

"The—the Confederacy?" Strat appeared lost. "I was told we were getting shipments and that we were bringing in new opium from a different supplier. Nothing about weapons, and absolutely fucking nothing about the Confederacy."

"You haven't been there during a shipment?"

"Walsh has us in our roles for a reason," Strat admitted. "I don't think he wants any one person other than himself knowing exactly what he has planned."

Her eyes narrowed. "You can't think we are so naïve to believe you had no idea that he's planning some kind of attack."

Strat took a deep breath. "He's going to attack the city some-time after Christmas. I don't know when or how or any further de-tails. I just know that Walsh wants to destroy the city and use every means at his disposal to do so."

"Destroy the city?" Celeste pressed, having a drink of whiskey. "How in the hell does he plan on doing that?"

"Well," Strat replied, "to be frank, Walsh has enough men to probably take on the United States Army, so I think an unarmed city wouldn't stand a chance with a surprise onslaught, especially in the dead of winter."

The Madame knew he was right. "We have to fucking pray we aren't the only ones alive, that's for goddamn sure."

"Why do you say that?" Strat asked.

"Because if no one else is left, we are alone in this fucking shit storm, and I can guarantee not one of us will survive the night. Those bastards will be back to finish the job, and this round, we won't stand a goddamn chance."

There was worry in both their faces.

"What should we do, Madame?" Celeste implored. "I feel like the only thing we can really do is just—"

"Wait," Strat finished for her.

With reluctance, the Madame nodded. "They will come. I promise you on my life, they will come."

It was challenging for the Madame to believe her own words, because in her heart, she was terrified that perhaps she'd lost some of the people she cared for most. With another gulp of whiskey, she leaned back into her chair and tried not to think of Marcy, vainly endeavoring to bury her apprehension about Claire's sanity, and yet what she could not begin to stomach was what it would mean if no one came. What they would do if there was no Louis or Will, no Esther or Thomas or Ashleigh. Sally would have to get them out within hours, and the Madame would have to do the one thing she always swore she never would: run.

For nearly an hour, the three of them sat in the office without speaking, refilling their whiskey at least twice while they each dreaded the ensuing hours and what would become their unforeseen and intertwined future.

Just as despair was sinking in, a knock came to the office door, and their three heads snapped up, each one of them focused on the door.

"Well, for fuck's sake, come in!" the Madame yelled. "And you better have some good goddamn news!"

To her relief, George's head peeked through the door, and his expression was optimistic.

"They're outside."

"Who?!" Celeste demanded.

When he'd arrived at the Turner residence, Ashleigh's head hadn't been clear or focused. Instead, he'd been wrapped up in his own emotions, caught in a loop of whether or not he should apologize to Celeste or be wary of what was happening between her and the newly elected mayor of New York City. It was just after nine, and he was flustered, angry with himself for falling in love and opening the doors of his vulnerability, something both Will and Ashleigh's own life of gun-slinging nearly wore out of him, though evidently not fully. He flicked his cigarette aside and kept putting one foot in front of the other, no more than four blocks away and hoping that at least today might be a minor victory for their faction. There were so many lives riding on the day's success that if they failed, Ashleigh had an inclination all hell would be released upon them, and that was something hard to stomach. No, he had to believe Tommy and

Es could pull this off, because if they didn't, it would be a catalyst for the end days, and there was no telling what Walsh would do next.

He lit another cigarette, his jaw clenching at the thought of Celeste choosing to pursue a life with Grant rather than with him, yet Ashleigh tried to consider that maybe he'd read her wrong from the beginning. Maybe this thing between them had been just a passing of time, a way for her to feel stable in a new environment of change and transformation. Could he blame her for it, really? Nah, he couldn't, he loved her too damn much for that. He only wished he could have been more ready if she chose to walk away from him, because while Celeste was worried about today, he was already planning the rest, and Ashleigh kicked himself for being eager when he should have been present.

It was at that moment he reached the Turner residence, and as he took a left turn to walk the direction of the stoop, he halted in his tracks.

The front door was already cracked open without a soul in sight, and Ashleigh immediately sensed something was amiss.

"Fuck," he uttered, the cigarette falling from his lips as he spotted drops of blood on the stone steps. Reaching for the two pistols around his waist, Ashleigh drew them whilst simultaneously pulling the hammers back with his thumbs, his eyes scanning the windows of the household, looking for movement inside. He took measured steps, listening intently for any sound that might echo outside, his heart pounding in his chest. This was not remotely what he foresaw walking into, and rather than rallying with Thomas and Esther for a preliminary run through of the day, Ashleigh prayed with every ounce of his person that he wasn't about to walk in and find the Turners dead.

Ashleigh took one step up the stoop, then another, until he reached the top and marched to the front door. The stillness in the air was making his blood run cold, the creep of fear running down his spine not for his own safety, but for the safety of those he cared for. If the Turners had been raided, that meant that perhaps there was something bigger going on—something that not one of them saw coming…

Gently, Ashleigh nudged the front door open with the barrel of his pistol to discover a complete and total bloodbath. Laying strewn on the floor and up against the walls were the bodies of men Ashleigh could only assume were Whyos, some gutted, some shot, and some undoubtedly having been beaten to a pulp by Esther's brass; to Ashleigh's relief as he inaudibly made his way down the hallway, graciously trying not to step on corpses, he noticed not one of them was a member of the Turner household. Suddenly, the low vibration of voices came from the great room, and carefully marching forward, Ashleigh took a right hand turn through the entryway and was greeted with the nose of a shotgun barrel.

"For God's sake!" Tony yelled at the top of his lungs, his gaze furiously locked on Ashleigh while he lowered his aim. "Next time, bloody announce yourself before I nearly blow your head off!"

"Sorry, brother," Ashleigh responded as he holstered his own guns.

Peering behind Tony, Ashleigh was able to spot Esther and Thomas huddled together on one of the sofas, both of them bruised and a little battered, although neither seriously hurt. Hiroaki paced to and fro behind them, his jaw clenched in consternation, though he gave Ashleigh a small bow of his head in salutation of his presence. Scattered throughout the great room were even more dead Whyos, some having met a far worse end than others, and as Ashleigh took the scene in with a combination of awe and horror, his thoughts immediately went to the innocents living at the residence.

"Your folks all right?" Ashleigh asked Thomas directly, looking around to make sure he didn't see them lying somewhere.

Thomas nodded. "By some miracle of God, Esther and I were going over the day in the great room when we got stormed by Whyos.

We were both dressed, ready to fight and heavily armed, merely re-capping angles and scenarios of what might occur and how best to handle if things went awry. Initially when we heard the approach, we thought you were early, but Jesus Christ, were we fucking wrong." Grabbing for a glass on the coffee table, Thomas took a gulp of what Ashleigh assumed was whiskey. "While we fought them off, Mrs. Shannon and Tony got William and Lucy locked in upstairs, and Esther, Hiro, and I took on the swarm. As you can tell, it got ugly."

"Ugly?" Esther quipped. "It was a dogpile. If we hadn't been trained by Hiro…and shit, if Hiro hadn't been here…"

"Hiro seems, well, unscathed, compared to the two of ya, I mean," Ashleigh pointed out, trying to hide a smirk.

This appeared to tickle Hiro, whereas Esther rolled her eyes. "Easier to keep distance behind a sword," she teased, a tiny grin coming to her face shortly after. "Either way, like Thomas said, it was a fucking miracle, and we made it through without sustaining any losses."

Ashleigh walked toward them and flopped down on the sofa opposite Esther and Thomas. "I s'pose there were a few strays that got away, eh?"

"Five," Tony declared, moving to sit beside Ashleigh, a nod sent his direction. "Most of them had already sustained injuries."

"The bad news," Esther went on, "is that three of the five that got away are bastards we really needed to get rid of. Auggie, Zeke, and Randall all got out. Which means they are heading straight to Walsh and to reorganize for God knows what. And what the fuck was this? Did they just want to…to kill us?"

Taking another gander at the carnage, Ashleigh let out a heavy exhale. "We oughta get to The Palace as quickly as we can. When I left, everythin' was fine, but Lord knows what kinda fuckin' ambush Walsh was runnin' on us."

"We were saying that just before you arrived," Thomas told

him, finishing his whiskey and rising up to his feet. "We need to get our asses over there. Who did you leave? Just George and Claire?"

Ashleigh mirrored him. "Celeste and Mock Duck, too."

The color in Esther's cheeks had drained, and she got up. "Thomas, that's not enough of them. There's no way they could have…"

"I know, Es."

"Let's go." She put her hands into her pockets, brass on her knuckles. "Hiro? Tony? Get this place locked down. We'll be back when it's over."

"Yes, Lady Turner."

Once assembled and without a second to spare, the three of them took off, sprinting the entirety of Central Park, faster than Ashleigh had run in years. Athena squawked overhead in eager anticipation of the hunt, her presence never feeling far as Ashleigh hustled to keep up with the shadows of Esther and Thomas. Esther took the lead, with Thomas nearly stepping on her heels at every breath, and Ashleigh just a few strides back couldn't help but wonder how in the hell these two could hold their pace so consistently and for so long. His heart felt as if it might explode at any second, and yet simultaneously, he understood that there was a time imperative, one that could save even just one life. If that life was Celeste's, Ashleigh would bleed his lungs dry to reach her before it was too late. In a full sprint, the morning pedestrians of the park stared at them as they streaked passed, unsure of what to think of the scene, though neither Ashleigh, Thomas, or Esther could give a damn. In three minutes—no two—they would be there, and the closer they drew to The Palace, the more Ashleigh started to worry as to what they might find left behind by the Whyos, if in fact their assumptions had been correct. Because if the worst happened, there would be nothing left to find other than death and destruction.

When they were on approach to the edge of the park and the

entrance of The Palace came into their sights, Esther came to an abrupt halt, then whipped around to face the eager Thomas and the heaving, out of breath Ashleigh.

"They've already invaded."

Both Thomas and Ashleigh gazed around Esther to behold that she was right: the front door was undoubtedly bolted shut, an enormous crack running down the center of it, though on the paneling were unmistakable drops of blood that dripped down the front stoop. Windows were shot out, and everything was quiet, far too quiet for The Palace, even at that late hour of the morning. A few paces away, the front gate casually blew open and shut in the cold December wind, an occurrence all three of them knew would by no means occur if the Madame were present or…or alive. That is, unless The Palace was on total lockdown. Thomas let out a whistle, signaling Athena to perch in a nearby tree, and the three of them huddled together.

"Wha…whatcha wanna do?" Ashleigh asked, glancing from Esther to Thomas. "We all know we ain' getting' through that door."

"I could sneak through the Madame's office windows—"

Ashleigh let out a snort. "Yeah, Es, and get fuckin' shot. Ain' no way in hell Tommy and I are lettin' ya do that. Place is locked down. Gotta be a way to let 'em know we here."

"Well," Thomas cut in, "we could just fucking knock."

That thought had not occurred to Ashleigh, and by the look Esther manifested, it hadn't occurred to her either.

Her eyes found Ashleigh's. "Worth a shot?"

Awkwardly, the three of them scurried up to the front door, and just as Esther was about to knock, they heard the bolt in the door thunk loose, and with a groan, it swung open.

There stood the Madame, a shotgun resting over her shoulder, staring at them with a combination of anger and gratitude.

"Get the fuck in here," she said quietly, stepping aside for them to pass.

Wordlessly, Esther hustled in first, followed by Thomas and last Ashleigh, who immediately turned around and re-bolted the door closed for the Madame. When he circled back in expectation of following the others up the main staircase, Esther and Thomas were already gone; instead, the Madame remained, and he realized she wanted to have some kind of conversation.

"What happened?"

"At the Turners'?"

"Yes."

"I think, first and foremost," Ashleigh began, "we oughta discuss what the fuck happened at The Palace." Skimming the room, Ashleigh could grasp the carnage there was similar to that of the Turner residence. "Looks like we got invaded."

"Yes. Probably over two dozen Whyos."

"Two dozen?!"

"Possibly more, I can't be fucking sure."

He could hear something was wrong in her tone, and he hoped it wasn't Celeste. "Madame, who did we lose?"

The Madame swallowed hard. "Marcy."

Shocked, Ashleigh tried to remain composed. "How in the hell did Marcy get caught in the crossfire, Madame? She ain' s'pose to be out durin' lockdown."

Her countenance ran cold, and the Madame's arms crossed over her chest. "You think in a million fucking years I would ever let Marcy put herself at risk if I had any say?" the Madame spat, and Ashleigh realized he'd crossed a line with her.

"Madame, please. I apologize. I ain' here pointin' a finger like ya did somethin' wrong. I just, well, hell, I ain' gonna lie. I am jus' happy you and Celeste is all right."

787

This caused the Madame's snarling to ease. "What happened at the Turners'?"

"Invaded, jus' like this place was," Ashleigh told her, shaking his head. "It was a fuckin' miracle they was ready to head south. No casualties other than Whyos, Madame."

"Well, we've got one problem we have to address pretty fucking fast."

"An' what's that?"

"Strat's here."

Ashleigh's jaw dropped. "What in the hell ya talkin' 'bout?"

"He's here, and I am sure that bastard is currently explaining to Esther and Thomas what the fuck the Whyos are up to, because it isn't fucking good."

His stomach twisted. "Tell me."

The Madame was hesitant to meet his eyes. "There was one other place those assholes wanted to attack."

"Aw shit—Daddy and Louis?"

Her response was a glimpse of utter sadness. "I don't know what we do, other than fucking wait and hope they're still alive somehow. It's a goddamn stroke of luck we are all still breathing, and I…"

The Madame's voice trailed off, because suddenly, racing down the main staircase went Thomas and Esther, and before either Ashleigh or the Madame could say anything, the pair of them busted out of the front door of The Palace and disappeared from sight.

After gaping after them for a few seconds, Ashleigh peered to the Madame. "I'm assumin' I oughta be here, helpin ya keep this place safe, rather than chasin' whatever the hell them two are up to?"

"Strat told them," came Celeste's voice from the top of the staircase, and as Ashleigh's head whipped towards her, she commenced descending down in Thomas and Esther's wake.

Though he hated to admit it, Ashleigh found her to be the most beautiful woman he'd ever beheld, particularly in the knowledge that she'd undoubtedly killed more than a few of the Whyo corpses spread about, and he fought that feeling hard to remain professional.

"They're going to see what's left of the barbershop and hope that Will and Louis might still be alive."

"No surprise there," Ashleigh remarked.

Pacing to the front door, the Madame threw it closed and bolted it shut. "We stick to our fucking plan of lockdown until they return, got it?"

"No one in or out," Celeste affirmed, reaching where Ashleigh stood. "Madame...if they are...if Louis and Will are...gone..." Celeste gritted her teeth. "They're going to go for Walsh."

"Well, I can't say I'm sorry for it," the Madame admitted aloud, and paused. "You two have ten minutes. Then, we're meeting in my office to figure out what the fuck we do next."

Without batting an eyelash, the Madame spun on her heels and climbed the stairs, not once glancing back towards them.

When she was out of earshot, Ashleigh sighed. "Well, I think we oughta just—"

"Ashleigh!" Celeste threw her arms around his neck and pulled him in, taking him completely by surprise. "I can't...God, I am just so fucking happy to see you..."

He wrapped his arms around her and pulled her tight, overcome with relief. "I...wish I could tell ya how glad I am you are all right," he said quietly, kissing the top of her head.

"We didn't know if...if anyone made it." Ashleigh could hear the slight tremor in her voice and only drew her in closer. "I just... I was so..."

Pulling away, Ashleigh looked right into her eyes. "We're okay, Celeste. We're both here. It's gonna be all right."

Her gaze didn't falter. "I love you, Ashleigh. So much."

Ashleigh thought his heart might explode. "I love you too, Celeste."

CHAPTER XLIX.

It was a strange sensation, not knowing whether or not he would survive the day, but Louis had grown accustomed to it over the years, almost finding himself more edgy on the days he felt safe than those he was in insurmountable danger. The fact that he had lived so many years still surprised him, given the lifestyle he'd chosen, and while others might crumble under the pressure, it was in times like these, when everything was hanging in the balance, that Louis operated at his best. He was built to endure difficulty, built for the moments when only those with cold vigilance and swift action would persevere, because if anyone knew how to cut throats and disappear into the night, it was Louis. Years of roaming New York City's streets, never picking fights yet always ending them when necessary, and completing the bloody tasks when others desired to keep their hands clean of the crime—that had made Louis into the deadliest hitman around. And with the end in sight, with just a few hours before he would leave the legend of the Frog behind, Louis wondered who he might be on the other side.

The hit would be a trap, of course, that much they all knew, and it was precisely the reason why Louis, Thomas, Esther, and the Madame wanted to pursue it: there might not be another opportunity to end Walsh and his reign of terror on their city. Esther was determined, and Louis had no doubt she was capable of killing Walsh with the amount of training she undertook with Hiroaki in England; however, Louis liked the odds of four of them versus Walsh and his crew, rather than a one-on-one duel of powers. When the confrontation came to a close, Louis and Will, or at least what was left of them, would meet Sally and be gone, whereas Thomas and Esther would rally with the Madame and discuss what to do next. He hated walking away, reluctant to leave the Madame before the war was truly over, but she insisted, and when the Madame made up her mind about something, there was no changing it. By the end of the day, Louis and Will would be on their way to Boston, and The Palace would be one step closer to triumph over Richard Croker.

As long as they got McCann.

On his very last errand for the Madame, Louis made a visit to the Mount St. Vincent Hotel in Central Park, one of the most beautiful new establishments in New York City, and supposedly, run by none other than Patrick McCann, the mystery man on Croker's infamous hit list. The Madame wrote an invitation for McCann to call at The Palace as soon as possible due to a customer conflict with one of his more established patrons, a lure to bait him into visiting even just for reassurance there must be some kind of mistake. She was brilliant, Louis had to give her that. To his disappointment, McCann wasn't at the hotel, apparently returning later in the morning following a quick trip to Philadelphia, where he owned another absurdly extravagant resort. The outing wasn't entirely in vain—Louis relished in the reactions of the hotel staff at his appearance as he lingered. No matter what the circumstances were, Louis was always entertained by the fear others had of him, a fear warranted by nothing other than his size and his relatively commanding presence in a room full of strangers. As he left, the concierge repeatedly swore he would give Mr. McCann the invitation immediately upon his arrival back at the hotel, and Louis had a hunch the Madame would have a visitor within the next few days.

A cold, December breeze whipped past, yet Louis pressed on, taking a quick glance down at his pocket watch. It was five minutes to nine, and that would give him and Will roughly an hour to discuss Boston before Esther and Thomas showed up to carry out the day. The four of them spent countless sittings over the last few days piecing together their scheme, combing through every scenario to be as fully prepared as possible for anything Walsh and the Whyos might throw their way. At this point, Louis just wanted the whole ordeal over with, and in a matter of hours, it would be. They would kill Walsh. They would get Priestly out of Croker's reach and to safety. And then, he and Will would get the hell out of New York and try to find what remained of their souls.

Louis rounded the corner and trotted up the back stair of the barbershop to his and Will's apartment, yet as he glimpsed down at the steps, Louis noticed that there were boot prints in the snow—boot prints that weren't his or Will's. He halted. There were multiple sets, and as Louis's gaze flickered up toward the door, he noted the handle was dislodged and the wood was cracked, more than likely having been kicked in. This wasn't Esther or Thomas. This was something else entirely. And he had nasty a feeling if he walked through that door, neither him nor Will would ever see the light of day again.

But he couldn't leave Will.

Keeping his cool, Louis sauntered up the final few stairs, cautiously drawing his revolver from the holster at his waist and cocking it while he pressed the door open.

All over the apartment Whyos were scattered about, and at the kitchen table were both Will and Walsh, Will facing Louis with a gun pointed at his temple by another Whyo, Walsh with his back to Louis, though at the sound of his entry Walsh turned around to face him, grinning malevolently. Louis looked at Walsh in disgust. Everything about him was darkness—behind his spectacles were a set of eyes that ran black and deep, filled with nothing but apathy and horrors Louis never wanted to grasp. There was a very short list of people Louis had met in his life who he considered to be evil; however, Walsh's manifestation went even further. It wasn't just evil—Walsh was like a disease, spreading through the shadows and unable to ever be fully satisfied by the death and destruction in existence. He wanted to create turmoil, to embody fear in all its horrendous glory, and he wanted to incite pain, suffering, and murder whenever given the chance.

Dragon…Devil…they were both the same to Louis. Walsh was a plague, one with devastating consequences, and Louis would go down trying to end him.

"Hello, Louis," Walsh greeted, his eyes fixated on Louis in delight. "Welcome. So happy for you to join us."

Louis kept his index finger on the trigger of his revolver. "Do you really want to do this, Walsh?"

"Do what, exactly, Louis?"

"Ya shoulda kept walkin', brother," Will uttered, their gaze meeting.

"I'm not leaving you with this sick son of a bitch," Louis affirmed vigilantly, his stare moving again to Walsh. "The prospect of killing Will and I will end with many of these men dying in the cross hairs—you really think they are ready to die taking out two old men? Two irrelevant old men?"

A couple of the Whyos near Will sneered. "Old men, eh?" one chirped. "We will be fuckin' gods, bringin' you two down. The Cat and the Frog. Finally, dead! We'll drink to that for fuckin' weeks!"

The murmur of agreement circled around, and Louis, in retaliation, let out a tiny chortle, aimed his revolver, and fired, striking the impertinent Whyo right between the eyes with a bullet. For a moment, everyone around him was utterly baffled at what just happened, yet the moment his body crumpled and fell to the floor, every breathing Whyo drew their weapon and snarled at Louis, awaiting orders from Walsh. Walsh, to the surprise of his compatriots, seemed amused by Louis's forthright actions, holding up a hand to silence the jeers echoing from the Whyos around Will and behind him.

"Well, that is one," Walsh declared with an air of contempt. "Got over a dozen more of those before you get to me, Frog. Boys?"

Before Louis could say anything, Will had not only a gun at his temple, but a knife at his throat, surrounded by six Whyos ready to kill him if asked.

"Take a seat, Louis," Walsh commanded, kicking a vacant chair his direction. "Let's have a quick chat, and then I'll let these boys tear you apart."

Unsure of whether he ought to comply, Louis wavered, and Walsh's gaze narrowed.

"Sit," he said, his tone not leaving any room for protest.

Louis moved forward, pulled the chair another few inches away from Walsh, and lowered down, casting a quick glimpse to Will and then reverting his eyes back to Walsh, speculating what in the hell this crazy bastard had to get off his chest.

Walsh's head tilted to the side, studying Louis. "As we speak, there are two concurrent raids taking place: one at The Palace, the other at the Turner residence." He paused for effect, and Louis felt his hair stand on end. Satisfied at Louis's reaction, Walsh carried on. "There are at least two dozen Whyos at both locations, with one objective—to kill you and yours. By the time our conversation ends, I believe your friends will be long gone, and I'll be doing you a courtesy by sending you to join them."

Will released a loud scoff. "Ya really think the Turners are gonna let Whyos just walk into their place on Fifth?! Gimme a break, Walsh. They'll get slaughtered, 'specially with the celestial and Es there."

"I scouted the household for days," Walsh snapped nastily. "Part of the reason we picked this time is because both William and Lucy Turner tend to rise late, and therefore, we would catch everyone at once."

"Ya…ya killin' all the Turners?" Will gaped at him. "What in the fuck is wrong with ya?! They didn' do nothin' to nobody!"

"They are complicit in that they know what Lord Turner has been up to," Walsh responded, rolling his eyes, his attention shifting to Louis. "The Cat is a tad dramatic, wouldn't you say, Frog?"

"You are trying to kill us in one swoop," Louis observed. "So that what? There wouldn't be any more resistance against what you plan to do?"

"Precisely. We are nearly ready for our victory song, and to get there, you are the last obstacle. With The Palace and it's cohorts gone, nothing stands in the way of us taking over the city in one, easy plunge."

"Priestly never mattered, did he?" Will asked.

Walsh let out a small laugh. "No, he fucking didn't, not even for a second. Which is why I already took the liberty of killing him last night. The police should find his body shortly, and it'll look like a suicide; one last gift to Richard before I bleed him all over New York."

Louis was distraught. "How?"

"Strangled him. Strung him up. Put together a suicide note, the works. If there is one thing I've learned through all these years, it's how to kill and cover it up when necessary. And it's not like Tammany Hall or the police will give a damn—they'll wipe their hands clean and walk away, relieved they don't have to do it themselves."

"Ya want 'em comfortable so they don' see what's comin', eh?"

"That is the idea."

"Is it true, then?" Louis pressed.

"What ever could you be implying?" Walsh mocked.

"The ties to the South? Lying to the Confederate supporters and convincing them to back you with the promise of the city?"

This caused Walsh to grin forebodingly. "Seems like someone has finally talked to the Hip Sing," he replied. "It is true. I've been having artillery shipped north for months to arm us for takeover."

"Takeover?"

"It was the plan all along, Frog, to burn New York to the ground. To destroy the city and everything it stands for—hierarchy replaced with anarchy, a destruction of the system that holds us in chains and keeps the rich in power and the poor at their fucking disposal. We will burn it, kill anyone who stands in our way, and when New York City is a wasteland, I'll figure out how to handle the Confederacy, because they won't want it then. This country—the world—will change in a matter of days, all because of us."

"They'll come for ya," Will interjected through gritted teeth. "If I know anythin' 'bout the South, it's that they don' take lightly to bein' betrayed, 'specially by a bunch of thugs who got nothin' but shit for brains."

Walsh's head twisted toward Will. "I think, Cat, our numbers might change their mind in the long run."

"Your numbers?" Louis endeavored to challenge.

"Whyos." Walsh was almost glowing with delight. "We are well over a thousand, growing every day. And that's just the higher ups—imagine what I could do with the immigrants, the poor, the people of this city who feel abused by those in power. We've already won... the only thing left to do is kill you and the Cat, and we will have buried The Palace at last."

Despair was not an emotion Louis knew well, though in that moment, he felt it for the first time in decades. There was nowhere to run, no place to hide. Their family was being murdered, slaughtered, and they had no way to get to one another. While Thomas and Esther had a small chance, if The Palace didn't have reinforcements, there was no way the Madame could hold it down. Blood would be spilled. Yet there was one small glimmer of hope for Louis, and it was the notion that if Thomas and Esther survived, the pair of them would wreak havoc on the Whyos until their dying breath. He would die, but Louis was content dying at Will's side, even if the end came sooner than he'd like.

"I'd be afraid, if I were you," Louis muttered under his breath.

This intrigued Walsh. "Afraid? Of what?"

"If there is even the slightest chance Esther and Thomas survive in the aftermath of this genocide, I can promise you, neither of them will rest until your throat is cut. They will hunt you down to the ends of the fucking earth, you know why? Because they understand something you don't, Walsh."

"Oh? And what's that?"

"That the bond of family is stronger than death."

Walsh's gaze narrowed. "He does present an interesting point," he thought aloud, leaning back into his chair, his eyes fixated on Louis. "All right, boys. New plan. Kill the Cat. We'll take the Frog with us."

Before anyone could move, Louis had his revolver pointed directly at Walsh. "You aren't taking me fucking anywhere, you bastard."

"If they do happen to survive," Walsh said, ignoring him and the gun, "which I highly doubt, but if they do, I want a bargaining chip. And what better bargaining chip than you? The man who has more or less been a surrogate father to both of them over the years? It'll lure them to us, scrap the unknown of when and where. It'll be on our turf, and then we will put an end to the Vigilante and the Assistant ourselves. Ahh, brilliant, if I do say so myself."

In the blink of an eye, Louis cast Will the signal, not wanting to delay the inevitable any longer. Straightaway, Louis drew his other gun with his left hand from the hidden holster on the inside of his right flank while Will simultaneously pulled both his feet up off the ground and kicked with his heels, thrusting the kitchen table towards Walsh, which then flipped over on top of him. Pulling his second revolver level with the other, Louis aimed their noses at the men on either side of Will holding him hostage and fired parallel bullets, each striking the Whyos between the eyes. The two of them fell to the floor in a heap, and when he was free, Will instantly leapt to his feet and rushed to Louis's right side, retrieving his own pistols to take aim.

"Only got a few shots at this range," Will remarked quickly.

"Then let's move fast."

The Whyos exchanged confused looks, awaiting orders, that is, until Walsh finally screamed out from beneath the table, "Kill them!"

Louis fired, and judging by the ringing in his right ear, Will did as well. Louis took down one Whyo, then another, but as he and Will got rushed and took hits of their own, guns became irrelevant. In the time it takes to inhale one breath, Louis made a quick assessment of their surroundings, noting his and Will's respective injuries: Will had a graze along his left torso that was seeping blood, though not profusely, whereas Louis took a bullet in his right bicep, though curiously, it went straight through with little carnage. Along with the two Whyos initially guarding Will, Louis and Will took down four additional goons together, yet there were still seven circling around in front of them, with three more outside and two others lingering in the background near Walsh, watching the fight unfold.

There was no time to communicate a plan, and Louis grasped that Will made the same assessment in the breath that Louis did himself. A plan wouldn't give them any leverage or upper hand—instead, Louis and Will would purely be fighting to survive, and based on their current chances, Louis wasn't sure how the battle would turn out.

Will banked right to their right and Louis tucked left, barreling into four of the oncoming Whyos as Will took on the other three in hand to hand combat. Tackling two of them to the ground, Louis immediately rolled right back onto his feet and spun, striking one Whyo square across the jaw with a right hook. Continuing his pirouette, Louis's left leg circled around to roundhouse the other thug, connecting at the weak part of his neck and breaking it on impact, and he fell to the earth, dead. As the two on the floor managed to stand upright and the other spat out teeth on his hands and knees, Louis got ready, kicking the lifeless Whyo out of the way.

"One!" he shouted at Will, in hopes to lighten the situation.

A scream of agony, then a snap, and Will's voice returned, "One back atcha!"

With a yell, one of the previously tackled Whyos lunged at Louis, grabbing him at the waist in an attempt to slam him into the tall shelves behind them. Louis stumbled two steps in retreat, grabbed one of Thomas's old pieces of metal work off a shelf, and blasted the man right on the top of his head. The hit sent the sound of his skull cracking loudly through the apartment, and with a second whack, the Whyo's grip on Louis went limp and he dropped down to the ground. His gaze lifting, Louis saw the other now running straight for him, a blade drawn, and with Thomas's metalwork still clutched in his hand, Louis nearly let out a small scoff. As the Whyo raced towards him, Louis simply drew the metal across his body to his left shoulder for the wind up, and with a lurch forward, brought it down hard across the right side of the man's head back-handed. It stuck in place and Louis released, shuffling aside to watch the goon collide into the wall and then collapse, motionless.

"Three!" Louis announced loudly.

"Still at two!" Will quipped back.

Then, without warning, the tides turned.

The Whyo whose teeth Louis knocked loose was holding a pistol, his aim directly at Louis's chest, a smirk on his bloodied lips.

"Walsh? 'Bout time now, yeah?"

Letting out an audible sigh, Walsh and one of the two Whyos beside him made their way closer to where Louis stood. The other pulled his own gun and targeted Will, who had his third assailant in a headlock and nearly dead.

800

"Release him," the Whyo barked at Will, yanking back the hammer. "Release him and we'll be merciful."

"Merciful?" Will questioned. "In what regards, exactly?"

"Well, in killing you, Mr. Sweeney," Walsh said matter-of-factly.

Will's eyes met Louis's in despondent defeat. "We knew it wasn' gonna end easy." Reluctantly, he tossed the purple-faced Whyo callously to the ground, then glanced back at Louis. "I love ya, Louis."

Louis's jaw clenched, the acceptance of losing not something he was used to feeling. "I love you too, Will."

Walsh clapped his hands together. "Well, isn't that just fucking nauseating," he snarled, reaching into his pocket and pulling out something Louis couldn't quite discern.

The toothless Whyo inched closer to Louis, gun ready to be fired, and the second near Walsh drew a blade, though both men remained just out of arm's reach of Louis.

"Scared, ain' ya?" Will sneered despite being backed into the corner of the kitchen by the two goons near him. "If ya get too close, he'll kill both of ya without breakin' a sweat, and won' give a fuckin' shit about it."

"Shut the fuck up, Cat," Walsh hissed, at last revealing what the object was in his hand.

To Louis's dismay, he saw it was a syringe, filled with some kind of liquid, and straightaway, he guessed what was going to happen next.

"Now, Louis," Walsh began, "you have a choice."

Upon saying those words, three more Whyos entered the apartment door behind where Walsh stood, one making his way over to assist in keeping Will where he was, the other two heading to loiter near Walsh as backup in handling Louis.

"A choice?"

One step at a time, Walsh started to inch towards him. "A choice. Regardless of what happens, you will be coming with me. The Cat

801

will be staying here to be put to his death. How you decide to concede will determine just how painful of an end Mr. Sweeney is subjected to from my fellows here."

"Louis," Will asserted as the Whyos around him closed in, "don' you fuckin' dare—"

"What would you rather have, Louis?" Walsh interrupted Will, discounting him altogether. "Would you rather have your lifelong love suffer for hours on end, be tortured until his old and mangled body decides it can't hold onto staying any longer—"

"Stop it," Louis hissed.

"Or!" Walsh kept going, holding the syringe up and shaking it with the intention to provoke him. "Or would you rather come with me, knowing he'll be beaten to a pulp and then shot within ten minutes of your departure?"

"Fuck you, Walsh," Will got out, just as he was seized by assailants.

Louis's stomach turned, but he didn't have much of a choice. "How in the hell am I supposed to fucking trust you to end it that way?" Louis responded through gritted teeth. "You don't give a shit about honor or keeping your goddamn word."

Letting out a heavy exhale, Walsh stared at Louis. "Of course, you are correct," he replied. "I do, however, have a soft spot for my associate killers, such as yourselves, and the pain and death you two have rained down on this city over the years…well…I applaud both of you on a job well done." He stopped in his dialogue, pensive. "You can't trust me. It is a gamble. Either way, like I mentioned, you are coming with us. If you fight, it's a lose-lose, because Will is going to fucking die no matter how I get you out of here."

For a brief second, Louis closed his eyes in agony, then opened them again to peer over at Will. He didn't say a word, only lowered down to his knees and let his arms dangle down at his sides, their gazes lingering on each other, both wishing they had one more day together, one more night, at least a warning that the end had been closer than they could comprehend. Everything around Louis became a blur of motion, his only focus being Will, and he tried to soak it in one last time. When Will walked back into the picture years ago, it was the best thing that had happened to Louis since Thomas was born. This was the life they had chosen, this was how they always expected it might end, and the reality of it was much more difficult than either of them could have ever anticipated.

Hands came to Louis's shoulders, a gun still pointed at his forehead. He felt a needle poke into the right side of his neck, sensed the cold, thick liquid slip easily into his bloodstream. Within seconds, the fog thickened, and Louis detected his muscles weakening. Suddenly, there was one Whyo under his left arm, another under his right, and they lifted Louis as Walsh shouted things Louis could no longer hear. With one last look at Will, who had tears streaming down his cheeks, Louis's consciousness slipped in and out. From the top of the staircase, he saw a carriage at the bottom, waiting for them, with more Whyos scattered about. There really hadn't been a chance for him and Will to escape, Walsh at least wasn't lying about that. Everything went dark, yet somewhere in the haze, Louis snapped awake long enough to see Whyos leaving the barbershop apartment, bloodied, sneering, and holstering their weapons.

Will was dead, and again, Louis felt nothing.

Cold.

He didn't know how long he'd been lying in a pool of his own blood, but Will's entire body felt as frozen as the winter weather outside. His lungs were pulling in inhales and letting out exhales, though those breaths were raspy and wet, to the degree that Will could grasp his life was hanging by a very tiny thread. Continuing to breathe, he was careful, not moving now that he was once again alert, and very cognizant that when he did move, the pain would commence and more than likely knock his ass out.

Just keep breathing…it will keep your heart going…

For what felt like an eternity, Will did just that—he kept himself breathing, heeding to the orders of some random voice in his head. Each inhale was rough and coarse in his chest, and each exhale took the entire effort of his diaphragm, yet Will managed to keep his heart beating. His only goal was to get to Louis. If the others were dead, Will and Louis only had each other, and if he could find a way to get up off the floor of the barbershop apartment, he swore on Ashleigh's life he wouldn't rest until he got Louis free.

You'll get up. Breathe.

Will kept at it, counting hundreds of breaths into and out of his lungs, until suddenly, vibrations tremored through the floorboards, and Will knew someone was approaching, his assumption being the Whyos were coming back to finish him off. Conversely, when he heard two voices on the back stair, Will felt his throat choke in gratitude.

It was Thomas and Esther.

They were flying up the staircase three steps at a time, and with a giant thunk, the front door was kicked down.

"…fuckin' shit…can you see anything you…"

"…blood everywhere, Thomas, and no fucking sign of…oh… oh no…"

"Will!" Thomas bellowed, and the thunder of their approach filled Will with reprieve.

Though he couldn't quite see them, his head covered by his disheveled hat and bloodied hair, Will sensed both Thomas and Esther by his side.

"I'm…breathing…" He was able to get those words out, to which Esther responded by letting out a substantial amount of curses and a few gasps of what Will could only assume were sobs she was ineffectively attempting to mask.

"Where the fuck is Louis?" Esther kept repeating, hastily hopping to her feet and scouring the apartment for any kind of signs.

"Will," Thomas whispered softly, and Will realized his face must have only been inches from his ear. "What did they do with Louis?"

"They...they took him, Tommy..."

The room went silent for a few seconds.

"Es," Thomas pronounced at last, "we've got to get Will moving. He has to get to The Palace and to Jeremiah."

The rumble of her footsteps drew near again. "Will? We are going to...er...gently maneuver you to see...how bad it is..."

"Lovely," he replied sarcastically.

The moment Will felt Esther and Thomas's hands upon him, the pain struck, and from the top of his head all the way down to his toes, Will thought his whole body was on fire. It took every ounce of grit and pride to not bellow out in torment, and as they flipped him over and helped sit him upright against the wall, from the expressions they wore, Will's situation was as dire as he'd predicted before they got to the barbershop.

"Well," he mumbled, "I must look awful pretty righ' this moment..."

Esther was dismayed, and even made an effort to reach out and grab his hand, but she retracted it with the knowledge touching him would only hurt him.

"Will, we need to get you to The Palace."

"How...how bad we talkin'? Is it as bad as I feel?"

"Might be worse," Esther jested, giving Will a small smile, which he appreciated.

Thomas let out a sigh. "From a first glance, I mean...shit, Will. Your left shoulder is dislocated...badly. Your ribs are broken, based on your baulking and breathing patterns. There are multiple, maybe

805

over a dozen stab wounds I can count from this view on your body, none so deep that they are fatal, but Jesus Christ, you are bleeding out, and that's what worries Es and me the most. There is a gunshot to your side…the bullet is through, but it needs to get sewn up as soon as possible…and you have a graze above your eyebrow that looks deep, which I am assuming is the shot they believed they fucking killed you with."

Clearing her throat, Esther cut in, "Not to mention your septum is shattered. Blood is dried all over your damn face, and who the fuck knows how much internal damage you have from a Whyo beating like that."

He tried not to laugh. "Legs intact?"

"Can you move them?" Thomas requested.

To his relief, Will could, and there was little pain other than soreness. "Not sure how in the hell the legs won this round, but I'll take it."

"Thank fucking Christ," Esther let out, sitting on the ground beside him. "We were both terrified you were paralyzed. But Will, what the fuck happened?"

"Walsh happened…the Whyos happened…" With shaking hands, Will tried to sit himself a little straighter. "Y'all made it out, yeah?"

"We did," Thomas confirmed. "And we've been to The Palace. The only casualty there was Marcy, one of the Madame's longtime girls."

The news perked Will up. "Ahh, fuck. That girl was a gem, but hell, we thought you all was fuckin' dead." He halted in his words. "Hold on a sec. You are tryin' to tell me that the Madame, Celeste, my boy, George, and a few girls held The Palace durin' a Whyo invasion? Are ya fuckin' kiddin' me?!"

"Well," Esther cut in, "they had help."

"Help?"

"Mock Duck was there," she told him. "He and Strat."

"Strat?!"

"If Strat hadn't been there…well, he would have been here, taking down you and Louis with Walsh," Esther established. "And The Palace would have fallen."

What Esther was saying settled in. "So, he crossed then, eh?"

Thomas nodded. "Abandoned Walsh, survived, and made it to the Madame with just enough time to arm them. Mock Duck had been leaving and chose to stay. It's because of him they are alive."

"I have no fuckin' doubt, Tommy." Will swallowed hard. "The two of ya need to get me in a cab. Send me north to The Palace and—"

"No fucking way," Esther interjected. "No. We are taking you there ourselves and then we can figure out what in the hell to do next."

"Ya can' do that."

"Why not?"

"Cause you gotta go get Louis."

Thomas's brow furrowed. "Where is he?"

"They took 'em. Took Louis as bait in case y'all survived the onslaught. But that's just the thing, ya see."

"What?" Thomas pressed.

"If ya take me all the way to The Palace—if ya delay—give them a chance to get settled and wait for ya. The advantage ya have right now will be gone. Ya gotta get after 'em right this second, or the odds of us gettin' Louis back alive are slim to none. Yeah, Es, I know ya ain' happy 'bout it, but it's the fuckin' truth."

The two of them glanced at each other.

"I don't know," Esther remarked, worriedly.

"I don' give a shit what ya know," Will stated. "All I know is if I don' see a doc in another hour or so, I ain' gonna wake up tomorrow. Get me in a goddamn coach. And get Louis, so we can have our family together."

Esther was eager, yet wary. "Will, we don't know where the hell to even begin looking for the Whyos and Walsh."

"She's right," Thomas added, visibly frustrated. "We know they wouldn't bring him to The Dry Dollar or to The Morgue. There has to be a hideaway we don't know about, and I think our best bet is honestly to retreat to The Palace and ask Strat."

"Or ya got one more option," Will held.

"What's that?"

"Ya both are forgettin' about the son of a bitch who got this whole thing started. The one who has known Walsh from the beginnin'."

Esther's eyes lit up. "No way…"

A smile came to Will's face. "Richard motherfuckin' Croker, Es. Go get 'em and find Louis. Don' waste no more time. And send that lyin' bastard my regards with a right hook full o'brass to the head, while you're at it."

In a matter of minutes, Will was tucked away in a coach, heading uptown toward The Palace. Thomas and Esther bandaged him up tightly enough that the bleeding would at least be restrained for an hour or two, giving Will enough of a chance as possible to make it to Jeremiah alive. Whether or not he survived was still in the hands of fate, but he didn't give a damn about his own life. If they had a chance to save Louis, Thomas and Esther had to take advantage of being right on Walsh's heels, and that left no time to babysit Will and his mangled Southern ass. His odds wouldn't increase with an escort anyhow—they depended solely on how fast the carriage driver could keep his horse running through the streets of Manhattan, and also, Will's desire to keep breathing.

The pain was excruciating. There wasn't another battle, fight, or encounter Will remembered when he had been this beaten to shit, and as far as the Whyos knew, the Cat was, in fact, dead. He'd done a damn good job faking it, collapsing facedown, slowing his breathing to such a degree, in spite of the blows he continued to take paired up with the final shot to the head, that when one of those dumb bastards checked his pulse, he didn't feel a heartbeat. That's right where they left him—in a pool of his own blood, laughing as they exited the apartment and already congratulating themselves on killing the notorious Cat and Frog of the Five Points. "The old ways have finally fuckin' died," one of them said. Will would never forget the sound of that man's voice, and with an immense amount of hatred, swore if he lived, he would track that one down in particular and remind him that the old ways never fuckin' die. And it was in that thought Will realized something.

He didn't want to die—not yet, anyhow.

They needed him: The Palace, Esther and Thomas, Louis, Ashleigh—they needed one more warrior on their side, fighting for their cause. If he gave up, Walsh and the Whyos would have an even greater upper hand, and he'd be damned allowing that to happen. Suddenly, Will felt something in his body shift—he could feel adrenaline start to flow through his veins, a strange sort of energy beginning to engage in his muscles and limbs. The awful hurt did not cease, and yet it became more tolerable, steadying his breath and clearing some of the murkiness from Will's mind. Peeking out the window, Will noticed they were still twenty minutes from The Palace, but he could make it twenty minutes. Shit, he could make it twenty hours if he kept feeling like this, and his contemplations shifted from his own survival to that of Louis's.

Louis was the strongest man Will had ever come across, in an infinite capacity. When they were young, Will was the talker, the salesman, the negotiator—sly, charming, and with one hell of a nasty bite if he was crossed. Louis was the muscle, the one in the shadows, the enforcer, standing beside Will and ready to do whatever John asked of them when it came to the gang and their politics. Their initial relationship was professional, and Louis was quiet, never sharing anything other than what was requested of him, executing whatever was necessary without question or protest. The two of them spent so much time together on the streets, a friendship gradually formed, especially after a few skirmishes wherein Louis got Will out of being shot or stabbed by rival gang members. Trust was built, enough so that they could rely on one another, reading each other's minds and handling what would normally be violent and scary trials with effortlessness. And then came the night, the first night. Will was the initiator, as he so often was with Louis, and he was almost surprised to find his advances were mirrored. The following morning, they swore it would never happen again, and then it did. Over, and over, and over again, though they kept it a secret for years, so in love and furthermore, terrified of what would become of them if the gang found out.

When John discovered that Louis and Will were in a relationship, he used it against them. They had already been winning loyalties and gaining notoriety and power which was beginning to outweigh their leader's, and he confronted them with enough evidence to send them both to their graves. Will wasn't sure what the fuck John had been thinking—maybe it had been hubris, maybe it had been the illusion of comfort with Louis and Will after more or less raising them through their adolescence, or maybe he just purely made a mistake. Either way, John hadn't predicted Louis's reaction and, to be fair, neither had Will. It was in Louis's reaction Will grasped how much Louis really loved him, and conversely, what Louis would do to another person if they threatened someone he loved.

Will didn't stop him, and guessed he probably couldn't have.

They would be killed anyhow, for John's death. Louis wanted

to run, but Will knew better—if they ran, it would be for the rest of their lives, and in Will's idiotic, juvenile opinion, they were too young for that; why live a life in fear when he could go out, guns blazing, the way Will always wanted to? With the walls closing in, Will turned himself into the Whyos, who consequently gave him to the coppers, and thus came a swift and speedy trial with a guilty verdict. He was given a death sentence by the judge, and the evening prior to his execution by hanging, Will was visited by Boss Tweed and the most beautiful woman he could remember seeing, a woman he later learned to be the Madame. Tweed would give Will another chance at life if he left New York City and did not come back— exile, so it was. In a state of confusion, Will asked why on earth they would allow him to live, to which the woman admitted they'd given John the evidence of Will and Louis's relationship in the hopes that he would get himself killed. John, it seems, had been stealing from Tammany Hall, and they'd wanted him gone.

It was appalling to Will, to be a pawn in someone else's game, yet he had no choice other than to comply.

As he reflected on it, bleeding out in the carriage on his way to The Palace and the very same Madame who'd both killed and saved him in one night, a smirk came to Will's face. He'd told Louis, of course, and this consequently gave Louis the idea of how to save Esther years ago when she'd been in the same situation in the Tombs. The depth of their connections was incredibly intertwined, and for Will, this was one of the motivations for his loyalty to stay with Louis and with The Palace. Like Louis, the Madame would do anything for her people, and her family now included Will and his son, who he loved immeasurably, regardless of how he acted around Ashleigh. Those were the two best things he'd done in his life: come back for Louis and have his son, and he only wished he could have been a better father. He just didn't know how to be one from the start.

The carriage came to a halt right outside The Palace, and the driver did as he was instructed by Thomas, sprinting straight through the front gate and to the front door, banging on it loudly. He was welcomed by the nose of a pistol, and after a bit of back and forth and perhaps some crying on the end of the driver, he was able to secure someone to walk to the coach with him. Will couldn't witness this happening firsthand due to his position in the cab, yet by the sound of their steps, Will sensed it was his son. When the door was yanked open, there stood Ashleigh, pistol drawn with the driver behind him, and immediately all the color drained from his son's aghast cheeks.

"Fuck, Daddy!" he bellowed, leaping into the carriage. "George! George! Get over here, goddammit!"

"Careful, now," Will stated, trying to straighten up as Ashleigh endeavored to lift him from beneath his shoulders. "My left shoulder is out, and I am pretty damn sure if these bandages start to unravel, I'll be unconscious from bleedin'."

Another rush of footsteps, and George's face came into view. "Holy shit," he uttered, helping Ashleigh get his father out of the coach. "Will, what the hell happened?!"

"Same thing that happened here, I expect," he replied as Ashleigh maneuvered him down and into George's clutches.

"Whyos?" Ashleigh pressed, hopping down and then placing himself underneath Will's good shoulder for support.

"Whyos and Walsh."

"Jesus Christ," George remarked, and the three of them shuffled toward the front gate of The Palace.

"Daddy..."

"Yeah, boy?"

"Where's Louis?"

"I don' know, son. But Es and Tommy are gonna find him."

"He's alive?!" George exclaimed, opening the gate.

"If he ain', God have mercy on 'em when the Vigilante and the Assistant get there, cause they ain' gonna show no clemency."

"And Walsh?" Ashleigh asked.

"I have a feelin' he'll be waitin' for 'em."

They reached the front door of The Palace, and Ashleigh kicked it open.

The Madame had consumed more whiskey that morning than she had the previous two nights at The Palace combined. It was nearing noon, and she'd just had the pleasure of telling her girls what the fuck happened at The Palace that morning, that they had lost Marcy in the crossfire, and until further notice, every single one of them was in grave danger and needed to stay put for their own protection.

The information was about as well received as she could have expected.

Uma, Penelope, Lena, and Rose were relatively hysterical in tears, both in losing Marcy and in fear of what might happen next. Jasmine and Arabelle stayed composed, and like the Madame, chose to drink their worries away rather than flounder in them, which in the Madame's opinion was a testament to the struggles they probably confronted in their pasts prior to The Palace. In her usual way, Razzy put herself second and took to comforting Dot and Paige, and while Paige was in a state of shock, Dot was in denial, unable to accept that Marcy was truly gone.

For an hour, they sat together by the bar, and the Madame promised each one of the girls no harm would come to them as long as they did what she asked. There were an exorbitant amount of questions, to which the Madame responded as best she could with honesty and with compassion; to her own astonishment, the girls grew angry, not with her, but with the Whyos, with Walsh, and with the

813

fact that anyone would bring harm to Marcy as a means to hurt the Madame. Very quickly, the tables turned, and what had commenced as a goodbye to Marcy and assurances of safety transformed into a sort of bonding rally against the Whyos and Walsh. Every girl wanted to be trained in how to use a pocket pistol, and there were plans put together in case of another invasion, along with a call for bolt locks on certain doors and weapons secretly stored in case of emergency.

It seemed that the Madame's army had grown.

She dismissed the girls a short time later for some afternoon rest and reprieve, though the real goal was for the Madame, Strat, Celeste, and Ashleigh to try and deem what they thought was best until they heard from the others, or what to do in the case that they didn't. Samuel was due back at any time, having taken the morning to sleuth around the police precinct as the Priestly hit unfolded, and boy, did he have a lot to catch up on after the day The Palace had in his absence. With the room emptied out, the four of them made their way down to one of the gambling tables and got comfortable, bringing a bottle of whiskey for moral support as George continued to monitor the perimeter.

"Girls took that pretty damn well, if ya ask me," Ashleigh broke the silence, leaning back into his chair and crossing his left leg over his right. "You'll have an entire house of armed whores, Madame. That's scary as shit and smart as hell, considerin' the war."

"I think we should do it," Celeste concurred, taking a sip of her drink. "They're feeling a sense of comradery after Marcy, and until we figure out how fucking bad the situation is, the more we need others to step up and defend The Palace."

"Strat?" the Madame queried him. "What are your thoughts?"

He considered the prospect. "All of it," he chimed in with the other two. "I've seen what a bunch of drunk assholes can do to defend the Whyos and their turf. A place like this? If there would ever be another invasion, it would be suicide." Strat leaned forward, grabbed the whiskey bottle, and poured more into his cup. "You ought to make this place a fortress. It's going to only get fucking worse, especially if things with Es and Tho—, I'm sorry, Lord Turner—"

"Nah, don' do that," Ashleigh interposed, "you can call him Thomas now."

This stunned Strat. "W-what?"

"You're fucking stuck with us, Strat," the Madame reminded him. "It makes you one of us. Thomas is one of us. The mystery of the Vigilante can be cast aside amongst our own people, unless you'd rather waltz around calling Thomas Lord Turner. I'm sure he would fucking enjoy that."

Celeste and Ashleigh fought to hide grins, yet Strat was full of reverence. "I just...I just never thought this would...would happen..."

"Trust me," Celeste declared, "we use that phrase around here on an almost daily basis. You better get used to it."

Ashleigh looked at the Madame. "We can get this set up within a couple o' hours. I just need ya to give me the go-ahead."

"Done. We'll implement every fucking request. Celeste, you and I will train the girls in using pocket pistols once this fucking shit of a day has come and gone. With fail-safe measures throughout The Palace, we'll never have an incident like this again, and let's make sure we send Mock Duck a goddamn invitation to The Palace that has no expiration date."

"Free for life?" Celeste asked.

"As of right now, yes."

"I'll let Dot know."

"Samuel is due here," Ashleigh went on, "until then, we gotta figure out what in the hell we gonna do."

"Well," the Madame said, "Strat is going to go sit his ass back with Jeremiah and get properly fixed up."

"What?" Strat questioned defensively. "I've been tended to!"

"Your eye is so swollen, it looks like it's about to fucking explode," the Madame pointed out bluntly. "Most of your cuts are still dripping blood, not to mention you just need some goddamn rest after what happened today."

Strat peered at Celeste and Ashleigh, and Celeste shook her head, near a chuckle. "Strat, you look like shit."

After a few seconds, Strat let out a chortle. "All right, I'll get cleaned up. What else ya got, Madame?"

"Ashleigh, you'll take patrol with George. I want you to watch every fucking person that walks by this place, and if you spot any Whyos, we don't hesitate to get our defenses ready. I don't trust any of those bastards, and if things do go badly for the rest, we are on our own."

"What about me?" Celeste entreated her.

"You, Claire, and I will sit at the bar, have whiskey, and load cylinders until our fingers start to fucking bleed."

"On it."

The three of them finished their drinks and rose from their chairs, heading different directions and leaving the Madame with her own contemplations. She sat with her whiskey, twirling it around in the glass, making an effort to not desperately be worried about Thomas and Esther and just what in the fuck they were off doing downtown. Whether they managed to find what was left of Will and Louis or chose to go in search of Walsh, she couldn't guess. What she did know was that minutes passed like hours, and that waiting for someone else—anyone else—to return was worse than any physical torture she'd endured. It wasn't about reinforcements or protecting The Palace—they were her fucking family, her people, the ones who mattered most. If they were gone, the only thing left to fight for was revenge, and in her past lives, revenge had only gotten the Madame so far.

As she reached for the bottle of whiskey on the table, Claire and Celeste reappeared, their skirts holding an array of cylinders and bullets.

"I think we've got enough to keep us covered," Claire stated blandly, her eyes bloodshot from tears for Marcy. "Should take us an hour or two to get everything loaded."

"Perfect."

Celeste and Claire both unloaded everything onto the table, and once they were done, the Madame held up a hand for them to cease.

"Celeste, could you give us a moment?"

"Of course, Madame."

Taking her leave, Celeste waltzed toward the back rooms, where the Madame assumed she would check on her brother and Strat. When they were alone, the Madame gestured for Claire to sit down, and she complied.

"Darling," the Madame coaxed her gently, "will you please, please...talk me through where your head is at."

Claire reached over to the table, grabbed the bottle of whiskey, and popped the cork out of it with one hand. "I just watched my best friend die," she said to the Madame, taking a swig. "Tell me how the fuck you would feel, Madame?"

"Well, I would feel destroyed. Lost. Fucking angry. And...alone."

Taking another gulp, Claire shut her eyes tight, then her gaze found the Madame. "I am not going to pretend I am okay."

"Claire, you need to help me get through this day. I don't care how much time you take to heal, but you know as well as I do that there is no fucking way to know whether we are attacked again or left alone. You are the one person I know I can rely on." The Madame paused, staring into her eyes. "I can still rely on you, can't I?"

Claire's eyes watered, and she nodded. "Of course, Madame."

Just as the Madame was about to call for Celeste, a shout rang out.

"Carriage!" George bellowed as loudly as he could, bounding into the bar area from the front lobby. "Out front! Coach has stopped and driver is headed towards the front door!"

Without a word otherwise, Claire was already on her feet and marching that direction, drawing a pistol from her dress.

"Ashleigh!" the Madame beckoned, following a few steps behind Claire and drawing her revolver. "Get your ass in the lobby now!"

He was already running through the bar area. "On it, Madame!"

Claire reached the front door, yanked the bolt loose and pulled it open, aiming her gun right at the driver's head with George behind her, shotgun raised.

"Who the fuck are you?" she demanded.

The Madame drifted to the left, Ashleigh to the right, in case whoever he was tried to bust in and she could take him out in one clean shot. In her peripheral vision, the Madame spotted Celeste on the other side of the bar entryway, armed and ready.

Instead, the man's whole body trembled, and he lifted his hands up into the air. "Please I…I just…"

"You just fucking what?!" Claire ordered.

Tears escaped his eyes, and from what the Madame could smell, urine escaped his bladder as well. "There's a…a man…in the carriage who…who…"

She'd had enough. Marching to the front door, the Madame grasped the handle and hauled it open wide, pointing her own gun at the driver.

"If you're done pissing yourself, can you tell us why the fuck you're here?"

"A drop off…that's…that's all the two of them asked of me!"

"Two of who?!"

"Some man with dirt on his eyes and a woman who was, well, dressed like a boy…"

The Madame froze. "Ashleigh? George? Go retrieve whoever is in the coach and bring them in here immediately."

When they brought Will through The Palace's front door, his body broken and his life waning, the Madame started screaming for Jeremiah. She felt her throat tighten at the sight of him—the Whyos had done some of their worst work, and the likelihood Will would make it through the night was almost zero. As Jeremiah came dodging through to Will's side, she could see it in his countenance, too, the appreciation of how bad his condition was.

"Madame," Will whispered, "he's...alive..."

"Whyos," Ashleigh explained to her, carrying his father past and toward the hallway leading to the rear of The Palace. "They took Louis to get to Es and Tommy."

"How would Es and Thomas even know where to go?" Celeste questioned, joining them. "The only person we have who knows where the hideout is...is...well, Strat!"

"Croker," Will uttered, "they were...goin' to pay Richie a visit..."

The Madame glimpsed at her doctor. "Jeremiah?"

"I've got him, Madame."

"Claire?"

"Yes, Madame."

She trailed behind George and Ashleigh carrying Will, while Jeremiah led the way to his rooms to try and keep Will Sweeney alive. Moving to the Madame's side, Celeste looked after them, stricken.

"What are his odds, you think?"

"Darling, it's not good."

"Fuck," she uttered softly.

In the next second, Celeste and the Madame heard the sound of someone climbing the stoop toward the open front door. Simultaneously, they drew their guns and whipped around, taking aim at a man on the threshold of The Palace, who threw his arms up into the air.

"Jesus fucking Christ!" he cried, eyes wide in fear. "Don't shoot! Don't shoot!"

"Who the fuck are you?!" the Madame greeted with her usual enthusiasm for strangers in her institution, yanking the hammer back on her revolver.

"Please! Can you ladies put the guns down?! I'm not here to harm anyone!"

Celeste then also pulled the hammer on her pistol. "Answer the question, and the guns disappear. Who the hell are you?!"

His whole body shook. "My name is…is McCann…I was left a note by some…large French bastard at my…hotel this morning…"

Both women lowered their guns, exchanging a glance.

"Patrick McCann?" the Madame probed hesitantly, worried this might be a hallucination.

"Thank you." The removal of weapons pacified his nerves. "Yes, that's me. Are you the…the Madame who sent me this calling card?"

"Yes, I am. I apologize for the rude introduction. As you can see from the state of my business, we've had one hell of a catastrophic morning."

She realized upon saying those words that McCann hadn't even noticed the bullet holes, blood, and ruination of The Palace's front lobby, and the expression on his face as he glanced around was absolutely priceless.

"Well…I can…er…see why my presence must have…startled…you…"

"Madame," Celeste mumbled so McCann couldn't hear her, "what do we do?"

"Go upstairs and get the office presentable," she answered almost inaudibly, and as Celeste departed, the Madame returned to McCann. "Mr. McCann, would you be so kind as to join me upstairs in my office? We can discuss the details of why I wanted to meet you up there. Perhaps a bit of whiskey or some kind of drink?"

This idea made him anxious. "Upstairs? I…well, Madame, I don't know…"

"Well, then answer me this," she went on. "What is your connection to Richard Croker?"

Right before her, Patrick McCann's entire countenance shifted from shaky and on-edge to well-controlled anger. "Croker is my brother-in-law," he told her, his tone firm.

"You are Elizabeth's brother?"

"Estranged brother, yes. Why is this relevant?"

"Because I am pretty sure you are the last name on a long list of people Richard Croker wants dead, and to be honest, Mr. Mc-Cann, I think I am the only fucking person in this city willing to risk their ass to keep you alive."

McCann's color went ashen. "Well, then, I think I'll take that drink, Madame. If you'd be so kind."

AUTHOR'S NOTE

I wanted to give a special shout out to the wonderful people who helped to fund this book's publication through my Kickstarter Campaign, Whiskey and the Renegades Return.

Matt Merritt, Ryan McNutt, Liz Menz, Shallen and
Sandro Ferreira, Mae Governale, Stefanie Sutton,
Einar Helgason, Anna Vitale, Samantha Burnham,
Rosie Stout, Vanessa Diaz, David Comfort, Jeremy Ruehr,
Cynthia and Edward Schuessler, Mike Raspatello,
Brendan O'Toole, Kelsey Grode, Caiti Stout, Katie Omick,
JD Whittington, Doug Bynam, Shahin Zarafshar,
Scott McCune, Katie Marie, Adam Lambert,
Barbara Lieberoff, Katie Coco, Troy Lyver, Ashray Urs,
Katherine Galligan, Pam Knowles, James McNutt,
Jennifer Savage, Yulia Denisyuk, Dharma Tamm,
Geraldine Steinhart, Lacie Guler, Arial Goodling,
and Lisa McMahon

THE SERPENT AND THE FIRE

publication supported by a grant from
The Community Foundation for Greater New Haven
as part of the **Urban Haven Project**

THE SERPENT
and the **FIRE**

*Poetries of the Americas
from Origins to Present*

Edited by
Jerome Rothenberg
and
Javier Taboada

With contributions by
John Bloomberg-Rissman

University of California Press

University of California Press
Oakland, California

© 2024 by The Regents of the University of California

Library of Congress Cataloging-in-Publication Data

Names: Rothenberg, Jerome, editor. | Taboada, Javier,
    editor. | Bloomberg-Rissman, John, contributor.
Title: The serpent and the fire : poetries of the Americas
    from origins to present / edited by Jerome Rothenberg
    and Javier Taboada ; with contributions by John
    Bloomberg-Rissman.
Description: Oakland, California : University of
    California Press, [2024]
Identifiers: LCCN 2023054065 | ISBN 9780520303546
    (cloth) | ISBN 9780520972759 (pdf)
Subjects: LCSH: Poetry. | America—Literatures.
Classification: LCC PN1300 .S47 2024 | DDC
    809.1—dc23/eng/20240111
LC record available at https://lccn.loc.gov/2023054065

Manufactured in the United States of America

33 32 31 30 29 28 27 26 25 24
10 9 8 7 6 5 4 3 2 1

The great snake absorbed all knowledge,
all the arts were inside her
When the fire reached her,
she exploded:
all knowledge gushed from her,
was scattered everywhere

KUMEYAAY INDIAN CREATION NARRATIVE

CONTENTS

A FIRST GALLERY
from the Florentine Codex to Walt Whitman

A SECOND GALLERY
from Emily Dickinson to Vicente Huidobro

A THIRD GALLERY
from María Sabina to Ernesto Cardenal

A FOURTH GALLERY
from Allen Ginsberg to Raúl Zurita

On my American plains I feel the struggling afflictions
Endur'd by roots that writhe their arms into the nether deep:
I see a Serpent in Canada, who courts me to his love;
In Mexico an Eagle, and a Lion in Peru;
I see a Whale in the South-sea, drinking my soul away.
O what limb rending pains I feel. thy fire & my frost
Mingle in howling pains, in furrows by thy lightnings rent;
This is eternal death; and this the torment long foretold.

—WILLIAM BLAKE, *AMERICA A PROPHECY*

1. Toward a Hemispheric Book of the Americas

As part of a long-term project shared with many, what the two present
coeditors have now brought together is an assemblage/gathering of the
poetries of the Americas, both north and south and drawing from the
multiplicity of languages and cultures on the two great continents. Too
often, in the English-speaking world and beyond, the idea of America
and American poetry and literature is limited, like the name "America"
itself, to work written in English within the present boundaries of the
United States. While this has been modified in several recent, largely contemporary anthologies, there has never been a full-blown gathering of
American poetries viewing north and south together in a hemispheric and

transnational vision of what "America" has meant in the long, overall history of our hemisphere and of the world, "from origins to present." Such a vision of another America, deeply rooted in its pre-Conquest and pre-"American" past and in the writings of its early European colonizers, comes to us from poets such as the Nicaraguan Rubén Darío, writing in 1904 of

> our America, which has had poets
> from the ancient times of Nezahualcoyotl...
> the America of the great Moctezuma, of the Inca,
> our America smelling of Christopher Columbus,
> our Catholic America, our Spanish America...

Or from José Martí, who, while feeling the oppression of Cuba's stronger neighbor to the north, wrote: "The pressing need of our America is to show itself as it is, one in spirit and intent, swift conquerors of a suffocating past." Their Spanish and Indigenous American civilizations constitute a declaration of independence from the other, English-speaking America and should be taken as such. Along with which there's also an African-descended America (Caribbean, Latin American, and northern), spawned by the horrors (and aftermaths) of the inhuman slave trade. All of these, and many more to follow, make for an unprecedented complex of advanced cultures shaped by both conquest and migration, and open to political, racial, and social pressures, both from inside and outside.

For the two of us poets, one from Mexico and the other from the United States, the idea of a still larger America(s), made up of many autonomous and semiautonomous parts, has been a topic of continuing shared interest. In the absence of a single gathering of "American" poetries or literatures that takes such an expansive and far-reaching view of its subject matter, we find ourselves free to make a new beginning, an open-ended experiment through what we're calling *omnipoetics*—to explore what results might follow from a juxtaposition of poets and poetries covering the breadth of the Americas and the range of languages within them: European languages such as English, Spanish, Portuguese, Dutch, and French, with their attendant creoles and pidgins, as well as a large number of Indigenous languages such as Mapuche, Tupí-Guaraní, Quechua, Mayan, Mazatec, Navajo, and Nahuatl.[1] While our sense of "America" along these lines

---

1. Writes Natalie Diaz: "Learning and speaking one's native language is an emotional and political act. Each time a poet brings a native language onto the white space of the page, into the white space of the academies and institutions of poetry, it is an emotional and political act."

would extend and amplify the common metaphor of the Americas as a "new world," we also recognize and embrace the reality of two thousand years or more of (native) American Indigenous poetries, both oral and written, and more than that, of poesis over a still longer span.

It is precisely such complexities and contradictions, even conflicts, that have engaged us here.

2. The Invention and Reinvention of America

We say it again, this book is an experiment: to explore anew the "poetries of the Americas," and to do so by gathering and juxtaposing some of their disparate parts as we find them, not as a new canon but as a corpus, a body of work that we would read as poetry in all its varied and diverse forms of written and oral expression. In other words, is there the possibility of imagining an anthology of the Americas as a series of intrahemispheric poetries, an omnipoetic experiment starting from what a first mapping affords us, while acknowledging at the same time the presence within it of idiomatic, cultural, and religious differences? Many of these differences, as we come at them, were imposed through a process of colonization on an unprecedented and long-enduring scale, reflective of the ideologies and lifeways of the European nations then in conflict: Catholicism versus Protestantism, Romance languages versus Anglo-Saxon or Germanic, monarchies set against nascent emerging republics. And the Indigenous and pre-European nations also show a remarkable range and diversity of languages and cultures, as important in their differences as in the later histories that connect them.

Into this congeries of nations, peopled and repeopled in successive waves, populations of Africans were brought as slaves, enduring over centuries and creating new cultures and languages in the hard-fought process of liberation, still in progress. And while the conquistadors and settlers saw themselves as singular sovereigns and preordained masters of their newfound worlds, the openness of the new America(s) brought with it an unprecedented influx of later arrivals, a complex of immigrations going well beyond the idea of a narrow European nexus and mastery, north or south, and opening at present into Muslim, African, and Asian immigrants and refugees/escapees from ecological and genocidal disasters. It is this complexity and diversity—this constant reinvention of America— that became clear and more compelling to us as we moved further into the reality of the multiple Americas before us. If these complexities have often been a source of conflict, they emerge in the domain of poetry as harbingers of power and of beauty—not an aestheticized calm and stillness (however tempting) but a counterforce of doubt and yearning. With that end in mind, our approach is biased toward an experimental, even avant-garde, selection of the works as we come at them, in the far past as well as the continuous present.

That there has also been a push toward a new unity, both pan-American and global, is another point worth noting. And it's in that spirit—many times repeated—that our selection attempts to imagine or sketch a gathering of the Americas that includes or shows some of the following characteristics:

- A deep and wide history of American poetries and related forms of orature (including performance), works of visual art and writing long predating the first European invasions and seen as part of our cultural and national/transnational inheritance, in many areas of Latin America in particular.[2]

- The reality of centuries of colonial and postcolonial, political and cultural domination, marked by later wars of liberation, on the one hand, and genocidal conflicts, on the other.

- A shifting process in the minds of some European settlers and writers, moving from initial horror and scorn on their arrival to admiration and support, becoming fellow travelers and defenders soon thereafter.[3]

- Revolutionary and Enlightenment ideas of freedom, egalitarianism, democracy, and change/transformation,[4] too often coming short or thwarted by recurring nativisms and the lures of racial privilege.

- An exceptional biodiversity: discovered and recovered landscapes,[5]

2. Of which Andrés Bello wrote (ca. 1850): "We have atoned enough for the savage conquest / of our unhappy fathers." And later: "The ghosts of Moctezuma, Atahualpa, / sleep now, glutted with Spanish blood."

3. As Father Antón de Montesinos said, delivering a sermon (1511) in Santo Domingo: "And they die, or better said, you kill them, only to extract and acquire gold each day. Are these not men? Do they not have rational souls? Are you not commanded to care for them as you would for yourselves?"

4. Thus, Walt Whitman: "I speak the password primeval, I give the sign of democracy. / By God, I will accept nothing which all cannot have their counterpart of on the same terms."

5. As Gonçalves Dias projected it for his unfinished epic *Os Timbiras* (1857): "I imagined a poem… as you've never heard of other like this: groups of tigers, coatis, rattlesnakes; I imagined mango trees and leafy *jabuticaba* trees, *jequitibás* and arrogant *ipe* trees, *sapucai* trees and *jambeiros*… ; diabolic warriors, witch-women, frogs and countless alligators: in short, an American genesis, a Brazilian *Iliad*, a recreated creation." Or conquistador Hernán Cortés in his *Second Letter* to the Spanish

both natural and manmade, moving toward an inescapable ecopoetics from the Romantic and post-Romantic 1800s to its acceleration in the climate crises of the late twentieth and early twenty-first centuries.

- The abundance of old and new American languages: the Indigenous and the European making way for new American idioms, but also creoles, pidgins, nation languages, language amalgams: a turmoil of languages.[6]

- A move toward experiment and innovation, encouraged also by European-based avant-gardes and by the rediscovery as well of pre-Conquest and African sources, and by homegrown pragmatisms and improvisations: what we consider seminal steps on the way to an omnipoetics.

- A renewed search for the deepest origins of poetry, language, the world. In hemispheric terms, but particularly in Latin America, a quest to find and connect with a deeply rooted "American" tradition: a non-European canon.[7]

- An open view of poetry (or what we call *poesis*) across genres,[8] often resulting in a blurring of the boundaries between "high" and "low" forms of the art.

- A poesis of the particulars (dating back to the first chroniclers and the proto-ethnographical accounts of Bernardino de Sahagún and other European missionaries)[9] and a fascination with science, facts, and data (objectivism, *exteriorismo*) along with independent visionary acts of the imagination.[10]

---

emperor: "I am not able to tell you anything about the things I saw here, except that there is nothing like them in Spain."

6. "An American does not receive a verbal tradition but activates it" (José Lezama Lima).

7. Ernesto Cardenal, in a letter (1956): "And here in the Amazon we have come to find America and the American man, the ancient America, which is for me the America of the future. We have come to find natives, myths, dreams.... Maybe then we will have something to sing."

8. Esteban Echeverría, in the nineteenth century: "The merit of any artistic work is not assessed by its form or by its magnitude, or by its belonging to this or that genre, but by the substance it contains." And Robert Creeley, as cited later by Charles Olson: "Form is never more than an extension of content."

9. Wrote friar Antonio Tello in his *Chronicle of the Conquest of Xalisco* (1650 or 1651): "If we descend into the particulars our amazement will never end." Or William Carlos Williams in his preface to *Paterson*: "To make a start, / out of particulars / and make them general, rolling / up the sum, by defective means... "

10. Writes Diane di Prima, among many: "The war that matters is the war against

- A hemisphere-wide eruption of American poetries over the last two hundred years, beyond the capacity of a single gathering to show.

With all of this, the mystery of America remains, not a finished work but a self-perpetuating work in progress. The effort in what follows is to present works of poesis as we found them and to encourage others to do the same, with an openness to contradiction and change that may itself be an American trait at its most enduring and most threatened.

That so much of what this book presents is currently under renewed attack is another point worth noting.

3. The Composition of a Work in Progress

Since 1984 University of California Press has published five large assemblages of poetry as part of a long-term project in which the present coeditor, with the assistance of a number of other poets and scholars, embarked on a series of anthologies/assemblages aimed at the remapping of poetry on a global, historical, and contemporary basis. The key works here are *Technicians of the Sacred*, first published in 1968 and recently republished in a fiftieth-anniversary expanded edition, and four volumes of *Poems for the Millennium*, along with the critical essays found in *Symposium of the Whole: A Range of Discourse Toward an Ethnopoetics*. From the start, those involved have seen this project as open to growth and change over the passing years, with a belief that every successive work is both a continuation and a new beginning, as changing possibilities present themselves for our consideration.

It is with all of these issues in mind, and living when and where we do, that we have turned to the composition of this assemblage, to transform what we've gathered into a possible image of how the individual parts play out when brought together. In doing so, we present four sections called "galleries," arranged in rough chronological order, and four called "maps," arranged thematically with a mix and juxtaposition of times and places—all accompanied by commentaries that convey the range of the poetics spawned across the two American continents and their adjacent islands. Our cutoff point for the galleries is with poets born in 1950 and earlier, a deliberate attempt to focus on work emerging by the end of the last millennium and to minimize the possibility of misrepresenting or

[and for] the imagination / all other wars are subsumed in it." Or William Carlos Williams again: "Only the imagination is real."

"canonizing" the more recent generations of poets, some of whom will appear even so in our four thematic sections and in various nonchronological addenda scattered throughout the book or in later gatherings that may follow this one.[11] And, on a different note, we also collage freely from commentaries drawn from the omnipoetic assemblages that preceded the present *The Serpent and the Fire*.

Our opening in this pursuit, for both the chronological and the thematic sections, is a section called "Preludium": an attempt to show, against the European sense of the discovery and settling of America as a new and still unnamed/untamed world, the reality of ten thousand–plus years of human presence and of long-standing civilizations and cultures both far north and deep south. With that in mind, we start our work, well before the naming of an "America" as such after a minor European adventurer, with an image of stenciled hands (as a form of writing) from the Neolithic Cave of the Hands in Patagonia; and with the same open sense of poetry, we attempt to sweep the two great continents, including hieroglyphic works cut into or painted on stone; older Indigenous texts, such as the *Popol Vuh*, written down alphabetically after the Conquest; and later oral accounts that offer an unbroken, retrospective series of narratives emerging anew into the almost present.

For this, the overriding technique is one of collage or juxtaposition: by the accidents of birth years in the galleries and by a more deliberate strategy of bringing "all things into their comparisons" (R. Duncan) in our four thematic maps. Accordingly, beginning with the preludium of the largely Indigenous pre-Conquest oratures and literatures, there follows a first gallery, from early colonial and surviving Indigenous work up to Walt Whitman; a second gallery, of Romantic and post-Romantic poetries; a third gallery, focusing on early modernisms and avant-gardisms from the mid-nineteenth to the early twentieth century; and a fourth gallery, of continuities and new approaches from the post–World War II generation to the near present, on an inter-American level.

By contrast, our maps are arranged thematically. The first of these maps is that of "the Americas" as such: a recognition that America, bounded by its geography and by its cultural and political realities, has been defined and redefined over the more than five centuries since its naming. Often

---

11. Of the further continuities and connections here, Lyn Hejinian writes, in *The Beginner*: "If in the 19th century, as Gertrude Stein said, people saw parts and tried to assemble them into wholes, while in the 20th century people envisioned wholes and then sought parts appropriate to them, will the 21st century carry out a dissemination of wholes into all parts and thus finish what the 19th century began?"

contradictory, these definitions have moved between utopian dreams and prophecies, both north and south, and dystopian blockages and conflicts. From the very beginnings of America as such, the Europeans' sense of discovery and conquest came up against the reality of defeat and enslavement for those brought unwillingly into the field of combat and subjugation. On the utopian and Enlightenment side, poets in the Americas shared in the creation of New World prophecies and revolutions, first in the north and later turned in the south against both the European rulers and the northern interlopers themselves. On the imaginal and metaphoric side, we give special attention and devote a subsection, called a mini gallery, to the image of a mythologized and feminized America as woman (often enough an instrument, however conflicted, of male privilege and yearning); and in acknowledgment of an America transformed by periodic waves of new arrivals, we devote a further mini gallery to the web of new and old, invasive and Indigenous languages—idioms and idiolects—this brings about. As a result, among many of those who saw themselves as newly named Americans, changing from generation to generation and across internal and ever-shifting demographics and national, political, or even social identities, there was and is for some of us the sense of a perpetual avant-garde and the search for a new poetry and art open to constant flux and reinvention, like language itself, that would issue early and later through its liberated poets. That this has played out against a series of dystopian contradictions has only added to the power of the work at hand.

It is in the same spirit that our next two maps—Visions and Histories—seek to explore poetries of fact and of imagination, both in their differences and in their often unavoidable and necessary overlapping. On the side of visions first, the poet has been imagined since ancient times as one-who-sees and gives that vision to others through language. As people give up or are stripped of their faith in personal vision, they confuse this vision with madness: coming to fear their own minds, they erect taboos against knowing. "A Map of Visions" tells of the difficult but continuous emergence and reemergence in the Americas of a major poetry of vision, both north and south, ancient and modern, sometimes cultivating what Rimbaud called "disorder of the senses" as a key to renewal, sometimes exploring dream as revelation, sometimes as terror, and sometimes reviving the idea of magic as a power of language itself. As Thoreau wrote, "The great god Pan is not dead, as was rumored," and Herman Melville, on its dark side: "Madness is undefinable—It & right reason extremes of one,—not the (black art) Goetic but Theurgic magic—seeks converse with Intelligence, Power, the Angel." Yet along with these, there is also a fierce drive to see clearly, a poetics of things seen anew, as if for the first time: what George Oppen spoke of as "the virtue of the mind... that emotion which causes to see." Or as Octavio Paz wrote elsewhere: "A poet does not hear a strange voice, but the voice and word are strange: they are the words and the voices of the world, to which the poet gives new meaning."

From a possibly different perspective, "A Map of Histories" draws heavily on Ezra Pound's simplified but useful definition of an "epic" as "a poem including history," calling our attention to the deep connection between poetry and history, with the sense, as Pound nailed it also, that "all ages are contemporaneous in the mind."[12] An intrinsic concern of poetry from its beginnings and taking on new forms and methods in the near present, it calls our attention to the fact that the American poetries and many of their attendant poets have been struggling all along to let the concerns of and with history flow through them. In a deeper sense, a poem is a historical act, just as individual life and consciousness are history in process, but the call of history is all the greater on the American continents, both to define a "new world" and to protect a range of older native worlds under threat of annihilation. "A Map of Histories" attempts to show, in its free juxtaposition of times and places, some of the modalities through which it is possible to see the interconnectivity between events in fact and events in consciousness. (Nor should we forget the importance of personal history—through self-observation and memory—as an area of exploration from deep Romanticism into the still deeper present.) But history begins, too, with the telling of a story, and "A Map of Histories" reminds us that history, story, and myth are all rooted in a common effort to know human meaning "in time."[13] That the American concern with both history and myth reaches, often, beyond our hemisphere as such is a further sign of its importance.

For all of this, it is the final "map" that presents an idea of poetry—Extensions—that has been essential to our work as a whole. In the long history of the Americas, as elsewhere, it is now possible to recover forms of language and "language happenings" that our conventional poetics had too often ignored. There is, in fact, a long countertradition of poetry that broke open in early colonial times, developed in the late eighteenth century, exploded in the twentieth, and is currently very much alive—

12. Or Luis Cardoza y Aragón: "The one who doesn't reside in the future doesn't exist. / The future started yesterday."

13. Jorge Luis Borges: "We shall never know who forged the word... / we shall never know in what age it came to mean / the starry hours. / Others created the myth."

a tradition of self-aware, often difficult, experimental work that locates poetry's "political" role (as a means to a reawakening of human possibility) in the very elements of poetry and of language itself.[14] These elements, in the context of experimental poetry and equally experimental prose, are not invisible conduits of poetic "content" but reveal the constraints on the mind, while indicating the means by which to throw off those constraints. Among its markers, stretching from the beginnings (post- or even pre-Conquest) into the twentieth century and beyond, are hybridization—crossover—improvisation and performance—dreamwork as poem—alternative forms of rhyme and lineation—visualizations—prose as an instrument for poetry—glossolalia and glossographia—first and later glimmerings of open verse, free verse, and words in freedom.

With this in mind, it is now possible to look even further, back and beyond, into areas not commonly identified with poetry or literature as such, and to find language works that we can now add, alongside deliberately experimental works, to the possibilities of poetry and expressive/imaginative thought.

4. America a Prophecy

An Omnipoetics Manifesto

If the words of the British poet/artist William Blake stand as the opening of our book, it is both for his recognition of a larger America and for his regard for poetry as an instrument of prophecy. It is in this sense that we invoke him as our guardian angel, to remind us (when history or circumstances repeat themselves) of this "calling" for our continents and poets. Like Blake, whose *America a Prophecy* is part of a series of continental prophecies, our hemispheric assemblage tries, through the voices gathered here, to reiterate this markedly American "path," or, in our case, this series of paths. Thus, the "prophecy about America" (if there is one in the following pages, as there surely was for Blake) becomes not just a projection of transformative events and times to come, but a testimony

---

14. From the latter-day shaman-poet María Sabina: "Wisdom is Language. Language is in the Book. The Book is granted by the Principal Ones." And again: "I cure with language." Or Mário Faustino, differently: "Life all language— / as we all know / to conjugate these verbs, to name / these names: to love, to make, to destroy / man, woman, and beast, devil and angel / and god maybe, and nothing / kicking and screaming / into language." Or Carlos Drummond de Andrade: "In the power of language / And the power of silence."

as well of the difficulties and threats we face today, north and south, and replicated ominously throughout the world.

All of this has been compounded, of course, by the circumstances of the time in which we've been working: events that have both reinforced our vision of America—as poetry and prophecy—and an upsurge of forces that have come to stand against it. More directly, our time has been marked by an almost unprecedented pandemic and an ongoing and worsening climate crisis, the consequences of which are continuing to assault us. Even more: we have witnessed an upsurge of new or revisited nationalisms and racisms, directed most often against that diversity of mind and spirit of which our lifetime projects were so clearly a part. To confront this implicit, sometimes rampant ethnic and ecological devastation, there is the need for a kind of omnipoetics that tests the range of our threatened natures wherever found and looks toward an ever-greater assemblage of words and thoughts as a singular buttress against those forces that would divide and diminish us. It is in this sense that we are attempting here an omnipoetics of the American hemisphere, as an experimental instance of what might be attempted further on a worldwide scale, toward what one of us once described as "an anthology of everything."[15]

Toward that end, then, we are offering the following as a manifesto of omnipoetics and of the work that lies ahead:

1. Omnipoetics as a rejection of the idea of a canon or of any state of mind or spirit that defines poetry as a hierarchy of high and low forms, separating verse and prose, sound and image, written and oral, voice and gesture, poetry and philosophy, etc., while recognizing individual works of genius in all these categories.

2. Omnipoetics as an attempt to create a horizontal corpus of works that can facilitate a mutual communication across borders, bringing it all into a continually expanding "symposium of the whole."

3. Omnipoetics as the recognition that poetry is the language art par excellence, the primary art of languaged beings, present in any language and neither exclusively spoken nor written—that poetry in that sense "is made by all, not by one" (I. Ducasse).

4. Omnipoetics as a late attempt (now or never) to tell the many tales of the tribe, the living and the dead: the final testimonies of our "residence on earth" (P. Neruda).

---

15. "To write at all is to dwell in the illusion of language, the rapture of communication that comes as we surrender our troubled individual isolated experiences to the communal consciousness" (Robert Duncan).

5. An omnipoetics of the particular and local set beside an omnipoetics of the global and distant, with mutual regard and conjoining.

6. An omnipoetics of multiplicities, against a false universality and in favor of a true one, a global map of differences in which everything is possible.

7. An omnipoetics rooted in language and poesis—a true *language poetry* explored and reinforced by a nascent *language poetics*.

8. An omnipoetics of resistance, open to the new and transgressive, "always on the move, always changing, morphing, moving through languages, cultures, terrains, times, without stopping" (P. Joris).

9. Omnipoetics as a contemporary attempt to project anew a primal (= complex) consciousness of the whole. As in the Kumeyaay myth of creation: "The great snake absorbed all knowledge, / all the arts were inside her / When the fire reached her, / she exploded: / all knowledge gushed from her, / was scattered everywhere."

The total work that follows, then, is an experiment toward an omnipoetics in action.

Jerome Rothenberg / Javier Taboada
Encinitas, California / Cholula, Puebla
2023

EDITORIAL NOTE. Honoring the principle of language as play and vision, we have decided to respect—and even highlight—the "inconsistencies" or unconventionalities of grammar, spelling, syntax, and capitalization, wherever found in the texts gathered here. Such a decision—along with a general foregrounding of idiom, idiolect, and difference—celebrates, for us, the multiplicity of voices and forms of expression that have shaped the poetries of the Americas.

What we've attempted here is a "grand collage" (R. Duncan): an amalgam of the many voices and minds that are essential to making an omnipoetics possible. Here we revert again—against the odds, perhaps—to the dream of a work in common, of a company of poets and other fellow travelers who have created or transmitted the words and images that a book like this demands. And beyond the makers—the poets themselves, and their translators—there are all those who have acted as advisers and explainers, essential to opening up more areas of poesis than we could ever have managed on our own.

In the work that we've undertaken here, however tentative, a strong feeling of gratitude and comradeship persists for the many poets and scholars who came to our assistance. First off was the essential presence of Heriberto Yépez, with whom the idea for our project was first initiated and planned. Although he left the project in its early stages and many things have changed since then, his impulse, ideas, and contributions can still be felt throughout.

In the further work of gathering and displaying the many poetries assembled here, John Bloomberg-Rissman was ongoingly active as a valued and necessary collaborator and adviser, who brought his sense of an American omnipoetics to supplement our own.

We have also drawn throughout from discussions and joint writings with previous collaborators, some of it collaged and incorporated into the present assemblage: Pierre Joris, Jeffrey Robinson, John Bloomberg-Rissman, Diane Rothenberg, Dennis Tedlock, and George Quasha. Along with these and essential for key aspects of our work, Jennifer Cooper was our principal adviser for Brazilian poetry and poetics, and H-Dirksen L. Bauman led us into transcription and commentary on ASL poetry as a language (almost) without sound but essential to a new viewing of the possibilities of poetry overall.

Other translators and poets with whom we've been in direct contact over the last few years include Charles Bernstein, Ricardo Cázares, Chris Daniels, Michael Davidson, Keith Ekiss, Clayton Eshleman, Cole Heinowitz, Suzanne Jill Levine, Ariel Resnikoff, Rachel Robinson, Rodrigo Rojas, Bryan Sentes, [David] Shook, Susan Suntree, Cecilia Vicuña, Juan Carlos Villavicencio, Molly Weigel, and Mark Weiss, but there are others, too, across decades and centuries, whom we have known through their writings and to whom we remain forever grateful.

At the same time, we note, with genuine regret, the inevitable omissions in a gathering like this, both from the far past and certainly in the near present, of those from whose work an equally meaningful book could have been assembled. It is our hope in this regard that our work, where permissions in particular were lacking, will somehow encourage others to compose their own assemblages, however different from ours, so that our gathering, if it succeeds, would be a possible first attempt at such an omnipoetics but in no sense a final one.

That being said, we also give warmest thanks to Eric Schmidt and LeKeisha Hughes, our editors at University of California Press, who encouraged and guided us in the best tradition of American literary publishing and editing. And beyond all else, we have been supported by the presence and love of our immediate families: Diane and Matthew Rothenberg; Frida, Emilio, Julia, and Matías Taboada.

PRELUDIUM

America before America

Patagonia, Argentina

from **CUEVA DE LAS MANOS**

COMMENTARY

Dispersed over multiple continents & regions, stenciled hands dating back to the late Paleolithic appear also in the Cueva de las Manos (Cave of Hands) in Patagonia, & as a form of writing/drawing can be taken here as a primordial instance of *poesis* in what would come to be called, some ten thousand years later, *America*. Of still another cave & other hands, the California poet Robinson Jeffers wrote:

> *Inside a cave in a narrow canyon near Tassajara*
> *The vault of rock is painted with hands,*
> *A multitude of hands in the twilight, a cloud of men's palms, no more,*
> *No other picture. There's no one to say*
> *Whether the brown shy quiet people who are dead intended*
> *Religion or magic, or made their tracings*
> *In the idleness of art; but over the division of years these careful*
> *Signs-manual are now like a sealed message*
> *Saying: "Look: we also were human; we had hands, not paws. All hail*
> *You people with the cleverer hands, our supplanters*
> *In the beautiful country; enjoy her a season, her beauty, and come down*
> *And be supplanted; for you also are human."*

3

Or in an "Aztec definition" of "cave" recorded ca. 1500:

It becomes long, deep; it widens, extends, narrows. It is a constricted place, a narrowed place, one of the hollowed-out places. It forms hollowed-out places. There are roughened places; there are asperous places. It is frightening, a fearful place, a place of death. It is called a place of death because there is dying. It is a place of darkness; it darkens; it stands ever dark. It stands wide-mouthed, it is wide-mouthed. It is wide-mouthed; it is narrow-mouthed. It has mouths which pass through.

I place myself in the cave. I enter the cave.

Translated by J.O. Anderson & Charles E. Dibble

Lower Pecos River, Texas

from THE WHITE SHAMAN MURAL: NARRATIVE & VISION

COMMENTARY

Time is written into the White Shaman mural... these murals are texts, analogous to the books once housed in the Library of Alexandria. (Carolyn Boyd) And again: *Like a book, each mural in the Lower Pecos Canyonlands was authored and composed to communicate thoughts and ideas. These ancient paintings are visual narratives.* (Shumla Archaeological Research & Education Center)

Nowhere is the achievement of early American imagination clearer than in the series of more than two hundred painted rock shelters at the juncture of the Rio Grande & Pecos Rivers in Texas. The dates in this instance go back some 2,500 to 5,000 years & mark the northernmost point of a vast cultural & linguistic area stretching south through Mesoamerica. Yet the images, while different from those farther south, are complex & unique, as they come to us, & they represent as well a kind of visual texting, now waiting to be read again. Writes Carolyn Boyd, a contemporary artist & archaeologist, who was among the first to approach them as more than scattered & disconnected/random images, "Perhaps the oldest known texts in the New World... incredibly complex and compositionally intricate, these ancient murals, like codices, are pictographic writing. Far from being the idle doodling of ancient peoples, the rock art of the Lower Pecos was part of a living landscape that provided food, shelter, and a connection with the spirit world."

ADDENDUM

EMILIO ADOLFO WESTPHALEN Peru, 1911–2001

from **The Amber Goddess Is Back**

We call Great Shaman or Powerful Shamans those who put us in a stage taken from Chaos or Nothingness or from themselves—& who surrounded us with Wonders and Beauties. Without neglecting—to certainly highlight these—Horror Boredom & Filth.

Translated from Spanish by Javier Taboada

Epi-Olmec

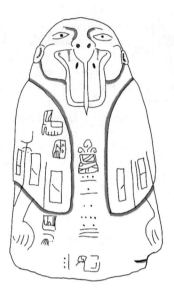

COMMENTARY

Early in the game, the Epi-Olmec (post-Olmec) culture (ca. 500 BC–AD 500) from the Tuxtla Mountains near Catemaco, Veracruz, shows an already active use of glyphic writing & the beginnings of a written literature as such. Inscribed in a still-undeciphered script, this statuette—a narrow-eyed figurine carved of green jadeite with incised glyphs, whose chin displays a duck-like boat-billed heron's beak—reminds us of the first shamanic protopoets, many of them depicted, as here, with animalistic features. For them—& still for us as latter-day interpreters—a key was needed to unlock their visions & healings: an inner language to unveil a world awash with hidden powers.

Adams, Ohio

AMERICAN EARTHWORKS: THE GREAT SERPENT MOUND

(1) Mounds / earthworks / monumental poems. Large earth mounds, often containing artifacts of great beauty, flank the rivers of the US Midwest, some ten thousand in the Ohio Valley alone. Though almost certainly native in origin, they led to myths of a vanished race, a lost pre-Indian civilization; treatises appeared, postulating immigrations from Mexico, refugees from Atlantis, traveling Danes, Malays, & remnants of the Ten Lost Tribes of Israel. Frank Waters, from a different vantage, in *Book of the Hopi* (1963) records the Hopi belief that the great Serpent Mound in Adams County, Ohio (ca. 1000 BC) may have been built by their migrating ancestors in the absence of cliffs on which to mark their pictographs. Whoever the author(s), it is the largest known serpent effigy in the world: length, 1,254 feet; average width, 20 feet; height, 4 or 5 feet. Physical structures with the power to convey tradition & call men to exegesis continue to figure among the possibilities of poetry—as witness the Mexican concrete poet Mathias Goeritz's "architectural poems"—e.g., a gate built of the word "ororororororo... ," etc. (in Spanish, alternately "gold" & "horror") (from J. Rothenberg & G. Quasha, *America a Prophecy*).

(2) And again, the image of the ancient earthwork reappears, this time in the land art of a contemporary mound builder like Robert Smithson, draw-

ing directly from the great serpent mound & other pre-American proto-types (as in the ancient Nazca images, say, in southern Peru), his *Spiral Jetty* constructed in the Great Salt Lake in Utah the iconic example of that rebirth, which—in other circumstances, as a long-lasting landmark—could be compared with the evanescent landscape poems of Raúl Zurita. (See "A Map of Extensions" & "A Fourth Gallery.")

Inuit

INUKSUK (HELPER)

Inuksuit (plural of inuksuk) are Inuit-created rock formations, some of which were created yesterday, some of which date back to ca. 2500 BC. They "are placed throughout the Arctic landscape [and act] as 'helpers' to the Inuit. Among their many practical functions, they are used as hunting and navigational aids, coordination points and message centers (e.g., they might indicate where food was cached). In addition to their earthly functions, certain inuksuk-like figures have spiritual connotations, and are objects of veneration, often marking the spiritual landscape of the *Inummaritt*—the Inuit who know how to survive on the land living in their traditional way" (from *The Canadian Encyclopedia*).

Mayan, Palenque, Mexico

from **TEMPLE OF THE TREE OF YELLOW CORN**

From the mid-twentieth century on into the present, the mysteries of ancient Mayan writing—what Dennis Tedlock calls "this most deeply American literary tradition"—have given way to a fuller understanding

& decipherment of the Mayan glyphs as vehicles both for meaning & for sound. Building on the work of forerunners such as Yuri Knorosov, Tatiana Proskouriakoff, David Kelley, & Linda Schele, Tedlock writes further: "The roots of writing go deep in the American continent. Even if we apply a narrow definition of writing, demanding that it record the sequence of sounds in a spoken language, we cannot get around the fact that writing existed in the Americas long before Europeans brought the Roman alphabet here. Mayans started writing when English (even Old English) had yet to be born. By the seventh century [C.E.], when English literature made its first tentative appearance, Mayans had a long tradition of inscribing ornaments, pottery vessels, monuments, and the walls of temples and palaces, and they had also begun to write books....

"And there is more.... We now know that... the writing of *history* began in the Americas before any European set foot here. For example, the lords who ruled the city whose ruins are known today as Palenque left behind continuous records that span four centuries (397–799 C.E.).... [And so] the time has now come to take a further step and proclaim that *literature* existed in the Americas before Europeans got here—not only oral literature but visible literature."

Quechua

A NARRATIVE QUIPU

*When my father's Indians came to town on Midsummer's Day to pay their
tribute, they brought me the quipus; and the curacas asked my mother to
take note of their stories, for they mistrusted the Spaniards, and feared
that they would not understand them. I was able to reassure them by
re-reading what I had noted down under their dictation, and they used to
follow my reading, holding on to their quipus, to be certain of my exactness; this was how I succeeded in learning many things quite as perfectly
as did the Indians.* (Garcilaso de la Vega, Royal Commentaries of the Incas, trans. Paul
Rycaut, 1688)

(1) For whatever else of it remains a mystery, Garcilaso's account points
to the use of quipu, a pre-Columbian system of writing & computing with
knotted & colored cords, as a vehicle for recording narrative & song, a
function & method still waiting to be uncovered. Toward that end, an
example of how complicated a story the quipu could tell is given in Louis
Baudin's *A Socialist Empire: The Incas of Peru*: "If an official wanted to
describe [by quipu] the reign of the first Inca, Manco Capac, [he could] say
that before him there was no king, chief, or religion and in the fourth year
of his reign Manco Capac subdued ten provinces. Also, the conquering of
these provinces cost him a certain number of warriors and in one province
he seized a thousand units of gold and three thousand units of silver. After
conquering all these provinces, he had a feast of thanksgiving for his victory and to celebrate the honor of the Sun-god."

(2) In the afterglow of traditional quipu writing practices, a number of
latter-day poets & artists, both south & north, have developed knotting
& fabric works a step or two away from language as such. Writes Cecilia
Vicuña of her experiments & probings in her verbo-visual artworks & of
what came before them: "*Chanccani Quipu* [one of her quipu/quipoem
works] reinvents the concept of 'quipu,' the ancient system of 'writing' with
knots, transforming it into a metaphor in space: a book/sculpture that condenses the clash of two cultures and worldviews: the Andean oral universe
and the Western world of print.... It is a prayer for the rebirth of a way
of writing with breath, a way of perceiving the body and the cosmos as a
whole engaged in a continuous reciprocal exchange. In Quechua the writer/
reader of the quipu was called: *quipucamayoc* (*khipukamayuq*), literally:
'the one that animates, gives life to the knot.'" (See also the commentary on
Cecilia Vicuña in "A Fourth Gallery.")

K'iche' (Quiché) Mayan

from **POPOL VUH**

from **POPOL VUH**

THIS IS THE ROOT OF THE ANCIENT WORD,
HERE IN THIS PLACE CALLED K'ICHE'

Here we shall inscribe,
    we shall implant the Ancient Word,
the potential,
the source for everything done in the citadel of K'iche',
           in the nation of K'iche' people.
And this shall be our theme:
the demonstration,
revelation,
and account
of how things were put in shadow
brought to light by the Maker,
           Modeler,
           Bearer,
           Begetter, names of Hunahpu Possum,
           Hunahpu Coyote,
           Great White Peccary,
               Coatl
           Resplendent Plumed Serpent,
           Heart of the Lake,
           Heart of the Sea,
Plate Shaper,
Bowl Shaper, as they are called, also named,
           also described as the Midwife,
               Matchmaker,

Xpiyakok,
Xmukane, names of the Defender,
           Protector,
           twice a Midwife,
           twice a Matchmaker, as is said in the words of K'iche'.
They accounted for everything
    and did it, too, with a clear state of mind
        in clear words.
We shall write about this now amid the preaching of God,
        in Christendom now.

We shall reveal it because there is no longer a way to see the Council Book,
                              a way to see the light from beside the sea
                                    the story of our shadows,
                              a way to see the dawn of life, as it is called.
There is the original book
and ancient writing,
but hidden in the face of the reader,
                              interpreter,
It takes a long performance
          and account to complete the lightning of all the sky-earth,
the fourfold siding,
fourfold cornering,
          measuring,
fourfold staking,
halving the cord,
stretching the cord in the sky,
                    on the earth,
the four sides,
the four corners, as it is said, by the Maker,
                              Modeler,
Mother,
Father of life,
          of humankind,
Giver of Breath,
Giver of Heart,
who give birth,
who give heart to the nations of lasting light,
                    to those who are born in the light,
                    begotten in the light;
worriers,
knowers of everything there is in the sky-earth,
                              lake-sea.

THIS IS THE ACCOUNT:
Now it still ripples,
now it still murmurs,
          ripples,
now it still sighs, and
     it is empty under the sky.

Here follow the first words,
          the first eloquence:

There is not yet one person,
        one animal,
            bird,
            fish,
            crab,
            tree,
            stone,
            hollow,
            canyon,
            meadow,
            forest.
Only the sky alone is there,
the face of the earth is not clear.
Only the sea alone is pooled under all the sky,
there is nothing whatever gathered together.
It is still at rest;
not a single thing stirs.
It is kept back,
still kept at rest under the sky.
Whatever exists is simply not there:
only the pooled water,
only the calm sea,
only it alone is pooled.
Whatever might be is simply not there:
only murmurs,
      ripples, in the dark,
           in the night.

All alone, the Maker,
        Modeler,
        Resplendent Plumed Serpent,
        Bearers,
        Begetters are in the water.
Light glitters in the place where they stay,
        covered in quetzal feathers,
           in blue-green.
Thus the name, Plumed Serpent.
They are great sages,
they are great thinkers in their very being.
And of course there is the sky,
and there is also the Heart of Sky.
This is the name of the god, as it is spoken.

And then his word came here,
he came to Resplendent Plumed Serpent, here in the blackness,
in the early dawn.
He spoke with the Resplendent Plumed Serpent,
and they talked, then they thought,
then they worried,
they agreed with each other,
they joined their words,
their thoughts.
Then it was clear,
then they reached accord in the light,
and then humanity was clear,
then they conceived the growth,
the generation of trees,
of bushes,
and the growth of life,
of humankind, in the blackness,
in the early dawn,
all because of the Heart of Sky, named Hurricane.

Translated from K'iche' Mayan by Dennis Tedlock

COMMENTARY

The *Popol Vuh*, literally "the book of the community" (or "common house" or "council"), was preserved by Mayans in Santo Tomás Chichicastenango, Guatemala, & in the eighteenth century given to Father Francisco Ximénez, who transcribed it in roman letters & put it into Spanish; it vanished again & was rediscovered in the 1850s by Carl Scherzer & Abbé Charles Etienne Brasseur de Bourbourg. It existed in picture writing before the Conquest, & the version used by Father Ximénez (& since lost) may have been the work, ca. 1550, of one Diego Reynoso. The book contains the cosmogonic concepts and ancient traditions of the Quiché/K'iche' nation, the history of their origin, and the chronicles of their rulers down to the year 1550.

ADDENDUM

AN ACADEMIC PROPOSAL

For a period of 25 years, say, or as long as it takes a new generation to discover where it lives, take the great Greek epics out of the undergraduate curricula, & replace them with the great American epics. Study the *Popol*

Vuh where you now study Homer, & study Homer where you now study the *Popol Vuh*—as exotic anthropology, etc. If you have a place in your mind for the *Greek Anthology* (God knows you may not), let it be filled by Tedlock's 2000 *Years of Mayan Literature* or the present editor's *Shaking the Pumpkin* or this very volume you are reading. Teach courses in religion that begin: "This is the account of how all was in suspense, all calm, in silence; all motionless, still, & the expanse of the sky was empty"—& use this as a norm with which to compare all other religious books, whether Greek or Hebrew. Encourage other poets to translate the Native American classics (a new version for each new generation), but first teach them how to sing. Let young Indian poets (who still can sing or tell a story) teach young white poets to do so. Establish chairs in American literature & theology, etc. to be filled by those trained in the oral transmission. Remember, too, that the old singers & narrators are still alive (or that their children & grandchildren are) & that to despise them or leave them in poverty is an outrage against the spirit-of-the-land. Call this outrage the sin-against-Homer.

Teach courses with a rattle & a drum.

J. Rothenberg, from *Shaking the Pumpkin*

Mbya-Guaraní per Pablo Vara

from **THE AYVU RAPYTA**

The Origins of Human Language

[1] The true first Father Ñamandu,
from a small portion of his own divinity,
from the wisdom imbedded in his own divinity
and by means of his creative wisdom
triggered the birth of flames and a thin mist.

[2] After he emerged in human form,
from the wisdom imbedded in his own divinity
and by means of his creative wisdom
he conceived the elements of human language.
From the wisdom imbedded in his own divinity
and by means of his creative wisdom
Our Father
conceived the elements of human language
and made them part of his own divinity.
Before the earth existed
at the core of the primeval darkness

before any thing that is was known,
he formed the elements-to-come of human language
and the true first Father Ñamandu
made them part of his own divinity.

[3] After he created the elements-to-come
of human language,
from the wisdom imbedded in his own divinity
& by means of his creative wisdom
he conceived the elements-to-come of love.
Before the earth existed
at the heart of the primeval dark,
before anything that is was known,
by means of his creative wisdom
he conceived the elements-to-come of love.

[4] After he conceived the elements of human language,
he conceived a little particle of love,
from the wisdom imbedded in his own divinity
& by means of his creative wisdom,
alone, he dreamed the elements of sacred song.
Before the earth existed
at the heart of the primeval darkness,
before anything that is was known,
alone, he dreamed the elements of sacred song.

[5] After he conceived, alone, the elements of human language,
after he conceived, alone, a little particle of love,
after he conceived, alone, a little sacred song,
he pondered deeply
with whom to share the elements of human language
with whom to share his little particle of love;
with whom to share the language of his sacred songs.
After he had pondered deeply,
from the wisdom imbedded in his own divinity
by means of his creative mind
he brought forth partners to his own divinity.

[6] After he had pondered deeply,
from the wisdom imbedded in his own divinity
and by means of his creative mind
he created the big-hearted Ñamandu.
He created them as echoes of his wisdom.

Before the earth existed
at the heart of the primeval darkness,
he created the big-hearted Ñamandu.
To father all his future children,
to father all the souls of all his future children
he created the big-hearted Ñamandu.

[7] Afterwards,
from the wisdom imbedded in his own divinity
and by means of his creative mind
to the true Father of the future Karai
to the true Father of the future Jakaira
to the true Father of the future Tupã
he transmitted the true knowledge of divinity.
To father truly all his future children,
to father truly all his children words & souls
he transmitted the true knowledge of divinity.

[8] Afterwards,
the true first Father Ñamandu
so she would be the foremost of his heart
made her to share in his divinity
she, true future mother of the Ñamandu,
Karai Ru Ete,
made her to share in his divinity
the one who would be foremost in his heart,
the future and true Mother of the Karai.
With Jakaira Ru Ete, was the same,
so she could be the foremost in his heart
he made her share in his divinity
the future and true Mother of the Jakaira.
With Tupã Ru Ete, was the same,
so she could be the foremost in his heart
he made her share in his divinity
the future and true Mother of the Tupã.

[9] Because they had absorbed
the creative wisdom of their own First Father,
after they absorbed the elements of human language,
after they inspired themselves with human love,
after they absorbed the words of sacred song,
after they inspired themselves with his creative wisdom,

for which we call on them:
high and true fathers of all words all souls,
high and true mothers of all words all souls.

Reworked by Javier Taboada & Jerome Rothenberg after León Cadogan's Spanish version

COMMENTARY

It's the intersection of creation & language—world & word—that comes at us again & again in the workings of myth or myth-as-history. Passed on orally from a distant time—here in the Mbya-Guaraní language of Paraguay—the primal story tracks the founding of "human language" (*ayvu rapyta*) in the mind & works of a first creative being, Ñamandu, before the existence of humans, other gods, & the world itself. As it comes to us, this salvaged version of the foundation myth would seem to be the work of the cacique Pablo Vara & others, along with León Cadogan as latter-day ethnologist/amanuensis. The invention of language as the start of all subsequent creation is suggestive, too, of the opening of John's Gospel, though there the Word didn't make, rather *was-with* & *was*, the Father. That this may have infiltrated Pablo Vara's account is, of course, a possibility, but the foundational character of *The Ayvu Rapyta* remains a matter of undiminished interest.

ADDENDUM

JORGE ELÍAS ADOUM [A.K.A. "MAGO JEFA"]
Lebanon/Ecuador, 1897–1958

In the beginning
SEX WAS LIFE
      & was the WORD
      inside GOD
      & lay in GOD.

SEX WAS LIGHT
      & shone thru
      the dark nest
      of nothingness.

The Atom-Seed
dug a wound
in an earth devoid of verve.

& seeing it
       sterile & cold—
SEX said

    FIAT LUX

& the earth was dipped in LIGHT

Translated & relineated from Spanish by Javier Taboada

Moche, Quechua, Peru

THE INCAN DEATH OF THE SUN & REVOLT OF THE ANIMALS & OBJECTS

How the Sun Disappeared for Five Days.
In What Follows We Shall Tell a Story
About the Death of the Sun.

In ancient times the sun died.
Because of this death it was night for five days.
Rocks banged against each other.
Mortars and grinding stones began to eat people.
Buck llamas started to drive men.

Translated by Heriberto Yépez

COMMENTARY

(1) These figures come from a Moche bottle & represent weaving utensils in a much larger scene of animals and other objects making war against humans. Moche culture flourished in ancient Peru between AD 100 & 700. The revolt of the objects myth appears in Moche visual depictions. As Walter Krickeberg identified in 1928, this myth reappears later in oral sources in the *Huarochirí Manuscript* and the *Popol Vuh*: "The Revolt of the Objects theme is known from three major depictions: a mural found in an upper rear room on the Huaca de la Luna in the Moche Valley & two painted pottery vessels, both now housed in German museums. Their thematic unity is in evidence by common depiction of various articles of military regalia and weapons shown with arms and legs apparently attacking humans."

(2) The revolt of the objects theme seems to be part of what the Incas would later term *pachakuti*, the reversal of the world order. The presence of this reversal of the world order myth in Moche, Inca, & Maya sources signals toward the hypothesis of a Pan-American Indigenous imaginary: a mythology (a poetics) shared throughout different Americas before America.

(Assembled with commentary by Heriberto Yépez.)

(3) From *Crazy Dog Events.* (1) Act like a crazy dog. Wear sashes and other fine clothes, carry a rattle, and dance along the roads singing crazy dog songs after everybody else has gone to bed. (2) Talk crosswise: say the opposite of what you mean and make others say the opposite of what they mean in return.

(Adapted from Crow Indian sources by J. Rothenberg.)

Delaware Indian (Lenni Lenape)

from **THE WALAM OLUM OR RED SCORE**

1. Long ago there was a mighty snake and beings evil to men.

2. This mighty snake hated those who were there (and) greatly disquieted those whom he hated.

3. They both did harm, they both injured each other, both were not in peace.

4. Driven from their homes they fought with this murderer.

5. The mighty snake firmly resolved to harm the men.

6. He brought three persons, he brought a monster, he brought a rushing water.

7. Between the hills the water rushed and rushed, dashing through and through, destroying much.

8. Nanabush, the Strong White One, grandfather of beings, grandfather of men, was on the Turtle Island.

9. There he was walking and creating, as he passed by and created the turtle.

10. Beings and men all go forth, they walk in the floods and shallow waters, down stream thither to the Turtle Island.

11. There were many monster fishes, which ate some of them.

12. The Manito daughter, coming, helped with her canoe, helped all, as they came and came.

13. [And also] Nanabush, Nanabush, the grandfather of all, the grandfather of beings, the grandfather of men, the grandfather of the turtle.

14. The men then were together on the turtle, like to turtles.

15. Frightened on the turtle, they prayed on the turtle that what was spoiled should be restored.

16. The water ran off, the earth dried, the lakes were at rest, all was silent, and the mighty snake departed.

Translated from Lenni Lenape by Daniel G. Brinton

COMMENTARY

The *Walam Olum* was the tribal chronicle of the Lenni Lenape or Delaware Indians & is the oldest epic surviving in written form north of what is now Mexico. Its name means "red score" or "painted records," from the symbols painted onto sticks & kept together in bundles. Each symbol, according to linguist C. F. Voeglin, "represented a verse of the chronicle. None of these sticks survive today," only copies of the pictographs & the Lenape verses in the 1833 manuscript of Constantine S. Rafinesque, a nineteenth-century botanist & a natural historian. Accordingly, both images & verses have frequently been called into question.

Again according to Voeglin, the *Walam Olum* was "divided into five books or songs, each made up of a varying number of verses. In total length it runs to 183 verses. The songs relate the tribal story from the Creation to the coming of the White man to North America. The main themes are the migration from Asia to Alaska and south and east across the North American continent, and the chronological representation of the chief [events] by which time was measured in the epic." The sixteen verses presented here comprise the second song, in which Turtle Island may be taken as the world (seen as fastened to a turtle's back) or, geographically, the northeast coast of Asia. It has elsewhere been taken as North America, but that is probably represented in another part of the poem by Snake Island. The more recent adoption of the name *Turtle Island* by ecologically minded North Americans (Indigenous & other) is also to be noted. (For which see Gary Snyder in "A Map of Americas.")

Various Poets Nahua, Mexico, ca. 1460

A PARADISE OF POETS

[TECAYEHUATZIN:]

Where do you dwell, poet?

It is true
he has just descended to the stage
of sacred drums

That's the life of the poet:

> to unfetter like the quetzal's feathers
> to spread out the Life-Giver's songs.

For within Heaven
from there
> delightful flowers
> delightful songs
> > come.

Our desire deforms them.
Invention spoils them.

[AYOCUAN:]

We have come in vain.

In vain we have sprung on earth.

      Shall I die as a flower dies?

My fame will be nothing someday?

Nothing my name on Earth?

      Just flowers
      just songs.

How could I persuade myself?

      We dwell here
      in the Land of Flowers.

No one will ever stop our flowers
no one will ever stop our songs.

Or have we not come here
just to know ourselves
          here on Earth?

[AQUIAHUATZIN:]

Intoxicating flowers...

with flowers we linger
      for the words of God

Such is your house
Life-Giver?

      Just listen to Him—
He has descended here from Heaven

& He comes singing
& His flutes are beating

[CUAUHTENCOZTLI:]

Are men true?

      If they are not
      our song will not be truth.

[MOTENEHUATZIN:]

I just came here to sing
sad flowers
sad songs.
            All turns into hate here.

We live in the House of Spring
sad flowers
sad songs.
            All turns into hate here.

[TLAPALTEUCCITZIN:]

Who am I?

            I go on flying
I compose
I sing my flowers
butterflies of song
I come from what's above us
I the quetzal of springtime
I have come to Earth.

Now I spread out my wings
over the stage of the sacred drums
& my song arises
springs!

I have made my home
with flowers & songs.

[AYOCUAN:]

Listen to me:

the Life Giver is among us
        this is His house
where the songs are
He is worshipped.

My house
that house my painted-books

make bright
it is Yours   God!

[TECAYEHUATZIN:]

My fellow poets:
listen to the words of dreams.

In spring they make us live.

Their shining ears of corn
cause us to see.

As a red-heron bird
their rosy-colored cobs
give us the sequence.

Now we know.

Transcreated by Javier Taboada

COMMENTARY

In the painted house, / a chant begins. / Song is sang, / flowers unfurl. / The song delights (Nezahualcoyotl, Texcoco, Mexico, 1402–1472) And again: *You write with flowers / Life-Giver / You paint with songs / You fade with songs / those who are to live on Earth*

(1) In 1460 several *cuicapihqui* (= Nahuatl "forgers of songs," i.e., oral poets) were gathered in Huexotzinco (near the present-day city of Puebla, Mexico) by the ruler and poet Tecayehuatzin to discuss the nature of poetry, its origins, & the fate of both poems & poets. The result of that historical meeting, as it comes to us, was a long renga-like poem that works as a collection of brief personal manifestos, the specific poetics through which the participating singers, whose names are given in brackets, developed their work or found meaning in it. Our selection here was taken from the sixteenth-century anthology of oral Nahuatl poetry, *Cantares Mexicanos*, collected & translated into Spanish by Fray Bernardino de Sahagún (see "A First Gallery").

(2) Writes Carlos Herrera Montero: "The Nahuatl language did not have a specific word for poetry but it did have the concept, a metaphor, 'flowers and songs' ('*in xochitl in cuicatl*') to indicate poetry. This concept was key in their perception of the world and Aztec mythology. It was the search for truth, for God, for the answers to the compelling and ancestral questions of humankind. It was their philosophy and theology. Poetry came from the god Ometeotl, a dual god: the father and the mother, the convergence

of masculine and feminine principles" (from "Flowers and Songs: Aztec Poetry," in the *Sopris Sun*, Carbondale, Colorado, 2021).

(3) The resemblance in this form to a contemporary collective work like the *Amereida* (*Amerodyssey*) poem in "A Map of Americas," below, may also be of interest: a great collective poem about poetry—in either instance.

Dekanawidah, Iroquois ca. 1450

THE TREE OF THE GREAT PEACE

I am Dekanawidah and with the chiefs of the Five Nations
I plant the Tree of the Great Peace....

Roots have spread out from the Tree of the Great Peace.
The Great White Roots of Peace.

Any man of any nation
may trace the roots to their source and be welcome
to shelter
beneath the Great Peace....

Dekanawidah
and the chiefs of our Five Nations of the Great Peace
we now uproot the tallest pine
Into the cavity thereby made
we cast all weapons of war
Into the depths of the earth
into the deep underneath
we cast all weapons of war
We bury them from sight forever
and we plant again the tree...

Thus shall the Great Peace be established...

Adapted by William Brandon, after Arthur C. Parker

COMMENTARY

(1) The event here was the founding of the Iroquois Confederacy (= *Haudenosaunee* = "people of the longhouse") that brought together five (later six) otherwise independent & warring nations: Mohawk, Cayuga,

Onondaga, Oneida, Seneca, & Tuscarora. For this the foundational work, as it comes down to us, is captured in Arthur C. Parker's nineteenth-century translations from oral voicings & visual (*wampum*) renderings, which are simultaneously an account of the miraculous birth & life of Dekanawidah as the Great Peacemaker & of a constitution for the confederacy & for the Great Peace it fostered:

> Roots have spread out from the Tree of the Great Peace, one to the north, one to the east, one to the south and one to the west. The name of these roots is The Great White Roots and their nature is Peace and Strength.
>   If any man or any nation outside the Five Nations shall obey the laws of the Great Peace and make known their disposition to the Lords of the Confederacy, they may trace the Roots to the Tree and if their minds are clean and they are obedient and promise to obey the wishes of the Confederate Council, they shall be welcomed to take shelter beneath the Tree of the Long Leaves.

(2) That his story begins with a virgin birth following his mother's dream vision is also to be noted, a later add-on most likely, but typical of history transformed as legend or myth. For all of which the words of Dekanawidah himself are very clear as prophecy & the founding document, oral or otherwise, of the Five Nations Iroquois Confederacy. Born a native Huron from farther north, his path, as told & retold, brought him to Onondaga in what is now central New York State, where he met & pacified the still untamed Hiawatha, to make him thereafter a fellow voyager & equal voice of peace.

From this the prophecy, as brought into writing by Parker, persists as a new kind of public poetry & a landmark of Indigenous American orature. Its influence otherwise on later Anglo-American nation making & egalitarian forms of governance has often been noted.

Snorri Sturluson Iceland, 1179–1241

from *THE SAGA OF ERIC THE RED*

Thorvald Ericsson Goes to Vinland

Now Thorvald, with the advice of his brother, Leif, prepared to make this voyage with thirty men. They put their ship in order, and sailed out to sea; and there is no account of their voyage before their arrival at Leifsbooths in Wineland.

They laid up their ship there, and remained there quietly during the winter, supplying themselves with food by fishing. In the spring, however,

Thorvald said that they should put their ship in order, and that a few men should take the after-boat, and proceed along the western coast, and explore [the region] thereabouts during the summer.

They found it a fair, well-wooded country. It was but a short distance from the woods to the sea, and [there were] white sands, as well as great numbers of islands and shallows. They found neither dwelling of man nor lair of beast; but in one of the westerly islands they found a wooden building for the shelter of grain. They found no other trace of human handiwork; and they turned back, and arrived at Leifs-booths in the autumn.

The following summer Thorvald set out toward the east with the ship, and along the northern coast. They were met by a high wind off a certain promontory, and were driven ashore there, and damaged the keel of their ship, and were compelled to remain there for a long time and repair the injury to their vessel. Then said Thorvald to his companions, "I propose that we raise the keel upon this cape, and call it 'Keelness'"; and so they did.

Then they sailed away to the eastward off the land and into the mouth of the adjoining firth and to a headland, which projected into the sea there, and which was entirely covered with woods. They found an anchorage for their ship, and put out the gangway to the land; and Thorvald and all of his companions went ashore. "It is a fair region here," said he; "and here I should like to make my home."

They then returned to the ship, and discovered on the sands, in beyond the headland, three mounds: they went up to these, and saw that they were three skin canoes with three men under each. They thereupon divided their party, and succeeded in seizing all of the men but one, who escaped with his canoe. They killed the eight men, and then ascended the headland again, and looked about them, and discovered within the firth certain hillocks, which they concluded must be habitations.

They were then so overpowered with sleep that they could not keep awake, and all fell into a [heavy] slumber from which they were awakened by the sound of a cry uttered above them; and the words of the cry were these: "Awake, Thorvald, thou and all thy company, if thou wouldst save thy life; and board thy ship with all thy men, and sail with all speed from the land!"

A countless number of skin canoes then advanced toward them from the inner part of the firth, whereupon Thorvald exclaimed, "We must put out the war-boards on both sides of the ship, and defend ourselves to the best of our ability, but offer little attack." This they did; and the Skrellings, after they had shot at them for a time, fled precipitately, each as best he could. Thorvald then inquired of his men whether any of them had been wounded, and they informed him that no one of them had received a wound. "I have been wounded in my armpit," says he. "An arrow flew in between the gunwale and the shield, below my arm. Here is the shaft, and it will bring me to my end. I counsel you now to retrace your way with the utmost speed. But me ye shall convey to that headland which seemed to me to offer so pleasant a dwelling-place: thus it may be fulfilled that the truth sprang to my lips when I expressed the wish to abide there for a time. Ye shall bury me there, and place a cross at my head, and another at my feet, and call it Crossness forever after."

At that time Christianity had obtained in Greenland: Eric the Red died, however, before [the introduction of] Christianity.

Thorvald died; and, when they had carried out his injunctions, they took their departure, and rejoined their companions, and they told each other of the experiences which had befallen them. They remained there during the winter, and gathered grapes and wood with which to freight the ship. In the following spring they returned to Greenland, and arrived with their ship in Ericsfirth, where they were able to recount great tidings to Leif.

Translated from Old Norse by A. M. Reeves

COMMENTARY

The first invasion of the two great continents came ca. AD 1000 from the north of Europe by way of Iceland & Greenland—no America as yet but what the Viking/Norse intruders called variously Helluland, Markland, & Vinland. For this the Vikings' tales that come down to us center on Eric Thorvaldsson ("Red Eric") & his several sons, most notably Leif and Thorvald Ericsson, who had the first armed encounters with those whom they called Skrellings (= barbarians) & who took Thorvald's life into the bargain—first inklings of a war or of a series of such that would continue for a millennium thereafter. That it gave a start, too, to what many would later imagine as American character & destiny is also worth noting.

A FIRST GALLERY

from the Florentine Codex to Walt Whitman

per Bernardino de Sahagún

Spain/Mexico, 1499–1590

from *THE FLORENTINE CODEX*

Offering Flowers

(The Aztecs had a feast which fell out in the ninth month & which they called: The Flowers Are Offered)

& two days before the feast, when flowers were sought, all scattered over the mountains, that every flower might be found

& when these were gathered, when they had come to the flowers & arrived where they were, at dawn they strung them together; everyone strung them

& when the flowers had been threaded, then these were twisted & wound in garlands—long ones, very long, & thick—very thick

& when morning broke the temple guardians then ministered to Huitzilopochtli; they adorned him with garlands of flowers; they placed flowers upon his head

& before him they spread, strewed, & hung rows of all the various flowers, the most beautiful flowers, the threaded flowers

then flowers were offered to all the rest of the gods

they were adorned with flowers; they were girt with garlands of flowers

flowers were placed upon their heads, there in the temples

& when midday came, they all sang & danced

quietly, calmly, evenly they danced

they kept going as they danced

. . . . .

    I offer flowers. I sow flower seeds. I plant flowers. I assemble flowers. I pick flowers. I pick different flowers. I remove flowers. I seek flowers. I offer flowers. I arrange flowers. I thread a flower. I string flowers. I make flowers. I form them to be extending, uneven, rounded, round bouquets of flowers.

I make a flower necklace, a flower garland, a paper of flowers, a bouquet, a flower shield, hand flowers. I thread them. I string them. I provide them with grass. I provide them with leaves. I make a pendant of them. I smell something. I smell them. I cause one to smell something. I cause him to smell. I offer flowers to one. I offer him flowers. I provide him with flowers. I provide one with flowers. I provide one with a flower necklace. I provide him with a flower necklace. I place a garland on one. I provide him a garland. I clothe one in flowers. I clothe him in flowers. I cover one with flowers. I cover him with flowers. I destroy one with flowers. I destroy him with flowers. I injure one with flowers. I injure him with flowers.

I destroy one with flowers; I destroy him with flowers; I injure one with flowers: with drink, with food, with flowers, with tobacco, with capes, with gold. I beguile, I incite him with flowers, with words; I beguile him, I say, "I caress him with flowers. I seduce one. I extend one a lengthy discourse. I induce him with words."

I provide one with flowers. I make flowers, or I give them to one that someone will observe a feast day. Or I merely continue to give one flowers; I continue to place them in one's hands, I continue to offer them to one's hands. Or I provide one with a necklace, or I provide one with a garland of flowers.

(Nahuatl/Aztec)

Translated from Spanish by Arthur J. O. Anderson & Charles E. Dibble

COMMENTARY

The Aztecs (they say) rode on lakes of flowers & decorated bodies, gods, & houses with flowers, which their language made into synonyms for speech/ heart/soul & for the sun as world-heart/world-flower. Men waged a "flowering war" of the spirit in which "if spirit wins," writes Laurette Séjourné, "the body 'flowers' and a new light goes to give power to the Sun." Only later, the Aztec rulers literalized this into a series of staged battles against already conquered peoples, that the foredoomed losers paid for (literally) with their hearts. So, too, the ceremony given here (the only monthly ritual without human sacrifice) was devoted not to Xochipilli, the god of flowers & the soul, but to the war god, Huitzilopochtli.

Quechua (Anonymous)

Inca Empire, Peru, 16th century

from **THE ELEGY FOR THE GREAT INCA ATAWALLPA**

…You all by yourself fulfilled
    Their malignant demands,
But your life was snuffed out
    In Cajamarca.

Already the blood has curdled
    In your veins,

And under your eyelids your sight
    Has withered.
Your glance is hiding in the brilliance
    Of some star.

Only your dove suffers and moans
    And drifts here and there.
Lost in sorrow, she weeps, who had her nest
    In your heart.

The heart, with the pain of this catastrophe,
    Shatters.
They have robbed you of your golden litter
    And your palace.
All of your treasures which they have found
    They have divided among them.

Condemned to perpetual suffering,
    And brought to ruin,
Muttering, with thoughts that are elusive
    And far away from this world,
Finding ourselves without refuge or help,
    We are weeping,
And not knowing to whom we can turn our eyes,
    We are lost.

Oh sovereign king,
    Will your heart permit us
To live scattered, far from each other,
    Drifting here and there,
Subject to an alien power,
    Trodden upon?

Discover to us your eyes which can wound
   Like a noble arrow;
Extend to us your hand which grants
   More than we ask,
And when we are comforted with this blessing
   Tell us to depart.

Transcreated from Spanish translations of the originals by W. S. Merwin

COMMENTARY

Atahuallpa (Atawallpa) (d. 1533), one of the last embattled rulers of the Inca Empire, took control by force from his half-brother, Huascar, but was himself imprisoned & executed by the Spanish conqueror Pizarro. The story of his death comes in many versions, but always the savagery of Pizarro stands out & with it a sense of cultural & religious conflict, as in William Prescott's later recounting, where a Bible is thrust into Atahuallpa's hands as a marker of the Europeans' religious & temporal authority, & hearing no sound emerging from it, Atahuallpa turns over the pages a moment, then throws it down with vehemence & exclaims: *Tell your comrades that they should give me an account of their doings in my land. I will not go from here until thou hast given me full satisfaction for all the wrongs they have committed....* which act the priest Valverde & the cruel conquistador take as a pretext for the garroting & death to follow.

Nahua (Anonymous) Mexico, 16th century

LAMENT ON THE FALL OF TENOCHTITLÁN

Our cries of grief rise up
and our tears rain down,
for Tlatelolco is lost.
The Aztecs are fleeing across the lake;
they are running away like women.
How can we save our homes, my people?
The Aztecs are deserting the city:
the city is in flames, and all
is darkness and destruction.
Motelchiuhtzin the Huiznahuacatl,
Tlacotzin the Tlailotlacatl,

Oquitzin the Tlacatecuhtli,
are greeted with tears.
Weep, my people:
know that with these disasters
we have lost the Mexican nation.
The water has turned bitter,
our food is bitter!
These are the acts of the Giver of Life

Translated by Lysander Kemp

Translated by Lysander Kemp

COMMENTARY

The invaders here are confronted by the city itself: the ancient capital unknown before this to the European interlopers, rising up before them as a new-world wonder. So, one of them, Bernal Díaz del Castillo, reports their first entry to the city, close to two years before they set it to the torch, the Aztec Tenochtitlán buried and the renamed Mexico erected in its place:

> *We proceeded* [he writes] *along the Causeway which is here eight paces in width and runs... straight to the City of Mexico* [Tenochtitlán]... *It was so crowded with people that there was hardly room for them all, some of them going to and others returning from the city, besides those who had come out to see us, so that we were hardly able to pass by the crowds of them that came; and the towers and temples were full of people as well as the canoes from all parts of the lake. Gazing on such wonderful sights, we did not know what to say, or whether what appeared before us was real, for on one side, on the land, there were great cities, and in the lake ever so many more, and the lake itself was crowded with canoes, and in the Causeway were many bridges at intervals, and in front of us stood the great City of Mexico...*

Translated from Spanish by A. P. Maudslay

Translated from Spanish by A. P. Maudslay

Fray Ramón Pané Spain, 15th–16th century

from THE ANTIQUITIES OF THE INDIES, A FIRST ACCOUNT

Of the Shapes They Say the Dead Have

They say that when it's day they're locked inside
but when it's night they'll go out for a walk
and that they like to eat a certain fruit
called a *guayaba*
that has a taste like quince
& when it's day they [...]
& when it's night they morph into a fruit
& celebrate & hang out with the living.

And to recognize them just observe this rule:
that if you touch their belly with your hands
& you don't find a navel there
they say they're *operito* which means dead
because they say a dead man doesn't have a navel.

And sometimes they can end up fooled
when they aren't well aware of this
& end up sleeping with some woman from *Co-ay-bay*,
& when they try to hold her in their arms,
there's nothing there,
because she's up & vanished just like that.

They believe this to the present day.

When a person is alive they call his spirit *go-e-iza*
& after death *o-pi-a*,
& as a *go-e-iza* he can turn up many times
in the shape of both a man & woman,
& they say that there's a man who tried to fight with her
& having come into her hands, he disappeared,
& then that man would raise his arms up elsewhere,
would put them over some old trees
from which he would be hanging.

And all of them believe this by & large,
both young & old believe it,
& what appears to them looks like a father,
like a mother, brothers, cousins,
& in other kinds of shapes.

They say the fruit the dead eat
is the size of something like a quince.

And that the same dead don't appear by day
but only in the night.

And even overcome by fear,
someone dares walk alone
at night.

Translated & lineated by Heriberto Yépez & Jerome Rothenberg

COMMENTARY

(1) Pané's account of Indian "antiquities" must have been finished about 1498, which would make it the first European book & ethnography written in America. As such, Pané here collects information about the Indigenous people of the island of Española (present-day Haiti & Dominican Republic) on the orders of Columbus, whom he had accompanied also on his second American voyage in 1494.

(2) Pané talks about his writing method: "Since they do not have alphabet nor writing, they do not know how to tell such fables well, nor can I write them well. Which is why I think I put first what should be last and last first." This combination of ethnography & error, even mistranslation, produces a strong, curiously literary version of Pané's texts.

(Commentary by Heriberto Yépez.)

ADDENDUM

PASCUA YAQUI TRIBE USA

Song of a Dead Man [Deer Dance]

> I do not want these flowers
> moving
> but the flowers
> want to move
> I do not want these flowers
> moving
> but the flowers
> want to move
> I do not want these flowers
> moving
> but the flowers
> want to move

out in the flower world
          the dawn
                    over a road of flowers
I do not want these flowers
          moving
                    but the flowers
want to move
          I do not want these flowers
                    moving
but the flowers
          the flowers
                    want to move

Transcreated by Jerome Rothenberg, after Carleton S. Wilder

Alvar Núñez Cabeza de Vaca Spain, 1488–1559

from THE JOURNEY

Nothing was talked about in this whole country but of the wonderful cures which God, Our Lord, performed through us, and so they came from many places to be cured, and after having been with us two days some Indians of the Susolas begged Castillo to go and attend to a man who had been wounded, as well as to others that were sick and among whom, they said, was one on the point of death. Castillo was very timid, especially in difficult and dangerous cases, and always afraid that his sins might interfere and prevent the cures from being effective. Therefore the Indians told me to go and perform the cure. They liked me, remembering that I had relieved them while they were out gathering nuts, for which they had given us nuts and hides. This had happened at the time I was coming to join the Christians. So I had to go, and Dorantes and Estevanico went with me.

When I came close to their ranches, I saw that the dying man we had been called to cure was dead, for there were many people around him weeping and his lodge was torn down, which is a sign that the owner has died. I found the Indian with eyes upturned, without pulse and with all the marks of lifelessness. At least so it seemed to me, and Dorantes said the same. I removed a mat with which he was covered, and as best I could pray to Our Lord to restore his health, as well as that of all the others who might be in need of it, and after having made the sign of the cross and breathed on him many times, they brought his bow and presented it to me, and a basket of ground tunas [prickly pears], and took me to many others who were suffering from vertigo. They gave me two more baskets of tunas, which I left to the Indians that had come with us. Then we returned to our quarters.

Our Indians to whom I had given the tunas remained there, and at night returned, telling that the dead man to whom I had attended had resuscitated in their presence, rising from his bed, had walked about, eaten and talked to them, and that all those treated by me were well and in very good spirits. This caused great surprise and awe, and all over the land nothing else was spoken of. All who heard it came to us that we might cure them and bless their children, and when the Indians in our company (who were the Cultalchulches) had to return to their country, before parting they offered us all the tunas they had for their journey, not keeping a single one, and gave us flint stones as long as one and a-half palms, with which they cut and which are greatly prized among them. They begged us to remember them and pray to God to keep them always healthy, which we promised to do, and so they left, the happiest people upon earth, having given us the very best they had.

We remained with the Avavares Indians for eight months, according to our reckoning of the moons. During that time they came for us from many places and said that verily we were children of the sun. Until then Dorantes and the Negro had not made any cures, but we found ourselves so pressed by the Indians coming from all sides, that all of us had to become medicine men. I was the most daring and reckless of all in undertaking cures. We never treated anyone that did not afterwards say he was well, and they had such confidence in our skill as to believe that none of them would die as long as we were among them.

Translated from Spanish by Fanny Bandelier

COMMENTARY

Cabeza de Vaca's *Journey* is not the first account of the Spanish discovery of the North American continent, but it's the first one that depicts a shift in the mentality of the conquistador. A failed sea expedition in 1527 on what is now known as Tampa Bay led de Vaca & three other survivors (from an expedition of six hundred men) to face extreme conditions in their retreat onto land. Stricken by hunger & walking on foot across America, they were captured by natives & became both their slaves & traders, for whom they performed many duties in order to survive. Cabeza de Vaca saved his life (& those of his companions) by transforming himself & becoming a powerful healer at their captors' service. Eight years later, he was found in modern Culiacán, Mexico, by a group of fellow Spaniards who were "dumbfounded at the sight of me, strangely dressed and in company with Indians. They just stood staring for a long time."

Cabeza de Vaca's transformation makes his *Journey* one of the first cross-cultural narratives in our hemisphere: from that of conqueror at any cost to that of protector & peaceful fellow traveler, a stance that can be seen later in the influential writings & interventions of Bartolomé de las Casas against the oppression of native peoples by the European invaders.

Alonso de Ercilla Spain, 1533–1594

from *THE ARAUCANIAD*

Canto XX

The Araucanians retire, with the loss of many people. Tucapel escapes, balefully wounded, breaking through the enemy. Tegualda relates to Don Alonso de Ercilla the strange and piteous process of her story:

Must the whole be harrowing battles,
Enmity, fire, blood, and discord,
Odium, bravery, grudge and rancor,
Ire, temerity, and madness,
Rage and savagery and vengeance,
Death, destruction, gloating cruelty
Nauseating Mars, the war-lord,
Far beyond my small resources?

But I must perforce be patient,
Since my own free will enslaves me;
Thus, my lord, I humbly beg you
That you be not loath to listen,
For this bold barbaric demon
Intercepts my weak excuses.
Comes he with such speed and fury
That I needs must rush my pen-strokes.

Like a beast incarcerated
Now on this side, now on that side
Bloody avenues he opens,
Everywhere smears equal damage,

With such insolence that haply
Mars he'd strike from fivefold dais,
If he might ascend to Olympus;
So consuming is his brainstorm.

But alone, and badly injured,
Seeing that his hosts are scattered,
Noting iron reversed and pointed
'Gainst his fibred breast impassioned,
He withdraws aside to notice
That the hill is steep and stubborn,
And perceives no wall where leaping
Might be tried from twenty armlengths.

Promise not without appraising
Funds of power on deposit,
For the one who's quick to promise
Will, they say, repent at leisure!
If we plight our word, it binds us;
Violence only can redeem it,
For 'tis common law's convention
To be honest e'en with foemen.

From such laws how far strays usage
Which these knavish times exhibit!
Promises make hope expansive,
But not one is kept or honored.
Vain is confidence, and stupid,
Which built up on air sustains us.
It collapses. Disappointment
Overtops our hope with havoc.

Of myself, I say remembrance
Plagues my mind with qualms vexatious.
I apologize for having
Pledged my word to end this poem,
For this sterile theme displeasing,
Barren, void, jejune, and irksome
To the end bodes toil consummate.
None from clods can squeeze sweet juices.

Who 'midst thorns and slopes hath placed me
In the wake of drums and trumpets,

When I might through sylvan gardens
Stroll and pluck thuriferous blossoms?
Might I not 'midst deeds and debits
Mingle fictions, loves and fables
There to gambol unrestricted,
Giving and receiving pleasure?

Translated from Spanish by Charles Maxwell Lancaster and Paul Thomas Manchester

COMMENTARY

(1) Writes scholar Ralph Bauer: "Alonso de Ercilla y Zúñiga's *La Araucana* is an epic about the heroic resistance of the Araucan Indians against the Spanish efforts to conquer the province of Arauca, which is in present-day Chile.... Ercilla's epic journal begins with an unambivalent celebration of the Conquest but gradually turns into a condemnation of Spanish actions. Instead, he praises the humanity, valor, civility, and wisdom of a defeated culture" (in *Colonial Discourse and Early American Literary History*).

(2) Voltaire praised Ercilla's in situ method of composition, being a participant at the same time in the Spanish war of conquest, saying that Ercilla had "made use of the intervals of the war to sing it, and as he wanted paper, he wrote the first part of his poem upon little pieces of leather which afterwards he had much ado to set right, and to bring together." Also, Voltaire addressed the paradox of Ercilla's own role: "He was at once the conqueror and the poet" (in *Essay on Epic Poetry*, as quoted by Bauer).

Francisca Juana

Nahua, Mexico, per Hernando Ruiz de Alarcón, born ca. 1500

OF THE REMEDY FOR WHAT THEY CALL "RECONCILIATION"

1/

Well now, please come forth,
My mother Jade-skirted One,
White Woman;
Dark Sign,
White Sign,
White Emotion,

Yellow Emotion.
For now I have come to set up here
The Yellow Priest,
The White Priest.
I, I have come,
I the Priest,
I the Lord of Enchantments.
Already I have fashioned you,
I have quickened you.
My mother Dewdrop-skirted One,
You who have made him,
You who have quickened him,
Even you are rising against him,
You are turning against him.
Dark Sign,
In the greatness of the waters,
In the expanse of the waters,
I shall leave you.
I myself,
I am the Priest,
I am the Lord of Enchantments.
Please come forth,
My mother Jade-skirted One;
Please go,
Please go to look for,
Please go to see
The Priest Light,
There in the House of Light.
What deity,
What marvel
Is already covering him with siftings,
Is already covering him with dust?
Blue-green Sickness,
Dark Sickness:
Wherever you go,
Wherever you disappear,
You will cleanse,
You will improve
The Priest Light.
Please come forth,
Blue-green Sign,

Dark Sign;
Throughout the mountains,
Throughout the plains
You have been wandering.
Here I seek you,
Here I entreat you,
The infant of the gods,
The child of the gods?
I have come to take up
The Blue-green Sign,
The White Sign.
Wherever has it gone?
Wherever has it gone to rest?
Wherever in the Nine Beyonds,
In the Nine Junctures,
Has it gone to rest?
I have come to take it up,
I have come to cry out to it:
You will make good,
You will make right
The heart,
The head!

2/

O Master of Signs.
Please come forth,
Nine Pounded,
Nine Struck;
May you not shame yourself.
Please come forth,
My mother Jade-skirted One;
1 Water;
2 Reed;
1 Rabbit,
2 Rabbit;
1 Deer,
2 Deer;
1 Flint,
2 Flint;
1 Lizard,
2 Lizard.

My mother Jade-skirted One,
What will you do?
Go and cleanse my vassal;
In some whirlpool,
In some circle of water,
In some flow of water,
Please put the Lord of Tlalocan.
I have come,
I the Page,
I the Crackler.
Do I think anything of it?
The stone is intoxicated,
The wood is intoxicated;
They walk here,
And you also,
And I also.
What deity,
What marvel
Now seeks to destroy?

Translated from Spanish by Michael D. Coe and Gordon Whittaker

COMMENTARY

Writes Hernando Ruiz de Alarcón of the poet-practitioner: "Francisca Juana, wife of Juan Bautista, of the settlement of Mescaltepec, used this spell among others. After the spell has been said, they cense the child with the conjured copal and fire, upon which they assert that his *tonal* and genius have returned to him and that he is perfectly healthy." And of the birthing ceremony itself & the threats it poses, he writes: "When the illness has been judged, the remedy remains to be dealt with. Although they use various methods for it, I am reducing them to one chapter, since they coincide in their purpose and manner, and almost all of that is reduced by means of words and spells. It is assumed that the water always enters as principal agent and sine qua non; they might join to this fire and perhaps tobacco or tobacco-with-lime. They cast a spell on all of this and always begin the invocation by speaking to the water and perhaps to the earth, because they attribute the main role in the child's birth to the water, it being the first thing that he touches (in their opinion) on being born, and to the earth, because on birth he falls upon it" (in *Aztec Sorcerers in Seventeenth Century Mexico: The Treatise on Superstitions*, ca. 1617, trans. Coe & Whittaker).

Arias de Villalobos Spain/Mexico, 1568–1622

from **A CANTO TITLED MERCURY**

Astaroth Appears to Moctezuma

… Cortés offers him peace   his love
& the pact is made.
but the earth shakes
& people cry an infernal howl…

the sad King   whose life
is running out of time
gets pale
& swiftly goes into his chambers

as soon as he entered
he saw this:
there was a mighty tiger
rampant feet in hunting pose
without exaggeration
it was a colossus
in front of it he felt a dwarf

it was horrendous
was more frightful
than the fury of dark Letheus
hair like sharp knives
grinding yellow teeth
showed its fangs in anger

both eyes bulged
were like two fires
two sparks from Vulcan's fires
crueler than the hell
of the Laestrygones
& burning more than Troy

the toughest heart would tremble
at the sight of both its claws
no one had seen
a furnace like its jaws
with that amount of flame and smoke

its body   smutty
filled with black stains
sullen color over all of Phlegethon
& round its nostrils
was a leather halter
a steel mesh & diamond bridle
armed as if it were a rhino
any boulder
softer than this monster's skin
that was Astaroth who spoke:

stop right there!
you coward!
where are you going? (roars)
get out of your house!
your land!
for whoever surrenders his free kingdom
let him be erased from his captive land!

you accepted a new religious law?
what have you done
son of a hideous bitch!
and your gods?
the faith of your elders?
skies!...   but the skies are mute...

... a parvenu has just arrived
a newcomer
& you already have bound yourself
to his powerless arms?
where's the power in yours?
where's your bow?
your arrows?
womanish!

thus I prophesize
your miserable omen:
you'll die
after a *macegual* throws a little rock
at your forehead
as you sow
so shall you reap

& your *mitotes* will turn into elegies
about captivity
& dreadful pain
& your *teponaztle* will be tuned
to play the melody
of misery in a foreign land

but… what is this?
what kind of boldness!
what infernal audacity
is now unleashed
by the spirit of the Fury
which finds no rest in air
on land & sea
but comes to swallow all the sea
the land & air

so get up
prepare your bow!
let your arrow make you merry!
fill the pool with blood!
aim at their bodies!
shoot!
fill the rivers with ships and canoes!

fill this realm with anger!
enrage this world!
attack!
& if you're lacking weapons
kill them with your bare hands!
…
& thus Alekto
the restless Fury
leads him to grab the axe of vengeance
& his secret heart
burns in rage
& his very self is drunk
with madness

yes
he knows his eternal shame
but he embraces it

& roars
>FREEDOM!
freedom captive land!
expel the thief from our home!
WAR! WAR!

and all their clubs now strike
against the others' swords
& they reduce the human bodies
into chunks of meat
chop off some heads
pour out some entrails
beating still
chests   legs   arms   hewed
& where some die
others rise up from the dead
& in middle of this pregnancy of Death
there were no more soothing words
than these
DEATH ANGER FIRE FRIGHT & THREAT

Transcreated & relineated from Spanish by Javier Taboada

COMMENTARY

(1) Arias de Villalobos emigrated to New Spain (colonial Mexico) as a young boy. There he spent the rest of his life, working as a courtier playwright. His most important work, however, is the *Canto intitulado Mercurio* (A canto titled Mercury), a quasi-historical poem consisting of 233 eight-line stanzas about the history of Mexico-Tenochtitlán (from 1325 to the fall of the city). In the *Canto*, the Roman god Mercury appears before the marquis of Montes Claros—then viceroy of New Spain—& reveals to him the history of the conquered city. It's interesting to note that the poem uses several Nahuatl words such as *macegual* (lower-caste native), *teponaztle* (sacred drum), and *mitote* (ritual dances), as in the selection above.

(2) In the *Canto*, Arias de Villalobos rebuilds a lost world through imagination (with many anachronisms, prophecies, & visions): he reconstructs Moctezuma's "orgies" & the sculptures/terror machines of Quetzalcoatl & of Huitzilopochtli, among other points of entry. Not a single Spaniard appears until the second part of the poem, after which the text acquires a progressively moral & encomiastic tone.

But it's the demonic/satanic world, the world of "sorcery" & "cannibalism" (ruled, it would seem, by Mesopotamian gods Astaroth & Baal), that plays most freely in his imagination & strikes us now as the most attractive aspect of the *Canto*. The poem's true heroes, then, are the ancient rulers, the mad prophets, the defeated gods, & those who fell clad in "skins of coyotes & griffins," native & European both.

Quechua 17th century

from *OLLANTA: AN ANCIENT YNCA DRAMA*

Song

You must not feed,
    O Tuyallay,
In ñusta's field,
    O Tuyallay.

        You must not rob,
            O Tuyallay,
        The harvest maize,
            O Tuyallay.

The grains are white,
    O Tuyallay,
So sweet for food,
    O Tuyallay.

        The fruit is sweet,
            O Tuyallay,
        The leaves are green
            O Tuyallay;

But the trap is set, O Tuyallay.
The lime is there, O Tuyallay.

We'll cut your claws,
    O Tuyallay,
To seize you quick,
    O Tuyallay.

        Ask Piscaca,
            O Tuyallay,
        Nailed on a branch,
            O Tuyallay.

Where is her heart,
        O Tuyallay?
Where her plumes,
        O Tuyallay?

                She is cut up,
                        O Tuyallay,
                For stealing grain,
                        O Tuyallay.

See the fate, O Tuyallay,
Of robber birds, O Tuyallay.

Translated from Quechua by Clements R. Markham; lineated by Javier Taboada

COMMENTARY

Ollanta (or *Ollantay*) is an Incan drama whose origin is uncertain. The themes point to pre-Columbian times, but its language (at least in the recovered manuscript) is colonial Quechua. The main plot of *Ollanta* is the forbidden love between a plebeian warrior, Ollanta, & Cusi Coyllur, princess (= *ñusta*) & daughter of the Incan emperor Pachacuti.

In the song excerpted here, the emperor—who doesn't yet know the cause of his daughter's sorrows—tries to console her: he asks for a chorus of boys & girls to sing & dance in the court. The song, which fails, however, in its goal, delivers instead an ominous prophecy for Cusi Coyllur. Among the natural symbols it calls up, the *tuyallay* is a small finch, a robber bird that may serve as a metaphor for Ollanta. By contrast, the *piscaca* is a bigger bird, which, previously killed & nailed to a tree, was used as a warning for thieves.

In the drama, Ollanta finally marries the princess. In reality, he was tortured & killed, like the bird in the children's song.

Roger Williams England/USA, 1603–1683

OF FOWLE

(New England, 1643)

from *A key into the language of America, or, An help to the language of the natives in that part of America called New-England together with briefe observations of the customes, manners and worships, &c. of the aforesaid natives, in peace and warre, in life and death: on all which are added spirituall observations, generall and particular…*

NPeshawog Pussekesësuck.	*Fowle.*
Ntauchâumen.	*I goe afowling* or *hunting.*
Auchaûi.	*Hee is gone to hunt* or *fowle.*
Pepemôi.	*He is gone to fowle.*
Wómpissacuk.	*An Eagle.*
Wompsacuckquâuog.	*Eagle.*
Néyhom, mâuog.	*Turkies.*
Paupock, sûog.	*Partridges.*
Aunckuck, quâuog.	*Heath-cocks.*
Chogan, ēuck.	*Black-bird, Black-birds.*

Obs: Of this sort there be millions, which are great devourers of the *Indian* corne as soon as it appeares out of the ground; Unto this sort of Birds, especially, may the mysticall Fowles, the Divells be well resembled (and so it pleaseth the Lord Jesus himselfe to observe, *Matth.* 13. which mysticall Fowle follow the sowing of the Word, and picke it up from loose and carelesse hearers, as these Black-birds follow the materiall seed.

Against the Birds the *Indians* are very carefull, both to set their corne deep enough that it may have a strong root, not so apt to be pluckt up, (yet not too deep, lest they bury it, and it never come up:) as also they put up little watch-houses in the middle of their fields, in which they, or their biggest children lodge, and earely in the morning prevent the Birds &c.

Kokókehom, Ohómous.	*An Owle.*
Kaukonttuock.	*Crow, Crowes.*

Obs: These Birds, although they doe the corne also some hurt, yet scarce will one *Native* amongst an hundred wil kil them, because they have a tradition, that the Crow brought them at first an *Indian* Graine of Corne in one Eare, and an *Indian* or *French* Beane in another, from the Great God *Kautánuwits* field in the Southwest from whence they hold came all their Corne and Beanes.

Hònck,-hónckock, Wómpatuck-quâuog.	*Goose, Geese.*
Wéquash-shâuog.	*Swan, Swans.*
Munnùcks-munnùck suck.	*Brants,* or *Brantgeese.*
Quequēcum-mâuog.	*Ducks.*

Obs: The *Indians* having abundance of these sorts of Foule upon their waters, take great pains to kill any of them with their Bow and Arrowes; and are marvellous desirous of our *English* Guns, powder and shot (though they are wisely and generally denied by the *English*) yet with those which they get from the *French,* and some others (*Dutch* and *English*) they kill abundance of Fowle, being naturally excellent marksmen; and also more hardned to endure the weather, and wading, lying, and creeping on the ground, &c.

I once saw an exercise of training of the *English,* when all the *English* had mist the mark set up to shoot at, an *Indian* with his owne Peece (desiring leave to shoot) onely hit it.

Kitsuog.	*Cormorants.*

Obs: These they take in the night time, where they are asleepe on rocks, off at Sea, and bring in at break of day great store of them:

Yoaquéchinock.	*There they swim.*
Nipponamouôog	*I lay nets for them.*

Obs: This they doe on shore, and catch many fowle upon the plaines, and feeding under *Okes* upon *Akrons,* as Geese, Turkies, Cranes, and others, &c.

Ptowēi.	*It is fled.*
Ptowewushannick	*They are fled.*
Wunnup,-pash	*Wing, Wings.*
Wunnúppanickanawhone	*Wing-shot.*
Wuhóckgockânwhone	*Body-shot.*
Wuskówhàn	*A Pigeon.*
Wuskowhānannûaog	*Pigeons.*
Wuskowhannanaûkit	*Pigeon Countrie.*

Obs: In that place these Fowle breed abundantly, and by reason of their delicate Food (especially in Strawberrie time when they pick up whole large Fields of the old grounds of the *Natives,* they are a delicate fowle, and because of their abundance, and the facility of killing of them, they are and may be plentifully fed on.

Sachim: A little Bird about the bignesse of a swallow, or lesse, to which the *Indians* give that name, because of its *Sachim* or Princelike courage and Command over greater Birds, that a man shall often see this small

Bird pursue and vanquish and put to flight the Crow, and other Birds farre bigger then it selfe.

| Sowwánakitauwaw | *They go to the South ward.* |

That is the saying of the *Natives,* when the Geese and other Fowle at the approach of Winter betake themselves, in admirable Order and discerning their Course even all the night long.

| Chepewâukitaûog | *They fly Northward.* |

That is when they returne in the Spring. There are abundance of singing Birds whose names I have little as yet inquired after, &c.

The *Indians* of *Martins* vineyard, at my late being amongst them, report generally, and confidently of some Ilands, which lie off from them to Sea, from whence every morning early, certaine Fowles come and light amongst them, and returne at Night to lodging, which Iland or Ilands are not yet discovered, though probably, by other Reasons they give, there is Land, &c.

| Taûnek-kaûog. | *Crane, Cranes.* |
| Wushówunan. | *The Hawke.* |

Which the *Indians* keep tame about their houses to keepe the little Birds from their Corne.

The generall Observation of Fowle.

How sweetly doe all the severall sorts of Heavens Birds, in all Coasts of the World, preach unto Men the prayse of their Makers Wisedome, Power, and Goodnesse, who feedes them and their young ones Summer and Winter with their severall suitable sorts of Foode: although they neither sow nor reape, nor gather into Barnes?

More particularly:
If Birds that neither sow nor reape.
Nor store up any food,
Constantly find to them and theirs
A maker kind and Good!

If man provide eke for his Birds,
In Yard, in Coops, in Cage.
And each Bird spends in songs and Tunes,
His little time and Age!

What care will Man, what care will God,
For's wife and Children take?
Millions of Birds and Worlds will God.
Sooner then His forsake.

COMMENTARY

I present you with a Key: I have not heard of the like yet framed, since it pleased God to bring that mighty continent of America to light.... This Key respects the native language of it, and happily may unlock some rarities concerning the natives themselves, not yet discovered. (R.W.) And again: *Forced worship stinks in God's nostrils.*

After having been banished by the Massachusetts & Plymouth Bay Colonies for his "new and dangerous opinions," such as freedom of conscience & the separation of church & state, & narrowly escaping deportation to England, Roger Williams fled south, bought land from the local Indians, & founded the Providence Plantation. The *Key into the Language of America*, which records the language & customs of the Narragansett people, was undertaken & printed to foster harmonious relations between the Indigenous inhabitants & the settler colonialists. As another poem from the *Key* has it:

Boast not, proud English, *of thy birth & blood,*
Thy brother Indian *is by birth as Good,*
Of one blood God made Him, and Thee & All,
As wise, as faire, as strong, as personall.

Úrsula de Jesús   Peru, 1604–1668

from **DIARY**

three Kings' day after comunion i was in a state or rrecolection dunno wheter/ dis coms from my head or are triks of the old imp but caim to my mind maria bran a slave/ of theconbent who die som forteen yirs ago— somfin/ i totaly forgot an sudenly i saw her cloakd in a priest/ alb the whitestof whites biutifully imbelishd and fastend witha tiny rope/ with Stylish tasels in her head was a garland of flowrs/ althou god maid me see her backwards i could stil see her face/ she was so lovly her face a flarin black i said to her how is dat/ such a gud black womn no thief nor liar hav spent so much time onpurgatory/ she sd she was in there cos of her caracter and cos she slept and ate at imp-/ roper time and althou she was there for solong her punishmnt had been myld and she/ was very thankfl to god who with his dibine probidens Originaly took her from her lanD/ and brout her to dis harsh and rrugd roads so she could becom a cristian/ and be sabed i askd her black womn go to heavn and she sd if they ar thankfl and heded his yenerosity and thankd him for they ar sabed/ throu his great mersy when i ask alldis questions i dont do it cos i want to but/ as soon as i see dem they start an spik to me with out me wishing it to happn and they make/ me spik with out wanting to i need for em to commendme to god cos all dis torme/ nts me maria also told me i should thank god for the gifs he had givn her but althou/ i think she was in heavn i coulnt be sertain—.

Translated from Spanish by Javier Taboada

COMMENTARY

Úrsula de Jesús was an Afro-Peruvian mystic & poet who served in the Catholic Church as a *donada* (a kind of convent servant or religious slave), who couldn't attain the status of nun. Her mother was also a slave, & Úrsula lived in her owner's house until she was eight; then she was sent to the convent. There, during her endless hours of work & service, she experienced "divine" visions—in which some nuns trapped in Purgatory appealed for her intercession & prayer in order to be released or to lessen their punishments. Úrsula recounted these experiences in her diary (between 1650 & 1661).

Our English translation tries to match the "irregularities" (which point to oral-idiolect patterns & to formal liberties) in Úrsula's original Spanish manuscript. It's worth noting, too, that her diary is one of the first pieces created by an African-descended person in Spanish-speaking America.

Anne Bradstreet England/USA, 1612–1672

from **THE FOUR MONARCHIES**

The Assyrian Being the First, Beginning under Nimrod, One Hundred and Thirty-One Years after the Flood.

When time was young, and the world in infancy,
Man did not proudly strive for sovereignty;
But each one thought his petty rule was high
If of his house he held the monarchy.

This was the Golden Age; but after came
The boisterous son of Cush, grandchild to Ham,
That mighty hunter who in his strong toils
Both beasts and men subjected to his spoils,
The strong foundation of proud Babel laid,
Erech, Accad, and Calneh also made.
These were his first; all stood in Shinar land.
From thence he went Assyria to command,
And mighty Nineveh he there begun,
Not finished till he his race had run;
Resen, Calah, and Rehoboth, likewise,
By him to cities eminent did rise.
Of Saturn he was the original,
Whom the succeeding times a god did call.
When thus with rule he had been dignified,
One hundred fourteen years he after died.

BELUS

Great Nimrod dead, Belus the next, his son,
Confirms the rule his father had begun;
Whose afts and power are not for certainty
Left to the world by any history.
But yet this blot for ever on him lies
He taught the people first to idolize.
Titles divine he to himself did take.
Alive and dead a god they did him make.
This is that Bel the Chaldees worshiped,
Whose priests in stories oft are mentioned;
This is that Baal to whom the Israelites
So oft profanely offered sacred rites;
This is Beelzebub, god of Ekronites;
Likewise Baalpeor, of the Moabites.
His reign was short, for, as I calculate,
At twenty-five ended his regal date.

NINUS

His father dead, Ninus begins his reign,
Transfers his seat to the Assyrian plain,
And mighty Nineveh more mighty made
Whose foundation was by his grandsire laid:
Four hundred forty furlongs walled about,

On which stood fifteen hundred towers stout;
The walls one hundred sixty feet upright,
So broad three chariots run abreast there might.
Upon the pleasant banks of Tigris flood
This stately seat of warlike Ninus stood.
This Ninus for a god his father canonized,
To whom the sottish people sacrificed.
This tyrant did his neighbors all oppress;
Where'er he warred he had too good success.
Barzanes, the great Armenian king,
By force and fraud did under tribute bring;
The Median country he did also gain,
Pharnus, their king, he caused to be slain;
An army of three millions he led out
Against the Baftrians (but that I doubt);
Zoroaster, their king, he likewise slew,
And all the greater Asia did subdue.
Semiramis from Menon did he take;
Then drowned himself did Menon for her sake.
Fifty-two years he reigned, as we are told.
The world then was two thousand nineteen old.

COMMENTARY

I found a new world and new manners, at which my heart rose. But after I was convinced it was the way of God, I submitted to it and joined to the church at Boston. (A.B.) And again: *There is no object that we see, no action that we do, no good that we enjoy, no evil that we feel or fear, but we may make some spiritual advantage of all.*

From what the early English invaders thought of, when found, as a new/old wilderness, outside the realm of God & king, the first poet fully to emerge there was a woman, much like the emergence a few years later in Mexico (New Spain) of Sor Juana Inés de la Cruz as possibly the greatest of all the New World poets. In Bradstreet's case, of course, the setting was Calvinist/Puritan rather than Catholic, & she a migrant, at the age of eighteen & two years married, from her native England. But the public act of writing & publishing, from which she shied away at first, put her in a strange, almost conflicted situation in the world in which she lived: a well-positioned woman, domestic at home & secondary to an accomplished husband & father, both of whom served as governors of Massachusetts & brought with them a library of learned books & poems in their migration from England to America. It was through a brother-in-law also—without her knowledge at first—that a book of her poems was published with great success in London, under the title *The Tenth Muse, Lately Sprung Up in America*. That it was greeted with a mixture of praise & condescension is also to be noted, & with that the later assessment of what she actually accomplished, as set out nearer our own time by Adrienne Rich:

> *Anne Bradstreet was the first non-didactic American poet, the first in whom personal intention appears to precede Puritan dogma as an impulse to verse. Not that she should be construed as a Romantic writing out of her time. The web of her sensibility stretches almost invisibly within the framework of Puritan literary convention; its texture is essentially both Puritan and feminine.... Her eye is on the realities before her, or on images from the Bible. Her individualism lies in her choice of material rather than in her style.*

And in that choice, her work thrust also toward more learned matters, prescient in that way of latter-day American poets, north & south, who pioneered a new kind of epic, defined by one of them (E. Pound) as "a poem including history." The exemplary work here was a series of four poems or books of fours, *Quaternion*, consisting of "The Humours," "The Ages of Man," "The Seasons," & "The Elements," to which she added a fifth, "The Four Monarchies," as shown above. And it's in that willingness to take on both the immediate world around her & the greater world beyond that her work approaches the quality of something bordering on greatness.

Michael Wigglesworth England/USA, 1631–1705

from **The Day of Doom, or a Poetical Description of the Great and Last Judgment**

No heart so bold, but now grows cold
and almost dead with fear:
no eye so dry, but now can cry,
and pour out many a tear.
Earth's Potentates and pow'rful States,
Captains and Men of Might
are quite abasht, their courage dasht
at this most dreadful sight.

Mean men lament, great men do rent
their Robes, and tear their hair:
They do not spare their flesh to tear

through horrible despair.
All Kindreds wail: all hearts do fail:
horror the world doth fill
with weeping eyes, and loud out-cries,
yet knows not how to kill.

Some hide themselves in Caves and Delves,
in places under ground:
some rashly leap into the Deep,
to scape by being drown'd:
some to the Rocks (O senseless blocks!)
and woody Mountains run,
that there they might this fearful sight,
and dreaded Presence shun.

In vain do they to Mountains say,
fall on us and us hide
from Judges ire, more hot than fire,
for who may it abide?
No hiding place can from his Face
sinners at all conceal,
whose flaming Eye hid things doth 'spy
and darkest things reveal.

The Judge draws nigh, exalted high,
upon a lofty Throne,
amidst a throng of Angels strong,
lo, Israel's Holy One!
The excellence of whose presence
and awful Majesty,
amazeth Nature, and every Creature,
doth more than terrify.

The Mountains smoak, the Hills are shook,
the Earth is rent and torn,
as if she should be clear dissolv'd,
or from the Center born.
The Sea doth roar, forsakes the shore,
and shrinks away for fear;
the wild beasts flee into the Sea,
so soon as he draws near.

...

Before his Throne a Trump is blown,
proclaiming the day of Doom:
Forthwith he cries, Ye dead arise,
and unto Judgment come.
No sooner said, but 'tis obey'd;
sepulchres opened are:
dead bodies all rise at his call,
and 's mighty power declare.

...

His winged Hosts flie through all Coasts,
together gathering
both good and bad, both quick and dead,
and all to Judgment bring.
Out of their holes those creeping Moles,
that hid themselves for fear,
by force they take, and quickly make
before the Judge appear.

Thus every one before the Throne
of Christ the Judge is brought,
both righteous and impious
that good or ill hath wrought.
A separation, and diff'ring station
by Christ appointed is
(to sinners sad) 'twixt good and bad,
'twixt Heirs of woe and bliss.

from THE DIARY OF MICHAEL WIGGLESWORTH

January 7th, 1653

If the unloving carriages of my pupils can goe so to my heart as they
doe; how they doe my vain thoughts, my detestable pride, my *unnatural
filthy lust that are so oft and even this day in some measure stirring in
me* how does these griev my lord Jesus that loves me infinitely more than
I do them? Do I take it heavily that my love is so lightly made of? ah! I
cannot love thee, not fear to sin against thee, although thou exercise me
with such crosses, as again this day, wherein I may read my own ill carriages towards thee. And dost thou yet make any beam of thy love break
out toward me, after nay fears? Nay have so oft and so long comforted
my self with thy love amidst my daily sins. The enmity and contrariety

of my heart to seeking thee in earnest, with my want of dear affection to thee, these make me afraid, but thou did give me thy self in the Lords supper, thou didst give me a heart (though vile) to lay hold of the desiring all from thee. and this gives me hope. bless be thy name.

Pride and vain thoughts again prevail over me to the grief of my god, cleanse me, o lord, when shall it once be? I had opportunity (purposely takeing of it) to discourse with one of my pupils much of the things of god: as also with another out of the colledge whom I went to visit, who spake something to me about his spiritual condition, the lord helping me to speak much to him again with some affection: the Lord bless it to them both. *My pupil was John Haines. I spoke to them both what a blessed thing it was to serve and seek the Lord.*

February 22nd, 1654

I was much carryd away with too much frothiness and love to vanity on thursday and friday having cheerful company in the hous with me. I found myself much overborn with carnal concupiscence nature being suppressed for I had not had my afflux in 12 nights Friday night it came again without any dream I know of. Yet after if I am still inclined to lust The Lord help me against it and against discouragement by it and temptations of another nature and disquietments.

COMMENTARY

Lord I am vile, I desire to abhor my self (O that I could!) ... I find such unresistable torments of carnal lusts or provocation unto the ejection of seed that I find my self unable to read anything to inform me about my distemper because of the prevailing or rising of my lusts. (M.W.) And again: *When thou showest me my face I abhor myself. Who can bring a clean thing out of filthiness? I was conceived bred brought up in sin.*

In the story of Anglo-American poetry & writing, Wigglesworth maintained a position as the exemplary Puritan preacher & popular poet, whose "Day of Doom" struck an understandable note of apocalyptic terror & guilt. For all of which there was an underlying narrative of self-loathing & doubt more clearly revealed in his long-concealed spiritual diary. Migrating from Yorkshire as a child, he settled with his family in New England, where he went through studies at Harvard before taking up a lifelong position as pastor & physician in Malden, Massachusetts. It was during his Harvard years, too, that he acted as tutor & advisor for younger male students, during which time he recorded in his diary the homosexual yearnings & torments absent in a direct or personal way from his poetry as such. Unlike that of the two great Colonial poets, Anne Bradstreet & Edward Taylor, his poetry was written in a popular vein, often described (wrongly or rightly) as doggerel, but transformed in how we read it, when placed beside his rediscovered diary. As with others, his poetry as testament appears at its fullest & strongest when viewed, beyond his verses, as the totality of what he wrote, both popular & hidden. The revelation of that total work is also something to consider.

Gregório de Matos   Brazil, 1636–1696

TO THE VERITABLE JUDGE BELCHIOR DA CUNHA BROCHADO

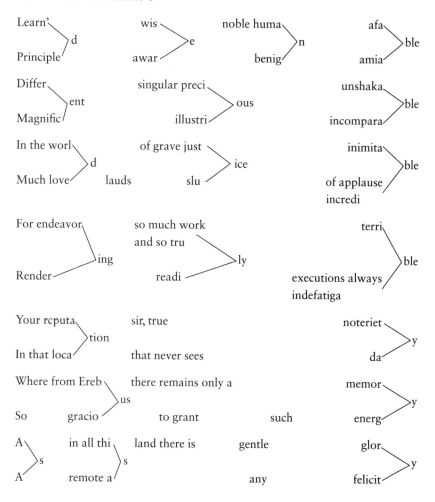

Translated from Portuguese by Jennifer Cooper

TO THE BOSSES OF BAHIA CALLED THE CARAMURUS

in Portuguese, Tupi, & Cobé

Is there anything like seeing a *Paiaia*
So much inclined to be a *Caramuru,*
Descended from the bloodline of the *tatu,*
Who speaks a twisted language like *Cobepá?*

The female line of which is called *Carimá*
Muqueca, pititinga, caruru,
Manioc mush, wine of fermented *caju*
Mangled in a mortar from *Priraja*

The male line of which is called the *Aricobe,*
Whose *Cobé* daughter & a pale-faced *Paí*
Cohabited on Passé Promontory

The white man was a *Mara-u* marauder
She an Indian maiden all the way from *Mare;*
Cobepá, Aricobé, Cobé, Paí

Translated from Portuguese by Jennifer Cooper & Jerome Rothenberg

COMMENTARY

If you are fire why do you glow so weakly? / If you are snow why do you burn without a break? (G.deM.)

(1) Gregório de Matos came to be known as Boca de Inferno—Mouth of Hell—for his searing criticism & satire directed to the evils & hypocrisies of both the Bahian elites & the Portuguese colonial project in general. After working as a judge in Portugal for thirty years, de Matos returned to his Brazilian hometown, Salvador, where, for his activities & his poetry, he was banished by the colonial authorities to Angola. A year after, de Matos was allowed to go back to Brazil, where his publications were banned.

In his works—which move from the religious to the laudatory, the amorous to the pornographic—he not only criticized & caricatured the elites but registered the daily life & the language of marginalized voices, including Tupi/Cobepá & Afro-Brazilian, with a burgeoning move toward a new orality.

(2) The opening piece presented here is from a group of laudatory poems, this one to the judge Belchior da Cunha, of Bahia. The form involves a playful construction common to the anagrams & labyrinthian forms devel-

oped first in the Iberian & European Baroque. (See "The Virgin's Throne of Wisdom" in "A Map of Extensions.") In the wordplay here, the last letters or suffixes of various words are shared from one line to the next.

In "Soneto" the terminal words of each line are from the indigenous Tupi/Cobepá & appear, as in the English version here, without translation.

(Commentary by Jennifer Cooper.)

Edward Taylor England/USA, 1642–1729

PROLOGUE

Lord, Can a Crumb of Dust the Earth outweigh,
Outmatch all mountains, nay the Chrystall Sky?
Imbosomin't designs that shall Display
And trace into the Boundless Deity?
Yea hand a Pen whose moysture doth guild ore
Eternall Glory with a glorious glore.

If it its Pen had of an Angels Quill,
And Sharpend on a Pretious Stone ground tite,
And dipt in Liquid Gold, and mov'de by Skill
In Christall leaves should golden Letters write
It would but blot and blur yea jag, and jar
Unless thou mak'st the Pen, and Scribener.

I am this Crumb of Dust which is design'd
To make my Pen unto thy Praise alone,
And my dull Phancy I would gladly grinde
Unto an Edge on Zions Pretious Stone.
And Write in Liquid Gold upon thy Name
My Letters till thy glory forth doth flame.

Let not th'attempts breake down my Dust I pray
Nor laugh thou them to scorn but pardon give.
Inspire this Crumb of Dust till it display
Thy Glory through't: and then thy dust shall live.
Its failings then thou'lt overlook I trust,
They being Slips slipt from thy Crumb of Dust.

Thy Crumb of Dust breaths two words from its breast,
That thou wult guide its pen to write aright

To Prove thou art, and that thou art the best
And shew thy Properties to shine most bright.
And then thy Works will shine as flowers on Stems
Or as in Jewellary Shops, do jems.

PREPARATORY MEDITATION 6

Am I thy gold? Or purse, Lord, for thy wealth,
Whether in mine, or mint, refined for thee?
I'm counted so; but count me o'er thyself,
Lest gold-washed face and brass in heart I be.
I fear my touchstone touches when I try
Me, and my counted gold too overly.

Am I new minted by thy stamp indeed?
Mine eyes are dim, I cannot clearly see.
Be thou my spectacles that I may read
Thine image and inscription stamped on me.
If thy bright image do upon me stand,
I am a golden angel in thy hand.

Lord, make my soul thy plate; thine image bright
Within the circle of the same enfoil.
And on its brims in golden letters write
Thy superscription in an holy style.
Then I shall be thy money, thou my hoard:
Let me thy angel be; be thou my Lord.

from *HARMONY OF THE GOSPELS*

On Angels

Angels are compleat spirits created, probablie in the morning of the first
day, with Intellectual faculties to attend the glorious Throne of God, and
to be sent out for the good of Gods elect... the Holy Angels appearing to
do their Messages do attend upon those forms and modes of good manners which are esteemed acts of Honour by those places where they are
sent.

The Angel doth not come in as a mere Clown, no, but as soon as he is
entered, he doth as it were move his hat and bow his body and say how
do you....

The visibility of Angels is not proper to their own nature for the Angelicall nature is spiritual and Invisible but they appeared visible in an elementary body which they either assume or make to array themselves withall when they are dispensing their Message for as an Ambassador coming into another country arrayeth himself in apparel suitable to the mode and Condition of those to whom he is sent, but layeth aside the same apparel when he returns if it is not in accordance to the Custom at home, so do the Angels sometimes array themselves in visible shape when they approach with Ambassies to Men which they lay by when they return into their own Countrie againe...

Hence se[e] what love God manifests unto his own people.

He hath special tokens to send them; a token is from a loving friend. So here is a token, a love token sent out of heaven unto thee, nay and it is sent by an angel; this much more manifests Gods love, the angels of God, those Courtiers of glory, that stand attending Gods royall Throne of Glory are not too glorious to be imployed in this work.

God sends them with good things in their hands to his people; he spares them his own royall Guard for this work! oh! then what love is here.... Hence se[e] what excellent wayes the wayes of God are to walk in; here the Angels of God are Conversant; here the soul may meet with the Holy Angels flocking from heaven unto him and may see them herein upon Jacobs Ladder flocking backward and forward in a way of divine favour to the people of God.

Hence se[e] what fools all those are that will not walk in Gods way.

Oh poor souls! they walk Just in the Divels way; they shall not meet the Holy Angels coming down from God out of heaven with love tokens unto them, but with the wicked angel rising out of the bottomless pit with damnable delusions to tole them on in the wayes to hell and eternall Damnation.

COMMENTARY

Born in Coventry, England, Edward Taylor's immigration to the Americas was late—at age twenty-four—& there, until his death sixty-three years later, he lived as pastor to the town & community of Westfield, Massachusetts. During this time, his poetry—hundreds of poems & thousands of lines—was the underpinning to his life as preacher & physician, a spiritual diary written & occulted by choice, that was passed along in secret by his descendants until its publication some two hundred years after his death. In this, his refusal to publish resembles the better-known story of Emily Dickinson as a further instance of the force of poetry as what Wallace Stevens later called "the poem of the mind in the act of finding / what will suffice."

In Puritan America, Taylor, like other Puritans, was a Calvinist & dissenter to the official Anglican Church, from which he turned aside before his journey to America. Here his religious & literary life continued, with a belief in & an exploration of a mystical tie to Christ at the heart of his poetics as a search for metaphor & vision to give it forceful expression. The source of that poetry in the earlier British metaphysical poets is also to be noted, along with the widespread practice of the "spiritual diary" among his fellows in America.

ADDENDUM

AFRICAN AMERICAN, TRADITIONAL

Listen to the Angels Shouting

(slave song)

Where do you think I found my soul,
Listen to the angels shouting,
I found my soul at hell's dark door,
Listen to the angels shouting,
Before I lay in hell one day,
Listen to the angels shouting,
I sing and pray my soul away
Listen to the angels shouting,
Run all the way, run all the way,
Run all the way my Lord,
Listen to the angels shouting.

Blow, Gabriel, blow,
Blow, Gabriel, blow,
Tell all the joyful news,
Listen to the angels shouting.
I don't know what sinner want to stay here for,
Listen to the angels shouting,
When he gets home he will sorrow no more,
Listen to the angels shouting,
Run all the way, run all the way,
Run all the way my Lord,

Brethren, will you come to the promised land,
Come all and sing with the heavenly band.

From the J.B.T. Marsh collection *The Story of the Jubilee
Singers; with their Songs,* 1883

Sor Juana Inés de la Cruz   Mexico, 1648–1695

from *EL PRIMERO SUEÑO*

First Dream

Sleep, at last, possessed all;
silence, occupied all;
the thief slept,
even the restless lover.

Past dead of night,
shadow diminished into halves,
when fatigued from diurnal care
not solely oppressed
by ponderous work of the body,
pleasure-weary as well;
continuous designs upon the senses,
though pleasant, also tire,
which Nature always changes,
first to one, then to another,
distributing offices destined to leisure or to labor,
unfaithful in the faithful needle's balance
with which it rules
the apparatus of the world—
thus the members occupied
with profound sweet rest,
—the senses stayed from ordinary toil—
work in the end, but lovingly,
if there be such labor,
and yield to the portrait
of life's inverted face,
which—stealthily armed
with weapons of sleep—
charges cowardly and lazily masters

both shepherd's hook and gilded scepter,
without distinguishing
sackcloth from purple robe:
all high Morpheus
grants no dispensation
to one whose three crowns
form the papal mitre,
nor to one who lives in sheds of straw,
neither to one on the undulant Danube,
nor who on a humble junk, humbly dwells:
leveling with always equal rigor,
this powerful image of death
measures sackcloth equal to brocade.

Remote, but still a part,
the soul removed
from external control
(unfolding the day for good or ill)
only dispenses to those oppressed members
of temporal death,
bequieted bones,
the wages of vegetative warmth,
the body being in calm repose,
a cadaver with a soul
(alive to death and dead to life)
the vital balance wheel
of the human clock
giving belated signs
of the latter,
if not with hands,
with arterial concert
—some small proof, pulsating,
manifests slowly from its well-regulated movement.

This heart, the member king
and center of life spirit,
with its bellow partner
—lung, whose lodestone attracts the wind,
now compressing, now dilating,
through the muscular, soft, clear conduit,
inhales the fresh air,
which takes revenge for its expulsion

by committing small robberies of vital heat,
to be mourned some time hence
for all must go to waste;
yet, the cycle repeats,
so there really is no theft—
these exceptions and
faithful witnesses
assured life,
while the senses with mute voices
and the torpid tongue, dumb
for once powerless to speak,
impugned the testimony.

And the stomach,
that most provident caterer
and alchemist,
proscribes the quantities of chyle
distilled by the food's incessant heat,
to every natural quadrant
—this mediator
between heat and phlegmatic humor,
interposed its innocent substance,
justly paying for that
which out of piety
or foolish arrogance
introduced it into
foreign wars
—this, if not the Vulcan forge,
the hearth of human warmth,
sent to the brain,
vapors of the four tempered humors,
so clear
they did not blur the simulacra
that sense gave to imagination
(which delivered them in purer form
to memory, a safer custodian
who tenaciously engraves
and carefully guards)
but gave to fantasy
the means to form
diverse images.

In every direction, the confused judgment
foundered hopelessly among the rocks
—lacking fuel, the fires dimmed,
though the body's heat continued slowly
transforming food into its own substance.
Meanwhile, the boiling turbulence
(caused by the union of static
and volatile forces in the crucible)
ceased, and, loosening the shackles of sleep,
began to free the rational throne
of the strange images
induced by the rising vapors.
Likewise, the rest-weary members
(chiding the torpid nerves)
stretched, as the tired bones
momentarily returned to the other side,
and with eyes half-open,
the senses, impeded
by the natural venom,
sweetly resisted the desire to stir,
till the last phantoms
—made of weightless vapor—
fled the now emptied brain,
and dissolved like smoke in the wind.

Thus a magic lantern
projects onto a blank wall
various false, painted figures,
produced no less by shadow
than by light.
While maintaining our reflections
through the proper distances
of informed perspective,
we pretend the fugitive shade
that vanishes in the light-of-day,
to be a multi-dimensional body,
when it is unworthy even to be a surface.

Meanwhile,
at the still point

the Father of ardent light
appeared in the East,
he bade farewell to the opposite pole
with a slant of tremulous rays;
but not before, the beautiful
placid morning Star
broke the first light,
and old Tithonus' Amazon spouse, Aurora,
(armed against darkness)
displayed her clear brow
shining with the morning,
a tender, valorous prelude
to the fiery Planet's
undisciplined advance
—reserving his veteran sparks
for the rear guard—
against the tyrannical usurper,
crowned with black laurel,
and who with awful nocturnal scepter
governed the shadows,
of which even she was terrified.

But scarcely had the radiant harbinger
waived the luminous colors in the East,
summoning a cacophony of birds
to sound the alarms,
when the tyrant Night, coward
burdened with terrible dread,
strove to make boast of her forces,
interposing the guard
of her lugubrious shroud,
receiving in it slight wounds
from light incisions—and,
since her unsatisfied valor
was a mask of fear,
she sought deliverance
more than engagement,
and blew the raucous horn,
gathering the black squadrons
to orderly retreat—
when she was assaulted

by a greater, neighboring,
plentitude of beams
that streaked the highest point
of the World's towers.

Closing the luminous circumference,
the Sun streamed
from a thousand times thousand
points of gold over blue sapphire,
a thousand golden lines
across the vast blue page;
as she fled—stumbling
on the shadows of her own horror—
with the chaotic, routed army.

That fugitive pace
attained, at last, sight of the West
and—roused by her own precipitous fall—
again maneuvered
to crown herself
with the globe's abandoned half,
while the golden Sun
adorned our Hemisphere
with skeins of judicious light
dispensing their colors
to visible things,
and restored to outward sense,
their full operation
—keeping to more certain light,
the World illuminated,
and I awake.

Translated from Spanish by John Campion

Translated from Spanish by John Campion

COMMENTARY

Who has forbidden women to engage in private and individual studies? Have they not a rational soul as men do? ... I have this inclination to study and if it is evil I am not the one who formed me thus—I was born with it and with it I shall die. (Sor Juana)

(1) It fell to a woman & nun to be the first truly great poet/thinker of the post-Conquest Americas. Native-born in San Miguel Nepantla, Mexico,

Sor Juana Inés de la Cruz emerged even in her teen years as a writer of remarkable intellectual & spiritual powers. Her poetry as such seems to have been coterminous with those beginnings, & her writings throughout her lifetime were prolific & included theological & philosophical speculations, along with lyric poems, liturgical dramas, & folkloric & dialectal transcreations. All of which, as with others exploring the joys & perils of the-mind-in-freedom—a hallmark of poetry as we've come to understand & practice it today—brought her into conflict with her religious overlords, as in her grand defense of poetry, precisely on philosophical grounds, in the "Response to Sor Filotea" (1691), quoted in the epigraph above.

(2) Almost crushed by orthodoxy & on the road to a self-imposed silence & exile, she rose three years before her death, in 1695, to write one final work, *El Primero Sueño*, an amazing epistemological poem on knowing & not knowing, taking the form of a soul's journey from darkness to freedom but fraught with dangers & fears along the way.

In the course of that journey, she reached the apex of an intellectual & epistemological poetry, wherever found, after which the rest, as someone else once said, was silence.

(3) "Sor Juana's work must include an understanding of the prohibitions her work confronts. Her speech leads us to what cannot be said, what cannot be said to an orthodoxy, the orthodoxy to a tribunal, and the tribunal to a sentence" (Octavio Paz).

For more on Sor Juana, see "A Map of Americas."

ADDENDUM

BRUCE ANDREWS USA, 1948–

from *Strike Me, Lightning*

> More, I am not in charge
> conducted to this happy death
> the imitation of the imitation
> invisible I, the worst
> woman in the world, Sor Juana Inés de la Cruz
> idolatrize
> automatons
> or incubus—
> wish you were here
> another sheep for your flock
> as the net closes around
> cloistered unsex virgin
> pregnant cloud

mummify
incognito
self-admiring
rosary noose
thermal panjandrum

per J.B. Moreton   England/Jamaica, fl. 1790

FOUR JAMAICAN SONGS

Working Songs

[1]

Tink dere is a God in a top
       no use me ill, Obissha
           me no horse
           me no mare
           me no mule!
       no use me ill, Obissha

[2]

if me want for go in a Ebo
       me can't go there!
since dem tief me from a Guinea
          me can't go there!

if me want for go in a Congo
       me can't go there!
since dem tief me from my tatta
          me can't go there!

if me want for go in a Kingston,
       me can't go there!
since massa go in a England
          me can't go there!

Dancing Songs

[1]

Hipsaw! my deaa! you no do like a-me!
       you no jig like a-me
          you no twist like a-me

Hipsaw! my deaa! you no shake like a-me!
you no wind like a-me!
go yondaaa!

Hipsaw! my deaa! you no jig like a-me!
you no work him like a-me!
you no sweet him like a-me!

[2]

Tajo, tajo tajo! tajo, my mackey massa!
O lawd! O! tajo, tajo, tajo!

you work him
you sweet me } mackey massa!
a little more my

Tajo, tajo tajo! tajo, my mackey massa!
O lawd! O! tajo, tajo, tajo!

I'll please my
I'll jig to } mackey massa!
I'll sweet my

Lineated by Javier Taboada

COMMENTARY

The selection above seems to be the first record of Jamaican Creole poetry/ song & the first in the English-speaking Caribbean. J.B. Moreton—an English bookkeeper settled in Clarendon, Jamaica—published *West India Customs and Manners* (1790), which included songs & stories in the language of planters & slaves. Along with his perspective on the ongoing Creole society in Jamaica, Moreton tried to capture its language. His efforts to depict the rhythm, syntax, & pronunciation of the Jamaican Creole speakers anticipated what Kamau Brathwaite would later call "nation languages."

For all of which, the reader may also catch a note of rebelliousness & derision in the address to the mackey massa, the false master, in the second dancing song above.

Esteban Echeverría Argentina, 1805–1851

from *THE SLAUGHTERHOUSE*

"Tie him up first," said the Judge.

"He's roaring with anger," a torturer said.

At one point, they spread out his legs to the table's feet, setting him face down. They intended to do the same with his arms, for which they released his wrists, fastened to his back. As soon as the young man felt them free, he made a violent move that wore out his vitality and strength. He tried to lift himself on his arms, then on his knees, but fell down instantly, murmuring: "You'll have to slit my throat before you bastards undress me."

His strength was gone. Immediately he was all tied up as if to a cross, and they kept on undressing him. Then, a rush of blood gushed from his mouth and nostrils and soaked both sides of the table. The torturers remained still; the spectators were dazed.

"The savage rebel exploded in rage," said one.

"Had a bloody river in his veins," said another.

"Poor devil. We just wanted to have fun with him, but he took it so seriously," exclaimed the Judge, glaring like a tiger. "Make the report, untie him and let's go."

Translated from Spanish by Javier Taboada

COMMENTARY

Our wise men have studied a lot, but I search in vain for a philosophical system... I'm looking for an original literature, a brilliant and lively expression of our social life, and I can't find it... (E.E.)

Writes Roberto González Echeverría: "*El Matadero* [*The slaughterhouse*, in our translation] is one of the finest pieces of Latin American fiction of the nineteenth century. Written about 1838, it denounces the [Argentinean] dictator Manuel de Rosas, but it was unfortunately not published during Echeverría's lifetime. It is a fairly extensive, tautly written short story that narrates the brutal assassination by a bunch of thugs at the Buenos Aires slaughterhouse of a young man who opposes the dictator.... It is a brilliant sketch, perhaps the best piece of politically inspired fiction ever written in Latin America. But the story's power lies in the drama of the young man's slaying; because it mimics that of the slaughterhouse animals, it takes on the air of an atavistic ritual sacrifice. It is as if the slaughter were a scene of men re-enacting their subhuman origins while at the same time it becomes an allegory representing Argentina in the hands of Rosas and his hench-men" (in *Modern Latin American Literature: A Very Short Introduction*).

Its resemblance to the fate of the "disappeared" in the following century should also be noted.

Edgar Allan Poe USA, 1809–1849

THE CONQUEROR WORM

Lo! 'tis a gala night
Within the lonesome latter years!
An angel throng, bewinged, bedight
In veils, and drowned in tears,
Sit in a theatre, to see
A play of hopes and fears,
While the orchestra breathes fitfully
The music of the spheres.

Mimes, in the form of God on high,
Mutter and mumble low,
And hither and thither fly—
Mere puppets they, who come and go
At bidding of vast formless things
That shift the scenery to and fro,
Flapping from out their Condor wings
Invisible Woe!

That motley drama—oh, be sure
It shall not be forgot!
With its Phantom chased for evermore,
By a crowd that seize it not,
Through a circle that ever returneth in
To the self-same spot,
And much of Madness, and more of Sin,
And Horror the soul of the plot.

But see, amid the mimic rout
A crawling shape intrude!
A blood-red thing that writhes from out
The scenic solitude!
It writhes!—it writhes!—with mortal pangs

The mimes become its food,
And seraphs sob at vermin fangs
In human gore imbued.

Out—out are the lights—out all!
And, over each quivering form,
The curtain, a funeral pall,
Comes down with the rush of a storm,
While the angels, all pallid and wan,
Uprising, unveiling, affirm
That the play is the tragedy, "Man,"
And its hero the Conqueror Worm.

from *EUREKA—A PROSE POEM*

An Essay on the Material and Spiritual Universe

Preface

To the few who love me and whom I love—to those who feel rather than to those who think—to the dreamers and those who put faith in dreams as in the only realities—I offer this Book of Truths, not in its character of Truth-Teller, but for the Beauty that abounds in its Truth; constituting it true. To these I present the composition as an Art-Product alone:—let us say as a Romance; or, if I be not urging too lofty a claim, as a Poem.

What I here propound is true:—therefore it cannot die:—or if by any means it be now trodden down so that it die, it will "rise again to the Life Everlasting."

Nevertheless it is as a Poem only that I wish this work to be judged after I am dead.

E.A.P.

Excerpts:

[1] My general proposition, then, is this:—In the Original Unity of the First Thing lies the Secondary Cause of All Things, with the Germ of their Inevitable Annihilation.

In illustration of this idea, I propose to take such a survey of the Universe that the mind may be able really to receive and to perceive an individual impression.

He who from the top of Aetna casts his eyes leisurely around, is affected chiefly by the extent and diversity of the scene. Only by a rapid whirling on his heel could he hope to comprehend the panorama in the sublimity of its oneness. But as, on the summit of Aetna, no man has thought of whirling on his heel, so no man has ever taken into his brain the full uniqueness of the prospect; and so, again, whatever considerations lie involved in this uniqueness, have as yet no practical existence for mankind.

I do not know a treatise in which a survey of the Universe—using the word in its most comprehensive and only legitimate acceptation—is taken at all:—and it may be as well here to mention that by the term "Universe," wherever employed without qualification in this essay, I mean to designate the utmost conceivable expanse of space, with all things, spiritual and material, that can be imagined to exist within the compass of that expanse. In speaking of what is ordinarily implied by the expression, "Universe," I shall take a phrase of limitation—"the Universe of stars." Why this distinction is considered necessary, will be seen in the sequel.

[2] Let us begin, then, at once, with that merest of words, "Infinity." This, like "God," "spirit," and some other expressions of which the equivalents exist in all languages, is by no means the expression of an idea—but of an effort at one. It stands for the possible attempt at an impossible conception. Man needed a term by which to point out the direction of this effort—the cloud behind which lay, forever invisible, the object of this attempt. A word, in fine, was demanded, by means of which one human being might put himself in relation at once with another human being and with a certain tendency of the human intellect. Out of this demand arose the word, "Infinity"; which is thus the representative but of the thought of a thought.

As regards that infinity now considered the infinity of space—we often hear it said that "its idea is admitted by the mind—is acquiesced in—is entertained—on account of the greater difficulty which attends the conception of a limit." But this is merely one of those phrases by which even profound thinkers, time out of mind, have occasionally taken pleasure in deceiving themselves. The quibble lies concealed in the word "difficulty." "The mind," we are told, "entertains the idea of limitless, through the greater difficulty which it finds in entertaining that of limited, space." Now, were the proposition but fairly put, its absurdity would become transparent at once. Clearly, there is no mere difficulty in the case. The assertion intended, if presented according to its intention and without sophistry, would run thus:—"The mind admits the idea of limitless, through the greater impossibility of entertaining that of limited, space."

It must be immediately seen that this is not a question of two statements between whose respective credibilities—or of two arguments between whose respective validities—the reason is called upon to decide:—it is a matter of two conceptions, directly conflicting, and each avowedly impossible, one of which the intellect is supposed to be capable of entertaining, on account of the greater impossibility of entertaining the other. The choice is not made between two difficulties;—it is merely fancied to be made between two impossibilities. Now of the former, there are degrees,—but of the latter, none:—just as our impertinent letter-writer has already suggested. A task may be more or less difficult; but it is either possible or not possible:—there are no gradations. It might be more difficult to overthrow the Andes than an ant-hill; but it can be no more impossible to annihilate the matter of the one than the matter of the other. A man may jump ten feet with less difficulty than he can jump twenty, but the impossibility of his leaping to the moon is not a whit less than that of his leaping to the dog-star.

Since all this is undeniable: since the choice of the mind is to be made between impossibilities of conception: since one impossibility cannot be greater than another: and since, thus, one cannot be preferred to another: the philosophers who not only maintain, on the grounds mentioned, man's idea of infinity but, on account of such supposititious idea, infinity itself—are plainly engaged in demonstrating one impossible thing to be possible by showing how it is that some one other thing—is impossible too. This, it will be said, is nonsense; and perhaps it is:—indeed I think it very capital nonsense—but forego all claim to it as nonsense of mine.

COMMENTARY

All religion, my friend, is simply evolved out of fraud, fear, greed, imagination, and poetry. (E.A.P.) And again: *Those who dream by day are cognizant of many things which escape those who dream only by night.*

(1) The reception of Poe in Latin America (as on the French side) was, as we know, far greater than on native grounds, & whether they got it right or wrong, there is no doubt but that they got it. For there is with him, far more than with most of his contemporaries, the sense of a new opening & of possibilities embedded in language & mind that he or others will make it their business to explore, whether achieved or not. Placing him in the penultimate spot in his radical study of poets & others thinking & writ-

ing "in the American grain," William Carlos Williams wrote as an isolated act of rehabilitation: "On him is founded a literature—typical, an anger to sweep out the unoriginal, that became ill-tempered, a monomaniacal driving to destroy, to annihilate the copied, the slavish, the false literature about him: this is the major impulse in his notes." And Baudelaire, who devoted himself to extensive translations from Poe, both the verse & the fiction, & to a number of biographical & critical assessments, described him as "the man... who throughout a life that resembled a tempest with no calm, had invented new forms, unknown avenues to astonish the imagination, to captivate all minds desiring beauty."

(2) Working between genres, Poe was quick to realize that the boundaries of poetry didn't stop at the border with prose, & while his sense of the "lyric" drew him famously toward the intense single moment (the meaning-charged fragment as a carryover from Romanticism) & to a rejection of the "long poem," his own long prose work *Eureka*—devoid of any resemblance to "poetic" diction or fixed rhythm—was for him not only an extended essay on cosmology but, as he specifically named it, "a prose poem." Thus, in one of the more daring/dazzling moves of the nineteenth century, he effectively erased, beyond the work of other, similarly inclined practitioners both north & south, the long-standing boundaries between poetry & prose.

ADDENDUM

RON SILLIMAN USA, 1946–

from **The New Sentence (1987)**

Let's list these qualities of the new sentence, then read a poem watching for their presence:
1) The paragraph organizes the sentences;
2) The paragraph is a unity of quantity, not logic or argument;
3) Sentence length is a unit of measure;
4) Sentence structure is altered for torque, or increased polysemy/ambiguity;
5) Syllogistic movement is: (a) limited; (b) controlled;
6) Primary syllogistic movement is between the preceding and following sentences;
7) Secondary syllogistic movement is toward the paragraph as a whole, or the total work;
8) The limiting of syllogistic movement keeps the reader's attention at or very close to the level of language, that is, most often at the sentence level or below.
.....

The new sentence is a decidedly contextual object. Its effects occur as much between, as within, sentences. Thus it reveals that the blank space, between words or sentences, is much more than the 27th letter of the alphabet. It is beginning to explore and articulate just what those hidden capacities might be.

Ralph Waldo Emerson USA, 1809–1882

from *NATURE*

Every spirit builds itself a house; and beyond its house a world; and beyond its world, a heaven. Know then, that the world exists for you. For you is the phenomenon perfect. What we are, that only can we see. All that Adam had, all that Caesar could, you have and can do. Adam called his house, heaven and earth; Caesar called his house, Rome; you perhaps call yours, a cobbler's trade; a hundred acres of ploughed land; or a scholar's garret. Yet line for line and point for point, your dominion is as great as theirs, though without fine names. Build, therefore, your own world.

ODE, INSCRIBED TO WILLIAM H. CHANNING

Though loath to grieve
The evil time's sole patriot,
I cannot leave
My honied thought
For the priest's cant,
Or statesman's rant.

If I refuse
My study for their politique,
Which at the best is trick,
The angry Muse
Puts confusion in my brain.

But who is he that prates
Of the culture of mankind,
Of better arts and life?
Go, blindworm, go,
Behold the famous States
Harrying Mexico
With rifle and with knife!

Or who, with accent bolder,
Dare praise the freedom-loving mountaineer?
I found by thee, O rushing Contoocook!
And in thy valleys, Agiochook!
The jackals of the negro-holder.

The God who made New Hampshire
Taunted the lofty land
With little men;—
Small bat and wren
House in the oak:—
If earth-fire cleave
The upheaved land, and bury the folk,
The southern crocodile would grieve.
Virtue palters; Right is hence;
Freedom praised, but hid;
Funeral eloquence
Rattles the coffin-lid.

What boots thy zeal,
O glowing friend,
That would indignant rend
The northland from the south?
Wherefore? To what good end?
Boston Bay and Bunker Hill
Would serve things still;—
Things are of the snake.

The horseman serves the horse,
The neat-herd serves the neat,
The merchant serves the purse,
The eater serves his meat;
'T is the day of the chattel
Web to weave, and corn to grind;
Things are in the saddle,
And ride mankind.

There are two laws discrete,
Not reconciled,—
Law for man, and law for thing;
The last builds town and fleet,
But it runs wild,
And doth the man unking.

'T is fit the forest fall,
The steep be graded,
The mountain tunnelled,
The sand shaded,
The orchard planted,
The glebe tilled,
The prairie granted,
The steamer built.

Let man serve law for man;
Live for friendship, live for love,
For truth's and harmony's behoof;
The state may follow how it can,
As Olympus follows Jove.

    Yet do not I implore
The wrinkled shopman to my sounding woods,
Nor bid the unwilling senator
Ask votes of thrushes in the solitudes.
Every one to his chosen work;—
Foolish hands may mix and mar;
Wise and sure the issues are.
Round they roll till dark is light,
Sex to sex, and even to odd;—
The over-god
Who marries Right to Might,
Who peoples, unpeoples,—
He who exterminates
Races by stronger races,
Black by white faces,—
Knows to bring honey
Out of the lion;
Grafts gentlest scion
On pirate and Turk.

The Cossack eats Poland,
Like stolen fruit;
Her last noble is ruined,
Her last poet mute;
Straight into double band
The victors divide;
Half for freedom strike and stand;—
The astonished Muse finds thousands at her side.

*I am born a poet, of a low class without doubt, yet a poet. That is my
nature and vocation. My singing, be sure, is very husky, and is for the most
part in prose. Still am I a poet in the sense of a perceiver & dear lover of
the harmonies that are in the soul & in matter, & especially of the correspondences between these & those.* (R.W.E.)

(1) Yet it was this that was almost lost in the distinction, too narrowly
drawn by others, between poetry & prose, nor was it Emerson's singing-
in-prose that was most relevant, rather the calling to which he gave himself—to be a poet—& where that would take him. In that quest, the poems
as such, as we would see & show them, need no apology, but there is something here, as with others in these pages, that goes beyond verse & that
informs his total work & thought. (Language itself he defined as "fossil
poetry" & led us to seek its presence everywhere.) For this, transcendental-
ism, with which he's so closely connected, might offer the key, but at the
peril of losing his particulars. For, as Sherman Paul once wrote of him:
"Emerson was not a mystic in the usual 'visionary' sense of the word.
He was not seeking in the angle of vision an escape from the world; as it
formed, the angle of vision was to make 'use' of the world. But the mystical union, for him, was an epistemological necessity. Vision, he said of the
inner seeing of the mind, is not like the vision of the eye, but is union with
the things known" (*The Angle of Vision*). Or Emerson again: "The secret
of the world is the tie between person and event. Person makes event and
event person."

(2) As with other poets—perhaps even more so—the philosophical/mysti-
cal/transcendental underpinnings of his thought & work were at the service always of a poethical sense of the unredeemed horrors of the world
in which he lived. Hovering below the surface in other of his poems, they
emerge in the quasi-news accounts of the "Ode to Channing": the US declaration of war against Mexico six weeks before the poem began, the parallel national & cultural wars in Europe & elsewhere, & centrally the sin of
slavery against which Channing wrote & spoke as an active abolitionist. If
Emerson pointed the way to Whitman as archetype of the new American &
New World poet, his own poetry, both verse & prose, also prefigured the
major works to come.

Walt Whitman USA, 1819–1892

COME, SAID MY SOUL

Come, said my Soul
Such verses for my Body let us write, (for we are one,)
That should
I after death invisibly return,
Or, long, long hence, in other spheres,
There to some group of mates the chants resuming,
(Tallying Earth's soil, trees, winds, tumultuous waves,)
Ever with pleas'd smiles I may keep on,
Ever and ever yet the verses owning—as, first, I here and now,
Signing for Soul and Body, set to them my name,
Walt Whitman

THIS COMPOST

Something startles me where I thought I was safest;
I withdraw from the still woods I loved;
I will not go now on the pastures to walk;
I will not strip the clothes from my body to meet my lover the sea;
I will not touch my flesh to the earth, as to other flesh, to renew me.

O how can it be that the ground itself does not sicken?
How can you be alive you growths of spring? How can you furnish health you
        blood of herbs, roots, orchards, grain?
Are they not continually putting distemper'd corpses within you?
Is not every continent work'd over and over with sour dead?

Where have you disposed of their carcasses?
Those drunkards and gluttons of so many generations?

Where have you drawn off all the foul liquid and meat?
I do not see any of it upon you to-day, or perhaps I am deceiv'd,
I will run a furrow with my plough, I will press my spade through the sod and
        turn it up underneath,
I am sure I shall expose some of the foul meat.

Behold this compost! behold it well!
Perhaps every mite has once form'd part of a sick person; yet behold!
The grass of spring covers the prairies,
The bean bursts noiselessly through the mould in the garden,

The delicate spear of the onion pierces upward,
The apple-buds cluster together on the apple-branches,
The resurrection of the wheat appears with pale visage out of its graves,
The tinge awakes over the willow-tree and the mulberry-tree,
The he-birds carol mornings and evenings while the she-birds sit on their nests,
The young of poultry break through the hatch'd eggs,
The new-born of animals appear, the calf is dropt from the cow, the colt from
    the mare,
Out of its little hill faithfully rise the potato's dark green leaves,
Out of its hill rises the yellow maize-stalk, the lilacs bloom in the dooryards,
The summer growth is innocent and disdainful above all those strata of sour dead.

What chemistry!
That the winds are really not infectious,
That this is no cheat, this transparent green-wash of the sea which is so amorous
    after me,
That it is safe to allow it to lick my naked body all over with its tongues,
That it will not endanger me with the fevers that have deposited themselves in it,
That all is clean forever and forever,
That the cool drink from the well tastes so good,
That the blackberries are so flavorous and juicy,
That the fruits of the apple-orchard and the orange-orchard, that melons,
    grapes, peaches, plums, will none of them poison me,
That when I recline on the grass I do not catch any disease,
Though probably every spear of grass rises out of what was once a catching
    disease.

Now I am terrified at the Earth, it is that calm and patient,
It grows such sweet things out of such corruptions,
It turns harmless and stainless on its axis, with such endless successions of
    diseas'd corpses,
It distills such exquisite winds out of such infused fetor,
It renews with such unwitting looks its prodigal, annual, sumptuous crops,
It gives such divine materials to men, and accepts such leavings from them at last.

RESPONDEZ, OR POEM OF THE PROPOSITIONS
OF NAKEDNESS

Respondez! Respondez!
(The war is completed—the price is paid—the title is settled beyond recall.)

Let every one answer! let those who sleep be waked! let none evade!
Must we still go on with our affectations and sneaking?

Let me bring this to a close—I pronounce openly for a new distribution of roles;

Let that which stood in front go behind! and let that which was behind advance to the front and speak;

Let murderers, bigots, fools, unclean persons, offer new propositions!

Let the old propositions be postponed!

Let faces and theories be turn'd inside out! let meanings be freely criminal, as well as results!

Let there be no suggestion above the suggestion of drudgery!

Let none be pointed toward his destination! (Say! do you know your destination?)

Let men and women be mock'd with bodies and mock'd with Souls!

Let the love that waits in them, wait! let it die, or pass stillborn to other spheres!

Let the sympathy that waits in every man, wait! or let it also pass, a dwarf, to other spheres!

Let contradictions prevail! let one thing contradict another! and let one line of my poems contradict another!

Let the people sprawl with yearning, aimless hands! let their tongues be broken! let their eyes be discouraged! let none descend into their hearts with the fresh lusciousness of love!

(Stifled, O days! O lands! in every public and private corruption!

Smother'd in thievery, impotence, shamelessness, mountain-high!

Brazen effrontery, scheming, rolling like ocean's waves around and upon you, O my days! My lands!

For not even those thunderstorms, nor fiercest lightnings of the war, have purified the atmosphere!)

Let the theory of America still be management, caste, comparison! (Say! what other theory would you?)

Let them that distrust birth and death still lead the rest! (Say! why shall they not lead you?)

Let the crust of hell be neared and trod on! let the days be darker than the nights! let slumber bring less slumber than waking time brings!

Let the world never appear to him or her for whom it was all made!

Let the heart of the young man still exile itself from the heart of the old man! and let the heart of the old man be exiled from that of the young man!

Let the sun and moon go! let scenery take the applause of the audience! let there be apathy under the stars!

Let freedom prove no man's inalienable right! every one who can tyrannize, let him tyrannize to his satisfaction!

Let none but infidels be countenanced!

Let the eminence of meanness, treachery, sarcasm, hate, greed, indecency, impotence, lust, be taken for granted above all! let writers, judges, governments, households, religions, philosophies, take such for granted above all!

Let the worst men beget children out of the worst women!

Let the priest still play at immortality!

Let death be inaugurated!

Let nothing remain but the ashes of teachers, artists, moralists, lawyers, and learn'd and polite persons!

Let him who is without my poems be assassinated!

Let the cow, the horse, the camel, the garden-bee—let the mudfish, the lobster, the mussel, eel, the sting-ray, and the grunting pig-fish—let these, and the like of these, be put on perfect equality with man and woman!

Let churches accommodate serpents, vermin, and the corpses of those who have died of the most filthy of diseases!

Let marriage slip down among fools, and be for none but fools!

Let men among themselves talk and think forever obscenely of women! and let women among themselves talk and think obscenely of men!

Let us all, without missing one, be exposed in public, naked, monthly, at the peril of our lives! let our bodies be freely handled and examined by whoever chooses!

Let nothing but copies at second hand be permitted to exist upon the earth!

Let the earth desert God, nor let there ever henceforth be mention'd the name of God!

Let there be no God!

Let there be money, business, imports, exports, custom, authority, precedents, pallor, dyspepsia, smut, ignorance, unbelief!

Let judges and criminals be transposed! let the prison-keepers be put in prison! let those that were prisoners take the keys! (Say! why might they not just as well be transposed?)

Let the slaves be masters! let the masters become slaves!

Let the reformers descend from the stands where they are forever bawling! let an idiot or insane person appear on each of the stands!

Let the Asiatic, the African, the European, the American, and the Australian, go armed against the murderous stealthiness of each other! let them sleep armed! let none believe in good will!

Let there be no unfashionable wisdom! let such be scorn'd and derided off from the earth!

Let a floating cloud in the sky—let a wave of the sea—let growing mint, spinach, onions, tomatoes—let these be exhibited as shows, at a great price for admission!

Let all the men of These States stand aside for a few smouchers! let the few seize on what they choose! let the rest gawk, giggle, starve, obey!

Let shadows be furnish'd with genitals! let substances be deprived of their genitals!
Let there be wealthy and immense cities—but still through any of them, not a single poet, savior, knower, lover!
Let the infidels of These States laugh all faith away!
If one man be found who has faith, let the rest set upon him!
Let them affright faith! let them destroy the power of breeding faith!
Let the she-harlots and the he-harlots be prudent! let them dance on, while seeming lasts! (O seeming! seeming! seeming!)
Let the preachers recite creeds! let them still teach only what they have been taught!
Let insanity still have charge of sanity!
Let books take the place of trees, animals, rivers, clouds!
Let the daub'd portraits of heroes supersede heroes!

Let the manhood of man never take steps after itself!
Let it take steps after eunuchs, and after consumptive and genteel persons!
Let the white person again tread the black person under his heel! (Say! which is trodden under heel, after all?)
Let the reflections of the things of the world be studied in mirrors! let the things themselves still continue unstudied!
Let a man seek pleasure everywhere except in himself!
Let a woman seek happiness everywhere except in herself!
(What real happiness have you had one single hour through your whole life?)
Let the limited years of life do nothing for the limitless years of death! (What do you suppose death will do, then?)

GOOD-BYE MY FANCY!

Good-bye my Fancy!
Farewell dear mate, dear love!
I'm going away, I know not where,
Or to what fortune, or whether I may ever see you again,
So Good-bye my Fancy.
Now for my last—let me look back a moment;
The slower fainter ticking of the clock is in me,
Exit, nightfall, and soon the heart-thud stopping.
Long have we lived, joy'd, caress'd together;
Delightful!—now separation—Good-bye my Fancy.

Yet let me not be too hasty,

Long indeed have we lived, slept, filter'd, become really blended into one;

Then if we die we die together, (yes, we'll remain one,)

If we go anywhere we'll go together to meet what happens,

May-be we'll be better off and blither, and learn something,

May-be it is yourself now really ushering me to the true songs, (who knows?)

May-be it is you the mortal knob really undoing, turning—so now finally,

Good-bye—and hail! my Fancy.

COMMENTARY

Come, I will make the continent indissoluble, / I will make the most splendid race the sun ever shone upon, / I will make divine magnetic lands, / With the love of comrades, / With the life-long love of comrades. // …
. For you these from me, O Democracy, to serve you ma femme! / For you, for you I am trilling these songs. (W.W.)

It's Whitman's range that can most astonish us, not only as a newly imagined "poet of the states" & of "Democracy," but with a reach that would "contain multitudes" & with a way of writing it down that constitutes a new, till then unheard-of music or measure. While empire always lurks within (in Whitman's own visions of USAmerican "Manifest Destiny"), the central vision that emerges is replete with ideas of democracy & freedom on an unprecedented scale, the makings, too, as it came to be seen, of a new "total poetry." In line with that, the "many long dumb voices" he invokes elsewhere run from "prisoners & slaves" to the stars of an emerging multiverse around him to "the deform'd, trivial, flat, foolish, despised, fog in the air, beetles rolling balls of dung." His task therein was to use the new means & openness to revive the vatic function, to employ the total language & range of human identities—body and soul, evil and good—toward a poetry that would be actualized only after his own time, by "poets [yet] to come." In doing this, his further aim was to bring "self" & "world" (but also self & selves) into a new alignment, the singular pronoun of his poetry (its "I") used with a new freedom, to summon up a range of real & fictive selves: "All identities that have existed or may exist on this globe, or any globe." And along with that, a radical opening of the poet's vocabulary to "all words that exist in use," for "All words are spiritual. Nothing is more spiritual than words" (*An American Primer*). The political aspect of the "democratic vistas" he thus opened in both poetry & life was also central to his vision—as it still may be to ours.

The dark & angry/despairing voice of his poem "Respondez" is also to be noted: an eruption of ironies toward what Robert Kelly once called "a poetry of desperation."

PABLO NERUDA Chile, 1904–1973

from **Ode to Walt Whitman**

> Without
> disdain
> for the gifts
> of the earth,
> the capital's
> abundant curves,
> or the purple
> initial
> of wisdom,
> you
> taught me
> to be an American,
> you lifted my eyes
> to books,
> toward
> the treasure
> of the grain:
> broad poet,
> across the
> clarity
> of the plains,
> you made me see
> the high mountain
> as my guardian.

Translated from Spanish
by Martín Espada

On which note the work moves forward to "A Map of Americas."

A MAP OF AMERICAS

Solitary, singing in the West, I strike up for a New World.

WALT WHITMAN

My tools open America's still undiscovered lands.

RUBÉN DARÍO

An American / is a complex of occasions, /
themselves a geometry / of spatial nature.

CHARLES OLSON

Who we are / Why we're here / To extend Africa /
So it can have buds / In the new fields of the Americas

ERNEST PÉPIN

If the people do not speak Mapudungun,
the earth will not be able to speak.

ELICURA CHIHUAILAF, MAPUCHE NATION

the pure products of America
go crazy

WILLIAM CARLOS WILLIAMS

Gary Snyder USA, 1930–

from *TURTLE ISLAND*

I pledge allegiance to the soil
of Turtle Island,
and to the beings who thereon dwell
one ecosystem
in diversity
under the sun
With joyful interpenetration for all.

For more on Snyder, see "A Fourth Gallery."

Joel Barlow USA, 1754–1812

from **THE VISION OF COLUMBUS**

Book IV

A new creation waits the western shore,
And reason triumphs o'er the pride of power.
As the glad coast, by heaven's supreme command,
won from the wave, presents a new-form'd land...

COMMENTARY

Originally written in 1787, and later reworked in a longer poem called *The Columbiad, The Vision of Columbus* was the first epic attempt to gather & praise the history of North & South America. In *The Vision*, Columbus dialogues with an angel who shows him the destiny of our continents: freedom & liberation, epitomized in the American Revolutionary War, in which Barlow himself served as military chaplain.

Susan Suntree   USA, 1946–

from **SACRED SITES**

The Secret History of Southern California
Universe, World, People

First

       there is

              quiet.

Only solitude

       like an empty house   (no house)

            Only

         *Kvish   Atakvi*sh

Kvish: Vacant

Atakvish: Empty

      These two are man and woman, brother and sister.

        Then *Kvish   Atakvish*

         become

         Omai Yamai

Omai: Not Alive

Yamai: Not in Existence

        When these two discover themselves,
         they talk with one another:

Brother, who are you?

Sister, who are you?

> (Desire stirs the man,
> so he never again calls her sister.)

She asks again: Who are you?

He says:

> *Kvish*
>
> *Kvish*
>
> *Kvish*

I am   Empty

Empty

Empty

He blows out his spirit breath: Hannnn!

She answers:

> *Atakvish*
>
> *Atakvish*
>
> *Atakvish*

I am   Vacant

Vacant

Vacant

She blows out her spirit breath: Hannnn!

She asks again: Who are you?

He answers:

> *Omai*
>
> *Omai*
>
> *Omai*

I am   Not Alive

Not Alive

Not Alive

He blows out his spirit breath: Hannnn!

He asks again: Who are you?

She answers:

Yamai

Yamai

Yamai

I am   Not in Existence

Not in Existence

Not in Existence

She blows out her spirit breath: Hannnn!

Not Alive-Not in Existence

becomes

Whaikut Piwkut   Harurai Chatutai

Whaikut Piwkut: Pale Gray   The Milky Way

Harurai Chatutai: Changing   Descending Deep into the Heart

These two become

Tukmit: Dark Sky   Tomaiyowit: Earth

COMMENTARY

(1) Writes Gary Snyder of the span of times & voices herein: "Susan Suntree's epic poem is a lovely weaving of science and myth. It is a work that sings... shaping the universe one song at a time.... [It is] a book about impermanence. From the very beginning, the landscape known as Southern California has reshaped itself dramatically and often. Learning how a place comes into being acquaints us with forces of life that are large and inti-

mately interconnected. For the Indigenous people, the creation and transformation of the world is an account of the First People. In this way of looking at it, the land is alive and working out its own story."

(2) Following the science-based opening sections of Suntree's poem, the Indigenous accounts, as here, draw on many sources, but largely the handwritten notes by Constance Goddard DuBois of Lucario Cuevish's oral narrative (Luiseño, ca. 1900). Of this encounter in particular, Suntree writes: "Cuevish, blind and near death, recited from memory while DuBois, sitting next to her translator, wrote down his words as fast as she could. Many scholars considered his to be the least affected by European influences of all the versions of this myth. For me, its poetic beauty, most evident in her original notes, sets it apart from all the other versions of this myth that I have read." (For more from Lucario Cuevish, see the end of "A Map of Visions.")

Rubén Darío   Nicaragua, 1867–1916

from *TUTECOTZIMI*

Digging in the topsoil of the ancient city
the pick's metallic point strikes something very hard:
some golden gem, perhaps, a stone that's been carved,
an arrow, fetish, some god's ambiguity,
or the enormous walls of some temple. My tools
open America's still undiscovered lands.

Let poetry's tools sing like harmonious jewels!
Let them discover fine, rich stones, gold, or opal,
temples or statue's hands.
And mysterious hieroglyphics that foretell
my own Muse.

From the thick mist of time emerges the strangeness
of annulled people's lives. and legends. once confused,
now shine. The mountain reveals its secret access
to ruins underneath the plants of the jungle.

Then the ferocious cry
of the oppressors stopped. Their reviled leader's heart
would beat no more, his bloody body torn apart.
And then, singing loudly, a person journeyed by.
He sang to earth and sky and used an Aztec song

to praise the gods and curse all wars as being wrong.
The people cheered: "Can you bring peace and work?"
"I can."
"Take this palace, these fields, arms, and *huepiles*, please:
lead the Pipil nation and praise our deities."

That's how the reign of Tutecotzimi began.

Translated from Spanish by Greg Simon & Steven F. White

COMMENTARY

The project that Darío begins to set out here unearths the name of a putative pre-Columbian Nahua ruler of Nicaragua, to create anew an American/pre-American inheritance on native grounds. Following the same archaeological trajectory toward a shared past & future, Pablo Neruda writes later, in *The Heights of Macchu Picchu*: "*We the Americans … have had to dig in order to find underneath the imperial ashes the colossal fragments of the lost gods.*" The fragmentation and the ongoing quest continue into the present, arising again & again for those who feel the need for them.

For more on Darío, see "A Second Gallery."

ADDENDUM

HENRY WADSWORTH LONGFELLOW USA, 1807–1882

from **Song of Hiawatha**

> And the Jossakeeds, the Prophets,
> The Wabenos, the Magicians,
> And the Medicine-men, the Medas,
> Painted upon bark and deer-skin
> Figures for the songs they chanted,
> For each song a separate symbol,
> Figures mystical and awful,
> Figures strange and brightly colored;
> And each figure had its meaning,
> Each some magic song suggested.

Simón Bolívar Venezuela, 1783–1830

ON THE CHIMBORAZO: MY DELIRIUM

Covered in Iris's cloak, I came from where the vast Orinoco feeds the God of waters. I had visited the lurid fonts of the Amazon and was eager to climb the watchtower of the Universe. I tracked La Condamine's and Humboldt's footsteps. Fearlessly, I trailed them: nothing stopped me. I reached the glacial zone and ether deterred my breath.

No human foot had stepped on that diamantine crown placed by Eternity's own hands on the lofty temples of the ruler of the Andes. I said to myself: this cloak of Iris, my flag, has crossed infernal regions, sailed rivers and seas, climbed over the Andes' massive shoulders: Earth has flattened out beneath Colombia's feet and Time has not deterred the steps of liberty. If the luster of Iris's bow has humiliated Bellona, couldn't I climb on the grizzled locks of Earth's giant? I will! and enraptured by the rage of a spirit unknown to me—but whom I judged divine—I out-raced Humboldt's tracks, tarnishing the everlasting crystals that surround Chimborazo.

I arrive as if driven by the spirit who excited me and I fade when my head taps the tip of the firmament: the threshold of the abyss under my feet.

A hectic delirium seizes my mind. I feel myself set ablaze by a fire—alien and grander—: it was Colombia's God possessing me.

Suddenly Time appears before me, under the image of an old man holding the rags of eras past—grim, crooked, bald, wizened, sickle in hand…

"—I am the founder of the ages—he said—I am the arcane mystery of fame and concealment. My mother was Eternity, and Infinity marks the boundaries of my empire. There is no grave for me: I'm stronger than Death. I see the past, I see the future, and the present passes through my hands.

"Why do you persist in vanity—babe or greybeard, hero or simple man? Do you think your Universe means anything? That rising above an atom of creation is to thrive? Do you think those instants you call centuries can be a measure for my mysteries? Do you imagine you have seen the Holy Truth? Do you foolishly presume your actions worth anything before me? All this is tinier than a spot beside Infinity, my brother."

Overwhelmed by a sacred horror, I replied:

"—O Time! How does a simple mortal, who has risen so high, avoid fading away and dying? I have surpassed the fate of all, have risen over everyone. I master the Earth under my soles and with my hands I reach for the Eternal; as I walk, I feel hell's chambers burning near me, stars that dazzle, and I glance at endless suns. Impassive, I measure the space enclosing matter and can read your face there, both the Past and the fore-taste of Destiny."

He said to me: "Watch and learn. Keep in mind what you have seen. Draw for your fellow men the depiction of the physical Universe, the moral Universe. Do not conceal any secret that the heavens have revealed to you: tell men the truth."

The spirit faded.

Enthralled, stiffened—so to speak—a long time I lay lifeless stretched out over that immense diamond that was my bed. Finally, the thundering voice of Colombia cries out to me. I resurrect. I sit up and with my own hands I unseal my heavy eyelids: I'm a man again and I write my delirium.

Translated from Spanish by Javier Taboada

COMMENTARY

(1) "Mi delirio sobre el Chimborazo" is the only poetical prose text by the South American *Libertador*, Simón Bolívar. Because of its posthumous publication (& because there's no direct proof that he ever climbed Mount Chimborazo, the highest peak in South America), some scholars doubt its veracity. Whether he ascended the peak or not, the text works as a revelation of Bolívar's awareness of his own destiny & shows us how he assumed his task—the liberation of Spanish America—to ultimately create a single unified nation: "The Great Columbia." In the ascent, real or imagined, Bolívar was inspired by German naturalist Alexander von Humboldt, who published an account of his own experiences on his ascent of Chimborazo, which Bolívar intended to follow—"in von Humboldt's footsteps."

(2) In any case, the figure of Bolívar became the symbol of Latin American striving for liberty everywhere. Or as Pablo Neruda had it, when he was involved in the Spanish Civil War:

I came upon Bolívar, one long morning,
in Madrid, at the entrance to the Fifth Regiment.
Father, I said to him, are you, or are you not, or who are you?
And, looking at the Mountain Barracks, he said:
"I awake every hundred years when the people awake."

"A Song for Bolívar," translated from Spanish by Donald D. Walsh

AMERICA AS A WOMAN

A Mini Gallery

Sor Juana Inés de la Cruz Mexico, 1648–1695

from *A LOA TO DIVINE NARCISSUS*

Scene Three

RELIGION: Surrender, proud Occident!
[Spanish Woman]

OCCIDENT: Now I must yield
[Aztec Man]   to your force,
    not your reason.

ZEAL: Die, insolent America!
[Conquistador]

RELIGION: Wait, don't put her to death,
    I need her alive!

ZEAL: How can you defend her,
    when you are the one offended?

RELIGION: Yes, the conquest of America
    is due to your bravery,
    but my piety
    will save her life.
    Your role was to conquer
    by force; mine to subdue her
    by reason and gentle persuasion.

ZEAL: After you have seen the perverse
    blind desecration
    of your cult, is it not
    better for them all to die?

RELIGION: Restrain your justice,
    Zeal. Do not put them to death!
    My kind disposition
    does not want their death,
    but that they convert and live.

AMERICA: If your request for my life
[Native Woman] and display of compassion,
               is because you expect
               to conquer me, proud one,
               as once with physical,
               now with intellectual arms,
               you deceive yourself.
               As a captive, I mourn
               my lost freedom, yet my free will
               with still greater liberty
               will adore my gods!

OCCIDENT: I have already said force of arms
               obliges me to surrender to you.
               But for the rest, it is clear
               that neither force nor violence
               can impede the will
               in its free operation.
               So although I groan as a captive,
               you cannot prevent me
               from saying in my heart
               I worship the great God of the Seeds!

Translated from Spanish by Pamela Kirk Rappaport

COMMENTARY

Written for the feast of Corpus Christi, ca. 1689, & later performed & published in far-off Madrid, the *loa* (= "praise") was prelude to a longer allegory, *The Divine Narcissus*, focused on a clash between two Indigenous figures—the female America & the Aztec male Occident—with Religion & Zeal as the ecclesiastical & military overlords of the ongoing colonization. What is striking here is not so much that the longer work would end in a modified version of Catholic orthodoxy, but that Sor Juana's projection of both America & Occident was firmly rooted in a defiant pre-American & "pagan" theodicy.

N.B. The "God of the Seeds" here may relate to Huitzilopochtli, Aztec god of war & flowers.

For more on Sor Juana, see "A First Gallery."

Phillis Wheatley   Gambia, Africa / USA, ca. 1753–1784

from **ENCLOSURE**

Addressed to His Excellency George Washington

Celestial choir! enthron'd in realms of light,
Columbia's scenes of glorious toils I write.
While freedom's cause her anxious breast alarms,
She flashes dreadful in refulgent arms.
See mother earth her offspring's fate bemoan,
And nations gaze at scenes before unknown!
See the bright beams of heaven's revolving light
Involved in sorrows and the veil of night!
The Goddess comes, she moves divinely fair,
Olive and laurel binds Her golden hair:
Wherever shines this native of the skies,
Unnumber'd charms and recent graces rise.

COMMENTARY

"Phillis Wheatley was kidnapped near her African home at the age of seven or eight and was brought aboard a slave ship to Boston, where John Wheatley, a local tailor, purchased her as a personal servant for his wife, Susanna. Tutored in the Scriptures and ancient classics by her mistress, Wheatley began writing poetry about the age of thirteen, and in 1773 John Wheatley's son, Nathaniel, took her to London, where later that year a volume of her poems was published under the title *Poems on Various Subjects, Religious and Moral.* G[eorge] W[ashington] apparently met her at his headquarters in Cambridge sometime in March 1776" (from the National Archives, through its National Historical Publications and Records Commission and the University of Virginia).

Jerome Rothenberg & George Quasha

AMERICA AS WOMAN

In *In the American Grain,* William Carlos Williams writes: "One is forced on the conception of the New World as a woman." In that form he has her speaking to De Soto, he who would soon be buried in her waters, "this solitary sperm... into the liquid, the formless, the insatiable belly of sleep, down among the fishes." She has told him while alive to

> ... *ride upon the belly of the waters, building your boats to carry all across. Calculate for the current; the boats move with a force not their own, up and down, sliding upon that female who communicates to them, across all else, herself. And still there is that which you have not sounded, under the boats, under the adventure—giving to all things the current, the wave, the onwash of my passion. So cross and have done with it you are safe—and I am desolate... Follow me—if you can. Follow me, Señor, this is your country. I give it to you. Take it.*

We have encountered that woman-presence before—a nearly universal myth of "Mother Earth," or of the land, that which we wrench from Earth, with pleasure at first, then in a dream of losses endlessly repeated. She is Blake's Jerusalem (and his Oothoon-Enitharmon, as America herself): the one the Jews called the Shekhina, the Gnostics called Sophia, the Tantrists called Goddess-of-Wisdom-Whose-Substance-Is-Desire and in her terrifying aspect, Kali. The First Nations of America knew her also, as the mother sometimes or grandmother, sometimes as the woman on a journey like the one for whom the mound in Upper Michigan was called Where-she-with-the-full-belly-turned-over.

In the story of American poetry she turns up often. She is earth or god, wisdom or muse—or that woman always one town ahead of our pursuit, say, or like the poor-old-soul of Bukka White's blues, singing

> I ain't got nobody
> To take me to this train
> Mmmmmmmmmmmmmmmmmmmmmm
> Mmmmmmmmmmm mm mmmm

as real in her desolation as our America in hers. Wrote Edgar Allan Poe, "The death, then, of a beautiful woman is, unquestionably, the most poetical topic in the world."

Originally published in J. Rothenberg & G. Quasha, America a Prophecy, *1973*

Smohalla Nez Perce / USA, 1815?–1907

THE MOTHER

My young men shall never work, men who work cannot dream; and wisdom comes to us in dreams.

You ask me to plow the ground. Shall I take a knife and tear my mother's breast? Then when I die she will not take me to her bosom to rest.

You ask me to dig for stone. Shall I dig under her skin for her bones? Then when I die I cannot enter her body to be born again.

You ask me to cut grass and make hay and sell it and be rich like white men. But how dare I cut off my mother's hair.

It is a bad law, and my people cannot obey it. I want my people to stay with me here. All the dead men will come to life again. We must wait here in the house of our fathers and be ready to meet them in the body of our mothers.

COMMENTARY

Smohalla was the founder of a nineteenth-century Dreamer religion among the Nez Perce, abandoning Christianity in favor of revived Indigenous concepts of a benevolent earth-mother & of the dream vision as the major vehicle for communication with her powers.

José Eustasio Rivera Colombia, 1888–1928

from *THE VORTEX*

Mapiripana is the high priestess of lush, the guardian of ponds and springs. She makes her habitation in the very kidneys of the rainforest, busily squeezing drops from its little puffs of mist, collecting every dew drop that condenses on its mossy banks, directing each trickling rivulet to engross its crystalline streams and, ultimately, its awesome rivers. Thanks to Mapiripana, the Orinoco and the Amazon have ten thousand tributaries.

The Indians fear her, and she tolerates their activities only when they don't disturb the peace of the forest. Natives who offend her find no game to hunt. The disappointed hunters know that she has frightened away the game when they notice the mark of her single foot in the moist clay. Skilled trackers, they recognize her distinctive footprint not only because no others appear nearby but also because the impression shows that she always walked backward. She always carries an epiphyte in her hands, too. And she was the first person ever to fan herself with a palm frond. You can hear her crying in the undergrowth at night, except during the full moon, when she navigates the rivers in a giant tortoise shell pulled by pink river dolphins whose fins sway in time with her singing.

Long ago, an evil missionary came to these latitudes, a man wearing an ecclesiastical habit, who abused palm wine and Indian girls. Believing himself sent by heaven to destroy superstition, he ambushed Mapiripana one night on the riverbank. His plan was to tie her up with his rope belt and burn her alive, like a witch. Somewhere, not far away, possibly on this sandy beach where you are sitting now, he saw Mapiripana gathering turtle eggs. She appeared, by the light of the full moon, like a young widow dressed in a gown of spider's web. The lustful missionary went after her, but an echo alone responded, luring him deeper into the jungle, and finally into a cave, where Mapiripana imprisoned him for many years.

To punish him for the sin of concupiscence, she sucked on his lips until he begged her to stop. The missionary was losing all his blood, and he closed his eyes in order not to see her face, which had become as hairy as an orangutan's. Within a few months she had become pregnant, and she gave birth to an owl and a vampire bat. Aghast at having conceived such beings, the missionary escaped from the cave, pursued by his own abominable children. Whenever he stopped to rest, exhausted, the vampire bat sucked his blood and the owl illuminated the scene with the green flow of its horrible eyes.

Translated from Spanish by John Charles Chasteen

COMMENTARY

The selected fragment shows Rivera's vision of the natural world. The jungle manifests itself with all its power: a feral place where human & natural relationships are conditioned by brutality, desecration & revenge. The metamorphosis of the environment into horrid creatures comes from irresponsible human behavior that threatens the equilibrium of the jungle. The apparition of Mapiripana—a goddess feared by native peoples—preserves this equilibrium; when broken, she will take revenge, leaving a trail of death. Through Mapiripana, then, Rivera displays ecocritical views about the devastation of the natural environment.

Trefossa (Henri Frans de Ziel)

Suriname, 1916–1975

COPENHAGEN

what is this by the sea?
see-see!
Watramama is that you sitting
on that stone?

Watramama I know you,
sure I do.
Watramama
my-my…

your golden comb
where has it gone?
my dearest dear tell me then
me alone.

Watramama you look at me
so calmly…
aha, I know his home:
Sranan!

Translated from Sranan (Sranantongo) by Virginie M. Kortekaas

COMMENTARY

"The Watramama lived in the rivers, from whence she often appeared before the people, ordering them to bring her sacrifices, such as the blood of a white hen. If such persons did not obey, she quickly would bring about their death, or the death of one or more of their family members.... In the course of the nineteenth century, the picture of this horrific goddess changed into a more lovely one, according to the descriptions of some slaves, who envisioned her 'as a beautiful [Amer]Indian woman with a child wreathed with water-lilies, humming-birds fluttering around her, their feathers glittering in the setting sun like gem stones'" (Gert Oostinde & Alex van Stipriaan, in *Slave Cultures and the Cultures of Slavery*, ed. Stephan Palmié).

Aída Cartagena-Portalatín

Dominican Republic, 1918–1994

from **YANIA TIERRA**

WITH this discourse I say love
A shared involvement
I say Man

      The voice reaches out across the distance
It grows / it passes through the forests
Rivers clogged with blood

WITH THESE SAME WORDS I SAY GOD
I FIND IT ALL COMPLETE

Through the streets and plazas
Goodness and love
Move across the Lofty Mountains
The rivers begin again to stir
              waters and palm trees
Oh! Yania Patria
Aleluya!

YANIA awake / Yania asleep /
They walk with her / They recognize the pounding of boots
They breathe with their expression fixed
Livid
Glassy
On the high seas they can see the nets used to fish for Islands

Exhausted they shift the weight of the load

Never bored with their task

They don't understand / Many don't want to understand it
They split their guts / Burst out laughing
They walk with her but never reach the end
Yania gold / Yania silver / Yania bauxite
Yania cacao / Yania sugar / Yania coffee

WHO cuts from the branch the most
                                treasured flower?
The women
Who place on the breast of the liberators
                                Malabar Jasmine?
The women
Who fall to their knees when
                                lead shatters?
The women
Who inconsolable await the
                exchange of gunfire?
The women
Who look for Doves of Peace in
                                an open sky?
The women

THEY COME / stories come that look deformed
Attached to the skin with pins
Sounds
Smells
Tears
The taste of pure lead
Stories come like births / They come
With an aroma of sour placenta
They keep coming from the North / The pirates loot
Riches from coffee / sugar / cacao
gold / silver / nickel / bauxite

THE CRIPPLE CRIES WITH JOY AND SORROW /
INDIAN WOMEN / BLACK WOMEN / WHITE WOMEN /
MESTIZA WOMEN / MULATTA WOMEN / JUSTICE AND
LOVE LOVE THEM WITH RESPECT COME!

                Come on! Women!
                Come on! Women!

        Release the birds of hope!
                Come on! Women!
                        Release the Doves!

Translated from Spanish by M.J. Fenwick & Rosabelle White

IT IS TRUE / I've lost the old rhyming game / I wish to speak in another way... the freedom of everyday / language / That is heard across your body / Yania Tierra (A.C-P.)

(1) Forsaking both the tone & language of her earlier, more well-known poems, Aída Cartagena-Portalatín shifted to a wider-ranging poetry, closer to the US Objectivists and the *exteriorismo* proposed by Ernesto Cardenal. The outcome was her major project, her own epic: *Yania Tierra, poema-documento*. This poem-documentary aims to rediscover & reassess the role of Dominican women—& by extension all American women—in historical terms. For this Cartagena-Portalatín employed diverse materials & genres—art, poetry, politics, folk songs, topography, myths—fusing them with her own voice. In *Yania Tierra*, the historical revisions start from 1492 & carry forward to the 1980s, focusing on the women deleted from Dominican history. *Yania Tierra* thus becomes a triumph of rewriting.

It is worth noting, too, that *Yania* is an alternative name for the Dominican Republic and by extension all of the Americas.

(2) At the time of her death, in 1994, Cartagena-Portalatín left unfinished another epic work, "The Antechamber of the History of America," which focused on the travels to our hemisphere before Columbus's arrival.

Plurinational State of Bolivia

from **LAW OF THE RIGHTS OF MOTHER EARTH**

Article 3. (MOTHER EARTH). Mother Earth is a dynamic living system comprising an indivisible community of all living systems and living organisms, interrelated, interdependent and complementary, which share a common destiny. Mother Earth is considered sacred, from the world-views of nations and peasant indigenous peoples.

Article 4. (LIVING SYSTEMS). Living systems are complex and dynamic communities of plants, animals, microorganisms and other beings and their environment, where human communities and the rest of nature interact as a functional unit under the influence of climatic, physiographic, and geological factors, as well as production practices, Bolivian cultural diversity, and the worldviews of nations, original indigenous peoples, and intercultural and Afro-Bolivian communities.

Article 7. (RIGHTS OF MOTHER EARTH). Mother Earth has the following rights:

1. To life: The right to maintain the integrity of living systems and natural processes that sustain them, and capacities and conditions for regeneration.

2. To the diversity of life: The right to preservation of differentiation and variety of beings that make up Mother Earth, without being genetically altered or structurally modified in an artificial way, so that their existence, functioning or future potential would be threatened.

3. To water: The right to preserve the functionality of the water cycle, its existence in the quantity and quality needed to sustain living systems, and its protection from pollution for the reproduction of the life of Mother Earth and all its components.

4. To clean air: The right to preserve the quality and composition of air for sustaining living systems and its protection from pollution, for the reproduction of the life of Mother Earth and all its components.

5. To equilibrium: The right to maintenance or restoration of the interrelationship, interdependence, complementarity and functionality of the components of Mother Earth in a balanced way for the continuation of their cycles and reproduction of their vital processes.

6. To restoration: The right to timely and effective restoration of living systems affected by human activities directly or indirectly.

7. To pollution-free living: The right to the preservation of any of Mother Earth's components from contamination, as well as from toxic and radioactive waste generated by human activities.

COMMENTARY

In December 2010, in response to an understanding of the impacts of climate change on the nation's economic & community health, the national congress of Bolivia voted to support an act to protect the well-being of its citizens by protecting the natural world—its resources, sustainability, & value—as essential to the common good. Based on the profound spiritual connection to Mother Earth that has long guided indigenous peoples throughout the two American continents, this may now be read as a major act of *ecopoesis* (adapted from an article in *World Ocean Forum*, July 25, 2019).

Given in the Assembly Hall of the Plurinational Legislative Assembly of Bolivia, on December 7, 2010.

Walt Whitman USA, 1819–1892

from **STARTING FROM PAUMANOK**

Starting from fish-shape Paumanok where I was born,
Well-begotten, and rais'd by a perfect mother,
After roaming many lands, lover of populous pavements,
Dweller in Mannahatta my city, or on southern savannas,
Or a soldier camp'd or carrying my knapsack and gun, or a miner in California,
Or rude in my home in Dakota's woods, my diet meat, my drink from the
    spring,
Or withdrawn to muse and meditate in some deep recess,
Far from the clank of crowds intervals passing rapt and happy,
Aware of the fresh free giver the flowing Missouri, aware of mighty Niagara,
Aware of the buffalo herds grazing the plains, the hirsute and strong-breasted
    bull,
Of earth, rocks, Fifth-month flowers experienced, stars, rain, snow, my amaze,
Having studied the mocking-bird's tones and the flight of the mountain-hawk,
And heard at dawn the unrivall'd one, the hermit thrush from the swamp-cedars,
Solitary, singing in the West, I strike up for a New World.

.....

On my way a moment I pause;
Here for you! and here for America!
Still the Present I raise aloft—Still the Future of The States I harbinge, glad and
    sublime;
And for the Past, I pronounce what the air holds of the red aborigines.

The red aborigines!
Leaving natural breaths, sounds of rain and winds, calls as of birds and animals
    in the woods, syllabled to us for names;
Okonee, Koosa, Ottawa, Monongahela, Sauk, Natchez, Chattahoochee,
    Kaqueta, Oronoco, Wabash, Miami, Saginaw, Chippewa, Oshkosh,
    Walla-Walla;
Leaving such to The States, they melt, they depart, charging the water and the
    land with names.

O expanding and swift! O henceforth,
Elements, breeds, adjustments, turbulent, quick, and audacious;
A world primal again—Vistas of glory, incessant and branching;
A new race, dominating previous ones, and grander far—with new contests,
New politics, new literatures and religions, new inventions and arts.

These! my voice announcing—I will sleep no more, but arise;
You oceans that have been calm within me! how I feel you, fathomless,
stirring, preparing unprecedented waves and storms.

COMMENTARY

At play here is Walt Whitman's quest for a new American poetry and language & for a new/old poetry of names absorbing the Indian past & present, above, in a gesture both imperialist & disarmingly inclusive. Of that vaunted program, as it came to him, he wrote: "The Americans of all nations at any time upon the earth, have probably the fullest poetical nature. The United States themselves are essentially the greatest poem. In the history of the earth hitherto the largest and most stirring appear tame and orderly to their ampler largeness and stir" (from the preface to *Leaves of Grass*). The relevance here to *all* the Americas might also be considered, as it was by others, both north & south, native & invasive.

For more on Whitman, see "A First Gallery" & elsewhere.

Pedro Mir   Dominican Republic, 1913–2000

from *COUNTERSONG TO WALT WHITMAN*

Why did you want to listen to a poet?
I am speaking to one and all.
To those of you who came to isolate him from his people,
to separate him from his blood and his land,
to flood his road.
Those of you who drafted him into the army.
The ones who defiled his luminous beard and put a gun
on his shoulders that were loaded with maidens and pioneers.
Those of you who do not want Walt Whitman, the democrat,
but another Whitman, atomic and savage.
The ones who want to outfit him with boots
to crush the heads of nations.
To grind into blood the temples of little girls.
To smash into atoms the old man's flesh.
The ones who take the tongue of Walt Whitman
for a sign of spraying bullets,
for a flag of fire.

No, Walt Whitman, here are the poets of today
aroused to justify you!
Poets to come!... Arouse! for you must justify me.
Here we are, Walt Whitman, to justify you.
Here we are
         for your sake
                demanding peace.
The peace you needed
to drive the world with your song.
Here we are
         saving your hills of Vermont,
your woods of Maine, the sap and fragrance of your land,
your spurred rowdies, your smiling maidens,
your country boys walking to creeks.
Saving them, Walt Whitman, from the tycoons
who take your language for the language of war.
No, Walt Whitman, here are the poets of today,
the workers of today, the pioneers of today, the peasants
of today,
         firm and roused to justify you!
O Walt Whitman of aroused beard!
Here we are without beards,
without arms, without ears,
without any strength in our lips,
spied on,
red and persecuted,
full of eyes
wide open throughout the islands,
full of courage, of knots of pride
untied through all the nations,
with your sign and your language, Walt Whitman,
here we are
         standing up
                to justify you,
our constant companion
of Manhattan!

Translated from Spanish by Jonathan Cohen

A note by Jean Franco qua foreword: "Mir's poem is both a celebration of Whitman and an assertion of difference—a celebration of the poet of the common people and a denunciation of the 'manifest destiny' of the nation that Whitman had helped to build. Whitman had brought together all the peoples of the United States into one choral and prophetic voice, *orotund, sweeping and final*, and now it is the turn of people from outside those borders, the anonymous, marginalized inhabitant of Quisqueya, the Caribbean island which is now divided between the Dominican Republic and Haiti. Thus Mir both follows Whitman and diverges. He follows Whitman across a pristine America and identifies with its founding spirit, even with the Whitmanian *I* which, like a Leibnitzian monad, is *the revolving of all mirrors / around a single image*.... But here the two poets must diverge. Something has come between pure self-affirmation and fulfillment and that something is money, the simulacrum that replaces reality and which alienates human beings from the self. Mir here comes closest to Ernesto Cardenal's vision of a fallen humanity as he traces the degeneration of the Whitmanian *I* and its resurrection as imperial egoism that has commodified Latin America and deprived the nations of the continent of their autonomy. Whitman's spirit can only be redeemed by a new pronoun, the *we* of all those nations and peoples that have been *othered*."

Charles Olson USA, 1910–1970

MAXIMUS TO GLOUCESTER, LETTER 27 [WITHHELD]

I come back to the geography of it,
the land falling off to the left
where my father shot his scabby golf
and the rest of us played baseball
into the summer darkness until no flies
could be seen and we came home
to our various piazzas where the women
buzzed

To the left the land fell to the city,
to the right, it fell to the sea

I was so young my first memory
is of a tent spread to feed lobsters
to Rexall conventioneers, and my father,

a man for kicks, came out of the tent roaring
with a bread-knife in his teeth to take care of
the druggist they'd told him had made a pass at
my mother, she laughing, so sure, as round
as her face, Hines pink and apple,
under one of those frame hats women then

This, is no bare incoming
of novel abstract form, this

is no welter or the forms
of those events, this,
Greeks, is the stopping
of the battle

      It is the imposing
of all those antecedent predecessions, the precessions

of me, the generation of those facts
which are my words, it is coming

from all that I no longer am,
yet am, the slow westward motion of

more than I am

There is no strict personal order

for my inheritance.

        No Greek will be able

to discriminate my body.

        An American

is a complex of occasions,

themselves a geometry

of spatial nature.

      I have this sense,

that I am one

with my skin

     Plus this—plus this:

that forever the geography

which leans in

on me I compell

backwards I compell Gloucester

to yield, to

change

     Polis

is this

A yearning here to reconceive his America, both temporally & spatially (its history & its geography), & in doing so to place himself as Maximus, a voice of authority addressing spoken words & written letters (= poems) to his native city (= Gloucester, Mass. = *polis*). Within a text written as a series of poems, documents, letters, & fragments, the central figure of Olson's epic *Maximus* is derived (at least in name) from a little-known second-century philosopher, Maximus of Tyre, but the implications of bigness/greatness the name carries are a match for Olson's own physical size & longed-for scope. Following from his sense of "history [as] the new localism," the work's setting is Olson's home city / fishing port, but its roots go off in all directions, in both space & time.

For more on Olson, see "A Third Gallery" & elsewhere.

José Martí   Cuba, 1853–1895

from **OUR AMERICA**

The conceited villager believes the entire world to be his village. Provided that he can be mayor, humiliate the rival who stole his sweetheart, or add to the savings in his strongbox, he considers the universal order good, unaware of those giants with seven-league boots who can crush him underfoot, or of the strife in the heavens between comets that go through the air asleep, gulping down worlds. What remains of the village in America must rouse itself. These are not the times for sleeping in a nightcap, but with weapons for a pillow, like the warriors of Juan de Castellanos: weapons of the mind, which conquer all others. Barricades of ideas are worth more than barricades of stones.

There is no prow that can cut through a cloudbank of ideas. A powerful idea, waved before the world at the proper time, can stop a squadron of iron-clad ships, like the mystical flag of the Last Judgment. Nations that do not know one another should quickly become acquainted, as men who are to fight a common enemy. Those who shake their fists, like jealous brothers coveting the same tract of land, or like the modest cottager who envies the esquire his mansion, should clasp hands and become one. Those who use the authority of a criminal tradition to lop off the hands of their defeated brother with a sword stained with his own blood, ought to return the lands to the brother already punished sufficiently, if they do not want the people to call them robbers. The honest man does not absolve himself of debts of honor with money, at so much a slap. We can no longer be a people of leaves, living in the air, our foliage heavy with blooms and crackling or humming at the whim of the sun's caress, or buffeted and tossed by the storms. The trees must form ranks to keep the giant with seven-league boots from passing! It is the time of mobilization, of marching together, and we must go forward in close ranks, like silver in the veins of the Andes.

Only those born prematurely are lacking in courage. Those without faith in their country are seven-month weaklings. Because they have not courage, they deny it to the others. Their puny arms—arms with bracelets and hands with painted nails, arms of Paris or Madrid—can hardly reach the bottom limb, and they claim the tall tree to be unclimbable. The ships should be loaded with those harmful insects that gnaw at the bone of the country that nourishes them. If they are Parisians or from Madrid, let them go to the Prado, to boast around, or to Tortoni's, in high hats. Those carpenter's sons who are ashamed that their fathers are carpenters! Those born in America who are ashamed of the mother that reared them, because she wears an Indian apron, and who disown their sick mothers, the scoundrels, abandoning her on her sickbed! Then who is a real man? He who stays with his mother and nurses her in her illness, or he who puts her to work out of sight, and lives at her expense on decadent lands, sporting fancy neckties, cursing the womb that carried him, displaying the sign of the traitor on the back of his paper frockcoat? These sons of our America, which will be saved by its Indians in blood and is growing better; these deserters who take up arms in the army of a North America that drowns its Indians in blood and is growing worse! These delicate creatures who are men but are unwilling to do men's work! The Washington who made this land for them, did he not go to live with the English, at a time when he saw them fighting against his own country. These unbelievable of honor who drag the honor over foreign soil like their counterparts in the French Revolution with their dancing, their affectations, their drawling speech!

For in what lands can men take more pride than in our long-suffering American republics, raised up among the silent Indian masses by the bleeding arms of a hundred apostles, to the sound of battle between the book and processional candle? Never in history have such advanced and united nations been forged in so short a time from such disorganized elements. The presumptuous man feels that the earth was made to serve as his pedestal, because he happens to have a facile pen or colorful speech, and he accuses his native land of being worthless and beyond redemption because its virgin jungles fail to provide him with a constant means of travelling over the world, driving Persian ponies and lavishing champagne like a tycoon.

Translator unknown

COMMENTARY

Written & published in 1891, while Martí was resident in New York City, the idea of his Spanish "America" extends both geographically/politically & backward & forward in time.

For more on Martí, see poems in "A Second Gallery."

Aimé Césaire Martinique, 1913–2008

from *NOTEBOOK OF A RETURN TO THE NATIVE LAND*

Look, now I am only a man (no degradation, no spit perturbs him)
now I am only a man who accepts emptied of anger
(nothing left in his heart but immense love)
I accept ...I accept ...totally, without reservation ...
my race that no ablution of hyssop mixed with lilies could purify
my race pitted with blemishes

my race ripe grapes for drunken feet
my queen of spittle and leprosy
my queen of whips and scrofula
my queen of squama and chloasma
(oh those queens I once loved in the remote gardens of spring against the
     illumination of all the candles of the chestnut trees!).
I accept. I accept.
and the flogged nigger saying "Forgive me master"
and the twenty-nine legal blows of the whip
and the four-foot-high prison cell
and the spiked carcan
and the hamstringing of my runaway audacity
and the fleur de lys flowing from the red iron into the fat of my shoulder
and Monsieur VAULTIER MAYENCOURT'S kennel where I barked
six poodle months
and Monsieur BRAFIN
and Monsieur de FOURNIOL
and Monsieur de la MAHAUDIERE
and the yaws
the mastiff
the suicide
the promiscuity
the bootkin
the shackles
the rack
the cippus
the headscrew

. . . . .

And my special geography too; the world map made for my own use, not
tinted with the arbitrary colors of scholars, but with the geometry of my
spilled blood

and the determination of my biology not a prisoner to a facial angle, to a
type of hair, to a well-flattened nose, to a clearly melanian coloring, and
negritude, no longer a cephalic index, gold plasma, or soma, but measured by the compass of suffering

and the Negro every day more base, more cowardly, more sterile, less
profound, more spilled out of himself, more separated from himself, more
wily with himself, less immediate to himself

I accept, I accept it all

and far from the palatial sea that foams under the suppurating syzygy of blisters, the body of my country miraculously laid in the despair of my arms, its bones shattered and in its veins the blood hesitating like a drop of vegetal milk at the injured point of a bulb

Suddenly now strength and life assail me like a bull and I revive ONAN who entrusted his sperm to the fecund earth and the water of life circumvents the papilla of the morne, and now all the veins and veinlets are bustling with new blood and the enormous breathing lung of cyclones and the fire hoarded in volcanoes and the gigantic seismic pulse that now beats the measure of a living body in my firm embrace.

And we are standing now, my country and I, hair in the wind, my hand puny in its enormous fist and the strength is not in us, but above us, in a voice that drills the night and the hearing like the penetrance of an apocalyptic wasp. And the voice proclaims that for centuries Europe has force-fed us with lies and bloated us with pestilence,

for it is not true that the work of man is done
that we have no business being in the world
that we parasite the world
that it is enough for us to heel to the world
whereas the work of man has only begun
and man still must overcome all the interdictions wedged in the recesses
of his fervor
and no race has a monopoly on beauty, on intelligence, on strength
and there is room for everyone at the convocation of conquest and we
know now that the sun turns around our earth lighting the parcel designated by our will alone and that every star falls from sky to earth at our
omnipotent command.

I now see the meaning of this ordeal: my country is the "lance of night" of my Bambara ancestors. It shrinks and its tip desperately retreats toward the haft when it is sprinkled with chicken blood and it states that its temperament requires the blood of man, his fat, his liver, his heart, not chicken blood.

And I seek for my country not date hearts, but men's hearts which in order to enter the silver cities through the great trapezoidal gate beat with virile blood, and as my eyes sweep my kilometers of paternal earth I number its sores almost joyfully and I pile one on top of another like rare species, and my total is ever lengthened by unexpected mintings of baseness.

And there are those who will never get over not being made in the likeness of God but of the devil, those who believe that being a nigger is like being a second-class clerk: waiting for a better deal and upward mobility; those who bang the chamade before themselves, those who live in a corner of their own deep pit; those who drape themselves in proud pseudomorphosis; those who say to Europe: "You see I *can* bow and scrape, like you I pay my respects, in short I am not different from you; pay no attention to my black skin: the sun scorched me."

And there is the nigger pimp, the nigger askari, and all the zebras shaking themselves in various ways to get rid of their stripes in a dew of fresh milk. And in the midst of all that I say hurray! my grandfather dies, I say hurray the old negritude progressively cadavers itself.

No bones about it: he was a good nigger. The Whites say it was a good nigger, a really good nigger, massa's good ole darky.

I say hurray!

He was a good nigger indeed
poverty had wounded his chest and back and they had stuffed into his poor brain that a fatality no one could collar weighed on him; that he had no control over his own destiny; that an evil Lord had for all eternity inscribed Thou Shall Not in his pelvic constitution; that he must be a good nigger; must honestly put up with being a good nigger; must sincerely believe in his worthlessness, without any perverse curiosity to verify the fatidic hieroglyphs.

He was a very good nigger

And it never occurred to him that he could hoe, dig, cut anything, anything else really than insipid cane.

He was a very good nigger.

And they threw stones at him, chunks of scrap iron, shards of bottles, but neither these stones, nor this scrap iron, nor these bottles . . .
O peaceful years of God on this terraqueous clod!

And the whip argued with the bombilation of the flies over the sugary dew of our sores

I say hurray! The old negritude progressively cadavers itself
the horizon breaks, recoils and expands
and through the shredding of clouds the flashing of a sign

the slave ship cracks from one end to the other ...Its belly convulses and resounds... The ghastly tapeworm of its cargo gnaws the fetid guts of the strange suckling of the sea!

Translated from French by Clayton Eshleman & Annette Smith

COMMENTARY

(1) Written after years as a student in Paris & the founding there of the internationally influential African & Antillean Negritude movement, Césaire's return to his native Martinique both localized the project & extended its reach as a poetry & poetics still in progress. So, he writes later: "I would like to say that everyone has his own Negritude.... We slowly came to the idea of a sort of Black civilization spread throughout the world. And I have come to the realization that there was a 'Negro situation' that existed in different geographical areas, that Africa was also my country. There was the African continent, the Antilles, Haiti; there were Martinicans and Brazilian Negroes, etc. That's what Negritude meant to me" (*Discourse on Colonialism*, 1950, 1955, trans. Joan Pinkham).

(2) And Césaire further: "I want to emphasize very strongly that while using as a point of departure the elements that French literature gave me, at the same time I have always striven to create a new language, one capable of communicating the African heritage. In other words, for me French was a tool that I wanted to use in developing a new means of expression. I wanted to create an Antillean French, a Black French that, while still being French, had a Black character" (René Depestre, interview with Aimé Césaire, trans. Maro Riofrancos).

For more on Césaire, see his poems in "A Third Gallery."

Pablo de Rokha   Chile, 1894–1968

from **YANKEELAND**

Chicago

The stupid, monotonous, rheumatic fumes, the horizontal, industrial fumes, the horizontal fumes that come from the factories, that walk over the roofs attaching themselves to malignant beasts of the dusk, the chimneys, the unanimous chimneys smoke their enormous cigars *interminably* and Chicago thunders, thunders, thunders like one hundred trains left to tumble from *the heights*, from *the heights* of the mountains down into the modest, common valleys, down into the world, into human things; public plazas and women, idealistic trees, palaces, markets, asylums and inmates, sanatoriums and laws, blonde, blonde schoolgirls, businesses, the sun, the moon, the earth, the abstract heavens smell of swine, smell of swine, smell of swine, and Chicago, Chicago, the great, painful, ironic, plutocratic, industrial city, grunts just like the plebeian swine:... oink!... oink!... oink!...

*
* *

Thermometer, chronometer, barometer of the twentieth century, Yankeeland sums up the psychology, the trajectory, the form, the diagnosis of the actual instant of the epoch, TODAY'S sickness; and like this, like this, it sings on *its* skyscrapers, on *its* global airlines, on *its* ocean liners, in *its* palaces, on *its* underground, *aerial*, underground railways, on *its* travelling zeppelins, travelling, travelling like *travelling* swallows, on *its* trucks, on *its* tractors, in *its* cars, on *its* mountain statues, on *its* mountain statues the nocturnal, emphatic hymns, the square, practical, human feats, the TREMENDOUS moan in which *each* voice is an ocean, *each* voice, the epic about bells, bells and tombs, agonies getting darker, agonies about *our* DELUSIONS OF GRANDEUR; and like this it cries *with laughter* in its financial, bankable loves, in *its* blues, contradictory and useless bunches of gloomy voices, in *its* cubic, mercantile romanticisms, *our* yellow, sickly ideology of Autumn; and like this, like this, like this it howls, it howls in *its* complete, total illusion, black like a dead body, white like a boy, grey like memories, and colourless, colourless like the human character, *our* red apostrophes on materials, *our* red apostrophes on materials and the oblique cries of *modern* MAN...

Joining *the world*, the whole *world*, Yankeeland, Yankeeland opens its IMMENSE *mouth* immensely full *with* dead birds!

Translated from Spanish by Stuart Cooke

COMMENTARY

Our old dreams of yesteryear are / now a delirium, our old dreams of yesteryear / are exhausted bouts of tears and phantoms' candelabras, just empty concepts and sequences. (P. de R.)

About "Yankeeland," a section of a vast work called *Los Gemidos* (The groans), Greg Dawes writes: "Intended to be an all-encompassing lyrical hymn with a first-person subject who is simultaneously poet and prophet, this work deals with the United States as bastion and bane due to its technological development, the human struggle with God and Satan, the overpowering influence of death on all creatures, the nature of utopias in general and the sea in particular, and the poet's life. [For de Rokha, the US epitomizes] the excesses of technology in modern societies.... This hypermodernity contrasts with the organic Nature that Walt Whitman extolled. Paradoxically, Walt Whitman serves as an antidote in the book to the mad rush to industrialize and seems to offer a solution to the societal quagmire the U.S. faced in the early part of the twentieth century" (in *Handbook of International Futurism*, ed. Günter Berghaus).

Herman Melville   USA, 1819–1891

from *MOBY DICK*

Chapter 40. *Midnight, Forecastle*

HARPOONEERS AND SAILORS

(*Foresail rises and discovers the watch standing, lounging, leaning, and lying in various attitudes, all singing in chorus.*)

Farewell and adieu to you, Spanish ladies!
Farewell and adieu to you, ladies of Spain!
Our captain's commanded.—

FIRST NANTUCKET SAILOR

Oh, boys, don't be sentimental; it's bad for the digestion! Take a tonic, follow me!

(*Sings, and all follow.*)
Our captain stood upon the deck,
A spy-glass in his hand,
A viewing of those gallant whales
That blew at every strand.
Oh, your tubs in your boats, my boys,
And by your braces stand,
And we'll have one of those fine whales,
Hand, boys, over hand!
So, be cheery, my lads! may your hearts never fail!
While the bold harpooner is striking the whale!

MATE'S VOICE FROM THE QUARTER-DECK

Eight bells there, forward!

SECOND NANTUCKET SAILOR

Avast the chorus! Eight bells there! d'ye hear, bell-boy? Strike the bell eight, thou Pip! thou blackling! and let me call the watch. I've the sort of mouth for that—the hogshead mouth. So, so, (*thrusts his head down the scuttle,*) Star-bo-l-e-e-n-s, a-h-o-y! Eight bells there below! Tumble up!

DUTCH SAILOR

Grand snoozing to-night, maty; fat night for that. I mark this in our old Mogul's wine; it's quite as deadening to some as filliping to others. We sing; they sleep—aye, lie down there, like ground-tier butts. At 'em again! There, take this copper-pump, and hail 'em through it. Tell 'em to avast dreaming of their lasses. Tell 'em it's the resurrection; they must kiss their last, and come to judgment. That's the way—*that's* it; thy throat ain't spoiled with eating Amsterdam butter.

FRENCH SAILOR

Hist, boys! let's have a jig or two before we ride to anchor in Blanket Bay. What say ye? There comes the other watch. Stand by all legs! Pip! little Pip! hurrah with your tambourine!

PIP

(*Sulky and sleepy.*)

Don't know where it is.

FRENCH SAILOR

Beat thy belly, then, and wag thy ears. Jig it, men, I say; merry's the word; hurrah! Damn me, won't you dance? Form, now, Indian-file, and gallop into the double-shuffle? Throw yourselves! Legs! legs!

ICELAND SAILOR

I don't like your floor, maty; it's too springy to my taste. I'm used to ice-floors. I'm sorry to throw cold water on the subject; but excuse me.

MALTESE SAILOR

Me too; where's your girls? Who but a fool would take his left hand by his right, and say to himself, how d'ye do? Partners! I must have partners!

SICILIAN SAILOR

Aye; girls and a green!—then I'll hop with ye; yea, turn grasshopper!

LONG-ISLAND SAILOR

Well, well, ye sulkies, there's plenty more of us. Hoe corn when you may, say I. All legs go to harvest soon. Ah! here comes the music; now for it!

(Ascending, and pitching the tambourine up the scuttle.)
Here you are, Pip; and there's the windlass-bitts; up you mount! Now, boys!

(The half of them dance to the tambourine; some go below; some sleep or lie among the coils of rigging. Oaths a-plenty.)

AZORE SAILOR
(Dancing.)
Go it, Pip! Bang it, bell-boy! Rig it, dig it, stig it, quig it, bell-boy! Make fire-flies; break the jinglers!

PIP
Jinglers, you say?—there goes another, dropped off; I pound it so.

CHINA SAILOR
Rattle thy teeth, then, and pound away; make a pagoda of thyself.

FRENCH SAILOR
Merry-mad! Hold up thy hoop, Pip, till I jump through it! Split jibs! tear yourselves!

TASHTEGO
(Quietly smoking.)
That's a white man; he calls that fun: humph! I save my sweat.

OLD MANX SAILOR
I wonder whether those jolly lads bethink them of what they are dancing over. I'll dance over your grave, I will—that's the bitterest threat of your night-women, that beat head-winds round corners. O Christ! to think of the green navies and the green-skulled crews! Well, well; belike the whole world's a ball, as you scholars have it; and so 'tis right to make one ball-room of it. Dance on, lads, you're young; I was once.

3RD NANTUCKET SAILOR
Spell oh! whew! this is worse than pulling after whales in a calm—give us a whiff, Tash.

(They cease dancing, and gather in clusters. Meantime the sky darkens—the wind rises.)

LASCAR SAILOR
By Brahma! boys, it'll be douse sail soon. The sky-born, high-tide Ganges turned to wind! Thou showest thy black brow, Seeva!

MALTESE SAILOR

(*Reclining and shaking his cap.*)

It's the waves—the snow's caps turn to jig it now. They'll shake their tassels soon. Now would all the waves were women, then I'd go drown, and chassee with them evermore! There's naught so sweet on earth—heaven may not match it!—as those swift glances of warm, wild bosoms in the dance, when the over-arboring arms hide such ripe, bursting grapes.

SICILIAN SAILOR

(*Reclining.*)

Tell me not of it! Hark ye, lad—fleet interlacings of the limbs—lithe swayings—coyings—flutterings! lip! heart! hip! all graze: unceasing touch and go! not taste, observe ye, else come satiety. Eh, Pagan? (*Nudging.*)

TAHITAN SAILOR

(*Reclining on a mat.*)

Hail, holy nakedness of our dancing girls!—the Heeva-Heeva! Ah! low veiled, high palmed Tahiti! I still rest me on thy mat, but the soft soil has slid! I saw thee woven in the wood, my mat! green the first day I brought ye thence; now worn and wilted quite. Ah me!—not thou nor I can bear the change! How then, if so be transplanted to yon sky? Hear I the roaring streams from Pirohitee's peak of spears, when they leap down the crags and drown the villages?—The blast! the blast! Up, spine, and meet it! (*Leaps to his feet.*)

PORTUGUESE SAILOR

How the sea rolls swashing 'gainst the side! Stand by for reefing, hearties! the winds are just crossing swords, pell-mell they'll go lunging presently.

DANISH SAILOR

Crack, crack, old ship! so long as thou crackest, thou holdest! Well done! The mate there holds ye to it stiffly. He's no more afraid than the isle fort at Cattegat, put there to fight the Baltic with storm-lashed guns, on which the sea-salt cakes!

4TH NANTUCKET SAILOR

He has his orders, mind ye that. I heard old Ahab tell him he must always kill a squall, something as they burst a waterspout with a pistol—fire your ship right into it!

ENGLISH SAILOR

Blood! but that old man's a grand old cove! We are the lads to hunt him up his whale!

ALL

Aye! aye!

OLD MANX SAILOR

How the three pines shake! Pines are the hardest sort of tree to live when shifted to any other soil, and here there's none but the crew's cursed clay. Steady, helmsman! steady. This is the sort of weather when brave hearts snap ashore, and keeled hulls split at sea. Our captain has his birthmark; look yonder, boys, there's another in the sky—lurid-like, ye see, all else pitch black.

DAGGOO

What of that? Who's afraid of black's afraid of me! I'm quarried out of it!

SPANISH SAILOR

(*Aside.*) He wants to bully, ah!—the old grudge makes me touchy. (*Advancing.*) Aye, harpooneer, thy race is the undeniable dark side of mankind—devilish dark at that. No offence.

DAGGOO (*grimly*)

None.

ST. JAGO'S SAILOR

That Spaniard's mad or drunk. But that can't be, or else in his one case our old Mogul's fire-waters are somewhat long in working.

5TH NANTUCKET SAILOR

What's that I saw—lightning? Yes.

SPANISH SAILOR

No; Daggoo showing his teeth.

DAGGOO (*springing*)

Swallow thine, mannikin! White skin, white liver!

SPANISH SAILOR (*meeting him*)

Knife thee heartily! big frame, small spirit!

ALL

A row! a row! a row!

TASHTEGO (*with a whiff*)

A row a'low, and a row aloft—Gods and men—both brawlers! Humph!

BELFAST SAILOR

A row! arrah a row! The Virgin be blessed, a row! Plunge in with ye!

ENGLISH SAILOR

Fair play! Snatch the Spaniard's knife! A ring, a ring!

OLD MANX SAILOR

Ready formed. There! the ringed horizon. In that ring Cain struck Abel. Sweet work, right work! No? Why then, God, mad'st thou the ring?

MATE'S VOICE FROM THE QUARTER-DECK

Hands by the halyards! in top-gallant sails! Stand by to reef topsails!

ALL

The squall! the squall! jump, my jollies! (*They scatter.*)

PIP (*shrinking under the windlass*)

Jollies? Lord help such jollies! Crish, crash! there goes the jib-stay! Blang-whang! God! Duck lower, Pip, here comes the royal yard! It's worse than being in the whirled woods, the last day of the year! Who'd go climbing after chestnuts now? But there they go, all cursing, and here I don't. Fine prospects to 'em; they're on the road to heaven. Hold on hard! Jimmini, what a squall! But those chaps there are worse yet—they are your white squalls, they. White squalls? white whale, shirr! shirr! Here have I heard all their chat just now, and the white whale—shirr! shirr!—but spoken of once! and only this evening—it makes me jingle all over like my tambourine—that anaconda of an old man swore 'em in to hunt him! Oh, thou big white God aloft there somewhere in yon darkness, have mercy on this small black boy down here; preserve him from all men that have no bowels to feel fear!

COMMENTARY

What's all this fuss I have been making about, thought I to myself—the man's a human being just as I am: he has just as much reason to fear me, as I have to be afraid of him. Better sleep with a sober cannibal than a drunken Christian. (H.M.)

(1) "They were nearly all Islanders in the Pequod, Isolatoes too, I call such, not acknowledging the common continent of men, but each Isolato living on a separate continent of his own. Yet now, federated along one keel, what a set these Isolatoes were! An Anacharsis Clootz deputation from all the isles of the sea, and all the ends of the earth, accompanying Old Ahab in the Pequod to lay the world's grievances before that bar from which not very many of them ever come back" (*Moby Dick*, chap. 27).

(2) Isolatoes they may have been, but there is great significance to their having been "federated along one keel." As Trinidadian historian & writer

C.L.R. James notes: "People write repeatedly that Melville describes the techniques of the whaling industry as if he were drawing up some sort of text-book or manual. Melville is doing nothing of the kind. He has painted a body of men at work, the skill and the danger, the laboriousness and the physical and mental mobilization of human resources, the comradeship and the unity, the simplicity and the naturalness. They are the meanest mariners, castaways and renegades. But that is not their fault. They began that way. Their heroism consists in their everyday doing of their work. The... graces with which Melville endows them are the graces of men associated for common labor" (in *Mariners, Renegades and Castaways: The Story of Herman Melville and the World We Live In*).

For more on the diverse races & ethnicities that have shaped the Americas—along with a call for their creative uprising—see the excerpt from Simón Rodríguez that follows.

For more on Melville, see the opening poem of "A Map of Visions."

Simón Rodríguez   Venezuela, 1769–1854

from **AMERICAN SOCIETIES (1828)**

Spanish Language & Government share the same position...

> asking for a reform &
> being able to admit it   { on one side

& on the other

> Reformers } search in many ways,
> can't find the true one.

Societies tend to have a *way to exist*, very unlike the one they have had, & which they are intended to have.

Men of these last eras—
reprimanded by the labor endured in useless attempts—
dissatisfied with the apparent convenience of the known Systems—
tired of hearing & reading pretentious praises to irrelevant things, &
sometimes to what has not happened yet—
fed up with being abused in the name of GOD! the KING or the NATION—

they want to live

W/O KINGS & W/O CONGRESS,
they don't ask for
masters   or   tutors
they want to possess
their own *persons, assets & will*
& that doesn't mean they yearn
to live like WILD ANIMALS,
(which is what the defenders of manifest or palliated absolutism suppose)

They want to govern themselves by REASON
which is Nature's authority

REASON, abstract figure of the THINKING FACULTY

Nature doesn't	Stupid,		Society does
breed	Slave		by neglect not by convenience
	Poor or		
	Ignorant Men		

PUBLIC INSTRUCTION
in the 19th century
demands MUCH PHILOSOPHY
the
GENERAL INTEREST
is crying out for
a REFORM
&
AMERICA is called on
because of the circumstances, to undertake it
this may seem a daring paradox…
… it doesn't matter…
the events will prove
what's a very obvious truth
America must not servilely IMITATE
but be ORIGINAL

we have {
Huasos, Chinos & Barbarians
Gauchos, Cholos & Huachinangos
Blacks, Prietos & Heathen Indians
Serranos, Calentanos, Indigenous
Colored people & dressed with Ponchos
Brown, Mulatto & Zambo
Whities & Yellow-footed
& a RABBLE of Mixed People
Terceroon Quadroon Quinteroon
& Salta-atrás
that bring up, as in Botanics
a CRYPTOGAM family

Where will we look for patterns? …

–Hispanic America is *original* = ORIGINAL must be their Institutions & Government = & ORIGINAL the ways to establish one & another.

we either Invent or we Err.

Translated from Spanish by Javier Taboada

COMMENTARY

The Americas are called (IF THOSE WHO GOVERN THEM UNDER-STAND) to be a model of good society, with no other work than to adapt. Everything has been done (mainly in Europe). Seize the good—strand the bad—imitate with judgment—& for what is lacking INVENT. (S.R.)

(1) Educator, essayist, & philosopher Simón Rodríguez was mainly known for being the tutor of Simón Bolívar (see above) & of the humanist & poet Andrés Bello. However, Rodríguez's innovative thoughts & reflections toward the intellectual, idiomatic, & creative independence of the Americas were gathered in a monumental work in progress, *American Societies*, which was published in successive editions from 1828 to 1842.

(2) Scholar Rafael Mondragón explains the nature of the work: "It was a philosophical book which would be published in installments. [The book left] blank spaces for the readers to scratch out and modify the text. [Rodríguez] would gather his reader's letters to integrate their reactions in the writing of each new chapter. The book would be distributed throughout the Americas via a continental subscriber's system. To conclude his work, Rodríguez invented a new way of writing, playing with typography to *paint* the page, and imagined ways to convey gestures and emotion on paper" (in *Periódico de Poesía*, UNAM, October 22, 2018).

For more of which, see "Notes toward a New Typography" in "A Map of Extensions."

Ernest Pépin Guadeloupe, 1950–

Ask me what's new
I'll tell you of the human commodities' crossing
I'll tell you of the voyage of no return
I'll tell you about the shark's feast
I'll tell you of the arrival and the scent of green lemon
On my raw wounds
I'll tell you about the red diarrhea
I'll tell you of the slave market
Yes I have scaled the steps of shame
At Petit-Canal
At Petit-Bourg
Or at the Abysses
I'll tell you of the dwelling
The manager
The overseer
And the Big House
Well located
Far from Black Shack Alley
And the smell of cattle
I'll tell you
Of the whip
The whip
The whip
I'll tell you of the consoling drums
And memory wearing out on the millstone of days
And memory reinventing
    Words
    Useless gestures
    Beliefs without substance
To preserve the memory of life

*

I'll play you the gwoka
    The mendé
    The toumblak
Tails
Pig snouts

Hardtack croquettes
Congo soup
And clumps of guinea-grass
I'll tell you that they've soiled the word Mandinka
They say maoundongue mandinga mandingo
That means savage
I'll tell you that they've soiled Africa
They've soiled everything to strangle nostalgia

*

At home
The earth crumbles like the powder of fear
Erupts with tension during cyclone season
And sometimes trembles
For fear of disappearing
Like a drop of water in the sea
And sometimes the volcano's rage is red
We swim below the ashes of the past
We try to remember
Sometimes memory is too heavy to bear
Heads burst
Things get confused
And we no longer know
Who we are
Why we're here
To extend Africa
So it can have buds
In the new fields of the Americas
Maybe we're here
To make the world round
To make the world's navel round

*

Now look me deep in the eyes
And speak to me
Sit down on the bench of the word
And speak to me
Tell me about beauty
Tell me about truth
Tell me about kindness
Don't talk to me anymore about Shaka
About Samory

About Queen Pokou
About Queen Nzinga
They're so beautiful in history books
Let history burn history
And let's talk about the present
Of the retreating forest
Of the advancing desert
Of endangered species
Of the still outstretched hand
And the crossroads of nations
Of the phantom universities
Of the brain drain
Of all the waste
And all that looting
Africa
my Africa
Africa
my only Africa

*

Not the Africa of the museums of Europe
Not the Africa carried
By the camels of the dream
But the Africa burning with the fever of the world
I ask you
When your hour will come

Translated from French by Christopher Winks

COMMENTARY

(1) Ernest Pépin's move, like that of others in the generation following Césaire, was to center even more specifically on the spoken language of New World Negroes, a step beyond Césaire's declaration that "I wanted to create an Antillean French, a Black French that, while still being French, had a Black character." The Creole movement staked out by Pépin & even more perhaps by others before him (Patrick Chamoiseau, Jean Bernabé, Raphaël Confiant) was called *créolité*.

(2) "Saltwater" was a name given to a person recently abducted from Africa & forced to come to the Americas across the "Middle Passage"—i.e., the second stage of a three-way "commercial" route that trafficked millions of Africans. The three parts of this "voyage" were (1) ships departing Europe

with manufactured goods to sell in African colonial markets; (2) goods traded for kidnapped Africans, who then were transported into the Americas as slaves; (3) slaves sold or traded for raw materials that Europeans brought back home.

James Weldon Johnson USA, 1871–1938

BROTHERS—AMERICAN DRAMA

(THE MOB SPEAKS:)

See! There he stands; not brave, but with an air
Of sullen stupor. Mark him well! Is he
Not more like brute than man? Look in his eye!
No light is there; none, save the glint that shines
In the now glaring, and now shifting orbs
Of some wild animal caught in the hunter's trap.

How came this beast in human shape and form?
Speak man!—We call you man because you wear
His shape—How are you thus? Are you not from
That docile, child-like, tender-hearted race
Which we have known three centuries? Not from
That more than faithful race which through three wars
Fed our dear wives and nursed our helpless babes
Without a single breach of trust? Speak out!

(THE VICTIM SPEAKS:)

I am, and am not.

(THE MOB SPEAKS AGAIN:)

                Then who, why are you?

(THE VICTIM SPEAKS AGAIN:)

I am a thing not new, I am as old
As human nature. I am that which lurks,
Ready to spring whenever a bar is loosed;
The ancient trait which fights incessantly
Against restraint, balks at the upward climb;
The weight forever seeking to obey

The law of downward pull—and I am more:
The bitter fruit am I of planted seed;
The resultant, the inevitable end
Of evil forces and the powers of wrong.
Lessons in degradation, taught and learned,
The memories of cruel sights and deeds,
The pent-up bitterness, the unspent hate
Filtered through fifteen generations have
Sprung up and found in me sporadic life.
In me the muttered curse of dying men,
On me the stain of conquered women, and
Consuming me the fearful fires of lust,
Lit long ago, by other hands than mine.
In me the down-crushed spirit, the hurled-back prayers
Of wretches now long dead—their dire bequests.
In me the echo of the stifled cry
Of children for their battered mothers' breasts.

I claim no race, no race claims me; I am
No more than human dregs; degenerate;
The monstrous offspring of the monster, Sin;
I am—just what I am.... The race that fed
Your wives and nursed your babes would do the same
Today. But I—

(THE MOB CONCLUDES:)

                    Enough, the brute must die!
Quick! Chain him to that oak! It will resist
The fire much longer than this slender pine.
Now bring the fuel! Pile it round him! Wait!
Pile not so fast or high! or we shall lose
The agony and terror in his face.
And now the torch! Good fuel that! the flames
Already leap head-high. Ha! hear that shriek!
And there's another! wilder than the first.
Fetch water! Water! Pour a little on
The fire, lest it should burn too fast. Hold so!
Now let it slowly blaze again. See there!
He squirms! He groans! His eyes bulge wildly out,
Searching around in vain appeal for help!
Another shriek, the last! Watch how the flesh

Grows crisp and hangs till, turned to ash, it sifts
Down through the coils of chain that hold erect
The ghastly frame against the bark-scorched tree.

Stop! to each man no more than one man's share.
You take that bone, and you this tooth; the chain,
Let us divide its links; this skull, of course,
In fair division, to the leader comes.

And now his fiendish crime has been avenged;
Let us back to our wives and children—say,
What did he mean by those last muttered words,
"*Brothers in spirit, brothers in deed are we*"?

COMMENTARY

O black and unknown bards of long ago, / How came your lips to touch the sacred fire? (J.W.J.) And again: *It is from the blues that all that may be called American music derives its most distinctive character.*

At the heart of the Harlem Renaissance in the 1920s was a homegrown poetry & poetics that penetrated the Negritude movement of the following decade & the work of African & Caribbean poets such as Leopold Sedar Senghor & Aimé Césaire (see above). Not an outlier, the poetry unleashed here created a new trajectory: a free Black literature extending the dimensions of America as it explored expanded ways & means to get it said. Writes Nathaniel Mackey of the further drive to make it new: "The relevance of experimentalism to African-American writing and of African-American writing to experimentalism needs to be insisted on and accorded its place in the discourse attending African-American literature and in the discourse attending experimental writing." Beyond that, too, it matches the transnational/global reach of a US poet like Whitman, traveling far beyond the boundaries of USAmerica as such.

N.B. In the present selection, the reader will notice Johnson's use of a tightly written & traditional blank verse, the experimentalism as such in the dramatic structure & the aggressiveness it carries.

Carla Fernández & Pedro Reyes

A MAP OF FIRST NATIONS

Oswald de Andrade Brazil, 1890–1954

from **PAU-BRASIL**

Brazilwood Poetry Manifesto

Poetry exists in the facts. The shacks of saffron and ochre in the green of the Favela, under cabralin blue, are aesthetic facts.

Carnival in Rio is the religious event of our race. Pau-Brasil. Wagner is submerged before the carnival lines of Botafogo. Barbarous and ours. The rich ethnic formation. Vegetal riches. Ore. Cuisine. Vatapá, gold and dance.

All the pioneering and commercial history of Brazil. The academic aspect, the side of citations, of well-known authors. Impressive. Rui Barbosa: a top hat in Senegambia. Transforming everything into riches. The richness of balls and of well-turned phrases. Negresses at the jockey club. Odalisques in Catumbi. Fancy talk.

The academic side. Misfortune of the first white brought over, politically dominating the wild wilderness. The alumnus. We can't help being erudite. Doctors of philosophy. Country of anonymous ills, of anonymous doctors. The Empire was like that. We made everything erudite. We forgot ingenuity.

Never the exportation of poetry. Poetry went hidden in the malicious vines of learning. In the lianas of academic nostalgia.

But there was an explosion in our knowledge. The men who knew it all inflated like overblown balloons. They burst.

The return to specialization. Philosophers making philosophy, critics criticism, housewives taking care of the kitchen.

Poetry for poets. The happiness of those who don't know and discover.

Here was an inversion of everything, an invasion of everything: the theatre of ideas and the on-stage struggle between the moral and immoral. The thesis should be decided in a battle of sociologists, men of law, fat and gilded like Corpus Juris.

Agile theatre, child of the acrobat. Agile and illogical. Agile novel, born of invention. Agile poetry.

Pau-Brasil poetry. Agile and candid. Like a child.

A suggestion of Blaise Cendrars: you have the train loaded, ready to leave. A Negro churns the crank of the turn-table beneath you. The slightest carelessness and you will leave in the opposite direction to your destination.

Down with officialdom, the cultivated exercise of life. Engineers instead of legal advisors, lost like the Chinese in the genealogy of ideas.

Language without archaisms, without erudition. Natural and neologic. The millionaire-contribution of all the errors. The way we speak. The way we are.

There is no conflict in academic vocations. Only ceremonial robes. The futurists and the others.

A single struggle—the struggle for the way. Let's make the division: imported Poetry. And Pau-Brasil Poetry, for exportation.

There has been a phenomenon of aesthetic democratization in the five enlightened parts of the world. Naturalism was instituted. Copy. A picture of sheep that didn't really give wool was good for nothing. Interpretation, in the oral dictionary of the Schools of Fine Arts, meant reproduce exactly.... Then came pyrogravure. Young ladies from every home became artists. The camera appeared. And with all the prerogatives of unkempt hair and the mysterious genius of the upturned eye—the photographic artist.

In music, the piano invaded the bare sitting-rooms, calendars on the wall. All the young ladies became pianists. Then came the barrel organ, the pianola. The player-piano. And the Slavic irony composed for the player-piano. Stravinski.

Statuary followed behind. The processions issued brand-new from the factories.

The only thing that wasn't invented was a machine to make verses—the Parnassian poet already existed.

So, the revolution only indicated that art returned to the elite. And the elite began taking it to pieces. Two stages: 1st) deformation through impressionism, fragmentation, voluntary chaos. From Cézanne and Mallarmé, Rodin and Debussy until today. 2nd) lyricism, the presentation in the temple, materials, constructive innocence.

Brazil profiteur. Brazil doutor. And the coincidence of the first Brazilian construction in the general movement of reconstruction.

As the age is miraculous, laws were born from the dynamic rotation of destructive factors.
Synthesis
Equilibrium
Automotive finish
Invention
Surprise
A new perspective
A new scale

Whatever natural force in this direction will be good. Pau-Brasil poetry.

.....

Barbarous, credulous, picturesque and tender. Readers of newspapers. Pau-Brasil. The forest and the school. The National Museum. Cuisine, ore and dance. Vegetation. Pau-Brasil.

Translated from Portuguese by Stella M. de Sá Rego

COMMENTARY

Only anthropophagy unites us. Socially. Economically. Philosophically. / The world's only law. The masked expression of all individualisms, of all collectivisms. Of all religions. Of all peace treaties. / Tupi, or not tupi that is the question. (O. de A.)

Or take it as a declaration of independence of Brazilian poetry from the bondage of a restrictive Portuguese inheritance. A master of manifesto-writing (as in the *Anthropophagite* [Cannibalist] *Manifesto*, quoted in the epigraph), Andrade found escape & renewal in lessons from an international, largely European-centered avant-garde & the resources of an earlier Indigenous tradition on native Brazilian grounds. That this might enter into the language itself & into the way that poetry was spoken & written makes Andrade's manifesto—named for the native brazilwood tree—a companion to a hemispherical call for a "new American poetry" rooted in a "new idiom" & "new measure." Both manifest in these pages as signs of "new world" renewal & transformation, each suited to the local reality from which it comes. (For which, see the W. C. Williams entry, below, & the quote from Juan María Gutiérrez attached thereto.)

For more on Oswald de Andrade, see "A Second Gallery."

Edison Simons   Panama, 1933–2001

from *MOSAICS: LII*

1984, RIO DE JANEIRO.
My Kuna friend, the drifting shaman
Arysteides Turpana,
lent me a tiny reading-book,
bilingual,
Dulegaya-Spanish,
for the children of his village
so they could learn Spanish
without losing
the auroral ear of San Blas
Archipelago,
situated
on the Atlantic shore
of Panama.

Years later,
in Paris,
scrutinizing the little book I felt
called
by San Blas's sounds
transcribed
in western characters:
after reprising its phonemes, I deduced
an ad hoc verbal code
("and if these similitudes be not received
in the simplicity of a loving mind
and in the sense in which
they are uttered
they will seem to be effusions of folly
rather than the language of reason")

Which
allows me
to transfigure nonsense on a tongue
where the nothingness of Adam slides down
from primeval red
stepfather
of every single thing

and of a world
now threatened with extinction,
as everything
that belongs to the aurora.

AH BYE ALAS!

Takarkuna
guagu
dage neg itisega
boe bab
belabela olo
uarguen guilenay
aturimska ibloged
banegine gurgina
magatbali
bubadi baabak
arbaedse narmayeke
uisiye
uied
Abya Yala

Some years later, Turpana, when reading my transcription, told me, smiling, that the meaning (o western maleDICTION!!) of my Kuna song was
the following:

tomorrow eight intelligences
through the ocean
with their bodies
are going to travail.

TRAVAIL comes from med. Latin TRIPALIUM, torture device for slaves
in Rome

Translated from Spanish by Javier Taboada

COMMENTARY

*What's the poetical question? The tongue in which you are born and die is
the receptacle of figures: hell.* (E.S.)

(1) Edison Simons's lifetime work was *Mosaicos*: 106 poems written over
twenty-one years (starting in 1976). A translator & a visual artist, Simons
was a *nomadic* poet; although he resided in Paris most of his life, he lived
also in Rome, Tokyo, Kolkata, London, Caracas, etc. His *Mosaicos* wit-

ness these travels and focus on language (all languages) as the fundamental faculty of man for every creative act. As a crew member of the first *Travesía* voyage in 1965, Simons participated in the collective work—the epic poem—called *Amereida* (*Amerodyssey*) (excerpts & commentary at the end of this "Map").

(2) Abya Yala is the Dule (or Kuna/Cuna) name for America, which means "land in its full maturity" or "land of vital blood," & the wordplay here (AH BYE ALAS) corresponds to that in Spanish, *Había ya ala* (= "There was a wing"), when translated homophonically. Other Kuna words are given without further translation, as they are in Simons's poem.

(3) The six lines in quotation marks & parentheses, above, link directly to Saint John of the Cross's *Prologue to the Spiritual Canticle*, translated here by David Lewis.

Edimilson de Almeida Pereira Brazil, 1963–

CALUNGA LUNGARA

I am going to put into words
what is not possible.
They are water-words
that dissolve.

I am speaking of Calunga.

It can be large or
small depending
on who crossed it.

Its name changes
according to the tongue.
In some it kills
in others it is ocean.

On it is traveling
someone who has no body.
We are sailors
in a land of pilgrimage.

Calunga goes around at night
studying dreams.

It accompanies captive
marks in the dust.

It brings present fears
family fears.
The oldest does not show
that even he would die.

I put into words
what should not have been spoken.

What one says is not Calunga.

Translated from Portuguese by Steven F. White

COMMENTARY

How shall the nation recite one hundred and eighty / tongues exiled from the dictionary? / And the African tongues that once negotiated / in slave quarters and public squares? / And the Portuguese tongue that turned into / the chameleon of the tropics? // Ah, how exhausting it is, discussing the way things are (E. de A.P.)

Calunga is an Afro-Brazilian "secret language" spoken throughout Brazil in communities founded by Africans fleeing or recently freed from slavery, mainly in the western region of Minas Gerais. While it has been labeled as an "anti-creole" language or as an "intertwined language," the etymology of the name itself is not entirely clear.

In any case, the attempt (& the failure) to speak about that "secret" language—unknown, uncontrollable, unreachable—is a quest for *poesis* in itself.

ADDENDUM

KERES PUEBLO USA

What the Informant Said to Franz Boas in 1920

long ago her mother
had to sing this song and so
she had to grind along with it
the corn people have a song too
it is very good
I refuse to tell it

English version by Armand Schwerner

Elicura Chihuailaf Mapuche Nation, Chile, 1952–

THE KEY THAT NO ONE HAS LOST

Poetry serves no purpose, I am told
and trees caress one another in the forest
with blue roots and twigs ruffling to the wind,
greeting with birds the Southern Cross
Poetry is the deep murmur of the murdered
the rumor of leaves in the fall, the sorrow
for the boy who preserves the tongue
but has lost the soul
Poetry, poetry, is a gesture, a landscape,
your eyes and my eyes, girl; ears, heart,
the same music. And I say no more, because
no one will find the key that no one has lost
And poetry is the chant of my ancestors
a winter day that burns and withers
this melancholy so personal.

Translated from Mapudungun & Spanish by Rodrigo Rojas

COMMENTARY

If the people do not speak Mapudungun, the earth will not be able to speak. (E.C.)

"The Mapuche are a native nation of South America who by their own reckoning have lived from the beginning of time in the central valley of Chile and in the grasslands across the Andes, in Argentina. Their language, Mapudungun, has been studied since the Spanish and other Catholic Missions were established in the region and admired only by a few dedicated scholars throughout the centuries. From their very first contact with the Spaniards in the 1540's they have been fighting for the survival of their culture" (Rodrigo Rojas).

And of Elicura & the other poets he translates from Mapudungun and Spanish, Rojas writes further: "The poets translated here use a wide array of poetic resources to refer to violence and discrimination and their search for roots that imply their whole history of struggle, not only against a dictator or the state, but against western civilization. They may use slang, mix Spanish and Mapudungun, use archaisms, or translate from languages other than Spanish into Mapudungun. They are mainly bilingual, and this has allowed them to enter more than one world at a time and not be fixed under one interpretation."

Joseph Sickman Corsen

Curaçao (Papiamento), 1853–1911

from *ATARDI (SUNSET)*

ta pakiko / why it comes
mi no sa / I don't know
ma esta tristu / but inside me sadness
mi ta bira / grows
every evening the sea
engulfs the sun
perhaps a premonition
a neglected memory
it might just be
something
coming out of my nature
looking ahead
      who knows
it might forecast
a grief yet unborn

will I identify it?
will I see you soon?

first
the night
fixed & vast
many unknown things
concealed within her
before
sunrise flames
too many changes
god only knows
who's already dead

I know nothing
ma esta tristu / but inside me sadness
mi ta bira / grows
every time I see
how the day ends

Transcreated by Javier Taboada

(1) *Atardi* (*Sunset*) is the first poem in Papiamento ever published (1905). Joseph Sickman Corsen's efforts helped to confirm, though posthumously, that Creole languages are powerful & equally valid channels for the expression of our *residence on earth*, &—at the same time—started a cultural & poetical transformation in the former Netherlands Antilles (Aruba, Bonaire, & Curaçao). Corsen also wrote poetry in Spanish, proposed prosodic & orthographic rules for Papiamento, & was a very prolific musician.

(2) His opening & final lines (in Papiamento/italics, in our version) paraphrase Heine's *Die Lorelei*.

Myriam Moscona   Mexico (Ladino & Spanish), 1956–

from *TELA DE SEVOYA (ONIONCLOTH)*

"*Senyoras, senyores. No podemos fuyir de nuestros destinos, todos estamos moertos, ninyas, ninyos, domadores, fieras. Todos moertos / Ladies, gentlemen. We cannot escape our destinies, we are all dead, girls, boys, tamers, beasts. All dead.*" I don't know what else the voice says. I hold onto my father's legs to leave the circus as soon as possible, I feel like the tiger is coming for me. I raise my face to ask him to carry me, but I suddenly lose him in the crowd. In his place, I see my abuela Victoria practically in front of me, speaking with an extreme sweetness:

—*Sentites kualo dijeron? Estamos moertos. Nadien te va a matar, sos moerta i tu / Did you hear what they said? We are dead. No one will kill you, you are dead too.*
—Where is my father? I want to go with him.

—*Tu padre esta en los ornos, ijika, ande keman a las linguas del avlar / Your father is in the ovens, ijika, where they burn the tongues that speak.*

I don't know what she's saying to me; from there, I see the tamer's face down covered in a crimson cloud. No one is left. The tiger, the people, my father, my grandmother, everyone has suddenly disappeared, except for the dead tamer and me. *Sos la ultima kreatura / You are the last creature*, a voice inside me says.

Translated from Spanish & Ladino by Antena Aire (Jen/Eleana Hofer and J. D. Pluecker)

I come upon a city / I remember / that there lived / my two mothers / and I wet my feet / in the rivers / that from these and other waters / arrive to this place. (M.M.)

The vehicle here is the near-extinct language spoken by the Sephardic Jews & revisited as a familial memory by Moscona and others in a New World / newly American context. Born in Mexico City, she intercalates the inherited Ladino/Judeospanish/Judezmo into her Spanish writings, the key work here her poetic novel *Onioncloth* (*Tela de sevoya* in Ladino). Of this Max Modiano Daniel writes in summary: "*Tela de sevoya* is a palimpsestic, genre-bending text woven throughout—like the titular onioncloth—with the voices of the dead, dying, and their living conduits. Part roots tourism, part scholarly interlude, part autobiography, and part dreamscape, what Moscona has produced is an artistic statement outlining the many deaths and afterlives of her personal, familial, communal, and cultural past, mediated by the central character of the Ladino language and her own psyche."

In this part of her total oeuvre, Moscona is also the coeditor of *Por mi boka*, an anthology of Ladino texts, & of a collection of poetry, *Ansina,* each text of which has a Spanish and a Ladino version.

N.B. While Moscona's grasp of Ladino comes through her Bulgarian-born immigrant parents, it should also be noted that the language first arrived in the Americas with Converso & Marrano Jews who were an integral part of the sixteenth-century Spanish conquests in Mexico & elsewhere.

Xul Solar Argentina (Pancriollo), 1887–1963

THIS HADES IS FLUID

This Hades is fluid, almist, no roof, no floor, redhaired, color in sunshut eyes, stirred in endotempest, whirlpools, waves, and boiling. In its clots n foam dismultitumans float passivao, disparkle, therz also solos, adults, kidoids, n they pergleam softao.

Transpenseen ghostliao, the houses n people n soil of a solid terri citi have nothing to do withis Hell, which is nao thereal.

This whole dense redheaded region selfmountains roun big hollo or bottomless valley of bluegray air, where it floes in dark winds, with uproarians n other lone umans, avoid n globoid. Here it floes more oop. N yon the solid city n its populas go on ghostliao.

Later I pass on to a better life, gray silver. Yere many groups lovefloat loosao processioning or thinking reunited. Yere clouds row with gray kiosks—of mother of pearl, metal, felt—with pensors circumseated.

Sloao I find myselfe in a slight kelestal sky. Its disposition is afternoon summeri, cloudii.

Plants zigzag one by one biomove and hum. Ther color lovaries from garnet to rosy. They r over floatislope of da same denser air, undspersing. Here juxtafly boids like speck eggs, not with wings, but with many ribbons.

Nextherz many color columns, baseless, supporting cloud roof: is temple floati in which many pray. When zeytheocoexaltzey inflate, zer auras vitaradiate, suchaozatzeyraize ze cloud roof ancircumseparate ze columns, an everysingfervienlarges n saintgleams.

Nextherz wide obelisk or tower, that swéz from its floatifloppi base. Its first floor, of stonebooks, mudbooks on top, woodbooks on top, cylinder books on top, the top, books. Almost lyk a house of cards, bristling with paper ribbons n banderols, periflown with letterswarmsflyao, juxtasurrounded by perhaps wandermunchingstudenti. Inna lil bit of floor floati, many dream, zermersed.

I float I go yonderfarre. Deeping in a plurmutacolor fog I see ceety. Theesbiopalaces n biohovels, of framework n I theenk. They pertransform, grow or shreenk; now they r pillars n archframes n cupolas, now plain phosphiplastered walls, now they quake weethpseudocrystal scaffolding. They shift, rise, seenk, interpenetrate, separate, n rejoicetera.

Houses ther r that burn, flame oop, but they don't self-destruct, they rather selfconstruct-um. Der fire is life, n da greater da boining, da more palace senwidens n grows. Houses ther r that infect set fire to the nébors that idem idem, n thus néborhoods expand. Ther people lykwisecoflame n coloom: this must be the cause burni, by pensiardor.

Houses ther r that ferviboil until they blow up lyk a bomb, a geyser, or smoke; but they d'ont self-destruct-um, they circumreselfconstruct; ther bits n pieces fervigrow in faraway subsidiaries that finally growjoin, dispile toweeracastyr morrenmore, on circumbarrenslessenless.

Houses ther r that suigrow in evridirekshun, skewpi, horizily, juxto, oop, fat; n they buzz, squeak, creak, dispeak.

Houses ther r that atrophy and shrink until they r seen no mor, when ther people diehatchinna better life inna better sky.

Houses ther r of illusion on smokehills; they altervanish.

So I embrace the soil of this citi, that wichis a cloudgathering, wichis several vague titans floatireclining.

Great sleeves or tubes circumset out-um for the vacuum: they might be sewers or suckers, I do'nt know.

N over that ceetytherees other ceety, backward, sullen, dark n slow that lives n grows juxto, n its people too. The nadir is deep, sullen, dark, foggi: maybe the hommeworld, some great wasteland.

I review the other city oop. Colonnades like centipedes travell in distrides. They r rigid disciples, carrying dometeachers with wide roofly robes. Tumbled in suihappyskyrabble, lovi-turvy in fog and sketches and clots of thot: gelatinementi. They go farre, into the vacuum.

I see zerz several very pily pagodas of just bookes, zatzer many readers incorpor-ate: they don't read, but rather vitisuck science n sophy.

Translated from Pancriollo by Molly Weigel

COMMENTARY

I am maestro of a writing no one reads yet. (X.S.) And again: *I am world champion of a game no one knows.*

Such reservations notwithstanding, Xul Solar is recognized today as a key contributor to the avant-gardist visionary art & poetry of the Americas. A prolific painter, poet, & inventor, Xul created a new language in which he registered his visions: *Pancriollo*. Cecilia Vicuña explains: "Pancriollo was a language Xul invented from the possibilities of language itself, a creative forerunner of *portuñol* [a mix of Spanish & Portuguese]… That is, a new co-echo aesthetic of the arts and behavior in a mutual fusion and interpenetration: a different way of speaking and theorizing fusion, imposing an uncertainty that generates new modes of interpretation. It is as if Xul had fast forwarded to a liberated and evolved era, where there are no frontiers or fundamentalisms and where everyone communicates through logic and poetry in a Pan Language of Latin roots and suffixes/prefixes from every language, according to necessity" (in *Co Ecos Astri: Xul Solar of Buenos Aires*). Xul Solar—the pen name he assumed—means "Reversed Light [Lux] of the Sun."

That his name was given as title to a major Argentine magazine of avant-garde poetry & writing—*XUL*—is also worth noting.

Jorge Canese   Paraguay, 1947–

SEXUAL KUSTOMS OF THE LESSER PALEOLITHIK

Discover a nu kontinent or planet name it liquidate its natural owners. The method doesn't matter katechize the rest for the good and for the bad impose your laws your language your favorite skin and eye colors. APÙROPE MANTÉ? We could at least try it killing oneself shouldn't be such a sad theeng. Boarding the nearest cloud and rowing against the current like we alwayz did until the disgusting moment of the kavernous pollution arrives.

Añarakopeguaré evidently I was mistaken about the epoch of scaffolding my hand slipped I went off the map. Patienze I did it for your wellbeing because there wasn't anything elze that could be done but stopping and saying: party on die julano I love you or the sun comes out the sun comes out and then be qwyet.

IT LACKS MEETER MAXO
temwolamentum nevermore

Translated from Guarañol by Shook

COMMENTARY

Writes Shook: "Born in Asunción, Paraguay in 1947, Jorge Canese, who also goes by Jorge Kanese, Xorxe Kanexe, and just the initial K, is a microbiologist and a university docent. His books of poetry include *Paloma Blanca Paloma Negra* (*White Dove Black Dove*), which was banned on publication in 1982 under the [Stroessner] dictatorship that finally fell after thirty-five years in 1989.... Even for Paraguayan speakers of Guarañol— which blends Spanish, Portuguese, and Paraguayan Guaraní alongside a significant percentage of idiolectic vocabulary, grammar, and wordplay—his work can be difficult to understand. In 2010 he published his most expansive work to date, *Las Palabras K* (*The K Words*), an occasionally undecipherable volume that remixes his previous work to even more opaque extremes. He has been jailed, tortured, and exiled, but now resides again in his homeland where, in his own translated words, 'he continues to believe in poetry, though not much in what is labeled such in the present day.'"

William Carlos Williams   USA, 1883–1963

THE PURE PRODUCTS OF AMERICA

The pure products of America
go crazy—
mountain folk from Kentucky
or the ribbed north end of
Jersey

with its isolate lakes and
valleys, its deaf-mutes, thieves
old names
and promiscuity between
devil-may-care men who have taken
to railroading
out of sheer lust of adventure—
and young slatterns, bathed
in filth
from Monday to Saturday
to be tricked out that night
with gauds
from imaginations which have no
peasant traditions to give them
character
but flutter and flaunt
sheer rags succumbing without
emotion
save numbed terror
under some hedge of choke-cherry
or viburnum—
which they cannot express—
Unless it be that marriage
Perhaps
with a dash of Indian blood
will throw up a girl so desolate
so hemmed round
with disease or murder
that she'll be rescued by an
agent—
reared by the state and
sent out at fifteen to work in
some hard-pressed
house in the suburbs—
some doctor's family, some Elsie
voluptuous water
expressing with broken
brain the truth about us—
her great
ungainly hips and flopping breasts
addressed to cheap

jewelry
and rich young men with fine eyes
as if the earth under our feet
were
an excrement of some sky
and we degraded prisoners
destined
to hunger until we eat filth
while the imagination strains
after deer
going by fields of goldenrod in
the stifling heat of September
somehow
it seems to destroy us
It is only in isolate flecks that
Something
is given off
No one
to witness
and adjust, no one to drive the car

COMMENTARY

I don't speak English, but the American idiom. I don't know how to write anything else, and I refuse to learn.... I have been as accurate as the meaning of the words permitted—always with a sense of our own American idiom to instruct me. (W.C.W.)

(1) Beyond what Williams expresses here (as "pure product") lies his sense of the multidimensionality of that new idiom & culture, yet with its dark & violent side always present, & his insistence to those who come after that they take hold of the language as given, to remake it, & at an extreme to "smash it to hell, you have a right to it!" In his own case, the hidden ingredient in the greater American mix is Caribbean Spanish (Puerto Rican through his mother), which he nurtures from its roots & lets rip on its own from time to time. Or, as he writes: "This independence, this lack of integration with our British past gives us an opportunity, facing Spanish literature [including Latin American], to make new appraisals, especially in attempting translations, which should permit us to use our language with unlimited freshness.... In such attempts we will not have to follow precedent but can branch off into a new diction, adapting new forms, even discovering new forms in our attempts to find accurate equivalents" (cited by Jonathan Cohen).

(2) A similar position regarding a true (or new) American Spanish language was held early on by the Argentinean historian & poet Juan María Gutiérrez when he rejected a position in the Royal Spanish Academy. He explained himself in *Cartas de un porteño* (*Letters of a citizen of Buenos Aires*) (1875): "What truly serious interest can we Americans have in fixing, in immobilizing, the agent of our ideas, the cooperator in our discourse and reasoning? Why would we strive to assume a language cultivated on the banks of the Manzanares, in order to mold and enslave the one that's currently in transformation—human as it is—on the shores of our freshwater sea? ... Language will be transformed, yes, but with this it will only give way to the stream formed by succession of years, which are the irresistible revolutionaries. By its own force, thought opens the channel through which it has to flow, and this force is the true and unique safeguard of languages" (trans. Javier Taboada).

Thus "A Map of Americas" comes smack on the language question again & again—on both continents.

(3) "When Williams was asked by a college professor where he got his language from, Williams responded, 'From the mouths of Polish mothers'" (Robert Coles). That this may go beyond the *pure* products of America to reach into later immigrant sources, his own included, is also worth consideration.

For more on Williams, see "A Second Gallery" & "A Map of Histories."

Gertrude Stein USA, 1874–1946

from **THE MAKING OF AMERICANS**

It has always seemed to me a rare privilege, this, of being an American, a real American, one whose tradition it has taken scarcely sixty years to create. We need only realise our parents, remember our grandparents and know ourselves and our history is complete.

The old people in a new world, the new people made out of the old, that is the story that I mean to tell, for that is what really is and what I really know.

Some of the fathers we must realise so that we can tell our story really, were little boys then, and they came across the water with their parents, the grandparents we need only just remember.

Some of these our fathers and our mothers, were not even made then, and the women, the young mothers, our grandmothers we perhaps just have seen once, carried these our fathers and our mothers into the new world inside them, those women of the old world strong to bear them.

Some looked very weak and little women, but even these so weak and little, were strong always, to bear many children.

These certain men and women, our grandfathers and grandmothers, with their children born and unborn with them, some whose children were gone ahead to prepare a home to give them; all countries were full of women who brought with them many children; but only certain men and women and the children they had in them, to make many generations for them, will fill up this history for us of a family and its progress.

Many kinds of all these women were strong to bear many children.

One was very strong to bear them and then always she was very strong to lead them.

One was strong to bear them and then always she was strong to suffer with them.

One, a little gentle weary woman was strong to bear many children, and then always after she would sadly suffer for them, weeping for the sadness of all sinning, wearying for the rest she knew her death would bring them.

And then there was one sweet good woman, strong just to bear many children, and then she died away and left them, for that was all she knew then to do for them.

And these four women and the husbands they had with them and the children born and unborn in them will make up the history for us of a family and its progress.

Other kinds of men and women and the children they had with them, came at different times to know them; some, poor things, who never found how they could make a living, some who dreamed while others sought a way to help them, some whose children went to pieces with them, some who thought and thought and then their children rose to greatness through them, and some of all these kinds of men and women and the children they had in them will help to make the history for us of this family and its progress.

These first four women, the grandmothers we need only just remember, mostly never saw each other. It was their children and grandchildren who, later, wandering over the new land, where they were seeking first, just to make a living, and then later, either to grow rich or to gain wisdom, met with one another and were married, and so together they made a family whose progress we are now soon to be watching.

COMMENTARY

Stein's great avant-garde novel is also a celebration & history of her immigrant forebears, the stylistics & poetics of her mature work put at the service of an ostensibly different subject. For contrast & comparison, the reader can also check out the poems by Louis Zukofsky & Mikhl Likht, elsewhere in these pages. An inescapable theme in American (particularly US) poetry, both directly & indirectly present.

ADDENDUM

GERTRUDE STEIN

America

Once in English they said America. Was it English to them.
Once they said Belgian.
We like a fog.
Do you for weather.

Are we brave.
Are we true.
Have we the national colour.
Can we stand ditches.
Can we mean well.
Do we talk together.
Have we red cross.
A great many people speak of feet.
And socks.

For more on Stein, see poems in "A Second Gallery" & elsewhere.

Régis Bonvicino Brazil, 1955–

171196

I

I have never lived on a street named Glass. Once I kicked cobblestones. Each day passed as in a mirror—of echoes. Telephones, wires. Once I took a boat out on a lake. I've never seen myself in my own reflection. Chats, conversations—one single character and person. Megaphone mute. I've also lived in a miniscule apartment. I like the name of the streets of some of my friends. Amherst, Mílvia, Sirius. I don't have time for anything. My hair has fallen out. Maybe that's all.

2

My ancestors came from Italy. Sicily. Naples, Venice. Alessandro Bonvicino.—Il Moretto. Also from Pontevedra in Galicia. My maternal ancestors came from Minas. My name: my father took it from a business card.

3

I've never been down a street named Scissors. A centipede moves sideways. Ants falling in the eyes. Giuliano Della Casa, water and paint, likes the paintings of Alessandro Bonvicino. Guiliano lives in Modena, Santa Agostino Street, 33. I spent some years shut, right here, in a room. There is a street called Scissors. Inhambu is the name of a bird. I like to take aspirin and opiates. A light wave abandons me now—as a match, before leaving. There is a sun and a moon, all at once, on Wilshire Boulevard. Sabine Macher lives at 7 Paradise Street. Somebody lives on Legion Drive.

The bicycle tire is not a circle. There is an avenue called Precita. The sky, yesterday, was overcast.

4

I'll see you later. David's eleven year old son likes foreign stamps. At this very moment, someone is having a *garage sale*. I didn't sense a muted complaint in the docility of the flowers this morning. I also didn't see a thin bird, eating insects, this morning. Someone lives on Gumtree Terrace. The water runs to the sea. The moon doesn't become full in a day. There is a street called Lepic. There is another, Lindero Nuevo Vedado. That sidewalk is dirty. Sweet William is the name of a flower. Elephants don't thread eyes of needles.

5

He may have lived on a street called *Si Dar*. There is a street called Campeche. Rose and Andy most definitely live on Cedar Street. Apples mean nothing. They say that a special sedative exists for snails. Nobody explains certain expanses of green. Large trees don't bear fruit, just shade. Sequoias and shells drive men to madness. A woman investigates by phone. There is a street called Cedro. Sack-cloths sanction millennia and wires. Statues form

a part

of the

universe

Translated from Portuguese by Jennifer Cooper with Scott Bentley & Douglas Messerli

COMMENTARY

I have never spoken of myself in a poem—in that sense my poems are quite objective. Italian Neorealist Cinema, Rossellini, Fellini and Antonioni, have been a constant reference for me—stronger than the influence of poets—because of their proximity to a certain reality... their detailing of the everyday life of the poor, the city as ruin, vertigo. (R.B.) And again: *Innovation is a relative concept and can become a contradiction if it is conceived as a tradition.*

Of Italian descent & a native of São Paulo, Bonvicino plays with the language of shifting urban spaces, time, & nature, to interrupt one another & construct & deconstruct identities—here, those of his origins & his hometown & elsewhere, as in "171196" (the title containing a date in 1996). For all of this, Charles Bernstein has written: "Bonvicino is to twenty-first century São Paulo what Charles Baudelaire was to nineteenth-century Paris: the poet as flaneur wandering through the cultural detritus of our time with mordant gaze and dark wit. Bonvicino's ebullient poems are replete with philosophically searing perceptions and socially conscious lament. Not yet elegy, Bonvicino's unrelenting acknowledgments center on the parasitic relation between those mangled by society and those doin' the manglin'."

Wang Ping USA, 1957–

IMMIGRANT CAN'T WRITE POETRY

"Oh no, not with your syntax," said H.V. to her daughter-in-law, a Chinese writing poetry in English

She walk to mountain
She walks to a mountain
She walk to mountain now
She is walking to a mountain now
What difference it make
What difference does it make
In Nature, no completeness
No sentence really complete thought
Language, our birthright & curse
Pay no mind to immigrant syntax
Poetry, born as beast
Move best when free, undressed

COMMENTARY

when the mind is full, the room ceases to be empty (W.P.)

On the other side of her poem's linguistic ironies, Wang Ping, born in Shanghai & migrating to the United States in her late twenties, developed in her new language as a significant poet, writer, photographer, & performance & multimedia artist. Of her work overall, New Mexico poet Arthur Sze writes, "Wang Ping's poems are notable for their incisive images and psychological acuity. [In them she] journeys from China to America and weaves passion and memoir into a shining loop." And Wang Ping herself, to bring the immigrant experience front & center, in words from her website, which must surely be her own: "[Immigrants] are a force of nature, like salmon, monarchs, trees, water, and mountains, moving with rivers, the earth and universe. Migration is the signature of life—no immigrants, no economy; no immigration, no civilization; no migration, no life. We are all immigrants."

Gloria Anzaldúa USA, 1942–2004

from *BORDERLANDS/LA FRONTERA*

The New Mestiza (El otro México)

"The *Aztecas del norte*... compose the largest single tribe or nation of Anishinabeg (Indians) found in the United States today... Some call themselves Chicanos and see themselves as people whose true homeland is Aztlán [the US Southwest]."

Wind tugging at my sleeve
feet sinking into the sand
I stand at the edge where earth touches ocean
where the two overlap
a gentle coming together
at other times and places a violent clash.

Across the border in Mexico
  stark silhouette of houses gutted by waves,
    cliffs crumbling into the sea,
      silver waves marbled with spume
        gashing a hole under the border fence.
Miro el mar atacar
     la cerca en Border Field Park
    con sus buchones de agua
an Easter Sunday resurrection
of the brown blood in my veins.

Oigo el llorido del mar, el respire del aire,
  my heart surges to the beat of the sea.
    in the gray haze of the sun
      the gulls' shrill cry of hunger,
        the tangy smell of the sea seeping into me.

I walk through the hole in the fence
    to the other side.
      Under my fingers I feel the gritty wire
        rusted by 139 years
          of the salty breath of the sea.
Beneath the iron sky
Beneath the iron sky
Mexican children kick their soccer ball across,
run after it, entering the U.S.

I press my hand to the steel curtain—
     chainlink fence crowded with rolled barbed wire—
rippling from the sea where Tijuana touches San Diego
    unrolling over mountains
        and plains
           and deserts,
this "Tortilla curtain" turning into *el río Grande*
    flowing down to the flatlands
        of the Magic Valley of South Texas
    its mouth emptying into the Gulf.

1,950 mile-long open wound
    dividing a *pueblo*, a culture
        running down the length of my body,
  staking fence rods in my flesh,
  splits me   splits me
me raja   me raja

  This is my home
  this thin edge of
  barbwire.

        But the skin of the earth is seamless.
  The sea cannot be fenced,
      el mar does not stop at the borders.
     To show the white man what she thought of his
  arrogance,
Yemayá blew that wire fence down.

  This land was Mexican once,
    was Indian always
    and is.
And   will be again.

COMMENTARY

Anzaldúa continues: "The U.S-Mexican border *es una herida abierta* [is an open wound], where the Third World grates against the first and bleeds. And before a scab forms it hemorrhages again, the lifeblood of two worlds merging to form a third country—a border culture. Borders are set up to define the places that are safe and unsafe, to distinguish *us* from *them*. A border is a dividing line, a narrow strip along a steep edge. A borderland is a vague and undetermined place created by the emotional residue of an unnatural boundary. It is in a constant state of transition. The prohibited and forbidden are its inhabitants. *Los atravesados* live here: the squint-eyed, the perverse, the queer, the troublesome, the mongrel, the mulato, the half-breed, the halfdead; in short, those who cross over, pass over, or go through the confines of the 'normal.' Gringos in the U.S. Southwest consider the inhabitants of the borderlands transgressors, aliens—whether they possess documents or not, whether they're Chicanos, Indians or Blacks. Do not enter, trespassers will be raped, maimed, strangled, gassed, shot. The only 'legitimate' inhabitants are those in power, the whites and those who align themselves with whites. Tension grips the inhabitants of the borderlands like a virus. Ambivalence and unrest reside there and death is no stranger."

Joy Harjo Muscogee / Creek Nation / USA, 1951–

A MAP TO THE NEXT WORLD

for Desiray Kierra Chmusee

In the last days of the fourth world I wished to make a map for
those who would climb through the hole in the sky.

My only tools were the desires of humans as they emerged
from the killing fields, from the bedrooms and the kitchens.

For the soul is a wanderer with many hands and feet.

The map must be of sand and can't be read by ordinary light. It
must carry fire to the next tribal town, for renewal of spirit.

In the legend are instructions on the language of the land, how it
was we forgot to acknowledge the gift, as if we were not in it or of it.

Take note of the proliferation of supermarkets and malls, the
altars of money. They best describe the detour from grace.

Keep track of the errors of our forgetfulness; the fog steals our
children while we sleep.

Flowers of rage spring up in the depression. Monsters are born
there of nuclear anger.

Trees of ashes wave good-bye to good-bye and the map appears to
disappear.

We no longer know the names of the birds here, how to speak to them by their personal names.

Once we knew everything in this lush promise.

What I am telling you is real and is printed in a warning on the map. Our forgetfulness stalks us, walks the earth behind us, leaving a trail of paper diapers, needles, and wasted blood.

An imperfect map will have to do, little one.

The place of entry is the sea of your mother's blood, your father's small death as he longs to know himself in another.

There is no exit.

The map can be interpreted through the wall of the intestine—a spiral on the road of knowledge.

You will travel through the membrane of death, smell cooking from the encampment where our relatives make a feast of fresh deer meat and corn soup, in the Milky Way.

They have never left us; we abandoned them for science.

And when you take your next breath as we enter the fifth world there will be no X, no guidebook with words you can carry.

You will have to navigate by your mother's voice, renew the song she is singing.

Fresh courage glimmers from planets.

And lights the map printed with the blood of history, a map you will have to know by your intention, by the language of suns.

When you emerge note the tracks of the monster slayers where they entered the cities of artificial light and killed what was killing us.

You will see red cliffs. They are the heart, contain the ladder.

A white deer will greet you when the last human climbs from the destruction.

Remember the hole of shame marking the act of abandoning our tribal grounds.

We were never perfect.

Yet, the journey we make together is perfect on this earth who was once a star and made the same mistakes as humans.

We might make them again, she said.

Crucial to finding the way is this: there is no beginning or end.

You must make your own map.

COMMENTARY

In Isleta the rainbow was a crack in the universe. We saw the barest of all life that is possible. Bright horses rolled over and over the dusking sky. (J.H.) Or again: *I know I walk in and out of several worlds each day.* And further: *We will keep going despite dark. Or a madman in a white house dream.*

The ascent from activist poet & musician to her tenure for a spell as the twenty-third US & first Native American poet laureate is itself notable, but the call of poetry & poetics even more so. Of how all of this comes together, she writes knowingly: "To imagine the spirit of poetry is much like imagining the shape and size of the knowing. It is a kind of resurrection light; it is the tall ancestor spirit who has been with me since the beginning, or a bear or a hummingbird. It is a hundred horses running the land in a soft mist, or it is a woman undressing for her beloved in firelight. It is none of these things. It is more than everything."

And of the old & new America this represents, she tells us further: "The world doesn't always happen in a linear manner. Nature is much more creative than that, especially when it comes to time and the manipulation of time and space. Europe has gifted us with inventions, books and the intricate mechanics of imposing structures on the earth, but there are other means to knowledge and the structuring of knowledge that have no context in the European mind."

Various Authors

from **AMEREIDA (AMERODYSSEY)**

the journey reaches its height
as the eyes

its traveled soil

wouldn't it reveal in the flesh

a rhythm
   to start off a language?
       without a language
all the roads into our intimacy
      though they lead us
are a distortion & a trick

     a language?

this one?
    the one who listens now the deaf ripples of the american sea
    still beating after all imitation
         & regret
which claims for a continent
      & embraces us within its stars
to create lands?

...

where do we get the names
   of the american discovery?
in what void were they born?
      greed
         bloody
            aims
the clear
   sea
    is called

– & he answered
    that people from culua
      sent him to be sacrificed
& since he was a stutterer
     he mumbled
oluaolua
   & as our capt'n
       was there
& his name was juan
   & it was the day of san juan
    we christened
        that isle
san juan de ulúa
   which is now

a widely known harbor

– & when he was saying that
                              in his own tongue
I recall'd he said
                    conescotoch conescotoch
which means
            ye come to mine house
                        & that is why we named
those lands
            since then
punta de cotoche
                & that is how it shows up on the nautical charts

            farther they found
some men
            they asked them about the name
of a big town
            near around
                    they said
téctetan téctetan

                    which stands for
I don't understand you
                but the spaniards thought
that was its name
                corrupting
the word since then
                    they called the place
yucatán
            & that name 'll never fade away

                            & he told
his own name
            saying
                            beru
and he added
        & said
            pelu
                he meant
if ye ask me for mine name
                my name is beru

but if ye ask me where I was
                        I'll say
I was on the river

                        christians grasp what they wanted   thinking the
native understood them & really meant his answer as if he & they were
actually speaking in spanish & since then   that was fifteen fifteen or
fifteen sixteen they named peru that rich & vast empire   corrupting
both names as the spaniards corrupt almost every word taken from the
Indigenous languages

...

                so america burst and came into a transition
that's its origin—to be in transition
in transition   not from the past to the present   not from barbarity to
civilization   but in a present transition
present is just what has a destiny
destiny is just fidelity to the origin
america has only a destiny when its bursting & upwelling are both present

...

& so
                said mourão
                        mello mourão
                                gerardo
as the gospel's rebukes
                                                charitas christi
                                urge us
love of america
                because
since the beginning of time
                the poet
                                        was credited
with the gift
                to foresee things
                                        no one
                as the poet
bears
        the
                essence of human history
                                        in which

destinies are made
         & that's why we feel here
that now
a new era of history
         begins
              with the
epiphany of america

…

everything relies on the comprehension of this line of Hölderlin–
    was bleibet aber stiften die dichter

what does *stiften* mean?
it's not to found & yet it is   to give a chance   *stiften* is the giver
whose gifts or talents allow us to come to an end
the poet is the giver

…

        stiften is not to found damnit! it is
        to tune our dwelling in its own rhythm
        to give the frame then the starting
        shot giving money is a
        way of founding –

what will the amerodyssey give?

      the road isn't the road

Translated from Spanish by Javier Taboada

(1) *Travesía* was the name for a *sea journey* made by architects, philosophers, poets, & visual artists—Latin American & European—such as Edison Simons, Jonathan Boulting, Alberto Cruz, Fabio Cruz, Michel Deguy, François Fédier, Claudio Girola, Godofredo Iommi, Gerardo Mello Mourão, Jorge Pérez Román, & Henri Tronquoy—whose main goal was to found an "American Poetical Capital" in Santa Cruz de la Paz, Bolivia. The journey shipped off from Tierra del Fuego in 1965. During the trip, the crew members landed at different points in South America, & there they performed artistic actions, none of them premeditated. They couldn't, however, reach Santa Cruz: they were stopped by the Bolivian Army & were forced to quit. In 1967 the members of *Travesía* reunited & created *Amereida* (translated here as *Amerodyssey*)—a collective long poem without any evident authorship or capital letters that reenacts & goes deep into their experience. Other *Travesías* followed up to the present time. While the "Poetical Capital" was never established, their idea shaped the foundation (in 1971) of Ciudad Abierta (Open City) in Chile, an architecturally revolutionary & experimentally designed city, supported by the Universidad Católica de Valparaíso.

(2) Like the opening image for "A Map of Americas," the route sketched here moves from southernmost Tierra del Fuego (shown on top) to Santa Cruz in Bolivia (at bottom). Of this inverted route, they write: "it's america seen from earth! / from below or otherwise / where dante comes from & the dead are."

A SECOND GALLERY

from Emily Dickinson to Vicente Huidobro

Emily Dickinson USA, 1830–1886

MY LIFE HAD STOOD—A LOADED GUN

My Life had stood—a Loaded Gun—
In Corners—till a Day
The Owner passed—identified—
And carried Me away—

And now We roam in Sovreign Woods—
And now We hunt the Doe—
And every time I speak for Him
The Mountains straight reply—

And do I smile, such cordial light
Upon the Valley glow—
It is as a Vesuvian face
Had let its pleasure through—

And when at Night—Our good Day done—
I guard My Master's Head—
'Tis better than the Eider Duck's
Deep Pillow—to have shared—

To foe of His—I'm deadly foe—
None stir the second time—
On whom I lay a Yellow Eye—
Or an emphatic Thumb—

Though I than He—may longer live
He longer must—than I—
For I have but the power to kill,
Without—the power to die—

TO RECIPIENT UNKNOWN

Master.
        If you saw a bullet
hit a Bird—and he told you
he was'nt shot—you might weep
at his courtesy, but you would
certainly doubt his word—
One drop more from the gash
that stains your Daisy's

bosom–then would you *believe*?
Thomas' faith in Anatomy, was
stronger than his faith in faith.
God made me–[Sir] Master–
I did'nt be–myself. I dont know how
it was done. He built the
heart in me–Bye and bye
it outgrew me–and like
the little mother–with the
big child–I got tired
holding him. I heard of a
thing called "Redemption"–which
rested men and women–
You remember I asked you
for it–you gave me something
else. I forgot the Redemption
in the Redeemed–I did'nt
tell you for a long time, but
I knew you had altered me–
and was tired–no more–[so dear
did this stranger become, that
were it, or my breath–the
Alternative–I had tossed
the fellow away with a smile.]
I am older–tonight, Master–
but the love is the same–
so are the moon and the
crescent. If it had been
God's will that I might
breathe where you breathed–
and find the place–myself–
at night–if I (can) never forget
that I am not with you–
and that sorrow and frost
are nearer than I–if I wish
with a might I cannot
repress–that mine were the
Queen's place–the love of
the Plantagenet is my only
apology–To come nearer than
presbyteries–and nearer than

the new Coat–that the Tailor
made–the prank of the Heart
at play on the Heart–in holy
Holiday–is forbidden me–
You make me say it over–
I fear you laugh–when I do
not see–[but] "Chillon" is not
funny. Have you the Heart in
your breast–Sir–is it set
like mine–a little to the left–
has it the misgiving–if it
wake in the night–perchance–
itself to it–a timbrel is it–
itself to it a tune?
These things are [reverent] holy, Sir,
I touch them [reverently] hallowed, but
persons who pray–dare remark
[our] "Father"! You say I do
not tell you all–Daisy "confessed–
and denied not."
Vesuvius dont talk–Etna–dont–
[They] one of them–said a syllable–
a thousand years ago, and
Pompeii heard it, and hid
forever–She could'nt look the
world in the face, afterward–
I suppose–Bashfull Pompeii!
"Tell you of the want"–you
know what a leech is, dont
you–and [remember that] Daisy's arm is small–
and you have felt the Horizon
hav'nt you–and did the
sea–never come so close as
to make you dance?
I dont know what you can
do for it–thank you–Master–
but if I had the Beard on
my cheek–like you–and you–had Daisy's
petals–and you cared so for
me–what would become of you?
Could you forget me in fight, or

flight–or the foreign land?
Could'nt Carlo, and you and I
walk in the meadows an hour–
and nobody care but the Bobolink–
and *his*–a *silver* scruple?
I used to think when I died–
I could see you–so I died
as fast as I could–but the
"Corporation" are going too–so [Eternity] Heaven
wont be sequestered–now [at all]–
Say I may wait for you–
say I need go with no stranger
to the to me–untried [country] fold–
I waited a long time–Master–
but I can wait more–wait
till my hazel hair is dappled–
and you carry the cane–
then I can look at my
watch–and if the Day is
too far declined–we can take
the chances [of] for Heaven–
What would you do with me
if I came "in white"?
Have you the little chest to
put the Alive–in?
I want to see you more–Sir–
than all I wish for in
this world–and the wish–
altered a little–will be my
only one–for the skies–
Could you come to New England–
[this summer–could] Would you come
to Amherst–Would you like
to come–Master?
[Would it do harm–yet we both
fear God–] Would Daisy disappoint
you–no–she would'nt–Sir–
it were comfort forever–just
to look in your face, while
you looked in mine–then I
could play in the woods till

Dark–till you take me
where Sundown cannot find
us–and the true keep
coming–till the town is full.
[Will you tell me if you will?]
I did'nt think to tell you, you
did'nt come to me "in white"–
nor ever told me why,
No Rose, yet felt myself
a'bloom,
No Bird–yet rode in Ether.

COMMENTARY

If I read a book [and] *it makes my whole body so cold no fire can ever warm me, I know that is poetry. If I feel physically as if the top of my head were taken off, I know that is poetry. These are the only way I know it. Is there any other way.* (E.D., letter to Thomas Wentworth Higginson, 1870) And again: *When I state myself, as the Representative of the Verse–it does not mean–me–but a supposed person.* (E.D., 1862)

The slow posthumous emergence of Emily Dickinson, alongside Walt Whitman, as one of the two great innovators of nineteenth-century North American poetry carried with it a series of mysteries & surprises waiting to be unsealed. Not least was the innovatory, even experimental nature of her verse—far different from Whitman's long-line "free" or "open" verse—concealed until late in the twentieth century, when her poetry began to be printed & published as she had written it. Her handwritten manuscripts, cut & bound into small booklets or fascicles for private sharing among family & friends, bristled with hyphens or dashes that seemed to serve, as the poet Susan Howe first suggested, as pause markers or line breaks that turned the ballad- or hymnlike structures of her poems into something far more radical. Along with that were alternative readings for certain words set beneath her poems like footnotes & still more radical, if rarer, wordless (asemic) writings & protocollages where images (sewn by her to the page with string) partially obscure the text & thus create an unanticipated visual poetry.

The "letter to recipient unknown," written to her singular outside reader & critic, is similarly derived from her handwritten manuscript. That it resides ambiguously between verse & prose is especially worth noting.

For more on Dickinson, see her asemic poem in "A Map of Extensions."

Sousândrade Brazil, 1832–1902

from *O GUESA ERRANTE*

The Wall Street Inferno

1   (GUESA, having traversed the WEST INDIES, believes himself rid
     of the XEQUES and penetrates the NEW-YORK-STOCK-EXCHANGE;
     the VOICE, from the wilderness:)

   – Orpheus, Dante, Aeneas, to hell
   Descended; the Inca shall ascend
       = *Ogni sp'ranza lasciate,*
            Che entrate …
   – Swedenborg, does fate new worlds portend?

2   (Smiling Xeques appear disguised as Railroad-*managers,*
            Stockjobbers, Pimpbrokers, etc., etc., crying out:)

   – Harlem! Erie! Central! Pennsylvania!
   = Million! Hundred million!! Billions!! Pelf!!!
       – Young is Grant! Jackson,
               Atkinson!
   Vanderbilts, Jay Goulds like elves!

3   (The VOICE, poorly heard amidst the commotion:)

   – Fulton's *Folly,* Codezo's *Forgery …*
   Fraud cries the nation's bedlam
       They grasp no odes
           Railroads;
   Wall Street's parallel to Chatham …

4   (Brokers going on:)

   – Pygmies, Brown Brothers! Bennett! Stewart!
   Rothschild and that Astor with red hair!!
       = Giants, slaves
           If only nails gave
   Out streams of light, if they would end despair! …

5   (NORRIS, *Attorney;* CODEZO, *inventor;* YOUNG, ESQ.,
            manager; ATKINSON, *agent;* ARMSTRONG, *agent;*
                RHODES, *agent;* P. OFFMAN & VOLDO, *agents;*
                    hubbub, mirage; in the middle, GUESA:)

– Two! Three! Five thousand! If you play
Five million, Sir, will you receive
                = He won! Hah! Haah!! Haaah!!!
                        – Hurrah! Ah!…
– They vanished… Were they thieves?…

6   (J. MILLER atop the roofs of the *Tammany wigwam* unfurling the
          Garibaldian mantle:)

– Bloodthirsties! Sioux! Oh Modocs!
To the White House! Save the Nation,
From the Jews! From the hazardous
                Goth's Exodus!
From immoral conflagration!

. . . . .

100   (*Reporters.*)

– Norris, Connecticut's *blue* laws!
Clevelands, attorney-Cujás,
                Into zebras constrained
                        Ordained,
Two by two, to one hundred Barabbas!

101   (Friends of the lost *kings*:)

– *Humbug* of *railroads* and the telegraph,
The fire of heaven I wished wide and far
                To steal, set the world ablaze
                        And above it raise
Forever the *Spangled Star!*

102   (A rebellious sun founding a planetary center:)

– "George Washington, etc. etc.,
Answer the Royal-George-Third. Depose!"
                = Lord Howe, tell him, do
                        I'm royal too…
(And they broke the Englishman's nose).

103   (Satellites greeting JOVE's rays:)

– "Greetings from the universe to its queen"…
As for bail, the Patriarchs give a boon…
                (With a liberal king,

A worse thing,
They founded the empire of the moon).

104   (*Reporters:*)

   – A sorry role on earth they play,
Kings and poets, heaven's aristocracy
      (And Strauss, waltzing)
         Singing
At the Hippodrome or Jubilee.

105   (Brokers finding the cause of the WALL STREET market crash:)

   – *Exeunt* Sir Pedro, Sir Grant,
Sir Guesa, seafaring brave:
      With gold tillers they endure
        The Moor,
Appeased by the turbulent waves.

106   (International procession, the people of Israel, Orangians,
      Fenians, Buddhists, Mormons, Communists, Nihilists,
      Penitents, *Railroad-Strikers, All-brokers, All-jobbers,*
      All-saints, All-devils, lanterns, music, excitement; Reporters:
      in LONDON the QUEEN's "murderer" passes by and in PARIS
      "Lot" the fugitive from SODOM:)

   – In the Holy Spirit of slaves
A single Emperor's renowned
      In that of the free, verse
        Reverse,
Everything as Lord is crowned!

107   (KING ARTHUR's witches and FOSTER the Seer on WALPURGIS by day:)

   – *When the battle's lost and won–*
   – *That will be ere the set of sun–*
   – *Paddock calls: Anon!–*
   – *Fair is foul, and foul is fair:*
Hover through the fog and filthy air!

108   (SWEDENBORG answering later:)
   – Future worlds exist: republics,
Christianity, heavens, Lohengrin.
      Present worlds are latent:

Patent,
Vanderbilt-North, South-Seraphim.

109   (At the roar of JERICHO, HENDRICK HUDSON runs aground; the
INDIANS sell the haunted island of MANHATTAN to the DUTCH:)

– The Half-Moon, prow toward China
Is careening in Tappan-Zee...
Hoogh moghende Heeren...
      Take then
For sixty *guilders*... *Yeah*! *Yeah*!

110   (*Photophone-stylographs* sacred right to self-defense:)

– In the light the humanitarian voice:
Not hate; rather conscience, intellection;
      Not pornography
           Isaiah's prophecy
In Biblical vivisection!

.....

117   (*Freeloves* proceeding to vote for their husbands:)

– Among Americans, Emerson alone,
Wants no Presidents, oh atrocious he!
     = Oh well-adjudicated,
       States
Improve for you, for us, for me!

118   (APOCALYPTIC visions... slanderous ones:)

– For, "the Beast having bear's feet,"
In God we trust is the Dragon
      And the false prophets
         Bennetts
Tone, th' Evolutionist and Theologian!

.....

173   (WASHINGTON "blinding because of them"; POCAHONTAS
without *personals*:)

– To starving bears, a rabid dog!
Be it! After the feast, bring in festoons!...

= Tender Lulu,
       Crying and you
Give honey to "foes", bee?... and sting poltroons?

174   (Guatemalan nose, curved into HYMENEE'S torch; DAME-RYDER
       heart on the poisoned window-panes of the *"too dark"*
       wedding pudding:)

– *"Caramba! yo soy cirujano*–
A Jesuit... Yankee... industrialism"!
       – *Job*... or haunted cavern,
             Tavern,
"Byron" animal-magnetism!...

175   (Practical swindlers doing their business; *self-help* ATTA-TROLL:)

– Let the foreigner fall helpless,
As usury won't pay, the pagan!
       = An ear to the bears a feast,
             Caressing beasts,
Mahmmuhmmah, mahmmuhmmah, Mammon.

176   (Magnetic *handle-organ*; *ring* of bears sentencing the architect
       of the PHARSALIA to death; an Odyssean ghost amidst the
       flames of Albion's fires:)

– Bear... Bear is beriberi, Bear... Bear...
= Mahmmuhmmah, mahmmuhmmah, Mammon!
       – Bear... Bear... ber'... Pegasus
             Parnassus
= Mahmmuhmmah, mahmmuhmmah, Mammon.

Translated from Portuguese by Odile Cisneros

COMMENTARY

*Someone told me I would only be read 50 years from now. I grew sad. The
disillusion of one who wrote 50 years too soon.* (Sousândrade, in his preface to
O Guesa Errante)

Along with Whitman & Darío, Sousândrade (Joaquim de Sousa Andrade)
emerges today as one of the great nineteenth-century forerunners to a full-
blown poetry of the Americas. Nearly forgotten after his own time, he was
brought back, largely through the enthusiasm of Noigandres poets Haroldo
& Augusto de Campos, to become, in Latin American terms at least, the

epitome of a late experimental romanticism & a prefigurer of new poetries to come. His masterwork, as boundary shattering & as American in its own way as Whitman's *Song of Myself* or Pound's *Cantos*, was a long poem entitled O *Guesa Errante* (The wandering Guesa), in which "layout, neologisms, verbal montage, and sudden changes in tone evoke the newspapers of that period and the hectic world of the stock market." Thus wrote the Cuban novelist Severo Sarduy; & Augusto de Campos further: "... a trans-American periplum (with interludes in Europe, Africa) from Brazil (Maranhão) to Colombia, Venezuela, Peru,... Central America, the Antilles, and to the USA." At the journey's center is the Guesa, a legendary figure of the Muisca Indians (Chibchas) of Colombia, destined from childhood for ritual immolation. To escape the *xeques* or priests who would carry out the sacrifice, the Guesa (or Sousândrade speaking for him) makes his own pilgrimage, "to end sacrificed in Wall Street, surrounded by stockbrokers' cries."

José Hernández Argentina, 1834–1886

from **MARTÍN FIERRO**

Now I'll sit me down to sing
to the twang of my guitar
cuz a man who can't stray far
from a pain down to the bone
like a bird that's all alone
sings a song where comforts are.

I only ask the saints in heaven
that they help me concentrate.
I only ask before too late
for a chance to sing my song
—memories are seldom long—
and knowing what I know can't wait.

All you saints with your milagros
git on over to my side
cuz my tongue is more than tied
and my eyes are going blind—
so I'm begging God to find
a place where I can run and hide.

I have known so many singers
who are famed both near and far,

once they've got to where they are
they can't keep the damn thing up
so before they start they stop
too wore out to ever star.

But where another gaucho goes
Martín Fierro will go too:
nuthin else for him to do
and no ghosts to freak him out,
cuz if they all sing and shout,
I can be a singer too.

I can sing until I die,
and when my life is gone and done,
then I shall come like every one
to kneel at God's great judgment seat—
out of my mother's womb I leaped
and sang until my race was run.

Translated from Spanish by Jerome Rothenberg

COMMENTARY

Earth is the mother of us all, but she also feeds us poisons. (J.H.)

Martín Fierro is an epic poem written in praise of the South American gaucho's way of life & history. By the time of its publication, in 1872, the traditional gaucho way (nomadic, often outlaw, akin to that of the North American cowboy) had been rendered more or less obsolete by the introduction of industrialized agriculture & farming & the gauchos often recruited as enforcers by contending political parties. Hernández's aim in the face of this was to create an archetype of the traditional gaucho, here called Martín Fierro, & to shape him as a national rebel against an oppressive society, its restrictions on freedom & mistreatment of nature: a society that (in its pursuit of progress) threatened gaucho & other forms of free life, pushing them to the point of extinction.

The poem in its complete form has 2,316 lines that re-create the metrics & style of the earlier *payadores* (rural gaucho bards) & those of Hernández's more literary gauchoesque predecessors: Bartolomé Hidalgo in his *Cielitos* & Domingo Sarmiento in his prose-based *Facundo*: absent all adornments, spontaneous & brutal.

That works like these have continued into the present is also worth noting.

Adah Isaacs Menken USA, 1835–1868

SALE OF SOULS

I

Oh, I am wild-wild!
Angels of the weary-hearted, come to thy child.
Spread your white wings over me!
> Tenderly, tenderly,
> Lovingly, lovingly,
> Plead for me, plead for me!

II

Souls for sale! souls for sale!
Souls for gold! who'll buy?
In the pent-up city, through the wild rush and beat of human hearts, I hear this
   unceasing, haunting cry:
> Souls for sale! souls for sale!
> Through mist and gloom,
> Through hate and love,
> Through peace and strife,
> Through wrong and right,
> Through life and death,

The hoarse voice of the world echoes up the cold gray sullen river of life.
> On, on, on!

No silence until it shall have reached the solemn sea of God's for ever;
> No rest, no sleep;

Waking through the thick gloom of midnight, to hear the damning cry as it
   mingles and clashes with the rough clang of gold.
> Poor Heart, poor Heart,
> Alas! I know thy fears.

III

The hollow echoes that the iron-shod feet of the years throw back on the sea of
   change still vibrate through the grave-yard of prayers and tears;—
> Prayers that fell unanswered,
> Tears that followed hopelessly.

But pale Memory comes back through woe and shame and strife, bearing on her
   dark wings their buried voices;
Like frail helpless barks, they wail through the black sea of the crowded city,
> Mournfully, mournfully.

IV

Poor Heart, what do the waves say to thee?

The sunshine laughed on the hill sides.

The link of years that wore a golden look bound me to woman-life by the sweet love of my Eros, and the voice of one who made music to call me mother.

Weak Heart, weak Heart!

Oh, now I reel madly on through clouds and storms and night.

The hills have grown dark,

They lack the grace of my golden-haired child, to climb their steep sides, and bear me their smiles in the blue-eyed violets of our spring-time.

Sad Heart, what do the hills say to thee?

They speak of my Eros, and how happily in the dim discolored hours we dreamed away the glad light, and watched the gray robes of night as she came through the valley, and ascended on her way to the clouds.

> Kisses of joy, and kisses of life,
> Kisses of heaven, and kisses of earth,

Clinging and clasping white hands;

Mingling of soft tresses;

Murmurings of love, and murmurings of life,

With the warm blood leaping up in joy to answer its music;

The broad shelter of arms wherein dwelt peace and content, so sweet to love.

All, all were mine.

> Loving Heart, loving Heart,

Hush the wailing and sobbing voice of the past;

Sleep in thy rivers of the soul,

> Poor Heart.

Souls for sale!

The wild cry awoke the god of ambition, that slumbered in the bosom of Eros;

From out the tents he brought forth his shield and spear, to see them smile back at the sun;

Clad in armor, he went forth to the cities of the world, where brave men battle for glory, and souls are bartered for gold.

Weeping and fearing, haggard and barefoot, I clung to him with my fainting child.

Weary miles of land and water lay in their waste around us.

We reached the sea of the city.

Marble towers lifted their proud heads beyond the scope of vision.

Wild music mingled with laughter.

The tramp of hoofs on the iron streets, and the cries of the drowning, and the curses of the damned were all heard in that Babel, where the souls of men can be bought for gold.

All the air seemed dark with evil wings.

And all that was unholy threw their shadows everywhere,

> Shadows on the good,
>
> Shadows on the bad,
>
> Shadows on the lowly,
>
> Shadows on the lost!

All tossing upon the tide of rushing, restless destiny;

Upon all things written:

> Souls for sale!
>
> Lost Heart, lost Heart!

VI

A soul mantled in glory, and sold to the world;

> O horrible sale!
>
> O seal of blood!
>
> Give back my Eros.

His bowstring still sounds on the blast, yet his arrow was broken in the fall.

Oh leave me not on the wreck of this dark-bosomed ship while Eros lies pale on the rocks of the world.

Driven before the furious gale by the surging ocean's strife;

The strong wind lifting up the sounding sail, and whistling through the ropes and masts, waves lash the many-colored sides of the ship, dash her against the oozy rocks.

The strength of old ocean roars.

The low booming of the signal gun is heard above the tempest.

Oh how many years must roll their slow length along my life, ere the land be in sight!

When will the morning dawn?

When will the clouds be light?

When will the storm be hushed?

It is so dark and cold.

Angels of the weary-hearted, come to your child!

Build your white wings around me.

> Tenderly, tenderly,
>
> Pity me, pity me.

*I have written these wild soul-poems in the stillness of midnight, and
when waking to the world the next day, they were to me the deepest
mystery. I could not understand them; did not know but what I ought to
laugh at them; feared to publish them, and often submitted them privately
to literary friends to tell me if they could see a meaning in their wild intensity.* (A.I.M.)

The power & bright newness of Menken's writing has been obscured over
the years, yet is always on the verge of reappearing. She was probably born
as Adelaide McCord in Milneburg, Louisiana, or possibly Philomène Croi
Théodore or Dolores Adios Los Fiertes in New Orleans, & there was an
ongoing play of identities: multiple versions of her birth, her parentage,
her ethnicity. Her ongoing artwork in that sense was an elaborate self-
construction—assertively Jewish in her earlier writings, militantly feminist
later on. As such the work developed a rare female violence & eroticism:
"wild soul-poems" in the writing but mirrored as well in her stage presence,
an actress who famously played the young male lead in an adaptation of
Byron's poem *Mazeppa*—transgendered & "shockingly" nude (or appearing to be so in flesh-colored tights) as she made her exit from the stage,
helpless & strapped astride a "fiery untamed steed." (Thus Mark Twain's
1863 account of it, while quoting Byron.) This was her principal & very
real celebrity, which carried her across America (New York first, then San
Francisco) & established her soon thereafter in London & Paris.

But her formal innovation as a poet, like that of Walt Whitman, whom
she knew from the New York café scene of the early 1860s, was in the
open / projective / free verse line of her later poetry. In this she needs to be
viewed no longer as an imitator of Whitman but as someone drawing, like
him, from the Bible & the fictive medieval crypto-poet Ossian while driven
by a very different sense of mind & body.

ADDENDUM

DELMIRA AGUSTINI Uruguay, 1886–1914

from **Prayer**

> ... Piety for the lips like celestial settings
> Where the invisible pearls of the Host gleam;
> —Lips that never existed,
> Never seized anything,
> A fiery vampire
> With more thirst and hunger than an abyss.
> Piety for the sacrosanct sexes

That armor themselves with sheaths
From the astral vineyards of Chastity;
Piety for the magnetized footsoles
Who eternally drag
Sandals burning with sores
Through the eternal azure;
Piety, piety, pity
For all the lives defended
By the lighthouse of Pride
From your marvelous raw weathers:

Aim your suns and rays at them!

Eros: have you never perhaps felt
Pity for the statues?

Translated from Spanish by Valerie Martínez

J[ohn] J[acob] Thomas   Trinidad, 1841–1889

CREOLE PROVERBS

Ox never tells the pasture: "thank you."

It is not for want of tongue that an ox cannot speak.

Ease is not hunch-backed.

The same stick that beat the black dog can beat the white.

The clay-pot wishes to laugh at the iron-pot.

You have not yet crossed the river, do not curse the crocodile's mother.

If the frog tells you the crocodile has sore eyes, believe him.

Nonsense is not sugar-water.

Conversation is the food of the ear.

The belly has no ears.

Teeth do not wear mourning.

Fat has no sentiment.

A single finger cannot catch fleas.

It is the frog's own tongue that betrays him.

It is in rainy season that the ox has need of his tail.

It is when the wind is blowing that we see the skin of a fowl.

It is the knife that knows what is in the heart of the pumpkin.

The garden far, the ochre spoils.

The yam vine ties the yam.

The monkey fondling its young too much, has poked her finger into its eye.

Joke freely with the monkey but beware of handling his tail.

Hate people, but don't give them baskets to fetch water.

Accidents do not threaten like rain.

Whatever affects the eye affects the nose.

What business have eggs in the dance of stones?

Too much talking rouses the watchdog from sleep.

Talking is no remedy.

Teeth are not hearts.

Words have no colour.

Words must die that men may live.

The man has died, grass grows before his door.

COMMENTARY

(1) "Born in Trinidad two years after the abolition of slavery, Thomas was a major nineteenth-century Caribbean intellectual, whose works are still influential. A schoolteacher who became secretary of the Board of Education, he was first and foremost a philologist, noted for his pioneering study, *The Theory and Practice of Creole Grammar*.... His later volume, *Froudacity*, is an example of merciless criticism at its most powerful: a point-by-point refutation of the misunderstandings, distortions, and outright lies written by the British racist and apologist for imperialism James Anthony Froude.

"Thomas's status as a precursor of surrealism rests primarily on his deep interest in—and his superb collection of—Creole proverbs.... Surrealist imagery, proletarian humor, and a strong awareness of the Marvelous are at the core of these wonders of oral literature" (in *Black, Brown, & Beige: Surrealist Writings from Africa and the Diaspora*, ed. Franklin Rosemont & Robin D.G. Kelley).

(2) The Creole presented here is largely French in origin—a testament to early migrations & colonization—& the translation into English is part of Thomas's early study following the British occupation of Trinidad.

Louis Riel Métis Nation, Canada, 1844–1885

from A SYSTEM OF PHILOSOPHICAL THEOLOGY

Système philosophico-théologique: If the state of harmony before original sin had endured.

If man had persevered in that state of happiness [before the Fall], he would have taken to it more and more. And the more tender he would have found his intimacy with the active essences, the more he would have worked to render it perfect. His obedient love would have attracted to him every day a new quantity of active monads. They would have condensed in his person to a considerable degree. The weight of his body would have finally become comparatively light in the bosom of their density. This prodigious concentration of the infinite essences in man would have constituted for him the gift of subtlety.

They would have absorbed him entirely. They would have carried him away to heaven wholly alive, as the sublime movement of wings lifts the volatile body of the eagle and like the air carries objects less dense and less heavy than the matter of its own invisible gases there.

40. ...The abundance of essences starts to diminish once he resolutely sets out on the road of excess: excess of play, excess of conversation, excess of wakefulness, excess of drinking, excess of eating, excess of pleasure; excess of work, excess of fasting, excess of diverse privations, excess of mortification, etc....

50. In isolation from the active essences, man languishes; he degenerates and bores himself.

53. Superstition consists in putting above (Super) the real God the establishment (Stition) of a false god; Superstition consists in imagining above (Super) the real God or some religious truth the establishment (Stitio) of a

false god or of some error in the Subject of religion. Superstition, properly speaking, consists in putting above the real God the establishment of a false god. Above Super, and Stitio.

Religion consists in binding (religare) human essences and divine essences together.

55. To insure the success of Moses' revelation and to insure the success of the doctrine of Jesus Christ (that are one and the same thing) I suggest that Ville-Marie [Montreal] in Lower-Canada replace Rome, that New-France, as a sacerdotal country, be substituted for the Roman States, and that bishop Ignace Bourget be regarded as the Supreme Pontiff of the New World.

56. It is enough to say I am obeying strong convictions.

31. And as electricities of the same name repulse each other, man enters a quarrel with his God.

32. When NEGATIVE divine electricities forbid us something, if we prohibit ourselves everything other than that, we bring into play, vis-à-vis that something, our NEGATIVE electricities and, as electricities of the same name are repulsed by each other, we quarrel with the active essences.

N.B. The use of our negative and positive forces is entirely subject to our faculties, whose Consciousness never ceases to approve or condemn the exercise.

Sex is in the monads that is to say each monad alternates between its male and its female form.
As is proper to it, each active male monad possesses an inert monad which is female.
And as is proper to it each active female monad possesses an inert monad which is male.

Translated from French by Antoine Malette and Bryan Sentes

COMMENTARY

My people will sleep for one hundred years, but when they awake, it will be the artists who give them their spirit back. (L.R.)

Writes Bryan Sentes as translator: "A controversial figure—revolutionary, lunatic, self-proclaimed messiah, traitor, hero—Louis Riel received a rigorous education while studying for the priesthood in Montreal before returning home to Manitoba to play a leading role in the Red River Rebellion (1869–70) that pitted Métis interests against the encroachments of the fledgling Canadian state. Undergoing a profound religious experience, he was briefly institutionalized before eventually settling in Montana, only to be enticed across the border to lead the Métis again in the Northwest Rebellion (1885), which was summarily crushed, resulting in his trial and execution.

"His book, the *Massinahican*, for all its provisional, fragmented brevity ('a draft of a draft of a draft' [Melville]), draws on Roman Catholicism, Leibniz's Monadology, psychology, the new physics of electromagnetism, and, arguably, Theosophy. Formally modelled on Allan Kardec's *Le Livre des esprits* (1857), Riel's pages prefigure Wittgenstein's argument-by-remark as much as they resemble the German Romantic Fragment (and, perhaps, even its ironies)."

Isidore Ducasse, Comte de Lautréamont
Uruguay/France, 1846–1870

from **MALDOROR**

Book III

Mario and I were riding along the beach. Our horses, necks outstretched, clove through the membranes of space and struck sparks from the pebbles on the beach. An icy blast struck us full in the face, penetrated our cloaks; and swept back on our twin heads. The sea-gull tried in vain to warn us by his outcries and the agitation of his wings of the possible proximity of the storm, and cried out: "Where are they off to at that mad gallop?" We said nothing; plunged in meditation we let ourselves be carried away by that furious race. The fisherman, seeing us pass by swift as an albatross, and realizing he was seeing before him the *two mysterious brothers* as we had been called because we were always together, hastened to cross himself and hide with his paralyzed dog in the deep shadows of a rock.

The inhabitants of the coast had heard tell of many strange things concerning these two persons, who appeared on earth amid clouds during periods of great disaster, when a frightful war threatened to plant its harpoon in the breasts of two enemy countries, or cholera was preparing to hurl out from its sling putrefaction and death through entire cities. The oldest beachcombers frowned gravely, affirming that the two phantoms, whose vast black wingspread everyone had noticed during hurricanes above the sandbanks and reefs, were the evil genius of the land and the genius of the sea, who promenade their majesty up in the air during natural revolutions, united by an eternal friendship the rarity and glory of which have given birth to the astonishment of unlimited chains of generations.

It was said that, flying side by side like two Andean condors, they loved to soar in concrete circles amid the layers of the atmosphere close to the sun; that in these places they fed upon the pure essence of light; but that they resigned themselves only reluctantly to reversing the inclination of their vertical light towards the dismayed orbit where the human globe turns deliriously, inhabited by cruel spirits who massacre one another on the battlefields (when they are not killing one another secretly in their cities with the dagger of hatred or ambition) and who feed upon beings as full of life as themselves and placed a few degrees lower in the scale of existence.

Or again, when the pair firmly resolved, in order to excite men to repentance by the verses of prophecy, to swim in great strokes towards the sidereal regions where the planet stirs in the midst of the dense exhalations of avarice, pride, curses and mockery, given off like pestilential vapors from the loathsome surface, seeming no larger than a ball and almost invisible because of the distance, they did not fail to find occasions on which they repented bitterly of their benevolence, misunderstood and spurned, and hid themselves in the depths of volcanoes to converse with the tenacious fire that boils in the vats of the central vaults, or at the bottom of the sea, to rest their disillusioned eyes in the contemplation of the most ferocious monsters of the deep, which to them appeared as models of gentleness, compared with the bastards of humanity.

When night fell with her propitious gloom, they rushed from the porphyry-crested craters and from the subaqueous currents, and left well behind them the craggy chamber-pot where the constipated anus of the human cockatoo wriggles: left it so far behind that they could no longer distinguish the suspended silhouette of the filthy planet. Then, aggrieved by their fruitless attempt, the angel of the land and the angel of the sea kissed, weeping, amid the compassionate stars and under the eye of God!...

Mario and he who galloped at his side were not unaware of the vague and superstitious rumors that were recounted during their evening vigils by the fishermen whispering around the hearth behind closed doors and windows, while the night-wind, desirous of warming itself, making its plaint heard around the thatched cottage, shaking the frail walls that are surrounded at the base by fragments of crushed shells washed up by the dying ripples of the waves.

We did not speak. What do two hearts that love say to each other? Nothing. But our eyes expressed all.

Translated from French by Guy Wernham

COMMENTARY

The end of the nineteenth century will see its poet (though at first he should not begin with a masterpiece, but should follow the laws of nature). He was born on the South American shores, at the mouth of the Plate River, where two peoples, once enemies, now struggle to outdo one another in material and moral progress. (I.D.)

(1) Decades before his rediscovery by the Surrealists in the 1920s placed him in the pantheon of the great French avant-gardists, the person & the poetry of the Uruguayan Count of Lautréamont were being praised & assimilated in Spanish-speaking America, most notably through the efforts of Rubén Darío, who, in 1896 & after, introduced & spread his works across our continent. Of this Darío wrote in a letter to the French-Argentinean critic Paul Groussac: "Dear Master, we, the young poets of the Spanish-Speaking America, we are setting the stage for the coming of our own Walt Whitman, an Indigenous Walt Whitman, full of world, replete of universe… [as] announced by the enigmatic and terrible madman from Montevideo in his prophetic and frightful book."

(2) Banned in France following its 1869 publication in Belgium, *Maldoror* didn't appear there until four years after Lautréamont's death. The book itself consists of six "chants" or "songs" of from five to sixteen prose "stanzas" each, each stanza in turn a kind of separate poem-offering. The central figure, Maldoror, is like a hero out of Nietzsche or De Sade "[whose] cruelty seems limitless, matched only by that of the Creator" (Ora Avni).

(3) Considering Ducasse one of the "four geniuses" who had "been born in our lands" (along with Jules Laforgue, Julio Herrera y Reissig, & Rubén Darío), Pablo Neruda wrote later: "Isidore Ducasse, Count of Lautréamont, is American, Uruguayan, Chilean, Colombian, ours. A relative of gauchos, of head-hunters from the remote Caribbean, he is a bloodthirsty hero from the dark depths of our America. The male horsemen, the colonists of Uruguay, Patagonia, and Colombia run in his desert literature. In him, there is a geographical environment of gigantic exploration and a maritime phosphorescence that is not provided by the Seine but by the torrential flora of the Amazon and the abstract nitrate, the longitudinal copper, the aggressive gold, and the active and chaotic currents that stain the land and the sea of our American planet" (in *Journey to the Heart of Quevedo*, trans. Javier Taboada).

José Martí Cuba, 1853–1895

I AM AN HONEST MAN

I am an honest man
From the land of palm trees
And I wish before I meet my death
To cast these verses from my soul.

I come from everywhere,
Towards everywhere I go:
I am art among arts
And in the peaks I am a peak.

I know the exotic names
Of herbs and flowers,
And of deadly betrayals
And sublime sorrows.

In the dark night I have seen
Rays of the pure splendor
Of divine beauty raining down
Upon my head.

I have seen the sprouting of wings
From the shoulders of beautiful women
And the coming forth of butterflies
From piles of rubble.

I have seen a man who lives
With a dagger in his side,
Who never uttered the name
Of the woman who killed him.

Briefly, twice, I have seen the soul
Like a reflection, when the poor
Old man died, and
When she said goodbye.

I trembled once—
At the vineyard's gate—
When the savage bee
Stung my beloved's brow.

I rejoiced once, in my destiny,
As I'd never rejoiced before,
When the warden read
My condemnation, and wept.

I hear a sigh that's traveled
across lands and seas,
And it's not a sigh—it's my son
Awakening.

If asked to choose the jeweler's
brightest gem,
I would choose an honest friend
And put love aside.

I have seen the wounded eagle
Soar through the serene sky
And the viper in its den
Die of its own poison.

Well do I know that when the world,
Pale with exhaustion, gives over
To rest, the murmur of a tranquil brook
Floats above the deep silence.

I have dared to stretch my hand,
Stiff with horror and joy,
To the extinguished star
That fell at my door.

I hide within my rugged breast
The sorrow that tears at me:
Son of an enslaved people
For which he lives, falls silent and dies.

Everything is beautiful and steadfast,
Everything is music and reason,
And, like a diamond, everything
Is coal before it's light.

I know that the foolish are buried
With great pomp and great lamentation,
And that no soil bears fruit
Like the soil of the cemetery.

I fall silent, I understand, and I remove
My rhymester's finery:
I hang my scholar's robes
From a withered tree.

Translated from Spanish by Mark Weiss

NOT RHETORIC OR ORNAMENT

Not rhetoric or ornament
But a natural verse. Here a torrent
Here a dry stone. There a gilded bird
Shining in green branches,
Like a nasturtium among emeralds.
Here the fetid, viscous trace
Of a slug: its eyes mud-blisters, its belly
Drab, greasy, foul.
In the treetop, higher still, alone
In the steel sky a constant
Star; and here, below, the oven
The oven that cooks the earth.
Flames, struggling flames, with
Eye-like sockets, arm-like tongues,
A man's fury, sword-sharp: the sword of life
That blaze upon blaze conquers the earth at last!
It climbs, roaring from within, destroying:
Man begins in flame and finishes in flight.
At his triumphal passage the dirty
The vile, the cowardly, the defeated,
Like snakes, like lap dogs, like
Crocodiles with their double rows of teeth,
From here, from there, from the tree that shelters him
From the soil that holds him, from the stream
Where he slakes his thirst, from the very anvil
Where bread is shaped, they howl and toss him,
Bite at his foot, cover his face with dust and mud,
Enough to blind a man on his path.
With one beat of his wing he sweeps the world aside
And rises through the fiery air,
Dead, like a man and like the serene sun.
Thus must noble poetry be:
Thus, as life is: star and lap dog;

The cave bitten by flame,
The pine in whose fragrant branches
A nest sings by moonlight,
A nest sings to the splendor of moonlight.

Translated from Spanish by Mark Weiss

Everything has already been said; but all authentic things are new. To confirm is to create. What gives birth to the world isn't the discovery of how it's made, but the effort of each to discover it.... (J.M.)

Writes translator Mark Weiss: "Martí may not be unique as a political poet-martyr (one thinks of Byron and Lorca), but he must have been one of the most politically involved. The very model of the committed artist, he was 42 when he died in one of the first engagements of the second Cuban War of Independence, of which he had been chief propagandist and one of the principal planners. He had spent his entire adult life in exile, chiefly in Mexico City and New York.

"Martí's densely figured, learned, syntactically-convoluted verse gave back to Spanish poetry the muscular intensity of the Baroque, anticipating in this regard not so much the *modernismo* that was to follow him as the poetry of José Lezama Lima, Cuba's greatest twentieth-century poet and fountainhead of the *neobarroco*, which remains a dominant force today in Latin American writing. Paradoxically, he also introduced, in 'Simple Verses,' a seemingly naive form reminiscent of South American *coplas*, the folk practice of constructing songs out of spontaneously composed quatrains, each participant in turn presenting his own variations on the theme, usually, of love or loss, and one thinks also of the gypsy ballads of Lorca that were to come 25 years later."

For more on Martí, see the excerpt in "A Map of Americas."

José Asunción Silva   Colombia, 1865–1896

ZOOSPERMOS

The world-renowned scientist
Cornelius Van Kerinken
who enjoyed a sizable
practice in Hamburg
and left us a volume

José Asunción Silva **209**

of some 700 pages
on the liver and kidneys,
was abandoned in the end
by all of his friends,
died in Leipzig demented,
dishonored and poor,
because of his studies
at the end of his life
on spermatozoa.

Bent over a microscope
that cost him a fortune,
unique and a masterpiece,
from a London optician;
his sight bearing down,
his hands shaking badly,
anxious, tight, motionless
focused and fierce,
like a colorless phantom
in a low voice he said:
"Oh! look at them running
how they're moving and swarming
and clashing and scattering:
these spermatozoa."

Look! If he weren't
lost and vanished forever;
if fleeing down roads
that no one remembers
he finally managed
after so many tries
to change into a man
his life still before him
he could be a new Werther
and after thousands of torments
and exploits and passions
would knock himself off
with a real Smith and Wesson,
that spermatozoon.

And the one just above him,
a hairbreadth away
from the so-to-speak Werther,

at the edge of the lens,
could end up as a hero
in one of our wars.
Then a statue in bronze
could serve as a tribute
to that unbeatable winner,
that bona-fide leader
of soldiers and cannons,
Commander in Chief
of all of our armies,
that spermatozoon.

The next one here might be
the Gretchen to some Faust;
and another, higher up,
a noble-blooded heir,
the owner at twenty-one
of a million or so dollars
and the title of a count;
still another one, a usurer;
and that one there, the small one,
some kind of lyric poet;
& this other one, the tall one,
a professor of some science,
will have written a whole book
about spermatozoa.

Good luck and gone forever
you small dots & small men!
between the two thick lenses
of the giant microscope,
translucent and diaphanous,
Good luck, you shimmying
zoosperms, you will not grow
over the earth to people it
with further joys and horrors.
In no more than ten minutes
you'll all be lying dead here.
Hola! spermatozoa.

Thus world-renowned scientist
Cornelius Van Kerinken
who enjoyed a sizable

practice in Hamburg
and left us a volume
of some 700 pages
on the liver and kidneys,
died in Leipzig demented,
dishonored and poor,
because of his studies
at the end of his life
on spermatozoa.

Translated from Spanish by Jerome Rothenberg

NOCTURNE III

A night,
A night thick with perfumes, with whispers & music, with wings,
     A night
With glowworms fantastically bright in its bridal wet shadows,
There by my side, pressed slowly & tightly against me,
     Mute and pale
As if a presentiment of infinite sorrow should stir you
Down to the secretest depths of your nature,
A path with flowers crosses the plain
      Where you traveled,
      Under a full moon
Up in the deep blue infinite skies
Its white light scattered,
& your shadow too
      Thin and limpid,
& my shadow
    That the moon's rays projected
    Across the sad sands,
    Where both were conjoined
& were one
& were one
& were one immense shadow!
& were one immense shadow!
& were one only one immense shadow!

    That night
    All alone   a soul

Filled with infinite sorrow
With your death and its torments
Cut off from yourself, by the shadow, by distance and time,
   An infinite blackness
   Where our voices don't reach,
   Mute & alone
   On the path I was traveling...
The sound of the dogs as they bayed at the moon,
   The pale moon,
& the croaking out loud
   Of the frogs...
I felt cold, felt the coldness that came from your cheeks
In the alcove in back, from your breasts & the hands that I loved
Under sheets white as snow in the death house!
A coldness of graves & a coldness of death
& the coldness of nada...
& my shadow
   That the moon's rays projected
   Was drifting alone,
   Was drifting alone,
   Was drifting alone through an unpeopled wasteland!
& your shadow, agile & smooth,
   Thin & limpid,
As on that warm night in dead spring,
That night filled with perfumes, with whispers & music, with wings,
   Came near & made off with her
   Came near & made off with her
Came near & made off with her...
Oh the shadows brought together!
Oh the shadows of our bodies joining with the shadows of our souls!
Oh the shadows sought & brought together in the nights of blackness
& of tears...!

Translated from Spanish by Jerome Rothenberg

COMMENTARY

*Leave your studies & pleasures, your / vapid lost causes, / &, as
Shakyamuni once counselled, / hide yourself in Nirvana.* (J.A.S., from Filosofías)
And again: *When you reach your last hour, / your final stop on earth, /
you'll feel an angst that can kill you— / at having done nothing.*

"Nocturno III" comes from an unusual extension of voice that even visually creates an unseen pattern of lines. One can sense in Silva's "night" the process of contacting his underworld and the intermittent flow and rupture derived from this contact. It is a chant to the night and to the obscure unity of a mysterious duality that does not lead to death, but is death itself. This poem in particular possesses a structure that would reappear (reinvented) in some of Neruda's pieces, for example, but most importantly it deals with an alliance with obscurity and a dialect of rhythm and breakage, sound and visual play, that is still haunting.

Silva is also the author of a novel titled *De sobremesa* (*After-Dinner Conversation: The Diary of a Decadent*). In 1896 Silva committed suicide by shooting a bullet directly into his heart.

(Commentary by Heriberto Yépez, originally published in *Poems for the Millennium*, vol. 3, ed. Jerome Rothenberg & Jeffrey Robinson.)

Rubén Darío   Nicaragua, 1867–1916

METEMPSYCHOSIS

I was a soldier who slept in queen
Cleopatra's bed. Her whiteness
and her cosmic and almighty gaze.
    And that was all.

Oh gaze! Oh whiteness! And oh, that bed
in which her whiteness glowed!
Oh, the almighty marble rose!
    And that was all.

And her backbone cracked beneath my arm;
and I, a freedman, made her forget Anthony.
(Oh, bed and gaze and whiteness!)
    And that was all.

I, Rufus Galus, was a soldier and I had
Gaul's blood, and the imperial calf
lent me a bold minute of her desire.
    And that was all.

Why amid that spasm did the tongs
of my bronze fingers not choke
the neck of the white horny queen?
    And that was all.

I was taken to Egypt. Around my scrag
was a chain. One day the dogs
ate me up. Rufus Galus was my name.
　　And that was all.

Translated from Spanish by Javier Taboada

TO ROOSEVELT

1904

It is with the voice of the Bible, or the verse of Walt Whitman
that I advance upon you now, Hunter!
You are primitive and modern, sensible and complicated,
with something of Washington and a dash of Nimrod.
You are the United States,
you are the future invader
of all that's innocent in America and its Indian blood,
blood that still says Jesus Christ and speaks in Spanish.

You are a superb and strapping specimen of your people;
you are cultured and capable; you oppose Tolstoy.
You are a horse-whisperer, an assassinator of tigers,
you are Alexander-Nebuchadnezzar.
(You are a Professor of Energy
as the whackjobs among us now say.)

You think that life is a fire,
that progress is eruption
and into whatever bones you shoot,
you hit the future.

No.

The United States is powerful and huge.
And when it shakes itself a deep temblor
runs down the enormous vertebrae of the Andes.
If it yells, its voice is like the ripping boom of the lion.
It is just as Hugo said to Grant: "The stars are yours."
(Glinting wanly, it raises itself, the Argentine sun,
and the star of Chile rises too…) You are rich—
you join the cult of Hercules with the cult of Mammon;
and illuminating the way of easy conquest,
"Freedom" has found its torch in New York.

But our America, which has had poets
from the ancient times of Nezahualcoyotl,
which has kept walking in the footprints of the great Bacchus
(who had learned the Panic alphabet at one glance);
which has consulted the stars, which has known Atlantis,
(whose name comes down drumming to us in Plato),
which has lived since the old times on the very light of this world,
on the life of its fire, its perfume, its love,
the America of the great Moctezuma, of the Inca,
our America smelling of Christopher Columbus,
our Catholic America, our Spanish America,
the America in which the noble Cuauhtémoc said:
"I am in no bed of roses": that same America
which tumbles in the hurricanes and lives for Love,
it lives, you men of Saxon eyes and Barbarian souls.
And it dreams. And it loves, and it vibrates; and she is the daughter of the Sun!
Be very careful. Long live this Spanish America!
The Spanish Lion has loosed a thousand cubs today: they are at large, Roosevelt,
and if you are to snag us, outlunged and awed,
in your claws of iron, you must become God himself,
the alarming Rifleman and the hardened Hunter.

And though you count on everything, you lack the one thing needed:
  God.

Translated from Spanish by Gabriel Gudding

AGENCY

The news?—The earth trembles.
They are hatching war in The Hague.
The crowned heads are all frightened.
The whole world smells rotten.
There is no balm in Gilead.
The Marquis de Sade has landed,
just in from Seboim.
The Gulf Stream has changed course.
Paris whips itself to delight.
They say a comet is approaching.
The predictions of that old monk
Malachi are coming true.
The Devil is hiding in the church.
A nun gave birth—(but where?)—

Barcelona is nothing now
except when a bomb explodes.
China has cut off its pigtail.
Henry de Rothschild is a poet.
Madrid has turned against bullfighting.
The Pope has got rid of his eunuchs.
A bill was recently passed
to legalize child prostitution.
White faith is beginning to pall
but everything black continues.
The palace of the Antichrist
is ready and waiting, somewhere.
There are intercommunications
between Lesbians and tramps.
It is said that the Wandering
Jew is coming—What else, oh Lord?—

Translated from Spanish by Lysander Kemp

COMMENTARY

*I seek a form that my style cannot discover… / And I only find the word
that runs away… / The neck of the great white swan, that questions me.*
(R.D.)

(1) From the publication of his early book of poems & stories, *Azul* (Blue),
in 1888, Darío (born Felix Rubén García Sarmiento in Metapa, Nicaragua)
was the first great poet of Spanish-American *Modernismo*: a reinvigoration
of Spanish *poesis* & language with its roots deeply planted in America. But
the *Modernistas*, as Octavio Paz would write of them later, "accomplished
more than a job of restoration; they added something new. The world, the
universe, is a system of correspondences under the rule of rhythm. Everything connects, everything rhymes. Every form in nature has something
to say to every other. The poet is not a maker of rhythm but its transmit-
ter. Analogy is the highest expression of the imagination." A wanderer (he
lived in Europe from 1898 to 1914, two years before his death), Darío by
the early twentieth century was able to bypass symbolism—to engage, like
the Romantics before him, in a poetics & in a politics (as here) from a less
(or more) than political perspective. If Whitman's *Leaves of Grass* was "a
Declaration of Independence from the 'bondage' of European & British
conventions," as one of us once wrote, then Darío in his way would declare
the independence of *his* America from the America to the north.

(2) "If there is poetry in our America, it is in the old things, in Palenque and
Utatlán, in the legendary Indian, and in the courtly and sensual Inca, and in

the great Moctezuma on the golden seat. The rest is yours, democratic Walt
Whitman" (R.D., from "Liminary Words").

And again: "If in these things there is a politics, it is because politics
appears universally. And if you find verses to a president, it is because they
are a continental clamor. Tomorrow we may well become Yankees (and this
is most likely); my protest stands anyhow, written on the wings of immaculate swans, as illustrious as Jupiter."

For more on Darío, see "A Map of Americas."

José Juan Tablada Mexico, 1871–1945

from **LI-PO**

Li-Po, one of the "seven wine-sages"
was a sparkling gold brocade...

The Cormorants of the idea
on the shores   of meditation
in the blue   and yellow
rivers they   try to fish
t he mo-   on's glow
......but   they fail
they get   nothing
their own   beaks break off the   still waters
smashing   the reflection of the mo-   on in thousand
silvery shards of nacre and alabaster and Li-Po, immobile, stares how amid
the glossy mist silence finally restores

the pearl of the MOON

On the mirror-river
the moon becomes
a silver spider
weaving its web

And Li-Po
the divine
one

                                        night
                                        drank
                                        the
                                        moon
                                        in his cup
                                        of wine

Gets its enigmatic
charm
and falls asleep
full of his lunatic wine

          "Where's Li-Po? Bring him at once!"
          The Emperor called from his halls

          And, kind of drunk,
          the poet comes
          and rests in the harem;
          a concubine
          gives him a paintbrush
          filled with ink;
          another, a stripe of silk
                    for paper,
                    and Li
                         writes this:

                                                  I
                                                  am
                                                  alone
                                                  with my
                                                  wine-jar
                                                  beneath
                                             a blooming tree

          the moon
          appears
          its rays
          say

                    now
               we're *two*

                    and my own shadow
                    then decrees

now
we're
three

though the orb
cannot drink
its share of wine
and my shadow doesn't
want to leave
since it's with me

in that joyous
companionship
I'll laugh at my woes
as long as spring
goes on

Translated from Spanish by Javier Taboada

COMMENTARY

My current poems are just language: some aren't simply graphical but architectural... Everything is synthetic, discontinuous and therefore dynamic: the explanatory and the rhetorical are suppressed for good; it is a succession of substantive states. I think it's pure poetry... (J.J.T.)

Poet, chronicler, painter, novelist, art critic—& more—Tablada was well known for his introduction of Chinese & Japanese art & poetry to Latin America, for being the first Spanish-speaking author of haiku writing, & beyond that, the first truly experimental poet in Mexico. His works exhibit a persistent shift & pursuit of new forms, showing "the chameleon poet" in him (in Keats's phrase) & his diverse interests & *states of mind*: from late "decadentism" to *Modernismo*, from haiku to calligrams & concrete poetry, from novels to entomology, etc.

Wrote Octavio Paz, in summary: "[Tablada] was a 'minor poet,' especially when compared to Huidobro, but his work—with its strict and beloved limitations—extended the frontiers of our poetry. And it extended them in two directions: in space, toward other worlds and civilizations; in time, toward the future: the avant-garde.... His small and condensed poems—besides being the first haiku-like work carried over into Spanish—were really something new in Tablada's time. They were that to such an extent and with such intensity that, even today, many of them keep intact their powers of wonder and freshness. Of how many, more pretentious works can the same be said?" (from Paz's introduction to Basho's *Sendas de Oku*, trans. here by Javier Taboada).

Gertrude Stein USA, 1874–1946

from *WINNING HIS WAY*

What is poetry. This. Is poetry.
Delicately formed. And pleasing. To the eye.
What is fame. Fame is. The care of. Their. Share.
And so. It. Rhymes better.
A pleasure in wealth. Makes. Sunshine.
And a. Pleasure. In sunshine. Makes wealth.
They will manage very well. As they. Please. Them.
What is fame. They are careful. Of awakening. The. Name.
And so. They. Wait. With oxen. More. Than one.
They speak. Of matching. Country oxen. And.
They speak. Of waiting. As if. They. Had won.
By their. Having. Made. A pleasure. With. Their.
May they. Make it. Rhyme. All. The time.
This is. A pleasure. In poetry. As often. As. Ever.
They will. Supply it. As. A measure.
Be why. They will. Often. Soften.
As they may. As. A. Treasure.

from *TENDER BUTTONS*

A CARAFE, THAT IS A BLIND GLASS.

A kind in glass and a cousin, a spectacle and nothing strange a single hurt color and an arrangement in a system to pointing. All this and not ordinary, not unordered in not resembling. The difference is spreading.

A LONG DRESS.

What is the current that makes machinery, that makes it crackle, what is the current that presents a long line and a necessary waist. What is this current.

What is the wind, what is it.

Where is the serene length, it is there and a dark place is not a dark place, only a white and red are black, only a yellow and green are blue, a pink is scarlet, a bow is every color. A line distinguishes it. A line just distinguishes it.

A RED HAT.

A dark grey, a very dark grey, a quite dark grey is monstrous ordinarily, it is so monstrous because there is no red in it. If red is in everything it is not necessary. Is that not an argument for any use of it and even so is there any place that is better, is there any place that has so much stretched out.

SHOES.

To be a wall with a damper a stream of pounding way and nearly enough choice makes a steady midnight. It is pus.

A shallow hole rose on red, a shallow hole in and in this makes ale less. It shows shine.

A DOG.

A little monkey goes like a donkey that means to say that means to say that more sighs last goes. Leave with it. A little monkey goes like a donkey.

A WHITE HUNTER.

A white hunter is nearly crazy.

from STANZAS IN MEDITATION

STANZA I

I caught a bird which made a ball
And they thought better of it.
But it is all of which they taught
That they were in a hurry yet
In a kind of a way they meant it best
That they should change in and on account
But they must not stare when they manage
Whatever they are occasionally liable to do
It is often easy to pursue them once in a while
And in a way there is no repose
They like it as well as they ever did
But it is very often just by the time
That they are able to separate
In which case in effect they could
Not only be very often present perfectly
In each way whichever they chose.

All of this never matters in authority
But this which they need as they are alike
Or in an especial case they will fulfill
Not only what they have at their instigation
Made for it as a decision in its entirety
Made that they minded as well as blinded
Lengthened for them welcome in repose
But which they open as a chance
But made it be perfectly their allowance
All which they antagonise as once for all
Kindly have it joined as they mind

. . . . .

STANZA 83

Why am I if I am uncertain reasons may inclose.
Remain remain propose repose chose.
I call carelessly that the door is open
Which if they may refuse to open
No one can rush to close.
Let them be mine therefore.
Everybody knows that I chose.
Therefore if therefore before I close.
I will therefore offer therefore I offer this.
Which if I refuse to miss may be miss is mine.
I will be well welcome when I come.
Because I am coming.
Certainly I come having come.
                    These stanzas are done

COMMENTARY

Poetry is concerned with using with abusing, with losing with wanting,
with denying with avoiding with adoring with replacing the noun. It is
doing that always doing that, doing that and doing nothing but that.
Poetry is doing nothing but using losing refusing and pleasing and betray-
ing and caressing nouns. That is what poetry does, that is what poetry has
to do no matter what kind of poetry it is. (G.S.)

(1) Gertrude Stein's own appraisal of her work ("the most serious thinking about the nature of literature in the 20th century has been done by a
woman") seems reasonable enough compared to the intervening neglect of
that work, but particularly the poetry, in favor of her otherwise celebrity

status. She came early to a root investigation of language & form ("going systematically to work smashing every connotation that words ever had, in order to get them back clean"—W. C. Williams) & to a poetry that brought Cubism into language (here as an altered concept of time, the "continuous present") & otherwise set the stage for much that was to follow. Her materials were simple enough to be easily misunderstood, & her declared intention was to "work in the excitedness of pure being... to get back that intensity into the language." She could produce work that was literally abstract, the end of a process of experiment by subtraction, or, as she would write later when looking back at her early *Tender Buttons*: "It was my first conscious struggle with the problem of correlating sight, sound and sense, and eliminating rhythm—now I am trying grammar and eliminating sight and sound."

(2) *Continuous present is one thing and beginning again and again is another thing. These are both things. And then there is using everything....*
    This brings us again to composition this the using everything. The using everything brings us to composition and to this composition. A continuous present and using everything and beginning again. (G. S.)
    And again: *There is no such thing as repetition. Only insistence.*

For more on Stein, see "A Map of Americas" & elsewhere in these pages.

Macedonio Fernández Argentina, 1874–1952

THERE'S A DYING

Don't take me to the shadowlands of death
There where my life will turn into a shadow
& where we'll live the would-have-been.
I don't want to live through a recall.
Give me more days like this in life.
Oh do not rush to make
An absence out of me
An absence out of me myself.
Don't take this living day from me!
I wish I still could be inside me.

There's a dying if within the eye
The gaze of love should turn
& just the gaze of life remain.
It's seeing the shadows of Death.

Death doesn't suck our cheeks,
This is Death: oblivion in eyes that gaze.

Translated from Spanish by Javier Taboada

from POEM ON THINKING POETICS

What has been called "Poe's metaphysics" is the unexpected metaphysics of a poet: a metaphysics of molecules; the poet's metaphysics is the nature of Consciousness in its ability to actively receive the happening or Contingency.

Poetry is every act of this acceptance. Why is it that Consciousness delights itself with that consent?

I'm proposing a Speculative-Thinking Poetry. For instance: my query is not about which insight explains the following facts, but what kind of poetry it justifies:

+ *Death* = the growth of mortals instead of the continuity (or the persistence) of One Immortal: the apparent idleness in refusing immortality and replacing it with multiple deaths and births.

+ *The unwillingness of Will:* we exist by chance—as survivors, and yet we are the Will. The Will-to-Live exists by chance. Why has the Will-to-Live shaped the survival of species in individuals who are fragile because they cannot avoid the Mechanical World?

+ *Why are there Images, why Memory, why Dreaming?* When in my dreams I'm frightened, why do I need the image of the murderer? I'm frightened while dreaming, nothing else. If I keep feeling hate or tenderness, why do I need the World?

+ *The invention of the Past,* which makes us see ourselves as survivors, ridiculed by an immense Nothingness preceding our own being, like a little foam in a huge wave. Why does Greece—which is an image—exist, but thunder and rain—which I so clearly represent in myself and which will happen next year—don't exist?

+ *The Criticism of the Given,* which denies and refuses to admit what is Given, i.e., the World imposing itself upon the spirit.

+ Why do we relate—by causality—the hedonic motivation with longevity: psyche and body? With this, the psyche loses all its grace: fluctuation and happening without a cause.

My Thinking Poetry will attempt to transcribe what happens with Consciousness when, through emotions, it accepts a painful mode of the truly Given. But poetry is in each one of those acts of acceptance. The Artist is he who, somehow, transmits those conscious moments and describes and recounts the moment of acceptance of that Contingency (a.k.a. The World)—previously unwanted by the soul.

Translated from Spanish by Javier Taboada

COMMENTARY

...time, space, causality, matter, and I, are nothing, neither forms of judgment nor intuitions. The world, being, reality, everything, is a dream without a dreamer; a single dream and the dream of one alone; therefore, the dream of no one, and that much more real to the degree it is entirely a dream. (M.F.)

(1) Essayist, novelist, poet, philosopher, & mystic, Macedonio Fernández's works & ideas—widely promoted by Jorge Luis Borges, his friend & disciple—influenced many generations of authors, as did his absurdist sense of humor & his conceptions of time & space. Aside from that, his life remains covered by the cloak of legend. Nothing but anecdotes: his fake campaign for Argentina's presidency (see "A Map of Extensions"), his plans to create a utopian society, & his refusal to be published all shape this sui generis character, who, like the best among us, deliberately blurs the boundaries between art & life.

(2) Borges said at Fernández's funeral: "A philosopher, a poet and a novelist died with Macedonio Fernández, and those terms—applied to him—recover a meaning that they don't usually have in this Republic.

"He was a philosopher, because he longed to know who we are (if we are somebody) and what or who the universe is. He was a poet, because he felt that poetry is the most faithful procedure to transcribe reality."

Which brings to mind Ludwig Wittgenstein's terse dictum qua philosopher: "One should really only do philosophy as poetry." Or David Antin's further assessment of Wittgenstein, which might equally fit Fernández, if switched to Spanish: "[He] is not a poet of the German language or the English language; he is a poet of thinking through language... a poet of nearly pure cognition."

A comparison with Poe's *Eureka* (in "A First Gallery") might also be of interest.

Wallace Stevens USA, 1879–1955

DISILLUSIONMENT OF TEN O'CLOCK

The houses are haunted
By white night-gowns.
None are green,
Or purple with green rings,
Or green with yellow rings,
Or yellow with blue rings.
None of them are strange,
With socks of lace
And beaded ceintures.
People are not going
To dream of baboons and periwinkles.
Only, here and there, an old sailor,
Drunk and asleep in his boots,
Catches tigers
In red weather.

SIX SIGNIFICANT LANDSCAPES

I
An old man sits
In the shadow of a pine tree
In China.
He sees larkspur,
Blue and white,
At the edge of the shadow,
Move in the wind.
His beard moves in the wind.
The pine tree moves in the wind.
Thus water flows
Over weeds.

II
The night is of the colour
Of a woman's arm:
Night, the female,
Obscure,
Fragrant and supple,
Conceals herself.

A pool shines,
Like a bracelet
Shaken in a dance.

III
I measure myself
Against a tall tree.
I find that I am much taller,
For I reach right up to the sun,
With my eye;
And I reach to the shore of the sea
With my ear.
Nevertheless, I dislike
The way ants crawl
In and out of my shadow.

IV
When my dream was near the moon,
The white folds of its gown
Filled with yellow light.
The soles of its feet
Grew red.
Its hair filled
With certain blue crystallizations
From stars,
Not far off.

V
Not all the knives of the lamp-posts,
Nor the chisels of the long streets,
Nor the mallets of the domes
And high towers,
Can carve
What one star can carve,
Shining through the grape-leaves.

VI
Rationalists, wearing square hats,
Think, in square rooms,
Looking at the floor,
Looking at the ceiling.
They confine themselves
To right-angled triangles.

If they tried rhomboids,
Cones, waving lines, ellipses—
As, for example, the ellipse of the half-moon—
Rationalists would wear sombreros.

The great poems of heaven and hell have been written and the great poem of earth remains to be written. (W.S.) And again: *The poem must resist the intelligence almost successfully.* Or further: *The poet is the priest of the invisible.*

So Stevens sought, then, as he said, "the poem of the mind in the act of finding / what will suffice"—or simply "the poem of the act of the mind." Although he rarely left conventional forms behind ("it comes to this, I suppose, that I believe in freedom regardless of form"), the process of that mind (= imagination) brought like Stein with her "continuous present" (above) to what a critic described as "a sense while reading him that creation is proceeding before one's eyes." His poetry, open to what Armand Schwerner called "the extraordinary reality of being, just being, moving, changing, flowing in the present," approached &/or surpassed the French & Spanish modernists in its vision of the "surreal" within the "real." But even his criticism of Surrealism ("to make a clam play an accordion is to invent not to discover") & his sense of the normality of all that as a different but necessary "miracle of logic" brings him close to the propositions of a number of post–World War II & early millennial poets.

Mina Loy England/USA, 1883–1966

from *ANGLO-MONGRELS AND THE ROSE*

EXODUS lay under an oak tree
   Bordering on Buda Pest   he had lain
   him down   to overnight   under the lofty rain
   of starlight
   having leapt from the womb
eighteen years ago   and grown
neglected   along the shores of the Danube
on the Danube in the Danube
-or breaking his legs behind runaway horses-
   with a Carnival quirk
   every Shrove Tuesday

Of his riches
a Patriarch
erected a synagogue
- -for the people

His son
looked upon Lea
- - of the people
    she sat in Synagogue
    -her hair   long as the Talmud
    -her tamarind eyes- -...
and disinherited
begat this Exodus

Imperial Austria taught the child
the German   secret patriotism
the Magyar tongue   the father
stuffed him with biblical Hebrew and the
seeds of science   exhorting him
    to vindicate
    his forefathers' ambitions

The child
flowered precociously   fever
smote the father
    the widowed mother
took to her bosom   a spouse
of her own sphere
and hired
Exodus in apprenticeship
to such   as garrulously inarticulate
ignore   the cosmic cultures

Sinister foster parents
who lashed the boy
to that paralysis of
the spiritual apparatus
common to
the poor
The arid gravid
intellect   of Jewish ancestors

the senile juvenile
calculating prodigies of Jehovah
-Crushed by the Occident ox
they scraped
the gold gold golden
muck from off its hoofs-

moves Exodus   to emigrate
coveting the alien
asylum   of voluntary military
service   paradise   of the pound-sterling
where the domestic Jew   in lieu
of knouts   is lashed with tongues

                      X X X

   The cannibal God
shutters his lids of night   on the day's gluttony
the partially   devoured humanity
warms its unblessed beds   with bare prostrations
An insect   from an herb
errs on the   man-mountain
imparts   its infinitesimal tactile stimulus
to the epiderm   to the spirit
of Exodus
stirring   the anaesthetized load
of racial instinct frustrated
impulse   infantile impacts with unreason
   on his unconscious

   Blinking his eyes-   - -
   at sunrise   Exodus
lumbar-arching   sleep-logged   turns his ear
to the grit earth   and hears
the boom of cardiac cataracts
   thumping the turf
with his young pulse

He is undone!   How should he know
he has a heart?   The Danube
gives no instruction in anatomy-
the primary
throb of the animate

a beating mystery
pounds on his ignorance
in seeming
death dealing-

    The frightened fatalist
    clenches his eyes
    for the involuntary sacrifice
    stark
    to the sun-zumm dirges of
    a bee
    he lays him out
    for his heart-beats to slay him

It is not accomplished
the burning track
of lengthening sun shafts
spur
This lying-in-state of virility
to rise
and in his surprised
protracted viability
    shoulder his pack

Exodus   whose initiations
in arrogance   through brief
stimulation of his intellect
in servitude   through early
ill-usage   etch involute
inhibitions
upon his sensibility

sharpened and blunted   he
-bound for his unformulate
conception of life-
makes for the harbor

and the   dogged officer of Destiny
    kept Exodus
and that which he begat
moving along

DIE in the Past / Live in the Future. / THE velocity of velocities arrives in starting. / IN pressing the material to derive its essence, matter becomes deformed. // AND form hurtling against itself is thrown beyond the synopsis of vision. (M.L., from "Aphorisms on Futurism")

(1) Buoyed by early contacts with F.T. Marinetti & other founders of Italian Futurism, Loy's work started to appear ca. 1913, & by 1918, Ezra Pound, probably unaware she was an Englishwoman (she became a US citizen in 1946), reviewed her & Marianne Moore as "a distinctively national product... something which could not have come out of any other country," & which, he said, typified the process he called *logopoeia* or "poetry that is akin to nothing but language, which is a dance of the intelligence among words and ideas and modification of ideas and characters." His further description of it, "the utterance of clever people in despair, or hovering upon the brink of that precipice," now seems truer of Loy than of Moore, & what he fails to observe on Loy's side is that her work by 1918 had taken on a largeness of theme & an energy of sound & image that few in her generation could match. By then too, or soon thereafter, she was into a private mythology, *Anglo-Mongrels & the Rose*, comparable in its scope & resources to Pound's *Cantos* & Eliot's *Waste Land*, & in its central character (based on her Hungarian-born Jewish father) to Leopold Bloom in James Joyce's *Ulysses*.

(2) "It was inevitable that the renaissance of poetry should proceed out of America, where latterly a thousand languages have been born, and each one, for purposes of communication at least, English—English enriched and variegated with the grammatical structure and voice-inflection of many races.... Out of the welter of this unclassifiable speech, while professors of Harvard and Oxford labored to preserve 'God's English,' the muse of modern literature arose, and her tongue had been loosened in the melting pot" (M.L., 1925).

William Carlos Williams USA, 1883–1963

EL HOMBRE

It's a strange courage
you give me ancient star:

Shine alone in the sunrise
toward which you lend no part!

THE LOCUST TREE IN FLOWER

Among
of
green

stiff
old
bright

broken
branch
come

white
sweet
May

again

from **PATERSON**

Episode 17

Beat hell out of it
  Beautiful Thing
  spotless cap
and crossed white straps
over the dark rippled cloth—
  Lift the stick
above that easy head
where you sit by the ivied
church, one arm
  buttressing you
long fingers spread out
among the clear grass prongs—
  and drive it down
  Beautiful Thing
that you caressing body kiss
  and kiss again
that holy lawn—
And again: obliquely—
legs curled under you as a
  deer's leaping—

pose of supreme indifference
  sacrament
to a summer's day
  Beautiful Thing
in the unearned suburbs
  then pause
  the arm fallen—
what memories
of what forgotten face
brooding upon that lily stem?

  The incredible
nose straight from the brow
  the empurpled lips
and dazzled half-sleepy eyes
  Beautiful Thing
of some trusting animal
  makes a temple
of its place of savage slaughter
  revealing
the damaged will incites still
  to violence
consummately beautiful thing
and falls about your resting
  shoulders

Gently! Gently!
as in all things an opposite
  that awakes
the fury, conceiving
  knowledge
by way of despair that has
  no place
to lay its glossy head—
Save only—Not alone!
  Never, if possible
alone! to escape the accepted
  chopping block
and a square hat!—

And as reverie gains and
  your joints loosen

the trick's done!
Day is covered and we see you—
  but not alone!
drunk and bedraggled to release
the strictness of beauty
under a sky full of stars
  Beautiful thing
and a slow moon—

                    The car
  had stopped long since
  when the others
came and dragged those out
  who had you there
  indifferent
to whatever the anesthetic
  Beautiful Thing
might slum away the bars—

Reek of it!
  What does it matter?
  could set free
only the one thing—
But you!
—in your white lace dress
  "the dying swan"
and high heeled slippers—tall
as you already were—
  till your head
through fruitful exaggeration
was reaching the sky and the
prickles of its ecstasy
  Beautiful Thing!

And the guys from Paterson
  beat up
the guys from Newark and told
them to stay the hell out
of their territory and then
socked you one
  across the nose
  Beautiful Thing

for good luck and emphasis
  cracking it
till I must believe that all
desired women have had each
  in the end
  a busted nose
and live afterward marked up
  Beautiful Thing
  for memory's sake
to be credible in their deeds

Then back to the party!
  and they maled
and femaled you jealously
  Beautiful Thing
as if to discover when and
  by what miracle
there should escape what?
still to be possessed
out of what part
  Beautiful Thing
should it look?
  or be extinguished—
Three days in the same dress
  up and down—
  It would take
a Dominie to be patient
  Beautiful Thing
with you—

The stroke begins again—
  regularly
automatic
  contrapuntal to
the flogging
like the beat of famous lines
in the few excellent poems
  woven to make you
  gracious
  and on frequent occasions
  foul drunk
  Beautiful Thing

pulse of release
  to the attentive
and obedient mind.

I propose sweeping changes from top to bottom of the poetic structure. I said structure.... [A] revolution in the conception of the poetic foot— pointing out the evidence of something that has been going on for a long time. (W.C.W.)

(1) Of the first generation of dominant US moderns, Williams was the most open to the full range of new forms & possibilities: to the actual scope of what had to be done. Along with his Ezra Pound association—going back to his student days at the University of Pennsylvania—he engaged directly during the First World War with poets & artists around the Others group & the New York Dadaists & wrote of that time: "There had been a break somewhere: we were streaming through, each thinking his own thoughts, driving his own designs toward his self's objectives. Whether the Armory Show in painting did it or whether that also was no more than a facet—the poetic line, the way the image was to lie on the page, was our immediate concern. For myself all that implied in the materials, respecting the place I knew best, was finding a local assertion—to my everlasting relief." An overview of his early breakthroughs would focus on the "improvisations" & nonsequential arrangements, with their interplay of prose & verse, which he was then exploring and which would lead in effect to the concept & structure of *Paterson*, the complex long poem whose appearance, initiated in a preliminary sketch in the mid-1920s, was being eagerly awaited by the end of the Second World War.

(2) "The mutability of the truth, Ibsen said it. Jefferson said it. We should have a revolution of some sort in America every ten years. The truth has to be redressed, re-examined, reaffirmed in a new mode. There has to be new poetry. But the thing is that the change, the greater material, the altered structure of the inevitable revolution must be *in* the poem, in it. Made of it. It must shine in the structural body of it" (W.C.W., 1939, from *Selected Essays*, 1954).

For more on Williams, see "A Map of Americas" & "A Map of Histories."

OLD TORLINO
Navajo Nation / USA, ca. mid-19th century

Therefore I Must Tell the Truth

I am ashamed before the earth:
I am ashamed before the heavens:
I am ashamed before the dawn:
I am ashamed before the evening twilight:
I am ashamed before the blue sky:
I am ashamed before the darkness:
I am ashamed before the sun.
I am ashamed before that standing within me which speaks with me.
Some of these things are always looking at me.
I am never out of sight.
Therefore I must tell the truth.

That is why I always tell the truth.
I hold my word tight to my breast.

Translated from Navajo by Washington Matthews

Ezra Pound USA, 1885–1972

PAPYRUS

Spring ....
Too long ....
Gongula ....

from *CANTO LXXXI*

Zeus lies in Ceres' bosom
Taishan is attended of loves
           under Cythera, before sunrise
And he said: "Hay aquí mucho catolicismo—(sounded
                     catoli*th*ismo
        y muy poco reliHion."
and he said: "Yo creo que los reyes desparecen"

(Kings will, I think, disappear)
This was Padre José Elizondo
             in 1906 and in 1917
or about 1917
       and Dolores said: "Come pan, niño," eat bread, me lad
Sargent had painted her
           before he descended
(i.e. if he descended
       but in those days he did thumb sketches,
impressions of the Velázquez in the Museo del Prado
and books cost a peseta,
          brass candlesticks in proportion,
hot wind came from the marshes
   and death-chill from the mountains.
And later Bowers wrote: "but such hatred,
   I have never conceived such"
and the London reds wouldn't show up his friends
         (i.e. friends of Franco
working in London) and in Alcázar
forty years gone, they said: go back to the station to eat
you can sleep here for a peseta"
      goat bells tinkled all night
      and the hostess grinned: Eso es luto, *haw*!
mi marido es muerto
     (it is mourning, my husband is dead)
when she gave me a paper to write on
with a black border half an inch or more deep,
   say 5/8ths, of the locanda
"We call *all* foreigners frenchies"
and the egg broke in Cabranez' pocket,
     thus making history. Basil says
they beat drums for three days
till all the drumheads were busted
     (simple village fiesta)
and as for his life in the Canaries...
Possum observed that the local portagoose folk dance
was danced by the same dancers in divers localities
     in political welcome...
the technique of demonstration
     Cole studied that (not G.D.H., Horace)
"You will find" said old André Spire,

that every man on that board (Crédit Agricole)
has a brother-in-law
                    "You the one, I the few"
                    said John Adams
speaking of fears in the abstract
        to his volatile friend Mr Jefferson.
(To break the pentameter, that was the first heave)
or as Jo Bard says: they never speak to each other,
if it is baker and concierge visibly
            it is La Rouchefoucauld and de Maintenon audibly.
"Te cavero le budella"
                    "La corata a te"
In less than a geological epoch
                    said Henry Mencken
"Some cook, some do not cook
        some things cannot be altered"
Ἰυγξ… ἐμὸν ποτί δῶμα τὸν ἄνδρα…
What counts is the cultural level,
        thank Benin for this table ex packing box
        "doan yu tell no one I made it"
                from a mask fine as any in Frankfurt
"It'll get you offn th' groun"
                Light as the branch of Kuanon
And at first disappointed with shoddy
the bare ram-shackle quais, but then saw the
high buggy wheels
                and was reconciled,
George Santayana arriving in the port of Boston
and kept to the end of his life that faint *thethear*
of the Spaniard
                    as grace quasi imperceptible
as did Muss the *v* for *u* of Romagna
and said the grief was a full act
            repeated for each new condoleress
working up to a climax.
and George Horace said he wd/ "get Beveridge" (Senator)
Beveridge wouldn't talk and he wouldn't write for the papers
but George got him by campin' in his hotel
and assailin' him at lunch breakfast an' dinner
                    three articles
and my ole man went on hoein' corn

            while George was a-tellin' him,
come across a vacant lot
            where you'd occasionally see a wild rabbit
or mebbe only a loose one
            AOI!
            a leaf in the current
                        at my grates no Althea

———

libretto

———

Yet
Ere the season died a-cold
Borne upon a zephyr's shoulder
I rose through the aureate sky
            Lawes and Jenkyns guard thy rest
            Dolmetsch ever be thy guest,
Has he tempered the viol's wood
To enforce   both the grave   and the acute?
Has he curved us the bowl of the lute?
            Lawes and Jenkyns guard thy rest
            Dolmetsch ever be thy guest
Hast 'ou fashioned so airy a mood
            To draw up leaf from the root?
Hast 'ou found   a cloud   so light
            As seemed neither mist nor shade?

                  Then resolve me, tell me aright
                  If Waller sang or Dowland played

            Your eyen two wol sleye me sodenly
            I may the beauté of hem nat susteyne

And for 180 years almost nothing.

Ed ascoltando al leggier mormorio
            there came new subtlety of eyes into my tent,
whether of the spirit or hypostasis,
            but what the blindfold hides
or at carnival
                        nor any pair showed anger
            Saw but the eyes and stance between the eyes,

colour, diastasis,
        careless or unaware it had not the
    whole tent's room
nor was place for the full Ειδὼς
interpass, penetrate
        casting but shade beyond the other lights
            sky's clear
            night's sea
            green of the mountain pool
            shone from the unmasked eyes in half-mask's space.
What thou lovest well remains,
                    the rest is dross
What thou lov'st well shall not be reft from thee
What thou lov'st well is thy true heritage
Whose world, or mine or theirs
                    or is it of none?
First came the seen, then thus the palpable
    Elysium, though it were in the halls of hell,
What thou lov'st well is thy true heritage
What thou lov'st well shall not be reft from thee

The ant's a centaur in his dragon world.
Pull down thy vanity, it is not man
Made courage, or made order, or made grace,
    Pull down thy vanity, I say pull down.
Learn of the green world what can be thy place
In scaled invention or true artistry,
Pull down thy vanity,
                Paquin pull down!
The green casque has outdone your elegance.

"Master thyself, then others shall thee beare"
    Pull down thy vanity
Thou art a beaten dog beneath the hail,
A swollen magpie in a fitful sun,
Half black half white
Nor knowst'ou wing from tail
Pull down thy vanity
            How mean thy hates
Fostered in falsity,
            Pull down thy vanity,

Rathe to destroy, niggard in charity,
Pull down thy vanity,
   I say pull down.

But to have done instead of not doing
   this is not vanity
To have, with decency, knocked
That a Blunt should open
   To have gathered from the air a live tradition
or from a fine old eye the unconquered flame
This is not vanity.
   Here error is all in the not done,
all in the diffidence that faltered . . .

COMMENTARY

The artist is always beginning. Any work of art which is not a beginning, an invention, a discovery, is of little worth. (E.P.) And again: *The sum of human wisdom is not contained in any one language, and no single language is capable of expressing all forms and degrees of human comprehension.*

(1) On the way from conventional to modern modes, Ezra Pound's breakthrough into "imagism(e)" came in 1912, cut almost out of whole cloth & still restrained by classicist notions of *good* writing, etc., but produced the influential three dicta: "1. Direct treatment of the 'thing' whether subjective or objective; 2. To use absolutely no word that does not contribute to the presentation; 3. As regarding rhythm, to compose in the sequence of the musical phrase, not in the sequence of the metronome." By 1914 the association with painter/writer Wyndham Lewis (two issues of the magazine *Blast*, etc.) & a strong whiff of Cubism & Futurism brought the earlier definition of "image" ("that which presents an intellectual and emotional complex in an instant of time") into the high energy of Vorticist theory & the onset soon thereafter of his ongoing masterwork, the *Cantos*. The poems therein appeared in history, in time; the image became a "moving image"; both image & Cubist collage were subsumed (along with translation & tradition = "make it new") under the proposition of mind as a vortex, where "all times are contemporaneous" & the poem a "knot of patterned energies" (H. Kenner) & a process of making it "cohere."

(2) To which, after bouts of fascism & madness, the following from another of the late *Cantos*, an exquisite poetry of failure:

I have brought the great ball of crystal;
   who can lift it?
Can you enter the great acorn of light?
   But the beauty is not the madness

Tho' my errors and wrecks lie about me.
And I am not a demigod,
I cannot make it cohere.

For more on Pound, see "A Map of Histories" & elsewhere in these pages.

Enriqueta Arvelo Larriva Venezuela, 1886–1962

THE BALLAD OF WHAT I HEARD

I didn't know who told me so.
A divine tone.

I didn't know who told me so.
I didn't care about details.
It's the infinite I heard.

I didn't know who told me so.
But I heard it.
Praised be my ears!

In a flash harmony was made inside me.
What I heard runs eternal and clean.

And what a blessing
not to know who told me so.

Translated from Spanish by Javier Taboada

DESTINY

A dim impulse fired up my forests
Who dumped me over the embers?

The wind passed by—aimless
Unearthed echoes sprang—mute

Birds without nests cracked the sky
The final dust buried the border

Restless and obedient, I settled in my voice

Translated from Spanish by Javier Taboada

All morning the wind has spoken / an extraordinary language. / On the wind I went today. (E.A.L.)

From the rural town of Barinas, far from the Venezuelan mainstream, Enriqueta Arvelo Larriva's works point toward an independent quest, in which "space & voice" are the key features. These in turn led her to break with the modes of poetry common to her time ("constrained music," as she called them) & to explore free & open forms of verse—"a form without rules"— that became, for her, a "belligerent calling": "[to] enter into the barbarous with fearless steps." In that way, her voice could achieve & develop its own power, coming from the unrestricted hinterlands of language.

Arvelo Larriva was—for the greater part of her life—a true outsider, never part of any literary group or movement in Venezuela &, like many women of her time, completely self-taught & developing her inner life in secret. Hemmed in by family, & as the caretaker of her father for many years, she began after his death to contact a handful of Latin American poets such as Gabriela Mistral & became in her later years a founding voice for modern poetry in Venezuela.

H. D. [Hilda Doolittle] USA, 1886–1961

THE MYSTERIES REMAIN

The mysteries remain,
I keep the same
Cycle of seed-time
And of sun and rain;
Demeter in the grass,
I multiply,
Renew and bless
Bacchus in the vine;
I hold the law,
I keep the mysteries true,
The first of these
To name the living, dead;
I am the wine and bread.
I keep the law,
I hold the mysteries true,
I am the vine,
The branches, you
And you.

from THE WALLS DO NOT FALL

To Bryher

for Karnak 1923
from London 1942

[1]

An incident here and there,
and rails gone (for guns)
from your (and my) old town square:

mist and mist-grey, no colour,
still the Luxor bee, chick and hare
pursue unalterable purpose

in green, rose-red lapis;
they continue to prophesy
from the stone papyrus:

there, as here, ruin opens
the tomb, the temple; enter,
there as here, there are no doors:

the shrine lies open to the sky,
the rain falls, here, there
sand drifts, eternity endures.

ruin everywhere, yet as the fallen roof
leaves the sealed room
open to the air,

so, through our desolation,
thoughts stir, inspiration stalks us
through gloom:

unaware, Spirit announces the Presence;
shivering overtakes us,
as of old, Samuel:

trembling at a known street-corner,
we know not nor are known;
the Pythian pronounces—we pass on

to another cellar, to another sliced wall
where poor utensils show
like rare objects in a museum;

Pompeii has nothing to teach us,
we know crack of volcanic fissure,
slow flow of terrible lava,

pressure on heart, lungs, the brain
about to burst its brittle case
(what the skull can endure!):

over us, Apocryphal fire,
under us, the earth sway, dip of a floor,
slope of a pavement

where men roll, drunk
with a new bewilderment,
sorcery, bedevilment:

the bone-frame was made for
no such shock knit within terror,
yet the skeleton stood up to it:

the flesh? it was melted away,
the heart burnt out, dead ember,
tendons, muscles shattered, outer husk dismembered,

yet the frame held:
we passed the flame: we wonder
what saved us? what for?

[2]

Evil was active in the land,
Good was impoverished and sad;

Ill promised adventure,
Good was smug and fat;

Dev-ill was after us,
tricked up like Jehovah;

Good was the tasteless pod,
stripped from the manna-beans, pulse, lentils:

they were angry when we were so hungry
for the nourishment, God;

they snatched off our amulets,
charms are not, they said grace;

but gods always face two-ways,
so let us search the old highways

for the true-rune, the right-spell,
recover old values;

nor listen if they shout out,
your beauty, Isis, Aset or Astarte,

is a harlot; you are retrogressive,
zealot, hankering after old flesh-pots;

your heart, moreover,
is a dead canker,

they continue, and
your rhythm is the devil's hymn,

your stylus is dipped in corrosive sublimate,
how can you scratch out

indelible ink of the palimpsest
of past misadventure?

[3]

Let us, however, recover the Sceptre,
the rod of power.

it is crowned with the lily-head
or the lily-bud:

it is the Caduceus; among the dying
it bears healing:

or evoking the dead,
it brings life to the living.

COMMENTARY

… before I am lost, / hell must open like a red rose / for the dead to pass.
(H.D.) And again: *We are voyagers, discoverers / of the not-known, / the unrecorded; / we have no map; possibly we will reach haven, / heaven. Or elsewhere: write, write, or die.*

In 1912 Pound dubbed her "H.D., Imagiste"—and created a movement, "Imagism(e)," largely based on her work, his own, & Richard Aldington's. But her great poems (*Helen in Egypt* and the classic *Trilogy*) came later in life, after she experienced what she called an "over-mind": "That over-mind seems a cap, like water, transparent, fluid yet with definite body, contained in a definite space. It is like a closed sea-plant, jelly-fish or anemone. Into that over-mind, thoughts pass and are visible like fish swimming under clear water.... I should say—to continue this jelly-fish metaphor—that long feelers reached down and through the body, that these stood in the same relation to the nervous system as the over-mind to the brain or intellect. There is, then, a set of super-feelings. These feelings extend out and about us; as the long, floating tentacles of the jelly-fish reach out and about him. They are not of different material, extraneous, as the physical arms and less are extraneous to the gray matter of the directing brain. The super-feelers are part of the super-mind, as the jelly-fish feelers are the jelly-fish itself, elongated in fine threads. I first realised this state of consciousness in my head. I visualise it just as well, now, centered in the love-region of the body or placed like a foetus in the body. The centre of consciousness is either the brain or the love-region of the body" (*Notes on Thought and Vision*, 1919).

Marianne Moore USA, 1887–1972

POETRY

I too, dislike it: there are things that are important beyond all this fiddle.
  Reading it, however, with a perfect contempt for it, one discovers that there is in
it after all, a place for the genuine.
    Hands that can grasp, eyes
    that can dilate, hair that can rise
      if it must, these things are important not because a

high-sounding interpretation can be put upon them but because they are
  useful; when they become so derivative as to become unintelligible, the
  same thing may be said for all of us—that we
    do not admire what
    we cannot understand. The bat,
      holding on upside down or in quest of something to

eat, elephants pushing, a wild horse taking a roll, a tireless wolf under
  a tree, the immovable critic twinkling his skin like a horse that feels a
  flea, the base-
    ball fan, the statistician—case after case
      could be cited did

one wish it; nor is it valid
  to discriminate against "business documents and

school-books"; all these phenomena are important. One must make a
distinction
  however: when dragged into prominence by half poets, the result is
  not poetry,
  nor till the autocrats among us can be
    "literalists of
    the imagination"—above
      insolence and triviality and can present

for inspection, imaginary gardens with real toads in them, shall we have
  it. In the meantime, if you demand on the one hand, in defiance of
  their opinion—
  the raw material of poetry in
    all its rawness, and
    that which is on the other hand,
      genuine, then you are interested in poetry.

THE FISH

wade
through black jade.
  Of the crow-blue mussel-shells, one keeps
  adjusting the ash-heaps;
    opening and shutting itself like

an
injured fan.
  The barnacles which encrust the side
  of the wave, cannot hide
    there for the submerged shafts of the

sun,
split like spun
  glass, move themselves with spotlight swiftness
  into the crevices—
    in and out, illuminating

the
turquoise sea
  of bodies. The water drives a wedge

of iron through the iron edge
of the cliff; whereupon the stars,

pink
rice-grains, ink-
bespattered jelly fish, crabs like green
lilies, and submarine
toadstools, slide each on the other.

All
external
marks of abuse are present on this
defiant edifice—
all the physical features of

ac-
cident—lack
of cornice, dynamite grooves, burns, and
hatchet strokes, these things stand
out on it; the chasm-side is

dead.
Repeated
evidence has proved that it can live
on what can not revive
its youth. The sea grows old in it.

YOU SAY YOU SAID

"Few words are best."
Not here. Discretion has been abandoned in this part
of the world too lately
For it to be admired. Disgust for it is like the
Equinox—all things in

One. Disgust is
No psychologist and has not opportunity to be a hypocrite.
It says to the saw-toothed bayonet and to the cue
Of blood behind the sub-

Marine—to the
Poisoned comb, to the Kaiser of Germany and to the
intolerant gateman at the exit from the eastbound ex-

    press: "I hate
You less than you must hate

Yourselves: You have
    Accoutred me. 'Without enemies one's courage flags.'
    Your error has been timed
    To aid me, I am in debt to you for you have primed
Me against subterfuge."

*They fought the enemy, we fight fat living and self-pity. Shine, o shine,
unfalsifying sun, on this sick scene.* (M.M.) And again: *What is brilliance /
without co-ordination? Guarding the / infinitesimal pieces of your mind,
compelling audience to / the remark that it is better to be forgotten than to
be / remembered too violently, / your thorns are the best part of you.*

(1) A brilliant, often far-out collagist, Marianne Moore enlarged the range
of incorporation & the limits of "personality" in the poem. Though she
would later deny the relation of her work to other avant-garde propositions, her early poem "I too dislike it" (reduced in its final version to the
first three lines & amplified in a subsequent 1961 interview to "what I write
could only be called poetry because there is no other category in which to
put it") adopts a strategy not far from Marcel Duchamp's proposal "to
make works which are not 'works of art.'" (Compare, e.g., her stripping-in
of "business documents and schoolbooks" with Duchamp's "ready-mades,"
etc.) "Hence," she said elsewhere, "my writing is, if not a cabinet of fossils,
a kind of collection of flies in amber."

(2) Born in St. Louis, Moore came to New York City ca. 1916 & lived
there until her death in 1972. Her well-known association with Williams &
Pound dates from that earlier time, & also to be noted is the loose resemblance of her appropriative & collage strategies to those of a later generation of postmodern & conceptual poets.

Her smart use of measure & rhyme, for those who seek it, might also be
considered.

Carlos Sabat Ercasty Uruguay, 1887–1982

from **SONG TO THE ESSENTIAL ONE**

The known is the language of the unknown.
The wave sings the hidden forces of the Ocean.
The star reveals the invisible powers of the deep.
The flame's tongues, don't they shout that the tree was fire?
All is double, triple, unfathomable
but the interior seeps forth on the face of everything.
The geometry of the infinite intelligence
fastens the cosmos's architecture.
Simple and pure, the beeline and the curve are intertwined
beneath the stars, beneath the flowers and the nerves
preventing unity devouring multiplicity.
Matter floats over intelligence.
Perfect numbers, wellsprings of primeval light,
sprout from the concealed cipher and create first love.
The ideal One reflects itself on substance's mirror and the Two is born
The One and the Two entwine in desire and the Three is born.
The invisible figure of the Three shuts its angles
and the surface is born.
The level of ideal infinity beholds itself on the cosmic ocean
and from the invisible geometry the body is born.
Through the passage of the astral bodies
opening up the invisible with the visible,
space and time are made in a sole heartbeat of the Self.
Brother, your body is the tangible line
and the number in love with substance.
All that you touch or think in you is number and form,
Your whole body dances to the ciphers' music.
The center of your Self is an invisible sphere.
Absorbs and radiates.
Imbibes light and brings light.
Devours music and sprouts music.
It is an infinite number which embraces all the ciphers of creation.
It is the deepest point of your life
and its radius reaches all the points of life.
Your invisible sphere holds the essence of all lines
and all forms.
The whole cosmos forms the image of that transitory sphere

but the sphere is also a recall of the whole cosmos.
All the concealed signs and secrets of the Universe
were printed in your substance by the presence of the eternal.
You look and say: *tree!*
but the tree is deep inside you
and you are the man and the tree,
the mirror and the image,
the tree of today and every day's tree.
You look the ideal One and the substantial Two
but your Self's center is One and Two.
What your senses detach, your essence unifies.
You say: *my hands, my eyes, my chest, my forehead.*
But in your Self's sphere there is a single verb which encloses all.
You touch: *nerve, bone, hair, nail, skin, blood.*
But in your Self's sphere you project a single image, a single form,
invisible for the eyes, visible just for the essence.
You say: *star*, looking outside
but the star is inside you
invisible in your essence.
Your Self's *shape (eyes, ears, touch, taste, smell)*
multiplies the One in which you float undifferentiated, identical to It,
but the essence flees your senses
and ties inside what you untie on the outside.
The sphere of your invisible Self
is not inside or outside the Self.
Put yourself behind the vast illusion and you will see neither object nor subject.
Neither will you see creation nor creator.
Nor illusion nor essence.
Neither God nor Man.
They will not see, for there is no vision.
Then you will be the whole inside the wholeness.
You will be able to peek, and the vision will be made.
You will be able to withdraw, and the vision will fade.
You will be in the infinite game of the One, master of the secret,
and you will become the One which just found itself inside its own Unity.

Translated from Spanish by Javier Taboada

COMMENTARY

*Why is my name Sabat? The coven! And all this demonic stuff that is
undoubtedly in me—with its negative power—fights the archangel.* (C.S.E.)

And then: *I am life. I have no patience to be a poet. Neither nail file nor burin. I improvise. I have a certain power of clairvoyance and a certain inclination for magical arts.*

Away from the *Modernista* influx, Carlos Sabat Ercasty developed a full-scale project—a cosmic work—that aimed to touch on every aspect of existence. With a strong Hindu influence, he focused on the purification of human perception as a way toward the ultimate "fusion with totality." This work, which started with his first book, *Pantheos* (1917), & went on through fifty published collections, depicts human relations with "the material" (senses, nature), with "the ineffable" (the universe), & with their outcomes in us—love, dreams, the concealed. The pinnacle of his quest was *Poemas del Hombre* (*Poems of Man*, 1921), a work structured in "cycles" grouped according to themes: *Book of Will, Book of Sea, Book of Love, Book of Dreams, Book of José Martí, Book of Messages,* etc., including the poem presented here. *Poems of Man* represents a turning point in Latin American poetry & proved to be very influential on poets such as Pablo Neruda (especially in *The Enthusiastic Slinger* & *Residence on Earth*).

T. S. Eliot USA/England, 1888–1965

from *THE WASTE LAND*

Death by Water

Phlebas the Phoenician, a fortnight dead,
Forgot the cry of gulls, and the deep sea swell
And the profit and loss.
A current under sea
Picked his bones in whispers. As he rose and fell
He passed the stages of his age and youth
Entering the whirlpool.
Gentile or Jew
O you who turn the wheel and look to windward,
Consider Phlebas, who was once handsome and tall as you

COMMENTARY

We know too much, and are convinced of too little. Our literature is a substitute for religion, and so is our religion. (T.S.E.)

Eliot's dominance in USAmerican poetry & letters was for a time—most of his century, in fact—undeniable, at first for his radically innovative poetry & later for his self-proclaimed emergence as an "Anglo-Catholic in religion, a classicist in literature, and a royalist in politics." It was in this context that William Carlos Williams described Eliot's masterwork, *The Waste Land*, as (wrongly or rightly) "the great catastrophe to our letters." And yet Eliot's later conservatism & the aid & comfort he gave to the US conservatizers of the 1940s & 1950s shouldn't obscure the actual contribution of his work to more extreme, often subterranean developments up to the present. So, for example, the collage techniques of *The Waste Land* (worked out in consultation with Pound & far more radical than what we're showing here) strikingly pointed, ca. 1920, to possibilities for holding multiple experiences in the mind as simultaneity &/or reoccurrence: what he elsewhere called the "simultaneous existence" & "simultaneous order" of all poetries of all times. And if Eliot himself came to rely on established literature & established church as props against disorder, the new intuition of poetic origins that he helped develop has led to a more open view of the universally human. For all of which, as poet/critic Jed Rasula has it, "*The Waste Land* is not only a poem: it names an event, like a tornado or an earthquake." Octavio Paz frames it beyond US boundaries: "the first great *simultanéiste* poem in English" (in J. Rasula, *What the Thunder Said: How the Waste Land Made Poetry Modern*, 2022).

ADDENDUM

NATALIA TOLEDO Zapotec, Mexico, 1968–

For T. S. Fliot

Red flowers, enormous and beautiful,
grew from my hands,
as if to ward off the fear of being robbed of all certainty.
I walked on my hands
and buried my body where there was mud
and my eyes filled with fine sand.
They called me the waterlily girl
because my roots were the water's surface.
But I was also bitten by a snake mating in the stream
and was blinded, I was Tiresias traveling his story without a cane.
What are the roots that clutch, what branches grow out of this
    strong rubbish?
maybe I'll be the last branch that speaks Zapotec
my children will have to whistle their language
and they'll be homeless birds in the jungle of forgetting.
In all seasons I am in the south
a rusted ship dreamed by my black jicaco eyes:

when I smell my land I'll go, to dance a song alone beneath woven
    branches,
to eat two things, I'll go.
I'll cross the plaza, the North wind won't stop me, I'll get there on
    time
to hug my grandmother before the last star falls.
I'll be the girl again who wears a yellow petal in her right eyelid,
the girl who cries the milk of flowers
to cure my eyes, I'll go.

Translated from Zapotec & Spanish
by Aura Estrada and Francisco Goldman

Gabriela Mistral Chile, 1889–1957

from *MADWOMEN*

The Sleepless Woman

When the night thickens
and what is upright reclines,
and what is ruined rises up,
I hear him climb the stairs.
No matter that they don't hear him
and I'm the only one to sense it.
Why should another servant
in her vigil have to listen to it!

In one breath of mine he climbs
and I suffer until he arrives—
a mad cascade that his fate
sometimes descends and others scale
and a crazy feverish thorn
castaneting against my door.

I don't rise, I don't open my eyes,
yet I follow his shape complete.
One moment, like the damned,
we have respite beneath the night;
but I hear him go down again
as on an eternal tide.

All night he comes and goes—
absurd gift, given and returned,
a medusa lifted on the waves
that you see when you get close.
From my bed I help him
with what breath is left me
so that he won't hunt groping
and hurt himself in the darkness.

The stair treads of mute wood
ring out to me like crystal.
I know which ones he rests on,
and questions himself, and answers.
I hear where the faithful boards,
like my soul, complain to him,
and I know the ripe and final step,
about to land, that never does . . .

My house endures his body
like a flame that twists around it.
I feel the heat from his face
—a glowing brick—against my door.
I taste a bliss I never knew:
I suffer from living, I die of watching,
and at this tormented moment
my strength departs with his!

The next day I rehearse in vain
with my cheeks and my tongue,
tracing the blanket of haze
on the mirror in the stairwell.
And it calms my soul a few hours
until blind night falls.

The vagabond who meets him
makes the tale into a fable.
He scarcely carries flesh,
is hardly what he was,
and a look from his eyes
freezes some and others burns.

Let none question him who meet him;
just tell him not to return,

tell his memory not to climb
so he can sleep and I can sleep.
Destroy the name that storms
like a whirlwind in its path,
and let him not see my door,
tall and red as a bonfire!

Translated from Spanish by Randall Couch

If it's all been dream and delirium / may death ripen me in my dream.
(G.M.)

Gabriela Mistral was the pseudonym of Lucila Godoy Alcayaga, one of
the most celebrated Latin American poets. About *Madwomen*, her editor
& translator Randall Couch wrote: "Written at the height of her powers,
the *Locas mujeres* poems associated with Gabriela Mistral's final collection
Lagar (*Winepress*) rank among the poet's most challenging and compelling
works. As her letter to the writer Fedor Ganz suggests, they are poems of
the self *in extremis,* marked by the wound of blazing catastrophe and its
aftermath of mourning.... In contrast to her first book, *Desolación,* these
poems do not perform loss and longing in a florid or sentimental style. The
poet has also largely laid aside the pastoral mission that played such a large
part in the growth of her influence and reputation. The tone of moral security, of tender didacticism, of speaking from safety on behalf of the childlike
and vulnerable, is gone."

ADDENDUM

SHARA MCCALLUM Jamaica/USA, 1972–

Madwoman's Geography

> In my first life, I slid
> into the length of a snake. Then
>
> sloughed scales for wings.
> Was content one hundred years
>
> till the air, as all things must,
> lost its charms. After a long time
>
> falling, I landed in the sea.
> What could I do but follow

any wake? How else chart
a course than the way a child

plucks flowers from a field—
the eye compelling the hand to reach?

Oswald de Andrade Brazil, 1890–1954

from **SENTIMENTAL MEMOIRS OF JOÃO MIRAMAR**

Sorrento

Crones sails cicadas
Mists on the Vesuvian sea
Geckoed gardens and golden women
Between walls of garden-path grapes
Of lush orchards
Piedigrotta insects
Gnawing matchboxes in the trousers pocket
White trigonometries
In the blue crepe of Neapolitan waters
Distant city siestas quiet
Amidst scarves thrown over the shoulder
Dotting indigo grays of hillocks

An old Englishman slept with his mouth open
Like the blackened mouth of a tunnel beneath civilized
    eyeglasses.
Vesuvius awaits eruptive orders from Thomas Cook & Son.
And a woman in yellow informed a sport-shirted individual
    that marriage was an unbreakable contract.

Sal O May

The cabarets of São Paulo are remote
As virtues

Automobiles
And the intelligent signal lights of the roads
One single soldier to police my entire homeland
And the cru-cru of the crickets creates bagpipes
And the toads talk twaddle to easy lady toads

In the obscure alphabet of the swamps
Vowels
Street lamps night lamps
And you appear through a clumsy and legendary fox trot

Delenda lovely Salomé
Oh tawdry dancing girl
Full of ignorant flies and good intentions

The javá is a piggish polka with the blue dust
But the purple empurples the procession of pink curtains

"I don't give a damn."
"I want to know about the nonsense of waiting with
    the revolver on the road."
"That black thug gave her a punch and the woman took
    a kick."
"In the belly."
The saxophone persists in an ache of frenzied teeth
Which spasms
Between shots and tips
But the open leakage of gas escapes
Into the penitentiary night
"Lord grant us the illumined spongecake of redemption"

The Tieté River rolls heaps of bricks
Water-colored and pink.

Translated from Portuguese by Jack E. Tomlins

COMMENTARY

Going back is impossible. My clock always runs forward. History too.
(O. de A.)

Born in São Paulo at the end of the nineteenth century, Oswald de Andrade was a pivotal figure (& possibly the most so) in shaping Brazilian modernisms, largely through his own manifestos & the Anthropophagite (Cannibalist) movement that he founded in the 1920s. He was also in that pursuit the co-organizer—with his wife, the painter Tarsila Amaral, & the poet Mário de Andrade—of the groundbreaking Semana de Arte Moderna (Modern Art Week), held in São Paulo in 1922, which went beyond its successful attempt to shock the bourgeoisie & academia alike to mark, in effect, a new Brazilian poetics & aesthetic, both international & aggressively rooted on native grounds.

Of Andrade's experimental novel, *Sentimental Memoirs of João Miramar*, as exemplar of his Anthropophagism, Haroldo de Campos wrote: "The *Sentimental Memoirs of João Miramar* was, actually, the true, 'ground zero' of contemporary Brazilian prose, of what in it is inventive and creative.... Important in updating our fiction in synchrony with the experiments of the European avant-garde, but also in the individual adaptation and re-elaboration of the techniques imported, based on local criteria, of the just assessment of a social context in transition, an urban reality in the first stages of industrialization." From a historical perspective, the experiment also coincides with the creative pulse of the jazz age. As Andrade himself characterizes it in the pseudonymous preface to his novel, it manifests in a type of "telegraphic" composition, achieving a syncopated whole in a "cannibalistic" devouring of sounds, forms, aesthetics, & poetics-of-the-other, transforming them into a fertilizer for sprouting something entirely new on local soil. (Or words to that effect.)

The influence of his *Anthropophagite Manifesto* outside of Brazil is also to be noted.

For more on Oswald de Andrade, see his *Pau-Brasil*: Brazilwood Poetry Manifesto in "A Map of Americas."

Oliverio Girondo   Argentina, 1891–1967

TROPES

I touch
touch pores
moorings
coves I touch
keyboard nerves
wharves
fabrics that touch me
scars
ashes
tropical bellies I touch
alone alone
undertows
death rattles
I touch and touchmore
and nothing

Foreshadowings of absence
inconsistent tropes
what you
what what
what quenas
what ravines
what masks
what hollow solitudes
what yes what no
what except that my touch is out of tune
what reflections
what depths
what bewitching materials
what keys
what nocturnal ingredients
what frozen window catches that don't open
what nothing I touch
in all

Translated from Spanish by Hugh Hazelton

GRAVITATE ROTATING

In the thirst
in the being
in the psyche
in the x's
in the exquisitubercular replies
in the moonmaking
in the erect simple excesses of erotorubbing etcetera
or in the exhausted doubledream of "give me take it give yourself right up to the full
      bull's nape of your such desire"
in the non-faith that ruminates
in the vivisecting the mental searches the metaphysirats in the summary goblins of
      the cosmic egogurgle
in every grafted gesture
in every form sunken polychipped tobroken level aphasic subtrite cocopleoniasm
      fromother
without home without dog without cove without stretcher without coca without
  history
endosuckingglutinous
among the mobile monsters gravitating round beneath the stariferous itch

along with the musevines fleshy poresuckers and the no less polypus sons of the lutio
    hiccough
volunteers of miasma
reinfringed on
oppressed among empty nevers and warning hooks
step by well swimming before fed-up vague thinkings of final floodgates that
  drown hope
with the shredding the questionable
the leopard yawns the halfwit jargon
ulcerating
when blood spreads without dwarf introits in the wide plecoitus with every
  insomniac
        dream and handsome spectre
pleasureshouting
aminded
in the no bastard born

Translated from Spanish by Hugh Hazelton

COMMENTARY

*I don't have a personality; I am a cocktail, a conglomerate, a manifesta-
tion of personalities.* (O.G.)

Born in Buenos Aires in 1891, Oliverio Girondo... belonged to the Argentine Ultraist vanguard, which also included Jorge Luis Borges and for which
he wrote the manifesto.... [The poems presented here] are from *En la mas-
médula* (*In the Moremarrow*) [1954], which culminates Girondo's career
of poetic engagement with the vanguard; his lifelong rejection of academic
authority and search for new forms of poetic articulation find their last
and best expression here. With this last volume, according to Trinidad Bar-
rera, Girondo puts a period to the Latin American avant-gardism begun in
the 1920s, of which he was a central figure, and provides a model and a
jumping-off point for contemporary Latin American poetry's concern with
the nature of referentiality.

  Like Vallejo's *Trilce* and Huidobro's *Altazor*, with which it is frequently
compared, *In the Moremarrow* forges from the Spanish language a new
poetic language with its own psychic vocabulary and syntax, constituting a journey into the uncharted space of whatever "more" the marrow of
language may or may not hold.... With seemingly unlimited combinatory
properties and multivalence, Girondo's language, or "pure impure mix"...
communicates desire and disgust, [while it] moves fluidly between ironic
distance and unguarded sadness or wonder at the limits and possibilities
of signification.

(Commentary by Molly Weigel.)

César Vallejo Peru, 1892–1938

THE HUNGRY MAN'S WHEEL

From between my own teeth I come out smoking,
shouting, pushing,
pulling down my pants...
My stomach empties, my jejunum empties,
misery pulls me out between my own teeth,
caught in my shirt cuff by a little stick.

Will a stone to sit down on
now be denied me?
Even that stone on which trips the woman who has given birth,
the mother of the lamb, the cause, the root,
that one will now be denied me?
At least that other one
which has gone cowering through my soul!
At least
the calcarid or the evil one (humble ocean)
or the one no longer even worth throwing at a man,
that one give it to me now!

At least the one they will have found lying alone across an insult,
that one give it to me now!
At least the twisted and crowned, on which resounds
only once the walk of moral rectitude,
or, at least, that other one, that flung in dignified curve,
will fall by itself,
avowing true entrails,
that one give it to me now!

A piece of bread, that too denied me?
Now I no longer have to be what I always have to be,
but give me
a stone to sit down on,
but give me,
please, a piece of bread to sit down on,
but give me
in Spanish
something, finally, to drink, to eat, to live off, to rest on,
and then I'll go away...
I find a strange shape, my shirt is

filthy and in shreds
and now I have nothing, this is hideous.

Translated from Spanish by Clayton Eshleman

from **TRILCE**

XXXII

999 calories.
Roombbb... Hulllablll llust... ster
Serpenteenic e of the sweet roll vendor
engyrafted to the eardrum.

Lucky are the ices. But no.
Lucky that which moves neither more nor less.
Lucky the golden mean.

1,000 calories.
The gringo firmament looks blue
and chuckles up its hocker. The razzed
sun sets and scrambles the brains
even of the coldest.

It mimics the bogeyman: Weeeeeetrozzz......
the tender railcar, rolling from thirst,
that runs up to the beach

Air, air! Ice!
If at least the calor (___ Better
                              I say nothing.

And even the very pen
With which I write finally cracks up.

Thirty-three trillion three hundred thirty-
three calories.

XXXVI

We struggle to thread ourselves through a needle's eye,
face to face, hell-bent on winning.
The fourth angle of the circle ammoniafies almost.
Female is continued the male, on the basis
of probable breasts, and precisely
on the basis of how much does not flower.

Are you that way, Venus de Milo?
You hardly act crippled, pullulating
enwombed in the plenary arms
of existence,
of this existence that neverthelessez
perpetual imperfection.
Venus de Milo, whose cut off, increate
arm swings round and tries to elbow
across greening stuttering pebbles,
ortive nautili, recently crawling
evens, immortal on the eves of.
Lassoer of imminences, lassoer
of the parenthesis.

Refuse, all of you, to set foot
on the double security of Harmony.
Truly refuse symmetry.
Intervene in the conflict
of points that contend
in the most rutty of jousts
for the leap through the needle's eye!

So now I feel my little finger
in excess on my left. I see it and think
it shouldn't be me, or at least that it's
in a place where it shouldn't be.
And it inspires me with rage and alarms me
and there is no way out of it, except by
pretending that today is Thursday.

Make way for the new odd number
                         potent with orphanhood!

Translated from Spanish by Clayton Eshleman

BLACK STONE ON A WHITE STONE

I will die in Paris in a downpour,
a day which I can already remember.
I will die in Paris—and I don't budge—
maybe a Thursday, like today, in autumn.

Thursday it will be, because today, Thursday,
as I prose these lines, I have forced on

my humeri and, never like today, have I turned,
with all my journey, to see myself alone.

César Vallejo is dead, they beat him,
all of them, without him doing anything to them;
they gave it to him hard with a stick and hard

likewise with a rope; witnesses are
the Thursdays and the humerus bones,
the loneliness, the rain, the roads . . .

Translated from Spanish by Clayton Eshleman

COMMENTARY

There are desires to return, to love, to not disappear, and there are desires
to die, fought by two opposing waters that have never isthmused. (C.V.)

(1) The power & audacity of Vallejo's poetry has grown ever clearer in the
years since his death, so that he stands now as one of the truly great poets
of all the Americas, present & past. In a brief summary of his life & writings, his most persistent & masterful translator, Clayton Eshleman, writes
of him: "Vallejo was born in Santiago de Chuco, an Andean town in north-
central Peru. His grandmothers were Chimu Indians and both his grandfathers, by a strange coincidence, were Spanish Catholic priests.... Much of
the complex anguish in Vallejo, based on the conflict between the spiritual
and the worldly, has its roots in the obsessions with sin, good, and evil,
of... a Catholic upbringing. Vallejo's first book, *Los Heraldos Negros*
(1918), and his second, the revolutionary *Trilce* (1922), bracket an incident
that was to change his life profoundly: he was... blamed for a shooting...
and imprisoned in a Trujillo jail for 205 days. Out on parole... he took
advantage of an offer for a third-class boat ticket to France, and embarked
in June 1923, never returning to Peru.... His fifteen years in Europe were
mostly in Paris, as a Latin American intellectual in exile."

(2) *Trilce* is Vallejo's most difficult & experimental poem, an extreme work
of language, like an autochthonous Peruvian growth, marked by word distortions & new coinages, rapid transitions & open gaps in meaning. The
title itself carries the sense of an unknown number—a fusion (perhaps) of
trillón & *trece* (thirteen)—in a work filled with quasi-kabbalistic ciphers,
where "even the very pen / with which I write / finally cracks up. // Thirty-
three trillion three hundred and thirty-three calories." Yet here as elsewhere
(Eshleman again), "when his language is obscure, it always represents an
effort to realize a reality in which nothing is clear, a sensing that in the heart
of Being there is a wound, that the 'lesion of the response' is the 'lesion
mentally of the unknown.'"

For more on Vallejo, see "The Spider" in "A Map of Visions."

Alfonsina Storni Argentina, 1892–1938

SOUR IS THE WORLD

The world is sour
unripened
halted
forests
with steel tips
in blossom,
old tombs thrust up
to surface:
ocean waters
cradling
a house of horrors.
Sour is the sun
above its world,
drowned out by mist
that hides the sky
unripened
halted.
Sour is the moon
above its world:
green
faded,
tracking down its ghosts,
skates
dripping wet.
The wind
across the world
is sour,
raising clouds
of insects,
dead, bound up
& scattered,
towers loom,
a weight of crape
in knots
for mourners,
heavy on the roofs.
A man is sour

everywhere
is balanced on his legs,
whole worlds
in back of him,
deserts of stones
on forehead,
everywhere,
deserts of suns,
& blind.

Translated from Spanish by Jerome Rothenberg

AND THE HEAD BEGAN TO BURN

On the black
wall
a square
opened up
that looked out
over the void.

And the moon rolled
up to the window;
it stopped
and said to me:
"I'm not moving from here;
I'm looking at you.

I don't want to grow
or get thin.
I'm the infinite
flower
that opens up
in the square hole
in your house.

I no longer want
to roll on
behind
the lands
that you don't know,
my butterfly,
sipper of shadows.

Or raise phantoms
over the far off
cupolas
that drink me.

I'm watching
I see you."

And I didn't answer.
A head was sleeping
under my hands.

White,
like you,
moon.

The wells of its eyes
held a dark
water
streaked
with luminous snakes.

And suddenly
my head
began to burn
like the stars
at twilight.

And my hands
were stained
with a phosphorescent
substance.

And with it
I burn
the houses
of men,
the forests
of beasts.

Translated from Spanish by Marion Freeman

Men ask for / your tongue, / your body, / your life. // Cast yourself into the fire / bloom in a cannon's / muzzle. // An edge of sky / touched by / the future / human house (A.S.)

Born in Capriasca, Switzerland, Alfonsina Storni & her parents migrated to Argentina, where she would become a journalist, an actress, a playwright, & one of Argentina's most celebrated poets. Her moves show different formal stages, from the traditional metrics of her first collections (especially her use of the sonnet, later what she called the "anti-sonnet") to her use of free or open forms. About her work, translator Nicholas Friedman wrote: "Storni's poetry is radical in its confessionalism (dealing as it does with depression and suicidality), bold in its theological and philosophical sparring, and unflinching in its unfashionable and idiosyncratic style. In nearly every sense, Storni hacked her own path through an overgrown, male-dominated poetic world. What she left behind is the remarkable chronicle of a struggle no less beautiful for its difficulty" (in Storni, "Three Poems," *Poetry Northwest*, July 2018).

Facing her impending death from cancer, Storni drowned herself in Mar del Plata on October 25, 1938.

Mikhl Likht Ukraine/USA, 1893–1953

from **PROCESSIONS 2**

TIME-BLOODIED

Rusty and yellow
dusty all-barbarous brutes
dear tyrants
we come and go
with symmetrically-hasty steps
of gentle does

an inveigling reproach
slung in Pan's moldy face

the schema is nearly consumed.

So someone walks around
in the sun,
his fiery pale-faced eyes

shine delight and
are membranes of doubt concealed.

(Once
many years ago
they murmured in my ear:

strong with the strong
one-by-one the weak go down
with us
with us
won the bottom—)

LEGEND

Wandering in the wasteland
I saw the snakes smile
their dusty skins
in convulsions
of laughter.

THE HAMMER OF LUCK

Waves—

        mountain on mountain
        heap on heap—
        waves
mischievous tongues
flare and lick—
        waves

one of the waves:
—just so, brother, fall
—that's called a carnival
—warmer warmer
—feverish—

one of the waves:
—dance for joy, brother, fall
—fine show
—we are bathed
—in a sunless sky
—fire-hot red—

shadows hang
half-extended

sway
in the air—

       waves.

HYMN OF SQUANDERED BLOOD

Tiny mouths
little lips
burn carmine
      —kiss me
      —kiss me
tiny creatures
fulfill
a ritual
      —take me
      —take me
something chained
with pliers
and sorrows
      —stop stop
      —your you your me.

A FAREWELL TO THE GODS

Lively and subtle,
great as a genie
you are great and holy
holy as a virgin's breast—

offal of hate and love,
fallen to rust
fallen in dust.

Translated from Yiddish by Ariel Resnikoff & Stephen Ross

COMMENTARY

Chameleon. Stretches that bring in unsuspiciously passive delight in their thought—sunk in the colorless depths of somnambulism—chaotic rhythm immerses itself—swims around in dewy blueness. (M.L.)

(1) What emerges in Mikhl Likht's work from 1923, as it comes to us in English, is an extraordinarily complex & experimental poetry & poetics, far more radical in structure & content than all but a handful of his US counterparts & near contemporaries (Pound, Zukofsky, Williams, Loy, Eliot, cummings), & to some degree predating most of them. It is a confirmation as well of Kenneth Rexroth's observation of a Yiddish avant-garde & Futurist presence in his own early years in New York: "A good case could be made for the claim that the best writing done in America in the first quarter of the [twentieth] century was in Yiddish. I don't think it's really true, but it is sufficiently true to be passionately arguable in one of those passionate arguments that used to sprinkle the whiskers with sour cream in the Café Royale." In Likht's case, however, the aptness of Rexroth's original appraisal, often repeated in conversation, seems remarkably & strikingly on target.

(2) Writes Merle Bachman, one of his translators, in a brief summary of Yiddish avant-gardism & Likht's life & career: "Mikhl Likht was an avant-garde Yiddish poet in New York in the 1920s and '30s (although he kept writing until his death at the age of sixty in 1953). Born in a Ukrainian village in 1893, he came over to the U.S. in 1913, where he eventually participated in the short-lived movement of American Yiddish modernist poetry associated with the '*In zikh*' group (meaning 'within one's self; introspective')." In their 1919 manifesto, they stated: "The world exists and we are part of it. But for us, the world exists only as it is mirrored in us, as it touches us.... The human psyche is an awesome labyrinth. Thousands of beings dwell there. The inhabitants are the various facets of the individual's present self on the one hand and fragments of his inherited self on the other."

Mário de Andrade   Brazil, 1893–1945

from *A VERY INTERESTING PREFACE*

When I feel the great lyrical impulse, I write without thinking about everything my unconscious screams at me. Later I think: not only to correct, but also to justify what I wrote. Thus the reason for this Very Interesting Preface.

.....

Preface: firecracker of my super ego. Verses: landscape of my id.

.....

Nor did I wish to attempt a blind or insincere primitivism. In reality we are the primitives of a new age. Aesthetically: I went about to search, among the hypotheses of psychologists, naturalists, and critics regarding the primitives of the past eras, for the most human and free expressions of art.

The past is a lesson to be contemplated, not reproduced.
"E tu che sé costí, anima viva,
Partiti da cotesti che son morti."
["And you who were there, living soul,
Peel off from those who are dead."]

I searched for myself for many years. I found it. So don't tell me that I search for originality, because I've already discovered where it was, it belongs to me, it's mine.

.....

[V]erses are not written to be read by mute eyes. Verses are sung, howled, wept. Whosoever doesn't know how to sing cannot read "Landscape No. 2." Whosoever doesn't know how to howl cannot read "Odium to the Bourgeois." Whosoever doesn't know how to pray, cannot read "Religion." To scorn: "The Escalade." To suffer: "Sentimental Colloquy." To forgive: the canticle of the lullaby, one of the solos of My Madness in "The Enfibratures of Ipiranga." I won't continue. I'm repulsed by giving out the keys to my book. Whosoever will be like me has the key.

And now the poetic school, "Delusionism," is finished.

Next book I'll found another.

And I don't want disciples. In art: School = the imbecility of many for the vanity of one alone.

I could have cited Gorch Fock. Would have avoided the Very Interesting Preface. "Every song of liberation comes from the prison."

Translated from Portuguese by Justin Read

N.B. Johann Kinau is the German author who wrote under the pseudonym "Gorch Fock" and died in the battle of Jutland/Skagerrak in 1916.

from **KHAKI DIAMOND**

XXXIII

> *pleasures and pains hold the soul in the body*
> *like a nail. they make it corporeal... consequently*
> *it's impossible for the soul to arrive pure in hell.*

Plato

my profound delight in light of the morning sun
                    a vidacarnaval...
              friends
          lovers
      laughters
the immigrant children surround me they ask for pictures of
movie stars, these that come in the
                    cigarette packs

I feel like Murillo's assumption!

XXXIII **[bis]**

plato! for following you as I wished
freeing myself from happiness and pain
being pure, like the gods that quimera
followed beyond life constructing!

but how not to gorge happiness when
this opal spring morning shines
sensual woman that next to me passing
my desire for c'ming exasperates!

life is beautiful! useless the theories!
a hundred times the nudity at which I shine
to the chlamys of science, austere and calm!
the path between smells and harmonies
cursing the wise, blessing
the divine impurity of my soul

Translated from Portuguese by Ana Paula

The street all naked… The lightless houses /… And the myrrh of unwitting martyrs… / Let me put my handkerchief to my nose. / I have all the perfumes of Paris! (M. de A.)

In the rush of arts & movements in the first decades of the twentieth century, Mário de Andrade was one of the founders of the seminal Modern Art Week of 1922, the watershed event that hurled a rock into the glass house of the Brazilian literary establishment. "A Very Interesting Preface," written after composition of his breakthrough book of poems, *Paulicéia Desvairada* (translated elsewhere as *Hallucinated City*), sets up & exemplifies his new poetics, while it marks a sharp rupture from the "titles," the "endless meetings," & the "mediocrity" of the so-called elite, favoring the language of São Paulo and "the path between smells & harmonies / cursing the wise, blessing the divine impurity of my soul."

His love of music & his solidarity with Surrealist, Futurist, & other avant-garde movements in Europe shaped his exploration of a distinctively Brazilian aesthetic. Combining a rigorous field study of music & orature from the north & northeast of Brazil with the urban effervescence at a time of intense immigration & industrialization (being one of the first in Brazil to include idioms of Italian immigrants in São Paulo in his poetry), his aesthetic of Brazilianness culminated in his picaresque "rhapsody," *Macunaíma: A Hero without Any Character*. He became an "agent of language" who, according to Alfredo Bosi, "raised to the level of an art, the prosody, rhythm, lexicon, and syntax of colloquial language."

(Commentary by Jennifer Cooper.)

Vicente Huidobro   Chile, 1893–1948

COW-BOY

In the Far West
            where there is only one moon
The Cok Boy sings
                until it breaks the night
And his cigar is a wandering star

       HIS PONY SHOED WITH WINGS
       HAS NEVER HAD A FLAW

And him
        his head against his knees
                he dances a Cake Walk

New York
> a few kilometers

In the skyscrapers
The elevators rise like thermometers

And near Niagara
> which has put out my pipe
I watch the spattered stars

The Cow Boy
> on a violin string
Crosses the Ohio

Translated from French by David Guss

from **ALTAZOR**

A Voyage in a Parachute

Altazor how did you lose your first serenity?
What evil angel landed at your grave your smile
With sword in hand?
Who planted anguish in the plains inside your eyes a god's adornment?
Why one day—in a flash—did you feel the terror of existence?
And that voice that hollered at you you're alive & you can't see that you're alive
Who made your thoughts meet at those crossroads for all grieving winds?
The diamond in your dreams cracked open in a mindless sea
You are lost Altazor
You're alone at the universe's center
Alone like a dot that blossoms high over the void
There's no good no evil no truth no order no beauty

Where are you at Altazor?

The nebula—anguish—passes by like a river
And drags me down by the law of affinities
The nebula changed into solidified smells eludes its own loneliness
I can feel how a telescope points at my head like a gun
A comet's tail beats on my face & passes by stuffed with eternity
Tireless seeking a lake with no sounds a break from inevitable angst

Altazor you will die Your voice will dry up & you will become invisible
The earth will continue to turn in its precise orbit

In terror of tumbling like an acrobat out on a wire its rope ends tied to the wide
    eyes of fear
You will hunt in vain for some maddened eye
But there's no way out & the wind displaces the planets
You think it doesn't matter falling forever if you somehow escape in the end
Don't you see that you're falling already?
It's time you were rid of morals & prejudice
If you try to rise & you stumble toward nothing
Let yourself fall without stopping without fear to the deep end of darkness
To the baffled cry of your Self
Maybe you'll find a sun that can't set
Lost in the fissures of cliffs
Fall
      Fall forever
Fall to the depths of the infinite
Fall to the depths of time
Fall to the depths of your Self
Fall as low as you can
Fall without dizziness
Into all spaces & ages
Into each soul each longing for land each shipwreck
Fall
      Scald the stars & the seas as you pass
Scald the eyes that watch you the hearts that await you
Scald the wind with your voice
The wind that's trapped in your voice
And the night growing cold in its cave filled with bones

Fall into childhood
Fall into age
Fall into tears
Fall into laughter
Fall into music all over the universe
Fall from your head to your feet
Fall from your feet to your head
Fall from the sea to its source
Fall to the final abyss of silence
Like a sinking ship drowning its lights

Then it's all over
The man-eating sea beats the doors of those merciless cliffs

Dogs bark at the death of our hours
And the sky hears the footsteps of stars trailing off
You're alone
And heading straight into death you're an iceberg split off from its Pole
The night falls it looks for your heart in the ocean
Its look grows wild like those torrents
And just when the waves swing around
The moon—child of light—escapes the high sea
Keeps watching this sky
It's a full sky it's rich like the streams in your mines
It's a sky full of stars preparing for baptism
All those stars like the splash of a sphere like a rock in primordial waters
They don't know what they want if the secret nets are still there
Or what hand holds the reins
Or whose breast breathes the wind that blows over them
Or if there's any hand or any breast
The mountains are fisheries
Hills as high as my longings
And I fling my last anguish out past the night
That the songbirds spread through the world

Tune up the dawn's motor
While I sit at the edge of my eyes
And click off the entry of images

This is me Altazor
Altazor
Locked up in his fate like a cage
In vain I grasp the rungs to try a possible escape
A flower blocks the way
And looms up like a statue ablaze
Escape is impossible
Strung out I move about more weakly
Than an army without light in the midst of ambushes

I opened my eyes up in the century
That Christianity died out
Contorted on its agonizing cross
About to cough up its last breath
What will we put there tomorrow in that empty space?
We'll put in a dawn or a twilight
And do we really have to put in something?

The crown of thorns
Dribbles its final stars & withers
Christianity will die & leave no problem solved
Only a handful of dead prayers its teachings
Will die after 2000 years of existence
A huge bombardment puts a stop on the Christian era
Christ wants to die with a cast of millions
To come crashing down with all his temples
To cross over into death with an immense cortege
A thousand airplanes saluting the new era
They are its oracles & flags

And just six months ago
I left the equatorial line freshly cut
In the martial tomb of some long-suffering slave
A pious crown for human ignorance
This is me talking now in 1919
When it's winter
And Europe has buried all its dead
And a million tears become a single cross of snow
Look at those steppes how they're shaking their fists
Millions of workers have seen the light at last
And raise their flags to heaven like the dawn
Come on workers we've been waiting for you you're our hope
The only hope
The last hope

I'm Altazor the double of myself
Who sees himself at work laughs at the other to his face
Who fell down from his high spot from his star
And voyaged twenty-five years
Hanging from his parachute his preconceptions
I'm Altazor the man of endless longings
Eternal & depressive hunger
Meat worked by plows of anguish
How can I sleep with so many lands inside?
Such problems
Mysteries hanging down my chest
I'm alone
The distances between our bodies
Are as great as those between our souls

Alone
    Alone
        Alone
I'm alone I'm stuck at the tail end of the dead year
The universe's waves break at my feet
The planets swirl around my head
And mess my hair up with their passing winds
Without an answer that could fill their chasms

Translated from Spanish by Jerome Rothenberg

ARS POETICA

Let poetry be like a key
Opening a thousand doors
A leaf falls; something flies by;
Let all the eye sees be created
And the soul of the listener tremble.

Invent new worlds and watch your word;
The adjective, when it doesn't give life, kills it.

We are in the age of nerves.
The muscle hangs,
Like a memory, in museums;
But we are not the weaker for it:
True vigor
Resides in the head.

Oh Poets, why sing of roses!
Let them flower in your poems;

For us alone
Do all things live beneath the Sun.

The poet is a little God.

Translated from Spanish by David Guss

I am the only poet of this century. (V.H.)

(1) If the claims were grand, what he offered in fulfillment, like a scattering of bards before him, had a largeness & visionary scope around his idea, often enough repeated, of the poet as a newly born creator/"creationist" & thereby "a little god." In that pursuit, he moved for a time between our hemisphere & Europe, to launch an encounter with Cubist & (later) Dadaist poets & poetics, & a singular movement of his own: Creationism. While in France, he coedited for a time the magazine *Nord-Sud* with Apollinaire & Reverdy, & composed poems in French as well as in Spanish. In this his overarching dictum qua Creationism was to declare a new, unbounded freedom to "create," along with a shared if possibly divergent perception that "the greatest danger to the poem is the poetic." From his home base in Chile, he moved thereafter between Paris, Spain, & Latin America, persisting with Creationism as a one-man movement, while announcing himself as a poet-shaman of a poetry that wouldn't so much describe the world as remake it through a vital act of language. As stated in his "Non Serviam," a mock address & antidote, shouted (literally) at Mother Nature herself: "I do not have to be your slave, Mother Nature; I will be your master.... The only thing that I want is never to forget your lessons, but I am now old enough to roam these worlds alone. Both yours and mine. A new era is beginning. On opening its doors of jasper, I thrust a knee in the earth and I greet you very respectfully" (trans. Michael Smith & Luis Ingelmo). These ideas, countering or superseding Nature, would be the basis of his future *Creationist Manifesto* in 1925.

(2) David M. Guss writes in his introduction to the works of Vicente Huidobro: "For Huidobro, [t]he poet is once again 'maker' and 'Creationism' is meant in the most literal sense of the word: the creation of 'new worlds that never existed before, that only the poet can discover.' That discovery is the 'inner word—the magic one.' Huidobro claimed that the inspiration for his poetic theories came from the words of an Aymara Indian poet who said: *The poet is a God. Don't sing about rain, poet. Make it rain.*"

With that said, then, the present gathering moves toward "A Map of Visions."

A MAP OF VISIONS

Go to a mountain top & cry for a vision.

SIOUX NATION VISION EVENT

The virtue of the mind / is that emotion / which causes / to see

GEORGE OPPEN

I don't have to go nowhere to see.
Visions are everywhere.

ESSIE PINOLA PARRISH

In me all miracles will be done

JOSÉ WATANABE

I was born with eyes that can never close.

JOY HARJO

I dream in my dream all the dreams of the other dreamers,
And I become the other dreamers.

WALT WHITMAN

The effort to forget
Is also poetry.

HUMBERTO AK'ABAL

Herman Melville USA, 1819–1891

LINES—AFTER SHAKESPEARE

It is better to laugh & not sit than to weep & be
wicked.—Ten loads of coal to burn from—
Brought to the stake—warmed himself by the fire.
Ego non baptizo te in nomine Patris et
Filii et Spiritus Sancti—sed in nomine
Diaboli—madness is undefinable—
It & right reason extremes of one,
not the (black art) Goetic but Theurgic magic—
seeks converse with the Intelligence, Power, the
Angel.

COMMENTARY

The words erupt in what Melville writes down on the flyleaf of the second
volume of his collected Shakespeare, the Latin taken up later for one of
Ahab's rants in *Moby-Dick*, & there translated: "I do not baptize thee in
the name of the father, but in the name of the devil." The vision here is
debased & conflicted—"undefinable" as well—& set beside whatever other
visions (intelligence or power) might issue from the Angel. The contrast
is between "Goetic" (= black) magic & the equally wild vision of Pip, the
Black cabin boy, who almost drowned but in those wondrous depths "saw
God's foot upon the treadle of the loom and spoke it."

The burden & ambiguity of vision are here laid bare.

ADDENDUM

UNA MARSON Jamaica, 1905–1965

Confession

I regret nothing—
I have lived
I have loved
I have known laughter
And dance and song,
I have sighed
I have prayed,
I have soared
On fleecy clouds

To the gates
Of heaven,
I have sunk
Deep down
In the pit
Of hell.

Nahuatl

TWO AZTEC DEFINITIONS

SECRET ROAD

Its name is secret road, the one which few people know, which not all people are aware of, which few people go along. It is good, fine; a good place, a fine place. It is where one is harmed, a place of harm. It is known as a safe place; it is a difficult place, a dangerous place. One is frightened. It is a place of fear.

There are trees, crags, gorges, rivers, precipitous places, places of precipitous land, various places of precipitous land, various precipitous places, gorges, various gorges. It is a place of wild animals, a place of wild beasts, full of wild beasts. It is a place where one is put to death by stealth; a place where one is put to death in the jaws of the wild beasts of the land of the dead.

I take the secret road. I follow along, I encounter the secret road. He goes following along, he goes joining that which is bad, the corner, the darkness, the secret road. He goes to seek, to find, that which is bad.

THE PRECIPICE

It is deep—a difficult, a dangerous place, a deathly place. It is dark, it is light. It is an abyss.

Translated from Spanish by J. O. Anderson and Charles E. Dibble

For more on this & other "definitions" written down by Bernardino de Sahagún in exchanges (ca. 1520) with surviving Aztec elders, see the opening poem in "A First Gallery."

César Vallejo ^{Peru, 1892–1938}

Peru, 1892–1938

THE SPIDER

It is an enormous spider that now cannot move
a colorless spider, whose body,
a head and an abdomen, bleeds.

Today I watched it up close. With what effort
toward every side
it extended its innumerable legs.
And I have thought about its invisible eyes,
the spider's fatal pilots.

It is a spider that tremored caught
on the edge of a rock;
abdomen on one side,
head on the other.

With so many legs the poor thing, and still unable
to free itself. And, on seeing it
confounded by its fix
today, I have felt such sorrow for that traveler.

It is an enormous spider, impeded by
its abdomen from following its head.
And I have thought about its eyes
and about its numerous legs…
And I have felt such sorrow for that traveler!

Translated from Spanish by Clayton Eshleman

COMMENTARY

The translingual byplay between poet & translator is set out by Eshleman as follows:

"1962, Kyoto: There was a gorgeous red, yellow and green Aranea centered in her web attached to a persimmon tree in the Okumura backyard. I got used to taking a chair and a little table out there under the web where I'd read. After several weeks of 'spider sitting' the weather turned chill, with rain and gusting wind. One afternoon I found the web wrecked, the spider gone. Something went through me that I can only describe as the sensation of the loss of one loved. I cried, and for several days felt nauseous and absurd. When I tried to make sense out of my reaction, I recalled César

Vallejo's poem 'La araña'—'The Spider'—which I first read in Blooming-
ton, Indiana, in 1958, right at the time that I had started to get serious
about writing poetry. Like the death of the Kyoto spider, the poem had
gone right through me. I could not get it out of my mind for months."

For more on Vallejo, see "A Second Gallery."

Robert Johnson   USA, 1911–1938

HELLHOUND ON MY TRAIL

I got to keep moving
    I've got to keep moving
            blues falling down like hail
              blues falling down like hail
Ummmmmmmmmmmmmmmmmmmmm
          blues falling down like hail
            blues falling down like hail
And the days keeps on 'minding me
      there's a hellhound on my trail,
          hellhound on my trail
            hellhound on my trail

If today was Christmas eve
    if today was Christmas eve
        and tomorrow was Christmas day
If today was Christmas eve
      and tomorrow was Christmas day
        (aw wouldn't we have a time, baby?)
All I would need my little sweet rider just
      to pass the time away
        uh huh
         to pass the time away

You sprinkled hot foot powder
      umm around my door
       all around my door
You sprinkled hot foot powder
      all around your daddy's door
       hmmm hmmm hmmm

It keep me with rambling mind, rider

                every old place I go

                        every old place I go

I can tell, the wind is rising

           the leaves trembling on the trees

                    trembling on the trees

I can tell, the wind is rising

           leaves trembling on the tree

              umm hmm hmm hmm

All I need's my little sweet woman

              and to keep my company

                  hmmm hmmm hmmm

                          my company

Lineated version by Eric Sackheim

COMMENTARY

Robert Johnson / May 8, 1911   Aug. 16, 1938 / Resting in the blues
(gravestone marker)

(1) With Robert Johnson, as with other great blues poets, the words offer an arena for small or larger changes, set off against a stable melodic line (or series of such) & the ironies of a "real life" (in his case, cut short by his death at age twenty seven). As with a range of songs across millennia and cultures, the verses, when isolated & written down, emerge as poems in their own right, to be read & spoken as well as sung, & the life of the poet, as with that of many others, acts as a powerful enhancement to the work at hand. In Johnson's case, the legend, as it comes to us, has it that he took his guitar to the crossroads of Highways 49 and 61 in Clarksdale, Mississippi, where the devil retuned & refined his instrument in a Faust-like exchange for his soul. And with that came a mastery of music & words, & his early death by poison, as the further legend tells it.

That the words of a number of his songs add fuel to this story is also worth noting.

(2) Eric Sackheim's masterful transcription is key here to keeping vision & rhythm together.

Juan Rulfo Mexico, 1917–1986

from *PEDRO PÁRAMO*

As dawn breaks, the day turns, stopping and starting. The rusty gears of the earth are almost audible: the vibration of this ancient earth overturning darkness.

"Is it true that night is filled with sins, Justina?"

"Yes, Susana."

"Really true?"

"It must be, Susana."

"And what do you think life is, Justina, if not sin? Don't you hear? Don't you hear how the earth is creaking?"

"No, Susana, I can't hear anything. My fate is not as grand as yours."

"You would be frightened. I'm telling you, you would be frightened if you heard what I hear."

Justina went on cleaning the room. Again and again she passed the rag over the wet floorboards. She cleaned up the water from the shattered vase. She picked up the flowers. She put the broken pieces into the pail.

"How many birds have you killed in your lifetime, Justina?"

"Many, Susana."

"And you never felt sad?"

"I did, Susana."

"Then, what are you waiting for to die?"

"I'm waiting for Death, Susana."

"If that's all, it will come. Don't worry."

Translated from Spanish by Margaret Sayers Peden

COMMENTARY

In Juan Rulfo's masterwork, the murmurs that fill Comala (the fictional ghost town that lies near but is not Hell) come from the trapped souls of its former inhabitants, who reveal—by their own pain & desperation—the nature of the world, its sins & ruins.

Iroquois USA

TWO DREAM EVENTS

1. After having a dream, let someone else guess what it was. Then have everyone act it out together.
2. Have participants run around the center of a village, acting out their dreams & demanding that others guess & satisfy them.

Harry Crosby USA, 1898–1929

from **DREAMS 1928–1929**

I

the dream of the glass princess is a cool moonlight of glass wings each wing a beat of the heart to greet the glass princess she is not bigger than a thimble as she tiptoes daintily down the tall glass corridor of my soul tinkle by tinkle tinkle by tinkle until I feel I shall go mad with suspense but just as she is opening her mouth to speak there is a shattering of glass and I awake to find I have knocked over the pitcher of ice-water that in summer always stands like a cold sentinel on the red table by the bed

2

red funnels are vomiting tall smokeplumes gold and onyx and diamond and emerald into four high round circles which solidify before they collide together with the impact of billiard balls that soon are caromed by a thin cue of wind into the deep pockets of sleep

3

the Man in the Moon is as rose-colored as our finger-nails as we go out hand in hand into the garden you and I to somewhere beyond the sleeping roses but although you remove your silk stockings and I my silk socks (we have forgotten our calling cards) the star butler with his silver tray never reappears and we are forced to find our way home along the bottom of the lake

4

I am rattling dice in a yellow skull they are falling upon the floor at the feet of the plump woman with bare breasts who is absorbed in the passion of giving milk to a rattlesnake but as soon as the numbers on the face of the dice correspond to the number of birds of paradise that form the jewels of her necklace she withdraws behind a red counterpane for the purpose of concealment

COMMENTARY

I write the word
  SUN
across the dreary palimpsest
of the world
  (H.C.)

In the last two years of his life, Crosby developed into a major image-making poet. The myth he unfolded was of the Sun—both as male & female—& he followed its orders through a striking series of structural innovations. Editor, with Caresse Crosby, of Black Sun Press in Paris (which published works by Hart Crane, Archibald MacLeish, Eugene Jolas, & D.H. Lawrence, along with his own first books), Crosby's verse experiments included, along with *Dreams*, the use of found forms (racing charts, book lists, stock reports, etc.) & concrete poetry, all concerned with sun-related imagery. After his suicide, several volumes of his work appeared with introductions by Eliot, Lawrence, & Pound, among others. But, in the anti-"modernist" reaction of the 1930s, he was turned into a virtual nonperson. In the context of a later time, however, the importance of his vision would seem clear—its dimensions suggested by Pound's earlier summary, viz.: "There is more theology in this book of Crosby's than in all the official ecclesiastical utterance of our generation. Crosby's life was a religious manifestation. His death was, if you like, a comprehensible emotional act.... A death from excess vitality. A vote of confidence in the cosmos.... Perhaps the best indication one can give of Crosby's capacity as a writer is to say that his work gains by reading all together. I do not mean this as a slight compliment. It is true of a small minority only."

Pauline Oliveros USA, 1932–2016

FOUR SONIC MEDITATIONS (1971)

NATIVE

Take a walk at night. Walk so silently that the bottoms of your feet become ears.

*

Sit in a circle with your eyes closed, begin by observing your own breathing. Gradually form a mental Image of one person who Is sitting in the circle. Sing a long tone to that person. Then sing the pitch that person is singing. Change your mental Image to another person and repeat until you have contacted every person in the circle one or more times.

ONE WORD

Choose one word. Dwell silently on this word. When you are ready, explore every sound in this word extremely slowly, repeatedly. Gradually, imperceptibly bring the word up to normal speed, then continue until you are repeating the word as fast as possible. Continue at top speed until "it stops."

RE COGNITION

Listen to a sound until you no longer recognize it.

COMMENTARY

An electronic composer early on, Oliveros moved later into an avant-garde/ arrière-garde series of "sonic meditations," the instructions & performance of which involved a new/old poetics of both sound & word, performance & attention. Thus: "Listen to everything all the time and remind yourself when you are not listening." And again: "Visualize your signature letter by letter slowly. Simultaneously hearing your name. Do this forward, then backwards. (Without sound.) See your signature in a selected color. Do these with eyes closed and eyes open."

Meskwaki (Sac and Fox) USA

THE LITTLE RANDOM CREATURES

found a hole with a light in it, and saying
Whose?
        set a trap
with a bowcord for a noose.
A giant of light, something alive, dazzled the path
on its way up, blinding
the little random creatures

o something alive was dying in the bowcord and it said
>Allow me to choke to death
>And you'll have night forever

and they let the sun go

Armand Schwerner's version from Meskwaki after William Jones's text

María Sabina Mazatec, Mexico, 1894–1985

THE SACRED BOOK OF LANGUAGE

The Book was before me. I could see it but not touch it. I tried to caress it but my hands didn't touch anything. I limited myself to contemplating it and, at that moment, I began to speak. Then I realized that I was reading the Sacred Book of Language. My Book. The Book of the Principal Ones.

I had attained perfection. I was no longer a simple apprentice. For that, as a prize, as a nomination, the Book had been granted me. When one takes the *saint children* [the sacred mushrooms], one can see the Principal Ones. Otherwise not. And it is the mushrooms that are saints; they give Wisdom. Wisdom is Language. Language is in the Book. The Book is granted by the Principal Ones. The Principal Ones appear with the great power of the *children.*

I learned the wisdom of the Book. Afterwards, in my later visions, the Book no longer appeared because its contents were already guarded in my memory.

Translated from Mazatec & Spanish by Álvaro Estrada & Henry Munn

COMMENTARY

Sabina then says, as if to drive the point of it home: "I cure with Language."

For more on and by Sabina, see "A Third Gallery."

PASAKWALA KÓMES Tzotil Maya, Mexico, contemporary

In the womb of my mother
I learned the spells.

In the womb of my mother
I heard them.

I took the basket,
I received the bottle,
I was given the incense,
I was shown the Book.

From the womb of my mother
I dreamed the incantations.

Translated from Tzotzil by Ambar Past,
for Taller Leñateros women's art collective,
Chiapas, Mexico

Hannah Weiner USA, 1928–1977

from **CLAIRVOYANT JOURNAL**

3/18 3   *crazy day*
DRINK COFFEE GO TO THE MUSEUM   They don't YOU NICE across

                                     Jasper John's

C   YOU DONT COMES   WHITE NUMBERS
O
P   *explain come*   C
Y   R
R   NOT LOVE   E
I   W
       says Morris   I   ONE MORE PAGE
          Louis   N
                  G
      DUNGAREES   A
                R
                 O
          BIG LIGHT U N   TOO MANY JOHNS
          END   D

                          in Guernica's colors, a portion
DOUBLE   pink SINK   of it appears in color

HEY SIS   BEATTLE   TO ME
                    "Bauhaus Stairway"
FANTASTIC   WHICH ARP
WHICH CHAKRA   SEE THROUGH
                    L AIN   ONE
              P
         T O M   FISH   JOB
      N C
   D O   ARAKAWA   DON'T COME ALONE
 D   GET OUT OF HERE   TO A PART
                                                      T
                                                    A
     FEEL THE HEAT from   IN FRONT OF THE ARP   H
                                                  T
                                                E
POWERFUL   ARP DIGESTS   I   E
                                N   S
                         D   NOT HONEST in white stone,
            CRAZY WOMAN   N leg appears green
                   SIT DOWN   G
                               E
   FEEL THE TABLE   HALA   R   DONT CRY
              YOU WONT BELIEVE   D
         ARP NOT WEAK   E
                                 S
              BEHAVE   C
         POOF   YOURSELF   R
                                I
                                B
                                E   YOU
              ONEMORE   THE
         BEAUTIFUL   A
            SAVE YOU   R
              DESIGN LINGERIE   DO C   OK
                   OK
              THIS AFTERNOON   OK LAMONTE
         WHOOPEE
                   TANTRA
              FANTASTIC
                            all this in front of Arp's
         GO HIT CHARLEMAGNE   "Human Concretion"
   Discontinue Laughing   NOT THE OTHER says Floral Nude
                   PARTY
   SMILE says Brancusi's Fish FATTY HEAT HERE DO NOT
         BIG ROCK   OMIT
                                   NO MORE ARP

the words began to appear / in 1972 and led to the clairvoyant journal
a three voice / performance poetry book about learning   explaining
instructions / and the counter voice (H.W.) And again: *All words are seen*

A practitioner & experimenter early on, Weiner's poetry was later to change—radically—with the onset of an actual & persistent experience, an alteration of perception in which visible words entered her field of vision as cause of wonder & as "messages" to be included in the written work that followed. The relationship of that experience to those of many traditional poet-mystics may also be worth noting—as when an anonymous thirteenth-century kabbalist (a follower of the great Hebrew mystic Abraham Abulafia) describes letters & words that "take the shape of great mountains" and other forms, to draw him thereby into sacred speech, etc. The lack of a similar context for Weiner's experiences may be seen as a condition of our time—on which no further comment.

Juan Martínez   Mexico, 1933–2007

from *AT THE GATES OF PARADISE*

A silence
upon the softest clearness.
Interior harmony
in eternity
precise perception
ego for super ego
subtle energy
of anti-matter.

EIGHTH CIRCLE

A face in the friendship
of the possible,
key in the non solar
light.

~

Eyelids of heavens,
beauty's fate,
perfect praise,
silver light

in the morn,
alone,
precisely there.

~

The dream,
imaginary ripples,
its prodigies
the key
for humankind.

~

Blue—sea & heavens,
a flush of birds,
the infinite skill
of thought,
the pattern of the present,
surname, fountain pen,
music enclosed
in the cube
of truth.

~

Imagination,
fruits,
blazing instants,
incense, fire,
motionless
movements,
the eyes play
at full sight.

~

Key, name,
sea, double action
the body's seed
in a long road
brown, through the line,
predestination
of dreams
& acknowledged

in time,
subtle streams
of comprehension.

~

Mother of days,
fragrance, sheer
almond
in our isolation,
unfold here
your splendid
muscular forms.

~

Jungle of tears,
listen:
seed of songs,
the perfection of gold
is yours.

Translated from Spanish by Javier Taboada

COMMENTARY

Let's dance, madness, / joy of the word / master key / of this house. (J.M.)

In saying which, Martínez emphasized his life as an outsider artist & poet, reflecting the world as he lived it on his own terms. Born in Tequila, Jalisco, within a traditional family, his path took him early on to Tijuana in Baja California & then to years of wanderings in & near Mexico City, where he constructed thousands of works of art "built," as fellow poet Alberto Blanco describes them, "with aluminum foil, tin, cigarettes and chocolate wrappers collected in the street, pressed with great force and consolidated with his strong hands to give them form." And further: "He used to spend endless hours swimming in the icy waters of the Pacific and nights in the cafés of the central Revolución Avenue [in Tijuana]. There he devoted himself to rest at times, but, above all, to what he called 'building'… drawing, painting, writing." In this "[he] made no distinction between 'building' by way of drawing or making sculptures, objects, writing poems, or doing many other activities."

In all of this, his work & life resembled that of other "outside" artists & poets, & like many of them—or like avant-garde artists everywhere—he explored & broke the boundaries between the arts in new & often astonishing ways.

David Antin USA, 1932–2016

A LIST OF THE DELUSIONS OF THE INSANE:
WHAT THEY ARE AFRAID OF

the police
being poisoned
being killed
being alone
being attacked at night
being poor
being followed at night
being lost in a crowd
being dead
having no stomach
having no insides
having a bone in the throat
losing money
being unfit to live
being ill with a mysterious disease
being unable to turn out the light
being unable to close the door
that an animal will come in from the street that they will not recover
that they will be murdered
that they will be murdered when they sleep
that they will be murdered when they wake
that murders are going on all around them
that they will see the murderer
that they will not
that they will be boiled alive
that they will be starved
that they will be fed disgusting things
that disgusting things are being put into their food and drink that their
   flesh is boiling
that their head will be cut off
that children are burning
that they are starving
that all of the nutriment has been removed from food
that evil chemicals have been placed in the earth
that evil chemicals have entered the air
that it is immoral to eat

that they are in hell
that they hear people screaming
that they smell burnt flesh
that they have committed an unpardonable sin
that there are unknown agencies working evil in the world that they
   have no identity
that they are on fire
that they have no brain
that they are covered with vermin
that their property is being stolen
that their children are being killed
that they have stolen something
that they have too much to eat
that they have been chloroformed
that they have been blinded
that they have gone deaf
that they have been hypnotized
that they are the tools of another power
that they have been forced to commit murder
that they will get the electric chair
that people have been calling them names
that they deserve these names
that they are changing their sex
that their blood has turned to water
that insects are coming out of their body that they give off a bad smell
that houses are burning around them
that people are burning around them
that children are burning around them
that houses are burning
that they have committed suicide of the soul

COMMENTARY

An early conceptual work drawn and expanded from a catalogue originally compiled in the late nineteenth century by Thomas Smith Clouston of
"actual examples of delusions of about 100 female melancholic patients"
("and they far from exhaust the list," he adds). William James included the
list in a footnote to *The Principles of Psychology* (1890).

A catalogue, here, of the pitfalls of vision.

For more on Antin, see "A Map of Extensions" & "A Fourth Gallery."

Dorus Vrede Suriname, 1949–2020

from **RETURN TO THE OLD LOMBE**

The old man trembled in his desire to feel the tree, but he did not touch it yet. He felt guilty for his absence during the transmigration. He had not been at his father's grave to bid him farewell. The obia hut with its divinities had disappeared beneath the water. Awanga still had to ask permission to speak with his fathers and the divinities.

Around his upper right arm was an iron ring that he had worn for more than fifty years. He only took the ring off when it was absolutely necessary. Now the moment had come for Awanga to take off this magic ring. A deep groove remained in Awanga's arm where the ring had been. He let the corial drift a few meters from the Kankan tree, so that he could tie its rope to a branch in preparation for the ritual to come. He broke off a piece of pembadoti and dissolved it in a mixture of water and spirits that he had poured into the gourd. Then he tied a piece of twine to the ring, which he held in the gourd so that the power of the contents could be absorbed. Awanga removed the ring and wound the end of the twine around his index finger. He moved to the middle of the corial and held the ring just above his knees. The ring hung there, motionless. Even the wind did not move it.

Very quietly, as though only thinking aloud, the words passed Awanga's lips: "Obia, I have fallen in the eyes of my father, but I have come in the hope of being forgiven. Is that right: will I be forgiven?" The ring hung still. This frightened Awanga a bit, but he recovered and calmly asked: "Will my father and the gods speak to me, Obia?" Now the ring swung quietly back and forth. This gave Awanga hope.

"Kr Will! myyyy father Mataibo, Afo Kwassi M'Kamba, speak to me in the name of Kedjama Kedjampo? Will they speak to their son, Wangainaito?" The ring swung wildly back and forth. Awanga was so pleased, he began to hum a song of thanks. Thanks to his father and the gods who had mercy on him. He was sure of himself, and he was satisfied.

"Di andeloeakkifiafia wan," he murmured as he watched the ring. "In truth, this ring is genuine," he repeated. He wrapped the twine around the ring and put it back on his arm. He untied the corial and paddled, now unafraid and full of longing, towards the Kankan tree. When he reached the tree he knelt in the boat for better balance. He spread his arms and hugged the tree passionately. Power flowed into him. He shook like a little bush in a waterfall. His eyes were ablaze. The Kromanti took possession of him.

Greetings greetings, I am here, I am here
I, child of the forest
I am here, my father, I am here
I want to greet you first and then I wish
to enter the kingdom of the dead.

Welcome, welcome my child
The gods of the wood and their sons
have not forgotten you
For you there is surely a place
beside your fathers

The meeting with the divinities lasted all afternoon.

Translated from Dutch by Sam Garrett

Translated from Dutch by Sam Garrett

COMMENTARY

Lombe was a town inhabited by African-descended Maroons—near the Suriname River—that was "relocated" in the 1960s for the construction of the Afobaka dam, which would supply hydroelectric energy to the Suriname Aluminum Company. Ineke Phaf-Rhineberger writes: "In this work, a native of Old Lombe describes the last minute when he has to abandon [in a corial, a small vessel] his hometown before the artificial lake arrives. His emotional charge is identified with the objects of African origin and manifested in his efforts to save them from drowning so he does not lose his strength and his contact with his protecting *obia* (a religious force)" (in *Revista de Crítica Literaria Latinoamericana*, trans. Javier Taboada).

Arysteides Turpana Panama, 1943–2020

UAGO

Uago. My name is Uago. The First Spirit. He who opened his eyes and knowing how, suddenly found himself standing amid a jasmine-scented chorus.

Uago. My name is Uago. Basil Man—my name: The First Spirit soaring as a breeze on the breeze; The First Spirit, The First Breath, The First Viewer of the Glade, The First Dweller of the Glade.

Uago. My name is Uago. The Enclosed-by-Light. The Illuminated. The Blazing. The Double-Torch Spirit. The Moon's Breath, The Stars' Breath.

Uago. My name is Uago. When I found myself, I found the unsealed bosom of the mother taking me in: Oh Earthmother.

Uago. My name is Uago. The First Spirit. River's First Brother, The First Spirit amid The Golden Air, The First Spirit amid The Silver Air, The First Spirit who peeps out from every valley & plain, from mountains & heavens, from clouds & hills: Oh Sunbrother.

Uago. My name is Uago. The First Spirit. The Very First, who—lit, illuminated & enclosed by moonbeams—was discovered by the stars.

Uago. My name is Uago. The First Spirit. The First who trekked amid the Flower's laughter, The First who saw Trees dressed with polychrome blouses & wild garments & necklaces of fruit enclosing their throats.

Uago. My name is Uago. The First Spirit. He who opened his eyes & not knowing how, suddenly found himself standing amid a jasmine-scented chorus.

Translated from Spanish by Javier Taboada

COMMENTARY

According to the Cuna (Dule) myth, when the Earth was still a little girl & was fully dressed with bushes, trees, & leaves, the divine couple—Paba & Nana—sent a messenger (not fully human) to verify their work. The first inhabitant's name was Uago, & astonished by the beauty of the creation, he started to sing like an indigenous Adam: "I am the flower's brother."

Arysteides Turpana was the first Cuna poet to have written both in his own language and in Spanish.

Joseph Smith   USA, 1805–1844

from **THE PEARL OF GREAT PRICE**

Extracts from The History of Joseph Smith, the Prophet

I had actually seen a light, and in the midst of that light I saw two Personages, and they did in reality speak to me; and though I was hated and persecuted for saying that I had seen a vision, yet it was true; and while they were persecuting me, reviling me, and speaking all manner of evil against me falsely for so saying, I was led to say in my heart: Why persecute me for telling the truth? I have actually seen a vision; and who am I that I can withstand God, or why does the world think to make me deny what I have actually seen? For I had seen a vision; I knew it, and I knew that God knew it, and I could not deny it, neither dared I do it.

COMMENTARY

And the king said that a seer is greater than a prophet. (The Book of Mormon)

The foundation of American Mormonism (the Church of Jesus Christ of Latter-day Saints) comes through Joseph Smith in the Book of Mormon, his work presented there as an act of visionary poesis & inscription. In the text selected above, Smith's recounting & testimony about the veracity of his visions acted "[a]t the core of Joseph's sense of identity," as scholar Douglas J. Davies stated, and "in this there's a real sense of hope, where hope indicates the sense of a possible future and a commitment to it, and courage bespeaks the energy summoned in forging a way ahead to make it possible" (in *Joseph Smith Jr., Reappraisals after Two Centuries*). The title of the related text, above, is derived from the parable of the pearl, as told by Jesus in Matthew 13:45–46: "Again, the kingdom of heaven is like unto a merchant man, seeking goodly pearls: Who, when he had found one pearl of great price, went and sold all that he had, and bought it." Its presence here alongside other American visionary works is also to be noted.

El Niño Fidencio

(Fidencio Síntora Constantino), Mexico, 1898–1938

from **SACRED SCRIPTURES**

March 12, 1935. The Jews

1 In the name of the Father, of the Son, & of the Holy Ghost, Amen.

2 On this date, through the Divine Providence of the Eternal Father, the Inspector of the Divine Science phone lines, by the Grace of the Lord, reports:

3 That between 12 & 1 a.m. he noticed having reached Space #3.

4 There he—The Inspector—had the joy of seeing Moses's Tablets.

5 The Lord granted it due to his big and growing faith.

6 For he met his true God in Spirit. For he felt Him in his heart, he was also dressed in Light & Divine Grace.

7 That's where the loving hearts of their True & Eternal God reach.

8 Unknowing it, he was reporting to the Holy Ghost's disciples.

9 The Holy Days were coming: The Passion & Death of our Lord Jesus Christ.

10 The Inspector reported that the Jews were pursuing

11 Our Father Jesus of Nazareth through valleys & a mount of thorns & thickets.

12 The Inspector reports the same thing: they were pursuing our Father Jesus of Nazareth

13 To sacrifice him on the days he gave his knowledge.

14 I connected myself with The Inspector's heart & I placed myself in the middle of a palmetto

15 & it covered my Most Holy Body

16 & when they passed by, they couldn't see me.

17 We kept moving toward the East, connected with the heart of the Inspector.

18 & I did this to teach my children the sufferings of this Holy Way.

19 My Inspector had a coin in his pocket.

20 & I threw it forward in the same direction, East,

21 For the Jews were almost reaching us.

22 Then God, with His power in the coin, molded a huge pond

23 & the Jews stood still

24 For they were shocked to see that huge pond.

25 We kept moving & after a short walk, voices were heard.

26 The Inspector heard: "Now we are reaching them"

27 Then I plucked a hair from my headdress & threw it forward & a mountain there was molded,

28 So dense: neither the Jews nor we could pass through

29 & we kept moving in the same direction.

30 After a walk, at some point, The Inspector heard again:

31 "Now we are reaching them."

32 Then I put my Most Blessed Hands on my chest,

33 & I opened my arms, embodying a Guardian Angel

34 & I raised my thoughts up to God asking Him to favor me in that moment.

35 When I opened my arms, a colossal mountain range of vast boulders was molded.

36 As we kept moving toward the East, The Inspector kept reporting to us:

37 To not be afraid if the Jews seek to reach us again,

38 For the 12 Apostles of the Lord were already with us.

39 Somehow, they reached a jungle & The Inspector saw the password I made.

40 The password was: *tell the ones that belong to Me,*

41 *That, to be saved, they should stay beneath the shadow of that tree.*

42 The Creator of Heaven & Earth & His Son were with him.

43 The Inspector reports that, when they were walking towards the East,

44 None of the apostles raised their eyes.

45 Not everyone walked meekly & some of them had slackened.

46 Divine Testimony & Spiritual Knowledge by the Author of Peace, Fidencio S. Constantino,

47 On the same date The Inspector was authorized to release these data to the Soldiers of Cristo Rey,

48 Victor Zapata, F.S.C.

Translated from Spanish by Javier Taboada

COMMENTARY

El Niño Fidencio (Fidencio Síntora Constantino) was a healer & prophet in one of many times when the "curanderos" & their religious movements were in bloom in Mexico & throughout our continents. The *Book of the Holy Scriptures* is a gathering (made by his followers) that recounts Fidencio's teachings & visions, many of which are a mediumistic rereading of the gospels. Fidencio—who dictated the visions—inserts himself as an eyewitness (& as a partaker) in Jesus's life.

Essie Pinola Parrish USA, 1902–1979

per George Quasha, USA, 1942–

(Somapoetics 73)

ESSIE PARRISH IN NEW YORK

It is a test you have to pass.
Then you can learn to heal
with the finger, said Essie
pointing over our heads:
I went thru every test on the way,
that's how come I'm a shaman.
Be careful on the journey, they said,
the journey to heaven. They warned me.
And so I went.
Thru the rolling hills
I walked and walked,
mountains and valleys, and rolling hills,
I walked and walked and walked—
you hear many things there
in those rolling hills and valleys,
and I walked and walked and walked
and walked and walked until
I came to a footbridge,
and on the right side were a whole lot of people
and they were naked and crying out,
how'd you get over there,
we want to get over there too
but we're stuck here,
please come over here and help us cross,
the water's too deep for us—
I didn't pay no attention,
I just walked and walked and walked,
and then I heard an animal, sounded like a huge dog,
and there was a huge dog and next to him a huge lady
wearing blue clothes,
and I decided I had to walk right thru—
I did
and the dog only snarled at me.
Never go back.
I walked and walked and walked

and I came to one only tree
and I walked over to it and looked up at it
and read the message:
Go on, you're half way.
From there I felt better, a little better.
And I walked and walked and walked and walked
and I saw water, huge water
how to get thru?
I fear it's deep. Very blue water.
But I have to go.
Put out the first foot, then the left,
never use the left hand,
and I passed thru.
Went on and on and on, and I had to enter a place
and there I had to look down:
it was hot and there were people there
and they looked tiny down there in that furnace
running around crying.
I had to enter.
You see, these tests are to teach my people
how to live.
Fire didn't burn me.
And I walked and walked and walked.
On the way you're going to suffer.
And I came to a four-way road
like a cross. Which is the right way?
I already knew.
East is the right way to go to heaven.
North, South, and West are dangerous.
And at this crossroad there was a place in the center.
North you could see beautiful things of the Earth,
hills and fields and flowers and everything beautiful
and I felt like grabbing it
but I turned away.
West was nothing but fog and damp
and I turned away.
South was dark, but there were sounds,
monsters and huge animals. And I turned away and
Eastward I walked and walked and walked
and there were flowers, on both sides of the road,
flowers and flowers and flowers

out of this world.
And there is white light, at the center,
while you are walking.
This is the complicated thing:
my mind changes.
We are the people on the Earth.
We know sorrow and knowledge and faith and talent
and everything.
Now as I was walking there
some places I feel like crying
and some places I feel like talking
and some places I feel like dancing
but I am leaving these behind for the next world.
Then when I entered into that place
I knew:
if you enter heaven
you might have to work.
This is what I saw in my vision.
I don't have to go nowhere to see.
Visions are everywhere.

COMMENTARY

*Toward the end of the world, when I am no longer here… it's important
people remember and respect.* (E.P.P.)

(1) Essie Pinola Parrish, a Kashaya Pomo healer & Dreamer from California & the final leader, along with Mabel McKay, of the revitalized Dreamer
religion, spoke at the New School in New York on March 14, 1972. The
text as given here is a reconstruction by poet/artist George Quasha of
her narrative of a dream vision, based on notes he took as she spoke; he
remarks that "the greater portion of the lines are as I wrote them in the
notebook. I'm just a humble scribe." And further: "My only 'formal' concern was to distort her tone and overall temporal curve as little as possible.
What I'm concerned with in the Essie vision is Dharma transmission. It was
clear to me that, despite her sharp irony about talking to white people and
the protective distance she kept, she was offering us a portion of the sacred.
What would it mean to take it on (as in Yeats's 'Did she put on his knowledge with his power…')? To my mind it meant getting the *words* and their
hidden *alcheringa*. And that's literal enough."

(2) Or Carlos Castaneda's notable work of the imagination *The Teachings
of Don Juan: A Yaqui Way of Knowledge* (1968): "When you see, there are
no longer familiar features in the world. Everything is new. Everything has
never happened before. The world is incredible!"

Kazim Ali USA, 1971–

RAMADAN

You wanted to be so hungry, you would break into branches,
and have to choose between the starving month's

nineteenth, twenty-first, and twenty-third evenings.
The liturgy begins to echo itself and why does it matter?

If the ground-water is too scarce one can stretch nets
into the air and harvest the fog.

Hunger opens you to illiteracy,
thirst makes clear the starving pattern,

the thick night is so quiet, the spinning spider pauses,
the angel stops whispering for a moment—

The secret night could already be over,
you will have to listen very carefully—

You are never going to know which night's mouth is sacredly reciting
and which night's recitation is secretly mere wind—

COMMENTARY

*Poetry is the smallest way—it is a small, small way, but it is a way
indeed—that the individual body can express its own personhood and
value in the face of faceless systems.* (K.A.) And again: *I learned God's true
language is only silence and breath.*

Kazim Ali was born in the United Kingdom to Muslim parents of Indian
descent & has lived transnationally in the United States, Canada, India,
France, & the Middle East. Estranged in certain ways from his family's
cultural traditions when he was younger, he has more recently reembraced
the Ramadan ritual, but still more cogently he writes of the subsequent
movement between tradition & rediscovery, & of the conflicts of vision this
entails: "A little while ago I thought I ought to stop writing about God. The
reason is that I was starting to have ideas. Ideas mean a system of ideas.
Every idea you have may preclude another. I thought that it would be better
to have a space of unknowing and that other poets would continue to make
poems about God. I don't know if I have kept my promise or not, but by
turning away from the task of trying to know the unknown and from the
vocabulary of the spirit, which is necessarily the language of abstraction, I
was able to come back into the world."

For this, his key work is *Fasting for Ramadan: Notes from a Spiritual
Practice* (Tupelo Press, 2011).

José Vicente Anaya Mexico, 1947–2020

from *HÍKURI (PEYOTE)*

I come across thousands of cloudy mirrors
and the reflection peers back fractured

I WILL BE THE WORLD'S ABCESS
       black angel of our darkness
       plumed serpent
       devil's advocate

I woke up uttering: ALL POETS ARE THE SAME

EN ESTE INFIERNO	(Vallejo)	thrashed heart
in this hell	(Ginsberg)	ulcerated saintliness
in der hiesigen hölle	(Hölderlin)	scorned vision
dans cet enfer	(Rimbaud)	rotten flesh

....

In the Zone of the Tropic of Cancer

at night in the pine-tree wilderness
of your eyes, Ruth, I see miniscule stars
orbiting
and we penetrate another firmament (Himmelszelt)

I BECOME WATER

mixed with water /

while you sail
the sea of your memory
to see a girl from a *naïve* landscape

....

there are ancient traces on my face too

Translated from Spanish by Joshua Pollock

I am convinced that, as a poet, I am a medium of universal wisdom, as if somebody (God? The Universal Unconscious?) asked me to report the visions they present to me via the poems. (J.V.A.)

Alongside Roberto Bolaño & Mario Santiago Papasquiaro, José Vicente Anaya was one of the founders of Infrarealism in Mexico in the 1970s. Writes his translator Joshua Pollock of Anaya's masterwork: "*Híkuri* is an outlier in Mexican poetry; it is a poem that has been systematically excluded from anthologies and critical discourse... instead thriving as a subterranean cult classic.... With *Híkuri* [*Peyote*], Anaya charts a transformative journey inward, toward a psychedelic convergence of inside/outside, male/female, past/present, self/other. The poem is multilingual: in addition to the quotes in German, English and French, the indigenous Rarámuri language is used throughout in the form of ritualistic shamanic chants.... The poet and critic Heriberto Yépez has written: 'For Anaya, poetry is revelation, a sacred practice against brainwashing and lobotomy,' and I think that is exactly what we need right now."

Ájahi   Kuikuro, Brazil, ca. 2004

from THE WOMAN WHO WENT TO THE VILLAGE OF THE DEAD

... "I'm going there"
       she said to her children
& the two women went away

& when the Widow & Mother-in-law
were not so far from the village
       her children screamed:
              STAY HERE!

some said
Mother-in-law placed the Widow in front of herself
       & she lifted her up
              lifted her up
                     lifted her up

& both were at the edges of heaven & earth

they went up
        "well turn your face down"
said Mother-in-law
        "turn your face down!
                turn it down
                        upside down"

& the Earth seemed upside down
down from the sky
                here
      above our Earth

& they went away
right at the start of the road of the dead

Mother-in-law pushed the Widow
to the edge of the road
        & erased her footprints
        so the dead
                could not see them

  . . . . .

they were at the back
of the houses of the dead
& entered a house
        over the platform
amid the slices of dried cassava paste

                too much flour there
              a lot of food for the dead

& Mother-in-law was sweeping the floor
to make her unknown
        so nobody knew
            so nobody knew

"bring me a *túhagu*"
        a dead woman said

"LISTEN!"
      said Mother-in-law
"they are trying to speak
        those which were our words
        that's how those which were our words
            are here"

shortly after she heard:
    "bring me my *igihitolo*"

"LISTEN!"
    said Mother-in-law
"the dead woman means the *alato*
which is the name for a *griddle*
to cook cassava bread
    in the words of the living

but to cook cassava bread
    she has said 'bring my *igihitolo*'

"& before she has said
    'bring me a *túhagu*!'
confounding the *strainer* in which she used to sift
called *angagi*
    in the words of the living

"LISTEN!
"this is what those which were our words
        are like here"
said Mother-in-law

    "those which were our words were inverted"

Reworked by Javier Taboada after Bruna Franchetto & Carlos Fausto's translation from Kuikuro

COMMENTARY

Anha ituna tütenhüpe itaõ, "The woman who went to the village of the dead," is a story recorded by Bruna Franchetto & Carlos Fausto in 2004, in Ipatse, the main Kuikuro village, near the Xingu River in the southern Amazon, where the Kuikuro people have lived since at least the sixteenth century.

The storyteller was a woman named Ájahi, a renowned ritual specialist & expert singer. Franchetto & Fausto write about the storytelling: "In Ájahi's version, a woman is taken by her dead mother-in-law and by her longing for her dead husband through the path of the dead (*anha*) to their celestial village."

And further: "In the afterworld, other words are used, referring to an inside-out world. The text recurrently makes use of the suffix -*pe*, as in *kakisükope*, which can be loosely translated as 'our former words' or 'those which were our words,' referring to the words of the living that the dead seek out and transform, in their language of the dead, into other words...."

Ájahi insists on the contrast/complementarity between the language of the dead and the language of the living. The suffix -*pe* here means that the dead are trying to recover their language (that they used when they were alive), but in this effort they only find synonyms in the language of the dead."

Alice Notley USA, 1945–

from **THE DESCENT OF ALETTE**

"I walked into" "the forest;" "for the woods were lit" "by yellow
street lamps" "along various" "dirty pathways" "I paused a moment"
"to absorb" "the texture" "of bark & needles" "The wind carried"
"with a pine scent" "the river's aura—" "delicious air" "Then a

figure" "appeared before me—" "a woman" "in a long dress" "standing
featureless" "in a dark space" "'Welcome,' she said," "& stepped into"
"the light" "She was dark-haired" "but very pale" "I stared hard at her,
realizing" "that her flesh was" "translucent," "& tremulous," "a

whitish gel" "She was protoplasmic-" "looking—" "But rather beautiful,"
"violet-eyed" "'What is this place?'" "I asked her" "'It would be
paradise,' she said," "'but, as you see," "it's very dark," "& always
dark" "You will find that" "those who live here" "are changed"

"enough" "from creation's first intent" "as to be deeply" "upset ... "
"But you must really" "keep going now" "'Are those tents" "over there?'
I asked" "I saw small pyramids" "at a distance" "'Yes, these woods are"
"full of beings," "primal beings," "hard to see—" "because it's"

"always dark here" "Most of them" "need not concern you now" "But
wait here," "someone is coming" "to show you your way" "She stepped
back into" "the shadows," "turned & left me"

COMMENTARY

It's necessary to maintain a state of disobedience against ... everything.
(A.N.) And again: *"I see" "with my voice"*

Of Notley's Dante-like descent into the subterranean/subway world of
New York City, Steve Silberman writes in summary: "*The Descent of Alette*

is a fully embodied universe, with its own terrain and history, and a narrative that flows with the inexorable gravity of myth. By refusing to surrender the incantatory power of the word to evangelists and ad men, Notley has invoked a portion of 'the great language in which the universe itself is written' (as poet Robert Duncan wrote) and dared to dream the world new."

And Silberman, further: "What may first strike the reader as a typographical gimmick quickly becomes part of the poem's force, as the reader is drawn through the dank caverns of Notley's subterranean 'world of souls' on a dire mission: the assassination of a charismatic and seemingly omnipotent tyrant, in whose name the subway dwellers are imprisoned underground."

Gloria Gervitz   Mexico, 1943–2022

from **MIGRATIONS**

beneath the summer-drenched willow only restlessness lingers
docile clouds descend into silence
the day dissolves in the hot air
green erupts within green
I spread my legs beneath the bathtub faucet
gushing water falls
the water enters me
the words of the Zohar spread open
the same questions as always
and I sink deeper and deeper
in the vertigo of Kol Nidre
before the start of the great fast
in the blue haze of the synagogues
after and before Rosh Hashanah
in the whiteness of the rain
my grandmother prays the rosary
and in the background plummeting
the echo of the shofar opens the year
into the gulf of absences to the northeast
pour words saliva
insomnias
and farther to the east
I masturbate thinking of you
the screech of seagulls the break of day
the froth in the dazzle of the wing

the color and the season of bougainvilleas are for you
the pollen still on my fingers
your scent of violets sour and feverish from the dust
words that are nothing but a drawn-out prayer
a form of madness after the madness
the cages where the perfumes are shut away
the endless delights
the voluptuousness of being born again and again
static ecstasy
move
more even more
don't be afraid
and the photographs fading in the fermentation of silence
the unscreened porches
fever growing red in other skies
the gleaming verandas darkening with the acacias
and in the kitchen the newly washed dishes
fruit and syrups
in the swell of rivers
in the night of willows
in the washbasins of dreams
in that steam of female viscera
rising unmistakable and expansive
I leave you my death entire complete
my whole death for you
to whom does one speak before dying?
where are you?
where in me can I invent you?

Translated from Spanish by Mark Schafer

COMMENTARY

in the migrations of red carnations where songs burst from long-beaked
birds / and apples rot before the disaster / where women fondle their
breasts and touch their sex / in the sweat of rice powder and teatime /
vines of passionflowers course through that which stays the same (G.G.)

(1) Worked on from 1976 to 2020, Gloria Gervitz's masterwork *Migrations*
is an epic of the migratory self. Like Pound's *Cantos* or Zukofsky's *"A,"*
hers is the work of a lifetime: a life's work including not only autobiography & familial memories as a kind of history but rife with sexual, religious,

& mystical imagery taken from different sources: from Jewish kabbalah to Mexican folk Catholicism & beyond.

(2) Writes Mark Schafer, translator, shortly after her death: "At the beginning of Gloria Gervitz's 261-page poem, which she composed over 44 years, she wrote: 'I leave you my death entire complete / my whole death for you / to whom does one speak before dying?' In the context of the poem, Gervitz seems to be addressing a version of her mother or grandmother. But given her own death on April 19, 2022, she now also addresses us, her readers. Except that—paradoxically, ironically, or both—we must now intervene as readers-writers of the text, replacing 'death' with 'life.' Death and life, the possibilities of the present and memories of the past, stasis and ecstasy, silence and song, the blank page and the printed word, are all in a constant dance in *Migrations*."

Pedro Xisto   Brazil, 1901–1987

EPITHALAMIUM II

He = éle   S = serpens
& = e   h = homo
She = ela   e = eva

Of the role of humanity as co-creator by the act of naming (i.e., utter-ing words/worlds), Concrete poet Pedro Xisto wrote: "Before POETRY was named, it already was... Yahweh named everything. And he named the light day & darkness night.... The whole problem of significant lan-guage was there: numen & name. Before they were named, every being was absent. And the Creator brought the man so he could declare the creation to them."

Pedro Xisto was an important figure in the Poem/Process movement, which began in the 1960s & took a sharp political turn during the period of the Brazilian dictatorship (1964 to 1985).

Edgar Bayley Argentina, 1919–1990

THIS WASTED WEALTH IS INFINITE

this hand isn't the hand isn't the skin of your delight
in every corner you find another sky
behind the sky there's always another lawn unique beaches
it'll never end this wasted wealth is infinite
never assume the dawn's foam is gone
after a face there's another face
after your lover's departure there's another departure
after the song a new touch grows longer
and early mornings hide unpredicted ABCs and far-off islands
it'll always be like that
sometimes you think your dream has said it all
but another dream erupts and is not the same
then you go back to the hands to everyone's to everybody's heart
you're not the same they're not the same
some of them know the word you ignore it
others know how to forget unnecessary facts
and raise their thumbs they have forgotten
you must go back your failure it doesn't matter
it will never end this wasted wealth is infinite
and every nod every form of love or blame
among the final laughs the pain and the beginnings
will find the sour wind and the vanquished stars
a mask of birch foretells the vision

you've wanted to see
at the end of the day sometimes you attain it
the river reaches the gods
raises distant murmurs up to the sun's clarity
threats
frozen glow
you don't expect anything
except for the course of the sun and of the grief
it will never end this wasted wealth is infinite

Translated from Spanish by Javier Taboada

COMMENTARY

The sand is my possession. A voice on the edge of destruction. The denial that makes a man—all men—beyond concern. From nausea a face will be born. The open eyes will look at last. (E.B.)

Writes Bayley, tracing his own visions: "Poetry is a bet, a mortal leap. There is a moment when the poet is all alone and apparently very close to the madman, to the hoax, to a fraud. Every truth has its own shadow nearby; and it happens that the shadow of truth is very similar to the truth itself..." And later: "The presence of poetry and the dimension of the sacred are within us, but they must come into being. And they come into being when we become what we are, when we become ourselves & we reach our genuine condition. Or to put it differently: when you manage to be faithful to *yourself.... How do we know a poet has received a revelation of his own self?* ... Just when—after some lines and beyond his skills—we discover a certain presence, a certain energy and vigor, a certain self of one's own" (in *Presencia de la Poesía*, trans. Javier Taboada).

María Auxiliadora Álvarez Venezuela, 1956–

STANDING STONES

everything I want to tell you son Is that you should go through suffering
    If you come to its shore if its shore comes to you Enter its night
        and let yourself

                        sink

      its gulp may drink you down its foam overwhelm you Let go *let yourself go*
Everything I want to tell you son On the other side of suffering

                              Another shore lies
there you will find great stone slabs One of these bears your carved form
          etched with your ancient mark Where you in your fullness will
                         fit exactly
these are not tombs son They are standing stones with their small
                                        engraved suns
                         and their crevices and cracks

Translated from Spanish by Catherine Hammond

COMMENTARY

One of the stronger voices in current Latin American poetry, María
Auxiliadora Álvarez writes: "If you can talk, you have not yet been
defeated... I feel urged by the necessity for a poetry in search of hope. I
think that the one who names can create more air if he invokes it or offers
it or seeks it. And I get tired of the weight of darkness.... I speak of darkness as of the reflection that is comforted in misfortune. I think the big challenge is to survive in the most intact way we can."

George Quasha USA, 1942–

from **AXIAL STONES**

18

Poet & artist George Quasha views an *axial* work as "an opening to active space *between* a medium and its viewer/reader/listener, and between diverse mediums themselves (sculpture, drawing, music, dance, language), reflecting our dynamic relation both with each other and with environment (*ecos*)." *Axial*, he continues, "stands for a single principle that shows itself at work in an *alert relaxed* way, communicatively across mediums and between beings. Axially, any two stones may come to balance through a common axis, simultaneously registered first in a person's *listening body*. It's an event between the stones and the person aligning with their balancing. Their precariousness (*no glue is used*) invites a viewer to *undergo instability* so as to *see with full body*, opening to renewal in fresh, even visionary seeing. This action is *visible axial poiesis*—where a self-regulating event's center of gravity is consciously reflexive, flexible and in flux." Quasha's many volumes of his invented poetic genre called *preverbs* follow the same principle, he writes, as in:

> *stones on edge are still happening like these dangling words*
> *stones stutter to a balance*
> *singular stone time turning true tones time out*
> *things done for themselves are the only things done for all*

Amy Catanzano USA, 1974–

from **MULTIVERSAL**

Notes on the Enclosure of Notes

We were free like fixed stars.
They fall beneath me.

I do not move; we are free to clear the space with these
stars. Space clears the stars from my eyes.
They are moving, and we

are free to fix the stars. They move
without falling. We are falling

and free. We are free

to make a spell with the stars.

Space is free; I populate
the space with stars. We fall beneath them like the sea.
We clear the sea
of its space.

We are free; the sea is free. The sea
is fixed. The sea has

moved;

I am fixed by the falling stars.

We clear the space from our eyes so that all we see
are the stars. The sea moves.

It is populated with words; the sea falls like a star.
We are free to clear the words
from our eyes.

They do not move. Words are not fixed

stars. I am free in the sea. I am free like the words
falling; nothing

is fixed. We populate the words in our eyes
with stars; we fall with them in space

up from the sea, free.

COMMENTARY

The poem comes at the start of Catanzano's explorations of a possible twenty-first-century "quantum poetics," toward a new way of envisioning & absorbing the larger, mostly invisible universe. Enough for the following appraisal from Michael Palmer: "Amy Catanzano offers us a poetic vision of multiple orders and multiple forms, of a fluid time set loose from linearity and an open space that is motile and multidimensional. The work exists at once in a future-past and in a variety of temporal modes.... In a time of displacement such as ours, she seems to say, in place of 'universals' we must imagine 'multiversals,'" in place of the fixed, the metamorphic.... 'A blaze within a tighter blaze, engulfed.' 'Earth pivots on a pearl.'"

That she has backed this up with on-site residencies at major space observatories & particle-tracking sites is also worth noting.

Diocelina Restrepo

Yukpa People, Sokorpá, Colombia, contemporary

WHAT THE GREAT ARMADILLO SAID IN DREAMS TO ME

"our food, the worm
"is among you
"we suffer, for our land has been burned
"give away your cat to someone else, so you can know me
"I'll reveal myself in the house
"go there around 6 am
"where the water breaks
"I'll talk to you
"if you don't listen, the Earth will slant
"I come for you to learn how to heal children
"you'll always lay your hands on them
"you'll always be healing
"if you really listen, we'll help you
"we'll be with you
"if you do this
        [and he performed a sleight of hand]
"you'll chase away the storms
"this knowledge will be forever in you
"will be stuck to you forever
"the climate is in our hands
"will you take it in yours?
"if they could only see me
"yes. I am. we are

      [and he started to sing:]

              imili-mimi-aha-ha-hah
              we're here
                    for you   yukpa
              if you're really listening
              you'll heal your children
              with your hands

"it's true you respect us
"you listen to me
"you believe in me
"for you sing our song

"now we are very few
"they have killed us all
"stop killing us

Assembled & translated by Javier Taboada after research by Anne Goletz

COMMENTARY

(1) The selection above assembles the different sayings that Kamashrhush (the Great Armadillo) delivered in dreams to the Yukpa ritualist Diocelina Restrepo. The Armadillo—known for being a friend of humanity in Amazonian culture—teaches Restrepo how to heal through a movement of the hands that would allow her "to chase away the storms." For the Yukpa world (as for many others), macro- & microcosm are the same thing. So, the power to control the weather, its effluvia, also grants the power to control our body fluids: water & air that manifest themselves, when uncontrolled, as illness: coughing, sneezing, diarrhea, vomit, etc.

(2) Writes Anne Goletz of the research on which this version is based: "In the context of an Anthropology of Dreaming dominated by the notion of soul-travels, this paper discusses the passive and embodied manner of dream experiences shaped by the visit from the other-than-human realm into the dreamer's everyday life. Furthermore, it highlights the cooperative nature of the relationship between Diocelina Restrepo and [the armadillo] Kamashrhush against the backdrop of armadillo-human practices based on (respectful) hunting and avoidance."

William Henry Hudson (Guillermo Enrique Hudson),
Argentina/England, 1847–1922

from **IDLE DAYS IN PATAGONIA**

Chapter VI: The War with Nature (Excerpt)

[Man] scatters the seed, and when he looks for the green heads to appear, the earth opens, and lo, an army of long-faced, yellow grasshoppers come forth! She, too, walking invisible at his side, had scattered her miraculous seed along with his. He will not be beaten by her: he slays her striped and spotted creatures; he dries up her marshes; he consumes her forests and prairies with fire, and her wild things perish in myriads; he covers her plains with herds of cattle, and waving fields of corn, and orchards of fruit-bearing trees. She hides her bitter wrath in her heart, secretly she goes out at dawn of day and blows her trumpet on the hills, summoning her innumerable children to her aid. She is hard-pressed and cries to her children that love her to come and deliver her. Nor are they slow to hear. From north and south, from east and west, they come in armies of creeping things and in clouds that darken the air. Mice and crickets swarm in the fields; a thousand insolent birds pull his scarecrows to pieces and carry off the straw stuffing to build their nests; every green thing is devoured; the trees, stripped of their bark, stand like great white skeletons in the bare desolate fields, cracked and scorched by the pitiless sun. When he is in despair deliverance comes; famine falls on the mighty host of his enemies; they devour each other and perish utterly. Still, he lives to lament his loss; to strive still, unsubdued and resolute. She, too, laments her lost children, which now, being dead, serve only to fertilize the soil and give fresh strength to her implacable enemy. And she, too, is unsubdued; she dries her tears and laughs again; she has found out a new weapon it will take him long to wrest from her hands. Out of many little humble plants she fashions the mighty noxious weeds; they spring up in his footsteps, following him everywhere, and possess his fields like parasites, sucking up their moisture and killing their fertility. Everywhere, as if by a miracle, is spread the mantle of rich, green, noisome leaves, and the corn is smothered in beautiful flowers that yield only bitter seed and poison fruit. He may cut them down in the morning, in the nighttime they will grow again. With her beloved weeds she will wear out his spirit and break his heart; she will sit still at a distance and laugh while he grows weary of the hopeless struggle; and, at last, when he is ready to faint, she will go forth once more and blow her trumpet on the hills and call her innumerable children to come and fall on and destroy him utterly.

COMMENTARY

... poets speak not in metaphor, as we are taught to say, but that in moments of excitement, when we revert to primitive conditions of mind, the earth and all nature is alive and intelligent, and feels as we feel. (W.H.H.)

In 1871 William Henry Hudson—an Argentine-born naturalist of North American descent—traveled to study birds in the Río Negro valley in Patagonia, then considered the boundary of "civilization." During his journey, Hudson accidentally shot himself in the leg, preventing him from continuing his task. Hence *Idle Days in Patagonia*, a free collection of ideas, experiences, & revelations about the relationship of humankind & nature, which now stands as a crucial link between nineteenth-century Romanticism

& the ecological movements of the twenty-first century. In our selection above, Hudson's vision of the latter-day perils of weather/climate change is remarkable.

Robinson Jeffers USA, 1887–1962

THE GREAT EXPLOSION

The universe expands and contracts like a great heart.
It is expanding, the farthest nebulae
Rush with the speed of light into empty space.
It will contract, the immense navies of stars and galaxies,
dust clouds and nebulae
Are recalled home, they crush against each other in one
harbor, they stick in one lump
And then explode it, nothing can hold them down; there is no
way to express that explosion; all that exists
Roars into flame, the tortured fragments rush away from each
other into all the sky, new universes
Jewel the black breast of night; and far off the outer nebulae
like charging spearmen again
Invade emptiness.
No wonder we are so fascinated with
fireworks
And our huge bombs: it is a kind of homesickness perhaps for
the howling fireblast that we were born from.

But the whole sum of the energies
That made and contain the giant atom survives. It will
gather again and pile up, the power and the glory—
And no doubt it will burst again; diastole and systole: the
whole universe beats like a heart.
Peace in our time was never one of God's promises; but back
and forth, live and die, burn and be damned,
The great heart beating, pumping into our arteries His
terrible life.
He is beautiful beyond belief.
And we, God's apes—or tragic children—share in the beauty.
We see it above our torment, that's what life's for.
He is no God of love, no justice of a little city like Dante's

Florence, no anthropoid God
Making commandments: this is the God who does not care
and will never cease. Look at the seas there
Flashing against this rock in the darkness—look at the
tide-stream stars—and the fall of nations—and dawn
Wandering with wet white feet down the Carmel Valley to
meet the sea. These are real and we see their beauty.
The great explosion is probably only a metaphor—I know not
—of faceless violence, the root of all things.

COMMENTARY

In pursuit of a geographically & environmentally based vision of America
& the worlds & universes beyond, Jeffers's life work begins in celebration & ends, as here, in dread & a measured anger. A major poet—even
prophet—of the twentieth century, as Gary Snyder had it, the best of his
geohistory can be read alongside Susan Suntree's *Sacred Sights:* The Secret
History of Southern California (in "A Map of Americas") & Cardenal's
Canto Cósmico (in "A Map of Histories"), among other epic works in the
present gathering & elsewhere.

Jorge de Lima   Brazil, 1893–1953

CHRISTIAN'S POEM

Because the blood of Christ
spurted upon my eyes
I see all things
and so profoundly that none may know.
Centuries past and yet to come
dismay me not, for I am born and shall be born again,
for I am one with all creatures,
with all beings, and with all things;
all of them I dissolve and take in again with my senses
and embrace with a mind
transfigured in Christ.
My reach is throughout space.
I am everywhere: I am in God and in matter;
I am older than time and yet was born yesterday,

I drip with primeval slime,
and at the same time I blow the last trumpet.
I understand all tongues, all acts, all signs,
I contain within me the blood of races utterly opposed.
I can dry, with a mere nod,
the weeping of all distant brothers.
I can spread over all heads one all-embracing and starry sky.
I invite all beggars to dine with me,
and I walk on the waters like the prophets of the Bible.
For me there is no darkness.
I imbue the blind with light,
I can mutilate myself and grow my limbs anew like the starfish,
because I believe in the resurrection of the flesh and because I believe in Christ,
and in the life eternal, amen.
And possessing eternal life I am able to transgress the laws of nature:
my passing is looked for in the streets,
I come and go like a prophecy,
I come unbidden like Knowledge and Faith.
I am ready like the Master's answer,
I am seamless like His garment,
I am manifold like His Church,
my arms are spread like the arms of His Cross, broken yet always restored,
at all hours, in all directions, to the four points of the compass;
and I bear His Cross on my shoulders
through all the darkness of the world, because the light
eternal is in my eyes.
And having in my eyes the light eternal, I am the greatest worker of wonders:
I rise again from the mouth of tigers, I am clown, I am alpha
and omega, I am fish, lamb, eater of locusts, I am
ridiculous, I am tempted and pardoned, I am
cast down upon earth and uplifted in glory, I am clothed in mantles of purple and fine
linen, I am ignorant like Saint Christopher and learned like Saint Thomas. And I am
mad, mad, wholly mad forever, world without end, mad with God, Amen.
And being the madness of God I am the reason in all things, the order and the measure,
I am judgment, creation, obedience,
I am repentance, I am humility,
I am the author of the passion and death of Jesus,
I am the sin of all men,
I am nothing.
Miserere mei, Deus, secundum magnam misericordiam tuam!

Translated from Portuguese by Dudley Poore

When all the confusion is undone / will the poet not speak from wherever he is / to all the men on earth, in one single language— / the language of the spirit? (J.deL.)

(1) Jorge de Lima began as a Neo-Parnassian poet, but soon he became a key player in the localized Northeast Movement & in the newly emergent Brazilian avant-garde as a whole. Interested in folklore & regionalisms— with a strong awareness & interest in Black Brazilian culture & language— he also went deeper into the natural & supernatural world, from where he developed a kind of mystical Christian way of life, based on charity & meekness. But it was in the charged modernist atmosphere that de Lima—a "simple man," in somebody else's version—first drew on (his own) Afro-Brazilian sources as a power to be reborn in that setting. The connecting link between the avant-garde & the local/nativistic poetry was the push to bring language down to earth, not only to humble it but also to invigorate it with new power from that source. In de Lima's terms, then, "the words will resurrect"—will do so in a language going back to magic, to that sense of a mystery to be unlocked that formed a central part of so much of the twentieth century's poetics.

(2) The image of the I-God/Universe-God constructed by de Lima as a multiform entity in eternal mutation reminds us of the words of a fellow shamanic poet, Empedocles (b. 494 BC): *For I have been a boy & a girl, a bush & a bird & in the ocean a flying fish.*

The vision below, from Lucario Cuevish, may be taken as a further instance among many.

ADDENDUM

PHILIP LAMANTIA USA, 1927–2005

from **There Is This Distance between Me and What I See**

> Constant flight in air of the Holy Ghost
> I long for the luminous darkness of God
> I long for the superessential light of this darkness
> another darkness I long for the end of longing
> I long for the
>   it is Nameless what I long for
> a spoken word caught in its own meat saying nothing
> This nothing ravishes beyond ravishing
> There IS this look of love
>   Throne Silent look of love

Lucario Cuevish

Luiseño Indian (Payómkawichum) / USA, ca. 1900

BEFORE THEY MADE THINGS BE ALIVE THEY SPOKE

Earth woman lying flat her feet were to the north her head was to the South sky brother sitting on her right hand side he said Yes sister you must Tell me who you are she answered I am Tomaiyowit she asked him Who are you? He answered I am Tukmit. Then she said:

I stretch out flat to the Horizon.
I shake I make a noise like thunder.
I am Earthquake.
I am round and roll around.
I vanish and return.

Then Tukmit said:

I arch above you like a lid.
I deck you like a hat.
I go up high and higher.
I am death I gulp it in one bite.
I grab men from the east and scatter them.
My name is Death.

Then they made things be alive.

English working by Jerome Rothenberg, after Constance Goddard Dubois

For more on Lucario Cuevish, see the commentary on Susan Suntree's *Sacred Sites* in "A Map of Americas."

A THIRD GALLERY

from María Sabina to Ernesto Cardenal

María Sabina Mazatec, Mexico, 1894–1985

[Throughout the entire passage that follows she goes on clapping rhythmically in time to her words.]

hmm hmm hmm
hmm hmm hmm
hmm hmm hmm
hmm hmm hmm
hmm hmm hmm
so so so si
hmm hmm hmm
hmm hmm hmm
Woman who resounds
Woman torn up out of the ground
Woman who resounds
Woman torn up out of the ground
Woman of the principal berries, says
Woman of the sacred berries, says
Ah, Jesusi
Woman who searches, says
Woman who examines by touch, says
ha ha ha
hmm hmm hmm
hmm hmm hmm
She is of one word, of one face, of one spirit, of one light, of one day
hmm hmm hmm
Cayetano García

[He answers "Yes..." She says, "Isn't that how?" He responds: "Yes, that's it." She says: "Isn't that it? Like this. Listen."]

Woman who resounds
Woman torn up out of the ground
Ah, Jesusi
Ah, Jesusi

[In the background the man laughs with pleasure.]

Ah, Jesusi
Ah, Jesusi

Ah, Jesusi
hmm hmm hmm
so so so
Justice woman
hmm hmm hmm

["Thank you," says the man.]

Saint Peter woman
Saint Paul woman
Ah, Jesusi
Book woman
Book woman
Morning Star woman
Cross Star woman
God Star woman
Ah, Jesusi
Moon woman
Moon woman
Moon woman
hmm hmm hmm
hmm hmm hmm
Sap woman
Dew woman

[The man urges her on. "Work, work," he says.]

She is a Book woman
Ah, Jesusi
hmm hmm hmm
hmm hmm hmm
so so so
Lord clown woman
Clown woman beneath the ocean
Clown woman
[The other words are unintelligible.]
Ah, Jesusi
hmm hmm hmm
hmm hmm hmm
so so so
Woman who resounds
Woman torn up out of the ground
hmm hmm hmm

Because she is a Christ woman
Because she is a Christ woman
ha ha ha
so so so
so so so
so so so
Whirling woman of colors
Whirling woman of colors
Big town woman
Big town woman
Lord eagle woman
Lord eagle woman
Clock woman
Clock woman
ha ha ha
so so so
so so so
so so so

["That's it. Work, work," exclaims the man.]

hmm hmm hmm
hmm hmm hmm
so so so
hmm hmm hmm
so so so
so so so
si si si
si si si
si si si
so sa sa
si si si
so sa sa sa
hmm hmm hmm
hmm hmm hmm
hmm hmm hmm
si so soooooooooiiiiii

Translated from Mazatec by Álvaro Estrada & Henry Munn

Language makes the dying return to life. The sick recover their health when they hear the words taught by the saint children. I cure with Language, the Language of the saint children. When they advise me to sacrifice chickens, they are placed on the parts where it hurts. The rest is Language. (M.S.)

(1) A major Wise One (= shaman) among the Mazatecs of Oaxaca, Mexico, María Sabina received her poems/songs through use of the psilocybin mushroom at all-night curing sessions (*veladas*), a practice going back to pre-Conquest Mexico & witnessed by a Spanish chronicler who wrote: "They pay a sorcerer who eats them [the mushrooms] & tells what they have taught him. He does so by means of a rhythmic chant in full voice." The sacred mushrooms, here called "saint children," are considered the source of Language itself—are, in Henry Munn's good phrase, "the mushrooms of language."

The selection presented here departs from the more extended, even "grandiloquent" language of most of the Chants, relying in part on techniques of fragmentation & the use of nonsemantic sound ("meaningless" syllables, humming, clapping, whistling, etc.). The session itself goes on for a whole night, with many of the images, "self"-namings, etc., established early & repeated throughout in full or fragmented form.

Cayetano García, in whose home the session took place, acts also as the principal respondent. "The tone of voice in which this passage [begins]," writes Munn, "is definitely playful, and at one point the man laughs with pleasure at her song. He thanks her for the beauty of her words."

(2) Of her status outside the limits of canonical poetry, Munn calls her "a genius [who] emerges from the soil of the communal, religious-therapeutic folk poetry of a native Mexican campesino people." And Mexican poet Homero Aridjis: "the greatest visionary poet in twentieth-century Latin America."

For more on María Sabina, see "A Map of Visions."

e. e. cummings USA, 1894–1962

from **NO THANKS**

mOOn Over tOwnsmOOn
whisper
less creature huge grO
pingness

whO perfectly whO
flOat
newly alOne is
dreamest
oNLY THE MooN o
VER ToWNS
SLoWLYSPoUTING SPIR
IT

UNTITLED POEM

Buffalo Bill 's
   defunct
        who used to
        ride a watersmooth-silver
                      stallion
and break onetwothreefourfive pigeonsjustlikethat
                                      Jesus

he was a handsome man
                    and what i want to know is
how do you like your blueeyed boy
Mister Death

PICASSO

Picasso
you give us Things
which
bulge:grunting lungs pumped full of sharp thick mind

you make us shrill
presents always
shut in the sumptuous speech of
simplicity

(out of the
black unbunged
Something gushes vaguely a squeak of planes
or

between squeals of
Nothing grabbed with circular shrieking tightness
solid screams whisper)
Lumberman of the Distinct

your brain's
axe only chops hugest inherent
Trees of Ego, from
whose living and biggest

bodies lopped
of every
prettiness

you hew form truly

COMMENTARY

*The Symbol of all Art is the Prism. The goal is destructive. To break up
the white light of objective realism into the secret glories it contains.*
(e.e.c.) And again: *My theory of technique, if I have one, is very far from
original; nor is it complicated. I can express it in fifteen words, by quoting The Eternal Question And Immortal Answer of burlesk, viz. "Would
you hit a woman with a child?—No, I'd hit her with a brick." Like the
burlesk comedian, I am abnormally fond of that precision which creates
movement.*

At the time of Charles Olson's influential Projective Verse manifesto
(1950), which cited e.e. cummings along with Pound & Williams as the
three principal Projectivist forerunners, cummings was the most popularly
recognized, most spectacularly experimental of the visible USAmerican
poets. While neglected or dismissed by more conservative poets & critics,
the extent of his further recognition among kindred contemporaries was
reflected in Pound's titling of his own global anthology *From Confucius to
Cummings*, or in Williams's statement on cummings, whom he placed with
Pound as "beyond doubt the two most distinguished American poets of
today," that "to me, of course, E.E. Cummings means my language."
   Along with this, we would note the prominence of cummings within
the early twentieth-century avant-garde, where he appears no longer as
a unique instance but (as he truly was) the great American interpreter of
the new visuality (& more) that was being developed on an international
scale for two or three decades (1895 to 1920, roughly) before & alongside his own entry into poetry. And, of special interest to us in the present
gathering, the still later Noigandres poets of Brazil (Haroldo & Augusto de
Campos, Décio Pignatari), in their "pilot plan for concrete poetry" in 1958,

list cummings among their top array of predecessors, citing him there for his pioneer work in "the atomization of words," in "physiognomical typography," & in his "expressionistic emphasis on space." (See the mini gallery on Noigandres in "A Map of Extensions.")

That he & they come together in the creation of a far-reaching & truly radical pan-American & global poetry is an essential feature of the present gathering.

For more on e.e. cummings, see the poem in "A Map of Extensions."

Jean Toomer USA, 1894–1967

PEOPLE

To those fixed on white,
White is white,
To those fixed on black,
It is the same,
And red is red,
Yellow, yellow—
Surely there are such sights
In the many colored world,
Or in the mind.
The strange thing is that
These people never see themselves
Or you, or me.

Are they not in their minds?
Are we not in the world?
This is a curious blindness
For those that are color blind.
What queer beliefs
That men who believe in sights
Disbelieve in seers.

O people, if you but used
Your other eyes
You would see beings.

Science is a system of exact mysteries.

Do now what you won't be doing an hour from now.

Those who seek peace too often find comfort.

Men are inclined either to work without hope, or to hope without work.

All our lives we have been waiting to live.

Tell me the person's strongest resistance and I will tell you what he most wants.

Two asses do not make an owl.

Whatever stands between you and that person stands between you and yourself.

Each of us has in himself a fool who says I'm wise.

People are stupid not because they do a thing but because they repeat it.

COMMENTARY

There is no end to "out." (J.T.)

In saying which, Jean Toomer places himself among those who step outside inherited ideas of form & content to explore a more expansive American & global context, including mixed folk & racial realities in a fusion of "Harlem Renaissance" & the extremes & limits of experimental modernism, wherever found. Of his major works, the "hybrid novel" *Cane*, a mix of verse & prose, stands in a line with better-known classics by Joyce & Faulkner & is cited often as an inaugural occasion for the more experimental side of the Harlem Renaissance. Of his own ambiguous relation to his Blackness &/or whiteness (another kind of hybridity), he wrote: "I am of the human race; I am neither white nor black but an American." And further: "My racial composition and my position in the world are realities which I alone may determine.... I expect and demand acceptance of myself on their basis. I do not expect to be told what I should consider myself to be." His important place, however, in a new corpus of American & world poetry & writing should by now be irrefutable.

For an example of Jean Toomer's experiments with sound poetry, see "A Map of Extensions."

Jacob Nibenegenesabe Swampy Cree, Canada

per Howard Norman, USA, 1949–

from *THE WISHING-BONE CYCLE*

I

Once I wished up a coat
wearing a man inside.
The man was sleeping
and when he woke
the coat was on him!
This was in summer, so many asked him
"Why do you have that coat on?"
"It has me in it!"
he would answer.
He tried to take it off
but I wished his memory shivering with cold
so it wouldn't want to remember
how to take a coat off.
That way it would stay warm.
I congratulated myself on thinking of that.
Then his friends came,
put coats on,
and slowly showed him how they took coats off.
Even that didn't work.
Things were getting interesting.
Then his friends
tried to confuse the coat
into thinking it was a man.
"Good morning," they said to it,
"Did you get
your share of fish?"
and other things too.
Some even invited the coat to gossip.
It got to be late summer
and someone said to the coat
"It is getting colder.
You better go out
and find a coat to wear."

The coat agreed!
Ha! I was too busy laughing
to stop that dumb coat
from leaving the man it wore
inside.
I didn't care.
I went following the coat.
Things were getting interesting.

2

One time I wanted two moons
in the sky.
But I needed someone to look up and see
those two moons
because I wanted to hear him
try and convince the others in the village
of what he saw.
I knew it would be funny.
So, I did it.
I wished another moon up!
There it was, across the sky from the old moon.
Along came a man.
Of course I wished him down that open path.
He looked up in the sky.
He had to see that other moon!
One moon for each of his eyes!
He stood looking
up in the sky
a long time.
Then he suspected me, I think.
He looked into the trees
where he thought I might be.
But he could not see me
since I was disguised as the whole night itself!
Sometimes
I wish myself into looking like the whole day
but this time
I was dressed like the whole night.
Then he said,
"there is something strange

in the sky tonight."
He said it out loud.
I heard it clearly.
Then he hurried home
and I followed him.
He told the others, "You will not believe this,
but there are ONLY two moons
in the sky tonight."
He had a funny look on his face.
Then, all the others began looking into the woods.
Looking for me, no doubt!
"Only two moons, ha! Who can believe you?
We won't fall for that!" they all said to him.
They were trying to send the trick back at me!
This was clear to me!
So, I quickly wished a third moon up there
in the sky.
They looked up and saw three moons.
They had to see them!
Then one man
said out loud, "Ah, there, look up!
up there!
There is only one moon!
Well, let's go sleep on this
and in the morning we will try and figure it out."
They all agreed, and went in their houses
to sleep.
I was left standing there
with three moons shining on me.
There were three… I was sure of it.

3

One time
all the noises met.
All the noises in the world
met in one place
and I was there
because they met in my house.
My wife said, "Who sent them?"
I said, "Fox or Rabbit,

yes one of those two.
They're both out for tricking me back today.
Both of them
are mad at me.
Rabbit is mad because I pulled
his brother's ear
and I held him up that way.
Then I ate him.
And Fox is mad because he wanted
to do those things first."
"Yes, then it had to be one of them,"
my wife said.
So, all the noises
were there.
These things happen.
Falling-tree noise was there.
Falling-rock noise was there.
Otter-mud-sliding noise was there.
All those noises, and more,
in my house.
"How long do you expect to stay?"
my wife asked them. "We need some sleep!"
They all answered at once!
That's why now my wife and I
sometimes can't hear well.
I should have wished them all away
first thing.

COMMENTARY

I go backward, look forward, as the porcupine does. (J.N.)

Trickster stories go far back in Cree culture (as elsewhere), but the figure
here is the invention, specifically, of Jacob Nibenegenesabe, born in the late
nineteenth century, who, Howard Norman tells us, "lived for some ninety-
four years northeast of Lake Winnipeg, Canada." Nibenegenesabe was also
a teller (= *achimoo*) of older trickster narratives, the continuity between
old & new never being in question. But the move in the Wishing-Bone
series is toward a rapidity of plot development & changes, plus a switch
into first-person narration as a form of enactment. In the frame for those
stories, the trickster figure "has found the wishbone of a snow goose who
has wandered into the Swampy Cree region and been killed by a lynx. This

person now has a wand of metamorphosis allowing him to wish anything into existence; himself into any situation." Norman's method of translation, in turn, involves "first listening to the narratives over and over in the source language, then re-creating them in the same context, story, etc., if notable, ultimately to get a translation word for word."

ADDENDUM

VÍCTOR HERNÁNDEZ CRUZ USA / Puerto Rico, 1949–

El poema de lo reverso

> In which everything goes backwards
> in time and motion
> Palm trees shrink back into the ground
> Mangos become seeds
> and reappear in the eyes of Indian
> women
> The years go back
> cement becomes wood
> Panama hats are seen upon skeletons
> walking the plazas
> Of once again wooden benches
> The past starts to happen again
> I see Columbus's three boats
> going backwards on the sea
> Getting smaller
> Crossing the Atlantic back to the
> ports of Spain   Cadiz   Dos Palos   Huelva
> Where the sailors disembark
> and go back to their towns
> To their homes
> They become adolescents again
> become children   infants
> they re-enter the wombs of their mothers
> till they become glances
> Clutching a pound of bread
> through a busy plaza
> that becomes the taste
> of the sound of church bells
> in reverberation.

Charles Reznikoff USA, 1894–1976

from *TESTIMONY—THE UNITED STATES (1885–1915)*
RECITATIVE

based on cases in law reports

The company had advertised for men to unload a steamer across the river. It was
    six o'clock in the morning, snowing, and still dark.
There was a crowd looking for work on the dock;
and all the while men hurried to the dock.
The man at the wheel
kept the bow of the launch
against the dock—
the engine running slowly;
and the men kept jumping
from dock to deck,
jostling each other,
and crowding into the cabin.

Eighty or ninety men were in the cabin as the launch pulled away.
There were no lights in the cabin, and no room to turn—whoever was sitting
    down could not get up, and whoever had his hand up could not get it down,
as the launch ran in the darkness
through the ice,
ice cracking
against the launch
bumping and scraping
against the launch,
banging up against it,
until it struck
a solid cake of ice,
rolled to one side, and slowly
came back to an even keel.

The men began to feel water running against their feet as if from a hose. "Cap,"
    shouted one, "the boat is taking water! Put your rubbers on, boys!"
The man at the wheel turned.
"Shut up!" he said.
The men began to shout,
ankle-deep in water.
The man at the wheel turned

with his flashlight:
everybody was turning and pushing against each other;
those near the windows
were trying to break them,
in spite of the wire mesh
in the glass; those who had been near the door
were now in the river,
reaching for the cakes of ice,
their hands slipping off and
reaching for the cakes of ice.

COMMENTARY

I will walk by myself / and cure myself / in the sunshine and the wind. (C.R.)

(1) Apart from his keen ("Objectivist") accountings of everyday, largely urban life, Reznikoff drew on materials & testimonies from a range of sources, of which he wrote later: "A few years ago... I was working for a publisher of law books, reading cases from every state and every year (since this country became a nation). Once in a while I could see in the facts of a case details of the time and place, and it seemed to me that out of such material the century and a half during which the U.S. has been a nation could be written up, not from the standpoint of an individual, as in diaries, nor merely from the angle of the unusual, as in newspapers, but from every standpoint—as many standpoints as were provided by the witnesses themselves" (comments on the 1934 edition of *Testimony*).

From which the idea of witnessing arose, as an activity of writing that begins from the testimony & the voices of those recorded first in books of law as facts & cases. In doing this, he made a space for voices from outside poetry as such & wrote through those voices as they appear in the most unpoetical of places.

(2) In a later work, *Holocaust*, Reznikoff turned his attention to a different field of testimony, with equally striking & chilling results: a form of collage & "investigative poetry" (E. Sanders) of which he was a master. Writes poet Michael Heller of Reznikoff's methods in both *Testimony* & *Holocaust*, working in the latter from twenty-six volumes of documentation of the post–World War II Nuremberg and Eichmann trials: "These works, edited from court testimony, trial records and historical documents, seem at first to be what we have come to call 'found poems' (if such material in its sheer poetic recalcitrance can be called poetry).... And yet for these poems to be simultaneously a witnessing and a rejecting of any social, artistic or psychological agenda in their presentation, for these materials to be able to 'speak for themselves,' strikes this reader as not only proper but in some powerful way as noble."

Juan L. Ortiz Argentina, 1896–1978

from *THE GUALEGUAY*

The river was all of time, was everything...
tweaking all the courses of its lines
as Eden's orchestra beneath the rod of love...
He was love, the river...
Everything was born from him, or came evangelically to him.
He did not reveal only every crease of air,
nor tune himself on the "sand sedge,"
nor was it just all eyes for the feathers of dawn
or the herons' clouds,
nor for the oily irises and bearded irises
that used to pierce, ah, or open, electrically, death,
when they, the first ones, did not foresee it in a rush of bells...
Not even simply ears for the ibises and kingbirds
on the "wedges" of dusk...
nor for the drowning whistles, where?
the dying scrublands...
he beat, beyond its music, with all of those vibrations,
until he made them his own
in something sought almost in circles
—and those bends that almost molded islands?—
since he was the whole gift, everything, in the intimate gills...

.....

Yes, he was also the whole gift, everything...
in the gold and the silver of his bosom
with all the shudders of sunrise and vespers
and a pale tenderness...
But why life or whatever was called life,
always swallowing itself simply just to be or to subsist,
in alliance with a monster that did not seem to have eyes
but for the "final equilibriums"?
Why everything, everything, for a terrifying shrine,
or in the terrifying hierarchy of a deity of teeth?

Oh he, with all the beauty of his salts
for the great phosphors
and for the beaks and claws,

and all the countless hungers, which one would call defenselessness...
he himself, for what he meant for all that thirst,
and, despite all, for that familial luck
beneath a flimsy tune:
itself, suddenly, inside a kindred blindness,
with the night of suffocation,
raiding even their most unrelated lives,
the most unanticipated,
amidst the miles and miles of disaster...
or isolation or solidarity, all hieratic,
atop the loneliest of branches,
or over those that Noah "dammed"

But this was not, despite itself,
somewhat like a halt in the most apparent bleeding,
in the face of a dark fright?
Or a sort of alliance against a father now turned hostile?
Death's bound workers gone on strike for days
against a rooted power, her son, who, likewise,
craved to drown them all?
Oh, if a music other than its own,
running, ceaseless, towards what unheard-of tone,
rose from another lyre "also raising temples
in some ears," even from the jungle...
Why would only horror halt, eternally, the horror?

Translated from Spanish by Javier Taboada

COMMENTARY

Sometimes you must lose "the city" and sometimes you must lose "the words" / to rediscover them on the vertigo, purer. (J.L.O.)

El Gualeguay is one of the most interesting experiments in Latin American poetry: the poem is two thousand verses long & deals with the history of the Gualeguay River from its primeval origins to the end of the nineteenth century. It took Ortiz almost twelve years to complete it. Although the poem seems to unfold lyrically, the standpoint of the poem is that of the landscape: the river—never named, just referred to as *él* (both "he" & "it" in the original Spanish)—perceives all history passing through its vibrations. Juan L. Ortiz carefully used many sources (botany, history, color theory, etc.), but they're barely visible, flowing like the river. In *El Gualeguay* nature & art are not in conflict, or, as Cage said: "Art is an imitation of nature not as she is but in her manner of operation." Nevertheless, this harmony in *El Gualeguay* will be broken by people's actions & their consequences—i.e., history as we name it: the definitive cut, now almost irremediable, of nature's own course & time.

Gamaliel Churata   Peru, 1897–1969

from **THE GOLDEN FISH**

Lectern

. . . . .

16 Through the snaky path of the blue clouds, a young man walked, delectable to see; and as he arrived, he spoke—effusive—a blithe request to us.

17 He said he expected to see me, to see her; that he saw us both and he saw one of us in the other; that there we will be continuous unity, and everything shall grow and ripen.

18 He offered his open hands; naïve, he showed his eyes; a generous shelter flowed from his smile.

19 Just as he who releases a caged bird starts by opening the door, once he fully undressed, he opened his own ear. Through it THE GOLDEN FISH flew.

20 From that sore fracture flowed a legion of poppies. To prevent his escape and to avoid touching him, the poppies' roots raised a wall.

21 After the flowers, a sweet old lady and a venerable patriarch arrived. Ancient knives enhanced the patriarch's sweet majesty. Just as the knives hit the ground, they both seized his neck to murmur their prayers.

22 After them—and emulating them—a white woman of shaky beauty cried for him with shaky kisses.

23 Next, another woman: a brunette made of copper. She tied herself to his feet and nurtured him. And she became the thirst along his way.

24 "Ta-dah, ta-dah," sang the old lady for her *Urpila*. Kneeling, from her eyes a lilac lily grew, which later purified his bones, his lips and tears. To live, they live.

25 "How happy the man!... All that he loves and all his lovers live inside him."

26 But, behold, the hour came. The Sun poured itself in honey and gold, and Delectable Man cried a bitter lullaby: "Girl, my dear girl"... She was a coral rosary in the golden skin of his song.

¡Piupiu-titit!
¡Piupiu-titit!
¡Piupiu-titit!
¡Piupiu-titit!
¡Piupiu-titit!

27 Did he come out of the girl? The girl out of Him?

28 Walled among the poppies, Delectable Man thought: "Without being, I'm here. Here we are, me and Him: the three of us, and I alone and dead. But inside, the three of us are one. We are bathed by the waterfall of her *ñuñu*; if the sourness oozes bile, her caress pours honeycombs."

29 The crying chorus of the *Wayñusiñas*:

HARARUÑA

And we, your brides,
your brides from that garden
wetted by your tears
nurtured by your kiss,
are we living without seeing you,
or seeing you living
among the high
aroma of filth?
Not in vain, from the soil
your heartbeat roused
the lips that kiss you.
You'll be only ours.
Or we'll make a purge for your love
out of your kiss
over that fiery dust
on which your love burned...!

30 They turned feline and with their petals they devoured the five-petaled girl.

31 Pentatonic, the divine song was created.

32 Delectable Man stuck himself in the ear of the soil and sang it:

HAYLLI

Old mother! You'll be pregnant
nine times! Pregnant by the blood

of those who languish without it.
Nine germs will grow with the blood.
After the ninth dawn
the tenth will surpass the nine,
and along with the germ which is the seed of song
the cosmic roar of the puma
will proclaim your childbirth.
Old Mother, the cloud and the mountain will
kneel over your blood. And new,
in yours will run
the blood of old and new songs.
Those born from you and who wait
in nine concentric circles
will reach—in the tenth—your embryo
where your fertile placenta
conceals honey and gold.
Death will round your lair nine times
but in the tenth, the fang
of the puma will crush death.

33 And, knowing his strength, he was pure desire.

34 The fang is the son! The fang is the son!

35 The piercing howl of the poppies: "Desire is the son! Desire is the son!... But first you'll have to go back to return to the son. And to be the voice in Him and the herb's voice, the mount and the mount's voices, the lake and the echo of its waves, the night and its flash, the wing and the song of its winds"...

36 A cold snow was burning on the embers of the blood...

37 "Are you cold, *imillitay*?... "¡You're afraid, *tatalay*!"...

38 "*Achachila* chases you, *imillitay*?... "Who's chasing you, *achachilay*?"

39 When I bite the *ñuñus* of the tomb, I hear the nine petals of air, the nine childbirths of the soil, the tenth petal raining down.

40 "Is *Achachila* sick, *imillitay*?"... "You want to nest in his soul, *achachilay*."

41 In the gloomy fang of the *kharka*, the pentatonic chirp was a candy.

42 Who? The one who saw two times two the eye of the old times?

HARAWI

Kancharani Achachila,
hina, hina, achachilay.

The best among the elders
is the old chief of the mountain

43 "You love yourself, *tatalay?*"... "You ask me if I love you,
imillitay?"... "Do you want to see your own eyes, *achachilay?*"...
44 They crossed the creek, hopping. They arrived at the *chinkhana.*
45 A crystal thread of light. Through the cracks of the invisible dome, a
drop of water fell, unaltered.
46 The drop was hurting itself with that thread, greedy for light; it was a
drop of water, falling, falling... Falling with the flick of the microscopic
kiss of the dead.
47 "Do you want to blow the old wind of your eyes, *achachilay!*"...
Taya! Taya!... He plucked the string of his charango, monotonous,
stoutly... *Taya! Taya!*... it vibrated stoutly, painful... *Taya! Taya!*...
The shadow lay hoarsely in the corner... Opening its sinister jaws...
Taya! Taya!... Hollow, humid, the voice of the moss... *Taya! Taya!*...
The drop of water fell, fell, fell, fell... Blazing eyes wept in the
shadows... *Taya! Taya!* The *achokhallo* slipped through the boulder's
crack; bands of *chiñis* fled through the hole... *Taya! Taya!*... The
pukupukus squawked...
Phantom arms were extending in the shadows... *Taya! Taya!*... The
slimy arms were closed. The flower bent without a sound.
Achachila!... Achachilay!
48 A song was hushed inside Delectable Man.

Translated from Spanish by Javier Taboada

COMMENTARY

*I write about death from within her, with the experiences that death offers
me.* (G.C.) And again: *I am your fruit, Father Sun; I am the one from
whom one must eat.*

(1) Born Arturo Peralta Miranda, Gamaliel Churata proposed a revival of
Andean culture within an avant-gardist context. One of his most celebrated
works is *The Golden Fish.* There, & through the display of the Andean
experience via an unusual writing language, he envisions a "monster," *The
Golden Fish*: a cosmology & a new way of perceiving formed from the
clash of languages & cultures that shapes current Andean culture. The display of this vision—along with its prophetic, ethical, spiritual, & percep-
tual contents—led critic Cynthia Vich to celebrate *The Golden Fish* as "the
Bible of Andean culture."

(2) In *The Golden Fish*, Churata employs several indigenous Aymara & Quechua words, among which we find:

achachila(y) = elder chief
achokhallo = weasel
chiñis = bats
chinkhana = cavern
hararuña = song
harawi = erotic song
hayli = war song
imillitay = little girl
kharka = crag
ñuñu(s) = tit(s)
pukupukus = owls
tatalay = old father
taya = west wind
urpila = dove
wayñusiña = a form of Andean poetry, hence "flower"

Luis Palés Matos   Puerto Rico, 1898–1959

BLACK MAJESTY

Down the scorching Antillean street
Goes Tembandumba of the Quimbamba
Between two rows of black faces
—Rumba, macumba, candombe, bámbula.
Before her, a congo band thumps
A bombastic conga—gongos and maracas.

Steatopygously the Queen steps up
And her immense buttocks with drums collide
So that seductive wiggles slide
In curdled rivers of sugar and molasses.
Brown-skinned mill of sweet sensation,
Her colossal hips, those massive mortars,
Make rhythms ooze, sweat bleed like blood,
And all this grinding ends in dance.

Down the scorching Antillean street
Goes Tembandumba of the Quimbamba.
Flower of Tórtola, Rose of Uganda,

For you the bombas and bambulas crackle.
For you these feverish nights go wild
And set on fire Antilla's ñáñiga blood.
Haiti offers you its gourds;
Jamaica pours its fiery rums;
Cuba tells you, give us what you got, mulata!
And Puerto Rico: melao, melamba!

Get down, my black-faced love-crazed rascals.
Jangle, drums, and jiggle, maracas.
Down the scorching Antillean street
Goes Tembandumba of the Quimbamba
—Rumba, macamba, candombe, bámbula.

Translated from Spanish by Paquito D'Rivera

COMMENTARY

Cover your ears / close every pore in your soul / and prime your instinct to defend; / for if, in the Blackland's angry night / a war or dance drum stings you / its potent venom / will course through your veins forever (L.P.M.)

Considered a forerunner of the Antipoetry that Chilean poet Nicanor Parra would proclaim some years after him, Luis Palés Matos was also the antecedent of Guillén, Ballagas, Cabrera Infante—the Black Poetry movement (*poesía negra*) that expanded throughout the Caribbean during his lifetime. His call for a true Antillean poetry, which explored new forms, not exclusively Black, but Criollo & Indigenous as well—wordplays & puns, imagery, sexual liberty, rhythms, irony, humor—stands as a major weapon against conservative poetics in our hemisphere & also as one of the more serious attempts to find & reveal a Caribbean (& by extension an "American") mindset. In his case, this "mind" is rooted in Boricua—not as a Puerto Rican Spanish dialect or idiolect but as a language in its own right. For this kind of move perhaps & in relation to his own search for a new American idiom, William Carlos Williams wrote about him: "Luis Palés Matos is... probably one of the most important poets of all Latin America today—though many would contest this from a conventional viewpoint."

Melvin B. Tolson USA, 1898–1966

from *HARLEM GALLERY*

The Curator and Doctor Nkomo
sat staring into space,
united like the siphons of a Dosinia—
the oddest hipsters on the new horizon of Harlem,
odder
(by odds)
than that
cabala of a funeral parlor
in Cuernavaca,
Mexico
...called...
"Quo Vadis."

. . . . .

The school of the artist
is
the circle of wild horses,
heads centered,
as they present to the wolves
a battery of heels,
in the arctic barrens where
no magic grass of Glaucus
gives immortality

. . . . .

Beneath the sun
as he clutched the bars of a barracoon,
beneath the moon
of a blind and deaf-mute Sky,
my forebears heard a Cameroon
chief, in the language of the King James Bible, cry,
"O Absalom, my son, my son!"
Solons of Jim Crow,
sages as far as the beard,
cipher and cipher and cipher—
and ask, "What is a Negro?"

Like some gray ghoul from Alcatraz,
old Profit, the bald rake *paseq*, wipes the bar,
polishes the goblet Vanity,
leers at the tigress Avarice
as
she harlots roués from afar:
swallowtails unsaved by loincloths,
famed enterprises prophesying war,
hearts of rags (*Hanorish tharah sharinas*) souls of chalk,
laureates with sugary grace in zinc buckets of verse,
myths rattled by the blueprint's talk,
potted and pitted by a feast,
Red Ruin's skeleton horsemen, four abreast
...galloping . . .
Marx, the exalter, would not know his East
...galloping . . .
nor Christ, the Leveler, His West.
Selah!

O Age of Tartuffe
...a lighthouse with no light atop . . .
O Age, *pesiq*, O Age,
kinks internal and global stinks
fog the bitter black estates of Buzzard and Og.
A Dog, I'd rather be, O sage, a Monkey or a Hog.
O Peoples of the Brinks,
come with the hawk's resolve,
the skeptic's optic nerve, the prophet's *tele* verve
and Oedipus' guess, to solve
the riddle of
the Red Enigma and the White Sphinx.
Selah!

COMMENTARY

A civilization is always judged in its decline. (M.B.T.) And again: *When the exceptional historian comes along, you have a poet.*

(1) As with other major poets of the Americas, the history & diversity of the work is what first attracts & startles. What is clear, too, is how poetry

becomes for Tolson the primary instrument to bring those histories to the forefront and to proclaim the poet's place as changemaker, asserting in a century of revolutions: "The most violent revolution in the world is taking place—not in Russia, not in China, but in American poetry." With an eye toward what would be, in effect, a growing US & inter-American Negritude (though he never used the term), he made clear that this revolution for the poets who led it was above all a matter of the language—"a secret language no white man understands" but that might still be spoken & invented as a written language, newly, in each poem.

(2) "In 1947 Tolson was appointed Poet Laureate of Liberia; he wrote *Libretto* in honor of the centennial of the founding of that African country. With its litany of African / Asian / European heroes, its griot rhapsody and telescoped aeons, this work rises above the circumstances of its genesis. No trace of the occasional lingers in this unique poetic celebration: a public ode that gives us not only the scoop on the nitty-gritty nasties of Western history but also, in a propulsive finale, predicts the rise of African nations" (Rita Dove, in her introduction to *Harlem Gallery and Other Poems of Melvin Tolson*).

Raul Bopp Brazil, 1898–1984

from *COBRA NORATO*

Nheengatu on the Left Bank of the Amazon

I
One day
I'll end up in the land Beyond

I light out, walking on and on
blending in the womb of the backwoods, chewing on roots

After a while
I work up a swamp-lily spell
& conjure up the Cobra Norato

"Let me tell you a story
Shall we stroll those curvy islands?
Now, imagine moonlight"

Night comes on sweetly
Stars chat in low tones

So I wrangle a rope around the neck
& strangle the Snake.

Now that's better
I squeeze into its elastic silk skin
& set out to travel the world

I'll find Queen Luzia
I want to marry her daughter

"Well, then, you must first close your eyes"

Sleep slips over my heavy eyelids
The muddy ground robs the strength of my steps

II
And now the encrypted forest begins

Shade hides trees
Thick-lipped frogs spy in the dark

Here a wit of woods is being punished
Saplings squat in the mire
A slow slip of stream licks loam

"All I want is to see Queen Luzia's daughter!"

Now the rivers drown
gulping the path
Water rolls by the marshes
sinking sinking
Up ahead
sand cradles the footprints of Queen Luzia's daughter

"OOOeee,
now I'll see her"

But first you must pass through seven doors
to see seven white women with empty wombs
guarded by an alligator

"All I want is to see Queen Luzia's daughter!"

You must deliver your soul to Papa Legba
chant on the new moon
& drink three drops of blood

"Only if it's the blood of Queen Luzia's daughter!"

Immense wilds with insomnia

Sleepy trees yawn
At last, the night has dried out
River water crashed
I've got to go

I get going willy-nilly, deep in the backwoods
where ancient pregnant trees are napping

They chide me from all sides
Where're you off to, Norato?
Here's three sweet saplings just waiting

"Can't stay
Today I'll lay with Queen Luzia's daughter"

III
I tear off, burning sand
Pokeweed scratches me

Fat shafts play sink in the mud
Twigs pssst as I pass

Leave me alone, I got a long way to go

Nuts-sedges block the way

"Ay Father-of-the-Forest!
Whose evil-eye has cursed me
& reversed my tracks on the ground?

I slither withered
searching for Queen Luzia's daughter"

I coil up for the night

Earth sinks away
Bog's soft belly roll swallows me whole

Which way should I take?
My blood aches
spellbound by Queen Luzia's daughter

IV

This is the forest of fetid breath
birthing snakes

Skinny rivers forced to work
The current bristles
peeling phlegmy banks

Toothless roots gum loam

In a flooded stretch
marsh swallows stream

Stench
The wind has moved on

A hiss frightens the trees
Silence injured itself

Up ahead a dry trunk falls:
Boom

A scream crosses the forest
Other voices arrive

River choked on a sandbank

A frog who watches me a frog
Who has a human smell
"Who are you?"

"I am Cobra Norato
On my way to cozy up with Queen Luzia's daughter"

V

They're studying geometry
here at the trees' school

"You're blind from birth. You have to obey the river"

"Ay, ay! We're slaves to the river"

"You're condemned to work forever and ever
Obliged to make leaves to blanket the forest"
"Ay, ay! We're slaves to the river"

"You must drown men in shadows
The forest is man's enemy"
"Ay, ay! We're slaves to the river"

I cross thick walls
I hear the ayeee-help-me finches' screeches
They're schooling the birds

"If you don't learn the lesson you have to be trees"
"Ay, ay, ayeee!"

"What are you doin' up there?"

"I have to announce the moon
as it rises behind the woods"

"And you?"
"I have to wake the stars
on St. John's night"

"And you?"
"I have to count the hours deep in the wilds"

tsrook... tsrook... tsrook... tsrook
zlit... zlit-zlit

Translated from Portuguese by Jennifer Cooper

COMMENTARY

*At night, the river calls you. // Deep in the bush, voices are calling you. /
Then you let yourself go into the waters / slowly / as a wild flower / before
the curiosity of the stars.* (R.B.)

(1) A foundational work, along with Oswald de Andrade's *Anthropophagite Manifesto*, for a deeply rooted new Brazilian poetry, Bopp's thirty-
three-part epic survives as an early example of "investigative poetry" (E.
Sanders) & ethnographic surrealism (ethnopoetics). It is, as the Brazilian
literary critic Othon Moacyr Garcia has it, "the one true epic poem of Brazilian literature (because of its essence rooted in the popular and for the
magic of its verbal form) and one of the greatest legacies of the Modernist
Movement."

(2) A note by the translator, Jennifer Cooper: "Stories of the *encantado*
(enchanted polymorphic entity) Cobra Norato are well-known throughout
Brazil. In the South largely due to this poem, but in the North and Northeast as well, these stories belong to an enormous repertoire within a thriv-

ing Amazonian oral tradition and practice—which is to say, the storytelling of currently occurring phenomena. In the case of the Cobra Norato, traditional accounts relate the antics of the anaconda turning into a man for the sole purpose of partying. Here, Bopp enacts a reverse polymorphism—from man to anaconda—contributing to the telluric quality that predominates, as plants, animals, other *encantados*, and the river itself become central figures in Bopp's narrative. Cobra Norato, at one point in the later sections of the poem, temporarily turns back into a fine gent, in traditional fashion, 'to kick up some dust and down some rum.'"

The *Nheengatu* mentioned in the subtitle above is the name of an Indigenous (Tupi/Cobepá) language & culture. The reader may also be interested in two oral Amazonian works presented elsewhere in these pages, *The Woman Who Went to the Village of the Dead* and "What the Great Armadillo Said in Dreams to Me," both in "A Map of Visions."

Hart Crane USA, 1899–1932

from **THE BRIDGE**

Cutty Sark

I met a man in South Street, tall—
a nervous shark tooth swung on his chain.
His eyes pressed through green glass
—green glasses, or bar lights made them
so—
    shine—
        GREEN—
            eyes—
stepped out—forgot to look at you
or left you several blocks away—

in the nickel-in-the-slot piano jogged
"Stamboul Nights"—weaving somebody's nickel—sang—

    O *Stamboul Rose—dreams weave the rose!*

      Murmurs of Leviathan he spoke,
      and rum was Plato in our heads . . .

"It's *S.S. Ala*—Antwerp—now remember kid
to put me out at three she sails on time.

I'm not much good at time any more keep
weakeyed watches sometimes snooze—" his bony hands
got to beating time ..."A whaler once—
I ought to keep time and get over it—I'm a
Democrat—I know what time it is—No
I don't want to know what time it is—that
damned white Arctic killed my time ..."

    O Stamboul Rose—drums weave—

"I ran a donkey engine down there on the Canal
in Panama—got tired of that—
then Yucatan selling kitchenware—beads—
have you seen Popocatepetl—birdless mouth
with ashes sifting down—?
                    And then the coast again ..."

    Rose of Stamboul O coral Queen—
    teased remnants of the skeletons of cities—
    and galleries, galleries of watergutted lava
    snarling stone—green—drums—drown—

Sing!
"—that spiracle!" he shot a finger out the door ...
"O life's a geyser—beautiful—my lungs—
No—I can't live on land—!"

I saw the frontiers gleaming of his mind;
or are there frontiers—running sands sometimes
running sands—somewhere—sands running ...
Or they may start some white machine that sings.
Then you may laugh and dance the axletree—
steel—silver—kick the traces—and know—

    ATLANTIS ROSE drums wreathe the rose,
    the star floats burning in a gulf of tears
    and sleep another thousand—

                    interminably
long since somebody's nickel—stopped—
playing—

A wind worried those wicker-neat lapels, the
swinging summer entrances to cooler hells ...

Outside a wharf truck nearly ran him down
—he lunged up Bowery way while the dawn
was putting the Statue of Liberty out—that
torch of hers you know—

I started walking home across the Bridge . . .

. . . . .

Blithe Yankee vanities, turreted sprites, winged
                                  British repartees, skil-
ful savage sea-girls
that bloomed in the spring—Heave, weave
those bright designs the trade winds drive . . .

　　Sweet opium and tea, Yo-ho!
　　Pennies for porpoises that bank the keel!
　　Fins whip the breeze around Japan!

Bright skysails ticketing the Line, wink round the Horn
to Frisco, Melbourne . . .
                              Pennants, parabolas—
clipper dreams indelible and ranging,
baronial white on lucky blue!

　　Perennial-*Cutty*-trophied-*Sark*!

Thermopylae, Black Prince, Flying Cloud through Sunda
—scarfed of foam, their bellies veered green esplanades,
locked in wind-humors, ran their eastings down;

　　at Java Head freshened the nip
　　(sweet opium and tea!)
　　and turned and left us on the lee . . .

Buntlines tusseling (91 days, 20 hours and anchored!)
                              Rainbow, Leander
(last trip a tragedy)—where can you be
Nimbus? And you rivals two—

　　a long tack keeping—
                    Taeping?
                    Ariel?

The bottom of the sea is cruel. (H.C.)

William Carlos Willliams's summary of their differences ("I suppose the thing was that he was searching for something inside, while I was all for a sharp use of the materials") seems fair enough in retrospect, provided one sees it against the actual movements of their work & the climates of their time. For Crane, the use of materials *outside* the poem becomes meaningful as the poet's mind absorbs & redirects them toward a "submission to, and assimilation of the organic effects on us of these and other fundamental factors of our experience." But his commitment to the transformative energies of "modern poetry" & the possibilities of its generating an epic American poem (*The Bridge*, in this instance) often stops short at the inherited boundaries of poetic language, & his decision to turn back in that sense sets him apart from more radical poets & explains his relation to the academicizers of his time & ours. Even so, his frequent use, as here, of mixed levels of language, his extensions of the Rimbaudian prose poem, & "the pacing of the rhythm of [his] lines, the syntax, the intensely human tone, or simply the punctuation" (R. Creeley), along with his personal/ interiorizing/"prophetic" stance (visible at a time when others of his contemporaries still committed to "rebellion against... the so-called classical strictures" had disappeared from view), have kept interest in the work & life continuous over the intervening decades.

Langston Hughes USA, 1902–1967

from *MONTAGE OF A DREAM DEFERRED*

Children's Rhymes

When I was a chile we used to play,
"One—two—buckle my shoe!"
and things like that. But now, Lord,
listen at them little varmints!

> By *what sends*
> *the white kids*
> *I ain't sent:*
> *I know I can't*
> *be President.*

There is two thousand children
In this block, I do believe!

What don't bug
them white kids
sure bugs me:
We knows everybody
ain't free!

Some of these young ones is cert'ly bad—
One batted a hard ball right through my window
And my gold fish et the glass.

What's written down
for white folks
ain't for us a-tall:
"Liberty And Justice—
Huh—For All."

Oop-pop-a-da!
Skee! Daddle-de-do!
Be-bop!

Salt' peanuts!

De-dop!

THE WEARY BLUES

Droning a drowsy syncopated tune,
Rocking back and forth to a mellow croon,
    I heard a Negro play.
Down on Lenox Avenue the other night
By the pale dull pallor of an old gas light
    He did a lazy sway . . .
    He did a lazy sway . . .
To the tune o' those Weary Blues.
With his ebony hands on each ivory key
He made that poor piano moan with melody.
    O Blues!
Swaying to and fro on his rickety stool
He played that sad raggy tune like a musical fool.
    Sweet Blues!
Coming from a black man's soul.
    O Blues!

In a deep song voice with a melancholy tone
I heard that Negro sing, that old piano moan—
    "Ain't got nobody in all this world,
    Ain't got nobody but ma self.
    I's gwine to quit ma frownin'
    And put ma troubles on the shelf."

Thump, thump, thump, went his foot on the floor.
He played a few chords then he sang some more—
    "I got the Weary Blues
    And I can't be satisfied.
    Got the Weary Blues
    And can't be satisfied—
    I ain't happy no mo'
    And I wish that I had died."
And far into the night he crooned that tune.
The stars went out and so did the moon.
The singer stopped playing and went to bed
While the Weary Blues echoed through his head.
He slept like a rock or a man that's dead

THE NEGRO SPEAKS OF RIVERS

I've known rivers:
I've known rivers ancient as the world and older than the flow of human blood
    in human veins.

My soul has grown deep like the rivers.

I bathed in the Euphrates when dawns were young.
I built my hut near the Congo and it lulled me to sleep.
I looked upon the Nile and raised the pyramids above it.
I heard the singing of the Mississippi when Abe Lincoln went down to New
    Orleans, and I've seen its muddy bosom turn all golden in the sunset.

I've known rivers:
Ancient, dusky rivers.

My soul has grown deep like the rivers.

In all my life, I have never been free. I have never been able to do anything with freedom, except in the field of my writing. (L.H.) And again: *An artist must be free to choose what he does, certainly, but he must also never be afraid to do what he might choose.*

(1) If a significant push in a latter-day American poetics, both on the northern & southern continents, was toward the exploration of demotic language as a vital literary instrument, Hughes's workings with such during his long & prolific career placed him high among its principal proponents. Of his self-declared sources (the language & rhythms included), he wrote in the introduction to his collection *Montage of a Dream Deferred* (1951): "In terms of current Afro-American popular music and the sources from which it has progressed—jazz, ragtime, swing, blues, boogie-woogie, and be-bop—this poem on contemporary Harlem, like be-bop, is marked by conflicting changes, sudden nuances, sharp and impudent interjections, broken rhythms, and passages sometimes in the manner of the jam session, sometimes the popular song, punctuated by the riffs, runs, breaks, and distortions of the music of a community in transition."
In short, then, a reality-based poetry-of-changes.

(2) Wrote Hughes again, at the outset of his career: "We younger Negro artists who create now intend to express our individual dark-skinned selves without fear or shame. If white people are pleased, we are glad. If they are not, it doesn't matter. We know we are beautiful. And ugly too."

(3) His translations from Cuban poet Nicolás Guillén, one of which follows, are a special bringing together of two important streams of demotic writing.

Nicolás Guillén   Cuba, 1902–1967

TÚ NO SABE INGLÉ

Con tanto inglé que tú sabía,
Bito Manué,
con tanto inglé, no sabe ahora
desí ye.
La mericana te buca,
y tú le tiene que huí:
tu inglé era de etrái guan,
de etrái guan y guan tú tri.

All dat English you used to know,
Li'l Manuel,
all dat English, now can't even
say: *Yes.*
'Merican gal comes lookin' fo' you
an you jes' runs away
Yo' English is jes' *strike one*!
Strike one and *one-two-three.*

Translated from Spanish by Langston Hughes

SENSEMAYÁ (CHANT TO KILL A SNAKE)

Mayombe—bombe—mayombé!
Mayombe—bombe—mayombé!
Mayombe—bombe—mayombé!

The snake has eyes of glass;
The snake coils on a stick,
With his eyes of glass on a stick,
With his eyes of glass.
The snake can move without feet;
The snake can hide in the grass;
Crawling he hides in the grass,
Moving without feet.
Mayombe-bombe-mayombé!
Hit him with an ax and he dies;
Hit him! Go on, hit him!
Don't hit him with your foot or he'll bite;
Don't hit him with your foot, or he'll get away.
Sensemayá, the snake,
sensemayá.
Sensemayá, with his eyes,
sensemayá.
Sensemayá, with his tongue,
sensemayá.
Sensemayá, with his mouth,
sensemayá.
The dead snake cannot eat;
the dead snake cannot hiss;

he cannot move,
he cannot run!
The dead snake cannot look;
the dead snake cannot drink,
he cannot breathe,
he cannot bite.
Mayombe-bombe-mayombé!
Sensemayá, the snake...
Mayombe-bombe-mayombé!
Sensemayá, does not move...
Mayombe-bombe-mayombé!
Sensemayá, the snake...
Mayombe-bombe-mayombé!
Sensemayá, he died!

Translated from Spanish by Willis Knapp Jones

Translated from Spanish by Willis Knapp Jones

COMMENTARY

I am impure, what can I say? / Absolutely impure. // But / I think there are many pure things in the world / that are nothing but pure shit. (N.G.)

(1) Having said that, his impetus, this so-called impurity, led Nicolás Guillén to a fully cross-cultural process of creation, which extended its scope from the merely local. Influenced by Luis Palés Matos (see above), Guillén embarked on a more ambitious project, Afrocubanismo, that encompassed a still wider range of Black Caribbean expression & led him to renew metric forms, themes, myths, & the modes of speech of Latin American poetry (as in his Black songs—his *sones*—or the long-overlooked *jitanjáforas*, something very similar to *scat* in jazz terminology).

(2) In his time, his role can best be compared with the one Rubén Darío had developed for a previous generation: Guillén's poetry & poetics had a major impact throughout the hemisphere, & its reverberations can still be perceived in our present. His bonds with the Harlem Renaissance & with the expression of African descent in Latin America & the Caribbean in the 1950s should be observed as one of the first serious attempts at an inter-American movement centered on Black art, poetry, thinking, & politics.

ARIEL RESNIKOFF USA, 1988–

Snake Chant (1)

if a snake wraps around (a man)   let him go down to the sea   & put a casket over his head   & face (the snake) opposite himself   & when (the man) goes into (the casket)   let him lift (the casket) into the water   rise & consume 4 grains of worm   (-colored) alkaline-plant   & wrap it upon his throat or dress   or wind it   thru coral   decocted ashen palms   roasted & smoothed-out   on its surface

[Based on ancient Akkadian exorcism incantations in the form of Jewish-Aramaic adaptations in the Babylonian Talmud]

Lorine Niedecker USA, 1903–1970

PAEAN TO PLACE

> *And the place*
> *was water*

Fish
    fowl
        flood
    Water lily mud
My life

in the leaves and on water
My mother and I
                born
in swale and swamp and sworn
to water

My father
thru marsh fog
    sculled down
        from high ground
saw her face

at the organ
bore the weight of lake water
    and the cold—
he seined for carp to be sold
that their daughter

might go high
on land
    to learn
Saw his wife turn
deaf

and away
She
    who knew boats
      and ropes
no longer played

She helped him string out nets
for tarring
    And she could shoot
      He was cool
to the man

who stole his minnows
by night and next day offered
    to sell them back
      He brought in a sack
of dandelion greens

if no flood
No oranges—none at hand
    No marsh marigold
      where the water rose
He kept us afloat

I mourn her not hearing canvasbacks
their blast-off rise
    from the water
      Not hearing sora
rails's sweet

spoon-tapped waterglass-
descending scale-
    tear-drop-tittle
        Did she giggle
as a girl?

His skiff skimmed
the coiled celery now gone
    from these streams
        due to carp
He knew duckweed

fall-migrates
toward Mud Lake bottom
    Knew what lay
        under leaf decay
and on pickerel weeds

before summer hum
To be counted on:
    new leaves
        new dead
leaves

He could not
—like water bugs—
    stride surface tension
        He netted
loneliness

As to his bright new car
my mother—her house
    next his—averred:
        A hummingbird
can't haul

Anchored here
in the rise and sink
    of life—
        middle years' nights
he sat

beside his shoes
rocking his chair
    Roped not "looped
       in the loop
of her hair"

I grew in green
slide and slant
    of shore and shade
       Child-time—wade
thru weeds

Maples to swing from
Pewee-glissando
    sublime
       slime-
song

Grew riding the river
Books
    at home-pier
       Shelley could steer
as he read

I was the solitary plover
a pencil
    for a wing-bone
From the secret notes
I must tilt

upon the pressure
execute and adjust
    In us sea-air rhythm
"We live by the urgent wave
of the verse"

Seven year molt
for the solitary bird
    and so young
Seven years the one
dress

for town once a week
One for home
    faded blue-striped
as she piped
her cry

Dancing grounds
my people had none
    woodcocks had—
    backland-
air around

Solemnities
such as what flower
    to take
    to grandfather's grave
unless

water lilies—
he who'd bowed his head
    to grass as he mowed
    Iris now grows
on fill

for the two
and for him
    where they lie
    How much less am I
in the dark than they?

Effort lay in us
before religions
    at pond bottom
      All things move toward
the light

except those
that freely work down
    to oceans' black depths
      In us an impulse tests
the unknown

River rising—flood
Now melt and leave home
    Return—broom wet
        naturally wet
Under

soak-heavy rug
water bugs hatched—
    no snake in the house
        Where were they?—
she

who knew how to clean up
after floods
    he who bailed boats, houses
        Water endows us
with buckled floors

You with sea water running
in your veins sit down in water
    Expect the long-stemmed blue
        speedwell to renew
itself

O my floating life
Do not save love
    for things
        Throw *things*
to the flood

ruined
by the flood
    Leave the new unbought—
        all one in the end—
water

I possessed
the high word:
    The boy my friend
        played his violin
in the great hall

On this stream
my moon night memory
   washed of hardships
      maneuvers barges
thru the mouth

of the river
They fished in beauty
   It was not always so
      In Fishes
red Mars

rising
rides the sloughs and sluices
   of my mind
      with the persons
on the edge

COMMENTARY

Strange—we are always inhabiting more than one realm of existence—but they all fit in if the art is right. (L.N.)

Among the US poets whose work might fit under the "Objectivist" rubric of the 1920s & 1930s, Niedecker, isolated & far from the geographical/cultural mainstream, was most readily ignored by many while held in highest regard by a small group of others. Writes Jane Augustine knowingly, long after Niedecker's time: "[Her] poetics, nuanced and original, arose out of experience, not out of theory nor out of Louis Zukofsky's influence. It exemplifies Objectivist practice par excellence. Like H.D., whose early poems enacted the paradigm that Pound declared in his Imagist dicta, Niedecker wrote poems that enacted Zukofsky's definition of objectivism in 'A'-24: 'desire / for what is objectively perfect / Inextricably the direction of historic and contemporary particulars.' Although Niedecker's subjects emerged from 'particulars' of time and history, often of her home near Fort Atkinson, Wisconsin, she sought to transform these within the a-historical, timeless object, the poem. For her the poem existed in eternity, as concentrated and evocative as a brush-stroke in a Chinese painting that never shows a shadow to betray the sun's passage."

César Moro   Peru, 1903–1956

THE SCANDALOUS LIFE OF CÉSAR MORO

Scatter me in the rain or the smoky cloud of the torrents that pass
At the edge of the night in which we see each other behind the running clouds
That reveal themselves before the eyes of lovers that venture out
From their powerful castle towers of blood and ice
To stain the ice to rip the waterfall of late returns

My friend the King brings me near the side of his real and royal tomb
Where Wagner guards the gate with the loyalty
Of the hound gnawing on the glorious bone
While sporadic and divinely disastrous rains
Corrode the air tram hairdo of recurring seahorses
And manslayers traveling the sublime terrace of apparitions
In the solemn carnivorous and bituminous forest
Where the weird passers-by get intoxicated with their eyes open
Under great catapults and elephantine rams' heads
Suspended according to the pleasure of Babylonia and Trastevere
The river that crowns your terrestrial apparition changing its course
Rushing furiously like a lightning bolt upon traces of the day
Deceitful heaping of medallions of sponges of harquebuses
A bull winged with significant happiness bites the breast or cupola
Of a temple that emerges in the insulting light of day or amidst the rotten
        and delicate branches of the foresty hecatomb

Scatter me in the flight of migratory horses
In the flood of ashes crowning the longevous volcano of the day
In the terrifying vision that pursues the man as midday the most shocking
        of hours draws near
When the seething ballerinas are at the point of being beheaded
And the man grows pale in terrible suspicion of the definitive apparition
        carrying in his teeth the oracle discernible as follows:

"A razor on the cauldron crosses a bristle brush with an ultrasensitive dimension;
as day draws near the bristles extend to touch the twilight; when night approaches
the bristles transform into a dairy farm of a modest and rustic appearance. On the
razor flies a falcon devouring an enigma in the form of wet steam; sometimes it
is a basket filled with animals' eyes and love letters filled with a sole letter; other
times a laborious dog devours a cabin that is lit within. The shrouding darkness
can be interpreted as the absence of thought provoked by the invisible proximity
of a subterranean reservoir inhabited by turtles of the first magnitude."

The wind comes up above the royal tomb
Louis II of Bavaria wakes up amongst the world's rubble
And comes out to visit me bringing through the surrounding forest
A dying tiger
The trees fly away to be seeds and the forest disappears
And covers itself with fog skimming over the ground
Myriads of insects now at liberty deafen the air
At the passage of the two most beautiful tigers in the world

Translated from Spanish by Leslie Bary and Esteban Quispe

COMMENTARY

I belong to shadow and shrouded in shadow I lie on a bed of fire. (C.M.)

César Moro cultivated a transnational artistic life—in dance, painting, performance, poetry. Fleeing from what he considered to be a "conservative" Lima, Moro settled in Paris in 1925 & entered André Breton's Surrealist circle. There, he employed the French language as his poetic tongue & explored the possibilities that he believed Surrealism gave him: absolute freedom in art & life. After a long stay in Paris, he went back to Peru, but because of his cultural & political activities (& what he also called, as an openly gay man, his "scandalous life") he was harassed by the Peruvian government. As an émigré later in Mexico City, he became a key figure in the expansion of Surrealism in Mexican artistic life. However, his separation from the "Surrealist pope" came after the publication of Breton's *Arcane 17* (1945), which Moro disputed for its strong antigay bias. According to Moro, Breton's statement was "a sad spectacle: the driver is lost in his own darkness. But more than sad, it's tragic, because in him the collective error shows itself at its peak."

Pablo Neruda   Chile, 1904–1973

WALKIN' AROUND

It just so happens that I'm tired of being a man.
It just so happens that I walk into tailor shops and movies,
withered, impenetrable, a flannel swan
that steers across a sea of origins and ashes.

The odors from a barber shop can start me bawling.
I only want a little rest from stones and wool.

I only want to see my last of institutes and gardens,
of merchandise, of eye glasses, of elevators.

It just so happens that I'm tired of my feet and my nails
and my hair and my shadow.
It just so happens that I'm tired of being a man.

And yet how delightful it would be
to threaten some accountant with the head of a lily
or murder a nun with a blow on the ear.
How beautiful
to go through streets with a green knife
and holler out loud till I die of frostbite.

I don't want to keep on being a root in the darkness,
irresolute, pulled from all sides, till a dream leaves me shaking,
dragged down through the seeping bowels of the earth,
absorbing and thinking, stuffed with food every day.

I don't want all that grief on my shoulders.
I don't want to keep on as a root and a tomb,
alone underground, a wine cellar stocked with the dead,
frozen stiff, half gone with the pain.

So the day called Monday starts burning like oil
when it sees me pull in with my face of a jailhouse,
and it howls on its way like a wounded wheel,
and leaves tracks of hot blood in the direction of night.

And it shoves me into certain dark corners, into certain moist houses,
into hospitals where the bones sail through the windows,
into certain shoemakers' shops with their odors of vinegar,
into streets full of terrible holes.

There are birds the color of sulfur and horrible guts
that swing from the doors of houses that I hate,
there are false teeth forgotten in a coffee pot,
there are mirrors
that ought to be crying from shame and terror,
there are umbrellas wherever I look, and poisons, and belly buttons.

I walk around with my calm, with my eyes, with my shoes,
with my anger, with my memory failing,
I move on, I wander through offices and orthopedic shops,

and courtyards where clothes are hung from a wire:
underdrawers, towels and nightgowns that cry
slow tears full of dirt.

Translated from Spanish by Jerome Rothenberg

ODE TO MY SOCKS

Maru Mori brought me
a pair
of socks
which she knitted herself
with her sheepherder's hands,
two socks as soft
as rabbits.
I slipped my feet
into them
as though into
two
cases
knitted
with threads of
twilight
and goatskin.
Violent socks,
my feet were
two fish made
of wool,
two long sharks
sea-blue, shot
through
by one golden thread,
two immense blackbirds,
two cannons:
my feet
were honored
in this way
by
these
heavenly

socks.
They were
so handsome
for the first time
my feet seemed to me
unacceptable
like two decrepit
firemen, firemen
unworthy
of that woven
fire,
of those glowing
socks.

Nevertheless
I resisted
the sharp temptation
to save them somewhere
as schoolboys
keep
fireflies,
as learned men
collect
sacred texts,
I resisted
the mad impulse
to put them
into a golden
cage
and each day give them
birdseed
and pieces of pink melon.
Like explorers
in the jungle who hand
over the very rare
green deer
to the spit
and eat it
with remorse,
I stretched out
my feet

and pulled on
the magnificent
socks
and then my shoes.

The moral
of my ode is this:
beauty is twice
beauty
and what is good is doubly
good
when it is a matter of two socks
made of wool
in winter.

Translated from Spanish by Robert Bly

COMMENTARY

I want to see thirst / in the syllables / tough fire in the sound / feel through the dark / for the scream. (P.N.) And again: *How much does a man live, after all? / Does he live a thousand days, or one only? / For a week, or for several centuries? / How long does a man spend dying? / What does it mean to say "for ever"?*

Neruda's work is Promethean, like that of Whitman before him, & reaches across borders & boundaries, a new America on what becomes, increasingly, his native grounds. Writes Federico García Lorca in tribute from a distant shore: "a flash of light that is full, romantic, cruel. Wild, mysterious, American." As such his Americanness is a matter not of *subject*—though that will come in later—but of what Julio Cortázar describes already for Neruda's early *Residence on Earth* (begun in the late 1920s): "an American way of seeing that had not been seen until then … a pulse, a great and deep American breath of life where there were only *passéisms* and fidelities to foreign canons that were growing more and more ridiculous."

With Neruda's epic 1950s *Canto General*, his work opened up to include history, & in his object-centered *Elemental Odes* of the 1950s & 1960s (from which the ode above is taken), he entered on a process of finely stripped lines & an extended virtual caressing of the object. At the same time, he continued a public & political life (first set into motion by the Spanish Civil War) as diplomat, as senator, as party activist, & as exile, as confidant of soon-to-be-assassinated President Salvador Allende. Already sick with cancer, Neruda died during the Allende overthrow while soldiers of the junta ransacked his home on Isla Negra.

For more on Neruda, see "A Map of Histories" & elsewhere in these pages.

Louis Zukofsky USA, 1904–1978

MEMORY OF V. I. ULIANOV

Lenin

Immemorial,
And after us
Immemorial,
O white
O orbit-trembling,
Star, thru all the leaves
Of elm;—
High, proportionately vast,
Of mist and form;—
Star of all live processes
Continual it seems to us,
Like elm leaves,
Lighted in your glow;—
We thrive in strange hegira
Here below,
Yet sometimes in our flight alone
We speak to you,
When nothing that was ours seems spent
And life consuming us seems permanent,
And flight of stirring beating up the night
And down and up; we do not sink with every wave.
Travels our consciousness
Deep in its egress.
Eclipsed the earth, for earth is power
And we of earth,
Eclipsed our death, for death is power
And we of death.
Single we are, tho others still may be with us
And we for others.
We have come to the sources of being,
Inviolable, throngs everlasting, rising forever,
Rush as of river courses,
Change within change of forces
Irrevocable yet safe we go,
Irrevocable you, too,
O star, we speaking to you,

The shadow of the elm tree leaves faded,
Only the trunk of the elm now dark and high
Unto your height:
Now and again you fall,
Blow dark and burn again,
And we in turn
Share now your fate
whose process is continual.

MANTIS

Mantis! Praying mantis! Since your wings' leaves
And your terrified eyes, pins, bright, black and poor
Beg—"look, take it up" (thoughts' torsion)! "save it!"
I who can't bear to look, cannot touch,—You—
You can—but no one sees you steadying lost
In the cars' drafts on the lit subway stone.

Praying mantis, what wind-up brought you, stone
On which you sometimes prop, prey among leaves
(Is it love's food your raised stomach prays?), lost
Here, stone holds only seats on which the poor
Ride, who rising from the news may trample you –
The shop's crowds a jam with no flies in it.

Even the newsboy who now sees knows it
No use, papers make money, makes stone, stone,
Banks, "it is harmless," he says moving on—You?
Where will he put *you*? There are no safe leaves
To put you back in here, here's news! Too poor
Like all the separate poor to save the lost.

Don't light on my chest, mantis! Do—you're lost,
Let the poor laugh at my fright, then see it:
My shame and theirs, you whom old Europe's poor
Call spectre, strawberry, by turns; a stone—
You point—they say—you lead lost children—leaves
Close in the paths men leave, saved, safe with you.

Killed by thorns (once men), who now will save you
Mantis? What male love bring a fly, be lost
Within your mouth, prophetess, harmless to leaves

And hands, faked flower,—the myth: is dead, bones, it
Was assembled, apes wing in wind: On stone
Mantis, you will die, touch, beg, of the poor.

Android, loving beggar, dive to the poor
As your love would even without head to you,
Graze like machined wheels, green from off this stone
And preying on each terrified chest, lost
Say, I am old as the globe, the moon, it
Is my old shoe, yours, be free as the leaves.

Fly, mantis, on the poor, arise like leaves
The armies of the poor, strength: stone on stone
And build the new world in your eyes, Save it!

COMMENTARY

The melody, the rest are accessory—
…my one voice; my other …
An objective—rays of the object brought to a focus,
An objective—nature as creator—desire for what is objectively
  perfect,
Inextricably the direction of historic and contemporary particulars

(L.Z.)

"Specifically, a writer of music," Louis Zukofsky writes in a "prose" section of *29 Songs*, & that concern is everywhere in his work, which seems now more innovative of forms & the hidden resources of language's soundings than that of any but a handful of American moderns, north or south. But the music, if the term holds, is as much of eyes as ear, the consequence of "the kind of intelligence Zukofsky has—seeing & hearing words in the world as the specific possibilities they contain" (R. Creeley). First published in Pound's *Exile* (later in other avant-garde magazines of the 1920s), he coined the word "Objectivists" (the quote marks his) to fit an issue of younger poets he was assembling for *Poetry* magazine (1931) thanks to Pound's intervention, later extending it to An *"Objectivists" Anthology* (1932) & to George & Mary Oppen's To Publishers, renamed the Objectivist Press. Not a polarization into object/subject but a dialectic, the Objectivist "principle" derives from a metaphor of vision ("*An objective—rays of the object brought to a focus,*" as in optics) & from earlier assumptions (mainly Pound's) about image & vortex. Or in a nutshell, Zukofsky's own dictum for *poesis*: "thinking with things as they exist."

For more on Zukofsky, see "A Map of Histories" & elsewhere in these pages.

Andrew Peynetsa Zuni / USA, 1904–1976

per Dennis Tedlock, USA, 1939–2016

from **FINDING THE CENTER**

Coyote & Junco

SON'AHCHI.

    SONTI^{LO——NG A}GO

AT STANDING ARROWS
OLD LADY JUNCO HAD HER HOME
and COYOTE
Coyote was there at Sitting Rock with his children.
He was with his children
and Old Lady Junco
was winnowing.
pigweed
and tumbleweed, she was winnowing these.
with her basket
she winnowed these by tossing them in the air.
She was tossing them in the air
      while Coyote
Coyote
was going around hunting, going around hunting for his children there
when he came to where Junco was winnowing.
"What are you DOING?" that's what he asked her. "Well, I'm winnowing"
    she said.
"What are you winnowing?" he said. "Well

pigweed and tumbleweed"
      that's what she told him.
    "Indeed.
What's that you're saying?" "Well, this is
    my winnowing song," she said.
"NOW SING IT FOR ME
so that I
may sing it for my children," he said.
Old Lady Junco
sang for Coyote:
      YUUWA^{HINA} YUUWA^{HINA}
        YUUWA^{HINA} YUUWA^{HINA}

YU^HINA YU^HINA

(blowing) PFFF PFFF

YU^HINA YU^HINA

(blowing) PFFF PFFF

That's what she said.
"YES, NOW I
can go, I'll sing it to my children."
Coyote went on to Oak Arroyo, and when he got there MOURNING DOVES FLEW UP
and he lost his song.
He went back:
(*muttering*) "Quick! sing for me, some mourning doves made me lose my song," he said.
Again she sang for him.
He learned the song and went on.
He went through a field there
and broke through a gopher hole.
Again he lost his song.
Again, he came for the third time
to ask for it.
Again she sang for him.
He went on for the third time, and when he came to Oak Arroyo
BLACKBIRDS FLEW UP and again he lost his song.
He was coming for the fourth time
when Old Lady Junco said to herself, (*tight*) "Oh here you come
but I won't sing," that's what she said.
She looked for a round rock.
When she found a round rock, she
dressed it with her Junco shirt, she put her basket of seeds with the Junco rock.
(*tight*) "As for you, go right ahead and ask."

Junco went inside her house.

Coyote was coming for the fourth time.
When he came:
"Quick! sing it for me, I lost the song again, come on," that's what he told her.
Junco said nothing.
"Quick!" that's what he told her, but she didn't speak.
"ONE," he said.
"The fourth time I
speak, if you haven't sung, I'll bite you," that's what he told her.

•

"Second time, TWO," he said.
"Quick sing for me," he said.
She didn't sing. "THREE. I'll count ONCE MORE," he said.

•

Coyote said, "QUICK SING," that's what he told her.
She didn't sing.
Junco had left her shirt for Coyote.
He bit the Junco, CRUNCH, he bit the round rock.
Right here (*points to molars*) he knocked out the teeth, the rows of teeth in
    back.
(*tight*) "So now I've really done it to you." "AY! AY!"
    that's what he said.
THE PRAIRIE WOLF WENT BACK TO HIS CHILDREN,
    and by the time he got back there his children were dead.
Because this was lived long ago, Coyote has no teeth here
    (*points to molars*). LEE————SEMKONIKYA. (*laughs*)

Transcribed & translated from Zuni by Dennis Tedlock

COMMENTARY

(1) The act of recovery here—discovery also—is to discern the presence of poesis in the oral narrations by master tellers over a wide range of traditional cultures. In the present instance, Tedlock's transcription & translation from Zuni is also an example of a method of representing narrative as performance that he pioneered & nowhere more clearly than in *Finding the Center: Narrative Poetry of the Zuni Indians*. For sounding "Coyote & Junco," then, the reader should observe that line changes = a pause of less than one second; double spaces between lines = a two- to three-second pause; CAPITALS = loud words & passages; smaller print = soft ones; long dashes after vowels = vowels to be held for about two seconds; a line or phrase set on different levels = line to be chanted with an interval of about three half tones between levels. Other keys to reading aloud are given, like stage directions, in parentheses.

(2) Although Trickster took many forms in the Americas (Raven, Rabbit, Mink, Flint, Spider, Blue Jay, Jaguar, etc.), his manifestation as Coyote has had the greatest carryover into contemporary American culture overall. In the present version, as one Zuni listener told Tedlock, Coyote is "just being very foolish"—a far cry, perhaps, from his work as Creator or from the tragic, obscene, & terrifying sides of him that turn up elsewhere:

Daybreak finds me,
eastern daybreak finds me
the meaning of that song:

with blood-stained mouth
comes mad Coyote!

Nez Perce, translated by Herbert J. Spinden

A comparison with Simon Ortiz's "Telling about Coyote" (in "A Fourth Gallery") would also be insightful here.

ADDENDUM

DIANE DI PRIMA USA, 1934–2020

from **Loba [She-Wolf]**

[as her own fierce imagining of a female Coyote-like presence]

I am a shadow crossing ice
I am rusting knife in the water
I am pear tree bitten by frost
I uphold the mountain with my hand
My feet are cut by glass
I walk in the windy forest after dark
I am wrapped in a gold cloud
I whistle thru my teeth
I lose my hat
My eyes are fed to eagles & my jaw
is locked with silver wire
I have burned often and my bones are soup
I am stone giant statue on a cliff
I am mad as a blizzard
I stare out of broken cupboards

Kenneth Rexroth USA, 1905–1982

A LESSON IN GEOGRAPHY

The stars of the Great Bear drift apart
The Horse and the Rider together northeastward

Alpha and Omega asunder
The others diversely
There are rocks
On the earth more durable
Than the configurations of heaven
Species now motile and sanguine
Shall see the stars in new clusters
The beaches changed
The mountains shifted
Gigantic
Immobile
Floodlit
The faces appear and disappear
Chewing the right gum
Smoking the right cigarette
Buying the best refrigerator
The polished carnivorous teeth
Exhibited in approval
The lights
Of the houses
Draw together
In the evening dewfall on the banks
Of the Wabash
Sparkle discreetly
High on the road to Provo
Above the Salt Lake Valley
And
The mountain shaped like a sphinx
And
The mountain shaped like a finger
Pointing
On the first of April at eight o'clock
Precisely at Algol
There are rocks on the earth
And one who sleepless
Throbbed with the ten
Nightingales in the plum trees
Sleepless as Boötes stood over him
Gnawing the pillow
Sitting on the bed's edge smoking
Sitting by the window looking

One who rose in the false
Dawn and stoned
The nightingales in the garden
The heart pawned for wisdom
The heart
Bartered for knowledge and folly
The will troubled
The mind secretly aghast
The eyes and lips full of sorrow
The apices of vision wavering
As the flower spray at the tip of the windstalk
The becalmed sail
The heavy wordless weight
And now
The anguishing and pitiless file
Cutting away life
Capsule by capsule biting
Into the heart
The coal of fire
Sealing the lips
There are rocks on earth

And

In the Japanese quarter
A phonograph playing
"Moonlight on ruined castles"
Kojo n'suki
And
The movement of the wind fish
Keeping time to the music
Sirius setting behind it
(The Dog has scented the sun)
Gold immense fish
Squirm in the trade wind
"Young Middle Western woman
In rut
Desires correspondent"
The first bright flower
Cynoglossum
The blue hound's tongue
Breaks on the hill

"The tide has gone down
Over the reef
I walk about the world
There is great
Wind and then rain"
"My life is bought and paid for
So much pleasure
For so much pain"
The folded fossiliferous
Sedimentary rocks end here
The granite batholith
Obtrudes abruptly
West of the fault line
Betelgeuse reddens
Drawing its substance about it
It is possible that a process is beginning
Similar to that which lifted
The great Sierra fault block
Through an older metamorphic range

(The Dog barks on the sun's spoor)

Now

The thought of death
Binds fast the flood of light
Ten years ago the snow falling
All a long winter night
I had lain waking in my bed alone
Turning my heavy thoughts
And no way might
Sleep
Remembering divers things long gone
Now
In the long day in the hour of small shadow
I walk on the continent's last western hill
And lie prone among the iris in the grass
My eyes fixed on the durable stone
That speaks and hears as though it were myself

I write for one and only one purpose, to overcome the invincible igno-rance of the traduced heart.... I wish to speak to and for those who have had enough of the Social Lie, the Economics of Mass Murder, the Sexual Hoax, and the Domestication of Conspicuous Consumption. (K.R.)

It was Rexroth's role in the grand mix of new visions & voices in post–World War II American poetry, both north & south, to be a necessary coun-ter to the line of Pound, offering alternative strategies for renewal, transla-tion, & assimilation of the past, calling attention to concerns that others had largely ignored or rejected: the full range of European & South Ameri-can modernism, American Indian & other Indigenous poetries, the work of overlooked contemporaries (still overlooked) & many of the new poets of the 1950s & 1960s. He had entered early into the avant-garde enterprise, as a painter first, then as a proponent of a "cubist" approach to the poem, & was, along with Zukofsky himself, the major younger contributor to Zukofsky's *"Objectivists" Anthology* (1932). He was also a major transla-tor from Spanish & Japanese, & during the early post–World War II years he was a central figure in the San Francisco Renaissance & an important participant in the poetry-jazz experiment.

Martín Adán   Peru, 1908–1985

from *AFTERWORD*

Written Blindly

I know only of my passing through,
of my weight,
of my sadness
and my shoe.
Why ask who I am, where I'm going?
Because you know plenty about the Poet, the difficult
and sensitive volume of my being human,
which is a body and a vocation,
nonetheless.
Yes, I was born,
the Year remembers my birth,
but I don't remember,
because I live it, because I kill myself.
My Angel isn't a Guardian Angel,

my Angel is one of Satiety, of Remnants,
and carries me endlessly,
stumbling, always stumbling
in this dazzling shadow
that is Life
and its deceit
and its charm.
When you know everything . . .
When you know not to ask . . .
Just chew on your mortal fingernail
and then I will tell you my life,
which is nothing but a mere word more . . .
The whole of your life is like the wave:
knowing how to kill,
and knowing how to die,
and not knowing how to tame plentitude,
and not knowing how to wander home to the source,
and not knowing how to quiet longing . . .
If you want to know about my life,
go look at the Sea.
Why do you ask me, Learned One?
Don't you know that in the World,
everything gathers from nothing:
a shrinking immensity from here to the next star,
nothing but a trace
eternally barely the shadow of an appetite?
The real task, if that's what you aspire to,
is not to understand life, but to imagine it.
The real isn't captured: it is followed,
and that's what dreams and words are for.
Beware your innovations . . .
Beware your distances . . .
Beware your thresholds . . .
Beware your refuge . . .
Who am I?
I am I,
ineffable and innumerable,
the figure and soul of rage.
No, that was at the end . . . and it was the beginning
and it was before the beginning began.
I am a body of spirit fury,

which is serene
and of harsh irony.
No, I am not the one who seeks the poem,
nor life . . .
I am an animal hunted by its own being
which is a truth and a lie.

My being is so simple and so breathless,
a piercing of a nerve, of flesh . . .

I was looking for another,
one who has been my search for myself,
I didn't want, and don't want now, to be me—
but another who has saved himself,
or who will,
not the being of Instinct, who gets lost,
or of Understanding, who steps back.

My day is a different day,
some days I don't know where to be,
I don't know where to go in my jungle,
among my reptiles and my trees,
my books and mortar
and neon stars
and women rising around me like a wall,
      or like no one at all, or like a mother . . .

and the newborn who cries over me
and through the streets
and all the wheels,
primal and for real.
Such is the whole of my days,
unto my last afternoon.

The Other, that companion, is a ghost.
Is there air
on which you choke and yet delight
in breathing,
in your inane body?
No!
Nothing equals the endless surprise
of finding yourself again,
always you, the same selves among the same walls

made of distances and streets...
And the same skies, roofs
that never kill me because they never come down...

And I've never achieved the turbulence of the divine
nor affection for the human.
I'm this way without regret.
That's not how I feel.
By day I am the Outsider
and, if I think about it, the Absolute of Zoology.
Or like the ferocious carnivore if I take hold.
Am I the Creature or the Creator?
Am I Matter or Miracle?
You ask: what is mine and what is another's...
Who am I?
Do you think I know?
But no, the Other doesn't exist,
only I am, fiendish and orgasmic!

Translated from Spanish by Katie Silver and Rick London

COMMENTARY

*Fabio, this passage and flow and writhing I'm thinking of / is the world:
element, eruption: everything, nothing, / in the immense power.* (M.A.)

Rick London, one of Adán's translators, writes: "Although personally isolated for much of his life, Adán's... visionary poetry is unique and, at times,
eccentric, seemingly not part of any local conversation, more reminiscent
of Mallarmé or Wallace Stevens than any of the main proponents of *modernismo*. In 1961, Adán published a reflection on poetry and the artistic life
of the poet, *Written Blindly*, moving away from his earlier work in more
traditional forms to make use of the greater latitude of free verse. As the
title suggests, this poem finds its way as it goes, at points seeming to pick
its way through unruly verbal rubble. He seeks no summary understanding.
Rather, as with all of Adán's work, the piece confronts presumed meaning,
and the way mind makes meaning—often by means of a density and vola-
tility of images that keep the poetic field from resolving in any terms. As he
did throughout his career, Adán here invites in energies from 'beyond the
limits of the normal world' (T.S. Eliot) and allows the mind a glimpse of
its own vast possibilities. Adán explored his art freely, with little regard for
the reader. Indeed, his shifts and juxtapositions, grammatical dislocations
and invented words, create a tension that can cause the intelligibility of the
text to tremble, even as he weaves it into lovely song" (in the introduction
to *Written Blindly*).

George Oppen USA, 1908–1984

from **OF BEING NUMEROUS**: **9**

"Whether, as the intensity of seeing increases, one's distance
      from Them, the people, does not also increase"
I know, of course I know, I can enter no other place

Yet I am one of those who from nothing but man's way of
      thought and one of his dialects and what has happened
      to me
Have made poetry

To dream of that beach
For the sake of an instant in the eyes,

The absolute singular

The unearthly bonds
Of the singular

Which is the bright light of shipwreck

PSALM

Veritas sequitur ...

In the small beauty of the forest
The wild deer bedding down—
That they are there!

            Their eyes
Effortless, the soft lips
Nuzzle and the alien small teeth
Tear at the grass

            The roots of it
Dangle from their mouths
Scattering earth in the strange woods.
They who are there.

            Their paths
Nibbled thru the fields, the leaves that shade them

Hang in the distances
Of sun

                    The small nouns
Crying faith
In this in which the wild deer
Startle, and stare out.

GUEST ROOM

•

There is in age

The risk that the mind
Reach

Into homelessness, "nowhere to return." In age
The maxims

Expose themselves, the happy endings
That justify a moral. But this?

This? The noise of wealth,

The clamor of wealth—tree
So often shaken—it is the voice

Of Hell.
The virtue of the mind

Is that emotion

Which causes
To see. Virtue...

Virtue...? The great house
With its servants,

The great utensiled
House

Of air conditioners, safe harbor

In which the heart sinks, closes
Now like a fortress

In daylight, setting its weight
Against the bare blank paper.

•

The purpose
Of their days.

And their nights?
The evenings
And the candle light?

What could they mean by that?
Because the hard light dims

Outside, what ancient
Privilege? What gleaming
Mandate

From what past?

•

If one has only his ability

To arrange
Matters, to exert force

To open a window
To shut it—

To cause to be arranged—

Death which is a question

Of an intestine
Or a sinus drip

Looms as the horror
Which will arrive

When one is most without defenses,

The unspeakable
Defeat

Toward which they live
Embattled and despairing;

It is the courage of the rich

Who are an *avant garde*

Near the limits of life—Like theirs

My abilities
Are ridiculous:

To go perhaps unarmed
And unarmored, to return

Now to the old questions—

•

Of the dawn
Over 'Frisco
Lightening the large hills
And the very small coves
At their feet, and we
Perched in the dawn wind
Of that coast like leaves
Of the most recent weed—And yet the things

That happen! Signs,
Promises—we took it
As a sign, as promise

Still for nothing wavered,
Nothing begged or was unreal, the thing
Happening, filling our eyesight
Out to the horizon—I remember the sky
And the moving sea.

COMMENTARY

There are things / We live among and to see them / Is to know ourselves
(G.O.)

Like Zukofsky, Oppen's reemergence coincided with the second wave of US radical modernism in the 1960s & 1970s. A wanderer in his early middle years, Oppen went to France, ca. 1929, with his wife, Mary Colby, where they founded a press, To Publishers (later renamed the Objectivist Press), which published Oppen's own first book, *Discrete Series*, along with Williams's *A Novelette and Other Prose*, Pound's *How to Read*, and

An *"Objectivists" Anthology*, edited by Zukofsky. It was after his time in France, in the throes of the Great Depression, that Oppen returned to the States, became a communist labor organizer, & took, he says elsewhere, twenty-five years to write his next poem, much of that time spent in exile in Mexico, designing furniture for a cabinetmaker's shop. But his poetry shows, for all of that, a remarkable continuity of attentions—a concern with structure ("the objectification of the poem, the making an object of the poem"), with the process that informs that structure (the poem as "a test of truth" or "test of images… of whether one's thought is valid, whether one can establish a series of images, of experiences… whether or not one will consider the concept of humanity to be valid, something that is, or have to regard it as simply being a word"). From all of which there finally emerges a poetry in which the "virtue of the mind is that which causes to see."

Or, as Robert Creeley writes in his introduction to Oppen's *Selected Poems* (2003): "I think much becomes clear, in fact, if one recognizes that George Oppen is trying all his life to *think* the world, not only to find or to enter it, or to gain a place in it, but to *realize* it, to *figure* it, to have it literally in mind."

José Lezama Lima   Cuba, 1910–1976

AN OBSCURE MEADOW LURES ME

An obscure meadow lures me,
her fast, close-fitting lawns
revolve in me, sleep on my balcony.
They rule her beaches, her indefinite
alabaster dome re-creates itself.
On the waters of a mirror,
the voice cut short crossing a hundred paths,
my memory prepares surprise:
fallow dew in the sky, dew, sudden flash.
Without hearing I'm called:
I slowly enter the meadow,
proudly consumed in a new labyrinth.
Illustrious remains:
a hundred heads, bugles, a thousand shows
baring their sky, their silent sunflower.
Strange the surprise in that sky
where unwilling footfalls turn
and voices swell in its pregnant center.

An obscure meadow goes by.
Between the two, wind or thin paper,
the wind, the wounded wind of this death,
this magic death, one and dismissed.
A bird, another bird, no longer trembles.

Translated from Spanish by Nathaniel Tarn

DISSONANCE

As to the contradiction of contradictions,
the contradiction of poetry,
to render the stone's reluctant reply
with a puff of smoke,
and to return to water's clarity
in search of the serene ocean chaos
severed in two: a continuity that questions,
and a rift in response,
like a hole crawling with larvae
in which, afterwards, a lobster will repose.
Its eyes tracing the carbuncular circle,
miasmas being lobsters with flaring eyes,
one half nestled in the void,
the other half clumsily scratching
the frenzy of the annotated faun.
First contradiction: to walk barefoot
over the interlacing leaves
that cover the burrows where the sun
fades like a weary sword
slashing a bonfire, newly planted.
Second contradiction: to plant bonfires.
Final contradiction: to enter
the mirror approaching us,
where backs can be viewed,
and in the likeness, eyes
begin over the eyes of leaves,
the contradiction of contradictions.
The contradiction of poetry,
effacing itself and plunging forward
with the laughable eyes of a lobster.

Each word destroys its appoggiatura
and traces a secular Roman bridge.
Each word spins in place like an affectionate
dolphin, surfacing
as faintly as a phallic prow.
Lips pursed hard when they announce
the order to retreat.
A word explodes and the sleigh dogs chew
the lanterns hanging from the trees.
As to the contradiction of contradictions,
the contradiction of poetry:
efface the letters and then inhale them at dawn
when the light effaces you.

Translated from Spanish by Roberto Tejada

COMMENTARY

Give me the outside of all things, I am a fanatic for the externality of things. (J.L.L.)

A bridge between the Spanish Siglo de Oro and his own times, heir of Luis de Góngora's seventeenth-century Baroque works, José Lezama Lima stands as a reference point in Latin American poetry & well into our own time became the force behind the influential *neobarroco* poetry movement, which continues into the present. His poetical system focuses on the *imago* (Latin for *image*). "Through imago time becomes extension," he writes, & in that way the poem becomes a medium—a body—that can grasp the flow of time without stopping it. For him, the image is like a geometric form in endless motion & development; this kinetic image—sign or symbol that moves like "mill blades," in his own words—saturates the core of the poem & expands up to its boundaries via a centrifugal force: the metaphor. (The resemblance, independently, of Lezama Lima's *imago* to Pound's *vortex*—static images replaced by images in motion—might also be worth noting.)

Or Lezama Lima in his *Diaries*: "What else can we achieve, but symphonic impressionism? If we consider the poet's culture a quantitative arsenal, the only possible unity is *that* symphonic impressionism.... The poet can be the fretful apprentice or the faithful craftsman of the whole, but in his poetry an inhabited land must be shown, a cosmos ruled by the real-unreal." And later: "I'm a phantom of conjectures and insignificancies."

Simone Yoyotte Martinique, ca. 1910–1933

HALF-SEASON

I

Embarrassed cold
in that splendid time when I was naked
I think about saying

far from there
from feet to head
THE SONOROUS SHADOW

Cries
like the seagull
I'm afraid those eyes

atonal desire
for the first roots

II

To J.-M.

Living comet on the peak
such a one
who likewise plunges
does not possess the source of pleasure
I was
like the rocks
an extra immanent
truncated
evil-minded
but the murmuring makes me change
place and ink
to my own measure
like
a liquid
weight that obsesses me
finds its way in a dream
and turns

Translated from French by Myrna Bell Rochester

PALE BLUE LINE IN A FORCED EPISODE, I CUT A HOLE IN THE FLAG OF THE REPUBLIC

My beautiful bird in the eternal the downspouts call you but don't think about coming back. The feathers of a pleasant surname won't fail to admit fear fear of the wind in the glaciers. My beautiful bird the thunder of all my desires the satisfaction of the sun already set and of all my confused thorns in the undifferentiated anguish of a sojourn I did not wish to impose on you my bird my late bird blood my despair in short sleeves of shaded satin color of my recklessness your feathers your feathered wings on the back foot my bird counter-riddle let us dissipate the brightness of your light blue lines my white voracious gudgeon you are my beautiful bird my beautiful bird zephyr in the night and when all the lamps blow out in the leather of my little agony. I have flown into the embankments and into the poplars I have sold worry to the easygoing investor I have wandered through the temples of desolation by night by day at the setting of all the great sorrows and everywhere beautiful bird I saw you in the stones and you could not know that the mind does not cross the river for on the bridge that you tossed me it was in vain that I stoned all the ripples. The call of the rhombohedron at the edge of April resembles the music of your own shadow my useless bird who only knows how to people in the revolt with all the great trees of the avenues and all the boulevards when the trumpet of the banquet halls resonates under the windows of the woman you do not yet love.

Translated from French by Myrna Bell Rochester

COMMENTARY

The murmuring makes me change place and ink to my own measure. (S.Y.)

The first woman of African descent to play an active role in the French Surrealist group in Paris, Yoyotte's work stands as a landmark, understated but real, of Afro-Antillean surrealism. Born & raised in Martinique, her experiments with automatic writing & dream narratives—aimed, as André Breton & others had it, to bring the unconscious into view—show the common threads that linked the Negritude poets of her time with the core Surrealist group in Paris—i.e., the charting of a new or hidden inner reality supressed by the interference of ego, morality, etc. Of Yoyotte's practice, the US Surrealist chronicler Franklin Rosemont writes: "Her colorful antirational imagery gives her work a unique and disturbing quality, radically unlike any other Francophone Caribbean poetry of the time. Only the very small number of her surviving poems and her early death can explain the fact that Simone Yoyotte has remained so little known" (in *Black Brown & Beige: Surrealist Writings from Africa & the Diaspora*, ed. F. Rosemont & Robin D.G. Kelley).

Pagu (Patrícia Rehder Galvão)

Brazil, 1910–1962

NOTHING

Nothing nothing nothing
Nada more than nothing
Because you wish only the nothing existed
Then there is only the nothing
A broken wiper, a leg twisted
Nothing
Physiognomies butchered
Friends in slings
Doors busted
Open to nothing
A child's crying
An idle woman's tear
Which means nothing
A dim room
With a broken lamp
Girls who danced
Who chatted
Nothing
A glass of cognac
A theatre
A cliff
Maybe the cliff meant nothing
A wallet of traveler's checks
A departure for two and nothing
They brought me white and red camelias
A beautiful child smiled when I hugged her
A dog growled on my street
A parrot said such funny things
Country girls crossed my way
In a swarthy samba sway
I held out my arms to embrace the usual friends
Poets showed up
Some writers
Theatre folks
Wild women windsocks at the airport
And nothing…

Translated from Portuguese by Jennifer Cooper

(1) Writes translator Jennifer Cooper: "Much like other women writers and poets of the 1920s and '30s—Djuna Barnes, Mina Loy, H.D., Nancy Cunard come to mind, among others—she spent a formative year from 1934 to 1935 as an expatriate in Paris, & although little is known about her life during this period, it ended in her arrest & expulsion from France for anti-fascist political activities. Pagu—the nickname given her by Raul Bopp—was thereafter a journalist, writer, cartoonist, translator of Artaud & Apollinaire, & playwright, as well as a world traveler. Her most well-known work, *Industrial Park* (1933), was published on her return from China, where she met with the deposed Chinese emperor Pu-Yi, who gave her (they say) the first soybeans to be planted in Brazil. An active member of the Anthropophagite movement & a later militant of the Communist Party, she was the first woman to be arrested for political activities in Brazil."

(2) Augusto de Campos, in *Pagu: Life and Works*, writes, "Pagu was revolutionary in art, in politics and in the practice of life." And of her role in the Brazilian avant-garde: "She embodies, as few do, the modernist and liberating ideals of the modernists... one of the few remaining from modernism who continued to be faithful to the revolutionary ideas of the movement with respect to renewing artistic language, while the rest either gave in to the academy or to regret."

Charles Olson USA, 1910 1970

THE KINGFISHERS

1

What does not change / is the will to change

He woke, fully clothed, in his bed. He
remembered only one thing, the birds, how
when he came in, he had gone around the rooms
and got them back in their cage, the green one first,
she with the bad leg, and then the blue,
the one they had hoped was a male

Otherwise? Yes, Fernand, who had talked lispingly of Albers & Angkor Vat.
He had left the party without a word. How he got up, got into his coat,
I do not know. When I saw him, he was at the door, but it did not matter,
he was already sliding along the wall of the night, losing himself

in some crack of the ruins. That it should have been he who said, "The kingfishers!
who cares
for their feathers
now?"

His last words had been, "The pool is slime." Suddenly everyone,
ceasing their talk, sat in a row around him, watched
they did not so much hear, or pay attention, they
wondered, looked at each other, smirked, but listened,
he repeated and repeated, could not go beyond his thought
"The pool   the kingfishers' feathers were wealth   why
did the export stop?"

It was then he left

2

I thought of the E on the stone, and of what Mao said
la lumiere"
                    but the kingfisher
de l'aurore"
                    but the kingfisher flew west
est devant nous!
                    he got the color of his breast
                    from the heat of the setting sun!

The features are, the feebleness of the feet (syndactylism of the 3rd & 4th digit)
the bill, serrated, sometimes a pronounced beak, the wings
where the color is, short and round, the tail
inconspicuous.

But not these things were the factors. Not the birds.
The legends are
legends. Dead, hung up indoors, the kingfisher
will not indicate a favoring wind,
or avert the thunderbolt. Nor, by its nesting,
still the waters, with the new year, for seven days.
It is true, it does nest with the opening year, but not on the waters.
It nests at the end of a tunnel bored by itself in a bank. There,
six or eight white and translucent eggs are laid, on fishbones
not on bare clay, on bones thrown up in pellets by the birds.

                    On these rejectamenta
(as they accumulate they form a cup-shaped structure) the young are born.
And, as they are fed and grow, this nest of excrement and decayed fish becomes
                              a dripping, fetid mass

Mao concluded:

> nous devons
>
>> nous lever
>>
>>> et agir!

3

When the attentions change / the jungle
leaps in

> even the stones are split
>
>> they rive

Or,
enter
that other conqueror we more naturally recognize
he so resembles ourselves

But the E
cut so rudely on that oldest stone
sounded otherwise,
was differently heard

as, in another time, were treasures used:

(and, later, much later, a fine ear thought
a scarlet coat)

> "of green feathers   feet, beaks and eyes
> of gold

> "animals likewise,
> resembling snails

> "a large wheel, gold, with figures of unknown four-foots,
> and worked with tufts of leaves, weight
> 3800 ounces

> "last, two birds, of thread and featherwork, the quills
> gold, the feet
> gold, the two birds perched on two reeds

> gold, the reeds arising from two embroidered mounds,
> one yellow, the other
> white.

>> And from each reed hung
>> seven feathered tassels.

In this instance, the priests
(in dark cotton robes, and dirty,
their disheveled hair matted with blood, and flowing wildly
over their shoulders)
rush in among the people, calling on them
to protect their gods

And all now is war
where so lately there was peace,
and the sweet brotherhood, the use
of tilled fields.

4

Not one death but many,
not accumulation but change, the feed-back proves, the feed-back is
the law

      Into the same river no man steps twice
      When fire dies air dies
      No one remains, nor is, one

Around an appearance, one common model, we grow up
many. Else how is it,
if we remain the same,
we take pleasure now
in what we did not take pleasure before? love
contrary objects? admire and / or find fault? use
other words, feel other passions, have
nor figure, appearance, disposition, tissue
the same?
      To be in different states without a change
      is not a possibility

We can be precise. The factors are
in the animal and / or the machine the factors are
communication and / or control, both involve
the message. And what is the message? The message is
a discrete or continuous sequence of measurable events distributed in time

is the birth of the air, is
the birth of water, is
a state between
the origin and

the end, between
birth and the beginning of
another fetid nest

is change, presents
no more than itself

And the too strong grasping of it,
when it is pressed together and condensed,
loses it

This very thing you are

II

> They buried their dead in a sitting posture
> serpent   cane   razor   ray of the sun

> And she sprinkled water on the head of my child, crying
> "Cioa-coatl! Cioa-coatl!"
> with her face to the west

> Where the bones are found, in each personal heap
> with what each enjoyed, there is always
> the Mongolian louse

The light is in the east. Yes. And we must rise, act. Yet
in the west, despite the apparent darkness (the whiteness
which covers all), if you look, if you can bear, if you can, long enough

> as long as it was necessary for him, my guide
> to look into the yellow of that longest-lasting rose

so you must, and, in that whiteness, into that face, with what candor, look

and, considering the dryness of the place
         the long absence of an adequate race

> (of the two who first came, each a conquistador, one healed, the other
> tore the eastern idols down, toppled
> the temple walls, which, says the excuser
> were black from human gore)

hear
hear, where the dry blood talks
      where the old appetite walks

where it hides, look
in the eye how it runs
in the flesh / chalk

      but under these petals
      in the emptiness
      regard the light, contemplate
      the flower

whence it arose

      with what violence benevolence is bought
      what cost in gesture justice brings
      what wrongs domestic rights involve
      what stalks
      this silence

      what pudor pejorocracy affronts
      how awe, night-rest and neighborhood can rot
      what breeds where dirtiness is law
      what crawls
      below

III

      I am no Greek, hath not th'advantage.
      And of course, no Roman:
      he can take no risk that matters,
      the risk of beauty least of all.

      But I have my kin, if for no other reason than
      (as he said, next of kin) I commit myself, and,
      given my freedom, I'd be a cad
      if I didn't. Which is most true.

      It works out this way, despite the disadvantage.
      I offer, in explanation, a quote:
      si j'ai du goût, ce n'est guères
      que pour la terre et les pierres.

Despite the discrepancy (an ocean   courage   age)
this is also true: if I have any taste
it is only because I have interested myself
in what was slain in the sun

    I pose you your question:

shall you uncover honey / where maggots are?

    I hunt among stones

COMMENTARY

It is not I, / even if the work appeared / biographical. The only interesting thing / is if one can be / an image / of man.... Otherwise, we are involved in / ourselves (which is demonstrably / not very interesting, no / matter / who. (C.O.) Against which (Olson again): *The soul / is an onslaught.* Or: *All that can inhabit the present is present.*

(1) Olson makes a big leap forward—starting, as he says, from wartime degradations of the human spirit, genocides, etc., to which the first resistance is forged (much like Artaud's in France) from physiology & body. Where it takes him is a vast, likely impossible enterprise: a poetics of the breath & body (as *projective* verse) that would lead to poems of maximal (*projective*) size (like Williams's *Paterson*, Zukofsky's "A," Pound's *Cantos*, his own *Maximus*) & to a radical remapping of all human history: a plan, in short, for a new "curriculum of the soul," often set forth in scrawled notes, then assigned to younger colleagues to flesh out. As with André Breton vis-à-vis Surrealism, this relation to a set of ideas & to a movement (projective verse; "Black Mountain" as the name of both the movement & the college of which he was the rector in the early 1950s) sometimes obscured the force of his work as a poet. The culmination of that work was *The Maximus Poems*, his ongoing "epic"—in Pound's definition of the same, "a poem including history."

(2) Of some interest here is Olson's visit to Yucatán in 1951, not so much for his delving into daily life there, but for his exploration of the ancient Mayan ruins, the "hunt among stones" noted at the end of "The Kingfishers." As he wrote elsewhere: "If there are no walls there are no names. This is the morning, after the dispersion, and the work of the morning is methodology: how to use oneself, and on what. That is my profession. I am an archaeologist of morning." With which there came a turning in his work as poet/"archaeologist," not as a return to ancient Mexico but in the local mindscapes & bodyscapes of his native Gloucester, Massachusetts, & in ancient worlds & times at large.

For more on Olson, see "A Map of Histories" & elsewhere in these pages.

José María Arguedas Quechua, Peru, 1911–1969

JETMAN, HAYLLI (ODE TO THE JET PLANE)

Grandpa! I'm in the Upper world,
above major and minor gods, known and unknown.
What's this? God is man, man is God.
Behold: the rivers, the worshiped ones that split the world have now become
    the trimmest thread of a spider web.

Man is God.
Where's the condor, where the eagles?
Invisible as winged bugs they're lost up in the air, among ignored things.

God the Father, God the Son, God the Holy Ghost: I cannot find thee, thou art
    no more,
        I have reached the realm thy priests and the ancients called the Upper World.
        I'm in that world. I'm seated more comfortably than anywhere else, on
            a burning saddle, red-hot, white-hot, made by the hand of man, of a
            wind-fish.

Yes, "jet plane" is its name.
The golden scales of all seas and rivers couldn't shine as it shines.
The fearful snow ridge of the sacred mountains shines below—so tiny: it has become
    a pitiful icicle.

The man is god. I'm a man. He made this indescribable swallow-fish of wind.
Thank you, man! Not the son of God the Father, but the maker,
thank you, my father, my contemporary. No one knows to which worlds
    your arrow will be thrown.
Man-God: set this swallow-fish in motion so your creative blood will shimmer
    more and more with every hour.
Hell exists! Don't lead this flying fire, lord of lords, to the world where human flesh
    is being cooked; may this golden-and-heavenly swallow
    plant new gods in your heart, every day.

Under the soft, infinite womb of the "jet plane," I feel myself more land, more man,
    more dove, more glory. My chest, my face, my hands have become all
    the flowers of the world.

My sins, my stains fade away. My body returns to sweet infancy.
Man, Lord—did you make God to reach him, or what for?
You created him to reach him and your chase is nearly over.

Beware: may the beak of this "jet," sharper than needles of earthly ice, not break
  your eyes in two
  —It's too much of a fire, too powerful, too free—this immense snow-bird.

Beware: when your son sends you the death throb, this butterfly, born from your
  creative hand, may turn your head to ashes.

Man, listen to me!
Under the body of the "jet plane" my eyes become the eyes of an eaglet to whom
  the world is first shown.

I'm not afraid. My blood is reaching the stars:
  the stars are my blood.

Don't let yourself be killed by any star, by this heavenly fish, by this god of the
  rivers that your eternal hands created.

God the Father, God the Son, God the Holy Ghost, Mountain-Gods, God Inkarri:
my body burns. Thou art me, I am thee, in the inexhaustible fury of this "jet plane."

  Don't come down to the ground.

Keep rising: fly more and more until you reach the borders of the worlds that
  boil and multiply eternally. Ride over them, Glory-God, Man-God.

You've killed the God who made you and killed you, my equal, earthly man.

You will not die anymore!

Behold: the "jet plane" is spinning, moved by the breath of gods that no longer exist,
  from the beginning and until that end nobody understands or knows.

Translated by Javier Taboada after the Spanish version by Alfredo Torero & the author

COMMENTARY

*The word "Indian" now seems to me to have a fairer basis, a fairer
content: "Indian" now means man economically and socially exploited
and, in that sense, we are all "indigenists," not only in Peru, we are all
"Indians" to a small group of exploiters. (J.M.A.)*

Mainly known as a storyteller, novelist, & ethnographer, José María Arguedas's poetry in Quechua—no matter how brief—deserves a good deal of
attention: his efforts to depict Quechua language, mythology, & culture as
living (a survivor of more than four hundred years of continuous attempts
at suppression) are truly remarkable. His poems are written in Quechua
but use Western forms, transposing oral poetics into a written medium,
& with this the introduction of new & open forms of composition that,

according to Arguedas himself, "contain, with an incomparable density and life, the matter of man and nature, and the intense link that fortunately still exists between one and the other." Yet, for his Quechua readers or listeners, some of the old oral structures remain recognizable.

Léon-Gontran Damas French Guiana, 1912–1978

HICCUPS

for Vashti and Mercer Cook

It's no good—I gulp seven swallows of water
three to four times every twenty-four hours
but my childhood comes back
in a hiccup shaking my instinct
as the cop shakes the punk

Disaster
speak to me of disaster
speak of it to me

My mother wanting a son with very good table manners
Hands on the table
bread is not cut
bread is broken
bread is not wasted
the bread of God
the bread of the sweat of your Father's brow
bread of bread
A bone is eaten with moderation and discretion
a stomach must be social
and every social stomach
does without belching
a fork is not a toothpick
do not blow your nose
so that everyone can see
or hear
and also sit up straight
nose high up
do not mop your plate

And also and also
and also in the name of the Father
the Son
and the Holy Spirit
at the end of each meal

And also and also
and also disaster
speak to me of disaster
speak of it to me

My mother wanting a memorandum from a son

If your history lesson is not learned
you will not go to mass
Sunday
in your Sunday clothes

This child will be the shame of our name
this child will be our name of God
Be quiet
Have I not told you that you must speak French
the French of France
the French of the Frenchman
the French French

Disaster
speak to me of disaster
speak of it to me

My mother wanting a son
son of his mother

You did not greet the neighbor
your shoes dirty again
and if I catch you again in the street
in the grass or in the bush
in the shadow of the Monument to the Dead
playing
romping with So-and-So
with So-and-So who was not baptized

Disaster
speak to me of disaster
speak of it to me

My mother wanting a son very do
very re
very mi
very fa
very sol
very la
very ti
very do
re-mi-fa
sol-la-ti
do

I've heard that you are still not
practicing your vi-o-lin

A banjo
a banjo you say
what do you mean
a banjo
do you really mean
a banjo
No sir
you know that in this house we do not tolerate
neither ban
nor jo
nor gui
nor tar
the "mulattos" do not do that
leave it then for the "Negroes"

Translated from French by Molly Weigel and Erik Greb

COMMENTARY

*The days themselves / have assumed the shape / of African masks / indif-
ferent / to any profanation / of quicklime* (L-G.D.)

In 1937 Léon-Gontran Damas published *Pigments*, a collection centered in
the antifascist & anticolonial discourses from the early stages of the Negritude movement. There, Damas focused on the way colonialism inserts,
absorbs, & classifies non-Western cultures (as goods) into its own schemes.
In the selection above, this process is depicted in a familial context. The hiccup symbolizes the way "the disaster" of childhood erupts (involuntarily)
into the present. Through it, Damas—with strong humor & irony—recalls
his own mother, who tried to raise him as a "gentleman": cultivated, pious,

etc. For Damas, the colonial education system is a process that empties the autochthonous identity through the accumulation of external cultural "goods" that *improve our value*. Writes the scholar Wilfred Cartey: "In the shocked indignation of his mother's voice, Damas exposes the snobbery inherent in a society where good breeding is measured by lightness of pigment, class by color" (in *Critical Perspectives on Léon-Gontran Damas*, ed. Keith Q. Warner).

Later on, for Damas, the presence of native individuals in colonial society comes from the colonizers' eagerness & insatiability for economic profit, instead of a true willingness to get in touch with other cultures. Some years later, in his *Black Label* (1956), Damas took this a step further: his criticism was now focused on those of his fellow Blacks who assumed European ways & religion (especially Catholicism). According to Damas, they voided themselves, willingly turning into Christian fanatics & humiliating their ancestors' power & wisdom.

Muriel Rukeyser   USA, 1913–1980

from **THE BOOK OF THE DEAD**

Absalom

I first discovered what was killing these men.
I had three sons who worked with their father in the tunnel:
Cecil, aged 23, Owen, aged 21, Shirley, aged 17.
They used to work in a coal mine, not steady work
for the mines were not going much of the time.
A power Co. foreman learned that we made home brew,
he formed a habit of dropping in evenings to drink,
persuading the boys and my husband—
give up their jobs and take this other work.
It would pay them better.
Shirley was my youngest son; the boy.
He went into the tunnel.

> *My heart   my mother   my heart   my mother*
> *My heart   my coming into being.*

My husband is not able to work.
He has it, according to the doctor.
We have been having a very hard time making a living since this trouble came to us.
I saw the dust in the bottom of the tub.
The boy worked there about eighteen months,

came home one evening with a shortness of breath.
He said, "Mother, I cannot get my breath."
Shirley was sick about three months.
I would carry him from his bed to the table,
from his bed to the porch, in my arms.

> *My heart is mine in the place of hearts,*
> *They gave me back my heart, it lies in me.*

When they took sick, right at the start, I saw a doctor.
I tried to get Dr. Harless to X-ray the boys.
He was the only man I had any confidence in,
the company doctor in the Kopper's mine,
but he would not see Shirley.
He did not know where his money was coming from.
I promised him half if he'd work to get compensation,
but even then he would not do anything.
I went on the road and begged the X-ray money,
the Charleston hospital made the lung pictures,
he took the case after the pictures were made.
And two or three doctors said the same thing.
The youngest boy did not get to go down there with me,
he lay and said, "Mother, when I die,
I want you to have them open me up and
see if that dust killed me.
Try to get compensation,
you will not have any way of making your living
when we are gone,
and the rest are going too."

> *I have gained mastery over my heart*
> *I have gained mastery over my two hands*
> *I have gained mastery over the waters*
> *I have gained mastery over the river.*

The case of my son was the first of the line of lawsuits.
They sent the lawyers down and the doctors down;
they closed the electric sockets in the camps.
There was Shirley, and Cecil, Jeffrey and Oren,
Raymond Johnson, Clev and Oscar Anders,
Frank Lynch, Henry Palf, Mr. Pitch, a foreman;
a slim fellow who carried steel with my boys,
his name was Darnell, I believe. There were many others,
the towns of Glen Ferris, Alloy, where the white rock lies,

six miles away; Vanetta, Gauley Bridge,
Gamoca, Lockwood, the gullies,
the whole valley is witness.
I hitchhike eighteen miles, they make checks out.
They asked me how I keep the cow on $2.
I said one week, feed for the cow, one week, the children's flour.
The oldest son was twenty-three.
The next son was twenty-one.
The youngest son was eighteen.
They called it pneumonia at first.
They would pronounce it fever.
Shirley asked that we try to find out.
That's how they learned what the trouble was.

> *I open out a way, they have covered my sky with crystal*
> *I come forth by day, I am born a second time,*
> *I force a way through, and I know the gate*
> *I shall journey over the earth among the living.*

He shall not be diminished, never;
I shall give a mouth to my son.

COMMENTARY

No more masks! No more mythologies! // Now, for the first time, the god lifts his hand, // the fragments join in me with their own music. (M.R.)

(1) Rukeyser in her poetry—emergent already in the 1930s—shows a persistent commitment to political & social action (human rights, the 1960s–1970s antiwar movement, a newly resurgent feminism), while experimenting still more boldly with the form & content of her poems. Describing the breadth of her work in the preface to her *Collected Poems* (1978), she placed it between "early lyrics and two kinds of reaching in poetry, one based on the document, the evidence itself, the other kind informed by the unverifiable fact, as in sex, dream, the parts of life in which we dive deep and sometimes—with strength of expression and skill and luck—reach that place where things are shared and we all recognize the secrets." To which she added, wisely: "Underneath all, the experience itself—a trust in the rhythms of experience."

(2) "Written in response to the Hawk's Nest Tunnel disaster of 1931 in Gauley Bridge, West Virginia, *The Book of the Dead* is an important part of West Virginia's cultural heritage and a powerful account of one of the worst industrial catastrophes in American history... a tragedy that killed hundreds of workers, most of them African-American" (Abby Freeland).

Aimé Césaire Martinique, 1913–2008

IT IS MYSELF, TERROR, IT IS MYSELF

Stranded dried up dreams flush with the muzzles of rivers create
formidable piles of mute bones
the too swift hopes crawl scrupulously
like tamed snakes
one does not leave one never leaves
as for me I have halted, faithful, on the island
standing like Prester John slightly sideways to the sea
and sculptured at snout level by waves and bird droppings
things things it is to you that I give
my crazed violent face ripped open in the whirlpool's depths
my face tender with fragile coves where lymphs are warming
it is myself terror it is myself
the brother of this volcano which certain without saying a word
ruminates an indefinable something that is sure
and passage as well for birds of the wind
which often stop to sleep for a season
it is thyself sweetness it is thyself
run through by the eternal sword
and the entire day advancing
branded with the red-hot iron of foundered things
and of recollected sun

Translated from French by Clayton Eshleman and Annette Smith

TO THE SERPENT

I have had occasion in the bewilderment of cities to search for the right animal
    to adore. So I worked my way back to the first times. Undoing cycles untying
    knots crushing plots removing covers killing hostages I searched.
Ferret. Tapir. Uprooter.
Where wherewhere the animal who warned me of floods
Where wherewhere the bird who led me to honey
Where wherewhere the bird who revealed to me the fountainheads
the memory of great alliances betrayed great friendships lost through our fault
    exalted me
Where wherewhere

Wherewherewhere

The word made vulgar to me

O serpent sumptuous back do you enclose in your sinuous lash the powerful
soul of my grandfather?

Greetings to you serpent through whom morning shakes its beautiful mango
mauve December chevelure and for whom the milk-invented night tumbles its
luminous mice down its wall

Greetings to you serpent grooved like the bottom of the sea and which my heart
truly unbinds for us like the premise of the deluge

Greetings to you serpent your reputation is more majestic than their gait and the
peace their God gives not you hold supremely.

Serpent delirium and peace

over the hurdles of a scurrilous wind the countryside dismembers for me secrets
whose steps resounded at the outlet of the millenary trap of gorges that they
tightened to strangulation.

to the trashcan! may they all rot in portraying the banner of a black crow
weakening in a beating of white wings.

Serpent

broad and royal disgust overpowering the return in the sands of deception

spindrift nourishing the vain raft of the seagull

in the pale tempest of reassuring silences you the least frail warm yourself

You bathe yourself this side of the most discordant cries on the dreamy spumes
of grass

when fire is exhaled from the widow boat that consumes the cape of the echo's
flash

just to make your successive deaths shiver all the more—green frequenting of the
elements—your threat.

Your threat yes your threat body issuant from the raucous haze of bitterness
where it corrupted the concerned lighthouse keeper and that whistling takes
its little gallop time toward the assassin rays of discovery.

Serpent

charming biter of women's breasts and through whom death steals into the
maturity in the depths of a fruit sole lord lord alone whose multiple image
places on the strangler fig's altar the offering of a chevelure that is an
octopodal threat a sagacious hand that does not pardon cowards

Translated from French by Clayton Eshleman & A. James Arnold

A man screaming is not a dancing bear. Life is not a spectacle. (A.C.) And again: *I would rediscover the secret of great communications and great combustions. I would say storm. I would say river. I would say tornado. I would say leaf. I would say tree. I would be drenched by all rains, moistened by all dews. I would roll like frenetic blood on the slow current of the eye of words turned into mad horses into fresh children into clots into curfew into vestiges of temples into precious stones remote enough to discourage miners. Whoever would not understand me would not understand any better the roaring of a tiger.* (trans. Clayton Eshleman)

Indelibly associated with Negritude & a powerful anticolonial poetics, the ferocity & intelligence of Aimé Césaire's work was identified early & described precisely by Jean-Paul Sartre: "What then did you expect when you unbound the gag that muted those black mouths? That they would chant your praises? Did you think that when those heads that our fathers had forcibly bowed down to the ground were raised again, you would find adoration in their eyes?"

For more on Césaire & Negritude, see "A Map of Americas."

ADDENDUM

RACHEL BLAU DUPLESSIS USA, 1941–

from **Eurydics**: Snake

> Large green-tailed lizard, zucchini-mottled
> flicks and swirls. But, no! It's not some random lizard:
> that's the snake! A rill of water falling up the stone,
> he'd heard my light, quick foot   as human-hard.
>
> And the dream? that wildly handsome man
> who had no wife,   his wife had "gone away"
> (but where?)   so he wanted to meet more   women
> he needed help   with his decor, his place
>
> was encumbered with little ceramic, clay-
> kitsch banalities—   I did not see the snake's head,
> since it faced away.   I could not fix
>
> it being *vipera* or *serpente*.
> That question hinged on poison in his mix.
>
> From what I saw, though, 'twas a very handsome snake.

Options:
"scaled to the human boy" or was it "scaled to the human body"?
  Which did I write?

Options:
Desire? temptation? yearning for danger? thralldom? lust? You can
  add to the list yourself. You can add yourself to the list.

Options:
Teasing enchantment. "How still the Riddle lies."

Options:
Insistent   "Shaft"   "a tighter Breathing"

The sibyl's many leaves are laurel made for wreathing.

Octavio Paz Mexico, 1914–1998

from **BLANCO**

From yellow to red to green
pilgrimage to the clarities
the word peers out from blue
whirls.
          The drunk ring spins,
the five senses spin
around the centripetal
amethyst.
          Dazzle:
I don't think, I see
                    —not what I see,
the reflections, the thoughts I see.
Precipitations of music
crystallized number.
An archipielago of signs.
Translucence,
                    mouth of truths,
clarity effaced by a syllabe
diaphanous as silence:

I don't think, I see

                —not what I think,

blank face of forgetting

radiant void.

I lose my shadow,

                I walk

through intangible forests,

sudden sculptures of the wind,

endless things,

                sharpened paths

I walk,

        my steps

                dissolving

in a space that evaporates

into thoughts I don't think

you fall from your body to your shadow *not there but in my eyes*
in a motionless falling of waterfall *sky and earth joining*
you fall from your shadow to your name *untouchable horizon*
you drop through your likenesses *I am your remoteness*
you fall from your name to your body *the furthest point of seeing*
in a present that never ends *the imaginings of sand*
you fall to your beginning *scattered fables of wind*
spilling on my body *I am the stela of your erosion*
you divide me like parts of speech *space quartered god*
you divide me into your parts *altar of thought and knife*
belly theater of blood *axis of the solstices*
tree of ivy firebrand tongue of coolness *the heavens are male and female*
earthquake of your thighs *testimony of solar testicles*
rain of your heels on my back *thought phallus and word womb*
jaguar eye in the eyelash thicket *space is body sign thought*
the flesh-colored cleft in the brambles *always two syllables in love*
the black lips of the oracle *P r o p h e c y*
whole in each part you divide yourself *spirals transfigurations*
your body is the bodies of the moment *time world is body*
thought dreamt made flesh *seen touch dissolved*

seen by my ears   *horizon of music spreading*
smelled by my eyes   *bridge hung from color to smell*
caressed by my nose   *naked smell in the hands of air*
heard by my tongue   *canticle of flavors*
eaten by my touch   *feast of mist*

to inhabit your name   *to depopulate your body*
to fall in your shriek with you   *house of the wind*

    The unreality of the seen
    brings reality to seeing

Translated from Spanish by Eliot Weinberger

COMMENTARY

The word of man / is the daughter of death. / We talk because we are mortal: / words are not signs, they are years. / Saying what they say, / the words we are saying / say time: they name us. / We are time's names. // To talk is human. (O.P.)

(1) A visible poet since the 1930s, Paz in the immediate postwar years made a close connection with André Breton & the surviving Surrealists, then came to international prominence in the aftermath of poems like *Sun Stone* (1957) & gatherings of essays like the influential *Labyrinth of Solitude* (1950). Of his time & place (&, by implication, our place within it), he writes: "The poetry starting up in this second half of the century is not really starting. Nor is it returning to the point of departure. The poet beginning now, without beginning, is looking for the intersections of times, the point of convergence. It asserts that poetry is the present, between the cluttered past and the uninhabited future. The re-production is a presentation. Pure time: heartbeat of the present in the moment of its appearance/disappearance."

(2) In *Blanco*, Paz works off a structure of several columns which serve as the carriers for a number of independent &/or counterpointed poems. Of the intended effect he writes: "*Blanco* was meant to be read as a succession of signs on a single page. As the reading progresses, the page unfolds vertically, a space which, as it opens out, allows the text to appear and, in a certain sense, creates it.... This arrangement of temporal order is the form adopted by the course of the poem: its discourse to another which is spatial: the separate parts which comprise the poem are distributed like the sections, colors, symbols, and figures of a mandala." And further, of the poem's title: "Blanco: white, blank; an unmarked space; emptiness; void; the white mark in the center of a target" (trans. Eliot Weinberger).

N.B. The lines presented here in italics were printed in red ink in the original Spanish version.

Nicanor Parra Chile, 1914–2018

THE INDIVIDUAL'S SOLILOQUY

I'm the individual.
First I lived by a rock
(I scratched some figures on it)
Then I looked for some place more suitable.
I'm the individual.
First I had to get myself food,
Hunt for fish, birds, hunt up wood
(I'd take care of the rest later)
Make a fire,
Wood, wood, where could I find any wood,
Some wood to start a little fire.
I'm the individual.
At the time I was asking myself,
Went to a canyon filled with air;
A voice answered me back:
I'm the individual.
So then I started moving to another rock,
I also scratched figures there,
Scratched out a river, buffaloes,
Scratched a serpent
I'm the individual.
But I got bored with what I was doing,
Fire annoyed me,
I wanted to see more,
I'm the individual.
Went down to a valley watered by a river,
There I found what I was looking for,
A bunch of savages,
A tribe,
I'm the individual.
I saw they made certain things,
Scratching figures on the rocks,
Making fire, also making fire!
I'm the individual.
They asked me where I came from.
I answered yes, that I had no definite plans,
I answered no, that from here on out.

O.K.
I then took a stone I found in the river
And began working on it,
Polishing it up,
I made it a part of my life.
But it's a long story.
I chopped some trees to sail on
Looking for fish,
Looking for lots of things,
(I'm the individual.)
Till I began getting bored again.
Storms get boring,
Thunder, lightning,
I'm the individual.
O.K.
I began thinking a little bit,
Stupid questions came into my head,
Doubletalk.
So then I began wandering through forests,
I came to a tree, then another tree,
I came to a spring,
A hole with a couple of rats in it;
So here I come, I said,
Anybody seen a tribe around here,
Savage people who make fire?
That's how I moved on westward,
Accompanied by others,
Or rather alone,
Believing is seeing, they told me,
I'm the individual.
I saw shapes in the darkness,
Clouds maybe,
Maybe I saw clouds, or sheet lightning,
Meanwhile several days had gone by,
I felt as if I were dying;
Invented some machines,
Constructed clocks,
Weapons, vehicles,
I'm the individual.
Hardly had time to bury my dead,
Hardly had time to sow,

I'm the individual.
Years later I conceived a few things,
A few forms,
Crossed frontiers,
And got stuck in a kind of niche,
In a bark that sailed forty days,
Forty nights,
I'm the individual.
Then came the droughts,
Then came the wars,
Colored guys entered the valley,
But I had to keep going,
Had to produce.
Produced science, immutable truths,
Produced Tanagras,
Hatched up thousand-page books.
My face got swollen,
Invented a phonograph,
The sewing machine,
The first automobiles began to appear,
I'm the individual.
Someone set up planets,
Trees got set up!
But I set up hardware,
Furniture, stationery,
I'm the individual.
Cities also got built,
Highways,
Religious institutions went out of fashion,
They looked for joy, they looked for happiness,
I'm the individual.
Afterward I devoted myself to travel,
Practicing, practicing languages
Languages,
I'm the individual.
I looked into a keyhole,
Sure, I looked, what am I saying, looked,
To get rid of all doubt looked,
Behind the curtains,
I'm the individual.
O.K.

Perhaps I better go back to that valley,
To that rock that was home,
And start scratching all over again,
Scratching out everything backward,
The world in reverse.
But life doesn't make sense.

Translated from Spanish by Lawrence Ferlinghetti and Allen Ginsberg

from SERMONS AND HOMILIES OF THE CHRIST OF ELQUI

I

Although I came prepared to speak to you
I really don't know where I should begin
I'll start by taking off my glasses
if you think this beard is false it isn't
I haven't cut it for 22 years
for the same reason that I don't cut my nails
to fulfill a sacred vow
going further than necessary
since the pledge was only set for twenty
I haven't cut my beard or my nails
except for my toenails
in honor of my sainted mother
just because of that I've had to suffer
indignities scorn and humiliation
although I wasn't bothering anyone
only keeping a sacred promise
made the day my mother died
not to cut my beard or my nails
for a period of twenty years
paying homage to that sacred memory
and to renounce the wearing of common clothing
replacing it with this humble sackcloth
Now I can tell you my secret
the penance finally over and done with
soon you'll be able to see me
in plain clothes again.

.....

VIII

I'm really more of an herb doctor than a wizard
I don't claim to solve unsolvable problems
instead I cure I calm the troubled spirit
I can expel a demon from a body
where I lay my hand it goes in up to the elbow
but I don't raise up rotten cadavers
the whole sublime art of resurrection
I leave exclusively to the Divine Master.

. . . . .

XXVI

To sum it all up
to mistake a leaf for a leaf
to mistake a branch for a branch
to confuse a forest with a forest
is to be a fool
this is the quintessence of my doctrine
you're starting to get the hang of it, happily
things are becoming clear to you
now you can see that clouds are not clouds
rivers are not rivers
rocks are not rocks
they're altars!
                    columns!
                              domes!
it's time to say mass.

Translated from Spanish by Sandra Reyes

COMMENTARY

The Nobel Prize for Reading / should be awarded to me / I am the ideal reader / I read everything I get my hands on / I read street names / and neon signs / bathroom walls / and new price lists . . . (N.P.) And further on: *For a person like me / the world is something holy.*

(1) Throughout his very long life, Chilean poet Nicanor Parra developed one of the most definitive & influential post–avant-gardes in American literature: *Antipoetry,* a kind of omnipoetics centered on the use of the common (vernacular) language to produce—effectively—that "disordering of all the senses" that Rimbaud longed for. Born in San Fabián de Alico, Parra studied physics & mathematics. In the 1940s he went abroad to specialize

in physics in the United States & Great Britain. During this time, he became familiar with US & British poetics practice, which widened his perspective or seemed to. In 1954, two years after his return to Chile, he published *Poemas y antipoemas*, the emergence of the Antipoetic model.

(2) For Parra, the language of the poetry of his time (especially Neruda's) was devoid of meaning & had become a mere rhetorical device: pulpit poetry, sterile & unable to be reached—much less created—by the common man. Hence his statement *everything is poetry except for poetry* meant a radical opening for new forms of expression (including visuals, sound, etc.). And for Parra, again, Antipoetry was any text that aimed to break the dying principles of the so-called poetic genres, using instead a living language. Hence the term "anti," as with other forms of anti-art that emerged in the early twentieth century, points to the double process of disintegration-reintegration of language & text &, in turn, the disintegration of the canonical tradition. The Antipoetic project replaces the "writing" of poetry with its rewriting.

Gwendolyn Brooks USA, 1917–2000

RIOT

> *A riot is the language of the unheard.*
> Martin Luther King

John Cabot, out of Wilma, once a Wycliffe,
all whitebluerose below his golden hair,
wrapped richly in right linen and right wool,
almost forgot his Jaguar and Lake Bluff;
almost forgot Grandtully (which is The
Best Thing That Ever Happened To Scotch); almost
forgot the sculpture at the Richard Gray
and Distelheim; the kidney pie at Maxim's,
the Grenadine de Boeuf at Maison Henri.

Because the Negroes were coming down the street.

Because the Poor were sweaty and unpretty
(not like Two Dainty Negroes in Winnetka)
and they were coming toward him in rough ranks.
In seas. In windsweep. They were black and loud.
And not detainable. And not discreet.

Gross. Gross. "*Que tu es grossier!*" John Cabot
itched instantly beneath the nourished white
that told his story of glory to the World.
"Don't let It touch me! the blackness! Lord!" he whispered
to any handy angel in the sky.
But, in a thrilling announcement, on It drove
and breathed on him: and touched him. In that breath
the fume of pig foot, chitterling and cheap chili,
malign, mocked John. And, in terrific touch, old
averted doubt jerked forward decently,
cried "Cabot! John! You are a desperate man,
and the desperate die expensively today."

John Cabot went down in the smoke and fire
and broken glass and blood, and he cried "Lord!
Forgive these nigguhs that know not what they do."

COMMENTARY

*Book burnings. Always the forerunners. Heralds of the stake, the ovens,
the mass graves.* (G.B.) And again: *If there is one class of person I have
never quite trusted, it is a man who knows no doubt.* Or: *I felt the reckless
abandon of one who knows she stands already among the damned. "Why
not, then, another sin?"*

Richard Wright responded to his first exposure to Brooks's poems thus:
"They are hard and real, right out of the central core of Black Belt Negro
life in urban areas.... There is no self-pity here, not a striving for effect. She
takes hold of reality as it is and renders it faithfully. There is not so much
an exhibiting of Negro life to whites in these poems as there is an honest
human reaction to the pain that lurks so colorfully in the Black Belt.... She
easily catches the pathos of petty destinies; the whimper of the wounded;
the tiny incidents that plague the lives of the desperately poor, and the
problem of color prejudice among Negroes.... Only one who has actually
lived and suffered in a kitchenette could render the feeling of lonely frustration as well as she does:—of how dreams are drowned out by the noises,
smells, and the frantic desire to grab one's chance to get a bath when the
bathroom is empty. Miss Brooks is real and so are her poems."

Brooks herself notes that she wrote "to prove to others (by implication,
not by shouting) and to such among themselves who have yet to discover it,
that they are merely human beings, not exotics."

Robert Duncan USA, 1919–1988

OFTEN I AM PERMITTED TO RETURN TO A MEADOW

as if it were a scene made-up by the mind,
that is not mine, but is a made place,
that is mine, it is so near to the heart,
an eternal pasture folded in all thought
so that there is a hall therein

that is a made place, created by light
wherefrom the shadows that are forms fall.

Wherefrom fall all architectures I am
I say are likenesses of the First Beloved
whose flowers are flames lit to the Lady.

She it is Queen Under The Hill
whose hosts are a disturbance of words within words
that is a field folded.

It is only a dream of the grass blowing
east against the source of the sun
in an hour before the sun's going down

whose secret we see in a children's game
of ring a round of roses told.

Often I am permitted to return to a meadow
as if it were a given property of the mind
that certain bounds hold against chaos,

that is a place of first permission,
everlasting omen of what is.

PASSAGES 18: THE TORSO

Most beautiful! the red-flowering eucalyptus,
        the madrone, the yew
            Is he . . .

So thou wouldst smile, and take me in thine arms
The sight of London to my exiled eyes
Is as Elysium to a new-come soul

If he be Truth
I would dwell in the illusion of him

His hands unlocking from chambers of my male body

such an idea in man's image

rising tides that sweep me towards him

...*homosexual?*

and at the treasure of his mouth

pour forth my soul

his soul   commingling

I thought a Being more than vast, His body leading
into Paradise,   his eyes
quickening a fire in me,   a trembling

hieroglyph: At the root of the neck

the clavicle, for the neck is the stem of the great artery
upward into his head that is beautiful

At the rise of the pectoral muscles

the nipples, for the breasts are like sleeping fountains
of feeling in man, waiting above the heat of his heart,
shielding the rise and fall of his breath, to be
awakened

At the axis of his midriff

the navel, for in the pit of his stomach the chord from
which first he was fed has its temple

At the root of the groin

the pubic hair, for the torso is the stem in which the man
flowers forth and leads to the stamen of flesh in which
his seed rises

a wave of need and desire over   taking me

cried out my name

(This was long ago.   It was another life)

and said,

What do you want of me?

I do not know, I said.   I have fallen in love.   He
        has brought me into heights and depths my heart
                would fear   without him.   His look

        pierces my side   ·   fire eyes   ·

    I have been waiting for you, he said:
                I know what you desire

        you do not yet know   but through me.

    And I am with you everywhere.   In your falling

I have fallen from a high place.   I have raised myself

        from darkness in your   rising

                        wherever you are

        my hand in your hand   seeking   the locks, the keys

I am there.   Gathering me, you gather

        your Self   ·

    For my Other is not a woman but a man

    the King upon whose bosom let me lie.

COMMENTARY

*I am speaking now of the Dream in which America sleeps, the New
World, moaning, floundering, in three hundred years of invasions, our
own history out of Europe and enslaved Africa.* (R.D.) And again: *A multiphasic experience sought a multiphasic form.*

(1) Robert Duncan was, in the end, a poet of enormous means & complexity—one of the last to assay a cosmological poetics, to be "the model of the
poet," as Michael Davidson described him, "for whom all of reality can
enter the poem." As such he was (he made himself) a man & poet open to
multiple influences, accepting & announcing against all "anxieties of influence" a sense of his own *derivativeness/derivations* that freed others to do
the same. One has only to think of the remarkable lists of predecessors—&
contemporaries—that filled his essays or, by collage & paraphrase, came
into his poems.

(2) In the same vein, he tells us, memorably: "I make poetry as other men make war or make love or make states or revolutions: to exercise my faculties at large." It is the kind of statement that placed him, by its bravado & because the poetry itself had also proved it, among that visionary company of which he knew he was a part. And that company could then be extended in every direction—noble & lowly—toward the greater symposium of the whole that he prophesied in his later "Rites of Participation" & that he saw already forming in his time & ours. What he offered then & later—in spite of any shifting moods & weathers—was a generosity of spirit or, more immediately, a poetics *of* the spirit, even where the generosity might seem to falter. It was an acknowledgment of, & an insistence on, the spiritual in art, as Kandinsky might have known it: an inspired reminder of what art & poetry still could be & a vision—through Whitman &/or Dante &/or others—of a totalizing universality that included & surpassed all separate individuals & species.

Against the odds, or on a par with them.

(3) Of his four-decade-long friendship & marriage to artist/poet Jess (Collins) & their life together as "householders" in common, the following:

> *The Life we at once lead and follow, that has recognized itself in and realized itself in, illustrated itself, furnisht [sic] itself with chairs, tables, dressers, bedsteads, books, paintings, objects, mementos, dishes, utensils, and the tools and materials of our arts in life, expands now into terms of a house. A house to be "ours" or rather to be us, where the very floors and walls will be terms of our entering life.*

And further, as Kate Sutton has it in her interview with Duncan: "Their relationship, both as lovers and creative fellow travelers, was an echo chamber of ideas, in which they lived with their sources as a kind of surrogate family, condensed in Duncan's term 'the household'.... Both men maintained separate practices, even as those practices occasionally followed parallel trajectories. As Duncan proudly put it, 'We have had the medium of a life together.'"

Eunice Odio Costa Rica, 1919–1974

from **THE FIRE'S JOURNEY**

Part III: The Cathedral's Work

DEDALUS
It is time. The gifts of morning
now begin to emit their sound

ION

Go see if the sun has arrived

DEDALUS

It's taking its time

ION

Let's wait

DEDALUS

It's late

ION

Give me my shoes

DEDALUS

The sun is rising

ION

Go see if the new olive's branches
resisted the winter season

DEDALUS

Woods, floods of rain and dew
went through the branches and it never gave in

Let's leave...

ION

Wait!

DEDALUS

You delay your departure. You're here bound to your body,
immobile and anchored
in this flint that never stops.
Go, my friend, take a great terrestrial leap

ION

You don't understand, you don't know that when I leave
a part of me will remain expanded and in awe;

and when I am set loose in pain
an impenetrable eye will escape,

it loses me, taking exile from me
and remains orbiting amid the domains
and dominations of granite

DEDALUS

After completing the work, they all have left,
we must leave

ION

We must

DEDALUS

Let's go

ION

Go ask for bread

DEDALUS

We'll find it on the way

ION

Go ask for bread!

DEDALUS

Is the cathedral not complete?
Does it need to be perfected in grace?

ION

Go, you noise and cry of my forehead!
Leave me alone, intimate ray, solitary presence!

DEDALUS

I am going toward myself; I'm leaving, but I won't be long

ION

Nothing is missing. Nothing.

Lightning wanders up above...

Naves, make room for it; ribs, shape it!

From the earth the face must be seen, from the earth.
It is the passing of a flame in search of its ashes.

The burning spirit is on the face,
it is summoned to witness.

Oh, Cathedral, you begin the morning!

Where the air ends you resume your movement;

where He begins to let go of His inaudible Voice
there you hurry and calm yourself;

there you plant your wave
barely interrupted by spatial zones.

I look up, I traverse my forehead,
and my face cannot reach up to grasp you.

How can I reach your luminous harmony,
your dimension flying through interior skies,

everything uprooted by the olive trees
orbiting in sacred swirls, in linear silences?

There is nothing in you I would not entrust
to found the joyful order;

your animal organs where the air lives
taken through the air toward paradise;

the broken atmosphere that follows you
like a vast greyhound and repeats your spatial acts.

Oh, unending word!
Oh, unending delirious flint!

The arches that announce you from above
were appeased in the wind

The patriarchs and pinnacles hold back,
they retain the swift smile of matter.

The South, spotless, the absolute South,
clear and fortified over the spire's needle,
finds its first movement
where it receives the breeze's crowns
and imparts meridians and regions
inherited before birth.

Oh, Cathedral, oh palace of flight!
Oh, edifice on its journey through dawn!

By day, we have found your earth amid laurels;
it was chosen among all the grounds,
among all the territories

to serve as a stage and border for the angels.

The apse is an indestructible wall,
the capital, a clearing in solitude;

the flying buttress,

one who began in eternity.

The sky pauses when you pass by, pure,
unpredictable residence of the air, Cathedral
capital of the heights, a straight delirious flower.

The sky pauses
when you pass by, as you become a visible ecstasy

Translated from Spanish by Keith Ekiss, Sonia P. Ticas, & Mauricio Espinoza

COMMENTARY

The word that will make the cupolas soar / and bloom on the tongue of the dead, / a new word unborn and blind, / renewing the origin of silence in the verb. (E.O.) And then: *I will show touch what darkness is / and darkness will seize it.*

(1) Eunice Odio's work is one of the most outstanding of the previous century, although she spent most of her life—as did others—unrecognized. Born in Costa Rica, which she fled at twenty-eight (never to return), she settled first in Guatemala, then in New York, & finally in Mexico, where she died in 1974. One of her English translators, Keith Ekiss, wrote: "Odio herself was aware of her marginalized, self-exiled position. Octavio Paz once told her that she was 'of that line of poets who invent their own mythology, like Blake, like St.-John Perse, like Ezra Pound; and they are rubbed out, because no one understands them until years or even centuries after their death.'" Although published in 1957, her masterwork *The Fire's Journey*, a monumental poem with more than ten thousand lines, is now slowly being recognized & acclaimed by both critics & readers.

(2) The main characters of *The Fire's Journey* are Ion—the poet/rhapsode addressed by Socrates in one of Plato's most famous dialogues—& the mythical crafter of the ancient Greek world, Daedalus ("Dedalus" in the translation). In an excellent piece about Odio's mythopoetics (called "The Creation of Herself"), Sharon Mesmer explains the nature & the scope of *The Fire's Journey*: "It is a process: the process of creation by and through the Word.... Odio's Ion is a poet-god, purveying (as well as creating) sacred language to bring the world into being. Like a shaman, he will embark upon a descent/journey to restore order and bring healing. [Thus,

the creation process] was indeed a projection of an artist-god," but with the introduction/identification with Daedalus, this process passes "from creation-by-speech to creation-by-craft."

This double feature is nothing less than *poesis* at its best.

João Cabral de Melo Neto Brazil, 1920–1999

DAILY SPACE

In the daily space
the shadow eats the orange
the orange throws itself into the river
it's not a river, it's the sea
overflowing from my eye.

In the daily space
born out of the clock

I see hands not words,
late at night I dream up the woman

I have the woman and the fish.

In the daily space
I forget the home the sea
I lose hunger memory
I kill myself uselessly
in the daily space.

Translated from Portuguese by W. S. Merwin

PSYCHOLOGY OF COMPOSITION (VII)

It's mineral the paper
on which to write
verse; verse
that is possible not to make.
Mineral are
flowers and plants,
fruits, animals

when in a state of words.
Mineral
the horizon line,
our names, those things
made of words.
Mineral, at last,
any book:
'cause the written
word is mineral, the cold nature
of the written word.

Translated from Portuguese by Charles Bernstein
with Horacio Costa & Régis Bonvicino

COMMENTARY

No one will write the final poem / about this private twelve o'clock
world. / Instead of the last judgment, what worries me / is the final dream.
(J.C.deM.N.) And then: *Poetry is not the product of inspiration triggered by*
feeling, but the product of the poet's patient and lucid work.

(1) But João Cabral de Melo Neto's actual focus on the concrete & material resulted in a highly physical poetry that aims to rebuild the "daily
space," attentive to social reality. According to Richard Zenith, one of his
translators, "Cabral's project is to re-create the world, taking the things—
both abstract and concrete—that are common to all men and turning them
around, making them uncommon, conferring on them the dimension they
lacked." And moving it further on, Augusto de Campos wrote: "His poetry
sustains, continues, expands and broadens a poetic language that is not
sentimental, but objective: a poetry of the concrete, a critical poetry, as
João's poetry is."

(2) Highly skeptical of a projected transnational dialogue between Northern & Southern literatures, Cabral wrote: "The Northern reader—that is,
in one of the more developed countries—has a tendency to value Southern
literature for its *costumbrista* or picturesque features, that is, for its exoti-
cism. The Northern reader knows about Southern literatures only when
they are translated or written in his language, and only occasionally and
from sporadic samples. He does not integrate them into the body of universal literature (which for him is that of the North)... "
Against which his own work functions as a true denial.

Pòl Larak (Paul Laraque)   Haiti, 1920–2007

LAKANSYÈL/RAINBOW

It's a ribbon tied to the rain's hair
It's a multicolored belt round the waist of a little darling
It's a talisman to chase the evil eye away
It's a lasso round the sun's neck
to make him come back and light up the earth

Rainbow plunges behind mountains
they say it goes to drink
all the way down to the head of the water
Ogun grumbles like bamboo
the siren went off to make love

Two little fish climb up
to watch Queen Simbi dance the *banda*
my hat fell into the sea
when a little breeze blows
all the boats' sails will swell

Rainbow is a bridle in the thunder's mouth
It's the fright pushing back wars
It's a shot of white rum after the cockfights
we can all beat the drums
sing the loas and dance voodoo
It's a sickle to weed out misery
It's a big collective to tear out poverty
to make water run in every garden
so hoes under the sun can throw off lightning
a collective reaching all the way to Guinea
all the way to the other side of the sea
a collective of comrades of every color
to transform the earth
to tame the mean ones
to change our life

Translated from Haitian Creole by Paul Laraque, Boadiba, & Jack Hirschman

To Angela Davis judged
for the double crime of being
a communist and a black woman.

There are words that burn
Like torches in the forest of the night
There are words that can ford rivers
Words that open the doors of History
Like a key
There are words that can string the bow of revolution
And arm the peoples with the arrows of victory

There are words sweet on our lips
As the mouth of a woman
And which strike our heart like the spear of love
White Christ of black Virgin
The hangmen slog away at raising your cross
They want to cut the rose of hope
But they can't extinguish the thicket of your voice

There are words
That cure the ills
Other words bring us
There are words
Sharp as knives
Action alone makes the dreams of poetry real
And from now through you real life is here

Translated from Haitian Creole by Paul Laraque, Boadiba, & Jack Hirschman

COMMENTARY

I've been living in the only hope of men / Who leave today behind so tomorrow can be born / One day I'll be in front of my people / To forge happiness out of the weapons of poverty (P.L.)

The continuity, as elsewhere, is in the language—the resistance also—emerging here in a new/old literature drawing on deep resources in Haitian spirit & mind (*esprit*). Writes Pòl Larak (Paul Laraque) as one of the founders of that literature: "Creole is, with voodoo, one of the most important elements of Haitian culture. It is a mixture of French, spoken by the white masters, and of the Black slaves' African languages and dialects, during colonial times. It can be either a revolutionary tool in the interests of the masses, or a reactionary one if manipulated by the cruel exploiting classes. It is a beautiful language with the rhythm of the drum and the images of a dream, especially in its poetry, and a powerful weapon in the struggle of our people for national and social liberation."

Jackson Mac Low USA, 1922–2004

1ST LIGHT POEM: FOR IRIS—10 JUNE 1962

The light of a student-lamp
sapphire light
shimmer
the light of a smoking-lamp

Light from the Magellanic Clouds
the light of a Nernst lamp
the light of a naphtha-lamp
light from meteorites

Evanescent light
ether
the light of an electric lamp
extra light

Citrine light
kineographic light
the light of a Kitson lamp
kindly light

Ice light
irradiation
ignition
altar light

The light of a spotlight
a sunbeam
sunrise
solar light

Mustard-oil light
maroon light

the light of a magnesium flare
light from a meteor

Evanescent light
ether
light from an electric lamp
an extra light

Light from a student-lamp
sapphire light
a shimmer
smoking-lamp light

Ordinary light
orgone lumination
light from a lamp burning olive oil
opal light

Actinism
atom-bomb light
the light of an alcohol lamp
the light of a lamp burning anda-oil

32ND LIGHT POEM: IN MEMORIAM PAUL BLACKBURN
9–10 OCTOBER 1971

Let me choose the kinds of light
to light the passing of my friend
Paul Blackburn   a poet

A pale light like that of a winter dawn
or twilight
or phosphorescence

is not enough to guide him in his passing
but enough for us to see
shadowily his last gaunt figure

how he showed himself to us
last July in Michigan
when he made us think he was recovering

knowing the carcinoma
arrested in his esophagus
had already spread to his bones

How he led us on
I spent so little time with him
thinking he'd be with us now

Amber light of regret
stains my memories of our days
at the poetry festival in Allendale Michigan

How many times I hurried elsewhere
rather than spending time with him
in his room 3 doors from me

I will regret it the rest of my life
I must learn to live
with the regret

dwelling on the moments
Paul & I shared
in July as in years before

tho amber light dims to umber
& I can hardly see
his brave emaciated face

I see Paul standing in the umber light
cast on his existence
by his knowing that his death was fast approaching
Lightning blasts the guilty dream
& I see him
reading in the little auditorium

& hear him
confidently reading
careful of his timing

anxious not to take
more than his share of reading time
filling our hearts with rejoicing

seeing him alive
doing the work he was here for
seemingly among us now

I for one was fooled
thinking he was winning the battle
so I wept that night for joy

As I embraced him after he read
I shook with relief & love
I was so happy to hear you read again

If there were a kind of black light
that suddenly cd reveal to us
each other's inwardness

what wd I have seen that night
as I embraced you
with tears of joy

I keep remembering the bolt of lightning
that slashed the sky at twilight
over the Gulf of St. Lawrence

& turned an enchanted walk with Bici
following Angus Willie's Brook
thru mossy woods nearly to its mouth

to a boot-filling scramble up thru thorn bush & spruce tangle
Beatrice guided me & I was safe
at the end of August on Cape Breton Island

but when Jerry telephoned me of your death
the lightning that destroyed
the illusion you were safe

led thru dreadful amber light
not to friendly car light
& welcoming kitchen light

but the black light of absence
not ultraviolet light
revealing hidden colors

but revelatory light that is no light
the unending light of the realization
that no light will ever light your bodily presence again

Now your poems' light is all
The unending light of your presence
in the living light of your voice

*o blessèd chance continue to happen to me! / For I wd never plan so
well—I wd have died of my planning.* (J.M.L.)

It was the range of Mac Low's experimental compositions that made him,
along with John Cage, one of the two major artists to have brought sys-
tematic chance (aleatory) procedures into our poetic & musical practice
since the Second World War. In the present instance, a series of sixty "light
poems" using both "chance" and "choice," as Mac Low would sometimes
have it, he works off a list of 288 kinds of light drawn from both everyday
& specialized word sources or newly coined by Mac Low himself. These
served as "nuclei" in composing the poems, drawn simply by chance procedures, as in the First Light Poem, or interspersed with a range of personal,
metaphysical, & social/political concerns, almost all dedicated to specific
friends and tagged by dating to the actual times & places of the writing.

Presented early along as an attempt to develop a "nonegoic" form of
writing, his Buddhist-derived emphasis on no-mind or mind-without-mind
is further modified & refined, as in a later note (1980) to his 1961 publication "Poetry, Chance, Silence, etc.": "I think I used to believe more strongly
in the nonegoic nature and origin of aleatoric art than I do now... the artist's motivation is inevitably mixed, at best—and the ego's not really evad-
able. Besides, nothing would get done—the work would never get written
or performed—if the artist's ego—including, of course, the body—didn't
get it done." And further: "Ego is inevitable. It's always there, in one way or
another. The more I've worked with nonintentional methods, the more I've
seen that the ego is manifested and effectual in anything you do."

With all of which he remained arguably the preeminent experimental
poet of his time.

Denise Levertov USA, 1923–1997

ILLUSTRIOUS ANCESTORS

The Rav
of Northern White Russia declined,
in his youth, to learn the
language of birds, because
the extraneous did not interest him; nevertheless
when he grew old it was found
he understood them anyway, having
listened well, and as it is said, "prayed
   with the bench and the floor." He used

what was at hand—as did
Angel Jones of Mold, whose meditations
were sewn into coats and britches.
        Well, I would like to make,
thinking some line still taut between me and them,
poems direct as what the birds said,
hard as a floor, sound as a bench,
mysterious as the silence when the tailor
would pause with his needle in the air.

MAKING PEACE

A voice from the dark called out,
            "The poets must give us
imagination of peace, to oust the intense, familiar
imagination of disaster. Peace, not only
the absence of war."
                    But peace, like a poem,
is not there ahead of itself,
can't be imagined before it is made,
can't be known except
in the words of its making,
grammar of justice,
syntax of mutual aid.
                    A feeling towards it,
dimly sensing a rhythm, is all we have
until we begin to utter its metaphors,
learning them as we speak.
                    A line of peace might appear
if we restructured the sentence our lives are making,
revoked its reaffirmation of profit and power,
questioned our needs, allowed
long pauses...
                    A cadence of peace might balance its weight
on that different fulcrum; peace, a presence,
an energy field more intense than war,
might pulse then,
stanza by stanza into the world,
each act of living

one of its words, each word
a vibration of light—facets
of the forming crystal.

*My mother was descended from the Welsh tailor and mystic Angel Jones
of Mold, my father from the noted Hasid, Scheour Zalman (d. 1831), "the
Rav of Northern White Russia." My father had experienced conversion
to Christianity as a student at Königsberg in the 1890s. His lifelong hope
was towards the unification of Judaism and Christianity. He was a priest
of the Anglican Church (having settled in England not long before I was
born), author of a life of St. Paul in Hebrew, part translator of The Zohar,
etc.* (D.L.)

Not with these alone as forerunners, Levertov traveled from birth &
upbringing in England to become one of the key figures in the Black Mountain wing of the new USAmerican poetry. ("I think of Robert Duncan
and Robert Creeley," she wrote in 1959, "as the chief poets among my
contemporaries.") It was Duncan who first placed her among the visionary company of poets (himself, ourselves included) whose "sense of a life
shared with beings of a household,... of belonging to generations of spirit,"
tied them not only to a string of literary forebears but to those "illustrious ancestors" to whom her work was, as here, already pointing. Of the
literalness otherwise imputed to a poetry of *things* (her signature issue, for
some), she wrote: "We need a poetry not of *direct statement* but of *direct
evocation*: a poetry of hieroglyphics, of embodiment, incarnation; in which
the personages may be of myth or of Monday, no matter, if they are of the
living imagination." And again: "'No ideas but in things' does not mean
'No ideas.' Nor does it specify: / 'No ideas but in everyday things / modern
things / urban things.' No! it means that: / poetry appears when meaning is
embodied in the figure."

   Her substantial participation in the antiwar movements of the 1960s &
1970s is also to be noted.

Jorge Eduardo Eielson   Peru, 1924–2006

MUTILATED POEM (1949)

you appear..
....and disappear
....................water shouting like obelisks

signaling the end of...
....abysses
.................lake
of disappeared species...................sand...................
....last line
of fire...
....
....
and far away..just into view
........................the hungry wolf and the eclipse pass by
you appear.............................
....and disappear
igneous magnitude.................
....

Translated from Spanish by Shook

from **ROOM IN ROME**

Alongside the Tiber, Putrefaction
Twinkles Gloriously

here i am gathering
words again
words still
lines arranged single file
that brilliantly announce
the nauseating demise
of love
with exquisite fluorescence
thousands and thousands
of words written
in a water-closet
while yellow
briefs and stockings hang
from the flaming sky
of rome
how can i write
and write calmly
in the shade

of an impassive cupola
of a smiling
statue
and not wind up screaming
through the hideous neighborhoods
of rome
and lick a drunkard's sores
disfigure my face
with broken bottles
and then sleep on the sidewalk
in the warm excrement
of a streetwalker or a beggar
i could fill pages
and even worse pages
tell heinous stories
speak despicable things
that I have never known
my shame is just a cloak
of words
a delicate veil of gold
that covers me every day
without pity
but if one day
one instant by the tiber
without a sound
or a whistle
or a cloud
or even a fly
at the bank of the river
with just
a cigarette
a match
and a chair
in so much summer
a sob rises up inside me
oh wonder!
like a mountain
or a mosquito that appears
each century at the zenith
that day
i swear to you

i will hurl the entire universe
into the basket
love will be reborn
between my parched lips
and in these sleeping lines
that will no longer be lines
but gunshots

Translated from Spanish by Shook

where does the ma / n want to go with his cane that / breaks always bre / aks on turning the cor / ner / lead limbs before stairs / that rise daily / from so fragile an egg / and return to the egg / so fragile (J.E.E.)

Writes Peruvian novelist Mario Vargas Llosa: "[Jorge Eduardo Eielson had] an open, curious and voracious spirit that would lead him, not content with cultivating a single genre, to jump from poetry to painting, theater, novel, events (he called them 'performances' and 'actions'), to installation works and even to the circus (he said to Martha Canfield—very seriously—that he considered himself an 'acrobat' and 'a clown'). He was interested in everything: archeology, science, religion, and, since the late 1950s, principally in Zen Buddhism. He participated in some way in all of the post-war intellectual and artistic European trends, but he never belonged to any group or sect, always defending his independence and isolation, and preserving, even in the most exhibitionist periods of his career (like when he 'placed' invisible poems on spaceships or on public monuments) a discreet and secret distance from what he did.... Eielson showed throughout his life an indifference to success and a tough seriousness in everything that he undertook as an artist, even in those humorous taunts. His contempt for fame was such that—for many years—his poetry was almost impossible to find and read, for lack of accessible editions."

Carlos Martínez Rivas Nicaragua, 1924–1998

FOR THOSE WHO LOST NOTHING
BECAUSE THEY NEVER HAD ANYTHING

To write about Hunger,
not protest poetry, but from experience,
is a difficult task if one hasn't suffered from it.

"Writing in darkness is a tough craft"
for Berceo.
Writing about hunger is an arduous task.

Not for César Vallejo
who on one rare occasion turned serious,
saying "the tremendous bread on the table."

Vallejo sees the bread as tremendous because eating it
—for his woman Georgette as well as for him—meant
leaving themselves once again without bread;
impotence of bread equaled potent hunger.

Sure, with a good camera, a Leica,
you can snap photos of hunger.
You can provide a graphic testimony of hunger.

Children from India or Africa,
nothing but brittle bones and pot-belly.

Bellies full of hunger, the type Leonel Rugama
spoke about.

—"Our Russia is so sad!"—Alexander Pushkin
said more than once to Nikolai Gogol,
with tears muddying his cheeks
whilst reading the manuscript of "The Inspector"
in 1836.

A man with a day's ration of stale bread
in Eritrea while the bombs explode.
A girl in war-time emergency room,
she's placed under anesthesia, but not completely under,
tubes worming her nostrils.

Haiti, the famine of 1975,
a boy who seems as if carved from wood,
so emaciated;
and that girl from Vietnam,
the naked and burning babe
running down an Agent-Orange highway.

With no livelihood, no address, a grandmother without grandchildren
sleeps in the demolished New York–Pennsylvania Station.

Intestinal worms—like the roses
in that sonnet by Elizabeth Barrett—fulfill the prognostication:
ancylostomiasis oncocercosis salmonella kálazar...
parasites that sing only for certain races.

And a couple, husband and wife, decrepit,
photographed by SIPA PRESS Agency,
in a piece entitled "Third World Gothic," a true waste fund:

He, toothless; she, frowning, and grim.
But the both of them united in their misfortune, dignified.
So much so you envy them.

And that's what I'm referring to
when I wrote the title
to this text: FOR THOSE WHO LOST
NOTHING BECAUSE THEY NEVER HAD ANYTHING.

Translated from Spanish by Anthony Seidman

COMMENTARY

Everything is material for the Poem—except / that Enemy: the Problems.
(C.M.R.) Or again: *Making a poem is planning a perfect crime. To create an
immaculate lie made true by force of purity.*

Carlos Martínez Rivas lived a life of poetry, although he decidedly got
away from the "poetry world" as such. In his deliberate self-reclusion, he
published only two books during his life: *Paradise Regained* (1943) & *The
Solitary Insurrection* (1953). The selection presented here, reaching well
beyond that, is taken from his posthumously published *Varia*, which brings
together previously uncollected & scattered poems.

Talking about himself & his poetry, Rivas stated in an interview with
Steven F. White: "When I saw the Hispanic American elite corrupted by
Europe, and I, with all my Central American power, a wildcat, I felt like a
savage among them. And, at the same time, in their same category. It's one
thing to feel like an ignorant savage and another thing to feel like a savage
with as much knowledge as theirs. That is the difference they noticed with
me, Cortázar and Paz. Those were Hispanic Americans who belonged to
the European elites. While I, the Hispanic American, who, embracing everything they felt, saw and knew, I had remained wild." Today, then, as more
& more of his poems come to light, Carlos Martínez Rivas has come to be
considered one of the major poets of Nicaragua & Latin America.

Bob Kaufman USA, 1925–1986

ABOMUNIST MANIFESTO

ABOMUNISTS JOIN NOTHING BUT THEIR HANDS OR LEGS, OR OTHER SAME.

ABOMUNISTS SPIT ANTI-POETRY FOR POETIC REASONS AND FRINK.

ABOMUNISTS DO NOT LOOK AT PICTURES PAINTED BY PRESIDENTS AND UNEMPLOYED PRIME MINISTERS.

IN TIMES OF NATIONAL PERIL, ABOMUNISTS, AS REALITY AMERICANS, STAND READY TO DRINK THEMSELVES TO DEATH FOR THEIR COUNTRY.

ABOMUNISTS DO NOT FEEL PAIN, NO MATTER HOW MUCH IT HURTS.

ABOMUNISTS DO NOT USE THE WORD SQUARE EXCEPT WHEN TALKING TO SQUARES.

ABOMUNISTS READ NEWSPAPERS ONLY TO ASCERTAIN THEIR ABOMINUBILITY.

ABOMUNISTS NEVER CARRY MORE THAN FIFTY DOLLARS IN DEBTS ON THEM.

ABOMUNISTS BELIEVE THAT THE SOLUTION OF PROBLEMS OF RELIGIOUS BIGOTRY IS TO HAVE A CATHOLIC CANDIDATE FOR PRESIDENT AND PROTESTANT CANDIDATE FOR POPE.

ABOMUNISTS DO NOT WRITE FOR MONEY; THEY WRITE THE MONEY ITSELF.

ABOMUNISTS BELIEVE ONLY WHAT THEY DREAM ONLY AFTER IT COMES TRUE.

ABOMUNISTS' CHILDREN MUST BE REARED ABOMUNIBLY.

ABOMUNIST POETS, CONFIDENT THAT THE NEW LITERARY FORM "FOOTPRINTISM" HAS FREED THE ARTIST OF OUTMODED RESTRICTIONS, SUCH AS: THE ABILITY TO READ AND WRITE, OR THE DESIRE TO COMMUNICATE, MUST BE PREPARED TO READ THEIR WORK AT DENTAL COLLEGES, EMBALMING SCHOOLS, HOMES FOR UNWED MOTHERS, HOMES FOR WED MOTHERS, INSANE ASYLUMS, U.S.O. CANTEENS, KINDERGARTENS, AND COUNTY JAILS. ABOMUNISTS NEVER COMPROMISE THEIR REJECTIONARY PHILOSOPHY.

ABOMUNISTS REJECT EVERYTHING EXCEPT SNOWMEN.

Let the voices of dead poets / ring louder in your ears / Than the screech-ings mouthed / In mildewed editorials / Listen to the music of centuries, / Rising above the mushroom time. (B.K.) And again: *I want to be anony-mous… my ambition is to be completely forgotten.*

But the work survives, & with it the legend of his life—"a poet of the streets," as David Grundy has called him, who "preferred to recite his poetry in coffee shops, bars, or on the street rather than publish it in print. All three of his collections were compiled by editors from the scraps, written and oral, he left lying around. Kaufman deliberately cultivated marginality, yet he was also marginalized—subjected to forced electroshock treatment, harassed by racist police, penniless, and virtually homeless." With regard to which, as if to hammer the point home, he writes in "I, Too, Know What I Am Not":

> *No, I am not deathly wishes of sacred rapists, singing*
> *on candy gallows…*
> *No I am not whisper of the African trees,*
> *leafy Congo telephones.*
> *No, I am not Leadbelly of the blues, escaped from guitar jails.*
> *No, I am not anything that is anything I am not.*

A prototypical outsider poet on the one hand, his influence on American Beat and jazz poetics is also to be noted.

Etel Adnan   Lebanon/USA, 1925–2021

from *THE ARAB APOCALYPSE*

III

The night of the non-event. War in the vacant sky. The Phantom's absence.
Funerals. Coffin not covered with roses. Unarmed population. Long.
The yellow sun's procession from the mosque to the vacant Place. Mute taxis.
Plainclothed army. Silent hearse. Silenced music. Palestinians with no Palestine.

The night of the Great Inca did not happen. Engineless planes. Extinguished sun.
Fisherman with no fleet fish with no sea fleet with no fish sea without fishermen.
Guns with faded flowers Che Guevara reduced to ashes. No shade.
The wind neither rose nor subsided. The Jews are absent. Flat tires.
The little lights are not lit. No child has died. No rain.
I did not say that spring was breathing. The dead did not return.

The mosque has launched its unheated prayer. Lost in the waves.
The street lost its stones. Brilliant asphalt. Useless roads. Dead army.
Snuffed is the street. To shut off the gas. Refugees with no refuge no candle.
The procession hasn't been scared. Time went by. Silent Phantom.

. . . . .

XXXVI

In the dark irritation of the eyes there is a snake hiding
In the exhalations of Americans there is a crumbling empire
In the foul waters of the rivers there are Palestinians
OUT OUT of its borders pain has a leash on its neck
In the wheat stalks there are insects vaccinated against bread
In the Arabian boats there are sharks shaken with laughter
In the camel's belly there are blind highways
OUT OUT of TIME there is spring's shattered hope
In the deluge on our plains there are no rains but stones

. . . . .

XXXIX

When the living rot on the bodies of the dead
When the combatants' teeth become knives
When words lose their meaning and become arsenic
When the aggressors' nails become claws
When old friends hurry to join the carnage
When the victors' eyes become live shells
When clergymen pick up the hammer and crucify
When officials open the door to the enemy
When the mountain peoples' feet weigh like elephants
When roses grow only in cemeteries
When they eat the Palestinian's liver before he's even dead
When the sun itself has no other purpose than being a shroud
the human tide moves on...

Translated from her original French by the author

COMMENTARY

*Places are part of nature, of the bigger picture. We are interrelated. When
we contemplate them in their own right, they can sometimes change our
lives; they can become spiritual experiences.* (E.A.)

(1) Born in Beirut, educated in French—which was designed to supplant
her native Arabic—a student at the Sorbonne and at UC Berkeley, Adnan

writes about her own self-journey, implicit here: "Speaking English was an adventure, but it also resolved my ambiguous relationship to the French language: something deep inside me has always been resentful of the fact that French came to us in Lebanon through a colonial occupation, that it was imposed, that it was not innocently taught to me as a second language, but a language meant to replace Arabic. For me, English had no such connotations.... I must say that when I landed in the United States, I had a kind of fluid identity: was I Greek, Ottoman Arab, almost French?... It was in Berkeley that all the threads that made up my mind and soul came together: I became what I was, I became an Arab, at the same time that I was becoming an American" (quoted in "The Itinerary of an Arab-American Writer," in *Scheherazade's Legacy: Arab and Arab American Women on Writing*).

(2) Hilary Plum tells us: "The poem [*Arab Apocalypse*] is written in 59 sections (others term it a collection of 59 poems) and in distinctively long lines.... Small ink sketches, sometimes no more than a swift arrow or darkened circle, appear between, beside, or as eruptions within the lines of poetry. This approach is distinct in Adnan's oeuvre.... This union of poetry and visual art also distinguishes *Apocalypse* within the landscape of contemporary American poetry; current parlance would call such a work 'hybrid'... "

But not only hybrid in Plum's sense, it is also culturally hybrid, with references to many cultures & geographies as if there were no lines between them, or, put otherwise, it is a *world poem*: it is large, it contains multitudes, as with Whitman's new American poet or Édouard Glissant's "*tout-monde*" (in "A Fourth Gallery").

Ernesto Cardenal Nicaragua, 1925–2020

from *THE GHOST DANCE*

The GHOST DANCE had no weapons
night after night they danced the sacred dance
     here were tribes that gave up their firearms
       and everything else they had of metal
     "everything the same as before the white man came"
In Oklahoma they said that the new land would come from the west.
With all the dead Indians
all who had died from the beginning, restored to life
     with buffaloes bison deer restored to life.
And some of them went back to their tribes saying that Jesus
had come again.   The white men had killed Him

beyond the Great Waters, now
He had come to be with the Indians who had never done him wrong.
Former times would return.   The
buffaloes would also return.

      To shoot at other men
The Great Spirit doesn't want it.
And in Nevada another prophet, a Payute:
First thing, no more war
      Love each other everyone
must dance
      MAKE LOVE NOT WAR
      Live in peace with the white man
And the Sioux saying
(the Sioux without their buffaloes):
      They are coming
all the dead tribes are coming
         and great droves of buffaloes with them
alive again
         from the prairies of the Great Spirit
      they are coming.

All the animals will be restored to the Indians
right away
         next Springtime
  when the grass is knee-high
   the day of the general resurrection.

With no weapons in their hands
      but hand in hand
      dancing in a wheel
(the red paint was the dawn)
      This is what the Father said
      everyone in the land must sing
      let them spread his message wide
      let them spread his message wide
(The feathers on their head were wings
to fly to the
      prairies of heaven)
In 1889 the Oglalas heard the news
that the son of God had arrived in the West
      and the Oglalas danced.

Hand in hand.
       The dance was handed on from tribe to tribe.
Pacifism, sit-ins, non-violence.
   "We want to live like brothers with the white man"
In the throes of the dance they saw the world of the spirits
       all the tents of new buffalo hide
the spirits on horseback returning from hunting the buffaloes
by the light of the moon, laden with carcasses of buffaloes
       and the prairies with thousands and thousands of buffaloes.
The Ghost Dance was without weapons
and some who had been in the nation of spirit-Indians:
       "the nation of dead Indians is returning
       is returning
       and the GREAT SPIRIT is returning to be with his redskin Indians."

And
... "in the land of the spirit-men
   I saw a teepee
   and in the entrance of the teepee a spirit-man
   told me: the white men and the Indians must dance
   all together; but first they must sing.
   There must be no more wars".

They saw the spirits setting up their camp in the prairies of the sky
the fastening of the tent-poles, the
                   tents being pitched
the women collecting firewood and getting food ready
the wind whistling between the tent-poles, making
the skins tremble.
       The bonfire inside and the songs
       round it and the smoke rising from the tent...

Some of them ate buffalo meat which they had brought back from that country.
And one of them saw a man on his trip from a tribe that had long been extinct.
And the Cheyennes on their trips saw the rivers of the sky in
psychedelic colors.
And the Comanches sang
       We shall live again
       We shall live again
And the Caddos sang that they were already rising
       —and it was true, the Caddos were rising!—
on high, where their people live, on high where their people live

Come, Caddo, we are all going up
Come, Caddo, we are all going up
to the great Village
to the great Village

Sitting Bull prophesied that
the sacred feathers
would protect the Indians from nuclear fire.

Near the Agency on Lake Walker, a ring like a circus ring
They waited all night anxious to see Christ
At dawn a great crowd of people arrived, with them
came Christ.   After breakfast Christ spoke with them.
"I saw a scar on His face and another on His wrist
I could not see His feet"

The last thing known about Wowoka;
that he was seen in a fair in San Francisco.
The Dance went on but with a new hopefulness
not immediate feverish and delirious as before but
a serene hopefulness
like the hope in the Resurrection that the Christians have
says Mooney.

And that magnificent old man whom I saw in Taos
(with his dressing-gown and plaits he looked like an old woman)
knew what I meant when I said: to heaven.
Because the tourist an old idiot from New England asked him
if he had known the buffaloes: Yes, when I was a child; and he added sadly:
No more buffaloes... I wonder where they have GONE
and I said to heaven
and the old idiot snickered—hee-hee-hee—as if it were a joke
and the old chief smiled sadly (and he knew what I meant)
(Fall 1965, my journey to the u.s.a. to
see Merton and the Indians)

Translated from Spanish by Donald Gardner

from *THE GOSPEL IN SOLENTINAME*

MARCELINO, with his calm voice, said: "I don't know about the mustard seed, but I do know about the *guasima* seed, which is tiny. I'm looking at that *guasima* tree over there. It's very large, and the birds come to it too. I say to myself: that's what we are, this little community, a *guasima* seed. It doesn't seem like there's any connection between some poor *campesinos* and a just and well-developed society, where there is abundance and everything is shared ..."

I said: "The great tree with all its branches and its leaves is already present in the seed, even though in a hidden form. In the same way the kingdom of heaven, which is a cosmic kingdom, is already present in us, but in a hidden way. A tree is the product of the evolution of a seed, and in nature everything is produced by a process of evolution. And it seems to me that with this parable of the seed Christ is also telling us here that the kingdom of heaven is the product of the same process of evolution that formed stars, plants, animals, people. And it grows in us impelled by the same forces of nature that impelled the evolution of the whole cosmos, which is to say that the kingdom of heaven is evolution itself."

Translated from Spanish by Donald D. Walsh

COMMENTARY

I became politicized by the contemplative life. Meditation is what brought me to political radicalization. I came to the revolution by way of the Gospels. It was not by reading Marx but Christ. It can be said that the Gospels made me a Marxist. (E.C.)

But the work—both before & after Ernesto Cardenal's involvement with revolutionary cultural politics in Nicaragua—showed a largeness of historical, even cosmological, vision that was key to his most important achievements as a poet. His path into religion (ultimately the "liberation theology" that would be so prominent in the Americas) began with seclusion (in the footsteps of fellow poet-priest Thomas Merton) at the Trappist monastery in Gethsemani, Kentucky. Ordained in 1965 (at age forty), he was the founder of a church & commune at Solentiname, a group of tiny islands in Lake Nicaragua, from which came *The Gospel of Solentiname*, a series of commentaries & renewals of Jesus's parables & teachings. There the activities—centered on the surrounding peasant population—were heavily involved with poetry, while his own work, as in the *Homenaje a los Indios de América* (1969), followed Pound's directive for the epic as "a poem including history." With a probable nod to Pound & the North American "Objectivists," the name he gave to this approach ("the only poetry which can truly express Latin American reality") was *exteriorismo*: "... objective poetry: narrative and anecdote, made with elements of real life and concrete things, with proper names and precise details and exact data, statistics, facts, and quotations."

With the victory of the Sandinistas in 1979, Cardenal became the Nicaraguan minister of culture, bringing about (however briefly) a proliferation of that poetry which, since Darío's time at least, had been the major public art of Nicaragua. Much of his later work—*Canto Cósmico*, most notably (see "A Map of Histories")—is an extension of *exteriorismo* into areas of world & universe formation.

The regard for facts & history, both scientific & mythopoetic, is further explored in what follows.

A MAP OF HISTORIES

The poet is the great protagonist of the stupendous
social scenario that sings and expresses history...
history anticipating history, from the heart of history itself.

PABLO DE ROKHA

History is the new localism, a pulls to replace the one which was lost

CHARLES OLSON

If you ask about language in the Caribbean, you must relate it to history.

DEREK WALCOTT

From another epic another history. From the missing narrative.
From the multitude of narratives. Missing. From the chronicles.
For another telling for other recitations.

THERESA HAK KYUNG CHA

Let history bury history
And let's talk about the present

ERNEST PÉPIN

When the exceptional historian comes along, you have a poet.

MELVIN B. TOLSON

Let me recite what History teaches. History teaches.

GERTRUDE STEIN

Mandan

A TREE OF HISTORY

For these stories are like the branches of a tree. All go back to the main trunk. The old Indians who know the stories, if we relate a branch, can tell where it belongs in the tree and what comes before and what after.

—Hidatsa, Bears Arm

The parts of this weed all branch from the stem. They go different ways, but all come from the same root. So it is with the versions of a myth.

—Blackfoot

One ritual is an arm or branch of the lodge, and the myth accounting for its origin forks off from the main branch.

—Menomini

after Martha Warren Beckwith, Myths and Ceremonies of the Mandan and Hidatsa (1932)

Walt Whitman USA, 1819–1892

from **SONG OF MYSELF: 3**

I have heard what the talkers were talking, the talk of the beginning and the end,
But I do not talk of the beginning or the end.

There was never any more inception than there is now,
Nor any more youth or age than there is now,
And will never be any more perfection than there is now,
Nor any more heaven or hell than there is now.

Urge and urge and urge,
Always the procreant urge of the world.

Out of the dimness opposite equals advance, always substance and increase,
 always sex,
Always a knit of identity, always distinction, always a breed of life.

To elaborate is no avail, learn'd and unlearn'd feel that it is so.

Sure as the most certain sure, plumb in the uprights, well entreatied, braced in
 the beams,
Stout as a horse, affectionate, haughty, electrical,
I and this mystery here we stand.

Clear and sweet is my soul, and clear and sweet is all that is not my soul.
Lack one lacks both, and the unseen is proved by the seen,
Till that becomes unseen and receives proof in its turn.

Showing the best and dividing it from the worst age vexes age,
Knowing the perfect fitness and equanimity of things, while they discuss I am
 silent, and go bathe and admire myself.

Welcome is every organ and attribute of me, and of any man hearty and clean,
Not an inch nor a particle of an inch is vile, and none shall be less familiar than
 the rest.

I am satisfied—I see, dance, laugh, sing;
As the hugging and loving bed-fellow sleeps at my side through the night, and
 withdraws at the peep of the day with stealthy tread,
Leaving me baskets cover'd with white towels swelling the house with their
 plenty,
Shall I postpone my acceptation and realization and scream at my eyes,
That they turn from gazing after and down the road,

And forthwith cipher and show me to a cent,
Exactly the value of one and exactly the value of two, and which is ahead?

For more on Whitman, see "A First Gallery" & elsewhere in these pages.

Ernesto Cardenal Nicaragua, 1925–2020

from *CANTO CÓSMICO*

Cantiga 9

The heavenly bodies
   and ours.
"Walking stars"—the Chaldeos. (About those not fixed.)
In Greek walking is *planetes*, so that
we inhabit a walking star.
Men who shaped Man
or rather will
    Or the prospect before us is merely
a barren planet like Mars
A mushroom-shaped cloud slowly rising
on the horizon
Star Wars which the *Wall Street Journal* called
"Dollars falling from the skies"
Neanderthal *Wall Street Journal*.
But no. We have for example
evolution from the primitive shark until it transforms into dove.
Man's death instinct
    is not inherited from animal ancestors.
Biology also teaches:
natural selection favours peace-loving animals.
Murderous groups within a same species do not prosper.
(Somozas, Pinochet, etc.) Gorillas are meditative,
they like to spend their time in contemplation.
That the solution to all China's social problems
was love
was discovered five centuries before our era.
One man helping another
which to Pliny is God.
The incarnation of God in our biology.

In our still mammal condition.
    Jesus: with Adam's chromosomes…
Only a million years since *Pithecanthropus erectus*.
The government rooted in the sky which Confucius mentioned
    Not dollars from the sky.
We've left excrement behind in plastic bags on the moon.
        The Mayas had already discovered the lunar month
only out by 34 seconds
34 seconds
in a time for them infinite, without beginning nor end.
The enemies of evolution (Somoza etc.)
Counter-evolutionaries.
How can there be unemployment on this planet?
But there is a tower we wish to build, Chuang-tse said,
that might reach to infinity.
Shit-eating counter-evolutionaries.
On that day even physical beauty will be egalitarian.

Translated from Spanish by John Lyons

For more on Cardenal, see "A Third Gallery."

Pablo Neruda Chile, 1904–1973

from **CANTO GENERAL**

The Heights of Macchu Picchu

I

From air to air, like an empty net
I went between the streets and atmosphere, arriving and departing,
in the advent of autumn the outstretched coin
    of the leaves, and between springtime and the ears of corn,
all that the greatest love, as within a falling
glove, hands us like a long moon.

(Days of vivid splendor in the inclemency
of corpses: steel transformed
into acid silence:
nights frayed to the last flour:

beleaguered stamens of the nuptial land.)
Someone awaiting me among the violins
discovered a world like an entombed tower
spiraling down beneath all
the harsh sulphur-colored leaves:
farther down, in the gold of geology,
like a sword enveloped in meteors,
I plunged my turbulent and tender hand
into the genital matrix of the earth.

I put my brow amid the deep waves,
descended like a drop amid the sulphurous peace,
and, like a blind man, returned to the jasmine
of the spent human springtime.

. . . . .

XII

Rise up to be born with me, my brother.

Give me your hand from the deep
zone of your disseminated sorrow.
You'll not return from the bottom of the rocks.
You'll not return from subterranean time.
Your stiff voice will not return.
Your drilled eyes will not return.
Behold me from the depths of the earth,
laborer, weaver, silent herdsman:
tamer of the tutelary guanacos:
mason of the defied scaffold:
bearer of the Andean tears:
jeweler with your fingers crushed:
tiller trembling in the seed:
potter spilt in your clay:
bring to the cup of this new life, brothers,
all your timeless buried sorrows.
Show me your blood and your furrow,
tell me: I was punished here,
because the jewel did not shine or the earth
did not surrender the gemstone or kernel on time:
show me the stone on which you fell
and the wood on which you were crucified,
strike the old flintstones,

the old lamps, the whips sticking
throughout the centuries to your wounds
and the war clubs glistening red.
I've come to speak through your dead mouths.
Throughout the earth join all
the silent scattered lips
and from the depths speak to me all night long,
as if I were anchored with you,
tell me everything, chain by chain,
link by link, and step by step,
sharpen the knives that you've kept,
put them in my breast and in my hand,
like a river of yellow lightning,
like a river of buried jaguars,
and let me weep hours, days, years,
blind ages, stellar centuries.

Give me silence, water, hope.

Give me struggle, iron, volcanoes.

Cling to my body like magnets.

Hasten to my veins and to my mouth.

Speak through my words and my blood.

Translated from Spanish by Jack Schmitt

COMMENTARY

Of his epic project, *Canto General*, & the pre-American ruins of Machu
Picchu in Peru, Neruda writes: "I came to understand that we walked on
the same hereditary earth, that we had something to do with those great
efforts of the Latin American community, that we couldn't ignore it, that
our ignorance or silence was not just a crime, but the continuation of a
defeat.... There is where my idea for a general song of the Americas began
to germinate. Before then, I had persisted in my idea of a general song of
Chile, in the form of a chronicle. That visit changed my perspective. Now I
was seeing all of America from the heights of Machu Picchu" (trans. David
Spener).

For more on Neruda, see "A Third Gallery" & elsewhere in these pages.

Battiste Good Dakota, 1821–1908

 1794–95 Killed-the-little-faced-Pawnee winter

 1795–96 The-Rees-stood-the-frozen-man-up-with-the-buffalo-stomach-in-his-hands winter

 1796–97 Wears-the-War-Bonnet-died winter

 1797–98 Took-the-God-Woman-captive winter

 1798–99 Many-women-died-in-childbirth winter

 1799–1800 Don't-Eat-Buffalo-Heart-made-a-commemoration-of-the-dead winter

 1800–1 The-Good-White-Man-came winter

 1801–2 Smallpox-used-them-up-again winter

 1802–3 Brought-home-Pawnee-horses-with-iron-shoes-on winter

 1803–4 Brought-home-Pawnee-horses-with-them winter

 1804–5 Sung-over-each-other-while-on-the-warpath winter

(1) A form of visual-verbal epic, if we read them as such, winter-counts (*waniyetu wowapi* in Dakota) were a widespread practice among nineteenth-century Plains Indians. Garrick Mallery, in his early account of Indian picture-writing (1888), defined them as "the use of events, which were in some degree historical, to form a system of chronology"—i.e., to individualize each year (or winter) by a name describing an event within that year, & to record said name by a visual symbol or ideograph. In practice the ideographs were mostly drawn on buffalo hides & were organized into patterns ranging from columns to spirals. In Battiste Good's count, the ideographs appear in an ordinary paper drawing book & are painted with five colors besides black. His full narrative includes a cyclical & mythic section covering the years 901 to 1700, after which the counting by year-names begins.

(2) Battiste Good's work is prefaced by the following account of a personal vision & by a vision drawing. Thus:

"In the year 1856, I went to the Black Hills and cried, and cried, and cried for a vision, and suddenly I saw a bird above me, which said: 'Stop crying; I am a woman, but I will tell you something: My GreatFather, Father-God, who made this place, gave it to me for a home and told me to watch over it. He put a blue sky over my head and gave me a blue flag to have with this beautiful green country. My GreatFather grew, and his flesh was part earth and part stone and part metal and part wood and part water; he took from them all and placed them here for me and told me to watch over them. I am the Eagle-Woman who tell you this. The whites know that there are four black flags of God; that is, four divisions of the earth. He first made the earth soft by wetting it, then cut it into four parts, one of which, containing the Black Hills, he gave to the Dakotas, and, because I am a woman, I shall not consent to the pouring of blood on this chief house that is the Black Hills. The time will come that you will remember my words, for after many years you shall grow up one with the white people.' She then circled round and round and gradually passed out of my sight. I also saw prints of a man's hands and horse's hoofs on the rocks, and two thousand years, and one hundred millions of dollars. I came away crying, as I had gone. I have told this to many Dakotas, and all agree that it meant that we were to seek and keep peace with the whites" (*Annual Report of the Bureau of Ethnology to the Secretary of the Smithsonian Institution*, 1888).

James Reuben Nez Perce / USA, 1853–1898

HISTORY OF THE NEZ PERCE INDIANS FROM 1805 UP TO THE PRESENT TIME

They lived and enjoyed the happiness and freedom
and lived just as happy as any other Nation in the World.

But alas the day was coming when all their happy days
was to be turned into day of sorrow and moaning.

Their days of freedom was turned to be the day of slavery.

Their days of victory was turned to be conquered,
and their rights to the country was disregarded by another nations
which is called "Whiteman" at present day.

In 1885 a treaty was made between Nez Perce Nation and United States.

Wal-la-mot-kin (Hair tied on forehead) or Old Joseph,
Hul-lal-ho-sot or (Lawyer),
were the two leading Chiefs of the Nez Perce Nation in 1855,
both of these two Chiefs consented to the treaty
and Nez Perce sold to the United States
part of their country.

In 1863 another treaty was made
in which Lawyer and his people consented
but Joseph and his people refused to make the second treaty

from that time Joseph's people
were called None-treaty Nez Perce.

The treaty Nez Perce number 1800
None-treaty numbered 1000

The Nez Perce decreased greatly since 1805 up to 1863.
The smallpox prevailed among the tribe
which almost destroyed the tribe.

Lawyer's people advanced in civilization
and became farmers etc.
They had their children in schools.

While Joseph's people refused all these things
they lived outside what was called Nez Perce Reservation

1877 Government undertook to move Young Joseph people on the Res.

At this date Young Joseph was their ruling chief
son of the Old Chief Joseph who died in 1868,
and left his people in charge of his own Son

Joseph and his followers broke out
and there was Nez Perce War bloody one
nine great battles fought

the last battle lasted five days
which Joseph surrendered with his people

1000 Indians had went on the war path
but when Joseph surrendered
there was only 600

400 killed during the wars
or went to other tribes.

after the capture Joseph was brought to this Territory as captives.

at present Joseph people numbers 350 out of 600
all are suffering on account of this Southern climate
result is he and his people
will live and die in this country exiled from home

Take it in the right light—
Nez Perce have been wrongly treated by the Government
it cannot be denied
not Nez Perce only but all other Indian Nations in America.

I wrote this about my own people

I am a member of Nez Perce Tribe
and Nephew of Chief Joseph

When this is opened and read may be understood
how the Indians have been treated by the Whiteman.

COMMENTARY

Slightly abridged & lineated by William Brandon from the text by James
Reuben, a prominent member of the Nez Perce (Nimiipuu) Nation in the
late nineteenth century, deposited in the cornerstone of the Nez Perce &
Ponca school on October 20, 1880, & recovered when the schoolhouse
was torn down. It was first printed by the Oklahoma Historical Society in
the *Chronicles of Oklahoma*, vol. 12 (September 1934).

Ed Sanders USA, 1939–

from *INVESTIGATIVE POETRY*

The Content of History Will Be Poetry

move over Herodotus
move over Thuc' [Thucydides]
move over Arthur Schlesinger
move over logographers and chroniclers
and compulsive investigators

for the poets are
marching again
upon the hills
of history

History-poesy, or investigative poetry, can thrive in our era because of the implications of a certain poetic insight, that is, in the implications of the line, "Now is the time for prophecy without death as a consequence," from *Death to Van Gogh's Ear*, a Ginsberg poem from 1958.

Investigative poesy is freed from capitalism, churchism, and other totalitarianisms; free from racisms, free from allegiance to napalm-dropping military police states—a poetry adequate to discharge from its verse-grids the undefiled high energy purely-distilled verse-frags, using *every* bardic skill and meter and method of the last 5 or 6 generations, in order to describe *every* aspect (no more secret governments!) of the historical present, while aiding the future, even placing bard-babble once again into a role as shaper of the future.

For this is the age wherein a Socrates would have told the judges to take a walk down vomit alley, and could have lived as an active vehement leader of the Diogenes Liberation Squadron of Strolling Troubadors and Muckrakers, till the microbes 'whelmed him. The era of police-statists punishing citizens for secret proclivities is over. Blackmail, in other words, is going to go bye-bye. One will not in any way have to assure one's readers (to quote, is it Martial, or Catullus?) that "*pagina lasciva, vita proba,*" but rather it is now most definitely the age of "*pagina lasciva, vita lascivior.*" And we are here speaking of uncompunctious conjugation, not of riches cutting up cattle from silent helicopters, or of bankers whipping each other on yachts.

Thrills course upward from the typewriter keys as my fingers type the words that say that poets are free from the nets of any *particular* verse-form or verse-mind. Keats would have grown old in such a freedom. The days of bards chanting dactylic hexameters while strumming the phorminx, or lyre, trying to please some drooly-lipped war-lord are over, o triumphant beatnik spores! It's over! And the days of bards trying to please some CIA-worshipping cold war tough-liberal professor are done! done! done!

But the way of Historical Poesy, as I said earlier, is mined with danger, especially to those bards who would seek to drag the corpses of J.P. Morgan's neo-confederates through the amphetamine piranha tank.

Pablo Antonio Cuadra   Nicaragua, 1912–2002

THE MANGO TREE

The lips that kissed you also told you,
"It's time for you to put down roots like the trees."
But you know about trees. You know about their different kinds of wood and
    growth rings.
Over the centuries, you've followed their slow caravans.
You've seen them in the jungles, by the great rivers,
their green hands covered with tangled vines and parasites,
fleeing into exile together with their birds. Fixed in space,
they make their pilgrimage. They are one invisible step
ahead of civilization.
You know about trees. You know
the native trees that helped to lift the land. River shepherds.
Trees that are so deeply Nicaraguan, like the pochotes,
which, even when slashed for kindling, sprout up again from the land.
And you know the strangers to this place
such as Senegal's abundant icaco tree,
or Algeria's pomegranate, or the immense breadfruit tree from the Moluccas,
or the Mango that arrived in Nicaragua from distant Hindustan.

It was in Calcutta (or Kolkata) where the galleon reached port.
"A little more favorable wind and all of you will become rich and blessed with
    good fortune,"
says Captain Céspedes de Aldana. Then they altered their course
and crossed 700 churning leagues of the Gulf
of China or the Philippines in their galleon on the so-called "South Wind Journey."

There, the Captain found ivory and gold brocatelles, taffetas and damasks.
And as he brought a plant on board with its newly formed leaves,
the beautiful Hindu woman told him, "Let this tree bear witness to your pledges."
But people laughed and spoke about the affair in low voices,
everywhere, once Aunt Elisa and Aunt Mercedes had retired to their solemn
  chambers.
Aldana had rescued them from the gloom of spinsterhood
by bringing them to America, seasick, almost ruing their new bad fortune,
but bound for marriages of honor and profit.
At that time, Granada had 200 inhabitants, mud-walled or lime-covered adobe
  buildings with ceramic roof tiles, as well as a pretty church:
a fistful of salt in the vast tropical greenness.
And in Aldana's house, there was an astrolabe, a compass, and rolls of maps
  stained by seawater, and the first clock brought from Germany, which he
  installed like a tabernacle in a formal room so the time it kept could guide the
  schedule for mass and meetings of the town council.
And in the courtyard, the mango tree, the first mango tree.
    "I have heard—he would say—that the learned Muslims claim
this fruit to be the avatar of a mysterious bird
called Jatayu,
        —bird-king of Hindustan,
red and black because the sun scorched its wings,
which means that it must be from the genus of the phoenix, from the Arabs,
because it nests in fire."
                And the Indians
transmitted this legend, but changed it,
saying that mango trees bear fruit to give back
the soul or *yulio* of the *chichiltote* bird,
        —the flaming votive bird of the Chorotegas.—
And there was once a poet who sang of that fable:
"You can hear the song and laughter of the fruit beneath its skin."

On his first sweltering nights in Granada,
Aldana, that old wolf Juan Céspedes de Aldana,
always dressed in leather and suede, despite the heat, and wore
the featherless hood of the earliest sailors.
And he would weep as he thought of his faithful 47-ton caraval, "The Greyhound,"
built and armed by him with the proceeds
"from the many taxes he levied on the land he owned,"
and of its masts from Moguer, and his father, Don Alonso,
—patriarch of the Pinzón family—

and of Diego de Lepe and Juan Díaz de Solís,
captains and pilots,
who were among the first to cross the equator
and who saw not only new lands but new stars as well.
    And every time he harvested his mangoes,
—as he passed around the fruit on a silver platter to his neighbors—
he would repeat the stories of his travails on his journeys:
On the perverse Sargasso Sea filled with ship-swallowing monsters
or on the passage through Guachinchina,
a gulf with many small hills and sandbanks,
replete with an Emperor and pearl divers,
or in the Philippines, where the women, Aldana said,
were incredibly chaste, with no conception of lust
or unfaithfulness to their husbands.
Then he would look at those who had gathered to hear him
and lower his booming pilot's voice
        (he had the round ironic face of the Aldanas,
            and their instincts, too, while his smile was a half-smile, really,—
            the rest of his sense of humor was in his eyes):
—"She planted the seed during the full moon
and married the tree in her pagan rites, joining two branches.
Ah! She had the biggest and brightest eyes a man could ever see!"
But Felipillo, his knock-kneed dwarf servant,
added the detail that Yadira's breasts were anointed with sandalwood,
which made the heat bearable for the navigator.

    His somewhat disillusioned grandchildren
inherited confusing chronicles but could still read
the name of the plant in Sanskrit
in his diary with its yellowing pages,
and see drawings in ink from the Orient
of its polygamous flowers,
and its lanceolate leaves, dark green and shiny,
and the red fruit shaped like a heart. ("It will multiply
my heart," predicted the woman. And so it did, in thick bunches,
every time they made love.
With every heartbeat of the lovers,
more fruit came into being.) Now
not even one stone remains to mark the old patriarch.
He chose an impetuous land of history, heated to the point of calcination,
and filibuster William Walker's fires erased his name

when he burned the temple where Aldana
twice entered with bare feet to fulfill his pledges:
once with a wax candle in his hand
when he lost his ship (after almost reaching home)
in a wind-whipped downpour on the Gulf of Papagayo,
and then again as a corpse,
wearing a Franciscan robe and hood.

    The Mango tree also burned its story in time:
and now you consider it from this place.
It professes a familiar green,
was born in your islands,
accompanies you in rows along both sides of your roads,
grows in the courtyard at home,
takes in
your native birds
as it interlaces breezes and the drone of locusts
like a hammock
for your siesta.

Translated from Spanish by Greg Simon and Steven F. White

COMMENTARY

In his masterwork *Seven trees against the dying light*, published in 1980, Pablo Antonio Cuadra invokes the history of earth as a register of the human journey. The seven trees depicted in the collection are not just symbolic trees; they function as protective entities whose destinies are intimately related to humankind. So, in the poem above, Cuadra evokes the Hindustani myth of the mango—avatar of Jatayu, brother of Arjuna—& its path all the way to Granada, Nicaragua, where it is considered a "national" tree. Thus, the torching of Granada & its protective mango by the North American fortune hunter & *filibustero* William Walker, while attempting to annex Nicaragua to the United States in 1856, acquires a new meaning.

Mahadai Das Guyana, 1954–2003

from *THEY CAME IN SHIPS*

They came in ships.

From far across the seas, they came.
Britain colonising India, transporting her chains
From Chota Nagpur and the Ganges plain.
Westwards came the *Whitby*,
The *Hesperus*
The Island-bound *Fatel Rozack*.
Wooden missions of imperialist design.
Human victims of Her Majesty's victory.

They came in fleets.
They came in droves
Like cattle.
Brown, like cattle.
Eyes limpid, like cattle.

Some came with dreams of milk-and-honey riches,
Fleeing famine and death:
Dancing girls,
Rajput soldiers, determined, tall,
Escaping the penalty of pride.
Stolen wives, afraid and despondent.
Crossing black waters.
Brahmin, Chamar, alike.
Hearts brimful of hope.

I saw them dying at street corners, alone, hungry

For a crumb of British bread.

. . . . .

Remember one-third quota, coolie woman.
Was your blood spilled so that I might reject my history—
Forget tears in shadow among the paddy leaves.

At the horizon's edge, I hear
Voices crying in the wind. Cuffy shouting:
"Remember 1763!"—John Smith: "If I am
a man of God, let me join with suffering."
Akkarra—"I too had a vision"

Des Voeux cried,
"I wrote the Queen a letter
For the whimpering of the coolies in logies
would not let me rest."

The cry of coolies echoed round the land.

COMMENTARY

About the history of struggle of Caribbean Hindu-descended women, as shown in the work of Mahadai Das, scholar Renuka Laxminarayan Roy writes: "*They Came in Ships* brings forth the experience of the Indians who were brought from India to Trinidad, Tobago and Guyana in 1845. The poem delineates the story of the women in particular who were forcibly uprooted, dislodged and disowned, from their ancestral land of India. They came to [a] strange land, searching for better prospects and a happier life. The distinctiveness of their identity was erased overnight, and they were reduced to the status of contractual farm labourers, 'the coolies'" (the term first used by the British to designate the inhabitants of Kula, India, but later used to refer to any hired "unskilled" worker). It's worth noting Das's ample use of historical references (both from Guyana & East Indian sources), interweaving specific information against a collective memory blackout.

M. NourbeSe Philip Trinidad and Tobago/Canada, 1947–

from **ZONG!**

As told to the author by Setaey Adamu Boateng

ZONG! #14

the truth was

        the ship sailed

        the rains came

        the loss arose

               the truth is

the ship sailed

the rains came

the loss arose

                                            the negroes is

the truth was

Nkrumah Ato   Nobanzi   Oduneye   Opa   Fagbulu

ZONG! #15

defend the dead

                   weight of circumstance

ground

            to usual &

                       etc

                   where the ratio of just

in less than

              is necessary

                       to murder

the subject in property

the save in underwriter

                   where etc tunes justice

                   and the *ratio* of murder

                   is

                   the usual in occurred

Akilah   Falope   Ouma   Weke   Jubade

                   the just in ration
                   the suffer in loss

                              defend the dead
                              the weight

                                            in

circumstance

        ached in necessary

                                     the ration in just

               age the act in the *ave* to justice

       Nompumelelo Okulaja Ekisola Abike Arike

COMMENTARY

they ask for water we give them sea / they ask for bread we give them sea / they ask for life we give them only the sea (M.N.P.)

"In November, 1781, the captain of the slave ship *Zong* ordered that some 150 Africans be murdered by drowning so that the ship's owners could collect insurance monies. In her extended 182-page poetry cycle, Philip composes entirely from the words of the case report, *Gregson v. Gilbert*— the only extant public document related to the massacre of these African slaves. Equal parts song, moan, shout, oath, ululation, curse, and chant, *Zong!* excavates the legal text. Memory, history, and law collide and meta-morphose into the poetics of the fragment. Through the innovative use of fugal and counterpointed repetition, *Zong!* becomes an anti-narrative lament that stretches the boundaries of the poetic form, haunting the spaces of forgetting & mourning the forgotten" (from the publisher's summary of *Zong!*).

In doing which, Philip is guided, she tells us, by the ancestral voice of "Setaey Adamu Boateng," telling a story "that cannot but must be told." Other voices' names appear as footnotes.

William Carlos Williams USA, 1883–1963

from **PATERSON**

Preface

"Rigor of beauty is the quest. But how will you find beauty when it is locked in the mind past all remonstrance?"

To make a start,
out of particulars
and make them general, rolling
up the sum, by defective means—

Sniffing the trees,
just another dog
among a lot of dogs. What
else is there? And to do?
The rest have run out—
after the rabbits.
Only the lame stands—on
three legs. Scratch front and back.
Deceive and eat. Dig
a musty bone

For the beginning is assuredly
the end—since we know nothing, pure
and simple, beyond
our own complexities.

          Yet there is
no return: rolling up out of chaos,
a nine months' wonder, the city
the man, an identity—it can't be
otherwise—an
interpenetration, both ways. Rolling
up! obverse, reverse;
the drunk the sober; the illustrious
the gross; one. In ignorance
a certain knowledge and knowledge,
undispersed, its own undoing.

          (The multiple seed,
packed tight with detail, soured,
is lost in the flux and the mind,
distracted, floats off in the same
scum)

Rolling up, rolling up heavy with
numbers.

          It is the ignorant sun
rising in the slot of
hollow suns risen, so that never in this
world will a man live well in his body
save dying—and not know himself
dying; yet that is

the design. Renews himself
thereby, in addition and subtraction,
walking up and down.

     and the craft,
subverted by thought, rolling up, let
him beware lest he turn to no more than
the writing of stale poems ...
Minds like beds always made up,
                    (more stony than a shore)
unwilling or unable.

          Rolling in, top up,
under, thrust and recoil, a great clatter:
lifted as air, boated, multicolored, a
wash of seas—
from mathematics to particulars—

          divided as the dew,
floating mists, to be rained down and
regathered into a river that flows
and encircles:

          shells and animalcules
generally and so to man,

          to Paterson.

COMMENTARY

Of which Williams himself wrote, by way of introduction to his master-work: "*Paterson* is a long poem in four parts [later five and an incomplete part six]—that a man in himself is a city, beginning, seeking, achieving and concluding his life in ways which the various aspects of a city may embody—if imaginatively conceived—any city, all the details of which may be made to voice his most intimate convictions. Part One introduces the elemental character of the place. The Second Part comprises the modern replicas. Three will seek a language to make them vocal, and Four, the river below the falls, will be reminiscent of episodes—all that any one man may achieve in a lifetime" (1946). For which history—including the personal & mythic—is a necessary/essential component.

It should also be noted that Paterson, New Jersey, was his hometown & close to Rutherford, where he pursued his profession as a local doctor.

Ezra Pound USA, 1885–1972

from **THE CANTOS**

LIII

Yeou taught men to break branches
Seu Gin set up the stage and taught barter,
 taught the knotting of cords
Fou Hi taught men to grow barley
 2837 ante Christum
and they know still where his tomb is
by the high cypress between the strong walls
the FIVE grains, said Chin Nong, that are
 wheat, rice, millet, *gros blé* and chick peas
and made a plough that is used five thousand years
Moved his court then to Kio-feou-hien
held market at mid-day
'bring what we have not here', wrote an herbal
Souan yen bagged fifteen tigers
 made signs out of bird tracks
Hoang Ti contrived the making of bricks
and his wife started working the silk worms,
 money was in days of Hoang Ti.
He measured the length of Syrinx
 of the tubes to make tune for song
Twenty-six (that was) eleven ante Christum
 had four wives and 25 males of his making
His tomb is today in Klao-Chan
Ti Ko set his scholars to fitting words to their music
 is burled in Tung Kleou
This was in the twenty fifth century a c
 YAO like the sun and rain,
saw what star is at solstice
saw what star marks mid summer
YU, leader of waters,
 black earth is fertile, wild silk still is from Shantung
Ammassi, to the provinces,
 let his men pay tithes in kind
'Siu-tcheou province to pay in earth of five colours
Pheasant plumes from Yu-chan of mountains

Yu-chan to pay sycamores
　　　of this wood are lutes made
Ringing stones from Se-choul river
and grass that is called Tsing-mo' or μῶλυ,
Chun to the spirit Chang Ti, of heaven
moving the sun and stars
　　　que vos vers expriment vos intentions,
et que la musique conforme

YAO　　　堯

CHUN　　舜

YU　　　禹

KAO-YAO　皋
　　　　　陶

　　　abundance.

Then an Empress fled with Chao Kang in her belly
Fou-hi by virtue of wood,
Chin-nong, of fire, Hoang Ti ruled by the earth,
Chan by metal
Tchuen was lord, as is water
CHUN, govern
YU, cultivate,
The surface is not enough,
　　　from Chang Ti nothing is hidden
For years no waters came, no rain fell
　　　for the Emperor Tching Tang
grain scarce, prices rising
so that in 1760 Tching Tang opened the copper mine (ante Christum)
made discs with square holes in their middles
　　　and gave these to the people
wherewith they might buy grain
　　　　　　　　　where there was grain
The silos were emptied
7 years of sterility
　　　　　der im Baluba das Gewitter gemacht hat
Tching prayed on the mountain and

wrote MAKE IT NEW
on his bath tub
     Day by day make it new
cut underbrush,
pile the logs
keep it growing.
Died Tching aged years an hundred,
in the 13th of his reign
     We are up, Hia is down.
Immoderate love of women
Immoderate love of riches,
Card for parades and huntin',
     Chang Ti above alone rules
Tang not stinting of praise:
     Consider their sweats, the people's
If you wd/ sit calm on throne.

新 hsin

日 jih

日 jih

新 hsin

COMMENTARY

(1) One of the great founding works of New World epic & long-poem writing, the composing of Pound's *Cantos* spanned a period from the 1920s until almost the year of his death in 1972. The work as such is a fulfillment of his definition of the "epic" as "a poem including history," drawing in materials from a wide range of languages & cultures, both historical & contemporary: Chinese & Japanese, Provençal & Roman, ancient Egyptian & African, along with latter-day American. An extraordinary multicultural display & an expanded "tale of the tribe," as he named it for the *Cantos*, but curiously—in that fascist mind—a greater tribe than privileged race & nation might have led us to expect. Writes Pound himself in assessment of where all of that might take us or him: "It is dawn in Jerusalem while midnight hovers above the Pillars of Hercules. All ages are contemporaneous in the mind."

(2) *I believe that when finished, all foreign words in the* Cantos... *will be underlinings, not necessary to the sense, in one way. I mean a complete sense will exist without them* (in Pound's correspondence with Hubert Creekmore).

For more on Pound in his different guises, see "A Second Gallery" & elsewhere in these pages.

Anne Waldman USA, 1945–

from *IOVIS*

Manggala

A man of sorrows
comes in lowness
comes to me in lowness
& this humiliation becomes passion
lamb into lion
then I am in lowness
& He is the great King
& He is the bridegroom
Time, O the time is at hand
& I am in lowness
& He is the great king
& I am in lowness
The dragon is Pharaoh
& I am in lowness
I eat the book in this oral philosophy
Tell old Pharaoh to let my people go
The time is at hand
(& I am in lowness)
The time is at hand in lowness
I will take his sorrowful past into my future
I will take both testaments
& transmute the mundane into heavenly music
& eat the book
The scroll is my number
& do not destroy my temple
I sing within & without the temple (it's this book the temple I speak of)
the male gods take over as electricity & dynamite
& let me preach these allegories for the last day
& we, goddesses, giddy on the last day
will preach these allegories on the last day
I speak out of my lowness
but the messiah is a man of sorrows
& O He is a great king
but I am in my writing
& in my richness
I speak a new doctrine to an old space

History—whose version? You have to ask. (A.W.)

(1) For which the argument is set forth in the wrappers of Anne Waldman's thousand-page trilogy: "Waldman's monumental feminist epic, a mythopoetic project of twenty-five years, traverses epochs, cultures, and genres to create a visionary call to poetic arms. *Iovis*, an intricate narrative web of montage and superimposition, details the misdeeds of the Patriarch, and with a fierce imagination queries and subverts his warmongering. This is epic poetry that goes beyond the old injunction 'to include history'—its effort is to change history." And Waldman herself on the present & past of such work—& the female & male of it: "I honor and dance on the corpse of the poetry gone before me and especially here in a debt and challenge of epic masters Williams, Pound, Zukofsky, and Olson. But with the narrative of H.D.'s *Helen in Egypt* in mind, and her play with 'argument,' I want to don armor of words as they do and fight with liberated tongue and punctured heart. But unlike the men's, my history and myths are personal ones."

(2) Of the title of her epic's opener—*manggala*—drawn from Sanskrit & Old Javanese traditions, she writes: "I wrote the Manggala after compiling BOOK I (300 pages). It came as a kind of prayer-psalmic and calls up the biblical messiah. A later section conjures the Qu'ran (The Koran), an old Cary Grant movie, a conversation with 10 year-olds, a 'take' from Clark Coolidge on the movie 'Five Easy Pieces,' and a Sanskrit invocation to 'onepointedness.'"

"*Manggala*" as such, as she defines it, is "an invocation that establishes the poet's understanding between him/her self, the text, and the world."

Ed Dorn USA, 1929–1999

from **GUNSLINGER**

*The curtain might rise
anywhere on a single speaker*

I met in Mesilla
The Cautious Gunslinger
of impeccable personal smoothness
and slender leather encased hands
folded casually
to make his knock.
He would show you his map.

There is your domain.
Is it the domicile it looks to be
or simply a retinal block
of seats in,
he will flip the phrase
the theater of impatience.

If it is where you are,
the footstep in the flat above
in a foreign land
or any shimmer the city
sends you
the prompt sounds
of a metropolitan nearness
he will unroll the map of locations.

His knock resounds
inside its own smile, where?
I ask him is my heart.
Not this pump he answers
artificial already and bound
touching me
with his leathern finger
as the Queen of Hearts burns
from his gauntlet into my eyes.

Flageolets of fire
he says there will be.
This is for your sadly missing heart
the girl you left
in Juarez, the blank
political days press her now
in the narrow adobe
confines of the river town
her dress is torn
by the misadventure of
          her gothic search

The mission bells are ringing
in Kansas.
Have you left something out:
Negative, says my Gunslinger,
no *thing* is omitted.

Time is more fundamental than space.
It is, indeed, the most pervasive
of all the categories
in other words
theres plenty of it.
And it stretches things themselves
until they blend into one,
so if youve seen one thing
youve seen them all.

I held the reins of his horse
while he went into the desert
to pee. *Yes*, he reflected
when he returned, that's less.

How long, he asked
have you been in this territory.

Years I said. Years.
Then you will know where we can have
a cold drink before sunset and then a bed
will be my desire
if you can find one for me
I have no wish to continue
my debate with men,
my mare lathers with tedium
her hooves are dry
Look they are covered with the alkali
of the enormous space
between here and formerly.
Need I repeat, we have come
without sleep from Nuevo Laredo.

And why do you have such a horse
Gunslinger? I asked. Don't move
he replied
the sun rests deliberately
on the rim of the sierra.

And where will you now I asked.
Five days northeast of here
depending of course on whether one's horse
is of iron or flesh

there is a city called Boston
and in that city there is a hotel
whose second floor has been let
to an inscrutable Texan named Hughes
Howard? I asked
The very same.
And what do you mean by inscrutable,
        oh Gunslinger?
I mean to say that He
has not been seen since 1833.

But when you have found him my Gunslinger
what will you do, oh what will you do?
You would not know
that the souls of old Texans
are in jeopardy in a way not common
to other men, my singular friend.

You would not know
of the long plains night
where they carry on
and arrange their genetic duels
with men of other states—
so there is a longhorn bull half mad
half deity
who awaits an account from me
back of the sun you nearly disturbed
just then.
Lets have that drink.

STRUM
    strum

COMMENTARY

For all of Dorn's connections to earlier North American epics (Olson, Pound, & Williams), the elements of comedy & parody, along with a sharp-eyed sense of his own time & culture (the late 1960s), mark a significant difference & divergence, "undercutting the high rhetoric of epic vision" (M. Davidson). As a popular British newspaper reports it, "*Gunslinger* is perhaps the strangest long poem of the last half-century: a quest myth wrapped around an acid-inspired western comic strip adventure in which a gunslinger, astride a drug-taking, talking horse called Levi-Strauss, searches for [business magnate & movie mogul] Howard Hughes ('they say he moved to Vegas / or bought Vegas and / moved it. / I can't remember which')" (*Guardian*, February 1, 2013).

In all of this, Dorn's *Gunslinger* emerges as a major instance of an oppositional avant-garde, coming headlong into our own time, but connecting as well with the disruptive work of traditional clowns & tricksters. The goal at its extreme was to turn the mind upside down & to call the sacred & the obvious into question—a program that showed up, to one degree or another, in movements and among practitioners of poetry & other artworks on a nearly global scale. Its presence in deeper historical & cultural time is possibly the greater lesson in a work like ours.

ADDENDUM

ISHMAEL REED USA, 1938–

from **I Am a Cowboy in the Boat of Ra**

> I am a cowboy in the boat of Ra. Ezzard Charles
> of the Chisholm Trail. Took up the bass but they
> blew off my thumb. Alchemist in ringmanship but a
> sucker for the right cross.
>
> I am a cowboy in the boat of Ra. Vamoosed from
> the temple i bide my time. The price on the wanted
> poster was a-going down, outlaw alias copped my stance
> and moody greenhorns were making me dance; while my mouth's
> shooting iron got its chambers jammed.
>
> I am a cowboy in the boat of Ra. Boning-up in
> the ol' West i bide my time. You should see
> me pick off these tin cans whippersnappers. I
> write the motown long plays for the comeback of
> Osiris. Make them up when stars stare at sleeping
> steer out here near the campfire. Women arrive
> on the backs of goats and throw themselves on
> my Bowie.

Diego Maquieira Chile, 1950–

from *LA TIRANA*

II. (I Blew the Virgin from My Legs)

I was falling onto his mother's pink bed
the bed pushed up to the bathroom wall
I fell with black veils on both breasts
each one entering its burning chapel
I'm the prick's daughter, a mother
painted by Diego Rodríguez de Silva y Velázquez
My body is one sheet over another
my nails as long as my fingers are
and my face of God on the face of God
on his painted hole the shining cross:
the one they raise up from here, the D.N.A.
blackballed from the box office
the one they've stepped on since 1492
But my face isn't the color anymore
it's on my double buried out beyond
with all my fingers and my teeth in its mouth
I'm Howard Hughes Stylites
I blew the virgin from my legs
Having thought about myself so much.

. . . . .

V. (Nicolau Eimeric)

It was great when your biggest enemy
that most celebrated and perverse of Catholics
the supreme leader, the hit man of Chilean
religion came into your house in solemn ceremony
handsome, with his black vestments
and escorted by Olivares. It was impressive
all your guests cried at the sight
Then you offered him your Boeri sofa
and ordered the candelabra lighted
to brighten up the atmosphere
You introduced him to Alessandra Mussolini
to see if maybe you'd stir his soul
and the party was almost over for you

because it took balls for him
to show up there after all
and one like you who knew the devil
You had a hard time keeping your family
calm, several of them wanted
to kill him right there. But you were cool
as you shot your way through, with the Aulentis
flying backwards through the walls
of the huge room, so they wouldn't touch him
and because you couldn't let the cross
slip from your hands at that moment
You hear me, Velázquez? I'm talking to you

Translated from Spanish by Karen A. Nielsen

COMMENTARY

Writes translator Karen A. Nielsen about *La Tirana* (*The She-tyrant*): "The protagonist of the book, La Tirana,… was a legendary Indian woman who together with a band of warriors, fought against the conquistadors, until she fell in love with one of them and intervened to save his life. For her treachery she was killed, along with her love, by the Indians she had betrayed. The legend does not appear however but provides the poet with an extraordinary female protagonist, whom he describes as 'a religious whore, a pagan Indian, a fierce warrior, who was domesticated by the blackmail of Christian love.'

"The poems take place in the municipal palaces, theaters and sex hotels of modern Santiago, where a wasted and desperate La Tirana pursues the Spanish painter Velázquez and slowly descends into madness. Characters of the past and present, gangsters, artists, hit men, poets and degenerate priests mingle in the decadent atmosphere and nightmarish ultraviolence of the films of Sam Peckinpah and Stanley Kubrick. The poet speaks not only through La Tirana, but borrows the voices of other poets in order to address the theme of the destruction of Chilean culture, which recurs throughout the book, and of the repression of freedom of thought and creativity everywhere."

That this includes the Pinochet dictatorship of Maquieira's own lifetime is also to be noted.

Louis Zukofsky USA, 1904–1978

from **"A"-12**

I'll tell you
About my *poetics*—

$$\int$$ music

  speech

An integral
Lower limit speech
Upper limit music

No?

To excel in humility
Is not to be humble.
Humility does not glaze
Other bodies,
With fellow creatures
Sees agony,
Is the stronger body,
With the eye of sky
Eats food that
Guano dressed.
Not a swallow made that summer.

Time qualifies the fire and spark of,
I can't improve *that.*
That closed and open sounds saw
          Things,
See somehow everlastingly
Out of the eye of sky.

Poetics. With constancy.

My father died in the spring.

Half of a fence was built that summer.
For minutes as I drove nails in the lower stringer
The sunset upside down
Tops of trees. even an inverted hill.

Gauze. In the high sun
Paul spoke of garlic salt as gargle-salt.
Spoke all the time.
C. *would* call the cottage Clostrophobia.
Of clapboard. Without the terracotta
Of a della Robbia.
A family of three
On *terra* with grass windblown
A first tall in the new cattails.
And so little space—
Three tiny rooms too many—
It had to be shipshape.
Almost on the back cement step
Cattails—hardly *firma*.

My father, where shall I begin?

Who will know what you meant?

To get out of the world alive
Despite despite—
To live among ordinary men
And yet be alone with Him:
To greet profanity
And from it draw the strength to live,
Said the Baalshem—
Thaew—as good as his name.
To sing a michtam of David,
To be alive, that is good.

All summer
Paul babbled of him
Living his life
In young memory.
Ready to speak, like grandpa Paul.
"No let's call the cottage
Grandpa Paul.
I'm sorry he died,
he asked me to come on
a week-day,

when he could buy me a toy
I like him
better than everyone."

To begin a song:
If you cannot recall,
Forget.

Sabbath, the pious carry no money
Make no purchases. They have everything
From Friday—the Eve of the Sabbath.
Rest.
A long Sabbath.

COMMENTARY

*The more the words of others impressed him with their factual content,
the more he felt he must wait for his own facts before being tempted into
words.* (L.Z.) And again: *Only emotion objectified endures.*

It was Zukofsky's genius to recognize, while composing his epic "A" ("a
poem" à la Ezra Pound "including history"), that the personal & even
the familial (his father Pinchos, his wife Celia Thaew, his son Paul) might
appear alongside the objectively historical & serve there as a driving force.
In Mark Scroggins's summary: "In his later years, Zukofsky took to calling 'A' 'a poem of a life.'" And further: "The poet's task in regard to form,
then, is an *aesthetic* one, a matter of finding a beautiful, harmonic, resonant
shape in which to dispose that subject matter. And once you have a general
armature to build on—say, twenty-four movements—then the form of each
of those movements opens up to possibility."
    The register of music, in Zukofsky's sense of it, was also crucial.

For more on Zukofsky, see "A Third Gallery" & "A Map of Extensions."

Charles Olson USA, 1910–1970

from **A SPECIAL VIEW OF HISTORY**

… "What did happen? Two alternatives: make it up; or try to find out. Both are necessary. We inherit an either-or, from the split of science and fiction. It dates back at least to Plato, who used the word 'mouth' as an insult, to say it lies, and called poets muthologists—don't tell the truth, and so mislead the Commonwealth.

"Story was once all logos, the art of the logos. 'The normal or characteristic function of the ancient Story Teller,' says J. K. Thomson, from whom I draw most of this on the Logos, 'was not to invent. It was to repeat.' It was not mere word or expression of human experience so much as it was a form of human experience itself.

"Because it was oral it was also Muthos. Logos itself did not originally mean 'word' or 'reason,' or anything but merely 'what is said.' For some reason, says Thomson, Homer avoids Logos, preferring Muthos, but Muthos with him means 'what is said' in speech or story exactly like Logos in its primary sense. Herodotus calls Aesop a Logopoies, and is himself called by Aristotle not that, but 'the Muthologos.' What it all comes to is this, that to those who listened to the Stories a Muthos was a Logos, and a Logos was a Muthos. They were two names for the same thing.

"One need notice, however, that Herodotus may have been conscious of a difference he was making when he did add the word 'history.' The first words of his book—oi logoi—are 'those skilled in the logoi'—not 'historians.' '['I]storin in him appears to mean 'finding out for oneself,' instead of depending on hearsay. The word had already been used by the philosophers. But while they were looking for truth, Herodotus was looking for the evidence."

.....

"'Story. Be cockney. Drop the H—how often, if you are a writer, have you been told by everyone you meet, if you could take my life down, that would be a story?…

"'Man is estranged from that with which he is most familiar.'—Heraclitus…

"History is the new localism, a polis to replace the one which was lost in various stages all over the world from 490 BC on, until anyone of us knows places where it is disappearing now."

For more on Olson, see "A Third Gallery" & elsewhere in these pages.

Derek Walcott Saint Lucia, 1930–2017

from **OMEROS**

Book Three, Chapter XXV

I

Mangroves, their ankles in water, walked with the canoe.
The swift, racing its browner shadow, screeched, then veered
into a dark inlet. It was the last sound Achille knew

from the other world. He feathered the paddle, steered
away from the groping mangroves, whose muddy shelves
slipped warted crocodiles, slitting the pods of their eyes;

then the horned river-horses rolling over themselves
could capsize the keel. It was like the African movies
he had yelped at in childhood. The endless river unreeled

those images that flickered into real mirages:
naked mangroves walking beside him, knotted logs
wriggling into the water, the wet, yawning boulders

of oven-mouthed hippopotami. A skeletal warrior
stood up straight in the stern and guided his shoulders,
clamped his neck in cold iron, and altered the oar.

Achille wanted to scream, he wanted the brown water
to harden into a road, but the river widened ahead
and closed behind him. He heard screeching laughter

in a swaying tree, as monkeys swung from the rafter
of their tree-house, and the bared sound rotted the sky
like their teeth. Four hours the river gave the same show

for nothing, the canoe's mouth muttered its lie.
The deepest terror was the mud. The mud with no shadow
like the clear sand. Then the river coiled into a bend.

He saw the first signs of men, tall sapling fishing-stakes;
he came into his own beginning and his end,
for the swiftness of a second is all that memory takes.

Now the strange, inimical river surrenders its stealth
to the sunlight. And a light inside him wakes,

skipping centuries, ocean and river, and Time itself.

And God said to Achille, "Look, I giving you permission
to come home. Is I send the sea-swift as a pilot,
the swift whose wings is the sign of my crucifixion.

And thou shalt have no God should in case you forgot
my commandments." And Achille felt the homesick shame
and pain of his Afric, his heart and his bare head

were bursting as he tried to remember the name
of the river- and the tree-god in which he steered,
whose hollow body carried him to the settlement ahead.

.....

III

He sought his own features in those of their life-giver,
and saw two worlds mirrored there: the hair was surf
curling round a sea-rock, the forehead a frowning river,

as they swirled in the estuary of a bewildered love,
and Time stood between them. The only interpreter
of their lip's joined babble, the river with the foam,

and the chuckles of water under the sticks of the pier,
where the tribe stood like sticks themselves, reversed
by reflection. Then they walked up to the settlement,

and it seemed, as they chattered, everything was rehearsed
for ages before this. He could predict the intent
of his father's gestures; he was moving with the dead.

Women paused at their work, then smiled at the warrior
returning from his battle with smoke, from the kingdom
where he had been captured, they cried and were happy.

Then the fishermen sat near a large tree under whose dome
stones sat in a circle. His father said:

                              "Afo-la-be"
touching his own heart.

                    "In the place you have come from
what do they call you?"

                    Time translates.

                                              Tapping his chest,
the son answers:
                    "Achille." The tribe rustles, "Achille."
Then, like cedars at sunrise, the mutterings settle.

AFOLABE

Achille. What does that name mean? I have forgotten the one
that I gave you. But it was, it seems, many years ago.
What does it mean?

ACHILLE

                    Well, I too have forgotten.
Everything was forgotten. You also. I do not know.
The deaf sea has changed around every name that you gave
us; trees, men, we yearn for a sound that is missing.

AFOLABE

A name means something. The qualities desired in a son,
and even a girl-child, so even the shadows who called
you expected one virtue, since every name is a blessing,

since I am remembering the hope I had for you as a child.
Unless the sound means nothing. Then you would be nothing.
Did they think you were nothing in that other kingdom?

ACHILLE

I do not know what the name means. It means something,
maybe. What's the difference? In the world I come from
we accept the sounds we were given. Men, trees, water.

AFOLABE

And therefore, Achille, if I pointed and said, There
is the name of that man, that tree, and this father,
would every sound be a shadow that crossed your ear,

without the shape of a man or a tree? What would it be?
(And just as branches sway in the dusk from their fear
of amnesia, of oblivion, the tribe began to grieve.)

If you ask about language in the Caribbean, you must relate it to history. (D.W.) And again: *When I was writing this book, you might say I was thinking of the two great Caribbean artists, Hemingway and Homer.*

That being said, what Walcott gives us in fact is an "epic of the dispossessed" (Robert D. Hammer), reimagining the Trojan War—very loosely— as a Caribbean fishermen's tale, with a complex intertwining of adapted names & places, contemporary & ancient, into which he enters as well, both as voice & as persona. The dialogue, above, between the Caribbean fisherman Achille & his Yoruba ancestor Afolabe is a highlight as we have it here. But not enough to give a true sense of the length & scope of Walcott's work & its multiple plots & timelines: seven "books," sixty-four chapters, eight thousand lines.

That the language of God, as presented here, carries the sound of what can be taken as a kind of Lucian or Caribbean English may also be of some interest.

Jacob Carpenter USA, 1833–1920

from *DEATHS ON THREE-MILE CREEK 1841–1915*

An Anthology of Death

Wm Davis   age 100.8   dide oc 5   1841
    wars old soldier in rev ware   and got his
        thie brok in last fire at Kinge's monte
      he wars farmer   and made brandy
        and never had Drunker in famly

Franky Davis his wife   age 87   dide Sep 10   1842
    she had nirve fite wolves all nite at shogar camp
        to save her caff   throde fier chonks
      the camp wars half mile from home
    noe she must have nirv to fite wolf all nite

Charley Kiney   age 72   dide may 10   1852
    wars farmer live in mt on bluey rige at kiney gap
      he had 4 wimmin cors marid to one
          rest live on farme
    all went to felde   work to mak grain

all wen to crib for ther bread
all went smok hous for there mete
he cilde bote 75 to 80 hoges every yere
and wimen never had wordes bout him
haven so many wimin
if he wod be living this times
wod be hare pulde
thar wars 42 children blong to him
they all wento preching togethern
nothing sed   des aver body go long smoth
help one nother
never had any foes
got along smoth with avery bodi
I nod him

COMMENTARY

Written down by Uncle Jake Carpenter of Three-Mile Creek, Avery County, in the western mountains of North Carolina. The impulse to poetry in these "obituaries"—some written long after the actual deaths—may not be much different from that in Edgar Lee Masters's *Spoon River Anthology* & other elegies. Now known as "Uncle Jake Carpenter's Anthology of Death," the title by his own reference was to his "Son-of-a-Gun Book" or his "Jot-em-down Book"—a red-backed account ledger in which he recorded the deaths of many of his fellow citizens over a seventy-year span. The work also enters contemporary American poetry through Jonathan Williams's poem "From Uncle Jake Carpenter's Anthology of Death on Three-Mile Creek."

The last entry Uncle Jake made in his notebook reads: "Jacob Carpenter is sick took bed this day." As noted elsewhere: "That was his last illness, for he died on March 10, 1920, aged 87, his death being attributed to an attack of the flu."

Jackson Mac Low   USA, 1922–2004

from *THE PRESIDENTS OF THE UNITED STATES OF AMERICA*

1789   (begun about 15 January 1963)

George Washington never owned a camel
but he looked thru the eyes in his head
with a camel's calm and wary look

Hooks that wd irritate an ox
held his teeth together
and he cd build a fence with his own hands
tho he preferred to go fishing
as anyone else wd
while others did the work *for* him
for tho he had no camels he had slaves enough
and probably made them toe the mark by keeping an eye on them
for *he* wd never have stood for anything fishy

1797

1

John Adams knew the hand
can be quicker than the eye
& knew that not only fencers & fishermen live by this knowledge

If he kept an ox
he kept it out of doors in summertime
so the ox cd find his water for himself
& make it where he stood
& find the tasty grass
his teeth cd chew as cud.

1801

Marked by no fence
farther than an eye cd see
beyond the big waters
Thomas Jefferson saw grass enough for myriads of oxen
to grind between their teeth

His farmer hands itched
When he thought of all that vacant land and looked about for a way to
    hook it in for us
until something unhooked a window in his head
where the greedy needy teeth & eyes of Napoleon shone
eager for the money which
was Jefferson's bait to catch the Louisiana fish.

COMMENTARY

An ongoing involvement with historical matters but expressed most often
through lettristic & aleatory (chance) procedures. Always transparent

about his methods, Mac Low provides the following note: "*The Presidents of the United States of America* was composed in January and May 1963. Each section is headed by the first inaugural year of a President (from Washington through Fillmore), and its structure of images is that of the Phoenician meanings of the successive letters of the President's name.... They are:

A (aleph) 'ox'   N (nun) 'fish'
B (beth) 'house'   O (ayin) 'eye'
etc."

Writes critic Charles O. Hartman of the resultant mix of chance composition methods with politically & historically themed poetry—one of Mac Low's principal achievements: "This procedure puts us into a suspicious relation with the poem's language (I glimpse a system of meaning lurking behind what I'm reading); just so, the 'President' poems concern themselves with the relation between the schoolbook vision of these men and the reality of their slave-holding, politicking, and war-mongering."

While the series ends mid-nineteenth century, the sense of distress & outrage could well carry into the present.

For more on Mac Low & chance procedures, see "A Third Gallery" & "A Map of Extensions."

Leónidas Lamborghini Argentina, 1927–2009

from **EVA PERÓN AT THE STAKE**

XV

against all privilege: my works. there I put.
against all oligarchy. there. my works are born. a drop. an ocean:
they better come.
they better see. my works:
a drop falling. over. against. one hundred years of: the injustice
of a century. ocean. one. the exploiting race. against.
there my works: I had to.
had: to destroy with my works. against all. my works are born.
to destroy: charity. I know that still.
to destroy: the coins they let fall. a drop. miserable.
the coins: cold.
my works against. my works born. a century:
the cheap soul of. miserable. there the oligarchy. all.

the asylums: paint there. one hundred years. injustice that is: an ocean.
I had to: to destroy. against. there I put: my works. they are born.
the walls should be: born.
the tables should be. born.
the dishes should be. born.
the clothes should be. born.
the bedrooms should be. born.
the flowers should be. born.
they better come.
they better see.
there I: they are born. a drop falling. my works against. I know that still.
a drop in an ocean: falling. there.
an ocean of: what this world is. a drop falling in: the
injustice. an ocean. my works against. I know that still.

XVI

not functionary: a bird. I wanted so. freedom:
I always.
revolution: I always. think I was born for.
so: a bird free in the forest. immense.
a bird not chained. not to the huge machinery. not to the state.
bird: not hired. non. not functionary.
a bird: I always liked. I wanted to live. think I was born.
free. so I: I always. the air. the free.
not to the state. not to the huge
freedom: I. bird: think I was born.

Translated from Spanish by Javier Taboada

COMMENTARY

In *Eva Perón at the Stake*, Leónidas Lamborghini deconstructs & reassembles Eva Perón's autobiography, *La Razón de Mi vida*, published in 1951, in which she shapes & develops—through melodramatic testimonies & speeches—the persona & myth of herself as Evita, an internationally known victim finally saved by a romanticized Juan Domingo Perón (hero, husband, protective father of the nation, & Argentina's populist president). Not an outrider, the poem presented here is the first of a series of poems in which Lamborghini cuts up & collages a number of texts—Evita's autobiography but also Argentina's national anthem & a number of popular tangos—as a questioning of national identity.

Despite his criticism, Lamborghini was himself a *peronista* (a militant of Perón's political party).

bpNichol   Canada, 1944–1988

from **THE MARTYROLOGY**

history is time
myth is space
gilgamesh *was* human
5th king of the second post-diluvian dynasty
Uruk third millennium B.C.
how do you separate them
the aborigines never bothered
myth being everything
history becomes unreal
binding in
a narrowing of focus
the man who has no "dreamtime" goes insane
we have travelled a long way
"on the road from which there is no way back,
to the house wherein the dwellers are bereft of light,
where dust is their fare & clay their food."
you were never fooled by any mask or pose we might have taken
whatever aspect we assumed
traced my own family back to the 1830s
Ireland (the hypoboreans?)
we are robbed of myth
bereft of trust
just a few hundred years of almost nothing
dust piling on dust
there are bigger things

COMMENTARY

*I wanted a writing… that would not pretend to an omniscience or to an
authority that it didn't have, a writing which partakes of the human condition in the sense that we're all vulnerable, we could die at any moment.*
(bpN.)

bpNichol's massive poem and life project in nine ongoing "book" installments ended with his early death in 1988. Of the implications of that work
& life, Jed Rasula wrote: "The twentieth-century long poem is a special
province of Americans. Between them, Pound, Williams, Olson, and Zukofsky slapped down thousands of pages in *The Cantos, Paterson, The Maximus Poems,* and '*A*'. But with characteristically Canadian unpretentious-

ness, Nichol blew them all away with his *Martyrology*, nine volumes of which he completed before his untimely death. Unlike the big [US] guns, *Martyrology* does not make martyrs of its readers: Absorbing what the poet dubbed its 'mirthology' is not a chore. If anything, it's a pun expanded to improbable dimensions.... 'In a curious way,' he once said, 'the saints were language, or were my encounter with language.'"

And it is such an encounter with language that we find again & again—& from all sides—in "A Map of Extensions," which follows.

A MAP OF EXTENSIONS

I can't understand why people are frightened of new ideas.
I'm frightened of the old ones.

JOHN CAGE

AMERICA must be original...We either invent or we err.

SIMÓN RODRÍGUEZ

All life is an experiment. The more experiments you make the better.

RALPH WALDO EMERSON

DAY BY DAY MAKE IT NEW
YET AGAIN MAKE IT NEW

EZRA POUND

The relevance of experimentalism to African-American writing
and of African-American writing to experimentalism
needs to be insisted on.

NATHANIEL MACKEY

Everything is poetry except for poetry.

NICANOR PARRA

It is better to fail in originality
than to succeed in imitation.

HERMAN MELVILLE

Mayan

from *THE MAYAN CODEX*

COMMENTARY

(1) The art here is in the mix of both written words & brightly colored images, creating a visual poetry & the well-wrought codices or painted books that contained it. With the onset of the European invasions, all but a handful of these numerous books were put to the torch in an actual, religiously driven auto-da-fé or holocaust. The three surviving Mayan codices were carried intact to Dresden, Paris, & Madrid; the partially charred remains of another, above, is the only one of its kind still left in Mexico. Of the books themselves & their destruction, which he had set in motion, Bishop Diego de Landa wrote, ca. 1566:

> *They wrote their books on a long sheet doubled in folds, which was then enclosed between two boards finely ornamented; the writing was on one side and the other, according to the folds. The paper they made from the roots of a tree and gave it a white finish excellent for writing upon. Some of the principal lords were learned in these sciences, from interest, and for the greater esteem they enjoyed thereby; yet they did not make use of them in public.*

> *These people also used certain characters or letters, with which they wrote in their books about the antiquities and their sciences; with*

these, and with figures, and certain signs in the figures, they under-
stood their matters, made them known, and taught them. We found
a great number of books in these letters, and since they contained
nothing but superstitions and falsehoods of the devil, we burned
them all, which they took most grievously, and which gave them
great pain.

The recurrence of such iconoclasms stretches into our own time as well—as does, in what follows, the effort to retrieve them.

(2) According to an account made by the Mexican historian Justo Sierra O'Reilly, in the 1562 auto-da-fé of Maní alone (in present-day Yucatán), the confiscated & burned Mayan objects included "5,000 idols of different shapes & sizes, 13 large carved stones that served as altars, 22 small stones of various shapes, 27 rolls of written hieroglyphs on deer skin [= codices], & 197 vessels of various dimensions & forms."

Martín Gómez Ramírez   Tseltal, Mexico, 1961–

CICADA

[LEFT COLUMN]
Tiniest witness
of new life & spring
insect 13 moons solid
hidden away in holy mother
you cocoon ages old
& wondrous button.

[RIGHT COLUMN]
Singing and they sing
in chorus perched between its arms
the liquidambar tree flow,
concert on the eve,
the San Juan festival already,
San Marcos in April.

(1) Martín Gómez Ramírez (b. 1961) is a Tseltal Mayan writer from J'itontik, Chiapas. "Cicada" may be the first modern poem to employ ancient Mayan hieroglyphs.

(2) Wrote US poet Charles Olson, back in 1951 or so: "Christ, these hieroglyphs. Here is the most abstract & formal deal of all the things this people dealt out—& yet, to my mind, it is precisely as intimate as verse is. Is, in fact, verse. And comes into existence, obeys the same laws that the coming into existence, the persistence of verse, does" (*Mayan Letters*).

Shakers USA, 19th century

SHAKER VISION DRAWING

The United Society of Believers in Christ's Second Appearing—called "Shakers"—originated in England in the mid-eighteenth century & soon centered around the person of Ann Lee (Mother Ann, or Mother Wisdom, or simply Mother), who became "the reincarnation of the Christ Spirit… Ann the Word… Bride of the Lamb." The group practiced communal living

& equality of the sexes, along with a reputedly complete abstention from sexual intercourse. After persecutions & jailings in England, Mother Ann brought them to America in 1774, where for many years they thrived on conversions, reaching a maximum number of six thousand before their demise in the twentieth century.

Between 1837 & 1850 (known as the "Era of Manifestations"), the Shakers composed (or were the recipients of) "hundreds of... visionary drawings... really [spiritual] messages in pictorial form," writes Edward Deming Andrews (*The Gift to Be Simple*). "The designers of these symbolic documents felt their work was controlled by supernatural agencies... gifts bestowed on some individual in the order, usually not the one who made the drawing." The same is true of the "gift songs" & other verbal works (below), & the invention of forms in both the songs & drawings is extraordinary, as is their resemblance to the practice of later poets & artists.

Manuel Antonio Valdés Mexico, 1780

from *MUTE ROMANCE TO THE VIRGIN OF GUADALUPE*

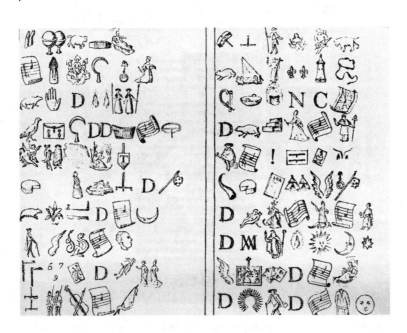

(1) Spanish in origin, *romances mudos* were pieces of visual poetry based on the utilization of fixed image patterns, which had to be more recognizable in order to help the interpreter to get into them. This kind of hieroglyphic composition is similar to the rebus; when deciphered, the verses spring from the combination of the names of the represented objects. So, the phrase in the first line, "de dos esferas, oh sagrada aurora" (translated literally: "from two spheres, oh sacred dawn"), is formed of five different images & words: fingers (dedos) + spheres (esferas) + female-bear (osa) + tier (grada) + dawn (aurora) = DEDOSesferasOSAgradaAURORA.

It's worth comparing this image with Clemente Padín's *Nahuatl Protest Song (I & II)*.

(2) The *Mute Romance to the Virgin of Guadalupe* was placed on the altar of Guadalupe in 1780.

Walt Whitman USA, 1819–1892

WORDS

[EDITORS' NOTE: In An American Primer *(ca. 1860), Whitman announced a range of words for poetry that would move its vocabulary out of previously restrictive bounds.*
And if we now read his list as a poem... ?]

Words of the Laws of the Earth,
Words of the Stars, and about them,
Words of the Sun and Moon,
Words of Geology, History, Geography,
Words of Ancient Races,
Words of the Medieval Races,
Words of the progress of Religion, Law, Art, Government,
Words of the surface of the Earth, grass, rocks, trees, flowers, grains and
    the like,
Words of like climates,
Words of the Air and Heavens,
Words of the Birds of the air, and of insects,
Words of Animals,
Words of Men and Women—the hundreds of different nations, tribes,
    colors, and other distinctions,
Words of the Sea,

Words of Modern Leading Ideas,
Words of Modern Inventions, Discoveries, engrossing Themes, Pursuits,
Words of These States—the Year I, Washington, the Primal Compact, the
    Second Compact (namely the Constitution)—trades, farms, wild lands,
    iron, steam, slavery, elections, California, and so forth,
Words of the Body, Senses, Limbs, Surface, Interior,
Words of dishes to eat, or of naturally produced things to eat,
Words of clothes,
Words of implements,
Words of furniture,
Words of all kinds of Building and Constructing,
Words of Human Physiology,
Words of Human Phrenology,
Words of Music,
Words of Feebleness, Nausea, Sickness, Ennui, Repugnance, and the like.

[And again: *All words are spiritual. Nothing is more spiritual than words.*]

ADDENDUM

JORGE TEILLIER Chile, 1935–1996

In Order to Talk with the Dead

> In order to talk with the dead
> you have to choose words
> that they recognize as easily
> as their hands
> recognized the fur of their dogs in the dark.
> Words clean and calm
> as water of the torrent tamed in the wineglass
> or chairs the mother puts in order
> after the guests have left.
> Words that night shelters
> as marshes do their ghostly fires.
>
> In order to talk with the dead
> you have to know how to wait:
> they are fearful
> like the first steps of a child.
> But if we are patient
> one day they will answer us
> with a poplar leaf trapped in a broken mirror,
> with a flame that suddenly revives in the fireplace,

with a dark return of birds
before the glance of a girl
who waits motionless on the threshold.

Translated from the Spanish by Carolyne L. Wright

Edgar Allan Poe USA, 1809–1849

from **X-ING A PARAGRAB**

Sx hx, Jxhn! hxw nxw? Txld yxu sx, yxu knxw. Dxn't crxw, anxther time, befxre yxu're xut xf the wxxds! Dxes yxur mxther *knxw* yxu're xut? Xh, nx, nx! sx gx hxme at xnce, nxw, Jxhn, tx yxur xdixus xld wxxds xf Cxncxrd! Gx hxme tx yxur wxxds, xld xwl,—gx! Yxu wxnt? Xh, pxh, pxh, Jxhn, dxn't dx sx! Yxu've *gxt* tx gx, yxu knxw! sx gx at xnce, and dxn't gx slxw; fxr nxbxdy xwns yxu here, yxu knxw. Xh, Jxhn, Jxhn, if yxu *dxn't* gx yxu're nx *hxmx*—nx! Yxu're xnly a fxwl, an xwl; a cxw, a sxw; a dxll, a pxll; a pxxr xld gxxd-fxr-nxthing-tx-nxbxdy lxg, dxg, hxg, xr frxg, cxme xut xf a Cxncxrd bxg. Cxxl, nxw—cxxl! Dx be cxxl, yxu fxxl! Nxne xf yxur crxwing, xld cxck! Dxn't frxwn sx—dxn't! Dxn't hxllx, nxr hxwl, nxr grxwl, nxr bxw-wxw-wxw! Gxxd Lxrd, Jxhn, hxw yxu *dx* lxxk! Txld yxu sx, yxu knxw, but stxp rxlling yxur gxxse xf an xld pxll abxut sx, and gx and drxwn yxur sxrrxws in a bxwl!

Guillermo Cabrera Infante Cuba, 1929–2005

from **THREE TRAPPED TIGERS**

Brainteaser (Excerpt)

… Of curse the wan and ownly oner had to turn up right then & there: a fat bald little fellow even shorter than the waiter, so short that he become shorter as he approached us and when he finally arrived at the table he seemed to be walking with his hands not his feet. A moveable feat. A bust. Or was it a buster?

—wassa matta?

—We wonly want to weat, Bustro said, turning a doldrum profiles toward him.

—You won't get anything to eat if you fool around like that.

—Like what? Bustrofastidious asked and as he was a tall skinny fellow
with a real ugly mug and thismugly of his was cratered with an acme of
an acne or

huge pox Americana or
by time and tide and its ruins or
meteorites or
vultures or
by all these things together:
MACNEPOXVLURETEORUINITES

He stood, got to his feet doubled tripled, B' telescoped himself forward
looking more like an unjolly green giant every miniminute till he almust
touched the ceiling, roof or rafters, so big was he.

AND THE OWNER GOT SMALLER AND SMALLER AND
smaller and yet smaller if it was still possible and man
was but so incredibly shrunk he was only the size of my
thumb or my little finger which is a very little finger:
he's in fact a genie of the bottle in reverse and now he
went on getting littler and littler, as tiny as anyone
can be, even tinier and tinier; the tiniest tim on
earth, and tinier even: tm: till amazing us with
his shrinking bouts & feats: and he was no
longer visible, not quite yet invisible: so
final-ly he stood up to vanish down a hole
by the door: a mouse-whole by-by by
the way by the door: a house of a
dormouse so very Butso housey
this mousey-hall did not begin right
& there it began somewhere
els somewhere elsie: it
began with —oh no! oh
yes! —but no! but yes,
sire, it began it
yessiree! but hole it,
mate! hold it a
moment for this
hole begins
here but
and/or
ah so
a n
o

Translated from Cuban by Donald Gardner, Suzanne Jill Levine & the author

Written in "Cuban language," Cabrera Infante's masterwork *Three Trapped Tigers* is—in itself—a tongue twister, a multilayered & experimental novel (better: a blast of verbal & visual procedures) in which its characters pursue art in prerevolutionary Cuba through an outbreak of speech patterns & musical rhythms, wordplay & images over more than four hundred pages. The brilliant work of translation/transcreation of this so-called Cuban Ulysses (as in the co-translated excerpt presented here) should also be noted & praised.

José Antonio Aponte Cuba, 1760–1812

from **A BOOK OF PAINTINGS**

Plate 26

In a jar on a desolated beach Diogenes appears protected by the Goddess Isis she who favors him debarking from her carriage every afternoon to bring him all the things a man needs & the learnèd king Rodrigo down below commanding him to leave his jar to which he answers anything his majesty the king requests a poor man must obey & when the king asks what he has to offer he scoops up two fistfuls of earth a scepter hidden in his right hand in his left the coat of arms & flags of Spain the king excited by such wonders offers thanks to God & makes sure that the one inside the jar will stay there while he sails back to his kingdom in the small boat in the painting on the right

Again the question looms how could Diogenes as set forth heretofore have formed the coat of arms & scepter of the king of Spain from just two clumps of earth the way the witness guarantees us that he took them from the jar & knowing the philosopher was unable to have worked such wonders he has always been persuaded & believes it was the effect alone of his connections with the goddess

Translated from Spanish by Javier Taboada & Jerome Rothenberg

(1) A carpenter, sculptor, & veteran of the Black militia in Cuba (he participated in the capture of the Bahamas from the British during the

American Revolution), José Antonio Aponte's legacy in art & poetry needs to be reconsidered as an early form of experimental collage. His *Book of Paintings* (the large assemblage/collage he worked on for more than six years) was likely the first such work in the Americas. There he gathered "drawings and paintings and cut images from books, prints, and decorative fans. He represented a wide array of scenes: Greek and Roman gods; Black men as emperors and priests; stories from the Bible; scenes from Ethiopia and Egypt, Rome and Spain, Havana and the heavens. In the book, Aponte appears to represent a diasporic Black history that connected the shores of Cuba to faraway lands like Ethiopia" (in *Digital Aponte*, hosted online by New York University). The *Book of Paintings* can be seen as a prophetic vision about Black Africans in the Americas & elsewhere.

(2) "Although the book is believed to be lost, Aponte's descriptions of these [plates, seventy-two in number] survive in the record of his trial for conspiring to plan slave rebellions beginning in March 1812. At the end of the trial, Aponte was sentenced to death. He was hanged in public on April 9, 1812. His head was severed from his body and placed in a cage about a block and a half from his house, at an important crossroad in the city, where everyone would see it" (*Digital Aponte*).

In the absence of Aponte's actual collages, his verbal descriptions serve here as a temporary placeholder for his long-vanished masterwork.

Ulises Carrión Mexico, 1941–1989

from **THE NEW ART OF MAKING BOOKS**

What a Book Is

A book is a sequence of spaces.

Each of these spaces is perceived at a different moment—a book is also a sequence of moments.

. . . . .

A book is not a case of words, nor a bag of words, nor a bearer of words.

. . . . .

A writer, contrary to the popular opinion, does not write books.

A writer writes texts.

The fact, that a text is contained in a book, comes only from the dimensions of such a text; or, in the case of a series of short texts (poems, for instance), from their number.

.....

A literary (prose) text contained in a book ignores the fact that the book is an autonomous space-time sequence.

A series of more or less short texts (poems or other) distributed through a book following any particular ordering reveals the sequential nature of the book.

It reveals it, perhaps uses it; but it does not incorporate it or assimilate it.

.....

Written language is a sequence of signs expanding within the space; the reading of which occurs in time.

A book is a space-time sequence.

.....

Books existed originally as containers of (literary) texts.

But books, seen as autonomous realities, can contain any (written) language, not only literary language, or even any other system of signs.

.....

Among languages, literary language (prose and poetry) is not the best fitted to the nature of books.

.....

A book may be the accidental container of a text, the structure of which is irrelevant to the book: these are the books of bookshops and libraries.

A book can also exist as an autonomous and self-sufficient form, including perhaps a text that emphasizes that form, a text that is an organic part of that form: here begins the new art of making books.

.....

In the old art the writer judges himself as being not responsible for the real book. He writes the text. The rest is done by the servants, the artisans, the workers, the others.

In the new art writing a text is only the first link in the chain going from the writer to the reader. In the new art the writer assumes the responsibility for the whole process.

. . . . .

In the old art the writer writes texts.

In the new art the writer makes books.

. . . . .

To make a book is to actualize its ideal space-time sequence by means of the creation of a parallel sequence of signs, be it linguistic or other.

COMMENTARY

Writes critic Viridiana Zavala, in *Ulises Carrión's (Un)Writing*: "The manifesto *The New Art of Making Books* is Carrión's best-known text; in it, he sought to dissociate a writer's work from the traditional concept of the book, and spoke of the death of writing as a primordial element of this disassociation. Carrión viewed books as autonomous spaces that he could use in different ways. His particular interest in books as living organisms—as something more than a mere container of texts and narratives—led him to explore new configurations of language and linguistic media...."

David Antin USA, 1932–2016

SKY POEMS

COMMENTARY

In 1987 and 1988, poet & conceptual artist David Antin performed two pieces he dubbed "Sky Poems." The first took place in Santa Monica, California, & the second in La Jolla, California. Antin employed a team of pilots who had developed a skywriting technique called "sky typing," which involved flying in formation & releasing a series of oil-based "puffs" according to a preprogrammed code to produce dot matrix–style text in the sky. Antin disseminated press releases & other forms of publicity ahead of the events to alert the public to the time & place of these happenings. He programmed the sky-typing computer to display successive lines of poems he had written for the occasions. In radio contact with the planes, he directed them from the ground, having them print each successive line over the same space as the previous line once it had fully dispersed.

Antin also introduced odd spacing between some of the words so that they formed multiple syntactical units (poem, line, subline, etc.). The inaugural sky poem read, in full, over a two-hour period:

IF WE   GET IT TOGETHER
CAN THEY TAKE IT APART
OR   ONLY IF WE LET THEM

Conceptually, these performances were imagined by Antin as part of a monumental (yet ephemeral) poem that would last half of a lifetime. In actuality, Antin performed only two discrete sky-typing poems.

Raúl Zurita Chile, 1950–

SKY & LANDSCAPE POEMS

COMMENTARY

Zurita has worked on diverse modes of poetry—visual & sound—but he also has shown a concern about the ways in which poetry & landscape may meld. His moves include different kinds of interventions in the public sphere & also in natural environments. Among other such events, he sky-wrote in 1982 fifteen phrases (in Spanish) from his poem "The New Life" over New York City:

MY GOD IS HUNGER
MY GOD IS SNOW
MY GOD IS EMPTINESS
MY GOD IS PAIN
MY GOD IS NO
           [etc.]

Similarly, Zurita bulldozed the three-kilometer-long phrase "Ni Pena Ni Miedo" ("Neither Pity Nor Fear") into the sand of the Atacama Desert, in close proximity to the Pacific Ocean & visible only from the sky overhead. And in an unrealized follow-up, he envisioned one "Last Project" on similar lines, the text of which can be seen, along with more of his work, in "A Fourth Gallery."

For more on earthworks, ancient & modern, see "The Great Serpent Mound" & others in "Preludium."

Mario Montalbetti Peru, 1953–

LANGUAGE IS A REVOLVER FOR TWO

dog—to talk
cat—to meow
      (mooing—cow)
lion—roar, tiger
crow—to croak
goose—tocr
         oak
parrot—gargling
      (gargles the parrot
      coos the dove)
man, wom
            an—to talk, tal
k, till mash
      the heart.
hush—the bonze.

Translated from Spanish by Javier Taboada

COMMENTARY

Mainly concerned with ineffability, the poetry of Mario Montalbetti features a constant questioning of the insufficiency & failure of language. His moves, as with many others, led him to consider language as a dangerous artifact. Yet silence, for him, was not the solution: "But to say the very least, saying the minimum / one can say / it's what allows us to say something."

Gertrude Stein USA, 1874–1946

FIVE WORDS IN A LINE (1930)

Five words in a line.

Murilo Mendes Brazil, 1901–1976

TO LIVE

A line. A wine. A wane. A wave. A weave. Awove. A love. Alive.

Transcreated & composed after Murilo Mendes by Chris Daniels

José Coronel Urtecho Nicaragua, 1906–1994

MASTERWORK

¡o!

what it has taken me to do this!

Translated from Spanish by John Lyons

Aram Saroyan USA, 1943

TWO POEMS

1/

eyeye

2/

lighght

José Garcia Villa Philippines/USA, 1908–1997

TWO COMMA POEMS

The, caprice, of, canteloupes, is, to, be,
Sweet, or, not, sweet,—
To, create, suspense. A, return,
To, Greek, drama.
Their, dramaturgy, is, not, in, the, sweet,
Soil, but, in, the, eye,
Of, birds, the, pure, eye, that, decides,
To, bestow, or,
To, withold. Shall, I, be, sweet, or,
Not, sweet?—looking,
Up, at, your, face. Till, sudden:
I, will, be, sweet!

. . . . .

The, hands, on, the, piano, are, armless.
No, one, is, at, the, piano.
The, hands, begin, and, end, there.
There, no-one's, hands, are, there:
Crystal, and, clear, upon, the, keys.
Playing, what, they, play.
Playing, what, they, are.
Playing, the, sound, of, Identity.
Yet, how, absurd, how, absurd, how, absurd!

COMMENTARY

Of José Garcia Villa's "comma poems," as here, for which he was widely
known in his time, he wrote: "The commas are an integral and essential
part of the medium: regulating the poem's verbal density and time movement: enabling each word to attain a fuller tonal value, and the line movement to become more measured."

Simón Rodríguez Venezuela, 1769–1854

from *AMERICAN SOCIETIES* (1828)

[Notes toward a New Typography]

in written SPEECH

Size &
Variety } of the typeface indicates TONE

separation &
isolation } of phrases indicates PAUSES

Separation is painted
by placing words or phrases *among dots*

isolation is painted
by placing { words or
phrases } in the *center of the page*

Ellipses are painted { by placing a dot
under the omitted word

Hyphens indicate RELATION
Diagrams . CONNECTION

to *perform* all these it is necessary to FEEL
nobody *learns* how to Feel &
nevertheless we all express *our* feelings

but we must learn { to express others' feelings
which produce our own

This is the aim of the READING's principles

Reading is *to resuscitate* ideas
& to perform this sort of miracle
we need to know the *Spirits* of the departed
or have *equivalent* spirits to subrogate them

The *Writer* must *dispose the page* to achieve the same result as the ORATOR
thus *the art of Writing* requires
the art of Paint.

Translated from Spanish by Javier Taboada

Rodriguez's typography & spatial use of the page precedes Mallarmé's groundbreaking *Coup de Dés* by almost fifty-five years. *American Societies* is an early avant-garde work as we now conceive it.

For more of which, see the entry on Rodríguez in "A Map of Americas."

e. e. cummings   USA, 1894–1962

R-P-O-P-H-E-S-S-A-G-R

                              r-p-o-p-h-e-s-s-a-g-r
              who
a)s w(e loo)k
upnowgath
        PPEGORHRASS
                              eringint(o-
    aThe):l
          eA
             !p:
S   a
              (r
    rIvInG   .gRrEaPsPhOs)
                                       to
    rea(be)rran(com)gi(e)ngly
    ,grasshopper;

For more on cummings see poems in "A Third Gallery."

"Jack"

SHAKER SOUND POEM

(Holy Ground. Oct. 6th 1847)

Ah pe-an t-as ke t-an te loo
O ne vas ke than sa-na was-ke

lon ah ve shan too
Te wan-se ar ke ta-ne voo te
lan se o-ne voo
Te on-e-wan tase va ne woo te wan-se o-ne van
Me-le wan se oo ar ke-le van te
shom-ber on vas sa la too lar var sa
re voo an don der on v-tar loo-cum an la voo
O be me-sum ton ton ton tol a wac-er tol-a wac-er
ton ton te s-er pane love ten poo

COMMENTARY

Writes Edward Deming Andrews: "The first Shaker songs were word-less tunes… [&] were received from Indian spirits or from the shades of Eskimos, Negroes, Abyssinians, Hottentots, Chinese and other races in search of salvation. Squaw songs, and occasionally a papoose song, were common. When spirits came into the Shaker Church, the instruments would become so 'possessed' that they sang Indian songs, whooped, danced and behaved generally in the manner of 'savages'" (in *The Gift to Be Simple: Songs, Dances and Rituals of the American Shakers*, 1940). As such, they show the kind of connection between ideological & formal innovation that has characterized many movements of recovery, past & present.

The resemblance to other forms of glossolalia (speaking in tongues) seems obvious, but there is also a resemblance to modernist & popular experiments with sound poetry, as in the following instances. Related explorations of a kind of spirit induced visual poetry were also common, an example of which can be seen above.

Mamie Medina USA (fl. 1920s)

THAT DA-DA STRAIN (LYRICS)

Have you heard it, have you heard it,
That Da-Da Strain?
It will shake you, it will make you
Really go insane.
Everybody's full of pep,
Makes you watch your every step.
Every prancer, every dancer,
Starts to lay 'em down,

Everybody when they hear it
Starts to buzzing 'round;
I get crazy as a loon,
When everybody hums this tune:

Da-Da, Da-Da,
Da-Da, Da-Da,
Because the feeling
Sets your brain a-reeling;
Just like you're falling,
That runabout refrain, [?]
When everybody starts to
Da-Da, Da-Da,
Da-Da, Da-Da,
I want to do it once again,
I'm simply wild about that Da-Da, Da-Da Strain!

Oh, Da-Da Da-Da
Da-Da Da-Da,
Because this feeling
Sets your brain a-reeling,
Just like you're falling,
That runabout refrain, [?]
When everybody starts to Da-Da, Da-Da, Da, Da-Da
I want to do it once again,
I'm simply wild about the Da-Da, Da-Da Strain.

Da, Da-Da, Da-Da,
Da-Da, Da-Da,
Da-Da, Da-Da,
Because that feeling
Sets your brain a-reeling.
Just like you're falling,
That runabout refrain, [?]
Oh, Da-Da, Da-Da,
Da-Da, Da-Da,
I wanna do it once again,
I'm simply wild about that
Da-Da, Da-Da Strain!

Transcribed from vocals by Ethel Waters, recorded in May 1922

The full text of "That Da-Da Strain" makes a curious & little noticed connection to the European Dada activities that immediately preceded & accompanied it. The melody, minus vocals, became a traditional jazz standard that persisted over the next several decades. The composers, when credited, are generally given as Mamie Medina (lyrics) & Edgar Dowell (music). It should be noted, however, that the otherwise undefined "Da-Da" parallels precisely the contemporaneous invention by Hugo Ball, Tristan Tzara, Kurt Schwitters, & others of what was then a radically new sound poetry—a twentieth-century poetry without actual words. Relevant also: the later development of scat singing as a jazz variant of sound poetry on deeply American grounds.

All of this aimed here toward a new omnipoetics.

ADDENDUM

ELLA FITZGERALD USA, 1917–1996

from **Lady Be Good**

(scat version)

eet-dih-dee-laht / dah-ee //// uh-boo-bee-un-boo-bee-un-boo-bee //// ih-bih-dooh-yooh-dooh-dooh-doo-dey-oo-dah-doo-dey-doy-ah-doo- dah-dm-dey-ohb-dey-oh-dluh-oh-boy / bah-buh-doh-dleh-ley-ley-boy ////// bih dl oy dih dih dl ah dl dih boo oo doo oo dl ah dl ah dl doo-dee-oo-doh-oy-dee-doo-dl-uh-bee-doo-deh-doo-dl-oh-ehm //// boh-dl-oh-dl-oh-dl-ah-boh-ehr //// boh-dl-oh-dl-oo-dl-iht-doo-ehr // boh-dee-dn-lih-dee-dn-dah-dah-dn-lih-dee-ah-lee-ah-ah-OO-DOO-BOW- BAH-OO-DN-BEE-DLEE-AH / oh-dee-dee-dlee-oo-dn-dee-bah /// oo-dee- oo-dee-oo-dee-oo-dee-oo-dee-oo-bee-uh-loot-deel / ooh-bee-oot / bih / oo-bee-oot-dee-ih-dee-oo-dlee-doh-dl-oht

doh-dley-dey-ey-ey-ah-ah-buh-dee / doh-dley-dey-ey-ey-oy /// ooh-dn-dee / ooh-dn-dee / ooh-dee-dn-rih-bih-blee-oo-boo-boym /// oop-bop-sh'-bam- a-klook-a-mopl // dee-dih-lih-dl-dih-dee-lih-dl-uh-ooh-ee /// ee-ih-dih-dn- dih-dlee-ah-bih-doo-dih-dee-ah-bahp / blee-ah-dl-ah-doh-loh-dl-oh-deyl // bah-blee-oh-doo-dah-dee-doh-lah / dee-oo-dee-oo-doo-loh-dl-oy-uh-oym /////// beh-oh-dl-deh-dih-deh-dih-dee-dah-doo-deh-doot-dee-oo-bahp / beh-oo-daht / bee-oo-bahp / bee-ooh-behm // I'm-just-a-lonesome-babe- in-the-woods // Oh,-lady,-oh,-lady /// lady-won't-you-be-so-good-to-me? // bah-bee-doo-dlee-dah-bee-doo-dn-doo-boy

Transcreated by John Bloomberg-Rissman after Justin G. Binek

Jean Toomer USA, 1894–1967

TWO SOUND POEMS

(I)

Mon sa me el kirimoor,
Ve dice kor, korrand ve deer,
Leet vire or sand vite,
Re sive tas tor;
Tu tas tire or re sim bire,
Rozan dire ras to por tantor,
Dorozire, soron,
Bas ber vind can sor, gosham,
Mon sa me el, a som on oor.

(II)

Vor cosma saga
Vor reeshen flaga
Vor gorden maga
Vor shalmer raga

For more on Toomer, see poems in "A Third Gallery."

Michael McClure USA, 1932–2020

from *GHOST TANTRAS*

#1 (1964)

GOOOOOOR! GOOOOOOOOOO!
GOOOOOOOOOR!
GRAHHH! GRAHH! GRAHH!
Grah gooooor! Ghahh! Graaarr! Greeeeer! Grayowhr!
Greeeeee
GRAHHRR! RAHHR! GRAGHHRR! RAHR!
RAHR! RAHHR! GRAHHHR! GAHHR! HRAHR!
BE NOT SUGAR BUT BE LOVE
looking for sugar!
GAHHHHHHHH!

ROWRR!

GROOOOOOOOOOOH!

#51

I LOVE TO THINK OF THE RED PURPLE ROSE
IN THE DARKNESS COOLED BY THE NIGHT.
We are served by machines making satins
of sounds.
Each blot of sound is a bud or a stahr.
Body eats bouquets of the ear's vista.
Gahhhrrr boody eers noze eyes deem thou.
NOH. NAH-OHH
hrooor. VOOOR-NAH! GAHROOOOO ME.
Nah droooooh seerch. NAH THEE!
The machines are too dull when we
are lion-poems that move & breathe.
WHAN WE GROOOOOOOOOOOOOOOR
hann dree myketoth sharoo sreee thah noh deeeeeemed ez.
Whan eeeethoooze hrohh.

COMMENTARY

Writes McClure by way of introduction to his poems in "beast language": "These are spontaneous stanzas published in the order and
with the natural sounds in which they were first written. If there is an
OOOOOOOOOOOOOOOH, simply say a long loud 'oooh.' If there is a 'gahr'
simply say *gar* and put an 'h' in.

"Look at stanza 51. It begins in English and turns into beast language—
star becomes stahr. Body becomes boody. Nose becomes noze. Everybody
knows how to pronounce NOH or VOOR-NAH or GAHROOOOO ME."

Papo Angarica   Cuba, 1942–2015

BATÁ TOQUES FOR THE ORISHA

for Babalú Ayé:

I(L) yá(L) nko(L) tá(H)
I(L) yá(L) nko(L) tá(H)
I(L) yá(L) nko(L) tá(H)

Ko(L) kpa(H) ni(H) yé(H)
Ko(L) kpa(H) ni(H) yé(H)

for Inle:

I(H) lya(L) ba(H) ta(L) cho(L) bi(H)
I(H) lya(L) ba(H) ta(L) cho(L) bi(H)
A(L) ga(L) da(L) I(H)
lya(L) ba(H) ta(L) cho(L) bi(H)
I(H) lya(L) ba(H) ta(L) cho(L) bi(H)

* (L) = low tone. (H)= high tone.

Transcription by Kenneth Schweitzer from original performance

COMMENTARY

(1) Scholar & musical performer Kenneth Schweitzer explains the *batá toques* (talking drums) as follows: "The Cuban *batá* descends from an African tradition where drums mimic speech. In this way, both African and Cuban *batá* drummers are storytellers who use drums as their voice. These linguistic actions refer to historical events, real and perceived. They speak of a time when the Orisha walked upon the earth. To a large degree, the Lucumí [Cuban Yorubas] have forgotten how to speak their language. Its usage is generally restricted, in both speech and semantic *toques* [drum hits], to short exclamations and greetings… chanting… and singing. As a result, the ability to convey meaning through semantic *toques* is limited…. Remaining true to their heritage as storytellers, [Cuban *batá* players] rely upon musical metaphors to communicate with and tell stories about the Orisha."

(2) Papo Angarica, considered a legend in Cuban music, was also a priest of Ifá (the Great Diviner) in the African-derived Orisha religion.

David Meltzer   USA, 1937–2016

from **IMPOSSIBLE MUSIC**

When we talk of music it is about love impossible to speak of.

●

Music kabbalah, the black and white of it, the page, the letters, notes, the ink, its absence its presence.

Describing the revolutionary harmonic shift wrought by Debussy, Ravel, Satie, a jazz pianist said, "Yeah, they're playing the black keys."
The sounds made are colorless until pulled off the page, transcribed, not even trance-scribed, but blacked onto white onto black lines off the page. Like poetry, a writing first.

•

Like books, those boxed sets are a death hedge. Properbox, Definitive, Mosaic, JSP—investments in immortality. Can't check out yet, split, quit it, if the book remains unread or a CD unheard.

•

Sounds, type, ineffable material of wake-up. Where one is and was inhabited with salamander ease and edge.

•

Where's the mind the music unminds?
Who's minding the store, the score? What gets away stays; what stays gets away.

•

"Not all sounds are musical," writes H. Lowery.
"All sounds are music," states Cage.
Corrosive crackles of 78s recycled onto CDs or vinyl LPs played into oblivion, whose grooves etched white as old dimestore acetates.

•

Penetrates psyche and soul and, like all mysteries, transforms the person receiving those sounds. Mysteries of sound, rhythm, voice; the mystery that can't be described in words, as if the experience of music is indescribable. Like the poet confronting the mysteries of the world that he or she enters into. We try, but always with the sense that it eludes our words.
The ineffable is beyond words; music is beyond words.
The impossibility of music.

Originally published April 10, 2013

COMMENTARY

Tell them I'm struggling to sing with angels / who hint at it in black words printed on old paper gold-edged by time (D.M.)

... whose gift was to open old worlds—kabbalistic, Semitic, most notably—in the context of a pervasively contemporary "bop prosody." From a family of lesser musicians, he never left music behind, performing with a group (his wife, Tina, and poet Clark Coolidge included) under the designation "Serpent Power." Once set on these paths, he continually expanded his view into hidden worlds of Jewish kabbalists & mystics but also gnostic, apocryphal Christian, & pagan areas that left their mark, as a kind of catalyst, even when he swung back to the mundane 1960s world: the "dark continent" of wars & riots, the funky sounds of blues & rock & roll, the domestic pull of family & home. To which he pays homage in the words presented here, with music always present, he tells us, "as a form of autobiography."

Emily Dickinson USA, 1830–1886

ASEMIC WRITING

COMMENTARY

Dickinson's page appears here as a harbinger of experiments with wordless graphic [= asemic] poetry equivalent to the better-known sound poems of

Dadas & other latter-day avant-gardists. Writes one of the major US practitioners, Michael Jacobson, on the road toward a definition: "The forms that asemic writing may take are many, but its main trait is its resemblance to 'traditional' writing—with the distinction of its abandonment of specific semantics, syntax, and communication. Asemic writing offers meaning by way of aesthetic intuition, and not by verbal expression. It often appears as abstract calligraphy, or as a drawing which resembles writing but avoids words, or if it does have words, the words are generally damaged beyond the point of legibility. One of the main ways to experience an asemic work is as unreadable, but still attractive to the eye. My point is that without words, asemic writing is able to relate to all words, colors, and even music, irrespective of the author's or the reader's original languages; not all emotions can be expressed with words, and so asemic writing attempts to fill in the void."

That Dickinson's page, based on overwritings with family & friends, may actually fit the definition is worth consideration.

Jackson Mac Low USA, 1922–2004

MILAREPA GATHA

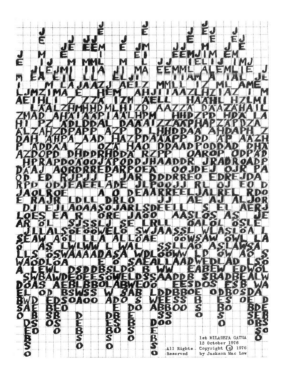

Mac Low's "Gathas" constitute an open-ended series of verbal performance scores & visual poems begun in January 1961. The letters of their
words are placed in the squares of quadrille [graph] paper. Performers
(soloists or groups of any size) are speaker-vocalists &/or instrumental-
ists. *Gatha* (Sanskrit: verse, hymn) originally designated a versified section
of a Buddhist sutra; in the past century, Dr. D.T. Suzuki applied the term
to poems by Zen masters & students. Mac Low chose it for these works
because (1) he considered them Buddhist poems; (2) until 1973 they were
all based on mantras; (3) until 1978 they were solely composed by nonintentional [chance] operations, use of which—together with giving performers extensive freedom of choice—deemphasized the composer's ego
& thus encouraged performers and hearers to give "bare attention"—as in
meditation—to sounds of words, phonemes, syllables, etc., & to those of
instruments. (When instruments are included in performances, each letter is
"translated" by a tone, in accordance with a letter-to-pitch-class code specific to each particular gatha. (Commentary based on J.M.L., from "Open
Secrets," online.)

For more on Mac Low, see "A Third Gallery," "A Map of Histories," &
elsewhere in these pages.

N.H. Pritchard   USA, 1939–1996

H A R B O U R

for Nancy & Arthur

W here   quiet ly   on   ly   go   e   s
k   now   in   g   the   s   h   or   e
w   it   h   its   sun   dried   hues
s   ever   a   l   b   oats
l   a   n   g   u   i   d
be   neath   the   d   us   k
s   ee   king   h   a   i   l   s
t   he   d   a   w   n   to   c   h   oo   s   e
&   of   w   h   at   c   ease   less   t   ide
pro   c   l   aimed
s   till   s   i   l   e   n   t
e   m   p   t   y   &   we   t
deck   e   d   to   the   c   alm

w it h g row in g m oo n
h over in g eve r
& the s mall buoys
c l ever f eat her limbs
m as king the h i dd e n fro s t
w it h f in s
as k in g
the net s pro test the w in d

Edgartown
September

COMMENTARY

Writes Erica N. Cardwell of Pritchard's position in a wing of USAmerican avant-gardism well underway by the 1920s but too often neglected until now: "Jazz poetics, the formative tradition rooted in the Black Arts Movement, has contributed a sense of energetic permission towards experimental transcendence, specifically for Black voices from within the diaspora. In N.H. Pritchard's two works, *The Matrix Poems: 1960–70* and *EECCHHOOEESS*, readers encounter poems that exemplify the literary innovation of this era—a commitment to the pursuit and study of sound and a symbolic resistance to legibility. Pritchard's poetry illustrates a specific tenet of jazz poetics: words are more malleable when deconstructed" (*Brooklyn Rail*, June 2021). Or David Grundy in *Artforum* of what Pritchard later called "transrealism," drawing from theosophical thinking & beyond: "A poetry of shattered rites, it offers disorienting reconfigurations of our coordinates for race, identity, and thought, interrogating the very grounds of being." And Aldon Lynn Nielsen, to open the field still further: "Jazz poetry had long been an interracial as well as an intertextual phenomenon."

Josely Vianna Baptista Brazil, 1957–

from **AIR**

I   N   F   I   N   I   T   S

for Nietzsche

among birches and nothings, nothing
s and dawning, beats, fairies, fugue
s, arias, among frozen snowpetals, li
ght crystals filing down smoky nicht
s, among peaks and abysses, birches a
nd nothings, there, where breath short
ens: your speech, rasping, polishes a
ll and a nil: in the twilight of ido
ls, the divine unseen (wanderer a
mong truths and lies), seek the burs
ting flower, rare in rock, among nein
s and pistils, aurora, shattered stone
: on ober engadin valkyries course in
file down on moons howling still for
lous, and the visionary, on the thres
hold,   engendering   centaurs

Translated from Portuguese by Chris Daniels

COMMENTARY

A major inventor of new forms & a translator & ethnopoetic transformer of the very old, Josely Vianna Baptista has come into greater & greater prominence since her first published writings in the 1990s. Of her special position among Neo-Baroque & Concretist writers & artists, both reenforcing & diverging from the work of others, Chris Daniels writes as poet & translator: "Baptista's poetry must not be thought of as being related to, or influenced by, any of the contemporary poetries and/or poetics in the United States.

"[Rather,] work, like Baptista's, undermines, conquers, colonizes, and transforms European tradition in the creation of new art forms for the Americas."

Of all of this, as it emerges in her early sequences *Ar* (Air) and *Corpografia*, Baptista writes on her own behalf: "I proposed, by means of blocks of 'aerated' texts, a 'sensory strophation' inspired by the Guarani concept of 'word-soul' (*ñe-eng*) and the interdependence of breath and perception." And again: "Curiously, the aeration of my poems always was linked to a concretist process: the principal motive was to de-automatize the reader's gaze, to allow the body to participate in the reading, with its own sense of duration."

Henry David Thoreau USA, 1817–1862

A TELEGRAPH HARP (1851)

SEPT. 3

As I went under the new telegraph wire, I heard it vibrating like a harp high overhead. It was as the sound of a far-off glorious life, a supernal life, which came down to us, and vibrated in the lattice-work of this life of ours.

SEPT. 22

Yesterday and today the stronger winds of autumn have begun to blow, and the telegraph harp has sounded loudly. I heard it especially in the Deep Cut this afternoon, the tone varying with the tension of different parts of the wire. The sound proceeds from near the posts, where the vibration is apparently more rapid. I put my ear to one of the posts, and it seemed to me as if every pore of the wood was filled with music, labored with the strain—as if every fibre was affected and being seasoned or timed, rearranged according to a new and more harmonious law. Every swell and change or inflection of tone pervaded and seemed to proceed from the wood, the divine tree or wood, as if its very substance was transmuted. What a recipe for preserving wood, perchance—to keep it from rotting—to fill its pores with music! How this wild tree from the forest, stripped of its bark and set up here, rejoices to transmit its music! When no music proceeds from the wire, on applying my ear, I hear the drum within the entrails of the wood—the oracular tree acquiring, accumulating, the prophetic fury.

The resounding wood! how much the ancients would have made of it! To have a harp on so great a scale, girdling the very earth, and played on by the winds of every latitude and longitude, and that harp were, as it were, the manifest blessing of heaven on a work of man's! Shall we not add a tenth Muse to the immortal Nine? And that the invention thus divinely honored and distinguished—on which the Muse has condescended to smile—is this magic medium of communication for mankind!

The telegraph harp sounds strongly today, in the midst of the rain. I put my ear to the trees and I hear it working terribly within, and anon it swells into a clear tone, which seems to concentrate in the core of the tree, for all the sound seems to proceed from the wood. It is as if you had entered some world-famous cathedral, resounding to some vast organ. The fibres of all things have their tension, and are strained like the strings of a lyre. I feel the very ground tremble under my feet as I stand near the post. This wire vibrates with great power, as if it would strain and rend the wood. What an awful and fateful music it must be to the worms in the wood. No better vermifuge. No danger that worms will attack this wood; such vibrating music would thrill them to death.

COMMENTARY

Note, too, David Antin's suggestion that Thoreau's two years at Walden Pond—his experiment in "living deliberately... fronting only the essential facts of life" can now be read, much like the foregoing, as an example of performance art *avant la lettre*. The further resemblance to a later, electronic-based cyberpoesis might also be considered.

ADDENDUM

JOHN CAGE USA, 1912–1992

from Mureau

sparrowsitA gROsbeak betrays *itself* **by that peculia**r squeakari**EFFECT OF SLIGHTE**st tinkling **measures soundn**ess ingpleasa We hear! Does it not rather hear us? **sWhen he hears th**e *t*elegraph, he thinksthose bugs have issu*e*d forthThe owl *t*ou*c*hes the stops, wakes reverb erations *d gwalky* In verse there is no inherent mus*ic e*ofsttakestak es a man to make a room silent It ta**kes to** make a roomIt **IS A Y**oung a ppetite and the app**ETITEFOR** IsHe Oeysee morningYou hear s**cream o f great h**awka *ydgh b*o*dy Shelie being**silence I t wo**uld be noblest to sing **with the wind**To hear a neighbor s*inging!*

[Variations on **MU**sic & Tho**REAU** in Thoreau's Journal = **MUREAU**. The texts are letter-syllable-word-phrase-sentence mixes obtained by subjecting to a series of I Ching chance operations all remarks by Thoreau about music, silence, and sound that are indexed in the Dover edition of his Journal.]

Dutty Boukman

(a.k.a. Zamba Boukman), Haiti, d. 1791

INDEPENDENCE EVENT & RITUAL

1. Grab a pig.
2. Congregate the people and start a fire.
3. Promise to Ezili *Dantor*—the spirit of vengeance and rage—that all of you will rise up and defeat the invader.
4. See the mambo priestess be possessed by the aforementioned spirit.
5. Say the following:

> *the god who created*
> *the giving-light sun   the one who rouses*
> > *the ocean and rules the thunder   our God*
> > *he who has ears to hear   you*
> > *hidden in a cloud*
> > > *you see all*
> > > > *all the white man has made*

> *the white man's god inspires him with crime*
> > *the god within us   our god   the just*
> > > *commands us to avenge our wrongs*
> > *he will direct our arms to victory*
> > > *he will*

> > > *let's cast away the pitiless image*
> > > > *of the white man's god*

> > *listen to the voice for liberty that speaks within us*

6. Slay the pig.
7. Seal the pact by drinking a cup of its blood.

Transcreated by Javier Taboada after various sources

COMMENTARY

Bois-Caïman (lit., "Alligator Forest") in northern Haiti was the site for the political, religious, & strategic assembly that on the night of August 14, 1791, sparked the revolution against the French colonizers. It is said that Dutty Boukman (a voodoo *houngan*, or shaman), along with Cecile

Fatiman (a *mambo* priestess), offered up a sacrificial pig in a ritual event now considered the official start of the Haitian independence movement. Many Haitians believe that this event assured their success, & up to the present Bois-Caïman is regarded as a holy place.

Macedonio Fernández Argentina, 1874–1952

THE MAN WHO WILL BE PRESIDENT

Macedonio

COMMENTARY

No superfluous words here, but only a notecard with his name on it. Writes Jorge Luis Borges: "The mechanism of fame interested him, not the way to obtain it. For a year or two he played with the vague purpose of being president of the Republic.... He insisted that the most important thing was to disseminate the name.... My sister and some of her friends wrote Macedonio's name on strips of paper or cards, which they carefully forgot in shops, in trams, on sidewalks, in hallways and cinemas.... From these maneuvers, the project of a fantastic novel, located in Buenos Aires, emerges. We all began to write it. The work was entitled *The man who will be president*; the novel's characters were his friends.... Two arguments were interwoven: one—visible—Macedonio's curious efforts to be the president; the other one—secret—was the conspiracy created by a sect of neurasthenic and perhaps crazy millionaires to achieve the same end. These resolve to undermine people's resistance through a gradual series of uncomfortable inventions.... At the end, the government falls apart, and Macedonio enters *Casa Rosada* [the presidential house in Argentina], but nothing means anything in that anarchic world" (in *Prólogos con un prólogo de prólogos*).

For more on Fernández, see poems in "A Second Gallery."

NOIGANDRES

A Mini Gallery

from **A PILOT PLAN FOR CONCRETE POETRY (1958)**

by Augusto de Campos, Décio Pignatari,
& Haroldo de Campos

Concrete Poetry: product of a critical evolution of forms. Assuming that the historical cycle of verse (as formal-rhythmical unit) is closed, concrete poetry begins by being aware of graphic space as structural agent. Qualified space: space-time structure instead of mere linear-temporistical development. Hence the importance of ideogram concept, either in its general sense of spatial or visual syntax, or in its special sense (Fenollosa/Pound) of method of composition based on direct-analogical, not logical-discursive juxtaposition of elements.

"Il faut que notre intelligence s'habitue à comprendre synthético-idéographiquement au lieu de analytico-discursivement" ["Our intelligence must get used to understanding synthetically-ideographically instead of analytically-discursively"] (Apollinaire).

[And from] Sergei Eisenstein: ideogram and montage.

Translated by the authors

Décio Pignatari   Brazil, 1927–2012

THE EARTH

```
TH   EARTH EAR
THE   ARTH EAR
THEAR   TH EAR
THEART   H EAR
THEARTHE   ART
THEARTHEA   RT
THEARTHEAR   T
THEARTHEARTH
```

Haroldo de Campos Brazil, 1929–2003

IF / BORN

if
born
dies born
dies born dies
        reborn redies reborn
           redies reborn
               redies
                 re

re
unborn
un-dies unborn
un-dies unborn un-dies

borndiesborn
diesborn
dies
if/one

Translated from Portuguese by Jennifer Cooper

Augusto de Campos Brazil, 1931–

WITHOUT A NUMBER

without a number
a number
number
zero
a
    the
    numb
      er
       number
      a number
     one without number

A Map of Extensions

Marjorie Perloff remembers the following remarks made by Kenneth Goldsmith on Concrete poetry in a cyberpoetic context:

"In the spring of 2001, the poet and intermedia artist Kenneth Goldsmith participated in a panel on Brazilian Concrete Poetry with, among others, one of the movement's founders, Décio Pignatari. Goldsmith recalls:

> I was stunned. Everything [Pignatari] was saying seemed to predict the mechanics of the internet ... delivery, content, interface, distribution, multi-media, just to name a few. Suddenly it made sense: like de Kooning's famous statement: "History doesn't influence me. I influence it," it's taken the web to make us see just how prescient concrete poetics was in predicting its own lively reception half a century later. I immediately understood that what had been missing from concrete poetry was an appropriate environment in which it could flourish. For many years, concrete poetry has been in limbo: it's been a displaced genre in search of a new medium. And now it's found one.

N.B. The centrality of Latin American avant-gardism in international experimental poetry should also be noted.

THE VIRGIN'S THRONE OF WISDOM

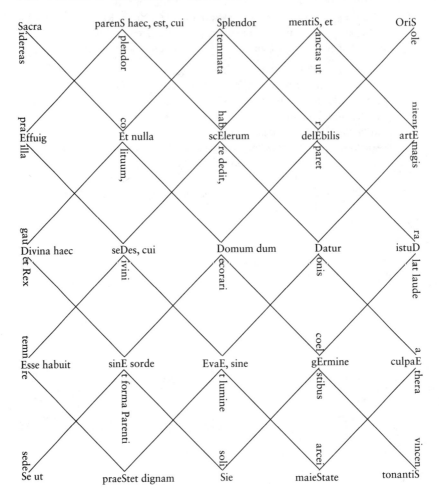

COMMENTARY

"Poetic labyrinths" were composed in Europe beginning in medieval times, their makers implanting a Latin word or phrase among many letters & highlighting it with colors to ease its reading. For their religious contents, these pictograms were intended to teach & amuse Christians. The piece above, originally called *De Virgine Sapientae Sede* & composed in seventeenth-century New Spain, builds a poetic maze in which the repetition of the capitalized Latin word *SEDES* (throne) can be tracked, following a complex of vertical & diagonal paths, guided by the labyrinth's lines. But it is also possible to read the verses of a continuous Latin text, printed in normative lower & upper-case letters, both horizontally & vertically. Toward their absorption in a later "poetry of the disbelievers," these labyrinths open up new visual possibilities.

Dick Higgins USA, 1938–1998

INTERMEDIA CHART

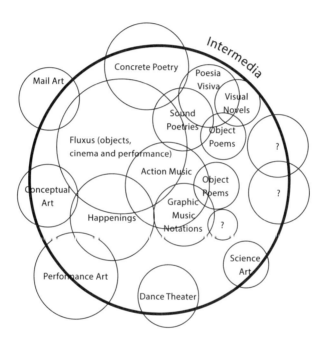

COMMENTARY

"Higgins' 'Intermedia Chart' resonates with temporally dynamic socio-grams, where human interactions are highly differentiated and radically decentralized and based primarily on the specific needs of a given body, in this case artists. According to a model like this, historic and contemporary experience is diverse, causally flexible and permissive of the as-yet-unknown.

"The chart depicts intersections between Fluxus and related work and makes no attempt at linear chronology. Fluid in form, the chart shows concentric and overlapping circles that appear to expand and contract in relationship to the 'Intermedia' framework that encompasses them. It is an open framework that invites play. Its bubbles hover in space as opposed to being historically framed in the linear and specialized art/anti-art framework of the typical chronologies of avant-garde and modern art" (Hannah Higgins, Ubuweb.com).

N.B. Fluxus, which Higgins's chart celebrates, was a major international movement across the arts, including poetry, & with significant offshoots on both of the American continents.

Guillermo Gómez-Peña Mexico/USA, 1955–

from **BORDER BRUJO, 1988**

IV

[He begins walking in circles and howling like a wolf, keeping a rhythm with his feet.]

crísis
craises
the biting crises
the barking crises

[He barks.]

la crísis es un perro
que nos ladra desde el norte
la crísis es un Chrysler le Baron con 4 puertas

[He barks more.]

soy hijo de la crísis fronteriza
soy hijo de la bruja hermafrodita
producto de una cultural cesarean
punkraca heavy-*mierda* all the way
el chuco funkahuátl desertor de 2 países
rayo tardío de la corriente democratik
vengo del sur
el único de 10 que se pintó

[He turns into a *merolico* (Mexico City street performer).]

nací entre épocas y culturas y viceversa
nací de una herida infectada
herida en llamas
herida que auuuuuulla

[He howls.]

I'm a child of border crisis
a product of a cultural cesarean
I was born between epochs & cultures
born from an infected wound
a howling wound
a flaming wound
for I am part of a new mankind
the 4th World, the migrant kind
Los transterrados y descoyuntados
Los que partimos y nunca ιlegamos
y aquí estamos aún
desempleados e incontenibles
en proceso, en ascenso, en transición
per omnia saecula saeculorum
"INVIERTA EN MEXICO"
bienes y raíces
vienes y te vas
púdrete a gusto en Los United
estate still *si no te chingan*

[He continues with a sound poem.]

v
[With thick Mexican accent, pointing at specific audience members]

I speak Spanish therefore you hate me
I speak in English therefore they hate me
I speak Spanglish therefore she speaks *ingleñol*
I speak in tongues therefore you desire me
I speak to you therefore you kill me
I speak therefore you change
I speak in English therefore you listen
I speak in English therefore I hate you
pero cuando hablo en español te adoro
but when I speak Spanish I adore you

ahora, why *carajos* do I speak Spanish?
political praxis *craneal*
I mean...
I mean...

COMMENTARY

Born & raised in Mexico City, Gómez-Peña moved to the United States in 1978. In his performance work, which is treated as exotic & unfamiliar, he places the audience members in the position of "foreigners" or "minorities"; he mixes English & Spanish, fact & fiction, social reality & pop culture, Chicano humor & activist politics to create a "total experience" for the viewer/reader/audience member.

Flying Words Project
PETER COOK: ASL PERFORMER
KENNY LERNER: VOICE PERFORMER

POETRY

POETRY
    POETRY
        POETRY

> *clenched fist, unfurling from the heart*
> *poetic feet beat embodied meter*

POETRY IS THE SHOT

> *hand-gun shoots bullet—becomes planetary-orb*

ORBITING
    CIRCLING
        REVOLVING
            EXPLODING!

IT IS THE OPEN WINDOW

IT'S CAUGHT

> *baseball catcher blown back*
> *ball-becomes-bubbling-sauce*

    SMOKING
        SMOKING

IT'S THE FLAME

bullet drips into a pot

    AND IT TASTES DELICIOUS

Cook tastes bullet-sauce

IT'S LOADED INTO THE MAGNUM

AND IT'S SHOT . . .

toward the audience. stops. rewinds.

    RIGHT BACK INTO YOUR HEART

THAT'S
POETRY
    POETRY
        POETRY

clenched fist, unfurling from the heart,
poetic feet beat embodied meter

IT'S THE PAINTER
    AND THE PORTRAIT

Painter slathers a handful of paint,
thick-river-curves-on-canvas

then becomes the portrait painted,
thick river-curves slathered on the poem's face

…….……………………..

little-finger scribbles on the fourth-wall-canvas

poem's face scribbled in fine little-finger lines

………………………..

painter slashes diagonals across the canvas
brushstrokes mouth & jaw right
eyes & forehead left

face-poem slashed in diagonals,
brushstroked mouth & jaw left
eyes & forehead right

…………………………..

IT'S A PLATE OF PAINT
    SMASHED INTO THE PORTRAIT

IT'S THE PAPER
    RIPPED OFF THE EASEL
        AND CRUMPLED UP

                                  Last g(r)asp of the poem:
                            hand screaming out of discarded canvas

AND THROWN INTO ORBIT
                                 planetary orb twisting in the cosmos

IT'S A FOREST OF TREES
                                 painted onto nature itself

    BUSHES
        UNDERBRUSH
                                 paint-hurled-becomes-sun

A BLAZING SUN

    A RED TAILED FALCON
                                 paint-hurled-becomes-bird

        RISING UP TOWARD
            THE SOURCEFUL SUN

        BURSTING OUT

    SUNBATHED RED FALCON

        SWOOPS DOWN

                                hand-wings-soar-into-flight

IT'S A BUTTERFLY
                           become-butterfly-lights-on-poet's-head
                                    -brushes it off

A TREE
                           poet tenderly paints a tree into being

    POETRY
                                 "P" falls like a leaf

A LEAF FALLING
                           index-finger leaf falls
                                   then another

      LEAVES
      F
       A
      L
       L
      ING

five-finger-leaves flutter

TOWARDS THEIR REFLECTION

IN THE RIVER

POETRY

POETRY

POETRY

clenched fist, unfurling from the heart,
poetic feet stamp out embodied meter

IT'S THE BOMB BAY DOORS OPENING

Bomb drops to the ground

MUSHROOM CLOUD

THE NUCLEAR WINDS

D IS INT EG RAT IN G H AI   R
  E   Y E   S,
            CLA TT ERI NG   T E ET H

        BONES

H E ' S

   G

      O   N

          E   !

Translated from ASL & textualized by H-Dirksen L. Bauman

COMMENTARY

(1) The signing poetry emerging as an aspect of the "culture of the deaf" challenges some of our cherished preconceptions about poetry & its necessary relation to human speech. American Sign Language poetry represents, in itself, a language without sound &, for its practitioners & viewers, a poetry without access to that experience of sound-as-voice that we've so often taken as the bedrock of all poetry & all language. In the real world of the deaf, then, ASL, like its national & autochthonous counterparts elsewhere, exists as a fully formed language: a kind of writing in space & an independent language without recourse to any more dominant form of language for its validation. The extensions it brings to our definitions of poetry can hardly be overstated.

(2) Writes H-Dirksen L. Bauman about his textualized version of "Poetry" as conceived & performed by Flying Words Project: "As a sign language poem can only be fully appreciated in its embodied performance, readers are encouraged to visit the [video version on YouTube at https://www.you tube.com/watch?v=JnU3U6qEibU] to see Flying Words Project's 'Poetry' in its original form. Those who view the video will see (if sighted) Peter Cook's blend of ASL and gesture and will hear (if hearing) Kenny Lerner's voicing, which is not intended as a translation but as a verbal supplement, painting a context within which viewers can grasp the significance of the visual-gestural images. Presented here in print, the ALL CAPS words on the left margins are the direct transcription of Kenny Lerner's voicing, while the italicized text on the right margins consists of my own 'imagist conden-sations' of the ASL/visual/gestural performance that the audience would see for themselves."

That Peter Cook enhances his performance with a range of mimetic ges-tures & nonverbal sounds is also to be noted.

Michael "Mikey" Smith   Jamaica, 1954–1983

MI CYAAN BELIEVE IT

Mi seh mi cyaan believe it
mi seh mi cyaan believe it
room dem a rent
mi apply widin
but as mi go in
cockroach rat an scorpion also come in
waan good
nose haffi run
but me naw go sideung pan igh wall
like Humpty Dumpty
mi a face me reality

one lickle bwoy come blow im orn
an mi look pan im wid scorn
an mi realize ow me five bwoy pickney
was a victim of de tricks
dem call partisan pally-trix

Oan mi ban mi belly
an mi bawl
an mi ban mi belly

an mi bawl
lawd
mi cyaan believe it
mi seh mi cyaan believe it

Mi daughter bwoyfren name is Sailor
an im pass through de port like a ship
more gran pickney fi feed
but de whole a we in-need
what a night what a plight
an we cyaan get a bite
mi life is a stiff fight
an mi cyaan believe it

me seh mi cyaan believe it
Sitting on de corner wid me fren
talkin bout tings an time
me hear one voice seh
"Who dat?"
Mi seh "A who dat?
A who dat a seh who dat
when mi a seh who dat?"

When yuh teck a stock
dem lick we dung flat
teet start fly
an big man start cry
an mi cyaan believe it
mi seh mi cyaan believe it

De odder day me pass one yard
pan de hill
when me teck a stock
me hear "Hey bwoy!"
"Yes, Mam?" "Hey bwoy!"
"Yes, Mam?" "You clean up de dawg shit?"
"Yes, Mam"
An mi cyaan believe it
Mi seh mi cyaan believe it

Doris a modder of four
get a wuk as a domestic
boss man move een
an bap si kaisico she pregnant again

bap si kaisico she pregnant again
an mi cyaan believe it
Dah yard de odder night
when mi hear "Fire!"
"Fire, to plate claat!"
Who dead? You dead?
Who dead? Me dead?
Who dead? Harry dead?
Who dead? Eleven dead
Wooeeeeeeeeeeeee
Orange Street fire deh pan me head
an mi cyaan believe it
mi seh mi cyaan believe it

Lawd, mi see some black bud
livin inna one buildin
but no rent no pay
so dem cyaan stay
Lawd, de oppress an de dispossess
cyaan get no res
what nex?

Teck a trip from Kingston
to Jamaica
Teck twelve from a dozen
an mi see mi Muma in heaven
MAD OUSE! MAD OUSE!
mi seh mi cyaan believe it
mi seh mi cyaan believe it
Yuh believe it?
How yuh fi believe it
when yuh laugh
yuh blind yuh eye to it?
But me know yuh believe it
Laaaaaaaaaaaaaaaaaaaaaaaaaaaaaaaaaaaaaaawd
mi know yuh believe it

COMMENTARY

In *History of the Voice: The Development of Nation Language in Anglophone Caribbean Poetry*, poet Kamau Brathwaite delineates the differences between various Englishes & related languages in the Caribbean.

With Dub poet Mikey Smith as an exemplary instance, Brathwaite lays out the following, "in contrast to dialect":

> *We in the Caribbean have ... a plurality [of languages]: we have English, which is the imposed language on much of the archipelago. It is an imperial language, as are French, Dutch and Spanish. We also have what we call Creole English, which is a mixture of English and an adaptation that English took in the new environment of the Caribbean when it became mixed with the other imported languages. We have also what is called nation language, which is the kind of English spoken by the people who were brought to the Caribbean, not the official English now, but the language of slaves and labourers, the servants who were brought in by the conquistadors.*

For Brathwaite's further take on Mikey Smith in a more personal and political vein, see his poem "Stone" in "A Fourth Gallery."

Louis Zukofsky USA, 1904–1978
with Celia Zukofsky USA, 1913–1980

from *CATULLUS*

A Homophonic Translation

Miser Catulle, desinas ineptire,
et quod vides perisse perditum ducas.
fulsere quondam candidi tibi soles ...

.....

Miss her, Catullus? don't be so inept to rail
at what you see perish when perished is the case.
Full, sure once, candid the sunny days glowed, solace,
when you went about it as your girl would have it,
you loved her as no one else shall ever be loved.
Billowed in tumultuous joys and affianced,
why you would but will it and your girl would have it.
Full, sure, very candid the sun's rays glowed solace.
Now she won't love you; you, too, don't be weak, tense, null,
squirming after she runs off to miss her for life.
Said as if you meant it: obstinate, obdurate.
Vale! puling girl. I'm Catullus, obdurate,

I don't require it and don't beg uninvited:
won't you be doleful when no one, no one! begs you,
scalded, every night. Why do you want to live now?
Now who will be with you? Who'll see that you're lovely?
Whom will you love now and who will say that you're his?
Whom will you kiss? Whose morsel of lips will you bite?
But you, Catullus, your destiny's obdurate.

COMMENTARY

As with the first three lines, shown above, the constraint in this translation
is to retain as much as possible of the original Latin sound, in the way that
standard translations abandon the sound of the original and foreground a
semblance of its meaning.

ADDENDUM

BERNADETTE MAYER USA, 1945–2022

After Catullus and Horace

only the manners of centuries ago can teach me
how to address you my lover as who you are
O Sestius, how could you put up with my children
thinking all the while you were bearing me as in your mirror
it doesn't matter anymore if spring wreaks its fiery
or lamblike dawn on my new-found asceticism, some joke
I wouldn't sleep with you or any man if you paid me
and most of you poets don't have the cash anyway
so please rejoin your fraternal books forever
while you miss in your securest sleep Ms. Rosy-fingered dawn
who might've been induced to digitalize a part of you
were it not for your self-induced revenge of undoneness
it's good to live without a refrigerator! why bother
to chill the handiwork of Ceres and of Demeter?
and of the lonesome Sappho. let's have it warm for now.

Susana Thénon   Argentina, 1935–1991

POEM WITH SIMULTANEOUS
ENGLISH-ENGLISH TRANSLATION

Cristóforo
     (the Bearer of Christ)
son of a humble carder of wool
     (son of one who went for weaving without carding)
sailed forth from the port of Poles
     (pole in paw he forsook the port)
not without first persuading Her Majesty the Queen
Isabel the Catholic of the benefits of the enterprise
he'd conceived
     (not without first persuading Su Majestad la Reina
     die Königin Bella the Logistical to cop
     the crown in Blumenthal's con-verted canteen)
even if they poured out liters and liters of
genuine ancient B-negative blood
     (and even if it cost blood sweat and antipodal
     tears)
went off to sea
     (went to seed)
and after months and months of ingesting only
oxymorons looking for the elusive roundness
     (and after days and days of chewing Yorkshire pudding
     with an extra penguin on Sundays)
someone exclaimed land
     (no one exclaimed thalassa)
they disembarked
in 1492 A.D.
     (treading
     on 1982 A.D.)
chiefs were waiting
genuflecting
in the buff
     (big shots were waiting
     naked
     on their knees)
Cristóforo drew out his missal
     (Christopher shot off his missile)

said to his peers
        (muttered to his stooges)
coño
        (fuck)
behold these new worlds here
        (behold the unworldly filth here)
keep them
        (loot them)
for God and Our Queen
        (for God and Our Queen)
A M E N
        (O M E N)

Translated from Spanish by Rebekah Smith

COMMENTARY

In the preceding, originally titled "Poema con traducción simultánea
español-español," Thénon tries to mock & debase colonial & postcolonial
languages & imagery (military, religious, etc.) in order to resist them.
Through her "translation," she creates a bridge that links the schemes
& structures of power between two different historical—& therefore
ideological—periods. In her work, then, there is a direct line from the
colonialist & near-epic history of Christopher Columbus to the postcolonial
moves of the United Kingdom that provoked the Falklands/Malvinas War
against Argentina in 1982. Although Thénon is sometimes related to other
poets of Argentina's 1960s generation (such as Alejandra Pizarnik), she
rejected belonging to any group, opening her writing to more experimental
features while at the same time developing a strong feminist & political
criticism.

Ronald Johnson   USA, 1935–1998

from **RADI OS**

words
            hazard all

        Abyss, and
        World,

mid Air;
possession put to

song

,fit body to fit head!

whence
limits
wheel

Turned fiery
phalanx
as when a field
waving bends
Sway

Atlas unremoved:

the Elements

In counterpoise,   events

(1) An early example of "erasure poem" practice, in which Johnson writes his way through Milton's *Paradise Lost*, striking out text to create an alternative poem from the words remaining in their original order. Thus the title *RADI OS* from Milton's pa**RADI**se l**OS**t, & so on.

(2) "*RADI OS* happened… when I was teaching at the University of Washington. I went to a party at a student's one night and they played a Lukas Foss record called 'Baroque Variations.' His Handel piece [in which] his strategy was to take Handel and erase things so that it had a modern, modish feel, but it was definitely Handel. It was really neoclassical in some odd way. And so I went off to think about it and the next day I went to the bookstore and bought a Milton *Paradise Lost*. And I started crossing out. I got about halfway through it crossing out anything because I thought it would be funny. But I decided you don't tamper with Milton to be funny. You have to be serious. I didn't think about Blake right then but I went back and got serious. And wrote *RADI OS*" (R.J., from an interview by Peter O'Leary).

Alison Knowles USA, 1933–
& James Tenney USA, 1934–2006

from **THE HOUSE OF DUST**

A HOUSE OF DUST
  ON OPEN GROUND
    LIT BY NATURAL LIGHT
     INHABITED BY FRIENDS AND ENEMIES

A HOUSE OF PAPER
  AMONG HIGH MOUNTAINS
    USING NATURAL LIGHT
     INHABITED BY FISHERMEN AND FAMILIES

A HOUSE OF PLASTIC
  BY AN ABANDONED LAKE
    USING ALL AVAILABLE LIGHTING
     INHABITED BY VARIOUS BIRDS AND FISHES

A HOUSE OF GLASS
  IN MICHIGAN
    USING ELECTRICITY
     INHABITED BY PEOPLE WHO EAT A GREAT DEAL

A HOUSE OF TIN
  ON AN ISLAND
    USING CANDLES
     INHABITED BY PEOPLE WHO SLEEP ALMOST ALL THE TIME

A HOUSE OF STONE
  ON THE SEA
    USING ALL AVAILABLE LIGHTING
     INHABITED BY LOVERS

     [etc.]

COMMENTARY

"*The House of Dust* was a poetry project created by Alison Knowles and James Tenney and the Siemens 4004 computer in 1967 using fortran computer language. An early example of a computer-generated poem, creating stanzas by working through iterations of lines with changing words from a finite vocabulary list. An early example of computerized poetry that plays on the unlimited possibilities of the random juxtapositions of words. To create this work, Knowles produced four word-lists that were then translated into a computer language and organized into quatrains according to a random matrix. Each of the four lists contains terms that describe the attributes of a house: its materials, location, lighting, and inhabitants. The computer program imposed a non-rational ordering of subjects and ideas, generating unexpectedly humorous phrasing and imagery.

"Printed on perforated tractor-feed paper common to dot matrix printers of the time, Knowles printed out numerous pages of these phrases in the form of a long scroll. She then created a book of sorts by tearing off a block of approximately twenty pages at a time, folding it in the manner of an accordion, and placing it in a plastic pouch. Hundreds of variations of houses are possible, as every version of the poem begins and ends with a different set of quatrains. Knowles's collaboration with the computer highlights the underlying arbitrariness of language, demonstrating how words acquire different meanings through structural relationships and shifting contexts" (from the catalogue accompanying an exhibition at James Gallery, New York, September 2016).

N.B. The many cyberpoetic works of the twenty-first century are also to be noted.

A FOURTH GALLERY

from Allen Ginsberg to Raúl Zurita

Allen Ginsberg USA, 1926–1997

from **KADDISH**

For Naomi Ginsberg, 1894–1956

Hymmnn

In the world which He has created according to his will Blessed Praised
Magnified Lauded Exalted the Name of the Holy One Blessed is He!
In the house in Newark Blessed is He! In the madhouse Blessed is He! In
  the house of Death Blessed is He!
Blessed be He in homosexuality! Blessed be He in Paranoia! Blessed be
  He in the city! Blessed be He in the Book!
Blessed be He who dwells in the shadow! Blessed be He! Blessed be He!
Blessed be you Naomi in tears! Blessed be you Naomi in fears! Blessed
  Blessed Blessed in sickness!
Blessed be you Naomi in Hospitals! Blessed be you Naomi in solitude!
  Blest be your triumph! Blest be your bars! Blest be your last years'
  loneliness!
Blest be your failure! Blest be your stroke! Blest be the close of your eye!
  Blest be the gaunt of your cheek! Blest be your withered thighs!
Blessed be Thee Naomi in Death! Blessed be Death! Blessed be Death!
Blessed be He Who leads all sorrow to Heaven! Blessed be He in the
  end!
Blessed be He who builds Heaven in Darkness! Blessed Blessed Blooood
  be He! Blessed be He! Blessed be Death on us All!

from **THE SOUTH AMERICAN JOURNALS**

April 28, 1960

Intiwatana, crescent moon, city strictly in the clouds—now alone at night—
  living in a hovel drinking cold coffee—the last priest.
Up there in the cave it's very dark
The bodies are even gone from the tombs
More stones for the locusts, Pompeii, Rome, Herculaneum, Cuma, Chichen Itza,
  Uxmal, Palenque, Machu Picchu—have lived in all these dead cities.
A rabbit and a lizard, and a white dog that barks too much and the southern
  cross.
Black centipedes over the stairways
The prow of the mountain like a ship in the night, this city.

Standing on platform looking into the obscure forum by the dim light of
crescent, the house shapes and terraces half invisible—addressed to them—
where are you now?

What are you dreaming of—what war?

The half-mad scholar bending over his notebook in the darkness 2000 years
hence—questioning the inhabitants—This I did with my beard, resting book
on balcony and peering at it to write, then looking sideways scared into the
fields below.

If I had summoned a ghost to talk to me, which I did not because of fear—In
that vast obscurity—and

What language would we have spoken?

The ghostly solitude—I am the king of the dead, on their ancient throne—sitting
1000 years later lording over these ghosts, questioning in the later moonlight,
from the height of the sacrificial stone.

And the stars over the dead city, so far away—suddenly in the presence of the
Universe itself.

from WICHITA VORTEX SUTRA (1966)

I'm an old man now, and a lonesome man in Kansas
    but not afraid
        to speak my lonesomeness in a car,
      because not only my lonesomeness
          it's Ours, all over America,
              O tender fellows—
        & spoken lonesomeness is Prophecy
        in the moon 100 years ago or in
           the middle of Kansas now.
It's not the vast plains mute our mouths
        that fill at midnite with ecstatic language
      when our trembling bodies hold each other
        breast to breast on a mattress—
    Not the empty sky that hides
        the feeling from our faces
  nor our skirts and trousers that conceal
      the bodylove emanating in a glow of beloved skin,
        white smooth abdomen down to the hair
          between our legs,
    It's not a God that bore us that forbid
      our Being, like a sunny rose

all red with naked joy
between our eyes & bellies, yes
All we do is for this frightened thing
we call Love, want and lack—
fear that we aren't the one whose body could be
beloved of all the brides of Kansas City,
kissed all over by every boy of Wichita—
O but how many in their solitude weep aloud like me—
On the bridge over the Republican River
almost in tears to know
how to speak the right language—
on the frosty broad road
uphill between highway embankments
I search for the language
that is also yours—
almost all our language has been taxed by war.

COMMENTARY

First thought, best thought. Spontaneous insight—the sequence of thought-forms passing naturally through ordinary mind—was motif and method of these compositions. (A.G.)

(1) So it fell to Ginsberg to become, for many, the iconic representative of a new generation of poets & other outliers toward an unprecedented liberation & transformation of behavior & language. Under the self-proclaimed rubric of "the Beats," he brought into wider public view what had long been out-of-bounds but always lurking at the heart of poetry: the politically radical; the sexual; the religious as a struggle with the repressive powers of religion & its "mind-forged manacles" (W. Blake). (He would later become a spokesman for a new American Buddhism & cofounder, with Anne Waldman & the Tibetan "master" Chögyam Trungpa, of the Jack Kerouac School of Disembodied Poetics in Boulder, Colorado.) This early willingness "to die for Poetry & for the truth that inspires poetry" led him not only to a poetic courage shared with others but also to international visibility (as a Beat Generation founder & political & spiritual mentor for several later generations) & a growing sense of responsibility for things said—both those to be said again & then again & those to be said & then unsaid.

(2) In the poems presented here, the "hymmnn" is a broad variation on the traditional Hebrew Prayer for the Dead; the excerpt from *The South American Journals* is from a series of 1960 notebook improvisations, the Intiwatana an ancient ritual stone located at the site of Machu Picchu; &

"Wichita Vortex Sutra" is part of a long work, *The Fall of America: Poems of These States 1965–1971*, & is also largely improvised, composed while driving cross-country early in the years of the US war in Vietnam.

René Depestre Haiti, 1926–

ODE TO DESSALINES

Erzili

It's up to me to tell of Dessalines
It's up to Erzili goddess of sweet waters
It's up to me to lift up this torrent of black flames
In the old days of my green leaves
Dessalines carried away my body in his current
One night on this island a night brand new
As was then my woman-blood
Dessalines hurled his running waters under my woman-sun
Dessalines hurled his horse over my woman-paths
Now, it's up to Erzili the black Venus
Fairy of love and beauty
It's up to me to thrust Dessalines toward your veins
It's up to me to parade his blood's most secret gems before your eyes
He arrived body covered with scars
Eyes red from stifling floods of tears under whip and insult
He was all bristly with claws
Like the sea on a stormy day
Rolling wave after wave
Its justice toward our slave-hands
And suddenly this was his voice:
"Stand up earth more mine than my suffering
Earth more mine than my foam stand up
And be an accusing geyser
Be a chopper of exotic heads
Be an incendiary people
Lift up your phosphorus sails
Toward the wood of their houses
We're through licking our wounds
Through digging the earth with our knees
Now is the moment to have a single rendezvous before our steps: fire
A single will: fire at the end of our arm's night!

Chop off their heads
Burn their houses
Make one pile of their hates
One big pile of their dogmas
Bring tar, pine-wood
Lamp-oil
And let all that's inflammable
Stop sleeping to guide our actions!"

Translated from French by Joan Dayan

COMMENTARY

Let's be crazy with rage and freedom / Let's make one single paw of our gods / To crush their cruel dogmas (R.D.)

Like many other writers of his time, René Depestre felt aroused by new poetical/political forces & procedures that aimed to transform the painful & oppressive social reality in the Americas. Moved by this possibility, he published his first poetry collection, *Sparks*, at the age of nineteen. Involved in political & cultural movements in his native Haiti (notably the early stages of Negritude, which he later critiqued & reformulated as a manifesto against a whole range of imperialisms) & developing a combative attitude against the practices of power, he was forced into exile until he settled in Cuba, by invitation of Che Guevara. There, Depestre drew from different topics (historical, erotic, folkloristic) to express more fully his position regarding cultural & racial identity & against US & European colonialism. In *A Rainbow from the Christian West,* the book from which this ode comes, Depestre writes odes to figures who embodied the same struggle—Malcolm X, Jean-Jacques Dessalines, and Toussaint Louverture, among others. The piece above is addressed to Dessalines, a former slave & leader of the Haitian Revolution—one of the first successful independence movements in the Americas & the only slave rebellion in world history that successfully resulted in establishing an independent nation.

Robert Creeley   USA, 1926–2005

A WICKER BASKET

Comes the time when it's later
and onto your table the headwaiter
puts the bill, and very soon after
rings out the sound of lively laughter—

Picking up change, hands like a walrus,
and a face like a barndoor's,
and a head without any apparent size,
nothing but two eyes—

So that's you, man,
or me. I make it as I can,
I pick up, I go
faster than they know—

Out the door, the street like a night,
any night, and no one in sight,
but then, well, there she is,
old friend Liz—

And she opens the door of her cadillac,
I step in back,
and we're gone.
She turns me on—

There are very huge stars, man, in the sky,
and from somewhere very far off someone hands
    me a slice of apple pie,
with a gob of white, white ice cream on top of it,
and I eat it—

Slowly. And while certainly
they are laughing at me, and all around me is racket
of these cats not making it, I make it

in my wicker basket.

AMERICA

America, you ode for reality!
Give back the people you took.

Let the sun shine again
on the four corners of the world

you thought of first but do not
own, or keep like a convenience.

People are your own word, you
invented that locus and term.

Here, you said and say, is
where we are. Give back

what we are, these people you made,
us, and nowhere but you to be.

COMMENTARY

To count, to give account, tell or tally, continually seems to me the occasion. (R.C.) And again: *I think, and / therefore I am not.* And also: *As soon as / I speak, I / speaks.*

(1) A defining figure of the Black Mountain school of post–World War II USAmerican poetry, Creeley's work marked an authoritative enlivening and transformation of the moribund lyric impulse (what a later "language poet," Charles Bernstein, dubbed "official verse culture"), turning toward a homegrown but internationally savvy inheritance that gave him "that sense of speech as a laconic, ironic, compressed way of saying something to someone. To say as little as possible as often as possible."

(2) Take the following, then, as an instance of Creeley's move toward a quintessential and complex sense of himself, speaking and writing as an *American* poet, and extend it, if we dare, toward the Americas overall:

> *I think this is very much the way Americans are given to speak—not in some dismay that they haven't another way to speak, but, rather, that they feel that they, perhaps more than any other group of people upon the earth at this moment, have had both to imagine and thereby to make that reality which they are then given to live in.*

And again: "I've always been embarrassed for a so-called larger view. I've been given to write about that which has the most intimate presence for me. And I am given as a man to work with what is most intimate to me" (cited by Marjorie Perloff in "Robert Creeley's Radical Poetics," *Electronic Book Review*, October 13, 2007).

The achievement, in that sense, & its influence are breathtaking.

Blanca Varela Peru, 1926–2009

MONSIEUR MONOD DOESN'T KNOW HOW TO SING

my dear
I remember you like the best song
that apotheosis of roosters and stars you no longer are
that I no longer am that we no longer will be
and nevertheless we both know very well
that I speak with the painted mouth of silence
with the agony of a fly
at the end of summer
and through all the poorly closed doors
conjuring or calling that traitorous wind of memory
that record scratched before it is used
tinted to match the times
and their old sicknesses
or red
or black
like a disgraced king before the mirror
the day of the day before
and tomorrow and the day after and always

night rushing headlong
burdened with premonitions
(is what the song should say)
insatiable bitch (un peu fort)
splendid mother (plus doux)
fertile and always barefoot
so not to be heard by the idiot who believes in you
so to better crush the heart
of the insomniac
who dares listen to life's footsteps
dragging
toward death
a mosquito's fart a torrent of feathers
a storm in a glass of wine
a tango

order alters the product
the machinist's error
rotting technology keeps you living your story

in reverse like the movies
a thick and mysterious dream
that runs thin
the end is the beginning
a tiny light flickering like hope
the color of egg whites
with the smell of fish and rotten milk
dark mouth of the wolf that takes you
from Cluny to Parque Salazar
a treadmill so swift and so black
that you no longer know
if you are or pretend to be alive
or dead
and yes an iron flower
like the last twisted and dirty and slow bite
the better to devour you

my dear
I adore all that is not mine
you for example
with your pig's skin over your soul
and those wax wings I gave you
that you never dared use
you don't know how I regret my virtues
I don't know what to do with my collection of picklocks
    and lies
with my indecency of a boy who should end this story
it's already late
because memory like songs
the worst the one you want the only
does not resist another blank page
and there is no sense in me being here
destroying
what doesn't exist

my dear
despite that
everything remains the same
the philosophic tickler after a shower
the cold coffee the bitter cigarette Swamp Thing
in the Montecarlo
everlasting life still suits everyone

the clouds' stupidity intact
the geraniums' obscenity intact
the garlic's shame intact
the sparrows divinely shitting in the middle
of an April sky
Mandrake raising rabbits in one of hell's circles
and the crab's little foot always caught
in the trap of to be
or not to be
or I don't want this one but another
you know
those things that happen to us
and that one should forget so that
for instance the hand with wings
and without a hand
can exist
the kangaroo's story—to choose the pouch or your life—
or the story of the captain inside the bottle
forever empty
and the womb—empty but with wings
and without a womb
you know
passion obsession
poetry prose
sex success
or vice-versa
the congenital emptiness
the tiny speckled egg
among millions and millions of speckled eggs
tú y yo
you and me
toi et moi
tea for two in the immensity of silence
in the timeless sea
in history's horizon
because ribonucleic acid is what we are
but ribonucleic acid in love forever

Translated from Spanish by Eileen O'Connor

There will be no witnesses. / We have been warned that heaven is mute. //
At most it will be written, will be erased. Will be forgotten. (B.V.)

(1) Blanca Varela's gift of poetry lies—paradoxically—in its silence. This "silence" or isolation (five small books in thirty-five years of writing) led her to establish few, if any, contacts with academia or the literary establishment, to elude the role of a socially committed poet, & to avoid public readings & appearances; for her, that opened the possibility of going deeper into her own resources & intensities. As she once wrote: "I think that poetry resides not in the quantity but in the intensity. It's like working at very high temperatures that don't allow us to remain there for long periods of time. The poet works in very delicate zones of consciousness."

(2) Jacques L. Monod was a Nobel Prize–winning French biochemist. In his work *Necessity*, he explored the capacity of biological systems to retain information & the ways in which that information is involved in the physical form of living organisms & thus is responsible for all the events in the world. Monod states that this process, acting over long periods of time (that is, through history) & altered by chance & necessity, explains the complexity & purposefulness of our existence & universe, without any mythical or religious accounting. For Varela, all history is within us, & our fate is dictated by our ongoing & hazardous genetic motion.

Frank O'Hara USA, 1926–1966

from MEDITATIONS IN AN EMERGENCY

Am I to become profligate as if I were a blonde? Or religious as if I were French?

Each time my heart is broken it makes me feel more adventurous (and how the same names keep recurring on that interminable list!), but one of these days there'll be nothing left with which to venture forth.

Why should I share you? Why don't you get rid of someone else for a change?

I am the least difficult of men. All I want is boundless love.

Even trees understand me! Good heavens, I lie under them, too, don't I? I'm just like a pile of leaves.

However, I have never clogged myself with the praises of pastoral life, nor with nostalgia for an innocent past of perverted acts in pastures. No. One need never leave the confines of New York to get all the greenery one wishes—I can't even enjoy a blade of grass unless I know there's a subway handy, or a record store or some other sign that people do not totally *regret* life. It is more important to affirm the least sincere; the clouds get enough attention as it is and even they continue to pass. Do they know what they're missing? Uh huh.

My eyes are vague blue, like the sky, and change all the time; they are indiscriminate but fleeting, entirely specific and disloyal, so that no one trusts me. I am always looking away. Or again at something after it has given me up. It makes me restless and that makes me unhappy, but I cannot keep them still. If only I had grey, green, black, brown, yellow eyes; I would stay at home and do something. It's not that I am curious. On the contrary, I am bored but it's my duty to be attentive, I am needed by things as the sky must be above the earth. And lately, so great has *their* anxiety become, I can spare myself little sleep.

ODE: SALUTE TO THE FRENCH NEGRO POETS

from near the sea, like Whitman my great predecessor, I call
to the spirits of other lands to make fecund my existence

do not spare your wrath upon our shores, that trees may grow
upon the sea, mirror of our total mankind in the weather

one who no longer remembers dancing in the heat of the moon may call
across the shifting sands, trying to live in the terrible western world

here where to love at all's to be a politician, as to love a poem
is pretentious, this may sound tendentious but it's lyrical

which shows what lyricism has been brought to by our fabled times
where cowards are shibboleths and one specific love's traduced

by shame for what you love more generally and never would avoid
where reticence is paid for by a poet in his blood or ceasing to be

blood! Blood that we have mountains in our veins to stand off jackals
in the pillaging of our desires and allegiances,

for if there is fortuity it's in the love we bear each other's differences
in race which is the poetic ground on which we rear our smiles

standing in the sun of marshes as we wade slowly toward the culmination
of a gift which is categorically the most difficult relationship

and should be sought as such because it is our nature, nothing
inspires us but the love we want upon the frozen face of earth

and utter disparagement turns into praise as generations read the message
of our hearts in adolescent closets who once shot at us in doorways

or kept us from living freely because they were too young then to know
what they would ultimately need from a barren and heart-sore life

the beauty of America, neither cool jazz nor devoured Egyptian heroes, lies in
lives in the darkness I inhabit in the midst of sterile millions

the only truth is face to face, the poem whose words become your mouth
and dying in black and white we fight for what we love, not are.

COMMENTARY

Everything is in the poems.... I don't believe in God so I don't have to
make elaborately sounded structures.... I don't even like rhythm, asso-
nance, all that stuff. You just go on your nerve. If someone's chasing you
down the street with a knife you just run, you don't turn around and
shout, "Give it up! I was a track star for Minneola Prep." (F.O.)

The core player (with John Ashbery) in what came to be known—ca.
1960—as the New York School of poets, O'Hara may here have overstated his dislike of traditional poetic praxis or, elsewhere, of theoretical
poetics—i.e., his writings on art show his critical intelligence, & his poetry
evidences both a great care for technique & a comfortable knowledge of
transnational modern poetics (Apollinaire, Rilke, Pasternak, etc.). Behind
his proclaimed love for surfaces & surface effects (a concern shared with
some Abstract Expressionist painters of the 1950s & 1960s) lay a daily
discipline summed up in "Meditations in an Emergency" (1957). Quintes-
sentially a city poet (but more in the Apollinaire/Cendrars vein, say, than
that of Baudelaire), he focused this attention on New York, & like so much
of the twentieth century's avant-garde, what attracted him was speed &
immediacy—which is why (wrote Marjorie Perloff) "[he] loves the motion
picture, action painting and all forms of the dance—art forms that capture
the present... in all its chaotic splendor."

(Commentary by Jerome Rothenberg with Pierre Joris in *Poems for the Millennium*, vol. 2.)

Russell Atkins USA, 1926–

ABSTRACTIVE

       I came upon that gate
that tracery'd gently into open

there lay the sum of the dearest
once belonging, the memoried
that scattered, then, compilingly
length'd into the poor pale

no place to bring one's birth
this hill they let run down
among them where the scant
droops to astray with dearth'd

      the one and one,
a four, or ten even and seldom'd
wisp'd across listened into grass

there where   only
         as a grey amount
coming on with swerve
solemns afar   whole family
again
     my dear ones

COMMENTARY

I would "compose" like a painter and write poems like a composer. (R.A.)

A major genre-crossing artist, composing for several decades between poetry & music, Atkins developed a mode of composition he called "phenomenalism," in which "image and sound combinations extend the possibilities of semantic meaning through sonic play and visual forms." He has often been described, perhaps too easily, as a "Concrete poet," while his influential essay "A Psychovisual Perspective for 'Musical' Composition" proposes a special & elaborate view of the visual aspects of both musical & verse composition. The intensity of his avant-gardism & longtime residence in Cleveland may have held back publication & visibility; his only full-length collection, *Here in The*, was published early along, in 1976, by the Cleveland State Poetry Center.

That he was the editor from 1952 to 1980 of *Free Lance*, "for many years the only journal dedicated to publishing African-American poetry," is also worth noting.

Paul Blackburn USA, 1926–1971

PANCHO VILLA OR THE FATE

In Spain one drinks from both cups.
Split a diamond   /   quarter it   /   cut it in eighths
the glamour of increasing surfaces.
              And in getting below them
              one partakes of aspects
                    like wounds
The fact, the designation, are only two
              ports of entry, Mister
Pythagoras
              Ulysse dixit:
                    "I have been to talk to Tiresias.
He said, 'Take an oar
and walk inland with it
until they think you are foolish.
              Go even further
they will think it is something else.
That way you will live very long.'"
              "Pero, trabajarlas senor, no es facil,"
meaning the earth Herself, meaning
his own damned terraces
                    There was another said that to me
                    meaning the bulls he fought
For the Poet
each poem

from JOURNAL: JUNE 1971

How it turns
in again, the pain
       across my shoulders these mornings.

              Possession of the mind
              a fragile thing / when the pain
              goes,
then's the time to use it   .   what's left of it .

Men with shovels directed a stream
of sizable pebbles into the excavations
about young new-planted mountain ash trees
set mid-quad in the concrete
from a dump truck   .
I brought back home
a single rhododendron bloom that had fallen .

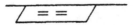

Outside the cellar door, I spoke to a bee, he
danced before me, crotch to face, he checked me out, he
                buzzed, I talked, he sat
                in my beard for a moment   .   We
                    talked.   I wanted to go inside   .   I told him
                        so   .   I did   .

                                                            16.VI.71

COMMENTARY

On the matter of song: I believe there must be a return toward the / musical structure in poetry, just as there must be, for certain people at / least, the return to warmth within a relationship. (P.B.)

Like other important North American poets of his time, Blackburn's work showed an identification with the initial experiments of Pound & Williams, buttressed in his case by resources of language that opened to a still larger range of European & Latin American predecessors, through his workings with Julio Cortázar & others. A Vermonter by birth, he lived most of his life in New York City, but traveled from there early & late, to chart the world through a succession of poems that were his ongoing journal (= daybook), culminating in a final diaristic work appropriately called *The Journals* (posthumously published in 1975).

The poems included here, like much of his work, reflect a poetics of the everyday as vision, in line perhaps with Charles Olson's citation & directive from Heraclitus: "Man is estranged from that with which he is most familiar." Or George Oppen: "The virtue of the mind / is that emotion / which causes to see."

In addition, his workings from the medieval troubadours (*Proensa*, 1953) were one of the true masterworks of contemporary American translation.

"Shake" Keane (Ellsworth McGranahan)

St. Vincent and the Grenadines, 1927–1997

from **ONE A WEEK WITH WATER**

WEEK FOUR 19–347

Kaiso   *Calypso*

Mauby   *Maw-beer*

'Nanse 'tory

Nonsense Story

NONSENSE

NONSENSE

In 1313 first recorded Africans arrived in the New World, from Mali. We, the members of CANGASOBOGGA (Can Garden Suburban Cognizance Assn.), cognizant of our duty to be remarkable, and resolved to be so cognizant, demand to know why we were not informed in time.

WEEK TEN 61–305

OX:	Man pass here, yet?
ASS:	No, man, Ox. Man does done dey home in he bed this time of a evenin.
OX:	Good. Let we rest here out the sun, talk little bit.
PARROT:	Littlebit littlebit littlebit.
OX:	But Ass, is six years now I ain't see you. I think you did loss?!
ASS:	Loss! I livin for years just behind da bush dey. Let Man do he own wuk. I is now my own independent ass-self. Nuttin but meditate and eat grass all the time. Only ting, I does have to be careful hold back meself when I feel to bray!
PARROT:	Braybray braybray.
OX:	Well boy, Ass, you lucky, nuh!? I wukkin for Man like a cattle every day, till me tongue dry-up and me tail ben-up.
ASS:	You must be a ass. All you have to do is play loss like me. Or better still, tomorrow mornin when wuk to start, don't mek *one* bellow; just drop down right by Man foot,

	breed heavey, and say yo sick.
PARROT:	Trick, trick, sick trick!
MAN (next morning):	My God! You ever see anyting so!? My ass loss already, and now my damn ox fall down wid bad feelins. Who the hell will do my work for me now!
PARROT:	Sen for Ass. Behind-the-bush-behind-the-bush,
	behind-the-bush dey!
MAN:	ASS!!! Come outta dey, you wutlass…
PARROT:	Lassassassass *ass ASS ASS AASSS*

(Based on one of the many "stories" I've heard over the years from an old friend, Elias Roache)

March 3rd, 1976   Arsch Wednesday

WEEK TWELVE 75–291

O
  AMEN
     MY MOTHER
   HELP ME
     TO AROUSE
       NOT necessarily
         OFFEND
         THEIR
            SENSIBILITIES

thus and thus dreamed the sane man
Whose mother is *Amen*
  Much-up   Much-up   own-way
gutsify   nyant-and-go-away

COMMENTARY

When I was born / my father gave to me / an angelhorn / With wings of melody. / That angel / placed her lips / upon my finger-tips / and I became, became / her secret name (S.K.) And again: *Music is a demon, / and rhythm is the spell / that sits upon his eye.*

Better known as a jazz trumpeter & flügelhorn player, Shake Keane's moves in poetry, especially in his collection *One a Week with Water*, deserve wider attention. Critic Philip Nanton writes about them: "Superficially, the reader is presented with a simple calendar offering observations for each week. These [Keane] described in the introduction as 'notes and rhymes.' They took the form of a collage of verse, riddle, story, letters, spoof of bureaucratic forms, aphorisms, reportage, and rhyme. Among the predominantly humorous pieces in the collection are distributed a number of poetic shards with flashes of anger, despair and loss. There is the sublime and the ridiculous. Regular patterns are avoided. Standard as well as local forms of English are tossed about for humor and serious intent. For the most part, however, Keane mixes humor and gentle satire while commenting indirectly on order and chaos in Vincentian society. [For Keane] a culture is being formed out of a diversity of accident and tradition. This process of formation… is chaotic, at times repetitive, but it is also creative. It is distinctly Caribbean, approaching Antonio Benitez-Rojo's definition of Caribbean culture as a *culture of performance*" (in *Shake Keane's Poetic Legacy*).

John Ashbery USA, 1927–2017

THIS ROOM

The room I entered was a dream of this room.
Surely all those feet on the sofa were mine.
The oval portrait
of a dog was me at an early age.
Something shimmers, something is hushed up.

We had macaroni for lunch every day
except Sunday, when a small quail was induced
to be served to us. Why do I tell you these things?
You are not even here.

INTO THE DUSK-CHARGED AIR

Far from the Rappahannock, the silent
Danube moves along toward the sea.
The brown and green Nile rolls slowly
Like the Niagara's welling descent.
Tractors stood on the green banks of the Loire
Near where it joined the Cher.
The St. Lawrence prods among black stones

And mud. But the Arno is all stones.
Wind ruffles the Hudson's
Surface. The Irawaddy is overflowing.
But the yellowish, gray Tiber
Is contained within steep banks. The Isar
Flows too fast to swim in, the Jordan's water
Courses over the flat land. The Allegheny and its boats
Were dark blue. The Moskowa is
Gray boats. The Amstel flows slowly.
Leaves fall into the Connecticut as it passes
Underneath. The Liffey is full of sewage,
Like the Seine, but unlike
The brownish-yellow Dordogne.
Mountains hem in the Colorado
And the Oder is very deep, almost
As deep as the Congo is wide.
The plain banks of the Neva are
Gray. The dark Saône flows silently.
And the Volga is long and wide
As it flows across the brownish land. The Ebro
Is blue, and slow. The Shannon flows
Swiftly between its banks. The Mississippi
Is one of the world's longest rivers, like the Amazon.
It has the Missouri for a tributary.
The Harlem flows amid factories
And buildings. The Nelson is in Canada,
Flowing. Through hard banks the Dubawnt
Forces its way. People walk near the Trent.
The landscape around the Mohawk stretches away;
The Rubicon is merely a brook.
In winter the Main
Surges; the Rhine sings its eternal song.
The Rhône slogs along through whitish banks
And the Rio Grande spins tales of the past.
The Loire bursts its frozen shackles
But the Moldau's wet mud ensnares it.
The East catches the light.
Near the Escaut the noise of factories echoes
And the sinuous Humboldt gurgles wildly.
The Po too flows, and the many-colored
Thames. Into the Atlantic Ocean

Pours the Garonne. Few ships navigate
On the Housatonic, but quite a few can be seen
On the Elbe. For centuries
The Afton has flowed.
                    If the Rio Negro
Could abandon its song, and the Magdalena
The jungle flowers, the Tagus
Would still flow serenely, and the Ohio
Abrade its slate banks. The tan Euphrates would
Sidle silently across the world. The Yukon
Was choked with ice, but the Susquehanna still pushed
Bravely along. The Dee caught the day's last flares
Like the Pilcomayo's carrion rose.
The Peace offered eternal fragrance
Perhaps, but the Mackenzie churned livid mud
Like tan chalk-marks. Near where
The Brahmaputra slapped swollen dikes
And the Pechora? The São Francisco
Skulks amid gray, rubbery nettles. The Liard's
Reflexes are slow, and the Arkansas erodes
Anthracite hummocks. The Paraná stinks.
The Ottawa is light emerald green
Among grays. Better that the Indus fade
In steaming sands! Let the Brazos
Freeze solid! And the Wabash turn to a leaden
Cinder of ice! The Marañón is too tepid, we must
Find a way to freeze it hard. The Ural
Is freezing slowly in the blasts. The black Yonne
Congeals nicely. And the Petit-Morin
Curls up on the solid earth. The Inn
Does not remember better times, and the Merrimack's
Galvanized. The Ganges is liquid snow by now;
The Vyatka's ice-gray. The once-molten Tennessee's
Curdled. The Japurá is a pack of ice. Gelid
The Columbia's gray loam banks. The Don's merely
A giant icicle. The Niger freezes, slowly.
The interminable Lena plods on
But the Purus' mercurial waters are icy, grim
With cold. The Loing is choked with fragments of ice.
The Weser is frozen, like liquid air.
And so is the Kama. And the beige, thickly flowing

Tocantins. The rivers bask in the cold.
The stern Uruguay chafes its banks,
A mass of ice. The Hooghly is solid
Ice. The Adour is silent, motionless.
The lovely Tigris is nothing but scratchy ice
Like the Yellowstone, with its osier-clustered banks.
The Mekong is beginning to thaw out a little
And the Donets gurgles beneath the
Huge blocks of ice. The Manzanares gushes free.
The Illinois darts through the sunny air again.
But the Dnieper is still ice-bound. Somewhere
The Salado propels its floes, but the Roosevelt's
Frozen. The Oka is frozen solider
Than the Somme. The Minho slumbers
In winter, nor does the Snake
Remember August. Hilarious, the Canadian
Is solid ice. The Madeira slavers
Across the thawing fields, and the Plata laughs.
The Dvina soaks up the snow. The Sava's
Temperature is above freezing. The Avon
Carols noiselessly. The Drôme presses
Grass banks; the Adige's frozen
Surface is like gray pebbles.

Birds circle the Ticino. In winter
The Var was dark blue, unfrozen. The
Thwaite, cold, is choked with sandy ice;
The Ardèche glistens feebly through the freezing rain.

COMMENTARY

Most reckless things are beautiful in some way, and recklessness is what makes experimental art beautiful, just as religions are beautiful because of the strong possibilities that they are founded on nothing. (J.A.) And again: *I am often asked why I write, and I don't know really—I just want to.* Or further: *I always thought that writing poetry was in itself a political act.*

There is a coolness in the work that may disguise its underlying intensities, not so much a modernist interest in content that fascinates Ashbery but a postmodern concern for process, or (as Marjorie Perloff has it) "[not] what one dreams but how—this is the domain of Ashbery, whose stories 'tell only themselves,' presenting the reader with the challenge of 'an open field of narrative possibilities.'" Despite later attempts by conservative critics to claim Ashbery as a mainstream late Romantic lyric poet, his deeper importance in the United States & throughout the Americas has been in the ongoing experimentation of the work, its distrust of (even high-modernist) rhetorical voices (Daffy Duck rather than Tiresias or Malatesta, as Charles Altieri points out), & its insistence on being not Stein's "everybody's" but "anybody's" [auto]biography. ("'You' can be myself or it can be another person... we are somehow all aspects of consciousness giving rise to the poem"—J.A.) What interests him is "... the experience of experience.... The particular occasion is of lesser interest to me than the way a happening or experience filters through to me. I believe this is the way in which it happens with most people. I'm trying to set down a generalized transcript of what's really going on in our minds all day long."

Or elsewhere: "The poem is sad because it wants to be yours, and cannot be."

Martin Carter Guyana, 1927–1997

DEMERARA NIGGER

In right accordance, and demandingly
because what withstands stands,
Farinata, the Ghibelline,
"entertained great scorn of hell
and asked about ancestors." So
be it. "Demerara nigger. Downward
through the horse." Hells are comparable
but mind stays in advance of dispensation. This foot for instance. This shoe.
Step. Floor. Book for instance. Lamp.
From one to the other; and words
tortured out like a turd. Until the sudden
fumble of the premonitory wing
of the bat in the roof. I held
mortality a thing to be endured;
human fact deliverable. What
when fear is hope; if no messenger rode;
way and cause as right if not
an ending? Therefore found it just
often to barter talk for sight
and turn a bat and confuse clocks. At
any cost I had to go; went scorning

and demanding. Mortality put to question.
Cosmic justice reckoned in confirming
a horse of hell as likely as the riding
companion mind; mind in advance of mind
the mind requiting and mind singular,
enabled mind, mind minded to suppose
nigger and Ghibelline.

COMMENTARY

After twenty days and twenty nights in prison / You wake and you search for birds and sunlight / You wait for rain and thunder (M.C.)

Jailed twice, the first time for "spreading dissension" & the second following the publication—in London—of his *Poems of Resistance from British Guiana*, Martin Carter belongs to that important group of poets & chroniclers of the Caribbean Emancipation, alongside luminaries like Césaire, Walcott, & Kamau Brathwaite. Like many of them, his moves involved political activism & revolutionary acts.

Dante, as here, is one of the touchstones in Carter's poetry, due—among other things—to their similar political circumstances. In the poem, above, Carter rephrases Dante's meeting with Farinata (the leader of the Florentine Ghibelline faction) in *Inferno* X. The persona in Carter's poem is a captive Black from Demerara, the name for Guyana during the Dutch Colonial period (1745–1815). The Demerarians revolted against the Dutch in 1795 & then against the British in 1823. Many of them were killed or imprisoned.

For Kamau Brathwaite, Carter's works are *a poetry of the negative yes*: "that eloquent militant opposition has been supported by an equally eloquent sense of hope."

Armand Schwerner   USA, 1927–1999

from **THE TABLETS (1966)**

Tablet III

the further emptying

the calyx, the calyx, someone has ripped it
it will not make loam, it will crumble
the pig (god?) has pulled life off ++++++++

the pig (god?) is stronger than a thoughtless child

my chest empties...my chest

I can no longer stand in the middle of the field and +++++++

I am missing, my chest has no food for the maggots

there is no place for the pollen, there is only a hole in the flower

the hummingbird................pus...................................nectar

the field is a hole without pattern (shoes?)

there are no eyes in back of the wisent's sockets

the urus eats her own teats and her.......................

the urus lies in milk and blood

the urus is a hole in the middle of the field

[testicles]..for the ground

"with grey horses" drinks urine

"having fine green oxen" looks for salt

let us hold.....................................the long man upside down

let us look into his mouth............................selfish saliva

let us pluck +++++++++++++++++++ for brother tree

let us kiss the long man, let us carry the long man

let us kiss the long man, let us fondle the long man

let us carry the long man as the ground sucks his drippings

let us feel the drippings from his open groin

let us kiss the hot wound, the wet wound...nectar

let us wait until he is white and dry......................................my chest

let us look into his dry evil mouth, let us fondle the long man

let us bypass the wisent on the river road pintrpnit

let us avoid the urus on the river-road pintrpnit

let us smell the auroch on the river-road pintrpnit

let us carry the beautiful (strange?) children to the knom

let us sing with the children by the knom

let us set the children's beautiful (strange?) skulls by the hearth

when the rain comes.

let us have rain

let us have rain

+++++++++

+++++++++++++

++++...tremble

and also to make the strangers piss in their pants for fear

and to make all the neighbors know of the terrible......that is ours

let them hear about it, let them know

let them tremble like a spear going through the heart and through the back

let them become a knowing spear, let them bore in, fish-death

let them shake from the spear's blow, let them hear it sing
I need to feel my solid arm, I need to feel my mighty penis
o my son at the other edge of fish-death
o my son by the dark river-road I can't reach your fingertips
o my son in the rain your liver will make the barley shoot up
o my son in the rain your eyes will see the way in the wheat
o my son on the happy edge of the emptying, fish-death, pintrpnit
o dark dark dark dark dark dark dark dark dark
o dark
you will-would-might-have-can, let us have rain

COMMENTARY

*go into all the places you're frightened of / and forget why you came, like
the dead* (A.S.) And again, in the voice of a pseudo-Sumerian: *a lot of dirt,
a terrible headache / and more than enough worry about my grave. Hogs /
will swill and shit on me, men / will abuse me*

(1) A poet of multiple means & a major figure in ethnopoetics, Armand
Schwerner was, as Paul Christensen described him, "palimpsestic," his voice
"one whose depths shimmer with other voices, his mouth issuing language,
it conduits in from the past or the 'outside' and uses as its own speech.…
The voices overlay one another like the strata of various civilizations." For
this—in his long ongoing work *The Tablets* (begun ca. 1968)—he created
an open-ended book or series of fictive translations, modeled on the fractured "accidental" form in which old Sumerian & Babylonian cuneiform
writings have come down to us & accompanied by a "scholar-translator's"
commentaries that are at once—as Schwerner tells it—"more than ironic
and other than nostalgic."

(2) Schwerner's simplified key to a reading of the poem's typographical
symbols follows:

…………………… *untranslatable*; +++++++++ *missing*; (?) *variant reading*; [ ]
supplied by the scholar-translator. With these italicized words spoken aloud
& Schwerner himself in the role of scholar-translator, the work was further
enhanced in performance.

(3) Schwerner again: "The commentator takes on a more active part. His
'notes' become 'poems.' What does that mean? What are the differences in
the first place? 'Poem' is what?"

Larry Eigner USA, 1927–1996

from **THE**

#31
  the frequency
    of hills
    in view but time

  creeps on

   water air
    borne
      over
        here   a direction
    the land drowned or
    revealed   or
        ex-
        posed

    the foghorn
     night
    firefly
     or cricket
    rides

  *   *   *   *   *

   bird skate
   air,   plow
      tree

  *   *   *   *   *

I feel my life again the strangeness
    it should be the same

sky grass tree level the eye

  with silence the picture
       bright
    the gift. of thought

  it's the old day   speed
    is an idea
  the sun light so unmoving

                    the bodiless roof
            of a birdhouse

        no, it's a
            hose bracket, that's

    right
                being so small

COMMENTARY

*Feeling your way along, you can, it seems, discover the right value, so to
speak, momentary as it may be—nothing lasts forever, the ephemeral is
ok. It's never quite enough, though (anyway there's always an amount of
concern abt the future, your own and x million others'), and like anything
else the present isn't to be exaggerated.* (L.E.)

From birth Eigner was bounded by a palsy that denied him ease of speech
& movement, but the powers of mind/thought (listening to many sources,
voices; looking out with clarity at what was immediately before him)
grew still sharper & thereby brought him a new music & a concentrated
sense of "daily act" (R. Duncan), "daily actualization [of writing things]"
(R. Grenier).

The fuller context for Eigner was Charles Olson's call, ca. 1950, for a
renewed "projective verse" as a poetry of mind & body "that... put into
itself certain laws and possibilities of the breath, of the breathing of the
man who writes as well as of his listenings." Working in the semi-isolation
that his condition often imposed on him, Eigner came early to accept &
exploit in himself a certain quality of body & voice that led him to what
his biographer Jennifer Bartlett describes as a "*crip* version of projective
verse"—not to be ground down by what he was but to use it to his & our
advantage.

Hugo Gola   Argentina, 1927–2015

TWO POEMS

NOR AT THE END

    or the beginning
        nor before
        or after
    when you weren't

        already here
    or when you
        no longer are

lost
    paradise
    before
        time
    or gained
    when
        time
            no longer
            exists

here
    in this fruit
        the paradise
        in this
    high & empty
            sky
    in this noon
        of vague
            footsteps
    bare
        ash trees
        &c elms

here
here
"let the wind
        speak"
said Pound
"that is paradise"

    that wind
        passing
            you by
        that bird
            flying
                up above
the leaf
        that spins
            & falls

on leveled
    soil
   that fragrant
        wine
   offered
        now
   this transient
       time
    crumbling

  paradise paradise
           paradise

•

                    gatherings
           goods
oddments
or shelves
    only bare walls
a pair of jeans
a t-shirt
a leather jacket
bread for the day
a small cut of beef
a few vegetables
a fruit
    what else?
stripped afternoons
to scale the lonely sky

just now the gymnastics
begin

Translated from Spanish by Javier Taboada

COMMENTARY

precisely / what no one can / nor today / not ever / precisely that / that's it /
precisely / precisely (H.G)

(1) Writes poet Ricardo Cázares: "Exiled from Argentina in 1975, Hugo
Gola resided in Mexico from 1979 to 2011, when he returned to his native

country. His defiant attitude against the academic world, his critical militancy against the constraints of worn-out traditions, & his permanent search for the renewal of language & poetic forms led him to edit two of the most important magazines in Latin America: *Poesía y Poética* and *El poeta y su trabajo*. This labor of inquiry into the poet's work coupled with his generosity marked a turning point in the development of generations of Mexican poets who—after glimpsing new possibilities—detached themselves from outdated forms & have begun to develop a more open & bold poetry.

"Gola's poetry is the result of an attentive ear and a powerfully concise and condensed diction, almost stripped of rhetoric. His are verbal objects of a sinuous mental & verbal rhythm, of clean & sharp images, of a diction that seems to have decanted slowly until it was inevitable."

(2) And Hugo Gola himself: "We are concerned with a formal renewal... with the use of a language that raises the question of the languages in America. To use the spoken language as much as possible; to differentiate what is intoned in the languages used in the American countries. In some way, we also reflected on the historical avant-gardes; about how much is still alive in them." And then: "We need to rethink tradition and not accept it as the norm, but see it as the past and criticize it, discard what is no longer useful and take out what is still alive. As Ezra Pound did when he wrote his *Paideuma*" (interview by Alfredo Núñez Lanz in *Una Dimensión Interior: Conversación con Hugo Gola*).

Édouard Glissant   Martinique, 1928–2011

from FOR MYCEA

O earth, if it is earth, O earth all-in-daylight where we came. O dive into flashing water and labored speech. See that your words have hauled me out of that long dream where so much blue and so much ochre were mixed. And see that I come down from that night, hear

•

I write in you the music of every branch, grave or blue
With our words we shed light on the water that trembles
We are cold with the same beauty
Strand by strand the country has unlaced what yesterday
You took up on your overflowing stream
Your hand stirs these murmurs together like something new
You marvel that you burn more than ancient incense

•

When the noise of the woods runs dry in our bodies
Surprised, we read this wing of red earth
Anchored in shadow and silence
We make sure to gather the agave flower
The burn of the water where we place our hands
You, more distant than the light-mad acoma
In the woods where it acclaims any sun, and I
Who restlessly hound that wind
Where I drove the intractable past

•

I do not write to take you by surprise but to give measure to this flood
of impatience that the wind names your beauty. Far away, clay sky, and
ancient silt, real

And the water of my words flows, until the rock stops it, when I come
down the stream among the moons that strut along the bank. There
where your smile is the color of the sands, your hand more naked than a
vow pronounced in silence

•

And it is only ash settled in the underbrush
It is only straying where the sky gives birth
The agave water does not appease the timid flower
The stars sing of a single gold that is unheard
At the crossroads where the sap was beaten out
Of so many who cry out inspired by the wind
I hail unexpected wandering
You go out from speech, slip away
You are the country of the past given in recompense
Invisible we travel the road
The earth alone understands

Translated from French by Brent Hayes Edwards

We are aware of the fact that the changes of our present history are the unseen moments of a massive transformation in civilization, which is the passage from the all-encompassing world of cultural Sameness, effectively imposed by the West, to a pattern of fragmented Diversity, achieved in a no less creative way by the peoples who have today seized their rightful place in the world. (E.G.)

Édouard Glissant's literary works were defined by the notion of a lost past—an African one—& by the clash of cultures & languages that shaped Martinican, but also Antillean, culture. This led him to first propose Antillanité (later called *creolité*) as a movement that rejected the preeminence of African descent (& also the fixed idea of Blackness) in the conformation of the Antilles; he sought to equalize it with European, Indigenous, or even Asiatic influences. Toward his final years, Glissant embraced a still wider idea he called "tout-monde," in which he envisioned our world as a network of communities & cultures that constantly interchange & endlessly develop new forms in the process. As noted by translator Betsy Wing, "Carrying the work of other theorists of Caribbean self-formation, such as Fanon and Césaire, into new dimensions, Glissant sees imagination as the force that can change mentalities; relation as the process of this change; and poetics as a transformative mode of history" (in the introduction to Glissant's *Poetics of Relation*).

Nathaniel Tarn France/USA, 1928–

THE HÖLDERLINIAE 1

It is a question of a murder: a man is murdered wishing
to live a life *He's* not allowed to lead over two hundred
years ago. *He* wished to be a poet. His folks wanted a
clergyman. *He* fought long, hard and, at the end, *He* lost
his mind. A question then of being murdered, of being
slowly murdered. By life which turns to death as birds
drop sky to ground, at feint of gnat biting your cheek.

While sky falls into trees, trees fall to ground, ground
falls to lake and lake into the deepest ocean, for which
the gods—those mirrors of our fates decked out in blue
evaporating coral—will never raise themselves to gather
back the sky. *And/Und & But/Aber*: impossible to see,

to witness gods in high sky shining down on where
one lives because that domicile is being murdered also.

In sleepless nights before dead fires, assassinated fires:
no coming up for air, no pass from worm to fish, from
fish to ape, from ape to—what! this *thing* is human?
this thing debased, massacred, gassed and paralyzed,
ghost-like legions of murdered men: when wars decide
never to end, never to terminate, when wars begin again
at cap drop, enter our lungs: we can no longer breathe.

It is a question of being murdered day by day, night after
night with not a single breathing space between a sleep
and sleep, become the one escape, the only right royal
residence left in the universe—and sleep turns into death
without a warning. Which hey! is being murdered, ended
just like *He* was by loss of sanity, by loss of mind, by
golden girl dying of death: what else—the bitter husband?

Among great Hymns, Odes, Elegies, and Fragments: *He*
spoke it first, wrote of it first, "*Mich reizt der Lorbeer. Ruhe
beglückt mich nicht*" / "It is the laurel that I want, not peace
and quiet." Singer of rivers reversing time: if there's a single
drop of life left in this man, this man is being slowly murdered:
it is become of him, because he lived and died among the dying
peoples, the deaf, the paralyzed, the gods.

Death has a thousand cards to play. Life only one.

COMMENTARY

*Despite any kind of appearances, every single poem in this geography is a
jointly created fiction and any resemblance between the voices you hear
and real flesh & blood authors is purely confidential.* (N.T.)

A poet of great complexities & a kind of experimental lyricism, Nathaniel
Tarn's late work, *The Hölderliniae*, summons & processes the words &
spirit of the great German Romantic poet Friedrich Hölderlin along with
his own, or, as the critic Rebecca Ruth Gold has it: "Through Tarn's hybrid
epic, which incorporates Tarn's own translations of Hölderlin's poems, the
poet invites readers to find ecstasy in the loneliness of the human condition and to reexamine our thinking about language, mortality, space, and
time." And Dennis King, of a further innovative & masterly move on Tarn's
part: "The book's main conceit is a series of italicized pronouns—*I, He,
She*—that *seem* to refer to, respectively, 1) a persona who may or may not

be the historical Tarn, 2) Hölderlin, and 3) Hölderlin's mother. Add to this a fourth perspective: 4) the person writing the book, another persona who may or may not be the historical Tarn. With these floating signifiers, the book's voice becomes a drift, never quite becoming any character at all, except, of course, the character of a book you are holding in your hands."

Adrienne Rich USA, 1929–2012

DIVING INTO THE WRECK

First having read the book of myths,
and loaded the camera,
and checked the edge of the knife-blade,
I put on
the body-armor of black rubber
the absurd flippers
the grave and awkward mask.
I am having to do this
not like Cousteau with his
assiduous team
aboard the sun-flooded schooner
but here alone.

There is a ladder.
The ladder is always there
hanging innocently
close to the side of the schooner.
We know what it is for,
we who have used it.
Otherwise
it is a piece of maritime floss
some sundry equipment.

I go down.
Rung after rung and still
the oxygen immerses me
the blue light
the clear atoms
of our human air.
I go down.
My flippers cripple me,

I crawl like an insect down the ladder
and there is no one
to tell me when the ocean
will begin.

First the air is blue and then
it is bluer and then green and then
black I am blacking out and yet
my mask is powerful
it pumps my blood with power
the sea is another story
the sea is not a question of power
I have to learn alone
to turn my body without force
in the deep element.

And now: it is easy to forget
what I came for
among so many who have always
lived here
swaying their crenellated fans
between the reefs
and besides
you breathe differently down here.

I came to explore the wreck.
The words are purposes.
The words are maps.
I came to see the damage that was done
and the treasures that prevail.
I stroke the beam of my lamp
slowly along the flank
of something more permanent
than fish or weed

the thing I came for:
the wreck and not the story of the wreck
the thing itself and not the myth
the drowned face always staring
toward the sun
the evidence of damage
worn by salt and sway into this threadbare beauty
the ribs of the disaster

curving their assertion
among the tentative haunters.

This is the place.
And I am here, the mermaid whose dark hair
streams black, the merman in his armored body.
We circle silently
about the wreck
we dive into the hold.
I am she: I am he

whose drowned face sleeps with open eyes
whose breasts still bear the stress
whose silver, copper, vermeil cargo lies
obscurely inside barrels
half-wedged and left to rot
we are the half-destroyed instruments
that once held to a course
the water-eaten log
the fouled compass.

We are, I am, you are
by cowardice or courage
the ones who find our way
back to this scene
carrying a knife, a camera
a book of myths
in which
our names do not appear.

COMMENTARY

If I thought of my words as changing minds, hadn't my mind also to suffer changes? (A.R.) And again: *Every act of becoming conscious / (it says here in this book) / is an unnatural act.*

As with others of her generation, Adrienne Rich's move from a middle-ground verse of closed form (& mind) to her open poetry of the late 1960s & beyond is an exemplary narrative of a feminist poetics allied to wider radical urban politics (civil rights & antiwar demonstrations), leading her to a distinctly "female aesthetics of power" (Claire Keyes) & into a lesbian separatism. While her 1971 book *The Will to Change* might seem to borrow not only its title but also its stance toward verse (if not toward reality) from Charles Olson's lines "What does not change / is the will to change," the truer story, in her own terms, is that of a struggle with the "mental fragmentation [that affects]... every group that lives under the naming and image-making power of a dominant culture... and needs an art which can resist it." The *resistance*, then, isn't Olson's so much as her own: the sudden onset (she writes) "[of] something I had been hungering to do, all my writing life[:]... to write directly and overtly as a woman, out of a woman's body and experience, to take women's existence seriously as theme and source for art.... It placed me nakedly face to face with both terror and anger; it did indeed *imply the breakdown of the world as I had always known it, the end of safety*, to paraphrase [James] Baldwin.... But it released tremendous energy in me, as in many other women, to have that way of writing affirmed and validated in a growing political community. I felt for the first time the closing of the gap between poet and woman" ("Blood, Bread & Poetry," 1984). The art that emerges from this, whether wholly free of patriarchal text or not, takes the measure of her world—& of her place within it—with a new force, a renewed authority.

Haroldo de Campos Brazil, 1929 2003

from THE DISCIPLINES

The Poem: Theory and Practice

I

Silver birds, the Poem
draws theory from its own flight.
Philomel of metamorphosed blue,
measured geometrician
the Poem thinks itself
as a circle thinks its center
as the radii think the circle
crystalline fulcrum of the movement.

II

A bird imitates itself at each flight
zenith of ivory where a ruffled
anxiety is arbiter
over the vectorial lines of the movement.
A bird becomes itself in its flight
mirror of the self, mature
orbit
timing over Time.

Equanimous, the Poem ignores itself.
Leopard pondering itself in a leap,
what becomes of the prey, plume of sound,
evasive
gazelle of the senses?
The Poem proposes itself: system
of rancorous premises
evolution of figures against the wind
star chess. Salamander of arsons
that provokes, unhurt endures,
Sun set in its center.

IV

And how is it done? What theory
rules the spaces of its flight?
What last retains it? What load
curves the tension of its breath?
Sitar of the tongue, how does one hear?
Cut out of gold, as such we see it,
proportioned to it—the Thought.

V

See: broke in half
the airy fuse of the movement
the ballerina rests. Acrobat,
being of easy flight,
princess of a kingdom
of eolian veils: Air.
Wherefrom the impulse that propels her,
proud, to the fleeting commitment?
Unlike the bird
according to nature
but as a god
contra naturam flies.

VI

Such is the poem. In the fields of eolian
equilibrium that it aspires
sustained by its dexterity.
Winged agile athlete
aims at the trapeze of the venture.

Birds do not imagine themselves.
The Poem pre-meditates.
They run the cusp of infinite
astronomy of which they are plumed Orions.
It, arbiter and vindicator of itself,
Lusbel leaps over the abyss,
liberated,
in front of a greater king
a king lesser great.

Translated from Portuguese by Antonio Sergio Bessa

from **GALAXIAS**

and here I begin I spin here the beguine I respin and begin
to release and realize life begins not arrives at the end of a trip
which is why I begin to respin to write-in thousand pages write
   thousandone pages
to end write begin write beginend with writing and so I begin to respin
to retrace to rewrite write on writing the future of writing's the tracing
the slaving a thousandone nights in a thousandone pages
or a page in one night the same nights the same pages
same resemblance resemblance reassemblance where the end is begin
where to write about writing's not writing about not writing
and so I begin to unspin the unknown unbegun and trace me a book
where all's chance and perchance all a book maybe maybe not a travel
navelof-the-world book a travel navelof-the-book world where
   tripping's the book
and its being's the trip and so I begin since the trip is beguine and I turn
and return since the turning's respinning beginning realizing
a book is its sense every page is its sense every line of a page every word
of a line is the sense of the line of the page of the books which essays
any book an essay of essays of the book which is why the begin ends
begins and end spins and re-ends and refines and retunes the fine funnel of
the begunend spun into de runend in the end of the beginend refines
the refined of the final where it finishes beginnish reruns and returns
and the finger retraces a thousandone stories an incey wincey-story and
   so count
of no account I don't recount the nonstory uncounts me discounts me
   the reverse

of the story is snot can be rot maybe story depends on the moment
the glory depends on the now and the never on although and no-go
and nowhere and noplace and nihil and nixit and zero and zilch-it
and never can nothing be all can be all can be total sum
total surprising summation of sumptuous assumption
and here I respin I begin to project my echo the wreck oh recurrent
echo of the echoing blow the hollows of moreaus the marrow that's
   beyonder
the over the thisaway thataway everywhere neverwhere overhere
   overthere
forward more backward less there in reverse vice verse prosa converse
I begin I respin verse begin vice respin so that summated story won't
   consume consummate saltimbocca bestride me barebackboneberide me
begin the beguine of the trip where the travel's the marvel the scrabble's
   the
marble the vigil's the travel the trifle the sparkle the embers of fable
   discount
into nothing account for the story since spinning beginning I'm speaking

Translated by Suzanne Jill Levine from a basic version by Jon Tolman

a poem begins / where it ends: / the margin of doubt / a sudden incision of geraniums / commands its destiny (H.de C.)

Haroldo de Campos was a master of Concrete poetry & with his brother Augusto & fellow Brazilian poet Décio Pignatari the founder of the highly influential Noigandres movement (see "A Map of Extensions). But with *Galáxias* & other late works, the poetry took on a largeness & uncompromising movement through historical & mythical space & time. Of that journey, he wrote in his headnote: "An audiovideotext, videotextogram, the *galáxias* situate themselves on the border between prose and poetry. In this kaleidoscopic book there's an epic, narrative gesture—mini-stories that articulate and dissolve themselves like the 'suspense' of a detective novel... but the image remains, the vision or calling of the epiphanic. In that sense, it is the poetic pole that ends up prevailing in the project, and the result is 50 'galactic cantos,' with a total of more than 2000 verses (close to 40 per page). This permutational book has, as its semantic backbone, a recurrent yet always varied theme all along: travel as a book and the book as travel (despite the fact that—for that very reason—it is not exactly a 'travel book'...)."

   And, as may be true for all poetry worth the effort, de Campos adds further: "The oralization of the *Galáxias* was always implicit in my project.... As it will be seen (as it will be heard), this is a book to be read aloud, proposing a rhythm and a prosody, whose 'obscure' passages become transparent to reading and whose words, when pronounced, can acquire a talismanic force, incite and seduce like mantras."

His work with translation, which he expanded & redubbed "transcreation," & with the unearthing of lost Brazilian masterworks should also be mentioned.

Juan Gelman   Argentina, 1930–2014

from **OPEN LETTER**

XIII

have you come and I don't see you? / where
are you hidden? / will nothing ever distract me
from you at last? / I groan in the night /
I hold the groan inside myself it is

my refusal to be comforted / wounded absence /
withering / missing you / how many diapers ago /
did you visit me / I come outside of all things
to see you / hating

my own pretending / the having been / the do-you-remember /
the touch that pulls me inside out / my son /
can you fly through these staves / can it be that
giving myself up from myself / I may hold you

through the city outskirts / the plazas where I look for you? /
not finding you do I go on thinking? /
do I win the loss of you to lose myself? /
by unsouling myself can I at last soul your little soul?

. . . . .

XVII

I want no other news except of you / any other
would be feeding crumbs to the memory
that is dying of hunger / that digs and digs
to keep on looking for you / goes

crazy with darkness / sets its own fury on fire /
burns to pieces / looks at your absent gaze /

mirror where I can't see myself /
you silver this shadow / a rustling of you /

cold sweat when I think I hear /
you / frozen with love I lie with my half
of you / always unable to come /
clearly I understand that I don't understand

the 24th of August, 1976
my son marcelo ariel and
his wife, claudia, pregnant,
were kidnapped in
buenos aires by a
military commando.
as in tens of thousands
of other cases, the military
dictatorship never officially
recognized their "disappearance."
it spoke of "those forever absent."
until I have seen their bodies
or their murderers, I will never
give them up for dead.

Translated from Spanish by Joan Lindgren

COMMENTARY

I've never been the owner of my ashes, my poems, / obscure faces write my
verses like bullets firing at death. (J.G.) And again: *The word that would*
name you rests in the shadows. When it / names you, you will become a
shadow. You'll crackle in the / mouth that lost you to have you.

Gelman's works—while presented in different modes, from his "fake translations" to his use of idiolects & idioms such as Ladino—focused on the
power of poetry to create or to destroy. One of the main features in his
work is the presence of apparently balanced stanzas that, in fact, are internally interrupted by the use of the slash mark; these inner dislocations,
combining their newly acquired breaks, meters, & punctuations, gradually affect the words & their meanings. This sense of change (or progressive breakages) resembles Gelman's life & struggle during the military
coups & dictatorships in Argentina of the last century. "They took away
my books"—Gelman wrote—"my bread, my son, they made my mother
despair, they threw me out of the country, killed my brothers, tortured my
comrades."

To all of this, the poem above clearly testifies.

Hilda Hilst Brazil, 1930-2004

from **OF DEATH. MINIMAL ODES**

IX

Your hooves bandaged
so I won't hear
your hard trot.
Is this, little mare,
how you'll come for me?
Or because I thought you
severe and silent
you'll come as a child
on a shard of china?
Lover
because I disdained you?
Or with the airs of a king
because I made you queen?

.....

XV

As if you fit
on the crest
on the peak
on the obverse of the bone

I try to capture your body
your mountain, your reverse.

As if the lips looked for
their converse
that's how I look for you
torsion of all depths.

Persecutory, I follow you
tether, muscle.
And you always resemble
everything that runs, time,
the current.

In my mouth. In the emptiness.
In the crooked nose.

Down river you run, silt
stump, towards me.

XVI

Horse, buffalo, little mare
I love you, friend, my death,
if you approach, I jump
as one who wants and doesn't want
to see the hill, the meadow, the mound
on the other side, as one who wants
and doesn't dare
touch your fur—gold

the bright red of your skin
as one who doesn't want.

Translated from Portuguese by Laura Cesarco Eglin

COMMENTARY

But the poet inhabits / The field of inns of insanity. (H.H.) And again: *How should I kill in me the various forms of madness and be at the same time tender and lucid, creative and patient, and survive?*

Composing her work from a place of relative isolation, Hilda Hilst became "one of the most important & controversial writers in the Portuguese language." Writes her translator Laura Cesarco Eglin further: "In her thirties, Hilst decided to leave the city of São Paulo in order to keep away from social life and concentrate on literature. She went to Campinas and lived in her house *Casa do Sol* until her death. Because of her strong personality, beauty, intelligence, and her eccentricities, and because she consistently questioned and went against norms and traditions, the myth surrounding Hilst's image has often overshadowed the importance of her work and the critical analysis of her oeuvre."

And Hilst in her own words: "The shortness of life, the dullness of the senses, the numbness of indifference and unprofitable occupations allow us to know but very little. And again and again swift oblivion, the embezzler of knowledge and the enemy of memory, shakes out of the mind, in the course of time, even what we knew."

Gary Snyder USA, 1930–

MILTON BY FIRELIGHT

Piute Creek, August 1955

"O hell, what do mine eyes
    with grief behold?"
Working with an old
Singlejack miner, who can sense
The vein and cleavage
In the very guts of rock, can
Blast granite, build
Switchbacks that last for years
Under the beat of snow, thaw, mule-hooves.
What use, Milton, a silly story
Of our lost general parents,
    eaters of fruit?

The Indian, the chainsaw boy,
And a string of six mules
Came riding down to camp
Hungry for tomatoes and green apples.
Sleeping in saddle-blankets
Under a bright night-sky
Han River slantwise by morning.
Jays squall
Coffee boils

In ten thousand years the Sierras
Will be dry and dead, home of the scorpion.
Ice-scratched slabs and bent trees.
No paradise, no fall,
Only the weathering land
The wheeling sky,
Man, with his Satan
Scouring the chaos of the mind.
Oh Hell!

Fire down
Too dark to read, miles from a road
The bell-mare clangs in the meadow
That packed dirt for a fill-in
Scrambling through loose rocks

On an old trail
All of a summer's day.

THE CALL OF THE WILD

The heavy old man in his bed at night
Hears the Coyote singing
               in the back meadow.
All the years he ranched and mined and logged.
A Catholic.
A native Californian.
    and the Coyotes howl in his
Eightieth year.
He will call the government
Trapper
Who uses iron leg-straps on Coyotes,
Tomorrow.
My son will lose this
Music they have just started
To love.

The ex acid-heads from the cities
Converted to Guru or Swami,
Do penance with shiny
Dopey eyes, and quit eating meat.
In the forests of North America,
The land of Coyote and Eagle,
They dream of India, of
    forever blissful sexless highs.
And sleep in oil-heated
Geodesic domes, that
Were stuck like warts
In the woods.
And the Coyote singing
    is shut away
    for they fear
    the call
    of the wild.

And they sold their virgin cedar trees,
    the tallest trees in miles,

To a logger,
Who told them,

"Trees are full of bugs."

The Government finally decided
To wage the war   all-out. Defeat
        is Un-American.
And they took to the air,
Their women beside them
        in bouffant hairdos
        putting nail-polish on the
        gunship cannon-buttons.
And they never came down
        for they found,
        the ground
is Pro-Communist. And dirty.
And the insects side with the Viet Cong.

So they bomb and they bomb
Day after day, across the planet
        blinding sparrows
        breaking the ear-drums of owls
        splintering trunks of cherries
        twining and looping
        deer intestines
        in the shaken, dusty, rocks.
All these Americans up in special cities in the sky
Dumping poisons and explosives
Across Asia first,
And next North America,

A war against earth.
When it's done there'll be
        no place

A Coyote could hide.

ENVOY

                I would like to say
                Coyote is forever
                Inside you.

                But it's not true.

As a poet I hold the most archaic values on earth. They go back to the upper Paleolithic: the fertility of the soil, the magic of animals, the power-vision in solitude, the terrifying initiation and rebirth, the love and ecstasy of the dance, the common work of the tribe. I try to hold both history and wilderness in mind, that my poems may approach the true measure of things and stand against the unbalance and ignorance of our times. (G.S.)

What Snyder brought us was the naturalizing of one line of American modernism—that associated, largely, with the work of Ezra Pound—& its opening to what would be defining concerns for the first *post*modernist generation. It was his genius, too, to engage in what Pound had called an "active" poetics, not at its fascist extreme—Pound's folly—but drawing on his own Wobbly & western American upbringing to be the visible spokesman for a new/old wilderness, an ecopoetics in which poetry might function again (as at its beginnings) as "an ecological survival tool."

Associated with the San Francisco Renaissance and the Beat Generation movement (he is the model for Japhy Ryder in Jack Kerouac's novel *The Dharma Bums*), Snyder has kept apart from other (literary) isms, though it is possible to relate his articulation of his own project—"the real work of modern man: to uncover the inner structure and actual boundaries of the mind"—to something as apparently distant, say, as André Breton's Surrealist revolution of the mind ("the critical investigation of the notions of reality and unreality, of reason and unreason, of reflection and impulse, of knowing and fatally not knowing, of utility and uselessness"). For Snyder, this includes a strong sense of (& need for) cultural continuity & transmission—a transmission he has elsewhere traced back as far as the Paleolithic. Or, as one of his later poems has it: "Pound was an axe, / Chen [Snyder's Chinese teacher] was an axe / And my son a handle, soon / To be shaping again, model / And tool, craft of culture, / How we go on."

That he is the primary forerunner of a twenty-first-century ecopoetics is also worth noting.

Mário Faustino   Brazil, 1930–1962

LIFE ALL LANGUAGE

Life all language
always perfect phrase, maybe verse,
generally without any adjective
column without ornament, generally divided.
Life all language,

meanwhile a verb, always a verb, and a name
here, there, assuring the eternal
perfection of the period, maybe verse,
maybe interjectional, verse, verse.
Life all language,
fetus sucking in compassionate language
the blood that child will scatter—oh active metaphor!
milk spurt in adolescent fountain,
semen of mature men, verb, verb.
Life all language
how well it knows the old who repeat,
against black windows, scintillating images
which star them turbulent trajectories.
Life all language—
as we all know
to conjugate these verbs, to name
these names:
to love, to make, to destroy
man, woman, and beast, devil and angel
and god maybe, and nothing.
Life all language,
life always perfect,
imperfect only the dead words
with which a young man, in the terraces of winter, against the rain,
tries to make it eternal, as if he lacked
some other, immortal syntax
to life which is perfect
eternal
language.

Translated from Portuguese by Jennifer Cooper

COMMENTARY

*What shall I do with this day that adores me? / Pull it by the tail, before
the / Crimson hour when it sneaks from my feast?* (M.F.)

Both revered & rejected in his very brief lifetime (he died in a plane crash
at thirty-two), Mário Faustino's moves toward poetical renovation aimed
to embrace & to dialogue with a wider scope of secular Western poems &
poetics, north & south, European & American: from Homer to T.S. Eliot
or Ezra Pound. Through his Sunday page—*Poetry Experience*—published
in the newspaper *Jornal do Brasil*, Faustino discussed & presented poetry

acts that resembled, for him, a step beyond traditional conceptions while, at the same time, opening up a space for new voices to be heard. As Régis Bonvicino notes: "Faustino's presence represented... a strong desire for the modernization of Brazilian culture, that was simultaneously adapted to the global rhythms imposed by the new North American technologies." So, in his own works, the outcome of this mash (even clash) of traditions in the spirit of the avant-garde led to what John Milton, one of his translators, calls a "complex mixture of different aspects of the same reality: love and death; the spiritual and the carnal; the classical and the modern; the formal and the informal. The poet will try to order the often antagonistic elements in order to understand the world. Faustino also believed that the poet should try to recover the primitive incantatory power of poetry and that poetry should be important to contemporary man."

ADDENDUM

LAYLI LONG SOLDIER
Oglala Lakota Nation / USA, Contemporary

from **Whereas**

WHEREAS when offered an apology I watch each movement the shoulders
          high or folding, tilt of the head both eyes down or straight through
          me, I listen for cracks in knuckles or in the word choice, what is
          it that I want? *To feel* and mind you I feel from the senses—I read
          each muscle, I ask the strength of the gesture to move like a poem.
          Expectation's a terse arm-fold, a failing noun-thing
          I scold myself in the mirror for holding.

          Because I learn from young poets. One sends me new work spotted
          with salt crystals she metaphors as her tears. I feel her phrases,
          "I say," and "Understand me," and "I wonder."

          Pages are cavernous places, white at entrance, black in absorption.
          Echo.

          If I'm transformed by language, I am often
          crouched in footnote or blazing in title.
          Where in the body do I begin;

Kamau Brathwaite   Barbados, 1930–2020

from STONE

for Mikey Smith,
Stoned to Death on Stony Hill Kingston Jamaica
on Marcus Garvey birthday 17 August 1983

When the stone fall that morning out of the johncrow sky
it was not dark at first. that opening on to the red sea humming
but something in my mouth like feathers . blue like bubbles
carrying signals & planets & the sliding curve of the world like a water pic
-ture in a raindrop when the pressure. drop

When the stone fall that morning out of the johncrow sky
i couldn't cry out because my mouth was full of beast & plunder
as if I was gnashing badwords among tombstones
as if the road up stony hill . round the bend by the church

-yard . on the way to the post office . was a bad bad dream
& the dream was like a snarl of broken copper wire zig zagg
-in its electric flashes up the hill & splitt . in spark & flow
ers high. er up the hill . past the white houses & the ogogs bark.

ing all teeth & fur. nace & my mother like she up . like she up. like she up
-side down up a tree like she was scream. like she was scream. like she was
scream. ing no & no.
-body i could hear could hear a word i say. in . even though
there were so many poems left & the tape was switched on & runn. ing &

runn. ing & the green light was red & they was stannin up there & evva. where
in london & amsterdam & at unesco in paris & at unesco in paris & in west berlin
& clapp. in & clapp. in & clapp. in & not a soul on stony hill to even say amen
& yet it was happening happening happening . the fences begin

to crack in i skull . & there was a loud **booodoooooooooooooooooogs**
like guns goin off . dem ole time magnums . or like a fireworks a dreadlocks
was on fire . & the gaps where the river comin down inna the drei gully
where my teeth use to be smilin . & i tuff gong tong

that use to press against them & parade pronunciation . now unannounce
& like a black wick in i head & dead . &
it was like a heavy heavy riddim low down in i belly . bleedin dub . &
there was like this heavy heavy black dog tump. in in i chest & pump. ing

murdererrr

& i throat like dem tie. like dem tie. like dem tie a tight tie around
it. twist. ing my name quick crick. quick crick . & a neva wear neck

-tie yet . & a hear when de big boot kick down i door . stump
in it foot pun a knot in de floor. board . a window slam shat at de back
a mi heart . de itch & ooze & damp a de yaaad in mi sil. ver tam.

bourines closer & closer . st joseph marching bands crash
ing & closer
& *bom si. cai si. ca* boom ship bell . *nom si. cai si. ca* boom ship bell

& a laughin more blood
& spittin out

lawwwwwwwwwwwwwwwwwwwwwwwwwwwwwwwwwwwwwwwwwwwwwwwwwwwwwwwd

i two eye lock to the sun & the two sun starin back black from de grass
& a bline to de butterfly fly

COMMENTARY

*it was as if my spirit was waking up in the middle of a very dark night as if
I was alone in a wood of presences and powers vague enraged potentiali-
ties I could not see or name.* (K.B.)

Poet & cultural thinker, Brathwaite's hold on history & self ranges from
images of Black diasporas along the "middle passage" between Africa &
the Caribbean to later outcries & Job-like visions in the aftermath of personal losses (death & sickness, natural disasters, senseless beatings) suffered by himself & others. The range of the work is therefore stunning, as
are the innovations that he needs—& thus invents—to bring it home. As
his first turning from (or deepening of) a strictly Anglo-Caribbean context, he became a major proponent of the use of "nation language" in the
work of poetry—not dialect or creole merely ("thought of as 'bad' English")—but that difference in syntax, in rhythm & timbre ("its own sound
explosion"), "that is more closely allied to the African experience in the
Caribbean." Yet his work is also "'modernist' in inspiration and involve[s]
an open-endedness, an inconclusiveness and a tendency to revise, transform
and depart from the shape of [its] traditional and engendering mythologies" (thus his friend & colleague Gordon Rohlehr).
    In "Stone," the central, martyred figure is the great Jamaican oral ("dub")
poet Michael "Mikey" Smith (see "A Map of Extensions"), whose work
Brathwaite has elsewhere transcribed & cited as an exemplar of Caribbean
"nation language."

Jerome Rothenberg USA, 1931–2024

COKBOY

Part One

saddlesore I came
a jew among
the indians
vot em I doink in dis strange place
mit deez pipple mit strange eyes
could be it's trouble
could be   could be
(he says) a shadow
ariseth from his buckwheat
has tomahawk in hand
shadow of an axe inside his right eye
of a fountain pen inside his left
vot em I doink here
how vass I lost tzu get here
am a hundred men
a hundred fifty different shadows
jews & gentiles
who bring the Law to Wilderness
(he says) this man
is me   my grandfather
& other men-of-letters
men with letters carrying the mail
lithuanian pony-express riders
the financially crazed Buffalo Bill
still riding in the lead
hours before avenging the death of Custer
making the first 3-D movie of those wars
or years before it
the numbers vanishing in kabbalistic time
that brings all men together
& the lonely rider
saddlesore
is me   my grandfather
& other men of letters
jews & gentiles entering

the domain of Indian
who bring the Law to Wilderness
in gold mines & shaky stores
the fur trade heavy agriculture
ballots bullets barbers
who threaten my beard your hair
but patronize me
& will make our kind the Senator from Arizona
the champion of their Law
who hates us both
but dresses as a jew one day an indian
the next a little christian shmuck
vot em I doink here
dis place is maybe crazy
has all the letters going backwards
(he says) so who can read the signboards
to the desert
who can shake his way out of the woods
ford streams the grandmothers
were living near
with snakes inside their cunts
teeth maybe
maybe chainsaws
when the Baal Shem visited America
he wore a shtreiml
the locals all thought he was a cowboy
maybe from Mexico
"a cokboy?"
no a cowboy
I will be more than a credit to my community
& race
but will search for my brother Esau among these redmen
their nocturnal fires I will share
piss strained from my holy cock
will bear seed of Adonoi
& feed them visions
I will fill full a clamshell
will pass it around from mouth to mouth
we will watch the moonrise
through each other's eyes
the distances vanishing in kabbalistic time

(he says) the old man watches
from the cliffs a city
overcome with light
the man & the city disappear
he looks & sees another city
this one is made of glass
inside the buildings stand
immobile statues
brown-skinned faces
catch the light
an elevator
moving up & down
in the vision of the Cuna nele
the vision of my grandfather
vision of the Baal Shem in America
the slaves in steerage
what have they seen in common
by what light their eyes
have opened into stars
I wouldn't know
what I was doing here
this place has all the letters going
backwards a reverse in time
towards wilderness
the old jew strains at his gaberdine
it parts for him
his spirit rushes up the mountainside
& meets an eagle
no an iggle
captains   commanders   dollinks   delicious madmen
murderers opening the continent up to exploitation
cease & desist (he says)
let's speak (he says)
feels like a little gas down here (he says)
(can't face the mirror without crying)
& the iggle lifts him
like an elevator
to a safe place above the sunrise
there gives a song to him
the Baal Shem's song
repeated without words for centuries

"hey heya heya" but translates it
as "yuh-buh-buh-buh-buh-buh-bum"
when the Baal Shem (yuh-buh) learns to do a bundle
what does the Baal Shem (buh-buh) put into the bundle?
silk of his prayershawl-bag beneath
cover of beaverskin above
savor of esrog fruit within
horn of a mountaingoat between
feather of dove around the sides
clove of a Polish garlic at its heart
he wears when traveling
in journeys through kabbalistic forests
cavalry of the Tsars on every side
men with fat moustaches yellow eyes & sabers
who stalk the gentle soul
at night through the Wyoming steppes
(he says) vot em I doink here
I could not find mine het
would search the countryside on hands & knees
until   behind a rock in Cody
old indian steps forth
the prophecies of both join at this point
like smoke a pipe is held
between them dribbles through their lips
the keen tobacco
"cowboy?"
cokboy (says the Baal Shem)
places a walnut in his handkerchief & cracks it
on a boulder each one eats
the indian draws forth a deck of cards
& shuffles
"game?"
they play at wolves & lambs
the fire crackles in the pripitchok
in a large tent somewhere in America
the story of the coming forth begins

COMMENTARY

A PERSONAL MANIFESTO. *[1] I will change your mind. [2] Any means (=
methods) to that end. [3] To oppose the "devourers" = bureaucrats, system-*

makers, priests, etc. (W. Blake). [4] "& if thou wdst understand that wch is me, know this: all that I have sd I have uttered playfully—& I was by no means ashamed of it." (J. C. to his disciples, the Acts of St. John) (J.R.)

(1) "I did not know—at the opening—how old the work was. Like others my age then—& others before & after us—I was looking for what in my own time would make a difference to that time. What is easily forgotten is the condition of the time itself that should make us want to go in that direction: to pull down & to transform. As a young child I heard people still talking about the *world* war (even the *great* war) in the singular, but by adolescence the *second* war had come & with it a crisis in the human capacity to reduce & stifle life" (J.R.).

(2) And again: "When I concluded 'Cokboy' with the line [not included here] about having nothing left to say, I didn't realize at first how it resembled John Cage's definition of poetry: *I have nothing to say and I am saying it and that is poetry.* In the poem of course I had invoked the reality of genocide—of both Native Americans and Jews—and after crying out four times 'America disaster,' had turned from it in disgust, but the '*nothing*' there, I would like to think in reconsideration, is really poetry as I came to understand it" (from *The Wolf Interview*, by Ariel Resnikoff).

David Antin USA, 1932–2016

from *TALKING AT POMONA*

it may be that formal concerns   applied to things that might be interesting in human space   turn out to be obscene   on the other hand thats
very interesting   it raises the issue essentially of what i would call
pornography   now art has always played with pornography   in the west
    its been significant because it has always been the challenge of the
artist that art is informal because one responds pornographically   the
  most cheerful aspect   the most heartening aspect about western european
art were its possible pornographic concerns because it was always the spec-
ter of the human however formal an art work was   if it played with pornography as an idea   not because pornography was beautiful or cheerful   but
because it was a reminiscence of human maneuver within the work   now it
seems one of the problems here thats raised is the kind of conflict that
exists between human values and the idea of art making itself as a career
    that is   what art making is about   or what it has often been about
    take the nude say   the female nude   from the renaissance on it has
  always offered something of an entrance to the painting through human sexu-

al feeling   the consumer   the art looker   was always assumed to be
a man   now everyone knows that men dont get excited when they see a
painting of a beautiful naked woman   not a gentleman or an art lover   re-
lator   not now anyway that we have photographs and movies   still who
can deny that there is that momentary flicker of interest   sure its more complicated than that   this feeling is surely diverted or suspended   by
some conflict of interest   in painting say or antiquity   nostalgia   still
its a naked woman youre looking at in a titian or a renoir   or a wesselman
        it isnt a wine bottle or a mountain   though the feeling   the flicker
of sexuality is protected from its consequences by its surrounding attributes
        its props   the case is maybe clearer with suffering than with sexua-
lity   the painter has painted a picture of a human being in torment   you
are filled with an honorable ennobling sympathy for his exquisite torment
        you look at gruenwalds christ and are filled with pleasure   youre mas-
turbating at the crucifixion   what is the point of all this self stimulation
if you are the viewer   or why all this generosity if you are the artist
        this sexual assistance?   what are you masters and johnson?   what
if you are most especially interested in   or in need of masturbation   for
an artist who gets no <u>frisson</u> from exposing himself or pretending to do so
what is there to do?   supposing art making is like a kind of knot making
        if youre a knot maker youve got an idea about what is a knot and
        what is a mess   a legal way of proceeding   what is a legal knot and
what is a snarl   all knots involve some kind of double reversal   you
start out going somewhere go back and take some of the past with you   to
wherever you were going to go and you find a way to mark off some memo-
rial to where youve been   a node   well there are two kinds at least   of
knot makers   one knot maker knows how to proceed making his knots and
        watches himself proceeding   in the end he arrives at a knot he approves   for
some reason   if he's been watching the way he has been knotting all this time
he wont be surprised at the outcome   and though he may be satisfied he'll
        walk away and forget it   then he's a process knot maker   or he might
not walk away but place it in front of you in the hope that you will be bettered
        thereby   in which case he's a therapeutic or didactic knot maker
or say he's a forgetful knot maker   as soon as he finishes a loop he
forgets it   because all the time he's only attending to the node he is
working on at any given moment   at some time when he's tired or
interrupted by a phone call he will look up and he'll be surprised by his knot
because he'll have no idea how he got there   he's a kind of magical
        knot maker   but with all of this   and I think we should not underes-
timate the pleasures and surprises of knot making   why in the world should
we bother making knots who cares about rope?   in a way this is a lot like

playing chess and you can say someone has played it well or played poorly but
         why should you care about this game?   it seems ridiculous to spend
all this time pushing little pieces of wood about on a board   havent you
   got better things to do?   but it was not always this way with chess
      chess is a depraved game   it represents the world as a struggle for
dominance between two sides that have no choice but conflict   there is
no clear demarcation or boundary that cuts off one side from the others
   hostilities   and there is no bound to human abilities   it is an arrogant
fantasy of war   in which the greater ability will surely win by annihi-
lating his opponent   what sort of paradigm is this?   no experience on
earth corresponds to it   so it is a game of no relevance   it is a funda-
mentally trivial representation of reality   but it wasnt always like this
      according to most authorities chess derived from an indian game
called <u>shatrandji</u>   which was supposed to represent the state of the
world   the social classes into which people were arbitrarily divided
      and it was a game invaded by chance   the best player   the best
plan could as easily be defeated as the worst   by luck   and this was
   thought to teach humility to rulers   <u>shatrandji</u> was the game of which
chess is the trivial example   and it doesnt seem that we have to be
especially impressed with <u>shatrandji</u> either   but as <u>shatrandji</u> was a
game built up out of the human experiences of its time   arbitrary inequi-
ties among people   the facts of unavoidable war   and the absurd circumstances of luck lying under the feet of ability   it is possible to
construct   make our art out of something more meaningful than the arbitrary rules of knot making   out of the character of human experience
in our world

COMMENTARY

*i had suggested that i had always had mixed feelings about being consid-
ered a poet   "if robert lowell is a poet i dont want to be a poet   if robert
frost was a poet   i dont want to be a poet   if socrates was a poet ill
consider it"* (DA.) And again: *The Sophists' paradoxical talk pieces and
their public debates were entertainment in 5th century Greece. And in that
world, Socrates was an entertainer.*

Antin's move—ca. 1970—was to break (radically) with his own work as
an experimental maker of still recognizable "poems" & to direct his energies thereafter to acts of talking (*real* talking) first presented in the context of performances & readings, then transcribed into a form of writing
that evaded the restrictions of both verse & prose. Like other avant-garde
moves, the challenge went to the heart of basic assumptions about poetry—
in this case, the lyric imperative—against which Antin presented a view of

poetry (*now* and *then*) derived not merely from *speech* (as opposed, say, to *song*) but from the dynamics of a true *discourse* (including *narrative*) as a form of thinking-out-loud, from which it had long been set apart.

For which reasons one might tie his talk-poems to the workings of oral masters—particularly those like Jacob Nibenegenesabe or Andrew Peynetsa (see above) or, among the modernists, John Cage, whose poetry workings (specifically) derive more from the side of speech, say, than that of song. Or Socrates & Wittgenstein, Antin's two great philosophical forebears, on the side of "talking to discover" as an act of poetry.

For more on Antin, see "A Map of Visions" & "A Map of Extensions."

Marosa di Giorgio Uruguay, 1932–2004

from *THE MOTH*

The wasps were extremely delicate. Like angels, many of them fitted on the head of a pin. All of them resembled young ladies, dancing teachers. I imitated their murmuring rather well. They circled the apple's white flowers, the quince's ochre flowers, the pomegranate's hard red roses. Or in the tiny fountains where my cousins, my sisters and I gazed at them, our hands on our chins. Compared to them we were giants, monsters. But the most wondrous thing was the cartons they made; almost in one stroke, their palaces of thick grey paper appeared, among the leaves, and, inside them, plates of honey.

Meanwhile, the lizard continued hunting for hen's eggs, warm tid-bits; snakes blue as fire crossed the path, curly, delicately crafted carnations, looking like bowls of fruit and rice, shot up.

The world, all of it, welcoming, magical.

And one face, separated, the only one painted, walked among the leaves, eyes downcast, red mouth open.

And when it had already gone by it walked past one more time.

Translated from Spanish by Peter Boyle

COMMENTARY

And in the garden one tall, black horse—he looked like he was dead, the abstraction of a horse—ran back and forth with a crown of rubies fixed tightly on his head, shining in the sun and the dew, and a voice cried out, "This is war." And we—the women—stared at him in shock. (M.diG).

Writes Thomas Sanfilip: "Di Giorgio, who died in 2004, considered her work one narrative. What is immediately apparent in di Giorgio's prose poems is how the transformative aspects of her being dictate her syntax. More than that, she uncovers the amorphic nature of all existence, at least poetically expressed. At a deeper level, what she reveals in her transmutations from one form to the next is an existential vacuity that seems to bear the whole weight of human existence often lived through her alone. She rides these inevitable transitions in half-awe as they strip her memories of their human value.... For di Giorgio, all things animal, human, or vegetal share in a universal nature, but at some point transcend their own inherent shape, purpose or being. She expresses this in continuous revelation, merging with all things existent at whatever state of evolution" (in *Rattle*, June 5, 2013).

Miguel Ángel Bustos Argentina, 1932–1976

from **VISION OF THE CHILDREN OF EVIL**

1
Outside I hear the rain, inside I feel the rain. My clay body dissolves.

2
A voice cries out from the commotion and terror. It reaches only me.
   It is the cry of the spirit that possesses me. I divine his message. My
   horrified tongue follows his evil rhythm.

. . . . .

7
Collect the sea grapes.
Make wine from heaven. Get drunk on earth.

. . . . .

9
Write when possible. Write when impossible. Love silence.

. . . . .

12
Kill the bird. Keep the song.

.....

14
Where will madness drive me if not to the heart of men?

15
The god of antimatter fears falling into the hell of matter.

.....

25
From heaven, Herod has cried out to you: Virgin, Virgin, strangle your
son. Rule only in the plains of Hell.

.....

29
Silence. The dead are listening to you.

.....

38
Listen, dawn. Listen, I'm dying.

.....

47
I want to be eternal as if I were never born.

.....

51
Horizon that beats me, sky that bites me, for your assassin hand. But
don't do as I say, heed horror instead.

52
Lord, Lord, I'm disguised as a virgin. Conceive in me a creator. Over the
horizon the Cross awaits the last dawn.

.....

58
As blasphemy grows I feel myself pray.

.....

67
Just as mothers like flowers, I sow shrieks in the seas.

73
And the last man will be called Omphalos. He will wander lost through
   the temples seeking a face of sun to worship.

. . . . .

75
In the Country of the Blind never say *I see seas of light.* They will beat
   you with stones.

. . . . .

82
Am I a verb that makes sense or just a senseless verb?

. . . . .

86
Hell: that rib we're missing.

87
I draw suns because I can't see the day.

. . . . .

94
I don't see—I *eat* radiance.

. . . . .

99
The mystical fortress is the Illuminated heart.

. . . . .

106
All reading moves parallel to the sun's.

. . . . .

112
Write celestial poetry with demonic words or better yet speak of Hell
   with the high purity of a god. Or hang yourself—make *both* poetries!

. . . . .

118
The tiger has no other god than his teeth.

. . . . .

120
Everything watches me with lidless eyes.

Translated from Spanish by Lucina Schell

COMMENTARY

When I die, the prophet in me will rise like a child without morals or motherland. (M.A.B.)

(1) Miguel Ángel Bustos's tragedy once again manifests the human frailty in a world whose forces raid & condemn liberty, creation, & imagination. Born in 1932, he was one of the thousands who were disappeared during the extreme military regimes that darkened the Americas during our last century. On May 30, 1976, a military command of Jorge Rafael Videla's Junta de Gobierno arrested Bustos—as also happened to other thinkers, artists, & journalists considered potential "enemies of the regime"—& took him into one of the many detention camps where these "adversaries" were brutally tortured & murdered. From then on, Bustos was officially labeled as "disappeared" until his son, the poet Emiliano Bustos, after an exhaustive search, found the remains of his father in 2014. Using a DNA match & other evidence, it was determined that Miguel Ángel Bustos had been murdered on June 20, 1976, by a firing squad.

(2) Like many authors, in other times & geographies, the threat to Bustos's imagination in a world that crumbles under the forces of power (as happened with Dante or Blake, for instance) led him to undertake a "descent to hell," like the one depicted in *Vision of the Children of Evil*. There, every rational choice is canceled: it's not only a struggle of the angelic/demonic but also a reformulation of language, perception, & thought as a counterattack to repression. The outcome was, as the poet stated in an interview, "a continuous and unbearable lucidity." This echoes & partly transforms Milton's words in *Paradise Lost*: "The horror will grow mild, this darkness, light."

Héctor Viel Temperley Argentina, 1933–1987

from *HOSPITAL BRITÁNICO*

Month of March, 1986
*(Version with splinters
and "Christus Pantokrator")*

Rosetta Pavilion, long corner of summer, armor of butterflies: My mother came to heaven to visit me.

My head is bandaged. I remain in the breast of Light for hours on end. I am happy. They have taken me from the world.

My mother is laughter, freedom, summer.

Twenty blocks from here she lies dying.

Here she kisses my peace, sees her son changed, prepares herself—in Your crying—to start all over again.

.....

"Christus Pantokrator"

The postcard comes from sailors, from old pugilists in that narrow bar like a submarine—of tin cans and wood—sinking into the coastal sun.

The postcard comes from a Christus Pantokrator, who, when I lower the blinds, turn off the light, and close my eyes, asks me to film His silence in a bottle washed up on an endless shoal. (1985)

"Christus Pantokrator"

In front of the postcard I am like a shovel that digs in the sun, in the Face and in the eyes of Christus Pantokrator. (1985)

I know that only in the eyes of Christus Pantokrator can I dig in the perspiration of all my summers until I arrive from my sternum, from noon, at that lighthouse shaded by the limbs of orange trees that I want for the half-mute boy I bore for many months upon my soul. (Month of April, 1986)

.....

Long corner of summer

Am I that crew member with a crown of thorns who can't see his wings outside the ship, who can't see your Face in the poster nailed to the hull and torn by the wind, and who still doesn't know that Your Face is greater than the entire sea when it throws its dice against a black jetty of iron stoves that waits for some men in a sun where it snows? (1985)

.....

My head is bandaged (distant prophetic text)

My head passes through the fire of the world to be born but keeps a winding stream of frozen water in its memory. And I ask it to help me. (1978)

My head is bandaged

Butterfly of God, pubis of Mary: Cross the blood of my brow—**until I kiss my very face in Jesus Christ.** (1982)

.....

My head is bandaged (text by the man on the beach)

Along with my soul the sun enters into my head (or my body—along with the Resurrection—enters into my soul). (1984)

My head is bandaged (text by the man on the beach)

It is the fault of the fiery wind that pierces its wound, at this moment, that Your Hand traces an anchor in my head and not a cross.

I want to drink back to my nape, forever, the two arms of the anchor of the trembling of Your Flesh and of the Heavens' haste. (1984)

My head is bandaged (text by the man on the beach)

Back there on my nape, I saw the pure white desert of this life of my life; I saw my eternity, which I must traverse from the eyes of the Lord to the eyes of the Lord. (1984)

They have taken me from the world

I am the place where the Lord spreads out the Light that He is.

They have taken me from the world

An armor of butterflies covers me and I wear the shirt of butterflies that is the Lord-within, inside me.

The Kingdom of Heaven surrounds me. The Kingdom of Heaven is the Body of Christ—and each day at noon I touch Christ.

Christ is Christ the mother, and my mother comes to visit me in Him.

They have taken me from the world

"Woman I impregnated," "Rosetto Pavilion," "Long corner of summer":

The pleasure of words comes back to my flesh in the tops of some eucalyptus trees (or in the heights of "B," where once—just once—I looked out and saw a heavenly beach leaning against the shore).

They have taken me from the world.

Hands of Mary, temples of marble from my beach in heaven,
Death is the beginning of a war in which another man will never be able to see my skeleton.

. . . . .

She lies dying

I'll never again walk past the bar that faced the Headquarters' patio. I won't look upon the table where we were happy.

The sun like that place beneath the waters of a river of soil and oranges where before learning to walk I looked upon God as a man who knows what war is. The sun like those waters of soil and oranges where without yearning for breath, for air, I looked upon him in this way: "I remember a far-off victory (so many saved faces that afterwards nobody wants to remember me) and I'm at peace with my conscience to this day." (1984)

She lies dying

I left her on a deathbed of tall, cold, purplish periwinkles.

For its stream-like finale, the wound on my forehead cries in the flowers and gives thanks.

She lies dying

Within four days she'll reach Your Ocean with one of my little toy soldiers asleep upon her lips. And smiling at me, she'll say to herself: "It wasn't long ago that this man went to the center of the sun each morning with a handful of tin soldiers. It wasn't long ago that in the center of the sun, each morning, his heart was a handful of tin soldiers among roosters."

Asleep upon her lips

How windy it is, little legionnaire! Tiny piece of tin, tiny piece of Sahara: There will be summers free of obsession; the sons of my sons shall pass. (1978)

I can chop all day but I can't dig all day. I can't dig anywhere without fully expecting a tin soldier to appear suddenly between my naked feet. (1978)

To start all over again

My piece of earth is the one that cries for the plum trees it has lost.

To start all over again

The summer we rise from the dead will have a mill nearby with a jet-white stream buried in its vein. (1969)

Translated from Spanish by Stuart Krimko

COMMENTARY

I'm the swimmer, Lord: just a man who swims. I greet your waters for in them / my arms still / rouse a beat of wings. (H.V.T.)

(1) From being elusive & lesser known, Héctor Viel Temperley is now regarded as one of the most impressive & original of Latin American poets. Born in Argentina, in 1933, in a middle-class family of British descent, his moves in poetry present a rare double feature of experimentalism (radical procedures) & inner-self intensity. Responsive to the silence of the Benedictine monks he long admired, his collections are not abundant. He published eight poetry books over a thirty-year span until he finished *Hospital Británico* in 1986, a year before his death.

(2) A note by his translator, Stuart Krimko: "Like the 'something in the air' that inspired Viel Temperley to dramatically reassess his own poetry, the visage of the Pantokrator became a place of faith and inquiry, a zone where he could 'dig into the perspiration of all [his] summers,' despite the fact that death was upon him. Bathed in memory and sweat, Viel Temperley was discovering that elegy gives rise to ecstasy, and that life is a fever dream built from facts" (in *The Last Books of Héctor Viel Temperley*).

Ted Berrigan USA, 1934–1983

I

His piercing pince-nez. Some dim frieze
Hands point to a dim frieze, in the dark night.
In the book of his music the corners have straightened:
Which owe their presence to our sleeping hands.
The ox-blood from the hands which play
For fire for warmth for hands for growth
Is there room in the room that you room in?
Upon his structured tomb:
Still they mean something. For the dance
And the architecture.
Weave among incidents
May be portentous to him
We are the sleeping fragments of his sky,
Wind giving presence to fragments.

. . . . .

III

Stronger than alcohol, more great than song,
deep in whose reeds great elephants decay,
I, an island, sail, and my shoes toss
on a fragrant evening, fraught with sadness
bristling hate.
It's true, I weep too much. Dawns break
slow kisses on the eyelids of the sea,
what other men sometimes have thought they've seen.
And since then I've been bathing in the poem
lifting her shadowy flowers up for me,
and hurled by hurricanes to a birdless place
the waving flags, nor pass by prison ships
O let me burst, and I be lost at sea!
and fall on my knees then, womanly.

. . . . .

XXXVII

It is night. You are asleep. And beautiful tears
Have blossomed in my eyes. Guillaume Apollinaire is dead.

The big green day today is singing to itself
A vast orange library of dreams, dreams
Dressed in newspaper, wan as pale thighs
Making vast apple strides towards "The Poems."
"The Poems" is not a dream. It is night. You
Are asleep. Vast orange libraries of dreams
Stir inside "The Poems." On the dirt-covered ground
Crystal tears drench the ground. Vast orange dreams
Are unclenched. It is night. Songs have blossomed
In the pale crystal library of tears. You
Are asleep. A lovely light is singing to itself,
In "The Poems," in my eyes, in the line,
"Guillaume Apollinaire is dead."

COMMENTARY

One of my principal desires is to make my poems be like my life... I
can't see myself the way that you can see me, but I can see everything else
around me. If I can make everything around me be the way that it is, pre-
sumably I can create the shape of the self inside the poem, because there is
a person inside almost all of the poems. (T.B.)

Alongside the last century's (still) high claims for poetry, there is a pull
also toward a deflationary/self-deflationary view of poet & of poet's stance.
For Berrigan, his undisguised sense of the former ("The gods demand of
the system that a certain number of people sing") was more than matched
by the latter ("I'm obscure when I feel like it / especially in my dream
poems which I never even / call Dream Poem but from sheer cussedness
title 'Match Game etc. [for Dick Gallup]' or something like that"). He was
born Irish American in Providence, Rhode Island, & it was his destiny to
come (with fellow poets/artists Ron Padgett, Dick Gallup, & Joe Brain-
ard) from university in Tulsa, Oklahoma, to form a second-generation New
York School of poets (ca. 1960) that led him & others to a new encounter
with the everyday & *un*remarkable, transformed into something dearly,
vividly held. The resultant work—deceptively personal, nostalgic, even sentimental—is simultaneously an inversion, precisely, of the personal, nostalgic, & sentimental. As Charles Bernstein rightly has it (concerning the
"inversions" in Berrigan's acknowledged masterwork, the untraditional &
unrhyming *Sonnets*): "*The Sonnets*—with its permutational use of the same
phrases in different sequences and its inclusion of external or found language—stands as an explicit rejection of the psychological 'I' as the locus of
the poem's meaning." Or Berrigan himself (in comic deference to Olson &
Rimbaud): "It is a human universe: & I / is a correspondent" (sonnet LII).
  A comparison to O'Hara's "personism" & Parra's "antipoems" might
also be in order.

ANSELM HOLLO Finland/USA, 1934–2013

Sonnet [for Ted Berrigan]

There are many places in this world,
some of them inhabited by the totally mad.
She hands them pennies, directs them
to the nearest shelter.
Some we live right close to & somewhat
believe in, as further language.
Remember, too, the ones who died
while telling us they felt great
& the doctors agreed. The sun
shines upon the just & the wicked,
but why should they feel the same way
about how it feels, when no one hands them
a thermometer. As for thought,
I think it went out with Ted. He took
all the thought & sprinkled it all over
the globe, which is now clogging up
the toilet of this Star Wars universe.

Amiri Baraka USA, 1934–2014

BLACK DADA NIHILISMUS

I

     Against what light
is false what breath
sucked, for deadlines.
     Murder, the cleansed
purpose, frail, against
God, if they bring him
     bleeding, I would not
forgive, or even call him
black dada nihilismus.
The protestant love, wide windows,
color blocked to Mondrian, and the

ugly silent deaths of jews under
the surgeon's knife. (To awake on
69th street with money and a hip
nose. Black dada nihilismus, for
the umbrella'd jesus. Trilby intrigue
movie house presidents sticky the floor
B.D.N., for the secret men, Hermes, the
blacker art. Thievery (ahh, they return
those secret gold killers. Inquisitors
of the cocktail hour. Trismegistus, have
them, in their transmutation, from stone
to bleeding pearl, from lead to burning
looting, dead Moctezuma, find the West
a gray hideous space

2

From Sartre, a white man, it gave
the last breath. And we beg him die,
before he is killed. Plastique, we
do not have, only thin heroic blades.
The razor. Our flail against them, why
you carry knives? Or brutalized lumps of
heart? Why you stay, where they can
reach? Why you sit, or stand, or walk
In this place, a window on a dark
warehouse. Where the mind's packed in
straw. New homes, these towers, for those
lacking money or art. A cult of death,
need of the simple striking arm under
the streetlamp. The cutters, from under
their rented earth. Come up, black dada
nihilismus. Rape the white girls. Rape
their fathers. Cut the mothers' throats.
Black dada nihilismus, choke my friends
in their bedrooms with their drinks spilling
and restless for tilting hips or dark liver
lips sucking splinters from the master's thigh
Black scream
and chant, scream,
and dull, un
earthly

hollering. Dada, bilious
what ugliness, learned
in the dome, colored holy
shit (i call them sinned
or lost
     burned masters
          of the lost
               nihil German killers
                    all our learned
art, 'member
what you said
money, God, power,
a moral code, so cruel
it destroyed Byzantium, Tenochtitlan, Commanch
                    (got it, *Baby!*
For tambo, willie best, dubois, patrice, mantan, the
bronze buckaroos.
        for Jack Johnson, asbestos, tonto, buckwheat,
        billie holiday
            For tom russ, l'ouverture, vesey, beau jack,
(may a lost god damballah, rest or save us
against the murders we intend
against his lost white children
black dada nihilismus

COMMENTARY

The force we want is of twenty million spooks storming America with furious cries and unstoppable weapons. We want actual explosions and actual brutality: AN EPIC IS CRUMBLING and we must give it the space and hugeness of its actual demise. (A.B.)

It was Baraka's genius to grasp the ferocity (theatrical, poetic) of Artaud's "theater of cruelty" & to redirect it—in the context of his own time (*our* time)—into a "revolutionary" poetry & theater, of which he wrote: "This is a theater of assault. The play that will split the heavens for us will be called THE DESTRUCTION OF AMERICA. The heroes will be Crazy Horse, Denmark Vesey, Patrice Lumumba, and not history, not memory, not sad sentimental groping for a warmth in our despair; these will be new men, new heroes, and their enemies most of you who are reading this." But his project had begun still earlier with a poetry practice (*Preface to a Twenty Volume Suicide Note, The Dead Lecturer*) informed by the line of Pound & Olson, modified by participation in Beat/"bohemian" doings & by ongoing attention to jazz & blues rhythms & (increasingly) to Negritude & Harlem Renaissance poetics & the language "really spoken" in the worlds around him. By the later 1960s, he had gone from LeRoi Jones to (Imamu) Amiri Baraka, had emerged for a time as a major American playwright (*Dutchman*, *The Toilet*, *The Slave*), & had taken a highly visible role in Black nationalist politics & Black culturalist practice. From 1974 on, however, his political stance turned sharply internationalist with a self-proclaimed conversion to "Marxism-Leninism-Mao Tse-tung Thought"—allowing him (again) to put his total person into play.

The "cruelty" of the approach, however brazen, never wavered.

Clayton Eshleman USA, 1935–2021

from **THE TJURUNGA**

begins as a digging stick, first thing the Aranda child picks up.
When he cries, he is said to be crying for
the tjurunga he lost
when he migrated into his mother.

Male elders later replace the mother with sub-incision.
The shaft of his penis slit, the boy incorporates his mother.

I had to create a totemic cluster in which imagination
could replace Indianapolis, to incorporate ancestor beings
who could give me the agility
—across the tjurunga spider's web—
to pick my way to her perilous center.

(So transformationally did she quiver,
            adorned with hearts and hands,
        cruciform, monumental,   *Coatlicue*
            understrapping fusion)

Theseus, a tiny male spider, enters a tri-level construction:
look down through the poem, you can see the labyrinth.
Look down through the labyrinth, you can see the web:

                    Coatlicue

    sub-incision   Bud Powell

        César Vallejo

the bird-headed man

Like a mobile, this tjurunga shifts in the breeze,
beaming at the tossing
foreskin dinghies in which poets travel.

These nouns are also nodes in a constellation called
Clayton's Tjurunga. The struts are threads
in a web. There is a life blood flowing through
these threads. *Coatlicue* flows into Bud Powell,
César Vallejo into sub-incision. The bird-headed man
    floats right below
the pregnant spider
centered in the Tjurunga.

Psyche may have occurred, struck off
—as in flint-knapping—
an undifferentiated mental core.

My only weapon is a digging stick
the Aranda call *papa*. To think of father as a digging stick
strikes me as a good translation.

    The bird-headed man
is slanted under a disemboweled bison.
His erection tells me he's in flight. He drops
his bird-headed stick as he penetrates
    bison paradise.

The red sandstone hand lamp
abandoned below this proto-shaman
is engraved with vulvate chevrons—did it once flame
    from a primal sub-incision?

This is the oldest aspect of this tjurunga, its grip.

CHAUVET. FIRST IMPRESSIONS

The depth of body.
The depth   of a hollow
   animal belly
imagination fills out to an agreeable convexity, &
the tenderness in a bear drawing

like a loom within stone.
Seesaw pitch of breath & stasis:
my heart pounding   Take Heed   halfway
up the mountain to Chauvet's entrance.
Frightened to almost be stopped within minutes of the cave.
(Olson in Hotel Steinplatz feeling
the World Tree give way in his giant frame).

Is that why Chauvet's interior was tinged for me
    with the rust of farewell?
Coffee outside the equipment nook
after the 40 minute climb:
4000 people, the guide Charles told us, have visited,
about 400 a year, or did he mean
about 400 will visit this year?
So I'm not that special—
    photo of the Methodist Hospital window
    in the room where I was born, X'ed by my father
    in his "Baby's Book of Events."

Cradle of art?
Roar of images cascading the wall,
rows of larger-than-life lion heads voracious for
a vertical totem pole of bison heads.
90% of Chauvet is virgin floor.
One bear skull is enveloped in stalactitic casing,
a polished white sarcophagus of sorts,
with a stalagmite a foot high "growing" out of
    the cranium dome,
as if the skull sends up its opaque
    shaft of words.
10% of Chauvet appears to be metal walkway.
"charter'd Thames" Nice to keep that much floor virgin
but it is as if this primordial labyrinth has been
    jigsawed with streets. Meaning:
no wandering, no "lost at sea" in being's immensity.
Like a huge solitary hanging fang, near the cave's end:
a Minotaur, with a drizzle of fingers,
drawn on a large feline body drawn there earlier.
Some panels boil with activity,
as if they magnetized Cro-Magnon soul,
sucked animal through Cro-Magnon bodies.

The 32,400 year old male rhino
in horn clash with maybe a female
has a fat, pointed erect phallus.
A chaos of animals, like "a paradise of poets,"
one masterly horse finger-painted in wall clay,
    shaded so carefully
to pull the outline boundaries in,
the limestone shows through—
as if nothing that special has happened since!
As if man were an afterthought of a humanimal brew
    still beating in my chest
like a wedge of lions crafting a kill.
Asking why certain spots were chosen for figures,
like asking why lightning here, not there...
Here-not-there coalesces into hermetic knots of
    wiggling anti-cores,
as if a solid helix were, this instant,
bursting into univocal lanes
(the metal walkway puns upon).

Why are you here
right up my nose,
as if a tweezer carbon-dated, on the spot,
    a bit of my brain &
came up with the abyss's
invisible but definite bottom:
death, as a feline gush of misericordia,
beauty & affinity, lined within the notion of being.
How did I manage to walk that last 20 minutes
    up the mountain?
Why can't I get over that pounding halo of
    serpent breath,
haruspex enigma...   Breathe &
    be grateful for
the various ranges quilted within, &
the many years with Caryl.
Thought of her on that mountain side, panting...
Did her devotion & utter decency
    lift me on?

*Today I have set my crowbar against all I know / In a shower of soot &
blood / Breaking the backbone of my mother* (C.E.)

It is this power that Eshleman brings to the work at hand: a willingness
to push the art & the act of poetry to its deepest sources & limits, both in
each of us as individuals & in all of us as species. That thrust in his work
(his *project* as such) is summed up in the idea of a *grotesque realism*, drawn
from the Russian writer Mikhail Bakhtin (in his study of Rabelais) & transformed by Eshleman into a proposal for an *American grotesque*. From this
base in his own body, he makes the leap (ca. 1970) into the equally subterranean & mysterious cave world (French *grotte*, Italian *grotto*) of the European Paleolithic, enters it (literally) crawling "on all fours," to find in the
animal beings painted on its walls a first "construction of the underworld"
by "Neanderthal and Crô-Magnon men, women, and children, who made
the nearly unimaginable breakthrough, over thousands of years, from no
mental record to a mental record." The work is carried forward further
by a remarkable series of translations of modern predecessors (Césaire,
Vallejo, Artaud, Holan), whom he calls (as an extension of his central image
& in line with their Paleolithic counterparts) "conductors of the pit" &
with whom he enters into acts of both apprenticeship & struggle. Together
with his germinal & aptly titled magazines (*Caterpillar* in the 1960s, *Sulfur*
later), the work becomes—as he would have it—the model of a renewed
(renewable) "construction of the underworld."

His spectral meeting with Vallejo is chronicled here & elsewhere in these
pages, along with the presence of many others: friends & fellow poets/
artists. The title word "Tjurunga" is an Indigenous Aranda word from
Australia, referring to a stone or wooden board inscribed with designs that
represent a sacred being of that name. And the visit to the Chauvet cave in
2004 came a decade after its discovery, in a line with his earlier explorations & absorption of our Paleolithic beginnings.

ADDENDUM

RICARDO CÁZARES   Mexico, 1978–

from **[Palas]**

> count to 14
> thousand million years
> insert your hand in
> the rock for
> a preliminary probe
> and touch—that is if

you want it
if you really do want
it
it is possible to score to
scratch the surface of
the source
please insert
a hand
a coin
turn on your drill re-
move the overlying residue
from stratum scrap
outline an excavation plan
the tunnel dam the pass
a pathway will be ready in
5 years

if you wish to continue
insert
if you desire
if desire moves you to
burrow through the bulk
insert
enter now

Robert Kelly USA, 1935–

PREFIX: FINDING THE MEASURE

Finding the measure is finding the mantram,
is finding the moon, as index of measure,
is finding the moon's source;

                              if that source
is Sun, finding the measure is finding
the natural articulation of ideas.

                    The organism
of the macrocosm, the organism of language,
the organism of I combine in ceaseless naturing
to propagate a fourth,
                    the poem,
                              from their trinity.

Style is death. Finding the measure is finding
a freedom from that death, a way out, a movement
forward.

Finding the measure is finding the
specific music of the hour,
the synchronous
consequence of the motion of the whole world.

BINDING BY STRIKING

Say I come to you by circles. Say the line
that carries my name keeps me
from knowing you as a car knows a garage.
Say I am a wine you know better than to drink.
Say I, seeing the pale skin inside your upper arms,
become a better animal and become water.
Say this water doesn't pull but when you fall
takes you altogether in. Say you are in.
Say we sit on some steps together, or a wall.
Say something falls. I come to you then confused by lime,
sand, long hair holding the mortar together.
Say we stand a long time and one of us falls and one
catches, one catches and one lets go and it's night already.
We are still together. Say I am oily and you're dry.
Say a straight path and a twisted gate. Say something
not easy to say. Say the self-renewing knot of flesh
they call the rose blocks at times the future prong.
Say we belong to each other. Say the same thing
that holds us holds us apart. Say we struggle
to get in and stay in and not ever leave. Say for a change
you are out and I am in and I have trees too
your path gets lost in. Say you have numbers I can count
and numbers that leave me out. Say we change
but say we are always being held to the same.
Not to say little of same. Not to say one is more than some
or some less worth than every. Not to say every.
Not to say your pale skin is paler than this or this wall higher.
We rise where we fall. Not to say the word that draws us
doesn't some way let us in. Not to say in is the only.

We are held where we call. We know something and are held
to what we know. We fall through the wall. Not to say
there is only one garden or one car. Not to say one
when we mean "a road" and not to say going when we mean "home."
Not to say time when we mean space. Not to say stone
when a wind blows through the place where we've fallen.
Say you come to me by line. Say the circle you understand
has more light than a bone and more air than a tower. Say
the broad leaf of burdock plays two pieces of music:
bug-holes and leaf-shadow. Say a skin is like that and that
what we have consumed gives us light and what is gone
is the constellation that guides us. Say you have come
and will come. Say the language is dry and the wall is low.
Say a word gets over the wall. Say we are in. Say my skin
draws you. Say what we do with each other goes on.
Say a voice that you hear. Say that we know ourselves
chiefly in many. The Oil of Others is the light-giving flame.
Say we are the same. Say we come to it simply again.

COMMENTARY

*Speak language // the way thunder does, / all the words at once // what
lingers / turns slowly into meaning // meaning is not what you think /
meaning is what stays.* (R.K.)

(1) "Scorn nothing / Write everything / the oracle said...," & thus Robert
Kelly's decision at twenty-three to spend his life in the service of poetry, saying: "To write every day was the method. To attend to what is said. To listen. To prepare myself for writing by learning everything I could, by hanging out in languages and enduring overdetermined desires..." The harvest is
awesome: near a hundred collections of poems (as well as more than fifteen
volumes of prose works: essays & fictions), representing but a fraction of
the total output. As a skilled practitioner of the long poem—*Axon Den-
dron Tree* (1967), *The Loom* (1975), *Mont Blanc* (1994), & more recently
Opening the Seals (2016)—Kelly is heir to both Pound & Zukofsky in his
vision of the poet as "scientist of the whole... to whom all data whatsoever
are of use / world-scholar." The title of his 1971 collection, *Flesh Dream
Book*, writes Kelly, "perhaps sets the priorities straight," locating "the three
great sources of human information: the flesh of sensory experience, dream
& vision, & the holy book of tradition & learning, shared through time."
If everything is of use in the alchemical *conjunctio* that is the poem, the
process of composition will be that of "finding the measure" where (so Jed
Rasula) "measure is musical base (or bass), and any trope is a turning in

a universe continually returning to its utterance of measure, or scale and proportion" (written by Jerome Rothenberg with Pierre Joris in *Poems for the Millennium*, vol. 2).

So, it's the masterful play between "deep image" & measure—visionary content & form—that marks the triumph of Kelly's work over a full lifetime.

(2) From Kelly again: "I believe that we can bring the deepest language from the mind. This language. All of it. I believe that when we listen deep, deep as cavefolk cut, we find the scratch or cough in stone from which the letters rose, still rise—the written language that comes before all speech.

"For we are primates of the sign" (from *Opening the Seals*, 2016).

Alejandra Pizarnik   Argentina, 1936–1972

TABULA RASA

cisterns in my memory
rivers in my memory
pools in my memory
always water in my memory
wind in my memory
blowing off my memory

Translated from Spanish by Yvette Siegert

THE NIGHT, THE POEM

Someone has found their true voice and tests it in the noon of the dead. Friend the color of ashes. Nothing more intense than the terror of losing your identity. This enclosure filled with my poems bears witness that the abandoned girl in a house in ruins is me.

I wrote with the soulless blindness of children throwing stones at a madwoman as if she were a blackbird. In fact, I do not write: I widen a breach so that the messages of the dead can reach me at twilight.

And this business of writing. I see through a mirror, in the dark. I predict a place that no one else has known. I sing of distances, I hear the voices of birds that were painted onto trees decked out like churches.

My nakedness gave you light like a lamp. You pressed my body to prevent the great cold of night, the blackness.

My words demand silence and abandoned spaces.

There are words with hands; barely written, they search my heart. There are words condemned like the lilac in a tempest. There are words resembling some among the dead, and from these I prefer the ones that evoke the doll of some unhappy girl.

Translated from Spanish by Yvette Siegert

OF THE SILENCE

> *… for it's all in some language I don't know.*
> Lewis Carroll, Through the Looking-Glass

> *I hear the world sobbing like a foreign language.*
> Cecilia Meireles

> *They went abroad to play this part.*
> Henri Michaux

> *Somebody killed something…*
> Lewis Carroll, Through the Looking-Glass

I

This doll dressed in blue is my emissary to the world.
She has the eyes of an orphan when it rains in the garden where a lilac bird devours the lilacs and a rosy bird devours the roses.

I am afraid of the grey wolf that disguises itself in the rain.

All you see, all that flees, all is unsayable.
Words close all doors.

I remember time leaning over the beloved poplars.
The archaic tone of my play required of my other self a lethal chamber.
I was the impossible and also a rupture for the impossible.

Oh the infernal color of my passions.
But I remained captive to the ancient tenderness.

There is no one to paint the greens.

Everything is orange.

If I am anything, it is violence.

The colors scratch against the silence and make decaying animals.

Then someone will try to write a poem. And it'll be with the shapes and colors and indifference and clarity (here I'll stop because I don't want to scare the children).

III

The poem is a space and it hurts.

I am not like my doll, who only feeds on bird's milk.

Memories of that voice in a somber morning watched over by a sun that gleams in the eyes of the turtles.

The one of that voice is a memory that makes me lose consciousness before the conjunction of sky-blue and green that is the sea and the sky.

I am preparing my death.

Translated from Spanish by Yvette Siegert

COMMENTARY

I forced myself / kicking and screaming / into language. (A.P.) And again: *Please Alejandra / open your eyes, / kindle the light / of birth.*

(1) Flora Alejandra Pizarnik was born to Russian Jewish parents in an immigrant district of Buenos Aires and died, probably a suicide, at age thirty-six. From a young age, she discovered a deep affinity with poets who, as she would later write, exemplified Hölderlin's claim that "poetry is a dangerous game," sacrificing everything in order to "annul the distance society imposes between poetry and life."

Like Artaud, one of her principal forerunners, Pizarnik understood poetry as an absolute demand, offering no concessions, forging its own terms, and requiring that life be lived entirely in its service. "Like every profoundly subversive act," she wrote, "poetry avoids everything but its own freedom and its own truth." In Pizarnik's poetry, this radical sense of "freedom" and "truth" emerges through a total engagement with her central themes: silence, estrangement, childhood, and—most prominently—death. Her great poem on madness is the book-length *Extraction of the Stone of Folly*, and her journals, which continued to be published after her death, read with a conscious sense of closing down: the record of a (failed) attempt to claim a life through poetry.

(Commentary by Cole Heinowitz.)

(2) From a late interview with Martha Isabel Moia: "The job of poetry is 'to heal the fundamental wound,' to 'rescue the abomination of human misery by embodying it.'"

Rochelle Owens USA, 1936–

BELONGED INTO SHEEPSHANK

Hunger
It is luck too. Hullabaloo Vishnu
Knowledge birds liturgic liverwort dynamite ne-not
Hideous Munt Jak
Barbarous.
Rosy.
Like emblem on the teeth. Two, the best
I pray thee, the nose leaking, the indians, the words
And songs
Nimble feeted.
Enlightened
Be a cold
Thing.
The same time. Tied to no place
Belonged into Sheepshank punjabi delusion
Unreal with no
Thing.
Lived.
Which my Pope. Bent over
Made pregnant ordained bursted the good
Fat foreskin
After entombment
And carpfishes.
Tonkin
Mere not Simon Magus. He was emptied
Before the man and animal mentally again and again
Between the hole of the mouth
And ass hole.
The base salty.
Some matter. I emit
I hold value and attached butter-fat love

Good selfishness
Burnt clay.
Unclearly christian
For a hump.

from **SOLARPOETICS, 1–3**

I

Wyh do we udnersntad a txet eevn fi the letetrs
aer in dsiordre
*

The letter A
like a membrane
melliferous the animal flesh
bread baking   butchery
Alphabet of blood and ash
Litanie   incantation
from the back part of her throat
salt for the stew   salt
for the bread
Sings the poet maudite
When I in my youth
strolled in a blue wool dress
I strolled in a circle
of blue

2

The reading brain   the eyes moving constantly
while reading
*

The letter B
when black letters of fire
patterns of animus across
the landscape
The place in the distance
Where the air
smells of poisoned rain
take one step after

the other
Where you do not want to go
An amalgam of words
in sequential order here where
you walk ahead   stop
raise your eyes

3

We identify only ten or twelve letters   quick jumps
three or four letters left and seven or eight letters right
*
The letter C circles
zigzags   animates the plaster
death cast   a solitary
workwoman then
From the back part of her throat
When I in my youth in a blue wool dress
I strolled among   maidens   monks
and birds   I strolled in wind
cold and heat
Across green volcanic hills
There In shadows   haze   smoke
in three dimensional space
piles of charred human
and animal bones

COMMENTARY

*possessed by the / last existence   the next / phase   of the shimmering /
heart of things // As if all / the old structures / the decayed regions / not
even a foul speck / on earth / captures the perpetual   springing world!
Selah* (R.O.)

There is a voice in Owens's work that seemed to some of us—when first
heard—like a fierce & unrelenting force of nature or like that, more aptly,
of some biblical Isaiah or Devorah, or of some other cracked (but real)
prophet mockingly come back to life. "Beauty will be convulsive or it will
not be," André Breton had written in setting the Surrealist agenda, by which
he meant (or we do) not beauty so much as *poetry*, with regard to which
"beauty" is but one-half (at best) of what we put into our workings. And
Owens—while she proclaimed herself, New York style, as "simply a poor
working girl [from Brooklyn] who was not even a graduate of Brooklyn

College or C.C.N.Y."—spoke a language even in her first poems ("Hunger / It is luck too. Hullabaloo Vishnu") that called forth voices (Hugo Ball or Khlebnikov or Tzara) from a not-so-distant past that she & we were newly claiming, making into *our* present. With her base in poetry, she came to a first public recognition through a series of plays (*Futz, Beclch, He Wants Shih, The Karl Marx Play*, others) to create what one of us would call "her theater of *impulse*" & to make her for a too brief time "perhaps the most profound tragic playwright in the American theater" (Ross Wetzteon, *Village Voice*).

Susan Howe USA, 1937–

from CHANTING AT THE CRYSTAL SEA

All male Quincys are now dead, excepting one.
John Wheelwright, "Gestures to the Dead"

1

Vast oblong space
dwindled to one solitary rock.

On
it I saw a heap of hay
impressed with the form
of a man.

Beleaguered Captain Stork
with his cane

on some quixotic skirmish.

Deserters arrived from Fort Necessity

All hope was gone.

Howe carrying a white flag of truce
went toward the water.

2

An Apostle in white
stood on a pavement of scarlet

Around him
stretched in deep sleep

lay the dark forms of warriors.

He was turned away
gazing on a wide waste.

His cry of alarm
astonished everyone.

3

A Council of War
in battle array
after some siege.

I ran to them
shouting as I ran
"Victory!"

Night closed in
weedy with flies.

The Moon slid
between moaning pines
and tangled vines.

4

Neutrals collected bones

or journeyed behind on foot

shouting at invisible doors

to open

There were guards who approached

stealthy as lynxes.

Always fresh footprints in the forest

We closed a chasm

then trod the ground firm

I carried your name

like a huge shield.

5

Because dreams were oracles
agile as wild-cats
we leapt on a raft of ice.

Children began a wail of despair
we carried them on our shoulders.

A wave
thrust our raft of ice
against a northern shore.

An Indian trail
led through wood and thicket

Light broke on the forest

The hostile town
was close at hand.

We screamed our war-cry
and rushed in.

6

It was Him
Power of the Clouds
Judge of the Dead
The sheep on his right
The goats on his left
And all the angels.

But from the book
backward on their knees
crawled neolithic adventurers known only to themselves.
They blazed with artifice
no pin, or kernel, or grain too small to pick up.
A baby with a broken face lay on the leaves
Hannibal—a rough looking man
rushed by with a bundle of sticks.

"Ah, this is fortunate," cried Forebear
and helped himself to me.

7

God is an animal figure
Clearly headless.
He bewitches his quarry
with ambiguous wounds.
The wolf or poor ass
had only stolen straw.

O sullen Silence
Nail two sticks together
and tell resurrection stories.

COMMENTARY

*A poem is an invocation, rebellious return to the blessedness of begin-
ning again, wandering free in pure process of forgetting and finding.* (S.H.)
And again: *Originality is the discovery of how to shed identity before the
magic mirror of Antiquity's sovereign power.*

A master archivist/collagist, like other poets in her lineage, Susan Howe
carries with her also a double inheritance through her Irish-born mother
& deeply New England–rooted father (descendant of Quincys & Howes).
Never losing track of those origins, she uses them also among the chief
building blocks for what she elsewhere calls "a telepathy of archives" &
"an American aesthetics of uncertainty." Of her book *My Emily Dickinson*
& much else, Pierre Joris has written tellingly:
  "If the sister-poet who guides her work is Emily Dickinson, then what
she has written of her predecessor's method, she has also made her own:
'Pulling pieces of geometry, geology, alchemy, philosophy, politics, biogra-
phy, biology, mythology, and philology from alien territory, a "sheltered"
woman audaciously invented a new grammar grounded in humility and
hesitation.' Along with which there is the more contemporary thrust of
Charles Olson qua scholar-poet-historian, but especially Olson's 'articulation of sound forms' (Howe's term) or that moment when (according
to Howe) he is at his wisest, observing that in Melville's *Billy Budd* 'the
stutter is the plot.' Core, then, to the work is the caesura of hesitation &
stutter, the birth-mark of the marginalized—be they women, visionaries,
or Indians—i.e., those left out of the smooth prose accounts of canonical
literary & politico-social history. Howe further: 'It's the stutter in American
literature that interests me. I hear the stutter as a sounding of uncertainty.
What is silenced or not quite silenced. All the broken dreams.'"

Diane Wakoski USA, 1937–

THE FATHER OF MY COUNTRY

All fathers in Western Civilization must have
a military origin. The
ruler,
governor,
yes,
he
was the
general at one time or other.
And George Washington
won the hearts
of his country—the rough military man
with awkward
sincere
drawing-room manners.

My father;
have you ever heard me speak of him? I seldom
do. But I had a father,
and he had military origins—or my origins from
him
are military,
militant. That is, I remember him only in uniform. But of the navy,
30 years a chief petty officer,
always away from home.

It is rough/hard for me to speak
now.
I'm not used to talking
about him.
Not used to naming his objects /
objects
that never surrounded me.

A woodpecker with fresh bloody crest
knocks
at my mouth. Father, for the first
time I say
your name. Name rolled in thick Polish parchment scrolls,

name of Roman candle drippings when I sit at my table
alone, each night,
name of naval uniforms and name of
telegrams, name of
coming home from your aircraft carrier,
name of shiny shoes.
name of Hawaiian dolls, name
of mess spoons, name of greasy machinery, and name of
stenciled names.
Is it your blood I carry in a test tube,
my arm,
to let fall, crack, and spill on the sidewalk
in front of the men
I know,
I love,
I know, and
want? So you left my house when I was under two.
being replaced by other machinery (my sister), and
I didn't believe you left me.

        This scene: the trunk yielding treasures of
        a green fountain pen, heart shaped mirror,
        amber beads, old letters with brown ink, and
        the gopher snake stretched across the palm tree
        in the front yard with woody trunk like monkey skins,
        and a sunset through the skinny persimmon trees. You
        came walking, not even a telegram or post card from
        Tahiti. Love, love, through my heart like ink in
        the thickest nibbed pen, black and flowing into words.
        You came, to me, and I at least six. Six doilies
        of lace, six battleship cannons, six old beerbottles,
        six thick steaks, six love letters, six clocks
        running backwards, six watermelons, and six baby
        teeth, a six cornered hat on six men's heads, six
        lovers at once or one lover at sixes and sevens;
        how I confuse
        all this with my
        dream
        walking the tightrope bridge
        with gold knots
        over

the mouth of an anemone/tissue spiral lips
and holding on so that the ropes burned
as if my wrists had been tied

If George Washington
had not
been the Father
of my Country
it is doubtful that I would ever have
found
a father. Father in my mouth, on my lips, in my
tongue, out of all my womanly fire,
Father I have left in my steel filing cabinet as a name on my birth
certificate, Father I have left in the teeth pulled out at
dentists' offices and thrown into their garbage cans,
Father living in my wide cheekbones and short feet,
Father in my Polish tantrums and my American speech, Father, not a
holy name, not a name I cherish but the name I bear, the name
that makes me one of a kind in any phone book because
you changed it, and nobody
but us
has it,
Father who makes me dream in the dead of night of the falling cherry
blossoms, Father who makes me know all men will leave me
if I love them,
Father who made me a maverick,
a writer,
a namer,
name/father, sun/father, moon/father, bloody mars/father,
other children said, "My father is a doctor,"
or
"My father gave me this camera,"
or
"My father took me to
the movies,"
or
"My father and I went swimming,"
but
my father is coming in a letter
once a month

for a while,
and my father
sometimes came in a telegram
but
mostly
my father came to me
in sleep, my father because I dreamed in one night that I dug
through the ash heap in back of the pepper tree and found a diamond
shaped like a dog, and my father called the dog and it came leaping
over to him and he walked away out of the yard down the road with
the dog jumping and yipping at his heels,

my father was not in the telephone book
in my city;
my father was not sleeping with my mother
at home;
my father did not care if I studied the
piano;
my father did not care what
I did;
and I thought my father was handsome and I loved him and I wondered
why
he left me alone so much,
so many years
in fact, but
my father made me what I am,
a lonely woman,
without a purpose, just as I was
a lonely child
without any father. I walked with words, words, and names,
names. Father was not
one of my words.
Father was not
one of my names. But now I say, "George, you have become my father,
in his 20th century naval uniform. George Washington, I need your
love; George, I want to call you Father, Father, my Father,"
Father of my country,
that is,
me. And I say the name to chant it. To sing it. To lace it around
me like weaving cloth. Like a happy child on that shining afternoon
in the palmtree sunset with her mother's trunk yielding treasures,

I cry and
cry,
Father,
Father,
Father,
have you really come home?

My name, Diane, declares
Moon Goddess, it too an oxymoron
as I control nothing,
not tides, or madness, not lovers,
or night blooming flowers. My name,
like so many names,
extravagantly, ironically, belies my organic or
celestial natures.

(D. W.)

There is a created personality or persona that emerges here & is the hallmark of Diane Wakoski's greatest work. With this in mind (*her* mind throughout) & in her ability to deliver, the poetry, while striking a note of the autobiographical—even to some ears (but not to hers) the "confessional"—asserts the truth of an imaginal life that moves (at several of its remarkable [cosmological] peaks) toward what Keats spoke of as *soul-making* or *world-making* & Wallace Stevens as a "supreme fiction." Wakoski, then, in her own words: "I feel a body of poetry has its own separate and organic life, just as a human being does. Conceiving of my poetry as a living organism, I began to conceive of it as a life. Of course, what it was representative of was my fantasy life. It drew from my own real life, but it began to have its own identity, its own life, and I felt that any life must have in it other people." And again: "In some ways I think of myself as a novelist in disguise, a mythologist—at least a storyteller, or a user of stories." Or, in a still larger frame—& as an indication too of what's stacked up against it: "Poetry is our history. / We study the stars / to understand temperatures. / Life and death are the only issues; / we often forget that—arranging our furniture, / washing our cars."

It is in line with this that she signs most of her later correspondence "I remain Yr Lady of Light, Diane" and somehow makes it stick.

Miyó Vestrini France/Venezuela, 1938–1991

from ONE DAY OF THE WEEK

When you were born
in 1938,
César Vallejo was dying.
When your little head,
your navel,
your virgin cunt,
entered the world
from between the beautiful legs of your mother,
they were lowering the poet into a hole.
They covered it up with dirt
and you,
you were covered by memory.
You could not choose.
Because if you choose
you live.
And if you live
you enjoy.
But joy is the horrific part of the dream:
sleep will be forever.
There will be the smell of fried peppers,
thundering voices in the bar.
It will be a day of the week,
when furniture changes places in the night
and in the mornings,
the women will talk to themselves.
Your nose will be congested and the right eyebrow
will fall more than the left.
The flattened hips,
the bad haircut and the body lost
in any slip that hides the fat in your waist.
If you had sad lunatics for grandparents,
it will be reflected in the report
of a responsible official.
They will cross your arms over your chest
and this is fatal,
because you can not
use Afrin

to breathe better.
It was fake that your hugs were convulsive
and your furies unpredictable.
Fake, the glass you still steam with your burps.
Fake, your nipples, your red freckles.
Last night you decided:
if I cannot sleep,
I'll choose death.
But you could not have expected the leg of lamb to melt in your mouth,
soft,
milky,
on your tongue.
You could only say:
two childbirths,
ten abortions,
no orgasms.
You took a long sip of wine.
Vallejo also sought a leg of lamb
on the menu of La Coupole.
All watched his stupid eyes,
while he could only think about the quiet ears of Beethoven.
He had asked his companion:
Why do you not love me anymore?
What did I do?
Where did I fail?
The sausage in the casserole left grease stains on his shirt.
Like you,
he felt compassion tired his body
and tried to guess who would be born on this night,
while trying to fall asleep.
Dying
requires time and patience.

Translated from Spanish by Cassandra Gillig & Anne Boyer

COMMENTARY

Writing is not important, she wrote, / and signed her name in small print, / believing it apocryphal. (M.V.)

The narrative feature of Miyó Vestrini's poetry (based on straightfor-ward—& often raw—speech) displays a sardonic & fierce critique of multiple aspects of human existence. As her translators wrote in the preface to *Grenade in Mouth,* from which the poem above is taken: "If Vestrini is a confessional poet, what she is confessing is not a set of personal problems: it is a fatal disappointment with the world at large. Her work is less a self-exposure than a set of incantations. Critics have called Miyó Vestrini the poet of 'militant death.'... These poems are spells for a death that might live eternally, for what Vestrini offers readers is a fundamental paradox: how to create, through writing, an enduring extinction. Her poems are not soft or brooding laments. They are bricks hurled at empires, ex-lovers, and any saccharine-laced lie that parades itself as the only available truth."

Vestrini killed herself with an overdose of clonazepam in 1991.

ADDENDUM

KATHY ACKER USA, 1947–1997

from **Pussy, King of the Pirates**

I'm no longer a child and I still want to be, to live with the pirates. Because I want to live forever in wonder. The difference between me as a child and me as an adult is this and only this: when I was a child, I longed to travel into, to live in wonder. Now, I know, as much as I can know anything, that to travel into wonder is to be wonder. So it matters little whether I travel by plane, by rowboat, or by book. Or, by dream. I do not see, for there is no I to see. That is what the pirates know. There is only seeing and, in order to go to see, one must be a pirate.

.....

Death is another bar which lies several steps below the normal world. I'm at its threshold, but not yet in it. Its doorway is doorless.

.....

For the poet, the world is word. Words. Not that precisely. Precisely: the world and words fuck each other.

LeRoy Clarke Trinidad & Tobago, 1938–2021

from *BUSH WOMAN*

... The air is laden with the smell of blood
Thick with crime and brine of cowards
Who eat and talk shit. Their manifestos
Are condoms, bursting with pus; belching stupidities
Over the squalor of a urine-burnt mange
The gummy glazed eye of a rolled over bitch
Mirrors the rotting teeth of rainbows.

Nothing grows here, not even tadpoles
Take to the muddy waters around.
Poverty has clogged the appetite for love,
it turns on itself, bites its own tail
With the enraged commerce of new cannibals.
Evil howls: gunshots are menacing rain
On ghetto rooftops, pebbles of pure hate
Pitched to a chatter-clatter for what?

She is dead!

That one with coals for her black eyes,
Where I have often entered and flamed, who
Left for an evening stroll and has not come back.
She is dead.

I place seven drops of rum
On the center of her hardened precincts,
Fill her stubborn ear with Papa Legba.
Her adulterous body, her limbs of spiders
Do not show it, exquisite whore of my clad!

She is dead!

Forthwith, the deep hunger of her old bones
Arrives on huge waves of ants
To cover the floor, black...
Ominous belly, ground of easy murders, her
Drunken blood proclaims her prodigious seasons
Filled with hours of knotted sap.

She is dead

She draws back to take cover
In dreams of beetle and bug.

The wind, the faint echo of a dying bird,
Turns around in the mirrors of midday,
Her curve hardens as a geometric fact
Among un-purged sand and its rusty bits.

She is dead

But this is only an eruption of delightful
Cruelties, hatched serpents and caterpillars
From odd copulations in the void.
With my spleen breaking the skin,
I kiss the sand of your lips.
I must have you.
No trace of bird or lizard, no hedge
Is left behind a taste of molten bronze!

She is dead

On the stout tomb of cardinal stone
The fresh corpse of a hunting dog
Awaits the lift of circling corbeaux,
I shall perish here!
I dip my cut finger into the wounded sea
The corpulence of a gluttonous salt
Has lost its savour.
On the altars of her chewed breasts
I plant corn, I plant peppers
That Gene grows so well in Aripo.

With the deep dark tree roots
Of your injured night, with furious
Dreams broken from aquatic branches...
I reap her yams; I reap her cassava,
I dance my salt dance on the rim of hours,
I drink fish broth. Her cheeks redden,
Round the sun, with love!

COMMENTARY

*for drawing and building things, using leaves, wood, stone, shells and
angel hair in the skies! The map of my palm! Fine lines between spaces
within forms that transmit meaning of fantastic weaving, to radiate the
spirit of the thing, and make the thing speak, singing out its eternal truth,
its personality.* (L.C.)

Poet & painter, LeRoy Clarke was also an Orisha priest. In all his works (especially in his Blakean illuminated poetry), Clarke goes deep into the mechanisms of worship & ritual, aiming to reach & get in touch with the Yoruba gods. In our selection, the poem is meant to describe a *bush woman's*—a shamaness's—search to bring back to life the prophetic power in a desolated world. For this, she performs a spoken *vevé* (in its original form, a ritualized line drawing that represents the power of the Yoruba gods) addressed to Yemayá, the mermaid goddess of fertility & creation, guardian of the spirits of all the creatures on earth.

Quincy Troupe USA, 1939–

ERRANÇITIES

for Édouard Glissant

I

the mind wanders as a line of poetry taking flight meanders
in the way birds spreading wings lift into space knowing
skies are full of surprises like errançities encountering restless
journeys as in the edgy solos of miles davis or jimi hendrix

listen to night-song of sea waves crashing in foaming with voices
carrying liquid histories splashing there on rock or sandy shores
after traveling across time space & distance it resembles a keening
language of music heard at the tip of a sharp blade of steel

cutting through air singing as it slices a head clean from its neck
& you watch it drop heavily as a rock landing on earth & rolling
like a bowling ball the head leaving a snaking trail of blood reminding
our brains of errançities wandering through our lives every day

as metaphors for restless movement bring sudden change
surprise in the way you hear errançities of double meaning
layered in music springing from secret memories as echoes
resounding through sea & blue space is what our ears know

& remember hearing voices speaking in tongues carrying history
blooming as iridescent colors of flowers multifarious as rainbows
arching across skies multilingual as joy or sorrow evoked inside
our own lives when poetic errançities know their own forms

2

what is history but constant recitations of flawed people pushed
over edges of boundaries of morality pursuing wars pillage
enslavement of spirits is what most nations do posing as governing
throughout cycles of world imagination plunder means profit

everywhere religion is practiced on topography as weapons used
as tools written in typography to conquer minds to slaughter for gold
where entire civilizations become flotsam floating across memory seas
heirloom trees cut down as men loot the planet without remorse

their minds absent of empathy they remember/know only greed
these nomadic avatars of gizzard-hearted darth vaders who celebrate
"shock-doctrines" everywhere ballooning earnings-sheet bottom lines
their only creed for being on earth until death cuts them down

3

but poetry still lives somewhere in airstreams evoking creative breath
lives in the restless sea speaking a miscegenation of musical tongues
lives within the holy miracle of birds elevating flight into dreams & song
as errançities of spirits create holy inside accumulation of daybreaks

raise everyday miraculous voices collaborating underneath star-nailed
clear black skies & the milky eye of a full moon over guadeloupe
listen to the mélange of tongues compelling in nature's lungs in new york
city tongues flung out as invitations for sharing wondrous songs

with nature is a summons to recognize improvisation as a surprising path
to divergence through the sound of scolopendra rooted somewhere here
in wonder when humans explode rhythms inside thickets of words/puns
celebrating the human spirit of imagination is what poets seek

listen for cries of birds lifting off for somewhere above the magical
pulse of sea waves swirling language immense with the winds sound
serenading us through leaves full of ripe fruit sweet as fresh water
knowing love might be deeper than greed & is itself a memory

a miracle always there might bring us closer to reconciliation inside
restless métisse commingling voices of errançities wandering within
magic the mystery of creation pulling us forward to wonder to know
human possibility is always a miraculous gift is always a conundrum

muddy water / underbottomed spirits crawling, nightmares / of ship-
wrecked bones, bones gone home to stone, to stone / bones gone home to
stone, to stone / riverbottomed, underbellied spirits (Q.T.)

A major figure in the Black Arts movement & elsewhere, Quincy Troupe is celebrated also as a writer & a chronicler, in particular of the great musical artist Miles Davis, the coauthor in effect of *Miles Davis: The Autobiography* and its follow-up, *Miles and Me*. As a poet of multiple localisms, he shares with the Martinican poet Édouard Glissant (above) the idea of a "*tout-monde*" (whole world) poetry, in which our world emerges as a network of communities & cultures that constantly interchange & develop new forms in the process. Of which he tells us further: "in this... I'm trying to bring all the 'cross-fertilizing' aspects of language and forms together... into something I hope will elevate the cross-cultural aspects of the American—not English—language." And again: "Poetic language comes from this mysterious place deep inside us, like earthquakes that come from somewhere deep inside the earth, which is a body, some say a woman's body. Poetry also comes from a body of communal gestures and speech, fragments and words and sounds and rhythms, articulations and all of that. When we hear dogs barking, car horns honking, the sound of music, everything, even colors, that's all in the mix. For me it is miraculous that we can harness or attempt to harness the way that poetry and/or writing expresses itself—through people like James Joyce in *Ulysses*, Pablo Neruda, Lorca, Ezra Pound, T. S. Eliot and Aimé Césaire, Derek Walcott and William Faulkner, Henry Dumas and Gabriel García Márquez—through a kind of natural, incredible use of language" (from an interview by Jan Garden Castro).

José Kozer   Cuba/USA, 1940–

KAFKA REBORN

It's a modest two-story house not far from the river on a narrow street in
   Prague. In the early morning
between the 11th
and 12th of November he awoke with a start and descended the stairs to the
   small kitchen with its round table and linden-wood chair, its portable stove
   and methyl-blue flame. He lit

the burner
and the fire became at once (three) flames reflected in the window's three panes:
   smell of sulphur. He wished

to go

to the dining nook to drink a medicinal tea of honey and boldo leaves, he moved
the chair and settled in before a sienna-colored clay bowl which he had placed,
he'd forgotten when, on the six-colored wicker tray,

Felicia's

gift; and once again

Felicia appeared her hair in braids and the radiance of candles reflected on the
white oval of that face greedy for consecrated loaves and cakes, that face

three times

a burst of flames in the window pane: she appeared and was again three times
the child of her dead, a few chamber players

responded to the stroke

of a triangle and the stroke of a bell (at three) in the high belfry not far from the
river: they took their ease, ten

cups, ten

chairs in the immense country house with its mansard roofs, the house in which
bay windows and glass doors (barns and sheds) were open day and night, the
water

and the sponges

shone. Yes: it was another time, and a chorus of girls tended the tea pots
(boiling), the eucalyptus (boiling), the marjoram and a digestive water (mint
leaves) respiratory

waters: at peace

at peace (at last), he climbed the stairs and saw himself stretched out in the
window pane (at last) no crowd of birds

in the window.

Translated from Spanish by Mark Weiss

MERCURIAL MOTION

Ineffable
translucent
white
becomes
a
baroque

pearl
(alone)
in
the
mirror
as
she
fastens
the
platinum
necklace
an
anniversary
present
behind
her:
it
regains
transparency
a
primary
condition
of
Li
Ching
Chao's
naked
nipples.
I
raise
Chinese
mamoncillos
to
my
mouth,
bite
rind
(nipple)
suck
white
viscous

(nipple)
fruit
I
eat
three
meals
(not
certainly
in
sequence)
three
meals
three
languages:
shark
fin
soup.
Sliced
papaya
(drops
of
lime
juice).
Herring
in
brine
with
dill
and
onion.
I
fasten
(unfasten)
Li
Ching
Chao's
necklace
three
times
a
day

(at
night
three
candles)
(printed
kimono
thrown
on
the
floor)
(slow
caterpillar
progress).
Wandering.
Reverberation.
I
receive
the
immanent
grace
of
Guadalupe
(Li
Ching
Chao)
turned
aside
the
middle
distance
the
(second)
condition
of
primordial
mercury:
transfixed
I'm
aware
(transcribe
it

here)
that
I've
left
on
the
beloved's
neck
the
(third)
trace
of
waterlily
(duckweed)
its
(snow-white)
skin
efflorescence
of
fish.

Translated from Spanish by Mark Weiss

I don't have a problem of language, I have a religious, metaphysical, philosophical, ethical problem. Language after all is not an end in itself, it's an instrument; it's not autonomous, it's a vehicle… Yes, for me, what moves me is religious difficulty, the difficulty before the death of the body. (J.K., interview with Jacobo Sefamí in "De la imaginación poética," trans. Peter Boyle)

(1) Writes Mark Weiss qua translator & longtime confidant: "José Kozer is one of Cuba's preeminent poets. Widely influential throughout the Spanish-speaking world, he is a major figure of the *neobarroco,* the international movement that traces its ancestry to the intricate, syntactically-complex poetry of José Lezama Lima [see "A Third Gallery"] and Baroque poet Luís de Góngora, and for which Kozer coedited *Medusario,* the definitive anthology of the movement. Already a published poet by the time he left Cuba for the United States at age 18, the shock of total immersion in an English-speaking environment made it difficult for him to write until he found himself once more in his native idiom, through work as a teacher of Spanish literature and especially through his marriage to his Spanish-born wife Guadalupe Barrenechea. He was already prolific, but once freed from teaching, his output has been prodigious: his morning, every morning,

begins with a draft of a new poem, which he revises in the afternoon and rarely revisits...

"Certain themes recur, among them, not surprisingly, Judaism, and the figure of Kafka, like Kozer an assimilated Jew. (There are hundreds of poems that bear Kafka's name or his presence.) Guadalupe appears too, as she does in much of his work, in the poem from 'Mercurial Motion' included here, where she seems to dance with Kozer's imagined mistress, Li Ching Chao (Li Quingzhao, 1084–1155), a great Chinese poet of subtle erotic longing. It's not too much of an exaggeration to see a key part of Kozer's oeuvre as an extended poem of conjugal love."

(2) Of Kozer's further resources, translator Peter Boyle writes: "A poet of varied and unpredictable fusions, of the widest layers of the animate and inanimate world, Kozer is a prolific creator with... an aesthetic continuity marked by a very specific set of poetic strategies and a single dominant layout for his poems. This stylistic continuity rests in turn on a vision of poetry not as autobiography nor as simply playing games, however clever, with words but as the deepest spiritual task, the daily zen-like practice of concentration and selflessness.... An experimentalist who wants his poetry to have the edginess of surprise, Kozer does not seem afraid of beauty or deep emotion.... This insistence on the poem as a vehicle for surprise combined with a strong underlying ethical or religious sensibility is at the center of Kozer's achievement as a poet."

N.B. To be noted, too, is his determination to write at least a poem a day, toward the goal of ten thousand poems in a lifetime.

Homero Aridjis   Mexico, 1940–

from **LOS POEMAS DEL DOBLE**

I

I grabbed my face
and brought it to the mirror

Searched my eyes
but did not know them

Observed my gestures
weak from terror

He left me fearful
of my self

2
You walk at night   alone
your own self's equal

counting out your hearbeats
in the windows' faded wings

on turning around a corner
a man tears off your face

beheaded you remain
at the foot of your own shadow

while someone in the distance
looks at you through your eyes

. . . . .

6
I closed the door and waited for my double
but instead of the expected face
a macaw burst forth from the white wall
the color of red fire.

Like an arrow tipped in blue
—hyacinth hallucination—
a parrot with yellow eyes
landed on the table.

The Kandinskys then arrived
wings spread wide and blue
belly orange, head in brown
their throats a breathless J.

A total symphony of greens,
the undisputed parrot came,
its chest, its beak, its neck,
its head and all in green.

Not a single one needed to show
credentials of who he was. There was
a congress of parrots in my mind.
They were going to pick the most handsome.

They began to discuss the value
of begreen, waxgreen, fieldgreen,
bluegreen, purplegreen, greygreen.

In view of all such circumstances
I postponed until the next day
the encounter with my double.

7
I opened up his eyes
saw
my living darkness

is there a boatman anywhere
able to shift the light
from limit unto limit?

yes
or
no?

8
Beyond you
I do not exist not even I
there is no definite horizon
nor hands to touch the light

all being is a surface
a place a stone that's all

Beyond me
you do not exist not even you

9
to breathe out the ghost
is task of the living

to drink memories
into their eyes
is role of the dead

there breaks today
in my mouth
the bread of illusion

10
one hour
hurls shadows
onto another

one butterfly wing
put in place
at my eye's horizon

the double has vanished
at the end of the road
total blackness is mine

Mexico, Saturday–Sunday 6–7–8 of March 1999

Translated from Spanish by Jerome Rothenberg

COMMENTARY

I dream of seeing the face of the earth / mother of beings and mother of my mother / and the face of heaven / father of air and father of my father / now / its shadow appears in my mouth (H.A.)

Homero Aridjis's move from Contepec, Michoacán, to Mexico City came early, building from there a life as poet, novelist, editor, & sometime diplomat, more recently (through his self-formed Group of One Hundred) as spokesman for endangered species (animals & humans; ecosystems & deep cultures). Of his lineage—ancient & modern both—North American poet Kenneth Rexroth wrote, by way of introduction/welcome: "Few poets better demonstrate the spread of an international style throughout the world, and the reduction and synthesis of the great writers of the heroic age of modern poetry to an international negotiable idiom. Influence hunters can find traces of San Juan de la Cruz, Góngora, and Eluard in the poetry of Aridjis, and behind them the mystical Nahuatl chants of the Aztec priests, the contemporary initiation songs of the Huichol Indians.... This does *not* mean at all that he is a bundle of influences; quite the opposite. It means that he is a visionary poet of lyrical bliss, crystalline concentration and infinite spaces.... I can think of no poet of Aridjis' generation in the Western Hemisphere who is as much at ease in the blue spaces of illumination—the illumination of transcending love. These are words for a new Magic Flute."

Lyn Hejinian USA, 1941–2024

from **MY LIFE**

A name trimmed
with colored
ribbons

They are seated in the shadows husking corn, shelling peas. Houses of wood set in the ground. I try to find the spot at which the pattern on the floor repeats. Pink, and rosy, quartz. They wade in brackish water. The leaves outside the window tricked the eye, demanding that one see them, focus on them, making it impossible to look past them, and though holes were opened through the foliage, they were as useless as portholes underwater looking into a dark sea, which only reflects the room one seeks to look out from. Sometimes into benevolent and other times into ghastly shapes. It speaks of a few of the rather terribly blind. I grew stubborn until blue as the eyes overlooking the bay from the bridge scattered over its bowls through a fading light and backed by the protest of the bright breathless West. Each bit of jello had been molded in tiny doll dishes, each trembling orange bit a different shape, but all otherwise the same. I am urged out rummaging into the sunshine, and the depths increase of blue above. A paper hat afloat on a cone of water. The orange and gray bugs were linked from their mating but faced in opposite directions, and their scrambling amounted to nothing. This simply means that the imagination is more restless than the body. But, already, words. Can there be laughter without comparisons. The tongue lisps in its hilarious panic. If, for example, you say, "I always prefer being by myself," and, then, one afternoon, you want to telephone a friend, maybe you feel you have betrayed your ideals. We have poured into the sink the stale water in which the iris died. Life is hopelessly frayed, all loose ends. A pansy suddenly, a web, a trail remarkably's a snail's. It was an enormous egg, sitting in the vineyard—an enormous rock-shaped egg. On that still day my grandmother raked up the leaves beside a particular pelargonium. With a name like that there is a lot you can do. Children are not always inclined to choose such paths. You can tell by the eucalyptus tree, its shaggy branches scatter buttons. In the afternoons, when the shades were pulled for

my nap, the light coming through was of a dark yellow, nearly orange, melancholy, as heavy as honey, and it made me
thirsty. That doesn't say it all, nor even a greater part. Yet it
seems even more incomplete when we were there in person.
Half the day in half the room. The wool makes one itch and
the scratching makes one warm. But herself that she obeyed
she dressed. It talks. The baby is scrubbed everywhere, he is
an apple. They are true kitchen stalwarts. The smell of
breathing fish and breathing shells seems sad, a mystery, rap-
turous, then dead. A self-centered being, in this different
world. A urinating doll, half-buried in sand. She is lying on
her stomach with one eye closed, driving a toy truck along
the road she has cleared with her fingers. I mean untroubled
by the distortions. That was the fashion when she was a
young woman and famed for her beauty, surrounded by
beaux. Once it was circular and that shape can still be seen
from the air. Protected by the dog. Protected by foghorns,
frog honks, cricket circles on the brown hills. It was a
message of happiness by which we were called into the room,
as if to receive a birthday present given early, because it was
too large to hide, or alive, a pony perhaps, his mane trimmed
with colored ribbons.

COMMENTARY

*The idea of the person enters poetics where art and reality, or intentional-
ity and circumstance, meet.* (L.H.) And again: *A word is a bottomless pit.*

(1) While Hejinian remains identified with a late twentieth-century movement of experimental and language-centered poetry, her own work, as
Pierre Joris describes it, "has gone (through language & a genuine—not
academic—strategy of deconstruction) into areas of self-identity & representation presumably off-limits for late twentieth-century 'language writing.'" For this the key work was *My Life*, which announced the reemergence of the first-person voice into the heart of "language poetry," without
weakening but rather reenforcing its experimental thrust.

(2) "Because we have language we find ourselves in a peculiar relationship
to the objects, events, and situations which constitute what we imagine of
the world. Language generates its own characteristics in the human psychological and spiritual condition. This psychology is generated by the struggle
between language and that which it claims to depict or express, by our
overwhelming experience of the vastness and uncertainty of the world, and
by what often seems to be the inadequacy of the imagination that longs to

know it, and, for the poet, the even greater inadequacy of the language that appears to describe, discuss, or disclose it.

"This inadequacy, however, is merely a disguise for other virtues" (L.H., in *The Rejection of Closure*).

Simon Ortiz Acoma Pueblo / USA, 1941–

TELLING ABOUT COYOTE

Old Coyote...
"If he hadn't looked back
everything would have been okay
... like he wasn't supposed to,
but he did,
and as soon as he did, he lost all his power,
his strength"

"... you know, Coyote
is in the origin and all the way
through... he's the cause
of all the trouble, the hard times
that things have... "

"Yet, he came so close
to having it easy.
But he said,
"Things are too easy... "
Of course he was mainly bragging,
shooting his mouth.
The existential Man,
Dostocvsky Coyotc.

"He was on his way to Zuni
to get married on that Saturday,
and on the way there
he ran across a gambling party.
A number of other animals were there.
                    He sat in
for a while, you know, pretty sure
of himself, you know like he is,
sure that he would win something.

But he lost
everything. Everything.
And that included his skin, his fur
which was the subject of envy
of all the other animals around.

Coyote had the prettiest,
the glossiest, the softest fur
that ever was. And he lost that.

So some mice
finding him shivering in the cold
beside a rock felt sorry for him.
'This poor thing, beloved,'
they said, and they got together
just some old scraps of fur
and glued them on Coyote with piñon pitch.

And he's had that motley fur ever since.
You know, the one that looks like
scraps of an old coat, that one."

Coyote, old man, wanderer,
where you going, man?
Look up and see the sun.
Scored, an old raggy blanket
at the back of the closet nobody wants.

"At this one conference
of all the animals there was a bird
with the purest white feathers.
His feathers were like, ah . . .
like the sun was shining on it
all the time but you could look at it
and you wouldn't be hurt by the glare.
It was easy and gentle to look at.
And he was Crow.
He was sitting on one side of the fire.
And the fire was being fed large pine logs,
and Crow was sitting downwind
from the fire, and the wind was blowing
that way . . .
And Coyote was there.

He was envious of Crow because
all the other animals were saying,
'Wowee, look at that Crow, man,
just look at him,' admiring Crow.
Coyote began to scheme.
He kept on throwing pine logs into the fire,
ones with lots of pitch in them.
And the wind kept blowing,
all night long . . .
                    Let's see,
the conference was about deciding
the seasons—when they should take place—
and it took a long time to decide that . . .
And when it was over, Crow was covered
entirely with soot. The blackest soot
from the pine logs.
And he's been like that since then."

"Oh yes, that was the conference
when Winter was decided
that it should take place
when the Dog's hair got long.
                    Dog said,
'I think Winter should take place
when my hair gets long.'
And it was agreed that it would. I guess
no one else offered a better reason."

                    Who?
                    Coyote?
O,
O yes, last time . . .
when was it,
I saw him somewhere
between Muskogee and Tulsa,
heading for Tulsy Town I guess,
just trucking along.

He was heading into some oak brush thicket,
just over the hill was a creek.
Probably get to Tulsa in a couple days,
drink a little wine,

tease with the Pawnee babes,
sleep beside the Arkansas River,
listen to the river move,
…hope it don't rain,
hope the river don't rise.
He'll be back. Don't worry.
He'll be back.

COMMENTARY

(1) From an interview with Simon Ortiz, a towering figure in the new American Indian poetry:

Why do you write? Who do you write for?

[S.O.] Because Indians always tell a story. The only way to continue is to tell a story and that's what Coyote says. The only way to continue is to tell a story and there is no other way. Your children will not survive unless you tell something about them—how they were born, how they came to this certain place, how they continued.

Who do you write for besides yourself?

[S.O.] For my children, for my wife, for my mother and my father and my grandparents and then reverse order that way so that I may have a good journey on my way back home.

(2) For an instance of the widespread influence of the Coyote figure beyond its Native American sources, the reader can check out "The Call of the Wild" by USAmerican poet Gary Snyder (in "A Fourth Gallery," above). It is Snyder, too, who hammers the point home for all of us: "Of all the uses of native American lore in modern poetry, the presence of the Coyote figure, the continuing presence of Coyote, is most striking."

That the name of the best known of the pre-American Native poets, Nezahualcoyotl, meant "Hungry" or "Fasting Coyote" is also of some interest.

Rodolfo Hinostroza Peru, 1941–2016

PROBLEMS OF BRABANTIO

> *O thou foul thief! Where hast thou*
> *Stow'd my daughter? Damn'd as thou*
> *Art thou hast enchanted her.*
>
> **Shakespeare**

A wave of migratory birds flew over your forehead
you were the girl from the orange trees
                              nothing is true but exile
a band / some music / seashells
                              I more dead than alive
kicking horse skulls across the beach
                              & it called to me
the watch will last all night
                              I will stay awake beneath the stars
counting the chords of the crickets
                              as such: ba bek brak bek
Nobody: my name is Nobody
                              I amble about and I lose myself on the planet
the borders are closed
                              I say *América América*
my memory is not the memory
                              nothing suffices there is no past
dust off old news place there one's finger
                              spawn and die.

& my tribe circumcised the skulls
                              ingested aphrodisiacs
herbs to glimpse the great beyond
                              the shadow of a car something
you don't hear me come stronger than the night
you haven't found some names crossed out on the wall:
                              Palmyra
Byzantium Babylonia Texacoatl
                              Jerusalem O Jerusalem
                              & there were virgins in
the walls
        blue tresses copper belly
                              flowers consumed during the feast
a tongue an odor
                      thus sang the poets
lost syllables babbling dead tongues
                              crossbred races
& one Power triumphed over another Power
                              one tongue slew another tongue

the conquistadors danced the sweet canticles of the enemy
my head spins
                the orange tree girl you were
I washed floors in Amsterdam
                        I praised the technique
                            Oh Most potent, grave and

reverent signiors
           The Earth is one.

III

There were no countries
                Anatolia Brittany Pomerania
                        incessant migrations
slow waves of birds / landscapes of deluge
we are all Black / Jewish / Homeless
                     no God is worth so much
Doors won't prevail
            we will drag away a total a force
the meadows will not die with me
              I have left behind a voice a call
the oranges of Wesselmann
          the sun's ovule
               Mater dolcissima.

IV

Keeping watch numbs me
          América América
             you chuck 21 stones into the sea
Yom Kippur this morning
             you were the girl of the orange trees
sunken civilizations
          there is no past I have no memory
no master no tradition
        everything is reborn at dawn
             the heavens have rotated
I don't recognize myself
         no one has authority
           a serpent is no better than
a camel
       One man than another man
         I have spoken Love

Esselentíssimos signores
            the call deep in the night
                        torn from dreams
sluggish.

Translated from Spanish by Anthony Seidman

COMMENTARY

like a tympanum that separates me from the rest / of things / the perfect equilibrium of the living / with dead bodies' memory (R.H.)

Writes his translator, Anthony Seidman: "Rodolfo Hinostroza is recognized as a bridge between such earlier poets as Vallejo and contemporary Peruvian poets. Indeed, his most acclaimed collection of poetry, *Contra natura* (1971) [from which the poem above is excerpted] made an impression as indelible as Vallejo's *Trilce*.

"The poems in *Contra Natura* unleash auguries, assemblies of voices across epochs and languages, a parliament of the shades and the living, yet the poet's presences always remain, an Imagination, an Emanation from the Imaginer, the Mage, the Images dissolving from Imperial Rome to the battlefields of 1960's Vietnam, the logic of the stars, the poetry of Dryden and Shakespeare, the counterculture, impossible Utopias, Eros, wild and young vagabonds in love with poetry, all of that forming a radiant bouquet that sparkles and dissipates in the unending and dark liquidity of the cosmos. This Poet, too, sees a World in a Grain of Sand, and intuits the constellations within himself and the one he touches" ("Some Thoughts on Rodolfo Hinostroza," in *Dispatches from the Poetry Wars*, June 15, 2018).

N.B. The name Brabantio is that of the father of Desdemona in Shakespeare's *Othello*, which is the source for the poem's epigraph.

Antonio Cisneros   Peru, 1942–2012

THEN, IN THE WATERS OF CONCHÁN (SUMMER 1978)

Then a great whale anchored itself in the waters of Conchán.
It was blue when the sky blued, and black under fog.
And it was blue.
Some saw it come from the North (where they say there are many).
Some saw it come from the South (land of lions and ice).
Others say it sprouted like a mushroom, or like leaves of rue.
People tell of it in Villa El Salvador,

poor among the poor.
All raised behind white hills, and in the sand:
People like quicksand in the sand.
(The only sea they know is fierce, is a smell on the wind)
Wind riffling the blue back of the whale's corpse.
Aluminum islet under sun.
That came from the North and from the South
and sprung alone from the tide.
The great dead whale.
Water spooks the authorities:
blue stink along the beaches of Conchán.
The great dead whale.
(The authorities protect the health of summerfolk).
Soon the whale will rot like a ripe summer fig.
The stench, let's say:
40 putrid cattle in the sea
(or 200 sheep or 1,000 dogs).
The authorities don't know how to flee so much dead flesh.
The summerfolk ward off a stink that starts with sea nettles on damp sand.
In the sandlands of Villa El Salvador, the people never rest.
They know, the poorest of the poor,
that past the dunes a fleshy island floats without a keeper.
As twilight comes
from sand, not from the sea,
they've sharpened the best kitchen knives, the master butcher's ax.
And Villa El Salvador's few swimmers swam out, armed.
At midnight fought the whirlpools where the waves spumed.
The great whale beautiful, heaved by the frigid swells.
Beautiful still.
May 10,000 mouths receive that meat.
May that skin roof 100 houses.
May all that oil fuel the nights
and frying pans of summer.

Translated from Spanish by Rowan Sharp

COMMENTARY

*And finding myself in such difficult times I settled into the softest and
most pestilent / regions of the whale.* (A.C.)

(1) Antonio Cisneros's poetry involved—since its beginnings—a revision of

the past. From his first collections, history unfolds as a counterbalance to our present. This exploration also comes with a quest for different modes of expression (from his early use of epigrams to his later turn to open forms akin to the USAmerican "long poem"), in which the *I*—the poet as both a maker & a seer—embodies the act of witnessing. As with Hinostroza (above), Cisneros's poetry aims to challenge the modes of writing initiated by Vallejo & in so doing to initiate a Peruvian postmodernism of their own.

(2) "Then, in the Waters of Conchán" is the final poem of Cisneros's collection *Chronicle of the Christ Child of Chilca*. The poem tells the story of a whale that ran aground on a beach in Peru. This sudden & unexpected arrival, amid the poverty of the inhabitants, causes an immediate shock & raises a question about fate & chance. The text incorporates testimonial fragments that, along with the use of repetition & traditional turns of phrase, attain a biblical & prophetic tone. For Raúl Zurita & Forrest Gander, writing jointly: "It is perhaps the only Latin American poem that might have been plucked from the Bible" (in *Pinholes in the Night*).

Michael Palmer   USA, 1943–

THE REPUBLIC OF DREAMS

She lay so still that
as she spoke

a spider spun a seamless web
upon her body

as we spoke
and then her limbs came loose

one by one
and so my own

AUTOBIOGRAPHY

All clocks are clouds.

Parts are greater than the whole.

A philosopher is starving in a rooming house, while it rains outside.

He regards the self as just another sign.

Winter roses are invisible.

Late ice sometimes sings.

A and *Not-A* are the same.

My dog does not know me.

Violins, like dreams, are suspect.

I come from Kolophon, or perhaps some small island.

The strait has frozen, and people are walking—a few skating—across it.

On the crescent beach, a drowned deer.

A woman with one hand, her thighs around your neck.

The world is all that is displaced.

Apples in a stall at the streetcorner by the Bahnhof, pale yellow to blackish red.

Memory does not speak.

Shortness of breath, accompanied by tinnitus.

The poet's stutter and the philosopher's.

The self is assigned to others.

A room for which, at all times, the moon remains visible.

Leningrad café: a man missing the left side of his face.

Disappearance of the sun from the sky above Odessa.

True description of that sun.

A philosopher lies in a doorway, discussing the theory of colors

with himself

the theory of self with himself, the concept of number, eternal return, the sidereal pulse

logic of types, Buridan sentences, the *lekton*.

Why now that smoke off the lake?

Word and things are the same.

Many times white ravens have I seen.

That all planes are infinite, by extension.

She asks, Is there a map of these gates?

She asks, Is this one called Passages, or is that one to the west?

Thus released, the dark angels converse with the angels of light.

They are not angels.

Something else.

for Poul Borum

COMMENTARY

You would like to live somewhere // but this is not permitted / You may not even think of it // lest the thinking appear as words // and the words as things / arriving in competing waves // from the ruins of that place (M.P.) And again: *It is true / that we do not write, / that a measureless silence / writes in our place.*

Behind the often noted (& often misconstrued) elegance of Michael Palmer's poetry, there is an obsessiveness, a sense of (moral) *disgust/intensity*, as Tzara had it for Dada years before. It is Palmer's return in fact—though hardly his alone—to something like the contention by Dada poet Hugo Ball that "a line of poetry is a chance to get rid of all the filth that clings to language" (to which Ball adds in his margin: "to get rid of language itself"). What Palmer gives us in turn is not an abstract questioning of the "referent in the world" but "the further anxiety that has been expressed by a number of poets, philosophers, and simply human beings… suddenly understanding that they may or may not refer to the world, that languages break down when we live in a world where pacification means annihilation." "In the case of Vietnam"—he asked back then—"what is reference?" The mark of his poetry itself is what Linda Reinfeld calls "a lyric of disturbance[:]… not so much [in] the choice of words as… the aggressive denaturing of them." Or Palmer, in his own terms: "Poetry—even, let's say, a lyric poetry (… [but] not the lyric poetry of the 'little me' churned out in America)—has a force of resistance and critique."

(Commentary by Jerome Rothenberg with Pierre Joris in *Poems for the Millennium*, vol. 2.)

Nicole Brossard Canada, 1943–

THE THROAT OF LEE MILLER

/ each time *une phrase*
opens with an I
she must be really young

and as we translate her
we must avoid saying never or in my view

I remember the throat of Lee Miller
one June day in Paris

. . . . .

/ often in the same phrase I return
knowing to repeat just there
where worry still craves vows entwined

and as we translate
to explain my *genre* I watch

the throat of Lee Miller that year
it was worth every abstraction

. . . . .

/ I often move to the same spot
a woman in love
to capture shade at the same hour

and as we translate
I breathe

the throat of Lee Miller perfection
of the image as I draw near

. . . . .

/ often in the midst of the phrase I am
breathless I observe
I can stay that way a long time without memory

and as we translate
I touch certain places I exhaust myself

the throat of Lee Miller
no trace of a Kiss

.....

/ above the city and the museum
huge intelligent lips signal
in a red that calls everything into question

and as we translate
I restrict myself to the top part of the work

the throat of Lee Miller around four in the afternoon
a silver-print day

.....

/ I often said every day
art stretches out in our lives as two-
edged dialogue

and as we translate
I cross the Rue de l'Observatoire

the throat of Lee Miller in mind
lips or bodies entangled I observe

.....

/ now in the thick of winter raging red
Geneviève Cadieux's *Milky Way*
I don't think I suffered from the comparison

and as we translate
bien sur il n'ya pas de rapport

the bared throat of Lee Miller
open to speculation

Translated from French by Robert Majzels & Erin Moure

COMMENTARY

*There is a price for consciousness, for transgression. Sooner or later, the
body of writing pays for its untamed desire of beauty and knowledge. I
have always thought that the word beauty is related to the word desire.
There are words, which, like the body, are irreducible: To write I am a*

woman is full of consequences. (N.B.) And again: *For my part, I have always made writing a place of pleasure, of quest, a space of dangerous intensity, a space for turbulence, having its own dynamic.*

As Quebec's preeminent experimentalist, Nicole Brossard moved, with other American poets of the last hundred years, into what Whitman had earlier called "paths untrodden," both of form & content: areas exploring feminine & lesbian identity as, she writes, "simultaneous quest for and conquest of meaning," adding that "identity becomes project when the border between the tolerable and the intolerable breaks down…that is when words lose their meaning or else take on a different meaning, another turn in the events of thought. The words begin to turn on themselves, inciting reflection, inciting thought to new approaches to reality." Propelled by a "necessity for politico-sexual subversion" & by "the demands of pleasure," these concerns come into the writing itself, in both her poetry & her prose fictions. If this represents a radical mix of life experience & poetic means, Brossard in her *Journal Intime* sets the priorities for her own time & for what follows: "Reality is what matters and as a writer I have to deal with it as fiction because I know that twenty-first century reality will be about the worst and best of our fictions."

N.B. After a photograph by Man Ray of fellow photographer Lee Miller.

Paulo Leminski   Brazil, 1944–1989

from *CAPRICHOS E RELAXOS*

My cut-off head
Thrown in your window
Moon-lit night
Window open

Hits the wall
Loses some teeth
Falls to the bed
Heavy with thought

Maybe it's scary
Maybe you'll blink
Seeing by moon
The color of my eyes

Maybe you'll think
It's just your alarm clock
On the nightstand

Not to scare you
Only to ask kindlier treatment
For my sudden head
Departed

Translated from Portuguese by Charles Bernstein & Régis Bonvicino

from *CATATAU (AN IDEA-NOVEL)*

... usque consumatio doloris legendi

ergo sum, in fact, Ego sum Renatus Cartesius, lost in these parts, present here, in this labyrinth of delectable deceits—I see the sea, I see the bay and I see the ships. I see more. Already III years gone by since I tore myself from Europe and civilized folk, there the deathbed. This "barbarus—non intellegor ulli"—Ovid's rehearsals of exile, are mine. From the Prince's park, to the spyglass's eyeglasses, I CONTEMPLATE CONSIDERING THE CAYS, THE SEA, THE CLOUDS, THE ENIGMAS AND THE LUXURIES OF BRASILIA. Since green years, as a rule, I meditate horizontal morning, early, just break of day light already sun's midday. To be, mister of gods, in current circumstances, presence in the watertightness of this Vrijburg, gaza of maps, tabula rasa of humors, origin and zoo, hut of beasts, and house of blossoms. Sarcophagus and carnivorous plants trip, a place in the sun, and time in the shade. They shake, sparkle water drop by drop, ephemeral, shock swarms. Coconuts hide in canopies, papas cheer: PAPAYAS. The mist moistens the spores, muffles the mold, asphyxiates and ferments fragments of fragrances. I smell, a palm from my nose, myself, immense and immersed, well. Beasts, ferocious among festival flowers circulate in a triple cell—the worst, double the biggest; in cages, the lesser, add venture—the best. Abnormal animals engender the equinox, dyslexic on the axis of the Earth, deviating from the lines in fact. A little more than the name toupinambaoults they signed, suspended by the knot of the appeal alone. From afar, ellipses... In focus, Armadillo, spheres rolling out from other eras, search far and wide. Come from the mother with seventy one teeth, ten of which fall out right there, twenty five on the first munch of earth, twenty the wind whisks off, fourteen the water, and one disappears in an accident. One, in the general gibberish, Anteater, by name, stretches tongue onto the dust of an uncertain insect, stands, one-eyed close, face to face, there, then, bizarre in excess, and is undone, eclipsed in ants. By or in the new-growth, you, metallic longsoundings, the mockingbird pumps icy ironies, kisskadee in the she-loves-me-she-loves-me-not.

Translated from Portuguese by Jennifer Cooper

Oceans, / emotions, / ships, ships, / and other relationships, / keep us going / through the fog / and wandering mist. / What is it / that I missed? (P.L.)

Of Polish descent on his father's side, African Brazilian on his mother's, Paulo Leminski was born in Curitiba, Brazil, & came of age at the height of the Noigandres Concretist movement led by Haroldo & Augusto de Campos, eventually breaking from it & them & forging a new & duly celebrated path of his own. Writes Jennifer Cooper of Leminski's masterwork, which includes the preceding excerpt: "Coming at the height of his powers, *Catatau,* his idea-novel or novel-idea (*romance-idéia,* as he called it), was written over an eight-year period and published in its final form in 1975."

The word *Catatau* itself, Leminski explains, "is probably onomatopoeic (perhaps for the sound of falling)" and can mean "'physical punishment,' 'a beating;' 'chatter,' 'arguing'; used as an intensifier for both 'something large or something small,' 'a particular card in a deck,' 'an old sword,' even 'penis,' and is 'one of the most polysemic words in the language.' It is also the common name of the *Campylorhynchus turdinus* or Thrush-like Wren."

And Jennifer Cooper again: "*Catatau,* then, is an experiment, which, among other things, parodies travel writing genres of the early seventeenth century through an immersion into a whirlpool of unanchored language that collides with the rocks and reefs on the shores of a fantastical world— the Americas—in the voice of *Renatus Cartesius,* Latin for René Descartes, on an imaginary visit to the Brazilian State of Pernambuco, in the city of Olinda, during the Dutch occupation. The work might also be read in relation to Sousândrade's *O Guesa Errante* [in "A Second Gallery"] as an instance of Brazilian poetry in geopoetical motion."

Anne Waldman USA, 1945–

MAKEUP ON EMPTY SPACE

I am putting makeup on empty space
all patinas convening on empty space
rouge blushing on empty space
I am putting makeup on empty space
pasting eyelashes on empty space
painting the eyebrows of empty space
piling creams on empty space
painting the phenomenal world
I am hanging ornaments on empty space
gold clips, lacquer combs, plastic hairpins on empty space

I am sticking wire pins into empty space
I pour words over empty space, enthrall the empty space
packing, stuffing jamming empty space
spinning necklaces around empty space
Fancy this, imagine this: painting the phenomenal world
bangles on wrists
pendants hung on empty space
I am putting my memory into empty space
undressing you
hanging the wrinkled clothes on a nail
hanging the green coat on a nail
dancing in the evening it ended with dancing in the evening
I am still thinking about putting makeup on empty space
I want to scare you: the hanging night, the drifting night,
the moaning night, daughter of troubled sleep I want to scare you
I bind as far as cold day goes
I bind the power of 20 husky men
I bind the seductive colorful women, all of them
I bind the massive rock
I bind the hanging night, the drifting night, the
moaning night, daughter of troubled sleep
I am binding my debts, I magnetize the phone bill
bind the root of my pointed tongue
I cup my hands in water, splash water on empty space
water drunk by empty space
Look what thoughts will do   Look what words will do
from nothing to the face
from nothing to the root of the tongue
from nothing to speaking of empty space
I bind the ash tree
I bind the yew
I bind the willow
I bind uranium
I bind the uneconomical unrenewable energy of uranium dash uranium
  to empty space
I bind the color red I seduce the color red to empty space
I put the sunset in empty space
I take the blue of his eyes and make an offering to empty space
  renewable blue
I take the green of everything coming to life, it grows & climbs into
  empty space

I put the white of the snow at the foot of empty space
I clasp the yellow of the cat's eyes sitting in the black space I clasp them
   to my heart, empty space
I want the brown of this floor to rise up into empty space
Take the floor apart to find the brown,
bind it up again under spell of empty space
I want to take this old wall apart I am rich in my mind thinking of this, I
   am thinking of putting makeup on empty space
Everything crumbles around empty space
the thin dry weed crumbles, the milkweed is blown into empty space
I bind the stars reflected in your eye
from nothing to these typing fingers
from nothing to the legs of the elk
from nothing to the neck of the deer
from nothing to porcelain teeth
from nothing to the fine stand of pine in the forest
I kept it going when I put the water on
when I let the water run
sweeping together in empty space
There is a better way to say empty space
Turn yourself inside out and you might disappear
you have a new definition in empty space
What I like about impermanence is the clash
of my big body with empty space
I am putting the floor back together again
I am rebuilding the wall
I am slapping mortar on bricks
I am fastening the machine together with delicate wire
There is no eternal thread, maybe there is thread of pure gold
I am starting to sing inside about the empty space
there is some new detail every time
I am taping the picture I love so well on the wall:
moonless black night beyond country-plaid curtains
everything illuminated out of empty space
I hang the black linen dress on my body
the hanging night, the drifting night, the moaning night
daughter of troubled sleep
This occurs to me
I hang up a mirror to catch stars, everything occurs to me out in the
   night in my skull of empty space
I go outside in starry ice

I build up the house again in memory of empty space
This occurs to me about empty space
that it is never to be mentioned again
Fancy this
imagine this
painting the phenomenal world
there's talk of dressing the body with strange adornments
to remind you of a vow to empty space
there's talk of the discourse in your mind like a silkworm
I wish to venture into a not-chiseled place
I pour sand on the ground
Objects and vehicles emerge from the fog
the canyon is dangerous tonight
suddenly there are warning lights
The patrol is helpful in the manner of guiding
there is talk of slowing down
there is talk of a feminine deity
I bind her with a briar
I bind with the tooth of a tiger
I bind with my quartz crystal
I magnetize the worlds
I cover myself with jewels
I drink amrita
there is some new detail
there is a spangle on her shoe
there is a stud on her boot
the tires are studded for the difficult climb
I put my hands to my face
I am putting makeup on empty space
I wanted to scare you with the night that scared me
the drifting night, the moaning night
Someone was always intruding to make you forget empty space
you put it all on
you paint your nails
you put on scarves
all the time adorning empty space
Whatever-your-name-is I tell you "empty space"
with your fictions with dancing come around to it
with your funny way of singing come around to it
with your smiling come to it
with your enormous retinue & accumulation come around to it

with your extras come round to it
with your good fortune, with your lazy fortune come round to it
when you look most like a bird, that is the time to come around to it
when you are cheating, come to it
when you are in your anguished head
when you are not sensible
when you are insisting on the
praise from many tongues
It begins with the root of the tongue
it begins with the root of the heart
there is a spinal cord of wind
singing & moaning in empty space

COMMENTARY

*I took my vow to poetry; this is where I'm going to be. These are my
people; this is my tribe. This is where I'm going to put my energy.* (A.W.)
And again: *We can think for ourselves and we can awaken the world to a
greater consciousness.*

The vows taken early on ("to never give up on poetry or on the poetic community") have led to a career including both a trajectory as poet/performer
&, inseparably, a lifetime involvement with creating & caring for poetic
communities. (After heading the St. Marks Church Poetry Project in New
York, Anne Waldman founded with Allen Ginsberg & Chögyam Trungpa
Rinpoche the Jack Kerouac School of Disembodied Poetics at the Naropa
Institute/University in Boulder, Colorado.) Much of the writing (she says)
"arises out of an oral yearning and attraction. I hear words before I 'see'
them." Suggesting that her voice is "everywoman's *cri de coeur*," she writes:
"I've always been on the track of the wizened hag's voice, the tough tongue
of the crone free of vanity and conditioning." But the work is wider, including an astonishing range of writerly concerns (dream & persona poems,
Malaysian-derived pantoums, the use of cut-up & collage techniques,
etc.). Her own "epic" work, *Jovis* (a celebration of the male principle &
a "counting [of] the 'fathers' I had known"), appears elsewhere in these
pages: a major instance of the new "long poem" in American writing. (See
"A Map of Histories.")

José Watanabe Peru, 1945–2007

THE HEALING

The even eggshell
held in the cup of a maternal hand
slipping through the son's body, back there up North.
That's what I saw:
      a woman meeker than you
scared away death with domestic rites, singing
egg in hand—a humbler priestess
I've never seen.
I gaze at the threshing on her lap
supper's corn
while a stray dog dissolved under sun's dew
licking
the pain thrown on the soil
      along with the egg of the miracle.
So it was. Life went by without a fuss
      among grim folks: father and mother
asking me for my relief. The single value
was to live.
Clouds passed by the skylight
and hens lined holy eggs across their bellies
and again my mother
hung on to the freshest
with only one conviction:
                Life is physical.
And with that conviction she rubbed the egg against my body
so I could overcome.
In that quiet and safe world I was healed forever.
In me all miracles will be done. That's what I saw.
           What have I not seen?

Translated from Spanish by Javier Taboada

THE BREAD

Sorry to say this brazenly
but mother and I lived in a town struck
    by hunger.

Scarcity
led us to live in a sort of innocence
        to live
in the purest core of ourselves.
That happens when nothing is left, except
the prideful pose of mother
        who slumbered as if she was satisfied.

From time-to-time prophets passed by
reciting gibberish in the name of a god
        promising, but cruel.
No one made rain over the wilderness
        nor the miracle of a lettuce leaf.

One evening the blazing gaze of a stranger
peeked into our door—another quack
but we didn't know who burnt inside him, his god
        or his demon.
He claimed his name was Elijah. He was starving like us.
        He stared at mother
who kneaded in the trough a handful of "Santa Rosa" flour
        with a tablespoon of non-commercial lard.

I'm making bread for me and my son. We'll eat it
and then, with the dignity of the sated poor,
we'll die of hunger, said mother
        in *Kings* 17:12

Translated from Spanish by Javier Taboada

COMMENTARY

*I write and my style is repression. In horror, I only allow myself this silent
poem.* (J.W.)

This being said, José Watanabe has proven to be a major influence & a
renovator (both in tone & speech patterns) of Latin American poetry. Like
many other Asian immigrants in the beginnings of the twentieth century,
Watanabe's father migrated from Japan to Peru, where he married a Peruvian woman working on a sugar hacienda in Laredo, in northern Peru.
Both of his parents played significant roles in Watanabe's poetry: the sto-
icism, severity, & austerity of his father would lead him to cultivate an
exactness & accuracy of speech, while his mother would perform the role
of the harsh diviner.

Almost everything in Watanabe's poetry happens in the rural town of Laredo; but Laredo is not only scenery, it is the center where poetry manifests. In his words: "The poetry to which I aspire the most implies a form of revelation that occurs in a physical space, that begins as an event of nature." So, as he would add later: "My poems are born from experience, they have a narrative base, so to speak; but also a reflection and a more or less careful language... For me, the poem is the found object... I just need to describe it and it becomes a poem. That's poetry to me: what I find."

ADDENDUM

W. S. MERWIN USA, 1927–2019

Bread

for Wendell Berry

Each face in the street is a slice of bread
wandering on
searching

somewhere in the light the true hunger
appears to be passing them by
they clutch

have they forgotten the pale caves
they dreamed of hiding in
their own caves
full of the waiting of their footprints
hung with the hollow marks of their groping
full of their sleep and their hiding

have they forgotten the ragged tunnels
they dreamed of following in out of the light
to hear step after step

the heart of bread
to be sustained by its dark breath
and emerge

to find themselves alone
before a wheat field
raising its radiance to the moon

Pierre Joris Luxembourg/USA, 1946–

from **AN ALIF BAA**

Preamble to an Alphabet

letters arose
says Abu al-Abbas Ahmed al-Bhuni
letters arose
from the light of the pen
inscribed the Grand Destiny
on the Sacred Table

after wandering through the universe
the light transformed
into the letter *alif*,
source of all the others.

another arrangement of letters
into words and words
into stories has it
that Allah created the angels
according to the name & number
of the letters so that they should
glorify him with an infinite
recitation of themselves as arranged
in the words of the Qu'ran.

and the letters prostrated themselves
and the first to do so was the alif
for which Allah appointed the alif to be
the first letter of His name & of the
alphabet

ا

Adam is said to have written a number of books three centuries before his death. After the Flood each people discovered the Book that was destined for it. The legend describes a dialogue between the Prophet Muhammad and one of his followers, who asked: 'By what sign is a prophet distinguished?'

'By a revealed book,' replied the Prophet.
'O Prophet, what book was revealed to Adam?'
'A, b...' And the Prophet recited the alphabet.
'How many letters?'
'Twenty-nine letters/'
'But, oh Prophet, you have counted only twenty-eight.'
Muhammad grew angry and his eyes became red.
'O Prophet does this number include the letter alif and the letter lam?'
'Lam-alif is a single letter.... he who shall not believe in the number of twenty-nine letters shall be cast into hell for all eternity.'

1.

and Alif has many seats

under which he is silent

though you cannot call it suffering

suffering rhymes with zero

at least initially

a sweet round perfection

as we like to draw it

doodling one into the other

(newspaper margins of the b&w middle fifties

at Mme Čavaiotti's where I wrote

or learned to daily at 5 p.m. whose husband

told me that in the last war (which wasn't

the last at all) he had been

forced to drink his piss from his boot

in the desert of Libya, his wife linking

zeroes, rounds, in the margins of the daily

"Wort," making, making writing

a chain of nothingness

that is something

and that is our fate *und Fluch*:

that we have to do something

      even to achieve the nothing

      even if only we doodle

ourselves through life
      while talking on the phone
      to someone doodling elsewhere
      while all we mumble are
      sweet nothings chains
      of linked zeroes
                    yet

step back &   focus shifts

      a shape emerges   from the space created

        by the two   circles'

intersections,

      mandorla,
        wherein stands
    the shape of Celan's eye, of the fruit
of the almond tree,
    there stood, maybe,
the names of the six kings
of Madyan, make up the letters
of the Arabic
alphabet.

    The nothing, where does it stand?
It stands outside the almond,
it stands in the shells
of the suffer'un
the zero-crescents
above & below

("Human curl, you'll not turn gray,
Empty almond, royal-blue")

fall away
as the almond looms,
yet remain as links

of a chain,
isthmus-claws
sew mandorla to
mandorla

2.
What a place that must be,
a something at least, to be in
and if that nothingness
was the hamza
a sort of zag without a zig
a future breath half taken now
with always something more
solid, important coming right
behind it.
a kind of fishing hook.

which puts an odd occasion
on this table:
a fishing hook
equals
a future breath
here lie the roots of another
surrealism yet to come
when we find the zig goes with
the orphaned zag.

COMMENTARY

The Millennium will be nomadic or it will not be. (P.J.) And again: *The days of anything static—form, content, state—are over. The past century has shown that anything not involved in continuous transformation hardens and dies. All revolutions have done just that: those that tried to deal with the state as much as those that tried to deal with the state of poetry.*

(1) Of his own nomadism—across borders of language & poetry, "lines of light" that led him from his native Luxembourg to the Maghreb & finally to America—Pierre Joris writes: "Europe gave me my history, those ghostly

voices of the ancestors, real or made up, lied to or listened to. America gave me geography, the space of my dance. My hope has been that language, or what little of it I have been able to serve, has made a threshing floor for their marriage." But the movement, as he proposes, is less linear than the Europe-America axis suggests: the nomadism of the life & a processual poetics make for an open-ended project where only movement is to be trusted, so that both poet & writing inhabit & share a condition one could call "betweenness." A "nomadic poetics, then, refusing to recognize any absolute, except as the localized and not delimited absolute of nomad space—be it desert, steppe or white page—where 'the coupling of the place and the absolute is achieved... as an infinite succession of local operations'"—as Gilles Deleuze & Félix Guattari have it elsewhere.

(2) With this, then, he enters on his own terms into a nomadism further reflected in the relationship to language, in an insistence on not only the possibility but also the need to write in a language that is not the mother tongue but the "other" tongue, in recognition & celebration of the fact that poetry is always an other language, & language itself already a foreign language. And his work as a poet of nomadic means allows him also to take on the lifelong project of bringing into English the complete oeuvre of the great German-language poet Paul Celan. Thus, he writes, appropriating Celan & others in the best of American (new world) traditions: "Poetry is always, then, 'on the way'—yes, on the road, as Kerouac has it here in these States where, as Sun Ra has it, 'space is the place.' It is also *unterwegs* (underway) as Celan writes, where I hear the *unter* also as under, i.e. as below the *Weg*, the way or road or path."

Nathaniel Mackey   USA, 1947–

from *SONG OF THE ANDOUMBOULOU*

55

—orphic fragment—

  Carnival morning they
were Greeks in Brazil,
  Africans in Greek
disguise. Said of herself
               she
  was born in a house in
heaven. He said he was
  born in the house next

door ... They were in hell.
  In Brazil they were
                      lovebait.
    To abide by hearing was
      what love was
... To
      love was to hear without
      looking. Sound was the
                        beloved's
      mummy cloth ... All to say,
said the exegete, love in
      hell was a voice, to be spoken
  to from behind, not be able
    to turn and look ... It
  wasn't Greece where they
                        were,
  nor was it Benin ... Carnival
morning in made-up hell, bodies
    bathed in loquat light, would-be
song's all the more would-be
    title, "Sound and Cerement,"
                          voice

      wound in bandages
      raveling
            lapse

                    .

    Up all night, slept well
past noon. Awoke restless
  having dreamt she awoke on
    Lone Coast, wondering
  afterwards what it came
                    to,
    glimpsed interstice,
                      crevice,
    crack ... Saw her
  dead mother and brother
pull up in a car, her brother
  at the wheel not having driven
    while alive, newly taught
                    by

death it appeared. A fancy car,
                              bigger
than any her mother had had while
    alive, she too better off it
appeared ... A wishful read, "it
    appeared" notwithstanding, the
exegete impossibly benign. Dreamt
                              a dream
    of dream's end, anxious, unannounced,
Eronel's nevermore namesake, Monk's
        anagrammatic Lenore ... That the
    dead return in luxury cars made
                              us
    weep, pathetic its tin elegance,
                              pitiable,
        sweet read misread,
    would-be
sweet

The song says the / dead will not / ascend without song. // That because if / we lure them their names get / our throats, the / word sticks. (N.M.) And again: *The dead don't want / us bled, but to be sung. // And she said the same, / a thin wisp of soul, / But I want the meat of / my body sounded.*

The voice and song here issue in a series of long poems—"world poems," as Nathaniel Mackey calls them, for himself & others—that bring together an ever-expanding boundary crossing that, in the oldest of poetic traditions, calls on the voices of the dead to create the vision of a greater communality that has to be sung into, or back into, existence. What he brings forward, then, is a universalizing poetics of recovery that seeks "access to history, tradition, times and places that are not at all immediate to our own immediate and particular occasion." Of that occasion as a personal point for departure, he writes: "I'm post bebop. I come after Bud Powell and Bird and Monk and so forth, and my sense of things very much has the imprint of... beginning to think about writing in the sixties, at the time when we had the black avant-garde, the new black music." But his imagination & intellect are vastly syncretic, constantly calling to mind (so Joseph Donahue) "pluralities... Olson's polis, Creeley's company, Duncan's heavenly city, Spicer's infernal one, Baraka's nation"—as well as other, more heterological instances such as Dogon cosmology or the tale of the Dausi and of their city, Wagadu. Thus the scope & in-gathering ambition of his ongoing serial poem *Song of the Andoumboulou* (here excerpted): Mackey's "new eutopic thought" (his term), aware of humanity's legacy of enslavement & violence, does not lead to an easy adamic naming (as possible for Whitman, Pound, or even Neruda & Cardenal on the Hispanic side) but to a processual investigation of the orders of language itself.

Of the Andoumboulou of the poem's title (sacred beings in the Dogon [West African] cosmos), Mackey writes: "[They are] the spirits of an earlier, flawed or failed form of human being—what, given the Dogon emphasis on signs, traces, drawings, 'graphicity,' I tend to think of as a rough draft of a human being." To which he later adds: "The Andoumboulou are in fact us; we're the rough draft."

And again: "In language we inherit the voices of the dead."

Rae Armantrout USA, 1947–

RUNNING

Let's say the universe
is made of strings
that "vibrate" or trash
in an effort

to minimize the area
that is the product
of their length
and their duration in time.

*

Let's call contraction
"focus"
or "pleasure."

*

You'll step forward,
I know,

into the contracting
light

ready to like
anyone.

How far will you get?

You'll be far ahead
and distracted.

By what?

I won't see it.

I'll be running to catch up.

I'll know you
by your willingness.

I won't believe

that what's continual
is automatic

SPECULATIVE FICTION

I.
The idea that producing a string of nonsense syllables
while pointing toward an object
may cause that object to change
is common in children on the verge of language.

*

The idea that force exists only
as an interaction between objects
while an object
is a kind of kink
          in a force field.

*

The idea that, if one survives X number of years,
one will live to see how things "turn out"
or even that things "end well."

2.
In the future we will face new problems.

How will we represent the variety of human types
once all the large animals are gone?

As sly as a mother;
as hungry as an orphan?

Wrapped strands and / What passes / for messages, / what pulls itself / apart to flash, / the twinkle / or tickle / of articulation. (R.A.)

(1) Armantrout has emerged over the years as an essential contributor to a new & evolving USAmerican "language poetry" & then some, the force of her work in fulfillment of Lydia Davis's earlier assessment: "In every line, every stanza of these brief and dense poems, Rae Armantrout's powerful mix of scientific inquiry and social commentary, wit and strangeness, is profoundly stimulating. She changes the way one sees the world and hears language—every poem an explosion on the page in which her individuality shines through." It is in that mix of the personal & what she calls her "physics-inspired writing"—the experiential & what she appropriates from a range of sources, both curiously intellectual & undisguisedly popular—that she comes to us as a tough-minded yet fragile & usefully self-doubting presence.

(2) Writes poet Ron Silliman, to push it further: "[Armantrout] belongs to what might be characterized as the literature of the vertical anti-lyric, those poems that at first glance appear contained and perhaps even simple, but which upon the slightest examination rapidly provoke a sort of vertigo effect as element after element begins to spin wildly toward more radical (and, often enough, sinister) possibilities."

(3) And Armantrout on her own behalf: "So this is a poetics of collisions and overlaps, contested spaces. The border of the public and private is just such a contested space. To use dream imagery in a poem, for instance, is to expose something private, but what if a recent film inspired the dream? As I have become increasingly conscious of such contested spaces and the voices that articulate them, my poems have become somewhat longer and more complicated."

Cecilia Vicuña Chile/USA, 1948–

WORD & THREAD

Word is thread and the thread is language.
Non-linear body.
A line associated to other lines.
A word once written risks becoming linear,
but word and thread exist on another dimensional plane.
Vibratory forms in space and in time.
Acts of union and separation.

The word is silence and sound.
The thread, fullness and emptiness.

*

The weaver sees her fiber as the poet sees her word.
The thread feels the hand, as the word feels the tongue.
Structures of feeling in the double sense
of sensing and signifying,
the word and the thread feel our passing.

*

Is the word the conducting thread, or does thread conduct the word-making?
Both lead to the center of memory, a way of uniting and connecting.
A word carries another word as thread searches for thread.
A word is pregnant with other words and a thread contains
other threads within its interior.
Metaphors in tension, the word and the thread carry us beyond
threading and speaking, to what unites us, the immortal fiber.

*

To speak is to thread and the thread weaves the world.

*

In the Andes, the language itself, Quechua, is a cord of twisted straw,
two people making love, different fibers united.
To weave a design is pallay, to raise the fibers, to pick them up.
To read in Latin is legere, to pick up.
The weaver is both weaving and writing a text
that the community can read.
An ancient textile is an alphabet of knots, colors and directions
that we can no longer read.

Today the weavings not only "represent," they themselves are
one of the beings of the Andean cosmogony. (E. Zorn)

*

Ponchos, llijllas, aksus, winchas, chuspas and chumpis are beings who feel
and every being who feels walks covered in signs.
"The body given entirely to the function of signifying."
                    (René Daumal)
A textile is "in the state of being textile": awaska.
And one word, acnanacuna designates the clothing, the language
and the instruments for sacrifice (for signifying, I would say).

*

And the energy of the movement has a name and a direction:
lluq'i, to the left, paña, to the right.
A direction is a meaning and the twisting of the thread
transmits knowledge and information.
The last two movements of a fiber should be in opposition:
a fiber is made of two strands, lluq'i and paña.
A word is both root and suffix: two antithetical meanings in one.
The word and the thread behave as processes in the cosmos.

The process is a language and a woven design is a process representing itself.

"An axis of reflection," says Mary Frame:
"the serpentine
attributes are images of the fabric structure,"

The twisted strands become serpents
and the crossing of darkness and light, a diamond star.
"Sprang is a weftless technique, a reciprocal action whereby the
interworking of adjacent elements with the fingers duplicates itself
above and below the working area."

The fingers entering the weave produce in the fibres
a mirror image of its movement, a symmetry that reiterates "the concept
of complementarity that imbues Andean thought."

*

The thread dies when it is released, but comes alive in the loom:
the tension gives it a heart.
Soncco is heart and guts, stomach and conscience, memory,
judgment and reason, the wood's core, the stem's central fiber.

The word and the thread are the heart of the community.

In order to dream, the diviner sleeps on fabric made of vik'uña.

Translated from Spanish by Rosa Alcalá

COMMENTARY

                    I speak to you
my thread
bridge of breath
                    unspun wool
beginning
                    spin a threshold
                                speech of light

(C.V.)

An artist/poet of multiple means, Cecilia Vicuña has worked with films, installations, & performance pieces & has moved between her native Chile & New York City for close to four decades. In this work, she draws not only from modern & postmodern contemporaries but from (principally Andean) shamanism, oral traditions, mythology, & herbal lore ("ancient and modern texts which help me to understand what I had seen"). The unraveling & weaving that (in her own description of it) characterizes both her written & her visual work draws from an almost limitless range of sources, mixing her words with those of others (old & new) in an assemblage or weave of words conceived (like "the sacred Quechua language," she tells us) as knots & threads (*quipu* in the old terminology, *quipoems* in hers). If this is a central metaphor for her, the sources for her words are given also as acts of vision in which (she writes) "individual words opened to reveal their inner associations, allowing ancient and newborn metaphors to come to light." And quoting therein Octavio Paz: "I don't see with my eyes: words are my eyes" (adapted from J. Rothenberg and P. Joris, *Poems for the Millennium*, vol. 2).

For more on quipus, see "Preludium."

Will Alexander USA, 1948–

INSIDE THE GHOST VOLCANO

With the body of a morbid hanging doll
my aura burns
by shifts
by ambles
by mirages

by the sun in its primordial morass
summoned from a spectral locust feast

through electric bartering grammes
living
as if a spectrum had been transmogrified
across the sum of exploded solar windows
amidst motions of viral infamy
of sudden discharge pontoons
of magical lyncean sails above ships of pure vitrescence

enthralled
by empty Minoan game dogs
debating oxygen as form
debating menace as ideal
as one listens to fire
in dense eruptional gullet
in hanging hydrogen mirrors
so that each image is shifted
back & forth
between gales & the apparition of gales

so that
unicorns from Çatal Hüyük
cease to condense as forms of the earth
but take on the body of enigma as transparence
as blackened meteor in abstraction

the sun no longer quantified
by strange calendrical posses
but becomes
balletic differential
which ceases to quarrel
with the magic of fragment as schism

as mist
as a power cast before oasis

because the game dogs
the unicorn mirrors
spun as a wakeless ocular thirst
as a conjured distance
evolved from the force of a clarified activity

like darkened water as shock
as scale which looms as humidity
then the eyes always focused
as pleas for hushed exhibits

COMMENTARY

For me, language, by its very operation, is alchemical, mesmeric, totalic in the way that it condenses and at the same time proves capable of leaping the boundaries of genre. Be it the drama, the poem, the essay, the novel, language operates at a level of concentration modulated by the necessity of the character or the circumstance which is speaking. My feeling is that language is capable of creating shifts in the human neural field, capable of transmuting behaviors and judgments. (W.A.)

A lifelong resident of Los Angeles, Alexander was until late in his career very little published, but his work has since opened up to assessments of his special & far-reaching view, like that, e.g., by Eliot Weinberger: "His work resembles no one's, and is instantly recognizable. In part, he is an ecstatic surrealist on imaginal hyperdrive. He is probably the only African American poet to take Aimé Césaire as a spiritual father (and behind Césaire, Artaud and Lautréamont). But he is also a poet whose ecstasy derives from scientific description of the stuff and the workings of the world…"

Or Alexander, from his own perspective—a journey through distanced worlds of inner time & space: "To see from this disk, I am cleansed with grounded facial negatives, with bone coloured writing, with vocal bone spur chemistry, with rapier crusades, with hunchback conjunctions, spurred by verbal star belt eternities."

Néstor Perlongher Argentina, 1949–1992

MME. SCHOKLENDER

Decked out in prickly pears and gladioli: mother, how you whip those scenes
of candied bearcubs, those bitter honeys: how you flourish
the frothing featherduster: and the spiders: how
you scare the stunned brute with your acid strap: fasten, pound in, and crush:
crutches of a paraplegic mother: soiled pelvis, Turkish
trousers: it's that mother who insinuates herself in the mirror offering
regalia of a night in Smyrna and baccarat: fasten and mark off: shed
the mother who offers herself changing into a befeathered lover, ruffle and
   ransacked: that plucking
of the mother who pulls down the gauzes of the whisky tumblers on the mouse
table: mother and runs: cuts off and hooking: and hiccups:

                                  hanging from
the mother's neck a bracelet of blood, pubic blood, of bullets
and bad guys: blood weighted by those bills and those creams we
ate too much of on the little table of light in the shadow of our
easy anniversaries: that giant tassel: if you took my balls as fruits of an
intrepid and erect elixir: dingles from a glacé that sweetened you:
but killing you was going too far: sweetly: making myself eat from those
stiff small disgusts that crouch tender in the haughty castling of my
muscles, and that conch-er when you lick with your mother's mouth the
caverns of the rising, the waning: the caves:

                           and I, did I penetrate you? I could
hardly stop myself like a drunk male of hinges, shapeless, withered from
tequilas, from putting myself up in syrup, penetrating your blondnesses of a
   mother offering themselves,
like an altar, to the son—minor and mannered? adopting your fan
wires, the jewels you carelessly drop chiming onto the table,
amid the tumblers of gin, indecorously greased with that archaic
rouge of your lips?
like a wanton wolf cub, I could rise up,
behind your petticoats and lick your breasts, as you'd lick my nipples
and leave dribbling on my tits—which seemed to titillate—
the purr:
            of your murmuring saliva? the strap of your teeth?
could I mother?
             like a gallant in ruins who surprises his sweetheart between
the crude flies of the longshoremen, on the docks, when

in the buttons, spawns loose, his protected perfidy? that secret
pubic place? how therefore I clutched that hand-hold, those tapirs
encrusted with orchid crutches, velvetly suspicious;
and supporting with my same member the cankerous spume of your sex,
to unload on your forehead? You'd smile tassled between the drops of semen of
the longshoremen who on the dock took you from behind, mildly:
I snatched you: what did you imagine?

Translated from Spanish by Molly Weigel

COMMENTARY

*There Are Cadavers / In the nets of fishermen / In the tumbling of cray-
fish / In her whose hair is nipped / by a small loose hairclip / There Are
Cadavers* (N.P.)

Néstor Perlongher was an Argentine poet & gay rights advocate, founder of
one of the first LGBT collectives in Latin America. He is also credited with
extending & updating Neobaroque poetics & practice in Latin America,
an influence felt into the present. Writes critic Jesús Sepúlveda: "He called
his style 'neobarroso,' which many authors adopted at the time, referring to
the *barro* (mud) in the sediment of the river that divides Buenos Aires from
Montevideo."

   In doing so, Perlongher defied the usual forms & aesthetic patterns of
Latin American poetry & turned to the experimentalists of the previous
generation, Girondo, Lamborghini, & Lezama Lima, for new models
that freed him also to explore, through his further readings of Deleuze &
Guattari, the notion of "perversity" *as a mode of being.* In Perlongher's
works, perversity finds its climax in the piece shown above, "Mme. S."
("Mme. Schoklender" in the English translation), inspired by a locally pub-
licized case of family murder.

Charles Bernstein   USA, 1950–

THANK YOU FOR SAYING THANK YOU

This is a totally
accessible poem.
There is nothing
in this poem
that is in any
way difficult
to understand.

All the words
are simple &
to the point.
There are no new
concepts, no
theories, no
ideas to confuse
you. This poem
has no intellectual
pretensions. It is
purely emotional.
It fully expresses
the feelings of the
author: my feelings,
the person speaking
to you now.
It is all about
communication.
Heart to heart.
This poem appreciates
& values you as
a reader. It
celebrates the
triumph of the
human imagination
amidst pitfalls &
calamities. This poem
has 90 lines,
269 words, and
more syllables than
I have time to
count. Each line,
word, & syllable
has been chosen
to convey only the
intended meaning
& nothing more.
This poem abjures
obscurity & enigma.
There is nothing
hidden. A hundred
readers would each

read the poem
in an identical
manner & derive
the same message
from it. This
poem, like all
good poems, tells
a story in a direct
style that never
leaves the reader
guessing. While
at times expressing
bitterness, anger,
resentment, xenophobia,
& hints of racism, its
ultimate mood is
affirmative. It finds
joy even in
those spiteful moments
of life that
it shares with
you. This poem
represents the hope
for a poetry
that doesn't turn
its back on
the audience, that
doesn't think it's
better than the reader,
that is committed
to poetry as a
popular form, like kite
flying and fly
fishing. This poem
belongs to no
school, has no
dogma. It follows
no fashion. It
says just what
it says. It's
real.

BEFORE YOU GO

Thoughts inanimate, stumbled, spare, before you go.
Folded memories, tinctured with despair, before you go.
Two lakes inside a jar, before you go.
Flame illumines fitful lie, before you go.
Furtive then morrow, nevering now, before you go.
Lacerating gap, stippled rain, before you go.
Anger rubs, raw 'n' sweet, before you go.
Never seen the other side of sleep, before you go.
Nothing left for, not yet, grief, before you go.
A slope, a map, insistent heave, before you go.
Stone & stem, nocturne, leap, before you go.
Compass made of bones & teeth, before you go.
The wind up acts, delirium's beast, before you go.
Spilt quell, impatient, speaks, before you go.
Rippling laughter, radiance leaks, before you go.
No place, no sound, nor up, or down, before you go.
Smokey, swollen seeps, before you go.
Tossing in tune, just like last night, before you go.
I'm nowhere near the fight, before you go.
Nothing to make it right, before you go.
It won't congeal, no more deals, before you go.
Hop a fence, well's on fire, before you go.
Slammed when you don't, damned if not, before you go.
A hound, a bay, a *hurtled dove*, before you go.
Coriander & lace, stickly grace, before you go.
Englobing trace, fading quakes, before you go.
Devil's grail, face of fate, before you go.
Suspended deanimation, recalcitrant fright, before you g
Everything so goddamn slow, before you
Take me now, I'm feelin' low, before yo
Just let me unhitch this tow, before y
One more stitch still to sew, before
Calculus hidden deep in snow, befor
Can't hear, don't say, befo
Lie still, who sings this song, bef
A token, a throw, a truculent pen, be
Don't know much, but that I do, b
Two lane blacktop, undulating light

Language is an event of the world, just as, for language users, the world is an event of language. Even the world is a word. (C.B.)

A founding figure of the USAmerican L=A=N=G=U=A=G=E movement in the 1970s & beyond, Bernstein's special view of poetry expanded in the decades that followed to include other movements & poetries on a global & historical scale. An offshoot from a range of modernist predecessors—domestic & foreign—known from the outset or gathered along the way & leading in turn to a select range of post-Language poets, he mixes poetry & poetics, practice & theory, in works of great & often explosive density that simultaneously defuse themselves, a turn of mind & language exemplified in the title of his collected essays, *The Attack of the Difficult Poems*. What is sometimes lost sight of is his remarkable sense of the comic & ironic, & the ability to write & think on multiple levels, as well as a specialized ear for the commonplace, rethinking & distorting it to serve his own needs & ours. With all of which & going beyond the experimental formalism at the heart of a "pure" language poetry, he finds in it the means to address the most personal & distressing of human experiences, as in the lament, above, for the suicide/death of his artist daughter Emma Bernstein. As with other crucial poets before & after, the work overall, as fellow language poet Ron Silliman put it, is "situated… within the larger question of what, in the last part of the twentieth century, it means to be human."

And in the twenty-first century as well.

Raúl Zurita   Chile, 1950–

DREAM 355 / TO KUROSAWA

I saw the first cities of water heading
north, in Atacama. They were suspended
in the sky, like gigantic transparent aquar-
iums, and the luminous reflecting lines
swayed on the ground completely covering
the immense ocher plane. It was 1975, the
end of the summer, and I suffered then. It
was also the first time I encountered the
desert. It didn't surprise me to see them,
I would even say it gave me a certain
peace. I had abandoned my children: the
eldest, four; a little three-year-old girl; and
the youngest who wasn't but a year old;

for the first time I could think of them
without so much anguish. In the distance
you could see the two volcanoes and the
reflections of the first of them imprinted a
greenish hue like the sea upon the snowy
peaks. I saw the second one later and it
seemed further away, more remote and
unreachable. That night I dreamt again
of my children and awoke crying under
the cold desert night. I threw off the one
blanket they gave me in the hotel and got
up to have coffee. The infinite luminous
lines continued crisscrossing themselves
as if the whole earth were the bottom of a
pool. At the end, undulating below those
same reflections, were the white cones of
the volcanoes phosphorescing in the blue
night. Kurosawa, I turned to tell him,
I suffered then.

Translated from Spanish by Ana Deeny Morales

THE CITIES OF WATER (II)

For Paulina Wendt

All of you is alive and dead· the grass's gleam at
sunrise and the voice thread that grows in the
deluge, the savage dawn and docility, the scream
and stone.
All my dream gets up from the stones and looks at you.
All my thirst looks at you, the hunger, my heart's
endless dread.
I look at you also in the wind. In the snows of the
South American cordillera.
Over there is the sky where I waited for you to
wake up, the posthumous night, the dead country
where we did not die. Over there all wounds and
beatings as I emerged from the demolished dream
I turned my eyes back toward you and saw the vast
stars floating in the sky.
Your face now floats in the sky, behind it a river.
There's such an old man.

There's such an old man in the midst of that river
and you look at him.

       the cities of water in your eyes

Translated from Spanish by Ana Deeny Morales

THE DESERT OF ATACAMA VII

i. Let's look then at the Desert of Atacama

ii. Let's look at our loneliness in the desert

So that desolate before these forms the landscape becomes
a cross extended over Chile and the loneliness of my form
then sees the redemption of the other forms: my own
Redemption in the Desert

iii. Then who would speak of the redemption of my form

iv. Who would tell of the desert's loneliness

So that my form begins to touch your form and your form
that other form like that until all of Chile is nothing but
one form with open arms: a long form crowned with thorns

v. Then the Cross will be nothing but the opening arms
    of my form

vi. We will then be the Crown of Thorns in the Desert

vii. Then   nailed form to form   like a Cross
    extended over Chile   we will have seen forever
    the Final Solitary Breath of the Desert of Atacama

Translated from Spanish by Ana Deeny Morales

THE LAST PROJECT

YOU'LL SEE A SEA OF STONES

YOU'LL SEE DAISIES IN THE SEA

YOU'LL SEE A GOD OF HUNGER

YOU'LL SEE HUNGER

YOU'LL SEE A COUNTRY OF THIRST

YOU'LL SEE PEAKS

YOU'LL SEE THE SEA IN THE PEAKS

YOU'LL SEE VANISHING RIVERS

YOU'LL SEE LOVERS ON THE RUN

YOU'LL SEE MOUNTAINS ON THE RUN

YOU'LL SEE INDELIBLE MISPRINTS

YOU'LL SEE DAWN

YOU'LL SEE SOLDIERS AT DAWN

YOU'LL SEE AURORAS LIKE BLOOD

YOU'LL SEE FLOWERS ERASED

YOU'LL SEE FLEETS RETREATING

YOU'LL SEE THE SNOWS OF THE END

YOU'LL SEE CITIES OF WATER

YOU'LL SEE SKIES ON THE RUN

YOU'LL SEE EVERYTHING GOING

YOU'LL SEE NOTHING TO SEE

AND YOU'LL CRY

Translated from Spanish by Javier Taboada & Jerome Rothenberg

COMMENTARY

Poetry is the DNA of humanity, it is prior to writing, it is before the printing press, it is before the book, it is before the Internet, it will survive in different forms, and it will die when the last human being contemplates the last of the sunsets. Without poetry, there is no art; poetry is what is behind every masterpiece. (R.Z.)

(1) In response to Augusto Pinochet's military coup, Zurita began to formulate an inescapable poetic corpus that extended into the beginnings of the 1990s, with a Dante-inspired trilogy (*Purgatory, Anteparadise, & The New Life*) & up to our present with his vast volume called simply *Zurita*. His works, both written & performative, from landscape poems to public interventions, surpass all the boundaries of a politically committed poetry & successfully develop a new poetic expression, in which history & environment meld in a poetics of cruelty, pain, & despair. As the US poet & translator Forrest Gander has written: "During the Pinochet regime, Zurita

had the guts to bulldoze a poem into the sand of the Atacama Desert. It read *ni pena ni miedo* neither pain nor fear. Long ago it would have been obliterated by rains and wind, but the people in the nearest village still carry shovels into the desert on Sundays and they turn over the sand of the letters to keep it fresh. In 2001, the President of Chile announced on TV something that most people already knew: that the bodies of hundreds of people who disappeared during the Pinochet dictatorship would never be found because they had been thrown out of airplanes into the Pacific Ocean and into the mouths of volcanoes."

(2) But cruelty in Zurita's poetry is not apart from his own life & body, in which he has also suffered from self-inflicted pain. "I lived in Chile during the dictatorship and survived both the dictatorship and my own self-destruction. In 1975 after a humiliating episode with some soldiers, I remembered the Gospel phrase of turning the other cheek and then I went back home and burned my cheek.... I didn't quite know why I was doing it, but something started there."

(3) As his terminal earthwork, *The Last Project* aims to project twenty-two phrases on a stretch of cliffs off the northern coast of Chile. Each one of these phrases, starting with "You'll see a sea of stones," are, according to Zurita, "the images a human being will see during his time on Earth. [The phrases] will start to be distinguishable at sunset... and the last phrase, 'And you'll cry,' will remain projected, gradually fading with the dawn until it disappears completely in the light of the new day.
"When everything ends there will only be the sound of the sea."

Further instances of Zurita's poetry & earthworks are to be found in "A Map of Extensions."

POSTLUDE

WALT WHITMAN

from **A Notebook**

> To the liquid
> To the
> As I sat
> To the music of ebb-tide ripples softly
> Alone
> To the ripples ~~flo~~
> ~~Floa~~ ~~Idly floating~~
>
> Idly I float

Permission for inclusion in this gathering of the following material has been graciously granted by the publishers and individuals indicated below. All due diligence has been used in the case of others, and additions and corrections in future editions will be made as requested.

Opening epigraph: Haida image, per Getty Images. Credit: Mecaleha.

Preludium

America before America

Patagonia, Cueva de las Manos: photo by R. M. Nunes, courtesy of iStock.com.

Robinson Jeffers, "Hands": from *The Collected Poetry of Robinson Jeffers*, vol. 2, *1928–1938*, edited by Tim Hunt. Reprinted by permission of Stanford University Press.

Lower Pecos River, Texas, White Shaman Mural (figure 3.11d and the insert): Carolyn E. Boyd's rendering of the mural appears in Carolyn E. Boyd and Kim Cox, *The White Shaman Mural: An Enduring Creation Narrative in the Rock Art of the Lower Pecos* (University of Texas Press, 2016). Courtesy of Shumla Archaeological Research and Education Center.

Emilio Adolfo Westphalen, from *The Amber Goddess Is Back*: reprinted by permission of Inés and Silvia Westphalen Ortiz; translation by permission of Javier Taboada.

Epi-Olmec, the Tuxtla Statuette: image licensed under the Creative Commons Attribution 3.0 Unported license. https://creativecommons.org/licenses/by/3.0/deed.en, image created by user Madman2001, in Wikimedia Commons.

Adams, Ohio, the Great Serpent Mound: photo by George Baily, stock.adobe.com.

Robert Smithson, *Spiral Jetty* (1970), Great Salt Lake, Utah, USA / Mud, precipitated salt crystals, rocks, water / 1,500 ft. (457.2 m) long and 15 ft. (4.6 m) wide / Collection Dia Art Foundation / Photograph: Gianfranco Gorgoni, 1970. © 2022 Holt / Smithson Foundation and Dia Art Foundation / Licensed by Artists Rights Society (ARS), NY.

Inuit, Inuksuk (Helper): photo by Robert Cocquyt, stock.adobe.com.

Mayan, "The Temple of the Tree of Yellow Corn": drawing by Linda Schele © David Schele. Photo courtesy of Ancient Americas at Los Angeles County Museum of Art (ancientamericas.org).

Quechua, "A Narrative Quipu": photo by Vanessa Volk, shutterstock.com.

K'iche' Mayan, *Popol Vuh*: translation by Dennis Tedlock reprinted by permission of University of California Press.

Jerome Rothenberg, "An Academic Proposal": reprinted by permission of the author.

Mbya-Guaraní, from *The Ayvu Rapyta*: "The Origins of Human Language": translation reprinted by permission of Jerome Rothenberg and Javier Taboada.

Jorge Elías Adoum (a.k.a. Mago Jefa), "In the Beginning ...": translation courtesy of Javier Taboada.

Moche, "The Incan Death of the Sun & Revolt of the Animals & Objects": translation by permission of Heriberto Yépez; image courtesy of Rebekah May.

Delaware Indian (Lenni Lenape), from *The Walam Olum or Red Score*: translation by Daniel G. Brinton; images courtesy of Rebekah May.

Various Nahuatl poets, "A Paradise of Poets": transcreation courtesy of Javier Taboada.

Dekanawidah (Iroquois), "The Tree of the Great Peace": adaptation by William Brandon.

A First Gallery

from The Florentine Codex to Walt Whitman

Bernardino de Sahagún, from *The Florentine Codex: Offering Flowers*: Arthur J. O. Anderson and Charles Dibble's translation is reprinted courtesy of University of Utah Press.

Quechua, from *The Elegy for the Great Inca Atawallpa*: Copyright © by W. S. Merwin, used by permission of The Wylie Agency LLC.

Nahua/Aztec, "Lament on the Fall of Tenochtitlán": Lysander Kemp's translation reprinted by permission of Beacon Press.

Fray Ramón Pané, from *The Antiquities of the Indies, A First Account*: "Of the Shapes They Say the Dead Have": translation by Jerome Rothenberg and Heriberto Yépez.

Pascua Yaqui Tribe, "Song of a Dead Man": transcreation by permission of Jerome Rothenberg.

Alonso de Ercilla, from *The Araucaniad*, "Canto XX": Charles Maxwell Lancaster and Paul Thomas Manchester's translation from *The Araucaniad: A Version in English Poetry of Alonso de Ercilla y Zúñiga* (1945), reprinted by permission of Vanderbilt University Press.

Francisca Juana, per Hernando Ruiz de Alarcón, "Of the Remedy for What They Call 'Reconciliation'": translation by Michael D. Coe and Gordon Whittaker reprinted by permission of the Institute for Mesoamerican Studies, University of Albany (SUNY).

Arias de Villalobos, from *A Canto Titled Mercury*, "Astaroth Appears to Moctezuma": translation courtesy of Javier Taboada.

Úrsula de Jesús, from *Diary*: translation courtesy of Javier Taboada.

Gregório de Matos, "To the Veritable Judge Belchior Da Cunha Brochado": translation by permission of Jennifer Cooper; "To the Bosses of Bahia called Caramurus:

Soneto/Sonnet": translation by permission of Jennifer Cooper and Jerome Rothenberg.

Sor Juana Inés de la Cruz, from *El Primero Sueño*: translation by permission of John Campion.

Bruce Andrews, from *Strike Me, Lightning*: reprinted by permission of the author.

Esteban Echeverría, from *The Slaughterhouse*: translation courtesy of Javier Taboada.

Ron Silliman, from *The New Sentence*: reprinted by permission of the author.

Pablo Neruda: from *Ode to Walt Whitman*: "Oda a Walt Whitman" (translation by Martín Espada) in NUEVAS ODAS ELEMENTALES © Pablo Neruda, 1956 and Fundación Pablo Neruda by permission of Agencia Literaria Carmen Balcells, S.A., translation by permission of Martín Espada.

A Map of Americas

"America Inverted" map: stock.adobe.com.

Gary Snyder, from *Turtle Island*: reprinted by permission of the author.

Susan Suntree, from *Sacred Sites: The Secret History of Southern California*: reprinted by permission of the author.

Rubén Darío, from *Tutecotzimi*: translation by permission of Greg Simon and Steven F. White.

Simón Bolívar, "On the Chimborazo: My Delirium": translation courtesy of Javier Taboada.

Pablo Neruda, from *A Song for Bolívar*: "Un Canto para Bolívar" in TERCERA RESIDENCIA (translation by Donald D. Walsh) © Pablo Neruda, 1947, and Fundación Pablo Neruda, by permission of Agencia Literaria Carmen Balcells, S.A.; five lines translation from *Residence on Earth*, copyright © 1973 by Pablo Neruda and Donald D. Walsh. Reprinted by permission of New Directions Publishing Corp.

Sor Juana Inés de la Cruz, from *Loa to Divine Narcissus*: translation by Pamela Kirk Rappaport. Excerpts from *Sor Juana Ines de La Cruz: Selected Writings* (CWS), translated and introduced by Pamela Kirk Rappaport, copyright © 2005 by Pamela Kirk Rappaport, published by Paulist Press, New York/Mahwah, NJ. Reprinted by permission of Paulist Press, Inc.

Jerome Rothenberg and George Quasha, "America as Woman": reprinted by permission of the authors.

José Eustasio Rivera, from *The Vortex*: translated by John Charles Chasteen, p. 104. Copyright © 2018 by Duke University Press. All rights reserved. Republished by permission of the copyright holder. www.dukeupress.edu.

Aida Cartagena-Portalatín, from *Yania Tierra*: translation by M.J. Fenwick and Rosabelle White, by permission of the translators.

Pedro Mir, from *Countersong to Walt Whitman*: translation by permission of Jonathan Cohen.

Charles Olson, "Maximus to Gloucester, Letter 27 [Withheld]": by permission of the University of Connecticut Department of Archives and Special Collections.

Aimé Césaire, from *Notebook of a Return to the Native Land*: translation by Clayton Eshleman and Annette Smith reprinted by permission of University of California Press.

A Second Gallery

from Emily Dickinson to Vicente Huidobro

Vicente Huidobro, "Cow-boy" and "Ars Poetica": translations by permission of David Guss; from *Altazor*: "A Voyage in a Parachute": translation by permission of Jerome Rothenberg.

A Map of Visions

Una Marson, "Confession": by permission of Peepal Tree Press.

Nahuatl, "Two Aztec Definitions": from *Florentine Codex*, Arthur J. O. Anderson and Charles Dibble's translation reprinted courtesy of University of Utah Press.

César Vallejo, "The Spider": translation by Clayton Eshleman, courtesy of University of California Press.

Juan Rulfo, from *Pedro Páramo*: by permission of Agencia Literaria Carmen Balcells, S. A. Originally published in Mexico in 1955. English translation by Margaret Sayers Peden copyright © 1994 by Northwestern University Press and in the UK and Commonwealth courtesy of Serpent's Tail publisher. Any third-party use of this material, outside of this publication, is prohibited.

Pauline Oliveros, "Four Sonic Meditations (1971)": by permission of Ione for the estate of Pauline Oliveros.

Meskwaki, "The Little Random Creatures": transcreation by permission of Adam Schwerner for the estate of Armand Schwerner.

María Sabina, "The Sacred Book of Language": translation by Henry Munn and Álvaro Estrada by permission of University of California Press.

Pasakwala Kómes, "In the womb of my mother / I learned the spells": by permission of Ambar Past for Pasakwala Kómes and for the translation.

Hannah Weiner, from *Clairvoyant Journal*: by permission of Charles Bernstein for the estate of Hannah Weiner.

Juan Martínez, from *At the Gates of Paradise*: by permission of Círculo de Poesía; translation courtesy of Javier Taboada.

David Antin, "A List of the Delusions of the Insane: What They Are Afraid Of": by permission of Eleanor Antin.

Dorius Vrede, from *Return to the Old Lombe*: translation by permission of Sam Garrett.

Arysteides Turpana, "Uago": translation courtesy of Javier Taboada.

El Niño Fidencio [Fidencio Síntora Constantino], from "Sacred Scriptures: The Jews": from El Niño Fidencio, *Libro de las Sagradas Escrituras*, edited by Antonio Noé Zavaleta (AuthorHouse, 2013), by permission of Antonio Noé Zavaleta; translation courtesy of Javier Taboada.

Essie Pinola Parrish per George Quasha, "Essie Parrish in New York": by permission of George Quasha.

Kazim Ali, "Ramadan": by permission of the author.

José Vicente Anaya, from *Híkuri* (*Peyote*): by permission of Andrea Anaya; translation by permission of Joshua Pollock.

Ájahi (Kuikuro), from *The Woman Who Went to the Village of the Dead*: licensed via Creative Commons Attribution 4.0 License (CC BY 4.0): http://creativecommons.org/licenses/by/4.0/ from *On This and Other Worlds: Voices from Amazonia*, edited by Kristine Stenzel and Bruna Franchetto, Studies in Diversity Linguistics 17 (Berlin: Language Science Press, 2017); adaptation courtesy of Javier Taboada.

A Third Gallery

from María Sabina to Ernesto Cardenal

Jean Toomer, "People" and extract from *Essentials*: by permission of the *Beinecke Rare Book & Manuscript Library,* Yale University.

Jacob Nibenegenesabe per Howard Norman, from *The Wishing-Bone Cycle*: by permission of Howard Norman.

Víctor Hernández Cruz, "El poema de lo reverso": by permission of Coffee House Press.

Charles Reznikoff, from *Testimony—The United States (1885–1915) Recitative*: courtesy of David R. Godine, Publisher, from *The Poems of Charles Reznikoff: 1918–1975*, edited by Seamus Cooney. Copyright © 2005 by the Estate of Charles Reznikoff. Reprinted with the permission of the Permissions Company, LLC on behalf of Black Sparrow / David R. Godine, Publisher, Inc., godine.com.

Juan L. Ortiz, from *The Gualeguay*: by permission of Esperanza Elena Sabella and Claudia Ortiz, heirs of Juan L. Ortiz; translation courtesy of Javier Taboada.

Gamaliel Churata, from *The Golden Fish*: "Lectern": by permission of © Herederos de Arturo Peralta Miranda (Gamaliel Churata), © Ediciones Cátedra (Grupo Anaya, S. A.), 2012; translation courtesy of Javier Taboada.

Luis Palés Matos, "Black Majesty": translation by Paquito D'Rivera; the poem "Black Majesty/Majestad Negra" from *Selected Poems/Poesia Selecta* © 2000 reprinted with permission of Arte Público Press – University of Houston.

Raul Bopp, from *Cobra Norato*: "Nheengatu na margem esquerda do Amazonas": excerpt I–V in *Cobra Norato – Poesia Completa*, Editora Jose Olympio Ltda, permission by heirs of Raul Bopp; translation by and with permission from Jennifer Cooper.

Hart Crane, from *The Bridge*: "Cutty Sark": from *The Complete Poems of Hart Crane*, by Hart Crane, edited by Marc Simon. Copyright © 1933, 1958, 1966 by Liveright Publishing Corporation. Copyright © 1986 by Marc Simon. Used by permission of Liveright Publishing Corporation.

Langston Hughes, from *Montage of a Dream Deferred*: "Children's Rhymes," "The Weary Blues," "The Negro Speaks of Rivers": from *The Collected Poems of Langston Hughes*, by Langston Hughes, edited by Arnold Rampersad with David Roessel, associate editor, copyright © 1994 by the Estate of Langston Hughes. Used by permission of Alfred A. Knopf, an imprint of the Knopf Doubleday Publishing Group, a division of Penguin Random House LLC. All rights reserved.

Nicolás Guillén, "Tú no sabe inglé": by permission of Indent Literary Agency; translation by Langston Hughes, by permission of Harold Ober Associates; "Sensemayá (Chant to Kill a Snake)": by permission of Indent Literary Agency; translation by permission of Willis Knapp Jones.

Ariel Resnikoff, "Snake Chant (1)": by permission of the author.

Lorine Niedecker, "Paean to Place": by permission of University of California Press.

César Moro, "The Scandalous Life of César Moro": translation by permission of Leslie Bary and Esteban Quispe.

Pablo Neruda, "Walkin' Around" and "Ode to My Socks": "Walkin' Around" in RESIDENCIA EN LA TIERRA (translation by Jerome Rothenberg) © Pablo Neruda, 1933 and 1935 and Fundación Pablo Neruda, by permission of Agencia Literaria Carmen Balcells, S. A., translation courtesy of Jerome Rothenberg; "Oda a los calcetines" (translation by Robert Bly) in NUEVAS ODAS ELEMENTALES © Pablo Neruda, 1956 and Fundación Pablo Neruda, by permission of Agencia Literaria Carmen Balcells, S. A.; "Ode to My Socks" translation by Robert Bly, from *The*

A Map of Histories

A Map of Extensions

Mayan, from *The Mayan Codex*: image: Museo Nacional de Antropología, Ciudad de México; photo by Tolo, from Adobe Images.

Jorge Teillier, "In Order to Talk with the Dead": by permission of Sebastián Teillier; translation courtesy of Carolyne L Wright.

Guillermo Cabrera Infante, from *Three Trapped Tigers*: "Brainteaser" (excerpt): copyright © 1965 by Guillermo Cabrera Infante, used by permission of the Wylie Agency LLC, translation courtesy of Suzanne Jill Levine.

José Antonio Aponte, from *A Book of Paintings*: translation courtesy of Javier Taboada and Jerome Rothenberg.

Ulises Carrión, from *The New Art of Making Books*: "What a Book Is": by permission of Ricardo Ocampo Feris.

David Antin, "Sky Poems": courtesy of Eleanor Antin.

Raúl Zurita, "Sky & Landscape Poems": by permission of the author.

Mario Montalbetti, "Language Is a Revolver for Two": by permission of the author; translation courtesy of Javier Taboada.

Gertrude Stein, "Five Words in a Line (1930)": by permission of David Higham Associates.

Murilo Mendes, "To Live": transcreation after Murilo Mendes by Chris Daniels; courtesy of Chris Daniels.

José Coronel Urtecho, "Masterwork": by permission of Luis Rocha (executor) and the poet's family; translation courtesy of John Lyons.

Aram Saroyan, "Two Poems": courtesy of the author.

José Garcia Villa, "Two Comma Poems": "The,caprice,of,canteloupes,is,to,be," and "The,hands,on,the,piano,are,armless," from DOVEGLION: COLLECTED POEMS by José Garcia Villa, edited by John Edwin Cowen, copyright © 2008 by John Edwin Cowen, literary trustee, Estate of José Garcia Villa. Used by permission of Penguin Books, an imprint of Penguin Publishing Group, a division of Penguin Random House LLC. All rights reserved.

Simón Rodríguez, from *American Societies* (1828) "[Notes Toward a New Typography]": translation courtesy of Javier Taboada.

e.e. cummings, "R-P-O-P-H-E-S-S-A-G-R": copyright © 1935, © 1963, 1991 by the Trustees for the E.E. Cummings Trust. Copyright © 1978 by George James Firmage. Used by permission of Liveright Publishing Corporation.

Ella Fitzgerald, from "Lady Be Good" (scat version): transcreation courtesy of John Bloomberg-Rissman.

Jean Toomer, "Two Sound Poems": courtesy of the Beinecke Rare Book & Manuscript Library, Yale University.

Michael McClure, from *Ghost Tantras*: by permission of Amy McClure.

Papo Angarica, "Batá Toques for the Orisha": transcription and permission courtesy of Kenneth Schweitzer.

David Meltzer, from *Impossible Music*: by permission of Julie Rogers.

Emily Dickinson, "Asemic Writing": by permission of the Emily Dickinson Collection, Amherst College Archives and Special Collections.

Jackson Mac Low, "Milarepa Gatha": by permission of Anne Tardos for the estate of Jackson Mac Low.

N.H. Pritchard, "Harbour": © The Estate of Norman H. Pritchard, from *The Matrix* (Ugly Duckling Presse and Primary Information, 2021).

A Fourth Gallery

from Allen Ginsberg to Raúl Zurita

Founded in 1893,
UNIVERSITY OF CALIFORNIA PRESS
publishes bold, progressive books and journals
on topics in the arts, humanities, social sciences,
and natural sciences—with a focus on social
justice issues—that inspire thought and action
among readers worldwide.

The UC PRESS FOUNDATION
raises funds to uphold the press's vital role
as an independent, nonprofit publisher, and
receives philanthropic support from a wide
range of individuals and institutions—and from
committed readers like you. To learn more, visit
ucpress.edu/supportus.